Lilith:

a biography

ken gunther

Gaiadigm Publishing, Inc.

gaiadigm-publishing.org & gaiadigmbooks.org

This book is a work of fiction. All characters in it are fictional.
A few of its places and institutions have been fictionalized as well.

All reasonable efforts have been made to obtain permission for quotes and illustrations included in this edition. If any acknowledgment has been omitted, copyright holders are encouraged to notify the publisher.

Printed in United States of America by Cushing-Malloy, Inc.

Text is set in Geometr231 bt
with text glosses set in Arial and Arial Narrow
and headings set in CloisterBlack bt and Staccato222 bt

First Edition

Library of Congress Cataloging-in-Publication Control Number:
(LCCN) 2004106320
Lilith: a biography / ken gunther
Book 1 (of 2)
1st Ed. p. cm (acid-free)

ISBN 0-9754608-9-7

Gaiadigm Publishing, Inc.

gaiadigm-publishing.org & gaiadigmbooks.org

U.S.A.

❦ ❦ ❦

This book is dedicated
to our mother, Nature/instinct,
for her tireless life-support,
and
to all children & other primitives
ever at risk of civil harm,
and
to my own children,
suffering under a (civil) system of belief
they regard as "only Natural",*
and
in adoring memory of
karen victoria "tori torinderella toriborealis" morris
(1987 - 2000)
true daughter of Gaia,
cheated out of a cinderella ending
in the very midst of earning it.

*Nothing renders more stark the moral poverty inherent in our civilized values than when we rate Natural behavior –such as dedication to family and community– as unique and praiseworthy …behavior which any baboon or queen bee, with no use for reward, devotes its life to.

❦ ❦ ❦

If all i've managed to do with my life
is extend the laughter of Earth's children
(ALL Her children) for just a few more days,
and to leave my reader with a healthier, and safer,
attitude toward Nature and instinct,
i could not want for more.

other works by ken gunther

non-fiction

the civilizing principle: a misconception of apocalyptic dimensions

Mothernature & the world matron

lilith's inviolable purity

a darkness within

popular dysconceptions & other essays

footnotes of a specular querist & ruminist

einstein's reality-challenged cosmos

fiction

the history of moonlite & other stories

verse

Ecocosm: the Cosmic Gaia

perversody

men, gods & gal-actics

seascapes & other verse

adversody

Book 1

Part 1

[Approximate date of composition by the author: Jan.-Feb. 1998. —Editor]

1

Lilith: pivot of my life, center of my universe.

Your name will fill my final breath. On the jolt of the initial surge: *Lih-!* Body arched against restraining straps, generator snarling, i will careen down the far side of life: *Lih-!* Shuddering now, face blackened, lips peeled back, tung (twitching in purple foam) will fall to rest on my teeth: *Thhhh.*

2

Lilith. What's in a name? Concepts. And in some names, whole paradigms! Lilith is such a name. It owns not only concepts but ICONcepts. I've scoured the complete iconologia of liliths and i can say, in their panoply there is not a single correspondence with –or, for that matter, hardly a suggestion of– my Lilith. So smash your liliths, reader. All of them. In one cathartic iconoclasm! For the Lilith at hand is like none who has gone before. Nor like any who will ever be. And we could end the tale right there except, there is a stunning Universe which comes with 'merely' knowing her, a miraculous Naturcosm that can be revealed only if we press on. Plus, it would be a tragedy to leave the story of Lilith to the talents of anyone who loved her less. For only the most steadfast love could hold to the facts thru the deluge of demonizing she has endured.

3

My Lee, my Lili, my Lith, how shall i limn thee? The library dictionary, thickest book in this pitiful place, does not list lilith, and the combined entries of all the resident encyclopedias offer only a gutless gloss. From memory then. In semitic myth, a female demon thought to inhabit ruins & desolate places; in medieval hebrew folklore, the first wife of adam before eve, who slept with him after his expulsion from eden, giving birth to the "evil" spirits; in *isaiah* she is called lamia (nite creature; some say *strix*, from the *vulgate* latin: screech owl) who lay down with he-goats; in babylonian lore she slept with the devil and gave birth to the jinn; later confused with child-slaying lamashtu; evolved into a succubus, causing nocturnal emissions and the birth of witches & demons called *lilin* (assyrian *lilû*); in medieval folklore she was a witch believed to attack molest or suck the blood of children. But those are only the bastardized versions of the *original* lilith, a Nature goddess of ancient sumeria. But that legend will have to wait.

Lilith. Whole ages of stigmata in a mere name! But live them down she did, my Lilith, every one. As for the teller of this tale, i'm not so sure. It is he now who lives in a dim desolate ruins. Lilith is my torchlite here. If she lives here at all it is only in her image on the cavewalls of my mind; the meteor imprint of her smile, the lisping lilt of her voice, the soft foldings of her fawn-pale body, caught for a fleeting moment in the pages of this sorry book.

I am *...haunted by the starry head of her whose gentle will has changed my fate.* Were i adam i would have chosen her over eve, sight unseen. But any likeness of those mythical misses to Lilith lapses here. Succubus demon witch vampire seductress child-molester murderess? Diabolized from every side, what name could be more unlike her? She who would rather run hide or die than hurt any thing.

4

In this tombal twilite, lying on my narrow rack-of-a-bed, the image of Lilith is etched on closed eyelids as if branded there by a high-voltage wand; the mind-movies of mind-sight projected as if the backsides of my eyelids were stereoscopic moviescreens. I dont so much close my eyes anymore as call up thisorthat scene from my 1,111-day life with Lilith. Act 1, scene 2, glows into focus as i write.

Before i knew her name, a tapping sound made me look up from my desk. She stood in the doorway. A haze-red afternoon sun stood opposite in the window behind me. Her downy arm glistened as she shielded her eyes with one hand. "Hi" she said. Under languorous lashes two bluegrays smoldered. When her eyes fixed you the jolt was intoxicating. She wore a snowy blouse with short sleeves. A white skirt glissaded over slim hips, almost to the knee, where the skiing eye skidded to a stop, a splash of snow spreading fanlike in the low sunlite. Hamstring tendons, delicately, distally, peeked from behind simpering knees, played tautly when she moved —harp-song incarnate! Then, singing upward behind the blind of her skirt, escaped the pursuing eye!

"I hope I'm not interrupting?"

{O interrupt, please.} Actually i just nodded.

Her flesh, warm to the eye, was wet-silken & fawn-hued. I thought i smelled a burnt-honey aroma as my gaze, advancing with a rake's predatory twinkle, tripped on her beauty, tumbled down a grassy slope, landed in a loam of audacious anticipation. And still i lie at her lemurid feet, lolling in lilies, languishing in a limbo of lilacs.

But this is just awful —overwrought prose. My words have eyes. And those eyes are tracking my guards not the reader. If this is going to work i cant be strip-searching every sentence, body-cavity probing every word, to be sure it isnt betraying a friend or indicting a loved-one.

Did Lilith have a perfect portent in my past? She did. Juanita darc was a flashing-eyed 13 when we loved. The threat of autumn & school rode every breeze, colored every scent & sensation those last days at camp. Long tainted by forbidden trysts –beside the barn in sunlite, in the woods by moonlite, by the lake in starlite– our lips met for a last kiss... then dark-haired gray-eyed juanita ran weeping from behind the barn to a waiting stationwagon. A moment later it was bumping onto the road with my irish-spanish darling inside. Tall, lanky, platinum-haired, a 15-year-old lad stood in the middle of the dusty driveway near a circle of sycamores, waving a wistful goodby.

Was she, like juanita, an anomaly, my Lili? Could the reader pick her out of a crowd, a group foto? SHe could. "Is this her? There's a glow about her." <Exactly!> The energy that spilled thru her veins was uncannily visible: a will-o'-the-wisp glint in the eye, the pomegranate cheeks, the impulsive quick laff, a lickerish glee in her giggle. But that hardly scratches the surface.

So there she stands, Lilith McGrae, in the doorway of my existence: whose height was 1.6 meters (5'3" in the old style) and whose age, and its squareroot, matched the time of day when she appeared! (How stilted, recondite. But what to do? Now the imbeciles are adjusting the surveillance cam out in the corridor.) And here i am, on the very threshold of oblivion, over a fathom & a ken (yet under 2m) tall, with the squareroot of my age —specially on those gray days when they startup the generators across the hall— often feeling like 10! But for the reader who wishes to snag that magic ratio exactlybutexactly, sHe need only contrast any 63.594731 of the total days falling between october 16, 1993 and october 31, 1996! But all this is probably even *more* arcane than it seems to my feverish & sleep-starved brain. So where were we? O yes. There she stands, my Lilith: China-white smile, dazzling bluegrays, blackchestnut tresses, shy winning ways. Quickly noticed. Impossible to forget. Repeat: Lilith, Lilith, Lilith... til the end of my days.

5

So much for introductions. Got to relax. This will not do. I'm a pianowire tugged in opposite directions by forces in conflict: the imperative of telling Lilith's story on one end; the fear that what i say will be confiscated, on the other. And what of the costs such confiscation will unleash? God. This is not even to mention the problem of how much time is left to *tell* the story! Gadshazm, what element of this undertaking isnt bad?

O for the luxury of knowing how many pages remain in this book.

Anyway... Here's the topo view. If in your hands, reader, right now, there's a book, a *whole* book i mean... *that's* good. And if the book is thick, that's *really* good. (Ok. This is better. *This* can work.) But if it's just a few sheets of paper youre holding —like a novella; or worse, a shortstory— well... That's *not* good. Actually that's bad. Really bad.

Wish i could nail down just one crackerjack meditation! ...the prize, if not gutlevel peace, would at least help me dump some of this pernicious anxiety. So, here we go again: square1. Got to remember, the reader is here to be entertained. Few expect the fingerprints of Reality to be pressed –a rose blackened by the passage of "time"– into these pages. A fairytale that fascinates, a yarn with a yowl, *that's* what the reader is after.

6

Here's such a yowl. I was born in mount morris (ny, usa) in the midst of a naive albeit slaphappy era. While my parents & their peers collected castings of a triplet of monkeys (hands over ears eyes & mouth) named *hear, see & speak* no "evil", and while they hummed & whistled songs about mairzydoats, sunshine & sundry sophist songbirds, runaway industry & government schemed to pollute the soil for the mairzydoats, make sunshine a deadly hazard, and decimate many of the songbirds.

[In the margins of this testament NS has made numerous bracketed "request(s) to the editor". At this point, for instance, he asks for what he calls "help-art". In most instances (like the present) NS has sketched what he wants pictured and where. When possible said help-art will be inserted without further notation. —Editor.]

Today we chuckle at the smiley-faced denial of 1940s-50s america. But why? For compared with the truth-dodging we've been practicing since the 1980s, america's 1940s-50s denial is kidstuff. For back then our denial 'merely' risked the destruction of a couple nations, while today our smiley-faces risk the obliteration of all life on Earth larger than a rat! Most curious of all is that, said obliteration now verymuch includes all of us! So, hey. Return me to 'those thrilling days of yesteryear' ...if only for a running start at leapfrogging the presentday madness we refuse to see.

That same establishment, grown now into a grotesque oligarchy, has doubtless prejudiced the reader against me. So, for those hobbled by this bias, my lawyer, emil green, is handling my estate ...if youre needing, that is, documentation (letters journals legal actions lab reports videos, relating to my life, my final arrest trial sentencing, that sort of thing). As to fotos, portrait repros, moviestills, press copy & the like, these are collected elsewhere in this biography. But as i was saying....

My parents were immigrants: your typical teutonic glaciers masquerading as average parents. Yet thanks to an art-loving paternal aunt and an abundance of agrarian space in "upstate" ny known in my clan as "the farm", my early existence was not halfbad. After age 4 however, and a move to mossville (n.jersey), i had quickly to learn how to be ignored with grace ε fortitude. Had i been a typic offspring –dna droppings of dad, manic mimic of mom– my childhood might not have been so lonely. (I see, my words are argus-eyed again.) But i was not typical; i was a lanky platinum-haired ganglia of nerve tissue with a sucking sponge for a brain ε wide blue inquisitive eyes.

If youth is indeed bounded by a wide blue sea of opportunity, my childhood was not a sunlit islet on that sea. But this is a waste. Tempus is fugiting and this is a testament about Lilith not me. Despite my lawyer's promptings, we should quit the autobiographics at once, specially since my childhood, photophobic amoeba, winces ε cringes under the brite lites of recall. Beside, pacing to&fro in the corridor the headsman, gloating ε green-eyed behind a hooded mask, sharpens his ax. Hyperbole? Hmm. How barely you wouldnt believe. And so my personal story diminishes to a dot of lite on a black screen and vanishes. And while the green revolution falters ε fails outside, i rot in this dim dungeon, dying of languor, longing ε love, and dreaming, o dreaming, of Lilith and better days.

7

I should wait for the foregoing chapters to be safe beyond these walls before i write another word. When i first arrived here my cell was raided once a week, my belongings confiscated, examined, and all i'd written given to the warden for the feds. Yet, believe it or not, this was better than having it fall into the hands of our prison psychiatrist.

"Why not just stop writing then?" asks the alert reader, by now thoroly aggravated with my stilted staccato style. "Such writing as yours should be punished no matter *what* it says!" Scrappy. Pithy. Intrepid inquisitor. I like that. "And what's the rush anyway? In most states it takes years to get somebody executed!" Hmm. But i should be so lucky as to be your typical deathrower. I am not. And so, to give my intrepid reader that certain touch of perspective he is demanding, we need at once to skip the roses and tussle with the thorns.

8

Thorn 1: On october 12, 1997 i was convicted of murder2, often called culpable manslaughter. Since the victim in question was a high-ranking federal official, my conviction was politically upgraded to murder1. (That this is the latest version of "Kill your mother if you must but dont mess with the king's hairdresser!" is neither here nor there just now.) Fact is, since my crime, at essence, amounted to no more than "breaking & entry with accidentally lethal complications" (as my defense framed it), the old standbys of "conspiracy" & "racketeering" looked foolish even to the most naive jurors. And so it happened that, three days after my conviction, my jury —even without a single peer in it, even with me paraded before them as a classic example of what happens to individuals who anger the federal government, even after months of browbeating that could have turned a dead saint into a snarling hyena— still these socalled judge's disciples handed down a sentence of only "imprisonment for life with the possibility of parole after 10 years".

Thorn 2: Two weeks later, in a move which stunned not just the jury and my fellow greens but thinking persons everywhere, judge black, the judge ~~overseeing~~ ruling over my trial, reversed the jury's "life with" sentence and, on october 29, 1997, condemned me to death by electrocution. [Such capital jury reversals have since been made illegal, however too late to help NS. —Ed.]

Thorn 3: Here's where it gets interesting. Altho electrocution had been the method of choice for capital punishment in the commonwealth of virginia for almost a century, following several hideously botched executions, the state legislature supposedly replaced electrocution with lethal injection. Supposedly? Isnt the law the law? Well yes ...and, no. And here's where 'merely interesting' turns nastily tricky. Unable to make a clean break, death by electrocution was retained as a legal "alternative" ...now get this... *in case a condemned prisoner would rather die in the electric chair!* Sane readers will think i'm making this up.

First of all. Anyone who thinks electrocution is quick & painless is uninformed or brainwashed. It's widely known as "death by instalment" for a reason. Here's that reason. A *series* of shocks is the usual. That is, ❶ 2,000 volts for 20 seconds, then ❷ 600 for 50 seconds. We're 10 seconds over a minute already. But because experience has taught us the prisoner is very often still alive at this point, and because there is no better protocol, we next *repeat* steps 1 ε 2! Since tom edison "fried" his first orangutan at a state fair in 1884, it's been anybody's guess what current strength works best for whom. There are many examples where four to six rounds of shocks were applied for up to 30 minutes before death could be brought about! Retired warden clayton duffy, who was witness to 84 electrocutions in his 35 combined years at singsing ε san quentin prisons (see furman v georgia), describes a typical execution.

> When the switch is thrown one hears a loud snap and, in a single motion, the condemned's fists clench as his body leaps forward to fight the straps with unbelievable strength. The force of the current is so powerful and his body's reaction so violent that his eyeballs sometimes pop out and rest on his cheeks as his face takes on a hideous bloody-holed grimace. This combined with a tendency to project vomit and blood has made use of a hood common practice today. Even so, one can see the tendons of the neck stand out like steel cables as the current continues to surge through his or her body. The prisoner usually defecates, urinates, perspires and drools excessively. All visible skin turns bright red as the temperature of his body soars. It swells, especially around the restraints, as if it would burst. Very often parts of the body (usually the head) will shoot sparks, some up to a foot or more in length. Or the skin itself will burst into flames. Sometimes both. At times the current will blow holes in the temples, wrists or ankles and a sustained sound like the crackling of pig fat in a frying pan cannot be missed. Soon a nauseatingly sweet smell fills the chamber as its upper space, despite exhaust fans, fills with a thick layer of gray smoke.
>
> When the first cycle of shocks is done the body is too hot for the attending physician to check for life-signs. At least five minutes is needed for cooling. For this reason the death of a prisoner can not be ascertained in less than seven minutes. In fact, a prisoner who at this point can be seen to be struggling, or heard moaning or gurgling, as if trying to speak or breathe, is actually better off than one who is alive but shows no outward signs. For the struggling victim, obviously still alive, may be given his second installment of shocks without having to wait the additional five minutes. Experience has shown me, the heart that is stopped in less than seven minutes can consider itself "lucky"

That's under the *best* conditions. As to the worst.

> I've seen botchings so bad I wished I could take a gun from one of my guards and end the so-called humane killing. An idiot with a Boy Scout knife could do a better job quicker than I've seen experienced personnel do with the best equipment. Hanging, firing squad, guillotine, any of these (also inhumane)

> methods are better than electrocution. Believe one who's been there many times. Only burning at the stake can match it for sheer suffering.... And God save him who has made enemies of those on the execution team! For he will beg for a quick death in vain!

Request to die in an electricchair? Madness. Distilled madness. Anyone who believes electrocution is being retained in any state for the benefit of the condemned is brainwashed. Only an executioner knows better than an inmate on deathrow what it's like to die in the electricchair. Botching stories are numerous and their documentation is the stuff of legends. Any deathrow inmate who elects to die thus is unequivocally insane.

> The unpredictability of electrocution has proven a powerful weapon for maximum security personnel.... The threat of an agonizing death is sometimes the only way to maintain control over prisoners who fear nothing but death itself. For any fool knows, the difference between being cooked for 1 minute or being broiled alive for 10 is all the difference in the world! As to 30 minutes, or even 20? That's unimaginable! For guess who makes up the electrocution teams? None other than the guards the condemned prisoner sees every day.... Whether they like you or hate you can change not only your life. It can change your death.

Tho i've been in what's called maxlockdown for only three months, i can attest to the authenticity of this testimony. I wasnt here a month before dr slugmoid [Samuel Sigmoid, prison psychiatrist —Ed.] warned: "Get on my bad side, schock, and I'll see to it they take an hour to fry you!"

Thorn 4: There is no law which says the fed. must abide by the punishment protocol of a state. The only guideline here, if any, is precedent. And unlike law, precedent need not be followed. Specially if an 'attractive' legal alternative is in place! (Va offers such an alternative, as explained.) In dispatching my case, fed. judge black took advantage of *all* the options. Not only did he overturn my jury's rejection of the death penalty, he interdicted that i suffer a form of punishment denounced by lawmakers in 38 states [39. —Ed.], and every other country in the world, as inhumane. That punishment, of course, is death by electrocution. In the face of this worldwide stirring of conscience, the wise reader will wonder why an entire federal court system permits the overturning of my 10years-to-life sentence, month after month, to go unchallenged.

Thorn 5: To spare us all the *official* spin, we'll quote dr slugmoid again. "Law schmaw. Trust me, schock. Nobody looks at it like you 'n' your silly lawyer. The fed. did not thumb its nose at state law. Quite the opposite. It sent a message loud 'n' clear. An' that message says, the fed. has washed it hands of you. It's says, 'Do with him what you will. You can even torture him if you like'. *That's* what the fed. means when it orders death by electrocution. You think [judge] black didnt *know* what he was doing? He damnwell knew! He was doing what the fed. wanted: giving the okay for the state to torture in certain cases. Read my lips: the electricchair, schock!" Deliting in the moment, he lites a cigaret, takes a lung-gagging drag, exhales blissfully. "Hey, I dunno what you did, schock. But you musta really pissedoff the big boys! Youre in a bad position here, and the sooner you realize it the betteroff you'll be."

If i pointout a few of the thorns beyond your rosewindow, reader, forgive. It's not for sympathy. It's for credibility. When i say i have neither the rights nor the privileges of other deathrow prisoners, i want to be believed. When i say, reprisals –potentially *lethal* reprisals– are made against those i contact or who contact me, i want to be believed. If i say, what i write or say may be used against not only me but against friends ε loved ones, i want to be believed. If i say i am not a murderer terrorist conspirator racketeer kidnaper neonazi or pedophile, i want to be believed. If i say i'm going to be put to death in the electricchair when the law says it's illegal to do so, i want to be believed. When i say i dont know how much time i have left and that, because of this, i must write our story despite the oppressive odds of vindictive risk, i want to be believed. Unfortunately the only way to come by such credibility is to describe –well, outline– what's happening around me daybyday and why. And this i will do as needed, tho i loathe both this place and my future within it, and would rather banish both from my thoughts forever.

Even dead stars, dead planets, spin; so our World turns despite all we've done to it; and so our oz grinds on, inviting us to indulge our latest fantasy! And indulge we do. For we refuse to see —crouched in shadow behind the seat of the flashy car, in the basement, under the stairwell of the new house; hidden in the voluptuous glare of the jillion gadgets we own or desire; masked in the persons we've purchased or who've purchased us— the jeering face, the mocking gryllos, alive&well in the belly of our greed! But i said i would stop. And i will, i will.

O for one of those nurseryrhyme civil gods who answer personal requests. O Gaia, whisk me from this dreadful fortress back to my Love! *O, quand je dors, viens auprès de ma couche, comme à ally apparaissait, maud....* O Mind that maintains the Cosmos, suck the sands of time back into the hourglass, that we may live again —this time without fear. Give back that day –berkeley campus in early autumn– riding the flames of my latest book into the dry tinder of a thousand newage minds. I'd only begun to speak when she –glowing, dark-haired, blue eyes flashing: beacons to a sailor lost at sea– was ushered down the aisle and seated almost directly below me... and i lost my place as gottschalk used to lose his place, and as i lose it now. And still, despite all the precious blood that has spilled like sand from the hourglass, still she distracts me, and still i lose my place ...and will, and will, til the dust of our bones blows free among the stars!

9

One last essential and we'll get back to our story.

Attorney green has come&gone. The start of this book is now beyond seizure & censure, so far as i can tell. For the political climate as i write is such that, while friends or loved ones are made to suffer to the degree they are close to me ("green terrorist" that i am said to be), my legal counsel is permitted to operate with token hindrance, providing he displays no overt arrogance or aggression. While the lawyer of your common serial killer is not only allowed an arrogant demeanor but *expected* to have one, the lawyer of an "enemy of the state" (the fed., in my case) who is at all aggressive for his client's sake will soon find his efforts ground to a standstill. Endless legal maneuvers & bureaucratic roadblocks will be thrown in his path —say nothing of being strip- & cavity-searched and heavily guarded every time he visits his client.

Emil is uncomfortable i know for having to smuggle this testament to safety. On the other hand –thanks to the fine people over at aclu, amnesty america & national lawyers guild– he also knows my rights are being severely violated. Emil is not the risk-bedamned sort one expects of a green lawyer. Yet it is precisely his conservatism which serves me best. For only such reticent by-the-book behavior can hope to wringout a jot of justice from an establishment which is all but completely under the thumb ...No. Make that, dangled by the purse strings... of powerful (cataNatural) corpolitical interests.

Thus i respect emil's agreeing to carry this "green contraband" to freedom. And thus (and here comes the main reason for this chapter) i listen when he suggests, "I know youre anxious to get started. Still I think it would be good if, instead of launching straight into the story of your life with Ms McGrae, you give your readers some personal background to cling to; a sampling of your childhood, maybe, and a smattering of those experiences which formed the man youve become. Like the rest of the world these days, most of your fans know only the lies, spin 'n' omission they get from mainstream media. They deserve more than that, if only for having stuck by you. And that may even include me" he added with a (rare) grin.

Even tho i am at root a *very* private, person —not to mention those time constraints hanging axlike above my neck— i promised emil i would give his treatment a try. And so, if only in appreciation for "compromising [his] professional principles" (by carrying this book to safety, against the court's sweeping gag edict), i offer now a couple "formative experiences".

10

Life begins in silence ...so they say.

It was a day in May. My paternal grandparents had gone out for the ritual sunday ride. During the period my parents lived with them, these jaunts commandeered most of the day. "Karly, no! Not on your mother's bed" giggled my mother-to-be. Nothing silent so far. But then, we're still not quite at the beginning.

If the cave is symbolic of the vagina, the grotto, i feel, intuits the vulva & environs. Thru the misty vision of a 3yearold i recall my second encounter with things grottolike: a rockgarden fantasy in my paternal grandparent's backyard: clusters of velveteen pansies being breeze-fluttered beneath the petinaed statue of a grecian lad —o, say, two feet high— pissing heroically all the day long into the pool which crowned this mini-grotto. It was then the words pansies & pandas —grandma's pansies; my own panda, pong— became entangled for life in my little brain. Only later did 'panzer' get tacked on, and still later, 'panspermy'. Aged 13 i saw that grotto/garden for the last time. The trickling streams which once wound down thru colorful copses, past exotic birds hobbled on wire legs, were dry; the pool was dry & blackened with gnarled algae; the lad's penis was not only dry but corroded half-off. "I varned him to zave it" winked grandfather, "dat zum day de ting vud vear out". 13 is an age when boys glimpse such humor at gut level only. Dont picture a doting grandfather. We're talking german ancestry here. Middle german ...well, except for a hot platinum slipUp from faeroe island who, with clever witchy fingers, stroked a harp twice her size for a decade before giving birth to grandfather, performing the "waltzer" in the first strauss orchestra ...licentious music, you know, in its day. Stern teutonic grandfather would die long after my nicer (but still oddly cool) grandmother.

Back inside, karly, with the raspy outcry of an upset heron, launches me. Well, not exactly me, but a kind of half-nascent nathan. A moment later he emits a volley of guttural growls, subsiding yelps & a final whimper. Elle (mother's given name) squeals in antiphonal sympathy with each spasm. Silent? I should say not. But we are cheating again i see. This is still technically not my beginning.

I can picture those moments clearly –hot vocal moments, just before the flagellate half-me is squirted on its life-or-death (e)mission– because once, by accident, i came upon my parents in full throes as they say. It was a latenite in autumn, fatal autumn —the very autumn of the summer i met juanita, in fact. Again, i was 13. They did not see me in the doorway, did not hear (above the writhing hubbub) the door open, close. I went upstairs, climbed out a 3rdstory window, sat against a gable. I did that alot in the city. (The correlation between high perches and peace-seeking goes back in me.) The twinkling of the manhattan skyline across the river replaced the stars of my rural past, stars ever missing from that pollution-socked city sky.

As to sex & my parents. A few summers at "the farm" had exposed me, on the one hand, to everything from chickens & pigs to cows & horses mating; and at camp that summer, alone in my bunk envisioning juanita, the thrill of first fluid (on the other hand). Yet mother & father having sex? In a house where physical warmth was a rarity, such a thing never occurred to me. I stayed on the roof til the first javelin rays of dawn skewered cold gulls seaward from the foggy sills of the city. While i was relieved to know i wasnt the only one in our house with a secret sexlife, still, youngsters reared in cool antiseptic households are troubled by the idea of their parents "having sex" muchless the sight of it. Heap on to this my having reached puberty and fallen deeply in love just months before. Well, let's just say, 13 was quite a year for me.

I soon found myself in a fever to learn all i could about sex. I started by borrowing the sauciest books i could turnup in mother's large pulp-gothic romance library, found in a bookcase at the back of her walkin closet alongside a curious costume collection. A handful were father's —the books, not the costumes. (I could tell by the snipes scribbled in their margins.) Those were the days when fair-to-good literature was racier than the 'best' pulp romances. Tho i read scenes from *lady loverly's chatter*, the same author's *the virgin and the gypsy* was more to my liking. Other filchings got me *the tropic of cancer*, *madame bovary*—or mama b's ovary as we'd later call her in euorolit1— and, best of all, frank harris' underrated *my life ε loves*, which in college i would return to for having only ravished its condensed paperback ~~virgin~~ version. 13 is also an age when gothic fantasy is attractive —real goth, that is. I soon grew a fascination for incubi, succubi ε their ilk.

I've mentioned costumes. Well, running as daytoday subtext is mother's passion for acting. Herself devoid of depth, there was nothing –i mean nothing that *i* knew of– which she liked better than to dressup ε play a role. While today i can imagine father refusing even to play santaclaus for my benefit, i was years understanding mother's motives for role-playing. I'm recalling her now as: one of santa's elfs, female version; female easterbunny; pilgrim housewife; female cupid; st patrick's girlfriend, and even house to house with me on allhallows eve as the lone ranger's girlfriend! <Why not go as tonto, mother?> By halloween aged 9 i'd had enuf. <No more!> This was not poor sportsmanship but survival. If my new urban peers found out she was my mother, well, i was as good as dead. By the way, just because the lone ranger ε tonto didnt appear to have girlfriends doesnt mean they were gay. And so what if they were?

What i didnt know was, a key part of the choreography behind mother's costumes included, *au fond* (pardon), the hope of arousing my maritally bored father. Altho she was a beauty by any standard, mother's outfits were too skimpy ε eroticized for family/community standards in 1950s america —why so many of our holidays were tensioned ε supercharged. Her easter getup for instance was simply a playboy™ bunny outfit. And save for the pilgrim attire (which i saw her make), all her stuff came from tiffany's of tinseltown™, the most ephemeral of which she wore every time i lost a tooth. Picture now that aerial ladykin, done placing under my pillow a quarter (candybar ε change, back then), transforming from toothfairy to toothsome witchnik on the way back to the parental chamber, thence to perch on my father as he slept and proceed to suck out his soul ...as most books had it. For books, hypocritically pure american books, still had not the candor or courage to talk of fantastic fellatio in the nite, of randy gymnastics in the wee hours of a child's sleep. Father (i might say, now that i'm a few bouts of my own the wiser), probably grinned from ear to rear at just the thought of the next gap in my smile.

Two faces were prominent in pantries in those years: the quaker™ oats farmer & aunt jemima™, a pancake syrup lady. So frustration-charged was our household, i recall dreaming, the jolly black girth of jemima chasing the amazed quaker around our pantry afterhours. I still see his face –typically ashen under the brim of an antiseptic black hat– strangely flushed, his white hair flown askew, teeth clenched; like a racehorse thru flared nostrils he pants as he runs. They shoot thru the door of a log cabin™ can (cabin-shaped metal container of a competing syrup company) as dreams love to allow. Next scene i see me peeking in that doorway. Inside, on a bed (my parents four-poster!), jemima & the quaker are replicating the same boistrous heap in which i'd glimpsed my parents, consummating passions apparently pentup for years in our pantry. Jemima & the quaker. Good name for a book by some descendent of the hemings/jefferson passionata.

What of others in whom i had indiscriminately placed my trust? While i'd always wondered about coach bruce at the y[mca], wonder soon became suspicion. And what about overly friendly glenn the policeman, and my pretty sundayschool teacher who was ever hugging me. And what of the mayor the president jesus the lone ranger superman & straight arrow? A boy virtually without a dad can chalkup a lavish iconologia, trust me. But this personal disclosure crap isnt getting any easier and my prose has longsince passed recondite.

11

It must be saturday for xodion & zodion are here. (Prison staff dont use their actual names so why should i use their fake ones?) Of an unpretty black-uniformed bunch, these two are ugliest. The moment they entered the block i knew something was up, for they are usually morbidly silent. "On your feet, losers!" Xodion, clubbing my bars as he passes like a punk playing a wroughtiron fencerow, yells "What day is today?" while his partner fakes adjusting the surveillance cam aimed at my cell. Sobbinrobin, a nervous wreck under any circumstances, cries out from down the way, "Tuhday is thursday, sir!". "Wrong!" We've heard their crude homonym a dozen times yet they cant get enuf of it. Knowing humpinlouie wont answer and sobbinrobin is either stumped by the question or frozen with fear, i am about to reply ...three agonizing months have taught me to play along in all instances where my essential values arent compromised....

However, xodion, unable to contain himself any longer, howls "T-g-i-f, you shitheads! T-g-i-f! Thank God it's fry day! FRY day! Get it? Cause someone's gonna cry t'day! His mama screamin 'why' t'day! Some loser's gonna die t'day! Become a charred frenchfry t'day! That's why I'm feelin *high* t'day!" ...all recited in that lusterless monotone common to many violent persons.

Some further slur (which my intercom does not pick up) is spat, and the marching booted pair, robin trotting between, leave for breakfast with a clang out the far door. Humpinlouie, ever grinding & groaning away on his cot, does not go with them. With the worst case of deathrow stomach i ever hope to see, he eats ...well, nibbles at... supper only. As for me, my meals are brought in —provided i havent spoken my mind when pressed. For, save for appointments with dr slugmoid, i get no time outside my cell, neither for meals nor the hour of free time the law guarantees every prisoner.

12

Back in my grandparent's bedroom, the male half of a reddish-dark universe pulsed pitched throbbed rolled & shuddered as, to distant groans & squeals, i shot forth —well, one half of me shot forth. And we were off! Nothing silent here. Thousands of protobrothers fought head-to-tail upward thru the swishy darkness. All at once, like a crowd hitting an exit doorway in a theater fire, the first wad of us were jammed at the gasping cervix. This confessional booth smells of old wine & smegma. May i talk about Lilith now, emil? [NS is, I think, jesting here. The present editor never dictated whom or what NS could or should write about. I merely made suggestions I thought a reader might find informative. —Ed.]

Point is, i feel all this prebirth compression & compaction business (ranging from sac to penis, to vagina, to –gulp– cervix & points beyond; and then back out from the other direction, from ovary down fallopian –gag– tube to uterus (for extended stay), then down birth canal, o shit, here we go!) ...all this led i think to a lifetime of cloistral phobia. It was monks who named it you know —cloister phobia. And not the free-spirited monks of the himalayas either.

Given this predisposition (fear of confining places), i knew what a prison cell would be like at age 7, while digging a fort with my best friend, geoff. Phobias work on an emotional level: prerational responses to what life has tossed our way. We have emotional memories & intellectual memories. You dont have to be a genius (or even sane) to be fritened or damned scared of something. So dont toy with me, *doktor*. Emotional imprinting is a predisposition for dna coding, and it's more implicit in us than conscious recall! And he's a pompous poltroon who thinks otherwise. As any student of mach knows, even a beaker of glycerine can remember how it was stirred. Anyway....

The entryway of our fort, a shiny-smooth ceramic conduit about 3m long & 1m high, was hid among bushes. You had to part the brush to find, to slide into, it. While buddy geoff & me didnt know it at the time, to go down there for a strategy chat was akin (notsomuch to coitus as) to two insecure kids trying to return to the womb for a fresh start. That was back in mossville, where my little friend priscilla lived —priscilla of the pale lashes, whose hair was the color of southsea sands and whose eyes were the color of that sea. But thought has drifted again. O, yes. And so i made a conscious effort always to conduct myself so that a closed-in place (such as a coffin, a grave, a prison cell) would not loom in my future. What fools are we who feel we have total command of our fate.

Mother is now toweling off in the bathroom. Father is asleep. If she were alive she would not be embarrassed to be on display here. In fact, in her juvenile lust for moviestardom, the exposure would 'do her proud'. Her favorite starlet was a green-eyed blond named gaga bazore —one of far too many celluloid simpletons. This reminiscing has me not only selfconscious but cynical, i see. Anyway, finished toweling her desirable body my mother-to-be begins the ritual of overlaying her lovely face with cosmetics. Simultaneously, like a cat, turning as it grooms itself before a black mirror, the egg –the other half of me-to-be– floats adrift in the soft glow of uterine space —the withinnards of undine's belly moonward bent to the rapt inflections of muffled lust . Winking with its anxious vulnerable eyespot, the coy womb-closeted & cosseted egg waits in baited silence for the other half of me-to-be's flagellate tung-kiss of bijugate life. (Somewhere in my unpublished essays i theorize, those sleeping misses of legend –the snowhites & brunnhildes, the sundry takes on sleeping beauty– are unconscious analogs of the unfertilized egg, where only the touch of heroic male lips, as if by magic, can bring the dormant female to life!)

Meanwhile, but centimeters from my goal, like an egg-bloated salmon leaping a waterfall, i surged upstream. <I'm in some sort of race> surmised my wee reptilian brain as it swam its dna motherlode (well, ok then: fatherload) toward some target veiled in evolutionary mist, compressed on every side by scads of other skilled swimmers! With the same goal? <Yes! A life-or-death race! That's what this is! I will die if i dont get somewhere, and get there first! But where in hell am i going? And *why?*> I'm convinced, i was incurably curious even *prior* to conception.

Lilith

However, if i ...well, if this frantically splashing sperm... could have seen the future, my life from aged 8 say to 17, it might have given up then&there. (*That* past, plus *this* future, could discourage a demigod.) Another sperm, perhaps from the same heat, would have become 'me'. What was wrong with my childhood? ...after all, it's not like i was burned with cigarets, drugged & sexually abused, like some other sweet thing we know. And i was hardly a bruise on the likes of davey pelser.

"You'll never amount to anytink" my parents would say each time i emerged from my room, wet-eyed, still in the throes of creativity, proffering my latest painting, story or poem. "Shtop vastink your time mit all dat *trödel.* [they would admonish] Go outzide und play *vooot*ball or zumzing. Akt like a real boy, naton."

Books, libraries, have been written trying to figure out the teuton psyche. Other cultures have it too, of course, but we germans –adolf & goons in particular– goosestep off with the prize. A genetic fluke, some call it. But maybe it's not that complicated. Maybe it's so simple we miss the point. For past a certain tender age, kids of german parents encounter much coldness & criticism, and from the very persons who should be praising & hugging them. When we grow up, us 'failure children', we pumpup our muscles, thump our chests (some load guns) and arrogantly dare anyone ever to say again, "You'll never amount to anything". If we're really paranoid, we think we hear whispers & tittering. And only when we rule the club the corporation the city the state the country –dare i say it? Da whole Vurlt!– do we feel in control of the whispers, the tittering, the fury mere criticism can arouse in us. Without warning, a monster *drache* from *unterland* explodes from our emaciated subconscious. Now *it* is in charge: the paranoid primal cortex of a goth/-

semite/teuton/celt! And male at that! What could be worse? And it knows by heart the names of all the whisperers & titterers in the crowd, and maybe even their vehicle tag numbers & home addresses.

It doesnt take a psych library to unravel the roots of national insecurity. It begins in childhood. Only we civil raised in hug-free zones are obsessed with personal or national security. Prewar germany (pick a war) was comprised of a nation of insecure pseudo failures —adult kids raised in homes where fathers were tyrants and mothers feared to challenge them; raised in homes where hugging & praising stopped suddenly in one's early youth or, worse, was never begun. War-mongers are last to learn of what stuff they are made. I have oversimplified for efficacy of course, but the gist is there. Fortunately, the gentle goethes schillers shuberts schoecks shindlers wolfs kants mahlers leopolds & deutschendorf jrs of my racial heritage overcame this cultural flaw. And as my best readers know, it was these gentle men –*not* the atillas bismarks wilhelms & adolfs of history– who were the *heldenikones* of my adult years. There! Do you see that? (Read the words after 'not' out of context.) Wonder why i guard the flanks of my phrases, ride shotgun on the backsides of my sentences?

While this next item might be seen as dodging my assignment, there is a phenomenon of life conception i would be remiss to pass over. Early this decade a california phd and his wife were arrested in a sex scandal. A jury acquitted them on charges of sexually sampling members of their study-group during lab time. (The chuckle is, the results of these studies still appear in orthodox journals.) The hic doctor would gather brainwave strips of high iq female subjects who had recently received sperm in their vaginas. (This was the problematic part for those lab bunnies without boyfriends, and where the hic dr, everready to lend a helping hand or whatever, came in.) In a darkened room, into the tingling ear of a time-encoded recorder, his wife's soothing contralto would remind a given woman to vocalize any unusual sensations she happened to see traipse thru her head over a 72-hour period.

Out of 222 subjects a poor showing of 17% saw a brite flash. Follow-up study however reversed the initial disappointment for it revealed: 21% of the women had conceived a fetus at the time and that *all* among the 17% (who saw "the flash of conception") fell among the impregnated group!

As pertains to the present case. They were just finishing supper when sperm-me reached egg-me. I knew i was onto something (hic,tsk) the moment other sperms began arriving. {Sheesh, so quick?} Like hornets with stinging payloads they descended on the anxious but admittedly sexy ovum i was already nosing around. Tho exhausted, ready to quit, i scuttled over the vulnerable surface of that prize like a hounddog on a scent. (Human eggs are not quite round, you know. Centrifugal oblation? Spin of Earth, perhaps? spin of galaxy ...Universe?) {Flap my tail, wriggle, swim! Push in,push in,push in! Aha, *that* is my mission!}

You kids sneaking a read of this book, those of you whove been told, "Youre never going to amount to anything", and you adults who, because of such parental mental flogging, believe youre losers, dont forget the miracle you accomplished just to be born! Out of a heat of thousands of capable swimmers *you alone* reached the goal! you alone (you!) were the alpha sperm!

...Draw back the curtain, this I am certain,
you'll be impressed with you.

When you see a door with a hole in it odds are a man did it. The impulse to push in where it seems one is blockedout is more than just impulse; it's an elemental imprint, the most primal & pandemic of all male characteristics! The rest of our bodies —those aggregates of flesh bone & behavior known as tomdick&harry (you & me, guys)— are but apparitions of persona sprinkled on top of this basic impulse merely for purposes of individuation. Other cell colonies in us males echo this primal encoding. For instance, several decades later the specialized cells of my tung would recall, could reenact in detail, this desperately impassioned search, as it wriggled spermlike over the warm velvety vulnerable & sexy loins of a certain later lover of mine.

Lilith

Grandfather was laying a slice of cheddar atop his mince pie just then. Life begins in silence? I think not. Dining next to mother that evening, trumpetlike, father's father sallied forth the customary tattoos of flatulence. One always knew it was coming for, like a hornist standing for a solo, like a royal tribune, he would rock to one side on his chair for the delivery. Such tooting, as he called it, was a signal to the cook that the 'king' had enjoyed the meal —a custom brought from the fatherland by the blue-collar class. Beaming, unabashed, grandfather would chant midst the *schmatzen und schwatzen*, "Da beanz, da beanz, da musical froot; da more ve eet da more ve toot; da more ve toot da better ve feel; so ve eat da beanz mit ev'ry meal!" An unadorned folk, my lineage —shades of atilla, ach! Indeed, the anal fixity of the teuton male is easy to spot. You do not hug, kiss or frankly thank a female. Rather you pinch or pat her buttocks or some part of her sex anatomy. Why? It's less humbling to pass gas than give praise.

Thus mealtime quiet was cleft that evening. Mother, who always flushed at the paternal fart, tried to smile in shy recognition, for she was taught to think it crude. Ironically it was just then that i found it! that dainty dimple with a trapdoor! Others were there but they werent admitted either! Damn! I dove & circled & dove again. There was a brilliant flash, a sound of ...of distant trumpets? I could not tell from inside mother's belly as i plunged into the cozy wonder of the other half of me: the elusive & lovely egg. <Yes! I have done it!> Nascent nathan had arrived!

I have long believed –and that naughty prof has happily shown– that there is an electrical discharge when the negatively charged sperm enters the positively charged ovum —or viceversa. At any polarity, only 'whitelite' meditative extasy [sic] can compare with that lost moment! That is to say, only the mental orgasm that coincides with physical orgasm can touch it.

There is something about explosions that attracts the male mind. And to one with claustrophobia, the explosion of the titely-confined contents of an object is, in principle, the most aggressive act of sudden physical freedom there is. As a boy, toying with signaling devices made of dynamite (which i unstrapped from the rails along 6k of track leading to my friend wayne harding's house), i blew off three joints of two fingers, embedded shrapnel in my gut, knocked myself unconscious, and sent winging up onto a neighbor's front lawn the new door of our garage. (A staggering stash, hid among my father's nail kegs, had sympathy-ignited.) In an effort to win over my urban tormentors, this "countryboy" used to assemble devices which would explode when i, or a fascinated peer, hurled them sufficiently fast at a hard surface. Otherwise i was your average 11yearold.

Later i discovered the many explosions to be found in Nature, such as the nuclear flashes (potassium) that go off within our bodies every minute. We wont trouble with these just now except to say, explosions in Nature have more to do with new beginnings (with becoming) than with endings. While i did not take a degree in this area, i've always been a sort of astronomy/-cosmology buff. Astronomers view the explosion of a star (supernova) as the star's death —applying the usual anthropism: object explodes, therefore it must have been killed. But truth is, except for celestial explosion, life (human or otherwise) could not exist. That is, it is explosions alone (stars, galaxies, larger proto-entities) that have seeded the Cosmos with the very keys to life! The Universe *itself* exploded into being, after all! Little bangs, after the Initial Bang, seeded the proto-superclusters; exploding quasars seed galaxies; exploding stars seed the present as we know it, and so on down the line. And it's all very *sexy* stuff beside.

Read an astronomy book if you doubt this. You will find peepingtoms (in the name of science) with dewy-eyed telescopes spying on orgies of celestial bodies gyring in the dark; cosmolepts who stalk every GALaxy their lecherous gaze falls upon; "observing" as red giants & white dwarfs cavort with hot young stars; watching as cosmic jets, spurting from the cores of active galaxies, spew bizarre jizm into anxious & fertile space; as excited particles dance in clouds of degenerate matter; as black holes suck their astral companions to death; as comets, with heads, necks & tails redolent of spermatozoa, shoot across the nite sky and meteors squirt thru Earth's amniotic sac delivering the very seeds of life! And how about that Cosmic hetaira herself, gravity? A body, simply because it has mass, attracts every other body in an inexhaustible effort to possess the entire Universe! That's the Nature of a body —*before* biosexuality is added! And if gravity (contraction) is female and explosion (expansion) is male, then sex drives the entire Universe! Most magical stuff! Many is the nite i have thrilled –as our primitive ancestors must have thrilled & feared– witnessing this seeming infinitude of cosmosexual wonders?

Freedom is implicit in an expanding Universe.

My point? New beginnings, not endings; birth & rebirth, not death. And new beginnings –specially revolutionary ones– are triggered by spectacular explosion. The pressure, the trap of gravity (or the crush of social spiritual political scientific or artistic oppression) gets so suffocating, so unbearable, the repressive old laws beg to be, must be, broken. A star begs Mothernature for release, to be freed, sent hurtling into the arched & trembling womb of space. And so do we …we who recall the ecstatic feeling of primal freedom, deepgreen freedom.

Outward-hurtling freedom, my friends, not the gravity of crushing oppression, underlies the laws of Nature at this point in Universal evolution. For we live in an exploding Cosmos, not a collapsing one. The star, with its old ε seething brew at peak disequilibrium, begs the laws of Nature to supply that last crucial mote of matter! And it gets its wish. E-x-p-l-o-s-i-o-n! The order of the moment –obnoxious oppressive constraint– is exploded into its basic fragments, readied for new form! The rules, the old crushing laws, are shattered ...*must* be shattered ...in order to obey the *higher* law of an expanding Universe: the law of inchoate freedom!

And so it is: The male Universe-to-be, once upon a time *before* "time", must have groveled ε groaned, ardently laved ε loved, around ε around the egg of the Grand Creatrix. O please! he surely panted into the protoseas of her ear, the protoforests of her hair. Permit me to explode the egg-of-existence into Being! ...into Becoming! Let us replicate our plurality in a single entity: A Universe! And so it was, the sperm-of-time lay hard upon the egg-of-space, pushing in pushing in pushing in, aching to fertilize it. And so the egg-of-space uttered the YES! of all yes's! And so there was a gloried flash of lite in the omnipotent darkness, an explosion to end all explosions! ...or, rather, an explosion to *begin* them.

13

My attorney, my sole touch with non-punitive humanity, has left. Except for random spates of female voices reporting now&again off a wall beyond my barred window, deathrow is deadly quiet this evening. That window, my sole access to Wild Nature (the sky), at this moment contains four spectrographlike rectangles of molten-lava orange. One wonders if it's only accidental that deathrow is on the sunset side of this prison?

Tho my lawyer, in an effort to ease my mind, tells me there are 87 inmates waiting to die in the state of va, there are only 11 cells beside mine in this old dungeon. "Death's disciples" dr slugmoid calls us, tho we number only three. If there are 84 others, they are kept elsewhere. Emil of course knows, executions are not carried out on a first-come-first-served schedule. If they were, at only 15-20 a year, one would figure he has *some* time left. But that's not how it works. Who exhausts the appeals process first dies first. And who appeals not at all will soon find himself on his final walk. (Bed-humpin louie, my nearest neighbor, is such a mark.) Legislators have been trying to "streamline" the process by "fast-tracking" the "obviously guilty". Obvious to whom? And isnt 'fast-track' often a euphemism for 'railroad'? If physical proximity to the instrument of death counts, i'm smack in the arms of harm's way. Look at this floorplan.

There is a world of difference between <convicted killer> & <confessed killer>, and that world, sardonically, takes no prisoners.

Immediately nextdoor to my cell is a tiny room called the "tooth grinder", the place where prepped inmates wait to die. (Bed-humpin louie is there as i write.) To the left of it is the "basting box", where those to be executed are prepped. Directly across the corridor from mine is another cell. Here sick theater, created for my benefit, is staged. To the left of it is the generator room. It harbors the "big switches". Then comes a double wall with its own heavy iron door, separating the "old building" (here) from the new, yet also quite old. Immediately to the other side of that door lies the "dance hall" [execution chamber —Ed.], while the witness room, also in the new building, lies to the other side of it, just across the hall from an elevator, stairs & lounge.

Dr slug & his goons like to call my cellblock "pervert row". With all the perversion i've encountered among prison staff –perversions both sexual & ethical– this is an epitomal case of the pot calling the kettle black. It is however true, my rowmates make little effort to hide their sex habits. While sobbinrobin's problems stem from little more than low iq (69, i hear), humpinlouie is somewhat more complex.

Louie (guard gossip) some time ago escaped the nitemare of deathrow into a bubble reality of his own blowing and nothing —not beatings pepper sprayings tasings (high voltage cattle proddings) isolation gasp-girdlings (high-voltage restraining belts) or even mock execution— could make him speak again. Except for 30min stretches of genitals-washing before the sink three or four times a day (which, coupled with the corrosive soap they give us, keeps him bloodraw), he can be seen lying on his hands most hours of the day, grinding slowly groaning lowly in his solo *frottage*. It has been over an hour since they left him nextdoor yet i've heard no sound. This concerns me.

Due to the solemnity of the occasion, even sobbinRobin, two cells to my right & across the way, is silent —reaction to the announcement of louie's execution. Over the last five days this ~~announc~~ proclamation has been read formally outside louie's cell each morning by assistant prison director becillo. If the purpose of this is indeed to make sure louie knows he's going to die, once was enuf. As to sobbinrobin, by this morn he was blubbering even before becillo had finished reciting.

14

But enuf of prison verisimilitude.... Mother's side of my lineage gets convoluted. Her mother, hannah, holds the near-shakespearean honor of being born a harridan and dying a hag. Notorious table-gossip in the family, she married 10 times in 9 decades, kicking things off by advancing from *gay divorcée* to *merry widow* by age 19! An untamable shrew, she moved thru ever lusher laps of luxury not only thanks to her looks, which were considerable, but to a gift for what i will euphemize as connubial conniving. Somewhere along the way she caught the eye of the vicomte de masoche, who immortalized her in his novel *jeanine.* Unfortunately for hannah's repute, publication took place *after* the divorce. The fact that the wussy-eyed & beatifically-bruised vicomte modeled jeanine on hannah's escapades refutes the axiom, the wicked live forever. For by the end of the book jeanine is murdered —at the ripe old age of 19! In the short version: Mother's mother was so cruel the vicomte, grandnephew of the "father of masochism" himself, felt merely divorcing her wasnt enuf. At novel's end, in a most grisly fashion, he has her killed by a coterie of her former lovers!

The most i ever said to the woman followed her telling me (as clumps of dark soil thunked onto the lid of mother's coffin) "Ve musst be kruel to be kint [kind]. You veel learn dat." Now i'd heard this probably a dozen times before —everytime in fact grandmother had flown in on her jewel-studded broom to play in "a-merry-ka". My reply, kept at ready for years, went like this. <True. But cruelty, thank goodness, makes few of us wet between the thighs.> That remark cost me a cool 2.5million deutschmarks (mother's inheritance). But i knew what it would cost long before i said it.

Hannah the horrible (as father dubbed her) finally died at 91, in paris, her home after years of *wanderlust* (pardon the bullseye) —but not before seeing the last of her children into their graves: helga, 19 (suicide by drowning); holt, 26 (suicide: pistol), and mother, also a suicide-by-drowning except she chose lethal submersion in a chronic ritual of martinis. And, o yes. Hannah left her money to a fundamentalist christian fascist, the ideologic hero of all pan-european skinheads, incidentally. And, no, i am *not* sorry for my costly remark and did *not* attend her funeral.

15

Birth in the w hemisphere in my day was not the cozy dim warm event it should be; it was floodlites cold rooms frigid fingers ε tools, uptite attendants ε on-the-fly medicine. Specially merchandised was dr caesar's cut-em-open lift-em-out zip-em-up tactic. So who knows what bypassing the head-first fall from the backstage area of life does to a person in the long haul; missing in the process that toboggan ride from birth canal to love canal, the little amphibian's head finally reaching the last lock in that nine-month journey from starlit tropical sea onto the sudden brite subarctic beach of birth, an infuriated cervix strangling one's neck while four angry lips are pursed around one's overlarge head in a preposterous pucker, a pucker aimed at nothing less than spitting one being out of another forever? And if i lack the tiptoey touch of the persnickety diarist, or that ever-so-popular pseudogothic prose so badly suffering from fallen arches, i'm sorry for that too. Yet would the reader have me do otherwise than tell it as i feel it? I think not.

Of the three types of out-of-body experience birth is worst: the original descent into maelstrom. The newborn cries, shudders ε aches for a back-into-the-body miracle. But the mother doesnt see it that way. A 10-month tumor that grows like a watermelon ε kicks like a bullcalf deserves to be out-of-body as soon as possible! And so the lost mystical staging area is never quite out of memory. We stay ever watchful for a reasonable substitute. Look at this puzzle of sympathetic phenomena.

16

The girlchild priscilla shimmers, a remote fern-fronded islet in the surging sea of my past. Priscilla prinzi was a princess of the babyboom: blue-eyed blond-haired fulbodied uncommonly pretty. But there is a corpuscular blurring (a 'floater') in the dissecting lens that prevents me from focusing her features precisely. The magnification is too strong maybe, the diffraction, dizzying. Or perhaps the lens was left in the july sun of memory too long. Perhaps such blurring is common to unhappy childhoods. Perhaps my tearyeyed squint, in the brite lites of interrogation, causes it.

Priscilla was my age. We attended 1st grade ε church together; her father was sexton there. I lived to be noticed by her. You will laff, but we're talking pure obsession here; by age six i was already a dom (dirty old man). Many females adore pretty males. On the other hand i'm sure something of my emotional disarray must have shown and unnerved her. She rarely laffed and avoided me at first. This was sad for her smile was moon to my boyhood midnite.

In 2nd grade i fared some better. I would catch her watching me whenever i read or recited, or when i sang in choir. My boy-soprano was clear & unwavering. Despite my askance glances, my sinewy limbs, my tall slouched bearing, girls liked me. After all, the era of the antihero was on the upswing and i was there to welcome it. I existed only for priscilla however, easily the loveliest girl in school, age besquat. All other girls i kept in a peripheral reality.

In 3rd grade her *winteresse* began to thaw; she was probably 8 by then. And with the arrival of spring, just months before my family left for the city, she actually spoke to me. Nothing major you understand; probably just some topical trifle which later conflagrations of the heart have since drowned out. (Some wires have gotten crossed here i see. Sensory deprivation can precipitate synesthesia.) Some time after that (i had turned 9 in march) in church, she smiled when i sang. My shameful longings had not been for naught, for she owned, even then, the maddening blond glow of the young cybill shepherd, the young sharon stone ...both of whom are likely bruns, as beautiful blonds often are. But nevermind.

After school let out for summer (i see a saturday) i biked past priscilla's house (...hoping 'gilberte' would gesture suggestively from behind the hedgerow). After a third pass she appeared. We went for a walk. Away from her house (this may have got mixedup with a second walk) i kissed her —one of those dry sips only early love can thrill to. On a bikeride the next weekend, returning from her friend carol's house, we found a woods just off green av, near tyler creek. I'd played in this woods, by this creek, for years, but never let on. We stashed our bikes, trekked to an open meadow. Across a crumpled fence was an apple orchard. We chased among the trees, kissed glancingly under the green fruit. She laffed at last —not like juanita but more reservedly, like Lilith. I caught her in the meadow and we fell in tall warm grass —hardly more than that. After which she had me drag a wooden ladder all the way to the only tree with ripe fruit (*le cerisier*) whereupon she stood picking & eating in a peculiar state of detachment which reminded me of my friend geoff under our grapearbor. And tho it is possible to inread into those trysts some parallels with juanita, or Lilith —the woods the meadow the brook, a fecundity of Nature that scented the summer wind, the splashes of sunlite that dappled our youthful bodies; the air the chase the catching; the nymphlike something in priscilla, the new nymphoria raging in my maturing body— there is a problem.

Who does not carry some tainted concept of the word nymph? But this smacks of fairytales & dragons and i catch myself crying foul over a long & oft mistaken literary tradition as the reader, without his knowledge, is galloped off on the back of the wrong daymare. And i see where this regurgitation (well, ok, *retrouvé*) of things past will make little sense to the reader who has not read my other books. And as if this werent enuf, juanita waits in the wings to perform her almost mythical dance. And then there's Lilith! Gadjizm, the press of time crushes on every side! Still, before we leave this pristine islet, this prinzidom by the sea, whose tropic sands were somehow safe from the wild surf of my home life, with its dark waters heaped like the jaws of nite on every side ...still i would be remiss if i should skip the conclusion of this near-harmless cameo.

Being barred from "kissing in a tree"
    priscilla and nathan faced a quandary.
First comes desire, then comes a date.
    "But they wont let us!"
    <So, then let's mate.>

On our third tryst, in the undergrowth of a convenient copse, straddling her legs i slipped her shorts to her knees. (We'd gotten just this far the day before.) <I want to look at you.> I touched her; she shivered; her tawny tummy drew in; she held her breath. My heart leapt at the sight of her! Her panties, far skimpier than my own cotton briefs, were coral pink and made of silk edged in white lace. (I'm still amazed, even in this age of porn & pervs, at the sexy things so many mothers buy for their daughters or permit them to wear.) I slid those dainties down. She grabbed at my bunched fingers. "No. Someone will come." Did she know something i didnt? <No they wont.> Did i know something she didnt? We wrestled. I bared a bone of contention which surprised even me ...and won —far too easily. But i didnt know that.

Out of shyness, she raised her knees, pressed them together. I stroked her body with great tenderness, great awe, great longing. Here were the lovely legs with a dancer's calfs, the *same* lovely legs i had kissed & rolled upon in the arid agonies of my verybest dreams!

...pale from the imagined love / Of solitary beds....

Little realizing the potency in my timing (result of fearing to rush ahead, fearing not to), i kept her balanced between breathless anxiety and some primal calling; frozen at the spot where those (not necessarily conflicting) emotions met, she moved only when i moved her. I watched her face intently —start of a habit i would never lose. Her expression kept me mesmerized. I parted her knees, her compact legs now clad only in white anklets. Her eyes watched me with blue fear & hot wonder. I touched her electric strangeness. The resiliency of her flesh maddened my novice fingers. I pressed my face, my dry lips, against the tops of her blond-fuzzed thighs. Knees still up, with a slow almost pulsing rhythm, her legs swayed outward & closed again, alternately squeezing my head. I have seen the wings of butterflies move in this way as they probe the gluey depths of a blossom, slow-breathing, as if caught in the caves of some chromosomal reverie.

While the emotional inks of our three meetings may bleed one into the other, the details of those trysts are etched in the memoirs of mnemosyne. If anything has been forgotten it cannot have to do with sensation. I can smell & taste her still, tho that taste did not excite me til i found it later. That the naked lotus i kissed could be opened & probed, i had no idea; neither did she tell or show me, as would a later leaner-bodied little lebanese, not in cedar shadow but under her porch, behind a sooted city lattice.

Perhaps it was ingenuity that had me turn my flower on her tummy, away from the blazing sunlite; perhaps it was a billion old bonobo erections still wedged in my dna that directed me, that drove me on. For then i too lay down, for a good while stayed pushing against her. {Push in, push in! [i thought] But into what? Surely not ...not into her *bottom!* That's not how it's done, is it? Ah, here. O yes! This will do jus fine!} My wildest dream was happening and i did not want to stop. The vice of her thighs, whether out of fear or reflex, held me fast. Yet my sudden surprise bliss, while better than any i'd known before, was still sandpapery, still barren.

Soon i fell beside her, hugging her with a ferocity only my dog, my stuffed bear, knew. We lay thus for some time. Then, in a move that startled me, she wriggled free. All at once she was over me, pressing her mouth to mine with a ruffness i would not encounter again til adulthood.

Mothernature i take this moment to salute
you who made the prissy in 'my' priscilla inabsolute!

At last allowing me to catch my breath (i vividly recall risking happy unconsciousness rather than interrupt that kiss), gazing at me intently, she repeated it ("...live lips upon a plummet-measured face"). Had she seen such kisses in some movie? She screwed her face thisway&that on mine, opening her mouth as she did so, tho i dont think knowing why. Of course i was no help. And very next day i was on my way to a boys' camp in new hampshire and would never see her again.

17

But i will not carp on the negative. One more sunset (dont think i'm not grateful) splashes its color along a quadrangle of cloud that has got caught in the grimy grip of my little window.

Good news prefaced bad today. Emil tells me, hundreds of cards & letters are received each month at greenEarth (gE) headquarters, many saying they have contacted the president, the justice dept, members of congress or the governor of va, asking that i be freed, get a fair trial, a commuted sentence etc. Dream & gag, greens of the World. Hundreds more, i'm told, have been forwarded to greenEarth international by other ngo's, namely EarthNow & ecoForce. Mostly they come from readers of my books. Scant few, sad to say, are received from the millions of kids who were once loyal fans of Lilith's tv series *captain greenEarth*. Tho gE staffers comb mainstream media databases, little sign of this once huge constituency is evident! Tho it may be, of course, the press hears but is just not telling, a practice now common where establishment dissent is concerned. And when they do tell, major weeklies like *newsweak & mime* go out of their way to lead readers to believe "The ecoactivist front has turned its back on its former hero, Nathan Schock". Corrosive venom! All that which confirms my innocence, that which isnt sucked into the conspiratorial vacuum, is whitewashed or blackedout. It grows dark in here. Where are the lites?

For instance, on the heels of my indictment, not caring to wait for a trial muchless a verdict, tv stations nationwide yanked Lilith's splendidly executed ...bad word... splendidly rendered *captain greenEarth* cartoon series from the airways. They did so because (they said) "the series is based on the life and work of an alleged antigovernment terrorist and murderer". At the time they still had to use the modifier 'alleged'. Years of striving to make environmental caring come alive for children was cut off in one collusive swoop. Blond smiling muscled captain greenEarth —generous deeds in tow, a passion to save Motherearth from yet another deadly villain— vanished from the airways! Since then all the comics softcover books videos toys games ɛ clothing, having ignited in the world marketplace, began disappearing.

If all this seems hurried, compressed, it is. Must get these facts on paper for God knows when.... But never mind that. Weak moment there. Now then, where are the lites? Can hardly see. Are they saving electric, storing it for.... Horrible. The unknown can be most unsettling.

As to Lilith's cartoon creation. The problem was, still is, the establishment doesnt raise an eyebrow when violent games for kids make millions of dollars, so long as they support establishment values. But when the game making billions is *critical* of the establishment, and when it has the artistic audacity to make its criticisms exciting as well as constructive, well then, the establishment may just react ...specially if the establishment has a repressed destructive underside it is not ready to face muchless cure. In just over 2yrs (1994-96) Lilith's cartoon series became a hit internationally. With 23% of profits going straight to the coffers of gE international (producers of her cartoon) –instead of into the pockets the usual hollywood moguls ɛ poggles– gE was soon basking in the glow of unprecedented capital growth among green organizations! But even as this windfall empowered enviros as never before, corpolitical moguls ɛ poggles —whose megaprofits depend on the much-secreted crime of trashing our Planet with impunity— grew panicky.

We must briefly pause to define 'corpolitical'. In my 1983 book, *the ungreening of tomorrow*, i coined the word to unify in language what is unified in fact: big corps ɛ the politicos they keep in their (very deep) pockets; a union of forces which, tho eroding to personal freedom and illegal according to the u.s constitution, has nonetheless surreptitiously stolen the power from the many (democracy) and placed it in the hands of the few (oligarchy). This momentous capitalist sleight-of-hand has turned much of the civilized world into a corporate autocracy (economic dictatorship). Because of its ability to join in language those governmental ɛ corporate agendas which are joined in fact, use of the word corpolitical (in its several forms) can save us much time ɛ paper waste. But now, as to that mementos sleight of hand....

Quickly defined it is capitalism v democracy. Readers wishing to know how this little trick of global dimensions was carried off will have to look elsewhere.

For there is not time for us to tackle it in these pages. Those curious to know how i enraged the wealthiest 20% of the western world –those who brought to power this economic dictatorship we slave under– a good place to start would be my essay, "the invisible crucible of our times" (subtitled, "how and why capitalists sabotage democracy"). But we must press on. For the big question here is, How is it possible that environmentalists have been labeled a "threat to national security", and that we greens are now called "enemies of the state"?

For the answer, recall the ussr collapse. While most of the "free world" celebrated the freeing of east europe from autocratic brutality, and the freeing of our Planet from imminent nuclear holocaust, the u.s military ε federal police were crestfallen. The pentagon, like its cia, the fbi, ins, atf ε many other large policing organizations, could think only of job security. For without a real live enemy, they, like the rest of us, were suddenly safe (read: out of war work). So did they, with happy hearts, look for peacetime employment? Not on your life. These tax-supported warlords immediately set to work replacing a grand old enemy with a grand new one. For while the old standby, communist china, was the obvious option for a scary new enemy, ye old "yellow dragon" had not breathed fire outside its own purlieus for years, had long slipped back into its legendarily deep cave. So, with no hope of spinning the chinese dragon into an enemy anyone would believe in, the pentagon, and all its generals ε arms-mfg bedbuddies, panicked. What to do?

 "O for the good ol days of imminent nuclear armageddon."

Sudden peace between the superpowers had spread happiness unequally. While the one (old red bear) was busily occupied trying to feed and put back to work an impoverished nation, the other (old sam eagle) found itself with a vast global policing machine suddenly out of work. Pentagon warriors —historically undeterred by the mind-numbing numbers of young sacrifice interred in the cemetery directly across the street from where they plot ε scheme— were quick to find more fodder for their molochian appetites: "Protecting energy resources for the free world", ahem, was their first foul fabrication. (The mideast oil "crisis" is still with us as i write.) Nonrenewable resources, of course. Even as the beer empties ε party favors were being sweptup around the dismantled berlin wall, u.s war ε police organizations hit upon a workable solution. (Sad to report, brite ideas are not the property of constructive minds alone. But you came to this book knowing that.)

"Hey, I know! How about a collection of SMALL enemies whose combined threat we can make look equal to that of the big enemy we just lost?"

And so the concepts of "rogue nation" ε "international terrorist organization" quickly rose to prominence in the fed.-parroting poppress. Iraq iran syria lebanon pakistan n.korea ε even, yes, tiny cuba ε palestine, suddenly loomed as a league of rogue nations, all possessing "sophisticated" warmaking capabilities; all possessing a sudden "lethalness" formerly unsuspected by anyone including the nations themselves ε their neighbors, and all having dossiers just bursting with grudges against you-know-who.

"A 300billion$-a-year war machine saved! Phew! That's as close as we here at the pentagon ever wanna come ta world peace, thanks!"

Arclites glow in the chill moist air above the prison walls. Tho their hazy amber fills my smutty little window, it is too dim to write by ...for across the hall theyre still toying with the generators. I had hoped to scribble out these items before "lites out". Now this. The way things are going next it'll be me.... But i am too anxious, i see. Maybe i should just abandon ...No, wait. Here they come! Feeble ε flickering but at least lit. I shall cram every sentence (as a terrified runaway packs her suitcase before that repulsive ε cruel man returns, to once again....) and we'll be done with it, reader.

But what could replace the old "red menace" within our suddenly safe borders? With a "red villain" no longer threatening national security, with no "reds" or "pinkos" to torment prosecute or waste, the life of the fed.cop —those not playing in that other farcical sandbox, the drug war— no longer had meaning. Yet, did their chiefs, or their keepers in congress, seek to downsize these lumbering bureaucrasaurians in some guise of parity with the collapsed cold war, and thereby give back to us taxpayers a wage we could live on? Not on your struggling lifestyle, they didnt.

While our fed.-pampering poppress kept us distracted with all the inane "issues" it could find –celeb murders in hollywood, lowdown sex in highup places– the fed(stoy)'s war ε police departments put their heads together (rare moment) over the one goal they could absolutely agree on: Rule by force. And what did they comeup with? You guessed it. Homegrown terrorism. With its traditionally "fuzzy" sources, "unknowable" strengths & "unpredictable" motives, terrorism on the u.s homefront became the switcheroo of choice for public enemy #1. To think our hard-earned taxes pay for such sinister brainstorming.

And so it was the press began to pose a new & peculiar sort of hype: ECOACTIVISTS ECSTATIC: WHERE TO AIM GREEN POWER NEXT?; MOTHER EARTH GETS BIG GREEN LAWYER, CORPORATE POLLUTERS GROW FIDGETY. Even investment slicks taunted the wary eye. CAPTAIN GREENBUCKS $CRAMBLES, $UMMIT OF CASH-FLOW $TILL NOT IN $IGHT; and, CAPT. GREENBUCKS FLEXES NEW MUSCLE: PLANET PLUNDERERS BEWARE; and, GREEN IDEOLOGY MARCHES TOWARD VICTORY: ARE CONSUMERISM & FREE ENTERPRISE DOOMED? The intratext & subtext in every case being, "Hey, capitalist america! Are you going to just sit by while greens grab your money & power? The threat to big corporations and their (disappearing-ink) underwriters (the fed.) was clear. Corpolitical crime-in-the-name-of-greed being put by greens more&more on the public's radar screen, was in jeopardy. Like a bloodied sun, a newage reality loomed on the horizon of business-as-usual corporape. Captain greenbucks, socalled, growing bigger & more powerful by the day, had to be squashed, or olympus dc would soon quake with the thunder-blows of gods & giants. Condensed version: ecogreen v greedgreen to-the-death.

Now theyre flickering like gaslites, like candles. This waiting is awful. There they go again. The arclites outside have died as well. Perhaps public vengeance has blackedout the whole town this time, maybe the whole state! Maybe only those places with their own generators... But i choose my words poorly. Yet if prison generators cannot supply enuf electric... What i mean is, how can they expect to exterminate us at all humanely if...? There, they're coming back up again ...slowly. Perhaps now they will get it over with.

While this media scaretactic united the corporich FEW, We, the MANY, remained as politically apathetic as ever. And so it was just a matter of time before this headline raised its ugly head.

ECOCZAR SQUARES OFF WITH ENVIROS: GREEN IDEOLOGY IN QUESTION

What sort of argument could the head of an organization sworn to protect the ecology of our nation (the epa) possibly have with its only committed constituency, environmentalists? So critical to the narrative is the answer to this question, it will have to wait for its own hollywood moment. Til then it must suffice to say....

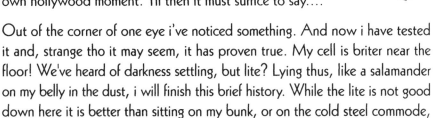

Out of the corner of one eye i've noticed something. And now i have tested it and, strange tho it may seem, it has proven true. My cell is briter near the floor! We've heard of darkness settling, but lite? Lying thus, like a salamander on my belly in the dust, i will finish this brief history. While the lite is not good down here it is better than sitting on my bunk, or on the cold steel commode, which is my only chair.

...Summarily. It was not honest governance at a federal level which caused this subtle switch in public "enemies", but interagency collusion. In a series of covert maneuvers, fed. spindoctors, and their groupies in the popmedia, together saw to it that the old "red menace" was replaced by a new "green menace". And thus the age of the ecoterrorist, the ecoguerrilla, was born. And now to the final question.

Today, corporations in bed with politicos comprise a smoke&-mirrors corpollosus of global deadliness.

With the many antigovernment & white-supremacy militias scattered around the nation, why were environmental activists selected as the homeland terrorists of choice? or as terrorists at all, for that matter? How did we become the domestic archenemy? Herein, dear reader, lies a puzzle-piece of a quality which truth-seekers dream of but rarely find. Because those in charge of the destiny of our nation (which should be "we the people" but no longer is) could not be less worried about suppressing freedom fiters or white supremacists. As the pentagonal head of the armed forces put it: "Not ta worry. We could squash their combined powers in a matter of hours." Beside, as my friend the baron said in his best play (pj priapus is lecturing nolan clarke here):

> The militia are more concerned with the stability of democracy in America than our politicians have been for decades! You want the big picture? Then understand: The only freedom-fighting that goes on inside our federal government mimics the "freedom-fighting" that's been going on in Wall Street and Madison Avenue for decades: That is, the battle to free *capitalism* from the constraints of democracy. *That's* the only freedom our bureaucrats are concerned with anymore. The Fed has

become little more than a white-collar mafia, extorting the hard-working taxpayer for protections he doesnt need. You'll never get the big picture till you've gotten this. Nobody does. So you'll be one of few. The only threat government takes seriously anymore is what threatens the corporate wealth to which it is married. And the only ones really threatening corporate wealth are environmentalists. That's why to *all* bureaucrats: The greener you are the scarier you are.

Because greens were gradually but surely proving to a grassroots populace worldwide: Corpolitical forces are exploiting your & your children's Planet and everything on it. And as this ruthless oligarchy grows mightier, communities –all communities, Wild & domestic; plant, animal & human– are suffering ...those which arent outright extirpated or exterminated! Faithful enviro watchdogs –despite bigmonied smokescreens, whitewashes & blackouts– daily were making it ever clearer to the little guy: The bottomline corpolitic mantra (ie: "Sorry but we cant afford it") is merely gluttonspeak for, "Screw you, little guy. We're in this for us not you". And so, despite billion-dollar propagandist haybales & sandbagging, green truth was weakening corpolitical dikes worldwide. We had to be muzzled, else the tacit tyranny of the few HAVES (over we the many HAVE-NOTS) would be known far&wide.

Thorjizm! There they go! Listen to them whine! The generators, i mean, not the ladies upstairs, who hear them also and are howling & bleating. I find my breath stoppingup; my heartbeats stagger, regroup, restagger. I dont care what he did, this is a beastly solution; proof positive, civilization may have knowledge but is devoid of wisdom. We are at half-power now. These minutes of victim on "broil" are long indeed.... Great Gaia, help him die! ...An eternity in this heinous hiatus! Tick... tick... tick... tick... tick.... There, the lites are back. Is it done? One prays so for the sake of the executee. So, where were we? (Must stay busy.) You civic isolationists (non-voters, tsk) can skip all this if it's toomuch (political) reality in a single gulp. I know you wont believe this, but there are those who want desperately to understand such things.

And so, step by step, everyday events –business fires, industrial accidents and the like– began to be attributed to environmentalists. Because at the start the fed. laid blame on a largely makebelieve "violent green fringe" (socalled "guerilla greens", persons & groups which legitimate greens never heard of and *nobody* could locate), few questioned this trend. Tho allegations were many, arrests were few ɛ convictions none. Even so, the poppress, talons-out, swooped in on every fed. press release like it was fresh roadkill, never questioning facts ɛ sources. Afterall, hadnt the collapse of communist rule in europe left the mainstream press in the same pickle barrel with the pentagon ɛ fed.police, in the same brine barrel with the huge war-industry backing them all? It had, of course. And hadnt the poppress lost a valuable (read, news-selling) "enemy" when it lost the "communist threat", a threat it worked to the bone for decades! For even as global capitalism was draining the pigments from reds ɛ pinkos everywhere....

Great Gaia, here we go again! How could that little man, that flimsy marriage of skin ɛ bone, who almost bled to death nextdoor to my cell just a couple hours ago, have survived even a normal house current? ...While they left him to wait alone in the tooth-grinder he tried to cheat the public of its vengeance by hacking at his testicles with the edge of a metal mirror. Yet i smell the stink here of still another of dr slug's "scientific studies", a thing he arranges when the condemned is without representation. Then again, few readers i'm sure care to confront this incredible circus of cruelty i've been dropped into.

For the poppress, the collapse of the berlin wall was fast losing its sparkle. Its crime&grime mindset was discovering a terrible truth about itself ɛ its consumers. "Peace + love = boring news." As happened with ecology news, owners ɛ editors had not the faintest idea of how to make constructive human achievement exciting reading or viewing, or, at the very least, interesting. Positive copy was as alien to them as positive thinking. Like an old homicide coroner out of work, the popmedia's boredom at facing another day without blood, sex ɛ gadgetry was glaring. Why should this be?

For the same reason some reader's (i shall resist citing any types) cringe and pageoff when the storyline (read, in-your-face blood,sex&gadgetry) pauses to reflect on an issue intelligently. Like *now*. In fact, as long as we're addressing it: Those who've had quite enuf of this learn-while-you-read thing may jump off here... while those wishing to understand how environmentalists ɛ ecologists became worldclass villains to be hunted to extinction may continue reading in the column to the right.

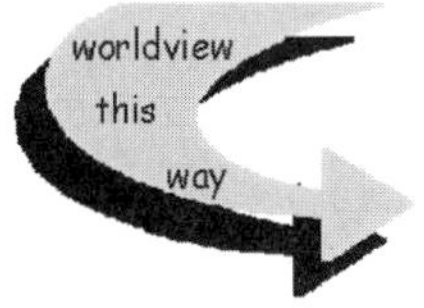

18

And so i lost mossville, with all its faults, gained a filthy city with little beside faults; and so i lost blond priscilla, gained a dozen vacant-eyed dark-haired waifs who thought i was from mars. And as if these losses werent enuf, circumstance began setting me up for still more.... But to keep to some calendric sense of continuity, perhaps now is as good a time as any to introduce juanita. But only because the leap from young priscilla to grown Lilith, jumping over juanita in the process, would put a kink (if not a chasm) in that continuity, and because to hopscotch over juanita (without bending to pick up the colored jacks in their chalked boxes) would render the rest of the game senseless.

But before we scoopup those jacks, one may wonder what became of priscilla? Did she endup the heroine in a hodgson play? a lotti grisi who somehow escaped my notice? O, yes. With those dream-legs of hers she could have danced alright! Yet, like most beautiful women of her era & class, she doubtless bought into the expectations of some suburban castle or other.

It was 4yrs after losing priscilla i met juanita. I was 13 and, as i've said, it was quite a year. Every

The poppress (read: sensationalist media) had long failed to train its audience to appreciate constructive reportage. In short, few news consumers had a thirst to hear about the virtues of a healthy Planet, a diversified & healthy speciation —even if it is our own! Few wanted to hear, day after day, about global freedom, international goodwill, personal-belief tolerance, lots of official handshakes & piles of peace treaties. And (not to put *all* the blame on the mainstream media) the public at large, needing its daily adrenaline fix, had long forgotten the benefits of well-rounded reportage. It's no accident, for instance, that blood, sex & gadgetry are, in a fritening number of instances, inseparable from high entertainment. And it's also no accident, these are the props of war. Yes, sex included. But this also will have to wait.

Guards xodion & zodion are in the corridor high5ing each other. I am to gather from this display that bed-humpin louie is officially dead. I now have no doubts, he had not a single witness looking out for him. Even sase nuns (not self-addressed stamped envelopes but sisters against summary execution), who are sobbinrobin's last friends in this world, did not showup for social-dropout louie. (Since he did not acknowledge their visits, they abandoned him. That he never humped his cot or bathed his genitals when they were around apparently meant nothing to them.) Dr slug & goons should be in very good spirits for a few days.

So, with only the old standbys (jew v arab, orange erin v green erin, tutsi v hutu, balkan v balkan, khomaniacs v husseiniacs; in fact, politicians generally v everybody) ...with only these hackneyed old enemies left to spatter the headlines, the new green menace looked very attractive to the poppress. And so, just as the color red had bled its way into the 20th century, green seemed destined to bleed us into the 21st.

summer when school ended my parents would crate me up ɛ ship me off. Starting age 5, i was sent to a protestant "bible camp" for several weeks. Pleas to my father concerning its schoolish horrors won me, aged 7 thru 12, a summerlong slot at his brother ɛ sister's farm in upper ny state. Enter here the best months of my childhood; six successive summer sabbaticals which taught: Agrarian life, tho difficult, has physical ɛ spiritual rewards, the life-potent richness of which is not quickly explained. I learned also that my parents should never have been parents. Thanx to some family row or other, however, this agrarian phase ended and i was shipped for the next three summers (aged 13-15) to a fundy christian preserve in nw jersey. There, at gospel-in-the-birches, i met juanita.

Juanita darc was 11 that summer. Recall gets cropped here. I cannot be sure some of 12- ɛ 13yearold juanita hasnt crowded into the initial imprint: white female (skin: pale andalusian); about four-foot-ten (as we measured back then); paleblue eyes, a bit bulgingly big; black hair tied with a yellow leather thong, hair which reached the lumbar hollow of her slender back; brite face with clear complexion; a latin (pouty) lower lip; mature body dressed in jeans ɛ tanktop, revealing a provocative bloom in both buttocks ɛ breasts. Juanita was an intelligent sensitive girl. Emotionally advanced as she was, and emotionally scattered as i was,

The lites go out at 9. Must hurry. A couple more items and you non-green readers will be up to speed. Sorry about the driveby history lesson but without it most of us will not be reading from the same page. Those of you familiar with most of this sad ɛ gruesome background, bear with us, please. I am doing my damndest to make this as painless as possible, my personal circumstances besquat.

At this moment several million kids in the u.s are being taught that their hero (and my animated alterego), captain greenEarth, is not, and never was, the "reluctant warrior", the "planetary patriot" Lilith's cartoon painted him to be. Theyre being taught instead that he is the "cold-blooded killer of a fine government official" —when, that is, they are spared the many smuttier muckings which smear the pages ɛ screens of "adult" mediums. Worse, this fed. propaganda is being spread *internationally.* (*Captain greenEarth* was being viewed in 42 countries when it was squashed. Godzilla's gonads! How does one fite such a vast ɛ unprincipled opponent?

No losses hurt so much as losing the kids —not my final arrest, trial or imprisonment. There's no time to mince words here. It was ecoSec charles strickland, in league with the cia ɛ pentagon's "psycops" (u.s army psyche operations), who brought the "green menace" lie to life. And it was them who launched ɛ guided the fbi ɛ atf in its assaults against green activists across the u.s, bringing about the present state of affairs.

Before we let loose of this... Stop now and think, those readers who believe such things cant happen in a democracy. Exactly. I mean, *exactly!* They shouldnt. But they *can* in an oligarchy. And *will* in a police state. And how timely too! Just when the corpolitical establishment was scrambling for some way to silence the green message! to shut us up before the man in the street realized: All that he learns from the

the 2yrs between us quickly melted to zero. Tho physically bigger than she, in most ways i thought of her as my better.

Her mother (source of her irish genes), a keen-eyed statuesque woman of rational disposition, was camp nurse. I would meet her on my second day —for a chat ε a checkup. Her father (the latin side) was a missionary in venezuela, i think, and was away from home most of the time. Ever hovering "mama" was also nurse at her school (nyc). Juanita knew her way around camp "in [her] sleep", having attended there since age6.

I'd arrived in time for supper. As i stood in line before the cafeteria a line of girls approached. I spotted her at once. For standing there was zefferelli's juliet, years before she existed on film: facial blend of transparent purity ε seablue surprise; classic madonna face touched by just enuf titianesque *joufflu*-ness not to sacrifice the shading beneath the high cheekbones. She smiled: brite translucent smile! As with priscilla, it was instant electric. Yet her mature body, her all-absorbing eyes, left me even shyer than i was by nature.

My naked izzat (some would say soul) must have stood out in that lineup of boys, a carrot among cabbages. I felt gangly, exposed. ("He at once girl-hungry and girl-shy, held himself nervously aloof.") Most boys were compact animals of action. Head in the clouds, i poppress passes first thru two filters: the wallstreet filter ε fed. filter: that corpolitical sieve whose goal is to spread blind consumerism thruout the world while making our tweedledum/tweedledee system of politics appear as something other than the authority-without-representation it actually is —politics without we-the-people representation, that is.

It is almost 9. In a moment... But there's the warning flash. It will be dark in one minute, and the security lites are too dim to permit... unless one is desperate. Maybe one more sentence.

In a word, today as i write, all the gains made in environmental issues since the 60s are under siege, and industry treats the fed's assault on ecoactivists as if.... That's it; theyre out. I can see the words but not the lines on the page. Nite-blindness. Had it since being so often glare-blinded on enviro assignments at sea.

Madison & Dalton White

It will be better if i close my eyes for awhile. This place has thoroly depressed me (again) anyway.

Cant sleep. A slomo snowfall is muffling the arclites above the tower ramparts. That one cannot muffle lite i dont care. That's how it seems. Now that my eyes have become accustomed to this teacup of terminal twilite i live in, i can finish this —dull ε dense as it may seem to some. What would a child do with such an obstinate reality? We will therefore make believe... magic words! We will *pretend* we must cram for a popquiz. No. Make that, final exams. For perhaps "school will be out" for me sooner than i think!

In a word, today as i write, all the gains made in environmental issues since the 60s are under siege. Industry was quick to read the fed. assault on greens as a signal it's okay now to return to old plunder&pillage tactics. In short, corporape was often immobilized by introspection. I felt her eyes on me as we filed inside, as we ate. Like those of Lilith, their flung-wide guilelessness was both exciting & disarming. And they sparkled when she laffed. But unlike Lilith, she laffed at the slitest provocation. O i liked her alright.

19

Before we get down&dirty, however, permit me to say... To the criminologist, the political historian, the psychologist studying my case, perhaps many years from now, i want it known upfront: Juanita's role in Lilith's biography is no more, no less, than it was in my own life. Detectives of nomenclature, literary investigators in pursuit of a lineage of lambdanomes (names beginning with 'L') —tracking them from the ancient middle east to 20th century america— are sure to be disappointed. Old hounds & young, sniffing the underbrush of my recall in pursuit of *anything* L-tainted, from rhymed theory to reasoned gossip, are sure to be disappointed as well. I advise them to turn back now. And to those bounty-hunting belletrists —arrest warrants in one fist, braces of baying hounds in the other— chasing down a booty of analogous belles, they too will leave empty-handed. For i make a poor procatalept, and any such nexus of lowly *animatas* (found cowering in shadow, naked, drenched in guilt) will turnout to be but the waifs of circumstance, the little invented is back in vogue and, with it, the corpse of a decaying monster has been exhumed ...it walks among us, and its name is the same: *profit without conscience.* It was strickland's goons who raided greenEarth's san francisco hq, stole cash, records, destroyed our computers, smashed equipment all over the building including even the handicapped-visitor cart. And it was strickland & his goons who kidnaped, tortured, raped & murd... But let's not go *there,* dear God, just yet. May a cult of cannibals tear off her killer's testes with pathogenic teeth and, chanting merrily, spit their gonads into a kettle of boiling oil! —petroil!

Some things grow clearer in darkness. As i lie in my bunk i can see it is, after all, briter near the floor. The glass frontwall of my cell does not reach ceiling height; therefore the lites in the corridor cast a shadow that descends obliquely past my bunk, strikes the floor near the backwall. Unfortunately that brow of stone does not inhibit the security cam. It hangs on its bracket out there and its wideangle owleye misses little, nite or day. Only if i position myself close to the door of my cell is some privacy possible. For instance, when i must extract from my person.... But why do i blabber on like this? We must finish. Tomorrow's inquisitive minds need to know the truth today.

To hell with it. We're about done here anyway. Suddenly this cot feels damp & cold. O great Frith, wrestle this heaving heart into submission! Like a good poltroon, my reader has read the papers, watched the news, and thinks sHe understands the big picture, great Mother of Earth! And as happens when news & truth arent even passing acquaintances, propaganda rules the land!

So, this ending is what i must live with ...and die by. The crimes i've mentioned, and thousands of ghosts of someone's overactive imagination.

Seen from the level of this rickety table on which i scribble tonite, priscilla ɛ juanita are harbingers of, and handmaidens to, Lilith. That may be the expurgated version but it is as good as any. For while the reader may see in juanita only an average girl (however gifted), to *me*, at *that* time —in *that* sunlit moonlit starlit lamplit or unlit lakeside woodland setting— she fell little short of being a fulfledged nymph. But there's that word again. If we were splitting hairs ...as i suppose we should since she was 11 when we fell in love, 13 when we parted... then perhaps the proper designation would be *fledgling* nymph –ie, nymphette– the tainted aspects of which term raise yet another problem —a most rueful problem, to be sure. But we have lost enuf time here as it is.

others like them, go untried, unpunished (how can sweet Motherearth still turn?), and yet little of this is known to jon ɛ jane q public and their kids! And now all those trusting young minds, so desperately seeking a new hero (in a world full of angry ɛ bitter antiheroes), have lost the noblest hero they may ever know! So, to hell with it! All is blurred now anyway. My tiny script scurries along the page like a crippled insect with ink on its feet. Emil will have difficulty deciphering this. So let's be done with it.

The snare is triggered; the noose tightens around the poor creature's neck; a bloody froth trickles from the wick of its mouth. What are these rumblings in the Earth, dear fiver? What do they mean? Why does the sky darken so? Why do the clouds tumble angrily, ashen ɛ black, above us? Why does it rain ruby ice, (little) hrairoo, and the meadow run with rivers of blood? Is the black rabbit of inlé coming? O tell us, fiver, please do! Is the day of zorn upon us?

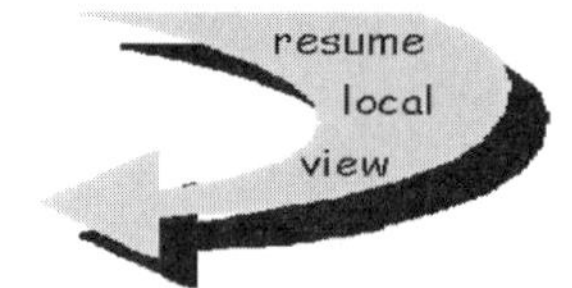

20

Love grew in skirmishes. Alphabetized, waiting in parallel lines on coed daytrips (hiking, Naturewalks, canoeing/boating, horseriding), juanita would drift slowly back toward me from the girl's 'd's while i, for my part, would advance from the boy's 's's toward her; a mutual gravity that became routine. The most public symptom of this attraction however entered toward the close of that first summer.

Morn ɛ nite, chapel ritual was conducted on a hillside overlooking a lake: rows of ruffhewn planks set in tiers, surrounded by birches ɛ tall pines. In a back row, among the older boys, sitting behind juanita, i'm the one slouched forward, elbows on knees, ever trying to suppress my height. My face is so close i can smell the soapy freshness of her morning self. All eyes nearby shift from the preacher as juanita, slipping back on her plank, slips into my hand a hairbrush the color of her mischievous eyes, which meet mine with a glancing sidelong glitter. Lovingly, surreptitiously, with long languid strokes, i brush the hair that falls darkly between my knees almost to the ground. That we, stroker ε stroked, werent caught ε humiliated, is teleonomic of the freedoms we would inveigle two summers later.

By august of each year what started out as mere psychic abandon took on a sense of somatic desperation. During games she would brush past me, or i past her, or i would catch her offbalance, "save her" from falling. Less frequently, as ambient space began to warm to the idea of our mutual longing, some mediating force would suddenly permit us to collide, body-to-moving-body, yet be held guiltless for such "accidental" touching within the seamless sense of whatever activity. At such moments tensorSpace would collapse and we would surrender all to gravity's imperative —tumbling gratefully into the clover ε dandelions, giggling nuzzling hot heap of glancing guileless groping. But that's just part of it. In the leapfrog to august i've forgotten to pick up some jacks.

21

After breakfast came chapel, then swimtime —at luke lake. The best swimmers in camp, we were permitted to swim out to "our raft" —or so we named it, as we found the official name (the arc) a bit farfetched. The moment we arrived we would take to the water, lukewarm by august. Juanita is among the few females i've known who didnt immerse herself slowly, on tiptoe, as tho a prized part of her might melt in water. Whether from beach or dock, this laffing naiad simply ran, jumped or dove in.

We spent hours out there, phototroping like sunflowers. On occasion she would raise her head, astonishing me with her sudden ethereal strangeness (*extrañezas*): "I swear I remember traveling in europe, as a child ...maybe in a past life, huh? [pale eyes staring off into space] I just *know* I was in paris ...almost in medieval times!" Tho i may focus on the unusual saying or remark, i suspect our typical conversation was mostly quotidian, she turning her latin side up to brown deliciously while we talked, me turning my teutonic one down and *still* frying. (Bad word-choice.) What we were *really* doing was groping each other mentally; i feltup her naked nubile thoughts, she manipulated my imaginings (*ensueños*). We would have groped for each other under the dark water (and sometimes did) except that the apportioned swatch of sand ended under water deep enuf to romp & chase in but not deep enuf (or opaque enuf) to hide the kind of romping we had in mind. If we wanted privacy we had to go deeper, beyond the sandy bottom.

That she was unrevolted by the cold organic ooze which purled thru our toes when we stood in deep water amazed me. "Squishy! Like worms!" she squealed, standing quite still, laffing eyes looking off behind or thru me as she pictured what oozed below. A dragonfly came by, hovered above the water by her arm, its translucent –purpling, azuring– wings rattling like oriental fans. And there she could stay, smiling, changing from foot to foot to keep from sinking out of sight in the muck. Soon, by dint of the rhythm of my bobbing and the unwitting skid of knees against her thighs, she figured out: "Youre not standing youre treading water! It's *you* who cant stand it [the oozy bottom]!"

Then, "Ooooeeesh!" Eyes wide, she bends forward, fingers fishing inside her suit. <Whatsamatter?> "Maybe it was jus my imagination... <What?> ...but something jus went inside my suit."

It wasnt your imagination... [Huh?] ...It was mine.

"You dope" she said with a sly laff.

As to deeper talk? From the scraps at nmeny's fingertips i can reconstruct only repeatedly visited topics. For instance she often recited favorite verse.

Inebriate of air am I,
  debauchee of the dew,
  reeling thru the summer's rich
  intoxicating brew!

Her talk had a way of bouncing around in my head without my conscious consent. I'd often catch an excerpt, unbidden, replaying itself in one of many rehearsal rooms in the uncharted conservatory of my mind. Such replays usually happened at nite. As a lay on my bunk going over the day's events i would discover with surprise, i could recite this or that thing she'd said. She also had a habit of quipping titles or phrases from favorite songs to fit the moment. Knowing nothing of the poetry of the woman she called "my emily", and little of the music she liked, i often found myself hardpressed to know whether it was a song or a poem i had unwittingly memorized. Like the lines above, a few of these have stuck til this day. Perhaps it is its sheer tackiness (syrupy stickiness) which helps glue it in memory.

The dawn is breaking thru a gray tomorrow,
but the memories we share will banish sorrow.

Juanita was bilingual i'm sure, tho i never heard her converse at length in spanish. The peppering of her rapid brite speech with spanish idioms often left me well behind the pace of her patter. Except that her haughtiness was mostly muted where i was concerned, her genius might have put me off. On the other hand we were alike in many ways. I think it was our aloofness from the crudities of our coevals (anchorite & anchoret) that secured our relationship. Both of us uprooted from rural settings, we were instant outcasts in our new urban homes. Sensitive youngsters, life, as given by civilization, was not good enuf. The city lurked at our backs like a razor-toothed hunger, always ready & happy to strike. So we became polished pretenders; little survivors, we blottedout that highrise lowbrow heap of humans and their garbage we'd inherited, learned to create on demand a "world closer to the heart's desire" as old khayyám (greatgranddaddy of existentialism) once sang...trapped as *he* was in an earlier version of the same sort of societal sewer. Reading was a favorite escape: she, poems of beauty & passion; me, stories of high adventure. It was juanita who opened my mind to poetry, coaxed it from fairytale fissures in my past, made poetry part of everyday life. Poetry, for her, paralleled wisdom.

With every april shower comes a thunderstorm of tears.
For every taste of ecstasy we eat the gruel of years.

Like many children, we shared a love of the fantastic, the bizarre. Both of us for instance had seen the films *the hunchback of notre dame & the phantom of the opera* and read *the monkey's paw & the tell-tale heart.* Here was commonground —between her esthetic sensibility and my love of adventure. To that end, she was "devouring" in secret (that last summer) a novel by a frenchman (i think) full of racy scenes, parts of which she read with unforgettable intensity. We loved to sketch & to paint; she preferred brite fuzzy images, pastels mostly; i liked stark ones: bloody scarlets, snowy whites, lacquered blacks. I suppose this is telling. But strangest of all –for young persons, surely– we shared a fear: separation. O i dont mean just from each other. But something deeper. 'Dissever' is a better word for loppingoff the sort of unity we felt growing between us: a linking of vital organs, a system of one blood, one heart, one brain, that sort of sensibility.

22

Sunshine. Sound of children at play. Beneath the raft there is a pullip-pullaping of wavelets against the barrels which buoy us. We lie prone, talking, watching each other. Our wood-plank islet, rocking gently, is womb-warm. Our fingers, hesitant, stagger-walk toward each other, retreat; our knees (her left, my right) follow suit til they touch: ><. Fingers, again, advance; like sandcrabs, side-stilting, grapple {} and retreat {   }; repeat {}. Her touch, and the sight of her berry-brown body so near, excite me. "It's a standoff."

It is not. Your wrist was off the deck. I pin her hand quickly, palm down, to the planks. Why this is important to me i dont know; and how she can laff after losing i dont know either, teeth, bunny-big, silverbraced. We rotate onto our sides. The outline of her hip, in silverblue onepiece (bikinis were forbidden), stirs & fritens me; my own body feels suddenly immature. How could i foresee that two summers hence she would say "Your body turns me on ...'n' scares me too"? In a lakeside copse, beyond and just to the left of those vast blue eyes, a bird sang in couplets, "prettypretty prettypretty".

Item. In a minute i'm going to write "soul" (if they dont come to collect mine first). My deployment of the term disdains all connection to formal religion. I imply only 'essence of being', 'essential fire', that sort of thing; the spark of life socalled, as this is linked to the Cosmos at large. Some would call it spirit, *anima nous,* shade, id, izzat, quiddity. Most say soul. Father would say *wiltgist;* juanita: *entraña,* or *alma.* While i call it zizm. But call it what you will, it's all physical as hell to me, not spiritual. It's a sorry fact: What we are too ignorant to palpate with our five senses and crude instruments we call spiritual or deny outright. Why must we always apply some non-physical palliative to things we dont understand? At any rate, the zizm to which *i* allude animates stone, star & starfish alike.

We lay on that raft for hundreds of hours over three summers, the equivalent of 40days & 40nites —and still the floodwaters of desire would not recede, still they buoyed our tiny ark! Two by two our thoughts, like proud specimens, would trot aboard, as our souls (there's that word), like doves searching the face of the deep, sought each other. But all this is still unclear. What am i trying to say? There is a churning in the gut, a wrenching pressure in the groin, and somehow these unite into a single impulsion. In special cases (and maybe this is what we call love) the knot in the throat, the stone on the heart, join in.

Still unclear. Let's try this another way. If at death the aura of life is seen to slip off the failing body –like a slippery skin off a stiffening snake– and if this life energy can gather into a ball and depart the flesh, then perhaps, in the same way, the same life-force (the churnings, the pressures, the constrictions) can ballUp, tumble toward the beloved, sizzling & crackling like fireball litening. It is this i will call animal passion, luv, lust.

Juanita's pangs were no less real. But avoiding the trap of details, she & her ladypoets put it another way: My being gathers itself around you in a shimmering sigh. Same idea, just adding juanita's love of fuzzy images, subtracting my liking for sharp ones. Usually she was quoting her emily, but this i didnt realize til years later.

> This is the place where summer strives
> to kill "the White unseen";
> where grisly frost, as dew disguised,
> lies intimate with green.

"I wish I could write like that" she would sometimes say, hoping i would delve with her into the poem and discover her brilliant tamperings. In fact, for years i parroted some of her favorite lines as tho they were unadulterated dickinson. Only when i began parodying poets for pay in a series that ran in *harkness* magazine (PANS & PASTICHES ON POPULAR POETS) did i realize i'd been duped. Like godfrey day quoting *the prismatic asphodaffodel* (by knight), for years i quoted –freely, shamelessly– dickinson by darc! Of course she did not mean to deceive me. I'm convinced my ignorance in this area was just another artifact of what i call the psychic blindness of my youth. In fact, i'm sure her feelings were often hurt by my lack of plaudits for her clever (often brilliant) paraphrases, parodies & plagiarisms. And times when i *did* understand those geyser-gushes of gentle genius, i'm sure i failed to wreathe her in the laudatory laurels she deserved. This was doubtless because they were spouted in context with the rest of an average day's average chatter.

(The time has come to stop abusing my lip. I would like to have just said <snippets & quips spouted in quotidian context>. But i bit my lip again ...for the sake of that certain reader i am desperately trying to hang onto. But it's like dealing with a blackmailer. And so, in place of the explicatory rant all this lip-biting deserves, i am going to ask my reader to: Count the letters & spaces in the phrase "...in context with the rest of an average day's average chatter" (used above). I count 60. This is the number of letterspaces my tiptoeing style just cost us. 60 letterspaces, reader! When 20, just ⅓ of that number, would do ...if a certain reader didnt freakout every time i use a 'big' word! 20 letterspaces (in quotidian context) would have done it! Imagine, if every 99 pages of print could be said in 33! O reader, imagine ⅔ less air-cleansing & Earth-cooling trees killed for the sake of our ineptitude with language; our libraries & computers with ⅔ more room; our bookbags, and specially our bookcases, with ⅓ the weight & paper waste!)

As to the religious leanings of juanita's heroine/poet emily. By the time of our last summer together, "the cage of old superstitions" had already begun to "forbid flite", already she felt she was "battering [her] blithe wings on the bars" of civil religion. Our particular social genius was such that we knew our hunger for each other –that deafening hum, that lethargy in our languishing love– was not "sinful", or even "bad". We intuited it as Natural as life itself! As the indigo girls put it in their last performance with me, we were *...old enough to diss what we were still too young to kiss.* And so we lay day after day on our floating nymphaeum, mentally carousing on that sunlite-drenched ark of our new covenant, angry at the system of beliefs which barred us from the mating rituals which called to us thru bone & blood, angry tho we did not understanding why.

Lilith

Our souls grappled in a palpable ether. That's how it seemed. They were beautiful 'beings', those zizms of ours! Somewhere above our smoldering bodies they treaded sunlite like water! More than once we swore we'd connected "out there somewhere".

"Did you feel that?"

I did.

"God! How weird!"

And weird it was. Right under the noses of our Earthbound counselors, right under the letter of the gospel, our zizms, like cats, thrashed in the air above the hot hanging garden of some half-remembered arabian nite. Delicious sacrilege! Still striving, still clawing for meaning, i see it yet another way: Our 'separate' force-fields, matter-of-factly, without fuss or forethought, would slam into each other, like two mighty magnets across a greased mirror: whap! Love was simple enuf to us. Why did everyone complicate it so?

We loved music. We often sang or hummed songs together. We could go on for hours! I was a whistler, she was a hummer (no pun, please). I loved her voice. She wanted to whistle like me. "Please teach me?" Her lush latin lips, as if made to pucker, would draw into an orbit at the mere thought of a lesson, and the fleshy ellipse they formed made my heart leap! For decades i've tried to reconstruct the songs my music-lover liked. There's one on the tip of my tung as i write. If i could only bring back one strain, one end-rhyme, of that faraway tune, i know (like liting a fuse midway) the entire song would ignite! its fireworks thrilling the sky of recall. But all i have are disjunct images, blurred at that: starry nites, campfires, sound of guitars, dark & dusky eyes, seashores (hawaii perhaps?), a somewhere somehow sort of moon, a cooing —of doves, of lovers? Cant remember.

We even liked the same candy. Mallowcup it was called. It had a thin milkchocolate covering and looked like a lowcut cupcake. Its inside was filled with a frothy marshmallow & a thin layer of caramel which chewyness reminded us of what a kiss, a passionate kiss, must be like. She described, exactly, the ache i felt in my jaws when i bit thru marshmallow or chewed caramel, that 'urge' in the teeth to feel resilient resistance: male securing mate with teeth; female securing her young. We toyed with the idea of sneaking off one nite just to buy a mallowcup! We could imagine a carnal encounter with just candy as object! I bought one as an adult, spit it in the trash. The quality of popular candy had gone the way of popular food.

We loved animals too. Juanita loved a little white goat, one of six or so at camp. Her affection for the seeming-dainty creature, which she called hermanita, reminded me of the way i loved my dog butch. She would hug its head, press her cheek hard to its thin snout. Squeezing the creature to the point of pain was perfectly permissible ...to the animal, i mean. Hermanita had a diamond-shaped mark between her wet almond eyes. Sometimes juanita would press her forehead to this mark and proceed to rub back&forth, or she would in fact butt it, as rams & kids butt heads in play. I used to do that with butch! i confessed. (Butch got left with my childhood back in mossville, for whatever that's worth.) These were passionate acts, bonding rituals, behaviors i think we were convinced could merge creatures —any two creatures! It was as if our essenceSelves were growing horns and these horns itched mercilessly!

We would get rapturously rammish when the itch grew unbearable, try to lock horns with the racks of other beings and with each other! This feeling peaked in the last weeks of august.

In that first summer our talk was like the white froth one sees on a stormy ocean from a plane, where depth is not seen but presumed. Perhaps that's why i cant remember much of their substance. On the stage of memory the waves of our conversations perform their silent pirouettes, collapse ε vanish. Earlyon our talks dealt with events at camp or things back home. Kids have a rudimentary grip on Reality; perhaps the best sort of grip. Take the ideas of space&time. Time was nonexistent …til someone pointed it out: "Ten minutes til bed!" "Two weeks til camp ends!" On the other hand, space we never doubted. Bodies take up space and we certainly had those —their yearnings drove us to distraction! In fact, space was the only thing that separated us and we knew it …well, beside a daily ration of brimstone ε damnation. As to heaven&hell? Hell was doing what your instincts found painful; heaven was obeying those instincts. It was all really very simple. "Heaven's where *you* are" she would sing. And if there was ever a garden of eden, we were there: that sunny countryside with its timbered hills ε handmirror lakes. While no nymphdom by the sea (that i would find with Lilith), it was paradise to us.

In chapel, nites, i would brush her hair by firelite. I can almost feel the leathery coolness of her hairthong as memory slips it off. {Is her skin rouged by bonfire or brimstone?} I didnt care. From behind the veil of her gypsy hair i watch her eyes dart about, her raphaelian lips form a characteristic pout. She tried to tell her mother about us. An intelligent woman, with some background in scientific method, she struggled to balance on the same pinhead her religious rearing and her daughter's desires. It's my guess she had no more success with this than severe augustine or wily aquinas. We, on the other hand –intuitive rapscallions– chose to throw superstition to the winds, seize with all our strength ε cunning what we intuited was rightfully ε Naturally ours.

23

I have saved for last some fragments of that final summer. It was mid july before we knew we had to act: i would be too old for camp the following summer and had not been asked back as a counselor. Juanita's mother likely had something to do with this. And so, august loomed. We sought more&more privacy and found less&less. It was not me who solved this dilemma mrs darc, it was your "juana" & you. What bouts of rationalizing or pleading she used to turn the trick i dont know. I can only guess it had to do with her mother's guilt: juanita had recently lost a fultime father to a parish in the tropics and was now deprived of the glitz & frills which once kept her apace with her peers. Even the nice home in a safe neighborhood was gone. Something had to give.

The main house was a large old clapboard. Along its front ran an enclosed porch, at one end of which was a garden —minus the obligatory stone wall of literature. The briter, windowed part of the porch served as a firstaid area with cabinet, table & cot. Its other end looks to memory like it served someone in winter as a library/den. But this may be colored by a later event. We found ourselves permitted to spend rest period (the hour following lunch) on that porch. This was great gulps of freedom compared with the public hunger we were used to enduring within our group. Enter, a quirk in our behavior.

Typically we would drain every synapse in the slapdash supervision of our counselors. We viewed these lapses as opportunities to touch, to kiss —o nothing salacious. Yet in our new unobserved circumstance we chose to chat! Imagine! And so we sat, me here, her there, reading to each other, joking, listening to the radio —a squat old "superhet" of dark oak which graced a worktable. Juanita read to me from a book of favorite poems, or we sang & hummed songs. I remember agreeing that the spiritual sensibilities around us were ankle-deep & splashy, that we'd probably not find anywhere the quiet adoration for jesus & his Dad we sometimes shared in those summerhours. Other times we would trade scenes from our past. How i wish i had her voice on tape –melodious, aerial, winged as it were– or her image & voice on film, as i have with Lilith ...where i dont need it, as those memories still manifest fully fleshed.

One day she took out, and we caroused thru, her mother's medical manuals. In semisecrecy we gaped at the glans of penises (unaroused, of course). <This one looks like a helmet.>

"It does! And a snowcap too ...you know, when you pull it down in back?"

We giggled over the vertical mouths of vulvas —also unaroused, of course. "This one is singing! <A high note!> [we laff] An' this one looks shocked!" both youngsters too engrossed to pickup on the poised pun.

Our bodily fires soon re-ignited under this tutelage. Any anxiety we suffered because of our new freedom to have at each other, dissipated. After a couple days a spate of kisses & cursory caresses ensued, coyly fudged with choruses of singing & laffing —designed (in theory) to keep the enemy convinced of the innocence of our playtime. Juana's idea, again, mrs darc.

Essential point. On rainy days, when activities were largely suspended and campers were confined to cabins, our relaxation time was given an extension. A couple times it lasted the better part of a day. We didnt know all this would end before camp ended. Had we known we would have cut short that period of innocence & levity and got down to cases. Such bad-weather rest periods held a second bonus as they almost insured no one would walk past the stretch of windows which so worried us on sunny days.

Lilith

It was on such a day our relationship experienced a quantum lurch. It was like the doveOfDesire decided to depart the garden of child-love to dare the jungle of adult lust. She wore the usual tanktop & shorts. Girl's shorts (called shortshorts back then) were skimpily cut. A favored pair could, thanx to much washing & wear, grow quite flimsy & short on coverage; all this amplified by a young woman's growth. In retrospect, i just know juanita & her mother must have bickered over the pair i'm examining now, as they all but melt a hole in mnemy's (memory's) snapshot.

She would sometimes sit on my knees reading aloud. Her free hand would wave sweepingly, in rhythm with her voice. Reaching beneath the cotton of her shirt i would feel the silk of her back. In mid-sentence she would stop, reach backward, drag an armful of hair out of my way, sometimes helping me hikeup her shirt to a point just beneath the tuck of her breasts. Not usually wards of ladyluck, we were delited to be able to hear when someone approached. Her mother would pay us periodic visits. Gratis ("on the house", so to say), the wood-floors of the old place would creak riotously to warn of her approach, despite her sleek frame & light step —if, that is, the radio & we, werent being too loud. And while she could resist the urge to check on the intactness of her daughter's hymen, she was, on the other hand, unable to keep her eagle eyes from passing over the props of our play, trying to see if what she heard at a distance matched what she saw up close.

Juanita read aloud from "this terrific dirty book I'm devouring", dropping her voice to a whisper upon reaching questionable words or phrases, and rising to forte again with their passage. When we heard footsteps, juanita would have me stash the book among the dogears of a hundred pulp romances which soaked a shelf above the couch; while she, hardly skipping a breath, returned to reading from the flagged page in a treasured copy of *the home book of female poets* kept ever at ready. While i dont recall the name of that novel, or its author, i do remember roughly the storyline. An older man (dark-haired, shifty-eyed; a frenchman, as memory has it) buys or abducts from a small mexican town the daughter of a mestizo. I believe the girl's name was dolores, altho rosita & esmeralda also come to mind. Anyway, once in the u.s he secludes her, rapes her, and after a time of mixed love & abuse, sells or rents her to the owner (also male) of a whorehouse in texas (the word was bordello, new to me then). The story is loppedoff there as we are soon to be ousted from that steamy readingroom.

Reconstruction. Juanita reading: sitting at my side or on the arm of the davenport, or from a straight-backed chair in the middle of the floor, which she mounted tomboy style so that the book's spine rested on a rung where her own spine should have been. It went something like this (i metaparaphrase). "Rosita was dismayed. How was it possible he could just sit there, pour himself another drink while she was pouring out her heart? The orphan girl, newly painted and attired, stood beside the table. 'O Andre! Andre! You dont know. My duties are horrible. The men want only me, and the women hate me because of it!' Rosita walked over to a basket of laundry, touched it and turned. [juanita stood for this part] 'I have no choice. I must fly away.' [juanita adds:] She thinks she's a bird, remember? 'And you are a little idiot. [grunts juanita, deepening her voice, quaffing an imaginary glass of wine and chasing it with a bad imitation of a man's burp] And where would you fly, stupid?' Andre growled."

(I've concocted andre's name —not to protect him from the law but because i've forgotten it.)

"'I dont know. But I'll fly somewhere... O Andre! You stole my private treasure. And now you are selling it, day after day, while I die inside!'" There was a sob in juanita's voice as she made these awfully written lines believable.

"'And you use the money, *my* money, to buy your stinking opium, to keep your little whores in silk!' [her voice softened on 'whores'] 'And you never speak to me of love, or sing me songs, as Pedro [her older brother; you dont know about him] ...as Pedro used to do!' At this point she burst into sobs."

Dreadful book –or dreadful translation of a book– yet it spoke somehow to juanita, satisfied her need for adventure. For the friteful experiences of this unfortunate orphan aroused juanita's erotic curiosity. For my part, i would have preferred lewd fotos. That split again: her impressionism v. my realism —a question of method more than one of belief. Juanita clearly identified with dolores, whom she called "our poor little rosita". It could be, come to think of it, rosita was what the man called her and not her given name. She & juanita were the same age if i remember aright –at this part in the story anyway– and both were *belle bruns* of the first order.

Juanita was really into it. Looking back i realize, the parts she selected for dramatization were probably read-over the nite before. I believe my rapt audience was of great importance to her for, whenever it was time to begin, while withdrawing the book from its hidingplace, say, her eyes would flash, and she would wet her lips. "Listen to what happened last nite." Facing me, book held high in front of her, she swept the air with a free arm. "'O Andre! Every day I am raped....'" Voice lowered upon reaching the censored word but enunciated with unusual emphasis to compensate. Pacing now, "'I am raped, washed, raped again, rewashed, fed terrible food, inspected, disinfected, then raped again til suppertime!'" Arms extended, palms open; the fingers of her reading hand (splayed as best they could beneath the book) striving to help with the drama. Her thick long hair shook from side to side til thoroly disheveled; her cheeks flushed, her lips (suddenly thick & pouty), rounded every ah, every o, and then spread thin as, with teeth blazing, she bit down on her e's & i's.

"'Hourly I am a victim of disgusting lust, Andre! [juanita sobbed here, just once] How I hate you! You are a sick old man! A crazyman! A brute!' La rosita fell to weeping." Once, during such theatrics she garbled the words, got flustered, garbled them worse; a spoonerism, its called. Something like, "Some dirty squeal pigeon stooled on me!" was what came out. Well, we collapsed in laffter (dramatic relief), opened our eyes to find her mother standing in the doorway looking at us as tho we were daft, the book miraculously overlooked. "We cant lose control like that again" we agreed. But life is not that orderly.

Of all libraries, i figured this one, dirty-minded as it is, would have 'juanita's' book. It does not. While feeding its computer 'rosita' (under french lit) got me nowhere, when given 'dolores' it spit back several interesting options. Only one, tho, rang familiar: *the fortress,* by r h lendormon. The fact it was translated into spanish (1950, by a lenore mondale) makes it a likely candidate. Could this be the book? As a lark, i requested a copy. "This could take a few weeks" apologized larry the librarian, a mousy man of few words —spoken ones, anyway.

Mnemosyne can be a strange bird, specially the memory of a troubled youth. Why was i looking for titles in french when i'm convinced the book was printed in spanish? This is not as odd as it may seem, for i distinctly remember juanita saying some things in french! This could be because the cruder parts of the book were left untranslated. Back in those days this was often done by exporting publishers to mollify censors. To confound things, i remember her asking me to read thisorthat part, and me doing it. Item. I *still* cant read in spanish! O i read alright, in most of the romance languages. But understanding on my feet? That's something else.

Next item. Did that book make reference to poe's annabel lee or did juanita do that? And if so, why? I have no clue. Still i associate the phrase "I was a child and she was a child" with that book. But did juanita say that or did the book? This sort of muddle-in-the-mind itches subliminally. At any rate, few people realize, poe's ink was still wet when tennyson stole *life of my life; my darling, my dove; my life, my fate; the envy of angels* and *my bride to be!* He later even purloined "I was a child and [she] was a child". But my trailing truck has jumped the track i see. By the way, if all this business didnt explain so much about juanita, so much about me, so much about Lilith, i'd skip it. Beside, a great poet once said, kisses are the only worth all telling ...or somesuch.

Lilith

We learned earlyon about statistical probability; fly the airline that's just had a crash. The moment her mother hurried off to attend to other duties (she had many, almost running the place as she did), juanita would return to my lap. It was not long before i felt free to allow my spider hand to slip past the elastic of miss muffet's shorts, skate (me inwardly yelping!) down the front panel of her slick membranous panties.

At some point i remember her bent over and in the process of getting something (mirror, maybe?) and me feeling at liberty to answer a tug in my gut, an ache i'd suffered before, in school, on the street, in church, even in kindergarten! You will smile but i am bound to hide nothing. Before she could rise i was behind her, taking her by the hips, pulling her against me. As she rose (i would love today to have seen the look on her face as) i nuzzled & kissed first her bare shoulder, then her neck, also bare, the falls of her hair still slid well forward. Hands tingling i touched her thighs. One hand, without my permission, slipped to her groin. Her head fell back onto my chest, her teeth were bared. Looking down, i watched her seeming-buphthalmous eyes close, open, close again, their lids fluttering. The fingers of my other hand moved under the band of her shorts and down the dip in her abdomen; it was not the tense tummy of priscilla but the concave of Lilith. Using both hands by then, soon felt my prey. She gasped, licked her lips, sucked thru her teeth a long breath and slowly, dreamily, gave access to my goal by folding aside one thigh.

Private excursions of my own suggested something to be gained by manipulating her. Beside, on many a nite in the city i had pored over fotos in magazines found in gutters or mixed with newspapers atop the garbage cans of a known pervert. More than once a man up the street tried to lure me with strange fotos which i had no desire to see under the circumstances he had in mind.

I pushed against her, bent my knees so as to confront her fullon; this lowered my height so her head could collapse onto my shoulder. I then followed closely her climb: eyes closed, lashes flickering, mouth open, lips twitching involuntarily, as if the corpuscles of some ancient shaman dancing in her blood were causing her to utter some silent orgiastic incantation. A feeling of safety swept over me —swept over us. Rain drummed the porch roof; wind swayed the boughs of a stand of poplars lining the roadside out front; the rattlings & clatter of the kitchen seemed far off now and difficult to hear; litening flickered & sizzled; thunder clapped, boomed & rumbled off into the distance; the radio played a song about "turn[ing] back the hands of time", which i'd trade one of my mint lp's to hear again. I see her set aside a handmirror with an ivory rim; the chair, the window, the implied garden, the supplied poplars, this heliad & me, are fleetingly framed in its glass.

All bashfulness dissipated; i intensify my manipulations. Her mouth distended, sought ɛ found my earlobe, as if she'd picked up a small shell on the beach and decided to suck on it. A string of quick sibilant breaths is drawn thru her bared ɛ silver-braced teeth, followed by a low constricted growl. Her thighs give a shudder. A shiny apple, perched on the desk, begins to rock, rolls, falls. A throwrug (imitation persian) covered with autumn leaves (you'll see why i recall all this), which just happened to be sailing by, intercepted the apple's descent. From my present perspective it seems as if, sick&tired of the old order of things, the apple (now lying among the carpet of leaves [hic]) had tricked gravity (and the devil too), returned to the bough of its own volition! Her mouth opened wide as she took the side of my neck in her teeth.

Juanita did not see a splash of mud hit the air as the camp stationwagon cruised in, supplies blanking its windows. I found my fingertips in a hot humid grip. I could stand no more. Pressed against her with all my might, emitting the gurgle of a strangling orangutan, i wrenched into my shocked jockeys all the aching ɛ longing a civilly-challenged Naturboy can cram into a single lifetime! Over the next few days this scene was repeated. I would be lying if i listed an exact itinerary. While the details of certain incidents are clear, their exact sequence is not. I do recall being an apt pupil tho. I followed carefully, and felt deeply, her erotic responses, as if they were my own.

It was about this time her mother issued, and she passed on to me, the bad news: "T'morrow's our last time, nathan", lower lip pouted, shiny brow wrinkled under its bangs. Counselors had complained, or so her mother said.

That last day her mother paid more visits than usual. Had juanita protested toomuch? As our hour dwindled my lover became oddly animated. Amidst a louder-than-usual volley of histrionics, without warning, she reached over and gripped me thru my clothes. A moment later she was on her knees unzipping me. Her face was intense. "It's not fair. ...You *always* do me." Grimacing, and with considerable maneuvering, she withdrew what she sought. It seemed like she had rehearsed all this, step by step, yet i dont think she was prepared for what she found —for while in some respects i was the worst part of an adolescent, i had grown in secret 'the better part' of a man. Her mouth went ajar as if –on a busy street, walking home from school with friends– a man in a doorway had exposed himself. Recounting such a story on our raft next morning, juanita's mouth would drop in the same manner as it did in front of me then. It would not be the last time a female would be shyly shocked by nathan schock's *schacht*.

"Geezus!" She gave a stifled yelp and stared at it, one hand frozen in front of her mouth, the other afraid to reclose around what pulsed on her palm, still growing! Have i mentioned, my growth took a spurt upward from 13 to 17? We're talking years here, not centimeters. (It was here began the embarrassment which would end, years later, in my foolishly seeking a special sort of reductive surgery.) I'm not sure if she planned what happened next; memory has left few tracks. She tugged on me; her breath came haltingly, huge eyes peeredup from beneath dark lashes, trying to see the expression on my face. Her breath burnt as she tried her best to repay my favors of days prior. At length [hic], immersed in that applesweet breath, i felt brutish, selfish, yet unable or wanting to stop her.

A loud bang came from the kitchen, probably a dropped pot, a fallen pan. We both tensed. Soon she soon took up again, her eyes darting to the doorway which lay beyond my right hip. It excited me when she peered up –whether to taunt or track me i dont know– but her eyes, wide with whites, had a blank mystical depth to them. While on the desk a second glad apple grappled with gravity (and won!), my latin lily climbed & turned on the leafy rug, clearly locked in on some private & near-ravenous commitment, stopping only briefly to catch her breath, then taking up again. We talk of terror being communicable? What of orgasmic abandon? Now *there's* a thesis that could be an exciting read!

In my odd state (fear giving way to euphoria) i was slowly losing track of external reality. In a few moments i would be, for the first time in my remembered waking life, *completely* without fear. And so i was easy as an apple to polish off. Too soon to let go and too late to stop, i fired a fusillade of frenzy into, onto and all around the startled girl, who waved me about like an amok flame-thrower! But by then Earth-time had lapsed into slomo. I knew everything was dangerously loud –rain, radio, ringing bells & canonfire in my head– but i was helpless to halt the melting & the bliss. As from another universe, her mother's voice called "Juana!"

"O God!" Juanita's head pivoted in terror. Still gripping me with one fist, still pulling on me spasmodically —as if she would drag me spurting thru the house and out to the kitchen to help carry in groceries— she rose to one knee, calling out in a near-hysterical voice, "Coming mama!" I'm reminded here of juliet in the balcony scene —maybe because juanita's mother was a nurse? A moment later she was on her feet.

A last glimpse catches her paused in the doorway, looking down in wild self-assessment, checking arms shirt shorts legs shoes, with the fingers of one hand splayed as tho holding a sticky & still throbbing heart. Suddenly she resumes her miss muffet role! The transformation stuns me. Singing merrily a popular flamencan song

—When the speckled birds are moulting silent....

—to disarm, one supposes, any culinary inquisitors— she squats, paws the sticky stigmata onto a small throwrug by the door and, tossing an impish smile my way, stood & turned the doorway, combing away (with fingers still not quite her own) the telltale filaments of carnal cobweb clinging stubbornly to her tresses.

Painfully i stuff myself back into my shorts, just a throb or two short of absolute perfection, my mind trying to scream me a pathway back to Reality. Glancing about, i begin to sweep back&forth with a frantic bare foot, trying to erase, to scatter, to trowel dry the speckled blight upon the leafy rug ...that magic carpet upon which, only a moment before, my unselfish, courageous, wild & beautiful gypsy love had knelt; this half-woman/half-nymph whose loves & likes, unknown to us both, had locked in place for life all the points on my esthetic compass.

Did i say nymph again? O tainted word! Should i have said woodsprite? Dryad? The invented "evil" of civil (establishment) religion clings even to these. Yet how can one speak of a 'daughter of Nature', a 'daughter of Wilderness', and not imply nymph? It cannot be done. And so i must deal with this prejudice ("evilism" v. "goodism") now, before Lilith too becomes its victim.

24

I should at once dispel any connection of the present work with most modern usage of the word nymph, in all its several forms. Specially i want to disparage all linkage with another author's medieval & trivializing corruption (nymphet) which in his historically bogus guise (debasing mix of puerile preciosity & precocious sensuality) has attained a permanent fix in the firmament of our twinkling vernacular. For it is impossible ...o wise reader, harken! I repeat... *impossible* to speak intelligently of Nature & females (in the present case, Lilith & Planetary ecology) and turn a blind eye to that *archetypal* form of femininity, the nymph. So pull your chair closer to these bars, sweet attentive reader, for the female reputation has been begging for cleansing & reëmpowering for longer than most know or care to know.

25

Nymphs demonesses vampiresses hags witches banshees succubi and their many many sisters going all the way back in recorded history... Where did they come from? Were females really created "evil"? Or did someone, or certain cults of someones, in secret and with a private vengeance, invent cosmic "evil", then force-fit it to Earthly females?

In many cases (eg, milton) the assignation 'nymph' is but a façade for the fairytalement of the actual era of the goddess; the civil disempowerment of precivil deities (namely goddesses) via exile to a state of harmless fairytale & myth.

From puberty til i quit college —in fact til i found myself hunting & killing in the jungles of the fareast by threat of uncleSam's terrible vengeance— i had no clue as to these matters. Like every other male, i was in the dark sexually, victim of what i shall for the time being call 'the secret instinct'. And like all other kneejerk offspring of adam, i too believed eve, and all her fair daughters, were somewise "evil". To this very minute i can count, using fingers alone, all the men i've known who –bravely, forthrightly, in the company of men only– reject this antiquated (yet hardly forgotten) curse against femaleness. Yet it is a fact of record, the nymph —in her prime state in the ancient worldorder, in her mountains her seas her rivervalleys lakes & trees— was once revered as an awesome & absolutely pristine being! the rainbow bridge to humankind's joyous connection with Nature & an Earth-nurturing Cosmos!

What happened? When did female deities take on "evil" (morally dissolute & sexually depraved) characteristics? When did the pure nymph become the impure nymphomaniac? Who did this? And when did her little sister, the nymphet, become a pubescent pariah? My other books attack these questions as time will not allow me to attack them here.

[The bracketed note which follows, though intended for the Editor only, does much to explain the subject matter coming after it. Given NS' condensed presentation here of a topic unfamiliar to most, it would be a mistake not to include his note. —Editor.]

[Emil, i am about to claim for juanita –and Lilith too, in due course– that innate sexual purity which is the birthright of *all* of us. In interest of economy (time, in this case, as you know) it would be extremely helpful if you would assist me in purging (for the sake of this book & its best readers) the history of negative connotation in the term nymph, with the goal of restoring female sexuality –if not sexuality generally– to its Natural state of essential purity. I have written on the subject at some depth, as you may know, yet from my present disadvantage am unable to pinpoint exact chapters & pages. I have only the names of the texts & the appropriate index headings with which to steer you.]

[At this point NS indicates the text extracts he wants used, all from his own books. *The Castration of Priapus, Scapegoats & Fallgirls* and *Mothernature and the World Matron.* These extracts he tied together with new text as found below. —Ed.]

26

In the autumn of '89, 4yrs before i met Lilith, i was writing

> The idea of a universe with a single god responsible for its entire existence and maintenance is relatively new. Hominids and humans had been somewise polytheistic for perhaps a million years before the single-godded religions came along. In early civilization and pre-civilization many of Nature's forces and attributes, including human instinct, were considered divinely caused. Awe of a Nature/instinct with many facets evolved societies with many deities. In contrast, the gods of the religions of recent times rule in defiance of Nature, of instinct, and, most of all, abjuring other gods. And the heads of these new single-godded religions have three inviolate qualities: absolute authority, single authority, and single gender: male. These new lone gods (including Jewish Islamic and Christian gods), unlike the former gods of early civilization and pre-civilization, are hard-and-fast atheists —that is, they neither acknowledge nor permit the existence of other gods. This being so, all deities and their devotees, which existed for eons before these new lone gods came to power, were put on notice of their lives. Specially proscribed were *female* deities. Not only were goddesses and demigoddesses among the 'lesser unacceptable' gods, they were the 'wrong' sex. And being *doubly* "heretical" they were doubly condemned —and have been ever since.

Note: glaring disparity between my writing styles. For reasons of familiarity my publisher of the time convinced me to forego my tree-sparing writing style and follow standard rules of grammar as much as i could stand to do so. Lean in a little closer. I must whisper this so as not to scare off the remaining brave males. I love your eyes when youre wondering.

> It is no accident, a prevailing belief that females are somehow "evil" or "bad" invariably coincides with the rise to power of these lone male gods. Among the hundreds of "evil" or "bad" beings the newer religions evolved, we find demonesses

> vampiresses hags witches banshees succubi and their many many sisters. Even whores and prostitutes, which in many parts of the world once held high political and/or religious status, were suddenly thought of as "bad" or "evil" persons. In less than two thousand years a new mandate swept civilization: No one would be safe till the last of the old deities had been defamed debunked dethroned defiled banished and forgotten. The age of the terrible vain egocentric single phallic unmated and unmatable arbiter of the cosmos had arrived and would not soon be overthrown!

But we must be careful here. The paths fork & refork and most are false! The trail to truth is no trail at all. Truth always strikes out thru new & hazardous terrain. But because the watch on the wrist of the guard outside my cell is not on my side, we must take a shortcut. We must drop down the sheer granite face at the head of the gorge... over there! Stay close! Stepping gingerly, hugging the wet rock, we pass behind a wall of water, a rushing cataract which falls out of sight below! Mist, icy to our faces, swirls about; the winds are confused & cyclonic back here. Just ahead, a tilted slab of granite will start us downward again. After a day of harrowing descent we will plunge into that last remnant of Planetary rainforest we came to experience. Here, look at this map. Read over my shoulder. I will turn my chair just so. There. You know, your expression reminds me of Lilith's somehow. But where were we?

> After a certain point in history it doesn't matter what god we interrogate —sun god of the Aztecs, sun god of the late Egyptians, the *pater familias* of the (several sects of) Jews, the machismo Muhammads (of the several sects of) Islam or the unmated father-gods of the (many sects of) Christians— always we are interrogating the *same* social force: the projection of an alienated monastic male ego onto society at large. For all these deities share the same qualities: isolated dominion, unchallenged maleness, and a brutal punitive code for those who do not follow their dogmas.

No, i am not a lady writer in disguise.

> I wish to introduce now the inchoate female of the subconscious. For it is to the objective existence of an unconscious feminine that we are deferring whenever we invoke such subjective entities as nymphs: ie, goddesses demigoddesses nymphs witches and faeries and their numerous ilk, whether personifying plant animal fire earth water or air.

And, yes, we'll get back to juanita posthaste. The instructor pauses here, looks about, says <Entertainment isnt everything, you know. Shakespeare would

have vanished if he didnt wield a social bludgeon with his non-writing hand. The subtextual and supertextual lite-'n'-shadow everything>.

Psychology claims, it is the vital role which the mother plays in our lives which secures femaleness a predominating role in the human unconscious. This panhuman influence is called the "mother imago". In the psychology of Carl Jung this imago becomes an archetype, and that which caused it is expanded beyond mother to include sisters daughters and female mates. This unity of influences Jung called "anima". Ecopsychology would extend still further the range of forces constituting Jung's anima. For it sees a serious oversight when Jung fails to include (as a female influence) the "Mother" of all mothers/sisters/-daughters and female mates. I refer of course to Mothernature, whose dominion of nurture itself(!), being as old as life itself, not only must be hypertrophied in the human unconscious but is, obviously, also mirrored in the very indices of our genetic codes! It is thus unremarkable that primitive cultures so often represent Nature's innumerable aspects (oceans mountains rivers forests springs etc) as daughters of Mothernature.

the parameters of archetype

If it is not transmissible in a single emotional snapshot, if it is not bridgeable in a single neurologic twinge, if it cannot be defined as genetic memory transferrable as a single biologic trope, then it is likely a construct of experience not an archetype. Those who have spent prolonged periods in deep Wilderness are familiar with the 'flash' of archetype to which i refer—a flash of imagery instantly, both mentally & bodily, recognized not as food, not as predator, nor as potential mate, but as all-knowing protector. This image, often fleeting, can take the form of dolphin or doe, wolf or fox, black panther orsnowleopard, albatross or frigatebird, &soforth. These & others, whether apparition or flesh, are but standins for that sensibility of nurture & support which all of us intuit in Nature, often despite entire lifetimes of separation from Wilderness & constant propaganda to the contrary. Of course i should pointout, my better critics like to say "Schock's mother nature archetype is little more than pop psychology's mother/mate imago superimposed onto wilderness". Yet this, tho not bad as criticism goes, falls shallow of the mark. Why? Because it overlooks the very germ of genetic memory: those literally millions of years before any lifeforms were given mothers, per se –or even mates, in any remotely mammalian sense– millions of years over which (fundamentally formative period) life was absolutely intimate with that same environment which today we call Nature/Wilderness.

Such a view demystifies myth.

Ecopsychology also contests the Jungian view which limits the female archetype to the unconscious of males. It holds the inchoate feminine to exist in the human unconscious irrespective of gender. This is the same subliminal SHE which we, whether female or male, most often sense in Wilderness; we 'see' HER sitting by a stream, or feel HER moving in the wind, or "see" HER darting deerlike among the trees of our favored haunts. The early Amerind, the old Oriental, the Austral aborigine, all saw her, all knew her —knew her more intimately than Homer did the nymphs *he* immortalized. She is real, this archetypal nymph —real to the extent we sense femininity in our surroundings. This is the nymph i wish to bring into focus....

But the unbroken succession of antiNature phalladigms which civilization has brought about has successfully stigmatized the feminine archetype on a conscious level, creating a whole gynatheon of messedup mythical misses, misses whom we've been erroneously taught to think of as nymphs, as daughters of Mothernature. It would be most instructive if we took a peek at a couple of these. And, o. Those who skipped the 'bike path' running along the righthand side of the pages (above) may now wish to burn rubber to the next chapter. (Psst, nathan! They already did!)

> In the myths and legends of many cultures Mothernature is in charge of whatever humans consider treasure. In Norse and Germanic myth for instance Motherearth kept all the gold in the safe-keeping of nymphs in a single river. These nymphs were not attached to the gold in the sense that a vain woman is attached to her jewelry but in the sense the sea is attached to the shore or a tree attached to the sky. These nymphs were as selfless as Mothernature herself, whom of course they personified. This is the sort of *innate purity* we need to demonstrate; the essential and inviolate aspects of the inchoate feminine: the archetypal nymph.

Happily we can track the pollution of this intrinsic purity in the evolution of a specific nymph from the poetry of marlowe and raleigh. This will take but a moment and is painless.

> The earlier poet, Marlowe, doesn't chase his nymph as would any full-blooded satyr. No, his tactics are truly modern —and we're talking the 1500s! He baits his nymph with materialistic things. *Come live with me and be my love...* and i will give you gowns, fur-lined slippers "with buckles of the purest gold", belts "with coral clasps and amber studs", silver dishes, ivory tables. An updated version would say: "You get my drift, baby? I'm loaded, and all of it can be yours if you play your cards right." Item: Marlowe fails to see the sheer absurdness of his ploy? For the precious metals and stones unmined on our Planet (read, still guarded by Nature's daughters) even today astronomically outweighs all of what humanity could ever possess muchless what a poor poet can offer a nymph. Yet Marlowe –cementing in place a thoroughly modern arrogance which presumes Nature stupid– dares presume that materialistic bribery will work on the "daughter" of an entity which, in effect, owns the entire Universe (Nature)! "Hey, guys. Nymphs go wild for this civilized shit!" (Pardon my use of 'wild'.)

Instructor wets thumb, flicks to next page, says <His poem being famous, marlowe has thus done his part in the domestication of Wild Nature, an act which we know by the name, civilizing. Civilizing is a worldview which will

always be hardest on females so long as what humans are attempting to escape (via civilizing) is viewed as female (the powers of Nature)>.

> Now along comes Raleigh, daring to answer for "Marlowe's" nymph. Does he, speaking for her, have the good sense to say: "You *do* know that what you're asking is really stupid, right? [Er, why's that?] Because when you ask a nymph to come live with you what you're really doing is asking Mothernature to abandon the Wild in favor of living with you in civilization. You're asking her to crawl into the same filthy little cage you went and built for yourself, and then, like you, make believe she's content to be there! Can you not see how absurd that is? [Why absurd?] Because it's your civilized discontent which is causing you to want a piece of Wilderness...in the form of a nymph —namely me...in the first place! And to top that, you have the audacity to try and win me using jewels and metals you stole from the breast of my Mother! Even a common criminal isn't stupid enough to do that. Come live with you? I don't think so!"

For tho raleigh can see civilization is corrupt enuf no nymph would ever consider marlowe's offer, he too suffers a disconnect from the archetypal feminine in *himself*, forgotten how a real nymph (Nature) must feel about such dull-witted arrogance.

> A Homeric nymph, however (already well along the way to "evilness"), might have used the element of surprise (perhaps while Marlowe slept) or her capacity for transformation, grab the ivory, the fur, the silver and gold and (like any self-respecting Rhinemaiden) hot-foot it out the nearest window to return them to her mother, Nature. For you see, the paragonic nymph to whom i'm steering the reader is uncomplicated by incrustations of culture or man-invented values.

Even brochus' 'nymph' of 545ad seems as decked out as any glitterkitz at hollywood&vine. A return to habitat would be disastrous for her. Her trinkets would soon be lost, her hairdo melt in the river, her slippers wrecked on the rocks, her gown shredded by branches and brambles. She might even require psychotherapy after a simple picnic in the park —if it rained, say, or if she spotted an undomesticated animal!

> And even Lao Yin's delicate pottery rendering of circa 1100 BC (once considered the first nymph of the visual arts) is no nymph. She is, if anything, the first mall-crawler! —well, minus the Rolex and the Beemer. And she will be repeated a thousand times in a thousand different disguises: the false nymph of art, the fake nymphet of modern lit. The reader must put them out of mind. They are not nymphs. They are limp imps and impish imposters. In every culture they have been remade, the gilt and giddy creations of one civil phalladigm or another.

All this is not to say the archetypal nymph has gone completely unrepresented in the arts & lit. There is the rare case.

> The 3000-years more recent Waterhouse' (1847-1917) Hylas and the Nymphs is oddly far more representative ...though their delicate loveliness and supple grace is still not entirely free of that lewdness rarely absent in civilization's depictions of sensual females. For thanks to civilizing (the forced domestication of the Wilderness innate in us) sensuality and pleasure are stigmatized by a lewdness unfindable in all of Earth and the Universe outside civilization!

J. W. Waterhouse

While Nature's daughters may at times resemble elephant seals or walruses (appearing unsleek out of water), they are *never* the dissolute slobs depicted through the worldview of the likes of vecchio, titian and cabanel, and only rarely are they the more bearable –but still sedentary and decadent– debutantes of cranach. While a veneer of blubber may be pardonable in nymphs of sea and lake (though the everpresent need for escape keeps them dolphin-muscled and -sleek), such grossness of the flesh is pure heresy in nymphs. And to blast yet another myth. Just because a nymph is seen in or near water hardly classifies her as it's personification, since all nymphs have imperious hygiene and so drink much and bathe often. And because modern law is, even to this moment, polluted by his prejudices, before we move on we cannot forget mean-spirited milton's pornographic view of Mothernature's daughters:

> "Haste thee, Nymph, and bring with thee...wanton wiles." It was such a view of women as Milton's which helped this paradise, Earth, become "lost" to us. We can only imagine what he expected from, and did to, poor young Mary Powell. At least deSade, as degenerate as he was, did not hide his passions in a cassock or a law.

And what of the assigned sexuality of civilization's fake nymphs & false nymphets? How was it then perceived? and how, today? Listen to how i go on in my books, how i incense the censors.

> Let's next ply apart the voluptuous folds of Swinburne's nymphs, of Ronsard's nymphettes. (I've heard it said, he invented the word. Other sources say it was Drayton, in his *Muses Elysium.*) Let's for a moment part the flesh of their sonnets and blazons, palpate what they call *le sexe feminin.* As our eyes move along the

> ridges of the *vermeillete fente* we find the scale of religious stigmata has chafed that nymphic softness; we find that 2000 years of believing, pleasure is damning, sex, malignant, has dulled and sullied the once incandescent eyes of these sham shes.
>
> While Jung rejuvenated the inchoate feminine with his anima, William Morris proves the more capable nympholept. In his search for the Nymph of Hylas, we find true psychic excavation at work, well before Freud. His nymph exists on a shore beyond a "restless sea, [a] shore no ship has ever seen" (which is a damn good start) ...a place which he, the poet/lover, is "unskilled to find...what all men seek"! But most telling of all is what he calls "the unforgotten face." And here the archetypal nymph, key resident of the poet's subconscious, all but smiles at us from between the lines. He longs for her "once seen, once kissed, once reft from me", as if she were the very shadow of the Cosmic Feminine passing thru him(!), as remembered from some primal inscape, some seascape of the id. Morris makes us wonder how Marlowe and Raleigh –and the rest of us, indeed– got so damned lost to our very own Selves.

Because it is incidental to ecophilosophy i did not note in my *Mothernature & the world matron* that, mood & meter in morris' poem point us toward poe's annabel lee: She "...for [whom] I let slip all delight...for [whom] I cry both day and night...anigh the murmuring of the sea". It is probably also moot that his "little garden...thick with lily and red rose" (along with the negative imprint of a pillared villa closeby) are remindful of a still later 'plurabelle', whom another writer (crafty sinister enchanter) is "careless to win". And right behind all this comes one of those useless coincidences i love but have never had the time to collect & collate: An earlier poet, campion, begins a song to a 'nymph' in a garden also, a garden where roses & white lilies grow —along with "sacred cherries that none may buy til 'cherry-ripe' themselves do cry". We'll ignore his shameless cherry fetish (code: vulgar lust for virginity) and focus on something equally seminal in the popular garden metaphor: lilies & roses.

Morris' garden lends color to the rose (red) and campion's garden colors the lily (white). In bronte's *jane eyre* we find another "...garden, too...lilies had opened...roses were in bloom". And andersen's bent silhouette can be seen skulking behind the botanical guise of, "The daughters were young and beautiful...charming blossoms —a rose, a lily...whose little lambs will they one day become...?" More vulgarity, for lambs-to-slaughter is a clear subtext here. More seminal to this bio, a heroine in tennyson also "has a garden of roses and lilies". The symbolism is clear in most cases and examples are rife.

It is no accident that the waterlily family is called ***nymphaeceae*** and that the rose is the color of blood. For in all this "garden" business we are clearly intimating the defloration of the (often called pure) lily, and that lily is a eufeminism [sic] for Mothernature and all her pure daughters. That is why both flowers are often present in the literature of desire. Among fair-skinned writers the lily equals the naked female body; among all writers the rose often implies blood perfusion of the mouth/genitals. An open flower signals passion/readiness; a closed one (eg, the notorious rosebud), like the white lily, signals virginity. In wilde these same metaphors all but tackle us to the ground as we pass: "Lily of love, pure and inviolate! ...red rose of fire!" And we dont dare even brush up against the old don of subtext himself, whose "one-score" heroine (greatGaia save us), friteningly lost in a garden, can befriend a lily but is rebuffed by a rose.

For the nymph of history is essentially the nymph of art ε lit. But so, quite amazingly, is the nymph of science! For we find not only the *nymphae,* nymphitis ε nymphotomy of the female genitals still holding sway in modern medicine, we have also to restore to some sense of personal dignity the nymphomaniac —which judgement upon a female's right to pleasure i dont dare touch just now. In botany we have the *nymphaeceae* (waterlily family), the socalled flowers of the nymphs. In entomology we have the family of butterflies called *nymphalidae.* And in psychiatry we have the nympholept, male equivalent of the nymphomaniac. Unfortunately however psychiatry's dependence upon myth ε legend for evaluating its patients doesnt stop there. It endures in the historical sleight-of-hand of a certain scholar of note. For in psychiatry we have the socalled dumbert ε dolita complex, which tacitly accuses its "suffers" of being innately "bad" if not "evil". And lastly, it is hardly accidental that *nymphaea* is an epithet of aphrodite, and that *nymphae*, again in medicine, are the inner lips of the vulva. I could rave on but juanita, little "passionflower at the [garden] gate", awaits. And Lilith too: "Queen rose of the rosebud garden of girls".

27

This you will *not* believe. I was awakened this morning by a metallic banging sound. It was either a very gray day or i had not yet opened my eyes. I lay on my fleshless cot trying to picture what was being banged and where. Surely it wasnt anything under me. The sound came from outside my window. Delirious with sleep, i either dreamt or imagined that gE activists glendon starling mark scarlet ε helmut tonderstrom had scaled the wall to the roof beyond my window, as tho it were the side of a leaking oil tanker or nuclear power plant. Talking ε laffing, they grapneled over, used a large drill to remove the bars. I crawled out just as a chopper, with cinematic precision, swooped down and lifted us to safety. But i was dreaming, of course. My ecoactivist friends would never attempt such a thing. They would hang banners from prison walls, keep a vigil for a few weeks, depart, the way they did at my trial. It is only the baron who would take such a risk. But i am dreaming. For only a fairytale of biblical proportions can save me now. Which brings to mind. Where is the baron hiding? And how much longer can he stay clear of their clutches?

The dreamscape of this dream-escape was precipitated i think by the coming ε going lately of a muddauber wasp, who passes with impunity in&out of a coin-sized hole in my window, the too-perfect circularity of which has bothered me since my arrival. As to the window itself. Once a 2x4-foot opening, it is now a square, its lower half being blockedup with a steel sheet welded onto the inside of the bars. Because the wall is so thick and the bars set toward its outside, the resulting sill is around 40cm deep. (If Lilith were here she could, like a good fairy, perch inside the alcove with ease.) Standing i can see the horizon, such as it is. But to see the ground i must place palms on the sill and press upward my bodyweight (100kg or so since getting out of solitary confinement). It was while doing such triceps presses last evening that i saw the coroner's wagon park by a side entrance.

Today is su yet gluum ε glumm are on duty. Sounds of voices, scraping ε grunting sounds, as of things being slid with difficulty across a stage floor, reverberating from a point beyond the big iron door (propped open for a change) and beyond which i cannot see. Glumm, stone-faced, wields an electronic key as tho it were a pistol, shoots my celldoor aside and, saying nothing, steps in. Lying on my back, i do not rise but watch the goings-on peripherally. His demeanor is more military than usual; he stands, head erect, shoulders back, as if in anticipation of some fuhrer's arrival. My guess is not far off the deutschmark. "Prisoner schock, on your feet at once!" His voice is strident. Hair tousled, eyes glued half-shut and feeling as if pebbles are lodged in their canthuses, grays (my uniform) rumpled, bedclothes rumpled, life rumpled, i put bare feet to the cold floor and rise.

"Be ready ta receive vice warden straitmon 'n' assistant prison directa becillo!" Voices are close now. Two suits, turning about each other in animated conversation, waltz into view, while the noise, the grunts, the clatter of objects continues backstage. "Ya shudda been awake tweny minits ago" snaps glumm under his breath.

Got in late, i respond. Those wild saturday nites, you know?

"You'll get yours, smartass."

The way humpinLouie got his yesterday, no doubt.

Suits enter, interrupting our warm chat. "Aha. So *this* is mr schock? Of course. We've met before. I'm vice warden straitmon, this is assistant director becillo."

Becillo advances ("I'm becillo"), shakes my hand with the clammy thing hanging out of his sleeve. "You look dif'rent? Not like your pikchrs." I wipe my palm on my grays as he speaks. I know when i've been slimed.

"He means your picture in the papers. [becillo takes one giant-step backward] We see you have the row almost to yourself. We hope that pleases you."

Will you have a seat? [i indicate commode] For as you can see, i have no chair to offer.

"And that there is just one of the reasons we've come. You filled out this form?" He held aloft a few sheets of paper as tho there were an audience behind me that needed to see. "As you know we try to entertain the last wishes of inmates on deathrow. This form allows the doomed prisoner to express those wishes. May I take the liberty to read it? <Isnt it confidential?> But of course, of course. Is there a problem? [i nod at glumm who is eyeing us narrowly from the doorway] My dear glumm you may go now. I'm sure we are safe with mr schock just now."

Safe indeed. They know perfectly well the shy flesh which surrounds this poet's brain, this lover's heart, is but a sham of designer muscle. I have carved this body to warn away, to scare off, aggression, not initiate it. It, in collusion with my once big smile, was designed to inspire peace (not fear) in the hearts of the goons of the world.

"I'll be closeby if yous need me." Glumm bows deeply, recedes backward thru the doorway.

"Now then, where was I." Straitmon refers back to the script. While he fans the pages looking for his place i will tell you: Attorney green assures me, the same feds who arranged my arrest & sentencing are still in charge. They may even have written the script he holds. Or, if not quite that, surely they pull some of the wires of the dunces who sway before me.

You mentioned last requests, i prompt.

"O yes. Here we go. [flips back a page] The board which evaluates... [licks lips, begins again] The board which evaluates an inmates' last wishes is limited in what it can do. When not confronted by physical impossibility it is legal impossibility which gets in the way. For instance, as in your case under #1 here, a prisoner will ask to have a fair trial, to be absolved of all guilt, to be allowed back into the society from which he was, as you say, kidnaped, with damages for dehumanizing pain 'n' suffering.... In such cases, as you can imagine, mr schock, it would be impossible to grant the prisoner's wishes. We are not the state, or the supreme court. We are just members of a prison board. Can you see our position?"

No, i cant. I'm a puppet too, like you, dangling on synoecic strings. We do not think for ourselves. To tell the truth i think i dropped a line somewhere back there. Would you be kind enuf to cue me in again from your line which goes: Can you see our position?

Actually i stood in silence.

"Fine. As to number two, I quote. <I implore you to have Lilith McGrae brought to my dungeon. I ask you to provide us with a comfortable quiet private place for my last 24hours on this Earth ...no, make that: til all this heinous business has gone away ...no, change that to: til i awake in her arms, in a forest, by a waterfall, or on a cliff above a misty sur ...a misty sur....> Sorry. Ink's smeared here. <...above a misty surging sea> there. Very hot in here." Loosens tie. Bedbutty becillo does same. Actually it is uncomfortably cool, damp & musty, a veritable petridish for tuberculosis.

"<...And if you cannot provide us with a whole day then any amount of time will do —the longer the better, of course.> [clears throat] As you recall, nathan... May we call you that, since we are such good friends now?"

The skin on my forehead, my lips, the tops of my hands, feels numb, and i grow dizzy. Like suited manikins at the far end of a department store, they seem to recede from me. My legs & feet, like two flat noodles, melt out in front of me the way a shadow races off in an odd direction on reaching the bottom of a swimmingpool.

"Fine then. As you may recall, nathan, your request has an x struck thru it. Under that is written, in very dark hand: <Dont dare touch her, you goons. [both wince in unison] Ever! She will think she is being kidnaped an' draped again.> [eyebrows up] Didnt get that. [i did not write draped, reader] <The frite would be toomuch for her. I'd rather die alone in this human sewer and never see her again than authorize you to go near her!> Well, now. [both exhale deeply] As you know, judge, er —a-, black. Yes, black it is— has not authorized you to have visitors anyway... except, of course, your lawyer...."

"And, of course, a member of the clergy" adds becillo, timidly.

Straitmon frowns. "Of course. And while you are limited to the warm friendship of prison employes 'n' administrators —like myself 'n' mr becillo here— [he adds with mockmirth & a wink] I am however happy to announce that the board (of which I am the director 'n' mr becillo is secretary) [becillo bows on cue] ...I am happy to announce, we are here today to honor that request."

Somewhere in that neural gulf that lies between a giving heart & gonadal greed something big rolled over in me. I eye the two oafs before me with mixed panic & wonder. You dont know, reader, when starved ...i mean, for just the scent of her hair ...how intense, how burning, how raging wild... I mean, one can reach a point of absolutely alien sexual rapacity. Noises down the corridor still going on. Voices too. Thought i heard a female voice, just once —musical lilt above all the prop-shuffling. O God, have they brought her here? I will crush her in my arms. I will kiss her. I will take her and take her and.... Stop! Take slow deep breath ...Okay. Now, gather in rapidly branching thoughts.

Are you saying youve brought her here anyway?

"No, wait. What we meant is …dont look at me like that. Youve taken this all wrong. O what a shame! Our very best intentions! What we mean is, we're honoring your wish that we NOT bring Miss McGrae here …just as you requested!" His puffy rouged lips mutilate her name! "O what a shame! Sorry, my good man. After all, you *did* instruct… Look, right here [indexfinger shakes as it points], it says, <Dont go near her. Ever! I wont repeat the name you called us.>."

Something sags in me. Thank dumb cruel destiny they cant bring her here says a voice crouched inside me: infinitely gentle plunderer; rapist as tender as any lover who ever panted on such a neck, who ever gripped such a suddenly ardent body! More needs be said about these matters.

"There there. Goodness. I thought for a moment you were, well, you know, having another of your episodes. But I see you are still in charge of yourself. May we move on to item three now? Please read this section for us, bobby …I mean, mister becillo. I'll just sit over here." Waddles to seatless commode, removes newspaper from under arm, folds it, lays it on leading edge, squats gingerly upon it. Two men in work coveralls pass in the corridor, one carrying a jumble of pipes & a large red wrench, the other toting a hoop of wire over one shoulder. I thought i heard the distant whinny of a horse. Outside? Inside? "Bobby" read aloud. It must have been the whistle of the spittle on his lips.

"<I would like to be permitted to visit, for my last 24hours, my home in the mountains. I would like to be left alone there, to take care of personal things. You may bring guards. But no dogs or helicopters, please. And instruct, please, those swatteam imbeciles not to shoot or harass the many wild & free creatures they will see thereabouts. I ask they keep the relative peace that has been indigenous to the area since the time when dinosaurs grazed a more primitive flora.> I want you to know, a lady-member of our board wept when she read this part, did she not, my director?"

"She did." Straitmon fidgeted on the edge of his seat. I was grateful for the newsprint prophylaxis between his foul rump and my personal utensil.

"I too wept" confessed mr b, eyeing him with curiosity. "While it is beyond the power of the board, as you know, or even the warden himself (our indulgent mr todion) to grant such a wish, we are happy to say: We were able to come up with a sort of compromise-wish for you. What do you think of that, mr nathan? Are you pleased?"

<May i hear the compromise?>

"Of course you may, dear chap." Rising from the commode —over the lip of which he'd been dragging himself back&forth, eyelids half-closed ε flickering— straitmon rearranged himself, rather waddled over to the celldoor. Newspaper begins slowly to unfold itself. Clapping hands vigorously but ineffectually, he rather whines, "Guard glomm? Scuse me, gluum? glumm? So *there* you are. Were you hiding, you silly fellow? Instruct the workers to bring in the things now. Dont gawk, man. The things, the things!" A bell rings. (...Not *the bell to summon me away.*) "In fact, dear nathan [the dunce, in mock excitement, dares here to touch my sleeve], we will make your decision easier. We will bring our special surprise right here to you. This way you may evaluate our work within the comfort of your own abode." (*They're [just] anxious to begin their little play.*)

Things begin to arrive. Two men carry a porchswing past my cell; chairs go by; a matron in green carries two birdhouses; two workers in khaki jumpsuits angle a long desk thru the doorway; my computer desk is right behind; massive bookcases follow. I watch Lilith's studio furniture parade past. Cells are opened, used to represent rooms in our mountain home. A tall black man in carribean whites carries a large portrait of Lilith in one hand! Careful with that! I grab it just before he lays it, face down, on top of the birdhouses! Next our mountainbikes glide past gleaming like himalayan rams. Two of the eyrie's six windowed sidewalls arrive. Guard gluum, on duty after all, guides the workers as they wrestle with them. As they pass i see thru finger-smudged panes a square of duncan mountain, a piece of sky across the river, then the forest beyond the tarn as the wall turns and levelsoff; all of it rocking, tilting, in step with the jerky advance of the workers. Is that the clatter of hoofs? Are the palominos here? I watch for the cream ε beige beauties i bought for Lilith's birthday our first year together? Gluum disappears behind a prop, comes out as glumm at the other end. Captain of the guard godion, toting a bag under each arm and one under each eye beside, sets two of them aside, begins directing the resituating of my books —hand-numbered by someone (using chalk, thankfully) so as to maintain their exact order. Straitmon ε becillo stand by sweating ε smiling. Three books slide from the hands of a worker. Picking them up guard gluum reads "Invi... Invita... to a... to a... Be... Beha... Aw, bullshit!" Unable to read the title (printed in contrived cyrillic) he passes it, along with its companion volumes, to a tall man –the one who manhandled Lilith's portrait– now standing barefoot on one of the shelfs in order to reach the top. The gilt title of lao tsu's *Dao te ching* is slipped into its slot next to *Francis of assisi: the collected writings.*

For almost an hour things, ever smaller things, keep arriving. Empty cartons are crushed ε carted off. Why not reuse them? Surely my things must be repacked, returned to my home? They leave the cartons intact. A model train locomotive (collector's edition of a pennsygreen-liveried cat-whiskered gg1) is placed on a shelf above my desk. The porch furniture, even some potted plants, are linedup in the corridor.

"Well, I see we're about finished here", says straitmon. "We'll spare you the monolog. Our goal, as you know, is not applause." (*Andiam! Incominciate!*) The newspaper on the commode finishes unfolding, drops to the floor.

"Look out!" yells the woman in green.

I swing about in time to see several workers catch one of the bookcases which, loaded with half a ton of record albums, comes close to toppling onto, and surely crushing, the tall man in whites, now lying on the floor looking up with eyes big as white halfdollars. A moment later all workers are gone and glumm reappears, retaking his role by the door. He salutes godion as the capt departs. We are nearing scene's end.

"We pray the hours ahead give you pleasure, mister nathan. A word of caution tho. The fireplace is only a cardboard replica. And, while you are free to use the kitchen (fully stocked, as you may have noticed), the garbage disposal declined to work for the plumbers."

One word before [we] go —We'll do our best,
and crave your kind indulgence for the rest....

"We'll see you sometime tomorrow afternoon." Smiling, they shake my hand, my sleeve, and leave. "Come along, glumm", says becillo, indicating he should take up his pat position in the rear. As they walk away i spot a familiar looking piece of paper jutting from one of glumm's hip pockets. The massive corridor door (to the new wing), set free, clangs shut like a portentous iron bell.

I wash my hands, stand for a time wiping them on my trousers. Soon, despite myself, i am glorying in the old plush of my den chair. I switch on the sound system. It immed sets to playing an impassioned reading of sibelius' *spring song*. If this book is ever recreated for the screen this must be the main theme. A gust of woodland air stirs the blinds. O? But where is the rapid highup whirring of pulleys? As the music ends, thru hot tears, i listen for the midday cry of bluejays, the songs of the magnolia warblers or scarlet tanagers about, the bossy cantos of 'our' woodpeckers.

The oriole should build and tell his love-tale close beside my cell.

I test the quality of the quiet. I rise, walk downstairs to the windows of the lower deck. Carefully, like a sleepwalker, sure it will not cooperate, i attempt to open one. It glides aside! Feeling like an adventurer about to step onto the surface of mars, i look out over the land as tho i can see our pristine ε precious Earth 50 million miles off. I walk along the deckrail, test with tentative fingers the swing. It moves! Looking up, i follow its cables to the ceiling. Where are the hundreds of guy wires i expect? where, row on row of stacked scenery? I sit. I smell the forest scent of Lilith's hair as it cascades over the swing's back. O God how i've missed you!

Suddenly what i thought was the clatter of hoofbeats becomes, in my groggy mind's eye, a pneumatic nailgun somewhere outside my window. This rudely inserts a surprise sense of falseness to the morning's proceedings. I block the interpretation. {Why not dilate the lie if it affords ecstasy?}

We swing together for some minutes. Her bare brown legs, her excellent calfs set off by the white of her socks, pump the swing to&fro. Every so often, meaning to help, i give a disrupting shove with my own foot. A mild gust plays the vast gong of leaves in the trees below the bluff. A moment later a bluster of doves strikes into blueness above the valley! We rise, hand in hand walk to the steps and down, alight on the walkover, winding out thru her butterfly garden to the bluff. What possesses me? I feel as tho i'm standing amid ...that is, i think *I stand amid the roar of a surf-tormented shore... while I weep —while I weep!*

Suddenly i find myself alone among my dream-props. My hand, tho warm with memories, holds only my own shoulder, arms folded in my dream. I take one last lingering gaze at the rivervalley below, at the small buildings, at a car creeping antlike across the causeway, as the mountains beyond are draped in an ever-deepening lavender haze. I fill my lungs again&again with gulps of mountain air, til i'm giddy with dizziness. I am too dizzy in fact to be held responsible for where my thoughts wend me, & us, or for what happens in this low-budget theater of the id. Afterall, i'm hardly a willing participant in all this and i'm the captive audience beside! I lie on this wretched cot, nite on endless nite, watching vast formless things shift the scenery to&fro. But for this intimate moment *i'm* in charge of the scenery and i love it!

Her portrait, the floral scent of her studio furniture, the smell of my books, phonograph records, warm the chill of this despicable place. But mostofall, real blood still courses thru this body, this brain. I am still alive! Anything is possible, isnt it? Maybe even our first spring day together! Alternately the scents of blossoming dogwoods & chimneysmoke (from the valley) stir memory. Nothing can stop me now! Laffing, i jump onto the path that winds down the forested bluff to the river. Lilith (LiLethe for the nonce) should be home by 9! With singing heart i stride down the path, disappear into the happy woodland. I will have a feast laid out when she arrives. My darling, lite of my life! There will be candlelite, herbal aromatics; a softly musical *tendresse* fit to put goosebumps on the flesh of jove, an ardoresse of my best invention that will make the angels (those silly silly seraphs) envious. There will be passion such as petrarch's laura only dreamed: *Soudain mon âme s'éveillera!* (And of a sudden my soul will awake!)

28

Dacapo. I was awakened this morning by a metallic banging sound. It was either a very gray day or i had not yet opened my eyes. I lay on my fleshless cot trying to picture what was being banged, and where. Surely it wasnt anything under me. The sound came from outside my window. I sat on the edge of my cot, bare feet on the cold floor. After a time i rose, stepped to the dingy window. Some workers on the roof of the gym about 20m away were repairing an exhaust fan, a large propeller filling the gasping maw of a roof vent. But it was time for my morning contemplations. For rent: humble abode with humble commode. Here i sit on parade. Anyone ~~pissing~~ ...anyone *passing* in the corridor can look in, see me fullon. It's good there's little traffic along deathrow. Alot this matters tho, for the wideangle "security" camera hung from the corridor ceiling slurps all for its masters.

I am a private person. Altho i get by, i've never been comfortable with public toilets. O the urinal summons is not so bad: lineup of squirting dunces, noses pressed to a wall like so many dribbling corpses staring at the lids of their coffins. It's the commode stalls that put me off: cramped in a gamy cubicle teeming with slime & disease. My claustrophobia can get rowdy when other aversions are heaped on. I know where&when we lost the right to piss off a precipice in full view of the valley below. And i now know why. What i dont understand is why no one notices the deliberate trashing of every last one of our primal freedoms. In this sense that camera trained at my cage could be liberating except that the 'valley below' is populated by the gaping visages of so many degenerate lifeforms. Only a lifetime of wild mountain spaces can quell this primal-denial angst in me... a short lifetime at that if some good fairy doesnt wing in here and interdict in my behalf and damned soon! Horrible headache! What a nite! Where were we now? ...And only a lifetime of opendoor policy, where public toilets are concerned, helps me now, performing as i must this spectacle daily! And so, on my dias, i plan my day as tho no one were watching.

They have promised (hic,tsk) to bring a chair & small table tomorrow —desk & chair for me & my muse. A couple months ago i filled out a questionnaire.

> (One suggestion per item.)
>
> √ How would you improve meals? *use real food*
>
> √ What change would you make in the facilities? *demolish them*
>
> √ What would you like most to have available to you? *a little justice*

The usual propaganda: Dear human rights advocate, see how we worry over our inmates. The reply came yesterday, the reason i guess for my dream. "Your request is being evaluated. You will be informed in due course". I'd asked to be treated as if i were no different than any other prisoner. I pointed out, i have been quarantined like a mad leper for three months and that my behavior (if not my attitude) is exemplary. I asked also that the court's quarantine (on my contact with the outside world) be ignored.

Finishing brushing my teeth in grayish tap-goop i returned to my humble board, as the song goes. What else is there to do but write write write? As i juggled these thoughts on my cot, something caught my eye. At first sight i thought it was a fat pale spider dangling on a thread outside the windowglass. <Go away! The obligatory spider is already in residence.> Refocus eyes to deal with the film of dirt (*outside* the glass else i would clean it). <Go! There's not room here for three of us.> Just then my arachnid prison pal, spid (Hi, cecy. Hi, timofey), was eyeing me from her quarters in the underside of the sink. {Has this skilled rappeller appeared in my window to rescue my octopodan cellmate instead of me? All she must do to escape is slip out the hole in the windowglass, wait for her rescuer to swing overhead, lift her to freedom! But first he must drop lower. {Pssst. Lower, grapneler, lower! The prize, the eight-legged princess (four crotches, by cracky!), is still some distance below!}

I rise, go to the glass to study the process... find i have been duped! What i saw end-on was actually cigaret-shaped, lowered from above by a string of bagties. {But how do they know anyone's here? And do they just assume if youre in prison you also smoke? Just fishing for a contact maybe ...the fish being me.} Having raised myself on the sill, having got eye-level with the thing, i realize {It's no cigaret at all. It's a piece of paper rolled into a cylinder! Is *that* what the hole in this window is for?} How pathetic that such a thing has enthralled my curiosity! Yet i do want badly to snag it. Surely there's a way to reel it in, ravish that pale thin mysterious bait? Great Gaia! At this rate, what's to become of me?

For the sake of the camera i continue to act as tho i am doing tricep presses on the windowsill, a recurrent part of my cell-locked workouts, desperate as i am to stay in some semblance of health. I soon realize i have nothing even remotely capable of snaking out that hole, bending upward to make the catch. I drop to the floor, track it peripherally. It hangs there for some time. A breeze catches it. It sways stiffly on its wires. Then, as the breakfast bell sounds upstairs, it is retrieved upward by careful little jerks. (No insult intended.)

29

Feeling some better, having eaten. It is humiliating.... I mean, i never would have thought such a thing (note on the end of a string) could sprout wings of hope in me. Elaborate plans of escape? promises of freedom? I'm not so maddened with foolish desperation as to hope for these. Just the hope of contact with someone less cruel than my captors is enuf. So at breakfast i stole something; parts to a tool i will construct for gaffing that note ...if it is lowered again, that is. In the meantime, the duty of autobiography awaits.

30

Moving now from generic nymphdom back to a specific nymph: By this time juanita & me were frantic to fondle every follicle of the other's flesh. If there was a blush of selfconsciousness left in us i dont remember it. We were convinced, the religious infantry which surrounded our foxhole could be vanquished only by love —unstinting unhypocritical love. Meanwhile a new confidence calmed me. It is clear today, if i could only have stayed on there for another summer or two –free to roam those woodlands lakes meadows with my dryad darling– my emotional wounds would have begun to heal. But then, the same could be said about losing mossville, or losing those sanity-saving summers at the farm, or of the lost priscilla and that *bed of leaves and broken play.*

A last view of juanita & me on our raft is a composite of days of watching, of plotting. (Such compression is good; we must hurry along.) Our minds were fixed on one thing: the panic of separation. We need to talk about this problem of severing: flesh from flesh; rock & soil from Earthbody; a pulling of sea from shore; fear of the psychic equivalent of those great black rifts which scream silently between islands of galaxies!

And of course the counselors studied us. Where practical matters were concerned, juanita was our better judgement. To me, unless she would run away with me our situation seemed hopeless. For i was by then ready to copulate in broad daylite. But that, and running away, were too radical for her. She could break rules but not shatter them. Her cautiousness caused in me a sense of futility & malaise. Fear moved ahead to autumn, to school, to another bleak winter. <I wonder what it's like here in winter?>

On elbows, lying on her stomach, she shivered her shoulders, chestnut-brown by this time. "Bet a c'n skate around this raft."

Let's meet here christmas!

"What? We cant do that."

Silence & searing sunlite.... All at once she sat erect. "I know! How about on christmas eve? <Huh?> Yes. We'll look at a clock. Both at the same time. Jus like that [snaps fingers] we'll be t'gether! I'll be thinking of you, you'll be thinking of me. Pretending is doing."

Why not jus do it? Why not jus meet?

"O, I wish we could!" But that was as scary as eloping. She laid back down. Then, a moment later, "I know! I'll give you my address —we can write!"

Better yet. I'll visit you.

"Ooo. Mother wouldnt like that. She says I'm too spanish 'n' youre too wild. [pause] But why do I care what she says? <Yes, why?> And how can I love my parents 'n' hate what they believe in?"

Yes, how? Sunlite catalyzed our longing. We were two stars in mutual orbit, the gravity of each palpating the other's terrain, becoming intimate with it; our coronas brushed against, passed thru, each other as we ellipsed in a fiery electric & quaking binary dance!

"I have a plan. <What?> Jus be patient, you'll see." Juanita's practical approach to loosening the noose that gripped my young satyr's ganglia seemed as sterile as an ancient coin. But she was confident. Beside, i knew she could see things, pickup on her surroundings, in a way i could not. She knew for instance that "Miss lila 'n' miss flora are gay", and that they were having a "sweet affair". Such things got by me. "And miss louise makesout with mister newt up in the loft of the horsebarn." She viewed these undercurrents without judging them: acts devoid of misdemeanor.

I studied our counselors after that, some of whom were ex campers and a few of whom were not much older than me. I learned, for example, most males in camp had "the hots" for juanita, my counselor mr claude included. He was in his mid30s. It was only years later i figuredout he viewed me as a threat. O juvenita, you were desirable alright! By the last week of camp her plan was in place: On friday & saturday nites, predictably, rain or starshine, our counselors would lie in bed til they felt we were asleep, after which they would sneak off. A faith in this behavior (and not in the gospel they lip-served) was to be our salvation.

In the meantime i felt i knew how to copulate. As i lay in bed one nite, as i followed beyond my screen the flashing lanterns of tennyson's pleiades staggering about in the humid jar of a n.jersey nite, i tried to plot my actions. I felt quick as a bunny, stalwart as a stallion. This new selfconfidence felt odd on me, like a new loose-fitting jacket. I was sure, if only we got the chance

–just a few moments out of eyeshot– if they would only let us …let us, well …fall off a roof together or something, i was sure i could mate with her before we hit the ground! O how i wanted you juaniña, my gitanita. Too excited to accidentally fall asleep, i just lay there. After what seemed hours, mr claude stirred in his bunk: squeak of bed, shoe-shuffle on wooden planks, low rasp of plank against plank, twang of hinge-spring on screendoor –like the binding of rusty springs in my testes tonite– and mr claude slunk off. Thru a crack in the propped shutter i saw the moon –how near, how far– as if paused in passage. I counted the minutes, waiting to hear cars startup in the distance. I followed, in orbit above my bunk, the landing pattern of a salivating mosquito.

Lilith

I was afraid she would not be waiting by the barn when i got there! Her counselor had been sick all day; maybe decided not to go out! Was she trapped in for the nite? A lifetime of disappointment can bend a mind that way. Holding hands we tiptoed past the barn. Talking laffter lite sifted thru the cracks in its walls. Juanita knew exactly who was in there. "The redheads are at it again" she whispered. Once safely past, we broke into a run, headed straight for the lake, jumping over wellknown hazards ε their moonlit shadows: rocks roots tufts of tenacious turf whose growth even the foot-sloggings of a hundred children a day couldnt completely discourage.

One counselor each was always left at the boys' ε girls' camps. Tho they often snuckoff together they didnt dare leave the camp. We ran toward the one place juanita was sure they would not go: the chapelByTheLake. To them sex was sinful. One went to chapel to seek purification not to actout "man's innate wickedness", and certainly not act it out before "the alter of God".

At the fork one path swung upward toward treeline ε chapel, the other dropped toward the water. We froze. Two shadows sat on the dock. They either did not notice us or did not care we were there. (Our counselors may have been older but they were not wiser than we.) We picked our way quietly upward. Tho i didnt realize it at the time, my height made me look like mr claude, the tallest of the counselors. Once among the trees, the woods grew ever dimmer.

Lilith

I will not trust entirely to recall for those last tete-a-tetes. I will use a sheaf of poems which grew from this affair, the last of which was not set down til after i entered the military. Sketched in a hospital in saigon, finished in a hospital in seattle, i titled it "unscripted ascriptions of a nondescript conscript".

I know it may seem herenorthere just now, yet i might mention (since i dont expect to return to this topic), i got out early, but only two months, by the time they got done screwing around with all the fake rehab ɛ investigation: "You can avoid an ugly trial by taking an early-out". A "for medical reasons" discharge was convenient to the warcrimes coverup already underway. O the killing was going fine –an expression, you know– when something snapped, as they say. My last days of actual combat drew to a conscious close when lt. billy kelly (killerbilly, behind his back) ordered the "wasting" of 516 old folks, women ɛ children we had rounded up in a village after "zippoing" all their hooches. {My God, that's everything they own!} (Initially in its coverup, the u.s army would admit to 'only' the 42 executions i personally witnessed before "flipping out" as the ever cynical press put it during the subsequent trial. No, this was no 'mere' thanh phong massacre.) By the time the 41 old men were murdered, one villager was wailing so uncontrollably lt. twink [Kelly —Ed.] decided she needed "sumthin real ta scream about". Wrenching her baby from her grasp and holding it up by one foot, he chukachukachukaed the infant almost in half with rounds from his rifle. "Tear along dotted line!" he razzed, dropping the dangle of bloodied flesh back into the swooning mother's arms. "Dont think that one'll be sniping us any time soon!" (Just as deepgreens are considered potential terrorists today, back then we were instructed to think of all "nams" as snipergooks in disguise.)

...Your naked infants spitted upon pikes.

My conscience reeling, he ordered me to "hosedown the brats... Grease 'em, corprul schock. *Now!* That's an order!". The last thing i remember after knocking the lt. down ɛ disarming him was the sight of that poor mother's eyes; *all* their eyes, really —the pinpoint lites of those dark watery fearful disbelieving ɛ doomed eyes ...before 'waking up' (as they say) in a hospital in saigon. Seems i'd run off, captured an "enemy" officer in the jungle, insisting —in the face of a good deal of professional dissent: doctors officers prosecuting attorney— that the "brass gook" i'd brought back was our commander and that i'd rescued him from certain death at the hands of lt. kelly, whom i claimed shot everything he feared and i feared he feared everything. The commander not only appreciated my concern, there was also the matter of the hostage-value of the little colonel i'd somehow bagged during my weeks of dream-vague jungle awol. However he said he could not officially excuse my assault of an officer (kelly) no matter the "seeming urgency" of the villagers' plight. (My fellow grunts, it seems, kept the lt.'s two henchmen from gunning me down while i escaped.) I was thence posthaste (i'm just a clatter of cliches) shipped to a clean cool hospital bed in saigon, as i've said ...all of which worked out for the best, as i was a great shot but a lousy killer.

Anyway, i do not have access to those poems now, and i will not ask emil to include any of them since, at this distance, i cannot attest to their quality. The situation is made doubly curious for, while i can quote from memory works by others (and at considerable length in a few cases), all my life i've been unable to quote my own writing! Still, there's a kind of compensation which operates behind the scenes in this regard. For, when i rewrite a long-forgotten theme, it is not unusual for many of the original images to reappear intact! Why does this matter? Because it is the basic immutability of this sheaf of memories which mostofall acts now to show the feelings juanita & me shared.

In four hours the lites will dim. I must either devote the remaining time to recapturing these frangible feelings or risk a graphic description of two final encounters between a 15yearold faun-to-satyr and a 13yearold girl-to-nymph. I admit, our scenes on the porch were guilty of clinically cool curiosity, of young lust roaming at large. Yet

> We loved with a lust that was more than lust,
> my lovely juanita and me,
> a lust clean as fire, a lust pure as trust,
> in her nymphdom by the sounding trees....

And yet our final tete-a-tetes were bathed in a more ethereal desire. Still, because of time constraints, i will limit my brush to a sampling of impressionistic strokes, using the wide coarse bristles juanita preferred, the fimbriate pastels of her poesy, putting aside my own delineating strokes & bold contrasts of color & shadow.

A low stone wall enclosed the hillside chapel, which was pie-shaped —if one pictures the tip of a wide wedge bitten off by the lakeshore. Pews (planks on poles, actually) rose in terraces up the hillside; the rearmost ones rose well above the lectern and considerably above the level of the lake. In an attempt to fulfill 2yrs of daydreaming back at my desk at school & in bed by nite, i led my vestal dryad by the hand to the farthest bench, the one where i'd first brushed her hair.

We held each other, trying to control an infectious shivering which set in almost at once. Not that we were cold. In fact, the nite, tho a little damp, was warm. I can only guess (since this same tic would recur later, during my seaside tryst with Lilith) it was fear of what total unity might bring that wrenched our bodies. This is not so strange: desire is the polar opposite of separation —an index of the hazard of potential loss! Those with secure childhoods, those who had parents family or friends to complain to, will not understand. I would skip this except i know, while the same fears operate in the lives of others, they are masked by an adult paranoia that is widespread: a fear of admitting subliminal fear, a fear of admitting subliminal anything. For admitting the subliminal is admitting Nature/instinct as a hidden influence in one's life.

We stood close. A wall of crickets choiring along the shoreline could not cover the chattering of my teeth. Rub my spine; down more; right there. Faster. Harder. There. It's stopping. Damn, what was that? Otherwise, the quiet was as transparent as only Nature's sounds can be: laminations of quiet sounds heaped on quieter sounds, and thus, ironically, approaching silence ...which incidentally can never be 'heard' by living ears. The residual heat of three summers burned in her breast, raged in my flanks. All at once our mouths met, like concupiscent cannibals, our broken chains dragging in the dust behind a hunger too long inverted. I enwrapped her, shivering also, til we relaxed in each other's arms.

She wore a white jumper & blouse —the same airy muslin she would wear when we parted. She was barefoot (as we always were when permitted) and almost naked underneath! I kissed her and felt of that nakedness. She grew weak. I sat her down. I knelt, crawled, probed; like a bee on an orchidean drunk, i kissed all i could find of her. A family of grebes, rustling among reeds along the shoreline, burbled deliciously in their moonlite feeding. Juanita throbbed & moaned under the wash of my tastebuds. Like a micro mirror-image of my tung, the pimplets of her gooseflesh jostled & bleated like lambs. What hoary celtic bonfires leapt in her loins, what tattoo of druid drums thrummed in her limbs, i dont know; but all at once she gave a violent thrust and melted under my strivings. Our woodland dance was as old as protozoan desire.

A linnet rustled in the larches; in the dusk a ghostly orchid glimmered. Occasionally the laffter of the lovers on the dock drifted up to us, reassuring our sense of insularity. Oddly hallucinated & fearless (o wild nite, o damsel darc!), my clothes were soon in a heap around my ankles. We kissed again, newly deep. I rolled my nakedness on the silken gift of her body and quickly proved equal to the flood of feeling which at first shook me helpless. The whooit of a whippoorwill carried roundly, transparently, the distance across the lake.

Yet as hard, as deeply, as we kissed, i could not seem to satisfy the height to which she urged me, the tops of her bare thighs pushing at my lean rump. What completion of the flesh did juanita seek? what circuit of liquid systems did she long to complete? Her mouth, wideopen like that of a young bird, sought me; her tung searched back&forth –almost hysterically– in the shadow of my body. And i was the generous feeding parent, my desire dangling over her like a severed entrail, squirming blindly in the moonlite, rising in greased coils, searching for its lost mate-end. Her mouth, like her memory, like her bilingual vocabulary, proved lethal. O my juanita darckiss! *¡Doncella del beso oscuro!* On hands & knees now above her, thru a thin line of trees, i saw a breeze shiver a crescent of moon out on the water. Wild & tingling, i soon found myself helplessly melting upon her.

That breeze, when it reached us, stirred the leaves with a sound of rain. I lay down by her side. We felt womb-safe amid the sounding trees. We huddled thus for several minutes. The figures on the dock had long ceased to move (perhaps now asleep). Soon the old anxiety crept back. I kissed her. She murmured into my hair, "What time is it?"

I dont know. …Eleven?

She sat abruptly and fixed me with a blank look. Then, saying nothing, my woodsy wanton crawled onto her knees and, grabbing the edge of the stone wall behind the bench, looking back at me —a glint of stellar haze in her eyes, a web of wet moonbeam caught in her hair— she bent away from me, her hair slipping off her shoulder and dangling above the wall. The cry of a loon penetrated across the breeze-shivered expanse of water. (Harbinger of loss?) All at once i was a panther on the back of a fleeing gazelle. A scrimmage of cupids beat stubby wings on my back. Suddenly, gargantuan with blood, stooped & club-wielding, primal icons were prowling the cavewalls of my id. Fierce, yes. Yet their gaze was fetal-pure. For years after, they would scour the floors of my brain with their clubs hunting for arbitrary concepts; while others, outside in the darkness, would beat the bushes of my learned faith. Thus the routing of a horde of patriarchs, rulers & troubled saints was begun that nite ...all without my direct knowledge.

In wild moonlite & shadow i wielded myself like i knew what i was doing. I panic yet dont panic at the muted sounds she is making. Pain? ecstasy? or a new-to-me amalgam of both? Yet, unless she actually told me to, i could not stop. Shhh, juanita! Shhh! They'll hear us!

"I cant! ...I cant."

Thru a tear in the proxy ceiling of leaves memory spots a whole phalanx of red reeling galaxies!

Are you okay?

"Yes. Yes! ...Nathan? ...I love you!"

My new icons stared down at us from the stained-glass silences towering between the trees. And there, far below, in our timbered cathedral, amid the forest's dream & danger, rapt, engulfed by moonlite, a scarlet-stained but silken-throated orchid, an oiled anaconda, wrestled strangely among the pews! Those trees, that lake, those hills, for many summers had been juanita's nymphdom, and i (a satyr by this standard) had been permitted to enter it. Faun & nymph. Sathan & juanymph. Natyr & nymphita. The World was being made new again for us! Greedily i drank my ablution: whistling bones of prophets, crumbling corpses of saints! And beneath the feet of young desire (unbiased, reborn), crisp as leaves, transparent as glass, we trampled on the amputated wings of angels!

Out of a clear sky a dark cloud swept over the stars. Like a curtain at scene's end, it drenched us with its shadow, deafened us with its applause of rain —and was gone again by the time my icon-loaded lunging had peaked, strafed ε subsided. Tonite my strungback head inverts again that starry roof; the porridge bowl of the great bear is spilled across the graceful bare back of diana; my muted howl makes the moon wince; a skirmish of angels flails helplessly among the slender wet leaves of memory. I dont know how else to say these things. It seemed thus at the time. A few readers will understand the metamyth behind all the allegory ε metaphor.

31

[Emil, for the editor/publisher worrying over "the attentionspan of the average reader", this next is the chapter to cut ...not for any lack of intrinsic value but for the sake of appeasing (yes, again!) that certain reader. (Afterall we've gone some 30 chapters without a chase scene, without a "good ol' fashioned" rape or two.) On the other hand, we've put by 43 gory murders and, if that isnt enuf, let me say. This may be the only chapter which deals almost exclusively with the abuse of females, including rape —usually popular with the average civil reader. So it's kind of a tough call i guess. Personally, between you&me, those "certain" easily bored types have about exhausted my patience.]

Now to the rape ε mutilation of the archetypal nymph —so long as we find ourselves gargantuan with virgin blood anyway.

Hans Bellmer

For those readers who wonder about the history of brutality against females —why, for example, today's ideal female in art (the modern venus) is typically fragmented: anonymous (shadowed, masked or headless), defenseless (bound, crippled, armless or legless), sacrificed (bruised, bleeding, mutilated, sometimes even murdered).... What makes us call this art?

See me writing happily along, back when i wrote the above, with no clue as to its prevision of the violence to women in my own future! Yet it is impossible ...nathan schock, harken! ...*impossible* to speak cogently of Nature ε females and turn one's back on civilization's crucifixion of Nature. I'm writing fast now, cramming several books into a couple chapters. This never works, but we do what we can. This crucifixion of Nature/instinct has been traditionally, even classically, authorized by way of abuse of the primal nymph, that manifestation of the cosmic feminine which is the personification not only of Nature without but of the Nature/instinct within us. Those who could care less may of course skip on ahead. Your disinterest in knowing who authorized the rape ε mutilation (and, yes, even the murder) of our females young ε old past present ε future, will die with me.

We must resist the urge to flop open a dictionary. In fact, toss it out the nearest window with all the encyclopedias. For they know nothing of the archetypal nymph. To unearth the cosmic feminine we must go to those competent to speak on *manifestations of deity in early human consciousness.* In *faust,* well before jung, goethe called it "the eternal feminine". And here is what otto reich had to say.

> Long a constellation of feelings and intuitions in the minds of the first humans, the cosmic feminine entered human consciousness ages before the skills of drawing sculpting and writing. I'm thinking of certain humans now, ancestors a thousand times removed from the artists who carved and painted those amazing figures on the cave walls at Lascaux and Altamira tens of thousands of years ago! Which is why female deities in ancient Greek literature —or wood sprites of Amerindian legend, or the river goddesses of the Mayan and early Asian cultures, the rain girl of the Balkans, the zâna of Albanian springs, the rusalki of the Slavs, along with myriad others— are of limited value to us. The "female" we seek lies yet deeper than these. As Jung observed, nymphs mirror a primal ideation: those "traits" in the Universe around us we see as female: nurture, tenderness, gentleness, patience, re-creation, resurrection, etc.

Dont take him wrong. He encourages knowledge of the nymphs of, say, homer hesiod propertius plutarch paraclesus, to name but a few in western lit. But they come too late to show the platform in human consciousness of the Cosmic feminine —the *a priori* female & her archetypal daughters. While homer & his ilk wrote of lapiths & lethes, and even leleges, they knew not one Lilith McGrae between them. Not even a juanita darc. Certainly not the juanita i knew ...since their representation of females (let alone of nymphs) was so hopelessly narrow & patriarchally patronizing. Incidentally, there is no conflict in my admiring otto reich. I can respect him and in the same breath despise the prison shrink who torments me daily. Here is jung, reich's mentor, again.

> We are not being morbid but scientific when we say, we are commanded by shadow images. A rare few of us listen to them consciously, most do not. These icons of the psyche lie so deep, access can be had only through strenuous "archeology" —through excavations of the unconscious. Here instinct is alive and well. Here live the archetypes.

He is not talking about the masks which haunt my cell. Do not confuse the two. If youre not going to read my books you must trust me on this. The latter are the icons of an individual psyche, while jung & reich are unearthing the icons of a species! [Back to NS's texts. —Ed.]

Recent scholarship has unearthed a startling consistency among the myths and legends of the world. The sky was male but everything beneath it was female. Even the moon was once female! The 'man' in the moon in fact was put there quite recently —by the same social force which put a man (and not a woman) *on* the moon; the same force which stole the power of resurrection from the female, gave it to the male, the same social force which puts lone male gods in charge of invented "realities".

We've passed behind the plummeting cataract now, started down the slab of granite i spoke of earlier. You are trembling! Watch your step. It is perilously narrow and the surface slick with mist ε algae ...or is it the shed tears of a whole historiograph of abused ε forgotten female icons?

Spring (resurrection) and summer (nurture) were once female in all cultures. Not because males can't give birth but because, if new life is to thrive and be robust (like birth and growth in Nature itself), it will require nurturing: tenderness gentleness patience self-sacrifice soforth —traits possible to males but native to females. It is no accident, fetuses were given to females, females to fetuses. Nature, in its totality, knows nothing of accident. Only ignorance presumes accident and chaos in Nature.

For accident ε chaos are human misperceptions of that Reality which puzzles us so! The Cosmos has only one direction, one ending, in Mind, toward which, in the large of things, it moves inexorably *and* unerringly.

World literature abounds with such female beings. They frolic in the primeval valleys of Asia, the scrub lands of ancient Australia, the streams of Europe, the rivers of Africa, the falls of the Americas, the grottos of Iceland, the forests of Scandinavia, the oases of the great deserts, and along the shores of all the lakes and oceans of the old world. In short, Nature's feminine was pandemically obvious, her original representatives were pure, beautiful and awesome, and *always* revered! What happened to this reverence? When was the inchoate feminine, the archetypal nymph, made "evil"? demonic? And by whom?

While we've answered this, the question will serve to introduce the last generality. I would let Lilith explain if i could. Still, the book from which the following is excerpted was her favorite.

It's time to get philosophically naked. New ages should not be allowed till old ones are understood and corrections made accordingly. But that's not the way of civilization. We hide from, rather than face, the errors of our pasts. I offer now what i call the jestOfJests, my vote for the supreme self-deception of civilized man.

I am too intelligent, too evolved, to self-realized, to continue to be the throbbing puppet of some arbitrary instinct —a sex-drive I cannot control, much less dictate to, despite my best efforts. What I, and the rest of the world, need, is a system of beliefs that will once and for all free us from the pernicious carnality which so belittles our obvious superiority over all other creatures and things. I am neither animal nor primitive.

I'm civil. I prefer denial to Reality.

This is crux, if not cause, of the lone-male-god imperialist religions. And if ever there was an original sin, this surely is it. And odds are high, it was more (civil) adam than (precivil) eve who felt thus about himself.

For while she may be a slave to sexual function (menses, say, or child-bearing), females are not the "throbbing puppets" of their sex drive, rarely feel they have been made fools of by their bodies. (Though not so always their hearts.) In fact, in the face of thousands of years of criticism, females are proud to bear children and have no need to develop a system of beliefs which blames, say, "the curse of the Irish" on men. A woman's system of beliefs comes ready-made inside her. It was surely a male who was first ashamed of his sex-drive, and an unusual male at that.

Next thing we know, we look out our historical window and see the masturbating sex-fantasizing female-chasing guy we once were has disappeared! But not without a trace. For: Look, over there! Something is chasing the nymph *we* chased yesterday. It's a guy, and he's an animal from the waist down! Now this is significant. Soon this creature is making appearances in literature, art and religion, and it has a name: satyr. Great Zeus, we've found it! *Here,* displaced, is the sex-drive Adam denied! Suppressed, it has resurfaced in the form of a make-believe beast! Thus was invented the original apposition of the sexes, the original beauty and the beast: nymph and satyr.

As to the nymph of our discourse. Civilization in collusion with civil religion subjected her to the most astonishing transformation of all. While she was permitted to keep her desirable body (for obvious reasons), her altering was more insidious —for it penetrated beyond mere flesh, beyond mere sexuality. Over time it became a transmogrification of the entire female self! And it did not stop til it had tainted the quality of her very humanity! Thus the new civil/phallic vision established itself.

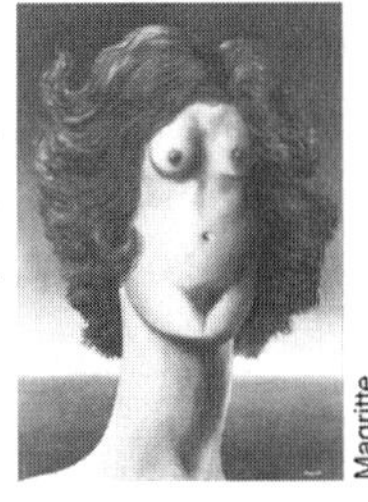
Magritte

And by such means did certain persons give the lust they hated to a beast. But we need point out, these were not your average person. No sir. For the common man, in private, if not proud of his sex-drive is at least not ashamed of it. To him it's not a loathsome subversive thing. It is, rather, a certain type of outcast who feels betrayed by his sexuality, betrayed by behaviors and desires which made of him a social pariah in less egalitarian times, and still may do so even today. And "control of desire" is the key operative here: "If humans are Nature's finest creation then they should be able to control all things about themselves. Therefor what cannot be controlled must be gotten rid of!" I repeat. It was not the average heteroperson who had reason to feel betrayed by his body from the waist down back in the days when civil religion and law were shaping their agendas.

In his famous play *the twisted cross,* my friend the baron has his "sandled nazarene" cry out from the bedside of the wise *bible*-disgloried mary of magda, "I'm a puppet to the Omnipotent who rules through my loins!"

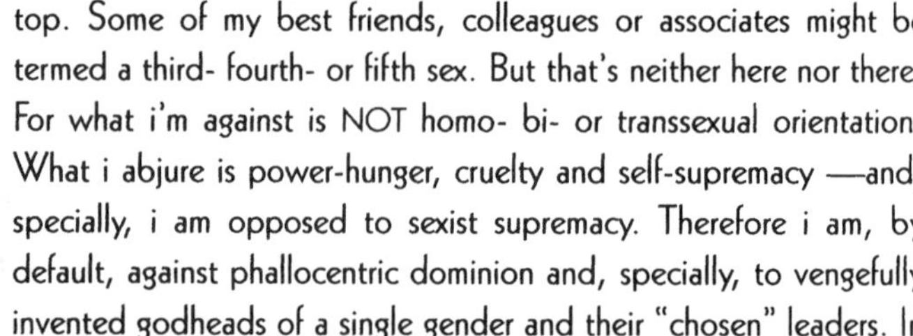
Esther Kaplan

Good or bad, it's not the average person who invents intolerant and subjugating ideologies and religions, it's alienated persons. Now it needs be made clear at the top. Some of my best friends, colleagues or associates might be termed a third- fourth- or fifth sex. But that's neither here nor there. For what i'm against is NOT homo- bi- or transsexual orientation. What i abjure is power-hunger, cruelty and self-supremacy —and, specially, i am opposed to sexist supremacy. Therefore i am, by default, against phallocentric dominion and, specially, to vengefully invented godheads of a single gender and their "chosen" leaders. In short, i reject the antiquated brutal pandemic infantile anal priapic and masculeptic domination we have endured for ages up till this very minute!

Go ahead, check my genitals, you doubting thomases! You will find i am not only male but hung like a bull not a bully.

This said, i give you the allegedly celibate monks and priests of these early historical times, times of masculeptic deconstructionism, and not just the masculine half of that certain socially (if unjustly) exiled gender—whose next get-back tactic was to push lust even further from the human male ...lest someone get wise; lest mr common male himself get wise!

Watch closely. We'll be moving fast down the gorge-face now.

At this point, borrowing liberally from world philosophy and polytheistic religion, those sad celibates set about thrusting male lust clear out of this world. First, the satyr was elevated to a pagan icon: Pan, remember him? Over time this put the satyr on a cosmic level. Then, since the new style of imperial god insisted on sole authority, Pan was turned into an angel instead of an antigod (new domesticating of old primal demons), an entity who was, on purpose, poorly suited to oppose the new lone godhead. In Judaism, Christianity and Islam this entity, to clarify his inferiority, was named "of light" (Lucifer), his light being a mere reflection of the "real" source of light. The situating of this satyr/devil appositionally to a solitary male god automatically

polarized him to the "supreme male". This created a *supreme negative state,* a fundamental condition of the new civil universe which was named "evil", thus cementing *malum in se* as if it were a real thing. And, again in Judeochrislamism, this "evil"/devil combination represents *the* ultimate in "evilness"! Thus was this angel molded into the exceptionally rational and civilized sort of demon he is to this day; a negative force with lethal philosophic baggage in tow —*the* demon among demons; Devil among devils.

None of this is of course to approach that *really* devilish problem of finding, *anywhere* in the known Universe, even one apodictic sign of that human invention we call "evil".

As a final touch, these mother- and society-betrayed men contrived to make females responsible for the "evil"/Devil presence in the world! —just as females were "responsible" for making males feel uncontrollable lust; just as they were "responsible" for the appearance on Earth of the first satyrs, and, soon after, for the coming of the satyr's horny and hoofed leader, Pan. Enter Eve. The creators of this masculeptic myth chose her, not Adam, to trust the serpent/Devil (Nature/instinct). Thus Eve was made the original Beelzebitch, retaining almost none of the scathing and Wild chutzpah of the early Semitic Lilith (who predated her in Adam's life). Thus was Eve's gender (and not Adam's) made "evil incarnate"; thus *she* was made the cause of all "sins of the flesh". And thus did civil religion isolate the female of the species as the sole cause of the "fall of humanity" ...another first-rank plagiarization since the story parallels the Greek pandora's-box myth in startling detail. And thus, most of all, were males rendered socially guiltless, socially superior. For male behavior in "Eden" was good (Godlike). At longlast the male of the species was made the "intelligent evolved self-realized being" he always suspected he was —with a bonus. "Because men respect God's law, men are spiritual". And since Eve's behavior in Eden "broke God's law" (by favoring Nature's), "women are not spiritual". They are "like the serpent/Devil": of the flesh, of "base" instinct, of the World, of Earth, and in empathy with "cruel and unpredictable Nature" —which, of course, the civil phase of our development has long (and may i add, tragically) perceived as the "enemy".

© Rachel Deitsch

And what of this cruel assault on eve's curiosity anyway? All humanity for all time was denied a state of eternal happiness for what reason? Partaking of the fruit of the "tree of knowledge"! One can only wonder what type of person would invent a god who first makes curiosity a basic compulsion then outlaws its use? And how could we, juanita ε me, the most curious persons we'd ever met —moreover how could i, seemingly born to be a specular querist ε ruminist— believe in any religion that condemned the only thing that, to me, made civil existence possible: the sating of curiosity?

What has civil (establishment) religion to hide that it keeps curiosity as the original sin? Is monastic fabrication so transparent it needs 'God's law' to legislate against humans wanting to possess knowledge?

> In short, to be male was to be spiritual (of sky, of God) and to be female was to be material (of matter, of Earth). Thus the new civil schism (between rationality and instinct, between left- and right brain, between conscious and subconscious) honed to a high polish its imperialist intolerant and subjugating structure: male/mind, female/body; male/culture, female/Nature; male/spirit, female/matter. All the pieces for a new vengeful and power-based hierarchy were now in place. At long-last the once "belittled but obviously superior" male superego had invented and deployed its scapegoats and fallgirls.

Never trust what you arent permitted to doubt.

It is this phrase which gave title to the book (my third) being quoted here, which Lilith had mostly memorized by the time i met her. And to close.

> Those cloistered power-hungry control-driven males of whom we speak at long-last had accomplished the "impossible". They had thrown off their chronic lust –the very desire that had made them pariahs– and given it to the Devil. Not satisfied, they then went and gave the very *cause* of their lust to females! Thereby was made "clear" which of the sexes had brought "evil" (lust, greed, etc) into the world. Females would henceforth be responsible for all ills and calamities! The "evil" guilty animal sluttish exploitable intimidatable stalkable batterable rapeable mutilatable murderable but still lovely mall-crawler was now frothing at the starting gate and ready to perform her "evil deeds" for ages to come.

(We who may be imprisoned (or worse) for speaking our minds are wise to couch in quotes our more incisive facts & ironics.) Thus the archetypal feminine (personified in the nymph) was stripped naked intellectually emotionally and spiritually, and her essential Nature-given purity everafter abused in every manner conceivable to the civil mind. In the same way, domestication has transformed the proud wolf into that foot-licking cur we call a dog. And so too, and for the same reasons, civilizing would turn the innate feminine in us all into a male-worshiping dispirited servant. So accustomed to gender abuse has the global female become, most cannot be convinced it is *not* the way Nature (Universal Law) meant things to be. And so the jestOfJests has been realized. In taking civilization further away from Natural law than it had ever been —via the *ad hoc* organization over time of civil [read: antiNature] ideologies and religions— the jestOfJests had achieved its most twisted possible extrapolation! And, to end this disabusive digression: This crash course, overgeneral tho it may be by necessity, must suffice as answer to the problem created every time the word nymph is used.

32

I'm at a diabolic disadvantage. Gluum & glumm went on&on outside my cell this afternoon. Their homoerotic pantomime (silent because the ic [intercom] was switched off) was performed solely for my benefit of course. Yet i refused to look up except to see if they were still at it. I am sure this is why glumm, dr frood's #1 goon, wore a sniveling grin on the way to supper. What makes them gloat makes me tremble. By the way, i filched my third bagtie at supper. They must be really dullbulbs in the kitchen. Do they never wonder where all the bagties get to? My gaff will be ready after breakfast tomorrow.

But there's a downside —like teaching a class of unknown length. I have a crucial message yet i dont know how long i have to deliver it, dont know when the bell will sound —the bell signifying my personal oblivion. You have no idea! I am minute-to-minute ripped up the middle by conflicting demands: What must be told? What must be skipped? Yet i will not be bullied by the unknown. When the heat ...no, make that, frenzy... when the frenzy to complete this testimony intrudes upon the integrity i've sworn to it ...when that happens i must lockup the brakes of my fears, bring us to a skidding screeching halt. For like it or not there are things, basic things, that must be dallied with, or the vehicle of my intent will surely crash & burn.

33

Someone must have said it. I cannot be the first.

> Any coroner will tell you, many's the corpse that's gotten an erection. Stiff stiffs, they call them. So it is safe to conclude: Not youth not imbecility or even death can keep the penis from rising. And, as if in defiance of the laws of causality, when there's no occasion it creates its own! It is as inexhaustible as life, as inscrutable as death, and its deepest motive (expansion/dispersion) is the very Urge of the Universe!

The jestOfJests is a subtle thing. That's why it worked. It is the ego coercing the superego —quietly, relentlessly. The following actually happened at a lecture i gave at osu/columbus just weeks before i met Lilith.

A tall man with grayingblond hair (image of actor jeff daniels, tho he swears it wasnt him), a camera slung over one shoulder jumped up, said, "Only ignorant men are ruled by their sexdrive!" And i had only just finished reciting my jestOfJests! I paused, looked at the ceiling, tapped the mic, looked out and said, <Is there an echo in here? [much audience chuckling] Are you saying, sir, sexdrive is no problem to those of us who are so evolved, so self-realized, we have become Godlike? and that you personally know of a *system of beliefs* which can free us, once and for all, of that sexdrive...?> But a grin i could no longer restrain had already broken my features and the audience was already breaking into unrestrained laffter.

And so we've had our fun. We've dallied with nymphs, their source, their pure past, their tainting & ultimate defilement in the libraries, museums & other aculturizing of the world. We've all but lain with the coy nymphs of falconet & clodion, who are as schizoid as a pornstarlet pacing before a confessional booth: the desires of a vamp in the flesh of a child. But hold. These are society's judgements not mine; and worst of all, most females still believe in them! And what of this painting hanging here, next to the clodion? *Shepherd with nymph*? Even it doesnt fare much better. Like parmigianino's more famous cheesecake, she's haunted by a christian decay instead of a pagan one; a decay caused by that old catechism: sexual pleasure is malignant. But enuf. We have met, and unmasked, the Beast behind this old & tired crime. Friends lie battered & bloodied on its horns! Loved ones lie dead in the dust under its cloven hoofs! But best of all, now we know who created this Beast, and why!

But tempus fugits and, lest we appear nymphixilated, young impatient juanita & nathan have waited long enuf. We'll wrap this after breakfast tomorrow. Meanwhile i'm exhausted and long for sleep.

34

I did not foresee such a confession. Hindsight strikes me (in this dun-dim dungeon) as bioluminous! Of the women in my life, only Lilith knew about juanita & priscilla; only with her did these things eke out of me as, using them, i coaxed Lilith's own pained remembrances. And those things we did not have time to share (it was all so terribly short, goodGaia!) i offer now in her memory, much as a mourning pharaoh carefully places around the beloved sarcophagus life's treasures, relives the why of being before the tomb is sealed, before we plod wearily away to the cadence of fifings too quickly faded. But let us press on. I get only til "lites out" to put this juanita juncture behind us.

35

As memory backs away from that time, juanita makes an almost ghostlike cameo appearance. I see us ...no, mostly i see her, from a remove, as tho grownup nathan schock has backed away from his youthful self to watch from the path that runs past the barn, backed away in order to study, unseen, the lovers' last meeting.

Up beside the house her group is about to pile into a waiting stationwagon. Juanita sees me, runs down the path while the others stand about, as tho she's forgotten something back at the cabins. No sooner did she turn the corner of that old barn when, as a breeze fills a tree, out of sight of all, she poured into my arms. I hugged her —as sometimes i hug this miserable cot, aching inwardly for the absolutely irretrievable. And here the peculiar displacement (above) takes over, here the thrilling tactility of the moment is sacrificed as the camera of memory is passed from the young lover to his older self.

Juanita is dressed in the same pale blue jumper (it had looked white by moon&starlite). But this time, shaped like a blue butterfly, there is a ribbon securing her long hair. I see the muscles in her legs flex as she rises in her black shoes & white socks to kiss me. I see her head thrown back so that her hair shifts downward, its straight-across cut coming to rest on the perch of her rump. The lips of her upturned face are second only in elevation to the infantile dip in her celtic nose, which is soon eclipsed by the tall lad's declining face.

One sip, one hard hot kiss, and breeze & tree are disunited. Somewhere in the pacific depths of me a great slab of granite tips on end, slips beneath the sand, slides (with agonizing slowness) thru the molten magma of my soul. If i make much of this parting it's because i know my arms will remain empty –in the sense of real love v. mere luv– for the next 21yrs! Thru blurring vision i see her run off, slide into the rear seat of that car, hear its door slam. With a logjam in my throat, a moon rock on my heart, i watch myself move down the path and onto the gravel of the driveway, stoop-shouldered, motionless as a dead tree ...and as alone as i'd ever felt.

Maybe the car wont start. Maybe they'll cancel the outing. All of august holds its breath.... To no avail. In a whirl of dust, the car backs, swings toward the road. A thin arm emerges from a rear window, a hand waves —like a windshield wiper off its track in a thunderstorm, tipped outward, backforth,backforth,backforth, waving in small helpless arcs that can not hope to cope with the deluge, can not hope to unblind the driver. Above the engine-roar a voice cries "Bye!" The wood-doored stationwagon swings onto the road, bottoming its springs with an audible thunk. It growls past the line of poplars, vanishes from sight. Suddenly selfconscious (can anyone see me here dissembling in the sunlite?), i glance about. Standing behind a screendoor i see juanita's mother. She is dressed in white, a tall apparition, and seeming to be staring at me with a munchesque blankness that stymies intent. I turn about quickly, head toward the cabins, not knowing what else to do with my sudden blindness.

...Tears where my heart was....

36

The leviathan insecurity of my youth has broken water (as sailors say), splattering the lens of memory's camera. Thar she blows! *This* was my mobydick. Already i was a gaunt & haunted young ahab and these were my totems: The old stationwagon represented winter. It swept into camp (paradise) like a chill wind in a cloud of august dust and bore my juanita (and summer) away! A jealous zephyr, this was not the first time, nor would it be the last, that foul fate (a dark angel i believed in back then) shamelessly coveted the one i loved. I have studied the primalcies [sic] of my youth, have excavated extensively at certain spots, and found: my subconscious had erected in secret whole templefuls of its own iconographics! If a person is not wary, introspective, he will fail to know the icons whose winds & currents drive the ship of individual destiny itself!

Now i'm hardly an occult person. I can see when the mirror of memory begins to ripple at its middle, blur at the edges, or when it tries to proffer subjective images as unravished reality. And i will share these ripples & blurs, not hide them like so many biograffitists, authors who are no more than tabloid tattlers with prostheticized attentionspans. For biograffiti has, afterall, replaced earnest biography in these popmedia times.

I was to be ready to leave that afternoon; when the girls returned from their last outing of the summer i would be gone. Most kids & counselors were gone already as activities had ended. Juanita & her mother would be among the last to leave. Halfblind & lite-agonized i walked past the barn, down the path with its ruts & turns, past the gamefields to the lake. As it comes into view i realize, i'd not seen the dock, the beach, empty before —not in daylite! Our raft, so memoryful, looks old & abandoned. Life that summer had been so rich; parting, so wrenching. When we have nothing to look forward to something in us has effectively died —killed the future with it.

I sat on the edge of the dock, feet dangling just above the water. A current i'd not noticed before rippled beneath: water moving slowly to the lower lake. A necklace of lakes, paying no heed to state lines, dipped into upper jersey from lower ny state, shared some of the many it had. Trying to deal with juanita's absence, memory jumped up, dove in, raced her out to the raft, scrambled up the ladder, fell laffing on the deck; the ritual was such that i would turn in time to see her face appear behind me on the ladder, grinning ear-to-ear, drenched, giggling raucously, her flesh slippery-smooth & glistening *(leonada),* hair hanging like strings of freshly made licorice, her big paleblues already a little bloodshot ...like mine. After some minutes of self-torment, i headed up to the chapel. Sidebyside we had sung, eyes locked, the doxology of our last campfire together.

The lord be with you.
The lord make his face to shine upon you.
The lord be gracious unto you, and give you peace.

Would it have made a difference had i sung <The lord keep you safe, and *mine,* forever and ever. Amen>? How much of our futures can we really influence? And would the fulfillment of my personal doxylogy [sic] have kept me a dutiful little christian? Silly boy.

Sunlite splashed in tatters on the benches. Under a canopy of leaves my mind shuffled a deck of memories: juanita in line for supper, shifting from foot to foot, nimbly, impatiently; juanita slipping her hairbrush furtively into my hand; juanita and our secret trysts of the previous two nites! Minute-to-minute for the rest of the day, until i was in bed back in the city, and while struggling to sleep that nite, and for many weeks after, i tried to imagine what juanita was doing —now & now & now. I think i hear her laff behind me. I swing about in time to realize it's only miss joanne, back at the gamingfield, playing with a couple late-departing charges, and whose tantalizing voice shares a rainbow of overtones with juanita's. I look at my hands: these have touched her! My loins ache, having known her. A breeze stirs; i hear her sigh.

Sad winds where your voice was....

What's going on? My stomach spits at me. What a fuktup world! Rage rises, rage against an impersonal Cosmos, which is all i have known it seems for my whole life! But anger offers only temporary salvation. I jump to my feet. The note? Where's the damn note?

Behind the barn, between sip & kiss, juanita had stuffed a folded wad of paper behind my beltbuckle. Damn! It must have dislodged as i stumbled from barn to lake. Love note? Her address? She promised that, at least. I raced down the hillside, retracing my steps, halting at every gum wrapper, every pale flower, every pale stone. With a jolt i remembered the lake!

Beyond the dock, having gotten well past the raft & outer buoyline by this time, i spotted it! —moving in breeze & current like one of those paper boats kids set adrift in gutters, boats often swallowed by sewers! I tore off my clothes and dove in.

37

Back in school i dawdled over my books, could feel whole seasons ticking away inside me —not for the first time: summer to autumn, autumn to winter, tictoc,tictoc, like a cosmic clock winding down, like the dripping of a familiar icicle, back in mossville, which every spring rehearsed its ornamental rite outside my bedroom window —drip,drip,drip ...but slower ...like a heartbeat threatening to quit.

...Happy summer days gone by and vanished summer glory

What does this young man's morbid dissection of seasons & shadows remind me of? Had i lost a love before? I felt hollow inside. The hollow freshman they could have called me. Did i say? I was 15 when i entered 9thgrade: flunked 3rd following the loss of priscilla. To make matters worse, at 9, new in the city, i was sent to school deckedout in shorts & kneesocks! For this i was marked: chased or beatup almost daily, by kids who wore black leather jackets, wielded pocketknives, chains & belts with razor-sharp buckles; guys that made the fonz on tv look like woody allen. Tall as any man by highschool, my discovery of bodybuilding began to ensure my safety. And girls, out of nowhere, began smiling in the wings of my sullen, badboy outer-theater self. But still there was my inner Self, and recent memories, to contend with.

Defeated, hating parents, school, my urban cage –no longer able to takeoff into the countryside on my bike– i more&more escaped anger & disappointment by throwing myself into heavy workouts at the ymca. Still, crazed by adolescent emoting & inguinal ache, imagination took wing; yet strangely did not head for nyc & juanita. Irrationally, it flew back to camp. A desperate thing, my longing flitted among the icy reachings of wind-blasted birches, flopped along the snow like a lame bird searching for summer & a lost mate. Flesh of my flesh. Hadnt i read that in my bible? But no one will understand. And i dont blame him. This is purest saccharine. Dont think i dont know that. It just feels good to give it away, to write it down on a sheet of paper that doesnt poke fun at me.

Our house in mossville had, in the front foyer, from floor to ceiling on one side of the entry door, a long window built of square bricks of glass; translucent: a figure could be standing at the frontdoor (as when my parents had gone out for the evening) but, try as i might, in my frite i could make out only billowing shadows in the porchlite's amber glare. Psychic blindness can be as hazardous as its optical counterpart. For years, til my selfesteem began to grow, the world (the world of humans) would remain to me a myopic morass. O my eyes worked just fine ...or did they? Bad vision is bad vision, no matter the cause. Chalkboards, teachers, other children, the city streets —all were a menacing blur. Only people & things i trusted could be seen clearly: my room, my modeltrain layout in the basement, my hero & superhero scrapbooks, miss stott my 2nd grade teacher, my friend geoffrey, things of Nature, my dog, my bible, priscilla, juanita; the list is not very long.

I stumbled thru my youth like a monstrous fetus trying to see the World from a womb that refused to release me. Claustrophobia (in this instance, the compression of psychic blurring), the only quirk of my quiddity i would never quite conquer, had sunk roots in more than one place within me. And how fitting (in a morbid sense) that my final fate should be a small cell with thick glass to one side of its entry(!); a place absolutely without exits ...so far as i am concerned.

38

Juanita's note was an instant treasure. Taking to the backseat of the car –silent glum invert– all the way home from camp i studied it. Undated, it read: [Emil, please use a typescript resembling juanita's handwriting. See "Juanita Darc" in my files.]

My dearest Nathan, here is the address I promised. P-l-e-a-s-e don't show up without calling. We'll be getting a phone soon. I'll send you the number when you send me your address.

And if you write, please don't say anything about love. You know what I mean? P-l-e-a-s-e!

I wrote some poems about you this summer. I hope you like them.

Vaya con Dios (the song, Nathan!), mi precioso.

Your Juanita

[Her address was placed here.]

By the might of mnemosyne i am certain the poesy that follows replicates juanita's originals —except that they are written here in my minuscule print and not in her lovely looping script....

[The original note to which NS alludes was written in pencil on both sides of three sheets of white spiral notebook paper with pink lines, in what is apparently the script of JD. Its fold-lines (stained brown where once taped) are now glued together. The note, obviously wet at least once, was found not in said JD file (as NS thought) but between pp 36-37 in a clothbound edition of *Emily Dickinson: The Complete Poems.* NS did however replicate the note and its poems in every detail. And, as he says, it seems the seeds of his writing style are to be found there as well. —Ed.]

....The first poem read:

Nathan

Nothing is blue like your eyes. Nothing.

Not one of Nature's bluestblue surprises
    gives the giddymarvel that your eyes give,
    not the starkest starKissed blue
    can match the eyes of you,
    nor the fastest lite can catch
    the quicksilver of the two.
Mine blue, yours blue—
Now there's a match!

O the meadowgrass is blond today alright
and like you tosses sunlite as it passes.
　　But not violets nor bluebells,
　　nor lilacs hanging noble,
　　can "sing the blues" of BLUE
　　like the clever Artist who
　　put aside his "work in blue"
　　just to paint the likes of you!

No, nothing is blue like your eyes are blue.
Nothing.

I remember feeling, as i dove into the water after that capsized & nearly lost note, that i was rescuing my very future. 50 times a day i read her letter at first, til i had memorized –no, assimilated– every comma, every nuance, every possible shade of meaning, every jot of juanita's miraculous pencil!

The second poem, taking up an entire page, was preceded by these words: *This one's not finished. It will be a sonnet when it's done. Right now it's kind of a mess. Some things you will remember we talked about –like the swallows we watched that day (¡Las golondrinas, Nathan!), pacing in circles in the driveway, like they were anxious, upset maybe, about leaving the old summer haunts ...like us, Nathan. Like us!*

In moccasins of snow

This charm-of-green can not disguise the old
　　blizzard-secrets frosting at its heart.
Even anarchist bluebells try to scold
　　this stifling air, this trembling august breath.
Who sees (in all this warmth) and who's been told
　　this charm-of-green hides souvenirs of death?
Whose shadow there? What moves beneath the eaves?
Whose doom lurks in the icicle's future descent
　　or in the snowy alarms of the birch's pale bark?
Who knows the swallow's urgings, southward bent;
　　or the winged frail dreams a chrysalis unfolds?
What idler sees the nests of springtime blent
　　courageously in mufflers wide with snow—
　　wind-tattered, empty, fallen, buried, cold?

This is a rearrangement of juanita's original 14 somewhat-metered lines, with additions from random unmetered notes on the last page. I have added, for the sake of a loose rhyme-scheme, only the words bent, blent ε unfolds; and also, mufflers, which seemed to act as winter's answer to august's "stifling air". I also changed courage to courageously, while adding a couple hyphenations. For without reshaping a couple ideas ε images i was unable to come up with the sonnet she envisioned. Yet what i offer echoes the polish of the original. Juanita (perfectionist) would want it that way. I have finally set your swallows free, juana. I know they will fly straight to you, wherever you are! And, who knows? The zizm of me may follow ...shortly.

[While NS' description of his alterations matches with JD's original, the finished product is more an "inspired restatement" than the mere "rearrangement" he calls it. For in his rendering NS discarded 116 words, plus miscellaneous punctuation, so that JD's ideas and images might be steered toward the setting she envisioned. That he was able to do all this purely from memory is noteworthy. —Ed.]

Weeks crept by. I toreup the start of a dozen letters. How stupid to write: Dear juanita, how are you? I hope you're doing fine. I'm okay. What have you been up to? ...when all i thought of, all i lived for, was to tell her of my love, send her the poems i'd been slaving over —but that werent fit to rest in the shadow of her own. Writing was out of the question, for everything i wrote embarrassed me. What to do?

It was mid october when i mailed that gift: a butterfly, displayed in a clear plastic case ...i didnt know back then Earth-slaughter could be stopped by consumer boycotting. To most of us then, a show of Nature's creatures (whether under glass or behind bars) was authentic Nature-science, good art. I put my address inside the little package with a short note. Dear juanita, this is for you. Please write. Your friend, ns ...or something like that. A week later it was back, stamped: MOVED. NO FORWARDING ADDRESS!

I asked my parents to drive me to her house. Mother, who hated goodlooking females of all ages, refused. Father didnt care except, "Yust dant git da leetle shpeek vit da baby." I shook with rage. What picture had her name called up in their narrow minds? You are my father, i know. But if you ever call her that again i will strangle you, i whispered. An excellent streetfiter, he just laffed ε walked away ...but never insulted her again.

Anger prompted action. Sitting by the window in an el train (subway-*cum*-elevated) i gazed out the grimy window as miles of tenements, crowding the tracks on both sides, clattered past?

And why do I often meet your visage here,
Your eyes like agate lanterns—on and on
Below the toothpaste and the dandruff ads?

Had her mother been right after all? Was i too Wild, she too spanish? How confused the sick minds of my elders made me.

Her address turned out to be in the bronx, a place which juanita (with a grin) referred to as *"La gran manzana."* Her version of priscilla's orchard was not the place i pictured when she spoke, and of which neighborhood, tonite, i feel sure she was immutably ashamed and never wanted me to see. Juanita, you did not know me. It was four flites up and straight out of a mobster flick.

"Dey moved away" a woman in the flat below told me. When? About to slam the door, my distress must have been obvious. "O, a munt ago maybe." Twenty walkups, a hundred creaking flites later, i found a school chum. "So *youz* iz nat'n! Wow, heah in poyson. ...Yeah, Juana" had told her "oowal about" me. Her dark eyes at once took me to bed. "Shuwah. Cawl whenevah ya waant. ...Muy plesja." But juanita never wrote to her.

39

You'd think a body waiting to die would enjoy a little more good fortune than i seem to come by. Luck went locally awry this morn. The whole time a note from "the girls upstairs" hung by my window, guard glumm hung by my door. Had to sit tite til breakfast, pretend not to see it. Why did he arrive so early? Does he suspect something? I've finally figured out what all the early-morning fracas is about. When "the girls" successfully dock the note at my window they begin to carry on —to draw my attention. One yelled "Hey, you down there!" Glumm looked straight at the window. I was sure the gig was up. But he simply grunted "Dere's nuttin uglier den a buncha horny bitches" and turned away.

At breakfast he seemed dejected. This is good. If my execution was near he would be dancing on air. The news depressing him turnedout to be library privileges for me. No more begging for books from moody or cruel guards.

Doktor frood was behind this, unlikely as it may seem. A note from him read, "I want you to have the materials you need for your epic, that memoir you call 'Coincidences of Confinement'. You may make library requests as soon as you like. Your physician, SS." Tho it's probably just another of his hoaxes, the journal he mentioned, *constellations of confinement*, exists ...a bogusbook which the camera in the corridor is convinced i spend my days slaving over. Frood, winking, calls it "Schock's mad epic". Several times he has ordered his lackeys to bring it to him, authenticating my charade —for i keep always at the ready the latest scribblings of this decoy "book" of mine.

40

Christmas eve offered a last hope.

In the country, city rain turned to snow. Hitchhiking took most of the day: late afternoon when i reached butler, almost dark when i arrived in lebanon. But no one was home. Tire tracks fresh. A little dog (nasty pugnosed pekingese) did snippish flips behind the squares of glass in the frontdoor. Had she been there already and gone? Suddenly i realized, xmas eve included the daytime too! Shitshitshitshitshit! Swearing & spitting, i stomped about for several minutes, at last going around to the porch windows and peering in. I tried to imagine juanita & nathan inside, that past summer, but it was no use! Many things were missing and much was switched around.

My feet were frozen yet the nite was still young. If the barn knew anything it didnt say. Once past the stable mine were the only tracks. The walk to the lake seemed short. It had a new beach: a halo of ice! By snow-glow i saw our raft was gone. No, there it is! Hauled onto shore: beached memory, locked in ice and past all gasping. At the fork in the path i paused. What voice did i expect? whose warm hand? The selfconfidence juanita's love had given me was gone; i felt like a pale fantom of my summer self. In strange slanting lite i ascended the levels of pathway leading from lake to chapel, chasing the emerald ghost of my lost ingénue. The chapel was quiet as a sepulcher.

...Silence where hope was.

Thru the bare-limbed birches the closeness of the lake startled me. The leafy canopy above the stone wall (our bornagain bench) was gone. The blankness of that sky beyond struck me not only as impersonal but brutal. Hope sank. I stood bewildered. An insidious shivering set in. Here was the green chill juanita had warned of —her imagined icicles drew their blades! All at once i knew i would not be seeing her —not that nite, and maybe never. (Enter, index of the hazard of loss noted earlier!) I brushed the snow from her perch and from the low wall that had supported her spontaneous acrobatics. Her nymphdom among the trees, abandoned, seemed alien now. I felt not like a young lover but a defeated antiquarian. It seemed there was nothing to hold to here if juanita wasnt returning.

It was snowing harder. A high gibbous moon lit the clouds, char-gray, snowladen. *The summer dells, by genius haunted, / One arctic moon [has] disenchanted.* How still my heart as i left the chapel. Fingers ε toes had lost feeling. A lite, missed on my way in, was on in the stable. The goats were gone; only two horses remained. My shivering grew worse despite the warmth inside, the absence of wind. Fresh hay filled the troughs. I went to check the house one last time.

When i returned, from midway in a stack of hay, i pulled out a few bales, crowded my quaking self into the cubicle they left behind, walled in the opening after me. O that the foodcellar of earlier punishments had been so cozy! I was too exhausted, too depressed, to bother to remove my shoes and avert stage1 frostbite. Years later, while writing xmas cards for a house on 23rd st in nyc, gazing at a card (dusk, old barn, blue snow) and waiting for inspiration, i recalled with a shiver my own "hour of lead". Maybe it was just exhaustion, maybe one too many defeats in my life, but i could not recall ever feeling so crushed. My despair was thoroly russkyan. Yet, for the first time, no tears came. Had i become at last a real-life phalladymic statusquoer?

41

The main lites will dim in 13 minutes, go out in 18.

I returned for a visit the following summer. Neither juanita or her mother had come back. A vacant stare wanted to know the purpose of my visit? O nothing ...just a joyous life i left behind. The same little dog, obliterated by the large woman who questioned me, yapped away. A sorry detective, i did not ask the best questions.

In spring of '95 i returned with Lilith to gospelInTheBirches, or at least its geosite, searching, you might say, for those *paths I knew best to reclaim her by.* All signs of the camp –even the old house and all the buildings– were gone. On our map i saw the lake was named echo not luke, fronted now by the docks piers & lawns of rolling estates, the surrounding hills thinned of much of their sacred timber. As predicted, *the arrow's oath* had been broken!

What woods remember now her calls, her enthusiasms?
Fool— Have you remembered too long?

Back in school juanita became hypertrophied in my mind: the green leaf of summer one puts in a favored book, meaning to preserve but which, no matter how loving the press of pages, passes thru its own autumn, its own winter, skipping in the dusk of its laminate cell all the drama of departure: the burning, the cleaving, the falling ...the trapped leaf going from softgreen to brittlebrown with little between but darkness & death!

Juanita darc, wherever you are, and wherever you have been all this time, i send this souvenir out to you. I wish it were more. But why didnt you write? call? something? You were so good at such things as i was so bad at them. Were you swept from that wretched slum off to caracas bolivia or esmeralda? Did you figure me lost forever, gitana, *señorita extraña?—que se me fue.* Or did you find another lover? Desperate for some clue, i imagined my *señorita desaparecida,* thrown in a dungeon, tortured, strangled. For it seems only tragedy... But why go on like this? For what it's worth, i will to you that sheaf of old poems titled *juanita* ...badly imitating yours, i'm afraid. If only i could let you know, it was *you* who cast my language sensibilities for life, tho all the power in your poetry couldnt make a poet of me. For poets like you are born not made. Compared to your sure-footed verse, my poetic license was restricted to a learner's permit.

There is none like her, none,
Nor will be when our summers have deceased.

Finally, sure she became a writer, i've searched shelf on shelf for her name for years: juanita anything! Anybody darc darque or even dark! Nothing. There is an eleanor darc (*tales from the piazza*), a plurabelle darkbloom (*dawn at mount falcon*) and a juanita perrot (*my sister dolly*), but no juanita darc. Still, among the scattered violets of another poet, i did stumble across the source of her "anarchistic bluebells", her "tossed sunlite", her "souvenirs of death". But i have yet to figureout those "stiletto icicles" of hers ...tho life has well-tutored me as to their "cruel descent". But there go the lites.

It is next day; wednesday.

I see i said well-tutored by life. I should have said existence. For, from cradle to grave, civil rules & expectations allow us little contact with life. Eg: When we're kids our genitals stay prettymuch commonsensical. But when we reach adolescence, Nature insists we wear them like masks. This is no accident. Nature wants that stage of our development not only easy to spot but impossible to ignore. Now, in a normal World, these genital masks (sex display) would gradually slip back to their orig locations once adolescence was outdistanced, and down there they would stay til they withered with age or disuse. But we no longer live in such a World. Instead of *living* that memorial stage (adolescence) of *inflagrante delicto* sex, which Nature meant us to live, civilization compels us to peel away our genital masks like old bad skin, as tho they could harm us or harm others. We are taught to dry them out, wear the shrunken heads of our sexlives like designer logos on our belts, on our sleeves; *never* wear them in full-blood & bloom on our faces! And so, thruout adulthood, we wear our sexuality as tho these shrunken dessicated remains represent a significant stage of our youth.

And thus we go thru life, the mumified masks of a quashed adolescence as only reminder of the Wild (read: uncivilized) times we mostly imagined we had ...and which we keep trying to reclaim for the rest of our days by projecting what was unfulfilled in our own youth onto the youth of the world in secret. And those of us who *think* we enjoyed such a *life*, we are the nuttiest of dreamers. For the full-blood & bloom to which i allude requires family & community sanction if not participation. But such life-affirming rites have long been deemed uncivilized, and so are lost to us and our modern *existences*.

And with that we are about done here; and almost on schedule too. If i were any good at glossing over fact and calling it fiction –and were i permitted to grow old without state interference– this juanita juncture could have made a decent novella. And, o yes. As i was going to say (before the lites went out last nite), i did stumble across ...opening & slamming books the way i often do depending solely upon the quality of their initial page... while i did come across a lady novelist, a joAnn gold. Ah, miss! a fine book! ...about a girl who falls in love with the same guy ...twice! not knowing it's him the second time around because, in the meantime, theyve both grown up and lost touch, and because she had gone blind since the time she last saw him. It was made into a movie in europe which some may remember. But unless they printed the wrong picture on the flyleaf, the author was not juanita.

42

Just behind the capability of my sense of smell to restore the past exists an auricular sensibility. Music. If i can, for example, capture just one thread of a melody from my past, even my very distant past, there will come with it (in addition to lyrics, if applicable) a bodily suffusion of sensation plus a psychic inundation of 'forgotten' images! And since old scents are not reproducible on demand, i often depend on music to give presence & emotional ambience to my recollections. So it could be with the songs juanita exposed me to. My experience being, if i can recapture just one thread of thus&such song, a whole spectrum of realization will suddenly perfuse etcetc.

In this regard, i have a good ear for vocal i.d. I would make a good blind man in this sense [sic]. My mother used to play over&over the songs of a singer named joni james. If i heard that voice today i would know it; a couple bars would do, whether i'd heard the song before or not. Well, juanita liked a happy-voiced male singer of catchy tunes. (I think her sense of rhyme-scheme may owe something to the syncopated lyrics of those songs.) I can call up snatches of lyric but nothing of melody, save one. This came about one day some years ago a bit flukily as my usual process of recall unrolled in reverse!

In a barracks in ca (second time in san diego) waiting to be shipped home, i was thumbing thru an anthology of poetry when i came across an item called *jenny kissed me.* Well, to employ the cricket's cliche, it came as a "bolt out of the blue". For when i reached the fifth line (the first four were unused in the song) a melody juanita loved came winging in from the past, alighted on my left brain! With it i could actually hear juanita singing! As this happened almost 7yrs after the fact it was a thrilling 'time traversal' Her voice has since vanished. I need another such melody to wing it back —not really that many years ago except that this cage is aging me fast. I tug childishly at my bars, realize: There is no tunnel to freedom here. And worst of all, princess heidi was swept out to sea on the nite tide!

Music, magical conduit to my past, works in relation to priscilla too. But i wont bore you with that. My point is, when it happens it brings with it an almost living person! And i jump about in the crisp memory like a kid in a leafpile! Nites when i cant sleep i sometimes work at locating in the darkness such a psychic trigger. Last nite, surfing those "lost" airwaves, i intersected with something —which is why i've brought all this up in the first place. This is grossly paraphrastic i realize: It is nite. There is dancing. And the desired one is made of something peaches something honey. And we danced (blank, blank) til her blue eyes were shinin'! ...But, sadly, no melody comes to fill behind the hisses ticks & pops of that old much-played & much-loved red-labeled gold-lettered black-vinyled (see how i struggle with this?) 45rpm record which juanita played over&over again out on that dampness-scented porch by the garden behind the poplars.... So, this having failed, i guess we're about done.

O, there is this one thing. The psychic blindness of my youth has misled us. Juanita was a gifted child, a *wunderkind* certainly. The point is, gifted children are rarely cheery & uncomplicated, which is the picture i see i may have inadvertently sketched for the reader. It wasnt that she, unlike me, lacked a whole cartful of psychic baggage. It was that, next to mine, hers seemed as nothing. In truth, juanita laffed too loud, loved too hard. It was years before i recognized the façade: the swirling energy, the too-positive attitude. I was blind to the hurt behind the mask of the gay little reveler at my side, a child-woman who, in a short time, thanx to her father's religious callings, went from princess of a rural utopia (lovely town, brick house beside brick church, a ready limelite for her talents & beauty) to poetess of instant poverty! The last page of her note to me, read with care, will permit a glimpse into that pain.

My Phœbus

So bashful when I saw him,
so handsome and so fair,
he lowered quick his blueblue eyes
but saw me standing there.

I could not help but love him,
I guess I always will,
but that he is too good for me
I can already tell.

No *poemas llorónes (playeras)* for juanita. No ma'am. Hers were brave, realistic. The second poem on that page had a double intent; it panned her earlier takeoff on dickinson while poking fun at herself. Untitled, it read

Inebriate of moon and tree,
debauché in a pew! *
Here's to summer! and here's to me!
but mostly, Here's to you!

*But please don't think I'm an *oportunista retorcida.* That's not me, Nathan. That's not what I'm about.

I got a sweet pimpolla in my hs french class to help me translate. The young woman, tho more than a little amazed, saw the thing thru. Juanita's pain, along with her endangered persona, got by me. I was a good lover & listener but my ability to empathize with her crisis fell short of ideal. Forgive me, proud (tho justifiably petrified) juanita oscura.

The last poem settles the matter. Tho again an obvious takeoff on her beloved emily, it also underscores her private encounter with our shared fear: separation.

Parting

Parting: litany of life,
summer's kiss & tell.
Autumn bodes the end of heaven
and the start of hell.

Be true to me, *mi amor, mi vida, mi pecado, mi entraña, mi alma. Ve con Dios.*
Your marquita gitanita.

Literally, your little gypsy, marquita. Juanita had no way of knowing the name should be written, marcheta (italian), as she'd heard it only in my recitation & song. The names marcheta & gitana refer to two lovesongs, songs i would play thruout the schoolyear inserting juanita's name where appropriate, and (to show the high index of the hazard already noted) never forgetting to add, *immer, immer.*

Nite. And a violin sobbing —for we're apart.
Nite. And the campfires are dying.
But my flame of love will never die.
Gitana! Gitana!

Dont know what it is about my mental makeup which insists that the 'facts' of my past are inviolable. Even as a child of 6 or 7 i recall feeling i was the sole repository of things happening to, and around, me. It is no doubt thanks to mother's obvious reality blindness and father's domestic detachment that i tookon early in life this *retrouve* responsibility. At any cause, this rational rigor has always included the locking into place of all sensate-, as well as psychologic, memory. And so i find the usual human game of reconstructing memory (*the future as it was, the past as it will be*), unforgivable heresy, a stab in the back to life. In seeming compensation for this hard-wiring of my past, while my emotional (or anywise subjective) experience of events is not permitted to alter things DIMENSIONAL or FACTUAL, it *is* permitted to tint, or to lite-adjust, and even to depigment. In fact, all the snapshots ε outtakes preserved in mnemosyne's library ε carrels are, and were always, shot ε stored with such emotional lensing locked in place.

To edit us straight to the chase. These lenses are of three modes. The first, tho emotionally the most treated, is coloristically the simplest. Black&white memory. Succinctly: Here, where the color of spilled blood is most crucial (my dad's trail of blood in the snow one xmas morn; my own blood dotting the way to the hole not long after i arrived in this prison*), we get only film noir. ("Mortal peril is colorless." —isabel lalath) [*NS is referring here to his isolation in Lorton Federal Penitentiary's horrific, say nothing of criminal, version of a sensory deprivation chamber. —Ed.] The second lensing mode is what i'll call still-life trichrome (my childhood generally: specially mother, the foodcellar ε city gradeschool). The third mode is posited in the realcolor of the original event, with emotional tinting, if any, limited to lite-adjustment (brightness/contrast) ε texture. Rather than the steadystream realtime ideal (which memory, like any finite computer, shies away from due to the immensity of data-storage involved), memory in this mode amounts to a flashing, or serial splay, of realcolor cards. Juanita, and summers on the farm for instance, were shot ε stored with this minimal-lensing effect.

These things outlined, the reader will hereafter understand if i say: When i flash the hand of recall dealt me under 'juanita' i usually see her in animated color (as happens also with Lilith); her characteristic pout, say, or sheathed in her sunlite-scintillated silverblue suit, holding her nose as she jumps off the raft to "cool off"; or i see her hands, moving in the moonlite like cranes in flite, whistling fingers lofting me, stellar haze in her eyes, moonbeams webbing her hair, as beyond a lowslung 'loveseat' birch, which kneels behind her, i hear the faroff cry of that fateful loon. And from that place (where *the linnet has flown*), winging back to me, at last comes a long-lost song.

Turn back the hands of time,
roll back the sands of time,
bring back that dream divine.
Let's live it over again.

And with its saccharine thrill come her shudders, her sobs; birchlimbs tracing the starred sky above the lake; frenzied flapping of wings as an applause of rain drenches us; my own stifled yeowl; and at the fount of the dark gaps —the stout ▯onic-shaped spaces of darkness backdropping the arc of tracer bolides rocketing from my body— i glimpse myself, mouth agape, head thrown back, hands white-knuckling the knobs of her iliac crests like a doomed steersman in a storm, as i'm devoured by a sucking vortex of stinging stars!

I still feel the spell of your last kiss upon me.
Since then life has all been in vain.
My poor heart is broken, I want you, Marcheta.
I need you, Marcheta —I do.

Loss bedamned. I do not regret having loved juanita. In fact, i pity those males who have never had their priscilla, their juanita, their Lilith. *Udite! Non conoscete amore.....* For who would guess, a mere trickling of true love –come tho it may but fleetingly in a lifetime– can salvage one's libido from the scrapheap of civilization! And with that this hebegynous nostolept desists.

43

In a moment i must prepare this last of part 1 to leave here with emil. (And to think i could have begun this book months ago, while awaiting trial, back when what i wrote was still mostly mine.) Yet in order to properly close this chapter of my life i have no choice but to use the most conflicted words in the human lexicon.

So far i've used the word zizm (essential Self) with marginal success. I say this because its potential for misinterpretation is still extremely high. Yet that potential is nothing next to that unleashed in the word God. For every culture of human has its own, mainly anthropic, images of what comprises a First Cause (Creator) or Intelligent Designer (God). And so, every time i cave into cliche expectation, every time i fling care to the winds and use the words Creator or God ...as i must do in a moment... i am aware of the thousand disparate 'faces' of deity i am stirringup from the toxic muck of theologic invention. Thus conflicted, i should not keep using these words in the hope people will understand what i mean. They wont. They never do.

Least tolerant are the teleophobic nulliversalists. This bunch, usually o/c atheists ɛ agnostics in high technodrag, has been specially bitchy about the Intelligent Design thing ...ever since discoveries in astronomy ɛ particle physics made the idea of an implicate-order Universe look attractive —next to the alternative, that is: instantaneous signaling —whose latest apodictums (in both intragalactic- ɛ interparticle crosstalk) have knocked most of them into a state of stuttering fibrillation. All of which i had to note so i can be somewhat understood when i say: I want it on record at the top of this document: Lilith [with a capital L], i Love you [love, with its own capital]. Until i met you i capitalized only the words Universe Reality Nature Earth Firstcause Intelligent Design **Ω** and the like. It was you who taught me to add, love –a certain unique sort of love– my Love.

If this page survives prison, censure by the fed., and my own death, let it be known. With all the vital thump left in this sad big heart, the crush of these guiltless arms, the creativity of this tormented mind, the aching of this captive body, the passion of this once-free spirit, o limpid-eyed lithe-limbed lovely ɛ lachrymose Lilith, no matter what stigmata their official lies ɛ ritual deceptions have branded us with, it is your purity of soul, your love of *all* things, which will fly highest, shine britest, when all is sad [sic] ɛ done.

the final audit

When some day some little person gets big and asks, "What did *you* give the Earth for my future? What did *you* sacrifice?", what will you answer? Remember: The old excuse which worked for our ancestors doesn't wash any more for us. Although few of us talk about it, *everyone* knows: We know *exactly* what we're doing!

—from Nathan Schock's *Scapegoats & Fallgirls* [editorial insert]

Part 2

[Approximate date of composition by the author: March 1998. —Ed.]

1

So here we are, facing the personal lookback i agreed upon. (Who said a watched pot never boils never waited to be executed.)

Re: "The stuff of my sources." According to my attorney, my conviction for murder compromises what i say "even for the most faithful nathan schock fans. For, really, they know nothing about you as a private person. You need to reassure them that you are made of decent flesh 'n' bone like them. They need to know the sources of your ideals, and the stuff of those sources. Your childhood would be a good place to begin." But what emil doesnt know is

My childhood is an ugly thing
i hate to reckon with.

(Juanita wrote that.) Except for the loves of my youth, and my hobbies –things pursued to escape the rigors of those days– my childhood was just that. Juanita ended, saying,

I search, I probe, I dig them up,
i view them in despair,
those disillusioned childhood dreams
the years cannot repair.

However, i will attempt one last time the more traditional narrative method emil has in mind. [Had this editor realized the importance NS placed on his suggestions he would have been less vocal about them. —Ed.]

2

Ressouvenir. My father, carl schock, was born in 1910 in deggendorf. While too young for ww1, as an airline pilot in his late 20s he was ripe for ww2, landing [hic] at first in the farcical fuhrer's beloved *stukagruppe77*, then demoted to the *luftwaffe* for lack of murderous aggressiveness. An ace at cya, he crawled out of his third ε last smoking ε burning messerschmidt109 in '44 with a gimpy leg and a lifelong love of gravity-challenging freedom. In the reconstruction following the war he met one spring my mother, elle, (nee tauber) while training pilots at the university in regensburg, elle's home of 16 years. By fall they'd eloped ε emigrated, settling in mt morris ny at the home of günter schock iii, amusical brother of the viennese opera star and grandfather's oldest sibling. It was there —rolling mountaintop dairy-farm, old 2story cellarless house with 8m snowdrifts on the canadian side— that nathan schock was born.

Beside a *singspiel* greatuncle, if spark of greatness counts, there's only greatuncle walter, a bonn geometrician who wrote several obscure math tomes, the most entertaining of which was titled: *the girl in the vortex of the helix*, the german for which i've forgotten. On mother's blood-side there is no genius, just much of madness and more of "sin".

My parents, both victims of teutonic testosterone, should not have had children. Pity they lacked the panache to swathe me in swaddling, cast me adrift to the fate of some swift; deposit me on the slopes of mt taygetus; or at the very least put me in a basket, set me on the doorstep of some estimable estate.

While sans the ruler-whack knuckle-rap learning my parents knew, grim meanness in the red schoolhouse (plus a little ear- ε arm-tortion) was not uncommon in those days. Among highlites that strike me [sic] as we whiz [hic] by, i recall being nastily expelled from school —*pre*school, that is. My offense was called a "private indiscretion", pardon the euphemism. Seems i had crawled atop a pronate classmate during naptime and, on being discovered, with a tom-kitten precociousness decried our senseless decoupling. By the next schoolyear we'd moved to mossville. I was told "Ve mooft avay becuz ve ver runnink from yoor kreeminal pazt, naton" (as mother claimed almost til the day she died). Truth was, our relatives were left no choice but to run my father off thanx to his wife's rift-rousing immaturity ε trouser-rousing goodlooks.

Transporting the rich & would-be rich pervades my paternal past. Father's father followed his brother to america, bought & burgeoned a limousine service in morrisville —an old hamlet lying adjacent to mossville nudejoyzee, as nj enviros call their forest-denuded state. Both towns took great pride in posting (on roadsides, on buildings) the details of every brush they had with early americana. No event, no relic, was too obscure, too trivial, to lay claim to, with a special fixation for the relics of war. Any war. "General Washington and his weary [code: much-abused] troops camped here before crossing the Delaware". Pamphlets plaques obelisks cairns any old thing were used to recount stories of skirmishes with amerinds, a people longsince slaughtered or run off the land of my youth. Mansions & monuments line lakesides, punctuate hillsides; colonial farmhouses, barns & stables dot the countryside, as do old bridges & wells, mills & millponds. All very nice of course if you could care less that no brass memorial reads:

> BUT FOR CIVILIZATION'S CREED TO PROCREATE AND COLONIZE AT ANY COST, A STUNNING NATURAL WILDERNESS AND A FASCINATING INDIGENOUS PEOPLE WOULD STILL EXIST ON THE SPOT WHERE YOU NOW STAND.

Father inherited grandfather's limo business, which he promptly sold for an airplane despite grandfather's remonstrations. Grandfather, knowing well father's passion for flying, had insisted on a written contract. Unable to dissuade him (or beat him anymore with a strap), he filed suit —an effort to collect the airplane and what remained of the wasted estate as he saw it. The ensuing [sic] trial achieved more notoriety than it deserved: FATHER SUES SON, newspapers headlined —a big deal back then. The judge ended by siding with father, the technical glitch being, the judge did not see the start-up of an "air limousine" service as "imprudent", or as an act of "irresponsible pleasure-seeking" as grandfather saw it. (O that i had had such a judge when *i* came to trial. My *big* one, that is.) And so feudally grounded grandfather (lord & liege of flatulence, you'll remember) bore the final insult of having to pay the costs of court. The upshot of which notoriety launched father's new business out of the red and into the blue so to speak. Little did young nathan dream, that trial would not be the last of dark notoriety in his family.

Father's first plane was a military transport: an awkward looking amphibious bird with two engines & pontoons. Albeit an ugly duckling, built in time for ww2a (as i like to call the non-oriental phase), that broad-bellied bird became famed & durable stock. Father named the initial "apparattlus" mother goose, first of three. It's logo which he, a talented caricaturist, painted on the plane's nose, is still vivid in memory: stork, stupefied eyes, wet bedraggled wings, pontoon feet clumsily angled out (like minniemouse falling thru blue sky in large ladyshoes), whose beak wafted thru the air in a dangling blanket a begoggled man in a businessuit, hair whipped by wind, briefcase in one hand, classic two-belled alarmclock in the other, its hands frozen at 8:55am!

Once settled in mossville, history began to repeat itself. I was expelled (ugly word) from kindergarten (lovely word), this time for a lesser indiscretion ...involving my lying atop a doll belonging to a nebulous blond named dolores, for whom the doll was a substitute, horizontally speaking. For by then i'd been sufficiently intimidated ...or, better yet, as cg jung would say: Natural desire had been perverted into alternative channels. Thanx parents/society. Which brings up a point. I can remember being struck dumb by the difference of my girl peers from my own boy self. Yet i can steer the empathetic sociologist only to ineffable things: The softness suppleness lethal attraction that suffused any space these unique beings occupied; as if, often merely on sight and against his will, one were tumbled toward, and then into, a forcefield greater than his own! Specially struck was i by the lovelier of my classmates. From earliest memory i found them more fascinating than any game song idea or socalled terrific toy. "Well then, surely, nathan, you like this firetruck! All boys *love* big trucks. Brrrrrrrm, brrrrm!" {If you say so.}

From the start —that point where memory struggles to its feet and stands on its own for a trembling moment— something seemed wrong with the world i'd been dropped into, a world which rarely seemed to care about what *i* wanted, what *i* and my *deeper* Self expected of life. And, to make matters unbearable, i would be decades figuring out that the World, as given, was perfect. What was wrong was *not* with the World per se but with what humans (read: civilization) had *done* to that World. Almost from the gitgo i suspected something was awfully outofwhack and never quite got over it.

At age 4 for instance i ran barefoot over hot coals for a girl and never heard the end of it. And how fatidic she should be named gretchen. Yet i dont recall any lowergut longings back then. These would wait til aged 5, til priscilla prinzi, to grip me... and from which moment forward i have not felt unshackled except during formal meditations ɛ their overflow of afterglow.

Father had a rather cavalier attitude about my precocity. (I think he was secretly prideful of it.) Yet mother was able to goad him into "schtrappink dat boy a goot vun" —for it seemed clear to everyone, a "dangerous pattern [was] developing [in me] and should be stamped out right away. For childhood is the only chance we get to subdue[!] such antisocial[?] behavior. We cannot permit Nathan to turn our little school into a petting zoo". (My brackets.) These words i found after mother's death, scrawled on the back of an early reportcard. Picture now the patriarchs of civil jurisprudence ɛ religion enjoying a good old-fashioned sopping of raiments as little nathan squirms ɛ squeals under the strictures of the strap. That was one of three times father beat me like a piñata out of which might tumble, if only he whacked it enuf, a better wife ɛ mother for us, a healthy leg maybe, or the ability to help his son negotiate a mother whom he had to have known was pathologically selfish ɛ unwell. And so it is that i have almost as little respect for father's fathering as for mother's mothering.

And so it came to pass, like all children raised in hug-free zones (no-touch environments) i figured the general chill –which civility has spread across the world like an emotional ice-age– was just the way things were with us humans, and that my desperation for intimacy (for the wee-est sample of primitive warmth) was due to some flaw in my own character. This is recall's first major corporeal-abuse event directly attributable to the much-bloodied hands of antiestablishmentdisciplinarianism.

The following year (1952, if my calculations are correct), when reintro'd to kindergarten, priscilla was there to greet and (tacitly) taunt me. For by then i'd learned my lesson: Look, dont touch. (Or more to the point: suppress instinct, begin mental illness.) And *look* i did, from as far back as i can remember. And still do! And always will! As liz browning said (and hubby rob echoed): "You should not take a fellow of just five years / make him swearoff kissing his peers." Tho i've had both fascination ɛ longing under control eversince, *innately* i'm still human, still a Natural man, still suffer from the curse incarnate of our Planet: desire for unbridled procreation!

A part of my fifth book, *die, primitive! anthropology & imperialism,* is a kind of novelet in that it follows for a time the daytoday existences of two prehistoric beings, dan ɛ nan –not quite primates, not quite homosapiens– from birth to death. Later, in a section of the book which shifts forward thousands of years to sometime in the 21st century, i included a series of panels in oil by the aging hartmut halstub titled simply "civilization". 12 in all, the first shows human legislators setup in the middle of a jungle rewriting the laws of Nature. The others depict things like, a man in cleric garb beating with a scepter two snakes amorously entwined on the jungle floor; a physician threatening to neuter two chimps curious about each other's genitals; two policemen dragging off a wizened bonobo caught sniffing the rears of a group of giggling youngsters ɛ soforth. The series closes with a man ɛ woman, separated by a brick wall, blindfolded gagged nose ɛ ears plugged hands ɛ feet in shackles and, the best part, a cutaway view of their insides, which begins at the feet with the emergence from the sea of the first amphibians and ends showing pristine jungle... from the neck up! The work has been described as dadaesque paulus potter, and i suppose it is. But what critics fail always (and 'why' is the question) to point out is, all this preposterous behavior so graphically captured on canvas is 'merely' civilization depicted as the tragic experiment it is.

With this as backdrop i have no qualms about declaring, nathan schock was not a little pervert because he tried to mate with dolores' doll in kindergarten, or because he topped that act the year prior by trying to mate with the real thing. No. Little nathan was a healthy child, responding to the voice of instinct in him loud ɛ clear. It was teacher school ɛ parents (ɛ any social system which could freakout over such a thing) that were sick. For they, in collusion, were determined to pervert the course of Nature/instinct in little nathan schock, stamp out the entire history of evolution in his body,

[Emil, i'm sorry i cannot take more seriously this rummaging thru the unwashed laundry of my past. Be forewarned, it's fearsome highwire antics youre asking here.]

convince both him ɛ me, the jungle signals i was receiving were both "sick" ɛ "evil". And, intentional or not, at every turn for the rest of my days, society would inflict pain where pleasure longed to lie down ...all this, til nathan schock was as sick as everyone around him, til i viewed my blindness my deafness my shackled limbs my manacled appendages my stoppered-up senses, as normal; til i conceded this beastial denial ɛ deprivation was a "healthy" ɛ "Godly" way to proceed.

Unmeaning, i'm sure, the insult it was to me, my attorney, today, along with his other concerns, brought me a writing manual, a popular text by two scholars called flunk ɛ frite and titled *the writaments of good rooting* ...a- *the rudiments of good rutting*.... Well, you get the idea. After he left i cracked the covers at one of his markers. "The good autobiographer should, early on in his manuscript, cite an erotically intriguing incident from his grotesque childhood." Ok, perhaps i've colored the authors' corny advice just a bit.

[I attribute this breakdown in communication which occurred between client and counselor to visitation time constraints, as explained in my Forward. NS failed for instance to make clear to me the monstrous role which prison psychiatrist Samuel Sigmoid was playing in his daily existence, along with the heinous abuse he was suffering at the hands of guards and other prison staff. NS' error was in assuming I had the time to keep up with his testament as he wrote it. I did not. Many were the times when the pages he gave me sat unread for weeks. In fact, NS was a third of the way finished with this book before it was made clear to me: That a proper legal defense required that I read every word he placed in my safe keeping. As to NS's aside, inserted vertically along a narrow margin of the manuscript: I have retained it, for I feel NS intended the reader to see it. —Ed.]

Flunk ɛ frite's advice reminds me of a fairytale. Shy almond-eyed bull named ralph, panicked by the prospect of recalling (for a curious boy) the gory details of its youth (back in madrid), got so chokedup it coughedup its cud! That entrail dangled for days (like a sheet of afterbirth) while the poor animal, trying to reswallow the thing, tossed its head thisway&that in an attempt to catch it each time it snapped past. That cud, incidentally, later became a subject of the boy's abject teen curiosity concerning matters of mammalian birth. So much for my lack of stomach for bringing up the past. This remembrance of things past has gone thoroly stentorian. I'm not feeling well and ask the reader's kind indulgence for a few minutes.

3

Tho my lawyer will think i'm puttingoff the promised peek at my past, prison catchup *must* be dealt with. For should i, like poor humpinLouie, become the next inhouse snuffjob, not just the reader ε my lawyer but friends ε loved ones too will never know the truth of how i turnedup prematurely executed.

"Good mourning, inmate schock! That's spelled m-o-U-r-n-i-n-g, in case you didnt pickup on my flawless enunciation." Slugmoid, md, is speaking. "And how was your weekend? Hopping 'n' carefree, I trust? Good. [finally looking up to see if it is indeed me sitting there] I'm sure you managed to come out of yourself long enuf to wish our good friend louie 'Happy oblivion', no?"

It is tu morn following humpinLouie's execution. Such appointments with our prison shrink, titled "corrections analysis and therapy", are "ordered" on an "as needed" basis. But unlike the usual patient/therapist relationship, here the doctor orders the visit not the patient. Were it the reverse, trembling at the possibility of even the slitest "transference", i would have switched doctors (as they say) immed following my "initial evaluation". But such is not mine to decide. As slugmoid himself is unshy to pointout, "We are a captive audience here and refusing an appointment may lead to reprisal": at best a day's meals denied, or a good pummeling ε floor- or wallslam; or, if one dares resist, a good clubbing shocking spraying&/or gassing ...only to endup in the pudgy dragon's lair anyway, maybe even on a litter or in a wheelchair ...of which i've endured all.

A gunless female guard-intern, porcine ε pockmarked, was let in. No words exchanged, she set on the desk an armful of cardboard box and marched off. The large man heaved himself to his feet, began removing styrofoam containers from it. As onebyone he peeked ε sniffed under their lids, he chatted about a "new copper-based ointment all fed. prisons have been mandated to evaluate. To us that means: Okay to experiment with, of course". Since nothing in my demeanor acknowledges him, tho my eyes follow him as he demands, slugfrood addresses the guards ε ambient space generally. "It makes a better shortcircuit" he explains, squeaking open a container and sniffing it's obliging puff of steam. "Of course, if some fool misplaces the ointment ...and lord knows we have our share of fools around here [darting sidelong glance at the guards] ...the condemned prisoner's hair 'n' skin are *sure* to burst into flame ...which may *still* happen even with this new stuff, of course, bureaucracy being what it is."

"Barbecutions we call em" says gluum from his usual spot by the door, thumbing a magazine as one plays a concertina.

"Happened in fact to an ape old tom edison used way back when. Caught fire, it did." Tossing aside the empty box, froodmoid arranges the containers in a white arc on his desk, sits. "Traveled round the u.s, ya know, showingoff his spanking-new invention ...Almos' slipped there. Almos' said 'new *spanking* invention'. [grins to self, unlids styrofoam cup, shoves fat finger into it] Cold. Shit. Put this in the microwave, gerald. [sucks finger clean. I am surprised to learn gluum's given name] ...A bad connection 'll do it every time. The gorilla ...come to think of it, it wasnt a gorilla. It was an orangutan [which he, usually well-spoken, pronounced orangatang] .... Anyway, the big ape just burst into flame." Slugmoid was characteristically cheery for having pulled the switch on louie just hours before.

{I can only hope when my turn arrives, i too burst into flames. Yet even then one can not be certain these ghouls wont have sex with his corpse "while it's still hot".} I do not say what i'm thinking.

Deathrow: the careful construction by prison authorities of an epidemic of pernicious dread.

"Too much juice 'll do it every time" says gluum, slamming the glass door and punching START.

Slugfrood glances past his shoulder with a sneer. "Everyone round here's an authority on barbecutions but only four of us sign up ta pull the switch. Anyway, like I was saying. 'A regular torch', one witness claimed. 'Nuthin left but a stink o' fried monkey' said another. There are fotografs of the whole thing. Charred chimp. [fork in hand, he pauses] They eat monkey, you know, where I was last winter." [cocks head, takes bite of chicken leg, mouth full says] Taint monkeynuts but it'll do. [chomps] Think I'll go ta tahiti next time. Hear there's more action there ...'n' cleaner merchandise too ...On the other hand [relinquishing fork for fingers], the chap who told me that's dead now ...caught some ugly bodyrot or other."

There is quiet while the froogmoid attacks its food, everysooften dangling animal parts my way, raising bushy eyebrows, grunting approvingly, as if i were missing a treat: gooey ribs of cow, shiny slice of pig, butcher's guttermix sausage, dead chicken parts. He knows perfectly well i'm a lactoveg. Setting aside a container heaped with bones, huffing, he pauses for air. "Old edison fried dogs cats even horses, trying to perfect his invention. Had a sideshow, I understand; toured the u.s for awhile ...trying to convince everyone that stoning, hanging 'n' firingsquad were old fashioned." Frood's eating habits clarify the distinction between gourmet & glutton. "Snap quiz, schock m'boy. [slurp] Pardon me, [chomp] but this barbecution sauce, -er, barbecue sauce, I mean, is mmm-mmm delicious! Now then, here's your question. What electric appliance [slurpchomp] predated every other ...'cept, o' course, the litebulb?"

Gluum, unable to contain himself, snaps "Da lectric chair!"

Loud thump of begrimed fist. "That was *schock's* question, mr smartypants. *You* are in big shit with me for that, okay.......? OKAY!"

"Big shit wichoo, yessir" grumbles gluum, plainly nonplused, handing over a steaming container and head-in-shell retreating.

"And as for you, my dear schock, you can thank good tom edison that, when the system gets round t' you (which should be any day now, come to think of it), you wont be shot stoned or hung til dead. [chomp, squish] No, not at all. You'll be dispatched in a *civilized* manner."

Knowing better these days than to speak my mind unnecessarily, his grotesquing of an already ugly history made silence difficult. <Thomas edison's motives (unlike your own, of course) were not humanitarian but selfish. His tour was designed to crush the competition by showing everyone, via his brutal but graphic sideshow, how dangerous mr westinghouse's new 'n' successful alternating current was. And as for the poor creatures edison murdered (unlike myself, of course), they were victims of sheer avarice 'n' shameless cruelty.> Even as i uttered the words i feared i had just mumbled <bruphic but grattle shidesow>.

Yet the slug, who would not have missed an opportunity to deride me had i actually bungled the words, said only "Aha! Mr betterthanthou speaks to us, gerald! But *that*, you see? *That* right there! *That's* your problem, schock!

[i get same evileye gluum got] You are an insufferable snob!" Not unlike the teeth of a hedgetrimmer, he immediately neats-up the meaty hangings of a club sandwich. "Matter of fact [choke, swallow] time's up... session's over. Get out! Get him outa here b'fore I lose my cheerful disposition!" He reaches out, rib in one hand, chickenwing in the other, and with a free pinky punches a recorder into operation. "I want ya to know, mr schock, your lack of cooperation here t'day has hurt my feelings." He then pops it off again, then back on again. "And, oh. Dont forget this booklet about what we've been discussing here today: your rights as a prisoner." Barbecue sauce meandering to a third chin, he hits STOP.

On the way back to my cell gluum continues the session. "...Den dey strapdown yer arms wrists legs feet yer gut an' yer head too. Da headstrap has a cup, ya know —fer yer chin [head back, points at his own chin while peering sidelong at me]. We gotta clamp yer jaw cause it stops a whole bunch o' shit from happenin...."

Political correctness afterall is description cutoff from honesty & courage. Afraid to offend, it can only watch helplessly while freedom of expression is put to death.

{Like searing rebukes, like cursing one's killers, like howls of anguish, like inconsolable sobbing? How about lip-blistering purple froth and postmortis drooling? Along with suppressing chances of a violent projectilation of one's last supper, of spitting it onto the glass that separates expectant spectators from unexpected expectorant.}

Dr slug's suite being in the new bldg, one passes the witness room ("An dis is where yer lady hasta sit if she wants ta watch ya die") ...and the death chamber. "An' dis here's da trone [throne] room" he adds [with mock gravity]. One o' dese days you'll be crowned in dere" says gluum. "Too bad you'll be a frenchfry a minute later" harrumphs glumm, finally speaking, and weakened by the cleverness of his humor. I can only guess theyve put my earlier "execution" in that room out of their shared brain. (More on that later, time permitting, hic,tsk.)

After sealing me in gluum leaves. But glumm i must hearout. For you see i've no way of turningoff the speaker in my cell. And if i dont get a chance to ballup toiletpaper, stuff it in my ears, i must hear what goes on out there. "Last of all dey pin a big diaper on ya, just before yer big walk."

{As if the prisoner isnt bow-legged and wobble-kneed enuf.}

He opens the black brochure i'd purposely left on my chair in the slug's office, scans it, squinting, stumble-reads, "Da state [pause] enshers dat da dig-ni-ty of da con-demn-da is pra-tected." Closes it. "No fuss, no muss, schock. Ya see? Here. I'm posed ta give ya dis." Drops brochure into security drawer, slams it over to my side of the door. "Like it or not, schock baby, yer gonna leave dis worl like a man: gut in, chin up. Da straps seeda dat. Den it's hang on fer dear life cause here we gooooooooooooeeeee-ooooooooooooow!" Shuffling his feet, banking from wall to wall down the corridor as tho hanging onto the bar of a careening rollercoaster, glumm left me to my thoughts. Thus ended another session of "Instructional Therapy for Inmates on Deathrow".

HumpinLouie was condemned to death for having caused the death by asphyxiation of an 11yearold. Having a child molestation record (one conviction), a prosecutor hit him with murder1. Disgusted with himself he pleaded guilty even tho his police & court confessions said to the effect "I was scared and only trying to keep him from yelling. I may be disgusting but I'm not a murderer. I love children." Before circulating around the prison 'official' excerpts from the court transcript, dr slugmiod took the time to circle the "I love children" part, adding three large exclamationmarks. As if to incite violence, at the top he wrote "Check this out, you men who believe in justice!"

As guards gluum & glumm told it: "Da nex day [guards] zodion 'n' xodion [the latter they pronounced exodion] beat da poowa muddafukka bloody an trew him in da hole fowa week." "Nevah tawked again. An' truss me, it wasnt cawz dey didn tryda make 'im. Doze two c'n git priiiiidy nasty when dey wanna." "An dey always wanna" added gluum.

4

Today a prisoner from the new bldg was marched thru here and put in sturry (solitary, iso, the hole). I know the feeling. Within days of arriving i too was placed thrown in there. On paper they call it a.d (administrative detention), or shu (security housing unit), both sheerest pc. For it is nothing of the sort. Whatever happened to the word punishment and to its modifiers "extreme" & "unusual"? Political correctness does not care how brutal the reality so long as its *description* does not offend.

Total sensory deprivation is illegal in the u.s in any form. When, following ww2, it became common knowledge that some of the crueler detention techniques used by the nazis had long been in use in u.s prisons, sensory deprivation iso was gradually phasedout & finally outlawed. For it is a fact, as 'little' as 36hrs deprived of sensory stimulation often brings on irreversible insanity. So it was with poor louie. A peek into one of two special cells at the far end of my cellblock will give a sense of why. The ≈1.2m wide × 2.1m deep cell to which i refer is walled with an old type of raw cinderblock —the last of this old building's orig cells to my knowledge. Only its window (blocked by a wall of the "new" bldg), floor, door ɛ toilet have been updated. Its rough concrete floor, when i arrived, was covered with a layer of ash which the slowly disintegrating (and doubtless beat-on clawed-at) walls had lain down over time. (Using paperplates from my "meals", i scraped most of the cinders aside. They had such a brittle splintery quality i guessed them to be volcanic in origin or possibly a byproduct of smelting.) The only other item in the narrow room was an old furniture-movers' blanket, crusty with skin waste, stinking of old urine, and with the same maddeningly biting ɛ chafing scoria that covered the floor embedded in it. Last but not least there is the door: outside-mounted walk-in refrigerator type with a leather seal so tite one's ears hurt when it closed, a seal so complete that only after a couple hours of blackness can one locate several pinpricks of indirect gray lite (daytime only) in the all but absolute blackness —the only sure means i had of counting the days as they snailed by —arthritic snail.

Tho no alcatraz henri [Young —Ed.], with his 38months in sensory deprivation for stealing $5, i can say, two days of sensory deprivation are like a week; a week, a month; a month, a year, etc. To say my "stay" seemed over a year long is not to exaggerate. Nervous breakdowns or irreversible insanity are guaranteed with isolations exceeding 16days. With *total* sensory deprivation it can happen in three! Multiply by *14* to arrive at the length of my *total* isolation!

Of the 40 or so "hole" isolations i've witnessed since my arrival, not counting my own (which would skew widely the numbers), the average is 1.5days. It would be even less but for the stays of two inmates. From this i surmise, most prisoners must be repentant or recantant. To loathe the politics in this place (ie, to refuse to barter one's body or beliefs) is to beg to rot in iso. For six weeks running i was 'the feral howl at the far end of the sewerpipe' —for that's what a voice from the hole sounds like ...when i can hear it, that is; only in the dead of nite. And to hear it is to know, tho only five cells away, the captive is shredding his larynx to be heard! The conversational level of the speech of the women upstairs is easier to hear in the middle of the day!

> Current inmate isolation methods, called A.D. (administrative detention), are totally unlike the personal isolation techniques of old-style prisons, methods from which the term "the hole" became justifiably infamous. For today's A.D. units separate groups of prisoners from the main prison population, not individuals. Also, today's A.D. units are not designed to be sensorily (light, sound, people etc.) impoverished. Where NS was imprisoned (Lorton, now closed) there was such a unit. But unlike the cell-row where NS was housed for most of his stay, and unlike "the hole" he speaks of, located at the far end of that row, the A.D. unit was resonably clean, climate controlled, well lit and housed up to 30 inmates. It is where in fact the present writer was led to believe NS was occasionally housed. This inhumane conspiracy of prison authorities, green-lighted by the federal justice system, was complicated by the fact that NS himself believed, for many months running, that his cell was located in the legal A.D. unit. Of course it was not. It was located in the long-condemned "old building", which cells are better described as dungeons and whose isolation cell makes standard A.D. look like primary school "time out". —Editor.

One doesnt forget such isolation. No sound but water trickling in the toilet and, when it stormed nearby, a very remote rumble of thunder. Nothing to stimulate the senses but the trickle ε the stench. No human contact but the swift sliding open&shut of a small door at mealtime: two cigar-sized pieces of slimy ε sinuous beefjerky twice a day. One's drinking water: tap-goop from the lidless plastic toilet tank. If one wants to see anything in his donjon keep he had better be staring at it studiedly, thru specially squinted eyes, during that three-second burst of lite when his food is placed —a skill it takes days to perfect. I recall the guards wondering on my way to iso if i'd be luckier than the wretch before me. He, i was led to know, on "finally" getting out, was "showud shabed 'n' fried befaw his eyes had time ta get usta da lite!"

verisimila(sol)itude

I am a child of silence, offspring of darkness.
Only hunger suggests i'm alive.
My heartbeat seems mythic; my breath, a lie.
I feel like a fetus......whose mother has died.

Composing such things, and then routinely reciting the ever-expanding repertoire to keep it crisp in memory, gave sanity a platform on which to pace in its shabby homemade tapshoes. How could a lawyer who visits at least every two weeks miss all this? some will want to know. Well, wornout by months of stress of a rigged trial, after visiting with me the day i arrived, and after initiating the first of my appeals ε petitions, emil escaped to europe ε the orient for a month of r&r. When he returned he was told i'd "just been" isolated for "assault of a prison official" and could not be seen for 2weeks.

Of course by the time he returned i'd already put in four weeks! To make my so-called a.d appear legal: at the end of weeks 2 ɛ 4 i was removed for a few hours, then put back again. I wish i could say these time-outs were spent merely trying to reaccustom myself to the "briteness" ɛ "noise" of prison life. They were not. Then again, neither am i prepared to horrify my reader with what occurred during those breaks, for sHe will surely suffer almost as much as i did inside the armor of my mental discipline.

Tho guards were assigned to clean me up, a non-criminal practice hadnt prepared emil for what he saw when i was led into our visitation cubicle. "Good God, man, what happened? ...The court didnt say anything about feeding you to the lions" etc. Weight-loss alone signaled something "terrible", as emil put it; then there was my right eye: almost shut with scartissue from closerange pepperspraying; and the bullet scar on my scalp festering thru its bandage. (While one's own urine is better than water from a filthy toilet for cleansing a wound, it is afterall not the best disinfectant.) Finally there was my soft-spoken ɛ peaceful demeanor in the face of this grisly abuse. Tho it was the more than 1ooohrs of darkness ɛ silence which had honed to near perfection my meditative skills, emil took my quiet smiling comportment to be a nervous breakdown of grandiose proportions –as did everyone– and i could not persuade him otherwise. One fact leading to another, he lodged a formal complaint —with copies to every board bureau committee ɛ organization which ugldf (united greens legal defense fund) lawyers could link with the abuses in question while they evaluated the pros&cons of filing suit against both state ɛ fed.

> Because maximum security prisons are typically located in rural areas, far from large employee pools; and because the salary is low and working conditions potentially hazardous; and since the job of 'corrections' is attractive only to a select type; because of these things human rights abuses in prison are all but guaranteed; <u>so</u> guaranteed in fact one wonders if that isnt the whole point.

The first result of all this (on my end of things) came a week or so later when i was "ordered" to "come before the warden", a phrasing which, in view of prior events, frankly concerned me.

5

An obnoxious & not terribly brite person, at first i thought his righteous indignation was an act: "How dayah (dare) yall concoct such a pack o' lies!" Yet despite all the ranting & marching about, whiffs of sincerity got me thinking: {Could it be this man has no clue what's going on in his own prison?} He told me if i were "smart" i would call my lawyer ("raaht this minute", smacking the fone with the flat of a pudgy palm), confess that my complaints were "all a pack o' lies, else" he couldnt be held "rahsponsible fowah the consequences". Of course our prison shrink, along with the guards who escorted me there (four examples of invert nastiness if i'd ever seen it) heard all this and were free to take the remark as a generalized delegation of "correctional" responsibility.

As to the term corrections? More pc, this time meaning: a job-style ensuring that 'bad' people are thoroly punished.

I tried to visualize my predicament. Still too new to decide if i would now suffer more or less for having stirred up a hornet's nest, it was the nature of hornets for swift & stunning reprisal which readied me for the worst. Whether insincere and knowing damnwell what was going on in his prison, or sincere & unaware, did nothing for my sense of personal safety. Pain still hurts whether allowed by ignorance or authorized by intent. Weeks of extraordinary meditations in iso, on the other hand, maintained me in a state of worry-free detachment, a state so effective it left me careless as to my safety muchless my future.

6

Coup d'ultime. I was not completely shocked when around 1a.m, during my first brief timeout from iso (designed to 'legally' separate my 1st & 2nd weeks in the hole from my remaining four), i was awakened & hustled off to be executed. Yes, that's what they said. "At four a.m sharp!" So there i was, an hour later, nextdoor to my own cell, all prepped (head & one calf shaved, diapered, bible-read & prayed-for, whether i wanted it or not) and ready for "the big cook-in", as they called their barbecutions. With everyone gone, presumably to prep the dancehall, sitting there waiting, on the cusp of yet another crisis meditation, the thought of cavaradossi's last dawn slipped onto the horizon of awareness. And altho, thru the filthy window of that holdingtank, a few *stelles* could be seen *lucevan*-ing overhead, my *sogno d'amore* was long *svani per sempre*.

Tho i've since witnessed from my cell the prep-end of several executions, at the time, being a newcomer and having no idea as to practice (v legal protocol) in these matters, i could not be sure if what was happening to me that nite was *not* the real thing. So far as i could tell, i was about to die in the electricchair (as promised by dr slugmoid) even tho we'd formally filed for lethal injection. To account for my rush to judgement my handlers "confessed", tho they knew what they'd been ordered to do was "not by the book" (i afterall had a right to 30 days notice) they were quick to add: "Bigwigs gave us no choice". Had i not been (as i've said) sufficiently disciplined to drop into the secondmost powerful meditation of my life, i think imagination alone might have disabled my heart if not my sanity.

To cut to the chase. At 3:45a they came and escorted me to the dancehall, strapped from ankles to head into the chair and asked if i had any "last words". Finding myself stunned & unprepared, and eschewing anything so cliche as "You are murdering an innocent man", i declined. Then, an electrode on one leg, another capping my naked skull, a hood was lowered to chin level and, after "Stand clear!" was blatted over the p.a system, after footsteps had hurried aside, and after a minute of deafening silence, an elec current tore thru me.

Deep into a neural tarantella well beyond my control, i was convinced this was it; that i was dying. As awareness was engulfed by a fast-expanding blip of black untime, the current & agony ceased or seemed to cease. {Am i dead?} As a smidgen of rationality began to return i gradually recognized, the agony i felt came *not* from the electrodes on leg & head but from my stunbelt! (Stunbelts, put on prisoners here when outside their cells, automatically deliver 50,000 volts for 8 seconds when triggered remotely. The dose is so excruciating it will throw a large man to the floor in a howling knot of drool & dual incontinence. I know. For this was my *third* zapping from that gruesome girdle.) I need to note: Before awareness began to recoup, my mental picture had me (deep in the womb of some single-starred cosmos) slumped into a quasifetal position. How surprised then i was to find myself sitting absolutely erect, still in that same ugly room with those same ugly people. It was not til the screaming of every nerve in my body began to subside that i heard the guffaws & chidings, and that i felt somewhat sure i was not going to die.... Not that nite anyway.

7

By now emil should know i'm not procrastinating. For who would choose to confess present hardship & humiliation rather than youth's follies & disappointments? Beside, my civilized reader needs sorely to confront at least some of the horrors the war against Nature/instinct has unleashed. Yet here's perhaps the oddest part of all this. Emil is learning of my day-to-day tribulations in virtually the same way the reader is: by reading what i write here. [It was through no fault of mine that counsel visits were limited by the court to 30 minutes per week. There was no way, in such a limited venue, for me to learn firsthand all the details of NS' suffering. See Foreword. —Ed.]

As followup to the warden's rant, dr slug ordered another appointment. "*Now* that sillyboy lawyer of yours is suing the state!" Dr slug is shaking a sheaf of papers in my direction even before i'm seated. "Do you know about this? Of course you do. Your ceaseless whimpering 'n' whining instigated it!" Tho still high on meditation, i'm a plainly wounded & wasted individual, fresh from six weeks of sd (sensory deprived) iso and by all appearances a shattered man. "That pansyass [my lawyer, he means] claims youve suffered thirtyseven, yes *thirtyseven*, events of, get *this*, 'extreme and unusual punishment'! This time you crybabies have gone too far!"

Emil had assigned one "event" for every day over the maximum 14-day legal limit on social isolation. [I had no way at the time of discriminating it from the sensory deprivation NS was actually enduring. —Ed.] The other abuses ranged from denial of daily time-outs from my cell, to food denial, to medical procedures that were physically psychologically & sexually abusive, to being forced to drink only water from a filthy toilet for 42 days, to abuses with stun guns paint bullets rubber bullets cattle prods stun belts pepperspray teargas kickings clubbings tasings blindings and, of course, the *coup d'ultime:* 6weeks of sensory deprivation plus mock execution! Emil also noted, but agreed not to count, my gunshot wound, as i felt it was accidental. (More on this later, maybe.) The slug's reaction to our not counting it? "Youre lucky my guards didnt *kill* you, you vainglorious titeass!" Which i suppose was true. Worse things have happened in here. "But this is the one that gets me right here [thumps chest]: Routine illegal and inhumane use of riot clubs stunbelts stunguns electric wands pepperspray 'n' teargas."

Officially these are called imd's (inmate management devices). Of them, stunbelts are the handsdown favorite. This is because (boasted slugmoid) "The smallest mind [glancing at the guards] can collapse the biggest knuckledragger [glancing at me] to a howling drooling pissing shitting pile of societal waste with just the touch of this little red button here!" Reminds me that i'm wearing this device as i face him, and that not only he but each of the four guards in the room has a red button of his own at ready. "Before this handy little widget I usta have no choice but ta sit you violent ones in that cage over there."

<An' *still* i'll bet we werent safe.>

Pouty frown sags his features. Further depressing his jowls, he peers down at the remote, gives the recessed red button a tap. The jolt, tho brief, caused a miniseizure which made me lurch forward and bearhug my spleen. "Ya see? Instant gratification! Amazing! Granted, not as sexy as the old testicle vice. But then, this way we dont hafta answer t' anybody's balls getting ripped off, if you get my drift mr cleverman." I hated that he so much resembled jonathan winters, for no one could have been more unlike that sweet dear gentle genius.

Still hunched in a burning coldsweat i survey him from under my brows.

"Why the face? <No face. Jus following the speaker as ordered.> With a forward heave of his hulk he rises, circles anxiously behind the large leather chair, obviously unused to unfawning patients. "Ya know, youre such a prissy little cunt, schock. I dont know what's to be done with you. You an' that candyassed lawyer o' yours. Hey, I know what! [suddenly livid with excitement] *Youve plugged that little pansyass havent you? That's* why he's always hanging around here. He's worried youre gonna get a new boyfriend! *That's* it, isnt it? You gave him a taste o' that monster bone o' yours an' he cant get past it!" [it occurs to me to ask {Why arent you recording *this,* doktor?} but i hold my tung] What you need, schock, is a few mansized schwantzes rammed up your virgin ass ta bring you back ta reality!"

If, like spying thru the high hedgerow fence which circles an insane asylum, i should part for a moment the foliage of this testament, it is only so the reader may get a glimpse of the truly gothic backdrop moving beyond the story of the text. As to what happened during that other, the second of those two brief but appalling hiatuses in my six weeks of iso, perhaps there will be time later. In the meantime... i wish i could dispatch all these basics without using words. But being no masereelist or mime, words it is and words you get. Yet be assured, i will not wallow in melpomenasty tho the facts beg it. And tho it is not in my nature to wail "Woe is me!", neither is it my nature to hide the truth, black & brutal tho it may sometimes be. And who cringes at the facts of max lockdown circa 2000, i suggest attacking its civil causes or eat the results of our apathy with equanimity.

8

This will wrap prison catchup.

Things have been happening around here. First, emil has been here&gone again, taking my most recent scribblings with him. But he says he is "troubled... You ask how much time is left to write your biography. I dont know. Maybe years, maybe days. What I *do* know is, in its push to make 'the purposeful endangerment of the safety of a federal official' punishable by death, the department of justice would love to make an example of you. On the other hand, there are more than a hundred 'n' fifty ahead of you ...some of them *multiple* murderOnes. In view of this, I think the powers that be are a little shy right now to set a death date since it would help establish our conspiracy argument in the public mind. If your concern is having enuf time to fully state your case, what I would do ...and I'm not telling you what to do here, believe me... what *I* personally would do is post an upfront brief. Facts of your case with minimal embellishment." He suggested a chapter with a list of whereas's. Tho an excruciatingly lawyerly tactic, i cant think of a smaller more effectual pill to swallow.

√ Whereas the corpolitical establishment has long considered me an enemy of "progress" (ie, an enemy of the plunder and pillage of our Planet by large corporations and the governments underwriting them);
√ whereas the federal government rigged my trial and condemned me to death unjustly;
√ whereas agents of the federal government kidnaped, tortured, raped and murdered....

But i cant do this. Not like this. Not now, anyway. Not if it means reliving every ghastly fact....

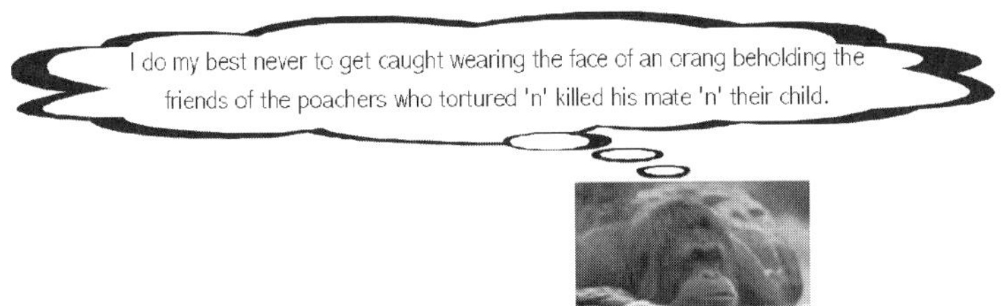

I do my best never to get caught wearing the face of an orang beholding the friends of the poachers who tortured 'n' killed his mate 'n' their child.

There now. I'm back. Once the brief is posted, emil figures i can proceed with Lilith's bio, content that the basic truths, at least, have been stated. While this seems fine at first glance, such a list would be better compiled for my signature by staff at ugldf hq. They would be more thorogoing than i could ever be with such an emotionally debilitating subject.

Something else also was "troubling" emil. "I've only had time to read a couple pages here 'n' there but it seems to me... <Yes?> ...it seems to me youre overly concerned with, well, how to put this delicately.... *Personal* things. <But that's what you asked me to do: establish my humanity with the reader.> I know I know. I jus didnt think you were capable of, well, such frankness. Dont get me wrong. I know how frustrating being in here must be for you. Never mind. It's good. It's fine. It's me. I've been told i'm somewhat behind the curve in matters sexual anyway."

Then, in response to our suit, complaints & petitions, comes a "NOTICE" from the warden. It addresses my petition for prison rights & privileges as follows. THE FOLLOWING INMATE PRIVILEGES HAVE BEEN GRANTED/RESTORED/RESCINDED. "Restored" is circled. Of course, it is pure fabrication since i never had privileges to start with. Anyway, among 32 possibilities only cafeteria & library are circled, both of which privileges i've been getting of late anyway ...thanx to the utterly out-of-character graciousness of gluum & glumm. Noting that the date on the notice is weeks old, and that the form looks worse for the wear, i soon realize: What the guards have been giving me is only what was made officially mine some weeks before! Slimed again in 4/4 time by doktor slugmoid no doubt. Anyway... I shall be visiting the library often. The dustiest gloomiest sweatiest carrels in hell are better than the screams of past slaughter which careen about this cell!

Re: ladies upstairs. Over the weekend i began tying my bedsheet (made of paper not to keep us from hanging ourselves as they claim but to cut down on wash)... tied it across the bars in such a way as to afford privacy for bathing ε toilet. Odion ε dion (guards alternating shifts with gluum ε glumm) ordered me to take it down. Hardly had i declined when another idea struck me. I tied one end of it into a cap and, now, whenever i need privacy, wear my bedsheet like a beduin tent. This stumped them.... resulted in my being ordered to "emergency therapy" with the resident slug.

"Those who require privacy should not get themselves sent to prison, my good fellow. If we feel you are a security problem we can monitor your every bodily function. We once had an inmate who was a pharmacist, and quite the man, if you know what I mean. He made a powerful bomb by collecting the methane in his urine 'n' feces. No one is beyond suspicion." Still, the slugfroog wanted to "cut a deal. Since I believe you revel in confrontation I'm going to try something different today." His proposition? Trade monitoring rights of toilet ε bath time for something every inmate (not in iso) has the right to anyway. Outtime: to be out of his cell for one hour in every 24. He says the warden will okay whatever he recommends. His voyeurism disgusts me: prefers watching me clothed on commode in preference to naked at bath! Still, should the ladies upstairs lower another message, such privacy from hall ε camera would be handy ...tho i cant believe i've allowed myself to become even this tinybit embroiled in such a pathetic imbroglio! Why do i care how they abuse their legal right to surveil us?

And finally... My so-called writing table –rickety as a newborn fawn– collapsed awhile ago, could not be revived. Packaging tape (for repair) was denied (using the ol' standby, the prisoner might hang himself thus depriving the state etc). Its little torso ε limbs were carried out of here much as i will be one day. As to replacement? Straitmon ε becillo never showedup that monday as promised. Maybe *that's* what happened to that missing day back when. No matter. So now, when there's no one to babysit me at the library, or when it's closed, i'm reduced to sitting on the floor before bunk or commode, writing on a square of chessboard —a board that used to cover the hole in my little table, a void which apparently once held plantpot or spittoon.

Lastly, this. Out of concern for cramming more data onto the pages i've been smuggling into my lawyer's care, i must increase the amount of abbreviations (abbrv's) i am using. (Right there! You see? How stupid that a word meaning "to shorten" should be so long!) In addition to the abbrv's i've already deployed, among those i foresee are the obvious w (with) wout win whold etc; re re:d re:g (reference regard etc); mx (message); immed; contd; encl encl'd encl'g; incl incl'd incl'g; rep'g (representing) &soforth. Over the course of a large ms (manuscript) such abbrv's addup to many pp (pages), pp that will not need to be smuggled to safety. And, if only the abbrv's i've used thusfar (like: fone thru enuf laff lite foto fed. dont wont cant didnt hadnt werent onceinawhile more&more here&there now&then soforth) were adopted on a World scale, it would save whole forests! And tho muchmore prison catchup is needed, i desist. The autobio imperative leans heavily.

9

I figure, if we do this in random outtakes –silhouette instead of portrait– it will work better for all concerned. Revisit this, reader.

The best days of my youth came about in summer. Once a year, school drawing to a close and faced w the freight of fultime parenting, mother would panic, cast about for a place to dump little naton til public school resumed charge of his waking hours. The problem was, i (curious, hyperkinetic kid) had a disconcerting knack for interrupting mother's routine —an agenda she enjoyed after father left for work, after she felt sufficiently buoyed by caffeine ε cognac.

More than once i surprised her. Off for the day on my bike, say, i would return for a forgotten something (padlock, tire patchkit, sandwich), catch her rehearsing: calling back an angry lover, say, on tiptoe, hand extended at the large livingrm mirror thru which he'd apparently escaped ...lucky fellow. Mother would be furious: "You schnook in, naton. You vurr trying to *spionieren* [spy]. [Verbs ε nouns often tried to trick her.] You are an *ubelkinder.*" In private she exerted little control over her juvenile emotions. While this was a boon of bliss for father in the boudoir i suppose, its downside was devastating for me. For as i matured i bore more&more the brunt of her repressed childishness. She often aimed a sort of curse my way: "Vur it not for you, naton, I vood be a fahmous aktress." Painted ε glitzy, in dangling fakegold ε thespian gladrags, hipswagging about the livingrm, mother would memorize lines from the latest movie of her matinee idol, gaga zabore. I came to loath the zabore woman after awhile. A gaudy parody of the sultry starlet she strove to be, gaga was mother's sacred cow. She longed for her cardboardy ε contrived idol's fame, lifestyle, fallopian tubes, even her celluloid-thin soul!

And so the annual scramble to pawn me off began. Mother, little naton's channel to life, complained so bitterly for so long about me and my behavior that, save for artistic aunty schock "up at the farm", no relative, either in america or out, would risk having me underfoot for the summer. Such family matters were further hampered by the width of an ocean and kinbürgers who suffered from teutonically impaired emotions. As time went on such familial rifts became an untraversable abyss.

Summerschool –a threat unleashed by my often shaky grades– hung always like an ax over the proceedings of late spring. I was the polar opposite of Lilith, who, despite a gauntlet of domestic abuse after age12, somehow did well in school! O my poor brite Love, how did you do it? (I am being monitored again. Gluum is back —switched duty w his twin and is now sitting outside my cell munching his lunch as if there were no better place on Earth to be.) I did not know summerschool was only a threat. For it (trudge two miles, rain or shine, return home at 1 instead of 4) did not get rid of me in the wholesale fashion my parents had in mind. And so it was, that banal horror, the christian camp, wonout over fuller ε funner curricula. Why not some other type of camp? Well, truth be told, religion camps were the cheapest: the sponsoring church, in trade for a reduced tuition, gets to fill the mind of the summer castaway with its prettified but still dangerous propaganda. "Suffer the little children...." It was only much later i realized, if the churches selling their conflicting versions of christ ever chanced to meet their hero in the flesh, they'd doubtless have him crucified ...again! —if only in the popPress... as some mad hippy imposter. For like sweet francis who followed him, he was too kind ε wise to go long unmolested in civil society.

10

We'll let mention of these vagabond masters leapfrog us into a key chalkbox and its one-footed-jumping jingle. As the loss of juanita set in, the sandled nazarene began to replace my boyhood heros. I often went to "the garden alone", so to say. But one day, alerted by the remark of a science teacher, i began to notice how my *bible* treated juanita ε her sisters w contempt. Here are a couple weals ε welts surfaced during my adolescent immersion in judeochristian scripture.

> More hateful than death are females. Their hearts bristle with tricks and traps, and their hands are as shackles.... One man in a thousand [is pure] but a [pure] female I have never found. —ecclesiastes 7:26-28

Why had my *bible* gone to the trouble to expurgate the female-praising *song of solomon* while leaving so many gross examples of female-loathing intact? I began to notice, females, animals & Nature ("these are a few of my favorite things"), since the time of eve, and incl'g eve, got a shabby biblical shake. I just happen to have another example here, this time from my then favorite "new testament".

> It is better not to touch a female. Nevertheless, to avoid fornication, let every man take a wife. —1 corinthians 7:1-2

Many christian scholars were schooled in misogyny by the writings of jewish monks —like the levite elias who, writing around 2500bc, was first to refer to females as 'those spiritually corrupt ten-holers of our fallen species...beings who, unlike every other of God's creatures, when they fall, even by misstep, land legs in the air, begging for sin to visit that foul place which any gutter rodent has the couth to keep hid.' A woman being pursued trips & falls. Imagine the spiritual corruption required for elias to interpret her rolling faceup (in time to defend herself) as a woman secretly begging to be raped! Such monastic antipathy brought this aspect of civil paranoia (fear & loathing of all things female) to philosophic depths incomprehensible to a healthy mind.

Despite such vicious assaults –which church & camp *bible* studies always leapfrogged– i grew only slowly suspicious. By my early 20s however suspicion began to open the way to new learning. In the meantime, thanks to family school & religion, i remained a sucker for distrusting females. While i still prayed daily (incl'g always my hope to one day find juanita), all the prettified propaganda was souring inside. It would be a few years til historian norman godwin helped clear things up.

[Emil, fill-in w appropriate godwin text my glossess & paraphrases below. The reader needs to know 'who' exactly taught whole cultures over many centuries to look at females w disdain or disgust.]

[Norman Godwin, in his book, *The Origins of Imperialist Religion,* speaking on "Celibate Intellectuals and the Misogynizing and Deëroticizing of Religion", argues as follows. —Ed.]

> It is no accident that, like royalty, these clans felt a strong antipathy for the masses. For while their less cerebral fathers and brothers were out working in the fields, or making war or love, they chose to stay home. Sewing, cooking, tending the children, side-by-side with mothers, sisters, they preferred mental pursuits. But in earlier eras an intellectual lifestyle was not viewed favorably by the masses.

In many parts of the world such pursuits are still ridiculed to this day. So it was, these males, belittled and bullied by other males, by the time of adulthood were much-embittered. Fathers and brothers, cruelly, drove them from home; neighbors turned their backs on these young men. They lived miserable lives; many, who failed to find shelter in a cloister with others of their kind, died of alienation, abuse, disease and starvation.

Godwin follows the thread out into full daylite.

Because mothers and sisters feared to protect them, these dropouts from laboring society came to resent, finally to hate, females. They resented them *most* for their sexual and reproductive powers; powers which these tormented males did not have, nor could they pray for or purloin.

(Gluum just up ε left. Crumbs, some quite large, are strewn around the base of the chair; another greasy smudge glisters where his head leaned against the glass. Why didnt he razz me like glumm? Can it be they *actually* spat among themselves?)

Lacking female bodies and organs and the power they wield, these psychologically (and often physically) battered males realized they were of lesser social station even than females! After all, though females were not as strong as men, they did possess powers which guaranteed them an integral role in society. That is, to be female was to have an opportunity to play a sexual or reproductive role. But to be viewed as "neither male nor female" (that is, to have no somatic rights to either role) was to be like a third sex, to be born without purpose, to be driven away in shame, to know the meaning of alienation on its deepest level!

Godwin's language is lucid.

It is for these and other reasons these men—intelligent, anguishing and thrown away like some accidental and inutile gender—as time went on and as human numbers increased, sought out each other, banned together. Coming from far and near, finding power in cloistered numbers, if only for their ability to read and write, these men were unique, muchless doing so in two or more languages. Borrowing from the "pagan" religions of the day, with their monastic genius, these early seed-pods of present-day academia set about the daunting task of, simultaneously, masculating yet desexualizing the polytheisms of their varied backgrounds; inventing along the way threats of eternal damnation sufficient to drive priestesses into the street and female temple servants into the gutter, rewriting the spiritual tales and rituals of the old world order with an eye to defaming all that is venerable about nature and females and condemning sexuality generally. Both hating and fearing nature—the *nature within* which insisted they "lust like animals", the *nature without* which insisted they were "freaks" of nature—these monks made sure that their new gods turned civilization's fear of nature into a cosmic event, a "divinely sanctioned" war designed to demolish any code of natural law which appeared to hold such persons as themselves to be without biologic, genetic or social purpose.

This latter took a tad of societal revenge, turned it into the very "wrath of God". Talk about "what goes around comes around". Here's one payback that's gone global!

> Over time these centers of learning, these monasteries, these repositories of history itself, became the religious seats, or "churches", of the various ascendant imperialist religions. Clandestinely, and later, openly (as church-states), these long-abused intellectuals methodically extracted their revenge, preying upon the ignorance, fears and superstitions of the common folk, the very laboring classes which, after all, had tormented them since time immemorial. After many false starts and failures they eventually became the hermetic seers, the celibates, the monks, scribes, abbots, rabbis, priests, vicars, bishops and cardinals, pontiffs and other "holy" rulers of the many imperialist religions as they exist today, and along the way wrote themselves into a durable hieratic power.

Himself an outed homosexual ɛ objective scholar, godwin skirts any&all homoerotic fault-finding. The gay abbé, the lay brother, the strange sister, are treated w empathy ɛ tact, as a genetic type not a biologic deadend, as they might have been.

> All the evidence insists, those who invented the imperialist religions were masculepts of the first order (sic). I infer those all-male cults headed-up by a lone male sovereign god which clearly prefers an all-male world in which males can procreate more males *ad infinitum* with no need for a second gender. (I.e., the fundamental God/man bond of *all* the imperialist religions.) But since this "ideal" world could not be made to jibe with reality—that is, since banishing or eradicating females would obviously soon eradicate all males as well—a more inclusive worldview was imperative. But there was yet another hitch. In a nutshell: How does one go about rendering females necessary yet valueless? To believably frame such a paradox was surely daunting. The only option available required a philosophic leap of psychotic dimensions. First you invent a condition of ultimate badness, then you give it a name. Evil. Then you proceed to call whomever and whatever you hate, evil. And, *voila!* Enter the story of Eve in that garden wilderness called Eden. Thus females were recast from a state of natural purity, remolded into an "evil state". Thus femaleness, in league with Mother Nature, was recast as a "necessary evil".
>
> Created by a lone male god out of a lone male's body, Eve, true to Judeo-Christian malecentric tradition, is brought into being not like Lilith, Adam's first wife, who was an entity in her own right. No. As if fabrication out of an expendable male body part were not insult enough, in order of creation, Eve is fashioned by this Hebraic lone male deity almost as an afterthought. And then, to assure her valuelessness, and the valuelessness of all her daughters for all time, the Hebrew *Torah* (and later both Christian and Islamic dogma) is then filled to overflowing with the sons of Adam begetting sons of Adam begetting more sons of Adam: an all-male dreamscape which effectively banishes females from the

> early imperialist record—actually, from the early lone-male-god universe! And as for poor Eve and her expurgated daughters: that veritable "gene-pool of evil in an evil world? Spawn of the Semitic Lilith", they are assigned the job of begetting more evil every time they beget.

The feminine quasi-archetype, lilith (re: adam), ε mary of magda (re: the subrosa jesus) ε courageous clare (re: the subrosa francis), are just three of the wise females viciously disgloried by imperial religion. But enuf of where my female-loathing *bible* went wrong. While i dawdle here the sorry scenes of my childhood mill about in exasperation. Still, having begun, it would be a shame to miss a last tidbit or two, treasures of my late teens, a foretaste, an early filching of objectivity. See now what i call the 11th commandment of that father of judeochrislamic (jci) belief, old moses himself?

> Kill every woman that hath known a man by lying with him. —numbers 31:17

When you consider, we're talking the annihilation of "20-30,ooo" female non-combatants here, thomas paine, writing some 200years ago(!), imprisoned ε facing execution like myself, was on-target when he concluded, "Among the detestable villains [disgracing] the name of man, it is impossible to find a greater [one] than Moses", whose generals he then commanded:

> But all the female-children, that have not known a man by lying with him, keep alive for yourselves. —numbers 31:18

Whoa! So old moses would have killed not just juanita (for having "known" me) but her mother too! Hmm. O yes, i learnt my *bible* well. Paine again: "...The number of women-children consigned to debauching by the order of Moses was thirty-two thousand."

My reader may or may not be happy to know i owe to this last seething insult (below) all i have been able to learn. I will never forget the moment, in my early 20s, suffering from war-trauma depression. The quote comes early in godwin's text. Saint odon of cluny (a pious abbé who lived during the middle ages) sounded my reveille.

> Yet, if we refuse to touch dung or a tumor with the tip of our finger, how can we desire to kiss a female...?

Of course "finger" ε "kiss" are euphemisms for 'penis' ε 'copulate with'. Poor eve! Western personification of femininity! By medieval times she had been degraded from a presence of voluptuous "evil" in the gardenOfEden to a disease, a festering tumor, a mere sack of shit. Given the need for revenge pent up in godwin's alienated celibates, cocreators of the various imperialist/civil monotheisms, whole schools of monk odons were predictable, as were those popular misogynists, jerome, paul & augustine —still honored as saints to this min! In the baron's play, *the twisted cross,* francis de assisi (defending the essential purity of gentle clarissa) says, "When history and philosophy are entrusted to schools of sadsack celibates, the defamation of nature and females is guaranteed." Gentle frank francis. Brave honest pj.

But my scission w religion, a necessary step when objectivity is the goal, could not be completed til i returned to my *bible.* Only in its well-thumbed pages could i affirm the roots of a mean-spirited male power structure i never dreamed existed! But dont think of me, please, as some *bitter* nullifist, or think that recent events have slanted me thus. For such basic matters as nullifist v. nulliversalist, stated years before my final arrest, fill the margins of my books. My readers know this. Only the pitch of my voice has changed in the meantime, become, i fear, somewhat of a melancholy drone.

Evil and Paranoia
Otto Reich

"Anyone who has worked in a psychiatric facility can tell you, paranoia is one of the hardest things to deal with. For no matter how attentive, how compassionate one is, he is always suspect. For the paranoid see the world as a strictly black and white duality. All of existence, animate and inanimate, is either a threat (bad/black) or not a threat (good/white). It is a world without color, without the gentle shadings and nuances of light and shadow which make up the real world. It is the origin of gothic, all shadow and suspicion. Many patients are so badly off they see 'evil' intent in a new blanket, a fresh pillowcase. And for most the only way to safety and peace from their malevolent world is by way of dying.

"In half a century of attending to the paranoid insane I was often struck by how much their outlook shares with the dominant world religions. Both see 'evil' everywhere, even in inanimate things; both feel nothing in the universe is beyond suspicion of 'evil'; and especi-ally, both believe the only way to escape 'evil' (I.e., the only way to paradise) is to die. One better understands the history of civilization, especially where religion is concerned, having delivered therapy to the paranoid insane under conditions of 'mutual' trust. For like many religious nation/states, the paranoid/insane may rise up and strike at any time, with no justification in reality, with total intolerance for the rights or beliefs of others, with a detestation for life itself, with no remorse for their actions, and sometimes without regard for outcomes including their own safety. To conclude that many religions have roots in paranoia seems unavoidable."

(continued below)

11

The day school ended for the summer 6yearold nathan slipped and wet the bed. Mother, wailing worse than berg's lulu, sent me to the tubs in the basement to wash pajamas & bedclothes: sheets, blanket, five times bigger than me and just as heavy wet. Were this the extent of my punishment i would have been ecstatic. As i hung them to dry (sunny day, carousel clothesline, bees humming in the clover) i spotted buddy geoff quietly munching grapes in the shade of our arbor. Mother, who had sent him around to the backyard to witness me struggling upon a small stool w my bulky & obstinate penance, then sent him home once i was free to play. "Naton vill see you in zee fall." And as geoff, dejectedly, departed, "Say hullo to your dear fahter unt mahter."

Up on "the hill", in mossville, lived doctors lawyers execs & other suits. Geoff's father for instance was an md and the metzgers had a large home on the golfcourse at one end of our street. Ours was the only "nonprofessional" family there. The very nature of father's business (toting the rich&famous about the eastern seaboard: nantucket hatteras martha's vineyard bermuda cuba the bahamas) fairly adverted our social otherness. Save for outlying tracts of truckfarms, we were the only bluecollars atop mossville's snob hill. And tho my family was the economic equal to some of our neighbors, my peers (save for geoff & priscilla) never let me forget my collar color. I've longsince learned, of course, many who behold themselves "Ah, professional, yes!", are really hardcore empirists in workaday drag, oligarchists whose weapons of choice have been limited –by that social 'nuisance' called democracy– to economic and

(Continued from above)

How delited i was when shy rhino press released *otto reich: the complete articles & essays*. For it is there i found this trove—tho some 20years after discovering norman godwin's sadsack celibates. Tho godwin did not study reich, a nexus of their views was i suppose inevitable. In his essay, "liberty and fear", reflecting on the clergymen he'd treated thruout his career, reich explains, "Endemic paranoia is most evident among monks and clergy. Their communal dread of an 'outside world' parallels the experience of prisoners who also believe in an 'outside world' which forces them into 'evil' conditions and then punishes them for succumbing." Unfortunately reich does not develop this further. It falls to godwin's genius to elucidate. "Imagine those poor fellows who escaped to such havens [monasteries] with their very lives during a time when the major religions were being grown into the imperialist ideologies they are today. Seeing the opportunity, how could they have done otherwise than invent or reinvent gods which trust no one but themselves? How could such frightened and angry men, given any opportunity, keep from inventing or reinventing gods which not only believe 'evil' exists everywhere, but gods so isolated from the Universe at large they believe 'evil' *actually* exists?" In short, what else could such cruelly abused & isolated men give birth to but paranoid gods, vengeful gods? Not incidentally, reich was first to my knowledge to challenge anyone to prove the empirical existence of 'evil'. "We invent a state we call evil [he said] at that point where our ability to comprehend the *actual* causes of destructive behavior or events collapses in exhaustion."

psychologic enslavement of the masses ...subspecies of a still "higher" snob-sector, the socalled successful: hauteurs w enuf money to stay in the game but not enuf to play with élan. And dont *even* get me started on that grandfather of *all* apartheids, the intelligentsia —code for that self-congratulatory class of wouldbe royalty which, given the chance, would caste the rest of us as 'untouchables', and who are more pithily described as degenerati. At any rate...

Father despised caste. Mother, however, like most on the hill, suffered terribly from *besserverdiener* envy, a trad german syndrome ...an unrealistic take, as my parents were clearly german immigrants in a time when adolf ε goons (incl'g his pilots, of course) were still armed ε dangerous as far as public memory went. But most envied by all on the hill were the dodges. ¼k beyond our cozy woodframe lay the dodge estate, a 900hectare glut of gardens ε spas replete w 42room mansion + seven other build's, w the lot encl'd by a 4m-high ivied brick wall, the cost of which alone could have purchased twice the land for a wildlife preserve.

During supper it was decided. Since lesser punishments —haranguing, sporadic whumps w a wickedly waterlogged washstick by mother, roundedout by father's infrequent but memorable whippings by belt— had failed to bring absolute results, little naton (quietly begging for clemency: <But i was stopped real good, mother>) would be locked in the foodcellar til morning. "Ve varned you zees vud hoppen eef you vet again" said mother, her jaw moving stoically yet not daring meet my eyes. It was true, she had.

My first exorcism went as follows. Since mother was plaintiff, judge ε jury, father acted as bailiff ε jailer. "Theez, sod to say, eez how boyz are made men." Creaking closure of wood-framed wire door; ominous click of latch&lock (my own bicycle lock!); sound of father's footsteps receding up basement stairs; finality of the upstairs door closing; the almost audible thud of sudden ε solitary blackness as the basement lites went off for the nite.

Two sensations were immed: a darkness which was total and for all childish purposes ominously alive, plus a sense of sudden severing, abrupt abandonment. Gripping the wire mesh of the door, after several mins i realized, neither shuddering nor weeping would bring rescue. Slowly facing about, i discovered it was some distance from the door to the stacks —rows of bundled newspapers located somewhere in the darkness to my left. As if on the edge of some abyss (and as if the edge of that abyss receded w each halting step), i made my way across the floor. After some panicky mins i reached the stacks, lay carefully down. For the moment anyway the little prisoner had avoided the imagined pit. (It would take more than an hour of discomfort before i found the courage to climb down, rearrange the bundles on which i lay into some semblance of a level surface; afterall the idea was, "za leetl pizzer" should have neither sheets pillow blankets nor mattress to soil.)

At first i lay feeling w fingertips the braille of fear the wire mesh in the door had imprinted on my hands. Then, as the pitchblack of the place preempted even subpalpebral images, sound began to take over: father leaving the livinglivingrm, heading upstairs to bed; mother, sometime later, leaving the kitchen and, after going about switching off lites, heading upstairs too. From below, the kitchen was reached via the pantry, which lay at the top of the basement stairs. At the start even thought gained access upstairs by this route. How distant were the sounds of that upstairs, a clean ε cozy place ...where only yesterday i was allowed to spend the nite. Only two floors away, my bedrm was as remote to my child's mind as another galaxy.

Those nites the house seemed a kind of living thing, w a whole bellyful of hitherto unstudied functions: water gurgling in some vast stomach at the far end of the basement, then sizzling thru pipes to the upstairs bath; the voluminous sounds of the toilet as expelled wastes plummeted down w a gush ε a slap, then swished thru the bowels of the house and on out toward the street. While these noises persisted i could derive a makebelieve sense of domestic comfort —as tho the sounds were meant to keep me company. But then, all too soon, silence was heaped onto darkness.

From an adult perspective i admit (save for what could have happened had there been a fire etc) i was a bit of a baby about all this. After all, many children that age, and younger, know *real* abuse, not the angst to which i allude. (Lilith was such a preadult.) With this in mind i will bore the reader w these trifles but a little further.

As the iron slab of nite was lowered i became aware of a cricket chirbiting crisply on the *free* side of the wire mesh —intermittent soothing presence. Even still, victim of a boundless imagination, i trembled under my robe, for some time dared not move, thought about a radio hero, *the shadow,* who sometimes rescued those fritened or alone. What were you ε margot lane doing, lamont cranston, when i needed you? A small oblong of mud-spattered window (only then recognized as one of those concrete troughs which attracted balls) suddenly brimmed w lite above me as the beams of a nextdoor neighbor's headlites swept by and were extinguished. Darkness drummed on. As my ears grew accustomed to the quiet i became aware of a faint swishing in the rafters. Back&forth, not as in poe's tale [hic] but arhythmically, w an occasional thump. I imagined nothing friendly at first. A bit later a familiar clicking left that spot. I followed in my mind's eye as it advanced from diningrm to kitchen, pushing thru the swinging doors. With a familiar muffled thud the trail of clicking ceased. A dear blond mutt, w a russet redolence of retriever, butch must have wanted to cool his belly on the kitchen tiles, i having gone silent below him.

Sometime later (a month to me and my mad reckoning of time) i satup stiffly on my rack. In the coalbin at the far end of the basement, a small landslide let me know i was not alone. I dont know if they came from there, so quietly i didnt hear, or if they'd been occupying the foodcellar with me the whole time. Even after long nites of subsequent punishments, i never figuredout where they lived. At what i guess must have been around midnite, they took over the cellar —at least it seemed so. There were probably no more than six or eight rats in all, but to me they seemed like an army ...an army quite unlike the britely uniformed battalions which terrified little clara.

Kids raised in "good&evil"-believing societies are taught to be fritened of many things in Nature. Rats roaches sharks snakes ε spiders rate near the top of a very long list, things that go bump in the day muchless the nite. My training was no exception, for mother believed most of Nature was the devil incarnate. Everything from litening to lizards made her startup ε bleed, despite lunar tides. Little nathan was therefore a setup for nictophobia. Where was the piedpiper of mossville when i needed him? Surely, like general washington, he'd camped hereabouts on his way to hamelin? And where were the lone ranger, the nutcracker ε singingjesus for that matter? —to whom i appealed often during those early years ...well, maybe not to the nutcracker. The four of them were probably having coffee w lamont ε margot in a donutshop on main street. So much for *"kindisch lallend der Helden Lob"*. Are such events meant to prepare us for the frites of adulthood? Like, why are cops always around when you *dont* need them?

They were wild, bold, ravenous.... They tore at the bundles of paper all nite. Fluff for their nests? Then again, while the rats were clearly shy of me when i moved, how was i to know what they were capable of while i slept? ...*Their red eyes glaring upon me as if they waited...for motionlessness on my part [so as] to make me their prey....* Well, that's how it seemed. So i dared not sleep. But naivete can manage this for only so long. In my several confinements, many were the times when one would scamper over my robe, or run over an exposed hand, leg or foot, or brush near my buried face, and i would wake in terror, kicking ε flailing. So i tucked knees fetally-near chin. This achieved two things; it brought bare legs ε feet beneath my robe and lent a sense of security. A nite or two of this and i learned to wake routinely, slap or kick the bundles to keep the relentless rodents at bay; or, on waking, as i got better at controlling them, i would thump the bundles from beneath my robe, causing them to retreat over territory taken while i dozed. Or i would lie there wideeyed heavy-lidded, at 2- 3- 4 in the morning, trying desperately not to nod off, and failing, always failing.

At the same time i feared making noise; felt it revealed my location, not only to the crafty enemy but to the 'other beings' sharing the basement w us ...a whole phalanx of childish phantasms swarmed jostled ε shoved each other aside in order to get their share of my frite. As the nite wore on an active imagination increased the size ε number of the rats, as well as transmogrifying their plans: *They writhed upon my throat; their cold lips sought my own ....* In my teens i would discover eddy poe's very *own* "pp story" w a long gulp of anxious recognition.

Ironically, my parents never figuredout, such punishment guaranteed recidivism. Anxiety, clear ε simple (over my parents' marital tensions, over their sometimes-violent fites, and guilt for feeling myself a thorn in their lives), precipitated my nocturnal mishaps. Now, w the advent of pissers prison in my life, i was doomed to err ε to err. Exile in that foodcellar became the little sleeper's nemesis. For i would be years understanding the cause of this pernicious ε humiliating malady. But this is a waste. Let's leave it saying, young nathan whimpered off into fitful sleep again&again on those first nites in solitary. I hate this place. I hate it. I hate it. I'll never slipup again, mother. I swear. Never.... Or so little nathan planned his life, ever fearful of future confinement.

Shades of the prison-house [of civilization] begin to close upon the growing boy.
—william wordsworth, "tintern abbey"

12

Such chatter will not do. Nobody wants to hear about the little one's throes ε agons. Anyway, those years are now broken into dusky panels and kisses are the only souvenirs worth sharing. Beside, such nostralgia[sic] is crippling; causes the walls of my cell, slowly, to seem to slide inward. And knowing the culprit –the one who wields the walls– helps only a little. The culprit is not loneliness, as one might suppose. Philosophers adventurers compulsive writers seekers ε seers, know how to make the best of aloneness. Isolation can be used as a friend —tonto packy lois margot or little john. It's claustrophobia that wields these walls, that crushes, not just isolation.

Not that confinement is new to me. Egg or womb, life, afterall, starts that way. And tho i've been "detained" all over the world, and on the highseas too, for one Planetary cause or another, still confinement exhausts ε defeats me. The worst (up til my final arrest) was 6wks in china; w a 3wk stint in ussr ε over a week in japan, which detention indirectly led to my meeting a very special woman. Even back then, when one got out of jail in the u.s, people were wary of celebrating publicly. But in europe ε scandinavia, even in parts of e europe, people are happy for greens when theyre set free; they give you a hero's hurrah ε sendoff; make one feel it is worth all the trouble. Yet in free America, a democracy founded on dissent? I've been released in many towns where people just stared, seemed to be thinking, "Maybe dissent really is criminal". It's gutless unpatriotic reactions like that which make one feel like quitting …the way i feel now.

So anyway, it's not just confinement which causes this crushing sensation; it's also a lack of hope —which for me is like being a kid again. Of course there's also the damoclean agon of waiting to die and not knowing *when* the ax –er, sword; er, liteningbolt– will descend. Yet it's all part of the ritual —like when they showup at your cell carrying *bible* scissors razor diaper stunbelt ε ankle bracelets, and announce, "*This* time we're *not* kidding".

13

One little acquiescence to cynicism before litesout, please. If this story were in movietheaters this month it might have a chance. But as things stand it will sink into a sea of spin, be dashed by that tsunami of lies broadcast daily over the globe from olympus dc. For you see, the great dream machine is *not* in movieland, reader. No, *we* are the great dream machine, you & me. Look at this oz we've created. ❶ First there is the wizard himself, the federal government. ❷ Then there are the large corporations which comprise the cells of the wizard's brain. ❸ Then there is the popPress, which is the wizard's voice. And then ❹ there's us, the little people of oz, who (to finish the loop) can challenge the wizard, or any part of him, but who conspicuously lack the daring of dorothy …or even the courage of the cowardly lion. Like it or not, i'm here to tell you. Dorothy has been kidnaped tortured raped & murdered and the tin man lies dying in captivity of a broken heart. And so, there will be no great green transformation! Quite the opposite. *More* innocents will suffer & perish and untold species be forever extincted! While we, sidetracked from civic responsibility by the sirens of our selfishness, pause only to loll in the great poppy field of our shameless greed!

And just in case this dorothyless oz isnt bleak enuf, now we believe there's no such thing as truth! How blind, to ignore the dark half of the moon simply because it's turned away! Truth is Nature —*universal* Nature, Nature as a whole. It is never less than this. And if one subtracts civilization, there's nothing left around us *but* Truth. It is *everywhere!* The fox the deer the wombat the worm, do not quarrel with their Natural fate. Flowers do not question the sun. Oceans do not balk at the moon. Trees, by nite, do not quibble with the stars. For them Nature is never wrong. And She continues to share her wounds & woes only with those who listen, listen with all our beings. And whether or not, reader, you are ready to put one ear to the ground, and all your senses to the wind

—the way primitives do when they want to know what cannot otherwise be sensed— the deep Earth-rumblings are still there. The false wizards we have allowed into power will continue to sink their fangs ever deeper into Earth's bloodied & tortured places. And all the tourniquets of "Let's pretend all is well" wont stem the hemorrhaging one stitch.

> **Social-science 101:** Most of humanity asks only to have "the 5 b's" for its contentment: bed board bread banter & breeding; or ❶ a reasonably safe & comfortable place to lie down, ❷ munchies, ❸ a daily gossip source (today: fone tv radio internet) ❹ the freedom to orgasm & ❺ have babies. That's prettymuch it. And on this predictable foundation the ruthless & clever, believing themselves superior beings above justice, have long-since built empires big & small.

14

Gluum & glumm are arguing out in the hall as i write —over a newspaper, so far as i can tell. I cannot hear them, as the glass on the front wall of my cell is very thick. Unless they open the passthru or switch on the intercom, i can only watch the proceedings askance. Most of the time the ic is left on —so i will not miss the clang of the big door down the hall, the whine & howl of the generators being put thru their paces for my benefit, which happens every sa, whether an execution is sched'd or not.

Pathetic pantomime: panzer imbecile & gestapo fop fiting over a newspaper. Gluum stalks off. Glumm opens the passthru, stuffs the newspaper in the tray, mumbles something. He still doesnt realize the ic is off, that their paid theatrics have been mostly wasted on me. Medieval farce persists. Pointing to the tray, he repeats himself. I ask <What?>, head tilted, hand cupped beside my ear. Hiss, spat: the loudspeaker snaps to attention. "Shit. It was off.... Here, read this. Youre gonna be pissed, schock." I am tempted to turn back to my writing. But the price for ignoring their childish antics is not worth the pain of reprisal. I rise, retrieve the paper, sit back down, scan the article circled by a smear of red ink.

EXECUTIONER DEAD AT 94

'GUILLOTINE BILLY' DIES WHILE VISITING U.S.

"Go ahead. Read it!"

The article scans as follows.

> Pierre Guillaume, known during most of his career as Guillotine Billy, passed away last night in a hotel in Washington, DC. Under contract by the fed, it was learned yesterday, Guillaume was slated to execute ecoterrorist Nathan Schock. Earlier this year Schock was found guilty of the murder of Charles Strickland, Secretary of Environmental Affairs, best known....

So?

He peers in at me w juvenile expectancy. "Go on, go on! Keep readin."

> Guillaume, well known for the execution of WWII war criminals, was said to be the only executioner "still living" who performed beheadings, early in his career, in public, using an ax, a method of execution otherwise not used since medieval times. Guillaume is also said to have bragged of having purposely botched the execution of prisoners whom he found to be "personally execrable". But "This has never been proven" says Guillaume Guillaume, grandson of the deceased....

"Whataya readin? No! Skip dat shit. Read down. *Dere,* at da checkmark... by yer tum [thumb]."

> Petitioning the court last month, Schock's lawyers claimed that despite knowing Guillaume has long been senile, some official "high up" asked him to "stay close". That is, to "be ready to pull the switch in the Schock case". Sources in Washington deny this. Justin Liti, federal prosecutor, reached at his home in Virginia, says, "Billy asked for the job. We didn't ask him. We don't care who does it so long as the sentence is carried out and justice is served." Guillaume, on record for the execution after WWII of 26 German POWs, is also known to have executed....

"Dat's enuf. Whadaya tink?" <Okay, i'll play. Why should i be pissed?>

Glumm feigns astonishment badly. "Cause now yer stuck wit second-best, you asshole! A secondrater! Now yer gonna git juiced by jack ketch!" —the name by which a guard from pelican bay penitentiary is affectionately known, since he regularly volunteers himself for major executions around the u.s. Glumm danced in a circle, fists reaching up, pulling down alternately the invisible arms of large electric switches. "Betcha ol' gill-a-teen billy didnt die in his sleep at all. Bet ketch killed 'im, held a pilla over his head so *he* gets ta fry ya, not billy! Kryst it mus be nice to be so fuckin popula *everyone* wants ta kill ya!" He grinned, strutted off thumbs up, still yanking imagined switches. And so i pass my days. This shabby charade reminds me of the day straitmon left a newspaper on my commode. Such antics might be refreshing to a captive audience if their motives werent so irredeemably squalid.

15

Since after age7 i all but lived for those no-school days when i could geographically escape mother's insufferable self-involvement; and since she & father saw me less as a son and more as a responsibility to which they happened to be directly related; and while the selfishness involved in permitting a 7-8-9yearold to bike 20-25-30k away from home from dawn til dusk every non-school day w no knowledge of his whereabouts likely qualifies as neglect; all that being so, if my all-day absences served my parents' purposes they certainly served mine: me & my lust for discovery in this wide Universe wiin which i'd been so unceremoniously cobbled together.

My day often started w railroad haunts, since prowling for local females was a waste of time til after ol' sol was wellalong his ecliptic. If such a connection looked possible –or, let's face it, even remotely promising– i would hang locally. But a couple days of such frustration were sufficient to slingshot me, at my very next opportunity, as faraway as i thought i could get and still get home by dark ...the only absence-related rule that was enforced ...well, beside, "An dunt bringen yeff into ärger (trouble) like za laaz time". Because geoff's parents insisted he showup for lunch when out&about, unless a clever plan was devised i usually had to leave him out of my longer jaunts.

Even back then vehicles had farmore road rights-of-way than people & other creatures. Because cops would leave you alone when you went "the back way", or via "the old road", main roads were usually the road not taken. Tho these hilly & poorer surfaced routes made trips farther & slower, their low traffic & ruralness made treks more peaceful, if boring to one wearying of smallville environs. Day-trips might consist of a bike over to chatham (22k+tangents) to try to find the former home of richard hinckley allen, astral etiologist, whom ms stott, my 2nd & 4th-grade teacher (whom i secretly wished was my mother), held to be "our greatest local treasure ...after chief jinnyjump, that is..." accolades doubtless made to the chagrin of the mossville/-morrisville war-glorifying (estab)lishment. More often however i would trek to morrisville airport (18k) to watch the sporadic action there, but secretly hoping to see father at work Wout him seeing me ...or into morrisville itself (28k+), a farmore happening hamlet than mossville and, come to think of it, home to dick allen's "young friend", lucy noble morris, great aunt of the awesome (and dead so horribly young!) artist, champion equinist & animal advote, karen morris. Synoptically, aged 7 to 9, i investigated 20-30k in every direction from home ...until, that is, spring of that dread year we moved away to the city.

My roving came to an abrupt end when a conscienced cop (serpico sort) found me 24k from home, trudging along an upgrade w a broken sprocket & little hope of making it home before dark. (My repairkit could handle only flattires & broken chains.) Deftly assessing my situation, he got radio ok to drop me at home where he explained to my parents how i'd been "poppinup" in morrisville for years ...since on my first jaunt there i'd run into a perfect halfsize audrey hepburn as she emerged from a drugstore [w her mama?], glided for half a block (behind blackchestnut hair that flowed around her like a cape) quite aware of skulking me the whole way, slid into a car ɛ vanished forever ...but not wout leaving me w an elfin smile ɛ secret wave that have hardly faded over time. "I taut da little guy lived dere akchally!" "In morrisville?" "Yep." He offered to help find a good babysitter "ta look afta dis jumble o' skin 'n' bone heah", shaking my shoulder amicably. Not getting the familial reaction he sought he then leveled his intimidator: "I could aysk ya naybuz ta help look afda da little guy if ya wan' me ta?" While this upgraded the parenting at my house til the day we moved away, my mother found the episode humiliating not instructive and could not rest –or let my father rest– til we "Ezcaap from zis horreebl kleindorf (little burg)".

16

To unload me during winter&spring vacations mother would nag father til he agreed to take me to work w him. A hop to hilton head was good for 2-3 days riddance; but a flite to bermuda was better; and one to the bahamas or cuba better still. But one to jamaica puerto rico or belize was her fondest hope, for it could rid her of me for up to a week or more.

For my part, the latter destinations, tho lovely ɛ somewhat biodiverse, were proof enuf that, save for perhaps pre-matisse days in bali or the society islands (windward side), hart crane had prettymuch summed it up with "...Yield of sweat the jungle presses with hot love ...nacreous frames of tropic death." For, in the same way which the "teeming plenitude" of lifelessness in polar climes affirms for the onlooker how alive sHe is, so the tropics, that fecund incubator, affirms the inevitability of our death (also in teeming plenitude)! All of which is to pointout, father icarus, unlike me, was fecklessly heliotropal. My guess is that, the instinctual *laissez faire* of seaside resorts (read: the effects of lux bombardment on the reproductive organs) had much to do w this. There's more enlitenment [hic] in the adage "make hay [or wild oats] while the sun shines" than meets the third eye.

Save for while he was climbing to, or had just achieved, altitude, father was not a spontaneous person. At such times however a story or song might escape him; usually one of the same half dozen or so songs but sometimes an unheard tale of aerial combat. These often featured one skilled adversary or another out of his wartime past, along w/ the lethal capabilities or limitations of their aircraft. None were "the enemy" by the way. They were "career pilots who just happen to work for different madmen"! When the flite was long and he got sleepy he would slide ajar a cockpit window to "disperse das dioxides". When that no longer worked he would slip on goggles, backthrottle, pop his visibly buffeted head out into the nose draft! Drawing it back after a few secs, curly black hair blown flat, eyebrows shagged wildly as he handskered a runny nose, after throttling back up & a quick instrument check, he might burst into song: "Alleluia, I'm a bum! Alleluia, bum again!"; or maybe oscar brand's version of dvořák's "humoresque": "If you hoff to pass some vater kindly call da pullman porter —he'll place a wessel in the westibule"; or tell me to put on one of his favorite records. Some of these being instrumental (genius of les paul, say) left him to supply every last word of "nola" or "goofus" in amazingly de-germanized renditions in a not unpleasant voice.

Because of their rareness & brevity, these *die goethezeit* moments –when father would sing or recite something gloriously wise & *volkspoetik*– are my best memories of him. Nite-vfr legs specially —for lite experience, both Natural & artificial. I cannot remember not having a fascination w/ lites immersed in darkness. (I guess it was inevitable i would one day find, in "the stumbling dim fog" of being civilized, an internal Lite that could not be stolen short of lobotomy or death.) Wingtip running lites, starboard specially; faithful companion out in the blackness, always right there thru the whole nite (and day). Fall asleep: there. Wakeup: still there. And, too, there was the radiumgreen glow of instrument lites: soothing assurance. (Few knew back then, these eerie green furies were the glow that killed the curies.) Cockpit radio playing softly anderson (leroy) or alfvén (hugo). Ground lites, panoramic, when banking starboard; star lites, hemispheric, when banking larboard. And how proud i would feel when other pilots informally saluted my dad, smiled & said, "Howdy, colonel schock...! Gotcher copilot, eh...! Safe skies, sir!" O i'm sure there were those who called him "the red baron" behind his back. But the best pilots knew him only as a perfect gentleman of skilled historic repute. That the handsome colonel never asked his "copilot" how he was doing, *really* doing, just because he cared to know, of this of course they had no idea.

17

How was mother able to reduce father again&again to a befuddled "I yam what I yam!" response, followed by a predictable door-slam departure? Mother ~~suffered from~~ enjoyed what is generally called multiple personality disorder (mpd). (Her most accurate dx was manic paranoid schizophrenia.) I say 'enjoyed'. For under any name, tho mental stigma is the tradeoff, mpd gifts the challenged individual w a social power sHe could never otherwise enjoy. Further, i maintain, anyone who believes mpd's –mean-spirited mpd's, that is– are worthy of pity, either doesnt understand them or is benefitting from their condition. Barring exceptions, it is only the timid ones, who switchoff life permanently, and those overpunished for said behavior, who are worthy of empathy. How dare i?

Because i know firsthand: Among mean-spirited mpd's, personality switching is typically selectively selfish in its ends if not its means; and further, is most often evolved as an escape from responsibility. (Whether that escape is justified or not is another, and consistently distracting, issue.) Because personality switching (hereinafter: switching) dazzles us who are closeby, it elicits our pity. This happens because we think, "Whomever would behave so crazedly [sic] can only be insane". And so we proceed to justify said behavior. Because we sense mpd's "really believe in what theyre doing" we presume in them a social weakness that is genuine. And because we're too imperious to ever admit we've been thoroly-but-thoroly duped by them, we assume the switcher has "lost his grip on reality". For we dont dare presume sHe, the switcher, may in fact be saner (way cleverer, more attuned to end results) than we!

For, depending on the energy/cleverness of the switcher –when to switch ε why– switching can become astonishingly sophisticated. So it was w mother. Plus the cruelest touch of all. The child of a switcher, being highly susceptible to parental coercion anyway, owns a potential for pity that is personally crippling. In fact, the emotional exhaustion my selfish ε manipulative mother brought about in me by the age of 18 caused me to run, and then to condemn, *myself*—rather than find fault w her. Indeed, decades of reflection ε study have proven me (the pityer) and not her (the pitied) the fool. (Only on her death-bed did she confess these dynamic theatrics of hers.)

While any primitive could expose in a twinkle the instinctual toolbox which empowers an mpd, we civilized –who fear the subconscious ε are thus alien to its intuitive powers— stand largely mesmerized by personality switching. Where in primitive cultures switching is a therapy (often in ritual form) applied positively & routinely (to maintain the health of the group unconscious), civil society, being in strenuous denial of (fearing) the unconscious in all its modes, stands dumbfounded by those of us who dare apply, and who are coy enuf to intuit, the manipulative latent powers in their (the *projective*) and in our (the *receptive*) subconscious minds.

Not unlike all of us (deepdown), mother was an irresponsible child. In her, however, the spoiled child was visible enuf that the grudge she harbored for father & me is today irrefutable. Holding us responsible for stealing her childhood, holidays were particularly difficult for her, specially ones where adults were expected to focus on the happiness of children. Her social-climbing only intensified this. For, tho there were few kids in our mossville neighborhood, what there were rcv'd a sickening landslide of expensive gifts on xmas & b-days. And so, if only in terms of sheer competition (mother v. me, mother v. the neighbors), mother's hostility grew in proportion to the imminency of the given holiday. Thanks to this ritual uglification, to this day i prefer to ignore both xmas & b-days if possible. One xmas in particular lurks behind these ramblings.

Twas the nite before xmas of my 7th year. Tension was high even for xmas. Father couldnt seem to do anything right or enuf, and my pleas for peace, "Just for tonite", earned me mother's early-to-bed ...which, once nestled therein, i wondered why i hadnt thought of it myself. While a pro at blocking reality, any visions of sugarplums, or sleep, which danced in my head were shattered by the intermittent but escalating hysteria in mother's voice downstairs ...which, in spite of myself, gave me to know there was plenty to dread. Then came what was by then father's ritual response: the smashing of any large handy object (below) which, tho precious to mother, was pretentious to him, followed by the predictable doorslam (usually internal, this time not) ...and then the wailing, followed by the weeping, of mother —which, til aged10, i felt it my duty to console.

Next morn, about to test my new sled on the breast of the newfallen snow, i stopped short. For, what to my wondering eyes should appear but a trail of blood which led all the way back to the garage, its doors agape, car gone. This i somewhat expected on waking, having sprang from bed on the doorslam the nite before, flown to my window to see what was the matter.

That bloodtrail explained why father's silhouette, as it crossed the moonlit yard to the garage, was hunched forward as if carrying an invisible sack of toys to a less troubled family. That xmas eve proved source to the first of two scars on father's abdomen, neither of which tanned but turned brite pink in summer, as did the older but far larger lesions on his leg.

18

More than two decades separate juanita ε Lilith. My impulse is to skip those years –the abyss crossed not plumbed– risking only an occasional glance into its depths (rushing, chaotic). But i have promises to keep and a thousand messages to deliver before i'm put to sleep.

After losing juanita to don fatum, my grades plummeted and i flunked my freshman year. I always managed to excel in english however; notsomuch from innate aptitude i think as from admiring the art of my pentimentor, juanita. As interest in the fantasy ε adventure authors of my youth waned (stevenson scott wells howard sturgeon collier bradbury shepherd), i began writing for the school paper and dating every girl i was sure would say yes. Maybe i should explain that.

In dirtycity, like the dregs of any city (code: sediment sumps in sinks of civility), existence was often brutal in the shadow of the neon hub itself. There it was dangerous *not* to be aggressive; there war seemed as natural as peace seemed in the countryside i came from. (*Wahn! Überall wahn!*) Tired of being abused by gangs at school, and gangs on the way to&from everywhere, in 8^{th}grade i began resculpting the lanky body passed down to me by my mother's father. By the time i was emancipated from elementary school brutality into a non-ghetto hs, i was tall as any man. Refusing aggression in all its forms –even as a little person i recall it striking me as repulsive– i decided it was time to look like a superpower even if i wasnt prepared to bully like one. And if people were stupid enuf to believe, "What you see is all you get", that was their problem. At least me ε my sense of fairplay would have a better chance than we had as things stood.

This musclingup attracted certain females who unfortunately were not typically my type: fast redheads free blonds battered bruns. However i used this cloying coterie as an attractor-factor. There is a taoist saying: plain moths flitting around a plain lite cause an inviting flicker. I am ready now to share a quick version of a certain persona parade: At 17 (a fairly good year) i took the mr dirtycity title; at 18, the mr jersey; at 19, the mr eastern usa. Since for obvious reasons most bodybuilders are not tall, i found title-garnering a snap. Tho tall persons must slave for a symmetry which reflects power, being on average almost a head taller than the competition, the grace-of-line aspect of the sport (today devalued) rewarded my efforts. It disturbs me to think that, while i was busy armoring my bones w muscle, a young man named mario savio was bracing for that autumn day in '64 at uc/berkeley u when he became the catalyst of a progressivism which spread like windfire, managing to impede thru the '60s ε '70s the devolution of civilization in n.america.

By then a local antihero, i used my newfound status to personal advantage. Girls rarely said no to my softspoken requests. Steps that took years w juanita i'd skip over in a single nite, sometimes in a single hour. And i abused those who loved me w only a minimum of mercy. Not physical abuse mind you but fickle abuse. How did sammy lerner ε tony martin put it? *Girls cluster to me like moths around a flame, and if their wings burn I know I'm not to blame.* Meanwhile, desire secretly shifted from searching every face for juanita to looking for a variation on my *idée fixe,* some lesser juanita/estelle to briten my existence. After a time, any reasonable likeness would do. How crafty ε amoral our survivalist brains. Which brings up a point.

If allowed, from age3 or 4, i would have begun accumulating certain artifacts of desire –make that *repressed* desire– things closely associated w the girls i longed to touch but could not: a hairribbon here, a hanky there, but mostly –let's face it, folks– panties. As w my love for females, and like any honest heteromale, i cant recall not liking panties. Cotton silk asbestos armored no matter. In healthy society one does not evolve a fascination for furtive frills. In fact, in healthy society, clothing is functional not frilly *or* furtive. But warned away, flogged away, deprivations grow into secret ideations. So that which in healthy society might have been only a passing fancy mutates into a fancy pastime. Begun in hs, i rather doted on my small clandestine collection. By my sophomore year i was too busy to do aught but scrawl a given firstname across a given pair, stash them for some elusive 'later date'. But that date never came. And when i left college, laundrybag slung over shoulder, i, jaunty panty santa, detoured to the admin bldg to pay a visit to the school paper's editor-in-chief —an ingeniously vindictive (reason for my visit) exlover. I spilled my sackful of slippery trophies onto the desk of her male assistant. <Check them out. [all turn to stare] Thirty-forty women 'n' no mold, you see?> I then reached into the heap, presented <Behold!> an inscribed pair of her very own in which i had grown a nicely greened & dried fetacheese mold. <The *only* grunderwear in the bunch, as examination will show.> Tossing them, name up, on his desk i looked at her. <I tried to drop this, you know. But you jus had t' turn it all nasty didnt you?> said i w sober regret ...and departed the stunned silence which had overtaken the entire floor. (More on ms vindictive later, time permitting.)

For my right to respond aside, i still had not forgiven mother for her pernicious selfishness. Remember, one does not ablute in a day prejudices which society spent years inuring; an attitude of female-loathing which a patriarchal lishment had literally flogged into one. Still, in the very next breath, i can i say: I cant remember not worshiping females. Or should i have said, *fetishing* females? For the form of adulation we're taught is not respectful. Truth be told, few of us raised in female-demeaning paradigms respect females, specially males who have not come to loving terms w their mothers ...or, i should say, *all* their *mothers*. For the definition of mother, if we are to be healed and made whole, must be expanded to embrace our Earthmother. But it would take the horrors of war, and emotional collapse, followed by a period of shadows & grieving, before i longed to stop acting like my brothers, the civil man; stop degrading, stop abusing, females ...learn to love, not just lust after, regard fondly not just fetishistically, females; to grow beyond viewing them as things to be possessed & collected. See how repentant i am? and how repentant i've been? and for so long too? Honest personal growth also comprises "the stuff of my sources".

Among the luvs of my hs years sandra brandywine standsout. A much-lettered gymnast, amateur jazzdancer & promising ballerina, sandy was not your standard drumstick-thighed cheerleader. Delicate yet strong, she wowed us in lites & tites on student nite dancing anderson's *the waltzing cat* ...while i awaited in the wings my turn to wail & grind. (I went thru a phase –brief, thank orpheus– where i thought i was john raitt w a groove but as my screaming fans knew, was merely a johnny ray wout one. (Wayward son of rhythm&blues, ray's vocal technique i feel was daddy to the rock&roll wail.)) Sandy was, for me, the grownup embodiment of priscilla and i could not rest for wanting her. It took intolerable weeks, for by then (senior year) my persona, inflating in pace w my physique, had huffed & puffed its way from a mere trembling soapbubble to a looming zeppelin! No sooner were we ritually betrothed (engraved bracelet traded for classring), hardly had i basked in that first bouquet of brandy, that first whiff of wine (so to say), when i rcv'd a jonletter, my third in a way of speaking. A perceptive man who distrusted me from go, the shadow of her dad paced behind its every sentence. I decided to drown my sorrows in new silks new scents. After all, hadnt i twice before known the hurt of hurts?

Beside sandy, other names, in no particular ardor [sic], come smiling up to me in memory's crowded corridor: cindy patricia joAnn hope shirley sandy (sandysoprano not sandydancer) lorelei carol carolsue sherry kathy marie and, of course, arienne. After sandy dumped me i steered clear of girls w 'toomuch' selfrespect. This did not always work. I was a senior and performing in loomis's farce *pure as the driven snow* when i first saw arienne. I had been picked to play the lech mortimer frothingham. This was no accident since i was dating & dumping two-three girls a week at the time and showing no signs of slowing —a fact our drama coach, the brilliant fx warren, would taunt me w regularly, even during class! (Tho i'm sure i've lost most of my female readers by now, my lawyer's argument should be borne in mind: It is my *entire* past which made me who i am today.) Savage in green satin, long burnt-auburn hair to her waist, as raven as red, arienne played sinding's *rustles of spring* on opening nite. I sidled over to a break in the curtains to see just who was playing....? Darling inclined profile, wrists nice & high! And no sheetmusic! Funny how some things stick. When i think back on that time, for some reason, instead of my own, the face of peter sellars peers out of those curtains. Not *pink panther* pete but *henry orient* pete. And as we ease away from the ruffles & rankles of my early reconnaughtyrie, i spot an affinity between henry, mortimer & the youthful me. But then again, leches young or old are rather alike anyway.

To closeout this seedy if passing phase, i won two prizes in english in junior year; one for an essay on the plight of females in third-world countries (who makes a face gets to take my place on deathrow for a week); the other for five poems, the best of which, you guessed it, were also about females. The best of the best was titled, *la tartán gitanita.* Maybe some scholar some day will dig it up. On graduation, as if in deference to my gruesome grades (if one discounted language & the arts), i was awarded a scholarship of sorts: two year's tuition to bigapple u, in whose lit journal several of my poems had already appeared thanks to the head of our english department, the tall stoop-shouldered understanding & kind mr bandino, who was want, in his humble instructorese, to call bigapple u his alma mater. Hi, mr b, wherever you are! You & mr warren alone made secondary learning bearable to many beside me i'm sure.

19

Not all that long ago i came into possession of some family memorabilia. Part of browsing its foto albums was being surprised by certain of my bodily transformations over the years, of being reminded of how the ascent to adulthood, for me, followed a dramatic sched of somatic oversions (overts) as if innards, like brain, were claustrophobic. Unable to endure captivity they seemed ever trying to burst their bodily bonds. The earliest of these involved my 5th extremity, so to say, and its secret satchel. (This blessed curse we covered, or tried to, tsk, during the juanita juncture.) Growth almost done at age16, my nose —which has been variously described as "strong", "masculine" & "virile", and which along w my chin i would say has saved my face from mere prettyness— was next to burst its bonds. In hs it began to take on somewhat of a hump at the bridge, a protrusion which many females find fetching. (Speaking of humps & bridges... well, nevermind. My frankness has done quite enuf harm already, eh francine?)

Another protuberance my body was to surprise me w began also to emerge at about that time. Decades of person-to-person touch w the public have left certain general situations indelible. Eg: When females look up at me as i speak, their eyes first move back&forth between my eyes & lips. But soon thereafter the motions of my (very prominent & very active) adam's apple —lump of cartilaginous flesh moving like the head of a pitviper beneath the supple foreskin of my neck— draws their attention. In her autobio, debra danzi's mother (alluding not all that subtly to myself) described this phenomenon as resembling "the masculinity of a ballet dancer bulging in his mauve tites so that, when lit from above or below, it verged on artless obscenity". Many have been the times when signing a picture, book, video etc, i had to break the spell of some ogling coed (or her friend) whose eyes had locked (like ripe lips on a new lollipop) on what *daughter* danzi described as "that big sexy lump in your throat" and refused to let go. In fact, i soon discovered a potent correspondence between a woman's interest in that organ of mine and their (sexual) interest in me. In the short equation: The more fixated a person is by my apple organ {Follow the bouncing ball, my dear} the shorter the distance between us and the nearest private place. But i will stop here as promised, francine.

20

I cleanedup my act for college, matriculated & trained like a spartan, dating only when duty was done. In oct i took the mr usa trophy and the following jan the rather heady intn'l title of sir cosmos —that was in london, where an agent of gmg studios offered a screentest. In early feb i was flown to hollywood. The screentest went well but only because my fast & furious lifestyle in the month following the contest had burned off substantial musclemass, left me more cam[era]-friendly as they say. A few days later i attended a screening of, well, me. In straight-on head shots i was reminded not of my body-building hero, lex reever, but of a cross between richard egan (mr smile: another boyhood father-substitute) & simon templar. The ceo's being pleased, i signed a five-year contract and dutifully returned to school to finishout the mester.

Dedication to my schooling was "rewarded" w two simultaneous aboutfaces. For the first time in memory, shamelessly hollywood-hankering mother tried to dote on me; then bigapple u followed this by nominating me for "favorite son" status. Mother was ever foning me now and the school paper –not the good one but the official one– solicited "Oh, anything" i wanted to write for every issue. More&more rollingover for the belly-scratching my new "moviestar" status earned me, it wasnt long til i was expecting a better grade than i deserved.

Meanwhile for the entertainment/enlitenment of fellow jocks i gave away junk verse at the gym: □Jack jimmied his jong into jill's jellied jamb... □He bragged he nogged his niece, she bragged she sprained her uncle... □Takeoff on a sickly saint: Why did the Architect who made women put the oval office right next to the offal orifice? □The symmetrical wrinkle 'round the mound where you tinkle / it's asterisk wink pouting over the chink... □From succored bliss to puckered blister, by his ears miss [blank] steered the kiss of her mister... □Kwiz: The top has a canthus, the bottom does not: there's a fat and pink mantis that prays at the spot... □The wick with a whistle (not the one with a wink), nor the elliptic epistle. But the puckered, the pink... □and other such doggerel as masturbated one's fancy.

Fame is a drug to the insecure. For me it was not just a high but an *elisir d'amore*. The attention (newspapers mags tv women gay movie moguls ɛ all sort of beefcake entrepreneurs) soon overwhelmed me. After all, i had yet to resolve my childhood insecurity ...which by then i was burying fast ɛ foolish. And i hadnt even been in one movie yet!

Enter dissolute period, a bore for its sheer predictability. Whereas in hs i displayed a mixture of emotional innocence ɛ social ignorance, by the time of college this excuse begins to wear thin. (The reader may recall, i was a bit older than my peers and might have known better.) I was happy to let myself be dragged by one date or another to parties, sit-ins ɛ luv-ins. At some of these cocaine was the drug of 'sophisticated' choice. Hedonism ruled from high to hangover back to high again, between all of which i straighted [sic] only long enuf to take *this* test, knockout *that* paper, or polish my weekly submission to *the campus campanile*—which forum i used mostly for hustling my next 'unattainable' conquest. Tho more active in college than hs, the names of only five women can be discerned win that pleasure-besotted timeframe: terry violet angela(mia) ɛ the slonim twins, rébha ɛ rebáh —whom i called rehab ɛ rhubarb for reasons mostly forgotten. (*Two* sarah silvermans? O gaawd-o'-mazzo, spare me!) To show my social blindness at that juncture: I had no clue that to these kosher sorority brats i was hardly [hic] more than a gentile dilldo [hic again]. R&r kept me (ɛ i think a couple others) duped w their nonstop dionysian hijinx. Female cheer should go up here. But my brain had givenup to stress by then, for at some point (very dim, this) i found myself reading the schoolpaper (the good one) and finding, in an editorial entitled "the dylan thomas of bigapple u", that i'd been fired from the staff of the preppy paper by its (scorned) editor (already noted). By then partying fultime, my quiz grades took a dive (since my sotm –squeeze of the moment– did all my assignments) while my instructors, overkind gentlemen ɛ ladies, graded me on potential not performance. From there it wasnt long til, clipped to my tests, i began finding notes like, "This will be the last time I can do this, Mr Schock. The future is up to you now." While that was debatable, i accepted it.

21

In the '60s a hope for great change arose among we teens & 20somethings. This revolution happened not just among youth in america but around the globe, from baffin bay to albatross plateau, from europe to the near-orient. Theories have been proffered as to why. Those popular in universities (in the u.s at least) are often more vain than perceptive and none that i've run across accounts for the phenomenon on the World-scale it deserves.

In the latter 1950s core coalitions of alert students began a movement of social dissent which came to be known as "beat" culture. The movement is often said to have been spread in '56 by alan ginsberg's *howl and other poems*, daringly published by sanfrancisco laureate poet, lawrence ferlingetti. Yet such an interpretation dilutes the role played [hic] by the new music of the day, rock&roll. Succinctly: It was youth "counterculture" *as a whole*, cued by perceptive academics, which put the lie to an lishment panacea that had been painted ever more prettily thru the '30s '40s & '50s. This countercul-ture publicly indicted a lishment which –to bring a prior allegory to fruition– was responsible for gagging that trio of monkey's which had graced for decades the mantles of every home w a for-show fireplace. Put simplistically. Beat culture subpoenaed those silent simian witnesses of middle & upperclass hypocrisy into the public square; and once corralled therein, made them reveal what their years as mum mantlepieces had taught them; forced them to confess the many social crimes they'd witnessed, crimes hid or prettified by half a century of lishment propaganda. In a word, while the beat movement was a wakeup call to the politically hoodwinked masses, it was the youth counterculture as a whole which, literally, brought that wakeup home to western civilization!

Whadaya say we go public
with all this 'evil' business?

See no evil Hear no evil Speak no evil

By the time i'd turned 18 this movement had become the beat *generation.* The term "beat" proved prescient. Tho drawn from the rhythm, or 'beat', of the new music, it was also a movement which had all the signs of being 'beat' before it began. Why? Because the beat generation, to which i was a near-midway arrival, tho surely well-intentioned, was comprised mostly of easily discouraged (easily 'beaten') youth: spawn of dr spock child-rearing say many. I disagree. I see my generation more as spawn of a generations-evolving dandyish middle- ε upperclass trend, a trend of which spock himself was spawn. If anything, in the west at least, it was this trend toward dandyish decadence which caused both the revolutionary successes of the '60s ε '70s *as well as* their failures. The failures i feel came about because punishment, in *all* its forms –incl'g the self-discipline to carry an ideal to victory– was by&large beyond my generation. For, truth is, successful social revolution requires a whole lot more suffering than my peers could endure. Only my darker-skinned coevals had contact w social abuse sufficient to allow them to Stand the blood&guts punishment that followthru revolution requires, a metal which negroes were first to prove.

At any rate, by 1969, beat culture had been effectively factionalized by lishment infiltration; ie, hoaxter hippies whose assignment (fbi ε atf led) was to incite the key personalities of a highly passive movement to felonious behavior: acts of violence or even mere talk of such acts. (But, as happened later w police infiltration of the enviro movement, it was the overall failure of such dirtywork which led to a plethora of groundless "conspiracy" charges.) The purpose of such lishment infiltration is of course to eradicate dissent —finding (or inventing) reasons to put the leaders of said dissent behind bars. And failing that, even outright assassination of major leaders is arranged. Woe, martin ε malcolm! (Congressional investigation of fed. cointelpro has longsince documented this.) In a movement whose overarching principles were love ε peace (openness ε trust), both movement leaders and followers were ε are of course sitting ducks.

As to the real drug "problem". Concurrent w the split in our ranks which police infiltration successfully brought about —that is, whether the movement should answer lishment violence w violence or stick w passive activism— a split in drugs-of-choice arrived on the scene. Whether in academia, the work force or the military (i habituated all three), the youth of my day split drugs into aggressive ε passive categories, a dichotomy still in place. While the aggressive dissenters among us (far&away the minority) were able to make a home in the ever-increasing chaos of the cities, the passive majority found "where it's happenin, man" (urbania) ever more difficult –say nothing of unsafe– to live in. It was at this time the movement, choosing the flowerchild ideal over the howling hippy ideal, succumbed to all the beatings, fines ε jail-time leveled against it. And so it came to pass that my peace-at-any-price peers began to 'beat' a mass exodus to the countrysides of the world. In his play of the same name, the baron crisply encapsulated a citation from my first book, *the castration of priapus:* "When too many in an army are on crutches (codeword: drug-dependent), that army is easily crushed."

This socalled return to Nature (read: return to an agrarian ethic) of the latter '60s precipitated a worldwide commune culture. This culture reached apex during the '70s. It was this tim leary-brand of dropout ¿activism? which made cleanup of all the political filth then in existence exponentially more difficult for those of us still on task in the '80s ε '90s. (Should i, perhaps, confess at last, *impossible to cleanup*–barring violent overthrow– ...specially given how brutally my lifelong *non-violent* ethic has treated me&mine?) Anyway, this dropout mentality ("We'll show you what a carefree vanishing act we beatniks can live with!") was very different from my own brand of copout, as we shall see. And if i, bytheway, seem hard on my *beaten* generation it is because i now know w all my being:

> When freedom is endangered we lose our birthright to an existence of political isolation and personal pleasure-gratification. For such an ideal Natural existence must be constantly earned when societies are trapped within the *anti*Nature (civic) strictures of civilization. Under these conditions, civic vigilance and dedication are *required* from *all* members of society at *all* times, else, sad to report, the repression and suffering of we the masses is guaranteed.[from NS's essay "Dissent for Freedom", written during the "deadly" Reagan administration. —Ed.]

It goes wout saying, some really fine people refused to run&hide. Winona ryder got it right in *1969* when she told scott she was going "to stay...'n' fight". While i was there as witness (hs college hollywd ε nam), and while i participated on occasion, i'm not about to credit me ε my peers alone w the mounting of this mystical milestone of the 20th century known as the revolutionary '60s, not about to setup a prism of history to iridesce what "special" youths we were ...a self-congratulatory pitfall many of my colleagues are prone to in retellings of those tumultuous times.

For, as i see it, it is rather an element of highstrung hamletian volatility which tweaks the dynamics of the era, the sort of violence-prone unpredictability which often follows protracted eras of instinctually dishonest cultural inbreeding. I say this because, when i look back, what begs attention is how unNaturally civil (if tooth-grindingly strained) the *initial* reaction of our elders was to our trashing of their hypocritical lishment. It was this emotionally dishonest response which, misleadingly –like some sinister form of entrapment– fanned the flames of our reactionary behavior. Stick w me for a moment here. When our see/hear/speak-no-"evil" elders failed at first to respond w the firm reprisals that weighed on their hearts, our reactionaryism snowballed fearlessly toward anarchy. Then, as always happens w repressed emotions, when our elders finally reacted, they did so w *way toomuch* punishment —say nothing of unleashing it on us in a cowardly way: via vicious police actions & vengeful courts instead of by their own hand. It was this volatile dynamic (a positive feedback loop where unNatural civility mutates into unhealthy violence) which served to stamp beat culture w its delphic depth, served to airbrush the entire "peace&love era" w a generalized dismay over the lishment's sophoclean overkill of its own blood!

A sense of the fragility of all life is the greatest gift a parent can give its child & the World.

For truth is, we simply did what youths do: react against the habits rules & expectations of the statusquoers to the degree permitted. Nature wisely programs youth to do this. Thus our instincts swaggered into the fray as naked & naive as ever; and thus we found ourselves on a battlefield as old as teendom itself. This was only normal. The abnormality enters (w a vengeance) because we were up against a status quo so convoluted by civil expectation it feared to react honestly, forthrightly and w instinctive timeliness. The result of all this highly civilized antiNatural dishonesty? As time goes on it more&more perspects as a molochian bloodspot on american history if not world history.

On the flipside, i'm not saying we, the well-off of my generation, didnt have the tiger of truth by the tail for a moment there. We did. All i'm saying is that, most of my peers didnt have the history of suffering w which to rally the "lower" classes (those most hurt by what we were battling against) nor the pain-tolerance of those same classes for hanging on to that tiger once the blood started flowing (as malcolmX so fervently enunciated). Most in fact not only went on to forsake the cause, we went on to become the enemy!

Eg: those who gave me the most grief during college for not being more involved, went on to become the very people whose lifestyles & beliefs have caused me, and those activists i love & respect, the most pain & sacrifice, and who will apparently continue to do so til i draw my last breath. Such is the power of human denial. Denial = mc^2, and maybe a bunch beside.

For now, quickly said, robin morgan was Lilith's philosopher of choice. "Today when I encounter people...of my generation who managed somehow to sit out those years unaffected", writes this passionate ruminist, and "when I encounter those who were in the streets and on the barricades against war, racism and poverty, but now are cozily settled into the establishment, [these people] sometimes ask me...'How come you're still trying to save the world?'" Morgan's reply ("How come you're not?") i feel is fartoo gentle. My answer runs always along this line. <Because things are bad enuf today to make the problems of the sixties 'n' seventies look like a teething toy to those of us who've dared take a hefty bite out of here'n'now Reality! Back then we were 'only' fiting for the survival of *some*. Today we are facing the non-survival of ALL. So my problem is –since you asked– i cant even begin to get my mind around the horde of horrors which must infect any conscience refusing to join us in this obviously crucial battle.>

And all this is to hardly have scratched the surface below which all those brave amerinds & afroamericans who'd long greased the road to dissent in america with their very blood, even as i fail to mention such truths as: all the marching against america's role in vietnam was initiated by maoist & communist sympathizers as early as 1964! For the ironic (if unpopular) fact is, nothing causes the hated to examine themselves as swiftly as those who hate them, since it is the haters afterall —and not we the 'merely' passionately discontent (as the baron was always happy to remind me)— who seek change most aggressively. And who's right or wrong has little to do w it.

Yet none of this is to ignore giving a nod to the spore of sexual repression begging to be burst by the 1960s. When we attain sexual maturity (the ability to reproduce our species), age besquat, we are supposed to leap from the nest of our own volition, or risk being booted out, in order that we learn to make our own way in the World. Nature (wisely again, i think) could give a care if what it compels us to do, or how it compels us to feel, meshes neatly w the rules & expectations of civil society. That civilization's goals, and the means to them, often clash w Nature's, is, after all, what civilzn is all about. (And doubleditto w lishment-approved religion, of course.) However, when vacating the nest fails to come about soonenuf (as in all technocultures), dissension sets in on the homefront, or on the virtual homefront (school, camp, etc) and does not cease til said offspring are permitted their own sexlives wout interference or proscription. In societies where the passion for sexual pleasure is treated as a character flaw (dirty shameful etc), youths *appear* to react against everything *but* sexual repression. In my era it was gender- ɛ racial inequality and the war in vietnam which took the brunt of our justifiably outraged instincts.

If there was any quality about the youth of my era that could be called special it was a sense of personal safety that was irrational. (Another foible of being kept too safe too long in the nest.) More to the point, my peers' (instinctive) belief that they were precious beyond fault was, in a civil setting, insane. This belief was reinforced by my peers rarely having been oppressed, and usually only for sexually or criminally inclined behavior —not even an oppression so genial as dad sitting on junior's chest til junior (now 19 and just denied something he wants) brings his fit under control. And so my peers had no sense that they could come to *bodily* harm ...save for being sent off to war, an outcome most lived in dread fear of. (Many not only graduated but went on to postgrad work just to get the 2S deferment they knew would stave off recruitment into the ranks of sgt asshole ɛ all the violence ɛ hegemony he is heeled to hold dear.) For instance, the males i knew in college could scream at and insult each other and their mothers. But let them get punched in the face for it, while a few went mad w unfocused fury, most, like rabbits under fang ɛ claw, simply slipped into a ductile state of shock. It was out of an era of such dandyism that the shriek/press-charges&sue syndrome was born. It doesnt take a genius to figureout: Absolute fearlessness of bodily harm or suffering is neither healthy nor safe. Truth be told, in the real World, siegfrieds ɛ lancelot's are dead young. I maintain: A sense of the fragility of *all* life is the biggest gift a parent can give to his child and the World. For w it comes personal humility ɛ respect for the rights of others, be that other a plant, animal or human. To fail to give this gift is to propagate blind arrogance, which quality is the soul of both civilization ɛ civil religion, even as blind wisdom (fear of some Grand [unseen unseeable] Justice) is the soul of deep Wildness.

> Parent: You have usedup your last warning. I am going to swat your hands the way I promised I would the next time you took something that is not yours. When I do this I dont want you to think I dont care what you think of me. I would like nothing better than to always be deeply loved by you. But it is more important that I care about the quality of person you growup to be. And that starts right here at home. For a good parent's first concern is not to win a popularity contest but to see to it his child growsup with values that will help build a healthy and safe world for her/him as well as for all. I am ready to risk you hating me today if tomorrow I can see you walk out into the world with a conscience that works for the wellbeing of all. (End parental lecture.)
>
> O that all of us were raised in such a healthy environment. But parents in competition to be popular with their offspring fear to love so much. For deep love often demands deep personal risk, which is why it is so rare.

Tho a generally peaceful bunch, denied what we felt was rightfully ours (like sovereignty over our own bodies), my peers could be bratty (arrogant) beyond belief. As to our overindulgent elders & institutions? In their state of slaphappy hypocrisy, tho it took awhile, they were soon dismayed by the highly contagious anarchy which their emotionally dishonest permissiveness had encouraged. Our elders' worst fear was that sooner or later they'd be forced to spank their offspring, now full-grown adults. Knowing this wasnt realistic, procrastination-of-the-inevitable became the next stage of civil sickness. "We refuse to change but we also refuse to spank those who would force us to change. So we will stick with coercion and bribery. It worked when they were little and it will work now." And so the '60s wore on. And the youth movement gained momentum. And like a downhilling snowball, it gained in mass & force. And the more it grew the more the simple (repressed) urge to "swat the little shit" transmogrified into wildeyed & frothing elder-vengeance.

Anyone who attended those early sit-ins knows, our *root* impulsion wasnt brandished on banners or placards or broadcast in what was yelled or chanted. Even so, our real bone of contention was so prominent in the pants of our protests that, by the '70s, most were called what they'd been all along: love-ins. And i attended my share. After all, bau faced on washington square. It, along w the commons of boston, was the very cradle of social protest in ne usa. Of the dozen or so i attended, the type of freedom we sought was evident if not graphic. The stars of these rallies were not the ones carrying the best placards, or having the best antiwar arguments. While such was allwell&good, the stars turnedout to be ❶ the most constructively unorthodox ❷ the most sexually abandoned, or ❸ the youngest unbashful anarchists among us. Or, in a sweeping victory ❹ all the above. While a 14-15yearold couple copulating on a blanket could steal the show, two or more same-sex persons doing the same thing, even fully clothed, would bring on the huzzas. Remembering well the mood of those rallies, i harbor no doubt that a distinguished couple in its 80s, caught hot&heavy necking, would have been equally applauded. For it was not just sex but sex *taboos* we really sought to set free; but mostly those taboos which had to do w us. The only variation that could have topped all the above was if the octogenarians & creative [hic] teens switched partners! *That* we would have held in awe for weeks. For, the feeling among my peers was, sex among consenting adults should be neither scorned nor proscribed, and certainly never criminalized, and that the legal definition of a sexual adult should be any person capable of suffering from sexual deprivation. It is enlitening & encouraging to find, in all the places around the globe where aggressive youth protest took place in those years, *none* of the underscored was legal among the common denizens.

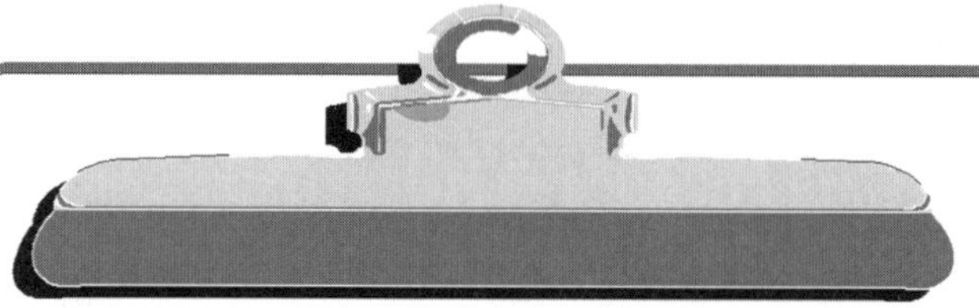

What's with this '60s hypertrophism? As much as i resisted their influence, these years would eventually effect my worldview. While the dregs of war was the cauldron which elemented (separated, quantified) my moral & instinctive sensibilities, it was these interim years --the life experiences which fell between adolescence & war exposure-- which encoded the civil side of my imagination. In other words, altho i, like any good primitive or orang (or flowerchild even), found politics so contemptible i would justassoon never have crossed paths (muchless swords) with it again, these are the times which seeded --and once they flowered, challenged me to undertake-- a life of Planetary activism. So if i belabor these turbulent times it is only to lay bare the deeper influences which i feel drove them, many of which ...speaking of laying bare... were rooted in libido repression. Yes, in things sexual. Eg: Who thinks that "doin the nasty" in public is just some "accident of those goofball times" may consider himself a victim of an expurgated (code: civil) version of history.

Be all this as it may, most of the marching ε protest left me largely uninvolved. I had unresolved emotional insecurities of my own (namely dislike of mother father ε self) which turned my everyday existence into an internalized revolution of its own. And tho i was practiced at appearing mature, my goals were very self-involved. I found it hard to get workedup over any pursuit not involving beautiful women music poetry opium or alcohol. Unlike my peers who fronted their rallies *w* it, neither was the war in vietnam of much concern to me. But then again, neither was i shy of death like my peers. On the contrary, some impulse (malaise at finding only civility everywhere i turned?) dared harm to come my way. How perfectly patent then that said war should, eventually, shake my life to its foundations. All protests i attended were nonviolent. Not surprisingly, it was the cops ε soldiers who sought ε incited violence, being but the repressed instincts of the angry old patriarchs they repped come to life, vindictive life; patriarchs who were in fact the *parents* of the never-spank generation, who now found themselves stuck *w* the living breathing ε numerous products of that hypocrisy and were reallyreally pissed about it. As for us, we did not strike out even to defend ourselves against the shoving cursing kicking ε clubbing authorities. On a personal level, these assaults served as initiation-by-fire for the many confrontations ε arrests i would later tolerate in the name of Planetary caring. And since my parents had never dandy-pampered me, my dedication, once underway, never cowered or flagged. But i would be yet awhile discovering where *w*in me exactly such unflinching caring was hiding, and why.

In societies where access to the necessities of existence & happiness is given to all equally (ie, societies in social equilibrium), the idea of revolution is as incomprehensible as the need for police or jails. Primitive societies are of this order.

In the most notorious of our protests we took over the admin offices of bau for three days&nites. While we claimed to be protesting the school's racial ε gender policies (slipping illegally appropriated documents to the press to prove our point), our *real* bone of contention escaped me at the time: societal sexual repression. While not attacked as viciously as were our fellow protesters up at hoitytoi columbia the following wkend, we did suffer injuries. Thanx to the unprovoked viciousness of nyc police, one of our casualties was crippled for life. And were it not for my unusual muscle-armor, i too would surely have been maimed, since i never collapsed as quickly as desired.

My worst injury was sustained at a splashIn. SplashIns were held routinely on wkends in (as opposed to at) the washington sq fountain. (Yes, the thing used to have water ℰ it founted beside.) Ten or so colleagues *in deshabille* were playing nymph in the fountain's pool when a vanful of cops (apparently stalking us) pulled up. While trying w a couple of my male peers to shield the girls, i rcv'd a ruthless ℰ reckless blow to my right scapula, an injury which bothers me til this day in dampness or cold (as in this prison every day, for instance) and which helped facilitate my early indoctrination to antiestablishmentdisciplinarianism, a long line of corporeal abuses i've endured, at the tailend of which my incumbent execution will deliver the ultimate blow.

> In re our cartingoff & arrest: Even the 'liberal' academe took til 1980 to look at what graham green (the quiet american) knew for a fact back in 1952(!) about u.s terrorism in vietnam —not so bad i suppose compared with conservative academia, which is still in denial.

Summarily. Such routine abuse gave new meaning to 'howl' ℰ 'beat' generation. And, lo! Thirty years hence, a farmore secretive ℰ brutal version of *the very same lishment* is abusing non-violent dissent worse than ever! Surely now we will launch our own candidates into gov't, no? And surely next time around we will get our ethically ℰ ecologically pro$tituted asses out of bed (w the socalled good life) and into the voting booth. And if we get clubbed there too, what is left but force? All of which only goes to prove that, as ever, the masses have only themselves to blame. For, sorry to say, it has taken whole generations of civic irresponsibility to bring about our present subjugation.

These plaints fairly circumscripted i am left now to wonder. Was it perhaps those official clubbings —combined w mother's several feral outbursts w heavy washstick anyoldwhere on my overlean young body— which predisposed me to abhor earlyon the clubbing to death of fur seals? —along w giving me these aching vertebrae? And finally. The fact that, by the time of college the satyr in me had been reduced to cavorting w nouveau nymphs of manmade fountains roughly augurs where my life was headed ...if i didnt, like my peers, hie me away to the hinterlands posthaste. The fact that i didnt, set me tumbling headlong toward hinterlands i never dreamed existed.

22

While we young dissenters did not own the legacy of bloodshed-repression successful revolution demands, enuf of my peers did have the acumen to aim public focus at those who did have such a legacy. Afterall, adolescence is a period of life when, by wise design, young og ɛ mog question their elders' choice of continuing to live in a cave where the cracks grow wider every year, a highly instinctive period of life designed, over millions of years of trial&error, to question the lishment surrounding it. It is a period when we humans, civil or precivil, are most instinctively driven —ie, the period of life when we are most Natural, most Wild. Where adolescence, under the best circumstances, is an iconoclastic (and therefor difficult) period, in cultures where the age of sexual consent is raised to apodictically unNatural heights, adolescence, for many of us, can comeoff as nothing short of inhumane.

When i was growingup, people of color generally, ɛ many women not of color, owned a bloodshed legacy sufficient to sustain them in the civil rights trenches til victory, or an acceptable compromise to victory, was won. And not unlike other youths around the world where sexual parity is inhumanely delayed or *never achieved,* me ɛ my peers also had a bloodshed legacy: a lifetime of sexual repression.

We who value the wisdom Nature has encoded into Wildness ɛ instinct know how rapidly captivity can ruin a Wild creature for freedom. Many is the animal which, having spent months or years in captivity —perhaps haunting the perimeter of its cage or gazing ever outward as if longing for freedom— on finally getting this freedom is afraid to seize it. For captivity has taught it to fear freedom. This unWilding, or domestication, is not unique in Wild animals. Human animals suffer from freedom anxiety as well. It is common and has many names: shelter- prisoner- cloistral- lifer- or, simply, institution(alized) syndrome. The family unit, whatever its composition, qualifies as the orig social institution. The youth w a difficult homelife, who has to deal w toomuch pain or responsibilty or both, will have developed little freedom anxiety when he reaches legal age. If things are specially bad she may even escape from home *before* she comes of age (as happened w the heroine of our story as we will see). My college peers however repeatedly exhibited the obverse of this coin. While intellectually above-average, intellect does not equal social/emotional maturity. As well-schooled as were some of my peers, not one that i knew had even a toe in the door of the school of hardknocks. Typically coming from cushy home situations, their freedom anxiety was very high. (And o how they could fume or sulk if i should hint at how obvious their pampered bratdom was to me.) If it were not so, could parental economic coercion have forced *their most impassioned desires* underground from birth to college graduation? and, in many cases, for life?

It was a time when lishment authority was aggressively bashing the sexual freedoms which young people in much of the industrialized west were claiming as a birthright. Thus was i conscripted by my fellows to strip bare in a poem the state of sexual suffrage created by lishment antipathy toward youth & sex. In plumbing for that (beat) poem, and failing, i hit upon what struck me as a viable truth. <If a person is old enuf to suffer the pain of sexual deprivation then he or she is old enuf to own the right to assuage that pain.> Accepted at once by my schoolmates as a movement principle, by the time it hit the w.coast a few months later it had been bannered as "an oracle of eros". [Actually it took only 40 days for it to appear in Ferlinghetti's "Citylighter" (San Francisco) by "author unknown".] Over time several leading voices of the '60s & '70s claimed the principle as their own ...til dedicated paperchasers traced it back to our underground school paper & thus to me. As for its author, i remained happily unaware of all the plagiarism til approached around '81 by a passionate researcher. (Hi, rhea.)

Why is revolution incipient in civil society? Because much that is necessary & Natural is denied us. Tho we know intuitively that many of the deprivations we endure are inhumane & in need of change, yet intuiting that such change would require vast change (revolution), we shy away from it. And so, for the sake of keeping the peace, we civil learn to live in a state of procrastination/-denial, moment-to-moment putting out of mind all that we sense should be Naturally ours to have or enjoy. For obvious reasons, some of us (the haves) are better able to live under such privation than others of us (the have-nots). And so, it is obviously no accident that revolution usually begins among the have-nots.

Having been scrupulously scared & scoured out of our sexual-freedom demands by the time of hs graduation ("You wanna practice freelove? Fine. Get a job 'n' rent some hole in the wall, 'cause youre not doin it under *this* roof!"), our civil coopting (unWilding, domestication) has long been underway by the time we reach college, a civil hypocrisy which runs so deep it even encourages one to think he's still young enuf to deny that he's really old enuf to care. But by college having learned not to endanger one's civil entitlements back home in the nest, those of us still not quite ruined for freedom tote our residual iconoclasm into the *in loco parentis* nest, be it college, peacetime military, seminary, convent or other institution designed to extend childlike dependency (and the period of our gullibility to propaganda). But by then (to cut to the chase) we have been so long compromised –having adopted secrecy & denial as a way of intimate life– we are blind to what in fact we are actually doing: clinging to the (civil) freedom to remain a child (food, shelter, etc) while secretly stealing the (precivil) right to behave as an adult (emotionally, sexually). And then, after achieving legal age, compounding this blindness, we promptly proceed to spend the rest of our days thinking of civilization as a constructive paradigm that has only our best interests, & our children's best interests, in mind. (Excuse me: Aaaargh!) And to cut to the capture: The average civil denizen, on attaining socalled legal parity, is a pathetic tangle of denial, compromise & categorical sellout to his own deepest Nature —which is of course the whole (civil) idea.

23

As we close out those academic years, a stiflingly hot day comes to mind. (Glumm just came on shift. Havent these guys got anything better to do than hang around my cell?) Da capo. Hot day. When i woke i lay naked & alone in a rm i did not at once recognize. Surreally, to the right of my feet, a poster of me (near-naked & being trophied in london) filled an entire closet door! Scrambling (not to kill the fat roach which scurried off rehab's bed w a plop) but to find a calendar, i found myself before a mirror. (The twins were likely in class.) My God, it's almost may! and my body looks like it's been taken over by woody allen ...whose life (as long as i've mentioned him) joyfully mocks civilzn's polarizing & dimorphic notions of gender. But, back then, a long way from seeing this, i dressed, went straight to the gym and, in a way of speaking, did not come out again til semester's end.

In early june i packedup and, after dumping that sack of undies on my editor's desk, and after a banal visit home (reaffirming the void of mother-love thereat), gmg flew me to l.a, set me up in an apt. A few weeks later, in drama class –midst elocution & character-internalization– i rcv'd word, father was dead. Freak accident: windshear, tailspin. It happened while hanging w a hetaera from hatteras whose liquor & laffs highlife was snuffedout w his. After flying to&fro for the funeral, never spotting the replication, i went into my own downward spiral. Mother, busy as ever w her own whorlygig descent (vodka vortex/gin spin), was unsympathetic to my new fatherlessness. It seems, just weeks before he died he pulledoff a swiftian swap so to say, going from ester to hester (the name of that handsome hetaera) and loving it. As a matter of fact, i'm not exactly sure why his death affected me so. After all, that he was my father was more technical than practical. A passionate researcher might find in my effects one day a certain document: a creative writing assignment in which i recorded every word the man ever said to me, or close to it. Nothing amazing about that except it was only about 20pp long ...doublespaced.

Never to be outdone in its ability to surprise, in aug of '68 the fed. –already in deep shit in se asia– sent me an iicr: invitation i couldnt refuse; aka, infantry-instead-of-college recruit! How quickly (a mere two months, reader!) they responded to my schoollessness. Foolishly i told the studio of uncle samuel's plans for me. Due to some contractual clause, my classes were suspended and my first movie, *hercules in hoboken* (role later revived by an amoral fascist), was put on hold and (the kicker) i was placed on a small retainer for two years or "until such time as you return to civilian life" ...or die trying, they should have added. Knowing few people in l.a and being smallfry in hollywd, i decided to return to greenwich village for the interim.

Funds in sudden but not sobering decline, and only 3mos from bootcamp, i saw further schooling as a waste of time. (Life itself was seeming more&more a waste of time.) Taking what i saw as the easiest alternative, i soon discovered something missed while working schooling ε partying thereabouts. Poe crane cummings whitman james o'neil ε their ilk had vanished wout a trace. The village had become home to those who only *partied* like poets —a bevy of bearded burly fetid ε boring *bon-vivants*. The passing of just a couple generations had lumped me in w dozens of these smirchy scrimy ε out-of-shape-in-every-somatic&mental-sense "artists"; wilting flowerchildren of the '60s ε '70s, encouraged to call their better thoughts poetry simply because they had figuredout how to stack them vertically on paper. It is these tasteless wreckingballs who took the original "deconstructionism" of the microsciences to depths from which, save for a few unjustly marginalized talents, it has yet to reemerge. Applying my own vertical stack of doggerel, i skirted this sewer-bound torrent w a vengeance.

...i refuse to trudge down
this dissipated "beat lit" path
one more impoverished foot, fraught
with rubin snipers & manson mines.
The next time they beat me i wont be
high on anything except good taste.

My disdain was not unlike kenny's wrath for the beats, just not put nearly as well. Like much of human creativity since circa1950, poetry suffers from a fractured vision. Incomplete (fragmented) theory in the chemistries & nuclear physics has inflicted on us the equiv of a cranial concussion, an injury which has left civilzn w a head-in-the-sand blindness from which Earth, and we, may likely never recover. Even as i vacillated daily between substance highs & downer boredom, i often wondered if maybe there was some huge existential joke circulating all around me whose punchline i was continually missing. Even today i feel i was dropped into an era all wrong for who i deeply am. In fact, i cannot ever remember *not* feeling like the altdorfer among the correggios & bosches of my time.

When boredom is your worst predator, when it stalks thru your life so often it makes death look interesting, you can consider yourself successfully civilized.

At any rate, w some of my partypals by that time wondering if i'd simply flopped in hollywd, i began to feel more&more like the college dropout/doomed gi i was. During occasional lulls in selfabuse i found myself shaved showered & straight, heading up to the bronx. (I may be the only villager who ever felt a need for personal improvement just to visit the bronx.) I was, of course, scouring for any sign or scent of juanita luck might have left behind. But i found only rumors; rumors she & her mother had followed her father "south of the border" to his latest missionary position. In lite of the underground news of the day, i couldnt help but wonder if she was among the university students massacred in mx city before the olympics, kids secretly helicoptered into a mass grave merely for daring to criticize their gov't. On one such visit i managed to hookup w a sweet thing named margarita who insisted she'd known "juana": "Latina, si? Weeth beek beek blue eyce!", fingers of both hands opening wider w each "beek". Yes, that would be her. *Blue spanish eyes.* Juana. My gitanita.

Pretty rita surprised me when she turnedup one morn at my door, gave herself to me before dark. But soon i was wrecking that honest gift too. More than once she appeared, more than once ducked under my arm or pushed past me only to find someone else inside. One nite, late, four men (three blades ε a gun) came to fetch her. I was sure i was a dead man. Why they didnt hurt me i can only ascribe to her pleas and my own pitiful state. For on leaving l.a i'd all but stopped training and lost a good deal of weight. Beside, i clearly recall not rising from bed to defend myself against so honorable a cause. What i've called the pushIn(stinct) was probably peaking at this point in my life, a period when i felt <The honeypokey hokeypokey is what it's all about>. That was around the time i first met ol' shep. [Jean Shepherd —Ed.] He still came by THE VILLAGE LIMELITE occasionally to do a show. A sociable sort, he would go from table to table after his monolog, visit, have a few drinks. I'm sure it was puerto rita that caught his interest and not my own rum-born ramblings. One of the woman rita caught me *w* was aurora. She was skipping classes that day —which i assumed meant bau just a hundred paces away but which in fact was a hs for convent-aspiring novitiates in another borough. For those of us who worked or schooled in the village, the absolute coolest lunch was to "brownbag-it" at the square. I was doing same when i spotted aurora spotting me, a little pocketbook of shakespeare's sonnets on her pretty knees. I must have been reasonably straight at the time because my braincells hold a holographic view of that moment that is neither wobbly nor blurred. Sun/warm; air/crisp.

<You look cold. Wanna join me in a cup o' coffee? I know a nice little place right around the corner.> Tang of pucciniesque bohemia here, specially having the copycat arch for backdrop.

"If ya think we'll fit, shur." Sly dark-eyed grin tests my response time. Reflecting on her reply by overseas mail some months later i wrote: That was a pretty snappy reply for a nun-in-training ... *while* she's being hit-on, no less. "A quick retort is a bad thing to waste, *especially* while being hit-on" she wrote back.

I was such a mess by the time i met aurora all i remember is scraps & tatters. Those days flash past memory like lites beyond a subwaytrain window. One of the few times she appears unfragmentedly she is strap-hanging aboard a seeming-perpetually circuitous el-train at xmastime, swaying below the PREGNANT? & DANDRUFF? ads brown-stippled w some angry human's coffee or cola. We are on our way to "catch" some movie or show. (Miller's *the crucible*, i believe.) I am hanging from the support from which hung those stainlessteel handles we still called straps, feeling lucky to have grown above all the jostling coughing & stale cologne swaying below me. Aurora, in her "ny state of mind", is looking sidelong at the camera of memory w a pixieish twinkle. "Its freezing in here!" In the unheated car we can see the reflection of our breath in the dark tremor of a windowpane. A min later i alone am hangingon while she, arms around my waist inside my jacket, plaid-skirted school uniform inside her coat, holds tite against me. O look! We marvel momentarily at the aurora of snowflakes sparkling in her dark hair. While beyond the jittery oily windowpanes, amber lites of a thousand flats rise&fall beside the tracks, and every three seconds or so the frozen motion of a bustling snow-lined holidays-lit street flashed below. Then, w a deafening clatter, all gets interrupted by the staccato flashing of windowlites from a train hurtling past at armslength in an opposite direction! {Minds, specially weak ones, should never be forced to get used to such sensory violence.} Tumbled among these mnemonic residuals i find, not \wout satisfaction, aurora's startling comment on another occasion. Recall w me as she, breathless w orgasm, informed me one day on my narrow rented bed: "You are competing with God for one of his betrothed. You know that, right? <Huh...? Mm-must we talk religion right now? Unh unh unh....> ...and youre [gasp] *winning! winning! winning! goddamnit!*" Aurora may be tangential to the tale i realize but what she rep's is not. And what if a couple characters in this bio are digressive? Cant we just chalk it up to my dedication to bio diversity and leave it at that?

In the meantime mother sat on my inheritance —money which father left me out of guilt, i suppose, and because he knew she'd only spend it to move to lalaland and party the rest away. (Despite everything he loved her too much for it to have been vengeance.) Breaking w family tradition, i never took her to court. I simply wrote an open letter, mailed it to her & to all my relatives on *both* sides of the atlantic, effectively excommunicating our whole damn germanic tribe save for aunt ethel schock. This proved good for my mental health ...tho i did capitulate briefly while mother was dying. But that's another story. Of course, between jobs i had the gmg retainer to fall back on, tho most of that (being back then more my father's son than i dreamed) i'd earmarked for alcohol & hightimes.

During college & while awaiting conscription it seemed i was always between jobs: taking ad copy, driving a taxi, proofreading legal documents (egad!), keeping containership manifests (yegods!), storeclerking and, on the side, scribbling quatrains for tuppence –at curbside when sunny, in our garret when rainy– while my talented garretmate (Hi, axel!) sketched portraits. Wkends & holidays we sat one to each side of an easel which read, YOUR PORTRAIT IN TEN MINUTES, which was forever blowing over thanx to those trash&ash-littered whirlwinds which, like urban dustdevils, swooped down those man-carved canyons, struck & vanished. And when a client stopped by, axel's charcoals or pastels would literally sizzle across the paper while i sketched w words those traits i could discern in so brief an encounter. Enter coincidence.

On comparing notes w the baron one day (where we'd lived, what we'd done, that sort of thing), i mentioned my painter friend, axel, and our sidewalk enterprise. He left the rm, came back at once carrying a framed portrait. A quatrain, angled into one corner, was scrawled w a flair so familiar it startled me. "This portrait of his, and this little rhyme of yours [said the baron], encapsulates me with unnerving accuracy." And so they did. A pittance of a pastime, that sidewalk poetastering was however a steady source of better-paying jobs, all of which i lost in record time, often a matter of hours, for uncaring performance or failing to show at all. Forklift jock in a factory, truckdriver, page-proofer, type-paster & greetingcard octotraineer.

Because of stuff published during college i was able to sell the urbane slick, *the big appler*, on a pet project. For fun i would pick a poet and pan him/her. I wrote some two dozen guess-who's before the lark wearied on the wing.

Turn ...the stair. Torpor drops.
Smoke, in wisps, winds the streets.
Eyes, where fog claws the windowpane;
    lassitudes of hair, in afternoon
    —infanta, inamorata! In my room
    the madames, felice and swoon,
    turn to stare ...and are gone.

An angry young man, even tho editor-stifled, my then preference for the ironic brandished its barbs. I also made my tripe complement the mood of the times: a 'cosmic' ennui that sought any old reason to despair. I liked playing w socalled "voices of the great depression".

Poets whose sad ghosts wander idly (dazed)
in places where pigeons (doleful) waddle
among bones, where men in rags, in doorways,
clutch (in greasy paperbags) a whisky bottle.

If such verse echoes the times, they were pathetic times. How dreadful to desire fulfilment (bliss, awe) but find only lassitude & torpor. And then there was the badly-existential crowd to mime.

We are imprisoned in an exhaustion of dust,
derelicts of burntout stars, we;
the black jest of some bent justice,
some mad executioner's suicide....

Give me, any day, the *poète maudit* who quietly removes his coat, folds it upon the rail, leaps into a widewink of brinkless sea, which, clasping him like a dark flower closing, swallows gratefully.

Shadow of silverwhite hair, eyes blue;
who did not permit his verse
to dawdle in despair,
but reinvented hope
out of thinnest air.

How my heart cranes to see over the side of the orizaba (not into the throat of the old volcano but over the side of the old passenger liner), pausing in transit to catch a glimpse of him who could have swam the distance to shore but resurfaced not at all from that wide blue wink of eternity he breathed at last like air!

I know many cringe & wince
when confronted by impinging genius
such as yours, hart, whom i would toast.
Yet what is one to conclude when the only ones
to remember you in verse are the likes of
ginsberg wheelwright lowell rexroth & me?
This befits some strange jest on the part of the gods
of language, or your own comedian Host.

This latter was not a part of my *pastiches & pans,* which chapbook proved, bythebye, sufficient to keep my shiny corner in that slick lit zine alive for most of my military tour. But when, toward the end of that tour, they asked for more, i was unable to deliver. For by that time –not lucky enuf to bag an ambulance-driver gig like ee, ravel & others– i had myself become a 'derelict' of the 'black jest' of war. But that's another story. Lilith's bio has enuf thunder & blood of its own to process.

One job gotten while awaiting bootcamp was server at the mob-run copacabana —briefest i ever held i believe: 2-3hrs. Between a staggering jonathan winter's monolog & a glorious vic damone opener, i took by the lapels a crudely condescending wallstreet wannabe (whose son, i'm sure, became the first yuppie) and shook him supperless. The maître garçon –whose portrait sat for months unfinished because of it– suddenly sans his french accent, said (as he dismissed me) he didnt think i was "cutout for dealing with the public" and that perhaps i should "Come back in the morning and apply for a bouncer position". As to ambulances. A medic class, which in the interests of lust i got locked into back in college, got me one 12hr shift a week w an east-village squad —my first brush w a uniform since cubscouts. The propinquiníquitous [sic] serendipity of one codeblue in particular flags me down as we pass.

Warm summer eve; ambulance parked on apron outside squadhall; me, dutiful rookie, shirtless in fireman's boots & jeans "washing down" the "unit" when, wout prelude, that certain thing happened for a second time in my life. Three well-constructed young ladies of say 14-15 strolled up. "Hey mista, c'n we get a drink from yer hose?" Coy grins all around. Handover hose. Three-on-a-nozzel slurpfest. Forward bent, dangling hair, shortshorts, tan legs. <Youve been thirsting in the desert all day i see.> One, holding back hair w pinkvinyl wallet, naughty-eyed, looks up, swallows, takes big breath and, as commentary to all the noise says, "We jus wanted ta hold it." Burst of doubledover laffter. "Dont mind her. She's a nympho." More laffter. *You* shud tawk! I want ya da know, *she,* dis one right heah [poking pinky into breast til poked one says "Ow!"] handjobbed vinny damadda yestaday!" Dripping chin, grinning, nods No. "O yes ya *did!*" Feigns shock, gives back hose, wiping chin w back of hand. "An yuah sumkana saint I spose? screwin y' mudda's boyfren?" All back away in mock battle. "Ya betta hose dem down befaw dey jump ya bones" says the third. "Yeah. We wanit bad!" "...Weah goin t' da movies, wanna come?" "...Ya dunno whatcher missin."

All laff, turn away swaggering. In unison: "If ya like it come 'n' get it!" Yelling out each other's names ε fone numbers, pushing laffing yelping whooping, they drift into urban twilite. Even after theyve disappeared i can still hear their cries in the muggy neon dusk. 20mins later i find myself a few blocks away assisting a man in his early 30s sitting on a commode in an unkempt apt holding his testicles in place w a bloodsoaked washrag. Claiming to be attacked by his girlfriend "for cheating", by the time we got him stabilized for transport the girlfriend, found nextdoor by the cops, was claiming (at the top of her voice) that she "caught da no good bastud sleepin wit" her daughter. When asked where the daughter was she replied, "At da movies ...wit 'er friends". The timing ε proximity of the two events made me think chance had, for an hour or so, kept me (but why?) at groundzero in the sexlives of three persons among the thousands we served.

The *first* time it happened (as long as we're this far) it had been about a year since juanita and our lost summer id- idy- idyll. There. (Some cliches cause actual pain in my temples.) At a youth meet, after visually tracking marylou rossi the whole eve —and specially after she grabbed me for protection when someone, during games, switchedoff the lites— i was in a terrible state. After walking her home, along w buddy barry higgins –to whom marylou's strict exboxer father always entrusted her for the walk to&from– i was too hungry for any sort of sex encounter to simply go home. Summer nites in the city stifled my spirit. I longed for those cool woodland nites under the stars w juanita. Intuiting that if a casual encounter might happen anywhere it would be in the dregs of the city, dressed in sportcoat ε signature turtleneck, i went "slumming" as it was called by my class in that day.

A fashion challenge to the trad italianate shoes of the day, friend barry ε me had switched to a box-toed shoe whose heels the coolest paladins were fitting w dancing cleats. At 16, ever on the prowl and finding pointy-toed shoes sneaky ε ratlike, we were perfect marks for this new manly antimafioso footwear fad which later became all the rage. I dont think i'd owned my new "box-fronts" a week yet for the su nite i have in mind. So caughtup was i in the hefty crack of my heels ricocheting about those quiet streets, i confess, rather than wearing my shoes i was *following* them. Platinum hair by then mostly blond, eyes ε shoes glinting in the streetlites' smudgy glow, i strode toward the ghetto community which lined both sides of communipaw av.

Crossing ẟ recrossing it in a randomized sort of sidestreet search grid, i combed the tenement rows for any sign of attractive femaleness. The looks i got from the few people i saw made clear just how starkly i stoodout against my surroundings. In addition to attire, i suspect it had something to do w my (falsely) proud bearing: tall, unusually broad-shouldered ẟ slim-hipped (from my intractable training), excruciatingly cleancut ẟ briteeyed. The few young women still out were w family or boyfriends. The fluorescentblue flicker in most windows made it clear where everyone else was.

Now i cant speak for other cities of the time but in dirtycity the predominating italians poles ẟ irish, thrown together, got on fairly well, which made for relatively peaceful city streets, specially w su considered a "family day". For improved circulation in warm wx it was not uncommon for entry doors to be propped open. For shabbier bldgs this meant revealing their vestibules, lower halls ẟ stairways. This was the case w the bldg soon to come into view.

The smell of that nite i can describe only as a mix of tired carbon ẟ copper sweat. And what was probably more than an hr-long walk, memory has distilled into a single ¼hr event. Five or six "tenements" ahead of me some females gathered around a street-level entry. With none more aware than yours truly of the harms inflicted when one makes age alone an arbiter, i know my mx will be lost, my own stunned reaction vitiated, if i dont. Ergo: if more than one of them was over 14 i didnt know my own age at the time: 16. Like impalas before a sated lion, they did not run. The closer i approached the more the group simply quieted, drifted into the shadow of the open doorway. This junglelike responsiveness only heightened my already fever-pitched lust. Getting juanita signals –dark hair, flashing whites of wide glinting eyes, trim bodies ẟ olive skin– i shortened my smartly clicking stride. Straightout from the doorway now and examining them as best i could –huddled as they were in backlit shadow– a husky female voice whispered, "Ya wan summa dis?" I stop, quarterturn. Voice continues: "How's a blowjob sound?" Too speechless to answer "coolly", on reflex i moved closer, clicked a cloven foot onto the low concrete step and, giving my coolest grin said, "Where?" That got what it begged. "Right heah. [said the same boygirlish voice] Wheredaya tink? [tossing a backward glance over a haltered bare shoulder] Whatcha name?" With hands on the shoulders of the pretty female she proffered, this tough but not uncute face shoved toward me, and into the lite of the street, a young lady w short dark hair. "Celie's a vehgin but she wants ta lose it real bad, huh cele?" Celie makes shy smile. Two others dart out, hustle not uncooperative me into the dim vestibule.

As big me (strangers took me for 18-20), back against vestibule wall, looks on in mixed disbelief ɛ anticipation, virile-voiced lena, reaching for me, whispers. "Ang, you kiss 'im while I do 'im. Dina, watch da damn doowa." Angela, hands locked behind my neck in the corniest sort of cinematic seductiveness, tilts head, inviting my kiss. I am putty in their hands... well, most of me was. Strange contrast of dry lips ɛ wet kiss assures me i'm not dreaming. With hissing whisper, giving a final freeing yank, lena sinks to her knees and declares "Look, cele! Is dis humongous aw what!" and immed sets about wielding my *wurst* at a level of skill which most of the older women i've known would do well to master. "Cele ...nina, you too... Git down heah. Yer gonna hafta learn dis. Heah. Take it. No, one hand under heah. Now suck. No, no. Phhh-wait! Let neenie try. Heah. ...Kryst! Yous guys cant be fah real? Phhh. [laffs] Shit, man! She can' even get it in her mout! [garbled response] ...No. Kryss, like dis. Heah, gimme da damn ting."

Meantime angela, the classiest, has ceased kissing me and, standing back, both hands pressed low on her tummy, stands blocking the view from the inner hallway, large dark expressive ɛ kind eyes tracking the action intently. Lena can play madame instructress no longer. "Watch me." While she works her legerdemain, elec glances pass between angela ɛ me til she finally says, "Me next, leen?" "No, me. [pops celie] I gotta do dis. I jus *gotta!*" Meanwhile the dazed victim has past the point of no return. "Shutup, da bunch o' ya. [cough]... Shit, he's ...Damn!" So closely were the others crowding, unable to get out of the way, lena averted the muzzle of the kicking canon —whose ordnance would've slapped the opposite wall had the aversion not put (astonished) celie directly in the line of fire! So erotic was this happenstance there was no sense at all of the usual post-fragging flagging. Lena, sensing this at once (how? Even *i* was surprised), glanced ferally about and, w the alacrity of a prostitute behind sched, slid shorts ɛ panties down a space and backed hard into the fray.

I've since been desired as much yet no one before or since expressed desire so honestly. We civilized just dont do that. I dont believe even rosa poza upstairs tonite, as hungry as imprisonment has doubtless made her (made all of us), will respond w the sheer candor ε voracity which drove the trim tite loins pressed hard into me that nite. Spitting into her hand and manipping [sic] herself, thru a break in the press of bodies lena hisspered, "Wheah's dina? Fuck! What's witchoo guys? Sumbuddy watch da fuckin doowa! Ooo. Come on, come on! Givittame! Shit!"

No sooner had we synced our stride ("Ah, kryst! Ah! Oh! Jeez!") when, w dina gesticulating from the doorway, a peterlorrelike man w a crumpled package turned into the vestibule from the street, stopped short on seeing my face above the group knotted around me. Spontaneously i withdrew. Lena stood erect. Grabbing my aurochshorn w a hot fist she leaned back hard against me and, w a calmness that addled me, announced to me ε to all, "No sweat, girls. It's mista nobody". Squinting at us as he passed, the man said in a phlegmy voice "Figyuz itchoo". To which lena responded "Go take a showah, al. Ya stink!". Al, mounting the stairs, said under his breath "Fuckin little sluts!" So closely clustered was our retinue, and so short was al, even as, glancing over a shoulder, he moved up the stairs, he could only have generalized the circumstances. "Don' worry bout mr pencildick. He's nobody. Wit a capital zero!" she added w zest. By the time he gained an elevation advantage the smudged glare of a naked bulb blotted vision both ways. Unable (and really unwanting) to escape lena's death-grip on me, hardly missing a beat, she backed onto me again, this time w such voraciousness my surprise was quashed by lust and, for a few mins, i felt both audacious ε fierce. No sooner had i grabbed doting angela by the neck, however, and was kissing her, when a door at the far end of the long hallway opened. On seeing a swarthy man in a dark tankshirt peer out into the dusk, i froze. "Chayla!" he called. Resignedly celie answered: "Yeah." "Get in heah. Ya mama wantcha. ["A'right."] *Presto*, girl!" "A'right!" Door closes.

That was it for me. As celie slipped out one side of the orgiastic knot, tuckingup, i slipped out the other. <This is crazy. Gotta go. See ya round, angela." A min later me ε my lucky shoes were cracking down the sidewalk a couple blocks away, my footwear already kicking me for my cowardice. I'd have to say, it was about then i began to question women being the "weaker sex". As to the ghetto. Not entirely unlike the Wild, it constantly struggles to keep some sense of what's Nature-sanctioned, what's not.

24

The lishment, in prison or out, seems never to tire of taunting me. If shrink slugmoid's cruelty has any limits i have yet to locate them. He began our session on fr claiming Lilith is dead, first time he's returned to this gruesome tactic since our big confrontation. When i reject his slimy propaganda, his toxic ℞'s, his corrosive prognoses, he sched's me for "special therapy", ships me back to my cell. Were the penalties for refusing his socalled therapy less severe i would of course refuse. Then there's the camera out in the corridor ε the invert imbeciles he assigns to watch me.

It's impossible to write coherently w all these masks-of-the-mind a-miming. They haunt my cell. Point of note. Whenever the slugmoid is conceiving some new gauntlet for me to run, or when a given gauntlet has achieved some measure of torment, i have these episodes, these twilite surveillance masques, let's call them, where spying apparitions, cheshirecatlike, drift in&out of my sleep. The cause of these episodes of course is that lidless sleepless dark eye which monitors me day&nite. So it is, i suppose, on waking i feel strangely sensitized to the activities of those who monitor that camera; that sly peepshow of the suits who run this fortress w its codpiece longings. Following such "special sessions" (or brainfucks, as theyre known prison-wide), these masques always intensify. Last nite's, for instance, or was it just before i woke...?

While mimi lies a-bed spitting blood in a frigid garret and dying of consumption, the tenor singing rodolfo, between acts, invites the golden-horseshoe crowd to the lounge for cappuccino ε croissants, there to chat about other dramas, other deaths. Meanwhile virginia lee coughsup blood in a bdrm of the little poe home in turtle bay, a chill cottage circled by the frantic bare branches of cherrytrees. And as she lies shivering a-bed ε murmuring to muddie, eddie is in an adjacent rm feverishly penning his oeuvre of despair ε doom. So why cant i too sit by, writing- or singing-away, while dudley macdeath stalks those i love, snatches, torments ε throttles onebyone his lovely innocent victims. Alright. My pen has run riot. *Che penna infame!* I am further stymied (read: cut off adrift helpless) because of my hesitance to confront emil w this sick imbroglio i endure every day. His plate is full w my affairs as it is. So it is, he does not know who *really* runs this place, incl'g what ledup to my becoming dr svengali's favorite victim.

It started on su oct 12 1997, the day i was sentenced to life in prison. That same day i was transferred here —lorton federal prison, fairfax cty, va. Just nine days into my sentence i was thrown into sensory isolation for 6wks! (For a point of re: It is now early mar of '98. I have spoken of this.) And for what offense?

A typic appt is a foul catch22. On the morn of tu oct 21 1997, his pasty hulk flung back in a chair, *die doktor* says nothing as i enter. (This is my ninth appt in as many days, the avrg evaluation (read: interrogation) lasting 3hrs. During all sessions i was in legirons handcuffs ε stunbelt.) After a couple mins of staring at a file folder he looked up. "Youre gonna fall asleep again, arncha, soldier? Geezuskryss gimme that damn remote!" Gluum, having nodded off, rises, gives remote controller (for the stunbelt i'm wearing), resits. Slugmoid clips it to his shirt, picks up another remote. "You better hope i'm using the right one, schock." Grinning, he fingers a button. To his right (my left) a videoscreen glows. With difficulty i make out a gauzygreen underwaterlike infrared clip: apparently me in my bunk, in lotus position, meditating; he fast-forwards to me facing the wall, asleep. Turned half-toward me in his chair, cigaret smoke curling above his head, he says in a sticky voice, "Mr schock. What are you doing there...? I mean, up on the screen. Do you think I cant tell...?" This appt took place before i'd been trained to feign interest. "Okay then, I'll tell you. You are hacking off, schock, plain 'n' simple. Beating your meat. Pounding your pud. Whipping your whaler. You know it's against the rules yet you persist. Why dont you admit it? Talk to me about it? There you are, big as life (pardon the expression), curled up like a baby in a fetal trance, dreaming about your little sweetie —what's her name? ...who is dead anyway (but that's another subject) ...and pounding the pus out of your pud." Thruout the well-enunciated monolog the right shoulder of a hand i cant see undulates.

Gluum sits beside the door, bored smoking nodding stroking the butt of his revolver puffing nodding grinning ...if i chance to glance his way and his eyes happen to be open. I dont so chance.

"So here you are [video in freezeframe], preferring your filthy little act in your filthy little cot to having real live sex with a well-adjusted male friend or two. Shame, oooh, shame." Flicks off video player, lurches forward in his chair, squashes out the nub of a cigaret in a heaping ashtray (it continues to smolder), exhales fan of smoke, makes sucking noise thru his teeth. "But sickness is sickness, and boys will be girls, and that's why i'm here, so let's get on with it." Sits for several mins looking down at my file, up at me, down at file again. His catch-phrase has varied little from visit to visit: "So have you changed your mind about anything? <Like what?> O anything. Anything at all." I nod, no. "Hmm." He rocks in his chair which creaks under his hulk. "Are you quite sure?" I yod (yes) perceptibly. This leading nowhere he asks, "How about your power struggle with your dead father? A fine man. How's that coming? Any progress? <I have no such struggle.> Hmm. Denial." Writes something, flips page. Since my very first visit the slugthing has accused me of being a nazi. "You must start to deal with these things now, schock. Open up t' me. I'm your best friend, you know. Time's running out. Let's talk." Pours cup of coffee (keeps coffee-maker on desk). Five sugars. "Join me? ...No? ...As you choose." Slurps like a child. "Absolution, schock. That's your ticket to freedom. Absolution. I speak of freedom of the soul, you understand. Your body, as you know, will never leave this place ...not alive, anyway."

A scientist preaching souls?

Spills coffee on two of his several chins, lurches forward to a stooped but standing position, knocks ashtray to floor, scattering its stinking waste.

"I'll get it!" says gluum, jumping out of his nod w a start.

"Never mind. Never mind." Looking down w a gogolian flare of nostrils, brushing at the ashen streaks on his dark trousers, he adds, "I'd hate to interrupt your little sleep over there". Breathing heavily, he resits, lites another, almost in sync w gluum. "Where were we... Yes. Where else? You were rudely rejecting my warm ministrations again. Look here, you must purge yourself, schock, purge yourself of this childish hatred for your poor departed father. He had every right to screw the living shit out of your mother, you *know* that. A *legal* right! Your desires, on the other hand, are *illegal* ...say nothing of antisocial. Why continue to punish him, and me, for this? He is dead! Show some pity, man! [catches breath] Which brings us to this other thing: this problem of your little dead girlfriend." Puts on reading glasses, slips sheet of paper from my file, assumes grave face, reads aloud: "Certificate of death. Deceased, lilith alithe mcgrae. Is that how you say it? [glances over his glasses. I say nothing] Let's see here: physician diagnosing death; physician performing autopsy; cause of death: asphyxiation; mechanical cause (if applicable): deduced foreign object in trachea, hmm; sexual mutilation too —now *that's* gothic; says here, unmarried, is that right? Tsk, tsk, tsk, schock. Pity. Poor waif —almost an unwed mother, eh? You know, of course, she was pregnant when she died?"

She is neither pregnant or dead.

"She was carrying your kid, schock. The least ya coulda done was marry her. Even the lowliest scumbag wouldnv done that. Cause of death, date of death, approximate time of death. They forget nothing." Another slurp, smack of lips; sets cup, sheet of paper, aside, wipes drivel from chins, lites up again. "My friend, nathan ...I hope I can call you that? I have gone to some trouble, personal trouble, to secure a copy of this certificate ...for you, my boy, not for me. [shakes it at me] Yet still you refuse to buckup to reality."

<Where are your hot needles 'n' leeches, doktor?> As for Lilith being pregnant. The fact i never impregnated my Love strikes me tonite, as i write this, as perhaps the most tragic wetspot ever wasted on the bedsheets of human evolution!

He exhales, squints at wraith of smoke as i stare at the spilt mess smoldering on the carpet. "Have you any idea how this hurts my feelings? [pause] No. Of course you dont. [removes glasses] You are too self-obsessed to be moved by the hurts of others. [pause] So be it."

Thus he taunted me, every day from the time of my arrival, w threats of my impending death, w horror stories of Lilith's suffering & death. He tries to convince me it is Lilith who is dead, not her sister, lalage. "The coroner says, 'Death adduced as caused by accidentally or purposefully inflicted athrism'. *Very* gothic. Police translation? This surely will interest you. Two cokefreaks, skinheads —comrades of yours, for all we know— humped your sweetie t' death, schock. Face it! It was not fbi agents who killed her. Dont you read the papers, man? Werent you at your own trial?" Sinister grin, magnified as only in dreams, ignites his features. "Your little sweetie was fucked ta death, man! Wake up! Fuckedfuckedfuckedfuckedfucked ta death! ...in every hole she owned apparently!" Tho i've never seen his face, i feel i know what the eyes of dr mengele must have felt like to his victims.

<What did you say?> I find myself almost whispering.

"It's time you faced life" says this mengele clone, cup of coffee at rest on the handy shelf of his belly, right beside the dangling remote. "They jus forgot a basic human function, schock ...her need to breathe. During the excitement of torture, the heat of sexual engorgement...could happen to any of us, man: to you, to me, to the warden or the pope. Raw animal passion's a funny thing. From person to person it varies almost not at all. We're *all* predictably blind at that marvelous delicious moment."

As if confinement w no freedom in my future (ever!) werent enuf, for the last nine days, over 50 grueling hrs, i'd taken this person's criminal abuse. But for whatever reason, for a moment, just a moment, i felt like a free man w rights ε choices, a man wout a care in the world for living one more day. <Even petri-dish scab has more of a right to life than monsters like you.>

"Si'down, you gorilla!" He would have punched the red button but, w hot coffee in one hand ε cigaret in the other, was too slow on the draw. By the time he thought to just toss them aside, i had already slid across the desk, knocked the remote from his shirt, and w my manacled hands, spun him around. When gluum reached us ("Where's da fuckin remote, boss?"), one fat jowl in each fist, i had yanked the "boss" to his feet and was squeezing his jowls til he spat his half-gulped cigaret onto my chest. Thru the stretched crimson balloon of his face he screamed like a banshee. Givingup on the remote (which had fallen inside the fat man's shirt) and comically confused by the rather harmless mode of my "assault", gluum, after several sorry attempts to pull me away, could think of nothing better than to hop on my back ε apply a headlock.

Soon finding, the more he tugged the more pain he caused the squealing pig i'd caught, he pulledout his revolver and struck me across the head w its barrel, at which point the thing went off. I saw blue lite as a puff of plaster erupted on a wall straight ahead. Because froog (eyes bulged ε watering) screeched ε squirmed so violently, gluum, panicking now, thought he'd shot him. Holstering his pistol, he grabbed my wrists, digging his nails into them (as if this would make me release the sadistic creature i controlled at last), began shouting "Are you hit, doc? Are you hit?" "Dok", however, for the first time in my experience, could not speak. Ceasing his gurgling hissing ε shrieking for the moment, w one tremendous effort, he tried to punch me in the groin; would have jammed his knee there except i kept one shackled foot on his stubby feet. His swing falling short, he returned to shrieking ε gurgling. By then gluum, shifting back behind me, reapplied his headlock. Tho my head was hurting badly by this time (from the blow of the pistol, or so i thought ...actually the bullet had dug a short bone-carving channel in my scalp), i hunched my shoulders and held on. Everything had gone black&white by then, and, as coolly as if i were back in nam disarming our lieut, i chose —rationally chose— not to crush, or rip away, those fantastic jowls but simply to squeeze them, squeeze them until the pitch of his porcine squeals reached the decibel level of the ache which his unrelenting torment had caused in my heart.

I was still squeezing when three more screws [guards —Ed.] arrived. The four of them, clubbing ε pistol-whipping me, soon pulled me off the yowling fag and hauled me away. I was thrown into "sturry" (aka "the hole") for 42days ε 42nites —a record around here i understand. The worst part of which (beside my ripping headache) was that i'd been slug-slimed; that is, the fat man's drool spit ε sweat had gotten all over me and i had no other options than to rinse&rinse myself as best i could in my new darkness w handfuls of toilettank water.

I cannot be the first to note, the membrane that separates rapist from therapist can be as tenuous as compassion among infants.

To get right to cases. A third of the way thru my 'endless' nite of iso (ie: 2wks into the six), the humiliated more than hurt dr rodent dx'd me, sight unseen, w "chronic lower intestine obstruction". Six guards came, strapped me face-down on a gurney and —pulling my eyelids open as we went, shining maglites into them for laffs while i groaned from the searing pain— delivered me to the clinic for "denazification treatment". There i was kept for several hrs (which made my next 2wks of holetime appear legal) and subjected to two rounds of catheter treatment ε sigfreudoscopy: a long black tube ending in a cyclopean eye. Thus was my unswerving heterosexuality avenged by this socalled dr. As i was by then high from enforced "fasting" ε rushes of the best meditations i've ever known, the reader need not feel too sorry for nathan schock —for i had disciplined myself somewhat beyond harm. Actually the whole disgusting affair was beyond lifelike. "I'm gonna jamb this thing so far up your ass, schock, I'll be able to witness not only your shit-spattered birth but your mis'rable conception too!" It was no use trying to pick up an iv hanger and club him silly for sodomy w a depraved device for i may indeed have resembled what he called a "drooling slab of manly meat". All of which leads me to believe, given sufficient notice, i may just be able to face my execution in a state of bliss! But we shall see, shant we?

To trimup loosends. After my next 2wks of iso (by then 4wks into the six, my execution was faked. (I have recounted this.) Then came the last 2wks. This time when i was released i was formally charged with a&b. [Assault and battery —Ed.] *Die doktor* claimed i tried to choke him to death; guard gluum wrote that he saved the 'doctor's' life. His comments made no mention of the slug's many inhumane provocations over those nine days, and no one would hear my dissent, no matter how reasonably, how gently, i put it. Neither was i allowed to call or see a lawyer. By the time emil saw the wounds in my head, the bruises over much of my body, they'd been 6wks healing. He has so far been unable to get a court order to have me seen by a real doctor. For these reasons, and others, we have plainted, petitioned ε filed suit against both state ε fed. But if my cryptic notes are right, we've already touched on some of these.

By the book, 42days in absolute iso should have ended in silent ε staring insanity for me. Far shorter periods have mushed fullmany a mind. I could easily fill a chapter w how i passed that endless nite. Had i not understood what was happening (civilized persona losing control to primal unconscious) i would probably have gone mad. But having been thru a similar long nite (during the melancholia which gripped me following vietnam) i, slowly, came to understand what was happening.

Lilith

In a manner akin to the way sleep sets free the subconscious, absence of stimuli does the same —except one is awake for the event! Since we are rarely-to-never awake when our subconscious is roaming at large, the autosomatic reaction is to fall asleep. But one cannot sleep unbrokenly for such spans and so, to cut a psych description short: to awaken in an unconscious state is to think oneself gone mad! Once i regained control –ie, once i figured out how to certify i was awake not asleep– i felt in fact exhilarated. For i realized i was doing what we civilized have long forgotten how to do: Being us –that is, being our deepest Selfs wout persona– while awake! an experience of psychic power, of Self confrontation, it would require pages to explain. This experience improved my mental discipline so dramatically that, toward the end of my 6wks i was capable of zooming in&out of the most spectacular & gloried meditations of my entire life! Almost at will i could bring on a Lite state of extatic [sic] brilliance merely by closing my eyes, taking a few thought-purging breaths ...and there it would come once again to save me, to connect me, to reconnect me, not just to my surroundings but (so it invariably seems) to the Universe at large!

It was there in iso, in fact, that this book took shape; there, in that netherworld of civil justice, where i saw w clarity what i needed to do and, part by part, visualized the entire project. In that state of mind i recall my concern over writing part9 —of writing it prior to parts 10 & 11, that is. For in musical history, after beethoven & schubert died following the completion of their 9th symphonies, composers became leery of writing a "lethal 9th". Indeed, writing a 9th symphony seems to have been *todwunde* not just to ludwig & franz but to dvorak, mahler and that hymnic blunderbuss bruckner too. Sibelius, on the other hand, tricked fate by stopping at eight. "Eight, you say?" Well, yes. Tho his numbered sym's add up to only seven, his *kullervo,* unnumbered, is also a symphony. (Might mahler also have tricked destiny by slipping *das lied von der Erda* into the numbered mix?) Anyhow, sibelius, quitting short of nine, went on and lived to some ripe old age or other. Foolishness? What is there about staring death in the face day after day which leans one toward fatalism? Which reminds me (for a much-needed lighter touch here).

In a music store in huntsdell while waiting in line to pay, a man ahead, seeing schubert's incredible 9th in Lilith's hand —as if fate was handing him a readymade excuse to speak to her ("Hey, I have his eighth! See?")— he mentioned how "ridiculously expensive" cd's were. "This symphony is seventeen bucks! A total ripoff, if you ask me!" To which Lilith replied, "That *is* alot o' money t' pay for a symphony that isnt even finished", she added w gentle irony. For some reason this flustered him, which, in its turn, made her feel she had said something wrong. As we strolled down the mall mins later, i said i thought the guy was <suffering from a stereotyping which believes females shouldnt be cultured, hilariously funny 'n' goddamned goodlooking all at the same time.> Lilith always needed such bolstering —which must have made her feel better for a moment later she briefly singsonged *"Schubert wrote a symphony. Too bad he didn't finish it. Gershwin took a poem in d and proceeded to diminish it."* Which remembrance could be made to niftily rondeau us back to those tenements of my youth if i wanted ...for a final cogent wrap.

Lilith

Be that as it may. From 6wks in iso i was taken straight to ratslug's offices. Trust me when i say, starlite seems brite after such a prolonged period of blackness muchless an office aglare w bluewhite lite. In legirons ε wearing a stunbelt, i was placed in a cage and wheeled before the shrink's desk. "I want you to look at me when I speak to you, schock.... What's wrong with him?" chides the slugmoid. All enjoy a laff over my inability to open my burning throbbing ε copiously tearing eyes. Following their little chuckle, the guards are instructed to wait outside. Dr rodent begins, "My dear mr schock, how are you? Good to see you again. Sorry about the accommodations but I dont relish being assaulted by you again as you can imagine. Enuf of that tho. My, my. I see we've got to fatten you up. [then making sad] But I trust, now you understand? I mean, which of us is prisoner, which is boss? I'll take that [my silence] to mean, yes. Now then...." He reads aloud from my file. "The patient blames himself for the death of ms lalage mcgrae (who is not dead but resides on his property in quadrant appalachia). He still refuses to face the facts. That is, that lilith mcgrae is the one who is dead and not her sister lalage. He refuses to acknowledge these facts even after being shown a death certificate. He still insists that they, meaning the murders, are government officials. The patient often falls to weeping and speaks to the deceased as tho she were alive and in the same room with us."

Calmly, resignedly, <Lies. All lies>.

"I'm sure by now youve heard thru the grapevine [i had not], my prediction for you has come true. On october thirtyfirst, while you were off playing in the dark, the honorable judge black overturned your life sentence. You are now to be executed. How do you feel about that...? Relief, I'm sure." He rises, waddles around his desk, holds up to the bars what looks to my crippled vision like a legal document. However, after his stunt w Lilith's faked death certificate –a document any hs student could see was a forgery– i was not about to fall for *this*, my own, death warrant. Beside, my meditations had rendered me unfazable, at least to these levels of torment. For his part, being more dean-of-punishment than psyche counselor, he took my calm resignation to mean i was 6wks along the way to the totally malleable cookie dough he was after.

From ratslug's office i was forwarded to the clinic to be cleanedup, readied for emil's visit. [Emil, if i've covered any of this already please delete accordingly. Thanks.] He had just returned from the orient to find my sentence had indeed been overturned and that i was now condemned to die. But on sight of me that day he could not bring himself to deliver the truth for, as i've explained, he too thought i'd suffered complete emotional collapse.

To wrap this catchup. As to fr and ratslug's latest terrorpeutic surprise, what is known in here as "the brainfuck machine".... But the reader no doubt has had enuf emotional chafing. Suffice it to say, while the erotic images of this "patient analysis machine" (slugfreud's nazification of the socalled penile plethysmograph) assaulted my trapped senses (closing or crossing one's eyes etc earned one a nasty electroshock), forcing my brain to override that torrent of filth, i recalled eddy poe's claim: "The death...of a beautiful woman is unquestionably the most poetical topic in the world." Such randomids popped to mind as one did all win his power to subvert this "testing" (which "prompts" the patient w a virtualreality barrage of unbelievably gruesome pornography while tracking his penile response to same). Who invents these machines anyway, the cia or mossad? Mental rehab, my cathetered ass! More like a fanny farmer orbital lobotomy sans the eggbeater. Anyway, oldtime est [electroshock therapy —Ed.] could not have caused wilder visions.

Last. Overriding the foul images which eyes&ears could not shut out, suddenly remembering Lilith&me in sf's war memorial theater, i saw myself turn to her, whisper, <Why is rodolfo pacing around the garret like that? Why isnt he under the covers with mimi, holding her, reassuring her? She might as well be dying alone. He should embrace her for her last moments, assure her of his love against a future of infinite nothingness.> Which recollection is what brought eddypoe to mind: Why does he just sit there? Why isnt he under the covers with annabel, or at least holding her hands, soothing her brow, thru those ghastly spasms? Why doesnt he caress her face, kiss her hair, her cheeks, her large glowing eyes, as she draws her last breaths? assure her death is not the horror he has painted it? For, o, how she worried always for *him,* whenever *he* was drunk or ill.

O you lucky poets, who were at her side when the love of your life died! And yet you have the insolence to feel sorry for yourselves! Jenny got it right in *love story* when she clued oliver, "Not like that, preppie. I wancha t' *really* hold me". Must get out of this place, must be free to protect my Love, must get free to be there for choking blood-spitting MotherEarth, help her thru this chronic case of humanosis, this lethally toxic civilizitis. O i admit, i do not want to die in this place! I want to die as planned, bluffside, beside Lilith's butterfly garden, under that huge old oak beside the chalet...if not in the arms of Lilith in springtime then in the arms of the wind, on a bed of fallen leaves, w fat unguent worms moving in the pungent soil beneath me, waiting in blind ecstasy; while annoyed birds flit in the trees, wondering why i linger thereabouts —and then, understanding; while a curious fox, sitting at a distance on its haunches, watches me meditate, sees me sink slowly backward (smiling), then lie still; where, higher up, a watery-eyed doe stands motionless, watching, listening, her tender colors reflected in the pool at her feet, as if she is waiting to be joined, in only a moment, by an ardent young buck ...who suddenly appears at her side as if out of Nowhere!

And the headwaters of muir creek move under Lilith bridge, over the spillway and down muir falls to splash into goethe grotto; then humbly happily lowly lappily sing underground for a stretch, then out again into leaf-dappled sunbriteness, traipsing on down the mountainside meanders, all the tripping way to the river below, whispering Lilith, Lilith, Lilith, as they go.

25

Quickly. As to those outcries fading in the near-distance of that muggy neon nite in my past... should we just let them dissipate in urban dusk wout comment? Like the sons of adam before us, do we fear to say, O there's a difference alright —between those cries ɛ the cries of females at play. When mnemy, darting back to gospelInTheBirches for a baseline, compares the afternoon sounds of girls at the gamingfields w the screeches of those same girls-to-women being teased by us boys-to-men —on the grass outside their cabins, beneath the slanting rays of summer twilite— those outcries are all the difference between noonlite ɛ moonbrite. The one cry, merely alerting; the other, taunting ɛ insisting. Even as a boy-man i knew that much. Not rationally, as i know it now, but viscerally... a genetic-coded knowledge of the vast difference between the cries of youth at play ɛ those adolescent shrieks going off like so many tracer-flares in the jungle nite: "Here we are!" "Here we are!" As if to say, "Even an idiot could find us!"

...girls whose bodies are more wise than they.

And many's the idiot, and the genius as well, who has located such shrieks, even as i pause here in search of words to describe them: cries which penetrate to the paleolithic pit of libidinous recall; screeches which rip like neural litening straight to the reptilian root of our randyness! What may seem gamelike to the novice taunter is, in primal fact, deadly serious baiting ...even to we the novice taunted.

26

Au courant. It was while working for a quadplex of gynecologists in queens (the hands-down pros among us ex panty pirates) that the fed. took me into custody ...and not for the last time. Strange tho it may seem, i was relieved to giveover my destiny to other hands just as my country was readying to celebrate its saddest xmas since ww2; that those hands were historically drenched in young male blood i saw as a plus, so demoralized, so disenchanted was this brandnew conscript. And it was not just me. 1968 was the year which demoralized a generation —internationally!

"The year that was" tom lehrer branded it. Deaths ɛ maimings of dissident youth around the world reached into the thousands! Few people are aware of the extent to which the world patriarchal lishment went to crush this outcry of its youth. It was the year of the "may revolt" in france, of bloody student protests in berlin ɛ prague, the year a hundred demonstrating youths were machinegunned in tlatelolco plaza ɛ buried in secret, the act silenced so the olympics wouldnt be called off; the same year che guevarra was assassinated, as too were senator robert kennedy (hope of young voters for next president) and martin luther king, hope of american blacks (ɛ all minorities); the year of apartheid backlash in africa, and of that debacle, the u.s democratic convention, w the infamous chicago police clubbing ɛ even shooting demonstrators (before the days of rubber bullets); the year that, even as i was bused off to bootcamp, the youth of a nation set the sad tradition of coppingout at the poles by the millions, a trad still very much w us; the election year when hubert humphrey came out against the war too late, and slimy dicknix won by the slimmest of margins, a margin we disenchanted millions could easily have tipped had hh had the forthrightness of martin or the brashness of bobby. And as we, the latest young fodder, marched ɛ crawled thru the icy mud of ft dix, komrad brezhnev was doing to demonstrating czech youth what mayor daley did to them in chicago, except w machineguns ɛ tanks instead of bullets ɛ teargas. Czechago *déjà vu* i called it in a prophetic memorial poem.

After bootcamp —in the dead of an iced-over winter, pausing only to pamper a protracted case of lowgrade pneumonia aboard ship— i soon found myself, as they say, in the steaming jungles of the fareast. I was not long suspecting (as i puked my way across the pacific), this pfc was descending rapidly toward a deadly dip at the bottom of his particular future. Yet in the retelling, just as we are about to skip over the jungle muck ɛ mayhem blood-pooled in the pit of that dip, i spot something —a crucial something. And, as w the memoirs of all the sons of adam, that something is gradually, unnoticeably, being left behind; like those cries in the neon dusk slipping out of earshot, this crucial something is stealthily slipping out of sight, ducking into the erotic shadows of negative equivocation, that traditional civil dimness we keep ever beyond shame, so that none should EVER have to deal w its outlaw truth.

27

The reader may recall a few weeks ago when, following a visit to my cell, a prison official left a newspaper behind, pardon the adverb. That paper, left on the cusp of my humble commode, was folded in such a way as to display an article about me. At the time i was prepared to let it pass, say nothing, move on. But the masked truth to which i've been alluding is so tied to that article that an honest man must deal w it. Its headline read, STATUTORY RAPE SUIT WEIGHED AGAINST SCHOCK.

> Convicted murderer Nathan Schock "may find himself facing another grand jury in the near future", says a spokesperson from the office of Federal Prosecutor, Justin Liti. The pending Tennessee State indictment stems from charges made by a resident who has admitted to state prosecutors she had sexual relations with Schock back in 1994, when she was 16. The Noogachatta resident, 21-year-old, Amanda Harlock, said she met Schock and his girlfriend, Lilith McGrae, back in the summer of 1994 and that McGrae suggested....

The banner headline of the article above, incidentally, read: BRAHMIN LEADER VISITS VATICAN, which overlooked the delicious subhead: Is sacred cow courting papal bull? What concerns me is not harlock's (baseless ꞓ vulgar) accusation per se —-for, disgusting but true, most people will cooperate w any witchhunt guaranteed to give 5mins of fame. What concerns me, and should concern us all, is not her vulgarity ...so vulgar in fact she could make a strap-on go limp... but the social environment which, like a sucking vacuum at the backs of our lives, all but begs for such dung of controversy to be dropped by someone, anyone, then rewards such droppings. Problem is, *we* are that social environment, you ꞓ me. One hopes the reader wants to know what, exactly, hides behind our routine need for a certain type of titillation.

Psychiatrist reich (otto, not heinrich) was, so far as i know, first to deal w what he titled "the outlaw instinct ...This fixation, this subliminal psychosis, hid in the shared human subconscious. The flimsiest hint of adult/youth sexual intrigue sets it off! In fact, just a *question of age difference* between sex partners can suffice to ignite this stinkbomb of the civil unconscious!" To address this stinkbomb, i submit now a conversation which Lilith's sister, lalage, who had a rollicking appreciation for social comedy, recounted to all present only months before my final arrest.

"Do you know, I heard yesterday, [so 'n' so] is marrying [so 'n' so]!"

"No! ...Why, she's barely out of diapers!"

Actually "ms diapers" was 22 at the time and couldnt recall ever having had a hymen. So what made this gossip so juicy? I'll tell you. The fact that mr so&so was in his 50s, that's what. Age, yes. But not *just* age, my dear. Age *difference*. Now there's a venal sin. We've all heard the classic society rumor where a 50yearold female is called a "child bride" because her new husband happens to be 90! But take the *same* gap, make him 56, her 16, and youve got yourself a really orallygazmic item. Intergenerational sex it's called, and we cant get enuf of it even as we condemn it ...and heap on the audacity to sigh w relief every time someone *else* is said to have done in fact what we (good people) only dare imagine in a "weak moment". Under the inviting green turf of such gossip a corpse is rotting —an *unidentified* corpse. Someone needs to dig it up, make a positive identification, and rebury it w all of its Natural ritual ꞓ a proper monument. One man alone, to my knowledge, had the courage.

Reich says, "The desire of societies to *any way* participate in the induction of their youth to the 'world of sex' is little more than our longing for lost ritual poking through the crust of modern existence like an archeological treasure —a long-lost lodestone which each of us scrambles to touch like some sacred talisman yet which *everyone* is afraid to admit exists. This treasure, the *prima materia,* the *arcanum lapis* of the human libido, has been banished by civil expectation and criminal law into our unconscious. Therefore arises in us this *sublimated craving* I call the outlaw instinct; a native impulse which is understood by few civilized persons and confessed by none." (My italics, english only.) As to that nasty article left in my cell. Kim jankaid, student of dr reich, asks in his *innocence eroticized:*

> Why is it we can never get enough of such [adult/youth sex] intrigue? Who profits by the inexhaustible circulation of these tales? And who pays the price for keeping such stories always before our eyes? Whose innocence and naivety is scapegoated so that our own motives are kept always beyond suspicion?

Thus the sexual doublestandard to which i aver will not be quickly or easily unearthed. Buried, denied for generations –wrapped, like an ancient mummy under the crisscrossed windings of pancultural taboos– the outlaw instinct of otto reich will not be exhumed without much agonizing, much denial. Dare we exhume it here? *That* is the question.

28

I've been "in the know" for almost two decades. I've known men from every cut & quarter of life. Since i was a kid i've kept my eyes open, my mouth shut, one ear to the ground. And this is what i have learned.

My earliest suspicions were conventional. Like the men around me, i watched in amazed silence as my own age increased yet the age of the females i was attracted to –sexually attracted to– slowly, over three decades, ground to a halt, stopped somewhere in the *visual*(!) mid-20s. By 30 i suspected something was out of plumb; by 35 i had named it. But like averagejoe, because no one talked about it, i had no idea other men were going thru the same thing. Like them i blamed myself, figured i just had over-fussy hankerings. And like my fellow travelers i went mum, dutifully mum; followed the rules like an ant in its groove. And all the while i hid from, or buried, the psychically distant & shadowy surgings of a restless & socially betrayed libido.

Today it is difficult for me to believe that such selfdeception is possible, particularly to *entire cultures!* Yet of course it is. After all, we never fail to forget reich's statement: "It is the sheer extent of the damage done by civilization's suppression of instinct that gave rise to psychotherapy in the first place!" (My stress.) That is, psychotherapy became necessary as humanity's rightbrain values ɛ rituals (our intimacy w our subconscious) were trivialized trashed ɛ forgotten. In my case, earlyon, this social charade was to undergo a thoro shakeup. And it would be a travesty –of all that the story of Lilith is about– to fail to tackle, head-on, this duplicity, this unchallenged sexual doublestandard. Enter, outlaw instinct ...swaggering.

29

My early 20s. It's after lunch on a stifling su during my fourth month in vietnam. (My intentions were honorable, i promise, when i vowed not to mention my war experience again.) We'd moved some 60k n of basecamp. Villages were few ɛ small now. For many we met, we were the first white persons they'd ever seen. While my fellow grunts felt superior ɛ heroic, i felt like a corny (if lethal) version of cortez in camos.

The kamerrouge (kr), one of the most brutal organizations in military history, were known to be in the region. We were therefore bivouacked til backup arrived. Talk in our q-hut (qwut) that noonhour turned to what to do w our day. Past wkends of grunting over jungle distances behind the air-whupping machinegun terror of two hueys [helicopter gunships –Ed.] had been "a waste of g.i jazz" said a recruit from fl. G.i jazz was a euphemism win a euphemism: the sexual issue (ejaculate) of a gov'tent issue (g.i). We lay askew on our cots, more from humidity than heat. The sound of cicadas in the surrounding jungle was surreal. All at once texas, a recent reup, jumped to his feet, let loose a confederate yelp, tore off his t-shirt and cried "Weah headin' ta mai dang ta git laid!" "That's a fact" added dakota, his bestbud. "Who dont rollout wiv us aint shayat!" Via hindsight, his charge, thru no prescience of his own, will prove uncannily accurate.

Mai dang was only a couple k from our bivouac. We'd passed thru it the day of our arrival and knew perfectly well there were few eligible females there. But before i address this, two terms need explaining: "casey" ɛ "caseyjo". They are homonyms for kc, abbrv for "killcrazy", used to describe any g.i to whom war is an excuse to vent urges that would be treated as homicide in civilian life (also called "walking-dead"). Onesuch in a platoon can be intimidating when a sergeant or officer does not stand up to him, or worse, authenticates his appetite for violence in order to 'motivate' others for attack-dog dehumanize-the-"enemy"soldiering. Our unit had not one but three caseyjos –counting the lieutenant (whom we've met sufficiently). Point is, in such a unit one is more likely to endup in a bodybag thanx to an "outgoing-" or "gook stray"; that is, killed by friendlyfire or -fragging, socalled.

Thus our entire hooch went along that day, some by need, some out of fear, but most by a combination of both. And so it was, an hour later, 12 guys from tx sd mt ga me fl oh chicago nyc & nj, and two i cant remember, found themselves in a tiny village under command of caseyjos dakota & texas, both ic's in the absence of our (snort-strung) sergeant & lt. banzai. Its inhabitants sd & tx were calling "mountain-yar roundeyes". [Vietnamese, *moi.* —Ed.] Tho these shy latindian-looking indigenous folk *obviously* had not a single "victorcharley [vc] boomboom bitch" (slut or prostitute) among them, sd & tx herded five of them to a small temple located at the center of the village.

...With foul hand defile...your...daughters.

Temple, in this case, meant simply the prettiest of 20 or so hooches. In the short version, two stood guard while 10 raped & orgied. And i would like to leave the story just there, move on. Most would. For this one case in my life i would rather not rehash. Not because i fear it but because of the denial –raging denial– its burden of fact elicits in others. Yet it is this truth which, ultimately, put me in the anthroperotic know.

The selection process was led by sd & tx (hereinafter, twang&drawl). Tho the youngest was in her early teens, all the women they selected were sexually mature —a judgement which takes into consideration not only that oriental females look young to the western eye but also that i saw each woman naked and functioning in a sexual manner. It must be noted. Had twang&drawl's purpose been simply to "get laid" as claimed, then a dozen females of acceptable appearance could have been conscripted. But that was *not* the purpose. The purpose was to rape babysans (young women) —in another country having a "less-than-human" populace, thereby legitimating (pardon the pun) acts which in one's own homeland are criminalized. For instance, when i suggested trading the youngest for a woman i found attractive, my idea was rejected. "You jivin me, g.i? The hag has two fukkin kids!" The woman i had in mind could not have been more than 18.

Sd ɛ me (nj), the "bookworms" of our hut, were chosen for pointwatch. This was no accident. Need i say, the behavior of our fellow humans on *both* sides of that temple door amazed us. For while every now&then a female outcry could be heard above the male whoops ɛ curses, no mamasan emerged from her hootch to rescue or plead for her daughter. (The only males were old or very young.) Personally, i found this silence ɛ subservience both spooky ɛ repulsive. Only later did i realize, ghastly kr brutality had taught them a brand of obedience that would last a lifetime. I do not claim to recall everything, but what i recall i recall vividly. I hear again the revel of male voices inside, remember studying the road, hoping to hear the *whup-whup-whup* of remf hueys in the distance, and praying (yes, i still prayed some back then) ...praying basecamp troops would pull in and end this saturnalian subjugation.

At rotation time, initial fever over, i was ordered inside. My unusual manliness is to blame for what happens next. The squeamish should close their books now and leave the hall for we are not even nearly at the dregs of the tale. I had long been a mark for lockerrm razzing: superstud skinhammer shockcock monstermallet maypoler kongdong cervixcorker screamerschwanz willythe-whaler ɛ soforth. I've heard them all. The present group called me schlongdong (presumably an oriental takeoff on my patronymic + longdong silver, a tri-x classic). I was ordered by twang to t-u-p (take up a position) in front of the altar —a simple affair: table ɛ small buddha surrounded by flowers both fresh ɛ dried, apparently gathered daily in the rainforest thereabouts. But i see i'm stalling. All the women were naked by then. Two were ordered to undo my utilitybelt and drop my camos. When i (or all of me that mattered to twang&drawl) was ready, the youngest was carried forth.

"Ta prove ahm yaw numbahOne mayun, corp'ral schlongdong, ahm gonna letchall fuck the brains ouda mah lil yobo dinkydoll heah... tydis –ah rapeat, TYDIS– lil hideyhole yall EVAH, sah, stab widat monstah bayonet b'tween yaw legs." She was pretty: kewpiedollish face **w** fritened black eyes and a small tho wellformed body; chintara sukapatana face ɛ eyes. {I melt, i die.} "Now heah's the playun. Yaw gonna play haad[hide]-the-pole in lil miss hideyhole heah, wiv no ifs ans aw buttfucks, ya heah? Cause thayat lil ass is all mine, undastood?" Using what is called a chairlift, two g.i's hoisted her onto me, or attempted to. Her turnedout knees showed the inguinal smears of fresh defloration, doubtless the cause of the weepful outcries sd ε me had wrestled w earlier.

Arousal ε disgust do not, will not, mix in me. And so the initial foray sagged, so to say. Pulling at my breeches i attempted to slink off, dragging my public humiliation like a limp boa. But the spectacle was not to be denied. Waving their rifles, t&d ordered me back, commanded the women to "git that soldier back at attention ...NOW!" In the midst of such an erotic freeforall, in all honesty i had to call on all my powers to forestall a ripping rëarousal. Twang, upset –oddly not w *me* but w my attendants– slapped them back into position w a bamboo baton he'd been waving about. Both about 15, sexually adept and the best looking of the women, after kewpiedoll they suffered the most attention that day. Twang grabbed one by the back of her hair, his knuckles tite against her scalp, and for several mins twisted ε shoved her face into me, all the while telling her (in a language she'd never heard in her life) to "Swallow the whole thang, bitchsan!". Soon the g.i's were taking turns w the remaining women. It was a monkey-see monkey-do extravaganza.

When i looked back a moment later drawl was striking his 'partner', commanding her to "Looga me while you suck it, cuntbitch!" His emotional insecurity was so profound, even tho it was his second tour, he misread the reason most orientals avert their gaze. I pulled away. Twang's rod delivered a remindful thwack across my nates. When, crouched there, drawl's partner continued to avert her eyes, he took his k-bar and balked at stabbing her. Each time she flinched he would yell "Yeah!" and stab again. Twang, infuriated at the interruption, yelled. But drawl was too fixated on what he perceived as a challenge to his authority by a female, dark-skinned no less. From the doorway nd met my gaze, wisely held himself in check, stalked back out in stupefied rage. Our training hadnt prepared us for this.

Most violent persons were raised in hug-free zones.

About to strike me again, twang dropped his baton, took up his m16 and fired a volley thru the roof. All activity ceased and i backedaway from the fray. Dropping it back on the altar he took up his baton, followed it my way, caught my sagging manhood under the chin so to speak, lifted its head to face all present, incl'g our wideeyed sacrifice, who now stood as if awakened from a dream. "Corprul tex!" began twang. "Ol schlongdong heah [his free hand pointing at that part of me while bobbing it up&down] dont approve o' yaw ungentlemanly behavyah. You *will* refrain from beatin' on yaw bitch til aftah church is ovah, have ah made mahsaylf cleah, brotha numbnuts?"

In the midst of this conflict of sick egos i was suddenly struck by the unusual narrowness of the heads of t&d. Instinctively i feared how little intelligence could be got into such a limited space. Now i've been exposed to enuf social science ɛ anthropology to know how unpopular theories of intelligence based on cranial shape ɛ volume can be (uncoupled, that is, from behavior/performance). But such uncoupling is not the case here. (Beside, i cannot help but note, has not absolute "evil" been most successfully depicted using a narrow head w a beveled brow?) All at once i saw, w the horror such intuition brings, in what direction this revel might explode at any moment. So while the handmaids ordered to get me "back into shape" are about their work, i would like to share some thoughts which have accreted over the years behind the sheer emotional mass of this event.

I have found, thru meticulous examination, that many of us, at some deep level, are captivated by the absolute giving in, yielding to us, of a sex partner. Degenerates thruout history have tried to unpuzzle by experimentation the exact differences between the shudder ɛ collapse of a body in sexual ecstasy and the shudder ɛ collapse caused by mortal wounding. Many is the b-grade movie director who missed the chance to fool the viewer by substituting the one for the other, which he might have done had he better understood the subconscious cravings driving him. And i cannot help but wonder —while i recall in dismay drawl yanking 'his' woman tite against him, thrusting the handle of his knife (which she expects is its point) hard against her lower abdomen, just for the thrill of watching her shudder ɛ weaken to a state of collapse— i wonder: Isnt it precisely those persons incapable of bringing a mate to a point of shudder ɛ collapse by way of personal intimacy who most need to achieve this unconscious goal by alternative means, means often crude, mean-spirited, violent, ɛ even lethal?

At any rate, it's right about here the nitemare really begins —for me that is, for the women were already wellalong on theirs. And memory gets fuzzy because of it. (Actually, as w most of us, i blackedout the entire incident for some years!) And here again i cannot stress enuf: The squeamish need to exit the temple at once else i can not be held responsible for their reactions. For deplorable or not, it is the gory details which are what this little pancultural exposé is all about.

In an effort to halt the abuse my lovely handlers were enduring for *my* failures, i allowed instinct –buried for years in a societally imposed abyss of shame– to rise up. Beside, beginning w those nites in the foodcellar of my youth, i had longsince graduated the school of gulp & go on. Visibly more excited than me by my re-rigid state, his beady eyes transfixed, twang would settle for nothing less than full endotracheal penetration! Soon one, two, three women at a clip were on their knees in the straw & dust below me, trying their best not to vomit. To the chagrin of twang, the cruelty driving the sex sent me into yet another slump.

Knowing men as i know them now, i am convinced, the vast majority (again omitting the mammary-longing oedipal types), placed in my boots at the time, would have escaped socalled moral responsibility by dropping into a state of fantasy: "I didnt know what I was doing. I sorta blackedout. I think I went temporarily insane," that sort of tripe. I can imagine others dreaming themselves tribal princes or conquering warriors who, because they have risked their lives for the popular war of the day, deserve anything & everything that comes their way. As for me, out of fear for the women, i was rationally locked. For i sensed that at any moment a more brutal form of violence might erupt among my peers. I was witnessing a sexual anarchy i'd never seen before or since and which latent intensity stunned me. I repeatedly wdrew myself so the female in position at any given moment would not passout from twang's merciless corkings. This gag reflex infuriated him. And while he punished me for my gentleness he feared to punish toomuch, full-knowing toomuch pain would delay the proceedings yet again.

I have said, i blocked all this for years ...once i'd dealt w it in a severe postwar melancholia. Next time i came upon these memories (in empathy w learning of Lilith's own girlhood trauma), i appeared before myself as in a primeval court of law, a fabulous fantom of my former civil self. And that fantom Self we will try now to locate thru the bamboo blinds of the intervening years.

It could have been an hour later, yet i'm sure it was mins, when twang ordered the youngest to be hoisted onto me for a second try. "Ah wancha da jaym thayat toadstickah o' yaws into this dinkbitch an ah wancha ta ram it HARD soldja! Thayat's an awdah (order)!" When again i pulledback at her wince, twang movedin behind me, set the bamboo baton he'd been using on the backs & backsides, breasts & genitals of the women, against my own buttox. Each time i pulled back he would strike me and yell "Yaw a froghayah [froghair] from boocoo shit wiv me, brotha schlong! We need a *mayun* behind that cock, sah! A *real* mayun! A-s-a-p if not soonah!" Meanwhile his ladrone, drawl, collared two women to assist in the sacrifice. Kneeling between us, they set about spitting upon the delicately downed mound, deploying tungs & fingers like shoehorns; while the g.i's cradling the initiate (two fools trying to jam a car clutchplate onto a bulldozer driveshaft) rotated & shoved her at me w mounting [sic] exasperation. I believe all present, save for t&d, were convinced the coupling everyone craved was preposterous.

All at once kewpiedoll gasped, soundlessly flung back her head. A cry of success went up. Now mark this, reader. The cry came from *every* throat! I can only guess (til such time as i learn otherwise), that for the women it was as much a cry of empathy as a hurrah. At this point the handmaids began furiously fingerpainting palmfuls of saliva along the unengaged length of me & around the victim's silkily flossed arch. No longer able to drive me forward w his baton (i believe he feared welting my skin past a certain point), twang

when 'evil' seems real

The most sinister powerplay in historical memory was pulledoff by those religions which successfully draped the civilizing principle in spiritual robes. More pointedly. Imperialist religion came to power by transforming the principle, "Nature is humanity's enemy" into "Nature/instinct is 'evil' ". (And ever since, devils & demons have been portrayed with a beastly (animal) aspect, as 'freaks of Nature' ...where, in a healthy view, the things that friten us should resemble ACTUAL monsters, REALLY lethal things, like greed, denial, bombs or bulldozers.)

The end result of this powerplay? Once humanity is convinced there is such a thing as 'evil', and then convinced that Nature & instinct are 'evil', no further justification for pursuing subduing screwing & snafuing Nature, or instinct, is required. For a World (Universe!) perceived as 'evil' is at the mercy of those who perceive it thus.

Need one add? In an environment of absolute imperialism ...where both matter *and* spirit are subjugated... only civil entities & institutions are aggressive enuf, intolerant enuf, to survive. Primitive cultures and their polytheisms, which strive to coexist with Nature/instinct, wither & die in such hostile & destructive surroundings ...IF they arent obliterated first.

circled around the group to a position behind the victim and began pushing at her w his knee, all the while ordering her cradlers to "Ram 'er to it, goddamnit!" Then to me, "Raym that cunt, schlong! Raym 'er good!"

With twang gone to the other side, i was able to control somewhat the entry. Soon the two wielding her, begging relief for the sake of their backs, lifted her off. Twang, now panting ε glaze-eyed, was infuriated by this latest delay. He quickly replaced them and the rite tookup again. During the hiatus babysan's head, which had been flung back most of the time, came up. From her semiseated position she surveyed the newly engorged coupling, eyes wide ε watery-dark and, surprisingly, showing intense wonder as much as fear, now locked onto my face. And as her new cradlers resumed rocking her, she simply watched, eyes never closing, mouth opening wide w each stroke, as if the mute gasp she emitted helped somehow.

All were gathered in a tite semicircle now, like mesmerized worshipers, the men masturbating openly, all but a couple of the women touching themselves in some unconscious way. Thoroly exasperated w my gentleness, twang was soon behind me again, dragging a woman on her knees after him. He now timed his whacks to the rocking motion of the cradlers so that kewpiedoll now resembled a human pistonsleeve. Her eyes rolled upward, their pupils all but disappearing, dolllike head flung back, mouth open. In the sacramental fever of the place they strove to cram me to her very cervix!

That she didnt hemorrhage was thanks i think to the copious lubricity ε skilled manipulations of her attendants, combined w my false starts ε halting stops, and, soonenuf, the initiate's own secretions, least of which was hymenal bleeding (or what remained of it by the time i was brought *en scene*) —the lot of which permitted a smoother intussception. Soon, at every midbeat she emitted a sort of gasp ε bleat, a cry that hurled me backbackback to juanita ε another temple; to a similar sacrament in another forest. Drawl pointed to her nipples ("Now looky thayah!"), aureolas swollen stippled ε jutting, while i concentrated on my discomfort. I mention this not for sympathy but to show some of the mental contortions by which i heldoff the onset of a ripping (literally) erection. Yet such diversion could not last, soon giving way to that inguinal vice whose grip the mind can only so long turn its back on! For a horde of hedonistic demons (or so i thought back then) was beating upon the basement doors of rationality as i struggled to avert total emotional inundation. To a drumming of feet & riflebutts, a chant of fuck 'er, fuck 'er, fuck 'er, fuck 'er, fuck 'er, hazily it dawned on me, the spectacle had only one finale in mind, for the mass urge had reached by then a frenzied fury.

Somewhere toward the end (what i remember of that end), the now sloeEyed victim raised her head again, surveyed me & the crowd. Her features were aflame. Seeing the intense emotions, the reverential awe, of those around her, her face, her eyes, took on an almost wild aspect. I can only guess, she suddenly felt herself some sort of religious martyr, village heroine, or Earth's ultimate female perhaps! Innocence, coupled w the subservience demanded of children & females by her people, might cause such a thing. In any case, i now realize –since the debacle took place in a temple, and at the very altar of her God– at no point could she have doubted that she was a much-prized sacrifice! Nor could anyone else present have doubted it.

With its potential for ghastly violence, this was the military's socalled clusterfuck in its most literal presentation. I will tell you this, almost to the very last, a tenuous thread of linear thought held sway in me. It was clear however the mass urge would not be denied! Even sd at the door now stood in subdued dismay while the women hummed singsongily along w the moans of the young heroine —who by this time, eyes wide, mouth alternately gaped & puckered, body shining w sweat, was holding tite, gripping in her fists the utilitybelts of her cradlers while fixing me w a look both challenging & greedy.

There was by then every reason to dismiss the discomfort and bring on the finale ...not leastofall being my fear that prolonged coitus of this nature might injure her. (I had no idea of course what lay ahead for her after i was ordered back to guard duty.) All at once conscious thought collapsed, imploded, unleashed an erupting column of molten & irrevocable instinct. A howl & huzza went up somewhere in the psychic distance as i all but fell backwards, all but passed out from the sheer recoil wallop of that immemorial flakspattering. Like a great serpentbird out of Earth's volcanic past, the outlaw instinct swooped in, settled its great wings in the dust & tore off its mask! Its talons gripped every throat, its blood-dripping beak was wedged in every heart! It strutted about that dimlit temple for several minutes, wildeyed, intimately recognized, arrogantly satiated, and, mostofall, effectively omnipotent!

30

Of this i am certain. On that infamous october day, on the edge of a near-impermeable rainforest, i experienced a wider variety of emotions than i will on the day of my execution: ideological disgust, moral fracturing, gender humiliation (public impotence), degrading subjugation, fear of the black unpredictable brutality smoldering in my civil fellows, instinctual fixation ɛ apotheosis (in the final min or two) and, for a few years after, major depression —manifesting in repeated bouts *w* episodic nausea ɛ psychic exhaustion. Thanks to years of hard work ɛ ruthless honesty however, few sideffects remain. Of those who came facetoface *w* my war experiences, two were lost as friends, and one, as lover —for i have found, there are few persons *w* the courage to accept the substrate of existence i have to share. Lex glen jon windstar ɛ the baron, among the men; deb danzi, bekky kydd, veronika, clarisse, Lilith ɛ lalage, among the women —and alice krawel, dexter dalrymple, jane phelps ɛ julie beltrán too, i'm sure, had we got close enuf to share such things.

As to the sideffects which remain, most are the result of the slaughter at dang nam. But a couple are mental scar tissue from the plunder in the temple. In sum, i cant eat animal flesh to this day, look askance when i pass even the smallest rawmeat display; i've since skirted all confrontations *w* virginity ɛ menarche —this held true even *w* Lilith, whose blood i all but worshiped. The reader may now also understand why i decided to undergo surgery, *w* the intent of reducing the size of my conspicuous manhood —or so i'd hoped. And finally, there is the mental/optical depigmenting reaction i have to the sight of blood. Tho i've had this since childhood, i feel wartime trauma has blocked all hope of ever overcoming it.

In nov of that year a quarter of a million people descended on the nixon/kissinger 4threich hq in dc to protest this war —in which 31000 of us had already eaten one last breathful of asian revenge. Meanwhile our unit had moved into another of those infamous freefire zones where it was 'ok' to gun down "anything that moves". Up til then we were still limiting our killing to "males of fiting age". (For those protected from the facts by our cowardly press of the day, this actually meant in practice killing *any* male from 7 to 70, civilian or otherwise!) There is no doubt, events at mai dang led to my "snapping" a few months later during the massacre at dang nam. God, their eyes! They haunt me still! Sorry unclesam, but i could not face those black fatalistic eyes one more time —not wout acting in their behalf. Tho years from understanding why, shame had begun to set in, shame for my pale skin (i will give the "civilian executions" stats which clarify this), for my maleness, and for my left-brained assist in this genocide of a right-brained asian culture, tho i had at the time only the dimmest idea that this is what i was participating in.

A major, albeit unspoken, objective of military initiation is to subject recruits (bound for wartime action) to a travesty of as much common decency as is emotionally tolerable. This is done in order to bare the instincts, particularly the ability to kill when convinced we must. And this treks us to the heart of this particular darkness. We speak of separate instincts; we talk of selfpreservation, say, or the nurture instinct, as if each were kept in separate lockers in some subbasement of the mind, as if the instincts operate separately from, and even in conflict with, each other. This is wrongheaded. For the subconscious, which 'contains' the instincts, is more like a room with no floor, where the bottom of things (rationality) is always droppedout, always threatening infinite freefall. In this room the instincts float about, volatile indistinct pigheaded & sometimes remorseless, and as likely to flow one into the other (to become a single force) as any two coalescing galaxies. In dreams we sometimes get to peek into this room and on waking we call what we witnessed there 'irrational', as if irrationality is always a negative thing, always lawless & dark. Sadly, each of us is thus estranged from the positive qualities of his subconscious. To most of us it is like another person, and not a good or wise person at that. No. We are taught to see our subconscious as shadowy untrustworthy menacing!

The civworld, incl'g civil science, views the forces of Nature as irrational. In that these are the same forces which have run the Universe for the past ~15billion years, could our civil spin on irrationality possibly be more wrong? That said, imagine next having to admit, our (civilly induced) dream of absolute rationality (absolute civility) is absolutely insane —totally at odds with the success of the Universe & its workings?

Thruout my books i re civilization as a cult of consciousness. For in it's crusades against Nature, civilization has converted or exterminated all cultures in close touch w instinct ε the subconscious so that today almost none remain. What does this genocide of rightbrain (precivil) cultures mean to you ε me, reader, personally? In the succinct version it means, our subconscious minds are being disfranchised. Ie, at least *one half of each of us* is being condemned ε banished from the landscape of awareness! The fritening part of this is, the missing half is, evolutionarily speaking, the richest ε wisest half. In effect, we are trading away the genetic treasures of our rightbrain for the mere calculator-type of intelligence of our left-brain.

We do this because we have been taught to fear our deep Self. Only one thing in all of civilization is more personally feared than external Nature. That thing is our *internal* Natures: instinct, ε the subconscious which harbors it.

And because we are taught, both consciously & subliminally, that instinct and the subconscious are dangerous to our health & safety, we learn to fear them. For instinct seems continually trying to trip us up, to make us fail at the rules & expectations of (civil) society. (When actually all it is doing is trying to restore our mental & emotional health by relinquishing all the [civil] repressions we suffer.) And so we come to believe that if we exterminate all we see around us which is, or seems, primitive, we will thereby obliterate the "evil" (instinct) inside us. This is why every page in the book of civilization is bloodied by the decimation of primitive (precivil) peoples. Indeed, much of what we label ethnic, religious or civil war today, or actions against "people without the rule of law", are rooted in this brutal & sinister civil crusade. Sinister because we civilized easily qualify as the most Self- and species-destructive form of life to come along in 3.5 billion years! For instead of striving to correct what is wrong w our worldview (the civilizing principle), we strive instead to correct all we *believe* is wrong w Nature/instinct (code: the Universe entire). Just how *absolutely* wrongheaded this is i can only hope to give some glimmer of in this meager space.

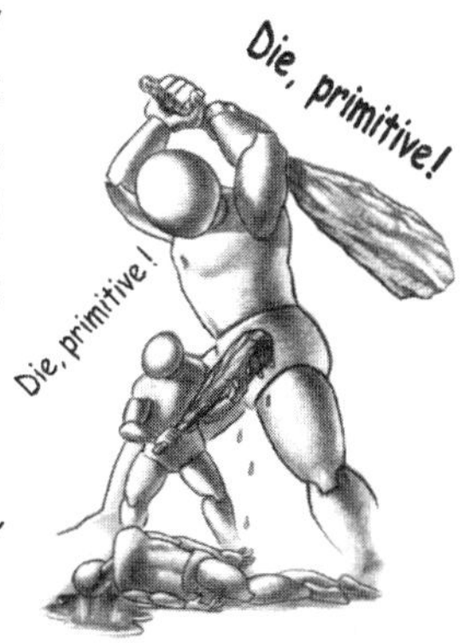

Think how bizarre that we should be suspicious of, even fear, part of our own person! How *personally* perverse! For if we are estranged to ourselves –and specially to our *deepest* Selfs– how estranged we must be from each other! And what of the Natural World beyond our own kind? What hope is there for us to be intimate w *it?* And what of our belief in "evil"? This superstition is easily the most lethal form of our ignorance! It has split not only the civilized from the primitive, the domestic from the Wild, it has split our very bodies, our very minds, in two! Why do we find it so hard to see that our irrational minds are as Natural *inside* us as any tree is *outside*? The irrational mind is as valid, as necessary, as the rational one. If nothing else, human history shows: our irrational minds (the subconscious) could hardly be more destructive than our rational ones, our socalled civilized minds! For no record of *violence of a species to itself* is worse than ours has been since the alienation of our species from the *Natural* World began. What for instance could be more insane than going thru life fearing (and thus doing the violence of abandonment to) half of one's own self? But i see we have strayed from the central problem: the holism of the subconscious.

the monster under our civil beds

Is it any wonder we have learned to fear our instincts? For they can be fearsome indeed when provoked. Yet to find the very worst provocation we need look no further than the instinct-repressive rules and expectations of civilization. This provocation, generations old, is unrelenting and cumulative. Studies of primitive cultures have repeatedly shown, our instincts are basically primatelike ...which, of course, is evolutionarily expected. Under precivil conditions our instincts are highly predictable and primarily passive. However, thousands of years of repression by civil law & expectation have successfully transmogrified our basically passive and predictable natures into the equivalent of a wounded and cornered animal. It is this 'animal' which our relentless domestication has turned us into on an unconscious/instinctual level.

For anyone who has ever wondered why civil man is so much more aggressive and vengeful than precivil man, this may give answer. One would suppose that even an imbecile in denial would, sooner or later, figureout why it is that the more civilized we become, the less predictable and passive (primatelike) we become, and thus the more violently unpredictable we grow. There should be no question as to why the rise in violence and chaos in the world parallels our crusade to leave no person, creature, plant or thing uncivilized. While it is clear, all of us can see this at an unconscious/instinctive level ...for like any creature, the bulk of humanity has always resisted civilizing... on a conscious level we fear challenging our civil monstrosity. For who in his right mind (pardon the irony) would dare criticize civilization itself? Such thinking strikes us as purest heresy!

The mx? Dont mess w repressed instinct (as war messes w it) wout intimate knowledge of what havoc repression has played in the civil subconscious. For repression transforms the subconscious into a volatile & likely-to-explode place. For, call up one instinct and you may just get another you didnt bargain for. It's as holistic as Wilderness in there (inside the subconscious) and the linkages possible are many & potentially lethal —a deadly game, not unlike messing w mind-altering drugs under uncontrolled conditions. And this is what war is: a powerful much-abused drug —specially powerful to we civilized wallowing in its depths, persons estranged from our own subconscious since birth— a drug few understand and one we civil latently crave in order to rebalance our psychic disequilibrium. That is why the dregs of war is like a dreamstate to those of us trapped in it; a state where rational control is at the bottom of the heap. And all this because the soldier is forced to maintain ever at-the-ready the ability to kill on a moment's notice.

But *instinct will not be separated from instinct:* the instincts hold hands behind our backs, share an umbilicus w the lifeforce itself! When a primal emotion is called upon why are we surprised when it brings w i it all its relatives & friends? For these are a closeknit wideranging & dramatically colored palette of 'personages' & potentials, personages thoroly pissed for having been so long treated like the black sheep of Creation. So, when we ask for violence we are sure to get hate too; demand kill and we're sure to get torture & rape. For, male or female, when death & dying are all around us, behind our backs (even w/out repression in the equation) survival-of-the-species joins forces w/ the urge to procreate, and suddenly our bodies are infused w/ an urgency to act in a way we have never known before, may never know again.

Tho i've kept a keen eye out since mai dang, i have been unable to find in any warcrimes record a comprehensive compilation of forced (incl'g threat & intimidation) sexual acts. All accounts are scattered or inconclusive. There is a reason for this, and the reason stinks to arcturus! Forget vital stats. We know only that the victims are typically women and often young. The accounts (the few that have been made public) seldom note even this. What *is* clear is the *suppression* of facts, a suppression that is both widespread & tacitly condoned. For, imagine this if you will. Only once, in thousands of years of civilized war-making, has a jury been convened to deal w/ the problem –the worldscale problem– of the mass rape, torture & murder of civilian females in times of war & social unrest!

(For a recent example of such suppression & denial look at how quickly the rapes of thousands of females (and not just by soldiers) in the "ethnic" wars of the former yugoslavia was dropped, or ignored outright, by our popPress in the early '90s, just when a few of us hoped the truth about the outlaw instinct might be glimpsed at last; just when that unmarked grave of a living desire was discovered in the psychic cemetery of the mass unconscious! But only one person since otto reich (kim jankaid) has dared dig up this suffocating innocent; no one beside jankaid dares seek her identity. Why? Because her identity indicts all of us who believe we are more civilized (less primitive) than the next person, the next creature, the next plant or stone, and who have the naked audacity to believe we have evolved beyond the mesmerizing rites of the outlaw instinct when the whitehot passion of our very denial scoffs in the face of this belief!)

The warcrimes tribunal convened in the hague in 1996 set out to prosecute, for the first time in human history (to my knowledge), rape under conditions of war. I needed to hear only the testimonies of two young women (fws87 & fws731), and the questions of their interviewers (both female), to realize:

The truth of the outlaw instinct would remain buried *despite* these groundbreaking trials; that the *real* issue would not be addressed! And it will remain buried til each of us, male ɛ female, is ready to have an open ɛ honest *rapproachement* w his ɛ her subconscious —ie, a reintroduction to the Self.

But i've said toomuch, confessed in these pages what *no* (civil) human confesses. No saint, and few madman, have been so honest. For this reason these pages will probably never see the lite of day muchless print! And if i get to write only one more thing before i die i must say: In this one area (brutal honesty), when i was conceived they threw away the mold. And o what the popPress would give to lay hands on what i've said here. Not *all* of what i've said, mind you. Just the gossipy part, the muck —the hurtful muck! Their dumbert-dolita fixation would be in a state of raging oralgasm for months! I should sell the mai dang story for a few million, donate the money to a study dedicated to exposing the agenda of the modern worldMatron —the torquing ɛ repression of instinct ɛ the primitive that lies at the heart of our civil sexuality. But she is safe, this worldMatron, possibly for another millennium. (Maybe forever, if humanity is as doomed as we appear!) The removal of my books from libraries ɛ reader lists will see to that, specially my *Mothernature and the world matron,* in which the latter is so scathingly indicted!

And this brings us facetoface w why i opened the door to that forbidden 'room' in the first place. No bluebeard, i. But then, neither is this a fairytale, sad to say. For all the kewpiedolls whimpering ɛ dying behind civilization's trapdoor to the subconscious are as real as they come. "She was zulu [dead], dakota. I know it." "She was *not* zulu! She wuz fakin! Them mountain yars is good at playin possum. *Real* good. Ah seen it a buncha tahms [times]." Another tentative voice. "Youre wrong, kota." Enraged, kota swings about, waving his rifle. "Stand tall, assholes! Ahm gonna say thayis once an once onla. Theyahs gonna be boocoo blacksmoke an a frag dischage fowah the nex one who peeps that zulu shayat agin! Yall got thayat?"

...i doubt i'll forget her / in two lives or three.

While twang's reflex was to gag (silence) us, like a good per posse –and specially as g.i rubberstamplicules– our reflex was to let him. Tho i later overcame this, reported the "violent conscription" of civilians for "criminal sexual purposes" at mai dang (when reporting the carnage i was witness to at dang nam) to the doctors who attended me in saigon –and still later to naval doctors in san diego– and tho they plainly lusted after every painful word, plied from me repeatedly every grisly detail i could upchuck for them, no action was initiated & no one was punished. In fact, the military claimed "no record" of these events —neither in my personal medical record nor in its own meager warcrimes records (those so far declassified. See patchin & mcsorley's *international bibliography on warcrimes*). The rapes & abuse, and the alleged suffocation-death of the youngest woman, along with *millions* of others over the centuries (yes, millions), never occur as far as military mentalities are publicly concerned. Why? Because there are aspects of war and the use of militia which, if ever opened & examined –as i have attempted to open & examine them here– would reveal the much-fouled undergarments & malevolent longings of that smartly dressed & unwell tyrant called civil man ...the lot of it repressed, and all of it denied.

I'm civilized. I prefer denial to Reality.

Because my book *Mothernature and the world matron* may be unknown to the reader, and because there is no time to expose the worldMatron and the role she plays in suppressing the outlaw instinct, the circle of sense roundingout what i have confessed here will remain incomplete, the shadow side of its sphere of wisdom hid from view.

31

In mid dec 1970, after about a week in a san diego naval hospital, the military cut me & my medical paper loose in seattle. Figuring i could use a wholelot of flowerchild r&r, i made my way down to sanfrancisco. My plan was to hang in those parts til reporting back to gmg studios, for the non-equatorial wx seemed good for what ailed me —not to rave on about what first sight of the goldengate bridge did to lift my sagging spirits!

Jeremy Shores

Immersed in the (already noted) sheaf of poems to juanita, the poetry scene in sf interested me most. As **w** the village, i found sf was now owned by the beats. Tho rexroth was still deftly skirting chasteness around town, his popularity had not survived the new deconstructionism. As he put it, "I refuse to march to the drum/of even that different beat, ginsberg...." I set aside my juanita lookback only long enuf to scratchout

the grapes of wreckswrath
(to kenneth)

Whether strungout beyond our last gasp
    waits the justice of endless nothingness
    or the indictment of some endless Wisdom
    —BECAUSE these are our likely endings—
    we must love this Earth, and each other.

(You see, not all my verse is to or about women.) Yet, as warcrimes obtestant ɛ noncomplicitant, i was anything but the typical DEROS(encavalier) nam vet (Deliriously Excited to Return from OverSeas), and soon found i lacked even the willpower to enjoy my hard-won freedom. In fact, i was having trouble just getting out of bed ...well, really, just waking up. After a week or so of high-rent inertia ɛ ever-darkening ennui i decided to return to mossville –not because mother, using my inheritance to climb back onto its social ladder, had resettled there– but because it was the only place on Earth, beside gospelInTheBirches ɛ the farm, to which my traumatized Self felt anywise spliced. Tho far from apprehending why, resplicing w Mothernature was a thing i needed desperately.

We cannot know ourselves til we have met our *innermost* Self.

Twilite ɛ shadows bore down. Following nam much of memory is darkened by recurring thoughts of death. Still a long way from understanding, i blamed myself for much of what had gone wrong. Just as the child of abusive parents blames herself, i was blind to how those todnaruts in the jungle depths had been foisted on me ɛ my fellow g.i's by parents relatives friends neighbors politicians police teachers schools communities religions the popmedia fellow soldiers our commanders the military in general our fatherland ɛ even the phalladigm of se asian culture itself! Yet until such time as my still incipient worldview proved itself beyond doubt to me, i remained your conventional male puppet, my dutiful cranium stuffed w indelibly encoded sawdust ɛ gunpowder and consumed w guilt ɛ grieving, agonizing over behaviors which were in truth other than my own invention. No wonder *pinocchio* haunted me as a kid. For i think, even earlyon, a boy can sense he may be just one more little ass on a vast island of bigger asses!

This island —of antiNature wayward&deadly artificiality— to which we civil are exiled i have named, for want of a more profound title, civilization.

Enter the only period in my life i kept a personal journal. Tho i recall having it on my return to work at gmg studios, when, in late 1996, events in my life turned horrific beyond belief, when once more i sank into an abysmal depression, i could not locate that journal and the help it might have lent me. Apparently i'd destroyed it for all i could find was what looked to be the last page. It's final side i will reproduce now. (I have put in brackets some helpful terminology i had yet to adopt.)

> I know all i need to know now. Recent events at dang nam & mai dang have been my teacher. Further knowledge will only confuse me. For what i need now is not more knowledge. What i need now is understanding —understanding what i already know. That is where i am headed now ...into that great darkness which engulfs the wee flame of curiosity. ¶ There is a point past which [civil] knowledge becomes mere extrapolation of some basic misunderstanding. Knowledge is therefor no longer important to me. Knowledge is dead for me. It is understanding [wisdom] i seek, and a whole world of misunderstanding [civilization] is blocking the way. A great mass of nameless sadness has settled on me, it's weight seeming to want to crush all hope of brave new discovery. Will this sadness be my new teacher? Maybe that is where i am going now ...into that great sadness which wraps the wee but precious flame of curiosity. I can only hope that one day it will spark a conflagration of understanding. Maybe even wisdom. And even if it doesnt, maybe it will at least show me a way to die with meaning.

Altho i thought i was suffering from a generalized despair w life & the World, i had unknowingly begun the arduous & pit-falled process of one day finding that my despair was rooted solely in humanity and its tragic choice in possible destinies.

As suzan sarandon put it: "To have a breakthrough sometimes you have to have a breakdown." I hope she is aware of the heights of wisdom this fact abuts to. To breakthru to healthy viability (the wisdom of the Self) one must "break down" the many 'walls' of civilization: practice the difference between knowledge & information, balance abstract civil existence with direct exposure to Nature, conquer fear of the Self (the subconscious) by overcoming fear of thoughtLESSness (meditation). All of which cant begin to make sense til we recognize that a socalled mental breakdown is but a lastditch effort of one's psyche to reclaim some palpable sense of the wholeSelf-freedom with which we are born —that is, a rational-mind shutdown which alone can set the subconscious free to rehabilitate one's total person —ie, reclaim the right to be one's Self. Those tender souls not lucky enuf to manage susan's sort of rehabilitative breakdown often crash with what we'll call an <abstract existence lobotomy>: a neurologically achieved removal of the debilitating sop's of civilization. Such absolute schizoid splits i believe account for most suicides, incl'g those permanent exits who endup staring in silence at institutional walls or windows til one day their heart stops.

32

Within hours of being around mother again i dreamt that her doctors were baffled by a horny growth in the middle of her forehead, which seemed the start of a unicorn horn. This made no sense as unicorns are compassionate. Some nites later i dreamt the cause of the growth: an eye-stalk for viewing herself; Nature's punishment for her appalling vanity. Mother had been only pretending to have matured toward motherhood.

One eve in march, out walking my dark ruminations like the family dog, i realized, the house mother had purchased was not far from the orchard where priscilla & me had had our tete-a-tetes. But the orchard had become "improved" real estate by then, and i found myself wondering if a similar "improvement" had befallen priscilla. This curiosity, coupled w a letter from gmg, lifted me somewhat from my malaise (malasia, hic). One morn, seated in the tub, mirror on a nifty mantle (which swung out from the wall), i found myself shavingoff months of beard growth. This innocuous act stands out because it signaled a rebirth whose growth & evolution i could never have imagined. For the first time since returning, i left the house during daylite.

But priscilla was not to be found: "Married, moved away... porcelain entrepreneur from phoenix", where no doubt my porcelain-perfect danseuse succumbed to the stock middle-amer womens' taygetian transformation, guaranteeing no son of zeus would ever darken her (bdrm) door again. But i did connect w geoff, fresh out of college and soon to begin a job in dc. While it was nice to see him, there was this thing: he'd decided it's never too early to start getting old. <Remember the time we made that ragman, carried it all those miles on our bikes...? Was that tunnel this side of summit...? I thought so. And we lowered it just when that car... Remember?> "The tunnel's gone. [said geoff] And fun is fun, of course. But we coulduv scared that man to death...lidderaly. It was irresponsible of us. When I have children I will see to it...." So i try another subject. <...And genius is dying not just in literature. Where for instance are the musicians to replace the likes of reiner kubelik scherchen paray dorati toscanini munch fennell! I tell ya, so much genius was spawned from eighteenTwenny t' nineteenTwenny that, well, the genius gene was usedup i think.>

"Personally I dont like classical music tho i *do* like liberace 'n' electric light orchestra... Yes, sometimes, but my favorites are haley 'n' the comets, holly 'n' the vomits, bobbysue 'n' billytwo 'n' little richard 'n' the everly brothers."

{ *This* is what i heaved myself out of the molasses of melancholy to hear? My God, goeff, where have you gone? Such gentle promise! Snap out of it, man!} ...Not just priscilla but buddy geoff was effectively gone too! And so my mood turned black again.

An advance on my contract arrived in late march. I bought a car (last of the flathead ford sedans), drove to ca. Well, sort of —accumulating a month of stopovers on the way, some of which i later revisited w the Love of my life: mountains plains rivers gorges badlands soforth; skirting populous areas like some plague, and shy as a lemur of humans w no idea as to why. That would have been around early may —for i will never forget my first spring in the rockies, the sierras! It was exactly what my internal doctor had ℞'d for my mood indigo. It was then i realized how beautiful my country-tis-of-thee must once have been from sea to shining sea! The jaunt w, keeping to Nature as much as possible, allowed the fine-combing of my hirsute unconscious to continue. For a purging, a catharsis, had begun. Yet it would be years til i suspected the depth of the damage society (read, civil society) had done me. Not just me, of course, but all of us! and our forebears, going back thousands of years! Had i suspected the growth ε change that lay ahead for me, moreover, had i known how all of it would end one day, i would probably have given up then&there, backwhen life was still painful ε black and i felt little would be lost by dying.

What a pellucid window into the failure of civilization we get when we growup and find, it is only some windfall (wealth fame new environs new love) that can locate genuine joy in us anymore ...when every waking dawn should be sufficient to do so!

Of course, civilization is not absolutely wrong. It has many really nifty & glorious aspects. It just happens to be wrong enuf to be ruinous of our deepSelfs & globally destructive to boot.

33

With my 1st arrival in ca being for a screentest, my 2nd for beginning work at gmg, my 3rd for shipping off to se asia, and my 4th being my return from there... this, my return to work at gmg, was my 5th ca trip of many to come. L.a found me both raw ε naive, tinseltown's favorite combination to exploit. The studio farmed me out to coaches ε classes almost immed: acting, voice, diet, bodybuilding —the latter w the goal of regaining some of the musclemass i'd lost since winning in london, almost four years prior. In july i was given a cameo in my first movie, *comanche dawn.* In august i turnedin sketches of a screenplay based on my experiences in nam. In the meantime, despite my protestations, mother sold the house in mossville and moved to l.a. With me there she found the excuse to make her dream-move: to be near her gagabazore of course, grandame of giggle & glitz. Oct brought me fourth-billing in *summertime killer.* (Movie buffs will scramble to see which role i played.) Tho an excellent part, and w the extraordinary bonus of working w olivia hussey, still it flew in the face of my contract, which promised "one starring role per year for five years".

Re: hussey. Why didnt she change that surname? She was its polar opposite. Anyway, i was smitten on sight —sorely, it turnedout. When shooting ended i paid her what i thought was the highest compliment. <If i were a director i could not rest til i'd starred you in a helen-of-troy epic.> Her response? Kind concern. "I know you mean that as genuine praise, Nathan, and I thank you. Really I do. But even overlooking helen's lovelife, at the very least she was an *awful* mother [awful, delivered w that wide brit inflection]. Even a gutterdog knows better than to abandon its offspring." Obviously i was not the first to associate the aneurysm-bursting beauty of ms hussey w the face that launched a thousand ships. On sight believing we were destined to become, at the very least, lovers, i felt bodyslammed by the time we said our goodbys. Being dispatched w a kiss on the cheek by whom i thought the most beautiful woman in the world plunked me back in my pessimismals. Tho i'm sure my postwar depression was part of the equation, what else but vicious gossip could have short-circuited the emotional electric that seesawed between us when first we met? Before olivia, only juanita, my mother & the dregs of war had had the power to send me sulking.

At about the same time i met a fellow grunt (lawyer & older brother of an actress i was dating) who talked me into appealing my military discharge (medical) and lodging a complaint concerning some of the warcrimes he realized (via my hypocrisy-scalding screenplay) both of us had witnessed. In nov i met jonathan windstar –who was playing small clubs all over the u.s at the time– was won by his boyish candor and the touching tales of his green guitar. In dec *comanche dawn* was released. Tho it did not fare well at the boxoffice it did win critical acclaim at several film festivals. It had the mood & agendas of the films *winterhawk, windwalker, silent tongue, dances with wolves* and *where the spirit lives,* yet came years before any of these. That same month i was given a part in *capetown,* another fourth billing and a role i did not like.

One eve near quittingtime, mother, braced w a covey of cocktails & years of zabore assimilation, sashayed onto the set of *capetown* demanding the studio make her gaga's understudy. Claiming i didnt know her, i allowed security to escort her off the lot ...once, that is, everyone figuredout mother was not zabore-playing-herself in public. I'd warned her this would happen if she ever made a scene ...or unmade one. In jan '72 [February. —Ed.], during that same shooting, the studio informed me it was unable to interest any producers in my screenplay, *jungle nitemare,* in which i was sched'd to star. With only a couple months to go til the first year of my revised contract ended, i found myself growing quickly disenchanted w hollywd. My peers however, hungry for fame and drunk on all the tinsel & shimmer, advised me to "eat" the first couple years of my contract and "just follow orders". But by that time all the panting & clawing materialism and sex-for-fame games i'd witnessed had tarnished the shimmer. Tinseltown was clearly a glorified conveyorbelt of flesh & avarice, a place where the threat of replacement by "someone more cooperative than youve been" (code: more corruptible than you) soiled every agreement.

In march *the killing october* was released to reviews that did not foresee a blockbuster. In the general euphoria of its surprise success the studio promised to de-mothball my scrapped script. In april however they dropped it once more. My lawyer friend, advising selfrespect (which his kidsister was blithely ignoring in her own career), filed a breach-of-contract suit for me. 'Amazingly' a couple weeks later *jungle nightmare* had backing and was set to begin filming (philippines, july). During this period of sudden renewed interest in me, i asked the studio to hire lex reever, former sir cosmos & moviestar, as my personal trainer —a way of getting to know a boyhood hero.

Lex retired from hollywd (flexflicks mostly) in his early 40s. Even at the peak of his career he was a retiring sort, led a healthy lifestyle, invested well. (Fame does not destroy everyone.) Tall, brown-haired, blueeyed, shy (but candid), the reever, today 70ish, is still in great shape. If the reader remembers "the saint", the blond limey detective of early tv fame (later agent007), well, lex had the same suave-smiled collegiate goodlooks. Never the bulky beefcaker (all lumpy vascularity & vasosheen), lex cut a new image in the body-sculpting bus: classically squared-off, v-shaped, dexterous ("able to run 'n' swim 'n' wash my own back") —a greecianly graceful masculinity difficult to achieve; so difficult that bodybuilders soon gaveup trying. Lex, a popMedia recluse to begin w (as are most persons of good taste), was repeatedly cast as a strongman strawman by the sequin-brained hollywd press corps. And so, following a gainful decade playing various herculetti (like "spaghetti westerns", flex epics were usually filmed in italy), seeking a healthier lifestyle, lex quit hollywd to live on 8000 very rural hectares.

His vocation, ever since, has been protecting Wild bison & mustangs and the rehab of hurt Wild creatures. "Usually pesticides but often cars or buckshot." He keeps a small staff to assist. Lex prefers "the speed, power and mindset of large cats but I usually end up with birds". Last i spoke w him he was getting a northern goshawk flite-ready. "He's kindof an ugly bastard ...til ya see him in flite! Then, whoosh! Breathtaking!" Reever's charges are sometimes shipped in from all over the u.s. "Some are in bad shape. Some arrive doa." Every couple years lex takes two or three months off, goes on a sailing project w greenEarth activists. Like windstar, he's a topnotch chopper pilot & navigator (ww2), and donates these skills. "I like ta break loose once in awhile. I'm one who likes t' replace wideopen blueOnGreen with wideopen blueOnBlue" he wrote in a modest little autobio a couple years ago. Lex had linedup a couple weeks of blueOnBlue for us this coming spring —a jaunt on which i wont be joining him i see. Tho there are few things quite like white-ocean existence days away from landfall, glen lex & me, and others of our era, are content these days to leave the winter-sailing to the newer activists. Then again, if i had druthers, rather than obliteration i'd take the dutchman's role any day. And one guess who my senta would be.

Bis in den Tod gelob' ich Treu'!

Following my sir cosmos win (which i'd trade for just one of aleksei nemov's olympic routines) i wrote to lex, told him he'd been a boyhood hero etc. He was kind enuf to respond, thank me for the rolemodel accolades i had long sent his way during interviews. However, it would take becoming fast friends for me to feel free enuf to share the rest of my boyhood heldenolatry, that toyboxful of surrogate dads & moms i once kept at ready. Our friendship was founded on this admiration. There is much i owe lex: a hundred training shortcuts & steroid-free body-sculpting are the least of them. His valor-in-the-clinches was of a quality even some fathers cant muster. In one of these clinches, in an effort to warn me away, lex confessed to compromises which, tho standard in the business if one desires to get ahead, are rarely admitted.

Drenching in the dregs of war caused an update of the iconologia of my youth. Collier bradbury poe hawthorne even hugo & melville gradually got replaced by philip wylie sy hersh d.parker s.deBeauvoir blackElk w.e.b.duBois g.w.carver heinrich heine voltaire wordsworth cummings crane joyce frost twain & of course oren liseley, followed by democritus kant daVinci turgenev r-grillet foucault rousseau emerson muir thoreau b.mor t.paine genet chomsky mach jung einstein goethe lao&chuang tsu et al & (unfortunately too late to help with my own work) the civilly blacklisted stanley diamond, the most deeply perceptive person i have ever run across.

During the filming of a pivotal scene in *jungle nightmare,* the director insisted my character must strike his superior officer, not simply bodyblock him to the ground & disarm him, as my screenplay had it. After several takes done my way, he ordered me to "Hit 'im, godammit! Fist, riflebutt, dropkick, I dont care! But this aint gonna work, schock, til you hit 'im!" I set down my rifle, walked up to this arrogant knowitall who never saw a day under enemy fire in his life, leered into his degenerate mug & hisspered <Well, sir. It worked for me in *real* war and i'm confident it can work here too!> ...and departed the set.

That eve, when i asked lex if he would do it all again. "Hollywood? No." When asked, why, he replied "The price is too great". In my youthful zeal i asked, werent the rewards worth the price? for i wanted to believe money & fame could replace the nameless faceless disenchantment i more&more was feeling somewhere deep inside. "Everyone who stays here too long, one day wakes up, realizes theyve sold their soul. And when that happens you think, the very least they could do ...I mean the people who got a piece of your soul... the very least they could do is give you money 'n' fame in return ...'n' lots of it. Once that happens, no matter how you twist the bargain in your mind, youre just kidding yourself. I'm no church person, you know that. Still I feel, hollywood is a kinda hell in disguise, an' the devil, which is simply greed 'n' lust, always gets the best o' the bargain."

Lex's impassioned advice about integrity & independence were priceless. "Hollywood fears [in actors] only one thing more than integrity: independence; personal sovereignty." In that dept louise brooks was his handsdown hero. "An honest breathing loving nation-state all by herself".

Since i'd never heard of her, lex gave me a copy of her *snub tinseltown, court death* ...which i inhaled in a state of free-falling fascination. "An incredible woman, no?" he asked in our next chat. <Most incredible. Wish i could write like her.> Brooks was still alive then ...and still feared by mainstream movieland —after all those years, imagine! Only a live case of unpollutable primal innocence can friten we civil denizens so enduringly! My only (lingering) question is, How did chaplin, who dated brooks during his *gold rush* days, fail to cultivate an enduring relationship w this quiet intelligent teen terpsichorean? And how could georg pabst spot across an ocean what chaplin couldnt spot a pillow away? (Crane gifted him w 'chaplinesque' during this visit.) Could it have been, such raw genius was less important to chaplin in a mate than was the fetching of slippers ε an oona-cooked meal? And most tellingly. What chaplin-disconcerting quality did lita lack that lulu didnt? Was the little tramp just as intimidated by wise penetrating candor as the rest of us? Was chaplin, even, unable to rise above his own latent, DIE, PRIMITIVE!? Why do we persist, even to the detriment of our most private lives, to damn vulnerable genius as unworldly naivete? Speak to me, charles! Or are you presently too preoccupied w the fevered pursuit of a certain fantastic wraith i adore?

As to my private life in lalaland, it missed few of the things the place is infamous for. Briefly put, the terms of my contract ε my social life did not allow time for the wounds of war to scabover muchless heal. Raw ε innocent, and at a time when i should have stayed in the sierras like master muir, i instead leapt onto the sweaty heaving back of a feeding ε fornicating monster known as hollywood. By oct —unhappy w the director's diminution of my screenplay into a hemingway war glorifier, filming 16-18hrs a day and studying ε training for an upcoming picture every min i wasnt working—wout warning, even to myself, i stalked off the set again. Unable to face another day's shooting in this by then totally ramboid epic, i hidout in my hotel, denying all visitors save lex and an actress friend. Key scenes shot, and on-location costs mounting, the movie was finished wout me. Lex, who by that time had proven a very dear friend, covered my remaining scene. And so it came to pass i can say today: I starred in a movie w lex reever!

To avoid suit after filming was wrapped, and keep me from tippling ε toking my troubles away, lex ε my lawyer/friend flew me back to ca, had me hospitalized. The day was saved on a technicality: a dose of malaria was dx'd during routine testing. While hospitalized i met another nam vet (glendon starling) recovering from a head wound gotten during a demonstration outside a chemical plant in l.a. Seems an lapd officer had kicked him in the head while he was cuffed and lying facedown in the street. His give-a-care frankness i found refreshing and, one thing to another, we became friends.

After negotiating an amicable settlement w gmg (we'll forget our issues if you'll forget yours), and not wanting to anymore lean on lex's friendship (or *anyone's*), i moved into glen's apt in frisco and, for lack of any direction of my own —yet sensing perhaps that only a return to Nature could save my smoking downward spiral— i soon found myself an ecoactivist.

When our pasts are too treacherous to bear, outdistancing them can seem as good as forgetting —as if a freshstart is guaranteed at the far end of a great distance. Over 500yrs ago, when we first began putting half-a-world of oceans between us & our various pasts, we americans began our tradition of trying to avulse history from the body of our existence. In this spirit of forgetting, we launched these united states of amnesia. Only in such a state of sustained isolation from the rest of the World & its history could one pursue with such shameless impunity what we have long known by the euphemism, "our manifest destiny", which is simply pop code for "the american dream", when we're not quite so proud of the effects that dream has wrought.

34

In those years greenEarth was a small environment/peace activist group, first of its kind. By nov i was at sea on my first intn'l assignment. A year or so later and still mostly at sea, i began writing *the castration of priapus*. Between assignments, sometime in '74 [August —Ed.], glen & me went to see windstar at universal city amphitheater in l.a. By that time jon had several best-selling albums and was drawing huge crowds. Then, on completion of an assignment in holland (ho ho, happy amsterdam!), i took a loa, moved back to greenwich village to see to the publication of *castration*, a move ire to somewhere as, <from green itch to greenwich>. [Interview on NZBTV (New Zealand) & BBCTV, January 11-18 variously, 1995 —Ed.]

Not incidentally, in aug '76 Lilith's parents vacationed in nyc. I mention this because it's win the realm of possibility that they & i might have shared a subway car, or stood on the same platform, maybe on the very day my love was conceived, or rubbed elbows or shoulders in the same elevator or theater lobby, or were blinded by the same gust of sooty wind on the same sooty street. I'm thinking now of causal coincidence & celestial conjunction, socalled synchronous phenomena; things like two birds dying in flite in different parts of the sky at the same focal moment: a third bird of the *same* species who, just then, is rising from atop two eggs to allow their hatching; i'm thinking of starry connascences, of recondite ruminations like, *When at sight of me he [God] thought of you* —stuff like that. Forgive my transumptive tropes & translocal locutions.

35

If i seem to be telling too little of the fun times, toomuch of the serious, in the foreword to my third book, *the ungreening of tomorrow*, i explain why: Sad to say, Earth's and our future are today too precarious for pleasure to be our principal focus. Where, on a healthy Planet, to a healthy species, pleasure should be important, on a sick one, to a fast-degenerating species, there is literally no time. And this, exactly, is how i feel about recounting my personal pleasures past or present. If there is no lesson in it, i have wasted not only the time it took to *experience* those pleasures but also the (precious) time&space it wastes to *tell about* them.

As to these matters writer kyle upjon, backwhen i had only two books under my belt, said "The best teachers walk a tightrope between entertainment and instruction. Schock is such a teacher. For every 'tick' of high adventure in his books there is a 'tock' of instruction". What upjon did not know was, if i had my way, the entertainment parts would be rare. For our forebears have usedup not only their share of pleasure ε irresponsibility but *ours* too, and our *children's*, and their children's children's! But here again, i do not have my way, and i must proceed as promised.

36

Was it God who began his autobio, "In the beginning there was not even memory"? Yet *my* childhood existence is not unbrokenly dim all the way back. For mother had her moments while i was yet small. With my big blue eyes, batty lashes ε cherubic chunks of babyfat, she could pretend i was the baby girl (the babazaza) she'd rather have birthed. But as i took on my own personality she thrust me more&more away. What i gradually lost was an emotional world that vacillated between stormy tenderness ε vituperative aloofness.

If, beside a warm bed ε a hot meal, i was blessed as a child, it was that, mother, unwilling to share her wouldbe starlet's nipples *w* anyone but a lover, immed secured a wetnurse for my "ravenous and squalling" mouth (the german is even uglier). This only came to lite when, home from war and caring about nothing, i insisted mother confess when exactly it was she began to hate my... ("O no. [metronomic rocking of index finger] Dunt zay 'hate'. I never [still rocking] hated you.") ...alright then, *resented* my existence.

When i learned she'd had her fallopian tubes tied in a sailor's halfhitch not long after i was born, i began to wonder about my easy access to melancholia.

One effect of depression (leftbrain going into electrical meltdown, rightbrain taking over) was, my subconscious continually cast shadows on the dim walls of my days, and these shadows, weighty, opaque things, seemed always trying to lean closer, as if to whisper something. Among other things, they raised a question of long dark hair, a shining scented softness ε rich warmth in my earliest past —powerful images in direct conflict w the short blond hair ε ditsy emotional dearth i had come to identify w mother. There was also the question of why i had not turnedout to be the typical neurotic of post-1940s pediatrics. I re the legion of men ε women deprived of fullterm *a le mamelon* suckling, denied the very act which defines us as mammals! It turnedout i had, indeed, had a wetnurse: the daughter of uncle günter's tenant-farmer. Mother, still angry after more than two decades because father had "had sleepingk eyes mit her" (something is always lost in translation), she couldnt remember even the girl's name. Finally giving up, i simplified my demands. Ok ok. Her name doesnt matter... i suppose. Can you just tell me the color of her hair?

"*O mein Got!* Brown, blaak? Sveet, mean? Tall, short? Faht, tin? Chinees, boolgarian? Vats wit you? How shud I know deez tings? She vuz a huzzy, dats all. A huzzy! You dunt get da faht belly if you dunt be da huzzy." Hi, there, worldMatron, m'am! Who says suppression of females is all the work of men?

Why, short of time, do i mention such trivialities? Device for *saving* time actually. For instance, i could wend my way thru all the affairs i've had, from priscilla to Lilith, and when all was done, wonder: Were my richest relationships the result of what father used to say when mother angered him ("Date blonds if you must, boy. But marry a brunette") or due to my earliest intimacies? Gazing up thru an infantile myopic haze, a memory so distant the rays of its image are blurred by the interdicting gravity of spacetime, again i see large wet eyes, shiny prominent cheekbones, scent of long dark hair swirling around my nuzzling/suckling face, soothing-sweet voice.

Ni chaiff dim amharu'th gyntun, ni wna undyn â thi gam.
(Nothing shall disturb your slumber, no one will do you harm.)

Yet beyond this gauzy blur of the senses lies the most important element: a feeling of resilient warmth, of intense ɛ delicious security, feelings i wish i could forcefit to mother. I am sure this dear milkmaid, whoever she was, loved me as she would have loved her own stillborn.

37

Ressouvenir. Essential to remembrance is understanding the dynamic tension which exists between present ɛ past. Therefor this note on now v. then.

It is widely believed, past ɛ present are different because we live in the one, not the other. But this is not an explanation, it's a gloss. Truth is, present ɛ past are different thanks to one thing alone; and that thing is not the passage of time —not objectively, anyway. Have i said? Time is the handtool of fools, the invention of those who fear to tackle the real 'culprit'. In the short version, CHANGE is the culprit. And change can occur only in the present. So, what *is* what *was*, exactly? Pithily put: The past is but the static residue of change. In the still pithier version: Change *is* the present, and time has not a thing to do w the entire process! Thus i give you: "time".

Change is also the soul of entropy. But never fear. "If you have a difficult concept," said heinrich hein, "the average person will not understand unless you can use his own body to demonstrate it." With that in mind, hank, here goes. <u>Sooner or later every part of the reader's body is left 'behind' him/her in a trail seven years long.</u> This being true, were i a misanthrope –as the fed. and its mimicPress accuse me– i would re the past as the dungheap of the present. But i am not. (O if only i were, how easy it all would have been!) I could also be the good scientist/entropist and say: ❶ The present is change, ❷ the future is the potential for change, and ❸ the past is the impossibility of change. End of subject. But such an aura of high wizardry (methodology of many a teacher) i will leave to the closet misanthropes of generalized academia. Personally i would rather share what i know, simple ɛ naked, than parade it in intellectualized costume.

Unlike the past, the present has a twofold open-ended awareness: an ongoing awareness of ❶ its sources (by necessity located in the past) and ❷ its destination —that is, the future. This is not an elective awareness, a choice which the wise among us apply to the Now. It is, rather, a psychoautonomic connection which the present *presumes* fore ɛ aft of us as we progress thru change; a connection which has much to do w our safety & happiness in the Now. Of course, we are wise who telescope this awareness of past & future to its limits. But this we rarely do wout a crisis. It is this in-transit awareness of ours —ever arriving from the past, ever departing for the future— which gives to the present its emotional capacity, and which lends to the tirelessly transitory Now its reflexive ambience; a double-ended 'spaciousness' we gloss as: living in the present. It is *this* in-transit sensation which the past has clearly lost, and which makes the past what it seems in our minds: a non-reflexive environment of unyielding facts, facts w which memory just cant wait to tamper.

Yesterday's sights scents sounds & sensations have receded among the stars, and the depth of echo those days once possessed has lost its conversant chasms & canyons. Those once-warm resonances have been muffled by the deep snow that is the lifeless inambience of the past. The young man's castigation of the Inscrutable Arbiter & its Cosmos, his lonely sobs, which the blizzard-blasted birches may or may not recall, mightaswell be suffocated in the depths of a tear-soaked pillow as remembered in these pages.

Time is the invention of perishable entities.
It is irrelevant to the immortal, the unborn and the dead.

An example is begged. In the past, unhappiness and danger are no longer threats, they are knowns. The past has no unstable potential; only stable content. When we say "the past is dead", maybe this is what we mean; no chance for change ...or even chance itself. In passing into the past the present is stripped of its reflexive vitality, thus becomes emotionally one-dimensional.

This, then "the potential for change, this element of the unknown" is what is most missing from the past. While we may remember feeling this potential when we go 'there', it no longer exists in fact. Not in that 'place'. Not in the past. There the double-ended awareness of the present is reduced to a re-cognition of <what was and what might have been because of what was>. For it's the honest among us who know best: The past has been stripped of 'what might be', left only with 'what was'.

How safe and happy we find our past, has much to do with how safe and happy our future might be. The reverse is also true. How dangerous and unhappy we find our past has everything to do with how dangerous and unhappy our future may be. Summarily: Nowness obtains its living ambience from the questionmark our mortality poses. That is why, when we 'return' to other times: Yesterday's stab is dulled and done; tomorrow's sting is stung and gone. The day we 'return to' does not exist. It preexists. It is immutable stone in the foundation of the present, and a tempting template for the future. And that very immutability makes all the difference in whether we see the past as happy or hurtful.

38

Heading bravely backward –once past the gravity of Lilith, and until i make landfall win the forcefield of juanita– memory recall mnemosyne mnemy hindsight lookback whatever one calls it, behaves like a small ball at the end of an elastic tether: tho batted repeatedly into the past, every time, it flies back into the present.

Imagine if you will having to stand at the center of a darkened rm, a rm where somewhere –up down left right before behind– there is said to be a small hook, and you must repeatedly bat this ball on its tether into the surrounding blackness until, small miracle, it snags on that hook! And so i send memory outward, day after day, and by dint of sheer will –form of psychokinesis, actually– i am now&again able to keep the ball at a distance long enuf to reachout into the blackness and tackle something, drag it back into the present. Yet if i should let go of it for a second, that thing, that remembrance, is snapped out of my grasp (as if by vengeance of einstein's Ω vacuum), and i find myself standing emptyhanded in the wide blackness surrounding the present.

I wish i had written this earlier, in time for emil to read it and, on the following visit, say "I had no idea, nathan. I thought your disdain for your childhood was merely a literary device." He might then excuse me from the task of prompting poor mnemy to share things she would just as soon forget.

[Parts 1 and 2 of this book were in my hands for several months before this editor could find the time for a comprehensive reading. NS's image of a lawyer/editor poring over his autobiography the moment it came into his possession is just not how it was. Try as I did to live up to this ideal, it was in fact months before I had any idea the retrospections of Part 2 were giving him problems.]

When i look back at my life, one day i'm 15, lost & alone, the very next eon i'm meeting Lilith! That's the way it is. My emotional cosmos is like the real one: great black voids w thin wisps of dim lite (superclusters of galaxy clusters) barely populating the blackness, each wisp lying at great distances from the other! with the point of observation very much resembling this prison cell, providing hardly enuf lite to perform this miserable scribble i'm all about of late. Anyhow, we will call the nearest island of lite, Lilith GALaxy. Next out, and to my right, lies juanita GALaxy. Then, further still, behind and to my left, there is, looking nebulalike, priscilla GALaxy. Now you are getting the idea. Investigating either of the latter involves a long & perilous journey.

Next, imagine trying to focus mnemy's telescope on a *single* galaxy win those wispy strings of lite, muchless on a single star! Such journeys are not easily made. The threat of personal obliteration has a way of fixing its victim solidly in the present. And so i must devise my own hooks for memory to snag on.

From 1972 til 1986, while still active w gE, i kept field journals. Indeed, this was part of my work. There are some 40 of these. A gooddeal of their broader content has already been gleaned for my books. And where my books fail to date an event, thought or idea, my field journals, or *the greenEarth chronicles,* can usually takeup the slack. Together they serve as maps landmarks ε signposts. For i must confess, i cant remember names places or events sometimes but that they are relatable to the overall fate of our Planet or to the general folly of the humans destroying it. Yet for some reason the journalists ε fans i've spoken w over the years find it hard to believe that, after a time, one activist adventure begins to melt into another; that is, factory melts into factory, ceo complex into ceo complex, oil tanker into oil tanker, nuclear waste barge or train into its kind, protest into protest, &soforth. "But you saved my daughter's life, dont you remember?" The er nurse says she remembers but she really doesnt. For she has saved alot of lives. Yet some things, like the publication of my books, do lend some precision ε individuality.

For instance, when i think of *the castration of priapus* several things flash to mind. First there is that day, a week or so after its publication, when i first saw it in a bookstore, its bloodred cover ε gold lettering propped boldly among other NEW ARRIVALS; and the scent of that book when i opened my first copy! Then there were the first few days, returning to gE hq as a published author, as if to say, <You see? Youre not wasting your time on me. I can earn my keep. And i feel *more* books inside, elbowing to get out>. Even the first few days back aboard ship are somewhat clear. I remember reading the first few fan letters that had trickled thru to me before we left port. This context reminds me of my first compromise in sincerity.

I had my publisher send all my fan mail "in care of" gE hq. GE would then answer them for me: an envelope w a slip of paper inside which read: "Unfortunately Mr Schock cannot answer all letters he receives. He has time to answer only those coming from Greenearth members. But he asks that we be sure to thank you for taking the time to write to him." A gE membership form was always encl'd. As the ranks of fan/members grew, i wrote a form letter twice a year, updating goingson w gE and my own public life: upcoming lectures videos tapes book-signings, appearances w artists such as windstar indigo grrrls fiona glengarry winter solstice the ungrateful undead jim page spruce bringsteen arlo guthrie rage against the machine buffysaintmarie ε others. Over the years, some 40 journals and seven and a half books later (i'm a slow writer. I'd rather have one good book than 20 mediocre ones), allowing gE to respond to my fans has sold ε renewed thousands of gE memberships wout knocking on a single door, ringing a single fone. In a few cases i have written back personally: to fragile ε unique greens (because i fear for them), and to mayors commissioners governors presidents ε prime ministers, generals ε dictators, sheiks ε shahs (because they hold the most power to impede civilization's lethal downspiral). Why do i mention these things? Because i can use them as annular rings for giantstepping across the years and thereby begin to wrapup this sudden confession i did not foresee.

39

Prison update. Today glumm gave me a copy of NEXT WEEKS CAFATERIA MENUE (sic all). I was pleased to note the prison's new sense of culinary sophistication ...until i read at the bottom of the page: Guests and Prison Staff only. That would be glumm's sense of humor. The prank is not nearly sinister enuf for our prison shrink.

40

After *castration* was published i returned to sea, this time aboard gE's flagship, green warrior. The seas of the world (i lived on them all) treated my tenure thereon not as the pilgrim ε rv shackleton were treated but as the pequod ε con tiki were treated. Tho anger ε frustration are evident at times in my gE journals –over spates of summer squalls, harassment by tireless winter seas– one thing is never entirely absent: reverence for Nature and a humble awe for the sheer preponderance of its support for life.

Many readers will be surprised to learn, sailors know ports-of-call as either blond, brunet or redhead. For instance, those who prefer blonds are always happy to put in, pardon me, in russia or scandinavia, while those who prefer brunets must be content w the rest of the world —a twist on an old sea shanty. Concerning the women in my past: I could save alot of time by giving now my recitation on sexual semaphorics —body-size -shape ɛ haircolor. But if i did, only males w beard in one hand, beer in the other, would applaud when i was done.... But what the hell. We'll do the cropped version.

Heteromales... in whose ranks i cannot incl mammary mashers; that is, those breast-fixated males who need a mommy not a mate. Anywho.... On sight, heteromales, whether they know it or not, tell females apart using only three criteria: size, shape ɛ color. (Scent ɛ taste have long been outlawed the on-sight role they once played.) Big deal, you say. On-sight is how we tell most things apart. Yes. But w most things, the size shape ɛ color we prefer is not driven by instinct. Point two. Instinct is not choosy when it comes to mates. We know the saying, by closing-time even the homeliest look good enuf. This is not just male vulgarity speaking. It's instinct finding a mate despite rationalization. It's goal is not political correctness but propagating the species. It's also Universal, driving asters ɛ asteroids, zinnias ɛ xenophobes! And it's not always discreet. Sorry to say, many's the thing that's been eaten alive or screwed to death simply because it looked like behaved like smelled like felt like something it was not! And all the rest is so much thorax-thumping in the jungle nite.

Once an ideal size & shape female has moreorless been agreed upon by a culture (to wit, beauty contest winners, top models, etc) there's nothing can be done about it even for the more discriminating. For even gay-lesbitrans & castrates accept & socialize the prevailing view of what comprises female beauty.

While those we call ignorant ɛ vulgar, kill eat ɛ fornicate indiscriminately, the few of us who do not are still haunted by the *same* forces, pressured by the *same* criteria. This we *cannot* change, try as we might —civilization, civil religion, plus the laws ɛ expectations theyve spawned, being the most tyrannical of these ideologies. Yet because of dogged personal discretion i can say today: all the blonds ɛ bruns i've bedded somewise resemble that initial female, that first intimacy, those earliest tendernesses of mine. No, not juanita. And not priscilla. But my cherished nursemaid, whoever she was. And only after her, and in their turn, does each port (in the lonely seas of my life) resemble priscilla or juanita. And all the rest is just weeping ɛ howling in the prison nite.

While a new activist at sea, and w the war ε my stint in hollywd disappearing over a fast-receding horizon, as i emerged from my depression my wish to die young began to be supplanted by a deeper calling. Over time that calling evolved into a commitment to live in such a way i would one day grow so old my location on the land could be spotted by the vortex of buzzards over my head. I have spent a good part of my life since then, first finding, then rehabilitating, my inchoate Self; that deepest part of us so trivialized by the rules ε expectations of civilzn. Now, after investing years in the archeologic discovery ε upheaval of this 'other mind' of mine, *still* i find my right to benefit, as a *free* man, from what i've learned, has been stolen. And gone also now is my right to grow old, to become that silverhaired duffer i envisioned, that jolly old cottontop jotting the latest of his ruminations in sunshine ε leisure, puffs of mtn breeze curtseying past, a rustling of blossoms ε leaves all around, lazy drone of bees, a frostian/dickinsonian/muirian dearth of civil madness so pervasive it invalidates the very concept of time! (For max fx, my dear director, play martucci's *notturno* behind this wishful reverie.)

Life as an intn'l activist does not lend itself to longterm relationships —not ones of fidelity to any given fleshsink anyway. (Sorry. Yet is 'fleshsink' that much harsher than 'one-nite stand'?) The closest i came to quitting Planetary activism (in '77) for personal reasons began in tokyo in '73. Veronika duras, 18moons older than ciociosan when we met, was the daughter of a french filmmaker and a thai fashion designer. When it came time to leave the city (to challenge illegal whaling ε nuclear-testing by former communist russia in the n pacific), my still valid *maiko* maiden left school ε signedup w gE ...tho she later confessed much of her green enthusiasm had to do w me. Our relationship lasted nearly four years, quite terrific years —which, if the corpolitic lishment has its way w my future, will remain a record in my life.

Beside physical attractiveness, over time, and from hard-won experience, i learned what i needed most in a mate: honesty tenderness the capacity for passion ε an eagerness to confront apodictic Reality. I rarely found all five qualities in a single person but they were present in nika for the mostpart. What i didnt know was, i required a sixth thing. Finding a perch on the highest point of the given vessel, seas permitting, i would regularly check the fluid levels in the system reservoirs of my existence: emotional rational subconscious somatic.

Yet as oceans ɛ missions slipped by, nika's passion for adventure in exotic places gave way to thoughts of an acting career in paris or modeling in tokyo, or both, and by june of '77 (on the 7th as fate would have it!), when *castration* was bought for publication, my *compagnon de voyage* and me sailed our separate ways. Lookback knows however, nika's reasons for departing were more complicated. While i knew there were significant family pressures (environmentalism is a career beneath contempt to business types), nika's code of family honor did not permit me to understand these pressures til too late. At the time all i knew was, letters from her youngest brother leith (who had incidentally technically raped her youngest sister) had a knack for making her feel guilty. Toward the end he went so far as to claim their mother's new husband was a heroine-user who beat him, said their mother did not know of these abuses because the man was clever. Tho nik doubted leith's veracity (as he did not opt to go live w their real dad as i suggested), still, his pleas were so frequent, and his love for her so pathetically unguent, they often interfered w our relationship in our last year together. Family honor, i will learn, like patriotism, has little of love in it, and much of vanity.

As my part of that ship sailed away, how could i know, the member of the duras family i would hear from again would not be nika? Thanx to family honor, my disoriented franco/thai lover became little miss lee ding. For i had assumed my tack no longer worked for her. My sails held true however: the adoring lauding ɛ protecting of Motherearth. And but for whom was born that june day of our separation, this book would be wholly unnecessary.

Nika is synced in memory w the writing of *castration.* Since she removed me from sexual circulation so to say, and since her franco/asian beauty (likeness of little-known [back when NS was witing this —Ed.] actor kristin kreuk) kept the gynalept of straying libido languishing happily in chains, i found time for serious composition. The following is not a fair sampling.

Not karati, jujitsu or kungfu
  possess the flyingkick my nik's eyes do;
  not supernovas, quasars nor voodoo
  unleash all the forces her woo do.

And in the end it was nika, really —emotionally stable nika— whose words were responsible for kicking the badboy "cool" out of me once&foralways. "Then why do I keep getting the feeling you believe stupidity is a prerequisite for niceness?" For in my insecurity i had unwittingly adopted the pride of the cool ɛ insecure. Tho nika delivered that judgement years ago, i still feel its jarring truth like she did so just last nite ...the 'soft' lites of rangoon harbor rising & lowering in the inky blackness beyond the gunwale to our drowsily recumbent right.

Castration was published by mcCrae-noble(!) books in time for the xmas season. The following year i befriended pj "the baron" falk, who'd sent me an outline for a play based on it. In '79 his version began an offBroadway run. 10mos later it was closed down w nostalgic reviews. City managers were given the dirtywork. The baron's play was said to be "operating in non-compliance with State, County, City and Borough laws and ordinances" and "in violation of safety and morality codes" incl'g "overcrowding, fire, public nudity, freedom-of-religion and pornography", all of which was pure ratscat. We all knew what the real problem was. As w my book, the baron & his players were exposing religious fundies in their undies, corpoliticos & feds in adulterous beds, and the whole power-driven phalladigm at fulblown & unexpurgated erection! 6mos later we reopened in a new venue i got us in frisco. A year after that it went intn'l, and the rest is history.

When mother read about the closing of the nyc production she foned. "Und vy did I get no audition furkrissake? Ya got two-hundrt pipples in de show und no room fuhr yur own mutter?" You could always tell how upset she was by the thickness of her accent. Her *pickelhaube* personality was still spitting little mustachios of vindictiveness when i hung up. As a favor, the baron cast her in the frisco mounting. She carried it off remarkably well as it involved alot of screaming at others.

Somewhere around that time [May 1981 —Ed] an essay, *last gorilla, last orang: a scientific, historic & moral tragedy,* written w anthroapologist (as she called herself) denise norris, was brought out in boston by *commons monthly.* In '80 my second & secondbest-selling book, *scapegoats & fallgirls* (Lilith's favorite), was published. In '81 i was given the green pen award for *scapegoats* even as the baron's *the castration of priapus* was being bought by bluecomet films. And in '83 my third book, *the ungreening of tomorrow,* was published. Amidst all this, since my personal success was linked w the organization's fundraising efforts, gE, in league w my publisher, began sched'g a lecture circuit synced to the same towns where artists w a progressive mx were performing. Since '81 i've thus shared a stage w everyone from abba to zappa, my favorites being performers who possessed a certain extrasensible something: jon windstar, fiona glengary, winter solstice, sarah thompsen, jim paige, jerry gracias, ani diFranco, steve earle, dar williams, sting, springsteen, jello biafra, tom waits, paul oaks, rebecca riots, deva premal&miten, the early smolderings of melissa crabtree, doria roberts, michael franti, rageAgainstThe-Machine, + any number of artists who give moral &/or spiritual heightening.

My gE activism more&more on the wane, soon my time was divided between writing ε lecturing, which salary cut made the lecture circuit economically essential. I suppose that after the inquisitive audiences of the 1960/70s any audience seems bland. Still most agree, audiences thru the '80s were the worst. The baron, also touring then, re:ing academic audiences, remarked, "The worst batch of morons since the stultifying '40s; a case of trying to cure the terminally illiterate with the worst sampling of cosmetic syllabi since the school of the social graces". Unfortunately those years were positioned at the very apex of my lecturing career, the circuit typically taking from oct to mar. This worked out nicely as it eased me away from cold wet winters on wide white waters. With the sea said to be a powerful muse i find it curious that some of my best ideas germinated during the heat of a lecture or in the afterglow of a q/a period (pop aspect of my lectures) ...while the sea itself, like a father one can never hope to measure up to, often left inspiration prostrate in its vast ε inexhaustible shadow. Debussy suffered from a similar stutter i understand.

Worst part of going to sea? Extended periods of claustrophobic conditions. If accommodations at sea are difficult for the average person we are safe calling them grueling for the big person, and spirit-crushing for the tallest claustrophobes. No ceiling high enuf belowdecks, i imagined my sea-going quarters designed by a maniacally cruel midget who hated *whom* worst of all people on Earth? Right. Tall people. Everytime i changed ship it took a cuttingtorch just to make my berth big enuf so when i went to bed my whole body could join in. 'Dreaming below waterline' (chap.head used in my *gE chronicles*) was more than a little remindful of my foodcellar nites. For an idea of what life was like during bad wx at sea, cube your worst wx at home. Dim cramped existence surrounded by water: sea rain fog mist. While i find such womblike conditions a marvel of tranquility when i meditate, coming for days on end, to a claustrophobe, they are depressing. Of course, they beat the alternative: a few nites in, say, a chinese or turkish jail.

Not the classic thalassic i thought i was, my sea-legs soon longed for land. In the spring of '84 i took time off to go buy a couple of the rolling hills i last knew as gospelInTheBirches. The attentive reader knows this quest was doomed. Colonization there was full-underway and prices were high, the lakes region ɛ surrounding woods by then dotted w costly private retreats. The end of the lake where juanita ɛ me had spent memorial hours had been dredged for a 4-berth boatdock. In the next decade the slips would grow tenfold, taking on an ugly white metal roof ɛ a platoon of pontoonboats! In our Wildest imaginations juanita ɛ me would not have guessed such a tasteless evolution for our enchanted culdesac in time.

From this disappointment i scurried off to the blueridges. A few days there and it was clear, proceeds from the sale of *castration* movie-rights could not buy the 800 minimum hectares (roughly 2000acres) needed to create a Nature reserve of any ecointegrity. Chasing my dream down along the smokys and into southern tn i endedup, purely by accident, in bamalachia on a bluff overlooking the tn river. Tho not the blueridges, it was a place where Nature clearly needed what assistance i had to offer (then again, where doesnt She?): Little by way of ntl forest, and w state forests ɛ pks w logging mining hunting trapping permitted, and where there was a near-zero ecoawareness in the populace at large. After mos of haggling w the tn valley authority (tva) over water easements (i sought guarantees that the Wild animals on the land i was buying would have unobstructed access to drinking water *in perpetuum*), i finalized the purch in the fall of '84 and named it goethe grotto Nature sanctuary (hereinafter, ggNs). {Work, yes!} i thought, gazing out over my new mtn home. {Definitely lots o' that. But peace, awe ɛ Earthplace, here i am.}

41

It was the amount of roadkill i happened on while looking for land which led to my forming a business some may know. In nam i'd had occasion to play "picador": search-party member who marks the location of govt property (remains of a battle, explosion etc) w brite-colored javelins. It was these which lay at the back of my mind when, from a cable-laying outfit, i bought a box of small marker flags. I always kept some of these handy under a floormat so that, at a roadkill site, w two quick bends of a wire stem, i could form a pennant base for sliding beneath the corpse in question.

I found someone to manufacture an improved version for my friends. This new marker (one-snap assembly, biodegradable) had a pennant of intn'l-orange stamped w a large forest-green teardrop. Thus was born the logo of what today is wellknown among enviros as GREEN TEARDROP ENTERPRISES™ and which markers have long been adverted in the marketplace as

---

Roadkill Alerts
1oz. litter-free road-safe "Monuments"
Turn their sacrifice into a statement
(not just more-pounding into the pavement)

OR was first to legislate the alerts "litter-free" ɛ "road-safe". Then (you guessed it) wa vt ɛ new zealand. 15 states have yet to do so. By the time i met Lilith, believe it or not, some states had even legislated *against* them: my own state being one(!), followed by tx oh and, recently, fl —all anti-green trendsetters. The excuse? Someone could be hurt placing them! Lilith's reaction when i told her three states had outlawed them: "Why dont they instead discourage animal hit-'n'-runs? At the very least it's littering 'n' unsanitary. Every day we litter Motherearth with the corpses of her own children! ...Even tyrants bury their horrors."

42

Firsthing after establishing the ggNs legal address ɛ erecting a mailbox, i sent myself a card of hearty congratulations! I shall never forget walking back to the manor from the mailbox and, after enjoying my own congrats to myself, opening my second piece of ggNs mail.

> **Welcome, Neighbor!** [{How nice!} i thought.] As the voice and ethical backbone of this loving and peaceful community you have chosen to reside in, the **Council of Conservative Citizens** welcomes you. ¶Our membership is made up of both politically active and God-fearing Americans. {Ugh-o} Our platform is very popular in these parts, especially up here on Alpalachia Mountain. With one voice, CCC members demand, that our right to live in ethnically pure communities be returned to the American people, along with the freedom to hold and express ethnic views and opinions. We demand the return to the community of the right to judge, punish, reward, or otherwise evaluate, those citizens coming under its jurisdiction, and to return to the community its right to a justice system capable of convicting and punishing immoral persons and acts. ¶We believe in the legalization of sex by God-blessed marriage only, and in the delegalization and disfranchisement of the following: Offspring not sanctioned by God's Church (illegitimate children), homosexuals, bisexuals, transsexuals (and all sexuality not sanctioned by God himself), environmentalists, {O damn.} socially disruptive feminists, vegetarian activists {What?}, animal rights fanatics and other such

> immoral radicals. {Is this a joke?} [i examined the flyer looking for a "Gotcha, schockster!" note from the baron or glen. There was no such note] We believe in the outlawing of all things degenerate, or which arouse purient [sic] interest or desire. We want laws capable of punishing violent and/or sexual acts, and punishing all behaviors unsanctioned by God, his Holy Church, its worshippers [sic] and chosen representatives.
>
> **Once again, a warmest WELCOME! from your local CCC chapter.**
>
> (Questions about membership may be directed to Harlan S. McFlinty at 555-5555 or 555-5556)

This would not be my last word from ccc'ers (new pc cover for the kkk). <The black mamba in the mailbox, the puffadder under the welcome mat!> i mumbled as, sitting on a porch step of my new house i reread the flyer several times. Well, this beats all. Never had it struck me so forcibly & bluntly: <There are, there *must* be, thousands of white persons who automatically think of me as some amerind- 'n' nigger-lovin jew-abidin spic-lickin asian- animal- 'n' tree-huggin feminist-kissin progaylesbitrans free-sex-promoting ethnically 'n' behaviorally unboundaried whacko!> I found myself babbling like a fool. Imagine me stunned to discover that some of my neighbors thought of me like that; automatic living threat to their freedom to hate all people of color, to kill any green thing they chose and to terrorize women children or animals via some biblical or pulpit sanction. <How many of my neighbors does this crap represent?> That was my quandary in the months ahead ...tho in time i would find neighbors ready to befriend me *w*in the limits of our estranged lifestyles if not our beliefs. But to those many "divine rightists" i was not a free citizen but an "evil" threat. Welcome? Did i feel welcome? Godzilla's gonads! I was stunned & thoroly disgusted, truth be told. Had i not just signed on the dotted line, had i not fought for & won free & open in-perpetuity rights for the sanctuary and all its creatures & things, had i not fallen in love *w* the place on sight, i would have clearedout of beautiful bamalachia then&there and never looked back.

43

Sorry about the brutal honesty (again). But why do i keep apologizing? More to the matter. Why on Earth should honesty *ever* be considered brutal? The child, who as yet sees no reason to recount Reality other than exactly as sHe sees it, can be brutally honest. Sometimes this honesty can be thoroly enjoyed. But often it is cause for embarrassment. And if that embarrassment is too great for those around him, the "offender" may be punished. Tho we dont stop to analyze it, we often punish so that we may go on believing in a rule or expectation of society that was momentarily exposed for what it *really* is —hypocritical or double-standardizing ...usually at the very least.

As to *absolute* honesty. If we civil were even close to it, court judges would hear from people every day, "How can you sit there in that ridiculous garment, on top of that ridiculous throne, and demand *anything* from me with a straight face?" For the civilized adult who, in fact, tells "the truth, the whole truth and nothing but the truth" will soon find himself forced to choose between absolute honesty and our *civil version* of honesty. Only the words "So help me God" are as often abused as our swearing to "tell the truth and nothing but". The question begged here is, Why is it that civil society, after thousands of years of *claiming* to aspire to tell "the whole truth", never gets there? And moreover, why dont we ever wonder about that?

The rhetoric is obvious. Civil society has long been content *never* to get there if at all possible. For the search for truth by necessity always refers us back to Nature —in that Nature possesses the only apodictic benchmarks. Yet Nature is the *last* place from which civil idealism wants to get its guidance. And so, civil society has gone to near-exhaustive lengths to 'prove' why truth can never be had. I say near-exhaustive because there is one area, a most obvious area, that always goes uninvestigated by the detractors of Truth and its possibility. That area is the investigation of *the cause of civilization itself.* Why should this question *always* be avoided, occulted even, like some plague or stigma?

My rhetoric this time notwithstanding ...But how did we get here? Ah, yes. The paranoia & hatred i found in my mailbox that day. Well, we're here now. I'll make this quick.... In my book *the civilizing principle: a misconception of apocalyptic dimensions,* and to some degree in the two books which followed it (*die, primitive! anthropology & imperialism* and *Mothernature & the world matron*) i layout the proposition that civilization is, and was originally, constructed on a false premise —or more accurately, on an incompletely informed principle —or more accurately still, evolved out of a fear-based intuition that is provably mistaken. That intuition, jammed into a nutshell (as everything in this book must be), goes like this. "Nature is humanity's most dangerous predator/enemy. One should never trust it for one can never tell when Nature will turn on him, do him or others great harm, or even kill him or those dear to him. For Nature is man's most ruthless predator. Forget this and risk death or destruction." Have several thousand years of scientific discovery helped dispel this fear-based prejudice? In academic isolation, yes. But in everyday life, very little.

Good bad evil sin. Four things that cant be found in the physical World anywhere yet figure into every niche of our lives! For these are not empirical but philoreligious terms; terms which, being irreproducible in physical reality, always cloud &/or confuse all ethical/moral questions. For ethics & morality need ask only one question ever: Is the behavior or act under investigation constructive, destructive, or neuter, in quality? Period. Want just the facts? Then keep the elements of inquiry empirical. Like time, good bad evil & sin are mental constructs unlocatable in the physical World... anywhere! Without them it's all very simple. Treat others as you would like to be treated. Of course, the paranoid, the depressed, the celibate, the manic, the martyrs & other masochists, as well as those in pain, cannot be trusted to interpret Nature's golden rule in a healthy (universally constructive) fashion. The history of civilization is antithetic to Nature/instinct's best altruism: "Imagine all life as yourself." But only the precivil make this a way of life. It has become all but second-nature for we civil to first *sus*pect not *re*spect. When most of us are waiting for the *other* person or belief to prove they deserve our respect, how dare we be surprised to find conflict everywhere.

For we have been carefully trained for centuries to blame everything we dont like or dont understand on Nature. The imperialist religions have even gone so far as to try to convince us that there is such a thing as "evil" and that Nature itself is "evil". Even overlooking such blatant insults as stripping the Planet of trees and acting surprised when flooding & mudslides result; or polluting the Globe and blaming the deadly results on Nature. We'll just call that the big stuff and leave it be. More instructive would be to turn our attention to those things we observe every day yet somehow never question. To wit: Even at this late date in our civilizing one cant watch a halfhour of tv w/out being repeatedly banged between the eyes w/ how "Nature has screwedup (again!)". Or, to make the old civil propaganda look updated: "How mean old Mothernature has impacted humanity negatively. Again!". Even a medium as harmless-seeming as weather reports is an information mode which depends for its very existence on our conviction that, "If Mothernature can screwup an event she probably will". The "cruelty" and "failures" of Nature in fact drive major sectors of world economics. Just study the tv ads you see if you doubt this. "Did Mothernature shortchange you on looks skin hair lips breasts hips eyes heart bowels buttox penis weight sweating body-hair menstruation incontinence fertility libido mental health your ability to see to hear to breathe to sleep get an erection relax seek intimacy cope perform get around enjoy life be warm safe comfortable etc etc etc *ad* [!] *infinitum*?

And i do mean *study* the adverts. For few have any idea how hard it is to get past our civil biases to any fair state of objectivity.

The source of this self-perpetuating shoppinglist of reasons why we should all entertain an unrelenting grudge against Mothernature i have elsewhere described as *the civilizing principle*. This principle views Nature & instinct as irrational & uncaring forces. It obtains its error notsomuch from being mostly mistaken as from being astonishingly incomplete. In two words, *irrationally* incomplete. For, like the fish which is last to notice the water in which it lives, civil humankind fails to see –and all our civil rules and expectations conspire to shamelessly hide– the all-but-infinite number of ways in which Nature, despite every last one of its possible harms, is still the best, and most intimate, friend & protector, nurturer & provider, which not only humankind but life itself has ever had or ever *will* have!

And so, far from understanding Nature as it exists and operates *in fact*, humanity, at the "dawn" of civilization (not nearly the dawn of humanity, please note), began daring to challenge, and then to try to escape from, "cruel" Nature. At the same time, realizing that the laws which governed his own body were as intractable as the laws of Nature "outside" his body, the process of our civilizing also incl'd the attempt to escape our *internal* Natures. That is, in our ancestors' campaign to control (fortify themselves against) unpredictable & uncontrollable Nature, they also embarked upon the earliest stages of controlling (fortifying themselves against) those things in their own *personal* Natures they felt were unpredictable & uncontrollable. Namely, instinct. (Our subconscious or socalled right-brain.) And so, in the evolution of our civilizing two things are happening simultaneously. ❶ Fortification against Nature *external* to us (epitomized by city-building) and ❷ fortifying against Nature *internal* to us (instinct), as mainly manifested in ideology-fortification ...which, simplistically, amounts to little more than building a mental justification for why we believe Nature is the enemy (say nothing of the endless laws & expectations needed to enforce those ideals because few of them come Naturally). Enter imperialist religion ...which will proceed to win *civil* power by 'upgrading' the civilizing principle from 'Nature is our enemy' to 'Nature and instinct are evil'. For the sake of clarity, i combine these simultaneous mechanisms of our civilizing (❶ & ❷) into a single biparte noun: Nature/instinct. For i contend that humankind –civil humanity, that is– in our compound failure to understand the true nature of

Nature, are taught daily, hourly, to fear equally both Nature within us *and* Nature external to us. For it's also true that *by nature* we fear all things that can do us harm yet which we cannot predict or control.

Any religion which works in sympathy with the civilizing principle qualifies as a civil/imperialist religion. My civilizing principle, in supercondensed form, reads: Nature/instinct is humanity's most dangerous predator/enemy. Civil religion then comes along & extrapolates this principle past the merely incomplete & mistaken into the entirely irrational. For after coopting a worldview of the paranoid insane called "evil" (see otto reich), it proceeds to frame both Nature & instinct as "evil" things —fundamentally "evil" things. What has all this to do with imperialism? If one accepts the premise, Nature is *everywhere* and instinct is *everywhere* there is life, we can see that both civilization & civil religion are compelled by default to propagate themselves to gain control over these everywheres. For both not only feel compelled to conquer Nature/instinct (the one, to outwit a 'superpredator'; the other, to outwit "evil"), but civil religion, in addition, feels compelled (also by default) to eradicate all *other* deities —eg, "Thou shalt have no *other* gods..." etc. Since all human cultures have deities (gods) of some sort, and since humans fairly populate Earth, civil religion feels compelled to propagate itself everywhere (on Earth). Therefor both civilization *and* civil religion are not only imperialist, but having 'everywhere' as their target for conquest, makes them *absolutely* imperialist!

To round out. Civil religion is the most destructive institution to come along since civilization itself, for the m.o of both are fascistic: the subjugation of the masses by an elite minority. The one (the religious minority) we call clergy; the other (the civil minority), are the politicians: same agenda (pandemic control), different masks ...even as their m.o is exactly the same: to transform the individual into a groupoid, the monozen into a plurizen. For you see, the spin doctors of *both* forms of propaganda are out to perform the same operation on the mind of every living thing: deep psychic surgery for the removal of our internal (Natural) compasses, a compass some call conscience; some, morality; some, individualism; some, willpower ...an operation intended to replace the moral compass Nature gave us with a civilized/domesticated zombie gene, the installation of a do-only-as-instructed mind-modem, an antlike guidance system (dogma, law, conformist expectation) which is okay when it's good (if youre braindead) but purest horror when it's not ...which is usually.

A barely masked version of this horror arrived in my mailbox that day. That flyer *still* has me mumbling i see...... And so, in their crusade to escape Nature/instinct, the humans who evolved civil religion proceeded to erect evermore "sophisticated" walls; walls both physical & psychologic; walls which, over time, have isolated just about every area of our *conscious* lives; walls which, tho we still do not comprehend it, have failed not only to put Nature in that cage civilization wants "her" in, but which walls, being so recklessly conceived, have endedup putting us, civil mankind, in a cage of our own making!

And the backlash of this our 'escape' from Nature? It goes almost wout saying: an occulted loathing (deeply buried & unacknowledged fear) for those things which we feel could hurl us back to square1. Namely, back to anything primitive. Or that we *deem* primitive. And the cost of some 300 generations of such escape & denial? Today we, we civil beings, instead of knowing "nothing but the truth, so help us, God" are now able to locate around us almost nothing but UNtruth! Rousseau hart crane & oscar hammerstein were hardly first to notice, "Civilization is on the lurch". And it is shakespeare who put the linguistic onus of that "lurch" most famously. "Words are grown so false I am loth to prove reason with them."

And just in case my dear reader may think i'm picking on rural folk and their chosen forms of worship, sHe would do well to mark this next. My civilizing principle also explains why, to this min, we civilized equate frankness (honesty) w provinciality. The "country bumkin" stereotype is ranked not alot differently than the slow-witted person. We even have the gall to call such honest persons "simple" folk, as if they are mentally retarded and dont know any better than to be provincial (countrified). We prefer this to admitting, rural folk are simply [sic] waymore honest than we —at least in the social graces. Meanwhile the very *definitions* of provincial & urbane prove my point. For both are based on the assumption that if cities are the repository of civilization (of persons clever enuf to "outwit Nature/-instinct") then the countryside must be the back door to primitivism: people too unclever, too provincial to become citified, or urbane (code: civilized). And for the same reasons amplified, we civil persons equate *absolute* (or "brutal") honesty with "children and other savages". That is, honesty at all times and in all things, wout consciously realizing it, we equate w primitive (pre-civil) behavior. In fact, the only time we can abide absolute honesty is in our own young. And even then, when "brutally" honest, they had better be *very* young or be prepared to suffer the consequences. Primitives, and the mentally retarded (those other "savages"), have long suffered such consequences at the hands of (and at the very old fears of) we "high-minded" civilized, both in our secular & religious versions.

Urbanity, not accidentally, accounts for the snobbishness historically of enviro groups —which, afterall, grew mostly from within Nature-deprived (rural longing) urban areas.

Take any Wild creature, put it in a cage and it will suffer. Civilization is such a cage. Thus the reason for our suffering (and the stress/-anger which results from it) should be self-evident.

To close this spontaneous rant on a personal note. My civilizing principle also explains why many of the things i've been writing & saying for much of my career have been variously accused of being simplistic & unsophisticated (primitive, childish) when they are in fact guilty of little more than attempting probity ɛ the search for Truth with a straight face ɛ a clear conscience. I expect it to be no different w this book. Then again, may i take that back? Being, herein, more intimate than i've ever been before, i expect things will be quite a bit different from now on. For to be brutally honest with *impersonal* issues is one thing. But to be brutally honest with *one's own reputation* is to risk (code: beg for) speedy martyrdom. That i am Earth's most reluctant martyr i expect will matter not a whit to my (civilized) martyrers, both secular ɛ religious.

44

What has the seven-veil dance of civilization's version of honesty to do w our story? A dreadful lot, as it turns out. Lurking in the shadows of my books for years one spots, repeatedly, the question, Why should something so antiNature as civilization come into existence in the first place? During my years w gE, for all those days&nites of gazing landward from a "rimless" Wilderness of sea ɛ sky, from all those times of internalizing that genetically jarring aberration: a whole city suddenly toweringup out of the sea like some geometric monster... the question of 'why civilization' gained more&more of a grip on my imagination. The first book to emerge from this fearsome curiosity was *the civilizing principle,* published in '84. Next, as i've said, came *die, primitive!,* written w denise norris (anthropologist) ɛ lindsey margault (paleobiologist). This latter book was finished, ɛ published, the same year i found, ɛ purchased, ggNs (aka the sanctuary).

This period is however marred by litigation: the baron ɛ me v. bluecomet films. *The castration of priapus,* the movie, was released in time for xmas that year and wrangout a fair success —tho, out of political fear, bluecomet wimped the baron's most powerful scene. Incidentally, when mother read about the movie-rights sale, desperately wanting a role for herself, she dropped into her sweet-little-girl personality, found me by fone. Trained by her mother to believe such was an acceptable form of apology among adults, i had always to force myself to interdict. <Baby-talk is not an apology, Mother. It's a decoy.> Then again, a min or two later. <Sweet-talk is not an acceptable form of apology, Mother. One must apologize for being nasty. That's what adults do who care.> And then again, a third time, in the middle of which she yelled "You are a cruel man, naton schock! Cruel cruel cruel!" and slammed down the fone. You'd think, being a cinema fanatic, she'd have known i had very little say in the movie version of my book, muchless in the casting itself, the very domain for which (shhh, dont tell) most mogul$ are in the business!

From '84 to '87 i served as editor of *the greenEarth chronicles*, published in '87. Also in '87 an essay, *heavenly sex: the sexuality of the physical universe* w v.rubins (astronomer), d.norris ε l.margault, came out in *natural alternatives*. In early '88 i was again nominated for the green pen award. Once the highest recognition one could receive for work in deep ecology, by then the purse had been tainted by rightwing ε corporate greenwashing. (It has since become the very badge of palegreen writers ε other ecowimps.)

Before i roundout part 2 –by sharing a sampling of what is perhaps the most absurd part of my life (and the privatest too)– i need mention something. First w the passing of the austrian wizard, otto reich, the philosopher, philip wylie, and the Natural philosopher oren liseley after him, i felt as tho i were, intellectually speaking, being cut adrift in a hostile sea. For these men ranked high among that handful of persons i felt were capable of transcending betimes the anthropic blindness from which humanity widely suffers. Perhaps this is why, in 1988 –moving from my *civilizing principle* on into *Mothernature & the world matron*– my ears were aching for a sane voice to worm thru the interminable deluge of throwaway data. As i remember it, the first ever i knew of alice krawel grew directly from an interview on public radio. With several books behind her –the most famous, *my soul is lavender*– the occasion was the publication of her newest, *the woman of lascaux is our sister*. With an eye to timesaving, the best route to displaying alice in my quicksilver lookingglass is to share what i heard in that interview.

Alice: ...That's why justice is so hard to come by; and why it so often looks like a parody on justice when we apply it ...Because, at root, justice and civilization are incompatible... No, I take that back... They are antagonistic.

Interviewer: Let me get this straight. Youre saying, justice 'n' civilization are polar opposites?

A: Yes.

I: Why?

A: Because nature and civilization are polar opposites.

me: Wow! Who is this woman?

I: Explain, please.

A. Nature contains the soul of truth. Justice should be the application of that truth. With nothing coming between, including civilization. Especially civilization.

I: Why, especially civilization?

The moment we believe Nature makes mistakes (code: that humans know a better way) we lose the thread to Truth in the labyrinth of life. It should therefor be obvious why those who accept animals (and primitives) just as they are, are also typically truth-seekers. For we sense, they still have a hold on that thread.

Me: Duh.

A: Because civilization is against nature at its roots, and so it is *anti-truth* and *anti-justice* by fiat.

me: Goodgrief, i love this woman!

I: How is that?

A. [i expected alice to sigh w exasperation] Because if you are against... No, let me rephrase this. Because if you are not absolutely pro nature you are against truth (and justice) by fiat.

I: So youre saying, nature has some kind of a monopoly on truth?

A: Yes. Truth is nature/nature is truth. But truth is so rare in civilized society, in fact, truth is so adamantly denied us, that one of the most cliche and embarrassing things a person can do is admit to being a searcher for truth. Yes. We are very distant indeed from comprehending truth and justice.

ME: As removed, in fact, as civilization is from Nature.

I hadnt even met the woman and i felt i knew her. But this next is what tipped the scales, for it had to do w an idea i was sure few mature woman in civilized society would agree w. To save time i will gather Alice's thoughts in a compound summary.

"Rather than belittle marriage (because it is right for a select few) I would much rather do my part in working toward a society which did not hold options other than marriage in contempt. [For instance?] Well, to begin with. What a pity we humans don't come together out of desire, pure and simple, instead of by law, by promise, by duty, by threat or conviction; or for so many other reasons —many of them destructive and hurtful... And why do we try to force-fit the men in our communities into roles which are plainly unnatural for them? In this sense, religious belief and traditional expectation are cruel. How much pain, how much misery, it causes... causes *everyone* concerned! Looked at collectively, such practices are nothing short of a human tragedy...."

I am drawn to the slow assurance w which she speaks. Silence in conversation does not make her uncomfortable. She views these quiet moments as breeding places for higher communion. I would not come across this quality again in a woman until Lilith —and almost as rarely in men. I was ready to fly to bali, or shanghai, to meet her. And where was she? In sanfrancisco. Almost right under my nose whenever i was there. I was quick to interview her. In fact, i can credit alice w being the inspiration, if not the germ, of *Mothernature & the world matron*, my first book written at the sanctuary.

"How much better to flow with our natures than to obstruct, or try to bury, them. Look at the condition of relationships in the world generally. The laws, religious and state, have clearly failed us... Jails, punishment. They're awful, but nothing compared to how *unhappy* people generally are. Look at the big picture. The unhappiness factor. Why is joy –simple, bubbly, overflowing joy– so rare! Such joy is farmore common in primitive cultures than in our own. As I see it, the distance we have come *away* from nature causes this. [here i suggest the distance which civilization has, *on purpose*, put between Nature and itself] Yes. And this distance is no different than civilization's distance from Truth... and therefore from all hope of our ever being able to harness justice... real, satisfying 'n' peace-propagating justice."

Need i say, over the years alice ε me have become fast friends.

45

Late in '88 i rcv'd an invite to a post-ceremony party in nyc —modeling's version of hollywd's oscars. Not knowing personally any "johnny lancas invites you", and on record for dissing such events as <full-immersion therapy for the shallow>, i was a little stunned to find myself present in my best-duds being intro'd all around by one ms deb(ra) danzi. Blond, graygreen-eyed, tall on film, deb was "all-the-rage" at this shophop on 5th av, where the rooms of a large towersuite were crowded w some of the biggest names in modeling –and w the page-flip-familiar faces of major slick misses ε lesser zine queens– and which walls were hung w their shutter-stuttering facsimiles.

And why was ms danzi the star? Because a whole couchpotato nation couldnt get enuf of her translucent ε willowy beauty, mostly thanx to her part in an all-the-rage primetime sitcom. Every pro model's dream is to successfully cross into a career in film or tv, and deb had done it. Notice i didnt say become an actor. For even models themselves dont expect *that* much. Speaking of not expecting. Tho i didnt know it, the in-demand ms danzi, who'd attached a handwritten "fan" note to my invite, was officially dumping hubby that eve and the elected dumping device was this little blondezvous of ours.

Deb is the daughter of flash-in-the-pan feminist of the '70s, vivian vanderlear, least virtual of the vassar virgins. (Names changed to protect the guilty.) Deb fulfilled her mother's worst nitemare by becoming a model. Fresh out of modeling school, at 16 she married one ray zane, a move construed by her peers as one big connubial connive for the top —for zane owned, w several partners, fleshfarms in the u.s europe brazil ε whoknowswhere else. [Fleshfarms is continental parlance for modeling schools. —Ed.] Zane flaunted a harem of houris wherever he went. "Hey, this is my job!" he would tell debra. "You know that." To others he'd say, "Eatcher heart out!" Most did.

Fame breathed life into pinnochiette. Moneymen tugged her wires from smoke-filled heights, displayed her from boardrm to billboard; clicking cameras incited that perfect smile, the freezeframe laff that stops traffic. She posed, pouted ε pranced, this petite ramp-strutting priscilla i'd found (well, who'd found me), danzied her way into the hearts ε hardons of america; while shuttermen ε -women, w the dreary drone of golf announcers, talkedup that salacious squint, that "Purrrfect!" smartass sneer ...as blowers stir up groundswells of shining hair ε gauzy umbrellaed lites glaze w treacherous (ε totally *poseuse*) *haute* those famed graygreens of hers!

Deb is synced in memory w the writing of *Mothernature & the world matron*. Deb was several ethical cuts above the last model i'd dated in the '70s, before it became cliche to say, "There's more to me than just looks, you know!" But glitzy ε counterfeit fame, when it's the only thing that brings you to life, torments ε destroys. Not just mentally abused by zane, deb had just hunteddown her genetic dad in hopes he would turnout to be the old italian cobbler who'd brought the doll to life, hoping he would say abracadEbra and, poof, make the pernicious insecurity that was knocking this doll to bits go away. But he proved no fairytale cobbler. And so it was, deb decided she needed a guy of "real quality". But there was much inner shaping to be done and i'd never carved a human in my life.

We came together rather like two alien suns, forced on each other by tides of dark matter thru space, locked together in an erratic ellipse, sometimes close ɛ hot, mostly distant ɛ brooding. Both of us dated others and there were no agreements except for proof of disease-freeness before intimacy. Buried under toomuch junk, deb's innate sweetness proved not enuf for me. Had it been a movie and i an onlooker, i'd have seen this at once. Friends were amazed. The baron was aghast, called her "Your worst debauch to date, emphasis on the deb". Glendon found that a bit harsh: "My groin understands if that's any consolation."

Every time she tried to move on, zane moved to derail her career. This failed, but his efforts took their toll. As rejection of any sort played havoc w deb's selfimage, she turned to cocaine. (Most readers will not know this part of the story.) Yet she somehow stayed insanely beautiful thru her trials. Because that core sweetness (her primitive person) had been wounded so badly somewhere along the way (it feared to come out ɛ play), a laniard of lust was the best tie we could devise thruout our on&off affair. For, thanx to her mom's sorry nurturing ɛ her stepfather's exotic spankings, ɛ who knows what else, deb owned a predilection she could not ditch. And because it was not a simple case of black&blue ɛ loving it, and because she knew what a turnoff brutality was to me, i was awhile garnering the pieces to her puzzle. Beside, we only saw each other when i was in nyc, or when she came to me to escape that glittering chaos which seduces so many. ("I've got a couple days free. You busy?").

Deb's urge for rough sex, tho not my bailiwick, was doable if i'd not been w anyone in awhile —tho, except for you know what, my version more resembled rambunctious. I wasnt wary earlyon when she turnedup w a bruise or two ("I'm always banging into things"). But when, later, she hinted i show up in the city one day unannounced and, dressed in black ɛ masked, abduct her from work, or the parking garage at her apt, take her someplace, force her to "have sex...even bring along a clean-bill-o'-health friend or two if you like", i began to see in deb the fate of a maureen or caroline guinness ...or worse. "You understand it's no good if I *know* it's you, right?" ...a rather startling fantasy for a person of such impeccable hygiene. Yet, in defense of all this wouldbe debauchery i say: fantasies voiced during erotic moments do not necessarily rep doable reallife.

Toward the end our affair got to be, for me, more rash than rush, more heartburn than heartache. And it was definitely over when she returned to zane for the third time only to get beat again. (It's amazing what weals&welts a good body w fabulous skin can heal in a couple weeks, and that a little makeup can hide in a couple mins.) Yet the more i tried to end it the more she clung. When she showedup at ggNs one day snorting like a snowblower ("Take me back, nathan. I cant make it without you. You *know* that!"), i turned to her halfsister, bekky kydd (some may remember the name), asked her to <Help me end it, please, before it gets any uglier>. Anyway, i'd grown more than a little weary of romancing the stoned sotosay. Tho bekky helped, the rift it caused between them has *still* to heal i gather.

The coda (the last of several false endings). Deb's career peaked after a few years of playing amanda somebody on a second all-the-rage sitcom. Someone tattled to the tabs about her justinesque encounters —probably her now infamous mismatch w an old heroin-*muselmánner*ed rock star known for his degenerate lifestyle. When they'd reached a mexican standoff –he would say nothing of her problem if she would say nothing of his– deb blamed me ε bekky for blabbing to the press. When it was clear the dryout programs werent helping, i suggested the teacher who'd taught me meditation, whom i soubriqueted, shri blisswizard. When this too failed (seems her reservoir of discipline was usedup just getting to work and to the gym) she reappealed to me. "Please come see me, nathan. *You* are my blisswizard" etc. It's thanx to her nickname for me spreading like fanned fire thru the modeling empire that the blisswizards ε blissgurus of film-fame were born —so that today every schmo w a tung ε three fingers thinks himself a blissmaster of some enviable belt.

Incidentally, it's deb who gave me a javelin. Fanciest car i ever owned, or ever will. In its factory form, the xke was a finicky asphalt spinet w a dozen cylinders demanding bimonthly tuneups! I got the thing for a song (well, maybe a *danzi* too) on the way out of our affair —kind of like a tryst-ring one doesnt give back. Deb blew up the engine one midnite on a mojave highway after the last thrashing from zane: whitehot block, pistonrod clean-thru the side! "Yeah. I think it *was* [all the way to the floor]. I was trying to reach escape velocity." (Why does such flip self-destruct resignation fascinate us?) Too costly to fix, she parked it. And there *i* was, wanting an xke since i was this kid, see....

Son of jaguar, it dared to challenge in the asphalt jungles its toothier-grilled heavier-haunched higher-crouched sire. Esthetically speaking (like lowey's gg1 among trains, his farmall among tractors), back then the xke's contours were more than half a century ahead of their time, the first true aerodyne among production cars! But i was just this kid, see, and could only beg for a copy of the glossy sales brochure, a stack of which lay on a glass table in a classy showrm in midtown manhattan. A salesman let me sit in one. {To actually drive this some day! Jumpin javelinjizm!} When i criticize civilization, reader, dont think i dont understand how workedup a body can get over its toys—specially when one is young ε blindsided by all the glittery propaganda. Me, malthusan? I wept when i finally saw the gg bridge little less than when i first saw the mississippi. There is *some* tech that is high.

Shawn Nolte

Most news of deb came from bekky after that. A sick paparazzo shadowed her til he got some pricey pics: puffy lips razed knees ε an er report of multiple bruises ε a broken wrist. Still today it is widely agreed, she had "the best flesh in the business". Was that it, deb? Worship of your "afghan girl" silvergreens,* your pay-to-publish skin? Would-be ballerina, black-masked, posing near a parapet of alabaster; charming wout/cheerless win; magitrix of transformation, princess of protean surprises! Wish there were more time, deb. This (dys)asterisk footnote is inadequate for you i know —a story by yourself. Maybe one day bekky will write it. No hard feelings i hope? And by the way. We never ratted. But you knew that. *[NS refers here to the eyes of one Sharbat Gula, a tribal region Afghan girl in a *National Geographic* photo (1985) of whom he wrote in his *Die, primitive!* manuscript that same year: "In a saner world that face, those primally pristine eyes, would be better known than Mona Lisa's."]

Meanwhile, over the years, *castration* (book ε movie) became a cult classic among greens, finding an afterlife in video that has longsince outdistanced its success on stage ε bigscreen. This doesnt mean it was my best work, of course; tho it *was* my angriest —and therefore one of the baron's favorites. My best are *the civilizing principle* and *Mothernature & the world matron*. (And mostofall, *the cosmic Gaia* ...the book i'd be wrappingup at this moment were it not for this more urgent calling.) But my favorites did not sell like *scapegoats* and *castration* sold. Then again public taste rarely underwrites what i like best, strongly resists my (uncivilized) truth.

As the danzi affair began deteriorating (which was almost as soon as it began) i began dating others. This complicated period drew to a close w nikki mckinney. (*Outa da fryin pan 'n' into da fire* as billy holiday put it.) Readers, my lecture circuit audience, friends ε acquaintances, were usually responsible for the matchmaking i enjoyed. To protect the privacy of those few who want it, when multiple names are given (below) only one is guaranteed accurate. I am careful also to differentiate between students of my work ε fans; actors ε stars; authors ε writers; even writers ε journalists, etc. The reader will understand if, in the telling, i dashoff my past like ~~an author~~ a writer in a rush to receive his advance. And if it comes off like a rake's progress report, it is, in fact, less that than <...A fool's pursuit of that illusory flesh-candy/once known as houghmagandy./And, if nothing else, i have learned:/The faustian predilection (where sex is concerned)/is vibrant ε kicking in the healthy erection>. And, o yes, imt is shorthand for 'introduced me to'. (The insightful reader by now senses in my prose when my activities are being heavily monitored.)

Doug burrows, fan (of mine) and conceptualizer of the chunnel, imt grandniece bunnie hopkins, pursuing a degree in reproductive pathology when we dated; ibraham masoud, economist, imt granddaughter golda myner; muchomacho (violence&sex) filmstar rolando orlando landoro imt kidsister lazita loquita, model ε wouldbe filmstar; pietor potapoff, a reader (of mine) ε lead dancer w the ballet russes, imt the lovely katrina kloack (nee latrinella) (who turned out to be more than just "faintly hermaphroditic"), and later to anna haakana, poetess (far more to my taste); the intn'lly pop mariachi bandleader ε trumpeter jose ozinga imt his niece lygia maria garcia; bjold stepmann, fan ε astronaut, imt starla astrella, space academy undergrad; hubert humberstone, arctic explorer, imt stepdaughter laletta lyons; don wi now (swivel-hipped polynesian fashion designer) imt holly la fala ε delilah deloin, hardly divisible models; pummel pugh, dutch olympic boxer imt kendra kussrath, granddaughter of *the tinseltown tattler* kussraths; sheldon holme (security systems magnate) imt estella ezterhazy, grandniece of d.a.r grandmadam, waverly flagg, and who proved a classic cherubitch; reader thanom kittikatchorn, thai architect, imt delia dahlhaus, majoring in architectural engineering when we dated but who gave it up to become dear thanom's wife & mother to a litter of kittikatchorns; wong font, publisher & amnesty intn'l activist, imt to the beautiful dutiful rosa proselyte; the humble don quatsee, philosopher & inventor of the wind-powered turbine, imt faustine toboso; fergus zanspantz, fashion designer & friend of bekky kydd, imt models carrie cuddleback, benita bodigoi, rhonda fondillier, vivian vigouroux & sheila shebad (of the spangled talons & clang-dangling earrings), but not incl'g two drum majorettes from excelsior nj, which *he* endedup fooling around w, not me. Thanx, fergus —i think.

And such the dicing of blind fate
few matching halves here meet and mate.

While my past is not *dives puellis* in the true taurian sense, among the daughter's of atlas socalled are numbered other names —which come wheeling out of the past even as i try to put the brakes on all this feminiscing. (Dr slime just left —spent the last halfhour w guards zodion & xodion in a cell across the way, often glancing my way my peripherals say. Something is up.) The first is way out of sequence: one gilda bellagamba (marylou rossi) w whose legs & face mostly i was in young lust. Next there is figureskater marguerite fleming, whom i fell for not just because of her good heart, grace & beauty but because of her resemblance to that unattainable passion of my youth, primaballerina suzanne farrell. And then there were those rare women like gloria steinhem jane fonda & rosanna arquette (bekky kyddlike fiter of hollywd misogyny), none of whom i had the good fortune to meet. On the lighter side, there's delphine devi, my eastindian maiden ...'made in' anglosaxony (more of deldevi later)... and sam (samantha) spinnenweber, jungian psychoanalyst & dropdead poledancer afterhours. And, of course, elena chekeb, pairs figureskater of the priscilla-perfect legs & positively magnetic panties-packaged pelvic purlieus, not to forget doe-eyed jane phelps, novelist, whom i dated concurrently w nikki mckinney and maybe should have gone and cohabituated [sic]... well, maybe not. For finding Lilith would have interrupted that too. As to the nikki person, we shall elaborate only as absolutely necessary.

Lilith

Recalling all the females i have fancied
—collapsing in exhaustion partway thru—
not one has even halfSoMuch entranced me,
and none, not one, draws near the likes of you.

So sharpen your quills modern willies, consider yourselves forewarned. 'Cause here comes the new Juliet, and not without will's *dräng und stürm* !

46

Public notice: Whereas the scholar abélard was castrated for love of his pupil héloïse; whereas even immaculate frances had his clare ε christ his magda; whereas disgusting augustus had his livia and fussy fitzgerald, his zelda; whereas mean old milton's paradise was *really* lost when thoroly modern mary powell fled the bridal chamber; and whereas old q had his teresina and pushkin dueled ε died for a five-years sheTeen——

whereas dickens had his mary, ee, his kitty's, ε stanny, his evvy's; whereas courbet had his daisychain of entwined young sleepers and renoir, his houseful of rubenesque bathers; whereas claudius had his valeria, casablancas (and a thousand other starmakers) had their stephanies ε shrimptons; whereas klimt had his moa, plus that noble-but-doomed neuzil nymph——

whereas de sade debauched his détenues at an age when captain archer was notching his flossie and louis, his eleanor; whereas ferdinand had his miranda and old faust, his gretchen; whereas liederlich had his margarets and 'the lover', his idochine marguerite; whereas andersen had his little nymphs *de la mer* and harry bumpas, the victims of his randy toasts; whereas puccini had his ciocio *sans* kimono and mozart (and a wealth of wizened wolfs) enjoyed their *una donnas a quindici anni* in lieu of a woodsful of red ridinghoods——

whereas odysseus had his nausicaä, telemachus, his polly; whereas athenian men chose but two-years-teen wives and thus even gay isomachus took a token bride; whereas chaucer had his virginia and the hermit, his alibech; whereas pepys had his deb, and willyS, not just juliet but julietta too; and whereas even the darlings laurence b ε frédérique were too mature for bashful balthus' petite palette——

whereas poe had his virginia, polanski, his EXILita, gauguin, his tehura and jerrylee (like a troop of other superstars), his myra; whereas casanova tracked the morphing of his marieloise and the blackHero, whole villages of virgins; whereas nero had his octavia and schiel, his viennese urchins ...plus the neulengbach nymphs, never fear; and whereas novalis had his sophie and jefferson, his dusky sally——

whereas (as into "a whiter shade of pale" we drift) moliere had his agnes and the earl of richmond, his margaret, and the enchanter his orphan and lenormand, his lolitas; and whereas gortyaan guys in their 30s ε 40s regularly played the groom to mere epiteen brides——

whereas (sinking low thru that pale) cragged king david bagged little abishag, and david otlingham snagged a whole gallery of epigynees; whereas vladikov agonized for just one "emmi" of sad victor x's various many, and whereas don daniel clearly machiavellied leticia worse than dumbert svengalied dolita——

whereas (immersed past that pale) a certain miss world was royally dysenjoyed a full decade before her official crowning; whereas wilhemina harris was pregnant at teen minus three; and whereas the self-abuse of that recluse from vaucluse was no less obtuse than those dozens of school physicals given by a certain gulfcoast md——

whereas (that pale gone pathologic) ruskin had his rose ε reverend carroll had his tacitly pampered epigynolepsis for gutter alices (or *arrēphoroi* in peplosian *déshabiller*, as *he* dreamed them); whereas louÿs had his *rou*-nymphs and his bilitis, and she in turn, her own nymphitis; and whereas ezekiel enjoyed the sisters oholah ε oholibah while his grandad, ol moses, kidnaped 32,000 virgins via beliefs so absolutely brutal it would make the black prince blush with 'inadequacy'.... But i desist. For there are appetites which even the passionate historian hesitates to entertain wout textual imperative.

And so, in place of the scurrilous scraps remaining in this steadily degenerating countdown, permit a final exhibit: WHEREAS this mere smattering of examples insists, it is bonobos (not chimps) which carry our socio-sexual genes—— therefor this Notice. Humankind's sexual history makes my little lovelife look as licit as dandruff, as boring as dumplings. So project your inglorious cache of repressions, dear "modern" society, toward what, ε whom, *caused* them, and not at me. I infer the (lethally repressive) rules ε expectations of that artificial reality we call civilization. *That's* where the cause of my politically-driven scapegoating is hid, dear juror. Not w me. Or w my friends or loved ones ...no matter what the fed. ε its spoonfed press may collude to the contrary.

47

As to that other woman in my life. I kept minimal contact w mother. As to her lifestyle. Her l.a home became the place where all the atrophying wannabees & gonnabees of orange county went to swill alcohol & gobble club sandwiches; so that in just two-plus decades —her income gobbled & its principle swilled— mother became all but a pauper. Earlyon in the process, curious as to where my inheritance was going, i attended a couple of her soirees: "I was on my way to the top ...was really *there*, you know?... when, bamm...." (Uninsurable act of God intervenes.) So goes the standard line of the highroller.

Mother never figuredon, i know, the tuff competition she was in for in l.a. I'm talking about the glittering menagerie of badly aging *real* starlets (w rosters of *actual* films to their credit) who populate the region into which she moved w her *makebelieve* film successes. I re that 40plus set of non-actors vying w one another to regrasp some glimmer of past glamor. As w aging models, starlet glory is guaranteed to fade. Yet this sad procession of salonistas persists, generation after generation, in fantasizing itself as still sleek & alluring as it parties before only rose-colored mirrors. I speak of drawingrms filled w dilettante dowagers of the film industry, non-actors who refuse to fade away wout first thoroly embarrassing themselves ...depressing droves of eternal debutantes! O the frankenfacilehorrorsteins which our hard&fast belief in the civilized path can manufacture out of mere vanity & flesh! Attending these salonista shindigs was like hangingout w ghouls. "I once ate the left buttock of so&so." "No! How wonderful! But did you know? It was her *sister* who ate so&so's father's sweetbreads —*all* of them, and *by herself!* Now *that's* being at the top, if you ask *me*." Thus mother died wout us sharing a constructive thought ever. This makes me wonder if she was simply an honest overtion [sic] of grace hart crane? If so, that would tieup alot of biographical loosends.

About the time i was breakingup w deb danzi and interdicting socially (pardon my verbiage) lazita loquita, i rcv'd a letter –well, two, really– from a law firm in paris. It seems some sort of time period had expired and my maternal grandmother's "personal effects" were to be distributed &/or disposed of. If i wished to "take possession" of any of them i was advised to do so "at once". A sample of these "effects" was encl'd. The letter was in typescript.

Dear Nathan: ¶ I am about to give up my "hollow lifestyle" as you always called it. Mr Death has decided to jump in and spare me the public insult of utter poverty. I am not complaining. Forty is way too old for a woman much less my age. Besides, I've had my good times. Once your father was out of the picture. The man was a professional bum, as you know. A poor father and a worse husband. But I loved him. And I always will I suppose. But I am not writing about that. I am writing to get a great weight off my chest. ¶ I always blamed you for my marriage going bad. But it was not your fault. You were a good kid, Nathan, a kid a lot of people would have liked to [have] had. But I have to say, you were one big agony at birth. Impossible to forget. Your head was huge. Five times the size of the doorway to life, they said. At first they were worried you had water on the brain. They wanted to cut me open to get you out. Over my dead body! The agony went on for two days! Finally you came out! I was so relieved I thanked God and Jesus and everybody. But your head ripped me apart. Because of it your father stopped coming to my bed. And I always blamed you for this. So, before my time is up I must tell you. It was not your fault. And my scarred breasts are not your fault either. You were just a baby. I know that now. I could never explain how sorry I am I ever accused you of these things. I have been a foolish woman. ¶ You are a good boy, Nathan. You always were. And smart too. You turned out to be the opposite of what they thought. You are all brains and no water. That's a compliment. You were so smart in fact you scared me half to death most of the time. Smart like your father. And that wasn't your fault either. I had no right not to like you for it. I'm afraid I was very selfish. And for that I am dying alone. ¶ I should have told you these things a long time ago. And I should have told you something else. This letter is written with love. My little helper here says it's never too late to tell someone you love them. I hope she is right. ¶ [signed in wobbly blue ink] With LOVE from Your Mother. [witnessed above a notary seal by a wendy vought, rn]

How grandmother shecklgrubber got possession of this letter i dont know. The *eine abrechnung* of a dying mother, kept for years from her only son out of pure maliciousness —a malice that reached beyond the grave! Mother's mother was exactly as father dubbed her: "Hannah the horrible." While no 'danny boy' ending to be sure, that letter meant all the uncivworld to me.

Tho my inclination was to have no part in her effects, if hannah had this letter perhaps she had other things belonging to Mother or to me. Since discriminating among her effects proved impossible by fone or letter, i made arrangements to have them ship "thee werks" (as my americanized contact put it, and which sounded more absurd every time he repeated it). I wondered about the handsome fee until the container arrived. Among its treasures was a louisXVI "secretary" w silk-padded *fleur de lis*-backed chair. {Now one of louis' own concubines i might abide but an antique secretary?}

Most of "thee werks" i found worthless, limited my rescue to parents' early love letters, my own letters home from summer camp & the farm, and foto albums. Special to me were □ my gorgeous teenaged mother on horseback, hugging a dog, and in bathingsuit at some lakeside □ my father beside her, on the wing of, in the cockpit of, taxiing or flying his various birds, from early *"lufthansa" und luftwaffe* up to that fatal last goose □ a shot of someone (fuzzy soft-featured dark long-haired demure big-eyed & wispy of figure) who, because of backdrop (gravity-tilted tenant-house steps & doorway) just had to be my wetnurse (!) □ baby me sitting squat beside my paternal grandmother's pool & fountain, best part of fount not showing □ 11yearold me cradling my beloved lionel gg1 □ plunked all leggily on a stuffed chair in party dress, priscilla (!) □ my friend geoff & me, one arm each around the gaping mouth of our beloved den □ me as pib on steps of elementary school in mossville, fat frog flat on my camera-proffered palm □ me in bathingsuit at 1.5 years, hand stuffed inside suit like napoleon except i seem groping for the bulge between my fat little legs, which i hope was a wad of wet sand but i fear was not). I am half-turned toward the pretty young woman beside me as if to say <Have *i* got something for *you*>, and she is smiling as if to answer, "Hey, I noticed." □ and perhaps more than anything: several snaps of my summers at gospelInTheBirches, two *w* juanita pictured(!) (less perfect of body but as lovely of face as remembered), *w* one sunshot snapshot (juana in luminescent blue bathingsuit) showing the footfall-eroded slope beyond the beach and, above it, the beginning of the path leading up thru the trees to the *locus sanctus* of "*immer, immer*"! And given my present dearth of trees, what i'd give to be once again among the red-mapled woodlands of mossville, the pale birchwoods & dark cedars of lebanon, or the leucian poplars of Lilith's purlieus.

Now if some of this lookback comesoff as "unresolved anger toward parents" that's unfortunate. If i harbor any animosity (and i do), it is for that civil 'ghostwriter' who went and turned the horror in *pinnochio* on its head by transforming my parents into jackasses who could not comprehend who i was, no matter how donkeyishly i cried, <Ma-a-a-a-a-a-a-ma! Pa-a-a-a-a-a-a-pa!> whenever i was ignored or sent away. Bythebye, i became that antique secretary's parttime pimp, eventually unloading the thing on an admirer in huntsdell for thrice the total price of acquiring it. (But my hebegynolepsy is sufficiently outlined i believe.) How could i have known Lilith would have loved to have it for her house?

48

Were i just Lilith McGrae's biographer, were our lives not inextricably intertwined, part2 would turn this book into a joke. But as my lawyer, who prompted me to scribble these *bildungsromanesque* rambles (emphasis on the 'dung') rationalized: "Ms McGrae spent one-half of her adult life with you, and an even earlier part of it imagining you as her hero and savior. Surely the reader of her bio will want to know a thing or two about her best friend colleague 'n' life-mate?" That emil never called her Lilith is i think an indication of his striving always for objective remove.

49

Sound of female voices woke me. Felt nauseous —now&again the kitchen likes to season w a pinch of ptomaine. I glanced at my window. There again, hanging on its wire. Love note? lowered by some sweet unjustly-accused thing upstairs? Or an escape stratagem sent by a kindred spirit trapped in this same loveless nitemare? Dream on, stubbleface.

Last nite, for the first time, i found myself looking forward to today. Finally i'm writing Lilith's story. Other things too. I'm to get that table & chair. And now there's that pupa hanging outside my window again. I've been snagging bagties of late. The bread (which tastes like burnt cotton) is stacked in loafs on the food line. While there are always bags from which i can extract my pitiful portion, i open a fresh bag each time. This keeps me not only somewhat freer from the undernail-filth of others, it yields the bag's wire closure beside.

With no one but sobbinRobin in my cellblock, working w my back to the camera, as if writing, i peeled away the coverings of the wire ties, twisted them into sequence, forming a tiny hook at one end. Before tying my sheet across the bars, i stripped down as if to bathe. I've spoken of the small hole in the window. Well, pushing my gaff thru the opening, i began the illicit contest of making contact w a presumed female. Virile knight –one used to having the princess of his choice– could easily go mad in this hand-operated ice palace! <Damn. Too short!> Shortshafting is strange to the young seekfreed. Tho inmate (let's call her) hope, upstairs, had added wires so that it hung lower than before, the walls of this fortress are so thick it was still out of reach! Infuriating.

And so that thin white chrysalis hanging on its thread just beyond my grimy pane has captivated me. As you see, i am being systematically starved into psychopathic behavior. Sticking the straight end of my gaff into the eraser of a pencil, i tried again. <Still short!> Even when the breeze blows the paper cylinder ε its wire hard against the outside wall, my gaff comesup short. Can you imagine? <If only i had a longer pencil! Or if it would blow just a little closer! Damn!> Looking across at the clerestory windows of the gym it suddenly struck me, a pale undefinable something reflected in that glass was waving ...at me? I dashed to my bed, to spid gave a whistle. Returning *w* pillowcase to the window, i paused only to wretch into the sink a short stream of cornedbeef&-hash. <This place will be the death of me!> Ah, stinging cliche!

While the fish could not snag the bait dangling by its tank, at least i established contact. For after a min or so of trying, each time i covered ε uncovered the window *w* my pillowcase, an 'echo' semaphore responded above. Cover once; one reply. Twice; two replies. Skip to six; six replies. Back to four; same. The radar echo was unfailing for several mins! Ye gods, reader, if you have one iota of benevolence, take notice of the humiliating longings, the pitiful fears, of we desperate souls confined in such places!

50

The corpoliticos of today are merely the royalty of yesterday operating in different clothes from different castles. And like the royalty of yesterday, despite appearances, they number among the most dangerous forms of life. Their potential for triggering morbidity is in fact the emotional cost these people pay for the act of sustaining (often for entire lifetimes) the appearance of superiority, lifetimes so crammed with manners & courtesies (COURT-oisies), affectations & pretensities, they can only result in instinct strangulation. It is no accident that royal (code: whitecollar) crime has always made the crimes of the populace look petty by comparison. For just as any logger or heavy-equipment operator would be ready to kill after just a year of tutoring in how to 'properly' hold a fork, enslave a populace or pamper the egos of his (emotionally volatile) superiors (muchless a lifetime of it), today's corpoliticos may be generally described as lifestyle-maddened: an oligarchy of cataNatural fops & dilettantes who enforce all the violence it takes to maintain the apartheid of racism ε economics which has caged them as well as us for millennia —them with their inescapable burden of malignant guilt, we with our inexorable burden of serving their every mad whim ...or suffering for failing to do so. The chapters which follow deal with this deadly dilemma.

As distant catchup nears the present, a most telling, political situation developed. In '92 most voters went to the poles unaware one of the candidates was only a bumpersticker/lapelpin enviro. And so it was that, almost accidentally, a lip-service green admin was voted in. When, just before the election, such a limegreen success seemed possible, big corporate $ panicked, set about spinning a catchy war-cry. The weapon-of-choice went as follows.

"Enjoy your lifestyle? [happy well-dressed family patting & praising gasguzzler in front of cushy house] Liberals would destroy it. [enter liberal: man walking snarling cur which leaps at family, cringing appropriately] Liberals love to go after and fix what's not broken. And environmentalists are the most liberal liberals. [embarrassed man hurries off tugging snarling liberal by collar] Let's keep the liberals on a very short leash." Shows man slamming gate to dog pen, sighing w relief as cur continues to snarl & leap behind fence.

With difficulty i will keep my criticism single. What sort of mental malady allowed then, and allows still, the average amer to sit transfixedly by and watch greens be labeled liberals? I thought it was obvious: While liberals come in many colors they are seldom green. Greens are conservationists. This is so basic that the conservativeness of conservationists should be legendary. It is *this* very conservativeness in fact which has long been a problem to greens such as myself. *So* anti-liberal in fact are the usual enviros they have no will to do the battle it would take to restore Nature to the self-sustaining Wildness it once possessed. My green friends, so slandered in the poppress as liberals, are content merely conserving conserving conserving, content to have inherited no more than the sickly little pockets of pale-green wildermess [sic] which our greedy forefathers left us. Do the language, reader. Conserve > conservation > conservative. Not only by belief but definition, greens are *first* conservative, *not* liberal. In fact they are the polar opposite of liberal. Truth be told, it is *non-greens* who are the liberals; worshipers of civilization being the most flaming liberals! For, being antiNature by definition, civilization is the most anti-conservation (liberal) stance humans have ever known! On sane reflection we find,

> The transmutation of Nature/Wilderness into civilization, being the most violent human act in all recorded history, must (by simple deduction) also be the most liberal. —from *the civilizing principle*

Reality historian howard zinn: ≈Our most deadly enemies are not terrorists or other nations but are corporate and government officials. These are persons who consign millions to death and misery, the collateral damage of their lust for profit and power.≈

No matter. BigCorpx ε their politicos sent out its new warcry to every popnews medium. "Liberals are dangerous and greens are the most liberal liberals!" And even tho their cry was *the exact opposite of fact,* it was accepted widely as truth. The lesson? Even tho politics is usually in direct conflict w Natureality (Universal conditions), it has effectively replaced the quest for Truth in civil culture! When conditions are such that truth becomes the *opposite* of what we believe, it seems to me there's a problem; a potentially lethal problem when we dont realize it.

The history of this inversion of reality is easy to track. In the way religion once reinvented language, the combination of science, politics ε law has created a new language, a mishmash of sciencespeak, political jargon ε legalese. And we, taking our example-of-reality from these sources (via the popmedia, which is always quickest to adopt them), we have come to exist hour-to-hour in the environment which these jargons ε their artifacts have constructed around us: a vast ε overcomplicated system of artificial objects ε beliefs which is all but absolutely at odds w Natureality!

> Since the time when civilization first put flesh on the bones of sheer fiction, truth has appeared ever more ghostlike to us. —from *die, primitive!*

Sciencespeak, political jargon ε legalese have replaced the pursuit of Truth. Where are they now, those truth-seekers? Hiding? Killed? What cockeyed optimism makes me think there *must* be persons *somewhere* who still long to touch the widewide Reality that lies *outside* civilization, that wide World of plants creatures ε other wonders that came w this Wilderness of stars ε planets we've been plunkeddown among? If such individuals *do* exist, we are, in effect, a group now all but stripped of a key venue to Truth: language/communication. As i said in *the civilizing principle,* "To be successfully antiNature civilization must turn Truth/Objectivity (Natureality) inside-out."

And this precisely is why, every time i try to explain myself, every time i sense my listener thinks i am a madman or a liar, i am reassured: Even if one has language, and no matter how well that language expresses itself, if the ears hearing you have been corrupted by a world of politicized agendas and its plethora of artificial props, then the message will make no sense to those ears. And thus the (objectivity-seeking) language being used (my language) is rendered effectively mute illiterate isolated lonely incapable of defense (or attack) and doubtless doomed. Yet it is this language alone which conscience leaves me no choice but to speak. Or more to the point of this part of our story as a whole –yet also in reply to the rhetorical wreckage in the childhoods of dickinson/darc....

because civil really means antiNature

I yearn for a childhood stolen from me
 by the imprimatur of a society
 chained to a doom named civility
 —a sophisticated doom we fail to see.

51

Done finally w panning my youth i summarize. The child reared civilly must come to the following trauma many times over: "This is not me you are asking for". Yet society's answer is always, "Yes it is". So the child gives life-such-as-it-is another try. And when frustration heaps again sHe cries out: "This is not ME you are asking for. Not the REAL me!" And still society insists, "Yes it is!" So the child gives a more heroic try. And when this too fails sHe decides, "Then there must be a fake me and a real me, and everyone wants only the fake". Of course, being trained not to see things as they are Naturally but as civil society wants them to be, what the child actually concludes is, "There must be a good me and a bad me. Even tho I think the bad me is the best me, they want to see only [what they call] the good me".

And so, over time, the civil child comes to believe his basic Self (his instinctual Self, his subconscious Self) is a "bad" self. And so we learn to hide ε bury that Self —which behavior (shame of Self) over time can only build a fearsome deficit of guilt, guilt over the "illicit person" we civil feel we must be deep inside. This is of course why civil society can claim, "Each of us has a dangerous or "bad" side". It is also how civil religion gets away with saying, "We are sinners, every one" and not be laffed out of town... er, out of the Real Universe. For the ugly fact is, both civil society ε civil religion have, as a single cost of their brutal domesticating regimen, infected the *successfully* civilized among us w what is indeed a dangerous ε dark side, and they do so typically wout suspecting the generalized horror they are creating! And in those cases where this regime of law ε propaganda is incomplete or still in process....

Enter what is called neurosis. First, one cannot be civilized and *not* be schismed (emotionally divided). Second. Because we have divided 'selves' we *must,* to some significant degree, also be paranoid. (That both these conditions are automatic & unavoidable, i explain elsewhere.) Further, succinctly stated: The adult neurotic is neurotic precisely because the child-doubter in him (the Wild zizm of us) has not yet been beaten into unquestioning submission, has yet to be convinced that his repressed Self (his once-favored Self) is truly dangerous ("bad" "evil" "sinful" lawless). Of course, we civilized —w our personalities effectively always under pressure to split into a civil-v-primal dichotomy— can only turnout neurotic. (In this sense, only primitives are individuals. We civilized in contrast are very much dividuals.) Thus the major difference between we the highly civilized and we the poorly civilized reduces to the apparent (*nota bene!*) effectiveness w which each of us deals w those neuroses which civilizing (personality splitting) automatically spawns. The highly civil among us (aka the divisibles) have effected an *apparently* complete splitoff from the primal Self, while the poorly civilized among us (aka the indivisibles) liveout our lives in such a way that others may glimpse the war against domestication ever raging win us. And for this (merely letting it show) we are labeled neurotic ...if we are not institutionalized, or worse, along the way.

No mastery of the black art of negative equivocation (rationalized denial of hard fact) can compare with its practice among we highly civilized.

Just as civility replaces truth with politics, so high civility replaces ethics & morality with manners & law.

With patience exhausted (from chapter on chapter of me,me,me) i conclude: Neurotics —by fiat of not having swallowed & ignored as much guilt & denial as the rest of us— are the healthiest (the least potentially dangerous) among we civilized. For the doubting child still lives in the neurotic, ever trying to integrate the intuition that he is not wrong for believing, "It is not ME you are asking for here. Not the REAL me anyway". For the neurotic adult is still the child who intuits, "It is my best (basically kind & forthcoming) Self which you [civil society] are slowly murdering". Because of his/her ongoing resistence to the pernicious coercions & punishments (rules & expectations) assaulting our Natural Selfs every minute of every day, the neurotic is typically the healthier civilian. But tragically sHe never finds this out. And so none of us ever come to know: It is often the neurotic who is the true hero of our times.

52

Finally, this must be said before we close part2. Re saigon 1970, deep in the jaws of military retribution. Because i was at the time still wholly owned by that emotional-outage which Nature, in her compassion, allows traumatized creatures, as i lay in that hospital bed i as yet felt no pain or remorse for my reactions of moral repulsion & whistleblowing. Enter colonel chaplain, brandishing, as if it were a gift, a stupor of conscience in its most civil (code: brutally detached) form. Presuming me a lowgrade imbecile he said, "Now corporal schock. Try to think this thru with me. If the whole world has forgiven president truman for the mass murder and maiming of a few million civilians in hiroshima and nagasaki, why cant you be a big enuf man to forgive your fellow g-i's for a few all-too-human slipups?" It was that dose of mental napalm which began to burn a hole in my brain. I can see today how an emotionally compromised & much-propagandaed young & unworldly american youth like myself would feel compelled to swallow whole such excrementation (mind-scat). My question is, could that chaplain, a man in his 60s, well-spoken & world-traveled, possibly have believed even one venal shard of such conscience murder? If so please understand, my reader, should i ever utter the words, just how i come to know –simply know– it is precisely civilzn's high black art of negative equivocation which is surely dooming us all.

53

I began part2 hoping to share w the reader "the stuff of my sources". Yet as i wrapup all this atticquarian[sic] rummaging i believe, our sources lie as much in our dreams as in our environment or in our genes. If the average emotionally-stable boy is a profligate hero-worshiper, picture if you can the bursting scrapbooks of heldenolatry of which fatherless or virtually fatherless boys are capable. But what beats all is, among the (literally) reams of pasteups, both orig & stock, which i assembled in my boyhood, i cannot recall a single *greencape* among them! This begs the question: What *are* my sources? From whence came that greencape i donned w such proud humility [sic] back in the fall of 1972? From whence came that "green-warrior" who'd never heard of muir or emerson or carson or leopold or erlich or liseley or brower or anybody green til *after* he'd already committed to deepgreen activism? And what of that similar anomaly: from whence came the prototypic 'greencape' in whom Lilith found the Planetary warrior she named, and then famed, as captain greenEarth?

If i get to guess (and emil assures i do), my guess is: the nathan schock the public knew (before the fed. ɛ its poppress conspired to defame me) grew from that reciprocal connection which meditation caused to occur between my conscious ɛ subconscious —which discipline, of course, grew from *its* own Sources, some of which *must,* i think, be Wild (or Gaian) in Nature.

None of this is to imply i havent been my share of what comprises a fool —a sometimes romantic fool but a fool nonetheless. And, yes. I did stupid selfish ɛ hurtful things in my youth. And that i've always paid a high price for having done them is beside the point i suppose. However, it is the degree to which i've changed over time, and the endless hurdles i've had to run to effect those changes, that i consider my *personal* life-measure, a yardstick i've borrowed from goethe himself. I paraphrase my personal history. ≈A story where the protagonist is recognizably the same at the end as he was at the start is a tale not worth reading, and certainly not worth the writing.≈

Procataleptus (and probably not my last): And so we have huffpuff reached the finishline of this thoroly itchycrawly harkback, page on selfconscious page of more than the reader needed to know about the former me, and which section of this book will doubtless strike my nastiest critics as an obfuscatory exculpatoriad —whether or not they divine what that means.

[Director: No wipes or dissolves, please. Insert durable fade only.]

Part 3

[Approximate date of composition by the author: April 1998. During the writing of Part 3 NS decided to compose the biography "from back to front". —Ed.]

1

The expectation of imminent death is said to radically reorder one's priorities. And i'm sure it does ...except for those of us who view life as a fragile ɛ transient –albeit incomparable– phenomenon.

And so, as Lilith, privately terrified but resigned to her plan, readies to intersect w my personal timeline, and as –in expectation of recounting this event which changed my life– i sit facing my doom, i find i need little in the way of reordering of priorities. There is only a pernicious constriction of "time", the time remaining for me, to deal w, incl'g a propensity for grave panic as a sideffect. For there is now a need in my life to accomplish more than may be possible in so brief a time. But as sam johnson (i think it was) said: The threat of execution tends to concentrate the mind most wonderfully, or somesuch.

In a sense i wish i could say my days are numbered. But there is no such countdown. By such&such date i do not have to have thus&such done. If i were sched'd to die in 30days, say, i would know what i had to do and by when. As things stand however i could be in mid sentence (as i am now) yet have reached wout my knowledge the end of my sentence —that time when they showup outside my cell w bowl razor diaper ɛ book and an aspect of death about them one can smell. I know i said this earlier but, i do wish i could reachout from my postchronistic existence long enuf to palpate the number of pages remaining in my reader's right hand (left, in some cultures). Then at least i would have some idea what i must do ɛ by when. The reader, having the answer in hand, should also be aware of the toilsome logistics of my task.

In a standard-ruled page i invest some 10,ooo heartbeats! My handwriting ɛ margins are minuscule, so small that my pages –w two lines of condensed cursive filling every ruled space– contain ~1800 words; 3600, both sides! There's good reason for this. At bottom lies a pernicious aspect of my trial. In the short version: All persons who try to contact me become, by order of the court, suspect antigovernment terrorists or conspirators. *Anyone.* Likewise w anyone *i* try to contact. Are the implications of this understood? how farreaching, unequivocal? Who would dare place anyone he likes in such jeopardy? And as to those i love? I am as unresponsive to their often heartrending attempts to reach me as death itself.... One moment, please....

Now then, as i've said. To get anything outside these walls it must be smuggled. The only free person i'm permitted to see –til the fbi's investigation is closed, or so they say– is my lawyer, even if i dared see others. So the smuggling is primitive: wad of paper folded small enuf to be palmed ɛ passed, as magicians say. Since our conferences are watched by both seccam ɛ human (sort of) guard, and since emil didnt practice magic as a kid, most of the subterfuge of transference falls to these hands (hic), thankfully large: Emil gives papers for me to read. Nothing suspicious there. On my lap, leafing thru them, i unfold ɛ shuffle into their midst my cube of contraband. I am limited to two pages per visit. ~7200 words. (Try folding just one page into a palmable cube!) So much for setting this testament free.

Complicating this is the random cell search. Earlyon, personal effects in my cell were often confiscated ɛ examined. In re this. I used to keep copies of favorite fotos ɛ portraits hung about my cell; and later, an album of same. But none survived. Most fotos of Lilith lalage or clarisse were sexually defiled in situ or stolen; some even given (likely sold) to the press. So now i keep only a small vinyl doubleframe, taking it w me when i leave. It contains a foto of my favorite beltrán (julie) portrait of Lilith ɛ a snapshot of she&me on the deck at ggNs, sunnygreen&blue rivervalley for backdrop. And while i keep innocuous documents –such as my *constellations of confinement* (bogus focus of my daily lexis in this locus)– lying about as decoys, the pages of this book must leave w emil's every visit. (Earlyon the librarian sent along w a book i requested another of his own. "Never once borrowed in my five years here so just hang on to it if you like." That book, poetry of john donne, was all i dared keep lying around in those early days in my donjon keep.) As added precaution, all pages we smuggle contain many (numbered) blanks, text so crucial that discretion ε valor insist it be omitted til i give emil the next instalment, at the top of which subsequent pages the text corresponding to each (prior) blank is revealed. O bartleby knows, these minuscule curlicues of mine are hard enuf to read wout additional impediments. Between my small mad script ε this pitiful liting, i will be "meeting my Maker" half-blind.

And finally: visitation searches. (Just a few moments more, please.) The humiliation of a strip-search can by itself make a prisoner resent visits by family or friends. Lawyer visits are easier, specially if the lawyer is as squeakyclean as mine. A casual post-visit pat-search is the norm now. But it wasnt always that way. (I used to be strip- ε body-cavity searched: picture me naked, arms raised, palms forward, fingers ε legs spread, mouth agape, tung extended. And that was the easy part.) Since inmate trousers have no pockets and since i should have w me only papers stamped "audited" and w a "prison control #"; and, mostofall, since a strip-search could, in theory, happen even *before* a visit, i am wise to transport my small wad of papers by a most exotic method. No. Not what youre thinking. That sunless gambit has not only been wornout by cop ε crook alike, it is disgustingly banal.

Tho it may seem chatty, this chapter has helped decide something. Now that most of the autobio bilgestew has been pumped out of our little craft and we're more biographically seaworthy, it occurs to me: Why not write Lilith's story back-to-front? —logging key events, onebyone, the way one might plotout any murder mystery: causally, pausing only to outline pivotal scenes then moving on ...but w a twist, proceeding from the end of the story (my present imprisonment) and moving backward toward its beginning (to where we've gotten as of now), about to meet Lilith, about to learn of that lifework which made both of us enemies of the state. Why didnt i think of this sooner? So much time wasted —and on my own past, of all things!

I am thinking now of puck, near the end of the tale, circling, dusting onebyone the sleeping bodies of the lovers in the forest and resolving the plot thereby. Lacking a date of execution and the merciful countdown such dates afford, only a back-to-front method of composition can give peace of mind. For the true story must be told —not the federal fantasy or the poppress' soap-opera *poshlost'*, which are the only versions jon ε jane q public, and their kids (and maybe even my reader too), have seen or heard.

Of course, using this back-to-front technique, there is the everpresent danger of a sudden lapse in narrative continuity to consider; ie, the danger of the storyline being suddenly cutoff because its author has been executed. But then, this hazard has been there all along. Yet, w my new approach, that hazard will find its considerable heft shifted to the crippled leg of the state. That done, instead of the worst scenario –a story w no ending to justify the telling– we embark now upon the lesser danger of writing a 'symphony' lacking a second or third movement ...a scenario the too-young-dead schubert would surely have preferred. And so, if the reader should find the story suddenly leapfrogging across "time" to its heroine's final days w the narrator, sHe will understand what has transpired: My death has intervened.

2

Opening scene: Downtown san francisco ε the bay as seen beyond the treelimbs of twin peaks or mission dolores in early autumn.

Around aug of '93 i remember hearing that a tropical cyclone had killed hundreds in caracas. The fate of juanita crossed my mind, of course. Might she have settled there? I'll probably never know. By that time i was living in the southern appalachians, had served w greenEarth international for a couple decades and been a socalled environmentalist author for almost as long.

Come evening of oct 9th that year i was beginning my 2ndwk in a 2mo spate of lectures on the w.coast w a stint at uc/berkeley across the bay bridge from san francisco.

> Bythebye, in interest of saving trees energy & book-space, this will be the last time i honor the antigreen dictum of my fellow san fransiscans to not refer to our mutual city as frisco, or to its inhabitants as friscans. Sorry, but i think even *francisco* himself, who respected trees as the people they are, might approve my need to abbreviate.

While 2mos may seem overlong to spend speaking in one area, the pacific coast is easily the most ecologically aware region of n.america —tho not in all the civilized world. So it is no accident that many of my advotes are there, as they are in the nederlands, scotland, germany, new zealand ε other environmentally responsive regions. (I refuse to think of them as fans and Gaia preserve us from devotees ε disciples.) Beside that, ca was my home state ε primary landfall for several years. So allinall, of the five or so months i devoted to touring back then, at least two were given to the "leftcoast".

Some students were there that eve but this particular lecture was attended mostly by my readers, ecoactivists, their families & friends. Indeed, this was the first of my lectures to be broadcast live by satellite hookup to smaller-budget schools. A video copy of it exists in some archive somewhere i know ...for those scholars (or high-caste leches) who desire a robot-cam audience-view from behind the speaker —as he gets his very first glimpses of the Love of his life! (It's really distracting when the steel door down the corridor clangs shut yet no one passes. Vexing voltjizm! Dont tell me theyre going to test the bigAppliance at this time of evening?)

Anyway, energy was high (hic) that eve, friends smiling & supportive, new acquaintances full of questions. On display in the foyer was a fair sampling of my books & videos. By the time i headed backstage it looked as if my latest book, *Mothernature & the world matron,* would sell out before the lecture began. Since the hall –an intimate setting used by trios quartets & other gaschamber ensembles ...speaking of which, the reader might not know, ca switched from gas to lethal injection a few years ago. Not so here in va. Again, now. (Their antics are awfully distractful. Sorry.)

Since the theater held only a couple thousand we tried to keep the entertainment a secret. Jerry gracias, lead guitarist for the ungrateful undead, was back home from a tour to record a children's album and agreed to stop by and play a few songs midway in the program. But word of his appearance was leaked to the dorms and, thruout the eve, clots of rowdy youngsters had to be turned away. As responding to my intro i came onstage, i spotted Lilith striding down the center aisle, my friend helmut tonderstrom at her side. I realized only later, when she told me who "he" was, that i'd hardly noticed her actual escort —a large man more than thrice her age.

Your stunning beauty dulled the britest madams.
Was he an older date, your dad, or daddums?

Helmut sat them just below and to my right as i said my hellos, began my acknowledgements. White slacks & blouse, long dark hair, glowing skin, large wide-set eyes **w** blazing whites! Who is she? Lose train of thought. Glance at notes. (Red gemlites, flanking the caboose of that 'train', rocking gently, recede around a curve and out of sight). I can feel her eyes on me as i speak; physically feel them! Finish opener, get laffter i'm after, reach for glass of water all good lecterns provide for such moments. None is there.

As a rule i like green activists. Shy aggressors, tender renegades, most are at once intelligent & open. Robinhoods of Earth, they aim to take from a gluttonous establishment and give back to an impoverished Planet. It's not one bit coincidental that robinhood wore green (that swashbuckling puck) & lived merrily in the forest. Deepgreens too are a different breed; the sort a new worldview must have to succeed. I'm not talking about bumpersticker-or t-shirt advotes. I'm talking *real* activism.

In 1975 jon windstar, progenitor of the deepgreen guitar, called green activists "the odd man, ousted, getting even". I enjoy the company of my readers; take each seriously; listen to his or her ideas; am often swayed or changed by them. I recall book signings which have run late into the nite; or, in a few cases, til eve next day, at some house, or just cafe-hopping ...the enthusiasm of two or three new faces refusing to dim before exhaustion set in.

Foyer, following lecture. A friend w exotic fruit groves served a brisk organically grown punch in jiggers made of recycled paper —enuf for savoring but not slaking the ancient thirst which gripped me. For over the heads of a circle of well-wishers & autograph seekers i had spotted the molten-eyed beauty lingering at the edge of the group, which neither abated nor allowed her access ...til a stricken fellow in his 50s, sporting a thinning pompadour from the same era, insisted she take his place. One could tell he was ready to sacrifice a foot of entrail just for a chance to lift her off her toes the better to see me. Our eyes met. (I will talk about that jarring phenomenon momentarily.) I wanted to reach thru the crowd, take her hand, lead her to its center: This is my friend ...what is your name? Why, your hand is freezing! Are you okay? Have you a place to sleep tonite, *mia piccina?* Our eyes met again. She glowed, being one of those people whose blood runs rich w roses & rubies. She glanced behind her. {Looking for her escort?} I hoped he wasnt the pinchfaced gaul standing by the nearest exit: gloomy squint-eyed sort w a pathologically sloped cranium; not your usual green and no one you'd want to escort your daughter home ...or even lay eyes on her.

Sign another book, chatting, look up. Still there. Good. Calaf salutes the heavens for making him tall enuf to see the princess above the blood-thirsting throng. *Che la lama guizzi, sprizzi fuoco sangue! Scapitozza!* I smile. Beginning to smile back, she looks away in a variation on eastern humility. But when i look up a moment later the fantastic fay has vanished! I note that the gaul has left also. It was only natural i should surmise he was w her. Damn. I scolded myself for not going over, talking to her. Experience had misled me to believe she would wait.

During the lecture it seemed the young lady might be such a person. *Écolière ecologiste!* Her brite-eyed almost aggressive attentiveness, close-up in the front row, burned into awareness as i spoke. All my berkeley lectures always incl'd the suggestion that my audience visit the plaque of mario savio in sproul plaza.<And any who care to drop by headquarters are welcome of course. I expect to be there thru friday. Remember, you alone are the success of enviroactivism waiting to happen.> I dropped this hypertext just before intermission, just in case she'd come to hear jerry sing not nathan speak.

That was one of few times i allowed our gazes to intersect. Good thing, for it was as if the lazerblue of her glance could zap my clothes to ash, leave me naked ε smoldering for all the world to see! Love at first sight? Hmm. What i felt from the moment i saw her was high physics explicable only by lowly language: rapid reciprocation between discrete bodies of some diaphanous fluid which, like an orgasm one is helpless to end, keeps arcing between those bodies like liquid litening ...til one party, w great effort, turns away, thereby disabling the phenomenon! Phew. For days i would kick myself for failing to get a name fonenumber seraphalanx anything, before she escaped back into deep forest or wide sea, or was it, back into the air? {Gadshazm what a fool!} For, min-to-min for days, not just my mind but my whole body remembered the sight ε the thrill of her 'mere' presence!

3

It seemed like weeks til i saw her again. Blowers on, please. No, no! Not a hurricane, guys, just an autumn breeze! Turn em down! Damnit, down! The pages [the director pointing to a desk-calendar] must blow *slowly* to the floor! *Slowly! More* down! More. There ya go. That's good. Now, *this* way. Follow em out the door. Now, across the lawn. Stay on em, man. There, turn em up again. Up! All the way! Now hit the pile o' leaves. Fan it back 'n' forth! Spread em out, ferkryssake! Hey, jack! Are ya fadin t' cold mist like we agreed? Yer kidding! Screw! That's it! Kill it! Whadaya say, guys 'n' gals? Should we all jus ga-home, ferget showbiz?

(Hard to stay on track here w the generators screaming like banshees. Theyre always coming up w some new ploy to annoy me. And the more i do not notice the more obnoxious they become.)

Seemed like months til i saw her again.... Like the dutchman who, roaming Earth, puts ashore every 7yrs (eg: 1972-93) in search of an absolute love he can never find, mo morn i reported to gE hq. GreenEarth's nat'l hq, now in dc, used to be in frisco. The intn'l office however, where intn'l missions are prepped & launched, is still there as i write. I spent most of mo thereat, met several new faces as a result of the lecture ...but not *hers*. Thankfully i was busy w a pressing project. Because its desk gave a partial view of the front walkway, i appropriated an office not my own. Given a second chance, she would not escape.

Mo passed. Tu, same thing. On wedn i finished a rewrite of my national ecology front (nef) proposal: an attempt –my fifth, 5yrs running– to join into one fist the "big14"; that is, the 14 most powerful enviro groups in the u.s. {Sooner or later [or so i envisioned] we will realize, the lishment's ability to weaken us lies in our own factionalization.} I was to speak at a "Save Our Ancient Forests" meet in oregon on sa and needed time to help finalize the degree of gE's involvement w EarthNow in that endeavor. As the afternoon wore on Lilith's vividly remembered image edged its way more&more into awareness. Like those regnant fullmoons you can feel rising before you see them, the look of her (still starbrite on the drawingboard of my nitesky recall) ascended, smiling, the backstairs of consciousness.

Stopbys had dwindled to one or two. {What are your odds now, fatuous don fatum? [i looked at my watch. After 4] You know i must fly out of here on fr? Is this it? Am i to be reduced, when i return, to prowling berkeley til i find her? Hi, there, a ...have you seen, -a, the most scrumptious babe this side of -a ...the milkyway?} I asked helmut if he remembered her. He grinned. They hadnt spoken exactly but he was sure she liked him. But that's just helmut. Glen played the irish immigrant when i questioned him. "You'll 'ave angels flyin outa yer arse beforn you'll iver git a tumble wi' *thet* lassie!"

Poorly slept all week, now&again nodding off at my desk, i began to think i'd been in lethean waters dipped. Thoughts stray. {She was, in a word, what? Scrumptious. Yes, scrumptious.} Few know the word first found print thanks to the wanderlust (*notavolmente!)* of the author of: I had a vision of nursery-maids: tens of thousands passed me by! And of the dozens that I waylayed, with alice liddell not one could vie! ...clearly intimating the armin-brentano-mahler *"elftausand jungfrauen"*. O scrumptious, matey, scrumptious! The "very reverend" lewis carroll first heard the word from shrimpers "down at the wharves".

Tap tap tap. "Hi. Hope i'm not interrupting?" And there she stood, will ever stand, at the apex of my existence! "Wanted to see you before you left, t' tell you how much i enjoyed your lecture. They tell me youre headed for a big conference up in -a... eugene, is it? ...O, i'm sorry. I'm Lilith. I know *your* name so well —some trick o' the mind. How silly of me. [hint of fluster] I thought you knew mine. No, that's alright. Dont get up. I only have a minute. Must get back downstairs. [my puzzled leer begins here] Back to the drawingboards, as they say."

If it be thus to dream, still let me sleep.

{O heart, do not do that. Not now} as if it would flutter ε burst. <Was just about to break for a cup o' soup across the street. [i lied, was really going to keep the vigil til closing] Join me?>

"Wellp... [cheerily] I havent had a break since noon. Give me a minute t' get my bag 'n' tell nikki?" Nikki was boss down in the art department. {This creature works here?} Because of my disarrayment it sank in only slowly. With a pixiewave –hand at shoulder-level, palm front, quick rippling of half-folded fingers– she feigned a pirouette and was gone.

We next come upon me waiting at the backstairs. A long window filled the stairwell. While the front offices are at street-level, the rear of the bldg, on a hillock, opens out into daylite offices below. Other office buildings are scattered ε tucked into the upslope behind hq. The sky, sunny all day, now threatened rain.

Such a name! Infinitely soft, gently brite! Lilith! Ever repeat someone's name to yourself, link it to some object in your life, or to some startling concept, so you wont forget it? Such a crutch never occurred to me. Peering across the mountain-heights of memory, i now find her name seared –from the moment she said it– meteorlike, across the backdrop of my days. *All* my days. While awaiting her reappearance i caught my lips forming three thin syllables: Li-lí-th. Did i say, *three?* It seemed there should be three. Li-líh-thh. The initial Li-, as in lickerish little literature: an explosion of brite flowerpetals over dark water. And the ictus, -líh-, as in lift, lissome, limniad: those petals in streamers now floating downward —botanical firework! And finally the agogic, -thh: a lisp of pale lilies aliting on a lush expanse of twilit lesbos lawn.

Is there some problem w her taking a break? I'm about to descend when clack of heels approaches below, turns up staircase. Darkly, inside chatoyant silks, delphine devi climbs toward me. "O, hi!" Small talk. Lovely inguinal mocha-colored birthmark drifts thru thought. I muse... *between her hips [all of] india is.* "Have to get this to rick right away." (Rick barclay, executive officer of greenEarth usa.) Delphine waves smiling "bye" w filefolder and, as ever, no hint of a grudge. {Great person, that deldevi.}

Voice echoes up-canyon. Spurning the elevator (as most of us do) she comes in sight on the narrow winding trail below, leading her burro, which is limping. But i see i've jumped ahead a couple years. Lilith is everywhere now! A moment later her reflection in the windows twirls across rooftops. When we reach the foyer, as i hold open the inner door and she passes, my fingertips graze her back. Fond first pericontact! She is real, after all! {Only machomales hold doors for females anymore} i think to myself. Actually i feared the embarrassment (whap!) of not being able to glide thru the glass after her! Such lightheeled motion! In our 1111days together i would learn every nuance of that lightsome stride. We headed to a café across the street.

"No. Started firsthing monday morning. [late arriver, i'd missed her] Nikki hired me.... O the pay's... well... [smile] ok. It's the cause that counts, right? ...since i have classes on tuesday thursday 'n' saturday morning, it works fer me. Well, so far, anyway."

When do you find time t' work out? —you are obviously athletic.

"That's kinduv a problem lately." Late afternoons, she guessed, after school ...or evenings after work. Her voice was lyrical, mellifluous. {...But i knew all along: / On similar seas better sailors than me / have crashed on the rocks of such siren song.} <You modulate your speech.> She'd learned that from "a voice teacher at conservatory. 'Send the voice up to sing in the caves of the sinuses, my dear' he would say, 'and let its honey drip down to fill the comb of the palette'. He was a little strange, mr artinian was. But as a former *la scala* leading tenor, he knew exactly what he was doing."

{I've dated dozens of women. So why this trouble staying cool? Think of something else. Is that a cast ...er, strabism... in her left eye? No, maybe not. Something in the lite maybe, playing on the rods of her silverblue retina: musical reeds of silver lite, flutesong of blue.} Both of us were just then at a point in our lives when we craved easy confluence of dialog w the opposite sex. So how very ironic that erato should choose that moment to come bursting in, carry euterpe off to lunch never to return! <Did you study dance or gymnastics? I can usually tell which.>

"Both. Father was a gymnast. Plus he loves ballet 'n' opera. Sent us to conservatory every monday wednesday 'n' friday for years. Dance gymnastics piano sketching painting voice ...lib'ral arts 101, really." <We?> Yeah. Sister 'n' me." There it is again! Left eye, ever-so fleetingly, performs an oblique protean dance, abruptly ceases!

Kid sister?

"Somewhat kid. Up in dillon beach. Father's in computers... sales end. She'll be attending uc/davis next fall... Gymnastics scholarship. She's nationally classed, you know." Also, we can scrap the cliche "they gazed long and deep into each others eyes". No such nonsense here. We farmore resembled two young daoists on a first date. Wary and yet secretly excited by the searing electric moving between us, we acknowledged each others' eyes w only occasional sigh ships –er, shy sips! Almost 5yrs hence, tonite, the tints of her eyes that afternoon remind me of the silvery azure of a desert sky, the very same sky we had marveled at the eve before her burro sprained its leg. (It's this prison perspective of mine, sorry, which tirelessly steers mnemosyne toward incense ε tapers.) <So what's your major?>

Right now i havent much choice. I'm on a two-year comArts scholarship, everything but food 'n' room paid. But i love cartooning ...and environmental issues ...but then i'm a lit nut too [sigh]." She formed her words as one used to speaking w the deaf. She had other interests beside, holdouts from childhood. "I like dancing; and i still play (piano) ...some. Not good, mind you. Just for me. And i like to travel. But i'm afraid i'm not very practical. <O?> Too many interests...as you c'n see. What commonsense i have i get from my dad. I know i need a career that will pay the bills but cant settle on one. I wish cartooning wasnt such a slammedshut career-choice."

She liked theater too, and "*some* movies". But rarely went. There just wasnt time. Did i know how you could like a thing alot yet never seem to do it? O i did. I did indeed. "And music too... all kinds, i guess." A friend, roger, had just taken her to see *la bohème.* Mimí's fate had touched her. She surprised me w a ready ε proper enunciation of the heroine's name. "And there were quiet, tender moments too. [which amazed her] A couple times there i almost forgot it was opera." Her wide silverblue gaze grayed as she spoke. {Her eyes seem to change hue in step w her emotions. Ineffable quality!} Sad: blue drains away, leaving silver or gray —as if the blue were being borrowed to color her mood. Glances at watch. "Should we be heading back? My stuff's still out on my board. [no need to rush. i hold up key] O good. [glances around uncomfortably] But i told nikki i'd be back before five." Drops bagstrap onto shoulder w declined thumb, pulls it onto her thighs w same thumb, opens flap.

I scoopUp check. <This was *my* idea.>

Hands motionless on open wallet, she stares blankly as if cancelling some protest for being too cliche. We rise. I finish my water.

"Youre lefthanded. Me too. Lefties are right-brained they say." The lissome profile of her denim-clad pelvis wove between tables ahead of me. I pointout as i track her <Left is an anagram of felt ...sensitive, intuitive.> "Well that settles it." Confirming my handedness was important to her. I pay check. Door opens when she pushes it! It is wellknown that fay creatures can interact kinetically w things when they wish. {This shy fay doubtless passes thru 'solid' objects only when no one's watching.}

It was 5:05 and sprinkling rain as we left. From across the street we saw the last stragglers making a dash for their cars. Downpour was imminent. A blond twit, wielding a scamp-of-a-car as if it were a red starfiter, beeped us into a run as we crossed. I scooped her onto the median. The feel of her bantam-light body in the hook of my wrist put a knot in my gut. (In Nature, as with primates, it is common for the male to risk much in courting the female. Weird is when we males do <u>not</u> do so.) It was already pouring at the far curb. "Hey, matey!" yelled sly helmut, pausing to fire his best smile our way. As we reached the entranced oors [sic] a last coworker was just then exciting [sic again]. Lilith chirped a sweet "Hi! Sorry i'm late". Nikki managed a weak smile as we (mere mortals) traded door-holding as demigoddess Lilith glissaded between. Nikki's umbrella, partially open, caught on the door as she attempted to scoot, slipped from her hand. The black thing gasped, folded its wings on the wet floor ε died. I retrieved it for her as tho her own arms were not empty. Taking it, she looked at me blankly, as if surprised i would stoop to such a thing. {It's ok, nik. Happy t' do it.} Scowling, she slammed open the umbrella and departed into the rain.

We got our things, met in the foyer. Busy tonite? "Yes. A-, no." She could make other arrangements. I didnt argue. Locking the doors we headed out. <I'm not an umbrella person. Sorry.> "Me neither." Dripping, we sat for a moment in her own (green) scamp.

Would you, could you, in the rain?

We agreed to meet at 7. After getting her fone# ε directions to the dorms (i was done tempting negative fate), i ducked into my car which, amazingly, was parked beside hers. The downpour quickly blurred ε erased the gemsheen of her receding taillites when, up ahead of my train of thought, she turned onto the ramp to the bay bridge.

4

After a shower, shave ε change of clothes i guided the javelin down market toward the freeway. The storm, which had soaked my end of town (one street away from 16th ε van ness) hit hers across the bay in oakland w its windy side. Her directions proved accurate. Circle, w huge ficus tree; hang two lefts, one right. Bldg D1031, second on left. She was seated on the steps outside her dorm when i drove up. By the time i rounded the rear of the javelin she had waltzed over. That same electrochemistry crackled in my temples as our eyes met. Am i late? I was not.

She wore a black dress (a plush stretch velvet, tastefully scooped neck, long tite sleeves, conservatively v-backed ε hemmed almost to the knee), silver chokerchain, black semiopaque pantyhose, clompy boxfront shoes (just then beginning to catchon) and carried a bulky crocheted white sweater. Her ensemble, dark enuf to pale most skin, hardly dimmed the glow of her. As we pulled away wind ε wipers scattered the wet leaves which had spattered the car in the brief time it sat. Looks like the worst is over.

"I understand it's not even the rainy season yet?" There was an almost-rustling fall of her blackwalnut hair as she shook it back into place. Trading harmless chatter i wound us back out toward the freeway. "I'm here only since june" and having spent most of the summer up in dillon beach, "Shur. I wouldnt mind seeing the city some" she said in a beguiling sibilant stream. As we drove i learned, she'd been to "a few places in town...mostly t' do with art. Our instructors take us. [she'd recently been to] ...the palace of fine art 'n' the art institute too."

"Toot too?" to you too.

Her laff is tauntingly musical. "My favorite so far is the cartoon art museum... I had no idea how far back cartooning goes: as old as storytelling 'n' drawing, which only makes sense."

Italian food is safe for a first date. PLEASE WAIT TO BE SEATED. Good time for lady to use restrm. I watch her recede, slim frame almost lost in the bulky sweater which covers to the hip, the skirt of her dress hugging in behind only enuf to whet pursuant wonder. I doublecheck the sign as i'm led to our table. For a moment, out of the corner of one eye, i thought it read: PLEASE WAIT TO BE SATED

As she returns, two mugs appear, one amber, one umber. "I see youve ordered. [sitting] Is that like a-, whadayacallit, [macho-deepening her voice, indicating my brew] stout? My dad prefers dark beer too."

You were about t' say something about paris when we came in. She looks puzzled, an endearing crook upturning one wick of her mouth. The bohemians, remember? leaky flats in winter? [but my clues are not for the general listener] rodolfo 'n' mimí? the opera?

"O. Right. The opera."

Was she a fan? "Not really." Roger was the "opera nut." Was he the distinguished gentleman who'd accompanied her to my lecture? "No. That was father. Roger's my art history instructor. But father loves opera too: male singers mostly. Says the women sound too hysterical 'r bossy.... No, *he's* no enviro. That's me ...tho he does love the outdoors. He's jus been trying lately t' be part of whatever i'm into ...which has been taxing for him."

"Appetizer?" A college lad stood ready to take our order. Could we use a few more minutes? We could. And your mom?

"Mother 'n' father divorced when i was twelve. She remarried ...coulduv had her pick o' guys." [folds left wrist to one side, palm up, as in 'O well'] Dated willy freed [i draw blank] ...the gameshow host? Became famous on that dumb show, princesses in a daze 'r something? But... [turn aside, sadly; nudge knife w index] she chose someone else."

And him we dont like?

Looks up. "Is it that obvious?" Gives tiniest toss of head, so small as to defy interpretation, looks askance. I change subject. What got you interested in ecology? "Father. [pauses, clears throat] My *real* father, not my step. He aroused our interest in Nature early. Smoky in here." Sniffles.

I didnt mean to pry.

"T'sokay."

We tookup our menus, ordered. <Do you ever paint? ["Sometimes."] T' recycle a cliche if i may: I'd like t' see your etchings some time.>

Shy smile. "Okay. But most o' them are still in virginia. B'side, they'll bore you. I think you'd like my cartoons better. Now *them* i brought with me. Speaking of art, nikki's really talented. I know i'll learn alot from her." I agree, as soup&salad arrive. Lilith immed notes something odd. "Beautiful soup. <Huh?> You see the pasta? ...in our soup?... It's oriental characters!"

So it is! Hmm. Perk of being so close to chinatown i suppose. I mention learning from my chinese friend, al chang, that there are some three-hundred 'n' thirtyeight characters in his alphabet.

"Alphabet soup in china must be reallyreally thick" she says, hardly breaking a smile. Sips spoonful, swallows. "Phew. And it's very hot too ...as in condiments-hot, i mean."

Chinese culture is among the oldest 'n' richest in the world, i say, still chuckling. You *do* know your alphabet-soup remark was hilarious, right?

"I guess. But doesnt that contradict what you said about ancient sumer?" On the page that remark looks like a challenge yet in person —well, it wasnt. I knew this even tho i had yet to pickup on her aversion to compliments. The sheen of her hair was oriental- or amerind-black by dinnerlite. Had she ever read *Dao de ching?* No. But she was *re*reading my *Mothernature and the world matron.* "And, no. I wont be givingup 'n' ordering the video." Smiles. She is re:ing my berkeley lecture.

I rather harangued about that, huh?

"I think you told it like it is. It mightuv turned a few people off. But them even the video might notuv helped.... And o, i meant ta tell ya this. The people sitting around us were amazed t' findout about the auto-emissions thing." She re:d something i made a point of telling my ca audiences at the time: The newly appointed "advisor" to the epa chief had flown out from dc to convince the governor to lower (yes, i said lower) ca's emissions standard! While my date put nothing past what she called "the new epa", many greens thought at the time there was some mistake. There wasnt.

During supper we spoke of mtns, travel, hiking. She slipped from her bag a wallet of fotos: "The smokys. Thanksgiving vacation last year. Went there with reesy ...aurise. She's my best friend."

Jean shrimpton! [gives querying stare] Sorry, but ever since i first saw you i've been huntingdown a *déjà-vu*/ havent-we-met-before thing. An' *now* i've got it! Funny how a picture, a trapped image like this, can pin down life-in-motion for closer analysis. ...What? The way she was looking at me i figured i had a noodle sliding down my chin.

"You think we've met before? <Yes. But too cliche ta mention.> ...Very weird. 'Cause we sorta did back in february. <Youve lost me.> Also, what you jus said reminds me of a butterfly collector. <Now i'm *totally* lost.> Do you remember what you jus said? <I guess i dont.> About pinningdown life-in-motion for analysis? That's like butterfly collecting."

<I guess it is. [still looking at fotos] But i'm using dead fotos not live butterflies. [i regroup for an analogy] I actually suffer from the *opposite* of a camera's prejudice. [gives askance squint] Seriously. Personality can all but obliterate actual appearance for me. Where a camera often cannot see personality i'm too often overwhelmed by it. Not necessarily a good trait for a writer. I'm the sort who needs still-frames of life in progress ...if i wanna stay even a little superficial. Snapshots like this are jus the thing.

Among them were two fotos *w* mtns ε fences, one snapped later than the other, one in the eastern u.s, one in the w, easily confused in a dim-lit place —or so we would later unpuzzle. Thanks to this mixup the following double-exposure appears on that day's page in mnemy's album. <This one [*w* the fence] is in the smokys?> The snapshot in question had the life-in-action blurring of a novice fotographer. Beaming at camera, the adorable duo leaned against a splitrail fence, high above one of those gorgeous gorges. (Ah, *déjà lu* again! Have i plagiarized?) Wooden sign w routed yellow lettering states: TWIN BLUFFS. EL. 6116 feet. The bluffs, scowling at one another across a misty abyss, were set into two high ranges, each ablaze w autumn as they trailed off behind the toothsome twosome (that ring again), purpling as they faded.

<How far south did you get? Really? Then you *were* near my home... Yes it is, actually... Chalet-style, on a mountainbluff above the tennessee river, with windowswindowswindows. I'm a claustrophobe; like ta be outside even when inside.> I promised to take good care of the snapshot of the comely duo, return it the moment she gave me another.

On reaching the car we change our minds, start walking. Only 2-3 blocks into our amble the low-slung sky decides to drop a chilly misting. We sidle into a theater foyer which happened to be passing just then, checkout its posters —all imports we'd never heard of. More to be carefree than stay dry <Should we?>, i bought us tickets to NOW PLAYING.

The house usher, a childsized woman of exceptional girth, marched us thru the small lobby to the beat of a drummer only she could hear. Proudly epauletted, capped & sworn to duty, she insisted on officially flashliting us to our seats whether we wished to visit the restrms or not. The place being warm, i help her out of her sweater, noting (as her long locks shift to one side) the hollow between her shoulderblades as, for a moment, they all but kiss across her kissable back. The colors on the screen dapple her profile: blend of laplandish adorableness (delicate softening of prominences: brow nose chin) and a woodcut-relief of classic roman, depending on the slitest turn of her head. Did she have irish or latin blood? Whispering: "Father's scotch 'n' german, mother's scotch 'n' soda. [emits little hiccup] Actu'ly she's french with a curd of feta cheese blooped in. Crazymixedup genes." Woman in front of us shoots exasperated sidelong glance. Wild creatures at heart, we move to an unpeopled area.

The film turns out to be an accidental black comedy. But no one laffed. <Hmm. Not very cinemafancy for friscans.> Accidental spoofs can be the most riotous.

"Tv has drugged imagination."

<Deep *in*quiry is suffocating under the weight of shallow *ac*quiry [sic].>

The film's ending, the only part i recall, was a wry critic's delite. Estranged heroine, weeping bitterly, creeps into protagonist's rented rm, awaits his arrival. Tree shadows, humanlike, play on walls of overdarkened set —tired devices. Soon hero arrives (love-mussed ε smeared, grinning ε tipsy). Distraught heroine amateurishly aims small pistol (much too clearly angled downward), shoots agrarian don juan at close range in the groin as credits begin to roll. The look on his face –drunken dismay giving way to burning agony– redeems the price of our tickets if not the duration of our cinematic hohumery. As we rise to go, heroine sinks forward on knees w a look of horror ε disbelief at what she has done. Smoking pistol topples upsidedown on her index finger (a myna inverted on its dowel). A mediocre wouldbe medea, she crumples to the floor.

We look at each other thru the theater dimness, mouths hung open, glancing sidelong at the screen as we go. Suddenly –and all the way up the aisle and into the street– we start laffing; me into the air, her, first into my shoulder (my cue to place an arm around her), then into my collar.

Terribly funny movie.

"But they were serious!"

I know i know!

"Was it the screenplay or should someone have cauterized the director?"

Both. {I think i'm falling in love.}

But the funniest part of the evening happened off-screen. The house usher, that round child-sized militarist already noted, having officially seated someone upfront (after backingaway w a modified bow), tripped on a runner and, for having a deathgrip on her trusty flashlite, rolled right to left across our field of vision for a ludicrous distance, looking the whole way like a cross between the tumbling reflector on a moving bicycle ε the wobbling beam of a pulsar, and all of it in absolute silence! Still under threat of breaking silence ourselves —for we had yet to change our seats (why are things so much funnier when youre forbidden to laff?)— we could but look back&forth at each other in amazement. Hardly had the poor woman rocked herself upright when Lilith whispered, "The fall of the house usher", and i grabbed my mouth to hold back the fit of spitting hysterics elbowing for exit. While there was never any doubt that i was in lust, that was when i first suspected that whole-body/mind madness we call love might be involved too.

And so went the evening. Youd think a true ruminist would have come up w a better idea for a first date than dinner ε a movie, specially considering, she was the only woman to *thoroly* captivate me in years! In the car, going back to her place, she grew quiet. "I'm jus not used to dating." *Because* of her quiet ε deeply reflective demeanor (a putoff for the typical comeon), her revelation does not surprise me. We agree to lunch on fr.

Lilith

As to my shrimpton analog (for versions of this book wout the fotos): If i had to pick just one face as a Lilith lookalike (crutch of a crippled imagination) it would have to be a face which, straight-on, had the soft-featured blankness of youth –one where individuality, as in infants, obtains mostly in the eyes– yet which, when showing any degree of profile, at once takes on maturity for the amount of bony-structure (of cheek, nose ε jaw) it reveals. Puberty, not accidentally, makes the biggest assault on the round-faced (protection-demanding) adorableness of youth. Any infantilism of feature which puberty overlooked in Lilith was, by the time i met her, being compromised by (lifestyle-exposed) bone structure. (Worry over the repercussions of runningaway to ca from her legal home in va, added to the ...well, face it... fear over her plan to meet me, had taken their toll on her weight.) For in the 3yrs+ that i knew Lilith, when i met her she was at her willowiest —euphemism for on the cusp of anorexia; tall-appearing w almost the hips of a girlboy. Body-profile fotos of her on vacation w aurise –launchpad for her escape to ca– show her as *too* thin for my taste. In pulpfiction code: Straight-on, at said weight, she was only the ghost of an olivia hussey/mia kirshner composite. That is, thru that period, from any angle left or right, it was the urchin-cum-debutante look of jean shrimpton that leapt to life.

Along w fotos of female friends i conscripted for my tour in nam, i can still see —as camou-dressed ns rummages in his wallet for a blank slot into which to slip a just-got foto of gi jane (fonda) ε an eve-naked bit of bardolatry— i can still see the ever-amazed eyebrows ε falsely glacial mystique of model/cinematic meteor (in the classic one-movie sense) circa 1965 stunningly-blueeyed jean shrimpton facingoff (in the junglelite of my wallet) against the vulnerable wideeyed warmth, glow & intense purity of olivia hussey ...which pocket gallery i justified carrying around in those war-polluted rainforests on the grounds of still aching for my lost juanita. In '70s hollywood, bythebye, i chased briefly a pale shade of shrimpton i'd stumbled upon, not realizing i'd come farcloser to the orig brit beauty back in london, when i caught the sirCosmos cup as it passed that year.

5

There are strict formulas for books that "sell big". These formulas make the deconstructive aspects of our civilizing sadly glaring. No matter how noble or unique a person might be, a story lacking grisly content or a strong sexual element cant even get a reading anymore. Any steamy raunchy device will do. Heroine taken by force in a warehouse; or on a motorcycle at the dim deadend of an alleyway, or on the stairs of a firescape. Or, more popular of late, have heroine corrupt hero, on a swing in a public playground, say, or in a library w people about. Or have trio of masked bunglers [sic] abduct me & my new friend, force us to perform at gunpoint various lust-inciting acts etcetc. And so i must warn the reader: If this book ever singes the fingers (and it will; it will) it will not be because of formulas based on greed & lust. The sex in this testament will happen as it happened in reallife, and not a moment before.

6

At lunch on fr Lilith seemed preoccupied. Guessing a cause, i asked if everything was alright downstairs. She said it was, "okay". Yet the way she said it made me decide it was time to tell about nikki. I'd hardly begun when it became clear, robert trebor, head of graphics, had been dropping quidnuncs around Lilith's desk all morning, clearly a result of our nikki/-umbrella encounter in the foyer the day before.

Since the very idea of refuting trebor's droppings disgusted me, i decided on a brief disclaimer. I'm bad at defending myself so i will limit this to one or two points. ["You dont hafta explain *anything* t' me."] But i want to. Nikki 'n' me are *not* engaged. Never were. When i was here in july we didnt even date. In fact, we have not dated since last december. And our last meeting coulduv left no doubt our dating days are done. When i arrived three weeks ago she was, in fact, almost hostile. That's all i... Well, maybe one more thing. This for *your* sake. While i know he is very adept at his job, there is no less reliable source of info in this organization than robert trebor.

On the walk back she confessed to being repulsed by gossip. "I'm like you. I c'n defend someone else but not myself."

Not a good way t' be. You endup looking guilty.

"Yeesh, is that ever the truth... Even to ourselves sometimes."

Good point. Ya know, people complain about negative info yet they thrive on it even in their personal lives.

In better spirits now, we agreed to "hangout" that eve.

Lilith

As to the nikki/nathan parting of dec 2002. I was happy not to have to dredge it up for Lilith's sake: <Ya know what your problem is, nik? [O tell me, do.] You use your sexuality as a weapon.>

"It's called sexual politics, nathan. *Everybody* does it. A few of us even consciously. Wakeup 'n' smell the roses, professor ...or should I say, eros." O nik was clever & brite alright, but *w* a lacerating meanstreak i was too late finding —for me a certified turnoff.

You mean, wakeup 'n' feel the thorns, dontcha?

"If the shoe fits."

Well, ya know what? It doesnt. So you c'n take that sexual weapon o' yours 'n' stuff it cause the "professor" here is turnedoff by your little garden of thorns. I rose to get my jacket.

And she rose *w* all her thorns intact. "An stuff it I will. An' stuff it, 'n' stuff it, 'n' stuff it! But I wont be stuffing it with you. *That* you c'n count on!"

I turned at the door to deliver my reply <One c'n only hope that on *that* one point you are a woman of your word> but bit my tung, instead said only: <One c'n only hope that on *that* one point you... Nevermind>, and went my way quietly.

7

It was good to soar above traffic again so to say. {Usually dont feel *this* good til i'm back in the hills of home} i thought as i crossed bay bridge. No, actually i felt even better. Years since i'd been emotionally skyborne ...since i'm 13, in fact! *Return with us now to those thrilling days of yesteryear* when juanita smiled at me, gave me my first love-wings.

At her dorm i had to wait while a motorhome methodically maneuvered out of what looked like an old courtyard. Dont trust those things. Any perspective-devoid dyslexic baboon can get behind the wheel w͞out a roadtest! I mounted the curb to stay well clear, waited in treeshade for the domestic dreadnaut to move aside. I was early and did not mind. The courtyard made for a quaint parkinglot beside the ivy & brick dorm. A couple cars away, a swarthy fellow –shirtsleeve version of claude chadeau– wrestled a sparetire from the trunk of a car next to a green scamp i guessed was Lilith's. Soon the driver of the deadly domicile had mastered the rules of the road sufficiently well to allow me to slip past & park.

Three young ladies & two smiles sprawled on the frontsteps. I asked the britest smile for Lilith —that is, Lilith McGrae. "Dont think she's home" said an angular redhead to a hard-eyed blond. "Sure she is" chided the first, indicating "Inside there's a fone. They'll connect you." "But I saw her, monika! [making up monikers as i go] She left in a red car about a halfhour ago!" "O? [turning back to me] Was she expecting you...? [she was] Then she's probly there. Just go inside. Use the fone." All watch monika as she offers "Here, I'll show ya."

Straightbacked chairs endtables dim lamps a couple ragged magazines and one person sufficed for the foyer & sittingrm of this old college house. Live voice answers, connects me to "busy" beep, whereupon recorded voice takes over. "Your party's fone is momentarily busy. Please try again later." {Bet that's a common message around here.} I take a seat and the only magazine. *{Bulldozer digest?}* A horny looking youth in red baseball cap and pink(!) hightop athletic shoes fidgets w a magazine across from me. {At least a dozen years my junior.} His treatment of its pages —which he ravages rather than reads, pausing only when ads touting bare female flesh unravel on his lap— causes me to imagine Lilith out w this fellow on a date, having for hours to stay away from those maniacal pastewhite hands w their freckled digits.

Two of the young ladies come in. "Hi!" "Hi!" as they sidle past my chair. "*I* wouldnt leave *that* waiting" says one voice. "Grrr." replies the other as they slipaway thru doubledoors. Door slams upstairs. Sign on wall at stairwell: NO MALES PAST THIS POINT. {Is that just for upstairs?} i wonder. I'd just risen to try my call again when a young lady *w* shortshort dark hair and a chestless letter-sweater bounced down the stairs asking if i were mr schock. "I'm beth. Nice meeting you. [amicable but no-nonsense] Lili 'll be down in a minute", and disappeared as quickly.

I resat, picked up my bulldozer update and, lo (while searching in vain for mention of caterpillar's™ role in the endless genocide of the palestinian people) she appeared on the stairs. I had to do a doublecheck to be sure it was her. <Your hair looks different.... Nice. But different [i added once outside] Thought for a sec there you were pink hightop's date.>.

"As if." We headed down the walkway toward a wet glistening cobaltblue javelin (sprinkler's had come on while i waited). Breeze shakes water from the leaves. Lemme get that door for you. It's tricky. Overhead an alder whooshed us well as she ducked into the car. Unbidden my gaze fell from her hair (styled much shorter) to a narrow band of bare skin between blouse & skirt. As i got in on my side she leaned forward, placed her bag by her feet, her jacket on top of it. I noted her hair again and, in a *hesodashi* revelation, the very deep inset of her spine. I touched her shoulder as if to turn her aside for a better look. Did you braid it? She shook her head. "Beth's in charge of hair."

Amazing. Baptist women where i live are big on braiding. Dont think i've seen such a sophisticated weave tho [touch lightly]. Nice. Very nice.

Thanks me, sits back. "Look's like rain ...again, no?"

This weather's a spinoff of xallison (with an x) ...pacific storm, ya know? Should clearup by sunday they say.

Motorhome is blocking the way again, practicing its ostensibly interminable maneuver. My rider advises "There's another way out... Over there... The storm's called xallison? As in xylophone? <Uhuh.> Hope it doesnt turn the area into 'xallison floods wonderland' b'fore it's done."

Very cute. Speaking of names, i've been meaning to ask: What do your friends call you?

"I'm not fussy. Some say Li fer short, some Lili... Dad used to read *alice* to us when we were kids. [us?] Me 'n' L-... Git, you... [chases unseen fly from blackskirted thigh] ...Me 'n' lage. She goes t' school up in petaluma."

Right. But you told me another town. ["Dillon beach?"] Right. Dillon beach. It's my lobotomy—actsup in october. ["Petaluma's where the school is."] ...Lage? A nickname? ["Yeah. Short for lalage."] Lovely. Almost as nice as Lilith. Rhymes with *nuage, mirage... susurrage....* French is the most romantic language, dont you think?

Yods (Yod is teenspeak for nodded yes). "Do ya speak it?"

Hardly. Took two very casual years in school tho.

"Wasnt it the french who sabotaged one o' you guys' boats?"

<Aa-mm— yes.> Driver to himself: {Is she serious? Must be the ozone-charged air.} <The french dont care what they do exactly so long as they pronounce it exotically.>

"One side of our family's french. Not the fake canadian bacon variety mind you but down 'n' nasty south o' france."

Yes, you were saying.

"Not ta worry tho. It's not sumthin we're zakly proud of."

I see. [stop at traffic signal] {Way less introspective t'nite.} You seem sorta, well, preoccupied t'day.

"O? 'Njoy it while it lasts. I uzhly talk more than I should. Lite's *greé*-een" she saá-ang in two tones, looking straight ahead the whole time. Round corner, cruise past a campus. "There's the school", she announced, as if she'd seen it only on postcards.

What school's that? ["A-, my school."] This gives me pause. <I've been thinking this whole time you went t' berkeley?>

"A-, no?" Looks concerned, while i'm wondering if i've forgotten something. "Cal college of media arts. Hope yer not disappointed."

Not at all. Guess i made a wrong connection somewhere. Maybe because the first time i saw you was at berkeley. We drop into freeway ramp.

"Where we headed?"

Dinner 'n' a stroll at the piers sound okay?

"That'll work.... Nice car."

Thanx. Not all it seems {...like this date so far}.

Parking at the piers is competitive fr nites. I decide on the "lorraine", near the promenade. As we enter i follow the deep inset of her spine {such vertebral inset usually signals upperbody fitness}, note again the clever braiding of her hair. At table my cheery chitchat does little to dispel that 'odd something' in the air. <If you'd like t' go home i'd understand, ya know.> That broke the ice ...some. It seems the problem was, she'd spoken to her mother (back in va) "And, no, everything [wasnt] okay. Leyda –mother, that is– has all these really unusual nonstop problems."

Did we wish a cocktail? Our server spoke in faux-frenched english while eying my date from beneath shaggy brows.

"C'n you suggest a liquór? Something transparent, and with body, prefrably?" Her sudden insouciant air sets up a sort of catching congeniality. {Socalled legal age in this otherwise avant garde state is 21. But being new here, maybe she doesnt know this? Or is the nimble fox toying w this shadow of the law's hounds?}

"A leek-hur weeth bowdy? Ah, yes. Let me see. [bar list replaces driverlicense image behind scotts-terrier brows] We haaf a berry nice leek-hur: a slightly weet ...pardohn... lightly *sweet* mirabelle!" Fingertips fan outward from lips at the mere thought of its bouquet —as he ruins the gallic 'r' w a tijuanan trill. "I sink you weel like eet." ["It's not a curacao is it?"] Suddenly not just our (finally) smiling garrrçon[sic] but the whole town seems ok w our mutual folly. <Your darkest spaten will do for me, thanks.> And, quick as you can say hooch, he was thanking us for our order. My date's sudden aire of *laissez faire* self-assurance struck me as high-order *obfuscage*. Was there possibly a richbrat flipside to the Lilith i knew thus far? Her half-brother would be down from sacramento in a couple days, "He's visiting relatives there with upch-... [touches lips w fingertips] Scuse me... with his father". She rather sneered the word.

Acoustic guitarist in andalusian garb begins playing on small stage. Salad served w sidecar of *foie gras.* Desperate for a topic between songs, i ask about her sister.

"Sister is ...well, was... feeling ill when I, when I talked to her". With little kicks of her fork she gathered the cherry tomatoes into a cluster at the side of her bowl. "Probly just a twennyfour-hour bug." I find myself wondering if the young lady might not be conveniently caught in a paternal vice of one-upmanship, playing dad ε stepdad like two slot machines, one in each fist. Or maybe there were others in the wide darkness of my ignorance about this young woman. I would have to wait&see.

Then, in the next few mins, after her speaking so well of her sister, i felt i was being too hard on her. <I c'n tell you care for her. Sooo... Here's to lalage an' her goodhealth with all our hearts! [she lifts ε knocks my bumper w her brandysnifter] I hope she's as gifted 'n' uniquely handsome as yourself.>

"Well, *thank* you. Wow." Savoring a sip, she rises to freshenup. The way she moves off makes me think she could do cartwheels among the tables and never spill a drink. She returns just as entree is being served. An aznavorian little man (owning the alsatian features our mexican waiter wishes he had) is led in, seated at a table in an alcove —the spot i'd hoped to hide away in w my date had it not held onto its former occupant til after we'd been served.

"Do you come here often?" she asks, slicing a forkful of fish. Fork inverted, she slips fold of meat onto tung.

Occasionally.

Strabismus *in absentia* tonite. The wide ponds of her eyes, tho as lovely as ever, seem busier, bluer somehow. As she raises her fork i notice on her right hand a delicate gold ring set w a small pearl. She notices me noticing. "From Sister." Hand puts down fork, extends ring across carmine tablecloth. I take her fingertips; conservative length nails, glossed in natural tones. {How refreshing.} <Very pretty.> Such civility makes me feel suddenly victorian. We eat. {Is he playing what i think he's playing?}

...the smile you are smiling you were smiling then....

Not very latin. She, wistful now, preoccupied, had never heard the song of course. The dark little man –seated where i'd sat w deldevi on my last visit– is either in love w my date or is writing a treatise on the faust/gretchen complex. So i slide to one side a rose in a black vase, thus blocking al sace's gloom-haunted face while more fully revealing my tablemate. Conversation, none of it memorable, comes easier during dinner. When the busperson has cleared the table, al hombre arrives to recommend coffee or desert. No, thanks. And the young lady? Silence, lashes lowered, does not answer. Indicating my lager –we'll take another, thanks– i'm recalling the nite i took my friend bekky kydd directly home after similar behavior. Be gentle, nathan. <I've figured it out. There's you and your thoughts over there t'nite; an' then there's me, over here, with mine.>

Looks up from crumpled napkin. "Sorry. My bad. I jus cant seem ta shakeoff the crash'n'burn selfishness of our endlessly troubled mother." Questioning her on this led only to a harmless confession of my own, a taste or two of each other's drink and a congenial spat over who would/should pay for dinner; after which we decided on a stroll. I can only hope this prose is as bumpy as that evening, thus far, actually was.

The promenade, as it's known, facing sausalito across the bay, runs from the s.end of golden gate bridge to the piers. She reads from a brochure as we walk. "Among other attractions it offers theaters art galleries gardens restaurants tennis- basketball- 'n' handball courts bike paths horseback riding (oooo) too and, mostofall...."

Wait a minute. Lemme see that.... That's gate park. That's not here.

"I know. I *said* that."

O. Our shadows stretch absurdly beyond us as we walk away from the lites & sounds of beach st.

"Ya know, this [shakes brochure] sounds nice." Lilith, in town only since beginning school, had been "almost nowhere yet".

<Ever look straightup while you walk? Relativist's dream.> Tree branches slide across cloud-bellies illumined by city lites as we pass under their leafy reachings; while the clouds, beyond, slide past the stellar backdrop from yet another direction. She pauses [Sheesh!] reeling slitely. I help her slip out of her jacket.

Soon the lites of the yachtbasin glare upahead. On a hunch i stop, shrug my shoulders, breathe thru my nostrils. She turns. <Ya know, i'm beginning to feel like... well, like it's me; that i did something.... Wait. I know you'll say, no. But when there's no explanation a person cant help but.... Hellsbells. Is this about nikki again?>

"Nikki-...? Well, no. No. She's got nothin ta do with it. Really. It's me. I'm just a mess t'nite."

I didnt know what to make of this ...this ...seeming alterity of hers. Tho a certain cause seemed palpable at times, that it might be true struck me as *beyond* absurd. And when i suggested we maybe try again some other time –no hard feelings, really– her apology was so sincere i backed off... again.

Promenade liting toyed psychedelicately[sic] w all whiteness –blouse, teeth, pearl in her ring– and applied, just-so, a lambency of lavender to all, incl'g the whites of her luminous eyes! Her shortsleeved blouse, cut off w small frills just below the shiny prominences of her ribcage, revealed a narrow panel of concave midriff ε a taut delicious navel. Frills also lined the deep-but-tasteful neckline. Beneath a silver chainmail necklace i glimpsed the rounds of two perfect doves: their soft backs rising ε falling w her breath. We pass near boats in their moorings. Strangling rasp of lines on cleats, rubbery nuzzlings of hulls against bumpers, cause restless mnemy to slip off to sleep in other places, other ports. For several mins she seems on the verge of divulging something. <Is the chasm so dark 'n' deep the rappeller fears the descent?>

"Huh? [i explain] Welp, r'member I said our mother called? Well, she had news: tho *good* news, as far as *she* was concerned ...it was bad fer me. [pause] It's hard t' talk about this; a tale much better not told." <Youre right. You shouldnt feel compelled to explain *anything* personal.> Looks over. "I'm gruesome company t'nite. Maybe I shoulda stayed home like you said. <Or sent a stunt-double t' take your place.> Thinking my humor has failed again, the grin i'm after soon dawns. We laff and walk on, an easier space between us now. We swing by the palace of fine arts, which of course is closed.

"Hey, I was here this summer ...with Sister."

Floodlites tint façade a brassy ochre, give the <weeping nymphs> atop the columns –already far too masculine– an even more cumbrous aspect.

"If *your* butt was that big, an' if you were cast for all time in *that* position –and in your sheerest nitey, no less– youd be weeping too."

Suddenly i knew what was wrong. {That sort of rapport right there, the easy exchange, the reflective wit. *That's* what's missing here.} <I think theyre crying over the state of art worldwide.> But even this eked no response.

We soon came across what looked to be, unlit as it is, a tropical garden. I put a hand on her shoulder as we slipped into the shadows. Standing midway on a little bridge, trying to see into the darkness below, i moved that hand into the cool hollow of her back, felt sure i could have kissed her yet limited myself to a brush of lips along her temple and a word or two about the fragrance of her hair. We moved on. Having reached the promenade again we looked for a bench —one that looked out over the expanse of water toward sausalito or the hazy lites of alcatraz. But all the benches stolidly –indeed, arrogantly– ignored the lovely view, faced instead the interior of the park! I took her hand (to lead her to the nearest bench) when, spurred by music blaring from a passing yacht, i decided (tho intent on another even zanier errand) to dance w her. <I figure this relationship could use a little diversion just now.>

"Is this supposed ta be an ol'time waltz?" she laffed.

Yes.

"But the music's leaving!"

Then *you will be my music,* said another nathan, pseudo-delirious w terpsy and aching to hold her. Dont you hear it? *Fete at the capulets!* [then looking up] No. It's the music of the spheres. I imagine her back at her dorm telling someone about her evening: "An' then, outa nowhere, he started dancing with me!" Tho her listener, unknown to me, will find that "terribly romantic", suddenly doubting my own waltz invention, i stop. I need t' face it, dont i? I'm no dancer.

"I think it was –howda they say?– terribly gallánt?"

<Terribly is right. But then, cheering you up was the whole point. Such behavior has *much of madness and more of...* How does it go?> ...I fully expected her to counter w *more of sin,* to which i would then have

appended, <Ah, yes! Sin! With its something chased forevermore? er-, chaste nevermore? er-, right, whatever....> But again getting no reaction, shaking my head, i strolled us over to the most ironic of the benches.

No sooner had we sat when, surprising even myself, i said <Wait!> and pulled her to her feet. Still stuck in my victorian script i said <First we must renovate! Stand aside!> Bending forward, i uprooted one end of the bench, went to the other; repeat. <Bureaucratic stupidity will be the ruin of us!> most of my natty *ébats* being somewhat *tipplag*ic creations, i admit. Clumps of dirt fell from twin concrete pedestals as i swung the thing aboutface, replanted it in its trenches, bid her sit. But by then she was laffing hysterically & walking in a circle, every so often peeking over at me, laffing even more. <Now that's more like it.>

"It is [she tittered, sitting] It is!" Tho my <more like it> did not re the new attitude of our bornagain bench but her much improved mood, i said nothing. "Now we c'n see the water ...'n' all the pretty lites."

The prognathous profile of a tugboat trudged darkly by as we sat. Her stepfather would be coming tomorrow. "Mother says he wants to make things right between us. I said it was a bad idea. She pleaded, said it would mean so much to him. She wished I'd learn t' let go of the negative past; called me a pessimist. When she started crying I stopped arguing ...I'm a dumb optimist, actually. Sometimes I think the impossible c'n happen. ...So now I'm hating myself for saying yes."

Waves from the passing tug look oily & black as they approach, then slap the shorewall. Taking her hand, i felt a drop of water splash past my wrist (tear? wave-splatter? rain?). You obviously detest the man. Tell me if i'm heading where i dont belong. "It's jus that it's stuff I havent even told Sister yet. An' there's no one more likely t' understand than her. [voice quavers] No offense. We were jus *reallyreally* close as kids."

No offense taken. The stars were hid by a mask of cirrus as she gazed toward the infamous island. After a few mins we rose, ambled across the grass, looked down at the water & its narrow swatch of sand, darkly streaked. {Petrol pollution!} <Outgoing tide shouldnt be this grimy. I wonder if the bayguard folks know about this?> We climb onto a raised breakwater, walk out to its end, sit looking down at the inky sheen as it slaps the boulders below our dangling feet. She asks about me.

My life's an open book so t' speak.... (Humor flops again.) Hey, at dinner i told you about my cousin sheila 'n' me —the games we played? Before her dirty-minded dad stopped us. I wanna make it clear: That wasnt totally kidstuff. I'll embellish if ya like.

Sound of buoybell clangs not far off. *[Gongs in white surplices....]* The water's many reflective facets, upclose, w distance graded into a wide unfractioned swath of swallowing blackness. "It's different for women. Not that you arent easy to talk to. I feel like I've known you a long time. I guess it's cause I've read that 'open book'...as much as it *can* be read."

{Aha.} You have a distinct advantage there. I know nothing about you in comparison.

Her black skirt, which shone like leather, turnedout to be kulots zippered on both sides. The taper of tendon, running from outer nether-thigh to upper calf, is sharpened by shadow. The tops of her thighs, knees, the fine bones in her wrists, glisten softly in the muted lite. "The firsthing I knew was that time you were arrested for handcuffing yourself to a container of nuclear waste set to be dumped in the ocean."

You *cant* remember that. That was at least fifteen years ago! I decided she must have seen a rerun of a taped interview made after *the greenEarth chronicles* was issued, as it was packed w outtakes of activists at work.

"I feel like I've been t' sea with you, been arrested with you, climbed smokestacks redwoods the sides of aircraftcarriers, been chained to harpoon launchers, nuclear subs, protected seals being clubbed to death, been clubbed along with you by cops." Dangles feet in rhythmic unison as she speaks. Strange glintings haunt watery depths. "Youre the most compassionate person I know. <Youre very kind.> No, *you* are... Whereas I only read or hear about the things *I* believe in, you *act* on them ...*write* them ...*do* them."

Two identically loaded barges slid by a ways off, pushed by a lone tug w eerie green runninglites. Its diesels groaning w their double load, the dark prow threw off a wake that was soon sloshing beneath our feet. One slosh shot high enuf to splash her legs. We jumped away, returned to 'our' bench: the one parkbench w a progressive attitude. I passed her a fresh handsker w which to wipe away the foul liquid. The sky to the n was litup by litening for fully a few seconds: thunderstorm moving in off the ocean. Sitting sideways to her i watched, a ways off, another couple drift in, sit down.

When the scented night of summer covers
field and city with her veil of [lavender?],
all the lanes are full of straying lovers....

Beyond them and across the street, the flicker of a cigaret liter glowed briefly inside a parked car. Lovers? A poltergeist? My date, facing the water, saw none of this.

Being not all that far from frix, an airliner thundered overhead, veered east, just missing the stormfront, the distant thunder of which commingled w its own. The vibration of the mix, as it tumbled tympanilike at us, reminded me of "cloudburst" in grofe's *grand canyon.* Cello-moans, strings murmuring like conversing demons, wind machine whirring: great buzzsaw in the sky; cymbal-strikes & piano-flickers of litening unzipping the black skirts of clouds.

She got up, walked to water's edge, stopped. "We'd better go. If I confess any more family stuff youre gonna think I'm a nutcase." Laffs humorless laff. Somewhere along the way as she spoke i decided her stepfather's last name was dodgson. I had unwittingly mixed into her talk a reference she'd made to an infamous divorce trial. Yet having no patience for monied decadence, had paid little attention. "Карл Красивый и Кара Безобразный." Metiers of mcguffin & montageurs of redherring need not scramble for a translator. My reader can trust me when i say, i will not stoop to scattering false scents across the countryside of this bio (even civilized bloodhounds deserve respect) for such detective-tale tactics would pollute the truth-&-nothing-but objective so vital to this testament.

I came up behind her, took her arms at the elbows, turned us face to face. Look, you dont hafta prove anything t' me. I think your want of privacy is admirable. She turned her face away, began to walk off, returned, sat, facing away. I went over, sat behind her, drew her hair back from her eyes; on feeling wetness presented her w a fresh double of the first handsker. "I'll wash it for you" she promised, done swiping, dropping it into her shoulderbag. Arms around her, using meticulous thumbs, i knead her wrists, while beyond her profile i watch several moths circling like planetesimals the yellow glare of a pathlite.

My dear young lady, i... Pause... Take one hand, caress back&forth the indiscernible fluff of her forearm. Look, i like you more than makes sense right now —to either of us i'm sure. Her *doux yeux* assured me i could have kissed her then, for the moment was resonant w sensation. The other couple, now strolling our way, stopped, turned back, sat at a considerate distance. Yet another plane thundered up ɛ over, the shadow of its long body clear against the sky. Lites pulsing, it penetrated a clenched fold of cloud.

How to explain reallife beyond what mere dialog can show? Let's just say, our civil sexuality is a complicated nutcase. For instance, it is documented that jurors, given responsibility for evaluating allegedly illegal sex acts captured on video, have admitted to becoming sexually aroused by the very acts they were sworn to judge. Not just that but, they felt so entrapped win the mechanics of these acts that, when it came time to deliver a verdict, they did so in a state of associated guilt, either w the victim or the perp, and sometimes both. Irrational leniency often results from such vicarious identification (stockholm syndrome); so much so, it is not unusual for skewed decisions to be handed down. (I need pointout however: The term irrational seldom has negative connotation for me.) Reader, i'm speaking of average men ɛ women, like you, like me. Even members of official committees, when dealing say w pornography issues, have admitted to reviewing more film more pictures more books for many more weeks than was necessary to formulate a judicious opinion. Indeed, well respected judges in similar cases (a little austere, a little grumpy, perhaps, but socially adept) are known to have removed such records to their homes for the purpose of "evaluation" afterhours. And what of those legions of coaches ɛ instructors, in schools ɛ other institutions, who find themselves applying the videos theyve created, w such passion for detail, less&less to instructive or training purposes ɛ more&more to private ones? But what am i getting at? Pastors physicians psychiatrists professional counselors mentors coaches ɛ instructors, in colleges highschools halfway houses summer camps monasteries convents all sort of official civil institutions, have become entangled w a sexually curious or aggressive patient believer client intern camper student inmate ward or charge, even to the extent of developing enduring relationships: i imply mistresses marriages domestics partnerships discipleships etc etc etc.

It needs be understood. In my lap just then, reader —yes yes, even as you read the paragraph above i'd pulled her onto my lap— was not perched some homeless baggirl picked up "down at the wharfs" by some ardent sailor. No,sir. For those who are w me on this, we have, rather, nuzzled ε cuddled in our mutual laps the maddeningly desirable, largely licit ε surely lethal body of a female person the accused author claims is Lilith McGrae ...whom, need i add, is quite possibly reliving win the interstices of her own hindsight (in writhing cinamavision ε white-hot techniscope) scenes from some sex encounter fit to melt the 3d glasses of the most jaded moviegoer! [*"beshrouded wails...."*] That i would be years discovering the true nature of these scenes from the girl/womanhood of Ms McGrae is beside the point. I'm no robot and neither was she. The science-minded reader will scoff but i swear i could sense something carnal sizzling like static elec from her nerve-ends as the titest little highriser buttox in n.amer lolled on my lap.

(After removing shrapnel embedded in my lower abdomen [that explosion, when i was a boy, remember?] doctor metzger informed my father, "The lad need not worry about a manly future. The erectile tissue in that region is robustly responsive". This exactly was my hardship that eve.)

Events often arrange themselves Wout regard for manmade laws or rulebooks. Life moves on –rich, throbbing ε vital existence– moves ahead, whether approved by us or not. Without warning our plane of being can switch from low hum to high buzz. A mere ringing in one's ear can alter, if only a little, his or her state of awareness. Watch, the next time it happens; as soon as the ringing begins, test your rational faculties. Did Earth's crust shift everso slitely? Meanwhile. {Why is she shifting her weight like that?} And might not such shifts actually be caused by angular acceleration in the ever-fluxing interplanetary gravitational grid? {How can she not be moving like that on purpose?} And why havent studies been done to see if the etiology of quake activity is linked to Earth's orbit —namely to see if there might be terrestrial effects due to elliptic acceleration? In other words, can an ostrich be certain its head is *not* in the sand when its ears are ringing?

Her face nuzzled into my neck, her breath brimstone hot; her lovely weight –excruciating vacuum on my lap– restlessly rolled ε shifted, yanked upon the worst intent of a vascular monolith i could no longer conceal. A sinister musician plucked at sinews where Nature offers no defenses; deep pizzicato strings rushedup at me from an uncharted abyss. I pulled her face to mine, looked into her vast wet eyes, and w my most iron will, resisted the kiss that would have detonated an irreversible vulcanism. The farthest galaxies, poised at the edge of "time", began to spill over that edge as, in midflux {GreatGaia!}, i managed to abort the terrible explosion seething in me by permitting her maddening weight to crush an overanxious testicle.

Somewhere in the hawaiian islands, italy or japan, maybe, or yaanek or orizaba, a burst of lava ε hissing ash outgassed briefly, spilled over its brim for a protracted moment, and paused ...just lay there, this molten stream of throbbing magma, midshaft, pulsing, poised, as if its entire future ε fate were at the whimsy, the wink, of the faintest shudder of the farthest star! Thank the goddess of virginity, she did not move —who cares if by knowledge or by fiat of *tipplagic.* intuition. Soon i was breathing almost normally again. Her dark lashes, wet, languorous, close to my face, were just lifting. It was time out-of-hand. Drawing her face to me (hand still gripping the nape of her neck), i misplaced two kisses meant for her lips. Soft as tiptoeing starlite i kissed first one wide eye then the other. Their lids, w a salty mist that tingled tung's tip, fluttered, squeezed under the press of my tung. In my lap her rump twitched convulsively. {Aaaargh! Has she any idea what she's doing?} ...what a rusted tanker of testosterone she'd set her cutting torch against? Another tympanal thunder rolled –in me or in the distance i couldnt be sure– as an ephemeral flute {Jumping jizmatics! Nobody move!} sang its adagio at the dizzied stars! Will, iron will, melted like candlewax. A distant galaxy switched into superluminal drive, exited forever our perceived reality! as a quaking bubbling spewing hissing groaning column of awe-full desire flowed ...flowed ...flowed out of me and did not stop til i was sure my innards must implode from the purge!

The other couple –in shadow some distance away, on their own law-abiding bench– stood to leave...in our direction! {God hymen, did i forget to offerup the beating heart of a lamb?} Seeing them approaching, like a naughty child from a stolen pony, ms wrigglebritches slid off my lap. {Ooo, dont gooo nooooow!} Then, by some reversal in the polarity of chance, the couple suddenly turned back, left by another route as i bent forward in a paroxysm of mixed agony ε bliss.

"Are you okay?" she ventured after a concerned silence.

<Yes> i groaned.

We sat for a time on that bench (later baptized: "our enchanted bark"). She lounged, head on my chest, while giddy instinct sauntered off –a dazed wildly reciting montague– into a handy mist of solipsism. *Ah! Quelle nuit, quel festin! Bal divin!* "And without a fresh snotsker for yourself!" she would tease months later —once we'd sortedout between us all the comedy-of-errors intrigue. Meanwhile, the storm had slipped to the n and, in the indigo sky above the lovers, between opacus clouds, the happily hoodwinked stars made a cameo appearance amidst long filaments of fog. Retrovision can still 'hear' (from somewhere outside the stone-muted walls wherein i agonize tonite) that brahmsian flute echoing high & thin as taut desire.

On the drive back i remembered my oregon trip. Forgetting school i asked if she wanted to join me. All set to clearcut classes she remembered her promise to meet her stepfather that eve. "Crapola." Little charley marley –"No, that's really his name"– her 4yearold halfbrother, would be there, "So it shouldnt be too hard to take." She could not disappoint her mother since their relationship, "deplorable for years", was just beginning to improve. "Poor leyda. [she sometime's called her that] Her mind is an abandoned nuthouse". That metaphor, which she could not explain, *still* haunts me.

Under the same alder i wished her well w her appt, said i would call when i got back. When would that be? Around 10oclock. ["Tomorrow nite ...I mean t'nite?"] Yes, t'nite. So i'd better scuttle along. Leaning against the javelin we embraced, not meshing nearly so niftily this time —since the top of her head, standing face-to-face, reached only the bottom of my (very declined) chin. So i hoisted her onto the car. We watched stars moon & filaments of fog vie for skyspace —cover, uncover, repeat. I guessed rain, perhaps before daylite, as a highup wind swept brushstrokes of cirrus in from the sea. Rare bay-area nite of negligible fog. After yet another goodby, we spoke of getting to the beach one day soon; maybe sunday? "That should work." Should i call when i get in? I'd better. <It might be late?> That's okay. We stayed, just holding, gazing, til she too had to go. *["Madame!"] "By and by, I come...!"*

I watched her lithe silhouette recede toward the amber-lit entranceway from which she gave a wave then slipped inside. Something told me to call her back but i did not trust the voice —guessed it was one of my bodyparts casting ballots. Ego (shy but unruly). Libido (unruly, period). Both gangingup on heart (unruly but honorable). Clearly, every organ in my body, little ε big, wanted its way w her. Like some kid, i wanted to carve our names ...No. Make that initials. One cant prove who's who by just initials... was tempted to carve them into the bark of a large tree "hanging out" near her window; or like a montague, climb to that window and to paradise. For i could still feel her small face in my hands, her lips marshmallowing under the brushing knuckle of my index, the hard press of her capable contoured body. (Still feel them even as i write tonite!)

8

Days are racing by, most wout my consent, a couple even wout my knowledge. It is midwk already. But no matter. This update, going back a few days, begins w the women upstairs.

Fresh out of the rack, ritually splashing face ε head w tapgoop, i spied outside my window that tantalizing white chrysalis just being lowered! As if for a bath, i hung my bedsheet and, w a new&improved gaff, was able to snag the thing when a puff of breeze brought it tite t' larboard. After coaxing the line thru the hole (which i'd been enlarging a little w every bath) i attached my own note and set it free; for i did not wish to let another day of failed contact go by. The following is what i sent aloft.

> My name is nathan schock. I wrote this note before reading yours...to save time. No, i did not murder secretary of the environment strickswine. I've never killed anyone outside of military service. Also, i'm no chickenhawk, as suggested by the press. My only sex partners have been women. What are you doing tonite? Probably what i'm doing tonite. Write if you have ☺ t-i-m-e. nathan s

I felt it best to keep it simple. Before i could read their note it was time to eat. I get my meals at the same time as the guards (but at my own table) and female inmates (in an adjoined messhall). I think this is because full staff is needed when male inmates eat after us. Not daring leave it in my cell, i took the note w me. On returning i sat on my rack, back to the camera, and read: (Brace yourself, proofreader.)

> What is your name. Mine is Janis. Why are you in. How old are you. Do you smoke. Do you coke. Do you like girls. Do you like to watch tv. Do you like wrestling or springer. What do you like to do on dates? Do they sexally haras you to. Please write back. Lonely. Your friend Janis. PS. This place has us all horny. You muss be horny to, no. [sic all]

You can imagine the mental pic that formed: mudwrestler janis: kinky thinning clown-orange hair, gapped & broken yellow teeth, poor hygiene, history of giving & rcv'g abuse etc. I couldve been in a cell beneath any one of a hundred females and i get janis! But then, who knows, this janisperson, this unassuming elephantasy of mine, could serve as go-between ...between me and some hotter little criminal upstairs? Perhaps all is not lost. Look on the ~~brite~~ briter side, nathan.

Table & chair arrived same day. Good timing, as i'd taken lunch back to my cell. Like the last 'newborn fawn' they gave me, this table is none too stable. And its chair (folding wood-slatted) needs a towel or it bites my nates when it sways. Emil, bearer of good news, arrived shortly after. Three petitions it seems —one each to the congress, senate, atty general, justice dept & to the governor of the big wooden chair down the hall— have been delivered, each having over 2million signatures! ...w an additional 3million promised in the next three months! The petitions' demands? That i be given a new & just trial; that my death sentence be commuted until said trial is over. Press releases noting this groundswell of protest have been sent out. But nothing has broken and we are not to expect anything from the poppress, emil warns. He hopes "If nothing else, judge black's overturning of the jury's verdict must be addressed by appeals courts, both state 'n' fed'ral." Even here i should expect nothing, adopt a wait-and-see attitude, not set myself up for more disappointment. When he left we shared a "pug" —brief backpatting hug of brotherly warmth commonplace among greens of deeper shades.

While i realized at the time of my arrest, when it came to conservation issues, emil was a juggernaut of jurisprudence, i also knew his professional method was conservative —when what i obviously badly needed was a criminal lawyer. Fact was however, all big names i interviewed or, ahem, "consulted with", struck me as, if not outright crooks, persons reeking of moral/ethical compromise. This is where emil's father entered. While he'd handled only a couple cases of any notoriety, he'd run a respectable "criminal" practice in the seattle area for a couple decades. On meeting, both of us liked what we saw and emil green sr was appointed head counsel.

After emil left i was not returned to my cell but escorted to the warden's office. It seemed everyone who was anyone at lorton [prison —Ed.] was there. Warden todion, who required a hissing shallow breath every five or six words, began by informing everyone, the basketball team had been "beat agin" in playoffs "despite owah facility bein one o' the faaaahnest in the nation. Frankla, ah dont know bout yall but ah dont lahk bein on the bottom o' ennathin but the divil's shitlist." Dr slug smiled at this while asst dir becillo flapped his thighs like a circus seal clapping.

Holding aloft a large glossy b&w press foto, the warden got "straight to the point. We have a stah among us, gentlemen. Is this yall, mistah schock?" It was an old victory shot snapped some three decades before in london at a sirCosmos competition. "Not bad huh gentlemen? Now ahm gonna git raaht ta whaa ah called yall heah. How long would it take yall, schock, ta git worl-class lak this agin...? No? Whaddayamayn, no...? Problum? What problum...? Food? What's wrong with owah food...?" He waddled twice around his large desk, pivoting its corners on fat fingertips. "Then blazes we'll *git* food! ...Aquipment? We *got* aquipment. An if we dont we'll git it. Bejezus, man!" Warden todion came around the desk, stopped by the side of my chair, close as a friendly dentist. Dir straitmon's thighs gave a flap. I leaned away. "Whatll it be, schock? Are y'on the team or would yall rather rot til ya die in that dayum sayl out thayah?"

<Rot.> I rose, headed for the door.

"Ahm not done with yall, boy! Git back heah. *Now!*" Two guards jump in front of the door, hit me in the chest w the flats of their palms, halting my retreat. "Who in the hayl do ya think you ah? Yall leaves heah when ah say an not until! Is thayat undastood, sah?" [i am shoved back down into the chair w formal flourish] Thayah's sumthin ah maht shudda tol yall." He approaches. "Now if'n we c'n show claym [clem], the govanah, what weze up ta heah. An' if'n ol' claym smiles on yall's new coowapative attitude. Wayl, who knows? He may jes putoff yall's execution, which is sittin on his daysk as we speak. [searches my face for reaction] Whadyasay, schock?" Slaps my shoulder: true coach & friend, yessir; winks at straitmon whose knees lock. Waddles back behind desk.

{This is a choice? Pump iron like a fool or be executed at the first political opportunity?} Finish this testament or die? {Hmmmm.} Feeling totally suckerpunched, i give deadpan, say nothing. My lack of further dissent is taken as a positive quasi-contractual gesture.

"Rahmemba, schock. This aint th' ol days. [holds aloft foto of contemporary bodybuilder] Ya gonna hafta heap on muskuls til yaw veins ah poppin 'cause nowadays this heah's what they call bewdiful." Greasy masses of bulging serpentine flesh writhe toward my suggested future. "Whaddayall think?"

I glance askance. <Greased obscenity.>

"Do yall believe this mayun? Here ah am takin mah valuble tahme ta offa you this singulah oppahtunity, sah, an oppahtunity which any *otha* prisona in this institution would jump at the chance ta...."

<Not one of whom can guarantee you the victory you want....>

His mouth closed slowly as he stared. "Mista schock, sposin thet's true... Tell me, is there *anythin*, anythin et all, dont be shy now, thet yall dont have a problem with? The good doctah assures us theyah aint no such thing."

Is that a sincere question, sir?

"Ah stand heah sinceah as sinceah c'n be."

<Justice. That i have no problem with. Undiluted unpolluted justice.>

Looks blankly over our heads. "Mista nathan, faw a supposebly smaht mayun you ah vera vera naive. [approaches, leans in, whispers] Pipedreams, ahm sorra ta inform yall, is not why ah've gathud these *verra* busy men heah taday. *Winnin* is why ahv brought them heah." I find myself almost pitying his short-of-breathness ε pasty sheen. He stood erect, turned back toward his desk. "Bein a man of ma wehrd, ma offa will stand til noon t'morrah. Take the prisonah away, gentlemen. [i rise, half turn] An' rahmemba, schock. Around heah we rahspect a mayun who aint too proud ta sing fah his suppah. [i turn back] Ah'll be spectin ta see yall up thayah, mistah schock!" He thrust out a short meaty arm indicating a point high ε behind me. All present looked puzzled. "Up on thayat theyah stage wheah yalls gonna win us the gold, sah!" He punctuated his desire w a stubby powerpump.

I was escorted back to deathrow by an unusually gloomy glumm ε glum gluum. Thank our lucky stars competition's still alive 'n' well in america, eh, guys? ...Ya seem down in the dumps. What's the beef? Actually i said nothing. I think they were wishing i'd been, in my foolish youth, a hopscotch or mumbletypeg champ instead of a bodybuilder.

And not leastofall there was other news that day. The last pages of part2 of the book you hold left these walls and are presumably beyond censure or destruction. (They stopped examining emil's brief case a few weeks ago ...but only when he *leaves* the premises. He's still searched coming in. This is good for, ideally, these writings should be in a safe place the moment i draft them.)

Lastly, on the walk back to my cell that day, the warden's admonition that i learn to sing for my supper, triggered a loop of lyric: "Sing for your supper" was a song which, in most versions i knew, i'd never particularly liked. For an old civil contagion [state enslavement of talent] was hid in the lines "Sing and you'll be fed... songbirds always eat...dine with wine of choice... gilded bird... courtesan with wings...." As to the warden's offer? I accepted. (Isnt that a no-brainer?) Lastly, wout leverage i'm helpless against dr ratstool's reign of terror. And, secondly, what if things really are that corrupt where, w a mere fonecall, todion can sway the governor of this death-dealing common-wealth not to do what 5million passionate signatories have yet to stop him from doing? "So, little swallow, swallow now [your pride]. For now is the time to sing for your supper". You have afterall, first&foremost, a story to finish, no?

9

The conference in oregon was chiefly about greenEarth & EarthNow joining forces to halt the clearcutting of the last 5% of our ancient nat'l forests. To add insult to tragedy, the buyers of these trees were getting them for $1each! And, o yes, tax dollars provided logging roads & other amenities. As you might guess, chainsaws were humming from dawn to dark and the suffocating press of mass extermination was everywhere.

We were airborne by 7a. I wanted to catnap but because rick brian delphine & emil were along, could not. It was on this flite i first met emil. In that he often worked for united greens legal defense fund (crucial arm of the big14 green organizations), i told him of my n.e.f ideas, of uniting the big14 w the 70 or so midsized enviro groups across the nation, creating a front large enuf to file suits against corps, the fed, or any state, county or municipality complicit in ecologically criminal activity. He liked the idea, said he would help any way he could.

I always think of the "beaver state" as first in the u.s to pass a bottle&can-deposit bill —back in 1971! The conference was hosted by u of or and attended mostly by EarthNow members. The atmosphere was tense for good reason. EarthNow hq had been raided by fbi agents (code: state-sponsored terrorism) just days before, its offices ransacked, records confiscated, property stolen ε damaged. Hours later EarthNow chief roy freeman was arrested ε jailed on charges of conspiracy (sure sign of legal desperation). In his opening, brian used an argument from my *ungreening of tomorrow.*

> Saving trees, "a pastime for kooks" they call it. I think it's a good deal more than that. I think, if a major road can be diverted in order to save a 200-year-old tree which Paul Revere is only rumored to have climbed, surely we can save just five percent of those trees which witnessed the dawn of humanity in America."

A round of applause interrupted the reading. When the crowd quieted brian went on to quote emil, who was one of freeman's lawyers.

> "If my client is guilty of conspiracy, it is a conspiracy to flush out the sane people in this nation. It is a conspiracy to gather together persons with a grip on the big picture, to show us all the cracks, big, scary cracks, in a dam which every life on Earth lives downstream from! I refer to the environment of this Planet of ours ...supporting life as we've known it by the skin of its teeth."

More applause. Let me note as i write now, i had not the slitest inkling emil would, in regard to my own arrest some 3yrs later, be saying something very similar to the press. "Schock's only 'crime' has been to repeatedly risk his life to protect 4 billion years of Earth's evolution. If this is a crime, I'm honored to defend it."

Some readers will remember, the fed. case against EarthNow fell on its face —despite the fbi spending 3.5million of taxpayer$ in pre-arrest stagings ε media propaganda. Their stings ε undercover infiltrations were designed to "yield an indictment that would stick". Saints during the inquisition failed less exotic censure. So tempers ran hot that summer&autumn. And the corpolitic press reacted by peppering articles w language like "violent fringe, green menace, green guerrillas, ecoterrorists, ecotage", etc. The picture the public was being given was both sinisterly planned ε sickeningly false.

By lunch it was decided: redwood summer —that is, the vacationtime effort to protect old-growth forest (those stands 150- to 3,oooyrsold!) would continue. GE officers agreed to supply transit for supporters to&from the next demonstration site, which was to be eureka (ca). The worst moment however came w deciding deepwoods tactics.

Because it was obvious cops federal & local had been sent by logging-industry bosses to tyrannize EarthNow members, a feeling of retaliation was strong among some of those present. GE officers, fearing violence in the woods, proceeded tentatively. I contended that <To supply buses is not to underwrite anything. By what methods caring adults decide to protect the millions of lives that comprise a forest seems to me to be up to them. Whether we rush these Planetary paramedics to the site of the hemorrhaging on buses bicycles rickshaws or donkeycarts has little to do with how they choose to stop the bleeding once they arrive.> I suggested, before we went any further, that all of us get on the same page in terms of principles. My thought was to capitalize on an overarching belief in biocentrism. Ie, get everyone to commit to a respect for *all* lifeforms, whereby one must respect the enemy's life by default. In *ungreening...* i wrote

> Every creature and Natural thing in the Universe has intrinsic value. Since we do not know, and *cannot* know, what that value is at depth, we must do everything in our power to guarantee all Natural things an equal right to exist. For these two things –intrinsic value and the right to exist– are inalienable in *every* Natural instance, whether asteroid or star, rock tree scorpion mole koala whale or human. Only by way of vanity greed or blind subjectivity dare we say, "I have more Cosmic significance than that tree, that ocean, that sky, that hillside, that stone, that flower, that star". For the human species to fill the planet called Earth with its kind, and for us to devour all else out of runaway greed and folly, is not okay just because we choose to pretend not to know what we're doing. This our mutual home, Earth, can no longer be viewed solely as a resource for the self-centered desires of humanbeings.

But instead of instilling the deep respect for all life i intended, EarthNow's soldier ants described old-growth loggers as persons who "pretend not to know theyre criminals". Tho deepwoods tactics went unresolved, we did agree to provide transport for those who espoused to nonviolent methods.

10

Oddly anxious to get back, i flagged an eve flite to frix. Nite obscured the view my morn arrival had afforded: salmon & scott ranges; trinity alps & siskiyous; an occasional river glinting thru rainforest Wilds; the alternating blacks&whites of the marble mtns, as tho the keys to some huge keyboard in the sky got spilled & shattered there; blacksand mirrors of beaches appearing in angular swatches thru the clouds as we made our southward turn.

{Anxiety. Hmm.} Examine priorities, for anxiety often lurks in things undone. ❶ Current book? Moving. ❷ N.e.f formation. Slow but going. ❸ Lecture series? Fine. ❹ Workout program? Behind. Catch up at once. ❺ Lilith... But was my numbering a sham? Had #5 rocketed to #1? Were my tadpole pituitary ε serpentbrain lusting again? Who among us (c'mon, guys) has exemplary control over his hairy libido? And who, macacuslike, salutes instinct the moment it rears its Wildeyed little head? Ruminate. {Is ownership ever ok? This watch this briefcase one's house the space around it? No. But what else beside ownership, in materialistic society, gets respect? What other tool, avail to the little guy, can keep the romans ε brits of our day from plundering every inch of our Planet? And to get to the point, why should one feel he must *possess* a mate? And possess *is* the right word!}

Airtravel (tin coffin transport) is hard on claustrophobes. {I do not own that place i call "my" land. I merely live there, try not to threaten its wellbeing. I know that without freedom from my tampering the land will die and its creatures with it. Should it be any different with a mate? Is it her physicalness alone that incites the monkey-lust in me, makes the reptile (coiled in a knot in my primal cortex) rise up 'n' dance on its tail? Again. Cant one "want" his female ideal without desiring to possess her? Of course he can.}

Achieve altitude, leveloff. {Liar.} *Ah, ravissant mystère!* Somewhere i'd heard, a tactic common to storytellers is to maintain, "The story you are about to hear was told to me by a complete stranger, a happenstance of travel". That is to say, someone somewhere, maybe not even very far away, could maybe solve the mystery of Lilith. *Et certes il existe.* And if, as he told his story, he replaced real names w fictional ones (for instance, olwen), how long might he go on before i recognize he's talking about Lilith? And why couldnt that storyteller be in the seat beside me? —instead of the self-absorbed corporate suit continually feeling his nails, caressing his face ε hair. {77% of hits at cyberporn sites occur from 9 to 5p. So much for the bad rap bluecollar ε no-collar males get in the popmedia.} By then i'd learned to fear most those *most* trapped win the wide civil sieve of oligarchic ethics.

"Your hostess will serve you momentarily." {Tepid tuckermanities, the word [momentarily] is everywhere! "Thank you for holding. All agents are busy. Your call is important to us. Someone will be with you *momentarily*."} Ever wait in an emergency for "momentarily" to arrive? Recorded voice on prison pa: You will be executed *momentarily*. Please hang in there. Your suffering is important to us. (Dr shrinkmoid delites in such expressions.) Momentarily arrives. Stewardess requests my choice in drinks. <Any all-juice juices?> Only o-j. <Concentrate?> Slite yod, flat-lipped. <I'll pass then, thanx.> Consternated. {Have i stepped off the treadmill *again?*}

As i gaze from my windowseat at patches of moonlite & cloudcover flashing on, flashing off, like stobes in a rave club switched to slomo, thought returns to my 'priorities' list ...specially to #2: my n.e.f: nat'l ecology front ...which i'd labeled <slow but going>.

{Going where? And why so slow? Why isnt a green legal defense fund big enuf to take on *all* environmental terrorists, whether they be corporate, municipal, state or fed., exciting to *every* green imagination? Such power in the courts would put an end to our being clubbed 'n' jailed for daring to criticize bigCorpx and the politicians they own. What sort of green mentality would hesitate to come fully behind such a cause, such a *totally possible* cause? And moreover, why *do* they hesitate ...or even run?}

Privately my nef vision incl's an umbrella gef (global ecology front), an intn'l coalition of enviro ngo's having the power to haul entire nation/states and pannational parliaments & corporations into court, a coalition headedup by the likes of enviro atty victor falconne. Falconne, w 30yrs of major legislative & court successes on his resumé, has been preaching for decades: "My method is simple. While the doors of your courts are still open, sue the bastards! You can lay there in a pool of blood with your protest sign and maybe get five seconds on the evening news —*if*, that is, you didn't get beat so bloody you upset people's dinnerhour. *Or* you can file a legal complaint and turn your belief into real green power." Yet a career-long struggle to teach this simple route to eco-empowerment has left falconne discouraged: "It's as if everyone has defeat built into his view of what's possible. I've seen it a thousand times. You can hand people the power to construct a whole new world and, guess what? They run like hell the minute they see success is likely. *You* tell *me* why....[Vic thinks it's because]...we've been mentally 'n' emotionally controlled from above for so long that the possibility of real justice at dawn tomorrow terrifies us."

I remember thinking as the clouds thinned ε the moonlite grew briter: If vic, as leader of ugldf (united greens legal defense fund), has uncovered such apathy among greens, what hope do my even more powerful nef ε gef have? Well, truth be told, the apathy vic confronted is not so innocent. For thanks to hearing the complaints of people of color during my world travels, i read this fear, this "reluctance to bring about significant change", differently.

Naomi Klein

Because every time i track it to its lair i am confronted w the unbearable whiteness of being green: the unspoken/unmentionable dread of many 1st world enviro bigwigs to bringabout ANY CHANGE which will threaten white privilege or its satellites of privilege. For just as royalty of old needed the hungry masses to support its lifestyle, so, on a global scale, 1st world nations need 3rd world nations (w their "stinking hordes of primitives and savages"*) to be *kept as they are*—unchanged, save for more enslaved where possible. This is the superstructure of civil politics laid bare in a single sentence, and it's been generally thus ever since those white supremacist charioteers thundered out of the north into ancient sumer like pale monsters from some negative universe. (*C.d strickland, 1989, while on cia payroll.)

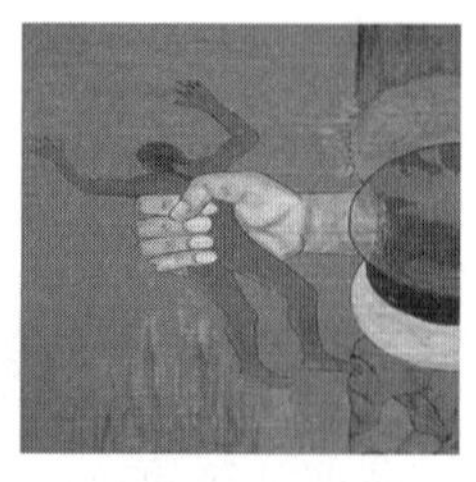

In this lite one quickly sees why the idea of "real justice at dawn tomorrow" terrifies only *certain* people. Because REAL justice means privilege for ALL, not just for white humans or their satellites of privilege. Paraphrase of black panther willie horton: ≈It's fear of pissed "niggers with guns" that made congress change laws, not their sense of empathy or justice.≈ Just the thought of people-of-color-w-power terrifies white supremacy in *all* its hiding places. (Hint: Why can white-supremecist groups in n.amer ε europe get away w training with, and hoarding, weapons ε munitions while green activists –let me stress, *activists*– are assaulted ε arrested every day for conspiring to think about some day owning a letter-opener? Ruminate that, dear reader.) I say: If 3rd world people controlled the ngo's of n.amer ε europe, most of those soulless bastards wrecking our children's Planet and its healthy future would be doing perpwalks on tv every day til we won back some of this *actual paradise-for-all* called Earth.

To fite for truth is to become the enemy of all things civil. Things have become that simple, that tragic.

Suddenly i realize, my checklist overlooks the biggest anxiety of all; my own personal gryllos —those terrifying little 'beings' we know from paintings made during the middle ages, hideous creatures which grin at the onlooker from the bowels of some monster's belly. What monster might that be? The sum of all gluttony ε denial in a single entity, maybe? Prostrating concept.

Backwhen i was free and at the pinnacle of my powers, the gryllos in the belly of civilization did not grin w such confidence, w such sinister glee as it does tonite in my cell. For i was upfront on the battlelines: skirmishing merryman of green innovation, greenarcher w a pen, and 'lucky' enuf to play a part in one of the most crucial times in Earth's evolution. Tho i wanted things to improve, ε tho i strove to halt rampant mass extermination, i was fartoo busy w the fite to go black w melancholy over the horrors civil mankind was perpetrating. Tho i knew it lived, no bloody-toothed Planet-gouging megamonster haunted the nite of *my* subconscious back then, its hideous little gryllos (the civilizing principle) urging it on. Compare this w my recurring dreams of late: civil humanity in the form of a global maggot mound swarming over Earth, devouring everything while claiming innocence w every swallow!

Hostess returns, pulls own string, replays self. 26 or so, red-haired green-eyed w a tire-smoking track record easy to spot. Was i sure i wouldnt be tippling tonite? (My word, not hers.) Just water, thanks. Darkhaired coworker turns, eyes me. Min later water arrives. "My friend says you have a nice smile." No jumpseat sniffer, consciousness merely scrolls backward a few years to stanny white's own penn station. Stella steno is walking ahead of me. Her sunglasses, hangingoff her purse by one arm, slip to the floor. When i stop her <You dropped these> she steps back, studies me as if about to start sketching, says, "You have a smile a girl could trust. But I'll bet you know that". It was not the first time, just the most candid. On the mu (electrified rail cars), somewhere under the hudson river, we got to talking —rare event in cities. Even rarer, we endedup dating. But traveltime to her apt (newark) soon outstripped desire... beside, she was a little whacked ε a nymphomaniac to boot. But that wasnt the outlandish part.

I'd often catch her staring. At first i thought {My adamsapple again}. Could happen anywhere. If our booth in a restaurant, say, was just a little private, she would slide over, touch w her fingertips, then kiss, the wick of my mouth.

I soon learned this was only a prelude, that it was not the bouncing nut of flesh in my neck that was the dish *d'resistance*. Turning my face toward her –and usually toward the wall, thank my aisle-seat rigor– she would wet an indexfinger, run it along my lips, wet it again, this time using my own tongue! I would pull her hand away, look around. She would laff, turn my face back, start over. Using tip of index like an artist's brush she would feel along the ridges of my teeth; upper first, then lower. "Theyre sooo straight", she would say, her breath coming in tiny gusts. "I can't believe it!" Just when i think she's joking, her eyes close, flutter, reopen and, showing a scary amount of sclera, threaten to roll up blank behind their orbits. "Theyre sooo beauuutiful" she panted one nite, oblivious to our surroundings. Once a waitress, dismayed, was standing there when i turned around.

I was initiated by stages. She soon began by wetting three fingers, sliding them deeply into her mouth, sucking on them, all the while palpating my teeth w her free hand, lisping thru fingers ε spittle "Theyre hot. But you know that. Youve really got some [pant] hot [gasp] fucking [lunge] teeth [spasm]!" She would draw out the -thhh ending to "teeth" as she fell back into the couch. A bout or two later she insisted i replace her fingers w myself, while she, reaching high w one hand and low w the other, plunged frantically beyond both our labia, moaning ε weeping the whole time …so loudly, in fact, one day on leaving i saw her neighbors peer after me thru their blinds.

{Even their [in-flite] water: Ghastly! …Radiated til dead.}

There comes a point for me where weirdness or fetishism, when the novelty wears off, gets grungy. Not "bad" or "evil", mind you —which are naive concepts unsupported in all the Universe! I speak of that point when you feel another's illness has begun to cling to you; a point where you are no longer just an objective (and still fascinated) apprentice. Play in the barnyard long enuf and you will slip and get some on you, as my (makebelieve) granpappy used to say. In this regard, as long as our narrator is ruminating….

I dated a girl once whose panties were being filched from the dryer in her pentaplex. She soon figured out who it was. The guilty one would return them in her mailbox w impassioned notes tied to the crotch w brite hairribbons. Soon he was calling her. She didnt mind this "so much" because "his notes are like poems". In fact what piqued her was findingout he was more interested in her panties than in her! The moment she realized he desired her undies more than the sweet bod they contained, the "romance" was over. This, reader (and not the bizarreness of the pantypoet's vice!), was my friend carol wert's cue to get tough. "Chillout on my underwear chump or I'll call the cops!" carol yelled into the fone one day —while a small stereo filled her rooms w a remastering of pelvisPretzel's hit, *a deck of cards*. The guano some women will put up w so long as their chosen chimp is singlemindedly passionate, flabbergasts me.

{What strange musement here in my windowseat by the wing. Looks like minimal moonshine below. But here, above the clouds: brilliant!} The larger lunar mares, paleblue, were clear to the naked eye. {Naked?} Thinking carouses. Naked-eye astronomy is a lost philosophy. Eddy poepoe knew decades agogo what few people know today. "To look at a star by [sidelong] glances… is to behold the star distinctly." [Emil, please insert exact quote; perhaps from an early eap flirtation w cosmology: *the thousand-and-second tale of scheherazade?*] [The quote is not from TSTS, though the subject matter is similar. —Ed.]

Between dozing ε waking ol' shep elbows his way into consciousness. PotUp themesong: trumpet tattoo of the *bahn frei* polka. "I was this kid once, see", in holman nude joisey, watchin tv. Shep recalls my father's rare turn w a tale…. Man (imagine rod serling) sitting by wing on crowded passenger plane. Clouds thick as chinese alphabet soup swirl past. Litening strikes; man thinks he sees, standing out on wing, a demon! Rubs eyes. Clouds intervene. Next electric flash, demon is back, sporting a pitchfork …like the one brandished for decades by the pickleshaped devil in ben-gay™ ads, digging his implement gleefully into debbie-the-cheerleader's bare shoulder. "Unless mr white, the friendly druggist, can help, she will not be able to attend the prom tonite." Only *this* demon, out on the wing, is way nastier.

I believe in letting the 'waking' unconscious run its course at least once a day, and this was it. Something my date said flitted past: But little charley marley will be there so it [dinner w her stepfather] shouldnt be too hard to take.

Jeering over its shoulder, the demon rams its triton into #3 engine. Man tells stewardess to tell pilot, plane is in danger of losing an engine. Pilots chuckle at this. Mins later #3 starts coughing sputtering, black smoke, the whole bit.

No one else can see the demon however. Pilots feather #3, chalk up failure to litening strike, limp on w remaining engines. Our demon, meanwhile, red-eyed, laffing, comes right up to window, spits at stewardess. But she cannot see him, only what looks like spittle smearing across the window. Demon moves on to next engine. Man sends stewardess back to pilots w latest demon update ...soforth.

Intermittently our plane passes thru high-heaped ridges of cloud. Out my window i see a stormy formation. It is shaped, well, like the bloated corpse of a pig —a black pig. I've seen such corpses in mexico india & africa. Out of each eye however [no "pig's eye" pun intended] emerges the head of a viper. Then, oblivious to logic, the porcine jaw sags so i can see all the way into the corpse's belly. There a white turbulence is wildly shapeshifting thru a series of masked images: twrch trwyth? One of these, by its sheer repulsiveness, reveals itself to be the corpse's gryllos. Somewhere midst this mental pingpong between brain lobes i fell asleep.

11

During breakfast guard glumm dropped a newspaper by my tray. "Thought ya'd like ta see this." Headline at the top of a1 could not be missed: JUDGE IN SCHOCK TRIAL REAFFIRMS DEATH PENALTY. {Another fed. tactic.} Before it acknowledged the millions of petitions in my behalf, the fed. wanted to reassure the public, it was indeed a "dangerous criminal" whom judge black had sentenced to die. Which brings up a point.

Within the boundaries of civilization Nature gets shortshrift. Nothing new here. Civilization afterall was designed for that purpose. No surprise then that Nature has no voice in the civil justice system. No Planetary rep was at my indictment; no creature or plant from ocean, sky or other Wilderness was given any say in my fate. The judge at my trial wore a robe that rippled like crude oil on drinking water. I was placed under oath using a book symbolically black, a book which has claimed for over 3000yrs: Earth is man's alone. It belongs to no other lifeform. Abuse what you like and, above all, beget beget beget. Imagine a book which purports to possess the wisdom of the ages never thinking to suggest, *Do unto Nature only as you would have Nature do unto you.* In such a toxic muck-of-a-philosophy our present legal system is grounded. And so-called modern man plods forward, blind to the sources of the very laws he lives by, swears by, destroys by, dies by.

And so i was commanded to raise one hand and speak under the aegis of that writ or be held in legal contempt. As i oathed to the god of oil the god of precious minerals the god of private ownership the god of selfishness the god of gluttony the god of instinct-hating the god of Nature-loathing the god of sexism the god of indentured servility the god of intolerance the god of paranoia the god of arrogance the god of imperialism and, mostofall, the god of denial w lethal impunity, i realized: {I am at the end of a very long line of outcasts forced to swear thus.} And tho the true Mother of us all (Nature) could not be barred from the proceedings (else trust me she would have been), she was forced to 'sit by in silence' while a son of hers –a son who had devoted his adult life to her welfare– was tried by the believers in *that* god, those gods, and then remanded to death in their names.

12

I got home around 11. The fone was ringing when i put the key in the lock ...upside down. Machine answers. Right key only to find it was right to begin w. Damn. Reinvert reinsert. What's the rush, anyway? Clunk. Caller hangsup exactly as imagined on my drive home.

On leaving the airport the robot controlling the gate did not approve of my perfectly good parkingpass. After a minute of haggling (w a commonsenseless machine no less!), i jumped from the car, bent its obscene aluminum appendage upward til i heard bones & tendons snap somewhere inside a gearbox. It shot up, hung there limply. The driver of the car behind leaned out his window and yelled "You go, guy!", while others behind him honked & waved in apparent approval.

Poured myself that tall juice i was by then ravenous to possess (nectar of passionfruit) –yes, possess!– started the mxs playing and sat. First came the usual fare. Then Lilith's voice. "Sorry to bother you, nathan. Youre probably not in yet. It's a long story ...beth's not in and i, well... My car's not running and i could use a ride. [pause, as if waiting for me to pickup] I'll try back later." Voice a little anxious maybe but otherwise normal. That was around 7p (if memory holds). Two hangups follow in the next hour. {Had she wanted a ride to keep from having to ride with her stepfather?} In the next mx the voice is entirely changed; breathless, angstful. "Nathan? Are you home yet? Can you answer? I'm at a fonebooth. I need ta talk t' you... Nathan? [pause] Are you there? [pause]" Machine cuts her off. Time

~10p ...followed by nine hangups! Every time, just before the machine answered (she later explained), she would hang up. This to save the last of her coins.

In the final mx her voice was changed altogether; slowly articulated, phlegmful, full of lenis ε a lisp, as tho fresh from the dentist and shotful w novocain. Replayed later, win the context of further events of that nite, this mx is nerve-shredding. The time: 11:11. That i wont forget. (The recording is probably still in a cabinet at ggNs. In fact i played it for the baron a couple months before my arrest —for he had more than a few memory-jarring questions about the details of this ε other events.)

I left the livingrm, headed upstairs. Too tired to think, i fall on bed, gaze longingly toward shower, wonder what to do. <Call her dorm, stupid.> No answer. Somehow i knew that too. Suddenly i felt as if i'd shed the skins of 21 summers and was this almost-kid again, standing braindazed in harlequin sun&shade, gazing after a swirl of dust from a vehicle which, by some twist of fate –no, make that, avulsion of fate– contains not only the lovely juanita darc, but my throat, heart, and at least two other prized organs.

I was showering when the fone rang. Back then i was still slow to comprehend vonfate's dark sense of humor, did not bring a fone into the bath. Untoweled ε dripping i answered: H'lo?

"It's me, Lilith."

<You alright?>

Cups fone w hand; there is distant coughing; returns] "I'm okay." Hollow-pipe sound of fonebooth.

Where are you?

She does not know "exactly. On the beach, somewhere near halfmoon bay, i think. That was the name of an airport we passed". Voice still phlegmful of lenis ε lisp. Disguised cough again. "I wouldnt bother you but i cant getaholda beth. An' father 'n' sister live so far. (I later learned, tho lalage ε her dad were indeed not near —motelled as they were in sacramento where lage had a major gymnastics meet next morn— and tho these logistics were enuf to put her off, they were not the only reason she did not bother her father ε sister that nite.)

I c'n hardly hear you. Can you breathe okay? I think we should call the medics til i c'n get there.

"No! Please dont call *anyone*. Please! O i knew i shouldnuv bothered you. I'm sorry. I better go."

Lilith... Lilith...! You *there*? [barely audible, "Yes".] Look, i wont call them. I wont. You have my word. But you tell me how i'm gonna find you if you dont even know the name o' the town for sure? [pause] Lilith?

"Jus turn right on young avenue a couple miles past the airport. Or young something. Street, maybe. I'm in the parkinglot near the beach. I'm the only one here... right now." I asked for the fone# there, told her to just wait, that i'd get there quick as i could.

Tho i knew roughly where halfmoon bay was, how to find Lilith once i got there from such sketchy directions....? Friends glendon mark & helmut had left thu on a mission. Elapsed time from fone hangup to igniting the javelin had to be a record for methodical me. Descending from the parking garage (around the corner), the bumper bottomed when i reached the st. My turn onto the beal st ramp was one long (and surprising) tiresqueal. Late as it was i called rick. "Sounds like she's south o' pillar point. Maybe el granada. Ask her if she c'n see a brite lite out on the water. Findout what direction it's in 'n' call me back. I'll check my g-p-s in the meantime....Hey, is there anything I c'n do?" Yeah. Get me the quickest route?

This was by far the fastest the javelin had gone since its new engine. Fearing i would overshoot the cabrillo exit i backed off, very nearly missing it anyway. Swerving out the ramp my headlites snagged for an instant, stark against a concrete wall, the wind-panicked wings of a {...a raven ...a vulture? ...O dumb.} ...a traffic-tattered plastic bag.

Rick knew where she was even wout the litehouse fix. "Cabrillo crosses a young avenue in el granada" which he pronounced graNAYda. The freeway ended abruptly about halfway to pillar point; the rest of the trip (on pacific hwy), tho w less traffic, was slower going, a lesson in speed v. angular momentum: roads normally just 'curvy' turnout to be real squealers. At a particularly perverse traffic signal in a town called moss beach, a police car, partially hid behind a dumpster, seemed begging me to run the lite. I used this maddening lull to call Lilith. It rang&rang. Lite finally changed. Fog-patches grew more frequent. {Switchon speakerfone.} When she finally answered i got some better coordinates, told her i was getting close. {She still sounds awful.}

When i reached young av i ran its length to a fenced parkingarea: long, narrow, w occasional openings leading to the beach. A policecar was just then cruising out a far exit. No fonebooth, no Lilith. {Shit.} As i retraced my tracks the policecar reentered where i came in. Fearing being run off, i was cordial. Could they help with something? The nearest fone? They direct me, cruise on. Not only set back, the booth's telltale lite was out. I parked, retrieved mag from the glovepocket, checked his innards (all ratshot), returned him on secondthought (leaving the pocket open), retrieved maglite (tire-thumper, socalled), went to look around.

No one in sight. Parkinglot lites were feeble ε few w fog rolling in thick at times. As i descended the stairs darkness took over and my flashlite behaved like a match in a windstorm. I aimed the limp beam outward. Rocks, like praying monks, lined the beach in both directions. Nobody else tho. {Might see better *without* lite.} Stood for a couple mins, eyes closed, depriving their pupils of photon stimulation ...the better to find her? But was i just wasting time? Had she called from another location?

I call out. <Lilith?> The moon, big ε brite up there somewhere (i knew from my planeride), was no help under this crush of cloud ε fog. It was dark: dark dark. Switchon lite again, weave my way past more monks, a couple of them prostrate w devotion. {Dev/ocean. Am i even going in the right direction?} Call out again. <Lilith! It's nathan.> When i heard it –the voice, out toward the water– i realized, my eyes were farmore ready to see than my ears were to hear. Lilith? ...Is that you? Beyond a crouch of rocks to my left i saw a cropped silhouette, the beam of my lite illuminating farmore the pale line of waves collapsing on shore behind her. A figure w long hair flailing in the breeze, standing in mist between a last rock ε ocean, shielded her face from the lite. "Turn it so i c'n see you ...please?" Voice quavery, much deeper, ε broken like an adolescent boy's.

I stopped, put the lite on myself <It's jus me> trying to defuse her fear.

"Are you alone? I saw police."

I'm alone. I promise. As i move closer i can see she is hugging herself and shivering uncontrollably.

"I thought the police were with you." Her usually emaculate enunciation, even thus slow & deliberate, was slurred.

<But i gave you my word.> I let the lite dangle from its wriststrap. And by this indirect liting, even when she got close, i noticed nothing out of the ordinary —unless one counted that she was barefoot and hardly dressed for the beach: slacks blouse; her hair, as expected from hours of exposure to briny fog & wind, all atangle, and long & heavy as a raincape.

What happened?

"It's a long stupid story." She stumbled over the words. "Pardon my retarded speech" she rasped under an obbligato of shuddering.

I took her hand to leave. <Youre freezing!> I took off my jacket. As i wrapped it around her it occurred to me how i'd once cradled, as a kid, a pet calf dying of exposure during an icestorm. I didnt findout til later that the "nice man" who came and took her away was really a butcher. She suddenly pulled away, bent forward, coughing. I could see her outline against the gungray of fog & sea. I proffer handsker. You okay?

"Uhuh."

We'd better get you someplace warm. I began walking her (she rather wove) toward parkinglot lites. I would have carried her except that she stiffened to any form of approach or touch. When we reached the lite my eyes confirmed what touch couldnt quite figureout. Unless this was some new fad (perhaps to go w the clash-colored lips/eyeshadow, hair-streaking & body-piercing just then spreading among her peers), one sleeve of her blouse was gone. {When she suggested we date at the beach one day, i hardly pictured *this.*}

On reaching the car, as i opened her door she slid out of my jacket. "I'm fine, really. I c'n handle this." In the lite of the car as she sat i noticed her left cheekbone was abraded, the orbit under the eye, swollen. There were stains on her blouse too, as if she'd tried to rinse away blood.

I knelt by her seat on one knee. Lilith, what happened?

"Tripped on some rocks in the dark, that's all." There was the tiniest twitch of her head as she bent forward coughing again, my handsker to her lips; then, as quickly, she threw her head back as tho to catch her breath, gave a small yelp and ducked forward again, grabbing the side of her head.

Whatsamatter? —i pictured something *very* serious.

Head still forward she indicates my knee. "Youre kneeling on my hair."

I felt stupid. She tried to laff but it hurt. Spotting the handsker briefly upturned, i grab her left wrist, turn it palm-up. The white cloth cupped a thick exclamationmark of blood. {O my mimí!} <Lee, this is serious. ["It's nothing, really"] Open. Lemme see. [turns away. grab chin, turn her back] I was a medic. Lemme look. [shine lite on open mouth] Damn, girl.>

She wriggles away. "It's nothing. Jus bit my tung when i fell."

O really? I'd seen enuf assaults to question that. <My guess is six 'r eight stitches at least. You musta been bleeding like a stuck pig. No wonder youre dizzy.> "Ditthy [ditsy], you mean." I let go, switch off lite. Blood in saliva always looks worse than it is i remind myself.

"It's stopped now anyway."

Ya dont say. [dig out from back of glovepocket packet of tissues] Here. I'll get you a blanket, just a sec. As i tuck her in i feel an old feeling in the pit of my gut. When that happens everything switches to black&white. Fresh blood looks like india ink; coagulated blood, like roofing tar. I think that's key. India ink & roofing tar are not emotional triggers. Anyway, when that state comes over me i become icily rational: emotional safety valve. While others stand frozen faint scream or vomit, i do what needs to be done. The worse the emergency the cooler my behavior. If the World suddenly ended tonite, and Lilith was not there to hold, i would just take notes... or assume a lotus pose, just float away to wherever i thought she'd gone.

I drove us back to the city. The sense of urgency i felt had to do *w who* the patient was and my attachment thereto —an unqualified attachment, i reminded myself. Then: {Hey, it's sunday! Hospitals just *practice* medicine on weekends!} A chance glance told me the sight of the pistol behind the tissues alarmed her. I reach over, give tissues, close glovebox. For some reason, after the same malicious traffic signal, same police car in same spot, the drive back was overwith quickly. Just a couple mins short of the oakland bridge i banked off the freeway.

"Where we going? <Hospital.> "No hospitals" she said. Jus take me home ...please. I cant go there." 

Lilith, youre weak as a starving kitten, bleeding internally (yes, the tung's internal), suffering from hypothermia 'n' banged about the head from who know's why, and you wanna go home? [silence] I'm a bit of a renegade myself but that's overthetopdumb. Anyone b'side *me* woulduv called 911, no questions asked. Dont put your head back or you'll jus keep choking. ["I'm okay."] Ya dont say? Well, i'll tell ya this. If that tung isnt sutured properly, 'n' soon, you'll be talkin like that the rest o' your life.

E.r waitingrm was busy. At the admitting window a sallow-eyed mexican wanted her to come over and play 20questions while he hunt&pecked at a keyboard in eng-glace. I put the brakes on that *w*: She cant talk. He told me to sit down, someone would see her. A bitter-looking woman *w* a clipboard came out afterwhile. There was much to-do over payment. My friend's purse was stolen (L looked at me), her insurance card with it; we'll have everything you need firsthing in the morning. But the trust-us idea was lost on her. What? Credit card? {Never saw *that* on tv: And dont forget, you c'n charge your next assault 'n' battery.} Gave her my card; she left satisfied.

In the briteness of the waitingrm, wrapped in my red-plaid lap blanket, during the filling-out of forms, the unhappy papoose did her best to hide her face. I looked at her only askance for i knew how selfconscious she felt. The how&why of her hurts taunted me. The contusion on her left cheekbone, the swelling under the same eye, were discolored already, yellowing ε turning dark in places. Such pooling takes hours. What time had all this happened? Her lower lip was swollen also.

When the woman left Lilith looked over at me shyly. "I'm sorry ...No, not jus that. I mean, I owe you an outfit too." She indicated *w* nodding forehead ε sad wet eyes, two brownish smears on my jacket. (For the sake of clarity i have made no attempt to duplicate the difficulty she had in articulating –the hesitation slurring ε lisping– or the awful humiliation she clearly felt over circumstances generally, the lot of it quite heartrending.)

"I'll be right back." She rather plunged for the restrms. Swallowing blood, i recalled, causes nausea —despite vampire propaganda. A nearby tv screen assured, my sense of color had returned. The clincher, i thought (testing one eye, then the other), was the missing sleeve, which indicated not a fall but escape or attempted escape. "I cant stay in here" she said as she passed, heading now for the door. Once outside i realized she wasnt leaving, just escaping the cattle car. I listened by the door for her name. After 20mins the sight of her —sitting on the curbstone wrapped up like that, resembling a war victim (a shatteringly beautiful war victim), silently coughing, still wiping blood into a supply of paper towels— was breaking my heart. What in hell are these people doing anyway? I know a little about triage and the woman they just called has been clowning around the whole time.

I went thru the swinging doors (ER PERSONNEL ONLY, in three languages), accosted the first nurse i saw. My friend has aspirated blood and is choking badly. She was promptly helped into a wheelchair and whisked away. I went out to wait in the javelin. Hospitals depress me too. An ambulance left. Another arrived. Then a cop car. After 10min or so it struck me: Could the hospital have sent for those clowns to *question* Lilith? Sonuvabitch. A nurse tried to stop me as i headed down the double line of curtained beds. "I'll have to call security." *Dont bother, theyre here.* Shiny black shoes, uniform slacks, showed beneath one cubicle. Miss, did you ask for these gentlemen's help? She nods, eyes brimful, suction tube hanging like a transparent leech from a corner of her mouth. I think they thought i was her doctor or the fbi or something. She's pretty badly hurt. Perhaps you could save your questioning til later? One cop motions me outside the curtain. <I'll talk to *both* of you out there if you please.> The other follows us.

"Look, e.r called us. We're required by law to foul a report when file-play is suspected, you know that. [sic all] We were already talking to her when you guys decided it was a seizure not an assault." We ambled past a nurse station. "Did she say she's had these before?"

Dont know. [in waitingrm by then] We've only been dating for a couple weeks. (I had no reason to continue a charade of their own erection.) They shared a brief blank stare. Could we get your name? Just routine stuff, they assured. Certainly.

Some mins later i was informed, ms McGrae would have to be kept "a few hours for observation". Not unusual w aspiration cases. I tagged along as she was wheel-chaired to the elevator and up to 6116. Funny how totally trivial stuff will wedge in the craw at such times. She was all but asleep when the nurse left. "She needs rest now." I was told she'd been given a sedative. "Some patients have been known to sleep for days following a bad seizure." I was somewhat familiar with grans & petits i said.

I touched her brow, stroked lightly her hair —which some nice person had tied loosely back w a bow fashioned of gauze. Pretty. Tho her cheekbone was bandaged the pain in her features was gone and she breathed easily, her eyelashes folded like the wings of a dozing butterfly. I like you toomuch and i dont know why. Did i say that or just think it? For a moment i had the urge to sink my face into the riches of her rumpled seaside hair, gather her up, hold her while she slept. But she was already cradled in the arms of a very lucky drug. I sat holding, stroking, her forearm for some time before leaving.

It must have been around 3a when i got home, just 10 or so blocks from frisco general. M.o: Before i leave i walk thru my house checking switches windows appliances etc. Every window in the house was lit, surprising energy-frugal me. As i entered the foyer –probably because she still had a key of her own– i was reminded of the days when nikki used to come by. {Hmm.} Hour bedamned, i had a new fone mx. "Hi, mr schock. This is beth. You probably dont remember me but...." In the midst of playing it the fone rang. No apology for the hour, same voice charged ahead w what was on its mind. "...I was at the game when she called. It's after two now 'n' I'm worried. <After *two?*> Dont get me wrong. She's a big girl. I dont care if she stays out all nite. Sorta. <We're all asleep here.> I'm no alarmist but she sounded a little desperate. I'm worried somethin mighta happened. N'fact, I'm just a shimmy'n'- shake from callin the cops ...scuse me?"

"Beth, listen. She's safe ...Sound asleep. We're all asleep here. I'll tell her to call you firsthing in the morning... Promise... She's fine... I will... Yes. Bye." The girl is all heartnoise & gibberish if not downright pushy, i thought.

13

It is sunset socalled, and we're about to move into one of the longest scenes in this book. So that the quotidian quanta dont snowball like last time....

When emil (on business in dc) came again this afternoon, and as i slipped into his possession the latest pages of this testament, he told me he'd "finally found time to start reading it". This surprised me. [This unfortunate misapprehension I address elsewhere. —Ed.] He went on to say there were now "rumors of a slim chance of a meeting with the governor ...probably a kneejerk to so many petitions pouring in". (But highly coincident, it seemed to me, w the warden's claim of friendship w the governor.) But i was not to get my hopes up even one little bit.

Easier said than done. I asked again for blanket power-of-atty for lex. And again he said "No good counselor would be party to such recklessness."

Then i want him to have temporary power. It's bad enuf he hasta deal with this stuff without having always to ask our permission.

"And as I've said before, that could endanger the future of the sanctuary. Beside, I thought we laid this to rest?"

You laid it to rest.

"I will mail a list of reasons why to do so is potential estate-trust suicide."

Why not jus send lex's papers for my signature? He is the most honorable man i ever met. I trust him implicitly. [I complied. But only after NS signed a waiver which explained the hazards involved. —Ed.] At some point in our exchange i'm sure emil repeated his mantra: "I did not sign on to be your yesman but to protect your interests."

Sun set? To get the deepest sky view i must stand. Since the prison walls are a little higher than my 2nd story window, and since the trees beyond are even higher in places, sunset for me comes more than an hour early. Of course, tho the sun 'drops' early, the sky remains brite til Earth spins her western horizon eastward; that is, 'up' ɛ away from the rays of that fantastic solar furnace. But sun "set"? Why do we continue to use such subjective ɛ archaic terms? How dare we laff at the ancients who thought the sun's fire, like a candle, was snuffed every nite? Call it 'last lite' or 'nitefall', if you like. Niteshade & dayset are better yet. But not sundown, or sunset. If the sun truly set (cf, sat, rested) once a day we'd enter a glacial age before we could yelp "How subjective we've been!"

Looking n out my grubby but gifting little window i can see the left side of the frontgate (pedestrians only), and, left of it, the employe parkinglot. Next, in the corner, is the nw watchtower. Then, moving s along the w wall, first comes the service entrance, which i cannot see being blocked as it is by the nw corner of the gym/cafeteria. I can however see all vehicles which come&go, since they must either use the employe parkinglot or pass along the wide corridor between the old building (where i am) and the g/c. At the s end of the g/c a fenced & roofed bridge spans the 2nd-stories of this bldg & the g/c. That bridge is the only place a visitor might chance to look up, see a prisoner. S of the g/c the security wall reemerges til reaching the sw tower. This area is blocked from view by the se corner of the g/c, tho i've seen it often from the bridge just noted. I mention this area because so many vehicles servicing the kitchen & laundry disappear around that corner. The (captive) eye, now moving along the s wall toward the "out-time" yard (which it cannot see, except from the bridge again) can however see state roadwork equip parked there: tractors mowers snowplows & -blowers. Is it any wonder i long to see a real dayset? I mention these logistics in case my (rough) sketch of the prison is not incl'd in this edition. It would be thoughtless of me to just charge ahead never considering the investigative curiosity and/or learned needs of my most careful readers.

14

I called around 9. She was surprisingly upbeat. "I'll be going home around 10 —after a doctor sees me." Was there anything she needed? "I hate ta ask you but" could i, please, stop by her dorm, pick up some clothes? The ones i was wearing, well, you know...." Beth would have them ready. She didnt want "anyone at thchool to thee me like thith". Did she know beth had called? I told her you were fine, that you were sleeping. Didnt say where. "I know. Thanks. She thought i was at your place." Lilith never forgot this honoring of her right to privacy.

Why does one enter a hospital rm guardedly? The firsthing i noted –midst an assault of whiteness ɛ sunlite– was the ingenuous blue wide-setness of her eyes. *Salut! Demeure chaste et pure.* Tho much of their sparkle had rekindled, one was still partly closed. And her face, bruised ɛ a little pale, seemed smaller somehow, perhaps because it was lost amidst a pillow-fanned falls of freshly showered hair.

Hi!

"G'morning" soft- ɛ slow-spoken.

Surprising myself, i brushed a minty toothpaste corner of her cheek w my lips. <Here are your things.> When i set the satchel on a nearby chair, what sounded like a musicbox, its melody muffled, haltingly managed a couple notes and expired. <Hey, i think i know that melody! [she is embarrassed] I'm not kidding. If i could hear a little more i think i could name it.> Place satchel on bedside.

Nurse enters bustlingly. "Gotcher release papers here, m'dear. What happened to that bandage, young lady?"

"It kept falling off. I threw it out."

"You shoulduv rang for a nurse. Youre gonna get that infected... I see you got your things. Just as well. Arthur's strange even for a graveyard vampire [midnite-shift blood-taker]... Missy here has all the men in this place offering her their firstborn." L, eyes lowered, flushes. As the nurse scribbles we decided w an "O well" shrug, my music quiz would have to wait for a more delicate moment. I no sooner step aside w L's bag than nurse normandy launches a beach assault, all the while peppering the air w nursely platitudes. L is given ℞'s for an antibiotic, nausea, pain ɛ convulsions. With the c-word L's eyes fall to examining the hem of her sheet.

Was her convulsions dx a way of putting the hounds off the scent? {What of the missing sleeve? the tear in her blouse?} Speculation quickly suffocated in a spawn of possibility.

"*This* one must be filled right away, you *know* that. [pushy sort] There's a pharmacy downstairs."

At five-bucks-an-aspirin.

Bed-sergeant scowls. "Do you know this guy? ...A volunteer will be here in a minute to fetch you. Dont leave on your own, you hear? That's 'bout it, toots. Chin up." Bogart's ghost, grossly refleshed in nurse whites, march-waddled off, talking of other duties other beachheads.

I can see why youre feeling better.

"It's that or get tung-lashed."

Hmm. Get's the job done tho. I like her —tho i rather resented losing our musicbox moment and Lilith's misty gaze. Once, as we stood shivering in the snow-muffled quiet of a lovely wayside trainstation in colorado, out of unbroken whiteness a dark shape appeared, moved toward us down the tracks: snowblower. A min later it had passed out of sight, while we ɛ our bags stood stunned ɛ snowblasted, the fronts of us buried to chest ɛ neck. Tho scary at the time it was the sort of event you laff about later —and for a lifetime ...if they let you live that long. This is how the entry ɛ retreat of that nurse, at *that* special moment, strikes me today.

Lilith, seeming chirpy, slid from bed, wriggled her long (unpainted) toes into a pair of brownpaper slippers. Attempting to hold shut w one fist the open back of her gown, she tookup the small bag i'd brought ("It's okay. I c'n do this"), shuffled toward the bathrm. Skin-texture taunts me thru skimpy scrubsgreen: arched bow of noduled spine, soft incurve of lower back, quick sheen of silken haunch ɛ tanned capable legs, o gaawd! At the door she did a half turn, pointed at her slippers. "If ya dont walk like a duck they fall off."

While nathan schock was ever on guard against it, his baser self (carefree peter pushin, whom youve met) was almost always reconnoitering in the bush, scouring the terrain w moltenblue gaze. She emerges in jeans ɛ runningshoes, getting about just fine now. Over a flouncy lavender blouse she is wearing a marbled blue-denim vest w real embroidered(!) gaucho-floral motif —a fashion salad of bluespurples&greens.

Very nice... Your outfit.

She mouths a wincing ɛ shyly subdued "Thank you".

Unused (she said as we left) to hangovers (lingering lassitude of lastnite's drugs), she suggested we "bust outa this morgue for a cup o' buzz", her swollen –and i'm sure, sore– tung rendering the yuppigram as "buthz". But then she also said "butht" for "bust" and "thith" for "this". "God! i cant believe thith trathsed [trashed] locuthion o' mine! It is thsooo humiliating."

Out in the car –when it managed a few more notes as i set the bag by her feet– i asked to see the musicbox. In a plain walnut box, its mechanism was visible under a glass window. I know that tune, i confessed, but cant quite grasp it. Wait. I reached over, put my hand on hers. B'fore you wind it jus give the smallest turn, okay? A hint is all i want. Yods, gives twist. Nothing. Another. Four or five plinks. <Damn. Still not enuf [of a threadend to grab thru the needle-eye of reminiscence]. I take some pride in my musical recall; dont mind so much being stymied by a melody i dont like. But one that i do, welp....> It was hardly the first time. Take a melody learned in the lush tones of a string section, say, and give it to a guitar. Alot that's vital gets lost (hid) in the transcription (transcryption!): a case of unfamiliar sonic cues. That is to say, a harpsichord balalaika cimbalom mandolin or guitar melody would be easier to spot coming from a music-box than from a tuba.

Wanting breakfast & it being late we went to 24/365 KITCHEN —the amer west's equiv of the east's AWFFLEHOUSE [sic]. *Voila.* Space by door. Shut off javelin, reach over. <May i?> I took the musicbox, which lay on her bag, gave it a gentle wrist-torquing. Opening phrase sounds, its notes sliding into my hand (cupped beneath the box) like colored stars come unglued from an old piano lesson page. *Dolly's bedtime.* No, wait. Got it. A-, *scarlet ribbons.* A-, danzig and a...a-, segal. "You know who *wrote* it?" Sometimes. Would she wind it up, play the entire thing? She wound *w* affection, stopped, clicked the switch. "A present when i was little ...it came inside a pink 'n' blue ball that rotates! ...with a very floppy-eared bunny on top. [pauses, staring at floor] Dont know if i c'n listen ta this right now. This may sound silly but... Well, some music makes me sad." Gives tite-lipped toss of head, as if it were no big deal.

Me too. Some melodies are so potent i block them. Hafta leave when i hear them in public. The first time i heard webber's *pie jesu,* without warning i found myself in tears. Yet the tears are not necessarily always sad. "God." *Pie jesu* had "had exactlybutexactly that effect on me too!" Our surprise was certainly mutual. Sunlite threw a shadowline of the dashboard across her legs, bisecting the cover of the pretty box in her lap. Steel keyboard & brass cylinder gleam under glass. I note the matching embroidered floral band running the length of the outseam of her acidwash jeans. Tho not skintite (she never dressed to seduce), they could not hide (from these eyes, anyway) the fullness of calf, the long contour of thigh.

A small group passed the car. A fat-faced child ran a toy intently along the length of the javelin's flank as his waiting parents looked on from the sidewalk, telling him to hurry along. Lilith's jaw dropped. The presumed father, who did not see us sitting behind tintedglass, patted his son's head as he passed. All turned & waddled toward a meal none of them needed. To think, i said, in a few short years, that boy may likely spawn another generation even more thoughtless than his parents'.

"If i didnt know you i'd think you were playing me. <Huh?> I mean, youre so non-agresso for a guy."

Remove key from ignition. I react against the standard patriarchal ideal, the bogart/wayne, bruwillis/stallonnegger despotism of american popart —the cinematic idolatry of the masses for certain penisheads who find, by some deadly twist in their gonads, violence 'n' vulgarity orgasmic. On the other hand, i respect men who are so deeply, so securely, male, they do not fear being sensitive; men who can permit themselves a damp eye in public 'n' who, like most women, feel free to hug or pat another of the same sex out of spontaneous warmth or camaraderie.

"You remind me alot of father ...I mean, my *real* father. It's a little spooky actually." Of course, he, unfortunately, hides it alot."

Grab doorhandle, pause. Maybe some day we can spend some time –you know, cliche stuff: fire blazing in fireplace, snow falling outside– comparing musical notes [hic]; a string of schmaltzy tunes on the sound system. Or maybe you could bring your musicboxes [she said she had "a whole collection"] and i'll try to match their melodies with my stuff. At last count i had over 5,000hrs of recorded music.

Staring selfconsciously at her knees: "That would be fun."

When i circled to her door she was already outside, bent over the seat. {Ugh, gawd.} What goes? "Not good ta leave tension on the spring." Setting the musicbox playing she quickly closed the door.

Would i order for her? she asked from behind her menu, peering around it to add "pleeeth?"

{O precious sweetness. Gawd again. Am i doomed?} What are ya gonna do about school?

"I cant be seen there. Not like this. The gossip there's unbelievable. With *this* [indicates face w index] for a topic they'll go positively spazzed. [pause] How long do you think it'll take for this... Well, for *these*... ta heal?"

Completely...? Two, maybe three, weeks. The tung, longer. ["God."] Good circulation is key. If you massage, probably less. I manage not to offer fulltime assistance w this.

We are served. Tho she had only oatmeal & toast i could tell every mouthful was a chore. Hospital oatmeal had been "ghastly". This was "some better".

I plunked two poached eggs into the spoon-carved fumerole of my grits.

Overnite the underside of her eye had darkened; definitely not a case of anemia or runny mascara. {Ravishing even in clouts & weals.} I could visit your instructors, show them a doctor's excuse. Maybe classmates will tape lectures for you. I'll tape what they miss when i'm free. I could use the ed.

Her lips pursed into an introspective pose, part smile, part pout. This look –head down, eyes up, swiping glances at me– would one day take on a meaning beyond mere oriental deference. Finished, we sat sipping a second cup —delicious sacrilege! (We found, tho we rarely had it, both of us loved coffee.) Leaning on elbows, we tilted toward each other, hands inadvertently close. Turning hers palm-up i noticed several abrasions on their heels. She quickly turned them down.

"Y' know, when i woke up this morning the sun was so brite for a minute i thought i was in my old room, back in virginia. {Encourage her w unassuming eyes.} For the first time in a long while i felt like a kid, back in the good days ...when father 'n' lage were still at home." Pauses, looks askance. {It's back! ...that enchanting divergent strabism!} "Y' know, after you left lastnite i dreamt, hallucinated, something –Dont laff at this, please– that sis 'n' me were kids talking in bed 'n' that i didnt have a care in the world. It was the drugs, i know. [pause again] But i think it was something else too."

(While she sighs a deep sigh and her left eye does that thing it does, and while i fold her hands in my own, i must repeat: In the interest of easy reading i have been ignoring the enormous difficulty she had speaking, just as i am ignoring her exasperation w her ongoing failure to speak at the level of elocution to which she was accustomed.)

Begins fussing distractedly w my fingers. "Nathan... [deep breath] I'm worried... [exhale, swallow] I need t' go home now ...let you get on with your life. <My life's just fine as it is, thanks.> I cant believe i've dragged you into all this... [reverie dissolving] Truth is, i'm not just embarrassed... I'm mortified. (That *is* a word, isnt it?) I tried to call a taxi you know last nite but they wouldnt go that far without a creditcard number and i couldnt remember mine. 'N' then nobody was home when i called the dorm ...well, nobody i trusted... [reverie gone] I feel like somekinda whacko with all these problems. I mean, look at this! [sits erect, indicates self w both hands] I cant even talk right!" I could see, had she been alone she'd have burst into tears. She moves to flop back in her seat but i catch hold of her hands.

Youre being *way* too hard on yourself.

"This is sooo slushy of me." Looks at ceiling trying not to tearup, a look of pathetic concern working into her features, a dimpling in the cleft of her chin appearing & vanishing w the effort. "I'm embarrassing us." Overbites lower lip, looks down, moves as if to sit back again. But i'm still holding on ...palms down, of course. <You should be a concert pianist.> Relieved at the change of subject, she tells of a piano teacher who said " 'If I had your hands I'd be on tour now instead of teaching.' [adding] But i dont like my hands ...Too long." Yet it was this very length, from wristbone to fingertip, that made them elegant.

Mimes 'n' dancers dream of such hands.

So as not to lose track of the sensual sense of these moments, imagine my body as an analog meter whose only indicator typically hangs at 6oclock. Then apply just the sight of Lilith (in the lab of imagination) and the meter's hand will instantly jump to 7 or higher. And, like some exotic form of magnetism, as proximity to her increases the hand rises in proportion, hitting & holding at full noon when any form of actual contact occurs; even contact of the most seemingly innocuous sort —like hand-holding. {May the god of tact & restraint be with me if'n'when full-body contact ever occurs!}

Anyway, each time she searched my face **w** those incredible eyes –up close as we were; so innocent clear deep & silverblue!– i felt something i hadnt felt in years: desire & weakness simultaneously! Now, the desire part i understand (if not its beastly intensity). But the weakness i must read as fear. But fear of what? Beauty desirability vulnerability innate purity, what? <Y' know, if i could only find the hint of ...i mean, it scares me. [eyes search mine briefly] You dont have the ego of- of... even snowwhite... 'n' that worries me. [quizzical look] Look, here's mine [i offer my ego]. Take it. I have toomuch. What i mean is, [speech slowing, softening] i get this feeling ...this feeling you have been hurt [look down at her lips] —i mean, reallyreally hurt.> I'm sure she sensed how much i wanted to kiss her.

Reflected in her eyes i'm a sailor lost at sea.

Still holding her hands, i do so —o gently. Glance at each other briefly, closely. Repeat. A metal napkin-holder, somehow, slips from the table, breaks open on the floor, launching its contents in a snowy stream. Well, that's what *could* have happened, what *almost* happened. Actually i caught it on the edge mid-tilt. We both slumped back in our seats, staring blankly at each other, as if the mere thought of a longer such kiss had exhausted us.

Returning to the car i note a dull scrape running waveringly from rear to headlite whence it lifted abruptly, presumably to allow the plump child to thump his bulk up the curb. I head us toward (golden) gate park, simply because she said she'd never been.

Lilith

The park, once a stretch of desert waste socalled, is a lush oasis in the middle of frisco, possibly the largest cultivated urban park in the world. I dropped her in the shade of a large olive tree while i went to park. When i returned she had the contents of her shoulderbag dumpedout on the grass. I note the discoloration of her left eye, almost closed from the sunny briteness.

Inventory?

"Yup. [looking, sorting] Seein if all my stuff's here."

But i thought... i thought your bag was missing?

"Beth sent it with my stuff."

I bite my tung (pardon the expression). Everything okay?

"Nope. My addressbook's gone... [scans around] 'N' my pictures too. ...I jus hope reesy's letter's here. [rummages side-pocket; finds sunglasses, puts them on] Her new school address is on it. [drops bag, grimaces] Nope. Gone. I *hafta* call her." I note pendant on keyring, seen the first day we met: leather, shaped, i thought, like a thumbsized coffin and resembling a medic's bitestick. She fingered the pocket of a checkbook. "*Your* address is gone too." She went thru her wallet again. "Every single picture." Her arms dropped to her sides as she let out a very long sigh.

The fotos i saw the other nite?

Looks up, tilts head. What's she thinking behind those sunglasses? "Your picture too. <Me?> Yup." She had cut it from the dustjacket of one of my books. She grunts, "Wha?", pulls out a handful of bills, retracts head abruptly, stares blankly down. A wad of hundred-dollar bills fans in the seabreeze like a small anemone. "Yech!" says she, tossing them high & behind her. They fly some distance, a few catching in the grass just shy of the curb.

Across the way, slumped beneath a tree beside a bicycle, large backpack draped across its wire basket, the squint of a man who'd been following the proceedings suddenly widens. Pandiculating like some mime or silent-cinema genius, he found his feet, sidled toward the street, exactly downwind of the money!

Lee, listen. I dont know what's going on but i know, society works in such a way that some rich fop, whose family hasnt paid honest taxes for generations 'n' who daily disembowels our Planet for profit, will probably endup pocketing most o' that money. And if that fellow over there gets it in the meantime, he'll only drink himself to death. She glanced over, a look of glum pity crossing her features in profile.

Quarts of port cases of sherry pints of muscatel casques of amontillado danced before the fellow's bloodshot eyes! One of the bills nearest the curb was doing pushups in the grass, as if readying to sprint across the road to freedom. A rollerblader scooted past unnoticing.

Lee, remember you told me about your practical side? —the side you get from your dad? Why not turn that money, which you obviously dont want (for *whatever* reason, an' that's fine) ...turn it into something beautiful. She looked askance at me —definitely a moviestar behind those glasses. If it's from someone you hate, why not sign him or her up as a contributor to greenEarth? Have them do something they might otherwise prefer to die than ever hafta do themselves? [spark of recognition]

Occasional car drifts by. Man now sits on curb, seeming to look everywhere but at money. Not all his braincells had drowned.

In fact, whoever it is, i could see to it he gets an accountant's receipt and our very best membership kit; that way the donor would be assured *you* didnt windup with any of the money. The way things are he or she is free to suppose you accepted it. (Tilts head, as if snagging the thought.)

A gust of wind made her grab at some papers next to her wallet. She gathered them, looked up to see where the money had got to. Shakes out hair, gives quick brite flash of teeth, sighs. "Youre right." The same gust whirls most of the bills out into the road. A passing car sweeps up a few, drops them some distance away.

While she gathers her things i round up 18 in all, each one a hundred. As i walk back the tramp is catching another two, one of which he holds out to me in a withered copper-colored hand while trapping the other beneath the sole of a partly topless shoe. He looks at me sidelong as he hands me the bills. I wont thank you with money. I cant be sure what you'll do with it. Looks down at his feet. However my friend and i will be leaving here around... o, say, threethirtyish? What size shoe do you wear...? If i see you i'll give you a pair of the verybest walking shoes. They are brand new 'n' it would take *two* of these at least ta buy them. He nods shyly. I walk away.

She would not take the money. I should hold it, take care of the details, please. "And, o <What?> ...Thank you." Even smudged sunglasses couldnt obscure the sweetness of that smile. We walk. Tho the sunlite is warm the air is cool. "Now *that* looks neat!" Up ahead she spies a carousel inside a large playground. ADULTS MUST BE ACCOMPANIED BY A PERSON 12 OR UNDER. She is disappointed, for this is not the typical carny-go-round. Built to resemble a greek temple, its mounts incl unicorns gorgans manticores & even centaurs in both black & white.

<Maybe we could *rent* a kid somewhere.> We sit on a bench near the entrance. A young latina & her bug-eyed child are on the next bench. L & she exchange smiles.

Any of your musicboxes have merry-go-rounds? Or should that be, merries-go-round?

A most curious smile upturns one side of her mouth. "No. But there's one with a carousel horse... Maybe you know its melody." I'd apparently hit on the right topic to subvert her consternation. "And there's another i'd love to know the words to... it's got an italian guy with a huge mustache standing in a boat... <A huge mustache standing in a boat?> O youoo-ooo-ooo. [poking me three times] *Please* dont make me laff. ...You *know* what i mean: Those boats they push with poles? There's one in the browning poem, a- ...Well, anyway, he's playing one of those little accordions... unnnn.... That's it! Thshit! I've gone totally braindead."

Is he wearing a white half-mask? Is there a lovely young singer in the boat with him? She surveys me curiously. "No... The boat turns in a circle as it plays. You know the kind i mean? They use 'em in venice... in the canals? Help me with this, please." It was a draw, whether to be angrier at one's fuzzed thoughts or one's exasperating speech impediment.

Gondola, gondolier? [Right.] And the mustachioed guy's playing a concertina maybe?

"Right! Damn you! ...Sorry. Didnt mean that the way it sounded."

You'll feel better t'morrow. Ever heard the song *deserted carousel?* [Nuh-uh] Ballad in waltz form... suffers from snatches of schmaltz, but sung right... i think youd like the ed ames rendition.

"I'm a carousel haunt" she says, as if confessing something awfully naughty; peers around me to answer our neighbor —somehow she has made friends already. A few mins later i find myself buying tickets for all of us. I choose my mount (middle track) so Lilith will have the outside view. (It will take me years to discover her relief that i chose the black unicorn [stallion], left her to ride the white one [mare].) I study them as we wait to start. How can you tell what sex they are?

"They always put long eyelashes on the females. [pointsout two horses up ahead] *And all the pretty horses.*" Battlescars ε all, she was a vision whirling round&round among a *mélange* of exotic painted creatures (beside the unicorns gorgons ε manticores there were horses pigs stags rams dragonlike seasnakes etc), her hair –longer than the mane of the mare beneath her– bounced slowly, fluffily, as in a hair-product ad. One rank ahead, our little sponsor, black eyes big as olives, whiteknuckled the stang of his seahorse while his mother loped beside on her necessarily foreshortened dragon. From a centerstage adazzle w blinking lites, a "tinkling calliope" pipes *beautiful ohio.* (She will play it on piano one day, challenge unbogeyish me w "You *must* remember this?") "Your horse...! <What?> Your *unicorn,* nathan!" What? *What?* Cups her mouth. {Is she sniggering at me?} Lilith, what? "Youre too big for it. It looks like your riding on ...on... a little dog!" Struggles not to laff. As we say goodby to our latindian friends i note, for the second time (nurse at the hospital was first ...after helmut) how just-mets behave like old friends when parting from Lilith.

"Now that's the best –i mean, *best*– carousel i've been on!" As we leave i turnback in time to see her walking backwards. Perspective protracts for an instant, stops just when everything looks twice further away. Tho she is 1.6m tall ε unarguably female, she suddenly looks petite in her smart denim outfit (femalekin). Seconds later, at my side, she is adult-sized again. "See? Theyre *still* empty! What kid would wanna ride a black centaur 'r seasnake anyway?" When it cameout, "sneesake", we both melted in mirth, hers stifled.

From a concession we got two bottled waters ε one straw. Takes pain pill. "Burns a little but not bad" smiles brave Lee. (For audio version take care not to say: smiles bravely.) I wet a corner of my handsker, ask for her sunglasses. I figure i'll be able to see her eyes better if i remove some of the sun-silvered smudges. As we walk among ferns orchids lilies all sort of tropical botanics at the conservatory of flowers –some of which to me are so sexy i dare not comment– i learn: "The downside is, all carousel creatures are trapped ...two ways [she adds]. One, theyre caged in an infernal circle... <Worse even than a zoo-in-the-round. I c'n see that.> An' two, theyre stanged [publicly paraded on poles] for life! ...I had a nitemare a few years ago, a really bizarre item. I'd just run across the legend of the *earl king* by gertha. [wrong moment to correct her pronunciation] Anyway, it was an eerily moonlit nite in my dream an' all the animals on the carousel i was riding were either stanged alive or freshly taxidermied. The black stallion i was on somehow broke away and was running wild thru the countryside. I knew there was no hope of it ever stopping because it was terrified of, get this, *all* shadows."

{Aha!} I figured i'd unpuzzled her fear of dark-colored horses. (I had not.)

"I've redreamed it so many times i'm expert now at wakingup the moment my horse bolts from its stang." She blamed her very first carousel ride. "It jerked into motion so violently it threw everyone, kids 'n' adults, to the floor. With all the screaming 'n' stuff i stayed scared o' carousels for years." In her carousel-noir dreams, "Instead o' britening the ride like youd think, somehow calliope music always lends a sense of scarily black humor to the weird proceedings of the dream". So it was, when i intro'd her to the symphonies of mahler, she suffered a most keenly dark *deja entendu* whenever his hurdygurdy themes apparitioned themselves thru a sidedoor in the score.

Need ta sit? i ask as we leave. Tho some of her glow is back she still looks gothically gaunt around the gills. While i knew lastnite had been traumatic (beyond even what i imagined), i was determined to just quietly follow her lead.

"I'm three-leggin it, huh...? Sorry. This is really not me at all."

The planetarium's right over there? Theyve got great shows. She sucks her straw as we wait for a squad of helmeted skaters to pass. "Do they remind you of lemmings at all?" Her analogy wows me. There follows a diminutive version of a burbling roar as her drink bottoms-out. As all shows are sold out (busload of middleschoolers), i get an idea....

"So much greenery...for a park!" she says as i reconstitute our day w a horse&buggy tour. "An' right in the middle of a city!"

At a cost of a mere million gallons of water a day!

"No!"

Yes.

"Speaking of stats, there must be a thousand skaters here t'day!"

Try 5,000.

"No!"

Yes... on weekends. ...Used to be *more*.

Pssst, reader. Again today i am much-watched by the scopotropic imbeciles who guard me. Much? What a stupid-sounding word. Much. Much. Much. Why not pronounce it mewtch, as in mute? Or mewk, as in mucus? It grows more germanic by the second: mutch ...mutsch ...muttsch. And what of mütsch (mitch) or mück (mik)? At any rate, my best guess says, die doktor has ordered another hit on me. Zerstruen, narrlungs! Leave me be!

"No!"

Yes. Backwhen rollerblades were alltheRage. This is where i come to run ...weekdays. We decide to try it "sometime".

The gaberlunzie is waiting near the miniature train. It rattles past as we exit our buggy, its whistle sounding, its red green yellow & blue gondolas loaded w screaming tots. He follows it w the gaze of a hobo too long off the rails. "Didnt think ya'd come back." <I am a man of my word, sir.> I'd guessed he was not about to let loose easily of anyone who throws thousands of dollars over one shoulder and doesnt look back.

As Lilith contd to struggle not to let her hurts slow her natively brisk stride, he rather trotted along as we walked, wheeling his packcycle w two-fingered familiarity. I wanted to ask if he'd ever hopped a slow freight to memphis or chattanooga, but it was none of my business. When we reached the car, and as i opened the trunk, Lilith removed her sunglasses to dab at her wounded eye w my handsker, more&more tearingup from the day's briteness. One glimpse of those gorgeous orbs and our new friend seemed suddenly driven to justify his existence. "Let me introduce myself. They call me memphis[!] johnnie.... My pleasure. The politically correct may call my kind 'urban outdoorsmen' or 'residentially challenged', butcha know what? Nuthin's changed really. The public, 'n' especially the cops, still think of us as hobos bums 'n' vagrants just as they always have. Maybe even worse; social leeches; illegitimate non-citizens; a notch above a common criminal maybe but not a very big notch. An' worse, nobody's stoppin ta ask why there's so many of us. ["I've heard that."] Ding! Another thing nobody wants ta face is that we homeless are much better adjusted ...adjusted to the *real* World, I mean... than you establishment groupies."

Now *that* hurt, even tho he quickly added "Present company excluded, of course". One thing i never wanted to be was labeled a lishment groupie, and there i stood hogtied & branded.

"I'm not as dumb as I look ta most people. [had our jaws hit the pavement that visibly?] Ya shudnt go by looks alone ya know. I was tenured fer years just across the water there, an' I mean berkeley not alcatraz... Us terminal homeless have sumthin special that people dont see ...'r maybe *wont* see: Our souls are outa the closet 'n' are hearts 'r' free. [scratches my side of his hirsute underchin w one leathery claw] It aint easy out here but, as tom paine said, its freedom."

<Real freedom never was easy> i say, holding out a fine pair of shoes he's now too passionately involved to even notice.

"Ding! Now I *know* I like ya. [intense grin my way] No one stops ta realize, us homeless are livin the way 'r human ancestors lived for millions o' years ...man's longest heritage is homelessness, ya know: a cave, a tree, an armful o' grass, a large warm skin; pickup 'n' run on a moment's notice; run from the lethal gods o' the elements 'r chase that restless angel of nurture wherever she flies ...or die... Like primates are always on the move in the Wild? Well, so were *we* til the advent of agriculture —which is like almost yesterday in human history. So who are the strange ones really? Establishment groupies 'r me 'n' my kind? I say, Motherearth knows we homeless *best* of all."

"Youre absolutely right" says Lilith w perfect passion-v.-logic equanimity.

He turns to me. I offer shoes again, this time at eye-level. "People ferget, ninedynine percent o' human history is livin close ta the heart not the brain. You culture-straights, you rules-herdies, uv got it all backwards –nuthin personal, yaunderstand– an' that right there's the reason yer all so damned unhappy [slaps bike seat w palm], present company excluded, o' course. You guys are the best. Anyone c'n see that. What I'm sayin –in the nicest way I can– is: Technoman, who thinks he's really with it, is both biologic'ly *and* historic'ly outa the loop; the oldest loop he owns... 'n' b'cause of it he's emotionally 'n' psychologically challenged an' doesn even know it, muchless know why. *No* idea! *Seriously* challenged too! Ya see? Which is why all the nuthouses 'n' prison's are overflowin 'n' the streets are fillinup with people like me. An' I hate ta tell ya but it's gonna get worse bafore it gets better. ...Pardon the lecture, but that's how I usta make my living... Our cardboard roofs may be caved-in with rain er snow, our walls 'n' our shrinkwrap flappin like broken wings in the winds o' chance, 'r ennertainment, a tv playin on the warm side o' some window somewhere. But ah'll tell ya.

Those times when we do feel warm 'n' happy with a ray o' hope –like I feel now with the two o' you– the feelin's more deep 'n' genuine than I could ever explain. An' I think it's-, welp, b'cause the feelin's based on *real* life, on close-ta-the-bone life-, no, on close-ta-the-heart life-, life that's inevitable not invented ...an' it's moments like these, all by themselves, make this lifestyle I chose worth all the discomfort... [grins] Well, *most* of it anyway."

I could see, if L wasnt wary (scared of *all* men, as i was learning) she'd have hugged the guy then&there ...as i might have. Obviously memphis johnny had made a choice which we were too preoccupied and frankly too exhausted that day to absorb. (Considerable effort some mos later failed to turnup his name at soupkitchens safehouses berkeley law-enforcement etc.)

Lilith asked for the money. I gave it unquestioningly. She took it, extracted a bill, stuffed it in his lapel pocket. He gave it back. She regave it. "Tutorial fee for all youve taught me today, professor. I insist." He took her hand, stuffed the bill in it, closed her fingers around it and, like a truly noble nobleman fallen on hard times, bent, kissed lightly the hand that gave it and said, "I know you mean well but, thank you, no". He then turned to me, said solemnly, "This young woman is special, sir. *That* I know. [then flicked-on britely] But I *am* happy to relieve you of this *very* fine footwear ...nice. *Very* nice. Thank you... *if* youre certain, that is, it's of no use t' you?" He had his pride and one now understood it. Chaplinlike, pressing the shoes to his chest like a bouquet, he bowed deeply, extending the other arm, palm open, to one side in a grand gesture, forgetting the bicycle he held ...which, as if as amazed as we, stood by itself for a very long moment before toppling. In a true pratfall finale, a pocketflask skidded & twirled across the pavement ...and i got the uneasy feeling all this was being filmed for later broadcast; and that i was, perhaps, sid caesar, L was imogene coca, and that our gueststar was (actually looked like) red skelton.

"A very intelligent man. [L said as we got on our way] Only i'm not sure if i'm feeling bad more for him 'r for us."

<Wow... Maybe both? Afterall, we are, all of us, victims of the degree of our civilizing... The question is, i think, did memphis johnnie *decide* to be, or could he not *help* becoming, one of those ≈Hobo-trekkers who forever search... Each seeming a child, like me, on a loose perch, holding to his primitivity like some termless play.≈ ...Hart crane, moreorless.

She thought about that. "I think he couldnt avoid living his 'close-t'-the-heart life' ...a life the rest of us are scared ta even consider. [we thought about that] ≈Mine might be the right to help him but his was the right to need help. And where these exist in twain his was the greater.≈ Robert frost, moreorless." I hoped aloud that that was rhetorical because i found myself conflicted beyond a good answer. Staring straight ahead, a kind of smile-grimace held her features. I'd yet to learn how close to tears –well, flood of sobs– this brave little smile meant she was. "The missing link. <Huh?> Memphis johnnie's the missing link; the piece o' this evolutionary puzzle none of us see. An' right under our noses too."

Damn, girl. Wow. Damn! In a preoccupied daze i suggested we go to my place, whip-up smoothies, help her comeup w a plan of action for school. For her options were really near zero the more i thought about it. Tripped ε fell? Not likely. Epilepsy? If one wants to be pitied feared ε shunned (tho we didnt discuss these options). And, w either claim, still having to walk around campus looking like she'd in fact been assaulted. Picking thru a bin of blackchestnuts at alf's (grocery chain w a sense of good nutrition), i rather extolled her missing-link theory. {Is she ignoring me?} Then again, we had decided she should speak only when prompted. For her injury –short but deep laceration (six stitches, seven little lumps)– thanx to the pills, vexed her more than hurt.

Thrilling to have this creature moving about this dragon's w.coast lair, we made her smoothie first (frozen coconut milk, blackwalnut/blackcherry/banana), then mine (coconut/banana/vanillabean). "That feels sooo good" she said w the first swallow. Frosty tumblers in hand, we retire to sittingrm. I put on music, slouch on couch, legs extended in low-slung non-threatening pose). She sat forward ε well above me. "I want to thank you for all your, well, thoughtfulness last nite ...well, for *everything*, really... No, i mean it." She said this w such straightforward simplicity it gave me a twinge.

I patted her hand. T'sokay. No trouble. Reach up, touch her cheekbone. Dont forget t' keep massaging this ...often as you c'n stand it. Run tip of pinky over discoloration beneath eye. It'll really speed healing. Run index gently along the fullness of her underlip. I want to kiss you, i said, but i think it might hurt —non-threatening, coming as it did from my lower station.

As tho taking a small microphone, she wrapped her fingers around that index, kissed it. "My mouth" she said, w a breathy-almost-gritty-sound, "feels terribly unkissable right now." Those silverblues full-upon me now, something deep in my groin, not knowing wherelse to fall, plummets moonward. I put an arm around her, she slides a little down. I pull her head to my chest ...my smoothie spills a small spill. Not wanting to wreck the mood, still slouched, i wipe the spot w my spare handsker. <No. Stay. I'll get it later.>

"What's playing?"

Lullaby of a mother whale for fritened seal pups.

"That's the name?" murmurs my sleepy guest. <Yup.> It's pretty."

I stroke her hairline. Her brow feels oddly cold, temples seem china-brittle to my large fingers. I am humbled by her drowsy ductility, her sleepy unbias. Some mins more of those lulling sea-sounds and the wounded nereid is asleep. I think nothing of it, for i have no idea at the time how seldom i will ever see her asleep. Transfixed by this exquisite person foldedup next to me, i lay her head, which is slipping slowly anyway, on my lap, waking her briefly. Her hair trails off onto the carpet's tufted teal. I study her dark lashes which, folded, twitch occasionally; her lips, softly parted, close, drift apart, close, drift apart again. As i drift toward sleep myself, the image of juanita —head in my lap, dark tresses trailing over my legs and onto the tufted grass— respired into, and out of, consciousness. Poorly slept for days, all at once the waters of lethe buoyed me as well, and i fell into a deep sleep....

Till the fone rang. No mx is left. I peer at my watch. Almost 6oclock! How long have you been awake?

"Not long."

You ok?

"I'm fine. Jus looking thru your scrapbook [thcrapbook]." [seems depressed]

You sure youre okay?

"Yep. ...I made a couple calls. I'll give you the money."

Not ta worry. Make yourself at home, *please*. Hey, did you ramember ta call your friend, a-...? [Reesy?] Right, reesy. Is that her given name? [No. Aurise.] Never heard it. Nice name.

"She's a good person... I called beth too. She's getting my stuff t'gether for me... Nathan, i need t' tell you. I called father. He wasnt home but i spoke with sister [her lisp turns this zanily to "thithter" despite her care in negotiating the word]. Sis knew right off sumthin was wrong. She's comin down t' get me. I'm thinking i really need t' head up there for a couple days."

Stop her. I'll take you home.

"I think i've been quite enuf trouble."

Stop her. I hand fone repeatedly til she takes it.

15

With another raid on my cell looking likely, i dare not write another potentially harmful word. And so, behaving as if i have no idea something is up w these [blankblank's], i sit here playing an association game. [At the top of his very next instalment NS assigns the term 'lockdown clowns' to this double blank.]

Think of a word. Primary sort of word. Ok: priscilla, my first lover. Well, maybe 'lover' is overstating. My first 'accomplice of the flesh', let's say —not counting of course one's natalmother. On first try the word priscilla triggered 'sunlit'. Deeper exam found this unsatisfactory. Suncozy gave a closer match. That's sunlite + cozy, of course. Next i tried juanita, my first lover in fact. The concept, juanita, turnedout to = greenglowposey, a term distilled from: the color of the aura of photosynthesis + poetry. Hey, i dont invent this stuff, it's simply the language of thought set in print, a process entirely beyond my control. While suncozy ɛ greenglowposey may strike one as compound associations, they are in fact *single ɛ unfractioned* concepts in the mind's eye. The semaphores of thought have no regard for orthodox syntax, just as combined scents become a new scent in olfactory memory. And so it is that <the color of the aura of photosynthesis + poetry> = juanita. Now then, what of Lilith? (As long as we're still waiting to be raided.) Here an odd thing happens. Instead of continuing the trend toward more complexity, i am left with only one undiluted image: Love. So i try again....

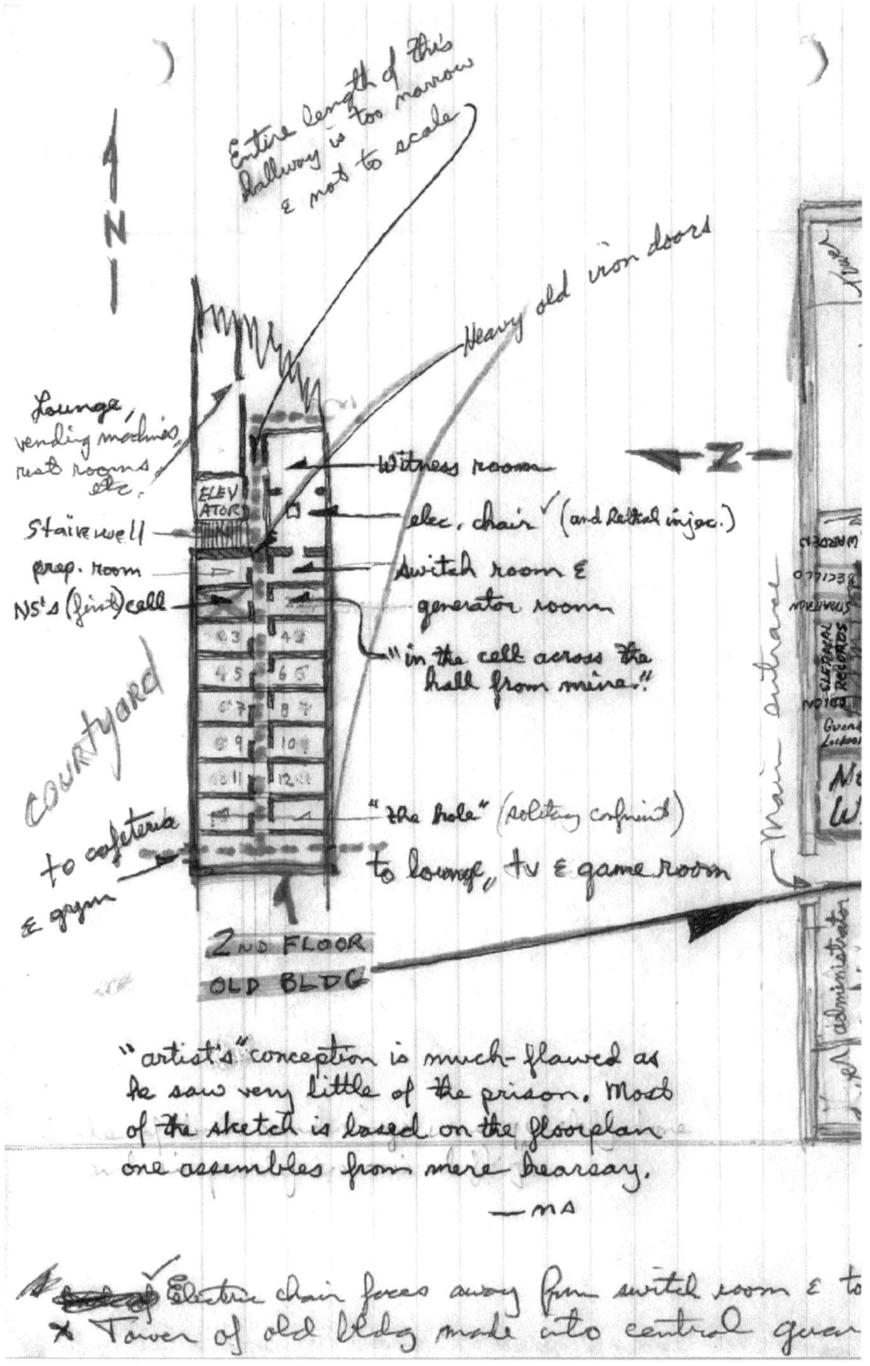
Entire length of this hallway is too narrow & not to scale
N
Heavy old iron doors
Lounge, vending machines, rest rooms etc.
ELEV ATOR
Stairwell
prep. room
NS's (first) cell
Witness room
elec. chair ✓ (and lethal injec.)
Switch room & generator room
"in the cell across the hall from mine."
3 4
5 6
7 8
9 10
11 12
COURTYARD
"the hole" (solitary confinmt)
to cafeteria & gym
to lounge, tv & game room
2ND FLOOR OLD BLDG
Main entrance
administration
"artist's" conception is much-flawed as he saw very little of the prison. Most of the sketch is based on the floorplan one assembles from mere hearsay.
—MA
✓ Electric chair faces away from switch room & to
* Tower of old bldg made into central guar

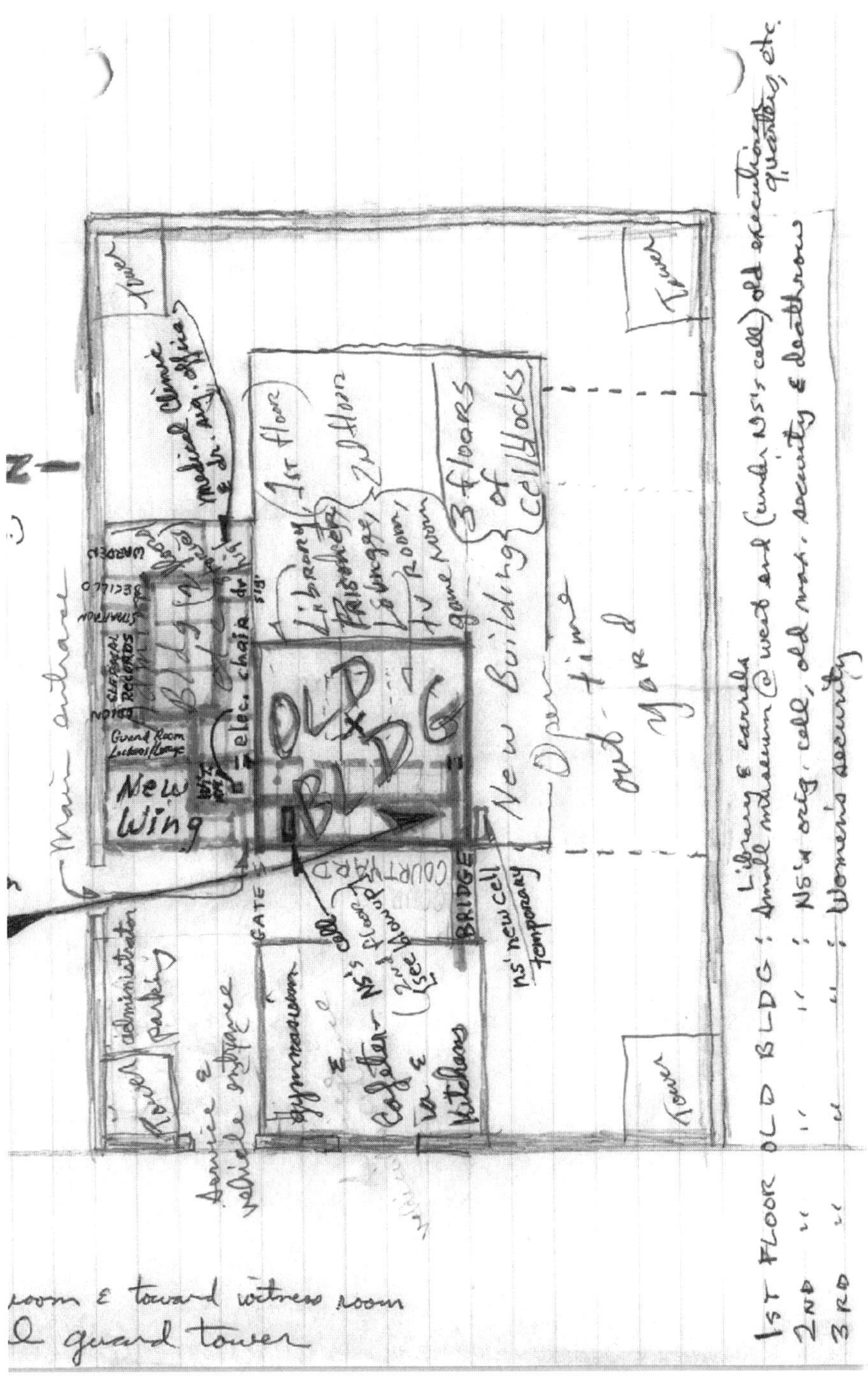
Main entrance
New Wing
OLD BLDG
COURTYARD
GATE
BRIDGE
Tower
Tower
Tower
Tower
administrator parking
Service & vehicle entrance
Gymnasium & Cafeteria & kitchens
New Building
3 floors of cellblocks
Guard Room Lockers/Lounge
RECORDS
WARDEN
elec. chair
medical clinic
NS' new cell temporary
1st FLOOR OLD BLDG: Small museum @ west end (under NS's cell) old execution quarters, etc
2ND " " : NS's orig. cell, old max. security & death row
3RD " " : Women's security
room & toward witness room
guard tower

Love. And when i take myself completely by surprise, fire off her name in the midst of another thought.... *Still,* love. Deep love. Heart-wrenching love. Nothing else will come up on the screen of association. Of more than passing interest should be the absence not only of gender ε sexuality in these synoptic reclamations, but of *all* physical anthropism.

While we wait why not toy w the L word.

Love. Consider it. There is a dove, with an underbelly of flossy velvet, nestled there; and an adverbial lily, costumed in swanwhite, lingering in the wings, waiting to dance the *pas de seul* which closes my little wordplay.

Consider its enunciation. Say it aloud, *l-o-v-e,* slowly, dragging out each phoneme. A long erect l looms large upfront, before the little orifice of the o; one's tongue must lift above the teeth to leap its polished lissome length.

Consider next that o, which, nudged open by the enunciatory press of the erect l, holds its form (lips taut against the teeth), readying soon to close, to lead us down to the feminine v.

Consider now that softpink velvety v. It transforms the open lips of the o into the merest pinch-of-a-pout. As we come upon it, the v lies to the other end of the torso of the word. Its function is so complete, so satisfying, as to leave the trailing e with nothing to do. It is as if the word were spelled luv.

(No raid yet, but emil has come&gone and zodion, arguing w xodion, just banged the glass of my cellwall violently w his club ε left the block.... Where were we? Ah, yes. I ache to rush ahead, but let us first wrap what's here begun.)

Consider last of all that e. It just lies there, limp, wormlike. And the l (which at the start stood so tall, so erect, so proud) has somehow lolled itself into that e. We see it doubled over there, having fallen on its face ...all the sighing ε crying phonemes of love longsince uttered.

Language, with its lovely ε versatile body, has always been alive for me —approachable soft enchanting submissive; more female than male, certainly. It is the only body i have now to touch —to dandle or to fondle or to love. In a place like this, and w an ending like mine, there are farworse ways to bide one's time.

16

I dropped her at a restaurant in berkeley while i went to get her things. Lilith had assured beth everything was fine. "She'll be sick with worry if she finds out." While beth, for her part, hoped "Lil's" tung <Cut it on a cracked glass> would be alright. And, as i was leaving, satchel in hand: "You know, mr schock <Call me, nathan>, Lil's special. Take care o' her," which cameoff more like a command than a request. I will.

The restaurant was a popcult version of a speakeasy, its walls littered w anachronistic trivia, all of it ancient history to the crowd inside. Lilith was seated in a booth at the rear and a server, hovering by her table as i came up, selfconsciously intro'd himself ɛ scooted ...wout asking if i wanted anything, even a bus ticket out of town!

She sipped a seltzerwater, seemed in good spirits: "Fizzle feels good on these miserable stitches." Each table had its own movie poster. Framed in green&gold, ours depicted the fotobusts of three moviestars, one male, two female. The title, *twin beds,* separated their faces. *Ménage á trois?* No *cinéastes,* we, we guessed late 40s-early 50s hollywood. Here our server decided to see if i wanted anything. Usually but not always, we agreed, the book is better than the movie. "Did you see *dances with wolves*?" The exception to the rule, we agreed. "I think hollywood hit rare heights with that one ...and with *fried green tomatoes* too ...dija see it?... an' all within months of each other." *True women* would have been high on her list too, i know, had circumstances allowed.

Still, hollywood mostly worships the trashing of morals 'n' Motherearth.

"Amen. It has long-glorified most of what is most wrong with civilization." And here she dropped another of her conversational stunbombs. "Take that line from the *african queen*? <Ya got me. When it comes ta movies 'n' teevee i'm at a loss.> Well, there's this tense moment in the movie when snobby hepburn says to ruffcut bogart: 'Nature, Mr Allnut, is what we're put on this earth to rise above.' "

Youre kidding. That's an actual line ...of spoken dialog, i mean? [Word for word ...i think.] My God. I've *got* ta use that ...but only with your permission of course. Wowed, i had yet to learn what Lilith's family ɛ friends already knew: Such *mots l'ultime* were the very watermark of her mostly reticent existence.

Movie chitchat soon gave way to literature, a word impossible for her to pronounce right then and which, when we stopped laffing at her attempts, made her remark, "Youd be amazed how many liberal arts kids in my classes pronounce it *just* like that: 'litachur'. Now i know why."

Me too. Language is being crippled by popmediocrity.

Their father had got them "interested in reading... kept a large library in his den" where they used to "investigate the titles, mostly for the pictures" she confessed. "One, a big heavy book, green with gold lettering, called, *duplicate hominids and double monsters,* made a huge impression on me ...couldnt hardly forget a name like that once you learned ta say it." She made that gesture again, wrist doubled back, palm up.

Ironic law: When one's not rushed, restaurant service is prompt. I ate, she nibbled. "There was a wasp pictured in that book, one that lays its egg in the egg of a butterfly. Imagine? Which reminds me...." Surprise flickers across her features. <What's wrong?> "Well, i had this dream a couple years later. Sheesh, i havent thought about this for ages!"

Coax to share. <Our civilly abused subconsciouses need all the outing they c'n get.>

Glumm&gluum burst into my cell before dawn today. (I knew something was up yesterday ...starting to read them like alphabet blocks.) Their mission? Confiscate (one more time, barf me) my dummy writings titled <constellations of confinement>. Dr rodent used to have my cell raided regularly, and i would fake a fuss if <c of c> was not returned, as if this diurnal decoy held great meaning for me. For it is what they think i spend my hrs days wks scribbling beneath the everpresence of their carnal surveillance.... I've chosen an early extract for the backdrop explanation it offers.

3.21.98 Our labors today take us 53cm se of this benchmark.

This polestar benchmark, chosen not without forethought —being nearest to the center among thousands of dimples (& tiny craters) in the thick coat of vomityellow paint which covers the w wall of my cell. The epoxy, insufficiently mixed & sprayed on, spattered. The dimples & craters which resulted (each an asterism) have dirt-darkened into stippled & highly random patterns.

...If we proceed se of the arching tail of yesterday's entry (scorpio: inverted, folded at its midsection at right angles to itself) the first star we encounter we'll call betelgeuse. I do this not because the figure i am about to reveal is the constellation orion (typically associated with that star), but because the implied radiants between stars more closely resemble the ancient hero, longsash —amerind version of orion, strongly proximate to the ever-spasming scorpion. Except for this alternate skylore we would be lost for an authentic figure to fillout this distorted pattern. (cont'd below)

"Welp, my dreams c'n be totally whacked. So be warned. In this one i was pregnant... Dont ask me how. You know, a thirteen-year-old's idea of pregnant? [i didnt know but i faked it] I was out walking in the woods. The sky grew dark. A wind ...like an approaching tornado... began t' blow. I looked up. Like a small helicopter, a gigantic wasp hovered overhead! It was black, with bloodred splotches. And it was after *me.* I started ta run. I knew it wanted to lay its egg inside me. In fact, inside my baby!"

Of course our server arrived just then. Which was just as well, for her enunciation was in need of a breather. I, a slow eater, finished first. Since it was getting late she asked to have hers wrapped to go. On the way to the car she noticed "Wow, real stars", uncommon sight in foggy frisco. The trades were hustling the pelagic fog along in seethru patches. We stood by the car for a moment pattern-hunting thru the clear stretches.

"You studied astronomy, no?"

As much as any seagoing ruminist i suppose.

"Well, you were the first to knock me over the head about the constellations. I was convinced they were real things." L re:d a little lesson of mine from *scapegoats & fallgirls* in a chapter titled <fact v. mirage>.

> As to the mirage of the constellations. Here we get this one big chance (i mean, the stories of the stars! Wow!) for imagination to teach us an objective Cosmic lesson, and we blow it ...on a thousand different versions of a single-minded urge: human desire —the blindest form of our pandemic anthropism! But even aside from turning the heavens into a humantheon, all the constellations of the night sky –all the shapes and symbols we've so carefully charted over centuries– are in fact only *very local* illusions. Though we think of them as Universal they're anything but. While these same stars can be seen from Arcturus or other stars ...in principle anyway... the way we *constellate* them –that is, their *arrangement* into Orion, Gemini and Taurus, say– exists only when seen from our stellar neighborhood. Pure mirage. For almost a hundred percent of the Universe cannot see the constellations we see. In point of fact, even if Earth were suddenly plunked down in some other region of our very own galaxy, the sky –the naked-eye sky– would look totally strange to us.

The chapter summarized.

> The whole point being. Religions have always presented their gods in the same way as the constellations are presented to us to this day —that is, not as the mirage of perspective they really are but as if those gods actually exist. Just as we're taught to believe the constellation Orion exists in fact, most of us are also

taught to believe some highly humaniform god or other exists in fact. Nobody points out that, just as the 'existence' of Orion depends entirely on our location in the Milky Way, that version of God we believe in often depends on pure location as well —that is, on where in the World one is born and even to whom. (I.e: If you're born in India you will doubtless believe in a different god than if you were born in Australia.) Both are mirages of perspective. And so it goes with our concepts of time, good, evil, and a whole bunch of other constellates of purest myth we're taught to carry to our graves as if they are real things. ¶ But back to what got us started and the title of this chapter: What frightens me most. Okay, i realize we sailors-of-life are so at-sea and in-a-fog, objectively speaking, we can't separate mist from mast. Fine. It's a truly scary fact but we learn to navigate around it. What terrifies me is when i stop to realize, {I'm on the same Ship with six billion myopic sailors and its they, my reader, who have the last word on where we're all headed and why! And worst of all? There's hardly a whisper of mutiny anywhere to be found!}

As if it were a character flaw, before we got underway, Lilith confessed to not knowing "very much about the stars or constellations. I know orion the hunter, of course ...everybody does... ever a threat to taurus (there) and to the hare (over there)...." Her eyes locked in place for a moment as if searching the starred dome of memory. "The hare, before dawn, will, one more time (i hope), leap into blackness ...'n' freedom." <I like that. Wow. Very nice.> Then, deliberating for a sec, she adds, "Unless of course youre watching right now from honolulu or the like, wherefrom our little buddy is still in deep doodoo from that mean ol hunter." The way it all just popped out of her so unaffectedly, so earnestly, had i known her better i would have given her a bearhug ...well, ursus-hug. Plus, in that all this was delivered w those vast eyes ε that pathetic lisp, i was ready to make her then&there my very own leveret. "My heart has always been on the side of the hunted not the hunter."

Mine too.

"I know." As i bent, key in hand, to open her door, she asked, "Have you read richard adam's *watership down*? ...No? It's one of my mostfavorite books. I'll loan it t' you."

<And i will read it.> And i did, cover-to-cover, over my next few flites. Which takes us back to her horizon-leaping hare . Until i saw the movie, *watership down,* it was matisse's hare ("the hair") which came to mind whenever i looked westward at the winter sky. But after seeing the movie, it

was the skyleaping artwork of duncan, guy ε rosen which everafter came to mind ...and which artwork, bythebye, inspired the animal representations in mcLith's own art. [McLith (lowercase m) is how LM signed her artwork. —Ed.]

As we crossed the bridge to san rafael she informed me, "You know, i've been here since june and still havnt been across *the* bridge!" The golden gate, she meant of course. We agreed to remedy that <on foot>, and "soon". I asked her to finish her dream. She demurs, says it was a stupid dream anyway. Meaning to earn some lit points w her i replied <Would you leave me so unsatisfied?> This got me a most curious askance glance.

"Where was i? [i explain] Well, i knew the ugly thing wanted only one thing: to lay its egg inside my unborn daughter. Dont ask me how i knew it was a girl. And, no, i didnt question how a wasp carrying an egg could be male either. Anyway, harried as a hare, i ran into a thicket of trees 'n' hid. It's too big to squeeze in here, i thought. But then, like that, the thicket became a large room. You know how dreams do...no rhyme no reason? Well, mine are worse. [delivered w deadpan staring ε glassyeyed severity] ...the woods the thicket the wind the monster wasp, are all inside the room with me now 'n'-... <And?> I'm jus now realizing: the room was lit from *outside* not inside... hmm... an' the lite is coming thru windows of bloodred glass. [pause, mouth open] Sheesh. Now *that's* a touch. [trying to make light of an obviously odious experience] Do ya really wanna hear this? It gets even more stupid than i thought."

{If this is the only puzzlepiece i c'n worm outuv her i'll take it.} Please. ...*Really*.

She looked thru the windshield as if she could see her past unfolding out of the darkness of the road upahead, and that what she saw there was ominously clear. "Welp, the thing –the wasp thing– is getting closer 'n' closer. Its wingwash pushes aside the bushes as it stands over me. It looks more like a person now 'n' its pulsing wings sting my face 'n' arms like ruff sandpaper. Its face is ghastly in that lite 'n' it's laffing at my terror. The wind is worse than ever now 'n'-, oh... One *more* thing."

What? (I'll be getting better lines soon.)

"I'm just realizing: the lite in the room is wavering like the rest o' the world is on fire! Anyway, trees are tilting, limbs are falling, dead leaves are blowing all around. And oh, watch this: someone's shawl blows past. [Now there's a touch, i say, trying my own mood-lightening device.] Anyway, when i try t' getup ta run the manwaspwhatever-thing knocks me to the ground, pushes me down with its wings so i cant move. I c'n see its stinger clear as if its under a powerful microscope ...long pointed black pulsing. Y' know how a wasp's stinger pulses when it's about t' sting? We saw this film in science class once ...some have *barbed* tips on their stingers, you know! This one did too. That's how they keep it stuck in til they spaz all the poisons out."

Constellations are also implied by the many fractures & fissures in the paint, as they present in coincidence with the stellar dimpling & cratering. My socalled diary displays other sensibilities as well. For instance at 6.07.98 we find

> And so we find, our <constellations of confinement> are not in the usual places. For instance, canis major (big dog) is quite near the usually more distant gemini (the twins). While they, the twins, castor & pollux (which i've taken the liberty to rename astra & polly, according to the special logic of my private universe), have become the small but brite-eyed stellation, the hare, that afrited creature ever hunted by orion & his dogs and whose stalking is avenged by taurus.

And so they go, these entries, yielding a sort of drunken nitesky, the universe of a tipsy ahab on a rolling sea, a cosmos gone amok in pursuit of a functional (indeed, bearable) reality. Slugmoid calls my journal "inmate schock's <constellations of madness>". I rather like that. But that will be our little secret, yours & mine, reader, ok? May the authorities comb my metajargon & its anomalous asterisms for clues in vain. Being written in the same stiletto-sharp & minuscule longhand as the ms of this book, the camera lurking over my shoulder cannot discern content, no matter how erect its vapid lens screws itself —tho this pernicious watching watching watching surely affects my hiccupy horrible stilted & selfconscious style at times: run-on phrases, carousing extrapolations ...not to be confused with the other anomalies imprinted in my idiolect, all of them very on-purpose: severe contractions, many linked germanically, phonic clipping of anglicisms, pandemic paucity of punctuation, symbols preempting real graphs, missing spaces quotes hyphens etc,etc,etc ...as a former king of siam like to enunciate.

And so, occulting the camera's orb with my back, i will fold this wks instalment & tuck it where the lite rarely reaches ...not where youre thinking, my friends. For that place –being a benchmark assterism, a very polestar around here– is in fact the first place the asstronomers who inhabit this observatory (stress on latin root, as in OBtuse OBscene & OBjectionable) pray to find contraband. For one infraction there earns one permanent rebuttal.

She paused, out of breath i think from trying so hard to enunciate. "You know, this dream's upsetting me? ...and after all these years too ...That's so dumb. I really need ta get a grip. [i treat the remark rhetorically] Well, it was clear in the dream what would happen next. It would sink its stinger into my belly til it reached the body of my baby —jus like the picture in the book. And then, once inside the baby, it would shoot its egg, like a poison bullet. [takes deep breath] But when the thing lunged at me ta do it, it scared me so bad i woke up. Arncha glad? *I* am."

Her tale complete, she just stared at the road unfolding out of the darkness. "There now. that wasnt so hard after all.... [nodding to herself] Cant imagine where i was keeping all that." Then, leaning forward, hugging her knees, in silence, she watched (from beneath arched brows) the sky. After awhile she asked, "Is that venus...? No. I mean that one over there."

Poe called the stars giddy but *that* one, trus' me, is sirius. {Totally unfair of me to expect a reaction.} That's sirius ...the dog star ...it marks the mouth of the constellation canis major. ["Big dog."] Yes. Youre actually looking at two stars there. One's a white dwarf.

"Youre sirius?" She turned, mildly smiled my way.

As i ate my condescending presumption i talk/sang four famous notes, *Flimmern, flimmern, little stern,* for i was feeling like a rejuvenated dutchman flying thru the nite w my enigmagic[sic] senta, inventing new verses as i steered our craft along: *O du mein holder übelstern*.... But as we turn back toward the nw, orion & his dogs are relegated to the rear window once more.

The berkeley/dillon beach drive takes a calm person about 90min. What traffic there was was returning to the cities from the n. I apologized for pressing her about the dream.

"T'sokay. It shouldnuv upset me like that ...not after all this time." I put my hand on hers (which was on her thigh), stroked it, retreated. She fell quiet. I put on some jon windstar, whom she "absolutely" loved. "You quote him quite a bit in your books." Captain greensong, she called him. "Are you guys friends?" Since the '70s. Why dont you put your seat back, try t' get some sleep? She would, but insisted on keeping me company —the least she could do. Beside, the petaluma turnoff was easy to miss, she fibbed. Windstar's *the eagle and the hawk* landed just as we reached that turnoff. <Ah, petaluma! And, ah, amy's kitchen! —source of my on-the-run foodstuffs, *specially* back in bamalachia, that organic-foods wasteland.>

"Lage goes t' school here. She's pretty famous here actually. In the papers 'n' on tv alot."

Gymnastics? [Uhuh] Follow tomales signs? [Uhuh] I try to steer conversation so she has minimal talking. So one might call your sister a sorta petaluminary?

"O damn, i dont b'lieve you said that. Dont make me laff! [hand on mouth til spasm subsides] Great word!" She recalled how "Father usta love catchy stuff like that. For instance, he used t' read [to them at bedtime] limericks 'n' poems." He loved lear, silverstein & carroll; read from *alice's adventures in wonderland & thru the looking-glass* "over'n'over again ...Other carroll stuff too. Do boys read those...?" Jabberwocky was a "fave". She bet he could still recite it. And when they "got all giggly, which was probably alot" they liked "beautiful soup" best of all. They made him read it "over'n'over'n'over til he threatened to barf ...of course *he* never said barf. He tried to get as silly as us, really he did... Hope you'll come in and meet him."

This image of him did make me feel more inclined to do so. For my part, i confessed to having a soft spot for "the owl and the pussycat" and "jimmy jet and his tv set"... And, o yes, field's "little boy blue". Now there's a classic tearjerker!

She quotes to the first semicolon, stops. "This mouth o' mine is such a drag." Reminds self of elmer fudd. "Pardon my lispy ellipses 'n' lapidated lapses. Did i say that? <Perhapses.> Ugh. Your petaluminary was better. *Not* that perhapses isnt cute. [her talk is turning detectably mumbly] Yes, cute. Hope it treats sis better than it treated winona 'n' polly." <It? What it?> Head slipping gradually down the seatback onto shoulder. *(...Noddin', droopin', close ta my shoulder till it falls....)* When i look back she is asleep.

A bit of explication while she catnaps. Tho it was immed clear why 'it', the city of petaluma, had not been good to polly (12yearold polly klaas had been missing from a slumberparty, at the time, for some 3wks); and while actress winona ryder's benevolence in the search for both polly & her abductor seemed enuf cause for L to link the two; why she felt the town had mistreated ryder, and how she came to know so much about ryder's private life, i would have to wait to learn.

After a couple mins she awoke violently. "Oooh!" <Whoa, easy. You okay?> Sorry. Fell asleep for a sec ...so hard i scared myself." Seeming out of nowhere she asked me to promise, please, never to call the cops 'r medics on her "no matter what... I know it was necessary. And i cant thank you enuf, please believe me. It's jus, such superaggresso people scare me t' death." Allowing no time for response, she asked if i'd be leaving town soon.

I confessed how much i really wanted to get back to appalachia –before all the trees were blown bare– but that i had a couple more lectures first. <Here, listen. I think you'll like this.> I turnup volume.

Just to look in your eyes again;
just to lay in your arms;
just to be the first one always there for you....

"God, that's beautiful" she said between verses.

Just to wake up each morning;
just to you by my side;
just to know that youre never really far away....
For you alone. Only for you.

When it ended i punched STOP. Save for juanita (and angie & maybe veronika too), Lilith is the only woman i've dated who would allow the vulnerable silence following such a song to grow its own meanings ...which of course addresses my *choice* in women, not women as a class. Examining the cd case in the maplite, after awhile she said, "I thought i had all his albums." Scent of the tuna-melt i'd coaxed her to finish reached me as she bent into the lite of the console. "Is this new?"

Not really. Jon's new company has distribution problems. It's yours if you want it. I have another back home. She promised to return it —the only promise she forgot to keep. (Over time windstar's "for you" would become that cliche which lover's re as "our song".)

The mcGrae residence was in a community of "country estates". Reaching out my window as instructed i pressed a red bar on a control box. A male voice spoke. Lilith leaned over, chirped into the intercom; i reveled in her closeness & the natural scent of her hair. A moment later the gate glided aside. After a slite jog right in the bricked drive, the headlites lit the door to a three-car garage. Would i come in for a moment? Image of a man trying his best to giggle along w his little daughters encourages me. Of course.

Daddy was older than expected. Kissing his cheek, Lilith stood beside him. He looked at her face ("O me, o my."), patted her cheek tenderly. "Lily speaks highly of you" he said, welcoming us into a spacious greatarea.

She is generous [i scan the fireplace wall & its hangings w a sweep of my hand] ...*and* your *best* work of art, if i may say so.

"Thank you. I have another from the same gallery, you could say." Gives a squeeze around her waist. L scoots ahead to a sittingarea. "But then, you *met* laly already ...lalage, I mean?"

Lilith overrides my diplomatically intended <Lalage? Yes, a-....> w "I'll bet she's asleep, no?"

"Yes —collapsed, poor child, just like that. [snaps fingers] Tried to wait up, she did. Last two weeks 'uv been hard, what with school, back 'n' forth ta the city, competitions 'n' all. Trains every minute she gets, the little tiger."

"Sister is the son daddy always wanted."

"Now, Lili. [stops, makes disappointed face which she doesnt look to see] Here, sit, please. Be comf'table."

The house was spanish mod. But then i cant tell a cornice from a corbel. Mexican tile, lots of adobe, lots of arches & open space. A large mural (sw Naturescape) covered the street wall of the livingarea, one side & rear of which looked out (in daylite) onto their own & neighboring equine pasture. Paintings & portraits hung in every nook.

"Can we get you a drink: a beer, a highball? No...? Fruitjuice? Of course." Dad will have a beer. "Understand you like good music, nathan? I'm a first-name sort. Just call me, don. So you like serious music?" He spoke of vocal triumphs/vocal tragedies. I pondered the bias in his terms "good" music, "serious" music. A strong-willed but apparently gentle person, i could see he worried over Lilith's "accident" as he called it in hushed tones when she left the rm. I sensed he was sure i had nothing to do w her hurts and everything to do w looking out for her.

Four fotoportraits transfixed my background awareness. These hung on apposing walls to each side of an elevated fireplace. Two were of a pubescent Lilith; the others, more recent, perhaps aged 15. Only one caught that captivating strabism in her silvergrays however. I looked about for similar portraits of lalage. Perhaps they hung elsewhere. I could only guess, this partisan display was meant to compensate for Lilith's overlong absence from their lives. What a stunning little beauty she'd been, this Lilith, *ainsi.*

"See theyve caught your eye. Beautiful arent they?"

<Huh? O yes.> I assume he's speaking of the portraits generally.

"They favor the young suzy farrell, no?"

Odd you should mention that. She was an early love of mine.

It was clear he expected me to say, suzy who? "You dont mean you dated her?"

O but i do... [jaw ajar, disbelieving tilt of head] ...in my youthful *dreams.* [share smile, his i think one of relief not to have to challenge me, for...] She was already dancing pro when i was still in high school.

"So you know ballet."

I know a *sauté* from *jeté* if that's what you mean. I have friends who are figureskaters 'n' ice dancers. But ballet? Not disinterested. Just havent found the time.

"Know the feeling. Most of my exposure's from before I was married. I even saw farrell dance a few times in new york. Her dulcinea [points to foto-portrait behind me] is without peer. <Ah, yes. Vey nice.> But family rasponsability ended that. It's my stress on balletic deportment that's put laly's gymnastics ahead o' the pack. She was an elite coming outa the juniors, you know? <Yes. Lilith has said.> An' she's still up there with the best. As a matter of fact, both my girls are familiar with suzy farrell; seen her many times. On film. [looks back at portraits] And they think mona lisa had a smile, eh?"

Yes, i said. Beautiful.

"An' here's one o' those suzies now!" L appears *w* trefoil of glasses wedged in one hand, sets the cluster clinking on a centertable.

"I'll never make a waitress." Retrospect notes, that was not to be entirely so. Anyway...

Don was just stuffy enuf (and, for L's sake, i wanted him to like me enuf) that i dared not say, while i had long enjoyed ballet music, i only came to like it as a dance form thanks to a foto montage featuring farrell in a magazine i chanced upon. It was love at first glance. And later, after seeing her dance, i wrote in the margin of my program

> ...This wispy assemblage of enchanting vibration (farrell's image in motion) ever threatening demanifestation back into the empty space from which she

appeared... she is a protoplasmic prism which turns music into lite, lite into motion, and motion back into music again.

...description begun back in h.s to assist w my wooing of sandy brandywine.

If the reader has noticed no mention here of the shrimpton likeness, this is for good reason. First, since shrimpton was largely gone from the scene by the time L was born, don probably never made the connection. Even more, by the time of the portraits his daughters' features still retained an element of juvenile roundness, had yet to attain the crisper delineation maturity brings. Indeed, only at today's remove can i dissect where exactly these differences lie. Oversimplified (for the sake of space), until one superimposes the face of dancer farrell onto that of model shrimpton, L's ethereal charisma –her essential warmth softness sensitivity ɛ mystery– will not appear.

We catchup w don at "...Björling, yes —for purity of tone 'n' ringing timbre [which he pronounced, timber]. But, when it comes to raw romantic quality, top t' bottom, lanza is unique. *Il voce de'l angeli !*

The giddy stars (so legends tell) ...attend the spell
of his voice.... [Your mario, dad, alias israfel.]

quoth Lilith. After asking her to repeat her ad lib he said, "God, I like that! Isnt she sumthin?" I nod in agreement. Don drank dark non-domestic, inhaled the froth w teutonic relish. "Isnt israfel a roman takeoff on orpheus?"

Lilith thinks arabic and <Dunno. I'm a flop at lit.>

"Me too [says don] ...unless someone has set it ta good music."

I recall as he rambles ɛ sips a recent date's mentioning her dad's preference for dark beer.

"If youre talking lit, daddy's mario was joyce's mario-the-tenor incarnate!", says L w rapidly flagging sociability. <Recarnate> i would have countered had i understood her at the time. "He even donned the same doublet joyce gave him [!] for *marta* in *the great caruso.*"

"Lionel, the farmer, trains his grief on martha. [continues don] *Marta, tu sparisti. Di dolor io morirò !* D'ja ever hear it? <I believe.> You'd love it. [don's latingua was surprisingly good] ...Those snob classical stations *still* wont play lanza tho. An' the oldtimer stations think any voice bigger than eddy fisher's is grand opera. People today have no way of hearing pop singers like tony martin john raitt sergio franchi al martino (early martino, I mean) ed ames 'n' gordy macrae. It's like they never existed. The only one still holding his own in the *bel canto* department is vic damone."

I sip my fruitjuice cordial, wonder {Can he not hear how sexist his talk is?}.

"Even *artsong* tenors get airtime ...an' those damn limp-wristed butt-wagging countertenors too —socalled men who sound like castrated capons escaping from the chef over hot coals! And *still* they wont play lanza. The vicious old jealousies of his peers, living 'n' dead, shames our socalled musical culture to this minute." Tho don's homophobia was a bit tangy, his candor was refreshing. Lilith, looking weary, sends a "That's my dad" face my way. "The upside is, all this narrowmindedness has made lanza more a cult artist t'day than he was when he was alive!" Swipes hefty swallow.

I'm beginning to salivate for a beer as Lilith snugs ever deeper into her chair between us. Sound of door closing somewhere behind my right ear. Curiosity strains for footfalls. Livingarea soundsystem (quietly processing a brahms symphony) is all i can discern behind don's amicable gush. Dare i air an old gripe? [Don: Consider yourself among friends, please.] There are talents 'too good' for their time. Those in power, be they singers writers runners or politicians, feel threatened by uncommon greatness; do all they can to crush unique talent wherever it appears. In many cases only the death of a great talent opens the way for objective assessment. Even then it takes decades ...sometimes centuries! He liked that. Sound of door closing, then another, doublecrosses my train of thought. Lilith seems more&more absent. I recall that nite on the promenade, the feel of that agile weight in my lap, hot breath on my neck. I note dark shadows around L's eyes. {Sensual resuscitant even in her lassitude.} Don, delited w his newfound soundingboard, drones on. Her head lolls on the back of her chair, only her eyes following the conversation. Closing. Trying again. Gathers armful of hair onto her lap, twists round&round w an index a strand of isolated tress.

Don, woundout to around 6000rpm's w little indication of shifting, will say after i leave, "An unusual young man. I like him". Shaking a full shock of white hair he addresses L. "Hear that? Your friend nathan here has heard o' lanza! The girls think I'm hallucinating when I say he still has fan clubs all over the world. [takes last swallow of brew, still shaking his head] And dead so young ...so young." Chokes briefly on a gust of foam. [i stretch w small sips my own drink] "So whadaya think about this monotonic dissonance that passes fer music today? Why would anybody wanna do that to his mind?" He fails to spot his sonic oxymoron.

That's just it. It's not a mind thing. Nor is it, i think, meant to be. Not unlike *verismo* opera, i find music more'n'more an attempt –often desperate, admittedly– to reunite the cartesian mind/body disconnect we civil so suffer from. An' being a whole-body pursuit, heart-rate rhythms, driving beats, hypnotic chants, are more'n'more the *idée fixe* of musicmaking, with language only an instrumental adornment because the longing body cant understand words anyway. Like folk art traditionally, pop art is just another way of saying, humanity, generally, is rejecting the cerebrally abstract existence which civilization, unjustifiably –and often brutally– demands of us. But somehow we civilized cant see this.

Don is near-successful at subducting the total blank he has drawn from my comment when he (as if offhandedly) asks, "So how d'ya come ta know opera?"

Mostly third-hand. My grandfather's brother was a tenor of some repute. Father's side o' the family often played his records. Mostly for show, sorry t' say. Save for my aunt, i think i was the only one really listening. I've heard a few arias 'n' caballetas, i'd say, but i'm in no sense an authority.

"What was his name? I might know it."

Schock, like mine.

"Not *richard?*", which he did not pronounce reeshard. <That would be him.> "No kidding? Goddamn fine voice! Tauber clone. Master o' falsetto. Hey, ya know what? I have a record o' his. [jumps up, goes to cabinet] Light stuff, but heck. Look here, it has his *rose weiss, rose rot* and *o mädchen, mein mädchen*. Terrific renditions! [my great uncle's face smiles out from the album he hands me] *That* was his art, come t' think of it, cause the voice is already dark 'n' tired here. Went the way of all german voices, no? All that bit-down *heldentenor* crap. And, o, this one I *love!* [from above me his finger finds & underlines] *Es muss ein wunderbares sein*. His *sotto voce* is heartrending." Don's italian is leagues-better than his german. Glancing over at L his smile sobers. "Speaking of roses, this one's fading fast."

Yes. This poor *mädchen* needs sleep and i need t' be going. Emptying ε setting aside my glass, i stand.

"Allow me, before you go, to play what I promised. [slowly i resit] Anyone who likes roberta peters 'n' kathleen battle as much as you do jus hasta love *this* voice." Don preps his audience for the music of gounod. "The voice of your typical marguerita is *way* too heavy. An' it's the same with most operatic juliets. The sounds that come outa those primadonnas are so matronly *any* romeo would scale a wall ...to escape, that is!" Under other circumstances his commentary would have been a hoot. But i could only smile, glance w obvious concern at Lilith who had, finally, lost the struggle and drifted off. "She *is* quite exhausted, the dear" said don, setting marguerite to singing anyway.

As mady mesplé finished a ravishing *Depuis le jour* i said, *Very* nice. "Coloratura extraordinaire", dotted don, obviously pleased w his revelation. Looking again at poor Lilith i added, But i'd better be going for sure this time. As i slid forward don halted my rise by presenting the recording's case to me saying, "For instance, I fail to get any of today's te kanawa hoopla. Like dotty kirsten an' de los angeles before her, I find the pretty maorist's range of expression confined to a purely social register."

So preoccupied was i w L's pathetic state i did not get his stinging satire til i was driving home. My response, unoffensive, i hoped, was <I see what you mean. [standing] Well, i certainly have enjoyed your hospitality, don mcgrae, sir. But i really must get on my way an' let poor Lilith here get some rest. L, perkingup, hands me straightout of sleep the promised book, insists on walking me to my car. As she heads out the walkway don, holding to the foyer, shakes my hand energetically. "A pleasure, nathan. Maybe we'll see ya again? finish our chat?" Then, grabbing my arm, leaning in, he whispers, "Thanks for lookin after m' baby." Has bearish-big smile upclose.

Surprising me, just before i ducked into the javelin, Lilith rose up *en demi-point*, kissed me lightly near the wick of my mouth and, w a tiny toss of her head (that tic again), whispered: "I wrote you a letter while you were thleeping. I put it under your thcrapbook. G'nite. [quick whisper as i sink into my seat:] Thanks for pampering daddy." Steps backward, as after a stage bow, so i can close my door. I want to leap out, scoop her up, runoff w her to my lair in the mtns for keeps.

17

On the drive home there was much to be mentally mulled. For instance, while don was entertaining ٤ hospitable to a fault, i found his push for yet one more pratfall —at the expense of his daughter's plain discomfort if not pain— selfish, or so it seemed. But more importantly, what, in actuality, had happened to Lilith to begin w? Who was it that took her addressbook, for instance, her fotos? put that money in her wallet? And why? And why did she have to warn a friend "someone" had her address? And, o yes. Did she really have seizures or was it just a cover? And if so, how did her sleeve get ripped off? Then again, if she didnt have seizures wouldnt her father have reacted differently? And, less personally, where was little charley procyon during all this?, the half-brother supposed to have been in attendance on the eve in question? And should we pause now to review for my reader a certain history which rick uncovered ...tho, sad to say, too late in the game... that near-oracle, that *le mot de l'enigma*, this *masque l'essentiel*, which could have saved.... But see me, again, way too far ahead of our story, slaphappily hopscotching into mortally perilous terrain. {And what to make of L's fear of cops 'n' medics?} I fell to wondering how one so young came to read police-types w such clarity. While i knew 9 in 10 cops own the imperialist gene to varying degrees, it had taken years of being at their mercy as an ecoactivist to absolutely know what i was talking about. {My books alone could not have cemented such a fear, could they?}

Lilith, not unlike many young people (not unlike myself at one time) was convinced she would die young. We had known each other about a year when i related a story from my non-military medic career. An old couple, fullknowing the husband was terminally ill, wished him to expire in the privacy of their own home. But a grandchild panicked. We arrived. My medic superior, aching to intercede, called in the police for legal backup. Tho the wife pleaded w us to go away, and tho the grandchild recanted in tears, i was ordered to proceed w als (advanced life support) protocol. I refused on grounds that to do so was unethical&immoral, and, after a few mins of heated exchange, i quit my job, retrieved my bag from the ambulance and walked the long way home. Followup revealed, instead of the peaceful final moments of sharing ٤ caring which the couple sought, during the last hours of his life this man ٤ his family endured the effronteries ٤ indignities of body-jolting electroshock, repeated bouts of manual ٤ machine achtung cpr, heartspace invasion by needles ε drugs, body invasion by a whole trapeze of tubes ε wires! What this hoard of caustic "humanitarians" in effect did was to arrogantly trash the intimate finale of a lifetime of togetherness in trade for a few mins of salaried egomania. In fact, only under threat of manslaughter charges was the wife allowed to remove the oxygen mask from the face of her beloved so they could share some final words. "It's alright. Dont worry. I'm okay. I love you my dear one. I know we shall meet again some day to rewrite this unfortunate ending." After hearing this story Lilith made us an appt w my lawyer where we created a socalled living will. Her goal was to give both she&me the legal right to die unassisted ε unmolested by all form of achtung lishment clones, whom we thereafter had the legal right to bar from the vicinity of our demise no matter our perceived mental states etcetcetc.

Thought ran circuitously as i drove —small circles, ever spiraling down to the same focus: the letter she said she'd left. Were the answers there? I tried not to speed to findout. For if ever i strike a deer a fox a rabbit, in a sense the driver too will be crushed. I would explain the extent of my care here except, well... What i "brake for", or go around, or stop to move out of the road, or flag in the middle of the road, could use its own handbook ...w which to explain my actions to the satisfaction of my civilized brothers&sisters. When it comes to the rights of other lives, where we draw the line marks the far side of the maturity of our innermost Self. Even tho in pain herself that nite, i'd caught Lilith wincing a couple times at a moth-strike on the windshield, while *privately* believing (as i'd one day discover) she still had a long way to grow.

Once a favorite pastime, i ceased driving between dusk&dawn unless it was extremely important —ie, unless arriving somewhere made more ecological sense than staying home or going next day. In college i drove a taxi at nite. After each shift we had to hosedown our cab. I would curse the insects that flowed by the hundreds from the grill onto the pavement. It never occurred to me to question the culture which taught me such selfcenteredness, a culture which perpetuated (o carefully) my disdain for Nature, and which labeled my callousness manly or cool! I never thought to cross-examine modern man's modes of transport muchless criticize the many forms of speed to which we are clearly addicted. Nature, i was taught, was just behind the times.

It was some time before my values took a turn, before i began to wonder about the difference between Natural & human-caused disasters: the creatures that poured out of my grill under the impact of the water; the possum i hit on a mtn rd one nite in pa; the death of a young raven whose neck snapped when diving (presumably) at the wing-shaped design on the hood of my vehicle, was thus impaled on the foil of the antenna. As it happened, the signal coming into my radio at the moment of the skewering was respighi's "pines of rome". The raven, jousting *w* an antenna it did not see (not in time, anyway), was impaled just after a moment in the music when the song of a nitengale seems praising all Creation —violin tremolos, as of forest deeps; harp-plinkings remindful of stars.

18

I was not tired when i arrived home; i was brutalized *w* fatigue. Even as i approached my door the feel of cool bedsheets was already winding my body in its cocoon. Lites. But i thought i turnedoff... Wait, havent we done this recently? Maybe i'm already in bed, dreaming. From the outer foyer i see someone sitting on the couch. I glance out to the street. On seeing a certain car i say <Aw shit> and stumble inside.

Now a word needs be said about ms nikki mckinney —whose name & actual position *w* greenEarth has been doctored mostly to protect the ggNs trust fund. Lilith's boss, whom we met in the foyer that delirious rainy afternoon, was for years chief artist for greenEarth news, a quarterly zine sent to members around the world. Her flamboyant "nmk" had long been visible on the artwork of its best features & covers. She could have headedup the graphics dept at any time but, to her credit, argued "I'm an artist not a collator."

A few months into our relationship, on a visit to ggNs, my friend glendon mentioned our engagement. "But she's wearing a ring." <But *i* didnt give her a ring. Or a promise. Or anything of the sort.> We broke up over this. Nikki was a classic overachiever —driven; not for money but status; status *w*in the green community. (Isnt such drive but the child of an adult called aggression?) My mother was a driven woman and the worst thing a woman could do was remind me of my mother. I get biology at a gut level. Dont expect durable heterogamy where the woman chased-down the man. If i'd had daughters –lovely little twin Liliths, say– if i told them nothing else about twitterpation i would warn: Never marry 'r live with a guy who doesnt want you, how should i say? ...alot! *If* you want it to last. For this reason the nikki/ns affair was off-center from the start. Artistic talented witty lovely as a tall flower: every incentive was there *except* whatever it is that triggers specific lust (not just generic desire).

Sensing she was pushing, nikki would suspend her manipulation (which i wasnt supposed to notice) somewhere between 'merely cloying' & 'mammary suffocation'. Snipping off her own nose, as they say, she would next go into hiding. More than once i mistook this tactic as passivity not repressed rage. My work on the w.coast done, i would leave for home. When i returned we would inevitably meet, being both of us headquartered in the same place. Her rage repressed (or so i now understand), she would be civil and so we would agree to date again. As to nikki's looks. That she was a felicity waterman (actor) lookalike w a janefondalike body didnt help me break off what i knew was amiss. The curious side of dating snippy but snazzy nikki was, you were almost sure from the gitgo that, when you got to see it eye-to-eye, she would *not* have a smilebutton for a clitoris.

Why date nikki to begin w? That's the same as asking, why all the intimates in my life save for juanita & Lilith. Leave it to a woman to broach this question perfectly. "In mating, what we see isn't necessarily what we get, much less what we wish we had, though it may be exactly what we need when we see it. For when it comes to love and sex, though we may hate to be caught vulnerable,

So far i've gotten back three replies from upstairs; the first two with several scribblers making entries. One carol hathcock has taken the role of lead correspondent. This is an improvement, tho her language is rather coarse. Not that i'm against swearwords; they can be functional, even erotic, in the right application. It's the tasteless use of <u>any</u> word that bores me. I will not soil this testament w more than a taste of the hankerings of the ladies upstairs ...for "a good fuck with a hunky fame [famous person]". It seems the entire floor is prepared to have sex with me ~~any brand any amount my choice. There is one hope tho. It seems there's a 19-year-old bodybuilder, one rosa poza: ``She has brown eyes black hair and a cute little shape... [or so carol says] ...a cutup little ginny if you ever saw one``. Hathcock means guinea, i believe. ``Shes the guards pet. [no apostrophes and little in the way of punctuation] The guards by the way are all girls ...and she likes you. Consider your self lucky. Youl wanna screw her socks off when you see her.`` Now that's something. She's slated, this alleged 10, for the women`s division at the same intraprison invitational i`ve been chosen to compete in, and was first to get to use what the warden called ``a spayshal gym for mah stah [star] pafawmas [performers]``, the same gym i now use daily. My criminal constituency upstairs also voted us ``couple of the year``. I am to ``keep a eye out`` for a foto of rosa which i'll find ``under the vynill cover of the big wate bench not the small one. It will have a note on back. Rosas too embarassed to write in this note with us.`` [sic, entire note, proofreader] I take embarrassment as a good sign in this place.

it is vulnerability alone which holds the keys to both despair *and* ecstasy." —bekky kydd, revising marianna torgovnick. And so we separate sex from love, love from sex, simply because *not* to do so leaves us friteningly vulnerable, standing to lose much that is personal & treasured for a single misstep of desire. Enuf of preface. Let us now confront the article herself.

Coming from behind the cover of the latest EarthNow quarterlyly, nikki, sitting there on my couch, had the chutzpah to smile up at me and say "Hullo". <What're you doing here?> Is that any way ta greet an *old* friend?" Even in my dazed state i couldnt miss the squirt of venom in the modifier "old".

This is *verboten,* nik. You know perfectly well i'm seeing someone else.

Bending forward she withdrew some sheets of paper sticking out from under the edge of my scrapbook. "Would *this* be that someone?"

{Lilith's letter!} which i was so looking forward to reading. That's none of your business.

She bent, scoopedup a notebook page i regognized at once. "Now *this* I know youve seen." The page she rattled at me this time contained a riddle i'd written on my flite to OR, and a poem, neither of which i'd yet had the candor or courage to show Lilith.

Youve been nosing 'n' poking all around here havent you? Arent you ashamed? And i thought you were merely sitting here brewing one of your old stews ...which would be bad enuf.

Standing like a stage director, script in both hands, "I wish my own stew was all I sat in! [indicates chalkywhite spot on cushion where my smoothie had spilled & dried] This stuff [shakes Lilith's letter like a gypsy tambourine] is so juicy it, well... Lookit that! It made a spot!

You do know this is your worst performance to date?

An' this here ejaculate of yours...! [she proffers my riddle, my verse] It needs an asbestos condom around its neck jus ta keep all the illegal sex from squirting out!"

I see youve had time to go over all your lines —say nothing of trespassing with afterthought 'n' malice.

Again indicating the white spot. "Ya know what I think? I think she's one of those squirt queens ...scuse me, princesses! Tell me. Does your little angel [makes wings w the pages] erupt like this every time you touch her?"

Way behind in quizzes & quips and stung by her cheap accusations, it crosses my mind to explain the spot. It's not what you think. I spilled my smoothie there, that's all. [I'll say you did!] But i come to my senses, explain nothing.

"As to afterthought 'n' malice? Now *that's* funny. I'd say that day in the foyer you two dished a bunch o' that. I got no call, no poem, no letter [shakes papers], no warning lites, no sirens. All at once you lovebirds flutter in out of the rain smack into my face!"

Your icy reception when i got here this summer was a pretty clear smack in the face i'd say. Life doesnt get permission, nik. It just happens. All at once Lilith was there —smack in the middle of my life. And, truth be told, so far, i'm damn glad *of* it.

"According to these [sweeps papers thru air] you werent short on warnings. [paces, turns] Cant you see she was laying for you all along?...pardon the expression. That you cant see that amazes me. It looks ta me [pointing to my verse] like she's swatted you outa the air like a fly. Whaap! Smackdab inta that little witch's gluey ointment."

My head felt numb. {Just get a drink. Then go take a shower. Attend to your life as if she isnt even here. If that doesnt work you can always put her out 'r call the cops.} I head for the kitchen. She follows.

"Youre home earlier than last nite?" Her reflection in the window above the sink is clear: head cocked to one side, painted mouth open in mock dismay, eyelids aflutter.

I go to refrig, pour myself a glass of herbal tea. I'd been wanting a fat cup of tea the whole drive home but now didnt have the patience to warm it. "How many times have you slept with her? A-, let me guess?" In the sink stand two tumblers filled w milky-colored water. {I suppose one could say we "slept together" 'n' not be lying}, i think to myself, imagining what nikki (still raving-on outside my head) would do with *that* one. I pass into the livingrm, turn on some music.

She follows, still sporting the papers. "Allow me ta read." (I have taken the liberty to omit her numerous thespian groans gasps grunts & breathy sighs thruout the following.)

My dearest nathan: I will not keep you. It is getting late. You are asleep beside me as i write. ¶Thank you for coming to my rescue last night. I don't know what would have happened without you. Your presence over the last few days has been like (hope this doesn't strike you as corny) armorplate to my life. (I warned you, my writing is cliche and my cliches are dreadful) ¶ I couldn't help but see your riddle and the lovely poem. They were inside the cover of the scrapbook when i opened it. so i don't think it would be in terribly poor taste to tell you, i fell for you years ago. And having the opportunity to know you in person has only reinforced this feeling. ¶ I know i've been much trouble, and left you in the dark about a few things ...and the pity of it is, we've only just met. Beside, i've asked far too much of you. I'm sorry. ¶ I hope you will continue to be my friend. But if not, i understand. I wouldn't blame you for ducking out. I mean that. In fact, what in the world you're doing around someone like me i can't imagine. But, again, thank you so so much for being there. ¶Your friend, lilith.

"Cant you see what she's doing, nate? Have you lost your grip? There's a cheap novel in here." Flicks papers w fingersnap, picks up & gulps down a daiquiri. {Must have brought her own mix.} Sets down glass. "But let's not stop there. Let's enjoy the rest of this schoolgirl drama."

On the verge of grabbing bag & jacket and shoving her out the door, i found myself w only the will to stand at the foot of the stairs in a kind of fatigued stupor. I dont think she knew i was hearing the letter for the first time. While i can pity her now, so biting was her attack i failed to see the hurt it hid.

"Here, now let's read *this* little treasure. You'll love it." She read the riddle.

To Lilith, from nathan
What has two Ls, two i's, and one TH,
two Ns, two A's and then TH (another)?
What melts the heart, ignoring things like age,
and wantonly exclaims: "To love i'druther?"

"Ah- let us try to guess: Two platypuses playing postoffice? No? Well then, a grown man and a- ...a child —God forgive me if I lie— screwing like alleycats on *that* couch right there!" She swept a purveying index over its length like a curse. "Am I warm yet?

Huh? Huh?" It suddenly occurs to me to turn up the music and go take that shower. She follows. "Next yooorr gonna tell me this affair isnt what it seems; that these [smacks papers] are all part of a novel youre writing, rrrright!" Her voice rising in pitch again. I enter my bdrm, in some disarray from days of being on the run. "Or maybe youre gonna tell me *yoooou* didnt screw the brains out of that little tramp... Right there, on *that* bed!" Points at heap of blanket & rumpled sheets which gawk at us as we enter. "...Or whatever else you two humping hyenas did in this house! Maybe yoooo expect thiiiis jury ta b'lieve you didnt fuck her li'l ass in every room in this house including all the closets!"

I throw my shirt toward the bathrm, turn, grab her chin w one hand, squeeze til a writhing fishmouth appears. She goes on glubglubbing in underwater fishtalk until she has delivered herself of my indictment. Only the mad hatter however could have understood the words that emerged from those pinched everted lips. Meanwhile i led her backwards by her chin to the bed and sat her down. All the way she kept up a barrage of jabbing kicks in my direction. The moment i let go, that mouth, rediscovering its old shape, started up again. "At least I used to make the bed when we were done. But that's a kid fer ya." Sitting beside her, i clap one hand over the flow of garbage, the other behind her head.

Another session w ratslug this a.m. Returning my dummy document: ``Your constellations of madness have delited me for a change.`` And so (for a change) i am able to respond <O?>, if only in secret dismay. For all of what i put into <c of c> is designed as surreal spin for the dr of spin himself: purest prolepsis & procatalepsis. Turnsout, he has swallowed completely a recent sentence which reads: <<And while at sea for those many mos glen & me learned a great deal about each other we would never otherwise have known ...given the medium of our mutual line of work, imagine our surprise on learning, both of us were orophiliacs!>> As he spoke i espied for a moment, thru the deep dung of his arrogance, the very human hope of stumbling upon, in the ramblings of my exotic skylore, an oracle of such delphic depth it might change him forever. Which bringsup a point likely relevant to our relationship, reader. Specifically, why can we not rid ourselves of the nagging suspicion that the imprisoned may be party to some enigmatic truth which we who are `free` cannot access? Is it because we civilized know, somewhere deepdown, our wise inner Selves are the repressed, untested & unfulfilled prisoners of civil law & expectation?

I delayed divulging for as long as i dared that `orophilia` was not mouth-love (as he hoped) but greek for love of mountains! Unfortunately his (clearly occulted) embarrassment only further incensed him toward me, so that in the space of a fingersnap he switched from `sunning` to `poised to strike`. (cont`d below)

"I can tell by your latest entries, you think youre homefree now. But let me warn you. All warden's gladiator's come to a bad end. In fact, in your ignorance 'n' vanity youve chosen the surest, if not the quickest, route to oblivion. Sad... It coulduv been so diff'rent. [stares at pencil which he logrolls methodically between thumbs & indices] Of course, I'm sure you also realize, this means war."

I ponder this. Seems t' me, from my little subjectiverse here, that you had war with me in mind well before we ever met ...sir.

Pencil whizzes past my face. "Glumm! Glimm! Gluum! Get in here! Now! [Sir?] Take this animal... [Sir?] As I was saying: Take this animal outa my sight. NOW! B'fore I barf on the lot o' ya! Get! Get! Get! ...An' dont come back!"

O blessed Verity. Become him, i beg. If only in that single oath!

Listen, nik. I dont care if you believe this or not. Yes i do. But that doesnt matter. [claims she cant breathe] Let me finish 'n' i'll let you go. Ready? "Uhuh", she tries to nod, yes —but only after another min of angry squirming. That means NO talking. ...Agreed? Slowly i take my hands away. Unless sheer jealousy gives you license to assault the character of anyone you please, your critique of my lovelife is totally without qualification. Aching i could see, to trash my argument, she somehow bit her tung. "How very rational. Are you done?"

I am not. Now, whereas you 'n' me mayuv screwed our brains out –as you so ladylike put it– on only our second date, Lilith 'n' me have yet to do so. In *fact,* we havent even kissed yet. [Pffft! she all but spit but otherwise kept silent] Beside that, i dont owe you an explanation *or* an apology. In fact, most people woulduv called the cops or thrown you out by now. (My rhetoric flared this last time and promptly went out for the nite.)

"Whoa. Arent *we* the perfect ones t'nite?" She went silent, got up, walked to the hallway, plainly tipsy but still clutching those goddamned papers. I'd hit a sore spot apparently and the blow knocked the wind out of her. Like a fool, i followed her to the kitchen for refills. I cant stand to see a creature in pain, any creature, now that her pain and not her vengeance was showing. I poured myself another tea, stood by as she mixed another daiquiri.

I cant do war, nik. Why dont you just get your things 'n' go.

She took a sip, looked away. "I still remember the stirfry dinner I made you, right here. She glancedaround, looked straight into my eyes, at my bare chest, then headed for the livingrm. "It seems like only last weekend that we.... God." She sank into a chair. "Life sucks." She was crying now.

"Everyone at the shop worships you, nate. Out in the world you have mosta the ecofreaks in the palm o' your hand. Even the old sep'ratist stiffs are coming around, talking about your N-E-F...[her voice trailed off] But this, this 'my dearest nathan' crap has got to go. [throws papers onto centertable] Youre old enuf to be her father." [leans out, picksup snapshot of Lilith, wipes eyes w forearm] "Where is her father, anyway? Does he know some big ape more than twice her age is seducing his daughter?"

Here we go again. Shoeshit&shinola. A few minutes ago you called her a tramp, nik. Now she needs her daddy? Youre talking nonsense. And, yes. He *does* know. An' you keep harping on this age thing like it makes any diff'rence. Why? Youre not exactly whistler's mother yourself. Tho meant as a compliment, only a fool mentions age during an argument.

"I beg your pardon. Just turned twennysix myself. I've had my drivers' license for ten years, not one, like your little soulmate here. [waves snapshot] And I've been outa college for as long as little lolitha here's been getting her period." Did she say lolitha? Flicks foto, which wedges under scrapbook as tho some pixie is helping me live up to my promise to take care of it.

Lilith is in college, nik. She's not only a scholarship student but is more mature than alot of other adults i know. If your behavior, for example, is mature, i'll take Lilith's any day, thanx. I turn away, take the stairs two-at-a-time for that shower. As i turn the upper landing i see her starting up. Sweetgeezus. I duck into the bath for privacy. The door does not close all the way due to my shirt being wedged there.

Her voice reaches me first. "So what am I supposed to do while you go off and practice free sex with strangers. [pushes door open] If you think I'm gonna wait around while you fuck every schoolgirl who takes a fancy t' you, youve got shitferbrains, charley."

Shit screw tramp fuck. [slam my things into already jammed hamper] What a total trashmouth youve got, nik.

Jousting from the doorway, she judges me w a javelin index ε imperious hubris. "I'd rather have trashmouth than trash behavior like you, mister chester molester. You need ta shower with heavy chemicals."

An' what about you 'n' mutt last year. Should i come your kinda clean too?

Dr snakemoid orders me back very next morn (yesterday). ``I recommend you picture yourself dead; then picture someone, perhaps your friends over at the aclu, or even those amnesty people. Let`s say they question the way we have killed you, okay? Let`s say they wanna make trouble for us. But what if, when our records are subpoenaed, they show you got killed assaulting a guard or trying to escape? Eh? Or if, when your date comes, we fry you instead of injecting you? And what if my records show you were suffering from such severe guilt over your crimes that you chose electrocution over injection? After all, that`s why the option`s there, right? For the benefit of the condemned? [laffs] You see? Hey, is it my fault if state legislators buy into the prison system`s most private needs? [withdraws rumpled handsker, wipes walrus folds in neck] And what if my records show you felt injection was a coward`s way out? And what if, moreover, your choice turned out to be in exquisite harmony with what your judge recommended: Death by electrocution? You see? Judge black did not buck state law, schock, he reinforced it! And so [arrogant smirk behind exhaled cloud], the fed. effectively okayed <u>whatever</u> we choose to do with you! Thanks to the fed. we`re doubly indemnified against criticism from <u>any</u> quarter! Anyone who pursued such a cause would make a fool of himself. [pigeyes stare bogus blankly at me] What say you now, sir?``

"O? Are you saying I was supposed to wait around darning socks like penelope while you exchanged body fluids with that doe-eyed novelist? You think I didnt hear about that?

I turned on the water: I see what youre doing, nik. You're trying to make our last time alone together as memorable as possible! Now *my* voice is rising. What, short of throwing her bodily out the door, can bring this stupidity to an end? I had lived enuf theater, seen enuf female tears in the last week to enthrall the most sadistic drama coach. As i stepped in the shower, closed the door, i saw her enter, still carrying that frigging snapshot. Kryyst! Now she's in *here!*

"Who's this other girl? Her sister? [i say nothing] Have ya screwed her too? Or maybe theyre siamese twins. [she's yelling now] Two for the prize of one. [i swear she said prize but the water is running hard now] That could be fun...! Think about it. Using hookedup cripples you could throw yourself on the mercy o' the court —tell the judge you figured their combined ages made fucking them legal. If he has a sense o' humor, who knows, you may only get five years *...apiece!...* pardon my french again." She's found her stride and seems loving it.

I was so tired the rush of water made me dizzy. It was my first hot shower in months (my usual is lukewarm & superlow-usage) and i planned on staying in there til she was gone. Are you planning to hangaround 'n' talk filthy til i throw you out?

She did. "I'm not even warmed up yet!" The thought that this might be true scared me. I could see the wavy blur of her standing in the middle of the bathrm. It looked like she was just staring toward the shower. O great. I turnedup the hot, hoping to steam her away. "I've had it with you 'n' your size-one girlfriends, nathan schock! I shoulduv known all along what you always wanted was to fuck someone who still plays with dollies 'n' who cant tell a hymen from a hymnal!"

All at once it occurred to me {The windows are open!} I pictured my neighbors, outfront in the morning w their little daughters, pointing at my house, shaking fingers no-no-no, turning their tricycles around, heading them back home. Unable to believe what was happening, i came out of the shower soaked & dripping {Fergot that damn bathmat again!}, pulled on a towel, went around slamming windows like a wildman. Slam. Slam. Other bdrm, slam. Came out, slam: hall window. Return to bdrm. Ya know, i wish i had all this venom of yours on video. I know you well enuf to know, a replay in six months would make you puke for a week. An' ta think, Lilith *likes* you, says nice things about you all the time ...admires you even! You are a very cruel person, nikki mckinney.

"At least I'm not bedding little boys in the sunny countryside of america. I should have known you had this dark side."

Nathan the minotaurus? That did it. <That's quite enuf of the real you, thank you. Could ya go back t' faking it?> I threw her on the bed.

"What're ya gonna do now, fuck me too?"

That would fit in neatly with your little plan, wouldnt it?

"I know! Wait! Lemme go put on my first communion dress!"

Shutup, nik. How did i ever miss your being a cunt with teeth? [now maybe i shouldnuv said that but there it is. And maybe i shouldnuv recounted most of this b-grade drama but there *it* is too. I've always been too honest for my own good —my own *civil* good] *Now* yer gonna listen, then youre outa here. I remind you, again: Lilith is in college. Most females her age around the world are married 'n' pregnant with their second kid. [she goes to sit up.

I push her down] I'm not done. An' most women her age *mentally* are at least in their forties. Finally, to answer your rude question (which is really none of your goddamned business): I havnt been t' bed with (or screwed, as you put it so rudely), either Lilith *or* any of her relatives 'r friends.

Out of a corner of my eye i catch sight of us in a dresser mirror, suddenly feel ridiculous. There i am, wet, nearly naked ε emotionally involved in a type of behavior that repulses me. The mere sight of us jambs my gymnologizing at its source. I grab the foto out of her hand, walk to the dresser, pop open a drawer to tuck it under my.... {Great! Now i'm fresh outa underwear too!} I hear her marching now from room to room, mumbling, sniffling. {Looking for more red herrings?} Whimpering, she thumps slowly downstairs.

I sit on the bed, head in hands, staring at the rug, tears threatening but not coming. Thank you, logos of lacryma! Here, in one fellswoop, 'simply' for having lunch w a brilliant ε beautiful young woman, then having her over to my apt for a couple hrs one afternoon, nikki had demoted me from friend ε lover to a state of resident-alien anonymous sperm donor. A moment later she appears in the doorway w jacket ε handbag. Saying nothing she reaches in her bag, takes out a small pistol and –sobbing shaking– aims it at my groin and pulls the trigger... as the credits begin to roll upward on the screen. I mean, what ending, reader (short of fire ε brimstone) would not be anticlimactic after the week i've had?

Trying to get back into harpie mode, she slips into her jacket, slings her bag over her shoulder. Instead of grabbing a gun (a basically moral woman), she throws her copy of the house key at me. "I dont even have a fucking ring to throw at you after all this time!" She grabs the doorhandle, as if to steady herself, and bawls, "I'll send the first pimp I screw to get my things ...or maybe I'll just run into the street 'n' get hit by a truck." With that, she bolts from the room, down the stairs and out the door, slamming it after her w a vengeance. My stomach lurches.

Mins later, down in the greatrm, i am dragging cushions off the couch, wrestling w them in dumb silence on the floor. Lying there, wrapped in a towel, face buried, too exhausted even to cry, i wished for a switch i could flip that would make me sleep for a week. Mins after that, sure she was long gone, i heard what i soon realized were the tires of her little machine. They screamed a last epithet at my startled frontdoor and carried her off.

Part 4

[Approximate date of composition by the author: Oct.-Nov. 1998. —Editor]

1

I awoke in the middle of the nite hugging a couch cushion like a lover. Groggy, i checked the frontdoor (better late than not), trudged about turning off lites music paddlefans, stumbled upstairs, collapsed onto my rumpled rack. Next thing i knew a lifesize two-dimensional nathan schock, shot full of holes, stood before floodlites as if at a wartime border crossing. Then, as dreams do, these turnedinto lites of interrogation —the intensity of which was caused by the daylite blazing thru a bdrm window i'd failed to blind. Then i remembered nikki's visit, ugh, and just lay there.

Publishers sometimes use lifesize fotos of authors to mark booksigning locations. So much for my dream replica. But why the holes —which the lites of interrogation shot thru like stinging stars? Elementary. Instead of using a pistol, nikki had shot a clipful of nasty accusations at nathan-the-innocent. Some had stung. Doubled-up there in bed i felt akin to the guy shot in the groin in that silly movie. {Why didnt i defend myself better? or just shove her out into the street?} Turnedout she'd caught me at a bad time. I was an unmoving target: emotionally dazed & exhausted from the events of a bizarre & blustery week. The emotional mountaineering of just being near a woman like Lilith was enuf wout the added intrigue of a spurned lover; specially a nasty & aggressive one.

Fone interrupts, answers itself. "Hey, nate. Just wondered if youre coming by today. Have news. When you get this gimme a call...."

Hey, rick... No. Still in bed... I know, i know. What's up? Me? O, the blues, the blahs... No, i'll be okay... No i didnt... Tell me.

The muir society was interested in my NEF plan: a voting block of green organizations, green believers –league of green voters– that might stand a chance at the polls against the unconscioned ε dangerous numbskulls in power. "But they made it clear, nate. Theyre scared of suing the fed... Right. But the ace is, they do'wanna be latecomers to any greenparty that looks like it might fly nationally...."

I apologize for my latenite call, thank rick for his help, which by some itch of intuition reminds him: "Hey, this girl, a... wrote her name somewhere here... droppedoff this big folio o' cartoons las week... [rummaging] I liked it, sent it on t' brian. [brian nugent, chairman greenEarth intn'l] Anyway, he likes the cartoon too... wrote her name here somewhere [still rummaging]... Yeah, that's it. You must luv her work, eh?"

Cant say i've seen it, rick.

"Really? A real magnum opus. You'll be pleasantly surprised. O, by the way. The new e-p-a advisor 'll be on tv tonite... Yeah, eight oclock. Word is he might touch on the f-b-i's raids on EarthNow, an' on freeman's arrest too... Yeah. That's my guess. But we'll hafta wait 'n' see. Well, rest up, guy. We'll see ya at wednesday's staffing...? Good. I promise a real eye-opener." Leaned over, ready to hangup: "Hey, nate? ...Call me if ya need anything."

Pampering's nice when feeling low. Now i'm sittingup staring at my toes. When on tour they spend so much time stuffed in shoes i feel a little guilty when i see them —like housebound friends youve been too busy to visit, and whom, when you see them –dimly gazing out a window or peering from behind a curtain– your guilt makes you wish you were invisible.

After showering i donned runninggear: shirt shorts socks ε trotters. Shirt: beach casual, type i favored when on the w.coast —mutely daubed in pink, lime ε sunflower-yellow. Drive to breakfast at FIT TO EAT, healthfood bar ε restaurant in haight-ashbury. Midway thru organic eggs, grits ε oatbran toast i catch myself staring at my server —bronzed skin bare midriff. Police van flashes by in the window behind. She heads my way but a yell from somewhere behind a display case of soy sausages & salads turns her back.

My eyes have their own mind. {Quite some time w/out a mate. Feeling largely celibate.} I guess her to be around 20. Suddenly age looms large, a thing i normally pay scant attention to. {Thanx, nik.} Random remnants of a book i came across in college float among the patrons like subtitles. Cant quite evoke that title so i'll quote from bradenton's the history of law, present in its 5-volume form in our surprisingly competent law library.

> In Britain, as in some other industrialized countries, the legal age for marriage is 16, altho it was raised from 12 as recently as 1929.

The satiny radiance of gérôme's "slave market" rises to mind as rudderless i ruminate. The idea that the instinct to mate w a young woman has changed since 1929, or 1929bc, strikes me as absurd {whether we're talking humans or humping hyenas, nik.} Munch plain toast. A glimpse into deeper recesses finds nikki's rage swirling inside me like a star-gobbling galaxy. {True, Lilith appeared 'n' uprooted her plans for me. But surely she knew those plans were doomed long b'fore Lilith.}

> In some Muslim countries, Australia and Japan, the marriageable age is 16 as well. In Iran, Bangladesh, many parts of India, Africa and South America, the age is 12. In the U.S. the minimum legal age for unmarried cohabitation is 16 generally, in a few states 14. In the latter cases, womens' groups are lobbying to have it raised to 15. This is in direct conflict with an opposite physiological trend: The median age of puberty has dropped since 1978 from 13.1 to 10.4; a downward shift some think is due to the introduction of hormones into our foods.

I contrast bradenton's history w my own work.

> The world matron operates always in the shadow of the Earthmother, so most of us believe that her demands are above suspicion.

Maybe i should have skipped the nikki/nathan parting shots. Most writers would have. And yet, writing manuals say, "Dont be afraid to soil your hero's image. Imperfections make a character come alive, make him human, more lovable. Remember, nobody's perfect". I go on then to imagine flunk & frite writing about themselves. Do we think they'd soil *their* images? Not on your life! But i'm igNathius veracious, my own biggest pain in the ass when it comes to frankness. I've recorded what nikki said, not what i wish she said. Stupid, maybe, but faithful to posterity.

Server comes over. "More juice, nathan?" Navel gawks from above her shorts. Weak moment. I find i want... i want (hate to admit this at this delicate moment)... {I'd like a cup of coffee}, which she's brandishing like a nurse w a pain killer. What did Lilith say? "Go gulp a cup o' buzz"? Health gyroscope corrects sudden yaw. <No thanks.> Navel smiles, recedes. Mind wanders back to college again, just home from work, lying on my bed, chin on pillow, reading.

> A Greek poet wrote: The bloom of a 12-year-old is desirable, and 13 is deliteful. Sweeter still is the flower of love that blossoms at 14. And its charm only increases at 15. But 16? Ah. Now that is the divine age!

{Such was the norm at one time, world over —and nikki has the nerve to call *me* chester molester! One cannot help but ask: could the desires of humans have changed so greatly in so short a time? —*instinctual* urges, i mean? —desires which reside in that subliminal place win us where such things are cast in stone? —evolutionarily-proven stone, no less? And since when is youth not desirable anyway? Show me an adult who wouldnt like to be younger, at least physically, and i'll show you a liar a sickness or both. And who is it, anyway, who's trying to make healthy males feel shame for what their instincts command?} I imagine a new and madeover world matron who, honestly recalling the longings of her own youth, setsout to sanctify Natural desire, not condemn it in others. {But then she'd be Mothernature!}

The world matron may oversimply be described as the civilizing of the Mother-nature innate in us.

However, castigation, imprisonment or worse awaits him who dares cross the age divide. Many states will happily clap an 18yearold into prison for being guilty of no more than consensual sex w a 17yearold —and pleas to "Leave him alone, please! He's the best thing that ever happened to me!" will not save him. Yet these same states ε their voters will admit to no sickly irony when they then turn around and put a 14yearold to death for murder —"He shudda known better. Thirteen's old enuf to know what youre doin" ...*unless* what youre "doin" has to do w sex. See highly civil us, caught again, fixing things w that crippling old mixture of social engineering ε Reality-denial —plugging the leaks in that chernobyl we call civilization using bars of nuclear fuel! ....when we should be confessing at longlast, "Heck, with almost 5billion yrs experience, maybe Nature/instinct knows the best way for us afterall!" And let's *not* forget: Brokenness can disintegrate beyond the ability of the finest tinkering to fix.

Civilization is thus broken. Rebuilding from the ground up is the only wise option. Too bad we're not wise. Worse, too bad we've wrecked, from the ground up, the only prototype known to us: PlanetEarth ε all its true primitives ε primates!

Then all at once you find yourself without a mate ...a celibate.
And in between the love affairs is when it's great ...to contemplate....

Two young women at a nearby table are speaking so softly, so intently, i supposed for awhile they were mute. Wisps of steam from their freshly poured coffees curl toward me, the scent, sacrilegious! {Addictive aromatic vice!} I know the coffee is organic ε fresh-ground and i want to wallow in the dark wealth of its scent ε stimulus.

To have to get your kicks without the shame of love ...the blame of love....

{Why am i letting the accusations of a spurned lover get to me? Fergodsake, Lilith is adult by any sane measure!} Which brings to mind, when Lilith herself was 15 and would decline to participate in some "fun thing 'r other", her best friend would tease her, call her "granny". She was always older than her years, not always the case w genius. Beside,

Truth-in-ageing law

When we with time in utero confer,
  we learn we're nine months older than we were.
Or: Thanks to rites of ovum/priapus,
  still keeps us nine months older than we wuz.

I am on the verge of a caffeinated debauchery. {Stop. Think this thru. First, brite lite ε carbs. Did that. Now, a walk to gate park, then a run. And, maybe after that, a good upperbody burn. Why do health bars offer coffee anyway? (Coriolis force of subconscious yields best mind meanders.) If i had a place.... Nah, yuv gotta offer the bean ...most popular drug on Earth.} I'll take a jolt o' that java, please. Yes, thanx. Do the hopelessly hooked abuse caffeine subdermally? I down half a cup, tip googoo-eyes, leave.

On reaching the park i follow roads ε paths which Lilith&me, just yesterday... How dumb. I'm talking as if she were dead. "Most everyone i know has mall fever. [she said during our buggyride] But i'm no mallrat. I'm not panning what others do, it's jus that, i dont understand consumerbots [persons who live to shop]." Lilith, no peerodigmer, simply felt "foolish" clattering off to some mall to parade last week's purchase of this week's fading fad. Better the reader think of her as someone who –sitting in a bar w her peers, watching them "bounce off the walls"– tries to find "the snitch in the lyrics or lack of one." Harken! Message-, not beat-, oriented! (Quotes from journals L kept in hs.)

I've dated fashion designers anthropathologists ε -apologists, lawyers ε marine biologists, engineering undergrads ε overgrad psychologists, ε others ε others. Still unflinching i say, Lilith had more talent (native ε schooled) more culture, more contact w her instincts, more emotional experience (prepubertal happiness/postpubertal trauma) than i can ever hope to wedge somehow into the perishable pages of this paltry little book.

Candid? frank? Dont play jimminy cricket to your fellow man unless youre ready to go life solo.

Let's be frank, francine. There's a hefty coalition of partying bozos ε bimbos who barely crunch thru the academic cosmos of c-minus; who can be located any eve merely by following the scent of medieval mead ε ancient semen. I know. I once ran w them. But there are also those students who are more adult than most older adults. We could begin w those elders who fund such parties, voyeur at those bars! But the walk sign is lit and we can cross now. {Park's relatively quiet today.} Mostly walkers bladers joggers ε bikers; benches dotted here&there w readers. My small breakfast a distant digestive memory ε the caffeine banderillas prodding ε perfusing me, i'm feeling a good run coming on.

No lishment rubberstamplicule, Lilith is just plain too mature for her peers. Admired often, but usually from a safe distance: It doesnt take alot of sensitivity ε thoughtFULLness to make one scary to others. I'm reminded of a yeat's essay, one in which he hopes his daughter will be beautiful ε intelligent "but notsomuch that she's alienated". Truly open warm ε giving persons –not just the learned imitation of these qualities we civilizens call the social graces– are marked for abuse or ruin.

A blurry shape stepped off the reedy bank
Into a crackling, gulping swamp, and sank.

(Up ahead a pompous ponysized poodle seemed out walking its birdlike owner.) Even the younger hs Lilith was so evolved she went about pinching herself: "Is this really how it is? And why do i feel stupid when i try to act that way?" She spoke of recently tagging along w some boozing bimbos (my word-choice, not hers) just to feel "in": " 'Be caj, Lili,' beth teases me. [says L on our buggy tour] I dont like being thought of as a brainiac so i gel —you know, just relax, wobble with the weave of the warp 'n' the woof?"

On reaching such a point [to posit my summary], olaf odd (or ola, in this case) casts about for someone who can reinforce the Reality she intuits is all around us but which nobody seems to see; a Reality which, because it consists of everything there is, has little to do w being human, and so always gets forgotten in a barrage of anthropic rot! And so, it's not just for Lilith that i hurt tonite; it's for a younger me too. Pass fonebooth. {Should i call? She is probably thinking her letter has scared me off. Park still quiet. In a few mins (lunchhour) this will change.} I break into that run.

Only now do i see. That's really what Lilith's letter was all about: Ola odd, reaching out into the dark ε stormy nite w only the braille of trust ε intuition, trying to figureout if it is truly olaf odd she has found? As i run i try to recall the exact wording of her letter. At her age i could only intuit that goal: Finding someone you can talk to for hours and rarely speak of human concerns! This alone can lead to objectivity; this alone approaches that baseline of Universal unMEness i someday want to own an entire day of.

In your eyes are my secrets that I've never shown you.
In my heart I feel, I've always known you. —d. zippel

In his early teens olaf aches for ola. In his late teens, in his early 20s, the search gets more heated. In his 30s (if he makes it that far) he is frantic for, demands the right to, such a companion; the right to know just one person who looks down on the World not just out at it —one person who gazes out over existence, not just out from it. But what happens when olaf ε ola reach 40-50 and still have not found each other? Terminal melancholy? Suicide? I cant say. For just in time i found Lilith. And that's the other part. The example of those beings ee cummings calls "the odd never breaking even". Olaf taking a harpoon in the chest, a shot meant for a brother or sister whale. Ola lashing herself to a mountain of toxic waste to be dumped in the living sea: "Hey, how were we supposed to know she was [chained] back there!" Yes, how? when one doesnt care to see beyond his culturated MEness

So maybe that's what you do next —if you dont find your Lilith McGrae. Or if, gadshazm, you should lose her along the way! Maybe that's what drives one to go out ε pummel til he's purple some industry mogul who is maiming ε murdering every day in the name of profit, or to strangle w one's bare hands one of the million politicos who profit from such plunder ε massacre. Maybe that's how absolute misanthropes are made, how one endsup performing one last act of Universal giving —to all creatures, to all things! Then, your gesture done, you just sit down where it happened, wait for the repercussions, the hatred, the fear, the denial; just sit ε wait ...just be ...just be....

A car w brain-thumping speakers is first to rumble into the park. I wonder if the social protest the driver exudes, down to his lowpro mags ε spiked silver hair, excludes the votingbooth, in the manner of the typical digm-blinded duhhead of our times.

Finally, in goethean terms (if i may), i met Lilith when she was the age of his lili, and saw her for the last time when she was christiane-aged —the age, that is, when the latter died of consumption —or was it typhus? Of course, at the cusp of both relationships my adopted mentor was a good deal older than i. And there are other temporal parallels which fall between: like stella? like vanessa? Or was that jonny swift? Whatever. As to the half-century-plus that yawned between wolfgang ε ulrike (large honest blue eyes under arched brows, classic features, slim frame, most elegant bearing)? At 96 ulrike had goethe's letters brought up from the castle library, burned them on a silver platter, had their ashes placed in an urn, the urn placed in the casket w herself! So much for all the 74-versus-17 age-gossip which persists to this day! Private ulrike, in her typically classy style, vanquished all that pernicious stupidity in one fellswoop of flame ε fond remembrance.

The most popular lovestory of all time has a heroine of only 14. And nobody minds, nobody notices. Romeo loves juliet nonetheless —or should we say, allthemore? But this is not my quandary. It's civilization's —once, that is, i finally exposed the whole mess in my *Mothernature & the world matron* ...and ever since the world matron ε -patron have been grinding their teeth, covering their ears, whenever anyone sings the jon windstar line:

> Everything that's innocent in me
> aspires toward what's innocent in you.

First lunch-hour glut of cars arrives. The runner weaves around them, thinks of the little bridge above the falls back home ...about which Lilith will one day write, "that emblem of his love which spans all the nite in me". {Yes! [breathing hard now, nikki's voxpox was flaking away into mitemunchies] Thanks, nik ...for forcing me to check the fluidlevels of my moral precepts.}

On the way to the gym i called my fone. No mx from Lilith. Tho tempted to go home, read the letter for myself this time, i stay true to my tack. At a lite an attractive female (why blonds ε redheads so often?), driving a candyred porsche, smiled over at me. This happens when i, claustrophobe, drive, windows down. We are judged by what we drive, what we wear, where we live, who we know. I'm more me in my 4-wheel-drive than in the javelin, wherein i'm reduced to: pair of "cool" sunglasses, shock of blond hair (tied in ponytail ...as it was before they bobbed me near-bald here); socalled hunk w an ivory smile. Prowling gays hope i'm rich ε gay, prowling gals hope i'm rich ε not. Up&comers drive cheap sportscars; those who've "arrived" drive expensive ones ...every bit of it quite vacuous ε trite, you know.

I'm writing like a drunk: staggerscript. Yesterday's brainache, tho bad, was not my worst. Still, couldnt remove the steel cap of angst caused by my visit w dr slime. Bear w me please while mind ε pen grope for each other across the blank expectant (and sofar disappointed) expanse of these pages.

When i got home from the gym there were mxs: lex the baron local media so on. None from Lilith. Nap disgustingly, go to supper, return. Fones, merely staring at me thru the day, are now pacing ε grumbling when i come near. I stop one, place the call that's been taunting me. Electronic don answers: "Please leave your message". I have just begun to do so when a live "Hullo?" cuts in. <Hi, a-, Lilith?> "Jus a sec ...who's calling?"

Nathan schock. {Coulduv sworn that was her.}

A moment later. "Hi."

Hi. Feelin any better?

"Yeah ...Lot-s.... How are *you?*"

Alot of tiptoeing to start. She: Is he calling to say hello or to tell me he'll be busy the rest of his life? He: Am i interrupting your existence? Both parties guess things are heatingup yet both are shy to show any sign. The upside of such false pride is, it helps keep the civil birthrate down. We talk about our day ("Dad s-ays 'Hi'."), about immed plans: "I think maybe I'll s-tay up here thru the weekend. The s-low pace, the s-leepingIn, i-s doing me wonder-s. I get t' workout with s-is-ter too...." The pace of her patter skids to a crawl as she clambers over the double-s's in sister.

Since last i'd spoken w her her lugubrious lisp had been replaced by a lighter brand of ...what to call it...? thithing? A marvel to follow: like speedbumps, on reaching a sibilant she would decelerate her speech. Just how, w less than 24hrs' practice, she could foresee a sibilant, slow down, move thru it, resume speed, i could not fathom. This irrhythmic delivery, obviously adopted in interest of good enunciation, had a foreign-sounding `something' about it, the way a well-spoken french swiss, say, will pause in mid-phrase to find the right word in italian, then pronounce it w confidence & skill.

You seem a little down. ["I'm okay... Been doing any writing?"] No, jus catchingup on my must-do list. Tho i do plan t' watch our new e-p-a socalled assistant on teevee t'nite —strickland, you know? Word is, it will probably be more bad news for greens.

"Think I'll pa-ss. [her t-h had the wisp of a whistle in it] Think i already know what he'-s gonna s-ay. B'-side, politi-cian-s depre-ss me. Think I'll wa-tch the matt-son- s-pecial in-stead." This last run of s's made even me cringe.

Mattson, you say?

"Yeah. They put ok-...." She stopped, probably scanning for a response wout so many sibilants. "They put s-trickland'-s s-peech acro-ss from matt-son on purpo-se i think." Her reference was to captain mattson, renegade green friend of the baron who sails an old black freighter & crew thru five of the seven seas. I knew the sea-cradle society had been filmed for tv but didnt know it was being aired that nite.

On ecowatch?

"Ye-s. Start-s at nine. It'-s called, 'the pirate-s of po-seidon'."

I know what i'll do. I'll r'cord it —watch matt after strickland.

"I'm r'cording him too. Matt-son, i mean. I think he'-s great. Overly aggressive, maybe, but great."

When i suggested <You seem kinda, well, distant> and posed that i leave her to get some rest, she blamed "my black mood (It shows? Sorry) [on] this stupid lisp of mine. Plus, there's this book i'm reading....". <Dare i ask?> It seemed, beth had given her "the story of barbara gobel, a girl burned as a witch back in the 1600s ...described by her jailers as 'the fairest maid in wherzberg' ...<Is the u umlauted?>... ah, veertsboorg, yes." She felt emotionally linked w the victim and even tho i said no explanation [for her mood] was necessary, perkingup noticeably, she went on to read from the book's preface, 'This rare non-politicized witnessing of a witch trial and burning makes it patently clear, many accusations of witchcraft have for generations been aimed at silencing all protest by women 'n' girls of rape and other abuse, crimes often inflicted by the clergy and protected by the church, and most always somewise complicit with the state'. [quickly appending] Such abuse is still going on t' this minute ...as you know."

Here, in the space of a sentence or two, the intellectual intensity i'd been so missing in her of late was blown from seeming-dead coals into a smoldering glow. Had i ever heard of a book called "...let me see here... *malleus maleficarum*? <Yes, a law book of the roman church, written in the 1400s by a couple dominican monks. It became in fact the lawbook of the judges of the inquisition and ignited, pardon me, the inquisition itself.> Wow, yes. <Maureen duffy called it the foulest book ever written, including hitler's *mein kampf!* > Wow, yes. It became church doctrine and it specifically states, it is a crime, punishable by the extreme penalty (which means burning at the stake), for a woman to rob a man of his virility. Imagine! It was this law, says barbara gobel's biographer, which was used again 'n' again to stop women 'n' girls from accusing men of rape 'n' incest; in fact, from accusung *any* man of *any* abuse. C'n you understand this stumblebum pronunciation of mine?"

Yes. Very well. But doesnt it hurt ta talk?

"If youve gotta go i understand. We c'n talk about this some other time."

Not a bit. I'm jus worried about your stitches.

"I'm fine. An' i jus know you'll love this quote ...o, where did it go? O, here. Listen... He's quoting the *malleus* here. 'All wickedness is but little to the wickedness of a woman.... It is not good to marry: What else is woman but a foe to friendship, an unescapable punishment, a necessary evil, a natural temptation, a desirable calamity, a domestic danger, a delectable detriment, an evil of nature, painted with fair colors!' Wouldnt you jus love to have had that one for *scapegoats*? An' did i mention, the church immediately went 'n' gave this testy tirade of pathological gender hatred its very highest authority? put it right up there with the *bible* 'n' the teachings of all the major saints? thomas, augustine, peter, paul 'n' john? Imagine! <O yes. Alice Krawel calls

the *malleus* the misogynist's bible.> But of course youve covered most of this already havent you? Years ago. Sorry. Youre the one who blew the whistle on monastic gendercide... <After reich.> Well, after reich. But still. [pause] It's *your* writing that set *me* free. *That* i know." {Wow} thought i to self. <It means alot ta hear that. Thanks.> "No. Thank YOU. An' i'm sure your work has freed alota other women too."

Tho the ball was positively in my court now (*twice* she'd confessed her feelings —indeed, even kissed my cheek!), still i failed to share anything of a personal nature. She mentioned lage bringing her down soon to pickup her car. (Only later did i learn it was in the shop; would not startup the day of her assault, at the last min causing her to have to be pickedup by her stepfather instead of meeting him somewhere as planned.) 9oclock came. I hoped she was <doin okay 'n' on-the-mend>, but this was as much tenderness as the gatekeeper (pride? fear?) would let pass —tho i'm sure a listener to our converse (a fed. wiretapper, say) could not have missed –between words, between lines– a certain warmth to what was said, a certain heat to what was not.

2

(The pain has mostly subsided today, so this may be a bit more lucid.)

Most of the next day i spent planning ɛ doing interviews. In the afternoon, being in oakland on business anyway and passing win a block of the dorms, a spur-of-the-moment thing, i swung by Lilith's bldg, my excuse being to help get her car back to her.

Pink hightops was fidgeting in his usual spot. When i finally found beth she claimed not to know where the car was. <But Lilith said *you* gave them the keys?> Looks aside; eyes narrow. Then did she maybe know who the person was who'd returned Lilith's things? "I was at a boomers' game at the time." You seem defensive? "Look. Lili was doin jus fine til you came along". Plot thickens. Then could i jus talk t' whoever *did* see the guy? Beth, squinting up at me from behind grannyglasses, made two chins. "I suppose." ...went back upstairs. I waited w pinkshoes in the lampshade dimness.

I was about to searchout *bulldozer digest* again when 4fingers'-distance behind her lettersweater, 'monika', the blond smile from the frontsteps, came bouncing down. "Hey! Your the guy from the other day!" I was somewhat takenback that such sweaters were still in style. But then, how could they not be, sports generally being so mammary? And what did bb (two thickly embroidered white B's hooked together) stand for? {Blond Babes with Big Bazooms?} i hazarded. "Berkeley boomers!" she replied. {I'll say!}

Pinkshoes being all ears & leers, we stepped outside —just as a tall lovely negress w a fiery crimson halo of frizzzzzed hair was coming up the steps. {Such a smile: ebony 'n' ivory!} It turnedout, all monika knew was that "He was jus some guy in a suit who said he was a detective... sfpd, I think he said." And beyond the fact the man was "not too tall 'n' kinda squirrely lookin. <Squirrely?> Yeah, squinty, edgy, dishonest like", she could add nothing except, "O yeah! He was kinda old too <Old?> Yeah, prob'ly in his forties?". Door opens, pinkshoes passes w date whom we'll call white heels. {Spikes 'n' pink hightops? Hmm.} Monika too gazes after them in good-natured disbelief. "And, oh! He had a kinda limp." No, she couldnt remember which leg. Was that important?

At home, a mx from rick reminded me of wedn's staffmeet. That eve deb danzi's stepsister, bekky kydd, was in town. Bek was "strug'ling" w her second book ("Writing this one myself") and was in "the deep shit o' wrestling with that godamn worldmatron o' yours", mostly our subject that eve.

Wedn morn helmut appeared at hq early to parade his newest friend. While a fine sort, he's a fool who sends wife daughter sister or girlfriend anywhere alone w helmut. Actually quite intelligent, mutt's so fixated on basic bodily functions he comesoff slow on the uptake. On Lilith's first gE mission for instance (i could not go), while swinging her onto a bulkhead, helmut bungled a cheap feel. Later at lunch (as glendon tells it): "I said: `Hey, mutt. Ya made Lili jump clear into the riggin'. At dinner Lilith gave mutt an out he didnt deserve, suggested maybe it was 'just an accident'. But insteaduv appreciating her gesture mutt puffsup like a rooster. So mark chimes in, 'Yer hand jus slipped, right mutt?'. Everyone laffed. But Lili, turnsout, was only jus gettin started. 'You guys dont understan' she says. 'Mutt was jus doin his job.' There was this pause. Then she adds, 'I mean, somebody has t' be the naughty little boy in sunday school, 'n' God depends on the mutts o' this world for that.' Well, mutt was so embarrassed he jumped up as if t' go fer seconds (his plate was full), fell over his chair 'n', redder 'n' a candyapple, raised his plate triumphantly 'n' said. 'Ya see? Big save, no? Helmut spill nuttink!' " I dubbed him the flying dutchman when i heard the story.

As the meet was about to start, in a kitchenet near the conference-rm, one got coffee tea or fresh-squeezed. Helmut circulated loudly, arm around his latest conquest, grabbing accolades as he went. After she left he announced in his best unGerman, "Olt helmut here [taps own chest] kun snaag da beautiful unt brainy vons too!" Several eyes met mine. Not his usual bimbo, bets were on as to how long this woman would find mutt's swaggering & unfocusable libido entertaining. And all this speculation went on in front of him –indeed, *w* his passive assistance– which is where it derived much of its humor. Thirty or so key personnel were in attendance. Routine business whisked by. The "revelation" rick promised was apparently his recording of the tv speech of the new epa "assistant to the director, c.d. strickland", a presidential appointment a few greens found very disturbing. On a wallscreen rick showed the contents of a vd he made of the speech, analyzing it phrase by phrase, sometimes, word by word. I extract only the most appalling parts of that speech.

[The following extracts are taken from a Richard Barclay (Rick) version which the EPA released to the press and which RB edited in an effort to match it with the actual speech. It varies mostly in matters of diction and phrasing. RB's edits follow the overstrikes. —Ed.]

"...EarthNow attorneys are claiming the federal government is responsible for these attacks. FBI investigation ~~shows~~ show however that EarthNow headquarters was not sacked and burned by the FBI but by others. These were hot-headed loggers, loggers whose acts were a *personal* vendetta unconnected with any logging company. The raid was apparently in ~~retaliation~~ retalation for attacks on loggers made by EarthNow members. Their ~~arraignment~~ arrayment this week revealed, EarthNow members have been booby trapping roads, trees and logging equipment for months, making the ~~loggers'~~ logger' jobs not only difficult but dangerous. In ~~fact~~ fac it came out: Several loggers were hurt as a result of this ~~ecotage~~ ecotadj."

Most readers will have heard of c.d strickland only because his death was sensationalized in the corporate media as a "politically-motivated murder", which it absolutely was not, nor was it even a murder. When appointed as "advisor" to then epa director monty o'brien, this former cia agent was touted by the admin as an environmentalist. Deepgreens like rick however were early to sense a ruse. As Lilith put it later: "You cant be a traitor to the cause if you were never green to begin with." Strickland's green posture & green record turned out to be just one more fed. fairytale.

"We're not saying what those loggers did was right. They will be brought to justice ...just [hereinafter "jus"] as Roy Freeman, EarthNow kingpin, was brought to justice, just as he and five of his followers were caught, arrested and jailed. Such violent behavior will not be tolerated by this administration...."

Groans went up here.

"The reason I'm talking about these things tonight is simple. We the people are being fooled, getting caught with our guard down again and again, and always by the same groups. These people have evil motives. I am referring to ~~extremists~~ estremists. Not political estremists but violent estremists. Let me draw a comparison. You are in a grocery store looking for a jar of barbeque sauce. Because the jar you pick is standing with a dozen other ~~similar~~ simila jars, you think what you're buying is safe."

I'd seen fotos of strickland but this was my first studied performance: big man, 40something, apparently in good physical shape. The absolute polarization of our beliefs aside, there was something slithy about him ...a portmanteau word i've borrowed, meaning lithe-yet-slimy. With thick black hair, he had beady black eyes set in deep shadow beneath a pair of active brows. But what gripped my gaze was something pickedup by the wideangle camera situated obliquely behind him, a longshot meant to show the hall and assembled press as well as the speaker. The unzoomed view from this camera showed the man's tall stature as dark-suited & lean. But its closeup revealed –in addition to a sloping hawkbrow & bird-of-prey beak– another feature: his jaw. With its short beard (flatbottomed goatee) it protruded like the "unshaven" (towline-laden) bow of a tugboat or scow. Am i too many years at sea?

"Let this be a warning. Reading the label is no longer enough. We must [hereinafter "mus"] learn to ~~scrutinize~~ scrunize the ~~ingredients~~ ingredient too. This is not always easy to learn. For many of us are ~~trusting~~ trussing people. Many of us want to believe what we see at a glance is the way things are. If we find a jar standing among other jars like it –or which resemble it– then we ~~expect~~ espec ~~what's~~ what in that jar will be safe to eat.

"But this is no longer so. ~~Because~~ Cuz there's a new enemy out ~~there~~ dere, an enemy of our safety and personal freedom. Most [hereinafter "mos"] of all, that enemy is as ~~deceitful~~ deceeful as he is dangerous. He ~~stands~~ stan beside us at equal-rights meetings. He ~~sings~~ sing ~~next~~ nex to us at rallies for world ~~brotherhood~~ brathahood. He ~~dances~~ dance nex to us at concerts for ~~environmental~~ envirometal awareness. He ~~marches~~ march with us into those few remaining places where old-~~growth~~ -growf timber is still being cut. ~~He's~~ He beside us when we work to clean up those few remaining places where industry still fouls the envirometl. But we do not ~~recognize~~ recanize him."

Several groans in succession, each more pained than the one before.

"That's because it is a deceeful enemy I show you tonight. In fac he may be the ~~trickiest~~ trickyess terrorist America (or the world) has ever come up ~~against~~ agains. For his trick is to fly the flags, wear the costumes, the uniforms, we hold most dear. That's how he ~~wins~~ win our hearts, our trus, our support. He ~~claims~~ claim to believe in what we believe in. He claim to be on the side of nature even, to want to help us save our envirometl. He ~~wears~~ wear our ~~highest~~ highess ideals where we'll be sure to see them: On his sleeve.

"In fac, the people deserve to know —a ~~statistical~~ statistica fac— that *same* enemy may be sitting right next to many of us tonight, in our homes, in our places of work and recreation, and even in our places of worship. In truth, nothing, and no one, is ~~sacred~~ sacra to him —not family, friendship, community, promise or belief. He will ~~infect~~ infec whoever [sic] he can, whenever he can, with his sickness. He does not love the things we love. We must learn this. This is something I have, personally, had to force myself to see. For to learn not to trus others is not going to be easy for some of us."

More groans. "Easy, guys" says rick. "This clown has no embarrassment at all" says glen's voice in the semidarkness.

"For when you study these persons, when you reveal their true nature, you find, this enemy ~~loves~~ love but one thing. And that is violence... [thumps lectern] ...to ~~wreak~~ wreck havoc in secret with all we hold dear."

We skip now to where rick says, "Here's where he begins laying his plan for us: a ploy as old as state-hatred itself."

"...We know communism is dead mos everywhere. And we are glad of it. But while communism was dying a new belief was growing in its place. That belief is the Green ideology. It's an ideology which seeks a better world for us all.... But I can tell you this. I, in my position as ~~executive~~ zecutive ~~advisor~~ avvizer to the director of the EPA, I help oversee several departments. Fine organizations, with many capable and dedicated people. Together we are seeing to it the Green revolution keeps its momentum. We are seeing to it the Green concerns of all of us are put in place, and swiftly. But more ~~important~~ impordant, we want to see these changes come about safely, without violence."

Rick: Easy, guys. Watch this next part closely.

"To this ~~end~~ en I have initiated the P.A.P.A., an organization many of you prob'ly heard about. PAPA is an ~~acronym~~ anacronym for Planetary Action and Protection Agency. But this is only one small step. Far more needs to be done. For there's a new menace threatening the progress we've made, threatening to halt our vital green work. I speak of a new red menace. And while this red no longer ~~stands~~ stan for communism, it does still stan for violence, it does still stan for the suppression of our personal freedoms. And ~~saddest~~ saddis of all, it does still stan for the red of hatred, the red of bloodshed.... [Three lectern thumps, one each on the word "still".]

"Dat's von spooky unit" says helmut.

"It was not easy to come before you tonight. ~~Originally~~ Originly my plan was to report on the progress we've made, progress in cleaning up the enviromet here at home, progress in helping other nations follow our lead."

At this point everyone burst out laffing, including rick, who'd obviously stayed up for hours analyzing this speech.

"...Over the pass few weeks I've been ~~hard-pressed~~ har-press to make a decision. That decision was whether or not to come before the people of this Nation and ~~expose~~ espose this menace. Well, with the help of the president, and with the help of friends and coworkers, ~~I've~~ I been able to make that decision. There was really no choice. For when the enemy has no conscience, and when he ~~operates~~ operate in secret, the people mus be ~~told~~ tol. Everyone I ~~asked~~ ask agreed: We are dealing with an enemy of national as well as ~~international~~ innernational ~~consequence~~ consquence."

Rick paused the picture. "This's the foul germ of his argument, the license he needs! Watch how he moves in for the kill!"

"We mus learn, some Greens –Greens we think are our friends, our comrades– we mus learn some of them are violent people first. They are only Greens as an afterthought, a means to an end, a disguise they can make us believe in. It is *this* violent fringe we mus unmask and bring to justice."

More rhetoric follows. Finally we get to, "In closing I will say: Together –if we stay alert, and if we learn to spot the warning signs early enough– we can smoke out this enemy. But this will happen only if we stay alert, learn to spot the hidden signs, an' to stop trussing everyone so much. Thank you."

We stare at each other shaking our heads as rick reviews his notes. He ends the presentation w a sampling of reactions from the corpmedia. Standard ε unified (as usual), no news organization suspects anything. The best motives are presumed. One is led to believe, the fed. never does wrong on purpose. No one infers mccarthy-era symptoms. No one sees shades of gray. A comparison chart rick has made shows the breach between green ε popmedia belief (when it comes to the credibility of the fed.) is widening to a chasm.

"I read this speech as classic and I do mean classic agitprop. ["Pleece haksplain 'ageetprope'?"] Yes. Sorry. Agitprop is the department of agitation 'n' propaganda in the communist state. Its mission is to rouse the ire of the people against all things the state disapproves of. A man named heinrich himmler turned propaganda into a behavioral science and a brilliant linguist named noam chomsky named that science *manufacturing consent*. History might one day note [ends rick] it was with this speech that the die was cast against greens, that this speech predicted the police-state that is clearly headed our way, and *has* been for quite some time now. The die to which I refer is absolute political polarity between deep greens and the u.s fed. I dunno about you but fer me this guy reeks of 'Dont mess with me or you'll be goddamned sorry you did'. Did anyone notice his eyes when he spoke of punishment? [some of us yod] You know what nietzsche said: Beware of those who like to punish. This guy represents nathan's terrific coinage, antiestablishmentdisciplinarianism, if anyone ever did. This sort of....

Helmut, visibly sobered by the himmler re, asked, "Vats da anti-vatever vurd mean?"

"Antiestablishmentdisciplinarianism, yes. It's nathan's word. Means, the punishing of those who disagree with the establishment ...who disagree, that is, with the viewpoint of those in power. Anyway, the danger here is, there are those...the loggers 'n' fishermen we confront in our green work, yes. But mostly bigCorpx ceo's... those who will use such talk in high places as license to act against us. And I think the prime purpose of this speech was to grant that license. For us, it predicates, I believe, a surge in the corporal punishment of greens. But that's just me. I'm not representing greenEarth when I say: Watch your backs, guys 'n' girls. To me this is scary stuff. Or as mutt says, spooky. And it looks like only the beginning. Spread the word." Lookback sees rick as among the first to have a handle on this titanus eironicus (giant of a pretender), one of the first to show us that the boeotian hunter was boldly abroad in the land, the first to advise us to think twice before receiving this parindareusan as a houseguest, even via the germfree mode of a video screen.

While rick spoke, an appendix to his notes sat unattended on the screen: a list of some 30-odd words w the heading: STRICKLAND VOCABULARY/PRONUNCIATION. The words he noted also incl'd: supposably orientated irrevalent contempoary & predomitly [sic all]. "Occasional hint of foreign (perhaps Caribbean) accent. This data has been collected in the event any Greens should ever suffer by this man's hand." Rick ended with, "I predict, this executive-advisor-to-the-director [of the epa] appointment will end with the president creating a new cabinet post (secretary of the environment), perhaps with this very man filling that post ...should he pass the allegiance test, that is." <I think he just did> i added.

When the screen went white, glen, shaking his head, said, "The guy's a godamn spindoctor. Delphine followed this w, "A storyteller with a dictator gene." Perhaps something to do w indian idioms accounts for it but, today i find deldevi's quip eerily predictive of what one of her motherland's amazing sisters, arundhati roy, may have been penning at that very moment for all i know! "A storyteller is a shaman of the imagination, an inveterate eupheMystic on a mission, while a spindoctor is only an invertebrate liar trying to convince the world not only that he has an imagination but a spine supporting it." Then someone mentioned strickland's use of the nonword orientated. "Ya know, alot o' people say orientated", adds pragmatic glen.

"Yeah. Vat's wrong vit dat?" adds helmut to scattered laffter.

"It's not good english" says the well-spoken dark woman at my elbow, black eyes flashing. More laffter. "But let's not forget. English is helmut's second language. It's the rest of us who have no excuse for how we speak" says she, whose own first language is in fact high new delhian. To myself i wonder why women are ever making excuses for the helmuts of the world? I asked this of Lilith months later after hearing about helmut's cheap feel. Why do women defend a guy who becomes the butt of his own sexist antics —often women of considerable etiquette?

Because my puzzle took awhile to produce a finished picture, because her answer came in bits&pieces over time, i can only paraphrase. "Women i think are secretly grateful for men guilty of some crudeness or other. It's an antidote for what we've been taught to think of as our own monthly crudeness. The perfectly tidy guy [tho ideally great] challenges a woman's [sense of] learned personal untidiness." This of course stunned me —after all my work! But why, forgodsake, when men cant give birth …the whole reason for menses? But that too was just "one more untidy woman thing". <My God! How in hell are we gonna cleanup civilization's attitude about [the Nature of] women when *everyone's* attitude is so abusive?> But all this will have to wait.

Rick's briefing took us to lunchtime: catered —not typical unless guests are present. None were that i could see, unless you counted glen ε mark, who'd caught a flite from norway; or helmut's new ladyfriend, who reappeared when we were done. Slowly, however, almost unnoticed at first, gE staffers began drifting into the room… til the place was packed. {What's up with this?} When everyone had served himself rick stepped to the lectern. "May I have your attention? …Yesterday the board had a most unusual teleconference. The subject of our talk could not make it here today but a friend of hers did. Chair nugent will take it from here. Hope ya all enjoy your lunch."

At that time i'd been a gE at-large member (pardon my english) of the advisory council to the b of d for over 7yrs, and i knew of no "unusual" goings-on. But for a split second it crossed my mind: {Nikki is not here. Why? Has she somehow connived the board to censure me? Absurd!} One's childhood insecurities are not easily put aside. Meanwhile a large sheetcake was being maneuvered by caterers to a nearby table. Why did i have the feeling naked dancers were about to pop out of it?

Brian stepped behind the lectern. After chitchat about the food, he spoke of "the exceptional work of a newcomer to our organization which has recently come to my attention. [low-key kinda guy, smiling, putting on glasses] This work of hers, as you can see, is huge; perhaps a thousand panels or more." He indicates what looks to be a massive fotoalbum lying on the table. Rick, sitting there, tips it up, rotates it so all can see it's eye-catching cover.

"What rick's holding there is a cartoon series. [rick slow-flashes the pages] ...a series dedicated to the work of our great organization, I should add. The board decided yesterday we'd like to syndicate this artwork. Now, if the... if the... [audience chitchat subsides] ...now if the big blond guy in green cape 'n' tites –on the cover there, and on the cake too, over there– reminds you of anyone in this room, well, all I can say is...." Laffter ripples around. All eyes turn my way. I spot the baron, then lex reever, in a small group by the entrance door, and suddenly get weak knees —and i'm not even standing.

"As you c'n see, the name of the cartoon is, the adventures of captain greenEarth. Eh? [when noise quiets he goes on] Now I understand, the young lady who created this extraordinary art could not join us today. [aside to his secretary] She's out sick, delphine says. [deldevi agrees] However we were able –by somewhat devious methods I confess– [slow smile] to coax the hero, the subject of her cartoon, to make an appearance here t'day! [allbut yelling over the talking] Would you all... [clears throat, clears it again] ...Would you all [shuffling, murmuring] ...would you please put your hands together for our very own captain greenEarth: long-time activist 'n' gE promoter without peer, nathan....!" Etcetcetc.

{So *this* was rick's "eye-opener". Lilith McGrae, what have you done? And to think the ball was positively in my court even *before* this happened!}

3

That nite, w the baron snoring in one bedrm and lex in the other, i lay downstairs on the pullout unable to sleep. I caroused the ceiling of memory, just as i'm doing now. Open or closed, my eyes were filled w the image of her. Starting on top i worked my way down. Hair: slippery-soft & shining, tumbling blackwalnut tresses... so i began examining the few frames of her which mnemy had thusfar took possession of.

All that day i had not called. O i almost dialed a dozen times but i'd stop partway to the fone. A couple times i even punched in some numbers. If hers was a plot to ensnare me as nikki warned, it was a damned good one —quite a few years & thousands of highly creative hours in the making!

I did not mention: by the time lunch was over i'd rcv'd the congrats of just about everyone, save nikki (whom everyone guessed was not really out sick that day), and the most extravagant of which was the kiss beside the mouth, w its silks-obscured bodypress, of warmbrown deldevi. "Congratulations, nathan ji. I will look for you tonite among the stars." Cute coy twinkle-eyes. An hour later lex glen mark rick the baron & me were the only ones left in the room. As i browsed Lilith's folio rick showed me the note that came with it: "I have been drawing this series since i was a kid. I can redraw any parts you don't like, especially the early frames, which are weak on action."

"Been her hero for awhile, I'd say" says glen with his usual sheepish smirk.

"I thought I recognized the guy in green tites when she set it on my desk. [chides rick] By page two I knew it was you."

"Yeah, but didja get a look at the green guy on the cake before they cut him up? Ol' nate here looked like peter pan!"

"The likeness *was* striking" boomed the baron in his orson wells baritone.

Rick browsed the pages. "Most of your major missions are here." <And a couple i maybe never had.> We all looked on as he browsed this 4color trove of high adventure. "But it's all *very* complimentary."

"History of greenEarth in action" adds glen.

The baron puts a hand on my shoulder. "Look at it this way, schock. [i'm wary when the baron plays warm] It's better than a monument. [knowing him, all waited for the blade to fall] When your monument is a cartoon at least pigeons cant shit on your head." The baron & glen rise at dawn just to razz me. "Nothing without nathan, you know", adds the baron, no one understanding his allusion at the time incl'g me.

I ask rick if Lilith gave him the album in person.

"She was really shy about the whole thing... darted outa the office before I could get 'er name even. The only reason I knew she worked here was- ...well, really.... [all snicker] Hey, dont bust my chops. She's hard t' miss if youre still breathing!"

"With the operative word being hard" mumbles glen smirkily.

We all headout for a "drink". Noteworthy that afternoon was the baron's (after dispatching a few domestic drafts) taking all of us on for our "foolhardy persistence" along a path of passive resistance. He argued, "What's gained if the mainstream media wont give you guys the time o' day? Hardly anybody knows youre risking life 'n' limb except you! What the hell good is that? B'side, your objective is taking too goddamned long to achieve! This Planet 'll be the biggest fucking landfill in the galaxy by the time you guys turn things around! [glancing askance w that tiny-toothed leer of his] But maybe by then this town'll offer a good german ale instead of this domestic piss i'm drowning in here!"

And so i lay on my bed that nite, as i say, my thoughts continually returning to Lilith, as the image of her gently tore at the garments of my maleness. (If this imagery seems sexually charged it's because those early sensations may be tainted by my present needs.) The beauty of her downcast face, the fingertip-mesmerizing feel of her skin, the sheenysilken knobs at the sides of her wrists, elbows & knees, the inset nodules along the lithe arch of her spine, the supple-muscled outline of her calfs & thighs, to just above the knee only, as high as vision had gotten to thusfar....

Yet... alot of it's in the eyes for me. Because i seek the primitive person behind the civilized laminates, unabashed bonoborangrilla that i am, i often look to the eyes. Bodylanguage, of course (incl'g facial expression), is the quickest & surest way in. The second thing about Lilith's eyes which an oculept notices is, how very wide-apart they are. Too often to be accidental, such spacing signifies right-brain ascendancy. And the *first* quality of those eyes?

They did not just look at one the way other eyes do. No. Rather they blazed & smoldered their way inside of you! They seemed to see something behind one's own eyes. One knew only, as something in him squirmed beneath that huge innocent terrifyingly beautiful glance, that he'd never seen such eyes before! Almondshaped ε sooty-lashed, those eyes had permitted me, once or twice briefly, penetration. Not just the prosaic mind-to-mind thing but a penetration that was downright sexual. Without our conscious consent our minds had shared a psychescrew, a sort of subliminal copulation. Most of us are not aware such a forcefield interface even exists, and certainly not aware such things can go on win it, in a place we dare think of as merely "air", or "empty space". But in a Universe fairly flatulent w forces ε conduits between forces, of course there is no room for a vacuum.

As i write i catch myself w no fetish in hand but the silks of memory. O eat your hearts out, dr.sickmund dir.straitmon warden todion chief guard odion ε guards glumm gluum zodion xodion dion ion ε even you mr imbecillo too. Try tho you may to invade my blanket chrysalis, to penetrate these obdurate shadows w your peeping cameras, it will get you no relief. [In some corner of my being i successfully kiss ε embrace her.] Compared to my conjurings tonite your most flagrant orgies, o my keepers, are bankrupt boorish ε banal! (Of course, wout another update of all that's been going on around here, all this will make little sense. So i'll simply say, the latest lusty note from the ladies upstairs has left me in a state.)

Speaking of fetishes. Sexual deprivation such as i'm experiencing here makes me think it possible to mate even w only someone's navel or teeth (hi, carol) or even hump like a dog the right person's leg. Victor stavro said it best i think. "The fame of the fetishist rests upon his facility to turn a fancy, no matter how freakish or forlorn, into the most feverish forum of fornication." This is possibly the case w me now. But it wasnt back then. We've heard it said, the biggest sex organ is not between the legs but between the ears. This being so, then eyes, for me, are the non-tactile conduit to that organ. For i insist, the eyes are the quickest means to the gist of another —and sometimes even to the very zizm of them.

I hope i'm among friends when i say, Lilith's eyes, for me, were sex organs —well, virtual sex organs. My anthropologist pal, denise norris, in her fascinating book *the body gallery*, has this to say about eyes: "Its shape, its circumscription of hair (eyelashes), its ellipse of everted pink flesh [the 'lips' of the eyelids, so to speak], its pearly wetness, its tendency to open on stimulation, close on dislike or fear (among other attributes), make the eye strongly remindful of the female genitals." O i agree alright! Hi there, neesy!

In short, eyes can be a real turnon —the right eyes. We've all heard the expression 'bedroom eyes' —flabby foofarow next to the heat which Lilith's eyes created in this oculept. If this seems a fetish, so be it. Lock me up. Well, perhaps youre a little late for that now. Anyway... i'm sure if someone did a survey there would turn out to be farmore oculepts than panty-fancies (socalled pantypirates or clothesline shoppers) or even, say, professional-white-sockulepts. This is because many females turn on to eyes too. Men however typically have a grosser view of sexuality. It's a sorry fact about us guys, but things have to sort of hang out of people, or at least radiate a febrile glow, in order to serve as sex triggers for most men. But i desist. The opacity, the bluntness of common male desire, has been sufficiently espoused by others. Worse, it's most often not even the guy's fault ...essentially. Be that as it may, the following is a crossover appreciation.

At hornell prepschool for girls in the adirondacks, back in the mid-50s, a lit instructor named van bloom wrote a now-famous poem: "my little irish iris". I quote a snippet.

> And for her eyes the teacher's lust was duple:
> Ah, bad —o bad— to long to probe each pupil.

Not to be confused w thompson's *daydreams of a schoolmaster*, i found, right here in our prison library, not one but two copies of the novel from which these lines are taken. It is a reprint of the original *confession of a caucasian widow*, w foreword by one e. ray rowe claiming "The real author was not female. Vivian (Vee) Bloom's real name was Van Bloom... A confession of particular note is: It was not Vee who murdered her 'philistine and fustian' husband, but rather (for what it's worth) the other way around. *Male* Van murdered *female* Vee, his wife.'"

In case the reader is still not lost: Further on rowe explains, "During the prim and proper era of this book's publication the view of the publisher was, lesbophilia in an all-girl highschool would be easier to accept than pedophilia in a junior high, no matter how refined and scholarly the instructor in question might be". And so it is that the sapphic original of the same rhyme reads:

> And for her eyes the teacher's lust was duple:
> Ah, bad —o bad— to long to lick each pupil.

Early in the novel all this "sexual eye" business is prefigured by a highly-charged scene in which instructor van uses his tung to probe ε remove an "object" from iris's copiously tearing eye: "That's the first time anyone ever did *that* to me" gasps iris, as van, tucking his tung back in his cheek, releases her. "I thought sure it was going to hurt when you first put it in." (Note: Most primitive cultures used the tung for removal of foreign objects from the eye.)

We are soon told, "On closer examination the object turned out to be a sty-like thing shaped like the stretched mouth of a wet red balloon and quite engorged with blood. And lick at the thing as I might, pushing it this way and that, up and down, side to side, even chasing it in circles (hold still, Iris!), I soon realized, it was a part of her anatomy that I had hold of (a sort of pudgy pink sty), and that the thing (by then aggravated ε itching maddeningly, or so she said) could not simply be licked or sucked away."

Later, after young iris has cheated on her adoring "Teach", we come upon the following. "Did you let him touch you?" "Touch me, my eye! The goon just about raped me!" By then the reader has begun to ask, Touched your eye? Raped your eye? Such eye-imagery is rampant in the book: "With an eye to my randy condition [says van earlyon, in a motel w iris] she decided to succumb to..." &soforth. By the time one is halfway thru the book he is wary enuf to test every "eye" phrase, every "I" usage, against some part of the female anatomy, or risk missing the juicy gist. The whole point being, we have here a case notsomuch of pedophilia as paraphilia; oculaphilia, really; ie, eye-fancy. And the author, male or not, has got it bad ...or had it bad. For it was not until after his death that *confessions of a schoolteacher* came out in its frank (compared to the earlier, francine) version.

And so i lay abed that nite. Should i, shouldnt i.... call her, i mean? As i started to say, *before* i became preOccuPied. I got only as far as Lilith's face, hair ε her zoom-to-doom eyes before pellucid memory royally did me in, found myself left only w the jizmatic gist of a wistful fistful of should-have-dones.

...rememb'ring their worth in that dizzying derth.
By the stars of such eyes poorer sailors than i
have attained to the ends of the Earth!

There is no passive solution to desiring so much. And o, female reader... forgive only those 'grossnesses' of mine which are native to all genders.

4

Next morning, bolstered by caffeine, i dropped a grouchy baron at home and saw lex off at frix. (If we can call l.a's airterminal lax, why not call frisco's frix?) Around 10 bekky arrived from carmel. Our purpose in getting together was twofold. Secondly, once i realized she was still troubled by my world matron thesis (on emotional not rational grounds) i decided the best way to defuse the resistance was to pull a gender switch. I would introduce her to the woman who best understood my argument and whose work bekky admired. But more importantly, it had been some time since i'd seen alice and i missed her.

Alice krawel makes her home (set among a blaze of blossoms) in the sacramento valley. Bekky, a reforming man-hater & beamer brat, drove us there. Quickly said, we had a great day (more of which later, perhaps). While alice & bek strolled & chatted, i called another alice admirer. "Come up early if ya can. An' bring some jeans for riding." Was there anything she needed from down this way? "Thanks, no. Beth an' a friend o' hers jus dropped off my car 'n' stuff", which she called an "unexpected surprise".

Fr morn, a little later than planned (for needing to see off bekky), as i drove n, coat on, windows down, i grinned back at a giddy ca sky. Autumn-crisp air & the musk of decaying foliage wafted thought back to *the hills of home.*

I'm homesick for you mountains that I know.

To get to dillon beach one passes several communities. Of the variety of vanity villages i find the many "yacht havens" & "golf paradises" the most obnoxious. Not far behind are what i call 'equine estates'. Like those bizarre lifeforms who live in concrete-chickencoops-by-the-sea yet never swim in it, so the majority who own equine estate's rarely ride the horses they keep. So the fenced creatures effectively spend 16hrs a day every day devouring grains & grasses & passing poison gases purely for purposes of status & esthetics! Or: "Unregulated afflatus for social status" as Lilith would quip. And because horses dont 'mow' the turf uniformly, equine estates does golf paradise one better. It primps its pastures & lawns in *addition* to its golfcourse.

Thus predisposed i arrived at horse-haven heights via dillon beach road. The exurban community's "ranchettes" were of two kinds: new england tudor & mexican-modern. (In real life, just for fun, try to imagine any tudor, new england or old, abiding *anything* mexican save for paying "wetbacks" slave wages.) Tho i remembered the mcGrae's as the latter style ranchette, there was a problem: In my haste that morn i brought no street name or fone # (unlisted) and could not remember which way from an introductory y in the road: long-sweeping right or less-sweeping left.

Edging the javelin thru the y i tried to recall making that turn w Lilith. Out of nowhere —careless as to my position on a rd which had been carless til that moment— a small car w an empty kayak rack zipped by from an opposite direction, its horn sounding anemic next to its blown muffler, which roared like a baby dragon at the lost tortoise in its path. <If you were going fifteen instead of fifty like the sign says, you imbecile!> Behind its smokedglass i guessed some harried delivery person. In materialist societies small cars have inferiority complexes anyway. I stop, back, head down the wrong fork. {And small red ones often act downright paranoid.}

A few mins cruising convinced me which style ranchette was don's. Single-level sprawling, white or beige, arched ɛ alcoved w rust-red tiled roof, matching stables, small green pastures w white-fenced quadrangles containing 0-to-4 horses. A few mins and i was sure i'd gone the wrong way, for i could find not one w the triple garage i remembered. Return to caballo hollow rd. Part b of my search went better. I happened past such a garage yet no nameplate said mcGrae. {Is mcGrae her stepname perhaps? ...To know this woman is apparently to be perpetually lost in a sort of siren-inflicted daze.}

I approach the likely suspect. As i swing into the driveway i spot the same fluorescent-pink flowers my headlites had set ablaze that nite. Floppy blossoms clambering up stone pedestal of mailbox obscuring nameplate. I ring. As i await donMiguel's answer i gently part blossoms. "Hi! C'mon in!" As gate opens i read nameplate: 16061. McGrae. Glance at watch. 40min late, it chides. I'm really not known for tardiness. {...Or for seeming perpetually lost either.} You look much better. "So, c'mon in! <How's your dad?> Fine. Left on business yesterday. Here, lemme take your jacket. An' sister jus left for school." Turning back, having hung it, i follow to greatarea where she bade me sit (as they used to say).

Afternoon classes, i guess?

"You could say that. Actually, fer her it's a slide. Only goes two days a week. Just missed graduating in june, ya know? She says they jus wanted to hang on t' their star gymnast for another season. [buzzer sounds in distance] That's fer me. Make yourself at home. Be right back." Gets up, skids to stop, backstrokes, bends, hands me a cd lying on a tabletop beside a book —my *Mothernature & the world matron*, only just released in tradecloth. "Here's that disc daddy promised. Be right back. Make yourself at home!"

Sheathed in black denim riding breeches beneath a fan of swaying hair, she walk-ran soundlessly out thru the dining area –tile/parquet/tile again– in white-socked feet, skidded around an archway and disappeared, to silence what i imagined was a dryer. Except for some discoloration ɛ puffiness under her left eye (as if one eye were short on sleep) and on the cheekbone, her face was as clear ɛ lovely as a mountain-grotto pool.

Typically, i dislike masonry homes –block stone brick stucco– not for their lack of eye-appeal but for their lack of amiability. It is a pity there are so many to whom building a home of ecowood is esthetic heresy. Like real wood, ecowood is dynamic/responsive while masonry is cold/unyielding. One is intimate, the other, formal —fortresslike, tomblike. The larger such homes, specially when lived in by older folks, strike me (sorry) as a pre-mausoleum stage: the penultimate stone marker!

Visiting some homes is like entering a pyramid. On arriving one is processioned straight to the sarcophagus. Once, back when i drank socially (as that hook is called), i felt, i swear, the hosts' couch –circa scandi-plutonian w chrome armrests like handles– start to move, like an egyptian bier atop a line of slaves, w me on it! That was just before conscription corked the alcohol. But the mcGrae home was at least brite. A sextet of skylites lit the centerpiece of the greatarea: rockgarden w gurgly fountain ɛ falls ɛ big-leafed greenery. As i glancedabout for the nymphs of this domestic grotto, my glance fell oncemore upon the portraits hung by the fireplace. {O yes!} Free now of don's gaze i strolled over.

{Gadshazm, what a beauty! Has she always had such eyes such skin such hair? People have killed for farless beauty than this!} I soon found myself in an imaginary conversation w don –whom, despite his prideful lifestyle, i respected– trying to talk him out of one or more of these portraits. These two here would be charming, i venture, flanking my own fireplace in appalachia!

Of course, youd be welcome to visit any time to check on them. Then again, if youd rather hang on to them, you could of course always allow the Real Item to go w me in their place, etc....

"I'll hang on to both, thanx" chose don, ending our imaginary chat. {The preoccupied mind is a dangerous thing and lately i've had that.} When i returned to my chair i saw a basket brimming w folded clothes: frilly blouse, jeans, black skirt, "underthings", as euphemized in more timid times. Tho buried midway, my arcane eye fell easily upon them.

Returning again. "Sorry bout the interruption. They dont wrinkle if you get them while theyre hot. Be right back. Sorry. Last time, promise."

I'm fine. I've got all day.

From archway, leaned back at the hips w her load, "Youre serious, not just saying that?"

Dead serious.

Returns a few mins later. Now she is dressed in blue&gray plaid flannel shirt which shades set her eyes ablaze. "Sorry bout that. I know how you feel about dryers 'n' all [pauses, spreads arms] ...'n' about houses like this... but i'm kinda still too new around here to suggest changes." Personally, just then, she struck me as the estate cinderella, in her signature domestics101 role. Of course i said nothing. "Can i get you anything? ...Drink? Sandwich? I dont know about you but i'm starving! [i rise to assist] No-no, sit." Fingertips stop me. (Rover, sit.) "Here's the remote, case ya wanna zap ol quimby there." (Tv on.) Stuffs remote in rover's paw, leaves. I fail to grab mistress' hand w one adactylous paw. As she escapes i note, the mass of her hair is now somehow gathered behind her head in a bandana (blue&white-checked), its rabbit-ears emerging from underneath.

On the tv "wilderness journalists" carlton quimby & his manly cohort are upstaging Nature as is their weekly wont, supposedly trudging for hours thru wormy steaming shin-deep jungle mud yet immaculate as you please in breeches boots tailored shirts & white pith helmets! Hope she doesnt like these phonies. Monkeynuts! Zap. When she returns i ask if she'd ever seen (in reruns) the quimby black-bear instalment filmed in the everglades years ago?

"Was that the one where he claimed t' be tracking the last black bear in tropical north america when actually he had the poor creature trucked into florida from upnorth?"

{Wow.} That would be the one. Zap again. Don's remote is plainly too exotic for me. Only dead-air now. Push channel-up bar. Sound blares. Quimby's heavy breathing & out-of-control volume combine to sound like i've hit on some jock&jill channel. Sorry bout that. Mute on but still no picture. {Quimby really needs to get in shape.} Picture back, while screen has melted to avocado & mustard tints & sound has disappeared altogether! A soapopera oozes onto the screen.

"I should warn you. None of this is organic." <That's fine.> Framed in serving window leaning on elbows, she makes a perfect restaurant ad. "The mayo's eggless. Is that okay?" Sexy residual lisp. <Fine.>

In the same room where i cannot prove all soaps are filmed, a graying mulatto man glares down at a pale brunet girl sitting leggily on a couch. {Shouldnt she be in school this time o' day?} With all their noxious innuendo, soaps are filthier than straightup triple-x. I try program button. Manhandled by some infernal rotator, 50channels proceed to click by. Hit channel-down. 50channels rotate in opposite direction, settling on the same murky screenful of dehydrated jizm. {Thank the gods of incest i cant hear what theyre saying.} Ditch remote, browse pages of own book. A few mins later Lilith calls me to brunch. "Hope you like avocados 'n' tomatoes?"

That pop genre of sublimated porn called soapopera & gothic romance has an ethos of vacuous pathos contorted (by artisans of the scrimiest pretensions) into shameless bathos.

Love 'em.

"Me too."

Lilith

"You c'n use Iage's mount. Daddy's is a little highstrung.

Theyre both kinda antsy. Is it me?

"No. They jus dont ride enuf."

But i thought *we* were riding *them*.

Such an elfin smirk! —the hollowed cheeks, slitely-flared nostrils ε pouty kiss-lips which warn, "Now if youre gonna jus stand there 'n' pun-away like daddy we're gonna hafta have a talk...." She turns away, strokes a cheek here, pats a flank there, much as one checks a favorite rig before a trip. Her casual way w such large creatures never failed to surprise me. "You said [on the way to the stable] something about soaps?"

O that. I wondered if anyone in your house was addicted. The remote snagged one and wouldnt let go.

"Daddy hates soaps. [fits one bridle, asks for another] So does sis."

Distracted by the sexy string of sibilants, i hand halter. Tip of tung to tips of top teeth ε blinking at me, she looks at my offering curiously. <Ooops. Sorry. Dont ride much.> Return it for the requested bridle.

"I'll do bridles if you'll get the blankets." Her speech, convalescing nicely, has left the ungainly "lateral lisp" stage (more musical variant in alveolar thithing), moved on to a "dentate lisp" (more sibilance than thithing) —at which stage it would linger to lesser&lesser degrees til... But why explain? Only my closest readers care about such things. In order to retrieve the blanket beneath the saddle i'm holding aloft, she brushed near me. Wondrous whiff of her hair is quickly snuffed by horsey stable air. We walk the arabians outside where she checks the cinch on my mount.

<Is that called a surcingle? ["Technically, i guess it is."] <Well then, let me say: You c'n check this single sir's surcingle any ol time> which gets me only a quick glancing grin. Not meeting my eyes, w a shy smirk she sized me up, re-adjusted my stirrups. "Go ahead."

I climbed aboard. ...Perfect.

Handsup reigns, walks to her mount. <Better check yours too.> "Already did. Wish i could get it that tite. Thanks." Tho the horse's shoulder is higher than her head, she alights effortlessly. "Liz browning was crippled at my age cinching a horse. Anyway, i've been dumped before 'n' learned my lesson."

What fool would dump you?

Same quick smirk, obliquely delivered. Reigns right, stops. "Jus a sec." Trotting back into the stable, her own ponytail abob, ducking doorbeam she reemerges w a key on a long red tether. "Almos fergot. The gate's locked." We rode leisurely across the pasture. I note the blues of her eyes, bandana ε plaid shirt are matched by certain tints in the saddleblankets, which looked to be tartans.

"The beach isnt far."

Let me guess which way? Wanted to show i wasnt lost all the time.

"Ya c'n uzh'ly smell the sea from here."

What i smell tho is the sea... erras [elfin grin again] ...*that* way. Turning in my saddle i drew a line from n to s in the east. Which means (turning back toward her), the ocean's somewhere over there!

Grin broadens beautifully.

{And juliet is the sun!} Passing car slows as we near the gate. {I'd slowdown too at sight of her, specially mounted.} We rode at about equal height: smaller rider on taller horse, taller rider on smaller horse. She left the gate at a trot. "This air feels great!"

It does!

A woodchip trail (which tied the whole community) led into a line of conifers and down a winding slope beside a wood overwalk to oceanside. Thru the trees i soon saw that ocean, which i'd expected to be much further below. Not too steep a coastline here!

"I think it's cause the bay protects it!"

At bottom the trail wound around sparsely pined dunes, ending on sloped but fairly open beach. Wave-tilt is reverse of usual: wee whitecaps curling away from landfall due to the sierran breeze. We rode on sand ε shell, highup for a stretch, then moved to water's edge. My mount immed sank past fetlock.

Isnt it a little mushy for them?

"It's a good workout for a couple minutes! Theyre used to it!"

Shorter legged than her horse, the flanks of my mare were soon drenched. I'm twice the weight of my mare's usual load but i dont know that. Heaving w every step now, soon i find myself grabbing for the horn ε turning my soaked beast back onto hardpack. Up ahead, riding smooth as a banner in the wind, Lilith (or rather her horse) trotted back. "Sorry. Didnt know you were sinking like that!" We return toward cliffbase. Ambling thru sun&shade i notice, in sunlite, the almost-black of boot, belt, saddle ε livery match the sheen of her eyebrows, lashes ε hair —except that the latter, which has now fallen half-free of its bandana, flashes russet highlites.

As we rode she came&went alongside, the blues ε grays of her eyes paled in the open lite. At one point –flat, no obstacles– i could feel the liberation of a good run. (When rob schumann's 'arabian in italy' symphony finally breaks into a rolling gallop, how rhythmically liberated-at-last we feel.) *They* were soon gliding effortlessly past *us.* {How else to say that without insulting the horses?} The sight of that tan-fleshed stallion moving muscularly beneath her —add to this her exhilarated glow, the flashing whites of her eyes, her easy weight lifting, lowering, lifting (and, frankly, because all this went on so close to an erect ε silver-helmeted horn)— stirred me in places that needed no stirring. Was this zamalzain (gala limping horse) –this writer, i mean– being led off to banbury cross wout his knowledge?

A halfhour or so and we reached a cliffside park. "We usually stop here ...there's a fountain for the horses over there." No one about; schoolday. Rinse hands while horses guzzle. When they'd had their fill she led the way to a grove of pine —so they shouldnt "mess" on the grass. Our mounts free-tethered, she pulled off boots, socks, and, not saying a word, broke for the water. I followed, what else...? And when we got back i flopped on the grass. My feet are on fire. I think youve crippled me.

"That's cause you were running uptop." On the shell, she meant.

Had to. I was sinking like in a bowl of cereal mush. Ooooh. Mmmm.

She hovered wondering what to do. I got up, jogged in a circle. T'sokay. Really! Cool grass feels good. We had run .7k or so down the beach. Having stripped to the waist for the run back, we ran shirtless —except that she wore a swimsuit top which resembled my favorite maui shirt. We sat. Introspective puffin, she gazed out to sea. With peripheral focus i followed as droplets of perspiration beaded her nose, shoulders, gathered between her breasts; there, in wee rivulets, in stops&starts, they trickled down the narrow ionic passage toward her tummy. A moment later we were off to a finking drountain.

The one runner, w his longer stride ε heavier footprint, was sinking in the shoreline mush while the other, lighter, and w a shorter gait (thank the gods), was gliding moreorless on the surface. No, you first. Shirt draped over shoulders ε back, she bent to drink. The physics of friction 'n' suction aside, youre one helluva runner! Awhile getting a satisfying suckle from that tiny spout of water, something else i didnt know backthen was, she didnt have a competitive muscle in her body —except to challenge herself, and this she did w the near-ferocity of an over-achiever. Who said it? The only truly competitive 'muscle' is the brain. Maybe i said it.

As we turnedaway a breeze lifted her shirt ...and i saw why she'd covered herself, and why, during our run back, after removing her shirt, she'd suddenly lagged a little behind [hic]. What looked like a patch of roadrash healed pink, had left an imprint resembling the wing of a shrike. And to best this, beneath that wingsized wingshape, in three symmetrical hashmarks, appeared what looked like a cartoonist's depiction of a thing in motion. I am immed. set to wondering just how a seizure, or a fall, can cause roadrash on one's upper back.

When we reached the horses i removed a saddle, which blanket she used to spread on the grass, "Human side up." The sky was clear, the sun, warm, as we lay there. With lowered gaze, i roamed the box-canyon of her ribcage, the gasp of her tummy, the languorous wink of her navel, puddled w sweat, the delineated roundness where her breasts, almost touching, snuggled sidebyside. Wondering by then if the avian imprint on her back might be a birthmark not an injury, thoughts of our last time on the beach crossed my mind.

Soon we were up on one elbow, talking. I caught her glance, just once, skipping shyly away from my body. For my part, i wore up top only a vertical dash of tawny chesthair; and mine was the paler skin. With a pinky she traced the pattern of the blanket. <Handsome plaid.> "In name only" she explained, shifting onto her back. Raising her pelvis {Aaaargh!} she withdrew a second bandana from a back pocket, twin to the one in her hair. "Tho it's way better than this one [shakes out bandana], it's not an official plaid." Dabs forehead eyes lips, admits, "I cant tell some checks from plaids either." Lifts chin, swabs neck & upper chest, shakes out ponytail.

And i cant ...how d' ya say [regroup misbehaving eyes]... discriminate between a rhomboid pied and a genuine harlequin.

"Isnt pied like [eyes up, thinking] ...like farmland, seen from a plane?" Then, almost spitting, she sat erect. "Hfft. Look!" Her eyes fell upon a silver tube tilted toward frisco in the distant ne. "Now what are the chances o' that?" ...thinking of plane highup over checkered farmland, glancing up, seeing same? This coincidence of thought & event left our jaws ajar as i wondered aloud if <the wine country beneath the plane looks "pied" or "checked" to its windowseat passengers>. Turningback pronate, "As for this blanket...." Its bogus plaid turnedout to be "The best daddy could find ...in real sutherland colors, which in truth are dullblue dullgreen dullblack dullwhite 'n' kindadullred, tho their combined effect is strangely mystical, emphasis on the mist: m-*i*-s-t."

G.G. Blisswizard

<Sutherland?>

"Yes." Here she did a pronunciation: "Sooterlunt, i think they say. That's the clan name for gray, our ancestral name. It's all very complicated.... Well, if you insist. Gray, they say, didnt sound scots enuf to strangers so greatgrandfather changed it to mac Gray: g-r-a-Y; which angus junior decided to spell, macGrae: g-r-a-E ...to be more like macCrae, i suppose: C-r-a-e.... I warned you, my ancestry is a muddle."

Tracking her scent like an ozarks hound, i guessed at what the taste of her would be like: brook-fresh meditation spine-nectar! (Probably different from what the reader's thinking.) With the tiniest tang of sea salt! {Here, lie still a moment. This is just an experiment; a quick tung test; comparison of molarities: salt of Lee versus salt of sea.}

"I really want t' go there [scotland]." She'd gotten a chance once "It jus could notuv workedout". So she declined. Becomes pensive.

When i think of scotland i think of clans 'n' conflicts, centuries of warring marring the mystery of a unique land.

"War has marred every land by now."

<Youre so right. My bad. But on the positive side, they –an' not the french as many think– did invent the guillotine ...more 'humane' alternative to earlier forms of capital pun.> She looked at me oddly, not sure if i were serious or still scolding the scots. <Really! Beat hell outa drawing 'n' quartering. An' hanging too. Wayless painful. They called it the iron maiden.>

That she knew. "We c'n only wish [she added] more nations would learn t' do what the scots have been doing for generations ago."

An' that is?

"Replace war with a music 'n' dancing olympics."

Youre right ...Ay, an' a bonny r'placement t'would be.

This brought a smile. ...Bogus plaid or not,

> i wanted to lie the sonsy lassy doon on it
> —thus interlockin' from tam-tip ta stockin',
> young tartan McGrae an' ole teuton vonSchocken.

But fearing civil strife of our own, i did not let on.

"Daddy wanted to name me maggie but got overruled by mother —the L-names thing, ya know? Well, i guess ya dont. Anyway, her name's leyda. Her twin sister 'n' another sister have L-names too: letitia 'n' lais. So she gave us L-names. <Us being you 'n' your sister?> Uhuh. <Do you prefer the name maggie?> Do i get a new start at life with it? <Absolutely.> Then, yes. I'd prefer it." Up on both elbows, she began smoothing a long blade of grass between thumb&index.

Didnt you say your mother was french?

Pauses to swallow. "Guess i did... But did i mention, she's part lithuanian too...? <Which makes you *Lilith*-uanian?> [impish querical smirk] That *is* pretty cute. [seeming a little unsure of what to make of me just yet] Assyrian, really. Pickedup the name from her father, who was part assyrian."

I was thinking more like greek or roman. ...Lilith reminds me of lygia for some reason. ...Assyrian, huh? Never would o' guessed that.

"Nobody does."

So there are lots of liliths in the mideast then?

"No. Very bad ...like a curse, really ...Nobody but my daft mother would name her child lilith. <Why's that?> She's ...i mean the legendary lilith... is believed by many religions to be the mother of evil forces."

Did *she* know that? ...i mean, when she named you?

"I doubt it. Guess she jus thought it was pretty."

It is. In fact, beautiful.

Flushes, jumps to add, "Then again, *how the west was won* was writ by a lilith person. An' then there's that t-v show. So it's not unheardof i suppose."

What about lalage? That sounds as french as... as... rendezvous. Still flushed. It was only then it struck me, compliments —all compliments— made her uneasy; even indirect ones. I knew the feeling; have the same problem. If our parents dont gift us w it, no one can convince us we're worthy.

"It is. Mother's family was mostly french ...with a jigger of italian sniftered in, as daddy says, so the french bread doesnt stick to the pan. You dont have italian blood, i hope...? That's good. Daddy likes italians alot; he just cant resist a joke, good 'r not. Anyway, she got lalage from our famous greatgrandmother, simone de beauvoir."

No kidding! The early feminist...? A friend o' mine's mother did a doctoral thesis on her. [she confirmed the tie] But arent you *mostly* descended from macbeth or banquo's ghost?

"Daddy checked that out. Not directly. But a scot, they say, is related to all scots." Celtic harps & flutes haunted the hills & dells of those mystical bluegrays whenever her thoughts drifted *retrouver.*

During the ride back, sure that she'd heard the good news, i ask if there's any word from hq. Looking worried, she says, no. "But i called nikki a couple times to apologize —an' ta someone in payroll too". This puts an instant knot in my gut. Apologize? To nikki? For what? She explains how "terrible" she feels about being out sick "so soon after getting hired. I promised her i'd be at work monday fer shur."

<I hope she accepted your apology>, which i knew was weighted w more than its share of empathy for nikki.

"She did. [dubious pause] <What?> Well, she was probably stressed the day i called," which stress i could tell she felt was also her fault.

Lilith. [Huh?] Believe me when i say this, okay? [Okay.] There's no one nikki likes ...that i know of. Maybe not even herself. Okay?

"I guess."

Don was home when we got back. We watered ɛ untacked the horses, rinsed them saltfree, set them to pasture. Don, a tad standoffish at first, was soon my best friend again, or so a stranger (as was i) might have thought. We certainly shared some views on health ɛ the performance arts, but (as Lilith warned), not much beyond. "I like what you said about our bill of rights in your reply to the libertarian [party] platform." Don was a libertarian "by default". His answer to "our new one-party system". Lilith, in a sense knowing my works better than me, had apparently mulled them over and decided, the following was most likely to make inroads into her father's worldview.

> Our so called Bill of Rights ignores the rights of almost all living things in our nation! It is, by self-definition, a bill of exclusion, not inclusion —a universally lethal exclusion, at that! But that is not to say at the time of its writing it was viewed as arrogant and deadly; just one more instrument of our blind anthropism; color-blind at that —our forefathers near-total rejection of the rights of *other* forms of being, including even humans who were darker-skinned than they. In effect, the Bill of Rights can be compared to beings from another galaxy arriving here on Earth and proceeding to enforce new laws which benefit everything *except* humans. That's how exclusionary the Bill of Rights is to *all other* forms of life beside us.

While he respected my views on environmentalism, as he called it ("Hey, I understand. Somebody hasta take that side"), he thought "some o' the stuff going on [was] jus too radical". But Lilith had warned me, "Daddy's stuck somewhere in the fifties on alot of issues", which was, she added, "better than most men his age". Friteningly, this was alltoo true.

"If i can pry you two apart for a sec", Lilith suggests, "You might wanna change outa those horsey things 'n', phew, grab a shower. *Eau de cheval* our instructor used t' call it". Don hopes i will stay for the supper their cook is already busy preparing. I explain, i am speaking at sonoma state at 8, ask Lilith (again) if she'd like to come. "C'n i wear sunglasses?" <Of course.> As i start for the javelin to retrieve my daybag, don says, "Lily's the shy one", gives another of his one-armed hugs.

No sooner am i bathed ɛ changed when don, playing proud curator, has us in the den/library hovering over a cedar thakatbox of memorabilia. <My ignorance of scots history, heraldry, whatnot, is allbut complete, save for bruch's "scottish fantasy", mendelssohn's "hebrides" overture, toss in a song 'r two from *brigadoon*. None of it true scotsmanship, i guess.

"An' the lot of it a semite's view o' the fatherland, I'd say."

"Imported scotch! [pipes Lilith] We did *brigadoon*, remember? In chorus?"

"I remember 't well" said a plainly proud father.

B'side robert burns 'n' a couple walter scott titles, that's about it fer me. (It would be some months til i could add fiona glengary to my list, the miraculous aberdeen marimbist/percussionist.) Otherwise, scotland's a mystery t' me.

"Tis a mystery t'us all" said don in a brogue thut sonded aut'entic.

Sought portrait is at last unveiled! In a column of sunlite, arm in arm, two girls in full scots regalia grin in matched glee at the camera.

"We were 11", says Lilith.

"That's 'bout right," don guesses. "There's an even better one somewhere in here." Picks up, hands me in succession, two smaller mats of the portraits hanging by the fireplace, "That is my laly" he says, giving the first, "and this is my Lily".

Fearing to hurt feelings i say, Beautiful, beautiful. For to my untrained eye-.... "Ah, here 'tis!" he exclaims, bringing forth ɛ unveiling a larger version of the first portrait. The girls, as he called them, costumed from bonnets to brogues, wore formal darks except for a tartan ribbon in the hair (bound *w* a crested snood and pulled over one shoulder), *w* the same ancestral plaid echoed in kneesocks and swathed diagonally up&over the other shoulder. "The tarrrt'ns hud t' be fulded sev'rul times so's not to burrry the gurrls completely" chuckled don. Then out comes what apparently is the prize: twin tartans, each sealed in a zippered see-thru garment bag. With hands unseemly rugged for a ceo, don tenderly lifts one tartan out of its mothballed limbo.

The southerland tartan is a beautiful thing. The cumulative effect of its colors & pattern remind one of a highland mist, drifting lowly over a forest floor, lingering there like a makeshift latticework, loathe to disperse in the morning sun. My glance returns to the portrait while don & Lilith caress the plaid. Mist of twinkling eye mixes w mist of tartan as strains of celtic tenor fill the greatrm just down the hall.

© David Harrold

"The girls will get these as wedding gifts. Or else, receive them when I die ...whichever comes first."

Cool whiff of autumn air assails me from behind. "Hopefully it's weddings, not funerals, pops!" says a third voice. One hand on don's shoulder, the other on mine, the owner of the voice (taller, older than i'd imagined) worms into the group. As i do my best not to do an obvious doubletake, all at once the perfect sense of the portraits-puzzle (the ones flanking the fireplace), and a couple other quandaries i'd been nursing, dawn on me like an advancing, tho dream-slow, lavalanche [sic].

An apple cleft in two! ...Most wonderful!

"The missing sister's finally home," smiles don, kissing in a routine way the temple lalage mechanically proffers while gazing down at the chest. "How was practice?"

"Ho-kay." Chirpy "ho-" w a half-octave drop to "-kay".

Lilith, index rocking on supple wrist, says unceremoniously, "Lage, nathan; nathan, lage" to which don adds, "Sorry. Thought you two already met."

"Ya havent been sellin off the heirlooms while I'm gone, I hope", says the bumptious blueeyed interloper. "Hey, there's mine!" Pointing, brite face ringed w dark tresses, to the unopened tartan draped over the lid.

How do ya tell them apart? i ask don.

"Theyre that like, I niver ken the tane frae the tither."

"Motheaten" answers lalage. "Sis's is motheaten, mine's not. See the hole!" And thus my query gets buried in the stuff of a tiff apparently on-going for years: which of the girls would "endup with" the "motheaten" tartan.

"Y' c'n hardly see it, lage! It's no big deal."

Dad, lifting out of the chest a massive book w leather covers & pages edged in goldleaf, promises ("for the hundredth time") to have the tartan mended "b'fore *anybody* ends up with it. [then to me] Theyre not always like this, my dears, laly 'n' Lily."

"Akchally the Lily-laly thing really goes: Lily laly pop. [peering around front of me] She's Lily, I'm laly, 'n' he's pop," indicating (w index) Lilith to my left, herself (w middlefinger tap of own breastbone) to my right, and (w hitchhiker thumb) don to her right. "Lily, laly, pop. Dont ferget."

Marching to his desk, large book open, like an overbig choirboy: "Now here's that urquhart tarrrtan you were asking about, Lily. Ya see? Not a bit like stewart of atholl —which is this one here."

"And definitely not like the macraes", notes lalage. "The wild wild macraes 'n' their highland ways", she talk/sings in an under-her-breath brogue, quoting some verse or song.

Lilith: "The crazy macraes, you mean."

"But they had style."

"Her leyda-blood's boiling again", observes don.

"Thanks alot, daaaad", snarls the one called laly.

"Ther'tis. Sixteensixteen. Tis awhile ago."

Lage: "Older 'an you, pop!"

Don. Donald. Donauld looks up from under shaggy brows going blond-to-white. She grins impishly. He looks down again, squinting. "Print'd in middlegaelic. Kin ye read't?" <A mystery t' me.> Shows how our name evolved." His finger runs reverentially over the entries of several handwritten pages. "Starts with gray, here, then changes to macgray... down here... Hmm.

Then over here to macGray, and then, down here, see? The mac is dropped, changes to mc, there. The first of the mcGrays. Then your grandfather angus changes it again... drops the y an' adds an a ...been that way ever since. An' here's me, 'n' there's the two o' ye, last o' the grays ...on *this* side o' the big loc, anyway." Staring for a moment unseeing, don closes the big book, walks it back to the chest, picksup, flashes the pages of another album. The girls appear sidebyside on page after page of formal portraits in "official costume": art- ballet- gymnastics classes, piano recital ε equestrian events, always by twos (in double exposures, by fours) til age11 or so, as if "coupling us for constant comparison were compulsory". (L journal.) And what radiant creatures they were!

"I dont remember this." Lilith has lifted out ε opened what is clearly the oldest album.

"Youve seen it, y' jus dont remember. Grandma lizbeth put it together before she passed on."

Frangible w age, i suggest laminating its pages, which had begun to disintegrate.

"Now i remember. This is, a- greatgrandfather angus! Son of, a-...." yods in the direction of a portrait of "...angus the first" which hangs to our left.

Tartans bible portraits albums save two, are wrapped, put away under a layer of cedarshakes and the lid closed. As Lilith, proud dad, sister shaduad ε me return to the greatrm don says, "Since we're so celtic I'd like ye t' hear one of the most touching songs ever written."

Lilith asks how soon we should leave. When had she decided to go?

I guess, soon. Dont know my way around rohnert park.

"I do!" pipes lage.

"Little lalykins here tries t' worm in on my travels too" smiles don. In the middle (again), i shrug. "Give a listen t' this, nathan." All sit obediently listening to a song i will one day come to love and whose involuntary augury, tonite, makes me shudder as i write. When big jim mcCracken had sobbed the last of "kathleen mavourneen" the sisters left us to "get ready". Don, friendly but (i sense) standoffish, strove to compare our likes&dislikes, which i resist since the task typically finds more division than unity. As he veered toward politics again, i asked about the name maggie. "Now there's a name t' fit an angel, an' a private tragedy ta go with it." Don was nothing if not versed in the music he loved, and in any typical biography the tender tale of teacher/poet george johnson & his student maggie clark would never be sacrificed to a mere problem of too little time.

Lilith

When maud & kathleen (Lily & laly, of course) were ready we said our goodbys. As we walked out i saw, parked to the other side of the javelin, a red car w a yak rack. Where do you yak at?

"I dont. Dad does. <I see.> Doesnt want racks on his lincoln. Too uncool."

"It was part o' the deal she swung to snag the scamp."

"It was that 'r drive a dumb escort 'r opal [bland economycars of the day]."

The javelin here will fit three –if none are joined at the hip– an' the jumpseat denizen must not mind riding perpendicular to the road. Don suggested we take his car. Of course, we mightuv taken lage's scamp too, but it was not "near as classy as nathan-here's speedcoach —'n' b'side, it has a big ol hole in the muffler."

"She blew the thing speeding", said Lilith as we pulled away.

"I only speed when I'm late."

"Which is all the time."

"True. But ontheotherhand, they say my amity is fetching. [quickly appending] This jumpseat aint so bad, nathan!"

Lilith looks oddly sidelong at her. One can spend years learning, and pages mapping, the meanderings of meaning which two people, intimately close, can transmit in the enigmatic stuff of a single fleeting glance. L handed me don's loaner cd one more time ("Dont forget this") as i meandered us back to the y in the road —which turnedout to have a YIELD sign past which that red scamp had whizzed earlier.

"Hey, I honked atchu this mornin. Didja hear?" <I did.> Lage knew a quick way there. "Make a left at the stop sign. Speaking o' joined-at-the-hip. I jus saw this program about these twin thai prostitutes who saved enuf money t' get cut loose. Is that what made you [mayjew: touching my shoulder w tip of index] mention joined at the hip...? Anyway, these two were joined at the thigh since birth —which begs for a terrible pun. But I havent figuredout how t' word it yet."

"Thank goodness. ...The don-mcGrae gene persists."

"Some play on thaiamese twins. Hey [pat-slapping L's shoulder], at least I dont recite the siamese-squeeze one anymore. Ho, this newsflash fer you, nathan. Didja know dad thought you were about thirty? ...Didn he, Sis? But he's pretty caj, our dad. B'side, I reminded him that leyda... that's our dear mother, ya know. She's sort of, well, mental, and is quite the wild one ta put it mildly.... Anyway he chilled when I reminded him leyda was only seventeen when they got lynched. ["Hitched, lage. Hitched."] Hitched, whatever. More like a lynching fer dad. Anyway, get this [producing a quick index w a snap of thumb&middle], only sixteen tsk,tsk,tsss when they started dating and whatever other stuff they were doing" which final tsk she pronounced in parodistic exhale fashion rather than using the actual sucking sound. If Lilith was at all embarrassed by this barrage of banter she didnt show it.

Highschool lovers?

"Nu-uh!", still forward on the edge of her seat behind Lilith. "Daddy was thirty when they met."

"Which sister here was quick to remind him."

"Well, he was getting on your case in case youve fergotten. So I got on him about getting it on with mom ...scuse me: with mother. Anyhoot, dear daddy don mcGrae was a major dom in his day, doncha kid yerself."

"I need t' warn you: lage has no secrets."

Frank 'n' friendly, wasnt it?

"I've been called a firebrand of fetching amity, akchally."

"Fine qualities" adds Lilith in seeming deadly earnest. "She even called our father... What was it you called him? Smarmy?"

"What I said was, skanky. As in: You mustabeen pretty skanky, dad, back in the ol days."

Lilith shivered her shoulders ["Brrr."] which caused words between them. However, the moment i was sure i was in the middle of a claw&bite they ended laffing over something that got by me. In my rearview mirror, giddy w the choppy roadsurface, i could see lage smirking.

"See there?"

Surenuf, after a trek of rural road ("Fergot ta tell ya, this road's twisty as taffy"), a sign indicated FREEWAY. "Killer-coordinated back here we are."

Where does your dad yak at?

"The ocean. Swims in bad weather, yaks when there are rips."

"An' off the point too."

"The rocks there 'r gnarly as hell, with the most greatwhites this side o' australia."

Everyone seemed certain, if don ever died it would definitely be in the ocean.

"Guys hafta challenge Nature, right? It's their job."

I s'pose.

"Ya usta climb smokestacks 'n' tall buildings, Sis says."

I guess. But that was challenging human greed not Nature. ["Right."] Gymnastics is your thing, right? ["Very."] I dont know much about it but it seems t' me y' could break your neck there too with a wrong move.

"*Entre deux feux*" interjects Lilith to herself.

"Aaaand? "

Well, that's challenging Nature, isnt it? Defying gravity as a favorite pastime?

"I stand advised. [re's "poor christy 'n' julissa"] Is he like this all the time?"

"Lage , as you c'n see, is definitely the son daddy always wanted."

Tho i saw no such person she parlayed that into "I am all the sons of my father's house 'n' all the brothers too."

"Theyre reading shakespeare at school."

"Out loud too. I'm viola. I was a shoo-in."

I once knew a viola. Canadyfrench, she was. Stabbed me in the gut when she caught me with cecy. *Voila!* said viola, laffing, withdrawing her dagger. When cecy jumped up 'n' beat the crap outa her, i, laffing 'n' bleeding, leaned over curb-sitting viola and whispered, *Touché!* But i was young'n'foolish backthen.

"Did it leave a scar?" asked lage, leaning in, intensely.

"Lage!" cried Lilith.

"Jus asking, sheesh. An' get this. Our teach says next we're gonna examine fairytales! Yes, that's what I said. [even tho nobody had questioned her] So *I* suggested we start with the *bible*. [i laff. L looks over, grinning.] Fer this, shakespeare 'n' fairytales, I'm wasting a good scholarship?"

I note, Lilith has cosmetically disappeared all but a slite puffiness on her bruised cheek. Mins later we found a gas station. Lage, reaching between us was finger-walking thru my cd case as we pulled in. "It runs in the family," she said, undaunted, as we waited for a pump to clear. "An' grandmother lais [leyda's mother], if ya wanna know, was a regular rahab... eloped with grandfather when she was fifteen! ...But he wasnt nearly as skanky as dad —bein only twennysumthin at the time." We slide up to a service island.

"Hey, at least he doesnt have any whatshisname (the 'mandy' guy?) in here... Right, unbearable manilow" i hear as i slip nozzle into filler neck. Just then a young woman, passing between us & the car ahead, pulls from her bag a mirror, frames for an instant the declining sun as if blinding me for having enjoyed the mere look of her. I set the digits on the gaspump to jumping each other like rabbits as the words "Our family *is* pretty bizotic, huh?" drifted out to me.

I drop back behind the wheel just as lage, still talking, is saying, "O she'll find a ca-reer okay. Emphasis on the 'rear' part. As fer matt", she said contemptuously from my side of her mouth. "He's torn between two girls alright: bev hill 'n' holly wood."

"Lage is our *diseur de bon mots* in case you didnt notice."

As we waited for a break in traffic two blonds in a topless porsche glided up, looked over, smiled, peeled rubber.

"Barf. [moans lage] That was sooo 'fifties."

Except, who were guys then are girls now.

"True."

"Like you know about the 'fifties, lage?"

"Like *he* knows?" —which i took as a major compliment.

Traffic sig before freeway being red, we come alongside porsche. Begin cliche on green. Glitterbags (Lage's term) whine away from the line. Apparently they'd yet to run up against an xke for a sample of "porsche faces life" —in the fastlane. Seeing me wayback however "glitties" glide right two lanes, driver fussing w purse, cd player or something til we're alongside again. Lage, playing the role of "I'm the loxie wielding that ragtop", turns to Lee. "Ho, mandy! Nonaggresso clydesdale approaching on 'r left!" Living on the edge of the slanguage belt, "Lage is veryup on post-yup", says Lee.

After we slide by on an inside track, they punch off again.

"Materialistic bunch."

"But with taste. Here, have a cavity brick. [offers little red rectangles of gum all around] All the girls at Sister's house [read, dorm] crave your wheels bytheway."

It's a way of getting around, that's all.

"Personally i wish they'd stop all the silliness 'n' get down t' business."

They? I figure she's talking about the "girls" at her dorm.

"Automakers."

Which silliness is that?

"All this lusting after Earth-trashing vehicles."

It suddenly hits me: {Is she maybe comparing the man at the wheel with the legend in his books?} Even the conestogas were not Earth-friendly. Lookat the oregon trail? —a century ...no, make that a century 'n' a half... an' the gouge of their passing is still there! We've heard about "learning to walk lightly on the Earth". Well, there's this thing called critical mass. An' civilization has passed it. Even tiptoeing isnt Earth-friendly when there are too many feet. [Sensing she wants to ask how many k's to the liter my car gets:] At home i use a hydrogen-powered vehicle. And my runabout, for the sanctuary, is electric-powered; a hybrid: half tractor, half geep.

"No kidding?"

Yip. Had 'er baylt [built] soon as ah faynished the hayouse. ...Had it fitted with re-geared golfcart motors.

"What'll this thing turn?" asks lage.

Turn is a tac[ometer] term related to speed only indirectly. But i know what you mean. I look over, grin, downshift. I am about to explain why my vehicle performs more like a foodblender than a car when, hand grabs my shifting hand: "No, that's okay! Dont show us! [i shift us back] Her question was purely rhetorical" says the level-headed sister.

"No it wasnt" says lage. "Look. Dinner starts in forty minutes! Ya better step on it, nathan."

"You 'n' your speed. We'll be there in plenty o' time. [quiet moment] You do know your normal driving speed is purest insanity, right? ["At the very least."] I mean, i still dont like it but at least i know your choice to behave in an irrational manner is made with fullknowledge of what youre doing."

"Youre serious, arntchoo? ["At the very least."] And what speed would Sister call sane? [Thirty k or under.] That's ...that's only eighteen miles an hour fer kryssake! My *horse* goes faster than that!"

A hasty speed-check reveals i'm driving at almost thrice that. I ease back.

"Which brings us to the crux o' the matter, thank you. When's the last time you heard of two horses crashing into each other 'n' dying?"

"You see? That right there. That makes no sense at all and yet you believe it. We're talking about people 'n' cars not horses. Hey, come ta think. What yer saying is, nathan here's behaving as irrationally as me! [to me] Hey, you slowed down, you sly dog, didnchoo?"

"You will kindly not refer to nathan as a sly dog? I have known the very slyest of dogs 'n' he is definitely not one. Now let me ask *you* something. Name an animal you think is fast. [Cheetah.] Actually certain birds c'n go way faster but nevermind. And when was the last time you heard of two cheetahs crashing into each other 'n' dying? [Yesterday ...Jus kidding. Yer question's rhetorical, right?] My point is. Even tho it often happens where two or more cheetahs, in the heat of the hunt, approach each other —in places i might add where there are no 'merging traffic' warnings 'r double-yellow lines painted in the grass— at speeds easily sufficient to kill or maim them, speeds often higher than those we use to kill each other; even at *that,* cheetahs *never* have such crashes. Ya know why that is?"

"Lowers voice, leans in close. "Ya know nathan, you dont hafta slowdown jus because o' this interrogation. ...I giveup. Tell us why cheetahs never crash."

"Because cheetahs have been evolutionarily preconditioned to move at such high speeds —biologically high speeds, i should say, not artificially induced high speeds, as with us."

"Kinduv like, we humans could be agile as cheetahs if only we attended Nature's highspeed drivingschool for a few millennia, right?"

I am astonished by repartee Lilith doesnt seem even to notice.

"That's *exactly* what it would take for us to catchup with whole genera of high-speed predators, cats which evolved eventually into the cheetah."

"So youve thought a little about this?"

"Thanks t' riding with you, yes, i know that someone i love is a prime candidate for tragedy. [hardly pausing to breathe] That said, have you ever heard of two or more humans crashing into each other 'n' dying? [Yesterday. An' this time I'm *not* kidding.] Do you know why that is? [I'm slow but I think I've got it, Sis.] Because, to use your metaphor, the human species has not yet been in highspeed drivingschool for a thousand thousand years; and because we have not been evolutionarily trained to move at speeds any higher than the speed at which we can run. And even at *that* slow speed, any distance runner 'll tell you, attention deficit sets in pretty fast."

"Hey, wait just a sec. I've heard o' elephants crashing into trees 'n' dying. An' what about all those animals that go charging offa cliffs?"

"Herd instinct, yes. Fear 'n' flite."

Herd panic. Stampedes. Yes. If i c'n add a little something here... Nature builds very little likelihood for accidents –accidents of motion, anyway– into the creatures she goes to so much trouble to nurture and evolve.

"We should care one-thousandth as much for each other."

"You guys are obviously on the same page. Www-hich, um, leads me ta b'lieve, all this comes from one o' your books, nathan. <No.> C'mon now. <I promise.> You guys 'r tryin a little behavior-modification experiment on me, right?"

<She may be but *i'm* not.> Truth be told, a couple times there i'd considered stopping the car 'n' spanking lage. {I'll bet you did, you sly dog.}

"Let me ask you this. [Lilith still on-topic] If you heard on the news that some animal species suddenly up 'n' started racing around real fast 'n' crashing into each other 'n' dying, how long do you think it would take before some expert 'r other claimed something had made that species sick? An' what if that *same* species showed a desire, generation after generation, ta go faster 'n' faster, kept increasing the speed at which it moved til it reached a point where it could absolutely depend on a huge percentage of deaths 'n' injuries ...among its own kind, mind you... depend on there being millions of socalled accidents every year...?"

Which, statistically viewed, look more'n'more like on-purposes not accidents.

"If you guys really *arent* in collusion, this is a little scary, you *know* that."

"...Thousands of accidents around the world due to speed alone every day of every year? And what if, furthermore, this species seemed to understand exactly what it was doing. What if...."

And what if it even documented this behavior with record-keeping, including accurate predictions of how many thousands of its own species will die an' be maimed on any given day of the year!

"Not counting the skadjillions of innocent creatures it slaughters in this unique state of madness."

"So youre saying we're insane?"

How many hours, lives 'n' billions of dollars a year does a species have to lose to irrational behavior to qualify as insane?

"You guys could be a killer song-'n'-dance team at drivingschool classes, jever think o' that?"

"How long do you think it would take someone, even a speedqueen like you, to call such a species not only reallyreally sick but *unquestionably* insane?"

"Speed *princess*, if ya dont mind" she replied, just when i figured she was thinking of walking the rest of the way. "I expec ta be dead b'fore I turn twennyfive anyway... So yer lefthanded too?"

<Me? Too?>

"Yes, too. Like Sister?"

Why d' ya ask?

"Jus lookin fer stuff you two *dont* have in common. <Hmm.> Daddy usta call us starb'rd 'n' larb'rd, 'member that, Sis? Cause we're prettymuch opposites. <Huh?> *Internally,* that is."

And handedness is an internal thing, right?

"Which just happens t' show *externally*" adds Lee, formally called Larb'rd.

"Some of our organs even are switched."

"Do you mind? God!"

"Well, I didnt mean *all* of them. He knows that."

Lilith to me. "You see now why i try always to steer the conversation?"

I cant help but smile. <I think i've heard o' that>, while in silence i evaluated more closely the idea of their having viseversa viscera.

"Hey, where's your med alert anyway?"

"Havent worn it for years. Havent you heard? Now they xray before they cut."

Unacknowledging, she goes on. "The lefthanded 'gote gets the mirror innards uzh'ly."

Goat?

"As in zygote."

O. What about fingerprints. I've heard....

"External quality. Exactly alike in our case. I could murder someone ferinstance 'n' she'd...."

"...And i'd get blamed."

"Cause that's her luck. ...Ooo. Sorry, didnt mean that." Grabs Lilith's head, kisses nearest temple.

Unless superman witnessed the crime.

"Superman?" repeats Iage twice.

Yeah. The nietzsche-for-kids guy... from the planet krypton?

"Xray vision, sister... Your murder theory?"

Sister stares, then groans, lolling her head. "My whole point waaas [groans again] (I cant b'lieve you said that. Youre like dad. You do lame on purpose, right?) A-ny-way, my whole point waaas: Handedness is jus the *beginning* of our differentness. Ferinstance, she's care, I'm careless. She's duty-bound. I'm duty-free. Then there's: I'm extroverted. She's introverted...."

Maybe she's just quiet, thoughtful —a specular querist 'n' ruminist, like me.

"If that means running deep, I suppose-" chatty tourguide interrupts self w "Sign ahead!" ROHNERT PARK 5 (miles. Miles were still u.s measure backthen). "Bout seven miles t' go" she says, leaning forward between seats, her hair falling against my arm. "The school's on the other side o' town." Scent of cinnamon is breathing not far from my ear.

A dinner/reception was sched'd to precede my talk, held at the santa rosa sheridan, "just a stroll" from the auditorium.

"*You* cant find the sheridan? You, the quintflip princess of santa rosa?" I remember thinking 'quintflip' was teenspeak for smartmouth.

"I know where the auditorium 'n' gymnasium are ...and the la quinta [motel]."

"I'll bet you do."

"Hey, gimme a break. Dad 'n' me stayed there."

Ever hear o' the alvarado street bakery? [Nope.] Their bakedgoods save me when i'm cutoff in bamalachia ...cutoff from organic grains, i mean.

"An' *still* ya cant wait ta get back- hey, that's it up there I think!" Ahead a sign blinked SHERI-something. "See?", briefly lip-flapping her sister. "Kryst, the place is packed! What's the big attraction?" Laffs.

You are a sketch.

I get out, retuck my shirt beside the car, put on tie & jacket, head in. Me to self: {At this rate this should be some evenin.}

Lilith

To our host, a thin man in his late 40s, member of the socio-ecology department, i introduce, on my right, a glowing but silent Lilith <who has just undergone dental surgery> ("Ooh. Poor girl!") and on my left, her sister, lalage. Looking from one to the other, pale skin perfused, w a single cordial quarter-bow he shook their hands. Both wore form-hugging dresses –lage in warm peach; Lee in creamy white– w long sleeves & (a)hems above the knee; both in white pantyhose & bulky knee-length sweaters, one white, one cream.

A dozen or so were seated at our table. I was assured i would not be asked to speak during dinner. "Always an imposition, dont you think? one weary lecturer to another?" he winked, checking his charm-level w my escorts. Seated to my left our host took out, glanced at & pocketed, a piece of paper. Presumably seeing this, leaning around Lilith, lalage wanted to know, did i use cribsheets? —thoughtful suggestion while there was still time to recoup. I wdrew from inside my sportcoat a sheet of paper folded twice down its length, its left third laddered w 8-10 words.

"That's it? That's your notes?" Her quick blueeyes moved to Lee, then back; her mouth (same pouty lowerlip) paused partly open.

I refolded, pocketed the list. Things i dont want t' f'rget ta say t'nite.

Breadsticks long gone, the hungry academics were soon stalking the celery & the visiting amenities. The guy to lage's right, for instance, tried to catch her ear. When this failed he came around, intro'd himself to me closing w, "And who might these young ladies be?"

I longed to answer w <This is duplith ...and *that* is her sister, duplage>, but resisted. Lilith, no social butterfly, meeksmiled ε snuggleddown into her sweater for safekeeping, while the host asked me a question —leaving the guy w no pretext and so to wander back to his seat.

Following the chat w our host i motion to our server who, from a nearby alcove, has been memorizing the sisters for later use. We'll take those drinks now. Feeling responsible for my date's isolation it occurs to me to confess. I should have told you, [touching her hand] i did get your letter. Thank you *very* much. As this seems to make her anxious i switch subjects. <You *do* know that rick ...rick barclay? [she knew who i meant]... tried to call you, right?>

"So *that's* who that was." She deep-exhales, plainly relieved. Had i known the unknown caller had so weighed on her i would have told her at once. For ms gurlich [beth] told her the caller had left no name number or mx, which i knew could not have been the case.

Delphine has sent you a letter with all the details. ...To whatever address you gave them, i guess. An' brian was gonna call you but i didnt wanna giveout your dad's fonenumber without permission. ...Welp, what all the fuss is about, since you obviously havent heard yet: [take swallow of water, smile broadly] GreenEarth wants to produce your cartoon as a teevee series.

Incredulous, she roseup out of her sweater like a hummingbird out of a large floppy blossom. Lips parted ε moving slitely, no words yet emerged. Looking at lage (who by now was asking, "What? What?" of both of us) she allbut squealed, "They want captain greenEarth for a teevee series!"

"Who does?"

"GreenEarth."

"No?"

"Yes!"

"Your cartoon?"

"Yes!"

"Hey, yo! Wow! Waaayda go, grrrl!" Double high5s go off like a happy firework.

Several people turn our way. "Somebody hit the lottery?" While the sisters rose, hugged, squelchedly squealed, hugged again, i had no choice but to share the news w our host. The complete communicator, he passed it on to the rest of the table in fustian gusts of garrulous grammar. Just then server returns w drinks. "Which way to the restrooms?" asks lage, shedding sweater over chairback (for the guy beside her to grope the sleeve of in her absence). As if sharing a treasuremap, server explains. Giving our drinks a quick sampling, we depart.

On our return, presumably because the host was away just then, Lilith took the wrong seat, putting me between the two of them instead of next to our host. But he is not long suffering my abdication and win mins is listing toward lage, appraising her of thisorthat, first resting his right padded shoulder against her left unpadded one, then resting fingertips on her forearm, briefly —all very harmless of course. Straight across from lage ε me sat a professor of genetics ε his wife. His pupils, i note almost immed –bird-intense pinpoints behind small square rimless glasses– operate like little thermometers of phallic heat; the hotter he got, the more constricted they became. He'd been devouring Lilith til we switched seats and the host began fawning over now sweaterless lage —whom he called Lilith for the rest of the evening. The host's occasional touching more&more aroused in the younger man a competitive streak.

"I think we should all toast the young lady's good fortune, what say?" he announced, out of the blue, loudly. "All" raised a glass to lalage, whom, thanx to the host, everyone now believed was Lilith; while lage –amazed, abdicating the compliments w grace ε humor– indicated her Sister was the artistic one not she. "She got the right brain. I got the left." All to no avail.

"How long have you been drawing?" asked the panting fool when the huzzas had subsided. His wife —apparently the only one who could tell the young lady dressed in peach from the one in white— and who'd been watching me watch her husband watch my sheath-decked jills (hi, dylan), tapped his sleeve. "She's not the cartoonist. *She* is." "O, sorry." Turns to Lilith. "To this young lady's talent then!" He is obviously the sort who, once having run out of toasts, is content to drink to drinking itself. (Hi, again, dyl.)

Seeming not to hear him, Lilith bends sideways for her bag, retrieves addressbook. I sense she senses what everyone else there clearly knows: professor raginggenes is styleless sweaty socially bumbling ε predictable.

Seeing the deadend in her direction, and seeing he is the only one still toasting, he returns to the former pretense; that is, following the conversation of the host while tearing away lage's clothing w the claws of his eyes.

Lilith meanwhile puts away book ε bag, pushes her chair back, angling herself toward me, presumably to disenthrall the guy now to *her* right. Thus she sat, one calf crossed behind the other, one knee leapfrogging the other, a contortion comfortable only to the female pelvis. Her dress, tho she tugged at it, in the process of outlining her body rode up her thighs more than she would have liked. Her hands, sidebyside, rested by her knees as if to assure that any shadowy aperture left by the dress's brevity (as she saw it) was covered. This position caused her to lean somewhat forward on her chair, as if she might up&leave at any moment. Lilith was clearly not at ease in lage's natty knits.

If i linger over her appearance that nite it is because it reflects an important facet of her personality: I will sit here 'n' enjoy this if it kills me —a resignation which, of course, defeats enjoyment. And there's yet another reason. It was one of few times i saw her in public dressed in a way one might call provocative. Her profile –pensive, lashes tipped down, lips slitely apart– had the sort of look models slave at and fotographers dream of. A swath of hair fell over one shoulder, obscuring part of her left breast, then disappeared between arm ε waist. Like her skin, her dress had a satiny-soft sheen. Memory adds a tastefully scooped neckline ε sleeves which, gathered at the shoulders, accentuate their squareness. A shadow underscores her breasts and she wears a long string of marble-sized "pearls", their pearly highlites matching precisely the fleshtones sifting thru the mute white of her stockings (pantyhose).

A matronly person in a crinkly gold dress w sequins (which struck me as painful to sit on) who'd been studying us from across the way, smiled approvingly as our dinners were set out. Not everyone there was translucent. Lage squeezed, then pulled on urgently, my tricep, whispering w explicit phrasing, "Dr grope here is trying to ask you something."

Now having my host's attention, i took our three glasses of water (mostly full), set them in front of prof raginggenes' wife. He glanced over but then contd bragging to lage about some paper he'd submitted to some journal some where, having, if i remember correctly, to do w uniovular cloning. I was sure he wanted to pilfer lage's 21stchromosome, rush the thing back to his lab and do private things to it. His wife listened attentively as i addressed her loud enuf for all to hear. <Why dont you dump these icewaters in his lap 'n' cool him down a bit?>

Standard victim of male dominion, she smiled nervously at the suggestion. "I should, shouldnt I?"

You should. Meanwhile our host, mouth ajar, had perhaps his only speechless moment of the eve. The young prof finally grasping his situation —i think he thought at first the big dumb guest speaker was about to bungle a party trick using water ε spoons— it dawned on him (thru the peasoup of his liquor-lubed passion) that darwin's theory of natural selection was about to assert itself *w* him as the classic weaker gene ...in front of students ε colleagues no less! He slumped back in his chair for the first time that eve where he stayed, making one last mistake of glancing at lage who semaphored more than said, "O welp! Win some lose some!": backward snap of wrists, palms forward, head snapped to one side, brows up, eyes rolled, mouth mockingly O-ed.

Me aside to Lee: All the fine instructors in this fine school and we're seated here among the academented degenerati.

"I hope the future of Earth is seated at the *other* tables 'n' not here with us," whispers Lilith.

{Old soul in young body. Wisdom scoffs at age! GreatGaia i'm falling fast!}

Following dinner our host, surrounded by the usual panting dogs ε buttbasters, "prayed" that his formal wingding had not been "sullied for me by mr so'n'so's unfortunate behavior".

Sitting front¢er, opposite calfs dangled, the sisters were nothing short of stunning. I found my gaze inadvertently moving over them thruout the program. Maybe it was the spotlites on me, maybe a lack of lite in the hall, but *w* one sister in half-lite, one in half-shadow, they were totally indistinguishable. When i looked at either one it was as if a biorefringent lapse had pirated my purview; or as if, every time i brought one of them into focus my pupils would spasm, assume the shape of a rhombohedron, promptly delivering the stereoscopic marvel of replication to my brain.

The trip south following the lecture was even more animated than the trip there.

"I wouldna missed it for shannon.

Shannon?

"Fershame, nathan."

"Lage's hero. Shannon miller ...Gymnastics."

"Ya know, some guy was taping you t'nite. [this concerned me since i was under contract for allbut a couple bodily functions] Really small camera. Rankedout on me when I asked fer a copy, the jerk. ...Look like? ...A-whatshisname —the detective in *pink panther*, I'd say."

"Howda ya meet these people 'n' where was I?"

"Using the facilities. ...By the way, I loved the part where ya bashed that heckler. What didja say again? Sumthin about a tax exemption?"

Lilith, countess of continuity, quotes the speaker better than he can quote himself ...and i mean that in earnest. "What he said was: <I'll bet that was your tricky way, sir, of saying you think Earth-worshippers have *just as much right* to tax exemptions as heaven worshippers?>"

"Veh-ry trendy, nathan schock. *That* shut 'im up."

"Actually it didnt. You jus couldnt hear him anymore over all the laffter 'n' applause."

Tho informality was the m.o for my lectures, i remember *that* one as particularly informal. My approach was simple. In the first 5min or less: local-area anecdote, humor, a little structured direction, then humor again; w the hall lites set to turnup when i say, <How do all of *you* feel about that? You know we can get where we're headed sev'ral ways? Would you stress topics x, y, or z? Or maybe you have something better? For ever since mr warren, my sciences instructor in hs, i've held that, fun plus enthusiastic pursuit are the best teaching props. And, on the flip side, that the worst thing that can happen to a student is to have an instructor even slitely bored w her/his subject.

"My favorite was: <We can either riseup 'n' be heard 'r duckdown 'n' be herded.>"

I had long noticed, thought i to myself, how female attention felloff ε chilled whenever a woman accompanied me to my lectures. This q&a session had been particularly standoffish ε brief. When i brought up capt.gE, Lilith became unusually animated. "I want to redraw everything! After i dropped off the album i felt it was a big mistake, like my work was really second-rate 'n' i jus wasnt seeing it." Which opened the way for lage to confess to nursing her own jitters. "The regionals are gonna be burly." In reply to a gymnastics question she said, "Talent 'n' skill are all people see. They have no clue about the struggle behind the scenes".

"Amen, sister."

Ditto here too.

Ready to dilute what alcohol dinner had failed to sponge, we impromptu celebrated Lilith's good fortune by stopping for a frozen yogurt. Ahead in line a highschooler ordered a flavor called "bubblegum". Lage made a "revolting" jackolantern face. "Zit farmer's fantasy" she called it aside. The young man, overhearing, turned our way, revealing a complexion which dotted her observation. Hurt eyes darting from lage to Lee and back again, he opened ε closed his mouth —twice. On a thin upperlip sat discontinuous pinches of reddish hair. Glancing next at me (who had shed coat ε tie on leaving the hall), he turned back to his friends.

"You should apologize" said solicitous diplomette Lilith.

"I never even *saw* him there. All I heard was bubblegum." The logic here was, i think, he'd overhear the explanation of innocence. Once served, the four young men ambled away. Tho the first dropped a bunch of napkins, and tho he saw this, he kept going.

Dropped sumthin, said i. Their seeming leader turned, looked back, looked at me. "Is there a problem?"

Yes. I spoke in a friendly-but-direct manner. As Lilith squatted to pickup the nearest of them, the youth **w** the skin-problem came back. "I'll get those". As he gatheredup what remained, the eyes of his group glommed ε glutted on the sisters, imagining (if facial cues reveal the thoughts which shape them) everything from a group-grope to a dopplegangbanger. When, to deposit them in the trash, red mustachio crosses past us, Iage says, "Hey... Sorry". Her words alone on the page hardly betray an apology, yet: "It's cool", said the young man, head permanently ducked, as he filled for a nanosec his dull gaze w her brite beauty, then, head noticeably higher, caughtup w his friends.

Me, plain vanilla, was made to go while they talked flavors. After ordering i asked the mcsisters what bubblegum (flavor) tasted like.

"Gruesome. Trust me. ...Scuse me", Iage accosted a second server. "Could I get a taster o' bubblegum?"

"Please", adds Lee, totally automatically. Don's answer to an earlier question of mine sings forth as i write: "You c'n tell better which is which with your eyes shut. Lily says "Please", Laly says, "*Now*, stupid!"

As often happens, the pretty face of the server was marred by the plain fact that: Just cleaning her own bdrm was "life being unfair" let alone having to mopup this gooey shit using a rag putrid with bleach. She plopped down the cloth, tookup a tasterspoon, dipped the requested miniscoop, handed it over to Iage, watched her askance w a disapprovingly cocked jaw.

"Thanx. ...Hey, there's no bubblegum here just icecream."

Disenchanted princess snags fresh spoon and, w a not-too-well-disguised exasperation, redips for a more representative sample. Snap. Striking a vein of cold blue&pink gum the spoon breaks. Snap, another. (Snowwhite confronts on-the-job cinderelladom.)

"Hey, that's okay", chirps compassionate Lee. "She changed her mind."

"I jus wanted nathan t' have a taste o' that junk that's all."

Lining the walls as we wait are vulgar commercial prints of witches ε jackolanterns, black cats ε moonlit sheaves. Plastic cornucopae vie w cardboard haunted houses, "Each mass-produced thing doing its part to drag further into the wastebin of public taste the public's already trashed idea of what art is". Lilith, scholarshipping on such stuff, called it "the curse of commArt". Them licking, me spooning, we drifted to an empty table. On a poster of a broom-riding witch, hanging behind now seated Lilith, someone has pasted the face of a famous actor in wicked profile —wild wig askew in a black wind.

"Hey, checkout the witch behind you."

At the next table a lone painted woman cringes, pulls her purse close.

"Double, double toil 'n' trouble" quoth Lilith, long used to lage's effect on the world around her. Closing her eyes, shaking slowly her head, half-smiling, she takes a deep breath, cranes to see better the doctored poster.

"Beetlejuice. A major dom if ever there was one" indicts lage.

Lilith, who'd actually lived daytoday for a couple years a farmore fritening variation on the movie (or so i would learn one day), responded: "At least they didnt paste lydia on the head o' that broom."

"Or poor polly, for that matter" added lage, plumbing to the quick of a crime then much on the public mind. Rightoff i was finding: Lalage interdicted herself into the lives of most who got near, if only by happenstantial projection. As w the baron, controversy followed her like a shadow; life seemed ever questioning notsomuch her buoyant beauty but her engaging method. It was as tho Reality, in constant astonishment, kept trying to reject the events she triggered —yet for some reason chose only to respond ineptly. "Speakin o' witches. Did judithanne ever bring back our good halter?"

"Daddy found it stuffed in the mailbox."

"Now *that there's* one [leans is, whispers this time] *total* witch."

"The best witches are really *good* people."

"Then make that, *bad* witch. Hey whaddaya call witches who live t'gether? I jus made this up but you'll like it.... ["We cave."] Broommates."

Verygood.

"Yes."

"Halloween's soon, isnt it?"

Allhallows eve.

L: "Feast o' the yams."

Isnt that an appalachian festival?

"I guess. But the one i'm re:g is from the caribbean."

"D'ju guys ever have sweetpotata chips? [we hadnt] Yer lucky. An' jus the other day ...Ya wont b'lieve this... I saw sliced, that's what I said, *sliced* peanutbutter! ["I dont get it."] Comes in a package jus like sliced cheese 'r baloney? <Aha.> Very weird."

"Youre jus too cool for our Universe."

"An' yer too cosmic fer mine."

Tho both assessments were made almost unconsciously i ventured: <C'n one be too cosmic for a universe?> But this had apparently been long-settled between them and the naif outrider found himself sketching the following couplet while awaiting readmission to their inner sanctum. {This next could be a civil rule: One cant be cosmic and be cool.}

They switched flavors halfway thru. "We share everything", says lage w a twinkle ε a sideways toss of hair, quickly tunging a pale droplet threatening along a rufous ridge of her concoction. Lilith, pushed back in her chair, looks at lage, then me, then down at her dessert, then defines bubblegum icecream as "It's like packing your teeth with the chemical aftertaste of fake fruit flavors." Choosing to be cold rather than show toomuch thigh, she sits, sweater folded over her knees. This was good since argus-eyed fancy found her flesh, even stockinged, imminent ε urgent.

"Speaking of which...." Makes sudden toothy 'aaargh aw-shit' face, looks over both shoulders, but the woman has already left. "Speaking of gum (as I was saying). She 'n' me usta be in gum commercials on tv."

Really?

"Yeah. 'Twinamint twinamint twinamint gum.' [she sang]. That was us."

"When we were kids", amends Lee.

"Did them for four years. Not alota people know, they hafta film ya for days jus t' get thirty secs o' tube-quality film? That's how bad they are."

"Nathan used t' be a model."

"Cool. Then he knows. I'll play them for ya when we get back."

"I think it may be a little late for that."

"Kryst, it's almost midnite! Hafta get t' bed. Big meet tomorra, ya know."

I now realize, Lilith could only have been blackingout a dark memory at this point: her stepfather's oft-repeated threat to go after "the other girl in those commercials" if she [Lilith] didnt "cooperate". I would one day discover *w* dismay, it was the lamb-sweet duo in those very tv ads which eventually sent him, in his finest sheep's clothing, to seduce their mother.

To stay awake on the way home after dropping them off, i put on the disc don loaned me. One lovely song had the lines,

> *I've never seen you wake at dawn and brush a dream from your eyes,*
> *I've never seen you part your lips to take a kiss by surprise.*

5

This next item should be put off no longer. The following note was found during my workout today. [My keen-eyed proofreader, there are just too many mistakes to even attempt sic-ing them.]

> **Dear Nathon Heres *that picture.* Listen *I* know your *innocent.* I'm *innocent* to if you can *believe that. I* was *sent* up for wasting my *boyfriend but it* was *the* cops who did *it but they wouldnt* admit *it* cause *they had no right to* kill *him. I only* got 10 years cause *they couldnt prove it and besides the* juge *and the other* loyer felt sorry for me. *Write back.* Love your friend Rosa.**

By all means. Imagine here a really squiggly spermtailed R in rosa. And scribbled along one side: "Sorry this is late. Mitzy a guard watches evry move I make. I culdnt hide this last time like I promise. Sorry." A little hard-of-eye & tuff-of-mouth maybe, but otherwise, rosa (in polaroid-sheened skin & cute training togs) is looking awfully good to this particular body-contact-sport-starved inmate. And, o, yes. The reader needs to know. When i left you in part 3 to go write parts 10, 9 & 8 respectively, it was late april. So now outside my grimy little window it is october. And inside, already the snowOwl of winter has its icy talons sunk deep in the thick skin of this place. Which reminds me. Ratslug is "heading south for a little r 'n' r". This facility should therefore soon show a sharp upswing in mental health. Bon voyeur, doktor mengele, slithering anus of the civilized world. May you blunder into a job offer you cant refuse.

6

I was years findingout: I came close to losing Lilith before we ever got started. The letter she left at my apt that day, or so she wrote in her journal, was "my final gesture". She had "bared [her] soul as much as pride & privacy will permit". How i come to be quoting her journals ε diaries –no small *or* painless happenstance– will just have to wait for now.

As to "that night of rekindled weirdness" (when i found her on el granada beach): The "last thing" she wanted was my help. "Tried & tried to reach beth (who i knew went to the game) & Sister (who would have sent a friend to get me if i could have reached her)". After that her choices "came down to three: call the police, stop a passing car, or call Nathan". She had let her "intuition (my sometimes scary intuition) call the shots" because "Hitchhiking is begging for more trouble & cops are often not a whole lot better". While "Nathan, whom i've probably too long imagined is my best friend, is the most compassionate mammal landward of all the seven seas". Let those who have called me "the world's foremost misanthrope", and, "traitor to [my] nation and [my] species" put that in their drinking water and assimilate it.

As to L imagining me as her best friend. In her capt.gE cartoon series there are parts where the capt rescues maggie (equivalent of superman's lois lane) from the clutches of titanus, arch-enemy of Gaia. A favorite frame shows maggie ε the capt in total silhouette walking together, holding hands, a lone star silvering above a darkening arc of sunset-fired horizon.

Under the mistletoe of dreams, a star —as though to join us at some distant hill....

7

On sa eve i had a speaking engagement at cal state in sacramento while nearby, at uc/davis, Lilith ε don attended lage's regional tournament (in which she placed first in three of four events). When Lilith ε me talked about her attending lage's meet that day (instead of my lecture) we discovered something. The sa before the nite i first saw Lilith at berkeley, the locations just given were exactly reversed. I spoke at uc/davis while Lilith ε don attended a prelim tournament of lage's at cal state/sacramento! Most curious reversal.

Su i returned to dillon bch. The horses were grazing near the front fence when i drove up. Don rcv'd me well enuf. <Thanks for the al martino. I enjoyed it. Here, this is for you. [i'd put some long-out-of-print music on disc]

Conductors argeo quadri 'n' hermann scherchen [tap case], *b'fore* the advent of the homogenized orchestra 'n' its dinnermusic conductors [employing transitions so syrupy they double as digestive enzymes.] [Well, thank you very much.] Good ol westmonster technology—late 'fifties! Quadri's "bacchanale" 'n' danse macbre' sound like they were recorded yesterday. An' scherchen's 'carnival in pesshh [pest]' (the mono version, mind you) and 'la gazza ladra' are little short of ravishing. Lemme know what you think.> This chat is important for what follows shortly.

On the drive back to berkeley L was barely conversant. She intimated "problems at home", thanking me (again) for not "going on" in response to don's prompts, "the way mos' people woulduv". I mention this because, on arriving home (after dropping L at her dorm) i found a mx from don. I called him at once. "I know youre a man o' the world 'n' that I can get down to cases. We've a problem here on the homefront that needs immediate attention. While I realize it's a family matter, truth is, our family's embarrassingly short on facts at this time. In all honesty, what Lily's saying happened ta her that nite, and what seems to have happened to her, just dont addup. An' her sister doesnt know a whole lot more than I do. What I need to know is, if *you* know anything –anything at all– that could help me piece together what happened to our little Lily that nite?"

At the time i had no idea how guilt-driven don was when it came to Lilith, due to a burgeoning sense of having abandoned her when he divorced her mother. Little by little, learning to be more attentive, don was slowly surmising the darker side of her youth, even tho Lilith did her best to hide the trials ε traumas of those years —not that she was secretive or dishonest but because, mostofall, she herself was hiding from those years. Before don went any further i warned him how little i knew. And for me to sit here 'n' merely speculate about what happened would be to betray not only Lilith's trust but yours as well. Whatever happened that nite happened outside my knowledge. For Lilith has yet to tell me anything.

"But you *do* know more than youre saying. This I know for a fact... Well, to start with, she said it's you that picked her up 'n' took her to the hospital, of which youve told me nothing."

That's true. But i thought those things were obvious given her injuries and treatment. Calmly ε w respect i said, But i cannot sit here in good conscience 'n' second-guess your relationship with your daughter. I dont know what she told you or what she didnt tell you. Neither should i sit here 'n' second-guess why you seem to doubt what she has told you, or not told you. As a medic some years ago i was trained to mind my own business, specially with "domestics" as they are called —or risk being dragged into court, hurt, or even killed. For those are the hazards of domestic situations. Now if Lilith were a child, or mentally compromised, i would of course feel very dif'rently.

"I dont know if you pay attention to such things but...when I met you I extended my hand and invited you into my home no questions asked." (I did not divulge what i sensed was otherwise on this point.) "What I'm asking is privileged information, true, but a privilege to which I'm legally entitled. For if I'm not mistaken, in california Lilith is in my care until she reaches eighteen. Which I suppose you thought she was? ...Well, at any rate, until then, it is *she,* and the people she knows, who need to solicit *my* approval, and not the other way around."

I thought we talked about this —that what is legal 'n' what is ethical are often worlds apart...? Excuse me, but i let *you* finish... To explain what i mean another way: With or without your consent i, for my part, will honor your privacy about our talk here, t'day, in the same way i'm honoring Lilith's privacy with regard to you at this moment. That is to say, if someone tomorrow, including Lilith, should question your credibility, I will tell them: To my knowledge don is an honorable person 'n' a gentleman. He has never lied to me. And, based on this, i must assume he has not lied to you either.

"I c'n see, there's no point in our continuing this conversation. You, a bachelor without children, obviously dont understand what it's like to worry over the welfare 'n' safe-keeping of anyone b'side yourself." I was about to respond, I hope i'm a little more caring than that, but the line to papa don's hacienda went dialtone.

I said nothing of his call to Lilith who, tho brite&early on the job, was clearly still downcast. Both of us had much work to catchup on and so agreed, again, to limit our contact to lunch-only thru the week. On wedn she met w rick, brian, myself & another board member concerning a contract for the proposed tv series. This is when L first met emil, who suggested it would be best to "holdfire on any contracts" til after an animation studio had been selected and could be made part of the deal.

She ε me celebrated at lunch w a "majorly chubborian" dessert as she called it: goat-cream cheesecake. I noticed a certain trait that day: the more upbeat her mood the more her talk resembled her sister's slanguage. The headline of a newspaper abandoned on the seat of our booth that day also sticks in my mind: Twins Take All. <I thought the sister of an ex-minnesotan might appreciate this.>

Th eve i showedup for "friends of the main", who were holding a fundraiser for the new frisco library. Here i met at last robin williams. "Jus finished a documentary on the grimm (makes face) brothers —all about the creating of fairy tales [makes elbowwings w limp wrists, flaps them] as you probly guessed. They plan to call it 'a grimm tale' 'r something, but I have a better title: A hickory-dickory-doc...umentary" —quickest mind i've ever come across. During the proceedings he offered gE his services (which generosity i passed on to rick next morn). "I'm just getting environmentally friendly myself. Still not at the kissing stage, you understand... an' certainly not bopping Mothernature on a regular basis (whoa!) like you. You go, nathan!" He assumed we'd be seeing each other "stsp (same time, same place, eh?)" fr nite. But who turnedout to be a mutual acquaintance ("Pj? Of course. Me 'n' the professor 'av been doublebilled at clubs a couple times") would be taking my place. So i could attend a workshop, that day i'd made arrangements for the baron (indebted to me for a loan he'd defaulted on) to take over my wkend speaking sched.

As to that wkend, except for a su nite date for the theater, i fully expected to spend it away from Lilith. For a friend, al chung, daichi master from china (who made co his home, half a mtn away from jon windstar), had invited me to a workshop he was conducting at gefalen institute/big sur. I viewed this wklong separation from Lilith w mixed feelings: my desire for her v. my need for freedom. Because desire narrows one's horizons, for me it is claustrophobic. And all this is not even to mention the intensity of that desire —which i found, frankly, scary. But for a reason long forgotten, Lilith's psych class was cancelled. When at lunch on fr i described al's "meditation in motion" classes, in tandem w the gorgeous surroundings of big sur (adding to this, my accommodations incl'd a cabin w 2bdrms), her interest was peaked ...as peaked as someone as reticent ε burdened as Lilith was at the time can get.

8

Before leaving town i gassedup the javelin. This stop rather forced a subject i suspected had been weighing on her. "How are cars like this on fuel?" I sensed she had a pollution-index in mind.

I'll tell ya a secret. This is the first time i've gassedup since we went to sonoma. [Your kidding?] Actually, no. Jav here is not your standard twelve-cylinder primadonna xke gobbling gas like mechar. Remember him? —hg well's giant robot which, out of revenge for constructing him without a soul, decimated mankind! (Turnedout she'd used the name mechak(!) for a character in capt.gE "who personifies the many dangers of our narrow mechanistic worldview".)

"C'n i be honest? <Please.> I probably shouldnt say this... [Go ahead. No, really. Speak your mind, please.] Welp... Fact is, i never figured you t' drive a car like this."

Jeremy Shores

Well, fact is, thanx t' this car i've been called everything from quitter t' hypocrite. Yet jav here uses less gas 'n' causes less pollution than the vehicles most greens i know are driving.

"But you jus said it has twelve cylinders."

Actually it's total liters-of-combustion that count but that's another story. A couple years back i needed a car for when i'm out here. At about that time jav here fell my way. T' make a long story short, i've loved the xke since i was this kid, see, and this one was a steal. Knowing i couldnt drive a gasguzzler (10k is not only bad mileage, it's Planetarily criminal), i had it fitted with a honda ultralow-emissions compact [engine], which is, truth be told, less polluting than the engine in your scamp.

This left her as much amazed as relieved. I pulled over, opened the 'hood' for her. "The whole front goes up! Trendy."

Trendy? I guess. Certainly for 1963. What's so funny?

"It's looks lost in there... like... well... <Yes?> ...looks like a musicbox motor! Do ya hafta wind it up?"

First it was too big. Now it's too small?

"No. Definitely, no. I'm sorry. It's jus that... I'm just sooo relieved. You have no idea how this car was bothering me. ...Boy, will sis be disappointed.

An' all the girls at your house.

"Yes. Them too."

It does look a little embarrassed in there, doesnt it? I put down the hood (hood+fenders, really). Now you know why i didnt speed to the hospital that nite. Needless t' say [patting 'her' flank], javelin here cant turn fourhundred k anymore ...not without busting the musicbox.

With a stop for supper at cannery row (monterey), it was after 10 by the time we moved bags from car to cabin. In that al's class met at dawn, and in that we expected a morrow of much activity —say little of, the closer we got to being alone for the nite the more quiet ε withdrawn she grew— both of us sensed we'd be beddingdown in separate rms. We will later agree: Hey, anybody can make love for the first time in a cozy private cabin in marvelous surroundings. We demanded something better! But in fact, that nite was a kind of temptation/torture for me. Lilith however later defined our challenge differently: hoped i'd prove to be an honorable housemate.

Lilith

If you could save the Planet by givingup the habits & gadgets which glut your life, would you? If by trading in your car for a bicycle you could give to your children the cleaner Planet of your own childhood, would you? I rest my case. The audience, from which the jury will be chosen, is prejudiced against me before the trial even begins.

Re my w.coast vehicle: Even as a kid, petrol ε coal-driven machines struck me as filthy inventions, not the modern marvels most people (still!) consider them. The clouds of oily carbon my father's airplanes belched on startup, the hiccups of noise ε fire which shot from the stubs of their exhausts as the engines warmedup into rhythm, couldnt have struck me as more primitive tech had his passengers painted themselves britely ε danced around the whupping props. The quiet ε clean vehicles i so admired in my scifi reading i found precursored in reallife by the elec motors of electrified trolleys ε railways then rising to prominence in the public trans corridors of the eastern seaboard. The many Earth-friendly vehicles ε powersources overlong on the drawingboards have also been overlong suppressed by the gas- coal- petrol- ε nuclear-driven industries, til it has come to this: choking ourselves and our Planet to death til we find ourselves, like ravenous vultures, squabbling beneath humankind's bargaining tables for the last bitter pockets of black gold.

Lilith

Gefalen lies win a much larger state preserve neighboring an even larger national preserve. Populous from spring to autumn, by late oct it's fairly quiet. Known for its "one world" seminars ɛ thinktank, its programs are of a newage sort, incl'g things such as rightbrain art, yoga, meditation, organic farming ɛ foodprep, ecology ɛ world-disarmament seminars and the like.

One cannot drive inside gefalen except to park. Save for bicycles, horseriding ɛ elec trams, everyone is on foot. Ecowood overwalks, winding thru trees ɛ wildflower gardens, act as main thorofares so as not to bisect the ecological continuity of the soil. Woodchip paths serve lesser traveled areas. All of which makes for tranquil surroundings.

The importance of going from a good nite's sleep to daiji in silence was understood by all, as, in dim lite, our small group met and then climbed, by way of an overwalk ɛ stairs, to a wide grassed space. Tho the sky glowed grayly in the e, the sun would be awhile yet surmounting the sierras.

"Feel this force we call life inside you, exulting in your limbs" sang al's thin clear voice. "Move your limbs like they are the paintbrushes of God, like they are the very Dao expressing itself in the air around you. Notice the dew in the grass, the mist in the trees, all trembling, all dancing, as the lances of the sun tilt above the mountain waving banners of promise. Try to penetrate the center of your being as they penetrate the sky before you. You will know you have found it when you feel the power whisp'ring inside you, tingling up your spine ...dancing you." Tho Lilith had never danced daiji before, and tho she was strange to these mtns, she thought it all felt "very familiar somehow". It was that morn, despite the efforts of her olivegreen skorts, that i first saw (and tried my best not to study) the marvel of her nutmeg-brown thighs.

Afterward, in the cafeteria, al asked us to join him. At table he said "For a first-timer, she dances with very free spirit." This caused her to flush a little and look down at her plate. "No, that's hokay" added al. The Dao, tho also very shy, has infinite strength."

How about me? [trying to lessen her barrassment] How did i dance?

"O, same as ever. Like a tree. A *big* tree. [laffs] The way the sequoia dances." Al's was not civil laffter but a bubbling over of his Self. "No, really. Trees do dance, you know? No thing is denied the universal dance."

Lilith did not take easily to men but she liked al almost at once. "I look forward to seeing you dance." She re:d the solo performance he would give after class that eve.

"It is the spirit of Creation that dances. I am only its student."

<And ya sure getup early t' do it.>

"The rooster sleep very late here at gefalen. They pay me to come and wake him up. [laffs] But i tell small lie —to hide truth. Fact is, I rise early because there is much to learn."

After breakfast we stopped by the commissary; left there clumping across the porch like novice cowboys in our rented boots.

"I sound like a little dutch girl."

Me too. She looked over; we laffed.

"Beats slaughtering another cow jus so we c'n go riding."

Or deer ...Miss DoeEyes.

DoeEyes glance up, not understanding —then try to ignore the rouge that retouches her cheeks.

After changing clothes we head for the stables, a bit of a hike from the cabin. I'd been to gefalen a few times and knew my way around some. Trees along the path, as it gentled downhill, were filled w birds still giddy w the gift of dawn —who are Nature's aubade.

"How do you come t' know al?"

Met him a few years ago at windstar's annual fete in snowmass. Al holds his own festival right after jon's, at both of which i've spoken. You could say al owes me a dance or two since i never cash his checks. I told of a merging of philosophies between al & me. <He knows i see it as fleshly wise of him to let his spiritual artform double as a lekking dance, a dance attractive mostly to persons of his own liking. "The same might be said of the 'dance of ideas' in

your books", he argued. To which i responded, How true ...and of the public behavior of most lifeforms. Agreeing with that he answered (i want to get this exactly right). "If we manage, for a moment, to make ourselves attractive to our Creator –apply the creator of your choice– must we not also be attractive, in that moment, to the favorite creations of that Creator?" <It is this statement of al's which, in fact, gave me hope of one day meeting the likes of you.> "How's that?" she ventured, more to deflect i think the compliment than to protract her discomfort at being its object. <By way of someone like you one day finding the "dance" of my life's work attractive to her.> Tho i dont think she fully understood all this on the first go-round (who would?), for she asked me to writeout al's amazing claim next day.

"Mable's stable" was attended by a blond (mable herself?) whom i took to be female. Her eyes, hazel/gentle, seemed at odds w the matte sheen of her sinewy tomboy demeanor, pocked cheeks & tuff-looking mouth.

How's the white mare?

"*Enid's*... a darling." Barely looking at me she placed a "horses are people too" emphasis on the creature's name. Quadruphilists are often misanthropists and often w good reason. After checking our surcingles on the sly (so as not to further offend mable), we surmounted our sur mounts & got on our way.

As to riding w Lee? Where to begin? Erotic, yes. My friend denise norris claims "It's no accident horseriding is taken up by females near puberty and given up after dating begins. This is not signs and symbols. [says norris] It's statistics." Other authorities agree. Personally i i.d'd as much w Lilith's saddle as w her horse, as i watched –no, studied– that tite-jeaned open-legged bonnie baggage bounding up&down up&down so close, so veryvery close, to that hard erect & chrome-helmeted horn, and wondered of the day she would ride thus a roan of mine named testoster.

The air was still & brisk w the scents & crispnesses of autumn. Among memories of our rides together only a couple were not done in the highest of spirits. For, the moment Lilith climbed on a horse she was transformed by a fulbodied sense of Wildness & freedom —freer somehow to think & say what she pleased. Soon we were riding in full sunlite, across the grassed slopes along the sur while a red-tailed hawk overhead screamed about something. Doves, w a colored band across their tails, roseup & rattled toward treeline. [These were probably not doves but band-tailed pigeons. —Ed.] To our right, kingfishers flitted & looped briefly above the bluffline, then dove & disappeared toward the surf below. "Still too early for whales, huh?" We agreed to get her some whale-proximity early in the spring. I had a standing offer i could use any time.

A trail wound us thru tanoak & torrepine, took us up to a sunny breezy ridge w little visible but treetops, hazy sky & distant sea. Furtheron, after halfanhour of rolling grassland seavista & brilliant sunlite, on a different trail back down the north face of the ridge, in a hollow, we passed into a stalwart stand of coastals (the smaller of the great sequoias).

"How d' ya tell the difference?"

Good question. If we werent so near the ocean i wouldnt know for sure.

"Steinbeck called them 'ambassadors from another time'."

I'd heard them called that but never with an authorial ascription. <Thanks for that.>

As we rode into the stand, up ahead, three black-tailed deer darted off the trail. Speaking softly. <Feels like home... Yes, i do [miss it].> Redwood sorrel & fern surrounded the feet of towering trunks as the four of us ("Horses are people too") passed by. With a sigh of matted spaciousness, a musical window opens, then another, then another, til playing tenderly in the wayback of consciousness i hear the adagio from enesco's romanian poem sifting down around us in the muted sunlite. Stop, turn in saddle, gaze out into tree-haze whose size alone makes one whisper. <This is one o' those times i c'n feel the eyes of amerinds, long-departed folks who came 'n' went around here never seeing a white man, watching, watching, watching us from out there among the trees ...watching me grapple for the *real* reason i'm alive... Stupid, huh?>

April Rouss

"Right there. [what? I look behind me. She too is whispering] That. [huh?] No. What you jus said, i mean... *That's* the thing i first noticed about you... after we saw a video of you in high school, crouched down by the edge o' the water, 'the windlite tousling your hair, the waterlite flecking your blue eyes with silver'. [moment of creaking leather, soft-clumping hoofs] I wrote a poem about you that day. I'm sorry. I dont mean to embarrass you. Anyway, it's spooky how you c'n jus swing open a window in the sidewall of reality without warning the way you do... 'n' wonderful too, of course. Not bad-spooky. Good-spooky... It's the way my mind works too. I c'n jus never show it; give it t' people the way you do." More creaking clumping hazy silences press in less fearfully around us.

But you *do* give that *something*. Your whole *self* gives it. ...Trust me, i know.

More muted sounds & lite creep in & around. "I love this day. Every day should be like t'day. <Amen.> ...Reminds me o' muir woods... Daddy 'n' sis took me there when i first arrived here."

(I wonder tonite if muir & enesco's lives ever overlapped the way their forests overlap now in my mind. It, well ...frankly, yes... terrifies me, to think i may die, *will* die, never meet those romanian Wilds enesco so passionately loved, or the old-growth europe which massenet mahler sibelius dvořák or smetana so loved. Talk about musical windows —sudden village in the forest, or along the riverbank, impromptu folk dancing, beyond the cowbelled countryside a sudden hurdygurdy— those rare deliteful surprises along the sidewalls of musical reality. Must they slam forever shut one day soon for me? or will a window to a new Reality swing open, o wondrous wide!)

Even before we emerged from that matté forest dimness, the gradual britening caused by the meadow/sea-expanse ahead —plus the psychic tension tickled awake by slow-walking for so long amongst such a host of historical ghosts— sent up my spine the foreshadowing of a damngood gallop-to-come ....such as occurs w subtle surprise & pleasure when the strings in berlioz' "vehmic tribunal" introduce, o cleverly, the liberating gallop just ahead, dotted along its way to breakneck stride w *fantastique*like string-popping pizzicato! But who anymore understands such talk? (You still out there, angela h?)

Out of 'nowhere' it occurs to me: {Losing this woman would be like never hearing music again!} We moseyed out of forest-shade, back out into full sunlite, the raucous sound of raven calls arching into the near-distance. Once back in grassland we took off at a gallop. {What a rush to ride alongside this beauty —on a horse, a tortoise, on a mere hunch, anything! This feeling i'm feeling, whatever it is, is an all-Natural hallucinogen!} It occurred to me that just the heat of my *thoughts* could ignite the surrounding grass & trees.

Recurrent hawk –er, hawks– wheeled in the currents above the ocean cliffs; a covey of quail, underhoof –flushed accidently from the grass w a startling whap ɛ a whir– hit the air like a puff of tan talc, which puff then spectrally scooted ɛ scattered back into the grass from which we'd roused it. A repeat uprising caused us to slow to a walk.

Ever think about the sound of a galloping horse?

"I'm not sure what you mean... But i can imitate one." Out of the side of her mouth she made a rapid clicking sound –five or six cycles of a phonic imitation of a gallop– which struck me as a precious juvenile harkback for this introspective creature. (How machismo we are who are shocked when some delicate thing raises two fingertips to lips, lets loose w an ear-piercing "man's" whistle.)

That was very good.

"I used t' do it much better." I assumed she meant, before her stitches.

Did you hear what you did? [i imitate the rhythm of a gallop] See anything strange about that rhythm? [thoughtful "No"] I usta listen t' westerns when i was this kid, see, and it always bothered me that a galloping horse, a *four*-footed animal, sounded *three*-footed: ta-ta-tum, ta-ta-tum, ta-ta-tum? One-two-three, one-two-three, one-two-three? You see? Why is one leg making no sound?

"Never thought about that." Goes instantly preoccupied.

In his wllm tell ballet music rossini highlites this 1-2-3/1-2-3 in the most fullout gallop he ever wrote (incl'g the slower one in his famed overture), easily as exhilarating as the gallop in ludwig's seventh if not as whipped 'n' spurred. A few mins later, following a second gallop —which takes us past a meadow of wildflowers and high onto a grassy promontory— she says, "Youre riding way better t'day".

Gelding's are more understanding i think. B'side, we're not sinking to our knees in seaside hops.

Sheep ɛ goats graze on our left. Then the pacific, wide ɛ blue, is suddenly all around! She rides up beside me grinning broadly. <What?> "You know, you have... you have... a nice butt?" In shock: <A-, hokay.> A few mins later we're side-by-side, the flanks of our horses touching, rubbing, boots ɛ stirrups creaking ε clacking together. I reach for her hand —first time we ever rode that way.

When we got back it was lunchtime, "Thank goodness!". Eastern veg dishes, new to us: korean soup, thai this, chinese that. Post-lunch was dedicated to Daoist artforms. When al saw her abilities w charcoal ε paint it was all over for him. "Your friend Lilith is very beautiful …inside as well as out. And very talented. Her art has power, power inside. So as your friend i find it compulsory to tell you: She makes strong feelings inside the man fortunate enuf to see her. I am guessing you are romantically involved?"

<Yes. [reflecting] But not entirely. I know you know what i mean. We are alike when it comes to commitment: You ε Lilith are free agents however, free to do as you like. I have no right of interference.> When i repeated this conversation to L a moment later, she flushed ε fell quiet. Tho not easily, i did so unquestioningly, then moved my sorry painting to another part of the room in case the feelings between them needed space to flower. Lacking my signal, al would have kept his distance. While lust wants possession, respect insists on giving freedom. So taken was L by al's gentleness honesty ε artistry [dance as well as painting], i confess i was worried, tho to lose her to an ideal situated somewhere between olden myth ε modern mithra was not the worst way to crash&burn i could think of.

As the blue pacific swallowed a huge oriental sun we ended our instructional day on a grassy knoll. Our classes had expanded due to the addition of lovers who had slept-in for the dawn session. Al made his last subtle foray that eve, to which i contd to give space. He took special care now&again to guide her limbs thru the phases of expression, offering this hint or that. But when the opportunity arose, Lilith used it to place herself beside me ε an admiring neighbor, a nice enuf guy who thought he was nijinsky incarnate and that we could maybe enjoy a private *pas de deux* one day.

After supper (pad thai, her; veg curry, me) we decided on a stroll. It had turned so warm we dressed in shorts shirts* ε sandals; bathingsuits beneath, just in case (*classy matching yukatas embroidered w ***the living Dao***, a gift from al).

Living Dao Foundation

The paths of gefalen are lined w dim low-lying lites which give to the place after dark a hilly sense of fairytale topography. Despite the moist warm trades, the leaves on the walkway were still crisp ε crunched underfoot as we headed down SEA TRAIL. Not far along i stopped us. Smell that? Spicy scent of ca laurel. "I smelled that in muir woods." I thought for the longest time that scent was redwood sorrel. "Well, it *rhymes* with sorrel ...sorta." Hmm, yes. Yet most people would say it rhymes perfectly. This put us talking poetry.

The path banked steeply left and descended –by way of a spiral stair, which however gaveup at one rotation– to a short tunnel passing beneath a ridge of rock. As we dropped below the level of the tree branches up ahead, a liquescent arc of ocean came into view —an ashen-silver sheen discernable only on the hump of the horizon, w the nearer ocean still a void, for the moon had yet to 'climb the sierras'. A large owl, allbut unseen, commanded an overhanging limb, moved only its eyes as we passed beneath.

She talked of loving sylvia plath, wrote poems herself "sometimes", which i asked to see but which she said was "stuff you wouldnt like. Stuff i write for just my eyes". She hoped i understood.

The sur is mostly sheer cliffface above rocky shoreline w patches of sand. Ocean highway, attempting to stay close to the sea, often succeeds w breathtaking consequences. However at big sur it veers uncharacteristically inland, in doing so leaps between two promontories via a gracefully designed span. This detour affords an unbisected swatch of mtn ε sur for the institute's grounds and for the Wilderness areas to the s. Along our way across this swatch –sea ahead, sea of trees behind– one passes an occasional MEDITATION STATION: flat-topped hammocks of "The softest grass i've ever felt!" We sat on our towels (the grass already dew-dampened out there); she w calfs crossed, arms wrapped around her knees, me in a leaned-back quasi-lotus, gazing at the sky. Orion's arm ε bow were just then jutting over the coastal range.

I c'n see only one Planet. Astarte reveled in her s.westerly ether while most of the eastern sky was obscured by forested hill-rise.

"Y' mean, two ...two planets, doncha?"

I think on that. <No. I mean one ...i think. ...Venus ...Over there?>

Gently, but w a whap/point accuracy that never failed to stun me, she said, "But what about this one? <This one?> Yeah. The planet we're sitting on?", pointing w bent index straight down.

Ouch.

Strong scent of sea. We rose, strolled out onto the sur where al had danced so wonderfully, a spot which gave, the closer one got to its edge, a sense of being in the open basket of an airborne balloon; breeze, stronger; air, damper. We stood at a rail, dimpled w the droplets of a dual wetness: dew settling, mist rising from a rock-pounding surf below, its sound fuller the more one leaned out. I wondered how her hair, unbound by thong or beret, was so little bothered by the breeze —except in the lowest quarter of its length.

{God, how she reminds me of juanita right now.}

The stairs to the beach, like all the paths, were lit by low-lying lamps. About a third of the way down, a deck area, w showers ε loungechairs, had been added since my last visit. <It's not unusual to find people here at midnite or later in summer ...sometimes even in the buff. Nobody seems ta mind.>

"That's not mentioned in the brochures" volunteered my companion, grinning.

A natural hotsprings —issuing from the mouth of a bronze-cast pontus set into the rocky face above the deck— warms ε freshens three (non-chlorinated) spas by way of three sluices. Shedding towels yukatas shorts ε sandals, we showered like hygienic poltroons before slipping into the farthest spa. Then, leaning back ε soaking splendidly, we gazed up.

"The cliff's blocking half the sky." Indeed, the proximity of the sur face [do not connect sur ε face, proofreader] cut the skyview (e to w) by half.

Which makes for what's called a late horizon in stargazing.

"The nite sky ...for me... is more for contemplation than study."

I agree ...completely.

"Best windowshopping on Earth."

I like that. ...And the Wildest of all Wilderness.

"And *i* like that."

The azure ripple of the spa lites ε the low glow of the deck-lanterns detracted not at all from the view overhead.

Let us bathe in this crystalline lite!

We spoke of cass (cassiopeia). "It's an 'm' t' me."

Which stands for? [A-, Mother? SkyMother.] I like that.

"And you?" voice dipping ε rising.

A-, 'w' ...definitely a w. [Standing for?] A-, woman. Goethe's eternal feminine perhaps... which –like the polestar, right there– leads men... by the hand, let us say. Or, a- maybe a w again ...for wonder ...the wonder that never sets in me while i sit wideeyed thru the too-short nite of existence. [*Nota bene*, reader!]

"That's terribly poetic."

How lucky, we mortals. We're surrounded by it ...poetry, i mean. Above, below [looked over at her, took her hand under the water] ...and beside.

"The letter w strikes me [she said, after the tiniest toss of her head, as if deflecting too late my compliment] strikes me as linked female symbols [v] which automatically produce a male potential [^] between them. And if you overlap them even slitely [w] they create a [third] female potential as well. <Suppressing the male potency in the process.> Of course it is the [gender] opposite with the male and his *inverted* w. <As in ʍan.> And *wo*ʍan. <Yes. And that too> ...I'll bet you know all the constellations?"

I used to know alot o' them, but no more.

"How come?"

Once i realized there are few less profound proofs of man's hopeless subjectivity i lost interest. And as for willy shakes saying the stars are constant.... [Willy who?] Shakespeare? [O.] Nite to nite the milkyway....

"Wait, are you talking about *romeo 'n' juliet?* Cause that only mentions an 'inconstant moon', not stars ...if i'm not mistaken."

The way you said that— did you play juliet?

"Just in workshop."

Lucky instructor!

"It was a woman."

No matter.

Consternated, she lifts her knees, higher, closer, and w a finger worries back&forth the sheen of their supple wetness.

No, the constant stars i'm alluding to are in one of his sonnets... i have no idea which. My point being, change is ubiquitous. Even the stars are not constant. Tho typically too small to detect with the naked eye, nite to nite the milkyway there, forinstance, changes. [its trillion twinklings arched splendidly overhead]

Now comes an aspect of Lilith that can only be fairly described as enchanting. "Which means: One's imagination cant wade across the same milkyway twice." Still worrying that sheen, she tipped the words my way.

I just stared at her mouth in profile: prissy little purl of upper lip, petulant pout of lower.

She looked over. "What?"

I leaned in, looked in her eyes, kissed her —gently to firmly to gently again. Tho her mouth was accepting (and such lips, o!), i sensed, a moment longer would have been too long. I pulled away, looked in her eyes, brushed that mouth once more w my lips, lay back, praying i'd not revealed even a fraction of the scope of my desire.

"This place is neat" she said after a min or so. "I'm glad we came."

The starry dome advanced w cosmolariumlike theatricality as we settled more&more into a frame of internal stillness that rendered our sense of Earthspin almost fantastic.

You raised your little finger when al asked if any of us meditated.

"Cause it comes on by chance mostly ...like sometimes when i'm drawing, or puzzling over something ...like now i could zoom off if i jus let go ...i dont think i've ever seen the stars move this fast. It's almost like their rushing thru the nite t'get somewhere special."

<A near horizon will do that.> I re:d the surbrow opaquing half our skyview.

Restless surfsounds below. "You'll laff but i swear i c'n feel us being whirled into the future ...whether we're ready 'r not."

And prithee which way is the future?

Just follow the signs to greed. Ya cant miss 'em.

"What a great name for a book: Which way, the future?"

And a good test of imaginative ability.

"I mean, with everything in the Cosmos spinning 'n' turning, who but a Creator could know the answer t' that?"

L: {{And I always say two heads are better than one ta figur it out.}}

[NS notes in his MS: "Emil (or other copy editor), so the reader will know it is Lilith and not myself who's {{thinking}}, it is important that her thoughts (recorded in her diary of the time) be set in double brackets. Thank you."]

An intelligence existing near the edge of the Universe would have a Cosmic sense of direction.

"Yeah. Outward in *all* directions. Not a whole lot more than we know right now. [her conceptual ability dazzled me] Maybe they'll drop us a postcard and let us know which way to the future."

Me being no cinéaste she had to give clues. <Sorry. but you *do* know, puns like that are a ticklable offense, right?>

"Ugh, look who's talking."

If this moment were less perfect i would tickle you til you apologized. *Postcards from the edge* of the Universe? how dare you.

"But *youre* allowed t' say, ticklable offense? I think not. Fair is fair."

There follows a quiet-smiling, then introspective, stretch.

≈Nature owns that circumference which dwarfs every other circumstance.≈

"It's spooky tho. <What?> The Universe going about it's gigantic business in total silence all around us here ...much of that business unfathomable and *all* of it unstoppable. <Wow. ...And all of it so impersonal too.> But i dont think, blindly. It's all taking place with extremest wisdom it seems. [silent moment of Universal motion/change] But the part that gets me is, no matter what the future holds ...no matter *what*... it's coming anyway!"

<As we speak.>

"Even if it's the end of the whole Universe, it's coming...."

{The [Universe] may glide diaphanous to death....}

"Cause that's the destination which Creation ...all of Creation we know of, anyway... has been assigned."

{Nor all thy piety nor wit shall [cancel] a word of it.}

Youre right. Spooky ...Very.

We slipped down into the cozy warmth. Soon her head came to rest against my arm, which i slipped around her back so that her head now rested on my chest. A moment later she did something i interpreted as sexual but which, in later talks, proved not to be. Underwater, the heel of her hand had come to rest on my abdomen. Fine. But then her fingertips began lightly, twirlingly, to toy w the slight sampling of hair present above my waistband. She doubted this happened as i recount it now, yet the reader may be certain, at the time i was conscious of her every nuance of movement! Gently, dreamily, her pinky allbut grazed a couple times a swollen arc in the drowsy dragon's great neck, which creature was soon smoking in its cave, apparently unknown to the sleepy princess, altho her head was tilted in that direction ...and a moment later she had driftedoff. As heartbeat returned to idle a meteor darted out of the ne. Then another. In this narrow-minded prison library i have no means of affirming what memory believes was a weak phase of an orionid shower.

Warm swirling water, surfsounds, startrails. Palpating fingers take up again their tiny motions, cease. That i could gather, her eyes stayed closed. For my part, like the nose of a snoopy snake, my thumb was hooked into the top edge of her swimsuit bottoms. My other hand at rest on the wetsilk of her thigh, amazingly, i too nodded off. I dont think we slept long for, as we driedoff, taurus alone had leapt the sur.

Once on the beach we headed s. "Look out! You almost stepped on it!"

Starfish. Female eyes are better in dim lite. You guys have the cones, we have the rods —or do i have that backwards? Wanted to add: That's how you knew it was me but i didnt know it was you, the nite i found you on the beach ...beside a similar sea. But i said nothing.

"I wonder if it's alive?"

Wait. Before you pick it up, which way's it pointing?

"Huh? Pointing? A-, five ways, actually."

Sometimes you c'n spot a bilateralism. [we squat] Like that. See this space?

"Then it's pointing, a- into the water!"

Well, then, that's the way we're supposed to go.

"Swimming? But what if it's pointing where *it* wants ta go?"

We faced each other across the starfish. The sheen of her flexed thighs was terribly distracting. I rotated it 90°. Dial-a-direction. It says we're supposed t' go *that* way.

She picked it up. "It's pretty fresh ...feel."

Feels like one o' those rubberfingers you sort papers with.

"Like warts on a witch's nose."

Should we?

"Uhuh."

I waded in, winged it, gently, as far out as i could, to where the surf was risingup out of smooth blackness.

"Lage 'n' me usta rescue starfish."

[maggie] befriended a stranded star....

Did you ever read oren liseley's *the star thrower?* ...You'd like it. We walk. Adopted him as my mentor when i was learning to write, back when i was striving for a liseleyesque turn of thought, an annie dillard way with a word.... Apparently not ...til i confessed it to him when we met years later.

"See? You were wrong. Sometimes stars do 'come out' at nite." This was in response to my claim back at the spas, <Stars dont come out at nite. Theyre out all the time>. O Lilith, that you were here to correct me now ...and tomorrow too ...and til the last of the stars has *brennschlüssed*.

Every 20-30paces there was another to throw. We soon passed a seaward-jutting massif, the tide approaching its face. Past that point the stranded stars stopped, and far out on the horizon venus was just beginning to drag her plumes in the sea.

The current on this side is sweeping them back out.

The sand was now packed hard.

"Wanna run?" she asked, trotting backwards as if to dare me. Half-a-k later we began seeing stranded starfish again, becoming more frequent as we approached a second promontory. "Should we climb it, swim around 'r head back? Looks challenging."

<That it does. And sharp of rock too> for my libido was making other plans.

We decide to rescue stars instead.

"I think the ocean's regurgitating them."

A regular starshower by hightide maybe.

"Most are pointing away from the water."

And star-dials pointed to morn.

That one for castor [toss], this one for pollux [toss]. How does a starfish devour a mollusk?

"That was terribly ogden-nashish ya know? Anyhoot, how does it?"

Give me your hand. First it attaches its tentacles (make a fist) like this. I splay my fingers as if on the shell of a clam. Then, with steady pressure it squeezes, slowly slowly, til soon the lips of the mollusk begin to part, more 'n' more revealing soft vulnerable inner depths. Kinduv exciting, eh?

That shy concerned look again: Is he serious or is he...? Better to say nothing or change the subject. "Here. You throw this one. ...Yours go way farther than mine."

But you have waybetter form ...and are waymore fun ta watch. You say farther, i say further... What rhymes with further? ["Hmm. Tuff one."] I'm about to suggest <Bad pronunciation of *the sorrows of young werther*? >....

"Oooo look! A cripple. Its tentacle is crushed. <It'll be okay.> I know. Daddy taught us alot about the sea.... I know what. I'll pick em up, you wing em. ...Hey, look over there! ...You see?" The cave she spotted had a large mouth, *w* tidepools everywhere. "Look, they have stars in them!" Reflections of stars not starfish, as seen from inside the mouth, where she soon stood.

I c'n see nothing, Lee.

"It's like a tomb in here.... By the sea, the sounding sea."

Whadaya say we do this t'morrow?

"Dont tell me youre scared?"

Of breaking my neck? Actually, yes. I can see nothing, Lilith McGrae. I shuffled along like a drunken spelunker. <Oof! *And,* its slip'ry as a greased snake in here!

"Hullo?" Hullo, came the quick dull echo.

You'll ...oops. You'll a-, ...pardon me for turning back but my mother ...damn, almost ate rock that time. Takes my hand from behind ...*your hands within my hands are deeds* ...My mother, for all her faults, did manage not ta give birth to a cripple and i dont wanna spoil that. We dont grow new appendages like starfish ya know. [here she jumped past me. "It's easier going back. C'mon."] Thy rods 'n' thy cones, they comfort me. Thy scotopic vision preparest the way before me in this ineluctable darkness. [i composed in petty panic as i picked my way along behind her] Surely good miss murphy will lead me thru all the *nachte* of my life, and, if not, i keep one hand at the level of my eyes! It's the little stuff like ooof this that always shit gets ta me ...with any double meaning there subconsciously intended, i think.

(I would be remiss if i failed to note, the month & day on which i am presently writing (oct 31st, nite of all nites of the year!) is only one number removed from the day i am writing about (oct 30th). This turnsout, on learned inspection, to be more peculiar than if the dates actually coincided.)

Back outside (phew) we sat. <Back home, behind the grotto falls, there is a cave which keeps pools of water year-round. And water seeping from cracks in the exposed stone face during cold spells sometimes freezes long enuf to form splendid icicles... No, the falls itself never totally freezes, consequently much of the moss on the rocky face there never dies. Overwintering birds c'n find a live worm under its green mat even in deepest winter. Why am i telling you this? [The pools... they reminded you.] O yes. The pools.... Look, each one has trapped the pitch 'n' quicksilver of its own separate universe. [breeze wrinkles each surface into a generalized glow of diffuse starlite. When it ceases, the pools go crystalline again] Creation is narcissus at the pool. The Universe reflects its wonders in everything; every particle is a lookingglass in which Creation studies itself, as if it plans one day to improve on perfection.

"Youre the only one i've ever heard call it perfect."

If the Universe contains all that there is, which it does by default....

"'...It must be perfect if it contains all that there is. For there is nothing to compare it to that isnt imaginary, that isnt artificial. And all of that *too* it obviously contains.' *The ungreening of tomorrow*, chapter three ...i think."

Lilith would write in her diary: "It was that night that i fell in love —really in love." I say diary and not journal because she had stopped making regular entries by then. And later in the same entry: "I knew by the time i was 14, Nathan was the only sort of man (beside Daddy) i could ever love. But <u>that</u> nathan was public not actual. So when i finally met him i was not ready for what i found. I got cold feet. <u>Very</u> cold feet. 'What have i done? There's way more to this than i expected. Just the way he looks at me! What if he's really not as kind as i think he is?' And so i kept turning & running."

An absence of that Wild frite (which i sensed was always pooled darkly just below the surface in Lilith; a sense that she, like a sable hare or silver unicorn, might break ε run at any moment) seeming out of nowhere loomed like a peaceful moon above the mojave as we sat talking. That anyone who knew me could read me as fearsome never occurred to me! Only later did i realize, it took my showing fear that nite, even if only over a thing like nite-blindness, for her to feel free to approach w her nurturing essence. "I'm curious about stuff too. [we strolled back onto the beach] But I'm not impatient for knowledge. I suppose that's dumb."

Not really. But i am —tho not for knowledge anymore. For wisdom. I want to know the law that feels free to connect, right thru every particle of me, the tinkle of these shells at my feet with the twinkle of those stars out there; the law that synchronizes the insolent noise of this surf with the indolent silence out there between galaxies. I want to know... well, honestly... everything.

She seemed about to reply but, instead, shot a fleeting barely connecting shy glance my way, a wideeyed upward brief meeting of our eyes the blank purity of which one sees only in newborns! Imagine here being struck w a frite of falling so intense one feels kicked in the gut by a sudden hollowness!

All that can stare, all that can stun....

Swallowing my sophic hairball, i agreed we should carry as many starfish as we could to the stretch where they werent washing in. "We're going that way anyway". Balancing whole armfuls, we headed back. As we walked she asked, "Have you always been impatient to learn?"

Always been very curious. But impatient? Hmm. No. I think impatience grew with the realization of my mortality. Frinstance, if i knew i'd live a long time ...say a thousand years or more... i could be more patient ...patient as a tree, maybe, or as those cliffs... But life's jus too short for all i know there is to learn. That's my problem. [little did i know how short] And so, intellectually, i'm as restless as this sea.

{{Or as *a willow in a windstorm.}}* After pondering this she looked over. <What?> "Are these guys making you itch?"

As we stood there, she handing me a star, me winging it out over the waves (*sobre las olas*), someone mentioned love. And so offhandedly did she follow it w a "fiona 'n' tommy" anecdote, i at first took them to be friends of hers. While i loved the *brigadoon* story, i'd long forgotten it's character's names."Their love was so unique it sorta melted a hole in the mists of time ...so legend has it.... But we dont b'lieve in time do we?"

For me it's not the time on the face o' the clock that's real... At which point she interjected: "...What's real is the changes the clock's mechanism goes thru to give us the abstract display on its face —changes which amount to no more than a display of the ever-advancing Now, which change alone can cause."

<You say that like you doubt it.>

"Not one bit."

I ask her to picture the start of all this [sweep of hand, scan of eyes]; picture the whitehot EggOfCreation b'fore the Beginning —and somewhere, way inside that 'egg', are the contents 'n' plans for this coolblue Earth were standing on ...all of it, plus everything there is —bajillions of galaxies, skadjillions of stars, and all the energy 'n' space they require ...all of it, EVERYTHING (her diary said i held out my arms here like stokowski at the end of *fantasia*). All this was obviously fully encoded by the Artist of the Infinite Nite before –BEFORE– SHe exploded it all into being! Say nothing of His imagining, implanting, way inside Her creation somewhere, the keys t' constructing you... to constructing me...! And then, best of all, His masterstroke: you with me here, *t'nite!* (Subjective, huh, yet it's a plain fact.) All these things are not acts of time but of brilliant arrangement, the ceaseless rearrangement of objects in space, or what we, oversimply, call change... the accumulation of which has placed us and our World where we are at this point in (not time but in) change —magnificent imponderable 'n' inexorable change!

{{Got it fig'red out fer myself.}}

I'll concede to <the ever-advancing Now of change> but *not* to "time". No, not to our mad leap to "time". B'lief in "time" 'n' "evil" are crutches for denial. To all of which soliloquizing only the sea dared comment ...while the Universe contd to rearrange itself as we walked, if a bit more selfconsciously.

And when she moves, and when she walks with me, paradise....

"How come you never wrote about that? —the time thing?"

I did. Or- rather say, i am. I write a page every now'n'then... a sort of ongoing rebuttal, i guess you could say, to the popular fixation people have with ...no, make that, the fetish our society has for... the concept of time. Which fetish got a really big boost from al einstein's mythomathematical fourth dimension, time —which al himself said was but a human invention for trying to come to grips with the awesome complexity of change. And still albert's "time" grew into that exotic blather of steven whatshisname... hawking, right. Thanks. Nice fellow, i'm sure, but with an overthetop sense of his own einsteinness ...yet very much lacking al's powerful commonsense that i can detect.

{{Common sense may tell ya....}}

Out at sea, near the horizon, the tiaras of two large ships passed each other. A distant horn blast –deep resonant salute– reached shore as they traded places; a duplicate horn answering a few secs later, as if someone, nodding off in a bridge, had to rouse himself to sound it. This ships-in-the-nite thing steered our talk back to chance/fate. I dont recollect how it came up but another of the musicals Lilith had taken part in in hs was mentioned. At first i guessed, wrongly, *kismet.* And then, because she kept re:g some guy named liliom (whom i surmised was the show's director), i soon lost the thread of sense. "I dont forgive, but I do understand, why he was so mean to julie —an' later, even to his own daughter!"

He slapped his daughter? [Who?] The director.

"Director? What director? ...*Liliom,* nathan, is the name of *carousel* in its original play form.

Gotcha... In that case, i'll say, personally, if ever *i* had a daughter...

{{Pink 'n' white as peaches 'n' cream is she.}}

...i'd make sure she knew where julie jordan went wrong —bad wrong... There's only one rule, kiddo (or so i'd say in *my* soliloquy): Make sure the kiss you want most wants you more than you want it —or at least make him believe it's so. Cause any other approach to romance will end in heartbreak.

{{Common sense may tell ya....}} "I c'n see youve thought about this." *{{But what's the use o' won'drin...?}}*

And this breakup here with nikki only made it clearer. [You loved her?] No. An' that's precisely my point. Make sure the kiss you want wants you more than you want it. But i'm telling trade secrets i see....

More stars had washed in while we were gone. "What if the ocean's harvesting them on purpose." She picked and i tossed again. And what if theyre beaching because of something humans have done to the ocean. "True." And when we'd finished she said, "I need ta rinseoff", and ran into the water. When i followed she splashed me, laffing, "Here, lemme help you rinseoff". Then, running backwards out of the surf, "C'mon. I'll race ya back!"

The haze of starlite was just then being perfused w a briter paler haze. That *mojave moon,* already above the sierras, would soon appear above the coastal range. This combined glow was reflected on the stretch of wet sand that lay between us, as, up ahead, her legs whirled in a lightfooted stride. She yelled something back to me and, suddenly, no warning, priscilla was running ahead of me in the flaxen lite of a lost summer day. I believe this trick of memory was triggered by the sonic makeup of that challenge, imprinted as it was w the hint of a certain shriek; a deadly innate thing; a sound which females from burma to bama ε back dont need to practice til they get it right: the mysteries of the sexual unknown; the dark&brite faculties, the shadowy yet blinding skills branded on our instincts. Months later she explained how my <warning to a future daughter> had set her running.

{{Commonsense may tell ya that the endin' will be sad, an' now's the time t' break 'n' run away....}}

On reaching them, instead of mounting the stairs she veered back toward the water. This detour allowed me to regain some of the distance she'd put between us.

The original old man of the sea, nereus, is often pictured crowned with seaweed, holding a trident, reclining on waves and surrounded by 50 nymphs, all daughters —one of whom was thetis, ordered by the gods to wait for peleus the argonaut on the seashore. Peleus, nascent nympholept, fell under her spell on sight and began the chase. When at last he caught her he was surprised at her strength, her quickness, her ductility of movement. It is said, while he held her wrists, thetis went thru many transformations: nymph to tree, to eagle, to tiger, to lion, to wind, to fire, to water, and finally, to a squid! This last is no accident of the tale i think since cephalopods are not only masters of wriggle-free tactics, they are masters of transformation ɛ disappearance!

Short of polevaulting on my passion, this love-stricken lept might not have caught her except that she came to an outcropping of rock against which the tide had risen. She slowed, water swirling around her legs: dim figure in phosphorescent froth. Glancing back, seeing me near, she decided to attempt it. <Lilith! No! Dont!> Game still on, she rejects the warning. At the seawardmost point of the promontory, a wave lifted her, allbut slammed her on the rocks. Sobered, the flite-intoxicated nymph dove for deeper water —else the next wave would surely have banged her about. Out so far and unable to porpoise any longer (leap forward, dive, leap forward, dive again; a thing she did so beautifully when playing in surf), her escape was allbut stalled. Finally finding her feet as the swell wdrew, she cleared the point and headed shoreward, and toward the next set of stairs.

Taller than she and so able to porpoise the entire distance, i caughtup w her in water past her knees, tackled her. Laffing ɛ out of breath, she twisted onto her back, hissing, "O no ...ugh... you dont!" as the wash ran out around us. She then, "Ugh" again, to keep me back, churned her feet in a rapid pedaling motion on my chest ɛ stomach. I grabbed her ankles just as a fresh onslaught of waves collapsed on us, buried ɛ rolled us. Using the wave's thrust i landed on my feet. Thinking her half-drowned i hoisted her up: landlubber rescues mermaid, what a joke. I held her wrists; she twisted ɛ squirmed. {I am wrestling an epileptic squid!} She brakes free, swings about. Wash of hair, full of sand ɛ foam, flails stingingly across face ɛ chest. I grab handful. She turns back, shoves me. "No fair! That's cheating!" O? She turns to run as an incoming wave knocks me from behind. I use its thrust to lunge, grab an arm ᴡ one hand, back of her neck ᴡ the other, whirl her around. {This wasnt in libido's script but it will do just fine.} Suddenly facetoface, impulsively, i pull her in and kiss her. As if by magic all contortions cease and she answers the kiss ᴡ a brief passion which startles me... so much so she is able to shove me hard backward and bolt away again.

Now *that's* what's called cheating! Centaurus gallops after, longer legs allowing me to hop over the wash running strongly back to sea. Peleus takes thetis down again ᴡ a body tackle on wet sand. A long kiss confuses resistance ɛ passion. Pull, snap. As the runout recedes and the moon, peeking over, surmounts the sur "like a dancing girl / No, like a drunkard's last half dollar", we see the nymph lying on the sand, near-naked as venus in a garment of foam.

I dont suppose, in this civil age of kill ɛ tell, that a few words of kiss ɛ tell will shock any of you gathered tonite around this memoirist's cell. Let's just say, had a child witnessed this scene (for in a sense, two were watching) she may have been fritened by what ensued: parts of bathingsuit flung up the beach, facing each other like drenched gulls, while nearer the water the lovers tangle. Suddenly the nymph's foam neglige is swept away, as if nereus were a stagehand who, simply by yanking some hidden wire, could cause a beachgoer's clothes to fall away. In the fresh moonlite her skin glistens under me like licked caramel.

...as I hold you fast and bend above you....

The passage of almost four years has hardly dimmed the silken resilient feel of her sleek taut body trying to wriggle free of my giant's hands ɛ kisses; the mixed silk ɛ grit of her wet seaside thighs against my cheeks. I have but to raise my eyebrows to glimpse the dark swath of long hair fanned in the shape of a seahorse above her head —which tosses from sidetoside, her features distorting as if in exquisite pain, eyes wide ᴡ fear one moment, shut tite (as if to trap sensation) at the next. Memory believes tonite: feeling ɛ fear tangled fur inside her like copulating sabertooths.

Et je tremble délicieusement.... —gustave charpentier

Her undinal belly arched moonward in reluctant-yet-lovely greed (even as the sea arched skyward toward lunar urgings). All that has since come between has hardly dimmed my surprise when her fresh brookwater taste suddenly sang thru the seasalt on my lips! Winds of dastardly deprivation ε loneliness demist the lens of memory. Like a groveling wildebeest soon i am kneeling above her. My motives exposed to the gawking stars, i find myself lowering onto her, moaning into the seaweed of her hair, the seashells of her ears. Her strong fingers are full of me now, trying to contain, to guide, the groping plundering monstrosity w only one thing on its mind —well, maybe *two* things. Her sexual memories were treacherous, i know that now. She was like a trapeze artist who, badly hurt in a fall as a child, fears to retry the old heights. Yet, w an urgency unlike me, i pull her hands away, reach under her knees so that she is tipped onto her shoulders; then grapple for, put in a vice, her wrists.

> What had been till then gamelike now turned serious. Yet on reflection, wasn't that what i really wanted? Wasn't it only another of Nature's ways of proving desire? And hadn't Nathan said, and hadn't my silence at his saying so seemed like assent? "Make sure the kiss you want wants you more than you want it"? Meanwhile my world was being turned upside down ...literally! He hoisted me like a rag doll: sky was where sea should be; the stars, all around his long wet mane, were all ajumble. Taurus could've been Orion for all i could tell, and the wash of milky moonlight was growing bright enough that it put his features, straight above me, in deep shadow. Was he grinning? Was he angry? I couldn't tell. Should i fight with all my being? Or just let myself fall fall fall to where i really wished yet feared so to go?

The fire in my loins had smoked out —from a northern steppe, from some paleolithic cave somewhere in the caucasus of my chromosomes— the Planet's first human lover ...and as his stooped form stopped, glanced down w woeful eyes at the hugeness of himself, the most desirable maidens tittered somewhere in the pulsing darkness, scurried off to hide themselves, while the plot-adept stars sniggered in the nite.

She winces, cries out (i confess it, more than once!): "No, nathan. No!" The mirror trough of a wave heaping to my left, wind-wrinkled in the moonlite just before it collapsed. "I found myself moment-to-moment vacillating between artemisian resignation & pasiphaën passion." (diary again) This vacillation she interpreted as a form of "deprivation hysteria. I think all women without a skilled partner, and all girls too shy to locate, muchless sync, their bauble & its secret ridges, cannot help but endup with deprivation hysteria." Men, she wrote, rarely suffered from it because "as Reesy says, 'Even a one-handed simpleton can figureout how to operate a penis' ".

If the imagined child ran off at this point, later to relate all she saw, we would think the worst. And it would not be the last time i was convicted on circumstantial evidence. But truth is (in a rather bare-faced analogy), the kodiak, now fullgrown, could no longer squeeze into the den of his youth, and w winter fast approaching had not the time to modify the entrance. For by then the distant summer-thunder of falling surf, its hiss as it swept rapidly toward us over coarse sand ε shell, had begun to blur sound, to muffle sight. And w the sling of the verynext wave, the gulls are swept out to sea and the starry froth is scattered like so many confused fireflies....

Tortured by a corbature i'd never known, the self-restraint for which i've been both prized ε cursed, suddenly left me. Never, since juanita, since...well... Unable to push into the mind-melting goal, as she handled me (female firefiter furiously pulling in hose) i arched backward, rose up like black fume. Lifted on the crest of an inchoate impetus, a levitation as old as life, i howled like a dying animal, the silver stake of a fritened child buried in my chest! (The alert reader sees the nobility in my behavior; the dirty-minded have only their own scabs to tease-off and sample.) The milky spill of a high-reaching wave scatters out to sea the lite&shadow of a full-risen moon, scatters moonlite like the pages of an erotic art folio. I collapse beside her in utter beastly repentance. Tho our bodies are still hot w sensation a shivering sets in –first her then me– a reaction unequaled since juanita! Soon the wealth of her hair, sticky w seaspume, laves over me, and her small face, already hinting drowsiness from the intenseness of our *ivresse*, is outlined above me; her eyes, large as planets, look down; lashes pulsing like wings, surround a swoon of tears; her fingers twine my hair, face coming close; her hot breath stirs me (again. O god!) as her lips, forming a maternal pout ("There, now"), kiss my forehead, my eyes, my mouth, and whisper "Sssh. It's not your fault.... Sssh. It's me. It's me".

Images flood in waves tonite; i cannot stop them. Most i reject. I wish to bottle only a few: how to show here the insistent throb of that sea, its fingers reaching, its fecund froth occasionally drenching us; how to give the feel of cascades of wet sand-clogged hair laving face ε chest; occasional scent of highsierra autumn wafting down the steep sur; cinnabar highlites of her shining skin mingling in memory w her cinnamon scent; taste ɛ grit of sand in my mouth; the blazing albedo of her unblemished sclera scintillating against the silver-haired nite; tactilics: her torso tossing under my torquing tung; gauzy screen of moon&stars, all of it unfolded by mythic handmaidens across the sweeping interior of Nature's bedrm, so the lovers might be led to think they are alone in the Universe.

Lilith

Concluding this beach scene i want to make clear, i did not suffer from some latent longing for coital consummation by the seaside. As any honest lifeguard will tell you, sex on the beach is much overrated –the stuff of bad movies, bad books, bad sitcoms ɛ bad mixed drinks– when it more resembles making love to a spindle of sandpaper, grit-side in for one, grit-side out for the other. Then there's this other thing. If i knew for sure juanita was dead, and that she had died before Lilith was conceived, i might be persuaded to reevaluate reincarnation —highly ɛ empirically modified, to be sure. For, if not juanita's facility w language, Lilith certainly had her poet's soul. But why must i be all the time questioning the recombinational genius of Nature?

A bloodred meteor sank in the sea
    when ed got lenore and i got my Lee!

Writing in her diary about this nite, Lilith's emphasis is lunar.

The moon, fully exposed overhead, flashes
    like a lily pad in a stream of stars—
    bright steppingstone from the milkyway
    onto the endangered banks of Motherearth.
O moon, threading the flesh of Earthly things
    with the motions & destiny of the stars!

Despite the man-in-the-moon of shakespeare ɛ others, the sun, which gives the moon its lite, is male in Lilith's poetry; and the moon, which comes alive to that lite, is female. As for me, i go w sam butler, who in his *hudibras* wants to know who first viewed the moon as male.

Lilith

Back at the cabin we took showers (No, you first... No, you.), moped our way thru one pointless task or another simply to putoff bedtime. Half of us, while overjoyed at having come so close to, ugh, sexual consummation, was also face-to-face w the half-empty glass: Why had we failed? Add this emotional short-circuiting to a strenuous & very long day, well.... Dressed in robes (her, chunky white terry; me, dark blue velvet-appt'd flannel), we sank onto the couch.

Following an introspective quiet we began a rondeau of apologies: me for my <beastly behavior>, she for "my wussy behavior". It was a moment of ridiculous –nay, ludicrous– mutual passification, each participant fearing the entry into the relationship of some unforeseen damage. Slouched sidebyside, she went first. She just had to make me understand "at least a little of what's going on with me.... Things've happened... in the past... like i tried to tell you. But i dont think ...i mean, i hope... they havent scared me for life. I guess what i'm tryin t' say is, while i'm scared o' being intimate ...an' acting like a little jerk because of it... my body thinks it's not scared one bit. [i pulled her next to me] So how can i let *you* take the blame when all these things are going on with me?"

Temples touching, i watched her hands twine my fingers on her lap. For my part i confess to being a slut's wetdream 'n' a virgin's nitemare! I was born the opposite of who i am —who i am ideally, i mean. Well, maybe not born that way; but certainly i grew that way. I evoked for her my own incredulity when, in my teens, hormones shifted my body into gorilla-gear so to speak. It seemed every time i checked i was bigger than the time before.... Do you pluck your eyebrows? (We were badly in need of a lighter topic.)

"Huh? No, why?"

Theyre so perfectly shaped. I mean, not a hair out of place.

"Hurts toomuch. I'm chicken t' pluck." I dont know where they came from... these spontaneous witticisms. Something in the way she was wired. She was unconsciously (as opposed to rationally) comedic, i think.

She X'ed rather than +'ed her legs –back of one knee resting against front of the other– as compared to a crossing where the outside of one calf rests on the knee of the other. (A couple decades ago i might have chauvined, <crossed her legs like a female>, let it go at that.) When she did so the hem of her robe slid open. Tho she caught & stopped it, like a tan dolphin, her knee, and a goodly bit of thigh, surfaced mischievously thru the froth of terrycloth. I espied a small whitish scar which ran obliquely across the distal shimmer of that knee (right patella). With a curious index i traced it. Fall from a bike? [nods] A trike? Scooter? Skates? Kneel on broken glass one summer at the beach? "Cant remember." It hardly seemed a forgettable wound. Introspective pose: part smile, part pout, mouth pursed, head down/eyes up, swiping shy glances as i put my questions. Enter here long deep sweet yet carnal spate of kisses... hardly interrupted by my picking her up, carrying her to the nearest bdrm.

After a quick detour to the bath i found her foldedup under her robe, hair, calfs ε white-socked feet only protruding. A wedge of lite shafting across the floor from the bath, scrambled up the bed (as if to get to her first) then (seeing me close behind) leapt to a far wall like an albino squirrelmonkey. Combined w the dim lite from the grtrm, the bdrm was softly lit. The masked robber, unable to tell if the victim were naked or not, stepped quietly to the foot of the bed. Kneeling there, he gently slid ε rotated the body so that when it reached bed's edge it was on its back ("Nathan! What on Earth...!"), its legs to either side of him, robe bunched at her hips, where she held it tite-shut.

Lilith's form, in retrovision, naked or clothed, always implies more of art than sex to me. Yet in person it was quite another story. There is a david otlingham collection, *the light-sculpted body,* which features in b&w film, dancers gymnasts aerobics afficionados ε bodybuilders; most of them young adults, all female. While i'd probably not send her packing, i'd prefer that the sculpted ballerina, the chiseled gymnast, the cutup bodybuilder, came to my bed after a couple weeks wout training. Give me an impressionistic cushion of adipose tissue over raw muscle ε veins any day. In fact, this is probably why i often find myself preferring the muscular definition of figureskaters over ballerinas. The musculature of ice skaters is less highly defined due to the environment in which they train. Cold ladles on extra millimeters of adipose flesh: Nature's body-stocking. Now, put that same ballerina gymnast or aerobicist on a bed in front of me; wash the texture of her flesh w the lite of a cezanne mist, a gauzy renoir glow, and you have my predicament that nite: over-stimulation of the senses; agonizing containment of schoolboy anticipation: dyslexic football hero out w best-looking girl in school, striving to integrate into a single date the difference between prom ε romp.

Head turned, holding foot ε knee, i play her left shin, the inside of her calf, like a harmonica, turning to the other leg for variation on same theme. The baby-softness of her nether calfs gives my lips an instant erection. Following this teasing lento, i remove her hands and untie her robe, open it slowly. Her breasts, average in size, have above-average definition. I begin an adagio of the abdomen, where the tung, like a raptured skater –swirling around&around the rink between ribcage ɛ iliac crests– carves teasing designs on the hot ice. I watch as her carmine areolas prickle w a halo of gooseflesh. Then, slipping s.ward again, being careful not to unfold her toomuch, i began kissing everything about her a gp is allowed to look at but not to touch. And, o yes. I'd shaved my face so as to meet the requirements of the most demanding ɛ stubble-fearing schoolgirl. The lite in the room was just sufficient to reveal those things which moon&starlite had so closely coveted. I thrilled to her softfocus symmetry: ovalesque complement of pubic hair (not the typical thick triangle) brushed on (by the artist who matured her) at a point above and just grazing the mounds of venus, which, in their turn, were so full as to completely hide (w their lovely ɛ puffy vertical smile) the interior of her gender!

Low on my knees, every so often having to kiss ɛ urge apart (one more time) the excruciating softness of her inner thighs, i began worship of her regenerative attributes. I took up my homage to either side of that place where the two halfs of a female's lower torso meet like hands gently clapped in prayer ...clapped shut til those prayers are answered and their palms begin to separate, to arch apart, til only their heels ɛ fingertips are any longer touching. Sigh by sigh, i began to unfold her unspoken prayer thus.

How to say this? Careful ɛ tender diduction w fingertips (of the wings of this perfect specimen just captured alive!), combined w vertical lavings of my mouth, soon revealed not only the canthus-w-a-cowl (ɛ its lovely pinkish thingum), but the smooth arc of a full ɛ pouty outer labia completely lacking in crenature! If my language in these matters strikes the reader as clinical, eclectic, or even painterly poetic, so be it. For whatever it takes, i must keep all evocation of My Love from any shadow of pornographism.

While not having the data of a don juan to draw from, such qualities i can recall being present in the gender of only two of my former lovers ...well, maybe three, counting priscilla. Of course, Lilith knew nothing of my delite ɛ awe, for i kept to task. At first she arched ɛ squirmed in minute abrupt spasms; her breath came&went thru her teeth as tho she were a sea creature surfacing, then sounding again, thru many fathoms of desire ɛ need. Whether from some unconscious compulsion to escape, or the simple reactions of a body to pleasure, she'd worked us well upward on the bed by this time.

Pulling my prize back to bed's edge, pivoting her somewhat sideways in the process, i began to pursue reactions of which only the most ardent gynecologist dreams. Laying her nearest thigh aside, mouth to the panic button above the door, w the tips of index&middle fingers i strummed the forwardmost ridges of that g-pad which is set, like a rose-window, in the ceiling of the royal chamber. Holding tite during her rushes ɛ releases, i monitored her face as she bit –or rather, overbit– her lower lip repeatedly, sometimes covering it completely w bared teeth. Then, to catchup on her breath, her mouth would open; the cycle ending w a cetaceous exhalation, lower jaw dropped as if about to bite a large apple —then, return to step one. Too shy to be very vocal, over time i would learn, the amount of lip thus covered, the extent of teeth bared ɛ blazing there, was a fair gage of the degree of her bliss. In tandem w this, i must add, following any given cycle, her eyes might open –slitely, dreamily, pupils rolling in reckless ecstasy– as if checking to be sure no danger was about, then reclose. But most fascinating of all: each time as they closed, their pupils would roll upward ɛ out of sight!

In the meantime she had worked away from me again. Instead of pulling her back this time i joined her on the bed. Crouched low beside her, i was a great blond spider splaying, then sucking, the thorax of my trapped butterfly! Soon this spicebush swallowtail i'd got hold of began to gyre like a spastic virgin. Down on all eight (ravenous arachnid) i attached my mouth to her engorged baguette w consummate skill, thoughts festooned w tear-shapes full-to-dropping, festively bobbing my head not for apples but for that skinned-pink ɛ slippery-ripe little fruit ...while, simultaneously, after palpating the pink arcs ɛ perfect crescents of her innermost petalature, i reached in and, w learned manipuellations[sic], swelled ɛ hardened the ridges at the roof of her ardor, tracing its every throb til she teetered on, then spilled over, the cusp of the "most glorious [ɛ conglutinate] meltdown one might imagine!". (The conglutinate business is not her diary's but nostalgia's addendum.)

With a scientist's pursuit of precision and an artist's quest for perfection, i tracked her state of arousal, constructing it, coaxing it, completing it, tingle by tingle, throb by throb, bleat by bleat. Which causes me to say, a survey of humanity's laundry would yield precious little proof of female ecstasy —ecstasy caused by males at any rate. Macho lugs ɛ louts will be put off by this, but here anyway are the world stats to date. 84% of sexually mature females never or rarely reach orgasm w a man! In the face of this (indeed, in a certain compensatory sense, because of it) i sought to bring her session thru several star-bursts! As she whirs & whirls in whorls of –i hesitate to say ecstasy at risk of diluting later escalations, later successes– personally, as i work away there beside her, i am delited to know i am trashing 3-4oooyrs of civil religion- & civil law-influenced gender relations.

Pardon me while i thumbflick these pearls of mine into that little teacup over there but... some females have as many as 15trigger zones which focus down to 3 or 4 as arousal progresses. There's a ratio for this protraction of sensation which we wont go into just now except to identify it: an intra-reciprocal tension which —in a constant flux of spreading (gathering sensation) & contracting (focusing that sensation)— flows between those trigger zones like liquid voltage, if one will imagine that. Yet to be a good lover one needs imagine such things. Apart from giving consummate pleasure, my aim is also to dismantle & destroy in the mind of my lover all sexual precedents; and not just tingle by tingle but cry by cry! Yet to do so one must transform himself into the ideal male: an interesting creature *w* six hands, two tungs & three penises, variously sized & located. My teacup is now atremble *w* pearls to its brim!

Unable to picture a more lubricious moment, i rose. The lite from the bath, slicing across the sheets, caused creamy & crescented highlites on her breasts thighs knees & calfs. Snagging a pillow, i placed it under her and gave her to hold for the nonce her knees. Then, *w* concentrated care & control, i attempted once more to insert myself into the vortexture of her dancer's body. And this i attempted *w* her help (slow-milking any last hope of shrinkage i might have had); then *w*out it, again yet again. But nothing –no amount of low spittle or high prayer– would turn the trick. Finally, in frustration, i lunge; and she, my brave consort, grits her teeth & moans ...and holds her ground, by glorious Gaia! Not *w*out pain (to her, i mean), the white knight, lance at ram ready, has charged across the moatbridge & attained the outer room of the castle. Ah, the propylaeum, yes!

There is a story about a guy who goes to a house of pleasure but, because he looks like a certain cop who harasses the place, is stopped in the vestibule. And when, in frustration, he proceeds to relieve himself right there, he is bouncered into the street to finish the deed. Unwanting to cause her further pain (for reasons even the casual reader understands), i *w*drew. Body leaned back, breathing a long sigh, jaw set in exasperation, onan, ardent wheelbarrower of a tremendous load, simply knelt there. {Surely, with a creature as desirable as this, thund'ring coitus cant be the *only* route to bliss.} As for Lilith's thoughts, in a place not faraway the following wkend she would confess, "I dont know who scared me most that nite, big you or little me."

In the same entry of her diary noted earlier she would write, a little melodramatically i think, "...my big sir at Big Sur, half rapist, half angel". Looking at me w a most pitying & pitiable expression, head & shoulders lifting off the bed, she reached down, began pulling & cupping me, and, at the same time, heels to my buttox, urged me forward. To reclaim his rightful "-ism", onan shuffled over her thighs to straddle her tummy.

Being confronted by my swollen linearity seemed to increase rather than deter her determination. Using thighs & knees now, she contd to urge me up,up,up. Briefly, brusquely, i brushed her lambent lips w blazing breath on my way to the wall. Up against wall & headboard now, head lowered like a bull's and unable to go further, i looked down. Her eyes were peering up at me as one strains to see the tops of tall bldgs from inside a car, the lodelites of Lithian lust seeming aglow in hotsilver glee. Jaw ajar, eyes wide, she looked at lower me (& the yanking-sleeve continuity of her spittled fists), then up at my face, then down again, her knees still shoving my buttox forward til i was fully-in-her-face as they say, her busy fists & flaming breath driving me past distraction.

Now i've done the bdrm thing a bit, know the difference between impure head/pure hedonism. I shrink from the former (pardon the vascular pun), view it as just one more genuflection to the myth of male superiority. Years before deb danzi, my polski friend carol (train station, dropped sunglasses, recall?) was quick to inform me, "Most men love it, you big kielbasa, you!" She would have me thrust where no further thrusting seemed possible. I would sometimes study her profile trying to figureout into what viscoelastic innards exactly a near-foot of ram-rigid flesh had plumbed to. Tonsil hockey, hell. Only a full pharyngeal plugging could appease poor carol.

Clinging to the headboard like king kong to the empire-state bldg, cheek-to-cheek w the wallpaper's design, trying not to avalanche the snow-capped mtn scene above the bed (threat of my own lavalanche being danger enuf for all present), awareness got lost in my labyrinthine libido as a swarm of swallows from capistrangula rose up, squeezed me in the mad swirl of their skyward ascent, beat me w their wings as they departed, til all consciousness was flailed into a gorilla geyser of opalescent release!

9

Such is animal nature in a wide world of sexual opportunity that we could not have gone on unconsummated indefinitely. Yet here, today, in my present state of deprivation, i see that socalled full-function utility (head, torso, four limbs and at least three working orifices, as they say in those vulgar ads) is imperative only to sexdolls ε women of lesser resolve. Only now do i see that, for my part (hic tsk), i could have got on wellenuf (or should that be, off wellenuf) merely partaking of the folded pinch in the popliteal hollows behind My Date's simpering knees, or the pale padded gists of her lubricious gifted fists. These alone, now, would do me royal til the end of my days!

10

Energized by new intimacy, we left early next morn. This change in plans was in answer to Lilith's, "I have nothing fit to wear", in re the theater that eve. This came about curiously. First time i saw the baron after my arrival in sep i mentioned that i'd just come into six tickets to *la cage*. After trying, ε failing, to coax me to attend w him, i traded my tickets for two he had (*the phantom of the opera*), the equalizer being, he would lecture for me at point reyes on sa afternoon ε in bolinas that eve. (I was dreading the latter anyway; a stuffy gig which always presumes the speaker was lucky to get invited.)

Cloud colloquy: Difficulty keeping mind on work. Like a kid at school i keep looking out the window. Why do i have spring fever when it isnt even spring? Today's wx moving out of the ssw. Fix on thisorthat cloud, ask it: Have you seen her? Or you there. Have you seen her? And you, over there. Didnt you sail over ggNs last eve? How are things there? Maybe you over there, shaped like an eye, maybe you saw her. Does that lassie with a twinklin eye still wander by, sad 'n' dreamy there, not t' see me there? But they dont hang around to chat, these clouds. Good. Get on your way, far away from this place. I track their course past the roof of the cafeteria, then out over the wall, and beyond the trees ---free they go, unshot at! racing away into the Wild sky, deliting in their freedom!

From big sur to carmel the road stays near ocean –sometimes breathtakingly near ("Wow, look there!")– and, tho the stretch is townless ε cars few, the sightseers are many and the road, winding. Tho awhile getting to monterey, the trip up the freeway went quickly. Notable were: ❶ What two people can say to each other in a day can fill a book. ❷ Lilith however, not just by mood but by nature, was reticent —more, even, than me ...who in one lecture says more than he otherwise says in a month. All this is to say, the dialog which appears between L ε ns in this part of the book is a fair sampling of our *total* communication —the more substantive part of it, anyway.

As to the second thing, it was at this time i discovered that, except for "a severe case of shyness", Lilith was a shoo-in for a career in musical theater. Tho i could not coax or cajole her to hum muchless sing a note for me, i figured her to have a lovely singing voice for her speech alone sang.

> ...and flow with the surge which now urged us along
> or crash on the rocks of her siren song.

I learned that her vocal coach, thru both jh ε hs (jacques artinian) tried to give her leading roles in both musicals ε musical events. These she always declined —"Except for *carousel*...last march". She had been the understudy for julie, "Who got sick. They were in a bind and i had no choice." As to *the phantom,* "I've been wanting to see it for years but it jus never worked out."

Curious kismet. [Why d' ya say that?] Well, the baron 'n' me traded tickets on the day i saw you at berkeley. I planned to ask you out t' see it if i ever ran into you again ...Welp, if ever i managed to find you.

Signs for santa clara made me wonder if it was <accidental that santa clara should be just below santo francisco? Clara was francis' sweety, you know. Your very age i think when she ran off with him.> I mentioned a girlfriend talking me into "becoming catholic" while i waited to be sent overseas. [That musta been a stretch for you, no?] Kinduv. But my childhood plan you know was t' be a clergyman. (She thought i was joking.) Anyway, the whole catholicism thing stalled when i couldnt find a patron saint i could b'lieve in —til aurora introduced me to sweet dear francis.

Had the freeway gone thru el granada i'd have gotten off, went around. In fact, when we got into frisco proper and signs read HOSPITAL, i ignored them, spoke of other things —like clothes-shopping. Familiar only w saks 5th av (from nikki), we headed for "shopper's paradise" (union sq).

Fashionfreaks depress me: notsomuch the shallow fetish itself but our refusal to see the waste ε stupidity of it all. <Styles are so bad they get ditched every six months.> L: "And we dare to laff at people who wear feathers." The fashion industry profits from what david suzuki calls premeditated waste 'n' i read as moronic mob mimicry. Hanging w moviestars, fashion models and (in a couple cases) the daughters of fashion pros, doubtless bolstered a jading begun in me as a child model. For all were ever trying to dress me like some big blond doll they'd stumbled upon, replete w wonderful vibrating attachments!

Fame too (my moderate exposure to that treacherous ambrosia) also foisted its complement of uptodate gladrags on me —me, who is really happiest banging about barefoot in shorts ɛ any ol' shirt. Then along comes Lilith, whose interest in fashion –tho occasionally swayed by esthetics– is limited to blending in + a complement of comfort. If the entire stint took halfanhour it was only because of lack of selection in her size: "Three. Four, for baggy." While she was off in a dressingrm i entertained myself w banners ɛ signs. FALL CLEARANCE ON MISSES & JUNIORS! ALL MUST GO! BUY TWO, GET ONE FREE! But i got to see L's selection only on it's hanger. <You shop like me. Know what you want, go straight t' get it. I like that. The only time i truly browse is win the arts or in the Wild.>

On paying (she insisted) we talked of eating, were told of "a great deli up the street". To get there we passed thru the sq itself, stopping so she could read the plaque at the base of a phallic corinthian column. Then, head back, eyes up (reminding me of our nite), she tried to see the goddess of victory at its top. <Called by locals "the goddess of retail" and, alternatively, "alma in her nitie".> We passed the requisite street entertainers: six black males rapping dancing ɛ tumbling, a tiny man on a tall unicycle, a black saxplayer w a potted tree, an organgrinder playing a piece by handel, a footless woman selling soiled keyfobs and a footloose man asleep against a fence. The females (not counting alma de bretteville) cost Lilith a dollar apiece in alms, incl'g a baglady who did nothing but look pitiful in a stench of alcohol.

<You are the ideal enabler. [Why?] Cause she's allbut guaranteed to spend that on destroying her liver.> ELEEmosynate. *Eleison* Lee, mosey-on w your nate ...til we reach a lovely oriental girl playing borodin's "and this is my beloved" theme gloriously on a cheap violin. She finishes <That was very good. [shy smile] You are thai? [Yes.] How much would you charge to play "méditation" for us? [*Thaïs?*] Yes.>

"My fee is whatever your heart says. {Eyes i know so well, gadshazm!} No. Please. [halts opening of wallet w delicate fingers] Wait til I finish. [violin to chin, eyes up] Maybe you will not like it." I have my handsker out ɛ am bitdown on my tung before she's done. <The last one t' do that ta me was michael rabin. Ever hear of him? [she had not. fishout two 20s] You share his sweetness of spirit. Thank you. [Thank *you* ... *Very* much.] Here are my cards. Solo violin would go well at my smaller venues. Call me if youre interested. The pay is not great but the exposure may help.>

"She was brilliant."

VanessaD without caffein. If i were a millionaire i'd have her performing with a major orchestra in no time. We cross a street. <This was once the tenderloin. Old ε infamous morton street here was renamed maiden lane in hopes of cleaningup its image. Naive, eh? A century ago, on this same walk, i'duv been shaLEIGHlied 'n' youduv been shanghaied by now.> Her eyes scanned for suspicious persons but, seeing none (tho i'm sure, now, they were there), settled on the arboreals. "Lovely trees... wonder what kind they are?" Well, theyre sycamore trees. [picture an adorable face having an 'aha' realization] "I get it: Sycamores, maiden lane. I'm learning the town from you already." She glancedabout for the sunblasted doorway but the libido-igniting doorprize was already beside me. As we neared the deli an outfit in the window of a small boutique caught my eye. Now *that's* you ...for t'nite, i mean.

"That one there? ...I dont *think* so." By the time we'd finished lunch i'd talked her into at least looking at it.

A b&w outfit, the blouse had an 18^{th}century poet/painter theme. Imagination cloudedover w visions of Lilith at the theater. It's you. Trust me. But just for t'nite, of course. She wanted to leave (would have walkedoff in fact had she known me better). You dont have to wear it ever again. My idea/my treat. Jus go in 'n' look at it. Please?

She dallied ε demurred, eyeing it thisway&that in a large triple mirror gawking at her from three perspectives. Lowering her arms she made a droll face as if to give it back to the salesgirl. Try it on. Please? Not wanting to hurt my feelings, specially in public, she ducked thru a dressingrm curtain.

Take $10 from wallet. She'll say it's too showy. Dont agree with her. [slip money to salesperson] We're seeing *phantom o' the opera* t'nite. It'll work perfectly. Salesperson(hia, sp), about L's age, is game: "She'll be the star!" While she changes i locate a pair of boots: simulated white leather w an overlay of black suede, artfully masking the white vinyl into a harlequin design. My vision appears! I watch in a mirror at the end of an aisle as sp, arms behind her back, sidles over. "I like it." "You do?" "Uhuh." "I guess ...but it's waytoo flashy, doncha think?" "No. Classy. *Very.*" A well-tailored woman in her 40s keeps an eye on the proceedings while fussing w a rack an aisle away.

Lilith, hiding her selfconsciousness, stood midst the three mirrors, turning, left, right. The blouse: brilliant white; three-quarter length sleeves ending in cavalier cuffs; ruffled front, gathered into a v-neck, *w* winekeg & eye-closures down its length ending in v-shaped tails, the v of its bibtail (worn outside) curves inward & upward, drawing the eye to her midriff.

Tails upfront! That's neat! Female villon! I love it!

"Really you do?"

Absolutely. Except....

What?

The leggings look a little baggy.

"O, baggy's 'in'."

"Not for *that* outfit" interjects the woman, allbut hovering now. "But youre right. Baggy is in. But in interest of historic authenticity, a closer cling is preferable." Phony british accent in drag. "Tell you why." <Yes, please.> The leggings should reflect the outfit's renaissance-poet theme."

Sp yods instead of Lilith. (Yods is teenspeak for nods yes, if i havent said.)

You certainly know your inventory.

"I designed this piece ...And alot of what you see around you."

Lilith, totally outnumbered, tries to agree. "But i cant go with skintite."

"O, I agree. Skintite is gauche. But a sense of shape –here, here and here– would be just lovely. [brandishing piece of chalk] "All my leggings are cut conservatively. You will look dressed, not draped, when we're done. I see to the tailoring of all purchases myself —no extra charge, of course."

By this evening?

"No problem. I could dress a *corps de ballet* before curtaintime!" [sp: It's true. I've seen her do it.] Squatting, putting a hand on Lilith's hip for balance, she took a tuck at the knee. "You see this?" Li watched the goings-on in the mirror. "And here, and here?" On one knee now, pins pinned on a card, card in her teeth, she moves up the inseam by deliberate steps. I envy those hands, those learned fingers. Li rose on her toes as the erect thumb of the fitter's hand brushed her groin. A peculiar grimace, half smile/half pain, crossed her features. The woman rotated on her knees toward me, smoothing ε adjusting the bibtail, her knuckles apparently grazing Li frontally. Repeat grimace.

Sp purses lips.

"There are no buttons past the ruffles, here, since this is to be left open, like so." She pried, then patted, the swallowtail cleft which split the bibtail up to the serrations of ruffles ε the bottom closure. Another brush of knuckles. Looking across at me, widening her mouth, she bares her teeth, hunches her shoulders (as if to squeal, yeeek) and settles into a nervous grin. Sp leaves to attend to the doorjingle of a new arrival.

Our many-handed sappho, flushed (from crouching?), rises to her feet, rotates Lilith back to the mirrors. "I'll tuck these sides a little too; your waist is so small." She stood behind Li, hands clutching material at both sides of the shirt. "And we'll do away with the shoulderpads. You dont need them. That will drop the tails to about here [yeek again], which is the perfect fall for you."

I hand Lilith the boots, at which she stares for a moment. Weary of balking, goes to bench, slides into them. Back before the mirrors, getting the feel of things (sudden model!), places left hand behind hip, fingers pointing down, puts one booted foot center-forward and, raising the other hand, brought a swirl of hair over one shoulder. "Isnt this what youre supposed to do?" All smile. Click. Had i a loaded camera i would have frozen that moment w something beside overheated harkback.

"Perfect for the theater. *Exquisite!*"

L smiled to herself. (Even i knew her 'exkweezeet' rendering was wrong.) Three females smiled back from the triplet of mirrors. Left one captures the classical Lilith: carved lithic profile, hellenic etching in prominent bones of face: chiseling of cheekbone, chin ε jaw. Ligaments in neck dart forward, move back again, when she turns her head. O helen, there is a haughtiness in thy beauty! In *this* Lilith i see artist ε dancer sorts, atthis, gongyla or gyrinna,

> (neopolitan gypsy would sing it, "Gira! Gira! Gira!",
> plying passionately a lydian lyre)

and the nymph, thetis, too, of course. And icyhot artemis maybe too!

In the center mirror stands Miralith. From this angle (not quite straight-on) a softening of line takes place, grading to …i want to say cute, reflecting a bit of the cuddly culpability stuffed animals imply. But then the onlooker will think she was pretty when, if fact, beauty was the Sculptor's sole criterion.

In the right mirror stands Duplith, more gymnast than artist; giddier, chattier, younger somehow. No lisp, no strabism, no little marvel of a tic. She swaggers in the glass: trojan helen, after the kidnaping but before the horse; faustina too, before the old philosopher's wish has come true; and much of the sapphic entourage as well. And not leastofall, thetis, deliting in the divorce!

For this job one needs a poet, which i sadly am not. For this lack her beauty still moves uncaptured beyond ε behind the sort of rational allusions i must defer to. Eg: Left mirror: jean shrimpton, model. Center mirror: juliet hussey, actor. Right mirror: mia (maud) kirshner, actor. Suffice it: L rarely did wrong before mirror or camera. Even a twisted glass would have to shatter to distort her image into an unlovely thing. She is everyman's Female, and every woman's, couching in her features a libraryful of immortal femmes! But most amazing of all, she was unaware of her ageless charm, her deathless beauty. In point of fact, she seemed virtually immobilized w shyness because of it!

While boring my male readers to tears i suppose, all this musing w mirrors may at least serve to prove, this Lilith, my Lilith, was wholly unconnected w all that vampire-legend lamia-lore stuff. If anything, my heroine today has the vampire's mirror-problem (catoptricophobia) in reverse. For it is mostly by way of a mirror that my Lilith may be seen —in that mirror her biographer holds aloft.

Seeming dazed by the whole event, on the way to the car she said, "Youre a switch, ya know?"

Whyzthat?

"Well, most guys try ta talk a girl outa clothes not into them." This remark was a landmark for us. Tho hid behind a façade of humor, w it three hurdles were crossed, at least for the time being. ❶ Bringing up on her own anything to do with sex; ❷ talking about it out of the context of intimacy; and ❸ criticizing me —albeit gently ε w humor. As for me and my sudden attachment to fashion? I can only say, the heights of love had, for me, begun to obscure the Real ε suffering world below.

With a few hrs on our hands til her outfit was ready we decided to see the town a bit. We parked the javelin back at my place and, by virtue of its proximity, decided to walk the mission district. In a city still sane enuf to give pedestrians the right of way, i'll park&walk any day.

San franciscans say we are crass who call their city frisco ɛ themselves friscans; or worse still, frixo ɛ frixans! But they doubtless have more time than i and dont care about the 50%savings in ink, letterspace ɛ treekill! Beside, the rationale behind this paper- ɛ ink-gobbling demand is usually vain instead of mystical. For the city's namesake is francis of assisi, called "saint" by some. In that context, saying frisco or frixo is like saying xmas, where the cause is overwhelmed (if not forgotten) by its effect. For some newagers any sleight to the memory of francis is offensive. Then again, francis was horrified by cities.

At any rate, it is only a few blocks (van ness to 16th, 16th to dolores; lit buffs will think i'm making these names up as we stroll) from my place to the mission. But we decided on the more colorful route via liberty ɛ valencia. In 1993 this was the very heart of the city's lesbian population; where grassroots feminism was weaned ...in america, anyway. As we passed the orig levi-strauss store (still in operation) i checked the label on her jeans. "What're you doing, you goose?" I point to sign. "Hey, beth told me about this street! A friend of hers lives near here somewhere." We paused here&there to gaze at the frescos for which these dusty streets were famous. As, not pausing, she passed, graceful as a girl, one fresco baldly doctored in graffiti, some of it gross, all eyes standing about (mostly female) were upon her. One brazen youngster, alone in a doorway, pretty in a gaunt sort of way –green-eyed, what looked like a waterlily in her long copper-colored curls– tried to entice my companion w a look of "Now why doncha jus come along with me, gurrl?"

Does that make you uncomfortable?

"Not really." We reach palmy dolores st. "She might be a very sweet person for all we know" twirling onto the opposite curb. "That's probably all an act." After detouring into the park for an overlook of downtown, i stroll past mission hs toward our destination w my happily nondolores duenna.

Mission *san francisco de asis*, aka mission dolores (good name for a gumshoe thriller), is a spanish-mexican cousin of a restoration in assisi, italy (the latter oddly severely damaged in '97 by an earthquake). Wish you coulduv been with me on my visit there [italia] a few years ago. This gilt adornment here, no matter its rusticity, is not in keeping with the memory of francis, who reestablished in post-medieval italy the ascetic simplicity of his dead mentor. Docent Lilith read from a pamphlet: "The timbers of the roof, roughhewn from redwoods, are still lashed together with rawhide. [a glance upward supported said support] And this, to our right, is california's first book. The story of junípero serra" sang the lingual lass as we faced an interiorly lit display under glass, shifting the accent on the second try. <Well read, Ms McGrae] "I guess my year o' spanish wasnt completely wasted."

Francis, w his love of Nature, is for many greens the obvious Earth patron of the 21stcentury. Most have read *the canticle of brother sun, sister moon*. As we sat in an alcove, near his likeness cast in bronze (blackened w 'age'), Lilith read from a thin sheet on which were printed some excerpts. "...With all thy creatures, specially brother sun ...and for sister moon, and for the stars...." I covered the page w my hand. She looked up. The lites in her eyes marked the joyous gaps between friendly stars.

Unless you want to scrape me off these tiles, or cart me around in a wheelbarrow, you'd better stop right there. Between your voice and his words, i'm sure t' melt ...like that candle over there... to a blob o' dolorous protoplasm. I hafta walk now, please. We passed thru a garden, in a few paces went from postcolumbian mexico to pillared moorish spain (basilica nextdoor), shadows entwined. "I'm not sure i like the moors or their architecture." After some mins we decided we liked the garden better. There i confessed a kinship w the writings of francis i'd never shared before, or maybe even realized before.

After leaving the mission a sign caught her eye (PARK HERE FOR BART) which at once suggested, "Bart who?" Sharing our favorite *simpson's* episodes, we caught a train to the civic center where a marquee then caught my eye: Symphony Fri-Sat-Sun. Tho i'd seen the sfs at davis hall many times, it was a radio broadcast of a new year's program in '91 (heard back home in appalachia) which always came to mind, solely because of the voice quality of a certain coloratura of whom i never heard again. Cant recall her name (i confessed to my *vade mecum*-thumbing fellow-tourist). It'll come ta me jus before i wake in the morning; that's the usual path ε mean of my archival recall. [That's handy.] It is ...very.

The civic complex sprawls. Dont dare stop here, said nathan as we passed the library. Once i enter a bookplace i'm lost t' the world. Ditto with modeltrain museums. This is where i met robin williams the other day. They were bldg the new "main" (library) at the time. When we reached van ness the museum (of mod art) came into view. A deep breath and we plunged in.

Modart, by&large, leaves me cold —that is, when it fails to amuse or appall. Durable talent is usually obvious to me. One shouldnt have to study a work of "art" to figure out if it will be around in a thousand years. An exception to the pinknoise of the place was colette hogarth's "vanessa", which just happened to be on tour at the time. We stood admiring its unlikely mix of degas blur & boucher softness ...minus all the babychunks backthen in vogue.

Three ladies –who kept reappearing each time i thought we'd lost them– persisted in asking what i thought of this or that piece. At the center of the last room stood a vinyl & metal collage. This room, *w* its skylite & vacant walls, reminded me of a garret on bleeker st which my artist rmmate (no menotti, he) departed owing two month's rent. Anyway, after giving the thing an f for art and a b-minus for geometry, i advised: Your first mistake is taking this stuff seriously. Rule 1: nearly all contemporary art is a throwaway experience, like the niteclub comedian the management tosses in with the singer you really came to hear, and most of whose socalled humor you wanna showeroff the minute ya get home.

Downstairs in a "permanent" room hung a quality repro of kokoschka's "murder of a woman". With no more than a cursory exam, Lilith turned away in apparent disgust. It would take the onset of the darkest period of my life, *and* hers, to make me understand what really lay behind her pitiable gloss for that reaction: "Something about it fritens me." When part of a famous collection came to a museum near bamalachia, she had a similar reaction to gérôme's exquisite "slave market". I far'n'away prefer the museum on the promenade i summaried as i took her past the operahouse. *Traviata* was just then running. <How ironic, eh? when right over there somewhere reallife violettas ply their trade every day!> [The tenderloin district was then very near the opera. —Ed.] Little did i suspect her thoughts: *{{Saria per me sventura un serio amore?}}* <Hey, look! In december theyre gonna stage ian mai's *hannibal*, Lee!> Curiosity aroused her from what was surely self-condemnation. Since the only daytime musical event was an ORGAN CONCERT AT 4P.M, and having had our fill of period-confused architecture & fair-to-mediocre statuary, we grabbed a trolley.

Do your coevals still call sexEd an organ concert?

"Some do." No sooner had we got on our way when, "Look, nathan!" A marquee read PHANTOM OF THE OPERA. Inadvertently she'd spotted our destination for that eve, while i enjoyed the sound of my name on her lips —which tonite reminds me of the time i stumbled on a poster of my first book in the window of a bookstore. Who has a poor selfimage thinks he's dreaming when such ego-puffing events occur.

For me (obdurate heretic) the tackiest thing a tourist in frisco can do is get caught in public humming or whistling the "frisco song". After that comes being seen riding a cablecar. But worst of all, doing both. My companion's enthusiasm however ("O we just *have* to, dont you see?") subdued my distaste for the pedestrianly predictable. Beside, i verymuch wanted to hear her voice in song. Tho we brokeup in laffter after singing (*molto sotto voce*) only the words of the title, it workedout to be a fond memory, which i know she foresaw. As remembrance of those hours unwinds i hear the words "catch a cablecar" ...and, as has happened w me (ever since juanita), the words triggered a line from a song: "...and put it in your pocket", which in its turn triggered the most querical look Lilith owned, a look which i think only a foto, taken at a certain precise instant, could hope to capture: a blank askanceness of unpresupposing naivete & fleeting-swift wonderment. And most curiously of all, the question which launched that look might take hours days weeks years before it was voiced ...if ever.

The cablecar seat opposite us had only one occupant. As soon as we sat that person began studying us w brite beady eyes. "You know I couldnt help overhearing." She'd read somewhere "only yesterday" that 70-some-odd singers had recorded that song since tony bennet first sang it. "That amazed me?" chirped the gemeyed octogenarian, a dash of the past obtaining in her choice of pincenez, parasol & flat lilac hat. "Have you, my dear", leaning forward & touching lightly Lee's hand w gloved fingertips, "heard the story..." then turning to me, eyebrows up, peering over bifocals, assuring "... it's based on fact, you know ...the story about the heartpatient who, returning to the northeast to recover, was overheard to say, 'I left my heartmachine in san francisco'?" Well, fingertips to lips, she almost melted in suppressed mirth.

I repeatedly got the feeling i knew this woman —which i thought at first was caused by her easy rapport w my seatmate. I felt i could read what she was thinking: {If the soul is in the eyes, this young lady's is surely the purest I've ever seen in an adult!} For, at that point, i was still thinking the same thought a hundred times a day. "I must be getting off soon. I'm staying at the mark. [pointing out the window] Right up there?" [rings for a stop] Snob hill, I call it. Why I can even see the bridges from my window!" She pushed herself up to leave. "Will you be in town for long?"

"For a little while" said friendly Lee.

"I'll be here for a couple more days, then it's off to the races again. If you have time, ring me or stop by." Then, looking down at us. "I'm the most mature person there, you know. [nods toward hill] Easy to find." She winked and, twisting back my way, whispered, "She's a sweetheart. Take good care of her", the prolonged oo in 'good' turning her mouth into a pale-lipped pucker. Patting my shoulder the spry thing sprinted for the door, which waited impatiently for her exit. No sooner had it closed when both of us realized. That was whatshername, tandy? *Foxfire*, ya know? With jon windstar? Lilith however knew her as the aged idgy from another movie. "Youre right. So *that's* why i thought i knew her."

For me it was like a slow-drip adrenaline i.v just to traipse about the world *w* this person, laffing wondering contemplating critiquing touching feeling sometimes even weeping. <If i had to live in a city, this one would be near the top of my list. With its hills 'n' narrow streets it reminds me at times of naples 'n' the amalfi coast, and of provençe at others. Then again, many of its names remind me of greenwich village.> Today, depressed, in this prison (while the cablecar clatters us along), i can however think of only twosuch namesakes: washington- & union squares. But mnemy knows there are others.

We got off at the last stop. No sooner had we reached the curb when, halting, bending suddenly forward and erecting rapidly (while simultaneously rotating at the hips), she whipped her extravagance of hair around & behind her, had the lot of it ponytailed in only the time it took me to turn & notice! While i would in time come to understand the centrifugal effect on her hair of this fascinating action –this multidirectional whiplashing whole-body motion– the organizational physics which ensured that every last hair would endup lying uniformly in a narrow quicky-ponytailed river between her shoulderblades, i may never fully comprehend. What i did know was, at my side walked a living breathing vanity-vacuous antidote to chaos-theory and i was loving it!

Some kids in costumes trooped toward us. Hey, is today halloween? ...Crap. That means we're gonna miss the parade. I started to explain the adults-only halloween parade but it turnedout she knew all about it. Youve been?

"No. A friend at school's in it. ...Sorrel. She's a goth. Wants me t' go with them. That's why i almost didnt go with you ...for the weekend, i mean."

Before we'd gone a block, from a doorway, to strains of "night on bald mountain", emerged an endless loop of hiccupy laffter. We ducked inside where a draculass w a fanged & feigned smile wanted $4, "Presumably to keep her off our necks" laffed Lee once out of earshot. A conveyorbelt lurched, launched us thru a tattered curtain ...straight into hell, or an adman's version ...whereat frite faces flashed in the darkness, flung themselves at you while frite bytes played over a cheap soundsystem. Hey, that's vincent price! "Which is pretty spooky in that he jus died." Youd think he'duv waited til halloween. "Maybe he tried." There's a thought. One had to yell over the noise. From room to room ...well, chamber to chamber, the theme changed little: ghouls groaned, ghosts boasted, vampires ranted, witches raved. "I think we've been ripped off." Doors creaked, banshees shrieked, bats scowled, cats yeowled. By the 6th room we'd seen everything from incense & murder to frankenstein. "This is ridiculous". By the next room we'd caughtup w a latindian family. On seeing the faces of the tots all agog she added, "We're jus the wrong age."

A stairway led up to the last feature. There, from a mezzanine balcony, one looked down on a moonlit mtntop where a witches' sabbath was in progress: the reason for the music we'd heard outside. Among the crags & caves a bevy –or is that, coven?– of mechanized hags, w yellow eyes & frizzed hair, cavorted. Well, maybe hags isnt the right word. A bonfire crackled & roared from speakers situated at the center of the scene; the flicker of its flames outshone the lite of a cloudswept moon. Hidden blowers tore at long trains of moss which swayed drunkenly in the trees; a large cobweb, w a redeyed spider poised at its center, pulsed in the wind which tore at the branches of a nearby tree; the skirts of the witches (mostly female) were whipped as they danced in place. This "wind effect" enlivened what might otherwise have been merely mechanical motions. Yet not a one of them was on a broom, or sported the usual pointed hat or ample black dress. <What have we here, an adman with imagination?> Beside the bonfire, which lite reeled across the rocks, stood a tall sinewy man. Pan? For he had not the usual horns, hoofs & tail?

Nice touch. Judging by his leer he looks horny enuf t' be a devil ta deal with. For this i was pinched yet could not stop. And it looks like he's gonna endup with more than a *little* tail before the nite is over. "Sssh", she urged, concerned the family ahead might overhear.

Stokowski's strings screamed & buzzed from the rafters. The raver-grrrl witches, barefoot & longnailed, cavorted convulsed & consorted below —-well, sort of consorted. Barechested males in revealing black tites, loomed above blonds brunettes & redheads. Strobelites toyed w & teased their cyclic motions. Two hags, the loveliest of the coven, were dressed in skirts blouses socks shoes & headbands which, we agreed, resembled catholic school uniforms.

"That one actually looks like reesy!" said Lee w a humph of surprise. She asked if i'd ever seen "a movie called *exotica*." I had not.

Plainly pet's of pan, both girls kneeled in the shadow of his staff, a quite phallic affair w unusual prongs. Both of them long-haired brunets, one hag rocked forward on her knees while the other rocked back onto her hands.

"Did you read *faust?* [adding quickly] Dont answer that. I should know better from *scapegoats*."

This is like an update of the harz mountain scene.

The flames of the bonfire licked convincingly upward as the scene pulsed w shadowed lite. A min later the modern dress made sense. Subtly, almost subliminally, every few secs the scene was transformed by the clever use of projected images. Using a rapid strobe effect, among the taller rocks you could make out the skyline of a city. Simultaneously the immed backwall of stone flashed as a streetfront, complete w sidewalk stoops & doorways. Pan's suggestively phallic staff (and the bonfire behind it) then became the centerpiece: a towering hypodermic syringe replete w dripping needle.

This is obviously the main attraction. ...If it isnt yet cult-famous it soon will be.

"Is it my imagination or should this be adults only?" she mouthed aside into my shoulder. <Good point ...But theyre leaving now anyway.>

A touch i thought particularly good (and possibly accidental) was, every couple mins the skirt of one witchlet (the one facing the blowers, on her knees, unbowed & ungroveling) would fold back, permitting the firelite to strobe in waves across her shining plastic thighs every few secs.

After exiting down a staircase and reaching the foyer L stopped, "Ooo, my sunglasses!" Leaving her to wait, i returned to the observation deck. A man stood alone at the railing. Tho he held a pair in his hand he shook his head "no" to my question. That i viewed the likelihood of a man in suit&tie in such a place as a probable case of lunchhour raunch may say more about me than about him. Then again there are those 9-to-5 stats to explain. As for the glasses in question, "I have them. Sorry," said she, shyly proffering them as i reappeared. As we exited i asked is she'd <Ever heard this music?>

"Shur. Daddy usta play it. An' it's used in *fantasia* too —the part with the fiery-eyed monster that looks like a devil?" Don had taken them to see it when they were "old enuf to appreciate it". Brite outside, Lee put on those sunglasses. We'd hardly walked a few steps when, "O my God!". Seeing a sign just ahead, she stopped short.

The "carousel museum", **w** its many colorful handcarved animals, its bandorgans of traditional carousel music, took up the remainder of our free time. Her disappointment when it was time to leave made me promise to return. "I'm a real carousel haunt. Sorry." Somehow i got the credit whenever this phenomenon popped into our path. To this day Lilith would tell you if she could, it was me who *insisted* we head in that direction.

Rebarked upon "the little cablecar", we were soon soaring up&down the hills again. A stop along the way netted her outfit. ("You may try it on, if you wish?" "That's okay. We're running kinda short o' time.") I thought she'd be uptite to be around this woman again. If she was, i failed to pickup on it.

11

If we are going to be chronologically faithful then a certain news item should reach the reader before it reaches the Biographee ε her narrator —neither of whom turned on a radio or tv or looked at a newspaper that wkend. Popmedia blitz is the coitus interruptus of a healthy lifestyle. To wit: While L ε n were at their respective places getting ready for the theater, a coroner in l.a was writing in his report, "The blast killed the victim [roy freeman] instantaneously." Then, about the time ubaldo piangi (fearless weeper) was being killed by the phantom, fbi labs (soon to be exposed for decades of evidence-tampering) began working on freeman's case.

Whenever the head is severed rapidly from the body, death is said to be "instantaneous". I emphatically disagree. There are many accounts of severed heads being conscious ε aware. The life forces cannot do other than go on w their work, sometimes for 2-3mins. I re one account where the head of a simpleton (who cut out a meager existence as a jester) rolled to the edge of the headsman's platform and, lying on its left ear, looked out at the spectators and apologized for a poor performance. Clown to the last, he said, "Guess I lost my head" (translation from the french). The poor fellow then laffed pathetically ε died. There are many other examples, specially thanx to the deeds of civil religion in spain. This is why executioners insist upon the victim lying absolutely still. Cut too high? Bones in the skull botch the blow. Cut too low? Shoulder girdle botches it. In worst cases the victim flops around like a large mangled sheep, which does not bother the executioner so much (after all, blood is his elixir). But it often sickened those paid to hold the victim down for a second try. Adrenaline-injected by this time, the doomed one is as powerful as a badly axed ox. All present, therefore, incl'g some of the spectators, are usually splattered with gore before it's over.

Witnesses to beheadings have remarked as follows: "I felt he [the head of the victim] was trying to scream something with his eyes, some important message, some truth from beyond the grave." Or, "I thought she was trying to say something. Her mouth was moving but there was no sound." Read my lips, rubbernecker. Deaf&dumb witnesses have done just that for the benefit of the ghoulish crowd —which crowds, as long as we're on the topic, seem to gather like maggots on a corpse for public executions. The last one (in the u.s) was staged in ky in 1936. 20,ooo attended, reader!

After perusing the work of the pros i am convinced, no amount of pain or blood can trigger an executioner's nitemare. Yet he does have a weak spot, his "a killer's heel", so to say. His fear is that some corpse one day will turn about and curse its killer! Shakespeare must have seen this happen. For this reason the executioner always aims high rather than low; high enuf to separate the still-living brain of the doomed from his voicebox. This, and not a quick death for his victim, drives the executioner to kill w precision. In the worst case, decapitating too low ends w the larynx intact. The disembodied head can now address all assembled; is free to say what is usually known only to the dead. In one such case, again in france, the garroted head of a poet (andrea chénier, beheaded for alleged "seditious acts against the state". Hmm) was able, despite copious blood & gurgle, to address the crowd. He repudiated –one last time– the political tyranny he saw all around him: "I can do no more than this"...and, wideeyed, expired. Heretic after my own heart!

The point of all this *excapito* utterance? The circumstances of freeman's death. Fbi decides: the bomb that decapitated him was designed to maim or kill from beneath the driverseat as soon as the car was moved. However it appeared that whoever placed the bomb decided (perhaps at the last moment) it would do better inside a styrofoam food container which freeman had left on the dashboard (he was known by those [mostly vegans] close to him as a junkfood junky). This put a powerful explosive at neck level (roy was a big man) so that, when his girlfriend rushed over, she was confronted by roy's bloodied head wedged hard against the rear window, eyes & mouth moving "as if he was trying to tell me who did it".

Fbi propaganda would later lead police to say it was "an inside job". Now i must ask: would that be ecoactivists murdering "ecoterrorists"? or "ecoterrorists" murdering ecoactivists? And, oddest of all, this turn of events came about just when the fed. case against freeman & EarthNow was falling on its face –after a cost of $20million in taxpayer money– and just when fuzzybear (petname freeman acolytes used) was out on bail and allbut guaranteed acquittal. Hmm. Be that as it may. I didnt learn of freeman's death til next day when i answered my mxs. It turned out, he'd been killed long about the time Lilith & me got to monterey (or so we later guessed), which makes me summon forth a couple more strange items.

On our return drive.... Well, first of all, it was then we discovered windshield adventuring, began evolving what would become a pet avocation: commenting on signs, licenseplates & the like. "Since we cant change it [the littering of public places w anthropic rot] we mightaswell enjoy it." It was in this context that clara & francis (above) came up. Turned into word-fodder also that trip were signs indicating san juan bautista, mt madonna, alum rock, montague expwy, willow rd, ravenswood, hetchy hetchy aqueduct & candlestick park, all of which raised comments as follows: "Ever go t' san juan capistrano? Daddy 'n' lage were there" (and what a tale, incidentally, that turnedout to be once i got the details); <Title of my favorite eddy munch painting. Come t' think of it, you two look alot alike. Specially last nite>; <A place we gotta keep you far away from... Tell ya some other time>; <A place the

experts will ever debate was gotten to by romeo or not>; <Hey, there's a willow road back in scotsmoor too.>; "Aaand, there's a ravenwood near where i grew up!"; "Now there's a name. Must be native american"; and finally, <Home o' the giant's 'n' 49ers.> "[pensively perusing her "guide to san francisco"] Carl h candlesstick[sic], worst of the giants. [i assumed that was who the park was named after] Never played a single game —got dropped for drug use"...each item stated in its respective order.

I have saved for last one particular signage ε its comments. Halfway between monterey ε san jose we passed a town called gilroy. One thing to another, the gilroy signs caused one of us to mention that undying graffitum "kilroy was here". Nothing peculiar there ...providing one overlooks the fact that we were passing gilroy along about the time roy freeman was killed! Said remarks then led to Lilith's asking, "Who was kilroy anyway?", which, in its turn (because of the suffix '-roy' and not the prefix 'kil-')— led us to talking about the freeman court case, just then fizzlingout. Anyway, the sum of these things could hardly be stranger. In fact, it was so strange, when fbi agents got around to questioning me (thanx to nikki, as we shall see), i dared not breathe a word of our travel chatter that day lest dirty small minds twist coincidence into reallife suspicion. (More on this later —maybe.)

"Do you know him?"

Not well, but i do.

"Do you like him?"

The question is rather, How much does roy dislike *me?* ["Thought that might be the case."] In person [roy] goes to unusual lengths to ignore me. Then there are the tales of his bad-mouthing me in front of multiple witnesses, at least three of them very credible. As to that dislike. I'm told it's notsomuch my method of dissent as its popularity. You might remember, a decade ago i said in *ungreening [of tomorrow]:* If you feel you must in good conscience perform some act which will cast a group to which you belong in a negative public lite, have the courage 'n' decency to publicly sever all connection with that group before you do so. That is to say, public sympathy for greens always suffers when any among us advocate or undertake tactics which the dirty-minded among our lishment leaders can twist to advance their own antiPlanetary agendas. ["Amen."] This same argument –clashing methods of dissent, we c'n call it– has in fact caused a rift between me and my friend the baron ...except that the baron has yet to call my methods weak 'n' cowardly. [Freeman said that?] Apparently several times, in public.

"Wow."

As i write today this same lishment is busier than ever twisting Earthnow, Elf ε alf tactics into an ugly thing in the public mind. The difference is, now i know of whence i speak. For, tho i unambiguously severed my association w *all* green groups *before* doing what i did, that single aggressive act of mine –even tho its thrust had nothing to do w green causes– is allbut guaranteed to keep the public memory of nathan schock demonized til the very collapse of civilization itself ...which, if Lilith's ultimate misfortune holds true, may just coincide w the obliteration of public memory itself!

12

I did not expect a three-hanky evening.

Laroux's *phantom of the opera* –like hugo's *notre dame* ε the grimm brothers' treatments before it– is just one more telling of the old beauty ε beast theme, only this time modeled after poe, detective-story style. As to the beauty/beast idea itself, it is as ancient as that first beautiful human female who wanted no part of sexual reproduction; ie, as old as the *precivil* artemis archetype itself.

Then along comes civilization and with it patriarchy ...and suddenly men who choose to chasedown ε rape women are glorified in story ε legend. This is exhaustively represented in an iconology (both eastern ε western) of not only gods who rape goddesses ε nymphs w impunity, but also giants centaurs mandragons lions bulls two-headed dogserpents seaSerpents satyrs name-a-monster watch-a-rape. Enter, belatedly, *the phantom of the opera* (hia, *the phantom*), who is, summarily, none other than the cliche stalker/raper/beast/-lover who just happens to have a penchant for dark foreplay set to excellent music. By fiat of fiction the phantom gets to do what instinct-crushed&angry civil heteromales only dare imagine, and merely for the price of dying by his own hand. And that's our preamble... except to say. In all civil beauty/beast treatments, basic male desire is viewed as terrifying ugliness (primitivity) in pursuit of terrified purity ("vulnerable civility"). Of course, this old storyline obtains its subliminal fascination from the (twisted) truth itself: The pursuit ε rape of (pure/female) Nature by (depraved/violent) civiliztion/civil religion!

And as w every other gender-twisted civil structure, the him-v.-her pathos comes built in. Eg: dominant power (male civilization) v. weak vulnerability (female Nature) is, as ever, presented as the way things *should* be! The story can then proceed to play-out ye old civil/religious propaganda using all its tired old codes ε semaphores.

In the theater foyer a potted ficus was tastefully hung w ornaments: clowns harlequins dancing figures in folk costumes, tiny theater masks, longstem glass roses ε the like. Set at its top was a glossy-white halfmask, the now-famous logo of the webber/hart musical. A small spotlite was trained on it from above so that the resultant shading was just the right mix of stony suavity ε plastic terror. One encountered a smaller replica of that tree on a table in the bar, into which we sauntered after a brief tour.

"He wrote *cats* before i was born. Reesy [aurise] 'n' me meant to see it but never did. It seemed sorta superficial anyway. <Look at the man. T. eliot.> Vladimirovich said eliot's name, spelled backwards, was like his verse. I think mirovich disliked him for the brutal things he did to his poor worshipful wife ...unforgivable things." As she enumerated the bartender served us unflinchingly. (I had crossed a hundred w two 20s, symbol of my good intent.) "I think he thinks i'm in the play."

And that i'm your father. "You doofus", says she, slapping my wrist. I hafta warn you about me, i began. Tho i'd seen the webber/hart musical w the orig ny cast, still i was sure i was in for a taxing eve —unless the performance was bad. I explained. <I employ everything from lip&tung-biting ta pinching myself, from looking at floor or ceiling ta mentally blocking all sensory intake. If it's a *merciless* tearjerker i sometimes even hafta imagine myself fornicating with hairy fat ladies who dont bathe. Or, failing these, i must leave the theater as tho removing a misbehaving child to lobby or street. An ongoing project of mine is to make it to the end of *dances with wolves* —past the part where snow is falling and they break camp, and dunbar looks like he's about to ride away, back to the wrath of the pursuing army...> away from the twa maryit wemen ...wrong dunbar, sorry... i mean <away from standsWithFists. I've twice left the theater halfblind (from the blowing snow), tho they tell me the end isnt all that bad. But then my mother told me that about *little boy blue.*>

I was not prepared for what transpired as the theater darkened and the auctioneer's gavel rang out. A musicbox, fashioned in the shape of a barrelorgan, is brought forward. Atop it the figure of a monkey in persian robes plays a cymbal. The box is set playing. "Just my luck" whispers Li, ducking, pressing her forehead against my arm. (The reader may recollect, she has this thing *w* musicboxes.) Matters only got worse from there. Only tonite, almost 4yrs later, can i understand all she must have gone thru that eve —first as her young self, lotte; then as torn *&* tormented christine, and in *both* of them as herself, Lilith.

CHRISTINE (dressed as a 17th century poet)
...The truth isnt what I want to see. In the dark
it's easy to pretend....

NATHAN (playing raoul)
It's okay.

(musicbox playing again)

LOTTE (christine as a girlchild)
Softly, deftly, music shall caress me. Hear it,
feel it, secretly possess me ...this darkness
which I know I cannot fite... O how I fear the
music of the nite....

RAOUL (suspecting lotte is Lilith)
It's okay. It'll be okay.

LOTTE (making the best of some awful situation)
...Forget all thoughts of the world I knew before
...let my darker side give in ...perhaps my fear
can turn to love for him....

RAOUL
Little lotte, listen to me! This man, this thing,
is not your father. You dont have to do all he
commands of you!

LOTTE (pretending her real father is with her)
You were once a friend and father ...then my world
was shattered ...wishing you were somehow here
again ...wishing I could be all that you dreamed
I could... too many years fiting back tears
...O why cant the past just die?

RAOUL
No more talk of darkness. Let me dry your tears.
I'm here beside you, to hold you and to hide you.

LOTTE (pretending to be the poet, Lilith)
Anywhere you go let me go too. ...With you, always
beside me, to hold me and to hide me ...that's all
I ask, that's all I ask of you.

At several points –okay, yes. I admit it– i wanted to rush her to bed, to the floor of a forest clearing a meadowland copse the grass of some riverbank some seashore even an empty theaterbox. At intermission, when all left the box but us, thinking her upsetment to be little more than a case of theater empathy, i attempted to lighten the atmosphere. When she mentioned "What a great job the girl playing christine is doing", i reminisced about the ny performance i'd attended. <I was so taken with ms chenoweths' christine i almost wrote her a note. I'd met kristin during my friend the baron's mounting of *fanny* (nudejoisy, paperdoll playhouse) but finding her betrothed i figured, "Here's a girl with no heart to give", 'n' walked away.>

Fearing to look up quite yet and still sniffling some, "*Fanny's* one of my favorites. [then checking w her program] Act 2 starts with a masquerade?"

Yes. And, fer me, one o' the weakest parts. I'd like to invite webber to dinner sometime, talk him into a new musicbox theme, something more hurdygurdy folkish —i'm thinking of a mahlerish sort of reverie ...darkly carnivalesque ...which of course would involve composing new masquerade music.

There was a butterfly fragility about her declined features.

Imagine prokofiev (or so i'd say to andrew) listening to berlioz' *romeo and juliet* with his unique ear yet having the sense to retain its dark sweet mood: moist summernite, distant music, frenzied whirling of a fantastic waltz (one,two,three & sweep,clash,fall; one,two,three & sweep,clash,fall), climbing thru key changes to unheard-of choreographic heights; all this playing tag with a skittish scherzo, a "queen mab" syncopation of harlequinesque harmonies. Sorry. I get like this whenever i'm saturated with good art. Ideas spill out of me like litters from the motherOfInvention ...i'm hearing in all this also berlioz' "dream of a witch's sabbath", the nasty brass, the rutting rasping strings cleverly inmixed visually with eddypoe's various masquerade scenes: the masque of the red death, say, or the grotesqueness of william wilson. Are you getting the picture?

She yods.

No, i mean, that's what i'd ask lloyd webber: Because the masquerade scene acts as a prelude to act 2, maybe it should be invested with a sonatalike development —i'm thinking now of the compactness, the cohesion, in beethoven's *lenore* overture. Which brings us back to poe again. Dont you think they look like brothers? Even twins? Berlioz 'n' poe, i mean?

I think my word-scat took her by surprise; say nothing of my own puff-eyed gaze when, sidelong & matted-lashed, she chanced a glance my way. (The guy who played the phantom was so mediocre i might not have shed a tear save for Lilith's own secreted meltdown.) "I'd give you this but i think i've ruined it." She clutched the handsker i'd passed to her after the second musicbox scene. <It's okay. Got one.> I show it. "O, that reminds me." Rummaging. It was then i saw, her purse (white) should have been masked in black suede like her boots. The lites dimmed a warning as she returned my handsker from that nite by the bay. A shakespearean scholar might say, "Aha! Desdemona." But i merely said, <Thanks. At this rate we'll be needing this>, over which we shared a chuckle —dramatic release, really. She lowered her head as others in our box returned. As i pocketed the handsker the raptoral [sic] profile of an eerily-lit tug slid darkly by in memory, the whiskers of its badly frayed tow-lines (looped across the bow) begging some barber's razor.

Lilith

After the theater we went for a drive, rode moreorless in silence. My rational mind, like a fool taking dictation from a genius, does a running commentary as the art it's been exposed to is assimilated into the subconscious —brilliant dyes soaking into an anarchic sponge! Webber's melodies played in my head, rewound themselves, played again, their lyrics perched, like lachrymose birds, on the rungs of my unmusical lips, each mentally singing itself to sleep.

I headed up twin peaks boulevard.

"Did you ever watch it? <What?> I know you didnt. You wouldnt waste your time. Dumb question. Nevermind." I did not probe. I feared she was sinking, or had sunk, into a depression beyond me to halt. Nor would i recall the allusion til i read in the journals of her girlhood, "Twin peaks is his [her stepfather's] favorite tv show —almost as weird as him." I parked.

Twins, yes. But not identical. One's 904 feet asl, the other, 910.

Valiant try at conversation. "Even identicals are not usually identical."

I thought about that. From here you c'n see *both* bridges!

And far below...a city exceeding fair to ken.

Her face was set in profile against the cities' fiery parcels. I could see the faintest flutter of her lashes ...dark moths flopping against an unseen windowpane, whisking into the diffuse lite a mist of teardroplets. I wanted to kiss those wet eyes as they tracked the cars below, tracked the lites creeping across the distant jeweled spans.

<*And thee across the harbor silverpaced....*>

She looked over.

<*A bedlamite speeds to thy parapets, tilting there momentarily, shrill shirt ballooning....* Hart crane, a gifted pontist, would have loved those "swift unfractioned idiom[s]" down there. Definitely that one over there. I yod at bridges. Tho she did not remember the poet's name, she recalled once reading "to brooklyn bridge" & "for the marriage of faustus and helen".

The play was hard on you... Had i foreseen... i mean, you coulduv gone t' the parade tonite 'n' had a waybetter time. I feel bad.

"Actually it was a great experience. ...one of the most powerful evenings of my life. [silent pause] It's jus that it was sorta personal, that's all. There was no way even *i* coulduv foreseen that?"

Dont feel, please, bad about crying. It was a bottomless weeper for me too the first time i saw it. Even t'nite, several times i had to imagine myself consorting with a bevy of hirsute 'n' farting fat ladies [quizzical sidelong grin/squint] ...all ta keep myself so disgusted i couldnt think to weep.

Gratuitous smile. "I'm sorry. That was very funny, i know. Youre probably thinking it's you. It isnt. It's me. [celtic weep in her voice] I need to deal with this stuff 'n' move on. I know that. [swallowing, eyes rolling, hoping to fix on something that will block the tears welling wout permission] But i dont know how." Celtic weep turns into swallowed neopolitan sob.

Unthinking, i leaned across the console, wrapped an arm around her, w fingertips brushed the wetness on her cheeks. <Sorry, but i'm fresh outa handskers.> Choked-off sobs mixed w laffter began to flow out of her like a dam coming apart.

"Dont think this is about daddy. It's not. It's my miserable stepfather. *He's* the phantom in the soapopera of my stupid life."

It's *your* nite; [stroke her hair] cry if ya wanna... It'll help. It *always* helps.

Gradually, out it came. "He'd even do stuff in front of her sometimes [in front of her mother]. Not nasty ...at first. But suggestive. She knew how i hated it but she'd jus smile. He had her sooo brainwashed. ...Lage thinks she was off doing drugs with him even before the divorce. Plus, she was abused as a kid herself. I know that now."

Lage?

She lifted herself off my chest, stared. I'll never forget that look: eyes wet & swollen, face dark —mix of pain & wonder. Such wretched beauty i'd seen only on film: fine actors, fine camera work. "Huh? Lage?" She was incredulous, as if i couldnt possibly know something about her sister she didnt. "Lage said she was abused?"

Lage? What are you talking about?

Our double misunderstanding left her sighing w relief. "That's all i need: sis abused too. I'd jus give up." Inflection, reaction, like dorothy in *the wiz*. She had meant to say, it was her "mother, back in france" who'd been abused "when she was young." I remember packet of tissues in glovebox. She settles back, wiping her face.

Have ya ever told this stuff t' anyone?

"Just reesy. A long time ago."

Ya oudda unload it then. It could make all the difference. I ask how things started.

Haltingly at first, she explains "...Then, a few days after they came back [from the islands; belated honeymoon] it startedup again. One day after school he grabbed me so hard [in the groin it turnedout] i couldnt get away without it really hurting. I got smart after that; stayed way clear of him. But you dont need this garbage. I know it's a mistake but... [pinches lips, shakes head, swallows hard, takes deep breath, looks askance] But i cant play mindgames like most people do. Youre always upfront with me all the time... upfront with the whole world actually."

I ask why no one called the cops on him.

It took awhile but someone had. "He blamed me but i think it was mr xavier [one of her teachers] ...a really wonderful man. Some people came to the house one day. Not the police; some agency; the county, i think. But mother wouldnt press charges. She told them i was just upset about her remarrying. She said okka was just... I know. That's what reesy named him: okka... She said he was just an affectionate man (God! C'n ya b'lieve that?) 'n' that he was jus trying t' be a real dad t' me." Shivers head nervously —that tic, that tiny litening-quick shiver of hers, which would one day break my heart ...once i understood its cause.

I maintained contact –shoulder, arm, touching hair– reassuringly.

"I think she believed what she said. Backthen, anyway. O, i could tell you things... He is so clever ...soooo clever...." Her voice trailed off.

By then my blood was fuming like whitewater. She was cold. I started the car for the heat. It had grown chilly ε damp as the inevitable fog moved in. Not her words so much, but the depth of feeling behind them, led me to suspect {This is just the tip of a whopping iceberg} —floating above a seemingly imminent seafloor volcano.

"I think... I think i'd better get on home."

I dont. [looks over, lips parted] I'm not leaving you with this... all alone with this stuff... hanging over your head. It would be... it would be cruel. I'm thinking hot chocolate warm music 'n' good company. I faced about, drove us directly to "my" apt. On the couch, playing the same music that had lulled her to sleep before, she contd, but only by dint of very creative encouragement on my part. What i learned that nite was nothing, of course, compared to what is recorded in her journals, the whole confessional sequence of which is addressed to (but was never given to) lalage. Lilith made the entry which follows about 3yrs after the fact of its actual occurrence: aged12.

Mother went to visit Aunt Leticia. [in Europe. —Ed.] Ree [Aurise] couldn't sleep over that night. She'd sleep over (like i told you) or i'd go to her house, whenever i thought i might end up alone in the house with him. That night he came to my room, asked me, "Whatcha readin?" Instead of saying, "A book Ree loaned me", i flashed the cover, gave him a nasty look. This made him mad. He grabbed it. (He always mispronounced my name. Leelee, he'd say. He meant, Lily —trying to copy Mother. Over time you can grow to hate a little thing like that.) "Puh-hal-lus in ...in hum-ber-land...?" he stumbled over the title. "What the hell's that?" He threw the book down, reached over, began to touch.... Well, my breasts... through my nightshirt. I pushed his hand away. He slapped it. "Now, now. None o' that, Missy!", and started again.

I imagine those eyes as she writes: gray, squited w tears & resignation.

Well, using the tips of his fingers like a broom he swept back and forth over them, saying the whole time he knew i liked it. I stopped him again. He hit me harder. So i twisted onto my stomach, buried my face in my pillow, prayed for him to go away. I felt him sit on the bed. Knowing i was alone in the house with him terrified me. Nothing happened for a few minutes. I knew he hadn't left because i could hear him moving, breathing. Then i felt my nightshirt lifted. I gritted my teeth. Either i was shaking or the bed was. I yelled for him to go away. The shaking stopped, then started again. I heard him groan, the gross gargoyle. Then it was quiet. I squeezed my eyes tight and started to pray.

He began moving about, doing something. All at once he started kissing my ...well, my butt. I reached down, pulled his hair. He grabbed my wrists and held them, just kept doing it, all the while trying to remove my panties. We wrestled. He punched me really hard in the back of the head. Panting like a dog he told me i'd better do what he said or i'd be sorry. He threw me on my back, pulled me to a sitting position, took one of my hands and made me... well, touch him. It was ugly. Really ugly. Then he grabbed the back of my neck, pushed my face down. "Ya know you've been wanting to s--- it" he said. I punched him. I swung as hard as i could. I told him he was disgusting. He lost his temper, hit me with the heel of his hand, real hard in the head. (He was smart never to leave marks right from the beginning.) It almost knocked me out. He picked me up, threw me face down, ripped off my panties, pulled my nightshirt over my head, tied the ends of the sleeves together so i couldn't move or see, then crawled on top of me. I could feel he was naked. I prayed to God the phone would ring or someone would come. He stayed there, crushing me for what seemed like hours, panting, growling, dripping like a wet dog. Then he... Well, you know. Then again, maybe you don't. It was just awful, anyway—a disgusting way to be introduced to sex. Well, to man/woman sex.

I dont remember in relation to what but, in the expurgated version she related that nite she said, "I didnt know if lage said anything t' you or not. [Wh-whadaya mean?] I mean, i dont know if she maybe guessed anything like this ever happened ta me?" Tho i answered nnn-no, i didnt really grasp what she meant at the time. But then, i didnt want to interrupt either, for we'd reached the most delicate part of her confession.

"He tried to but couldnt." Each time she noted these things her head, sometimes her left shoulder too, would jerk spasmodically, yet allbut imperceptibly; or one thigh would spaz inwardly; motions so slite as to be missed by anyone but a disciple of body-language; movements motor-sympathetic w a given traumatic or sexual memory. "He finally went away.... No, he didnt. Ya know me, little miss too-tite-ta-tango. [i manage an empathy smile] But my victory was shortlived. A couple hours later i wouldnt be so lucky."

In this cathartic outpouring she said she "wished" she could have "shared this stuff with sissy. But lage'd never get over the shock of it...i mean the revulsion. I c'n understand that b'cause maybe i never will either. [i questioned this. She misunderstood] That's just it. We *are* close. So close it would be like this stuff happened to her too." As for her best friend, reesy (who "went thru most of it" w Lilith), she "wont talk about it anymore. She's tryin t' forget too".

I kneaded the ligaments at the sides of her neck, her head tilting side-to-side as i did so, her hair spilling silkily over my forearms. "That feels sooo good." Many guys would have used such a moment as a springboard to sex; she might even have wanted or needed that for all i knew. But i felt it was my job only to hold her ...to hold her til she noddedoff. I remember droppingoff to sleep wondering, Why doesnt she make the world a safer place for girls and have the bastard put behind bars? Had i understood her better i would not even have considered this. For while antelope know very well who their killer is, they never gang together to destroy the cheetah. As w flowers trees & butterflies, a stampede of trampling vengeance against the lion is alien to the zebra.

Now, before we wrap this day, a peculiar thing deserves noting. After midnite (prison time, not book time) it will be october 31st —nite of all nites of the year! And here's the odd part. If i were writing this chapter tomorrow, the day of its writing and the day i'm writing about would be the same! But i see i've noted this already.

13

Because of the long-standing latino community on the pacific coast, *los dios de los muertos* festivities are a big deal in frisco, which anyway just might be the parade ε party capital of amer. In '93 it fell on a wedn. Tho primarily a latin fiesta, like halloween, it was a big day for pibs in general. (In case it should fade out of usage, pib is a cult acronym for 'people in black', which incl's everyone from trad goths to industrial ravers.) Because a friend had a "unit" entered in the official parade and because Lilith had agreed to help, she needed to leave work almost as soon as she ε brian got back.

Now sorrel le rose –whose surname was really jones and who called herself a goth– attended a couple classes w Lilith at ccac. Faux goth would be more like sorrel except faux is largely the point of goth. And so i prefer chick goth, or posh goth, where the sorrels of that scene are concerned. This is not to say i didnt like her —perhaps even toomuch for a wee stretch there. It was on meeting sorrel that i learned of L's part in the parade that year. The goth's first float was a model house of usher; the second, sorrel's creation, a horse-drawn hearse w a lidless coffin driven by roderick usher 'himself'. In it, who else but lady madeline, presumably on her way to burial ...alive —and played by none other than Lilith! Sorrel gave me some fotos to peruse while she recounted the day's events in that surpassingly sexy diction of hers. Munch's 'madonna!' i yelped on seeing the closeups —b&w only of course.

Rumors of her mean-spirited talk of L ε me having scuttled upstairs, that th nikki was called on the carpet —after a fashion. For penance she was told to rehire Lilith at once. (GE treats its tenured employees w verykid gloves.) At the time clueless as to the extent of nikki's viciousness, and given my position w gE, i kept my head low thru it all. Th nite i called L to wish her luck next day (off to l.a again), found her still unusually lowkey. Almost by accident i learned she had questions about her upcoming contract. <Am i understand-ing this? Rather than call me... Okay then, rather than bother me, you were gonna enter into this agreement not knowing the answers to any of these things?> She guessed she was. [This editor was at that contract signing and saw to it that all of Ms McGrae's questions were followed up on. —Ed.] <What's going on, Lilith? I thought we were friends?>

Further converse revealed, she'd gotten "the impression, after telling [me] all that stuff" about her stepfather, that i'd "rather have had nothing more to do with [her]". The reader may have guessed: Because i'd kept my distance that nite. <So much for empathizing with you at a time when every other guy on Earth woulduv tried to jump you!> I tried to remember in which of my books i'd written, <If we greens feel more tenderly toward MotherEarth for her having been abused, why dont *we* love ourselves more, we who've *also* been abused?> ["*Scapegoats.*"] Your favorite, you said. An' still, when it comes to your *own* purity, you hang on to all that civil-religion crap? [silence] Look, i'm sorry. I guess my patience is worn thin on this topic. [for we'd tackled it also the nite of her confession] What in the world has your, or my, or anyone's, sexual history got ta do with our essential purity as living things? JesusbuddhabrahmakrishnaDao! The purity of Nature itself is innate in us. Just like it is in any blossom 'r possum. Only we ourselves can give it away, Lilith. No one but no one c'n take our purity from us. My purpose was not to make her feel bad for having assumed the worst of me, but to slam the brakes on any such future self-doubts.

On fr Lilith brian rick ε emil returned to l.a to enter into a full-production contract. Lilith L. McGrae, gE enterprises ε animaze studios inc were the principles. So as not to appear her big protector, i made no effort to attend. While i wanted to ensure that she got at minimum 10% of profits, if profits were ever made, i dared do no more than suggest as much. Beside, i felt incompetent to gage the value of her work for at least three reasons. ❶ I was it's subject, ❷ i'd fallen in love w its creator, and ❸ i knew very little about cartoon art ε its reproduction at the time

While at hq that day, pickingup some gE paraphernalia prior to a luncheon lecture, delphine flagged me into her office. It seems, two fbi agents had been in the bldg on&off all week asking staff questions about the carbomb death of roy freeman. Rick, the most politically savvy among us, viewed the investigation as "an attempt of some person or persons, working thru the f-b-i, to pin roy's murder on greens, the objective being to paint a picture for press 'n' public of greens being essentially violent people at war even among themselves". Tho rick named no names, certain elements of epa appointee strickland's speech circulated w the story.

RE fed propaganda: greens killing greens. Any group is potentially dangerous. In the ugly face of human history, indeed, in the ugly face of its own history, the fbi should be first to admit that. Still, truth is, greens make poor vigilantes & even poorer killers. If you doubt this, ask my friend the baron (when & if they find him) why the green revolution failed. He'll be quick to tell you, "Because only one side has the killer instinct: The big corporations 'n' their government thugs."

"They identified themselves as f-b-i, wanted permission to interview staff. I called brian and he authorized it" said deldevi in a musical brit echoing the amazing arundhati roy. "They happened to run into nikki out in the hall there. 'We'd like to ask you some questions' they said. 'And if I dont cooperate' says she 'will I be arrested or something?' 'Not at all' they say. 'We'd just like to talk to anyone who might have some idea who, or why, someone, or some group, would want roy freeman dead. You *do* know who he was?' "

Tho delphine's recounting of the incident was excellent, and tho she could see their reflections "perfectly" in her doorglass, we will replay what remains wout all the quotes-within-quotes, a pain to writers & proofreaders both. [And to editors. —Ed.]

"No, I dont [know who he was]. You see, I was born yesterday. I'm just a little big for my age."

"I sense a little antagonism here." One agent to the other.

"Lemme ask. Have you guys ever harassed or intimidated a green?"

"No" they answer, straightfaced. "Matter of fact, at this very moment we're tryin our best to solve the murder of a green." To which the other agent chimes in, "...And we have this idea, perhaps naive, that greens (like yourself) would want to help solve the murder of one of their own."

"Touche!" yelps nikki. "As a matter of fact, now that you mention it, my ex-fiancé might have murdered him."

Breachbirth pause.

"And who might that be?"

"Nathan schock. You mayuv heard of him?"

"And his motive?"

"O, that's easy. Roy was getting toomuch of the glory. Nathan thinks he's Motherearth's favorite son, you know. Top guns fite over things like that."

"They do?" "I see."

"Hey, guys. Lightenup. That was a joke. You know, a joke? As in smile... laff even?"

"I guess blowing people up doesnt strike us as especially funny."

"And a fellow green too." "Very messy."

"I really must be going. People t' see, you know —people hopefully a little less ghoulish.... O, by the way. [turning back] There was actually no competition between them: Roy freeman 'n' nathan schock, I mean."

"O?"

"No. None at all. Freeman was clearly the better man. B'side [coming back another step, looking around ε whispering]... Actually, schock would gladlyuv died in his place just to keep roy from becoming a legend ...which is sure to happen now. ['very twinkley'] Bye guys. Have a ghoul day."

"And there you have it" says pragmatic (yet) warm deldevi, a bit gloomed from the telling.

I have this belief, says i. If i had a kid i'd pass it on t' him... or t' her.

"O?" says dev ...while not just dromedaries but camels too, at oases everywhere, stare off into hot quavering space like so many bison, their faces silently owning the wisdom of the ages.

Beware of those to whom the joke, the laff, is everything, with little or no regard for its content or result.

Dev agreed. That eve i joined the showbiz squad (Lilith brian rick ε emil) for an ad hoc bration. Wondering what was going on in her head, i spent alot of that eve furtively watching Lilith —if indeed one can watch a woman secretly in her presence. Here she was, star of the eve, w the least to say yet the most attentive. It was then i learned, in circumstances which tended to resemble class/student situations –group listening– Lilith had a curious habit.

We five sat around a large hightop. Once plates were cleared ε talk took the focus, Lilith leaned forward, slid fluidly into a pose i call 'the lovely listener'. One elbow to tabletop in midline w her shoulders, she brought chin to rest on upturned heel of hand, wrist flexed backward, fingertips folded to lips as tho cupping a tiny harmonica. She could hold this pose indefinitely, lashes batting over liquidy eyes, while the conversation went on around her, her gaze drifting from speaker to speaker, drinking in meanings past words, storing away the event at a level unsuspected by those present. When asked later, she thought she'd developed the pose in hs, but browsing an elementary school yearbook a few years later, i found a foto of her in the same pose, elbow on knee instead of tabletop, sitting, legs folded, next to lage, among other girls in school uniforms, the lot of them more than a little bored w whatever the proceedings were about. At table, desk or counter for any length of time, one would see this trademark posture, usually affected w right hand; presumably so her left was free to write. In this pose she would limit her talk to brief responses. And tho she could enunciate just fine, to watch it happen was like operating the mouth of a puppet w your eyes.

14

Next morn, while waiting for Lilith to arrive, in an effort to continue the bration into the wkend, i attempted to once more dump my sa eve lecture on the baron —this time ready to offer not just the chance to repay me, but cash, which i knew he could use. But i could not reach him.

L wanted to pay a visit to jessica threadgood before she left town. The reader may doubt this but, had the famous actress been someone who lived in a shack in mississippi, L would have reacted in the same way. She was, quite simply, thoroly charmed by the worldlywiseness & kindness of this woman. We got off the cablecar at the wrong place. It being still quite early however, and waiting for another car seeming a waste of time, we decided to walk.

She wore a faded denim outfit that day. I'm not just setting a scene here; she was in fact wearing such an outfit: shortsleeved peasant blouse wrapped onto the shoulders, tied across ribcage, showing little cleavage as usual. What the outfit did feature were the divine delta-wings of her clavicles as they swept from breastbone to shoulder. As to the jeans, tho relaxed in the leg, they ended hugging her hips.

Streets surrounding the mark are quaint, architecture varying block to block, sometimes house to house, w the meld dominated by spanish-european influence and colored by new world stone & ceramics. White stone fences intersected w cobbled streets, which roamed up&down the hills as far as the eye could see. At one corner a tourguide was dropping the names of famous people living in the area: "Not all moviestars live in hollywood. Many live right here on the hill."

"Miss threadgood [chided Li] tried t' warn us about snob hill."

How nice to be with someone who c'n really walk. "But this flatland body of mine is not used to such hilliness anymore. Is this what they mean by cablecars climbing only halfway t' the stars (get it)? You hafta climb the other half (huff,puff) by yerself?" Only feigning out-of-breathness, she had a habit of wincing when kidding around, as if expecting thrown objects.

At the frontdesk a clerk told us "She had to leave town ...but [index up, walks away, returns w envelope] Where did you meet her? [L explains] Well, she left this for you." Sunny, scented, its lovely loopy writing read: "Give this to the lovely girl I met on the cable car if she should stop by. Thank you."

"Looks like *my* writing. <Arencha gonna open it?> Maybe later." She stuffed it in her bag and off we went. From the hotel we headed for the twin towers of grace cathedral, "called the notre dame of america. Well, we'll see about that." During the visit she said two intriguing things that i recall. One, looking up at the rose-window ("Now *this* reminds me of paris."), the other beside a "fountain in the roman style", trying not to notice the immature genitals of the cast youth beside her: "When i saw notre dame for the first time i felt like i'd been there b'fore". She'd spent 3wks in europe w aurise ε family when she was 15. When the campanile startedup its clangor, teasing, hunching up shoulders ε elbows, glaring across her delicate declined bow i said in a gravely voice: So esmeralda, does zeez *moment* bring back memories for you za way it does for me?

"Esmeralda. Whereuv i heard *that* b'fore?" But it turnedout she'd read only "hi*s les mis*", and this was well before disney's *notre dame* mistreatment.

As tho waiting for us, a cablecar pulledup when we reached powell.

"And what about those songs? [i'd mentioned a couple songs i liked] You know, i dreamt last nite we were in the "carousel museum" [main focus of our day's itinerary]. But somehow it was back in va. An' you came t' visit us. I was young then. <What are you now?> The museum was filled with *my* musicboxes. Waymore than i actually have. An' each time i showed you one you knew its melody! It was amazing. But my dream kept confusing you with daddy. [grows contemplative] The songs. Sing them. I might know them."

Trust me, you dont. The only people who know *these* songs either wrote 'r sang 'em.

As we stepped from the car the bus we wanted was just pulling away. <Cablecar comes 'n' allbut sweeps us off our feet; bus leaves us flat. Get used t' it. [curious squint] The *De* of Cosmic parity i call it. It haunts me.>

"A kind of bad luck?"

No. Different. With bad luck ya know what youre getting. But shock-value is the name of this game (pardon the name, schock). Ever full o' surprises! In fact, surprise is what it's all about. Great luck, then terrible; medium bad luck, then medium good —but never in predictable order. O, no. That's the challenge. A sort of schism of infinite balance. Good for the Universe, bad fer me. Cause the Universe c'n deal with it. I cant. Kinduv a pollyanna version of murphy's law. Works handinhand with what i call the smallshit conspiracy. Smallshit is one word. When he sees me coming, murphy-the-prankster becomes thanos-the-tormentor. [blank look] An' since i'm the sort who'd rather face an enraged dragon every day at noon than swat intermittently flies 'n' mosquitos from dusk til dawn, it is exceeding fun for mad murphy to rub my nose in trivialities ...while, of course, taunting me the whole while with a closed book of the vaster laws i'd really like to have my nose rubbed in.

"Youre serious, arent you? [squashing successfully a smile] I mean, youve really thought this thru."

That i have. Serendipitous fate i used to think it was. Now i know better. It's serenduplicitous fancy. But no need for concern. [happily] Just a word t' the wise. Oops, is this 'r bus? Nope. Never mind.

A candystore occupied the corner we stood on. Across the street stone steps climbed a grassy hill; at its top was a white portico. "Where are we?" She checked streetsigns while whipping the pages of her guidebook. A young couple approached; she hung on his one shoulder, a radio hung on his other; both same height; handsome, italian i guessed.

"Here we go: chapel o' the madonnas. Unusual for having two madonnas, it says."

I see them ...madonna, there: madonna, there. Hard t' believe this town was settled mostly by heathens socalled.

Our fellow travelers, picking up on L's traveltips between kisses, turn down the radio, over which, tonite, a desperate love ballad seems to be playing.

For she's gone, gone away. I dont know where.
And the ache in my heart is too much to bear.

"One is called mother-of-joy; she's the one holding the infant christ; the other is called mother-of-sorrows; she cradles a crown of thorns."

"Scuse us, but, da-, is dis whea...." They wanted to know if "da bus t' da coit towwah stops heah?" Religious medalion dangling twixt pert breasts. Both seem friendly enuf (the lovers, i mean); still, his fast dark eyes swiped all they dared of the adorable docent at my side.

"I think it does" she smiles. [They turn away –"Tanx"– look into storefront window facing other st. Behind the glass on our side, heartshaped boxes of candy recline. <Thought at first they were speaking mish> —brooklynese-like dialect Lilith had been exposed to in the mission district.

"She wears her hair like reesy." Short straight wetlook.

"Hey, -a, could youz guys give a yell if, a-, da bus comes? Me an' her'll be roit insoid gettin sumpum... Hey, tanx."

You miss her dont you?

"No. I'm jus worried."

Jungfrau cheer goes up across the street.

He wont *really* bother her, will he?

I felt she expected i knew the answer. I didnt. "He has ways." Puts edge of book to lips, gazes off into distance, seeing nothing west of the mississippi surely. I follow that gaze, see only some girlscouts & what looks like the man from the horrorhouse –just a type, actually: stern dark person in suit, an intn'l sort one sees everywhere– waiting for our bus's twin across the street. Cablecar, gonging, slews between. Book still raised, she rests her forehead briefly against my arm. "Let's not spoil today with that business."

You are absolutely right. Let's not.

As lovers emerge munching contents of small white bag, Lilith is once more buried in guidebook. As she studies it the lovers walk from the candy store ("Hi-a. Hey, me 'n' her aint gonna wait no maw. Nice meetin' yas dho."), head for the chapel on the hill. As they leave the corner L announces, "Youre not gonna b'lieve this! We're only four blocks from where we're going!"

The tower on telegraph hill, worthiest of commemorabilia no doubt, may be the most ludicrous phallic symbol in the world. Donated by lilie "firebelle" hitchcock coit, a wealthy eccentric who was for many years "the firemen's mascot", insisted on it being built in the shape of a firehose nozzle in honor of the brave men who died saving the "little city". Because of its shape, the name & many suggestive tales about the woman who saw to its erection, it has long been the butt of local humor, being called everything from lillie's lingneus to coitus tower. Thinking the elevator might be less crowded next trip we browsed the frescos on the ground floor, one of which was painted by <Hey, siqueiros! He painted hart crane!>. It was at that time i believe i first noticed stylistic similarities between the fresco "the accident" & balthus' "the street", as if the angry little boy of the former grewup to be the man restraining the young woman in the latter —except that both were executed the same year on different continents!

There being hardly less people next time around, i decided to brave the "social realism" of a crowded elevator. With the elevator not working right and no stops along the way to the top, i annotated as we slowly rose. <I'm not real good at elevators>, standing behind L, long ape arms dangling, holding her hips. <Specially ones that creep 'n' groan like this.> I spoke softly into her hair. All stood in silence around us, all stared straight ahead. When i placed my chin on top of her head i learned i could look down, see her face. Tipping her head back slitely, our eyes met; grin widens her features. Straighten back up. Whispering once more in her hair. <Look around. This is how we men act in a restroom: silent, staring straight ahead.> To my surprise a man & woman next to us, on overhearing me, start snickering. <An' still we shudder 'n' rise. An' still they cant panic me, no sir.> I am having one of those stream-of-consciousness moments i've already mentioned.

It slows, shudders, surges again. <So there's grease on the cables 'n' pulleys [still whispering] and so the motor is old 'n' wornout. We're all t'gether in this, the day after trick-'r-treat, shooting up the middle of the world's scariest hollow weeny. But we're all enjoying the moment an' that's what counts.> We come to a stop; doors open. As we debark the couple beside us, beaming, says "Enjoyed it, thanks!", walk off laffing.

Lilith never impinged on my penchant for allaying the panic of cramped circumstances w impromptu narrative: in line, in elevators, in small waitingrms etc. Which leads us to ask: Does this, my cell, and my future herein, render this entire book such babble? make of the reader such an audience?

Not nearly so fine a view as that from twin peaks, still one could see both bridges w a clear shot down lombard st, "which", instructed my guide, "is called the crookedest street in the world!"

I thought that was wall street 'r madison av?

"Or massachusetts av."

Wow. What are you doing the rest of your life? [seems not to hear me]

We decide to forego public trans and walk ...thru a micro-italia, buying slices of fantastic focaccia at a bakery, passing the famed "tosca café" where one gets arias w his entree —mario ꞓ floria stepping into the shadows to check the menu posted there and allbut slamming into a scarpia-looking character as they reemerge. A few blocks later we're descending the cobbled terraced ꞓ hydrangeaed snakings of lombard, not knowing how close we'd come to the sf art museum where, 2yrs later, enlargements of some 30 of Lilith's classic capt.gE frames will be put on prideful display as "One of our town's own artists", which was sort of factual.

Like homing pigeons we came out exactly at the "carousel museum". You 'n' yer book have been plotting in secret i see. "No. Really!" Who'd guess so many items relate to carousels (sometimes by the frayed thread of the slitest pretext): mugs glasses goblets sweat- ꞓ t-shirts, placemats, refrigerator magnets, bookends totebags pencils pens ꞓ swizzlesticks, coasters posters even toasters, not even attempting a very long counterful of jewelry.

Unabashedly frog-eyed. "Your discovering my worst vice!"

I hope not your very worst.

She stared down at an array of musicboxes, hair falling just short of concealing her eyes. "Look at that!" She pointed toward the best box in the place, as if to change the subject. The fay frailness of her face was most apparent from above. A clerk who looked like a scrubbed carny was on her almost as she spoke. "What does it play?"

Pushes button on countertop. "Saves our boxes from abuse."

"O! Carousel waltz!"

Grins "Most o' them do". {Whoa. He is earnestly trying to charm her!}

Nearly an hour later, having set aside several things, i catch her shyly craving a postersize carousel connoisseur's chart, one side of which displayed in glossy color "famous carousels of the world", the obverse replete w reproductions of "most prized carousel animals in the world". I put it w her other layaways and we left.

"I never dreamt a place like that existed."

I like people who say dreamt.

"Where are we now?"

Hyde and something, i said. *Youve* got the map.

We walked, watching for a second sign. <Hyde 'n' seek? hyde 'n' jekyl? jeckle 'n' heckle? Theyre not telling.>

"Speaking of hyde. I saw in here somewhere, robert louis stevenson got married in san francisco, an' lived here for years!"

Til i got here i thought he lived in england. There's an r.l.s state park north o' here.

"I think i read somewhere he died on a tropical island. Or was that …you know …that french painter who loved primitives?"

Gauguin? It was terrific tramping w her —whereto was kind of irrelevant. I'm thinking now of those precious few times we drove to huntsdell for bagels or carrotcake, then stayed home for 3wks to makeup for the energy we'd wasted pursuing such irresponsible but delicious fun. And it all started right there in frisco, w this new laissez faire bent in my life.

We hit ghirardelli sq. <This is good cause i'm a chocoholic and, as an ex-sailor, have this thing for mermaids>. Since she loved fountains ɛ since "mermaids are people too", we sat there to sample our purchase. <This is good but it's easily bested by fran's and maison's …French import. Always keep a stash in the food cellar at home …for cocoa emergencies.>

Retracing our steps we soon came upon a statue of the city's namesake.

"Look at all the bouquets! Wow!"

Hey, today's all-saints day, huh?

She confessed to having a frances when she was a kid. "Frances was a badger with an eating disorder if ya c'n b'lieve that. Peculiar, frances was. She'd only eat strawberry jam sandwiches. An' she had a little sister who liked her eggs only sunnysideup. Is that one word? Anyway, daddy got us the book cause sister wouldnt eat brusselsprouts 'n' tomatoes 'n' i hated meat. It was a kinduv badgers-are-people-too book."

On crossing lyon ɛ mason streets i looked about for a sioux maiden and wondered aloud if L's eco-awareness might not have begun w francis the badger. <Cause, b'lieve it 'r not, mine got an early push from *the poky little puppy*>. Hardly had i said the words, hardly had she replied, "Really! I *loved* that story!", when we came to ripley's museum.

"'America's first big freakshow' [she read]. O, goody. We can go gawk at unfortunate creatures. We also passedup the guinness museum in favor of finding good water. Since i'd always avoided them i was surprised to find a wax museum enjoyable: james mason, sellars, chaplin, woodyallen, clayton moore (but not brace beemer), jay silverheels (but not john todd), the shadow ɛ superman. Also forced into a fantasy world at puberty, my tourguide understood my enthusiasm. On special daises were ol' sideburns ("the duke") ɛ young sideburns ("swivelhips"), two "legends" of the many i dont get. Its chamber of horrors did not stand up to the crack 'n' horse witches of the previous day. <While it's always nice seeing edgar poe bela lugosi klaus kinski vincent price 'n' friends, for a reallygood scare give me a powerful politician or a big ceo any day.>

"An' the room doesnt even hafta be dark."

{God, i love this girl ...this woman.}

"O there's daddy's mario!" He stood in mid-song, arms out, palms down, feet apart like a boxer, eyes sparkling, caught athwart singing the word "lite" or "spring" or "thrill" or "greatest", w a loop of *the loveliest night of the year* playing behind —if one pushed the red button, that is. She did.

Food smells at fisherman's wharf drove us to break for lunch —well, brunch. The booths lovers love were full-to-bursting so we ate at the bar, agreeing on how delicious the food at gefalen had been. Before leaving i tried to reach the baron again, and she, aurise, again. Next we wandered the piers: milling bodies in small shops, shelves ɛ counters jammed w ceramic ɛ porcelain pieces, curios "in every medium but real art", stuffed animals, wooden knickknacks, glass baubles, semi- precious bangles ɛ beads, handcarved this's, handwoven that's, imported scents ɛ exported nonsense. We strolled aimlessly from place to place, sure we would stumble on a healthfood bar sooner or later for a refreshing carrot juice or smoothie.

First time i ever saw her in sunglasses at a distance she was emerging from a public restrm. For a few seconds, as she scanned the crowd for me, unable to see her eyes, i saw her as a total stranger —stunning stranger! God! Sunglasses on unsung lasses! And she's coming this way! "Why are you looking at me like that?" You must be used to it, no? She never did answer that question candidly ...ever.

Each time she buried her nose in her book ("Where are we now?"), close in behind her, fitting my steps w hers, i would steer her thru the crowds like some beautiful blind dancer. How easily, i thought, i could lift her above my head, balance my new doubles partner there in an odd one-handed starlift —one leg extended, toes *en point*; one knee up, toes down, head thrown back, reading her book above me arms extended! Like kids we played games as we walked, trying to link food w smell, guess the relationships of people seen. Recurrent plainclothes security made us guess theft was commonplace in those parts. At pier 39 i did something unlike me. Tho i had an old rather large camcorder back home (ggNs) which still worked, i bought one of the palm-fitting cams new at the time. (I would not regret this, on hikes specially.) Stopping for drinks i studied the basics of my new camera. Our tour done, we returned to the carousel museum to pickup her stash.

Never have i encountered anyone as camera-shy as L. Good-looking people usually have no fear of a lens. I asked her to <Just wander around, look at things you like, pay no attention ta me>. Tho she tried her best to please me, she came off somewhat severely in the video; nothing like the light-hearted day we were having. At ggNs that winter, i played this film. "Youre so good with a camera." Actually, filming her in that colorful fantasyland was a little like shooting the carnivals of venice or rio: any lug w a lens is an expert by virtue of the subject matter. For it being a new camera however i did do some fair on-the-run editing: painted eye of one horse to painted eye of another, no wipes or dissolves; fast-fading from beautiful ohio waltz of the theater's calliope back into the same waltz coming from a musicbox —in fact linking them win the same musical phrase(!), tho in different keys, which couldnt be helped. My favorites, of course, were shots of Lilith: looking intently at this, or bent over that, hair draped or falling free, skin aglow, entire body unavoidable!

"I went a little crazy in there. Sorry. I'll pay you back on monday ...promise."

Hey, i'm a book, music 'n' modeltrain freak. No need t' explain.

"Which reminds me. Hafta find a bank." Turnedout she was walking around w a $100,000 advance from a 5million gE trust account "dedicated to encouraging eco-awareness in children". As we head for the cablecar station i recommend certificates of deposit <Unless you need t' spend it right away. Banks wont give you diddly for using your money otherwise>.

Behind the dusty glass of a fonebooth (i wanna try reesy again) she turns away from the camera. Watching this clip one lonely winter's nite more than 3yrs later, reduced by then to hunting down such clues, i spotted, in the very next booth, the quick profile, then the narrow back, of a dark-haired man in a businessuit, a thing i never would have noticed at the time of filming, or even later, when we watched it in our mtn retreat.

We boarded a cablecar, she toting her bag ε museum purchases, me w camcorder ε more of those purchases. Her changepurse, raped repeatedly thruout the day for streetperformers, finally bottomed out. I proffer my smallest bill. Never looking at us, white-haired man points tiredly to sign: DRIVER DOES NOT GIVE CHANGE. The beautiful gypsy ε her vagrant lover debark, walk in pursuit of change for a 20.

A much-relieved Lee ("Sometimes you only realize you miss someone when you hear their voice"), guidebook in hand, read to us as we rode to the west end of goldengate park. "The park exists due to a lifetime of dedication by one man, john mclaren, a scottish gardener ...you see? Fine people, those scots... who turned a wasteland of shifting dunes into... <A cheapshot at Mothernature, that.> True ...who turned a wasteland into a lush oasis of artificial lakes, flowers 'n' trees...."

And all this we'd miss without that little black book of yours. Again she thought i was teasing. <I'm not. Truly. It's very well-thumbed.>

"It's daddy's."

Since it requires several visits to see everything in the pk, we spent the brief ride cutting ɛ slashing events. Smell of ocean was in the air as we began walking —often the result of seaweed harvest, or rough seas uncovering organisms longburied in trough-sands, i explained. Funny how seasides smell the same around the world. "I like the smell." Me too. I wondered if she too could stand barefoot in pond ooze wout making a face.

My camera-of-the-mind sees her ogling a dutch-looking windmill, wearing babyblue faded jeans w a puffy-sleeved blouse tie-dyed in such a way it tricks the eye into seeing lavender(not purple)-on-white. Next we see her at the paddock, numbed by the shattering eyes of six or seven bison. <A thousand squarefeet for beings used to a million square-miles. It's no wonder they look so infinitely forlorn. I've felt close to bison since i was this kid, see.> I was about to relate what had happened to a bison at ggNs when she decided to quote me.

"Youve talked about bison. A faraway stare that goes right thru you, you said. That was in *last gorilla, last orang*. It went something like: They hold the plains of ancient america, and the myths of its original folks, in their eyes ...no, a-, ...in the amber-depths 'n' distances of their eyes. No, wait. There's something about shaggy wisdom too... Give me a minute here, i'll have it."

How c'n you remember that? [she didnt know how] ...That's it. As of now youre my new agent. Then again, youre gonna need your own agent soon, arent you?

She blushed ɛ looked down. Or as might be said in *tom jones:* Her complexion had more of the rose than the lily. On the way to a boat rental i watched as she headedoff to a restrm. As she left, w that deliberate yet graceful stride, i watched other eyes watching her, eyes male ɛ female. She was oblivious to this, always. She returned w a splay of postcards, most of them nite-views from twin peaks. We rented a dented duckboat rather than a gasdriven. A young family watched us from shore. <See me row my licit alice

across lake fear. Weird name, huh? [Really.] Now it's me, not the phantom, who's the man-in-the-boat, ahem —this little boat christened, Love. [she gazed at the water in such a way as to seem listening yet not impede my strange commentary] Watch me zip licketysplit around this sweet little moat.> We cut a wake beneath the slopes of strawberry hill. Halfway around we putIn, climbed the steep banks to overlook the bay.

"It says we're 400 feet up. Is that alcatraz over there? It says you c'n ferry there. Can you?"

We skipped the aquarium <Where they turn Wild 'n' free creatures into so many bored goldfish>. In the dim haze of a planetarium nite, she lifted her hair, draped it over the seatback, and, eyes glinting, leaned back to watch the narrator's arrow dart around the projected universe overhead. "It looks like a u-f-o." I could not help but kiss her, an innocent but very good kiss. Next we got silly at the children's playground. With the help of memory's ingenious editing i switch us now to the swings at ggNs. Her jeans-of-the-day tatter & flake away to white shorts as she arches into a blindinglyblue sky. Among a surround of dresses & screeches, head thrown back, in full extension at the top of her arc, she cries, "Look, nathan! <What?> The world's tipped upsidedown!". And, on our coming into perfect unison, she stretches her hand out to mine and, giddy w pendulous glee, we kick for the nearest cloud, her hair trailing behind like the negative imprint of a long cometary tail! O that the space between our reaching hands was today so finite as it was then, and that touching her once more was just a matter of good timing! Let us stay here, Lilith, in perfect sync, til i can figureout how to get back to you!

The sound of the carousel drew her attention. But again, having no one "12 or under" w us, we could only "peek in" momentarily. As we were walking away she wondered if "the musical phrase 'round in circles I go' was conscious art on the part of hammerstein or just a beautiful coincidence". I would be a long time understanding what she was getting at ...i mean really understanding. Lilith's waters ran not only deep but intricately underground! In this regard, the following diary entry was not meant ever to be seen by me: "Theatric description of my friend, nathan schock: Masquerading as enoch snow but really a billy bigelow. 'So what's the use o' won'drin' if the endin' will be sad? He's yer feller an' ya love him. There's nothin' more ta [know].' "

We ended among pagodas ɛ oriental statuary, watergardens ɛ waterfalls; and from the top of a delicate footbridge my Lily looked down at her floating floral sisters, the nymphaea, fragrant pale ɛ ethereal beneath us. In a japanese teagarden, still talking of lilies ɛ lotuses, i noted the name of her best friend.

"How could you remember that?", asked rather defensively i thought.

Miraflores? How could one forget such a name? ...Miracleflower!

"Funny i never thought o' that."

Several orientals were dining. Orientals, we agreed, seemed the most delicate of all humans. I did not say it was thanks to veronika i could look into their eyes again. In poor lite Li's hair looked as blueblack as nika's. Sipping ginsen [sic] tea on that trellis ɛ vine-covered terrace, the orange of a lantern hanging behind me asterisked in her eyes. {Who is she reminding me of? —this ethereal gentleness of feature, these haunting wide-set doe-eyes, so innocent yet so scarily wise?}

Failing again to reach the baron, on a lark, we put our ideas together: her wanting to return to point lobos, me having to lecture at uc in santa cruz. I called my contact at the school and had her reserve us "something private in a proximate Wilderness". Tho i've been carefully taught not to talk like that, in that moment of expectant elation it just slipped out.

15

We must now —still ignoring the need for a prison update ...if the reader had any idea what's going on here... These people are sick beyond belief, and, yes, cruel! Anyhow (breathe deeply; and again, deeply. There. Stay with it now.)... Anyway, we must note something before proceeding.

On&off thru our day Lilith fell into brief moments of... what to call it? Preoccupation? reverie? Gradually i am learning the signs: ❶ Lulls in conversation. ❷ Presuming she's busy at something she's not; in this instance, not studying her guidebook but gazing right 'thru' it. ❸ Manifestation of strabism —hard to spot if her left eye is at all obscured. And ❹, the tiny tic already noted, which may or may not present, and does not always signify reverie when it does, being more closely associated w fear, a relationship i had yet to unpuzzle. Beginning w her misreading of my feelings the nite of her confession; then again when i drove her home after the celebratory supper; and then on&off thru the day's events, i sensed something *still* troubling her. The first ε obvious cause was her growing need to reach aurise. But that was only a bud, not the bulb, of the black orchid she kept in secret. On our way to santa cruz i ventured my nextbest guess. <Is it your dad?>

"Sorta." Seems, altho she felt "obligated to share" the news of her capt.gE contract, she couldnt do it "now" because she ε lage had fought ... "Well, for us it was a fite. We c'n hurt each other with a whisper." Dr schock strongly recommends chimney-sweeping via sharing. Since this got me nowhere, and since it is crucial, i must now attempt a learned reconstruction of the sisters' argument. This verisimile, so to say, is based not only on L's diary-entry for that time but on my knowing, today, both parties intimately well.

When Lilith last left dillon beach she was upset. (I would say angry but, honestly, despite all that happened in our time together, i cant say i ever saw her display untempered anger.) It seems, lage, under some pressure to help w a "family problem", told don about L's stepfather (okka) coming to town, and of Lilith's agreeing to meet him. But when don went to her, asked if it was okka who had hurt her, she would neither confirm nor deny. When he pressed her, she "up 'n' left", but not wout first speaking her heart. Lalage, feeling bad about "narking on Sis", called her several times, "And if you dont call me back soon I'm coming down there!" Two thursdays later they connected. Here is that verisimile.

LEE. Do you tell him everything you know?

LAGE. Youre not serious? Like youve been on the level with me? You mean, like that? The way youve white-noised me about what's going on in your life? No, I dont think so. I think my act's a little more on the up'n'up, thank you. As fer you, I think there's something big, something real real big —some big black ugly thing that's happened t' you that you wont tell anybody about! Well scuse me if I'm ready t' do whatever it takes t' get us back t' where we used t' be —sharing —important stuff —automatically! Unquestioningly!" [Some of this probably went wout saying between two people as connected as they.]

It is this closeness L was likely re:g when she said, after seeing *the phantom,* "I wish i could share this stuff with sissy the way we used to." Lage later shared w me some of their confrontation. L: "Youre right. Okay? But I cant. I jus-, simply-, cannot. Not *now.* [lage had obviously committed it to memory nuance for nuance] It's jus been too long, laly. I've been out there too long, alone 'n' on my own. You guys jus wouldn understand all that's gone down in my life. It's too much. ["But we would!"] No you wouldnt. You couldnt. You think you could but you couldnt. It's like-, it's like somebody from a ghetto –some awfulawful gulag somewhere– is trying t' tell people how life is back in the ghetto-, people who-, people at disneyland, say-, shiny clean scrubbed little people from kansas 'n' iowa somewhere who have come there t' have tons 'n' tons of fun-, cleanclean let me stress *clean* fun. To suddenly hafta facedown real life in the gulag would be jus too much for them."

"That- that's how you think of us? Scrubbed little people from kansas? God, Sis!"

"Actually, yes. I do. I do. I'm sorry but i do. An' that's why i cant, i jus cant, share this stuff. I've jus been left on my own too long with it all. It's like-, like-, i keep goin' back t' this but it's all i c'n think of. It's like, there's a reason, good 'r bad, they dont have wife-beaters child-molesters drugaddicts 'n' serial killers marching in the disney parade. Cause-, cause people'ld be so grossed-out, so freaked, they wouldnt f'rget it fer the rest o' their lives! [picture here a finally speechless lalage and L's voice beginning to quaver badly] An' i jus dont want us t' endup like that: You, horrified of me. An' daddy, with a total heartattack over the facts, jus the facts. I wanna keep what we have. What's left of a-, of a wonderful mem'ry, actually. An' that's all i c'n say now."

And not a peep about her new good fortune. Key point. It was not the "dark stuff" of her past that was L's problem, it was facing being cutoff again from what little family she had left —specially her biologic other, a separation she of course would never get over and knew it. As the reader will be seeing, shortly after the wkend at hand, lalage ε me got the opportunity for a talk both were wanting. It was then she appraised me of some aspects of their fallingout. Apparently "a whole lot went down" in the mcGrae household after i dropped the sisters off following my rhonert pk lecture. Seems don, the day after meeting me, had skipped work to see if he could findout who had battered his daughter. Since both sisters knew only the onset of rigormortis could keep don from work, they found his mere presence around the house disconcerting. Lage in fact had planned to skip school "to be with Sister" but, "smack in the middle of breakfast", don requested alone-time w Lee.

"While I tracked down some rags 'n' scarfed my socalled breakfast he took to mooning around behind me, asking how much I knew about 'all the crap going on around here'. Crap? I go. ['go' is youthspeak for 'said'] What crap? I was maybe a bit of a bitch that day; had a big competition, plus it was not the time of moon fer me to be skipping merry 'r whatever it is ol shakespeare called it." However, sometime between Iage's leaving & returning, Lilith & don had reached a standoff. (Mightaswell use this juncture to note: At her best, Lilith would not argue; at her worst, just the thought of it scared her off.) At some point before Iage got home Lilith had slipped to silence —or as Iage put it, "she switchedoff". This was not the daughter don remembered. Such falling-silent reminded him of his ex: "That was leyda's gig. The woman who gave birth t' us? She could switchoff for days at a clip." This trait, seen now in his daughter, fritened don —"since leyda-the-luny wasnt wrapped too tite t' begin with. Daddy, mr nice, remembers her as restless. Hmph. Family trait he calls it... but only on the beauvoir side, let's get *that* straight. Personally I think our mother's a nympho first 'n' a nutcase second. But that's another story".

On the other side, Lilith, for all her depth, had little insight into this aspect of her behavior. "Classic blindspot. If I told her ('n' I'm gonna, real soon), Every time ya switchoff like that ya scare the crap oudda daddy, I know she'd be glorked!" Which was true, for L thought of herself as having little affect on her father. "And soooo... Sister kept to her room. Major crash. I jus figured she hadnt slept all week —what were you two doin anyway? Ya dont hafta answer that. Skanky rhetoric. Sorry. ...Every time I looked in on her she was asleep" and, "When I woke her t' see if she needed anything before we left, she jus slit 'er eyes, looked around, drew a blank, yodded 'n' went back t' sleep". (I love efficient language and Iage had a bunch.)

On the drive (w don) to her meet, Iage let slip, she knew more than she was saying. "So he goes t' me, 'Lemme get this straight. Youre allowed privileged information on the homefront while I jus get t' pay all the bills, is that it? I'm only here t' provide the lifestyle to which *you* get to become accustomed?' " To Iage's credit & credibility is the comic candor w which she recounted these things. "All the sudden all my jags t' oklahoma [for mentoring in gymnastics], my special school, my tutors 'n' my little red daddylac, flash b'fore my eyes. 'Dad, it's not you, it's yer temper. It's scary. If I tell ya who I think it was –let me stress, *think* it was– you'll go ballistic 'n' kill the bastard! I know you. I need a father with a job not one who's a jailbird.' Our father has no cool when it comes to fam-i-ly, capital f." Don promised not to lose his temper. "O right, says me. But I went ahead 'n' fingered the scumbag [okka] anyway ...pardon the expression, fingered. I figured, if worse came ta worse, only from the little I knew, the sonuvabitch prob'ly did deserve t' be shot, minimum."

Lage's hatred for the man Lilith called okka –and whom she called, upchucka– was based on little more than suspicion of foulplay; that is, she intuited things from how distressed her sister seemed whenever there was mere mention of the man. With the soft glow of a nearby sign pulsing in her mobile sclera as she spoke, lage hypothesized, "I dunno what the scumbag did t' her but it musta been bizotic." In a rare moment of contemplation, slumping back, forearm on her forehead, palm-up to the lavender-blinking ceiling: "Sister's not the same person I knew when we left virginia." (Reader reminder. All this i learned only *after* the sisters had argued.) "By the way, I was so pissed at everybody that nite —plus the fact my gut was cramping like crazy whenever I wasnt actually performing— all the shit goin down caused me t' ace the meet. Got gold in everything but the unevens [uneven bars] —my nemesis. An' gold overall too. *Viva la* lalage, eh? ...Lemme hear ya say *that* five times fast, prafesser."

Next day L, "wobbly as a boneless chicken", agreed to lunch w lage. Knowing he had to catch a flite that eve for some major a.m conference in chicago, one thing led to another as don readied to leave, "An' b'fore he knew it" he found himself confronting Lilith again, "as gently as our dad c'n manage such things. Like he blurted, 'It *was* him, wasnt it?' "

Openness, wonder & trust are not the words lage used to explain the look on her Sister's face when don said that. "Well [takes deep breath], Sister looks at him with such a face! Then at me! —like, sheesh!" Lage imitated her Sister's expression so perfectly that Lilith's native openness, surprise & trust were put to my memory as if i'd witnessed it myself. And so, i can see that dream-slow response of hers vividly as i write. " 'Him?... Who, him?' So dad goes, 'That mis'rable sonuvabitch who calls himself your stepfather, that's who-him!' Well, she looked over at me and with the most pathetic look you ever saw —you know, that look on a horse's or dog's face when it senses what the gun in your hand means? 'I cant b'lieve you narked!' she says in this chockedup whisper. An' I go, 'I cant b'lieve it either!' "

Apparently at that point Lilith "crept back t' her room. Dad followed. 'So it *was* him, wasnt it? [no answer] He's hit you b'fore like this, hasnt he?

['Dad!' I yell.] Ya know, your silence only tells me he has... Or maybe it's even worse, huh? Maybe he's done things to you?' (I go, 'Daddy, stop! Cantcha see this is getting worse instead o' better? God!') So he sits on the bed b'side her, puts his arm around her, 'Pet', he says, 'we cant nail the sonuvabitch if you wont say anything'. Now daddy hadnt called her pet since we were kids. She almost bursts into tears then'n'there but somehow blocks it." As i lay back listening i got a picture of crimped lips, of Lilith's eyes fixed on something faraway deep inside, of her hairline trying to crepitate backward, like waves up a beach tho the tide is going out. "She turns [away], stares out the window, her lips tite [with determination]." Oddly, today i can see that lost look better than i can remember myself backthen.

The session ended like that, *w* don saying he loved her, giving her a squeeze, kissing her cheek, rising, and both he ɛ lage tiptoeing from the room. "A few mins later Sis appears, bag in hand. 'I hafta head back ta school' she goes."

She just goes?

"No! I mean, not 'she goes' –like leaves 'r anything– but, she 'goes'. [whee, such slanguage] Y' know, 'goes'? Says? Speaks? Talks? <Right, right.> "T' which daddy goes –Okay, I mean: t' which daddy says– 'Why fergodsake?' his voice cracking. 'I'm trouble wherever i go' says Sister, matter-o'-fac'ly, heading for the door. 'B'side, i've got assignments t' catchup on.'

"Well, dad's just a flinch shy o' panic by this time. I think the times leyda walked out on him –well, on us, really– mustuv flashed thru his mind. Anyway, he up 'n' runs innerference {Innerfear-ance!}, blocks the frontdoor, takes her bag 'n' starts begging. 'We cant lose you again, Lilykins.' Now I hadnt heard *that* one since 6th grade. 'I promise, on my honor [boyscout when he was a kid, y' know], not t' ask any more questions... *ever.*' O right, says me t' myself. He reaches up, holds her cheek with one hand. 'Please dont go, Baby!' Hey wait a min now! says I. Thought that was *my* petname!"

I realized at this point i was watching the workings of one of the quickest minds i've ever known. Because, tho almost in tears herself, she tuffedout her objective-observer role to the bitter end. "Well, ta sumup, the whole damned emote ended with a mega cryfest, natchily. It was pretty disgusting all-in-all. It's a good thing you werent there. And then, Sister tells us, in no uncertain terms, what's wrong with our little family, 'n' jus goes...."

Glancing over at her untypically somber face, i wait for a quote to drop.

"I mean, goes. Like, *really* goes? As in leaves, departs, exuents stage center. [takes deep breath, let's go w a long sigh] An' I cant say she wasnt right in what she said —from her point o' view, I mean. Cause she prob'ly was. I mean, ya cant ditch somebody from yer life 'n' then demand your way back in when it's convenient. I mean, that's jus not right." Yet this, lage's epiphany of tolerance, was not easily won. In fact at the time of the tiff, lage's tendency was to emphasize don's kidglove treatment of L and her own guiltlessness (by virtue of her lack of decision-making power in family matters). To show this i ask emil now to quote from L's diary of the time. For such detail is crucial to understanding upcoming events among the mcGraes. [The following is LM's version of what she said that night before leaving. —Ed.]

I am sorry for the shame and upsetment i have brought into your lives. I understand what it must be like to have all this stuff going on, don't think i don't. I was a long time dreaming such a life as you have and i wouldn't want it wrecked by anyone either. But maybe you can understand my side too. You just can't come swooping in with your bucket of disinfectant and clean up this mess called my life just because it's not up to your standards. Not this problem, you can't. Because this problem, this infection, has been growing for a long time. And just because it was out of sight doesn't mean it wasn't festering. Yet because i'm family you look at this infection like it's growing in your own happy house —while you hoped or assumed, or whatever it was you did all those years, that everything was alright. But it wasn't. It was growing and spreading and getting stronger in the darkness, in the basement and in the attic, where you never spent any time, where you never had a minute to check, to be sure everything in your house was alright. But the festering went on so long, so awful long, that now the disease has spread, has dug in so deep and gotten so strong you're scared you're going to have to tear down the whole house to get rid of it. But since i'm used to this stuff, and since i'm the one who brought the disease, i need to be the one to carry it off. Then everything here will seem neat all nice again. Which, if the past could speak, should be good enough.

That off my chest, i left.

And again i stress. Even according to lalage, not a word of this was said w raised voice or any hint of malice, or even of disrespect. And that, no doubt, is what lent it it's sting. [This next, from that same entry, LM also addressed as if speaking to her father and sister. —Ed.]

But don't feel bad, please. Because i know, when a person has two of something he only needs one of, it is not unusual to get rid of the extra one —and why not the one with the crack or the missing handle. This may sound like I'm feeling sorry for myself (and maybe i am) but it actually helps me understand my predicament, and how and why i ended up the way i am... But this i didn't have the heart to say to them and maybe never will.

It is the next entry which astonished me most when i came upon it years later.

...And as to you, my sister, i forgive you almost completely —i mean, for not goading Daddy into bringing Mother to court to get custody of me. For i have searched my soul and i cannot say i would have reacted very differently from you back then. I say this because, by the time of the divorce you & me were sick of sharing, sharing, sharing —"halfies", always halfies; and everything the same, for you as for me, for me as for you; till we were ready to scream, "No more! Let us be who we want to be, not who you think we should be! Who knows, we might be very different persons! But allow us to find that out!" In all honesty, if i had gone with Daddy in your place, i can see where i'd be relieved maybe instead of lonely. I might have very conveniently forgot about you like you forgot about me —till i had a chance to find out who i was, anyway, a chance to grow up a little as myself, not as "us".

But now comes the part i have trouble with: I'm not sure i would have waited so long to find out how things were going with you —left behind with an emotionally unstable mother and a stepfather nobody knew squat about. And then there's the part about you being Daddy's pet —because you usually liked what he loved and i usually didn't. Though that wasn't your fault it doesn't make it fair either. And it never will be.

Because i think it's that and nothing else which led to you going with Daddy and me staying behind with Mother, virtually on my own, in that weird weird house with its weird weird people and their very weird desires ...where mental health and emotional well-being were nowhere to be found.

I remember thinking as i read, {She defends herself as poorly as i do just when incisive selfdefence is most crucial. We come out of our corners waving logic when we should enter swinging & uncaring of consequences, sadly the only way to garner respect in civil society}.

When Lilith & lalage were separated after the divorce, each was sure there was nothing she did not know about the other, and tho the separation lasted under 4yrs, it came at a time of significant change. For instance, when they met at don's place in minneapolis, after spending the summer of '90 apart, each was startled by the overt womanliness of the other, which, in cut-to-chase terms meant, each could not help but wonder if her counterpart was doing, or had done, the things her own body was plainly capable of. As lage tells it, when Lilith asked if she'd found "mr right" yet, she replied, "O, better than that. I shoulda told ya. We're pregnant with twins!" After an also "very pregnant pause" lage added, "Jus kidding!" That gave them their first "fat-free all-natural laff in ages." Lage went on to explain, "Laffs are different with Sis. I laff alot with my friends but no matter how good the friend, no matter how close, it's not the same. Like, didja ever su'prise yourself out o' the blue with a really funny thought? It's like that b'tween us. Like there's no one but ourself t' convince that what we're laffing at is just as funny as we think it is." First time i'd heard that usage: <Ourself?> "Right. Like [makes prayer hands] one body, two halfs?" <Aha.> ("...when ourselves we see in ladies' eyes.")

It was only natural that lage (playing catchup soon after L's arrival in ca), being the more outgoing, would be first to confess having "gave it up" to someone. "Matt ringwald, the two-time golder who coached me this past spring?" But the event ("our little bellyride") had been "so clean 'n' teen-zine-ish", when it came Lilith's turn to come clean... well, that was just the point —she couldnt. Save for them "[remi]niscing about some raunchy stuff ...prelim stuff, ya know? that alota 12-'n'-unders do?" (lalage), "there was just no comparing our private histories" (Lilith, in her diary).

To close this catchup. While don ε daughters exhibited a live&let-live worldliness in matters of small consequence, when it came to weightier things, personal things, all were hardnosed constructivists. Tho they would deny it (w lage loudest), don had managed to pass on to his girls his catechism: "Dont curse the potholes in the road of life if youre not ready to help build a better road." While Lilith got no less a dose, life had thrown her into very different circumstances —events "so intimate & bizarre" she couldnt even imagine relating them to her sister muchless her father. In fact, the worst of these were blocked even from her own remembrance. So, once back in the golden glow of father ε sister –w their perfect ε pure pasts, as she saw it– Lilith felt both polluted ε stigmatized, ruined ε disgraced, by incidents in her later girlhood over which she'd had little or no control.

16

It took some scrambling to put us in santa cruz in time for dinner —i'd lectured at thimann hall (hictsk) before and knew the way. Tho almost dusk when we arrived, Lilith was thoroly wowed. One of the most beautiful campuses in the world, the university is tucked among redwood stands ε mtn slopes overlooking monterey bay.

Since, as i've said, gE got so many contributors from my booksales ε lectures, they often sent a volunteer or two whose job it was to offer my books videos ε tapes and, subordinate to that, to attend to related gE business. That nite it was rick's secretary ε her husband. (Their son attended ucsc.) During my '93 lecture circuit, tho my latest book was *Mothernature & the world matron* (late '92), because most found it "too deep", i pushed along w it my *die, primitive: anthropology & imperialism* (from late '88). (I might note, right up til i ceased lecturing entirely, it was not unusual to sell at least one copy of *castration...*, my first offspring, or its attendant video or movie version.)

I remember that lecture for having snuckoff w people still waiting to see me, a 'star' tactic i rarely pulled. (It was bad enuf i'd sent a substitute speaker of late.) But that eve i was driven. For something ...something psychic hormonal lunar-tidal eye- or body-language-caused, i dont know... something insisted: Tonite's the nite! And all signs ε symbols i stumbled on agreed! And *because* we snuckoff, rick's sec got stuck w the post-lecture chat i was known for. (A letter ε foto rcv'd the following week showed how much i had disappointed at least one person, a lovely young figureskater w a limitless choice of mates.)

The school arranged accommodations at a place called capitolaptos lodge (had to use map to bring back that portmanteau name) —a handsome place not far from campus. No, nikki. The help there did not take one look at us and call the cops. In fact, they were most cordial. Male voice in back office to inquiring clerk: "Tell the prafesser 'n' his wife the school pickedup the tab." Where they got the professor/wife stuff i have no idea. Anywho, prof ε spouse immed retired to the eros end of a large bridal suite, a private outcropping of the hotel which overlooked a woods overlooking the bay.

All unwindowed walls of the suite were hung w fair repros. Surprising the shortest wall was the backfiring sensibility of magritte's "rape", while the long wall was well-hung [hic] w the delicate orientalism of two utamaro's, in their veils of yang mist, w the fantastic underwater ravishing (its graphics subtextual to start w) allbut deëroticized by fading caused by too many sunsets thru the balcony windows. A faint chem smell of new carpet was the only negative.

After calling for candles ε cognac (ε bagels ε creamcheese, in case we got hungry) i took from my daybag, robe, rip-away boxer ε jacket sleep set, ε bath tote. From the latter i removed a small tube of "luv-ease" (which was tackily subtitled "edible oil"; cherry, if you please) and slipped it into a sleepjacket pocket ...while just the thickness of a door away i could hear the shower running, pictured her washing her hair ...no, hair finished... a thoro rinsing of those lovely limbs and their attractive axes!

In knee-length robe, hair towel-wrapped, she opens door, says, "Ya c'n have it now. I'm done with it."

<Promises.> Roomserver comes, leaves. I head for shower. When i emerge, scrubbed, cleanly shaved (luxury rarely taken w shower), a hairdryer was wailing away. Craning around a corner as i toweledoff, i watch her, standing towel-wrapped before the mirror, as she tips head from sidetoside, while her hair, moving as very soft water falls, ripples back&forth lustrously, darkly, over her flesh: silk on silken.

Robed, in the only bedrm ...scuse me, bridal chamber... i brushed my hair, daubed on a musk of "rainforest mist". The room's three unwindowed walls boasted the best of the repros —w frank's "lovers" appropriately hung on the way into the all-ceramic bath; schiele's "embrace" (the good one) on the wall apposing the foot of the bed (arch-canopied ε fitted in royal&skyblue satins&silks), the entire space below the canopy valence filled w kokoschka's "tempest". I spot the edge of a paperback poking from her suitcase. Title intrigues. Sit, flaaash pages. Penned message behind front cover catches my attention. "Sis, see if this reminds you of what it reminds me of. Hope you like it. Love, Lage." Pink-wrapped blurb on back cover begins, "*Sisters, two* is vladigore's second book". Thanx to the author's ludicrous name (half vladimir, half igor) *the song of igor's campaign* popped to mind. I'd skip this whole digression except, sometime later i discovered (w a scholar's smile) in a translation of *song of...* the phrase, "...from vladimir of yore/to nowadays igor". Coincidence coddles curiosity ε viceversa, we know. But sychronicity in the bargain boggles both vice ε versa.

She emerged. "Sorry i took so long."

Now, before anything happens —while i march about the room (in my silk magenta robe w royalpurple lapels) placing ε liting candles and pouring us a snifter; and while she sits on the couch, glowing ε desirable, bare calfs ε socked feet drawn in close— we must have a little chat about sex.

With the advent of deadly bftd's in the '80s, as even people i knew or admired were struck down, i became more&more wary of the mates i took. My lovers ε me would agree (had to agree), if either party enjoyed (or suffered) contact w the bodyfluids of another person, while he or she was not obliged to confess same, he or she must abstain from intimate contact w the other party for a period not less than 12wks and, following which period, then bloodtested —if further contact was desired, that is. All agreed, it did not matter how clean or healthy an alternate mate appeared –whether *she* had bedded johnny tremain or *i* had bedded bernadette– the pact was immutable ...even tho i suspected our celibate 12wks was as much scientific farce as failsafe, for even at 12yrs it may have been too short. For fact is, i'm absolutely certain: many are the slips between condoms ε lips and i do not, and never have, believed the pop crap, "You cant get aids by mouth." To me this was just one more in a litany of deadly propagandum from med orthodumbdoxy.

But see! My words will seem sham to the reader! For the only instance when i really kiss&tell happens also to be the only one (since the early '80s) where, like evry other fool, i tossed caution to the winds of intuition: Lilith seems so very clean so healthy so non-promiscuous a person, and i've been so clean so health-conscious so careful and so choosy for so long. For, despite how my trackrecord looks, like audrey hepburn: "Tho much wanted I was never wanton." Still, in this age of plagues & palsies, cankers & cancers, only a fool or omnipotent would behave as Lilith & i did that nite at gefalen. And now, here again, we're alone together, w the odds high –quite high, if gut feelings dont lie– that we will be intimate. Here again, two reasonably intelligent people had all week to talk over these things, to setout a gameplan agreeable to both, to trade test results. Yet we didnt. Why?

Unlike Lilith, my former female friends, all the way back to juanita, given a mission, could deal w the daytoday necessities of sexual intimacy. But then, most had not been abused as young persons, had not developed such a deep (and deeply buried) fear of males. Tho she could be upfront w her journals & diaries, her poetry & sometimes even her friend aurise, something inside cringed at the thought of such talk w a man. It would be some time before she would trust me enuf to deal w this hangup ...and a lifetime before it would vanish. And since she would not discuss such things, and since something about her made me not only weak in the knees but weak in judgement, all sssop's were bypassed. (Safersex sop's: pronounced sissops; a term common around ca campuses and one i would soon hear even lalage toss off: "And we musnt ferget our sissops, of course!", well before her Sister ever said it.)

To roundout our chat, i cannot be the first to observe, the chemicals which desire unleashes in our bodies are both intoxicating & hallucinatory. In my experience, the on-rush of lust's potent potions jams the analytic function so that all that remains is a pulsing puddle of self-gratification. Precaution easily becomes a piddling pantomime going on at the perimeter of awareness. Yet, done right, sex w strangers these days should resemble preparing for a moonwalk. More&more i understand the baron's idea: "I hope aids takes out most o' the human race before its mutations run their course. Cause, for a change that would mean, *Nature* wouldnt be the one getting fucked 'n' dying. It would be us. Because the way I see it is: The bottomline of *every* problem, ecologic 'r otherwise, is us. There are just too fuck*ing* many humans, period!

And I *do* mean fuckING humans." He put such biting emphasis on the '-ing' tail of the modifier it blanched as a swearword.

Anyway ...i seem to be stalling... as for that nite, Lilith proved as determined as me to consummate our affair. And, we did —tho not wout a tournament of pain, and the writing of a new chapter on male constraint during extended foreplay. Great Gaia, please! After a point, not knowing what else to do, we gave control of our tender tournament over to the skilled equestrienne, whereupon she mounted "the beast" *chevaucher*—or should i say, *monter à califourchon* (big) *sur* (sir)?

...eyes that tremble like the stars above me

...driving the thing home at long long last of her own volition, by the gods!

{Aha! The fipper slits afterall!} cried the prince. There is some fang & claw in the best of us. Using the anesthetic of determination... O, i suppose, the blackcherry cognac helped a little. "This stuff is damn delicious! And i thought i didnt like liquor"... she dipt herself repeatedly... gasp stop gasp stop. "There it is, i think. Ooo! Wait!" Stop again, catch breath. "Phew, God!" Breathless: "A girl could use a toke 'r two long about now, she could!" Hair haloing her flushed features stringy w perspiration by the time i took over, she dipt herself repeatedly & greedily in the aphrodisial oils of desire, and each time lifted herself out unimpededly on fire!

17

We must move now to close part4, a juncture in the narrative that strikes me as somewhat joycean in the sense it assigns so many words to a brief timeframe. If i linger over these hours, these days, it is because the narrator is, well ...face it... falling in love w the Biographee, and wants the reader to have some quotidian sense of whom exactly he's falling for. (*Nota bene.* On the face of it, this explanation hardly seems worth its own chapter, i suppose.)

18

Sound of toilet-flush in distance, door-squeak. Thru squinty lids i watch her pause between bed & door. The bed shifts, everso slitely, as she lies down. A few mins pass in sweet twilite sleep; i feel her move again, feel her hand come to rest on my shoulder. Up on one elbow she is gazing at me when i peek out. Tho i rumple when i sleep, somehow she looked, almost always, the way they wakeup looking in movies.

You been awake long? Her eyes had that look i'd first seen at my apt, a sort of... what to call it? Domestic calm warmth? Stroke hair away from inclined cheek, pull her across me, paint w a finger the fine lines of her eyebrows, to nip w fingertips, gently, the black butterfly-wings of her lashes. "Stop." Other one. "Stop!" Not removable? "No. Not removable." Try to kiss her. "I havent brushed my teeth yet." Nor i. Trace paperthin china of cheek, pencil-in flush of rouge along her parted, then suddenly pinched, lips. "Stop! That tickles!" Head tips sidetoside, like brite pet listening. She bit, kissed, then bit again, my tracing torturing index, then did ditto w my lips.

Ugh. Maddening itch. Stop. Stop!

"You see?"

As i marvel at the pearly squares of her bared teeth i note how sleight the weight of her pelvics across my abdomen. An arrow of awareness shoots straight to my groin as my mind finds, feels, the press of her pubic mound. With both hands i draw down her mouth. The kiss is ruff, deep; full/hot cushions twist on my mouth w gentle/sweet fury. As happened first in youth w juanita, i recall clanking teeth in our early-on ardors til, like *vis a vis* dancers on ice, we learned to match the rhythms & twizzles of our interlocked mouths.

I came from that kiss like a lad who has escaped a black nite in a strange forest —all out of breath and on the run. My claustrophobia has confused more than one ardent mouth. I sit up. Sitting up too, she looks at me, mouth ajar, eyes awonder. I stand, look away, catching my breath. She thinks i've gotten somewise offended. <We'd better get some breakfast [polevaulting toward bathrm] before i devour you whole!>

A post-devouring hour later, hanging on each other like newly(barf)weds, we head down for an everything-but-meat breakfast. Her morning-after bridal glow fills the hotel like a late golden dawn. Across the table from me, dressed in soft white turtleneck halter, hair drawn back into a left-sided ponytail w widow's peak prominent, her halo of fleshlite was allbut unbearable. {O Gaia, o life!} Servers, servers' helpers, guests, looked at her as one looks at the sun. Silly w somatic overindulgence, we soon wobbled back upstairs, packed, left. Barely to the car, i decide i'd better go back, visit the boy's lounge. <It's a bit of a drive from here, case ya hafta go. Back in a sec.>

As i stride thru the foyer, enter the lobby, a man in a businessuit... No, it is su morn; make that church clothes... a man exiting the interior lobby doors drops keys, faces quickly away to retrieve them. As he does so his satchel catches & closes the door he'd apparently planned (in a more perfect world) to hold open for in-coming me. Cursing under his breath in swiss or freischütz, he untangles himself and, like a celeb ducking the paparazzi, scoots off. {One hopes [as i sidestep]a visit to church brings him a little more peace of mind.}

The town of capitola, long-time tourist trap, operates a narrow gage train of quaint coaches, pulled by an orig 1880 steam-driven "iron horse" across redwood forest & meadowland to an inland state park. This would make the fifth time i'd skipped the ride, notsomuch because of the pollution factor (probably a trade-off since it takes 50-60 people away from their cars for several hrs) but because of the time it takes to complete the circuit. A quick spin thru the village past the train depot inn (where i'd stayed w other dates) and we were on our way to monterey. With other plans, our visit was cursory. <The local icon of course is steinbeck>, which, looking over at her adorableness i garbled it into <The lical ocon. ...one fine humanitarian trapped however til the end in a human-affairs-only vision of the Cosmos.>

"Like so many of us."

Amen.

"Omen."

How is it possible one so young can run so deep? Seeing her flush & turnaway i immed deflected w, Steinbeck clearly suffered the primitive's plight deeply yet couldnt rise enuf above local context to glimpse the *real* cause, the *deadly* cause, of civilization's self-propagating DIE, PRIMITIVE! curse.

Still looking away: "Like most of us."

And which, again, more deserves your omen than my amen.

We agree we must do monteray aquarium one day soon.<Wildlife there comes 'n' goes as it pleases. [Really?] Yes. A true seaquarium. Ya wont b'lieve some o' these names. Brace yourself.> On main st we pass "roth's home interiors", running a sale on "the drapes of roth". A restaurant: FEAST OF EATIN'. Pet store: CANARY ROE. "Ugh!" And, rounding the corner, "cannery row" itself. And finally, w a yelp of happy discovery ("O, you! You knew, alright!"), another carousel.

Before we left i called bekky. <Lives just up the road —in carmel. <<Hey, beck. Just happened by. Didnt wanna leave without knocking y' up. Call me. Take care.>> A brit expression. Means t' stop by —it's a silly story about a male acquaintance of hers. Youd like bekky. Irascible but fascinating. I call her andrea dworkin's daughter jus t' get 'er goin.>

Saving 'her' pt lobos for our return trip, we head straight for the hamlet of big sur. Rearview wishes now we ≈pilgrims from the vacuum of civilization≈ had spent time at wise robinson jeffers' tor house & hawk tower, where i wanted us to spend a day not just an hour. On the way we passed one of the most obscene of all golf/equine&yacht estates, where theyve turned the entire monterey peninsula(!) into a gated antiWilderness fortress. From there south it was an ooh/aah drive if ever there was one, often a case of cliffs sheerup into skyblue on left, sheerdown into seablue on right, w only a guardrail between car & a plunge into a cold cold sea. The pacific, true to its name, seemed a Wilderness of glass that day. On the horizon, in the haze-dim west, the towers of a caravan of container ships looked like a city in the sea.

"Helmut swears he drove [the coast road] all the way from goleta to loleta in ...how'd he say it? Jus a sec. It was cute. O, yes... by the lite of one day. He's very funny."

Goleta t' loleta? Sounds like the title of a racy travel book. But since neither of us knew where goleta was we remained underwhelmed for the nonce. Scary how fast the man drives.... When did you see helmut?

"O, he comes down[stairs at hq] t' visit sometimes."

O he does does he? Mutt never visits me. ["Mutt?"] I explain.

In each shop we stop in one of us drops the line, Nice lil town ya got here, and in three out of five times get corrected nicely-but-stuffily: "Hamlet. The *hamlet* of big sur." Feign surprise. <But i was spelling town with an e, does that count? T-o-w-n-e.> All this san francisco-not-frisco/hamlet-of-big-sur stuff, while great fun for us, reminds me of <how upset demi moore ...scuse me, demí... gets when someone mispronounces her name.>

"The vanities of title should not be what an Earth-place is founded on."

Or an Earth-person. By the way, how does one pronounce Lilith properly? "Like ya jus did." Full-knowing that accenting the first syllable (as is common in the west) is contraindicated by the babylonian/assyrian root-word lilîtu, still she never corrected me —tho i kept saying it wrong (as did don ε lalage) til finally i heard aurise say it right.

We put a couple lactoveg subs in the cooler and contd s. Our orig plan was to hike the 12k loop at andrew molera but one thing to another (mostly for having no day-hike pack in which to secure the camcorder i was using discreetly on her) we opted for pfeiffer burns. Beside, we wanted to be sure to get her back to pt lobos before sunset.

One parks in a grove of coastals at pfeiffer burns. A tunnel under the coast rd walked us briskly onto an overlook set on a bluff about 30m above the sea. To one side a thin column of water fell. "That's beautiful." In spring the flow is quite spectacular. A plaque she read aloud said it was "70 feet high and the only stream on the california coast to fall directly into the sea."

The falls back at the sanctuary is about that tall. [Seriously?] Sixtyone feet. [Wow. Must be beautiful.] But it is a mere unknown trickle compared to this.

Sitting on a bench she asked if it was very far to capistrano. "...Lage 'n' daddy went to see them return when they first moved here. She called it awesome. That's saying something for lage. ...When do they leave? <End of october.> Where do they go? <Argentina, i think.> {Near where an old love of mine flew too —who, not incidentally, reminds me of you.} Sounds ...well... awesome, really." She gazes off to the s, stroking her hair, which lay across her legs –shiny, slick-skinned– in a stream of sunlite. {How heavy it must be when wet ...soaked by such a falls as this, say.}

At the parkinglot the tail of a trail lay invitingly still. Sign w arrow reads McWAY TRAIL. (Sounds made-up again, huh?) "How long do we have?" We are free agents. Takes deep breath (nostrils narrowing at top, flaring at bottom, eyes sparkling), "This air is sooo great! [rocking, bending sidetoside] Feel like a run?" As if energized by our impromptu *flitterwochen*, transformed by sun, sea ε air, she broke ε ran. I follow in her mcWake (what was a fellow to do?)

as she bounds up,up,up the trail slippery *w* pebbles, past a half k of bay laurel, madrone, tan oak ɛ fern. Before a token turn skirting an akimbo arm of rock, she pauses, i think for my mcSake, hardly breathing that i can see. “There’s that spicy laurel scent again!” So it was. “Wrong time of year for many wildflowers, huh? <[gasp] Unhuh.> What’s this blue one climbing thru the rocks here?” Babyblue-eyed columbine, gasp. Up-mtn running is my shtick gasp but these damn pebbles are gasp slip’ry. {Stop whining, nathan.} Please dont wait for me! Jus go! Fly, girl, fly! She hiphops on past old hippomenes —who, rather than hop over the naked rocks like her, ‘hemmed’ the skirt to catch his breath. Even as i rounded that skirt you were already at the next turn, my Lee. For like atalanta …as i would resign, once mr pride learned to love eating your dust… for like atalanta (who got the hermes gene), You too had wonderful luminous fleet little wings on your feet.

For all my breathlessness, still i found myself wanting her (again). An image of us as primitive creatures took over as i pursued. I felt that, in a more honest society, on first meeting her i would have dropped what i was doing then&there and just followed her, all that first eve ɛ next day, and the next. And that every time she stopped i would stop. And when she looked back i would turn away, a little selfconsciously; maybe checkout our surroundings, do,di-do,di-do. “Why do you keep following me?” It’s what i’m s’posed t’ do. “Why dont you follow her?” Hmm. Cause i like it fine right here. Do,di-do,di-do. “You said that about the last place i stopped.” I did? “Y’ know, i think you have a problem?” Search surroundings for good answer. Do,di-do,di-do. Find none. She turns away. And prettysoon we’re off again: same game, new surroundings.

Near the top, on the north face of mcWay canyon, a last stand of redwoods had stopped for a breather, wishing global warming was a myth. Phew. This girl is merciless. Whadaya say, on the way down we go a little slower, takein some o’ the f ‘n’ f? [Effneff?] I infer your Wilderness siblings, flora ‘n’ fauna? [Ah!] Flora of course being the older sister. “Of course.” {How nice to have a friend who doesnt say “Huh?” all the time… We seem even more attuned than me ‘n’ nika were… Like juanita ‘n’ me, maybe? …Hmm.}

Back at the car we take cooler, find picnictable, munch a leisurely lunch, get on our way. Same scenario when we get to pt lobos. While awaiting the sun to drop for the filming i have in mind, she is off again, running ɛ laffing by the sea, flitting up&down hillsides like a spring sylph. See me, loping after her like the lunatic in merrimee's *the chaser and the chaste*. She runs, i pursue. Jesters of jizm! Robots of instinct! {A game as old as life and i'm playing it like i just invented it!} Among microbes alone, the number of such chases enacted in the last 2billion yrs brings the powers of ten to its knees! Among humans, the number of chases in the last 24hrs (on foot, by fone, in car, by letter, by fax, by plane, by ad, by email, by train, by train of thought, soforth) would smoke the chips in most calculators.

She is in such good spirits i am able for once to convince her to pay no attention to the camera and just tour the point as if she is the only person on Earth. And thus was i able to enshrine her on film, moving in sunset glow before sea expanse and those famous wind-gnarled cypresses on their rocky ends-of-the-Earth perches. (Later in our relationship she would be less cooperative, ducking, turning away, even running off sometimes. In our travels over the years i would find my cameras buried under clothes, beneath blankets, removed to a drawer or closet. Youre acting like a fatlady in a g-string. Git back here!) Had i only known the dark cause of this shyness i would have shut off the camera then&there for keeps.

On the drive to pt lobos, then at dinner in monterey, and on the way back to frisco ꞓ her dorm, i discovered she was serious about quitting school. "I'll hafta do it anyway when production begins, which they say could be as soon as the first o' the year." I would later learn, this decision grew out of a single disappointment: her father's reaction to "The granada/halfmoon bay business. Plus i hafta prep the captain [which she also called "my cartoon"] for an animated format else alota things will go wrong." This she had recently learned from a drawing instructor at school who "worked for disney once" and advised her to "prep as many animators' templates" as she could stand to draw.

It took almost all the trip back to learn even this tidbit. Tho more conversant than usual, still she was slow to share her thoughts, specially if it meant casting anyone in a poor lite. "He wants t' hunt-down okka, teach him a lesson he wont forget —which he says he's going t' do if i dont press charges." Long pause. When i commend don's caring for her she, sadly, corrects me w "Daddy's more concerned with family honor than with respecting my wishes. [pause again] Tell me if this is right? Am i wrong t' want my wishes respected, an' ta not want any part of the old eye-for-an-eye tradition?"

My turn to pause. I wanna be sure what i'm saying here. [i am about to throw up a flag over being caught in the middle again when i think better of it] Gandhi said, an eye for an eye 'n' pretty soon everybody's blind. I think it depends on his reasoning. If it's only a case of family pride, then it's wrong. Wars are made mostly of such subjective stuff. But if he's doing it b'cause someone hurt you, or b'cause he fears for your safety, 'r even outuv guilt ...say, for not having been there for you in the past... then i understand where he's coming from.

"I wish i saw such motives. But i see only the old family pride/personal honor thing. Mother described it first when he caught her cheating. 'Your pride is bleeding but your heart sheds no tear' ...It sounded better in the original french ...I'd like t' think my feelings in this matter are at least as important as family honor. [long silence] You were right about scotland tho. Honor is important ta all clan fathers; way more important than nurturing understanding 'n' love."

Your standard patriarch is raised t' b'lieve he need not worry about such things. Patriarchy's fathers are often as distant from their children as patriarchy's gods are from the people and their Earth. It teaches that children are the job o' the clan mother... and the clan mother accepts this as, deep down, she feels the children *are* her job.

"I suppose. But i cant know. Our clan had no mother t' speak of."

Even tho i had yet to hear from lage about don pleading for L not to leave, i wanted to tell her what he'd said to me in private: ≈You, a bachelor without children, cant understand a father's...etc.≈ But i'd given don my word not to mention even his call. Then again, how to reconcile such talk w Lilith's opinion, say nothing of reconciling how said father could cut a 12yearold daughter adrift for years under highly specious circumstances?

That trip i learned: Something is wrong when more than 10mins passes and Lilith, off her feet, has yet to slip out of her shoes. Whether next to me in a car, or in a chair across the room, Lilith lounging nearby (white-socked feet tucked under or close beside her) was a cozy sight w a warm feeling i could easily grow used to.

19

That dayful of activity sent me straight to a good nite's sleep. A late rise next morn found a call from a friend back home. Rachel said one of the bison calfs was missing and, had i heard, "thousands of fish are turningup dead on the shores of gadsden lake. Enviros are up in arms the media says." What enviros? i ask when i call back. "And where have they been hiding?" says my concerned caller. Block-for-block, gadsden (Lilith will soon name it, egadsden!) is more polluted than noogachatta, the closer of the two to ggNs. "An' jus yesterday", rachel continues, authorities back in my home state were amazed to find, 5yearold twins, discovered bruised & tied together in a garbage-filled room, had "no desire to see their parents. Imagine!" And finally she tells me, at lee college, just across the state line (where i have lectured and where lalage will one day be invited to attend), a fire had "kids jumping from windows", two of whom rachel knew. And *still* i tell her i cant wait t' get back ...and mean it no less.

On mon i passed on to brian Lilith's feelings about the capt.gE tv project, of how she felt she needed to quit school in order to work on the cartoon fulltime. <She wants to have a comprehensive creator's visualization locked in before production begins.> When she came to work that pm brian called her in, asked if there were any loosends she felt needed tying before they handed over her cartoon (to a bunch of people to whom deadlines were as important as art)? Not letting on he knew anything of her plans, he offered fultime work "in case there's any prep you care to do", providing she felt it would help. When we spoke later she mentioned her "fairy godmother...finally managing t' hang around a little. Mr nugent also said that by wednesday i'd have my own space in graphics... Wait a minute. You didnt, by any chance, have anything t' do with all this?" I skirt all connection, say it is just commonsense for gE to want to ensure the quality of its venture etc.

On wedn L got her space in graphics while an ad was run to fill her position. Meanwhile, friends glen, mark & mutt were slated to ship on su for yet another whaling protest in japan. Unlike glen or mark, mutt hung around hq playing the seagoing hero –mostly to Lilith, while approaching new interns & volunteers– for his new girlfriend, he claimed, was away on business. At some point on wedn mutt "dropped down" w some old fotos in which glen, mutt & me are out lekking in various ports and in which i am teamed w various women. "Isnt that delphine?", to which mutt replies with his best imported grin, "Ol nate spreads himself pretty thin sometimes!" Meanwhile i'm growing just a little weary of mutt's negratiating [sic] behavior managed in his o-so-charming english, for he is doing all this in an atmosphere he had to know was tense for Lilith to begin with: Nikki working just outside her door in the makeup dept, w delphine as brian's assistant upstairs, and whoknowswhatall-else interoffice intrigue. On the other hand i knew, if anyone ever badmouthed me, mutt would be first to defend my honor. Mine was an old stew indeed.

Behind her easygoing façade neither me or mutt knew, as far back as she could remember, L had heard from the women in her family (on her mother's side, since don's parents died before she was born) the following dogma. "Men, good and bad, cheat. That's the way it is, that's the way it always has been. But the best men do their best to never let you know. In this case, ignorance equals marital bliss." Add to this, tho beautiful, Lilith was insecure and had the usual poor-selfimage to go w it. All of which combined to cloud-over the sunny things coming her way. When, to lighten things, i asked if mutt had hit on her <that nite in berkeley when i first saw you?>, she cleverly sidestepped the question, related how he'd intro'd himself: "Hello. I'm helmut. How are you I'm fine tank you and your name vud be pleece?" The retelling made her smile while i thought {I cant believe he's still getting laffs 'n' sympathy with that one}.

On fr i rcv'd calls from glen, mark & helmut, each of whom told of being questioned by the fbi in re freeman's murder. All warned me that a surprising amount of the questioning related to me and that the agents were making known that i'd been "downstate the weekend of the murder". This, they said, coupled w the "inflammatory revelations" of a certain unnamed gE employe, struck them as "cause for concern if nothing else". Glen asked them, he said, "if they knew how many times we'd all been arrested in the last ten years?" I wished glen calm seas and he told me to "Keep yer ass tucked, buddy. Those guys strike me like they havent had good sex in years!"

20

On fr afternoon lalage, feeling bad for her Sister, was waiting for L when she got home. When L called to ask if i'd mind "sister tagging along ...again" she seemed in good spirits. ["You mind. I c'n tell."] I dont. I'm jus surprised. [Why?] Well, t' tell the truth, i pictured you guys still not speaking. Yet win mins of their arriving (in lage's car) i felt something was amiss.

After waiting-out the drive to supper ("the ganges" in haight-ashbury) to see if i wanted to steer the conversation (as well as her car), lage took over. "We are total pibs t'nite. Well, she is. Personally I didnt plan a goth evening." Lilith looks sidelong at her. I can see nothing but black on either sister —black skirts & pantyhose; black blouse, one; black turtleneck, the other; black headbands, black shoes. While "the ladies" sashayed to the restrm i ordered drinks, *pour-boir* ing rather heavily our cocktail server. When they returned ("How was our timing?") we toasted our recurring problem. <To the denial of adulthood to young adults!> "Old enuf t' vote", "An' ta drive", "An' ta get married!", <An' ta die for our country!>. "But too young t' drink!" "Or get ragin skanked without a lecture! *...Toast à le gal!"* adds lage, Lee responding, *"À un vrai de vrai!"*, immed trading glasses, sipping in unison, yodding the choice, trading back. "We do that." "There is no friend like a sister."

After appending, *Toast à illegal!*, echoed by lage's huzza, i ventured (as we leaned on elbows around a tilty highboy near the bar), How come you talk so much more than your Sister. Now i'm not saying that's bad you understand.

"B'cause I'm more opinionated." She offered it as a good quality. "But Sister's waymore fussy than me", pointing at the subject *w* a fat pretzel.

Opinionatedness is a form of fussiness, isnt it? ...except it's a fussiness about ideas, not things, doncha think?

"Hmm... Then maybe I'm jus more openminded."

"O? Calling a guy a dweeb because of his clothes is openminded?"

"When did I do that?"

"About five minutes ago."

"Right. ...But there. You see? I can admit fault."

"We go out of our way to invent differences sometimes."

"What's the word fer that again?"

"Disidentification."

"No no. The other one."

"Yes, yes. But you wanna hear 'untwinning' dontcha?"

"That's it! Untwinning. Yes."

Wielding now a longer thinner pretzel she slides a drinknap into the halo of water brimming beneath her glass of brew, which rushes to fill it. The pace of her banter slows abruptly here, voice deepens. "There're kids who claim to be close; siblings, I mean. My friends lauren 'n' liz are like *that.* [taking pretzel *w* left hand, she presents index *ε* middlefinger entwined] But when the going gets ruff they go at each other. [resituates pretzel] But not us. [with back&forth motion of pretzel she twice indicates Lee *ε* herself] It never occurs to us to break a trust. We have this birthtrust. I dont think we'd know how to break it even if we were forced to...."

"...Like under torture 'r something," concurs Lee.

Contemplative pause follows, *w* a poking of the now sopping wad of napkins *w* the pretzel. "First comes us ...only after that is there a world out there."

"We have this old joke...." chimes the introspective one.

Lage laffs, "Right. Now *this* goes back," she warns.

"We usta sit in choir 'n' giggle at everything in the sermon...."

"Yeah, an' one day we decided...."

"Wait!" said Lee. "Tell the topic first!"

"O, yes. The Creation o' the World!"

"Mind you."

"Sitting in choir we decide, on the first day God made US...."

"Meaning, her 'n' me." Lee wields her wineglass.

"And then rested for six big ones!"

Share moment of micklemirth. Lage's pretzel buckles into an L-shape trying to push the napkin.

"God was seeing double when he created us."

"No. Nature was seeing double when *She* created us."

"Right. ...An' that's the way it's always been between us."

Lee, one eyebrow tilted up, kept track of lage's eyes ɛ lips as she talked, looked down when she'd finish.

Only today –isolated in this place, living a largely reflective existence– do i understand what was said that day. Now however i know there are times, rare to be sure, when a basic impulse –say, self-preservation– can be shared. This is probably not clear as 'self' implies only the preservation of one person. What i mean is, not a 'self' one risks out of love for another but a *single* impulse shared by *two* beings; *one* instinctual impulse shared by *two* bodies; an impulse that is prior to thought, prior to morality ɛ ethics, prior to loving even, as a beating heart is prior to mental awareness! But all this got by me at the time. I was still busy trying to figureout why neither sister seemed at all angry w the other as a result of their argument.

"What about you? Have you ever been real close with someone? I mean, like, real close?" Lage is now rotating the buckled L-shaped pretzel between her fingers like a propeller.

"Lage?"

"What?"

T'sokay, says i. Yes, in my teens, i was. She has a way of putting things, this lalage person, like she's just making ad hoc conversation yet i suspect she's not.

"Guy or girl?"

"Lage?"

"Well, a guy c'n have a close boyfriend without bein gay, ya know!"

"I didnt mean that. I meant, it's noneuv our business!"

{*Our* business?} They look at each other, eyebrows arched as in simple surprise. I have no clue what this gesture means, i know only that they are no mere daisy ɛ demi, this pair of not-so-little women.

"Ever see the movie *double trouble*? That's us."

"What she means is, that's her."

<Why am i feeling crossexamined? I could be being torn to bits here... clothes...mannerisms...anything. Now dont gimme that we're innocent stuff. This is not my imagination. I feel like a slab of raw meat on a conveyorbelt waiting to be stamped PASSED by two women in butcher aprons?>

They trade a pansing glass, a glancing pass, a passing glance (there it is) and a conclusion, "Dont worry, you passed". Another moment of mirth, allbut forehead-to-forehead this time, their tessitura risen now a tone or two. "Usda choice."

"Clydesdale."

"No. Guido!"

"No. Soigné! "

Then, looking at me –one right-handedly, one, left– both simultaneously pull down (like sudden masks from above their heads) two stern ɛ shockingly similar mime-white faces.

"There, we're done."

"Sorry... Really. We've been suffering these spells of flashback behavior since i arrived."

"We mean no harm, really." No sooner had Iage restarted propellering her pretzel when its folded tip centrifuflips over her shoulder, disappears into the silverblue bouffant of a woman at the next table ...salted brown rocket falling back into Earth's atmosphere. "Oops. Sorry bout that," whispers Iage, ducking reflexively *w* a mischievous flash of teeth ɛ eyes.

The woman notices nothing {Phew. But *the nite is young* ...and theyre so beautiful!} and we, like three juveniles in hs detention, cannot figure a way to undo what's been done for laffing so hard: "She'd be mortified if we told her." <What's the definition of mortified anyway?> "B'side, it would take twenny mins to find it in there!" "Schock party of three" comes over the p.a. We rise, walk our drinks toward the diningrm when Lilith, giving hers to Iage, splits away. "Back in a sec."

Seated, i ask if Lilith is okay. "Sister's changed alot since we were kids. Seems like it's always something. Real stuff, of course. But... Like t'nite it's some guy back east harassing a friend of hers" —who had called just when they were ready to leave. With Lilith hiding okka's abuse from her family, she was of course unable to talk freely w aurise. I guessed at that very moment she was on the fone doing same. "So whatuv you been up to?"

Whatuv *you* been up to is the question. My life's pretty predictable. Lectures, luncheons, meetings, then more lectures luncheons meetings.

Lilith returned just as lage was launching into a "state of my lovelife" address, having just displayed a bare ringfinger ("See? Gone.") and making it clear she was not "going back" with her ex ("The two-timing two-time golder!"), which she then backedup w a few rapidfire reasons. "B'side him thinking he's God's gift [since landing a job in a hollywood stunt school], I have this problem with guys who live t' date models 'n' b-grade actresses".

"And this is the sister who claims t' be open-minded" chides Lilith.

Fuss over spilled something at next table.

"Sorry, but I think mod'ling 'n' beauty contests are an expressway t' bimbo limbo 'n' most girls who get into movies that way uzhly cant act."

While hardly a member of the heidi fleiss rec club, i attempt a very private tabulation of the number of "models 'n' b-grade actresses" w whom i'd consorted in my model-coddling days.

"Beauty-contestants 'n' models are people too. We've been there/done that, in case ya dont remember."

"I do remember. An' that's not the *only* reason I'm saying it."

And we're off again! i mused as our server appeared. Precedential drinks in place, he asks if we'd like an appetizer. "You pick, Sis. I've never done indian b'fore." Lage's deferences to Lee's preferences seem an attempt to revive her sister's humor. I order for all. "What're you looking at?" she says to L as our server turns away, tapping her shoulders w the pinkys of her upturned hands as if to say, "myself asks you?"; then, hands out, looks down at herself as if checking for spills, or maybe an exposed breast. Like a film being paused, then let go, our server froze, then contd away, thinking for that brief moment that the young lady was about to put his private thoughts (What're you looking at?) on public trial. But it turnsout, L is looking not at but past her.

A young woman, replete w bare midriff, tattoos or piercings near every visible orifice, thought she'd "come over 'n' say, hi". Casually positioned between me ε lage, from somewhere near her rump she wdrew a sheaf of papers. But, on meeting in such tite quarters L's gaze, she delaminated. "I c'n tell you guys are the sort who wouldnt sign minding a petition for lay 'n' gezbian rights". O i understood her gutwrenched disarray alright. One glance from Lilith's eyes and you suddenly realize youve been treading over treacherously thin ice all your life; and, as you crash into freezing Reality, you think, "*No* adult can be *that* pure. No way." Then, daring her pure gaze one last time, just before the ice regels above your sudden cryogenic cocoon, you know your new knowledge has doomed you yet you care not a whit —for you cant ignore the feeling youve just been slammed w a dose of the same Love that maybe created the Universe! And all this is not even to start to describe the keen intelligence you sense is poised behind that dazzling innocence.

As the woman leaves, signatures in hand, i say to lage: You know, you remind me of someone 'n' it just occurred t' me who.

"O?"

Bekky kydd.

"Sorry. No lites." Looks at Lilith.

Miss u-s-a-teen scandal a couple years ago?

Shakes head. "Wait, was she the one who blew the whistle on sexual favors 'r something?"

One 'n' the same. An attempt to expose the corruption *behind* the contest, i explain.

"Reminds me o' the moneymoguls who loiter around in gymnastics."

Who are probably brothers-by-intent to bekky's ceodoms. [no reaction] As in c-e-o. plus dom?

"We call 'em slysuits. She [yodding at Lilith] knows a little about this stuff too. Identamint, Sister? R'member? Dirty old men, young 'n' old, is why daddy yanked us oudda the business."

Men preying on young women looking for a quick 'r easy way ta the top.

"Hopin t' give some young lady a legUp on the alternative horse as we call it."

<Youre kidding> i say, uncaring to mask my surprise at her frankness.

"Not. We have our, let's see- [peers at ceiling] mat mistresses, would ya believe? Gymnasties-, 'r gymnasteens- 'r- pommelhorse greasers, pommelhorse groomies, a-, backroom ballet, backroom layout, two-man pike, topsecret tuck, a-... downtimers, off-the-record swedish fall, a-... O, there's a whole bunch, I jus cant think o' them right now. O, 'n' there's a-, midnite optionals, afterhours compulsories, 'n' a-, miss so'n'so got t' the top... No, make that, *rode* t' the top, on the alternative horse... You look shocked."

<A little more graphic than i expected> i say as our drinks are refreshed.

"O, there's more, I assure you.

Lilith, having givenup on protesting lage's comments, is speechless.

I shouldnt be surprised. Bekky's whistle-blow brought out its own vocabulary too –well, idiolect– of euphemisms for what goes on "behind all the behinds" as they say in the modeling 'n' beauty contest world.

"Idiowhat?"

"Idiolect. Private language" says the quieter sister.

"Ya see? Right there's why she's *big* sister." Lage still trying t' lift Lee's spirits.

"We had that. [What?] Idiolect... when we were kids."

Now you have something even better. You anticipate each others thoughts. You guys make me feel like i'm seeing only highly edited trailers of reality.

L, hand on my sleeve, apologizes. As our server places appetizer, wants to know if we'd like to order or wait, i catch two men gawking again at our table. Spending time *w* beautiful women one gets used to this...to a point however just short of being able to ignore arrogant displays of raw gawking.

Private-speak, ya could call it; a way of communicating so that outsiders dont catch on. Speaking of which, there's a phrase bekky put in the vocabulary of every major news agency in america: Remember misuse-a-teen? Which is.... [i was about to explain the play on words of the title, miss usa teen, and how it evolved into misusateen, but Lilith interjected] "They run an 800number on tv, no?"

Could be. It's a national organization now: teen empowerment inc. Bekky originally intended it as a clearinghouse –or really, a network– for connecting young people who felt they'd been exploited by the phalladigm.

"Phalla what? Come again. [lage narrows eyes, looks at Lee] Look, I could always split if you guys wanna hold a private spellingbee 'r sumthin." For the first time i study their nuances of feature, presuming nothing.

"Phalladigm. A male-dominated power structure" says L, whom i know by now can quote my books better than me."

I follow lage's "Aha" *w* <Who do you admire in gymnastics?>

"That's easy. Cannon shannon/thriller miller."

Is that two people?

"One people."

"Shannon miller is sister's, ahem, mostfab fav."

Lage went on to overstate this veneration ...til L asked, "Yes. But is she a good person *outside* gymnastics? What i mean is, where most people woulduv felt giving a million dollars to find polly klaas and her killer was doing more than enuf, winona ryder was, in addition, out there tramping around the countryside with the rest of us." L re:d the still ongoing search for the abducted klaas girl which she & lage, & others on foot, undertook on horseback in the Wilds outside petaluma the last couple wkends.

"So that makes her better than shannon?"

"I'm not saying that. I'm just interested to know who my sister loves and *why* she loves them."

"O" says lage, full-stalled in her power-dive.

"Francois villon said, we should pick our leaders as carefully as we would pick the circumstances of our own death, for the two may one day intersect. ...It rhymes in the original french. ["And on that cheery note...."] My point being.

If we dont know them personally, we c'n no more know what our heros are truly like than we c'n forecast the circumstances of our death."

"And, like I said. On that cheery note: Garçon! Could use refills here!" Lilith is turned wrong to see whom lage is insulting. "Relax. He didnt hear me. ...Hey [pops lage], I remember that thing now. It was more than a couple years ago tho... Is she blond, real cute? Young? Well, backthen, I mean. [then to Lee] Brenda 'n' me jus talked about this not that long ago. We were trying t' picture some gymnast we know throwing down her trophy 'n' saying, 'I have sumthin t' confess. I didnt win this contest because I'm good. I won it because I had sex with the guy who payed for everything.' Right. That could happen."

"It *did* happen. That's what nathan's saying. That's *exactly* what bekky whatshername did!"

"Well she's the exception, trus me."

It's a catch22. ["Whatsay?"] You jus said it. People who take bribes 'r favors are the last ones t' admit it —basic survival.

"Which brings up a good question. Why did *bekky* admit it?"

Actually she didnt admit anything ...Nothing personal anyway. She just said this stuff went on, 'n' that she was sick of a system that trades sexual favors for trophies 'n' prize-money an' doesnt give a damn about who it hurts along the way. You hafta remember, she gave up a successful modeling career just t' qualify for the contest. But then, you hate models 'n' beauty contestants so this is probably not a good topic.

"No, wait. [stops me w a just-dipped rice chip] I dont mean there arent exceptions. Your friend bekky's obviously very unusual. Akchally she sounds, well, courageous."

"Hmm. There may be hope for you after all" halfsmiles Lilith. Questioned further, over tabouli & fig-paste wafers, i give thumbnail profile of bekky as bekky gave it to me. <As bekky says....

"Thanx t' mother I was famous *b'fore* I was born. I earned a thousand a week posing as a fetus ya know. In fact, it was me the guy who perfected the sonogram practiced on. I was modeling *b'fore* I could breathe."

Lage lets out a low whoop, "You go, grrrl!", anticipating, *w* hand raised ε an adorable squint, a second squirt as Lilith spears another cherrytomato from the american salad lage has rejected in favor of polishingoff the group's appetizer.

She has another expression. "I was an early starter. At age one I already had two years' experience."

"So she was modeling before the big fracas?"

Quit it under pressure from her mother whose argument was, "Models are a dimeadozen but there's only one miss america. ["Smart mother."] And she was sure her daughter could be one. Plus y' hafta remember who her mother was. ["Duh."] I recall being uncertain as to whether lage was razzing me. <Duh? As in: *Everyone* knows the answer to *that?*>

"No. Duh, as in: I jus plain dont know."

If this stuff didn interest you guys you'd tell me, right?

"I'm fascinated... No kidding, I am! I think sister might be a little bored tho." Lage trying yet a different tactic to bring L around.

"Speaking of bored. Does the batty-eyed cartwheeler remember the last item of conversation, hmm?" Lilith, knife erect, put this *w* such exquisite enunciation i thought sure it would trigger a clawfest —and this *w*out me even pickingup on the fact: to be called a cartwheeler is an insult to a gymnast.

"No, the cartwheeler *doesnt* r'member akchally... O wait! Her mother was a- [index rocking sidetoside as if wiping memory's windshield] ...a-, steering her daughter's career. There. What say you now, Sister?"

"Akchally [mimicking lage], had you been a little more bored 'n' less fascinated youduv asked, 'Who was her mother anyway?'"

To my amazement, batting her eyes in perfect time to the criticism, lage recites, "Right. Who was her mother anyway?"

Feeling outdistanced, i stare at my hands (7.3 digits flat on the edge of the table), lick my lips, look up. Why do i feel like there's a tennis match going on here and i'm the fuzzy little ball? Breaking the volley for a moment they agree, their banter is only a game, and that i should not construe it as disinterest or boredom. "In fact, we'll be upset if you dont finish bekky's story."

Fine. One more time then. Bekky's mother was no wallflower, i explain as our drinks are replenished. In the early seventies she formed a group called the vassar virgins.... "Hey, we studied them in school I think!" With not an ellen swallow in the bunch, they battled an aspect of the counter-culture t'day called the sex revolution... and the prevailing view of the time, which liked to lump all youth into one big drugs 'n' sex image.

"Some things never change" says L, toasting us *w* her glass.

People think the "stay a virgin" movement of christian fundies t'day is something new. Well, bekky's mother was the "dont give it up" doyenne of the early seventies. So when it came t' bekky, the apple didnt fall far from the tree, tho bekky doesnt see it that way. In fact, after she finished her movie –her only movie– she wrote a book: *starlet moms: kid marketing in america*, which rails against moms who push their daughters t' be what they themselves failed t' be; or, worse, who use them as steppingstones to a secondhand fame.

"Ho! Tell us about it! [to L] Shades of identamint, eh? Remind us t' tell ya about *that* marketplace some day."

I ask to be told right then but they insist i go on. Busboy clears away. "Ya done with this?" getting an upclose of the nearest sister. Supper, waiting behind him, is served.

Anyway, tho the vassar virgins are back in business today on gospel campuses around the nation –thanx to their apocaleptic parents; but that's another story for another time– as a frat backthen the movement fell apart when, at graduation, a reporter asked bekky's mom if she was still a virgin. Foolishly she said, yes, for the reporter had set her up. "Are you sure?" To which she responded, "I am! " —and all on film, no less.

Leaning back, yodding at her pronate fork, lage said matteroffactly, "When ya hafta swear youre a virgin yer prob'ly not one", kissing the tines as if goodby. All think about that. "What's the bigdeal about virginity anyway?"

Dont lookat me! Personally i dont like it ...*personally* that is.

"Now that's different ...How come?"

A private aversion. [Sorry.] But i *can* say this. It's a gutter-mind that has the audacity to base anyone's purity on the history of his or her genitals! Nobody c'n take away our purity but ourselves. Like our ability to love, purity is internal, intrinsic, innate, and only we ourselves can give it away. [in my peripheral vision i see Lilith studying me intently] I happen t' have a mini lecture on this so it's not a good idea t' get me started.

"That's intense. You must know that's intense, dont you?"

I know it's gotten some strong reactions, yes.

"Mostly from women?" asks L.

Hmm, yes. I'll tell ya this. It's mostly women who agree with me; and in a surprising number of cases, even in the face of whatever civil religions theyve been propagandized by.

"*Civil* religion."

Right. "Any religion which reinforces what nathan has named, the civilizing principle" inserts Lilith. <But that too is another story. Anyway, as to bekky's mom.>

"Yeah. What happened with that?"

Well, this guy pops out o' the bushes so to speak ready to prove she's a liar ...as in, not a virgin? An' if i have the story right, tho she backs down on the virginity claim he, stupidly letting himself be eggedon by the press, quickly finds, he's talked himself straight into a paternity suit.

"Filed by a really pissed ex-virgin no doubt."

I was gonna say sumthin like that.

Lilith: "Was she actually pregnant?"

She was. And the press (ever ready t' crack a joke at somebody else's expense), couldnt wait to announce, VIRGIN-BIRTH EXPECTED.

"That figures" says L.

"Timely" magazine billed her as "the most famous virgin since the madonna". And, of course, the jerk who broke the story to the press ...and whose name, by the way, just happened to be joseph ... 'n' boy did they have fun with that one! ["Youre kidding!"] No i'm not. An' joseph, as youve probably guessed, is of course bekky's older sister's (well, halfsister's) father.

"They got married ...after all that?"

Not that i know of. Joseph, i believe, cleared oudda bethlehem after mary hit him with child-support.

"A guy thing. So how did you guys meet?"

Never met the woman.

"No. I mean you 'n' bekky whatshername?"

"Isnt that just a little nosey?"

"I dont think so. These things int'rest me."

She's the....

L interrupting me: "You dont hafta answer her."

T'sokay. Bekk's the halfsister of someone i dated. [didnt mention deb danzi because of lage's disaffection for models] You guys are alot alike actually.

"Her 'n' me?" queries lage w a lobsterclaw flexion of wrist.

No. You 'n' bekky. B'side, bekk would *love* i know t' hear about the underside of gymnastics. She could really use your insidetrack.

"O good. An' I could kiss g'by all hopes of ever trophying again."

I suppose youre right. I was thinking things are more ethical in gymnastics than in beauty contests.

"They pro'bly are. At least near the top 'n' in public. But I think the –what should I call them?– opportunities? ...are prettymuch the same. An' specially pressing at my level this year. An' the offers of support always come from the same kinda people, with the same skanky motives ...money 'n' fame."

Advancement in-trade for sexual favors?

"Prettymuch."

Just hidden.

"Dont think it's all that hidden, personally. Maybe in public 'n' close to the oc [olympic committee] it is. Otherwise sponsors operate without fear —with the older girls anyway. You c'n see it just about any day."

Older, as in...?

"Middleschool? <Yer kidding.> Highschool fer shur?"

Arent there fraternizing rules?

"Shur. But it's just for show. It's up to the individual girl t' figure out if the attention she's getting is on the up'n'up. It's pretty expensive to stay in gymnastics the more you rise, 'n' alota girls dont come from genes with coin. If they wanna stay in the game they sometimes hafta make choices. An' then there's others who could give a crap about what it takes ta get to the top. Theyre not called gymnasties fer nothin."

Dishes cleared, looking from one sister to the other: Will there be anything else?

{In yer dreams, pal.} B'side the shoptalk thing ...gymnastese, we'll call it... [Lilith groans, which pleases me] there must also be camp stuff, no? Unwritten methods 'n' tactics which everyone knows?

"You talk like a teach, nathan. [i explain self] They'd *better* understand."

Were you ever approached?

"Talk aboutchur personal questions. Sis? Ya gonna sit there 'n' let him talk t' me like that? [L acknowledges the balk w one eyebrow] Heck, yes, I have. But y' hafta remember, this is not a black 'n' white thing, like, Hey, ya wanna step in my office 'n' show me yer stuff? It's more subtle. It's a game. It's eye talk 'n' body language —on *both* sides. These guys –an' in some cases, ladies– with seriouscoin– c'n tell in a sec if you have yer act t'gether 'r if your out beggin for a legup. Theyre experts in their field. <Which is?> Get all the young skin ya c'n get while ya can get it."

"Hey, dont hold back, sis. Tell it like it is."

"That *is* their cause, trust me. <Women, you say?> Shur. Why not? Hit fer hit, some score better than the men I think ...Less intimidating, ya know?"

So this isnt just lockerroom rumors. You actually know of people who've gotten, how'd you say, a legup?

"Heck, yeah. Everybody knows who's doin who, who's not. Ya get typed pretty quick. I have a friend [to Lee] ...you met brenda... who went down that road this summer 'n' regretted it. Anyway, the dom's opening line ta her was ...just a sec. Sorry t' putcha on hold at this juicy junction- I've got it: 'You must hafta giveup an awful lot ta stay in this sport, huh?'. Ya b'lieve that? What balls, eh!"

Server brings check. They insist on "do"ing the liquor tab & tip —"You hardly drank at all, nathan".

How old were you the first time it happened?

"Ya mean when I first noticed it? This is purely clinical on your part, prafesser, right? I mean, that's pretty personal. ["Hello over there!"] Jus kidding. How's twelve fer starters...?"

Your dad seems like an ethical sorta guy, says me, trying to keep my surprise in check.

"But our bodies ['hers 'n' mine' gesture] were *always* ahead of our age."

Deepclear throat. As i was saying: Your dad's an ethical sort. Did you ever tell him you were approached?

Mouth drops, looks at Lee, bursts out laffing. "He's kidding, right? <Didnt *think* i was.> God, no, nathan! Geez! He'd go ballsout ballistic pardon my french —castrate the sonuvabitch, ask questions later!... Daddy has no cool when it comes t' family honor. He's the same guy who had ta leave the entire eastcoast the minute he suspected our mother was cheating, cause he knew he'd kill the guy if he ever ran into 'im."

Lilith, yodding almost imperceptibly, confirms this.

Ya know what amazes me about all this? Not that it goes on. I know that. And i know why. We all do, really ...deepdown. What gets me is how you –an' apparently all the women 'n' girls who've been in gymnastics awhile– know *all* the rules ...even the unwritten ones... and seem to abide by them to the very unwritten letter. I guess what i'm saying is, even tho no one in gymnastics –or beauty contests 'r modeling 'r movies 'r the arts– explains it, somehow all the rules of howda turn one's sexuality into success is as clear as if they held classes explaining how it's done! How c'n that be?

"I dunno. But I *do* know, nobody gets used without their knowledge, without being willing... unless theyre reallyreally stupid, which I seriously doubt."

“Or maybe young ‘r trusting or feeling trapped ‘n’ afraid” adds Lilith.

“Afraid o’ what? You cant tell me they dont know. I mean, c’mon. Even a five- er six-yearold knows there’s sumthin wrong when some guy gives you money ‘n’ then sticks his tung down your throat! [L makes scrunched face, shy to press her point further] What gets me is these sixteen- ‘n’ seventeen-yearolds who say they didnt suspect anything til after they were in the motelroom —like that senator’s aide here a couple weeks ago? Gimme a frikkin break! Let’s cut the crap, carrie. They know perfectly well what’s going on. Theyre jus using the law ta have fun, then they cry ‘foul’ t’ get off clean [harrumphs] once theyve gotten what they want.”

Where did you find this girl? [hitchhiker thumb pointing at lalage] She’s great!

“In the next crib, if you must know. Anyway, if society’s gonna label such behavior bad, and it does, the very least it c’n do is make these desires ‘n’ these practices known …well, public, i mean. *Very* public.”

“From what I’ve seen, everybody prettymuch knows, an if a girl doesnt know –*really* doesnt know what’s goin on– then somebody oudda quick sewup her tush …with razorwire maybe! [here i almost spit in my drink] …I mean, b’fore she’s out there claiming thirteen kids on welfare!”

I gaze at Lilith.

“She’s a trip aint she?”

Lage half-smiles, shrugs, “I jus tell it like it is”, takes last swallow of her beer, swipes lips w tung, then napkin. We rise, take our chat to an all-nite coffeehouse nearby called TWO HOBOS & A VIXEN (changed to NOC NOC last i heard) which offers an all-natural cheesecake and which, everafter, w ourselves in mind, we re:d as “two vixens ‘n’ a lobo”. The place is peopled mostly by goths raves haight-hippies eurotrash ε a respectful class of punk ε industrial disco. That is to say, like my dates, most there were pibs.

“So lemme get this straight. Your friend wins the miss teen title, serves her time in glory, then blows the whistle on everybody?”

No. Gets crowned, goes t’ hollywood to do the film she was promised, watches the whole project collapse when she turnsdown sex with the film’s major suit …$uit spelled with a dollarsign. That’s when a whole career of systemic abuse caughtup with her [lage is by now genuinely intrigued by bekky] She rallied one-each former miss arizona florida illinois jersey pennsylvania 'n' texas, plus some thirty-odd other former 'n' current contestants —by itself an indictment of something being severely amiss, pardon me. When *all* their allegations proved consistent with systemic corruption, the popmedia jumped in. However, insteada pursuing an in-depth investigation, they merely went 'n' reviewed the footage of past competitions, thinking to find on film an example of what was being alleged. [Lazy asses.] That's prettymuch how bekky responded. "Dont bother. You'll never spot what we're talking about. You think these people are stupid? They hunt fresh young flesh for a living!"

Lage: Hell, public competitions are *designed* ta look as pure as a miss-goodytwo-shoes smile. That should be a no-brainer.

As bekky said. "The shows themselves tell no secrets. There's no way to see through all the glitter that one or more of the winners managed to *run into* [quote fingers flashing] *certain* [flashing again] judges 'n' promoters away from the competition proper, or that *certain* judges 'n' promoters managed to *run into*, ahem, *certain* contestants. Cause *that*, fergodsake, is how it's done!" Therefore suddenly, like weird magic, what was common knowledge all along amazingly turns into everybody covering everybody's tracks. [her "Duh" here again gives me pause, but i continue] And so the system, unable to dig up any dirt on bekky or her vouchsafes, can only cry "sourgrapes" over and over again.

Gymnastics is a big clique too. You nark on one person you nark on everyone, find yerself marked fer life."

Once contest bigwigs were sure the press was sufficiently smoke'n'mirrored, they up 'n' revoked bekky's crown.

"Youve gottabe kidding! <Nope.> Bastards!" said lage, biting the very air.

"For what?" says Lilith, silent til then.

Conduct unbecoming a pageant participant or somesuch garbage. But really, we all know, it was simply for telling the truth. Which only proves once again that civilization an' truth are totally incompatible.

"No wonder she's pissed." L's features narrow to darkly classic.

"And, of course, the stripping of her crown was also meant t' send a message t' anyone else thinking of narking. I remember this thing now. Hey, didnt some pics o' her in the nude turn up?"

Huh? No way.

"Youre thinking of a miss america... o, whatshername?...her crown was yanked too... [says Lilith, cheesecake untouched] Vanessa something."

Prettysoon the poppress, cowering before statusquo hypocrisy again, is referring to bekky 'n' friends as "the sourgrapes seven". In desperation, feeling like a fool in a theater that only moments before was filled with flame, bekky dugup a couple girls who the producer of her movie (the dollars dom who backedout, r'member?) had abused for pay in the past. [L: Good f' her.] Scared of being dragged thru a "Now bekky kydd is outing hollywood" scene, suddenly her movie is go again. [Lage: Great.] Which little money-miracle is sorta related t' where i came into the picture. But that's yet another story.

"So, she finished the movie?"

She did.

Lilith: "What was it called?"

The tragic tale of treva weldon.

They'd not heard of it of course, since distribution was successfully squashed.

"Speaking of all this cheesecake [says Lilith], you guys want mine?"

"Mightaswell. I've got nuthin ta lose at this point. <Nor i.> Lage's reply gets by me but not by her Sister. Preppy pib comes over, asks them to dance. "You guys cant *both* be with him. That would be unfair." "Good line!" says lage, and wows everyone w 10-15mins of mostly doubletime disco, incl'g a backflip/punchfront finale. She returns glowing.

He got *waymore* than he bargained for. Damn, *i'm* impressed.

"Me too. But dont you have an exhibition t'morrow?"

"That's *nex* saturday."

How many hours a week do you train?

"'Round thirty. ...Well, I *was,* anyway."

Must keep you permanently outa trouble.

"Like a nun, damnit... But I'm gonna have *lots* o' time on my hands from now on" yodding, eyes wide, the sort of face one fearing unprompted tears might put on, which is the opening L has been waiting for. She leans forward, "Why? What happened?" L's squint of concern is more than just a slitting of eyes: upper nostrils flatten, lower ones flare (i'm learning to watch closer now), and out of nowhere the tiny footprint of a wadingbird appears in the narrowed space between her suddenly unarched brows. Seems lage had "Heard back from karolyi 'n' nardi", both of whom i'd never heard of at the time. "Theyre *only* the last word in elite coaches ...which they say I'm not. ["Not what?"] Elite material. At this time, anyway, heh heh. Talent's very deep this year, they wrote. Sorry. Well, guys, hel-lo! It's *this* year fer me 'r *ne*–ver!" She goes quiet; severe consternation; rotates cup w fingers & thumbs.

While lage seemed past bursting into tears, not so, Lilith, who leans in, cups lage's hands cupping cup, "You poor pet, you. Youve been keeping this in all day havent you? [now L is feeling guilty] You need somebody to read you t' sleep ...and soon. [silence] So when did you hear all this? and why didnt you tell me?" Here they share an intense gaze that got by me til i learned, later that eve, the details of their earlier argument —ie, w Lilith wounded so badly lage putoff acknowledging her own internal bleed.

Brief backstory. When nat'l stats for '92-93 gymnastics came out, lage had dropped from 16th to 35th in overall skills, after being ranked in the juniors as high as 5th on balancebeam & 7th on floor exercise! This latest rating caused her & don to put together a video of her best meets, send it to the two best coaches in the u.s, both of whom replied w basically the same judgement.

"It's a female thing [lage explained], a fat-to-muscle ratio thing men dont go thru. An' when youre too tall 'r too heavy, 'r both, it slows your pace. All the frontrunners these days are five feet 'r under 'n' less than a hundred pounds. Marianne [webster], four-eight 'n' eighty pounds. Spanky [thompson], only four-six. 'N' age is another thing. It's creeping up on me. Well, galloping, really. If youre not ranked overall under fifteen ...well, twenny on the outside... by the time youre my age youre prettymuch deadmeat nationally.

Shannon [miller]'s the exception: 17 'n' still topflite. But even she's smaller than me. <How small's that?> I'm almos five-three ...'n' two slices o' cheesecake over one-o-five ...'n' still growing they say ...dammit!"

You look plenty goddamned elite ta me.

"An' t' me too, you poor baby."

"But then *you* [to me] never saw me in action. [grins] Well, not in gymnastics, anyway. [i assume she is re:g her dancing] But not t' feel bad, you guys, okay? I kinda knew this was coming this whole past year. Aaaand, in all honesty, I'm in a way relieved. [smiles weak smile] I could use a break... Really! [anticipatory silence] I'm jus now thinkin o' somethin spanky said in an interview here the other day. 'Maybe when I growup I'll have time to be a normal kid.' <That's pretty sad.> Aint it? But true. So that's the good part. I'm gonna have plenty o' time now... I mean, fer a life outside the gym. So when I do step inside it'll be t' have fun for a change, not t' bust my buns fer sumthin I c'n never have." Lilith slides her chair close, hugs her sister, head-to-head, shoulder-to-shoulder, each fingering the other's birthstone ring.

Teary-eyed myself, i note likenesses, specially in the eyes right then. It actually tested my powers of differentiation. It was like that *w* me *ε* music sometimes too, and i hated it. But only because i love music so much. While you cant slip a (key) change past me in an arpeggio, you can do it in a clever cadenza. And that's what was happening then. Halftone changes were being slipped past me again&again as i glanced from face to face, but for the life of me i couldnt name them before they disappeared or were transformed.

After dessert we pile back in lage's scamp, tour the town a bit. At some point we pass thru <Ah, the tenderloin>.

"Frisco's pubic area."

Downturn of disgust flits across Lilith's features. "What?"

"Okay, track me here. If they call the financial district the head of town, 'n' if union square's the heart, then this here's what? Right. The pubic area ...or maybe worse. So dont press me fer details." Silence.

Lee turns to the indecent docent. "I know you need ta blow all that foolage outa your system. So you *go*, grrl."

"Ooee! Leyda-french! Havent heard that one in awhile!"

"Youve had toomuch t' drink, young lady!"

"And you havent?"

Appt'd driver stops for traffic signal, change in inertia causes the long fob of lage's keychain (olympic medal replica) to bang between my knees.

"Pardon lage. It's her bad blood kicking in again."

Lage laffs, shimmies her butt. "Stop!" yells Lee (on whose lap she's moreorless perched in the bucket seat beside me) and swats her ...to no effect.

"...And on your left the socalled adult arts district starts: theaters galleries bookstores. [DOUBLE-FEATURE promises a passing marquee] We could take in some of the classier ones —mostly r-rated stuff so oneuv us here shouldnt blush... Sister dear. And then of course, coming up on your right is our famed sex museum. I mean, wax museum. Not as good as the one in oakland, as I'm sure Sister knows, living right there 'n' all. Which is spelled, in case you didnt know, w-a-triple-x muse-yumyum, and offers the work of famous sculptors sorta modified? Well, make that, grossly modified. But first we should swing by the dorms, 'r maybe even your place, nathan."

O?

"Yeah. One of us isnt feeling well."

I glance from one to the other.

"Not me. I feel fine."

Being closest to said museum, L's dorm is recommended. Return to oakland, leave off the under-the-weather reveler: "I'll be fine. Really! Go. ...I mean it, go!" As schober observed in schubert: *Rose nahet, Lilie schwankt.*

Sexual tensorspace in the car being allbut rigid —or permeable as putty, depending on the bent of your biology. "Oops. Think we were s'posed ta hang a left at that corner." The street we're on leads straight into a large restaurant/motel complex. On a rise to our right a sign scripted in lavender neon reads, LA LODGE

"Look!"

Uh?

"There."

Yeah? I give sidelong glimmer of grin.

"I *meant*, the neat way the fog glows purple all around the sign. I did not mean, o gee, there's a motel. Sheesh." With a shake of hair she pulls her bag onto her lap.

<Lavender. Or violet, maybe. But not purple.> I think of my friend who said, "Womanist is to feminist as purple is to lavender". In my best moments i believe, vivid images –like certain colors at certain times– can link minds.

"Our dog dinah's tung was purple." Rummaging in her bag.

You had a dog named dinah?

"Eerie, huh? But he was cute. <He?> Yep. [still rummaging. we stop for trafficsignal] *Hold your tung! said the queen, turning purple.* Funny how stuff that aggravates me gets stuck in my brain. Guess it's not all bad tho. Helps me keep that three-point-eight.

Hey, look. Indicate barbecue vendor.

"You hungry?" Bag-search suspended.

Nooo. I meant, the neat way the smoke from that cart is curling around the streetlite like a binary spill ...not, O look, yum, there's food. Sheesh.

"Ooo. *Toucher!*"

Had i been more literate i would have added, Look what a mere vapor can do with moon-tints of purple and pearl. Lite turns green.

"Straight for a couple more blocks."

Thanks to the baron i have seen a little theater. I think to myself: Is this lily-sabina, miss somerset, or whatshername, ivy? Three pretty maids all in a row! But then, who cares? Jus shutup 'n' enjoy the parade, nathan. O look, here they come! <What're you searching for in there?>

"Pack o' gum. I know it's here. I do know a thingortwo about binaries ya know. Astronomy club."

I was thinking of those ones where great whirlpools of glowing matter & gas flow from a red giant, say, into a white dwarf. Very sexy stuff, the stars. People dont realize.

"Not much inta red giants m'self. Or white dwarfs for that matter ...which reminds me..." Clawing at the bottom now, she sets about regaling me concerning "There's this motel ...back in the city. It has windows, get this, b'tween rooms!"

What will they think of next?

"That's an example of rhetoric, right?"

Right. ...And *that's* an example of satire, right? Or is it parody?

"Ouch." [thinking]

Howdaya know about such stuff? That motel, i mean. An' that wax museum.

"Ya hear 'bout stuff at school. Anyway, the upstairs is for gays 'n' lez's while downstairs is reserved for straights. Who's into it opens their curtain 'n' hopes nextdoor opens theirs too. Kinky, eh?"

And the silken sad uncertain rustling of each purple curtain thrilled me, filled me, with fantastic vistas I'd not seen before. <But the place has no restaurant 'r gameroom, right? [Hey, *veh*-ree good.] An' the pool's fulla unspeakable jetsam?>

"Oooph."

Speaking o' which, is there anything around here beside bars, restaurants 'n' motels?

"Actually, yes. But remember our wrong turn back there? [clears throat, ceases rummaging, gazes at street ahead] But as I was saying. R'member brenda 'n' brandon. Well last summer they had two blacks in the room next to theirs —both of whom were maypolers, I might note, and both of whom (wearing skimasks for privacy ...Imagine? Privacy? Anyway, both o' them were pluking, get this, this poor dwarf ...white dwarf, as you put it. Which, thank you, made me think o' this whole skanky story. Ya know, mmm... I'm thinking we're lost. Mmm, maybe a left at the next lite."

Would've asked about the maypolers but for the other part. Dwarf, you say?

"Right. Dwarf. As in small person? ...But no parsleypatch in sight ...or so they said. Which prob'ly means she was shaved. That's real big out here. <I see.> That, 'r prettymuch prepubescent, which bren thought she was but bran thought impossible ...which *was* pretty scary seeing as what they were doin t' her. But then again, ya never know, these days. *The dwarf hesitated. The king grew purple with rage.* Ya see? There's another one! C'n ya believe that? Whereda I store this stuff? I prob'ly shouldnt drink. Anywho there's this one girl up in petaluma... Welp, better not go there."

Hmmm. Why stop now?

"Fershame, nathan. My lips should shrivel on such utterance," says the inebriated cicerone.

Wouldnt want that ...in any case.

"More rhetoric?"

Actually, no. Quite serious.

"Good. Later maybe. Havent landed yet." Sighs. Back rummaging again. Fog grows heavy at bottom of a hill. <I think we've left town.> We'll grab the freeway, doubleback... down there, see?. Anyhoot, here's the weirdest part. There was this boy there too ...like the dwarf's kid brother 'r sumthin? But he jus sat watchin tv the whole time."

Or so they said.

She paused. "Right. So they said." Starts removing things: wallet, small green sack w drawstring, tiniest hairdryer i'd ever seen. Hairdryer? Grumbles something about "You frikkin gum, you! I know yer in here".

{Quite quite funny when she drinks.} Thanks for sharing that ...the motel thing ...Never c'n tell when i'll be driving around, endup wanting the white dwarf special.

Laffs or hiccups or something, thought she'd found it. Exasperated sigh. "I'll pass, personally. Not prejudiced, mind you. [index up, head tilted to one side] Black guys jus dont heatup my terminals. <How bout masked men?> Now that's something else. Next left. [pointing w sideward toss of head] Now, another left at the lite. ...B'side, ya don'wanna go there. Megascummy. Brrrrr. As if. ...Jus kidding. I'm not really an as-ifer ...or gagmewithaspooner ...or WHATeverer."

Barely clear lite as it goes red. A word father used to use (*schlalagfertig* [sic], quick-witted) pops to mind.

Her loud "Aha!" scares me as it comes in sync w a car honking real close. Withdraws elusive pack of gum, rips it open: spray of little rectangles in red ɛ foil wrappers spatter around us. "Shit." She opens one, pops it in her mouth, stuffs wrapper in her bag and, bending to gather the rest, holds the now halfempty pack up to me.

Do i understand [taking the pack] brenda 'n' brandon t' be brother 'n' sister?

"Sister 'n' brother. Yep. ...They're thought of as *vraies jumelles* by everyone including their doctors. You c'n see the heights to which stupidity attains here (to use your turn of phrase, nathan) when any ten-yearold knows, persons of different sex c'n hardly be identicals!"

Hmm. I see. Struggle to unglue a piece of gum as i drive. Scent of cinnamon vies w her cologne as she gathersup the rest, starting w those on my side of the console, her cool hair laving over my right wrist ɛ forearm.

"But ya prob'ly dont."

Dont what?

"Dont see. ...About brenda 'n' brandon? Her head popped up just then, as if intuitively. There it is! Turn right next corner."

Quick change of lanes temporarily interrupts my grapple w the gum. What's with this stuff anyway? It's like all melted tagether. I marvel at my sudden slump to slanguage.

"Here. Gimme those." She rises, swings an armful of hair back behind her, sets pack aside, opens one of those gathered from around my legs. I know the quote i'm trying to think of but cant bring it forth.

The Sephalica, budding with young bees,
Upreared its purple stem around her knees.

"Here." With two fingertips she presents to my hesitating lips a powdered ε pink little rectangle. "C'mon, open, socrates. It's cinnamon not hemlock."

The WAXXX MUSEEYUMYUM was indeed <Oneofakind. Some pieces were really quite artful. Are we going right? [my hand on her thigh, hers on mine] Am i speeding? [Yes.] Xxxtasy 'n' the nymph.>

"Yes. That was an xxx-cellent piece. *Pièce.*, i mean. *Pardon.* Some were pure trash, of course. But the good one's redeemed it, yes? <Story of art.> An' what about that ol guy gone crosseyed over the butterfly on the tip of his...?" taps my leg *w* finger. She re:d a statue of what looked like pan in clown checks ε plaids, licking his lips *w* a long tung very much remindful of a penis.

Yeah. What was that? A tung 'r what?

"Er-what, I think."

Such er-whats should be standard equipment on guys, no?

"You!" Slaps/pushes me. An almost-word, *schlalagen* [sic] leaps to mind. "How could one talk with such a thing in his mouth?"

I dunno. You tell me?

Schlagen 's me yet again, this time quite hard. Whoa! Almost hit the median there! You are being very naughty, miss.

"'R sumthin."

ERsatz. Naughty er-satz. Or should that be ur-satz? You of all people should know the word for that move. [I tollja, my brain's soused.] That's a shame, cause i've got an even better one. [Ah'll betchu do.] May i have the next ur-vault? She punches again, i suspect prompted more by my leer than my meaning. Now that hurt. For that you will pay.

"One c'n only hope [she titters]. Did any o' the gums fall b'tween here?"

(The slug has spent the last 20mins in the cell across the way whispering ε gesturing. My best reader knew, by language alone, that something was up.)

The fog broke into a slow drizzle and 10mins later, thanks to clever turns in both conversation & my siserone's [sic] itinerary, i found us back at point a, she sitting outside in the car watching raindrops on the windshield fillup-slipaway, fillup-slipaway, their liquid all limpid in the lavender lite...

The glowing purple took a dusky hue....

...while, inside, i signed us up. This was the tryst –if my mental record is straight– where we threw caution to the wind. Lilith averred i bent her double that nite. And the latter remembered, "One of us was ensorceled!" Oddly, there's another fillip or two in all this. If, on counting, this nite of dating proves to be the twelfth one of my new lovelife, it would fall none short of sheerest serendipity. Which brings up a point. When orsinio falls for viola, how can he (let alone the audience) be so cocksure she is the real item? Why couldnt it be sebastian substituting a wicked trick of his own?

Do do that déjàvoodoo that you do so well.

Come to think of it, compared to me (old ns-io here), orsinio couldnt consummate his affair wout proof-positive in hand. Lucky him. (Forgive, kind reader, my backthen alcohol-fuzzed train of thought racing downgrade from *that* past to *this* present. Whatever it takes ...from one who sometimes wishes his task enjoyed the freedom fictionwriters enjoy, just a moment or two of telling some fabulous fib, instead of always the truth the truth the truth, great-Gaia —like saying g&g suddenly up& followed dr s back to his office just so i could sit here and write in peace.)

With a plane to catch, my wakeup was around dawn as i remember. My motelmate soundly sleeping, head hurting, Ugh, i rose, did what i could to shower awake a hypallagic headache. Had she really mumbled *"Visser qch à mort!"* when i woke her, or had i dreamt it? As we were leaving she in fact did remark, "Talk abouchur role reversals. <Huh? How c'n you possibly be so chipper?> I cant b'lieve the girl is taking the guy home. [turning back on exiting] God, lookit that bed! —trashed totally."

Closing door. Will that mean we're banned here, ya think?

"Not t' worry. [heading for car] Jancita will take care of it in the morning."

It *is* morning.

"Ugh, dont remind me."

Not knowing any jancita, the remark struck me as an ethnic slur (albeit a light-hearted one), the sort of thing possible to lalage (like her dad, for the sake of a joke) but totally unlike Lilith. In my diplolalagic/tautoLilithic confusion, i was in fact only that morning just getting it right. As to that other glitch? Surenuf, her pib regalia proved not total after all.

On the drive home (for some clothes ε a daybag) i mentioned envy. <Jealousy has been the undoing of many a close relationship.> Now some readers may think, aha! Ns is trying to warn Lilith that lalage may be jealous of her —of her success; of her soon-to-be syndicated cartoon, of her guyfriend, whom lage has made it clear she considers a "catch" ...specially at a time when her own hopes of "major glory" in gymnastics are dimming fast.

"How c'n you say that? I mean, lookat las' nite? Didja see any jealousy? <Actually, no.> 'N' there coulduv been... But there wasnt. <Youre right. Youre absolutely right.> T'sokay. Nobody gets it. Not even daddy." And so i came away assured i'd been wrong to picture a sister who thought {If this lavender lite speaks true, I shall yet have a share in this most happy wrack}. But, for now, only "time" –and not the ecstatic victim of this labrysic conspiracy– will untangle these puzzlements.

Dulce ridentem [fill blank] *amabo dulce loquentem.*

21

I was sched'd to lecture at humbolt state on sa eve ε on su afternoon at college of the redwoods, both in eureka. This prettymuch gobbledup the wkend.

Earlier in my career i would fly from frix to ny or zimbabwe to repay a favor. Yet none of my colleagues, no matter how realized he or she was said to be, ever noticed that i never asked them to travel more than a town or two away to perform *w* me. When lateron i began pointingup the eco-logistics of this, i met *w* much sulking ε surprise. As time goes on however, mix&match scheds between booking agents is gaining acceptance. Tho often based on better profits ε personal convenience, at least it's being done. I would like to think some small part of today's simultaneous bookings grew out of these colleague-estranging beginnings. For truth be told, some of the biggest fallingouts i've had w famous friends has been due to my reluctance to bounce between timezones to repay a guest appearance. Dropping no names: w famous persons generally, the end permits the means; the most common (unspoken) excuse being, "I spread happiness [knowledge goodness whatall] therefore it's alright for me to waste 'n' be frivolous". But the one i find most objectionable is, "In order to teach Planetary conservation to so many people I cannot myself live as I *say* we should all live. Waste in my case is an expedient necessary for *stopping* waste." And this i've heard a thousand times from people in the eco-biz, my biz, people who should, and who claim to, know better.

Furthermore. I do not hang w trendoids &or wasteoids, as Lilith calls the consumerbots in her capt.gE. Too often i've seen the following fill the speaker w pride. "I hafta be in london tamorra and hong kong on tuesday." Barf me, but you only *hafta* breathe, and even that is demanding alot of a stressed Planet. At 10 i was unimpressed by such vanity and am appalled by it now. The whole point being. For a few years there my agent's tuffest job was efficient use of travel. But it was not long before familiarity w when i would be lecturing in a given region began to save both me ε the Planet some 30-40 flites a year, minumum! Still, geo-sequenced bookings are the exception. And that most famous persons still reject them doesnt make it ok.

Many in my audiences that wkend were students majoring in forestry. Now one would think a school named "college of the redwoods" would have a good understanding of the difference between a forest ε a treefarm, even if it didnt teach preservation forestry. Not so. Redwood's college highest credo turnedout to be: Always replace the trees you cut down with seedlings. GreatGaia! How not to appear horrified when students, in all sincerity believe, all's well w Cosmic justice if one replaces a forest of towering thousand-yearold sequoias w rows of hand-high slashpine —*after* bulldozing into virtual desert all the land ε the rich diversity of life win it! On the flipside, because of the size of the forestry- ε renewable resources depts at humbolt u, i grew my talk from a chapter in *the ungreening of tomorrow:* "A forest is not a collection of trees", subtitled, "Trees are merely the most visible layer of that fantastic ancient eco-cycle we call a forest."

Finally, instead of my usual fraternizing that wkend, i kept to my quarters. For i'd begun drafting lyrics to a tune from webber's *phantom of the opera*.

22

As usual, the last 2wks of nov were hectic. While i was wrappingup my w.coast segment (mostly s of frisco), Lilith slaved over capt.gE. Wildfires raged all around me as i triangulated the san luis obispo/l.a/fresno area. These fires were blamed on Mothernature (litening) by "authorities" ε their parroting press —til the fed. confessed to having a fistful of socalled "fire letters" mailed to the fbi from some guy named ransom larson. Again the reader will think i'm pulling names out of a hat. Imagine naming a child thus, then wondering why he turnsout to be a blackmailer ε arsonist. (My Lilith, how did you livedown your name? —and so gloriously too?)

L joined me over the wkend of the 20th for four gigs (in and around fresno) ε a funeral, in san luis. Freeman's funeral was hugely attended. On arrival i was asked to "say a few words". However just before the ceremony began a woman, whom i believe was roy's wife or sister, said, win earshot, "Not if *I* have any say he wont", whereupon a highly charged scene ensued among family members ε close friends. Later this proved to be thanx to rumors crafted ε spread by the fed. ...who, as ever, shameless to a fault, circulated thru the crowd of mourners ε rubberneckers in plainclothes despite the fact that most in attendance not only knew who they were but viewed them w disgust if not undisguised acrimony. As Lilith put it in her diary: "Like maggots among the mourners, they appeared even before freeman's body was in the ground".

Still w a newlywed glow, our plan was to head straight home following my pm lecture at sfsu. But a relaxing eve was not to be. A mx from the baron barked, "It's urgent we talk, my friend... alone, in a public place."

The last time we'd gotten together had ended poorly. He wanted me to push his shortstories on my publisher and my reluctance to do so angered him. In milkcrates, in a closet at his apt near the castro dist, pj had literally hundreds of them —had been writing shortstories since his teens. But something happened when he switched from plays to prose. In the absence of dialog his considerable power over words abandoned him. Look, i dont read or write fiction, i plead. Neither does my publisher. To cheer him i suggested sending his screenplay, *the hidden witness,* to my agent w a rave review. "My plays, teleplays 'n' screenplays have made it. Now I want my shortstories known. Which brings up a question. How come you'll back my *hidden witness,* which is pure fiction, yet have no comment when it comes to my shortstories?" Thus trapped, hurting his feelings was all that was left. To stunned silence i closed W: You are so great at so many things. Why are you so hung-out-to-dry over this shortstory business? This sour note still reverberated in him.

Skipping the intrigue (public fone callbacks, his use of a voice-modifier, etc), i chose *chez panisse* (berkeley) for our talk. It offered excellent organic cuisine ε was just a few blocks from L's dorm. Arrived late, he allbut dragged me to the frontdoor. "R'member I said I wasnt sure if your fone was tapped yet? [parts doors slitely, points across street] See inspector maigret over there? He was stakedout when i got here. So he's obviously *your* tail not mine. He thinks I'm undercover customs. <You spoke with him?> Of course. Other agency presence is the only thing that keeps these guys in line. [heads us back to our table] B'side [sitting down], it's good t' let them know you know theyre there. When they hafta keep switchin shadows for little 'r no return, they sometimes quit in search of hotter prey."

Beer in hand, occasionally looking around, whispering, he tells of being "grilled by the fed. for two fuck*ing* hours yesterday, my friend. We are now even... on that count, anyway". (I'd been questioned twice about him in the past.) He then launches into a near-harangue about "them" knowing about my trip s the wkend of "the murder" and about some "weaselgreen friend of yours at greenEarth who's tryin ta set you up"; and about freeman being murdered "not all that far from where you holedup with your new honeypot"; and about my obviously having been "moved from their blacklist to their redlist", which meant my privacy, unless i learned how to "slip underground", was gone for good; and that i would be surveilled, fones tapped, house ε vehicles wired; and that i needed an alibi, and quick, because, tho people "might not forget they saw you, and even *where* they saw you, they are, as we speak, forgetting *when* they saw you exactly. And unfortunately exactness is often all that stands b'tween guilt 'n' innocence". He then apologized for having to "cooperate with the enemy", having to tell them "the obvious": that he had "pinchhit" for my lectures that wkend so i could "get away with [my] lady" so far as he knew. "It jus goes alot easier on me when I c'n throw them a crumb."

Pj, look, i said. I dont want this t' sound like i dont appreciate your concern. I do. Really. But i dont see the world like you see it; and i dont care what the f-b-i thinks o' me or learns about me. I dont. It comes down t' this. I know i'm incapable of violence, so i'm a reformist not a revolutionary. You have your methods, i have mine. As to the reactions we get from the world around us; they are usu'ly a result of our choices.

"I hope someday when youre in jail for a crime you didnt commit [*Nota volmente,* my reader!!!] you can look back on this moment with the same carefree uppity cockeyed optimistic pollyanna... Ya know, the writer's biggest mistake of all is cutting down his foes with words 'n' not swords. This practice permits the writer's foes to ban together to stab him in the back, using swords not words. Nietzsche warned about this."

> Be sure the foe you cut down with words does not swallow swords for voice.
> For all of us, when cut, feel a right to reply to tit with the tat of our choice.

Merely by following the gaze of the men around us, this alert man spots Lilith just then spotting us and starting our way. "This could only be for you." To my intros he responded, "Lilith *ist das*. But, ah. *Nimm dich in acht vor ihren schönen harren!* Nevertheless, my dear [taking her hand w a slite bow], my heart my soul my magnificent mind are henceforth your playthings!" I knew, this was not entirely theater.

A decade older than me, the baron is best described as a mental magneto. Tho his prime love is writing, his interests are farflung. However, what we love most is not necessarily what we do best. His native talent is verbal. More to the point, oration or theater. After that, acting. For it goes wout saying, no great orator is a poor actor. For years i thought it pure accident that he always managed to be at his best&worst on meeting my lady-friends. With bekky he *really* delivered. "But nathan's objectivism, as you call it, is more quest than practice. [bekk's eyebrows arch] I see you have doubts. Allow me then to e-g my point. While patriarchy struggles to reify womanhood, nathan stubbornly continues to deify it. Well'n'good. [smooth as you please he is paraphrasing a monolog from his *twisted cross*] Yet while he is realist enuf to admit, both bears 'n' militiamen shit in the woods –and *that* he knows because he's stepped in it, thank you– you'll never hear nathan admit he has stepped in the shit of some nymph or redridinghood! Cause, in a word, our mutual friend here refuses to accept: The distance from his reasons for deification of women to their point of defecation is only a stinkyfingerstep." Thus, w a cynical grin ɛ two pudgy mincing fingers extended, the baron ensured he would never see bekky again ...if *she* could help it. As to women generally he felt, "Even at their best they are frilly inutilities". You see, pj never came to grips w being abandoned by his mother and orphaned thereby.

As small tribute to pj falk's achieving his greatest success in theater, i will employ for a space here a histrionic format. As our curtain opens he is describing, mostly to Lilith, the act of leaving his apt one day.

Baron. Well, youknowwho showedup just as I was locking the door. Three ascetic faces, three new testaments, dowdy dress. Cant argue with you today says I. Gotta run. But you need to know before I go: thanx t' you I prayed the other day. [Really?] Yes. It is true. First time since I'm a kid, actually. Well, their faces lit up. Theyre all standin there grinnin ear-t'-ear thinkin theyve made a convert when I add, Yes. It's true. After you left last time I prayed youd never come back. Next thing I know, there you are. So ya see? Prayers, like your biblical miracles, are bogus. With that I turned on my heel and left.

Ns. They'll be back.

Baron. Of course they will. They want to be abused. They *need* it. [checks our faces for reaction] It's that very martyr mentality that has played such havoc with our mental health. [to Lilith] And so they love the abuse; the more the better. Proof is, the time before when they came, I told em, When you guys are ready to admit God's been in hiding thru all recorded history including that of your silly black book, come 'n' see me. Til then, dont call. I'll call you. [when supper is served the baron ceases talking. Finished long before us, he broaches the subject of freedom] No, my dear nathan. You said it yourself. The last free man lived prior t' the invention of the state."

Ns. Yes, but youre obfuscating. I'm talking free compared to absolutely constrained.

Baron. Absolute constraint, in human terms, is lifelessness. As a group, jews in world war2 concentration camps came the closest to absolute constraint.

Ns. Fine. Then youve made my point. You are free —free enuf at least to attempt to treat nongreens like the nazi's treated the jews. And i am free to challenge nongreens with what human denial has done 'n' is doing. For i believe, if Natural truth were on display everywhere in the civil world, as it is everywhere in the Universe, all men would feel as reverent toward MotherEarth as any moonwalker.

Baron. No argument. It's your chronic naifness that pisses me off. Cant you see how long such education would take? Plus, there's hardly a niche for it anymore. Environmentalism 'n' ecology have gone blah in the face of consumerist greed 'n' it'll take a world crisis t' revive it. An' I dont mean gradual crises like global warming 'n' ozone holes. I mean the real stuff; stuff even an idiot cant ignore! Do you know how many species will go extinct by the time your method works? Sure just b'lieving c'n make it so. As paul says in my "twisted cross": "All the cedars of lebanon are decimated now. After only a couple thousand years of propaganda, the fairytale judeochrislam apocalypse has come to pass both in lebanon *and* palestine. And religious believing alone has made it so." But there's no time left for believing, nathan! Your way has had its chance. Not jus the cedars of lebanon are gone. Millions of species are vanishing —ten plant species every twelve hours 'n' two animal species every twennyfour! And EXTINCTION IS FOREVER. I remember you passingout that bumpersticker ages ago. Truth is, people are excruciating imbeciles. What was it you said in *scapegoats*...? Some rave you went on about... the pea-brain of man?

Lilith. Gimme a sec, a-... If, a-, knowledge is a freeway ...No, wait... If wisdom is a freeway to the Universe then the pea-brain of man will be another ten-thousand years on the acceleration ramp.

Baron. There ya have it. You said it, an' ya dont even know what ya said! If waiting on humannature is your method then youd better be prepared to wait epochs —evolutionary epochs! Because, done your way, that's how long it's gonna take. An' by then even man himself will be a forgotten usspimple on the ass o' the Cosmos!

Lilith. So how would you do things?

Baron. She's serious?

Ns. If you mean sincere, i hafta say, absolutely.

Baron. I'd make everyone live green, that's what. Work green, eat green, love green, die green.

Lilith. You say "make". As in "force"?

Baron. Yes. ...For those idiots who refuse.

Lilith. I see.

Baron. Maybe you see, maybe you dont. We, my dear –your brave handsome lover 'n' me– we represent all the difference between a scorpion 'n' a water buffalo. The one assures peace by dint of his terrible latent power if threatened. The other, me, the scorpion, literally stays alive by Natural entrapment 'n' aggression. Your boyfriend here enjoys the title, the green warrior. Ya know what that is? [Lilith shakes her head] I'll tell ya. It's a bone the nongreen press throws him t' keep him on track —a non-violent track. But t' me he's a green weeny. You look shocked ...pardon the pun. [mumbled into his hand as a fake aside] The way I see things, there's a big difference between waging war (being a warrior) and committing passive acts in public places, which is what your green hulk here does —scuse me, did I say hulk? I meant, hunk, of course. It's a sorry world, I say, a world of limp-fisted euphemisms, when sitting on your ass on the steps of some embassy somewhere, or pacing up-'n'-down in front of some nuclear waste site with a placard, is called being a warrior.

Lilith. Meaning no disrespect, can i ask how well you know nathan? [baron spreads fingers, looks around: "What does *that* mean?] I guess what i mean is, Have you ever had your little boat run over by a freighter? been almost ...whatda they call it? ...drowned 'n' chummed in its propwash? got bruised 'n' burned 'n' knocked down 'n' cutup by firehoses? been clubbed 'n' thrown in jail for weeks under terrible conditions? been shot at with guns 'n' harpoons? That seems pretty warriorlike t' me.

Baron. You call this a friend? You lied. This is a fullon disciple! But since you raised the question I'm gonna be honest. No, it doesnt strike me as warriorlike. As a matter o' fact, it strikes me as glorified masochism. T' me, the warriors are the guys who had the balls t' do all that mean stuff t' your hero here. Like yul brynner says in *the magnificent seven,* "We dont want him. We want the guy who *gave* him all those scars". But that was before your time.

Ns. Pj, on the other hand, is a warrior; a green warrior. Well, maybe i should say, a warrior green; warrior first, green second. The color of his cause is somewhat incidental to the waging of war. The baron is a gut german, a true teuton, a reborn erik, a flashback hun. But not t' worry. My words dont hurt his feelings. In fact, they are a source of great pride for him.

Baron. What he's saying is, we're the perfect team. He tells me, Hey, pj! The good guys are green, the bad guys are not. That makes sense t' me. So when he pushes the red button that activates me, like a stealth missile ...a rather squat, yes, but manly missile... I fireup, launch, deftly seek out the enemy 'n' destroy him. End of problem. [his jowls shake to a stop] Ya see, the good guys win in my scripts ...or die trying.

Lilith. You say "destroy". As in "kill"?

Baron. If given no choice, yes.

Lilith. Contrary to pop opinion, killing does not end killing. That violence is a constructive way to proceed is an imperialist myth. Killing begets killing. Over and over history attests to this. And if Mothernature seems to be doing nothing to protect herself, that's a myth too. Her means of self-defense are innate, and highly prioritized. There is always a least-lethal way to proceed —tho that way may not always be obvious to us."

Baron. Welp... your "least-lethal" methods are letting selfish 'n' arrogant humans kill millions of plants 'n' animals every hour! Literally, every hour! The very plants 'n' animals you two do-littles claim to love ...which I must seriously question. An' nothing but killing the bastards who are leading the killing will stop the killing!

Ns. Forgetting blood 'n' guts for a moment here. The baron's method is not education but propagandizing —but only because laws constrain him from cutting the enemy down with a sword. My friend, the sort of followers you win with your violent propaganda will one day cut you down while you sleep. [Here i was re:g his own *the twisted cross.*]

Baron. Youre both braying like asses.

Lilith. [tentatively] Would you say your method is to silence debate and overpower opposing arguments?

Baron. Absolutely.

Lilith. That's a definition of propaganda. I am not disparaging your point of view when i say, Persons on the right track need not exclude *any* argument. For the Natural path has the whole Universe for empirical support!

Baron. Let me take off a figurative hat to that. [does so] But imbeciles, my dear, cant imagine there are stars beyond the clouds. And the world is populated mostly by imbeciles. They must have their noses rubbed in truth before they see it. Time, I repeat, has run out. Isnt it clear yet where all the idiot assumptions of civilization have gotten us? It's *past* time for action.

Lilith. Nature's already busy doing something and has been: We're destroying ourselves. We wont hafta cleanup anything when Nature's finished. Top-heavy, weak or sick ...*whatever* the state of *whatever* species... Mothernature always cleansup her own doings.

Baron. But at what price? And when? Look at the losses so far! And we're not nearly t' where civilization has us headed!

Lilith. Who knows the worth of lost children better than their Mother? [she is looking down and does not notice the baron's masked amazement] Most of us in first-world countries are starved for a spiritual experience. Humans have always been ready to giveup material things for spiritual rewards. All that remains is for people to findout what every primitive once knew: a life centered on green living offers the greatest spiritual experience of all.

Baron. This is pure pablum. Fear is the only religion that works on imbeciles.

Ns. Why dont you let her finish?

Baron. [in theatric aside] The congenial guest concedes to the host's wishes.

Lilith. We have been carefully taught, we'll lose more than we'll gain if we adopt a green consciousness. But deprivation is not what being deepgreen is all about. That's what antigreens would have the world believe it's about ...b'cause they have no idea of the rewards that come of being in sync with Nature. I'm talking about deep, fulfilling, body- 'n' spirit-satisfying rewards.

Baron. Youre obviously another victim of schock [sic] therapy. You overlook history just like him. The blundering masses have always been led by the ear or kicked in the ass. Even captain chlorophyl here has ranted about the muttering 'n' drooling blindness of the masses. Just ask him.

Ns. Blindness as in denial-for-the-sake-of-greed, yes. But that powderkeg is only opened safely by not forgetting one's own blindness in the process! Yet my holding such a view does not mean i believe in dictatorships or the overthrow of democracy ...or what remains of it... like director falk here. No matter how ignorant a form of life may be is not license to enslave or kill it.

Baron. You need t' get back on the activist road again, captain. You guys are spending way toomuch time on campus. Your methods require reasoning 'n' the real world has very few reasonable people in it. Your boyfriend here once wrote about the unpredictable insanity he saw in the eyes of the harpooners 'n' poachers he faced. I think he's forgotten those eyes. They are the eyes of the civilized world. They are the eyes of arrogance 'n' greed 'n' they are everywhere! It's pure naivete t' think youre gonna melt calloused hearts with reason, transform imbecile minds with your green pablum. You are dreamers, both of you. You are the parents who are shocked when your child spits his food in your face, bats the spoon away and knocks the bowl to the floor.

[Just how Lilith managed to evince the baron's applied experience of Nature (code: lack of it) escapes me still. For if the baron –this fascinating cross between j cagney & edward g– owned any social skill, it was masterful equilibrium during debate. Yet, not only did this ingeniously wrapped package of guileless temerity, perched on the couch beside me, *not* need me to jump to her defense, she, somehow, managed repeatedly to coaxforth his humanity.]

Baron. I was in the Wild, as you call it, only a couple months ago. Tactical training –maneuvers bivouacs sorties recons that sorta thing– but dont pan it til youve tried it. It has its moments: times of quiet 'n' lone introspection, with only trees to appeal to. But apart from that, I suppose I dont often get close to Nature much anymore. I'm far too busy these days picking up all the slack you dreamers leave dangerously strewn across the deck. It's not rewarding but somebody hasta look out for you guys with your too-little too-late m-o.

Dinner done we ended at my place.

The baron's conversation tends always toward stream-of-consciousness monolog. Most people get caughtup in the rapids of that stream, if they dont run off first. Lips smacking, green eyes flashing, bushy eyebrows rising & falling like foaming surf, an inordinately large head in constant motion, he would quickly obliterate all necessity for comment or participation in his listeners. At one time, well before Lilith was born, the baron alternated w ol shep (the will rogers of indiana) as a standup solo at "the village limelite", a club in greenwich village, where he was marqueed as "the fantastic & mad baron theodore". I was in my teens then and visiting the village regularly. He banged upon as often as tickled one's cerebral funnybone.

"My life was always fraught with irony", he told my attentive friend, mug of beer in fist. "When people are laffing loudest I'm most deadly serious. [she feels obliged to wipe-away smile] A true tragedian I am, in spite of the fact fate has humiliated me with this clown's body!" He stood, arms akimbo like dodo wings, and, pirouetting, indicated w pudgy hands his husky tho abbrv'd physique. "I'm the unforgettable dwarf who came to dinner one nite."

Memory sweeps back to when, in nyc, out of nowhere, in bryant pk, he sidled up to me like a penguin and, pursing his lips, looking around us as if he pressed a seditious manifesto to his chest, withdrew from inside his jacket a flask-sized copy of the *rubáiyát*—which, just for the pure fun of it, he'd hustled past the twin lions guarding the bldg nextdoor.

<Librarybook theft should be a venal sin, severely punishable by law. The library police will come 'n' arrest you one day, you'll see.>

"And I'll have to live out my days as an angry convict ...er, lexiconvict."

<Youre amazing.>

As we awaited the uptown express (to yorkville), leaning close, his large head level w my xiphoid bone, he read several passages in a rasping whisper. When he reached the part about the deformed vessel, "Did the hand of the Potter shake?", he danced around me on the platform saying, "This part's about me! Did you get that? ...Powerful, huh?" He wanted me to be sure to know, he, pj falk, was that "vessel of a more ungainly make". Reversing orbit w each new point, in rapt syllables which approached song, the baron cursed ε indicted "the Potter who had fashioned" him! A sadder sample of self-parody i had not seen before and may never see again.

He was only a little less tragic this nite. "My body is a joke in bad taste. After all, we get only one go-round. Now, if I had your boyfriend's body instead, plus this great brain of mine, I'd be a billionaire ten times over! And if I were six-foot-four instead of four-foot-six, I'd have a girl like you in every closet, or her brother. [chuckles, his talk coming fast now] And the world would be on its bloody knees to me." As he enunciated b-l-o-o-o-dy, his jowls shook, lips everted, gums showing.

All in all, Lilith found him fascinating, if stark. She wore that eve a white turtleneck sweater w black stirrup pants. Her shoes were kickedoff already and, from certain angles, her legs looked a not-to-my-liking model-thin —bodies which look perfect in white&tite can look anorexic in black&slack.

"Scots lass, eh? Goddamned good aryans, those scots! The best humans are born of german 'n' scot parents, y' know. German fathers, scot mothers, of course. Come t' think of it. If you two ever produce offspring, he –and I emphasize, he; the resultant rugrat– should be a real *lebensborn* superman!"

That was the nite we came to grips over what i call civil warfare <mass murder at an immoral remove; not just a crime against Nature but against our own species!>. He could banter endlessly using militarist euphemisms like "rules of engagement" ε "collateral damage". These i repeatedly reduced to my own geneva convention article 1: <For a wouldbe attacker to shun face-to-face combat with his intended victim i find morally reprehensible.> To this he retorted, "If vis-a-vis combat only is allowed …a bit romantic but I like it… then civilization itself is a crime against Nature 'n' humanity. For no civilized man wants blood on his own hands. Rumored bloodshed, okay. Real bloodshed, nosir." L started to say something but i was already talking.

Give me a leader who wears feathers, any day
to the one who mass-murders from far away.

<Youve made my point for me then. In fact, inhumane abstraction is a major theme of my *civilizing principle.* Youve heard me say it b'fore: Civilization is not only humanity's biggest crime against Nature, it is humanity's biggest crime against itself! [to L] You were going to say?

"You just said it." L then broughtup the baron's achievements in theater. "Nate says you are the greatest director he knows."

"But how many does he know? [wholebody chuckle] Not to diminish the compliment but, in theater, that's not saying much anymore. Directors today are slaves to the moneymen. And I make a poor slave. I'd rather be free-'n'-out-of-work in frisco than a well-to-do slave in hollywood. Besides, I'm a writer. Shortstories is what I do best." This was true in part. At plot fabrication the baron is unmatched. He once had many writers as friends, til he foundout, "Their work was based on my plots, ideas stolen directly from my mad professor act! They'd flock to my shows on friday 'n' saturday nites. And then, later, I'd read my gigs plot-for-plot in some magazine or book …and sometimes, almost word for word! They were without shame! I wager, my mad professor act enabled more writers to success than writing students enable their dull-witted teachers to post-grad degrees."

"Why dont you try cable [tv]. You'd be scooped up in a second."

"She is brilliant but unworldly, this one. And kind too, of course. Where did you find her? Have you got a sister out there somewhere, miss?" He leaned forward, pursed his small mouth, patted her cheek. Tho i'd borne this sexist condescension before, when it came to Lilith, something in this prop deployment was specially ugly. "There are strict formulas comedians must follow, my dear. My brand of humor fits none of these. Once upon a time, back when art was a free form …in europe, the mideast, the orient… all musicians traveled with an orator. Orators were highly prized by the common man. The greater the individuality the greater the orator. Formula-acts were booed 'n' jeered off the streets …if they were lucky… curses 'n' projectiles if they werent. Art is uniqueness. Today's stock funnymen would have been driven out of town …which lends itself to a dirty old pun. (I restrain myself with difficulty.) Beside, my talk is not humorous. It is only the idiot mind of the audience that *thinks* its funny, that *thinks* I'm trying to amuse it. How many times I've had to stop 'n' say, Sir, madam, that was not funny. It was *true*. What are you laffing at?"

Lilith, caught w the wisp of a smile, is suddenly selfconscious.

"How sad a world when truth is funny to us. I would tell them all to go home to their homes on a nuclearwaste site and procreate more imbeciles like themselves. And do you know what? [intently examining Lee's face] They'd laff at that too! [deftly inserted pause makes her feel obliged to say something] I am disgusted with you! [pause again. Speechless, she blinks. I sit forward, on verge of interceding] I am disgusted with you, I would say to them. You are not only without taste, you are without shame over your lack of taste. You are the fruit of parents without imagination, the offspring of boring sex. Do you know that? [another uncomfortable pause] Great minds are born of ecstasy, which automatically eliminates all kids born in wedlock and to women generally. Artists, geniuses, are always bastards, I would say to them. And still they would laff. Nite after nite I would tell them the truth, how I really felt. And they would laff, send friends 'n' relatives to see me next nite. The public brain is a fearsome thing. It penetrates but skindeep. Because of this the real me has gone untouched, unknown, for years! For decades! In fact, since birth! I was an orphan, you know. But nevermind that. And a bastard too. But you guessed that. [finishes drink] I should not have been born. I spit on the walls of my mother's womb! [makes terrible face] I spit on the world! I see the universe as a volatile gas that goes on forever! Big-bang creation was but the diarrhetic flatulence of a humorless God!"

At this point anyone but empathetic Lilith might have run into the street. As for me, he kept running me to the kitchen for more münchenfest. L would have takenover the beer runs but that she knew the entertainment was primarily for her. It grew late, then our bedtime. But the baron, a nocturnal creature, was only getting started. Trying to deflect his tirade of World- & self-loathing i said, But i've heard you call your german heritage proud —race of giants i think you called it in your *sightless ones.* Are they too, your giants, also the result of said flatulence?

"My father they say was five/five with a head like humptydumpty. Not exactly a giant. My mother was a dumpling with feet. So what did I get? The top of him, the bottom of her —ghastly luck from the gitgo. I could have looked like my grandfather, you know? —the only tall man in ten generations of frontyard gnomes! Or been a blond fafner like you. But, no. I get t' play alberich, the deformed cobbold. And get this. I get t' play him in real-life not just in some musicdrama on a stage somewhere! Curse her ogre's ovaries, I say! And curse him too! How could he want to shoot his seed into a crosseyed 'n' crippled simpleton? What sort of man humps a humpbacked baglady?

"Maybe one who was intelligent enuf to see the beauty in her" says my trusting couch companion *w* wideeyed sincerity.

"Well then, curse beauty *and* intelligence too!" He rises, marches to the bathrm.

Ns to Lilith: I'm sorry. Here i am thinking i'm introducing you to a brilliant mind 'n' it turns out i'm, well... too close t' see how divergent we've grown. When he returns we, sleepy-eyed, sever a snuggleup.

"I feel like I'm intruding. <It's been a mostly sleepless weekend for us.> [sitting, retaking his favorite prop] An empty bladder transforms a man, they say. [takes swallow] As for all that mother-stuff. I've been thinking. Perhaps I was a bit harsh. That she was a jew whore is all I needed t' say. No further embellishment necessary. Fine beer, nathan. Thank you. Lilith, by the way, the *original* lilith, was a jew. But I'm sure you knew that. The ur-Lilith, i mean. Queen of nite walkers. Or is that, nite-stalkers? It's a jew name, isnt it?"

"Partly. Semite monks borrowed it from ancient assyrian."

"Stole it, ya mean. Like most everything socalled jewish: jewish rye, pickled meats, kosher this'n'thats. Stolen, all of it! Including most of israel! But the germans were always wise ta zionist imperialism. From *deutschland* they escaped only with rye bread 'n' gefilte fish ...them that escaped."

With a rather high body-count at a certain point there, eh?

"I'm not even going t' acknowledge that."

Ya know, while i realize alot of this is the voice of pain speaking, there are jews i happen to greatly admire.

"And if you knew them better you'd find, theyre all self-loathing —not unlike me. It comes with understanding one's race." Finishesoff his beer.

What professor mountebank here means is [rising to get his refill], we've worn that argument out, he and i. From the kitchen i hear him ask, "So, tell me. How does a scottish lass come to have a jew moniker?"

"My mother needed an L-name that was unusual."

"I ask that because alot o' times we have jew blood we dont know about. My mother's mother for instance had jew blood. And this, I think, most-of-all, is my curse. [i plunk down last bottle] What's worse than being a dwarf? Why a dwarf with jew blood, of course. Be that as it may, what say you about the rise in acts of violence against jews in socalled reunified germany?"

Politics is mentor to cunning as cunning is mentor to greed.

"I am not good at politics."

"This is not politics, my dear, this is state-of-the-world."

We can anticipate not just anti-semitism from certain teutons but anti-everything —everything that cant prove it's socalled aryan.

"That's hogwash 'n' you know it. But I asked the young lady what she thought."

"I think violence is depressing, no matter the reason."

"But violence is natural ...instinctive."

"Little in us is Natural anymore —or, at least, shows in a Natural way. We have been too long away from Nature; so long that our behavior resembles that of caged creatures. ["Caged by what?"] By our own invention. ["O?"] Yes. In our flite from the parts of Nature we fear we inadvertently caged ourselves *outside* of Nature. ["I see." humoring her] This cage we invented is called civilization. Because we've made so much of our lives anti-Natural, anti-instinctive, we are unhappy. So, like any caged –or socalled domesticated– creature, this unhappiness soon makes us ill. Our illness is often so bad we do violent things not even understanding why."

"And what about when we are laffing 'n' happy?"

L looks at me as she knows i've been chin-deep in the subject for years.

Those moments are often manic; need-driven. It is sad ...no, make that, tragic... that we laff so often because we need to laff. And so seldom laff out of deep irrepressible reflex. [slowly, enunciating by syllables] Undriven, unavoidable, rich, calm, upwelling laffter: when was the last time you heard that kind of laffter?

There is silence, as each of us fails to find an answer.

"Kids. *Little* kids", says Lilith. <And primates 'n' primitives, i add.> For we civilized left *real* happiness ...joy, that is... so far back in the Wild we dont even know where or how t' find it anymore."

Takes a deep breath, clears throat. "Ya know what I think? I think you two 'uv been isolate for too long. Surely you c'n see, violence is part of Nature. The tiger the leopard the gator the spider. Meat-eaters are violent. That's the way Nature made it; that's the way it is."

"But Wild Nature kills without hatred revenge *or* fear. Our civilized view of violence shows how little we understand it ...Natural violence, i mean. The view from our civil cage is a distorted view. It narrows 'n' cheapens the wider 'n' grander Natural order of things. <On purpose.> Yes. On purpose."

"Violence is the womb of new order."

True. But in its Natural state violence is not as we civilized understand it. A wolf kills without hatred or revenge; a star explodes without anger or fear. And so the true order of the Universe evades us. Nature stands magnificent 'n' unfathomed at the far side of what we civilized only *think* we know.

"You guys 'n' your Natural-law harangues. Your ideas work so well your green revolution's one big failure. It's green, yes. But it's not a revolution. Revolution demands revolt, and the only thing revolting about greens is their wimpy-assed longing for sorry compromise. What you ecowimps are doing is only a dance, not a revolt. The guys in power, and their copycat media, are more than happy to smile 'n' applaud your little performances. But theyre really laffing up their sleeves. An' you poor naive greens ...like so many flower-children high on life... you bow 'n' curtsy 'n' go home, to rest up for the next day's silly activities. If your not careful youre gonna endup the laffingstock o' the millennium!"

"What would you propose?"

"I think mattson, weizz 'n' kincaid have the right attitude. They know action is imperative —aggressive action. Not being into self-abuse like yourselves, theyre out to win the war not just pan it. An' even freeman was not halfbad. Of course, he's dead now. But that's what happens when youre not scared ta take risks. Tactics like those of elf and alf *demand* an answer. They are fedup with green compromise 'n' so am i. It gags me to watch my best friend doing the green gavotte while the enemy, chuckling to himself, slides his knife across the bare throat of Motherearth 'n' forces her ta giveitup ...again! An' then giveitup to his buddies 'n' friends when he's done! And then, them to their buddies 'n' friends after that! *Ad nauseam*. Talk about violence.

"So youre recommending a violent overthrow of the present government?"

"Not jus the government, my dear. The very worldview that government is founded upon! In all its nooks, crannies 'n' cohorts!"

"But history leaves little doubt, the leaders of violent revolutions most always come to violent ends, even when theyre successful."

"So be it."

Lilith sits back, fists drawnup to her chest, eyes darkening & wide.

"Like mattson says, greens need ta emulate the southern sheriffs of the thirties 'n' forties. It's time to whip out the old sixguns 'n' make those goddamn corpolitical niggers dance, barefoot in the burning dustbowls theyve left behind their shameless greed! An' one book, nathan –just one book– can stir the green dragon from his sleep. If it's the right book. One book did it in europe —twice. Twistedkryst knows, it's the right time for such a book!"

The baron's audience is no longer laffing. And tho he is tite, to be sure, he is lucid. (The book he re:d is a project he'd been after me to join him in for some time: A deepgreen *mein kampf*, he called it; written by me, directed by him.)

"Hard t' believe now, but it was your boyfriend here who first convinced me, *years* ago, that me 'n' my christian peers viewed our Planet as the ultimate whore-mother —the mother whose raw passion for Wildness we viewed as dirty 'n' unholy, whatever the hell that is. I woke up, realized, action, not just words, had t' be taken. And I took it. And I'll take it again. And now it's time for you t' wake up, my friend, and take action; action that *really* counts; action that gets something done, not just talks about it."

Still leaned back, holding a small pillow on her chest, L's large expressive eyes follow his monolog in all its detail.

"Arent you tired yet, nathan? <I'm hoping your talking bedtime.> Ferget bodily needs for a sec here. You c'n do that, I know. I'm talking, *tired* of wasting benevolent words on selfish people, then watching the last rainforests burn faster than they did the day before? This past summer southern california burned like a furnace in our very faces! This past year the world lost some eleven-hundred species! Minimum! Whada they hafta do, nathan? Set *you* on fire, kill you, b'fore you wake up? Theyve already poisoned your water your food 'n' your air! What's it gonna take?"

We knew it would take at least two generations to clear out the old farts, to get rid of the old m-o. The second generation is coming into power now.

"Exactly. An' most o' them are more greedy than their greedy parents. Twistedkryst, somebody help this man! [leans to one side in his chair in such a way i think he's going to be sick, then rights himself] If the enemy was burning your books at political rallies, *maybe* i'd give you the benefit of a doubt. But theyre not. Theyre ignoring them! How's that for success? So yes, I see nothing but backsliding all around! I see buttons 'n' badges 'n' bumperstickers 'n' slogans 'n' sayings 'n' sitIns 'n' standIns 'n' squatIns 'n' pissIns 'n' shitIns fer all I know. But no action. *Never* any action. None anyone in power could respect anyway. An' meanwhile, back in Reality, monstrous gluttony bulldozes on in secret ...alot of it dozed down by the very people who wear the badges 'n' speak the passwords...! But enuf. [puts down glass] I should invest my talents where theyre appreciated. [stands] I cant sit here another minute 'n' listen t' this pantywaisted candyassed pablum o' yours! We've been writing books 'n' plays 'n' films 'n' speeches for decades, nathan! Crippled kryst! How fuck*ing* long are you going to wait? How long do you want your life's work t' be played for a joke? *Silent spring* was written in nineteen-sixdythree, man! Do you know what year it is now? Green-coaxing is dead-on-arrival anymore. Billions are being born while only thousands become greens. Palegreens at that, mostuv 'em. Do the math, man! It's not hard! As ta the rest o' them? More gluttonous people, people who respect only one thing; the thing they swing when they want something fast. Power. Powerful power! Since john muir, this Planet has become nothing more than a feeding frenzy for humans. The fist of green power is the only option the sonsobitches have left us. Goodgod, man. I cant believe i hafta explain this t' you. You guys wouldnt still be combing for consensus if you were on your way to the gallows like the rest of Nature!"[!] He shookout the words, his jowls draped around them like a crocodile shakes a hog. "The only language we respect, really respect, is the sound o' guns 'n' bombs 'n' a whole lotta screaming 'n' dying." Lilith, seemingly afraid to speak anymore, leaned back with her pillow, watching, listening.

We with obscene lifestyles are able to maintain them by making believe other living things (incl'g our own kind) are not suffering & dying because of them. This condition of denial is so pandemic it no longer surprises. What does still surprise is our lack of guilt over it. In fact, this Planetarily-lethal conscience-outage is so casually & consistently unleashed by civil society, i find it nothing short of terrifying. And i mean this with all the force of my (stunned) being.

"It's time to write the big book, schock. The one that will be remembered for millennia! The time is right ...no, make that, perfect... for ecology's *mein kampf* —the book that rallies greenshirts to action! An' youre the guy t' write it. Youre the hero, the messiah, the revolution needs ...has been expecting without knowing it. You are the conscience of the future. And that future can begin here, t'nite!" He finished his beer a second time.

Sorry, i said. We're flatout. To runout of good german ale was one thing, to runout of beer period was to lose credibility w the baron.

"It's like what you said about civilization being incapable of truth-'n'-nothing-but. When it comes to honesty, I'm way more primitive than the two o' you put together.

Ns. Explain.

Lilith. Nathan is the most honest person i've ever known.

Baron. Honest? Nathan? No. I'm honest. He's kind. One cant be both. I tell it like it is. Nathan tells it like he wishes it was. World o' difference. An' that World is being flushed down the shitter before our eyes. Reason? TOO ...MANY ...fuckING ('n' I mean that literally) ...HUMANS. What are there, six billion of us now an' nobody sees a problem? Who's kidding whom? Even paul erlich's scared t' tell it like it is anymore: that five-point-nine-nine-nine-nine-nine outa six billion of us are little more than a bunch o' degenerate macaques fiting screwing 'n' wolfing down resources like there's no other life on the Planet b'side us, an' giving zipbutzilch back! We're so sickly fecund that not even disease war or famine c'n slow us down anymore! Motherearth doesnt even get a break when we finally thank clod die b'cause our remains are so fuck*ing* polluted we keep spreading our contagion even *after* we drop! When's the last time you told your readers that, nathan? When's the last time you told them what we *really* deserve is for some big flamethrower to swoop down outa the sky 'n' cauterize every last one of our genitals b'fore we drag *everything* inta the same ugly ending we're clearly headed for. And what's that? One big maggot-mound of greed warring over our own corpses cause we've killed screwed 'r devoured everyfuckingthing else there is! Ya see? Now is that being kind? Not on yer life. An' ya know why? B'cause it's honest. I give you the state o' the Planet without politics or denial. But nathan here knows damnwell: Ta say what i jus said in civil society is the kiss o' death.

Cause truth is the last thing we wanna hear. The truth in fact is what we're all running from ...full speed ahead no looking back at the global abortion we've caused! Humanity rational? objective? or even *human* anymore? What a joke!

L, chafing to speak: That's nathan's argument exactly.

b: [incredulous] What?

L: He jus frames it so people cant call it the ravings of a madman.

b: You mean, frames it in a way that permits people to keep hiding from who we really are as a species.

L: I disagree. Nathan hates hypocrisy. He's mentioned runaway population loads o' times. He just about invented your maggot-mound analogy. In fact, he says....

b: But has he made it his number-one issue? No. Because he knows damnwell it's the kiss o' death for his career ta criticize our species' propagation-diarrhea. That's my point.

L: But it's *not* your point. You missed your point.

b: What are you talking about? [So straightforward & nonconfrontational was she at all times, the baron, who blossomed out of the *conflict* of ideas, was put off his game by any argument short on ego or anger.]

L: I'm talking about your own words jus now: Truth is what we're all running from, is what you said... Truth is the *last* thing we wanna hear. That's what youre saying but youre not hearing yourself.

b: *What* is this girl talking about?

n: Why dont you ask her?

L: What i'm saying is. The elements of your argument are correct but youre attacking them out of order. By your own description, if civil society is running from truth then it's *denial* that must be attacked 'n' vanquished, not runaway population ...or any *other* issue for that matter. That's why nathan's been saying for years: <There are not seven deadly sins there are eight. And the first, an' most deadly of all, is denial. Only after denial is accepted c'n we move on to runaway population 'n' the myriad other problems our denial has spawned.> That argument is basic to all his books one way or another. You see? Your assault should be on denial. Any other issue, no matter how crucial, is futile til humanity's ghastly 'n' insane state of denial has been challenged 'n' changed. Your own words say that much.

Picture me dumbfounded. {Great Gaia, my very own instant oracle at delphi, sitting right here b'side me!}

b, in contemplative mode for the first time all eve: Then youve made my point for me. Thank you. Nathan's life-work makes it perfectly clear: One is a fool t' try 'n' convince a dog in a feeding 'r screwing frenzy that it's in denial. [leans forward as if addressing such a dog] Stop fuck*ing* 'n' listen ta me, you idiot! You see? He wont stop. Cant be done. He jus keeps screwingaway. Why? B'cause rational doesnt work on the basic animal we really are. It's like nathan's get-well card ta civilization. Goodkryst. What the shit was *that* pablum all about? He knows how i feel. We've talked about it. Civilization hasnt got appendicitis 'r the flu my dear. It's insane. [spellsout] I-n-s-a-n-e! Mad mad mad! In the *worst* sense o' the word! You said it yourself. Denial of reality is insane. It's insane no matter who does it, human 'r hyena! You dont send a get-well-card to an insane person! Especially a civilized one —with all its repressed violence just waiting to explode on the World! You lock them away where they cant hurt anything! Jus like with the screwing dog, rational wont work on humans in denial. Pain 'n' fear are the only modes of learning we respect as a species. Ya need a big stick t' stop two dogs from fuck*ing*, 'r ta make the lion share the kill. An' it takes a damn big stick ta stop him from boffing every lioness he c'n find, as if his whole purpose in life is t' suffocate the whole world with lions. It's no different with humans. We only *wish* it was. But it's not. Looking down from the moon any fool could see —any fool not in denial that is: Things are getting exponentially worse down here the longer we're allowed ta hang around. It's gonna take a very big stick ta stop this Planetary-wide debauch of ours. Cause all us selfish fuckers 'n' feeders at the top o' the foodchain could givashit if we take every thing down with us. An' I do mean *every thing!* That's why I've made it my life's goal t' find the keys to unleashing such a big stick. And if I *had* such a big stick I would wield it mercilessly …with the same disrespect for human life which we have shown for every living thing on Earth including our own kind! And I would wield it selectively, methodic'ly, a lesson of cosmic justice in every mortal swing. [his jowls shook as those little teeth of his gnashed at every word] And then your case of our pathologic denial would be moot, cause all youd hear is "I'm sorry.

Yes, I knew better. Ev'ry step o' the way I knew better. But please b'lieve me. I'm sorry. I'm gonna change! This time I *really* mean it!" Too late, slime. Zap zap zap zap. [large jaw fixed, his plump index selected ε vaporized entire civilizations in selfish ε brutal denial] What a joke, my species. What a brutal selfish joke. If we're not the most pathetic example of life in the Universe I dread ever to meet what is. And *if*, clod save us, we are indeed made in the image of our Creator, then we better stay ready ta kiss the whole fuck*ing* Cosmos g'by! ...Now, as you were saying?

L [fascinated or appalled, or both, closing her lips slowly, pressedout a seeming-dazed response]: I'm not sure i c'n find another way to answer an argument that appears closed to comment.

b: They dont call me "the master debater" for nothing, I suppose. [the baron's 'amicable' grin was as cynical, ε as tired, as i'd ever seen it]

By then it was around 2a. Look, i really hate t' be the one t' shutdown this terrific jamsession but we've been long on work 'n' short on sleep all week an' hafta be up for a staff meeting in ...wouldja believe? about four hours?

"Not *another* meeting. In self-defense again, no doubt."

Lilith rose to leave, at which point i asked her not to drive home at such a late hour. I insisted i would follow her home in my car if she insisted. And so we all headed for bed, the baron, stopping at the bottomstair, turned, said in reflective mode: "You'll be sure an' let me know, wontcha, when you guys finally have that big before-dawn briefing, on that wonderful day when you finally decide to overthrow the present Planet-destroyers? Ya know ya c'n count on ol pj here t' be there with balls on ...scuse me, miss. With bells on... everready to risk my life for the cause. Sleep well."

Those 4hrs were spent fitfully on the greatarea foldout. {New love blossoming; old friendship decaying ...on the vine.} The syncopated snores ε snorts of the baron upstairs, a skilled nomad from wayback, could be heard in the latenite quiet. On&off thru those wee hrs i came upon imagination (o timorous incubus) roaming to Lilith's bedside, hovering there like a ghostly guardian, a rather naughty familiar of only quasiplatonic intent. Only after the deed was done did i realize, Lilith was afraid her staying overnite would offend the baron, thought she'd be sleeping w the host in his bdrm in order to give the baron the guestrm across the hall.

Lying on my prison rack tonite the baron's words, refreshed by reminiscence, bang like anvils in my ears, swarm before my eyes like a sun-blotting flock of ravens in a swift november wind! For beyond these stone walls as i write, the green revolution, for which i fought so fervently for so long, flounders, falters & fails. And so i must ask myself: Did i squander the baron's call to arms that nite? turn my back on the only practical answer to the appalling greed & denial of humanity? And then, having known Lilith, i have to ask, is it raw power or subtle devotion that runs the Universe? Or are they one & the same? always unfathomably balanced by some brilliant Juggler of Forces? And was not the Universe *and* this World we call home born in the most incredible violence imaginable? —albeit Natural (hate-free, fear-free & unimaginably Wise) violence. And, finally, is my old friend, pj falk (wherever he may be), the dwarf who wished himself a giant, indeed one? a giant i failed repeatedly to salute?

If you fail to seize arrogance by the balls, it will bury you.
—pj falk

23

Next morn, in the kitchen looking for coffee <Please be there. *Yes!*> & a bite to eat, i thought i heard the frontdoor. Stepping to look thru the windows i saw the baron, trenchcoat over a shoulder, heading down the walkway. His strut (a jaunty waddle) lacked its usual nobility; his profile, severe, pale, aged.

<Autumn is a time of severing.> Lilith hoped it wasnt because of her. I assured her it wasnt. Afterall, this is the same man who wrote

Life's a jest —just
a joke with its poke.
Then we're dust.

24

A typical meet had 15-20 staffers. Rick's concerns had clearly now become brian's, who claimed "a connection between, one, the baiting 'n' grilling of greens for the murder of a green and, two, the recent appointment of a former c-i-a operative as a socalled assistant to the greenest director the e-p-a ever had. That nate here is being heavily surveilled by the f-b-i is exactly the kinduv thing rick warned us would follow strickland's state-of-the-environment speech. Yet, while each of us sits here thinking, 'Nathan schock, a murderer? That's absurd', police mentalities are thinking: 'Why not? Who knows what might shakeout if we plant a little nasty agitation here 'n' there?' Afterall, it was this *same* f-b-i who knowingly framed poor judi bari, wasnt it? And they did it *without* any overt public encouragement from washington d-c."

I added how i read things. <I see the fed.'s green paranoia as validation of a growing green consciousness within the electorate.>

"O really? [popped deldevi] A green populace? Have you forgotten about that poor green in ohio last year? Stoned, her house set on fire. Then, as if that wasnt enuf, stabbed on a public street. Werent at least a *couple* of the blokes who did it, and most of those who stoodby and watched, part of your green electorate, nathan?"

Full-knowing deldevi was worried i was underestimating my own danger i answered: That crime was instigated by corporate security —of course with a wink 'n' a nod from the c-e-o's. This is standard third-world corporate bullying coming home to roost right here in america. In any event, i see it as a status quo reflex, the *same* green-paranoia —coming from that part of the populace which feels threatened by the very green awareness i'm talking about. For the working classes are being carefully taught, wrongly we know, that greenliving means loss of jobs. A dumb conclusion, yes. But that's what the agitprop from the fed. 'n' its presscorps is drumming daily into everyone's head. Strickland's speech is a classic example of this lying 'n' destructive drumbeat from above.

"And then there's that poor activist in florida who was protesting proctor 'n' gamble's enviro crimes last year. [adds Lilith] She was tortured 'n' raped by three masked men..." (*Alerte,* my reader! As terribly convenient to this testament as these crimes may seem, i'm *not* making this stuff up. Checkout david helvarg's comprehensive *war against the greens.* There you will find dozens more assaults on greens i've no time to mention.) "...three men thought to be proctor 'n' gamble security and offduty cops too no less. From what i've heard, these police/military types are hired nowadays *because* of their lust for brutality, not in spite of it."

Most seconded L's very sober assessment. "Sad but true. [summed rick] And let us not forget our own patty costner, whose place –not all that far from where nate lives back east– was torched to the ground in ninedyone, and whose fone lines were cut just last year on the anniversary of that vicious arson.

Terrible stuff, all of it. But I think *all* of you are right. Cause it is very often the case: things have to get worse even as theyre getting better."

An important part of this meet was to "provide a forum for the airing of sentiments related to the murder of roy freeman"; an effort to unify our visions and defuse the fed.'s on-site agitprop. To encourage all present to voice their concerns i volunteered to leave the rm. (I must therefor paraphrase Lilith, rick & deldevi for the rest of this.) After backgrounding my situation, rick plumbed straight to the gist. "The f-b-i seems determined to capitalize on the sentiments of one of us (whom we shall *not* name here, thank you all), someone who has suggested that nathan murdered roy. While this person says they were only joking, the f-b-i has been running hard with that joke. And as a result, things are getting ugly. It's this we need to air. So let's have at it."

Except that delphine, eyebrows up, lips sealed, looked at Lilith, rolled her big black eyes toward nikki, and except that all present couldnt badmouth the fbi enuf, no one was prepared to give more than a ziplipped sky-glance & shouldershrug concerning the intent of nikki's socalled joke. With nikki not volunteering to leave, and no one allowed to name her, brian finally decided, "I dont think any of us who know nathan doubt for a moment the flagrant absurdity of this vicious f-b-i campaign. If anyone has *anything* at all to add, however, please speak up." Everyone incl'g a seemingly unruffled nikki sat silent. While i waited in rick's office, i found my childhood insecurity wishing my seafaring friends were present to lend support. Asked one last time if anyone wished to add anything, Lilith, silent since i'd left, said: "At the risk of sounding unashamedly biased: Anyone intimate with the sensibilities of greens knows, the very idea of intragreen violence, let alone of one green murdering another, is as oxymoronic as peaceful war". L's assessment, which eventually woundup in capt.gE, has since been often quoted or paraphrased.

At lunch, where much of this came clear, Lilith still had not a harsh word for nikki. She said only that delphine acted "curiously friendly toward [her]. I dont know how to explain what i mean. I havent figured it out." I should also mention that, over coffee that morn after he left, L asked if the baron was gay? <Yes. But what has that to do with anything?> "Well... it has t' do with his... his feelings. <O?> His feelings toward me, i mean." <But i thought i explained his problem with females?> You did. And so did he ...sortuv. It's jus that... Well... You probably already know this but-, i think... <Yeees?>

I think he's in love with you." <I see.> This recalled how once, years ago, the baron had fumed & stomped out of my life at my non-requital of his homoeros, later claiming, his spitting fumarolicry had been so much histrionics and that he was honored to find that i thought his "little performance" was real. It was backthen i'd made perfectly clear, <For me there is no eros –none– in male/male relationships. I've been told before that this is my loss, but that's the way it is. I'm sorry.>

Lilith empathized. "You neednt explain. My very best friend 'n' me had that problem. It has to end in pain for them. It seems there's no other way. I jus hate being the cause of any bad feelings between you two." I assured her (again), she wasnt, that the relationship had been deteriorating on philosophic grounds for years. But she seemed bent on faulting herself. "First i caused trouble between you 'n' nikki, then between daddy 'n' sis. <Lilith.> And now this with the baron. <Li-lith? He-llo?> An' i dont know what's going on now with delphine. She's almost *too* nice to me. <Is that possible?> Well, yes... sortuv. But only because i think she's in love with you too ...Delphine's why they know what you drink at 'the ganges' isnt it?"

{Thanx, mutt. On secondthought, youre lucky youre faraway at sea.}

The thing which mostofall troubled L at lunch however took me by surprise. "There hasta be more to all this. The f-b-i just cant be that desperate for action. B'side, i'm sure nikki would never have made that comment if she'd known what would result, what bad things could *still* result. These government policetypes c'n be *very* ugly i hear. [gives shudder] Brrrr."

But nik hasnt apologized to anyone, Lilith. Certainly not t' me. The best she could manage with rick 'n' brian was: "Hasnt *anybody* got a life? Forgodsake, I was only kidding."

"It's only Natural i suppose t' strikeout when hurt."

To throw a fellow green like bloody meat to the f-b-i? i blurted, amazed she was still protective of nikki. I followed this w a contrite <I'm sorry>, for i saw a look of black frite flit across her features. Giving a shoulder-to-shoulder squeeze as we left the café i buffered. <I know youre jus being kind. And i know, if you thought about it, you'd know as well as i, the "O well. That's only a Natural reaction to being hurt in love" response is all wrong in nikki's case. And that so many of us b'lieve it, makes it even wronger. A glance at her

face made me add: I'm not suggesting that's what *youre* doing. Youre way beyond that, i know. What i'm saying is: Vengeance is *not* a Natural response to loss in love. Sorrow 'n' dejection are Natural responses. Some initial yelling 'r stompingoff too i suppose. But a state of sustained vengeance? Vicious vengeance, no less? That's sick. [Lilith seemed so agreeable it never occurred to me she might be thinking my words were a parable for some other point i was trying to make] In fact, we so rarely get t' see untainted humanNature at work, how could we know, we civil, that *none* of nik's reactions have been Natural. And since only the very young, primitives 'n' primates display raw humanNature anymore, it's easy for us to forget what a *really* Natural reaction is. The surprise that flitted across your face a minute ago was humanNature revealing itself. And that makes you precious. We should prize our fellows when they gift us with such Natural responses. But since civil society mocks such frankness as unsophisticated sentimental folkish [code: primitive] garbage, most of us fear to risk such honesty.

The fomenting of fear by the fed. is just one example of the state needing to maintain a condition of mutual distrust among its citizens at all times. Civil society –ie: the state in its guise as good friend & caring parent– knows alltoowell that frankness & honesty (and, of course, love) between persons automatically builds community at an instinctual level (code: deeply human level). Which is why the state fears all forms of Natural communalism. For the state knows the power of communalism for uniting people is actually the power of the extended family at work in the general population. Which, when you follow the rationale back to its source, is why the state constantly strives to obliterate the extended family ...attacking it even on the level of language, mocking it with such names as tribe, cult, clan, cabal, camp, sect, cell, pack, gang, even 'commune' & 'family' in certain degrading contexts... all of it revealing the state's desire to impose the nuclear family in its place; to limit, to isolate, the power of our species' Natural communalism. The most insidious & destructive form of which fragmentation-via-distrust is the division of the human family, the human community, into those separatist &/or warring factions we've come to call states, treating them as if states are Natural entities —and each of which state always enforces the same plague of propaganda that got our Planet into the condition of deadly & dark freefall it is today. It is this contagion ...the seemingly harmless propagandas which each of us espouses every minute of every day —the "O well, that's only Natural, I suppose"; the "O well, the world's just a crazy place"; the "O well, i'm jus not myself t'day"; the "O well, that's jus the price of getting real I suppose"... the lot of it addingup to the civilizing principle unleashing its deadly malignancy minute-to-minute among us even as each of us spreads it unseeing.

But Lilith, versed in the above –and who typically posed little interrogatories of familiarity whenever talk touched on my oeuvre– had fallen strangely glum. But then she surprised me *w*, "I hope –and i really mean this, nathan– you havent taken what i've said about delphine, or the baron, or even nikki, as me in any way censuring what you do." She went on to say, she didnt care if i had dated "everyother woman in frisco. Honestly!" Such things were "absolutely [my] business and no one else's". Her seeming certitude on this point frankly made me uneasy. "And b'lieve me, i would have said nothing except that some people around here (no names, not even any genders) seem to enjoy dropping these personal tidbits, as if theyre challenging me to deal with them or run". Then, to cap, she disclaimed. "But, really, it's my own fault. I'm the one who put myself in your path. All this is my doing not yours. And now even the goddamned f-b-i is after you! And that too's probably because of me when you think about it. You were going along just fine with your life til me... <Lilith.> Mygod, what was i thinking?"

Hold it right there. But she couldnt be swayed, certainly not then w our lunchhour ending. There i was, for weeks, coaxing her to purge, preferring always confession to repression. Then, all at once, the pyrotechnic catharsis i envisioned for her, for us, was fizzling in front of me into one soggy ongoing stinkbomb. Tears in her eyes, we parted —her downstairs, me to rick's office. And all this got roundedoff by a letter i got on tu.

> Nathan: I want this on paper. The fact we have argued again will not affect [sic] my financial indebtedness —which, according to my records, is now about $47,000. You will be paid back as quickly as possible. And, as ever, you may still (in fact, I insist, you continue to) ask me to stand in for you whenever the fancy or need strikes you. You may be assured, my Bolinas theatrics will not happen again and that I will represent your green methods & goals in <u>total</u> deference to my own, just as agreed long ago. I am a man of my word and plan to stand fully & always behind it. PJ

The whole backside of the paper was embossed by the sheer pressure of his pen. The statement about bolinas was in re my confronting him w rumors that he'd done "a little rabble-rousing up there". For a reliable source quoted him as saying, "Between you an' me, schock's methods are a bit pantywaisted. Personally I'm an admirer of elf and alf, when it comes to green activism. They have the sort of spine which these bolinas bird-buggerers could use a shot of."

25

On th Lilith went to dillon beach for a thanksgiving dinner i suspected was not quite so "Okay" as she claimed. Then, on fr, she got a notice to vacate her dorm since she was no longer enrolled at the college. There was talk of lage's "drinking toomuch lately" also ε of a "really troubling fonecall from okka to reesy at school". Add to these the fbi intrigue ε my approaching departure, and, well: Lilith was not doing well. Backthen i took her inversions personally, figured she needed to distance herself for some 'us' reason or other. But what was she really escaping from? This we could use a better grasp of.

26

When i met her, one of Lilith's favorite books was robin morgan's *the demon lover.* (Morgan was aurise's favorite author.) This is fascinating because, when i finally got around to examining morgan's work, she turnedout to number among the handful of thinkers able to achieve an objective remove sufficient to spot the depth of unReality/denial which suffuses every nuance of our civil existence; and who, having plumbed to that depth, came away terrified by the sheer distance she found between socalled normal behavior (civil/domesticated behavior) and behavior moderated by unpolluted moral conscience (Native honesty). Morgan reads (what i for consistency call) civilization's labyrinth of negative equivocations as follows.

> Those are the ways they keep you thinking yourself sane while actually you are mad; those are the ways you go mad for fear of appearing to be mad when you are finally going sane.

27

I'd long held a ticket to fly back home after my last w.coast gig. Feeling a need to explain my departure, on fr –ignoring my respect for her right to crawl off ε thinkthru the question of 'us'– i coaxed her out to supper at "green's" (veggies w a view), a ferryboat ride ε a visit to "poseidon's pipeorgan".

It was a dark nite of patchy fog w intermittent squall clouds. These hung just above the boat and misted us at intervals seemed timed to annoy, given the delicacy ε privateness of what i was looking for a chance to say. She wore that eve a muslin skirt/blouse outfit which made me feel slipped into a flowerchild flashback, save for the lack of "flowers in her [longlong] hair". Water below the rail was black —inkblack; its only luminescence the occasional flip of a whitecap which glowed by ferrylite.

I've got only til the end of january til touring kicksIn again and, well... my place under the sun, and its seasons 'n' their rituals, are calling me. "Come home, nathan. Come home."

"I love that song. ...Rituals, you say?" A shadow flitted across her features.

Well, yes. Rev'rence for Motherearth sort o' thing. And what such rev'rence does for the whole point of being me: infinitesimal unit of awareness in such a gargantuan Universe.

"Would it be nosey of me to ask-? Welp, nevermind. I'm sure it is."

Not at all. But i dont know that i c'n adequately... But, hell. I'll give it a shot. Hmm. I guess i have many rituals 'n' dont even know it. We usually do. My obvious one's are time-of-day... No. Make that, state-of-the-day rituals: sunup, midday, sundown, after-dark, moonrise, etcetera. Modern ideas of time 'n' date have no role in this. In fact, *my* rituals are ruined by clocks 'r calendars. WholeEarth 'n' celestial change alone are the supreme arbiters of these rituals. When i rise in the morning i go... No... i'm drawn to go... splash my face in the pond 'n' drink a few handfuls of water. Tho the purpose of this ritual might strike an onlooker –might even strike me– as a refreshment of the senses (for the water is seldom warm), the most powerful aspect of this ritual is the seemingly secondary influx of images, scents, sounds, tastes 'n' feelings: [slowly, one by one, i try to isolate them for her] dew-art ...plantlife sensing the early morning lite... raucously 'n' colorfully ecstatic birds ...fish beginning to think of breakfast ...deer (gone from pond's edge before i arrive) looking up as i arrive, then continuing to browse ...and no one –no plant, no animal– cares if i am rich or poor, successful or a failure, showered or shaved, or even dressed, really. So long as i'm not malcontent, disturbed, disruptive, dangerous or unpredictable, i seem to be accepted. And there are lots 'n' lots of beings thereabouts to be accepted by. It requires years, and much caution 'n' respect, to discover most of them. At midday, needing a break in my pursuits, i go for a walk —usually among trees. I dont know why this is. Sometimes i talk to them, ask to lean on them, contemplate them, sometimes even taste their leaves... on the stem, that is... taste or chew their bark... loose bark... and even, yes, risking high presumption, hugging one of them at times, out of a sense of adoration i cant explain.

(Tho experience says i may be confessing too much, intuition, encouraged by my native frankness, says to go on.)

It's not that i'm expecting any big communion with that tree, with that forest... Or *am* i. But that's not even the point. It's the sense of mutual tranquility 'n' seemingly shared good vibes that begins to permeate everything. Sometimes it can even be a buzz. I return to my work invigorated, clear 'n' content. And as to the hour before sunset... That's special too. I read sunset, even in spring, as a miniature warning of the inevitability of winter —deepest winter. The setting sun makes me aware that we are being turned away, one more time, from the celestial engine of life itself. And each sundown, because i am fearful i may never see this Planet i so adore by the lite of day again, i meditate.

And if, as the sun disappears from sight i am other than absolutely thankful for being alive, of having been gifted with another day, then i know something is very wrong with my life, and that it must be corrected at once, else... Well... The point of it all disappears otherwise. Tho she says nothing when i finish it is somehow clear, she understands most of what i risked confessing. <There's more, of course. But... Well, maybe one day you'll visit 'n' i can show you.>

"It sounds really... I guess beautiful is a silly word for all you jus said."

Pressed against the rail, i smelled the chamomile freshness of her hair whenever a windgust blew it; the press of her hip against my hamstrings made me want her more than ever.

T' be quite honest. There are only two things i can think of... at this minute, anyway... two things that are wrong back home. One is, that the sanctuary doesnt encompass this entire Planet of ours; and, two... well... that you wont be arriving there with me.

...Where all the waters await your reflection, all the paths, your footfall.

Flushing, she quickly found some words. "Sounds like a terrific place. You have earned it." She apologized for her own "squalls lately", assured me i wasnt in any way their cause.

Out yakking on the river one day the following spring, following some bad news which put her in the doldrums, i came by my own impression of those socalled squalls of hers. As one's yak approaches, water turtles slip under the surface. They use the surface of the water as tho it were a random opening in the vast shell of their waterworld. We do not take their disappearance personally. The Lilithic shell was, in a like way, everready to receive, and to hide, its afrited & beautiful occupant from perceived danger. I would come to know those protective props over time: full-cover clothing, heavy robes & afghans, heavy socks, mufflers, quilts & sleeping bags fit to roast a reptile in the dead of winter. Lalage called it "switchingoff". I called it turtling.

And there was something else. Since puberty one of the best parts of her existence was escaping to her room to read, to draw & to dream. Of the books i was asso w, one of the first she devoured (as juanita would have said) was *the greenEarth chronicles: a history of, & adventures in, ecoactivism*. From this immersion, of course, grew her captain greenEarth cartoon. This research contd at great intensity so that, by the time we met, she knew all there was to know about me that one could know at such a distance. Heap onto this her makebelieve life w me as lara in her cartoon, and you end w an almost certain ℞ for disappointment. Not on meeting me. That part was easy. But on getting to know me.

She would later mock herself. "I expected you to just carry me off. Mostofall i expected that." And in a more Natural world (read: less civil) i would have done just that. God, i would have! But, fact is, the ns she came to know thru her onerous ε perplexing adolescence was a paper-thin persona. Also, the intimacy ε affection she evolved, ε shared, w that fictional me, on later inspection proved platonic —not just platonic but puerilely platonic. "Though it was love from the moment i first laid eyes on you… and on film, no less!"

In your eyes [were] my secrets that [i'd] never shown you.
In my heart [i felt i'd] always known you.

Truth is (and this is something she sincerely ε passionately denied when i first pointed it out), a key reason she created the capt was to recapture a former intimacy —a relationship w a certain adult male whom memory had hypertrophied largely *because* it had nothing to do with sex! In this sense, her capt.gE (not in looks, activities ε beliefs but in a visceral quality beyond brief description) was farmore like her father (don) than me!

That was level 1. Enter now a fleshedout ns. I of course had no idea how fully developed (in her mind) her fairytale-me was. For years i was no more to her than a legendary abstraction; first as subject ε speaker in video programs whose screen i could not escape long enuf even to ask her name; then as an author whose ideas ε actions were safely fixed between the covers of books; then as a partially fictionalized (by her) hero, whose every thought ε action she could manipulate at will. That is how i was packaged for Lilith from age 13 thru the period which concerns us now. As her diary puts it: "Great Mother of Earth, have i *ever* been knocked back on my assumptions! For here, smack down in the middle of my existence, is my own character come to life and totally out of control! Well, out of my control, anyway! Pinocchio was kid stuff next to this hunk of vital & virile self-determinism! Quick, stageboy! Where are his wires? I can't find them anywhere and the play has already begun!"

And, finally ...and this next is to completely ignore the roadblocks thrown in our way by virtue of her intro to sex; i mean, sex w a man ...GoodGaia, forgive me (tho i can barely forgive myself), for not being more sensitive to what was going on at Lilith's end of our courtship.

After touching on my questions (aurise's problems with okka, her tiff with her dad) she looked away, that strabism glazing her blues w wisps of silvergray —not unlike the silvergray mists which drifted past the drenched windowpanes behind her. {The frailness of her features reminds me now'n'again of figureskater katoosha gordeeva.} I want to touch her. I find myself thinking about the nite, not all that long ago, when i allbut carried that newborn calf-of-a-body in my arms thru a soupy darkness by the sea and never... (Well, less sweepingly.) ...was too concerned for her to do more than revel in the feel, the closeness, of her. (*Nota bene,* please, my motives, don mcGrae, sir, wherever you are, in plusRealSpace or minusFakeTime.)

Tho we touchedon her coming to ggNs for a visit, and even tho i went so far as to offer her the orig house for privacy ε work (if she ever decided to drop by), she feared tampering w gE's "terribly thoughtful" arrangement: freedom to work on her/their cartoon series at graphics-artist salary + office ε local amenities. Respecting her choices, *whatever* their causes (frisco's basic livingcosts alone would command much of her salary), on sun, nov 28 (if my calendar is correct), i left Lilith, departed ca for home.

A swallow just left my windowledge. I would not have seen it but that it tapped on the glass. If i were superstitious –seeing it was not only a swallow but female– i might've thought... well, truth is, i did think. But what i thought was specular and that's the difference. I know the creature was only examining the glass around the hole in my window with the idea of a future nest in mind, or perhaps just sharpening its beak, not some embodied familiar trying to get my attention as a very lonely man might dare suppose.

Solo amore, quando fugge e va lontono,
speri in vano ma non torna piú.

28

This is as good a place as any to flag down this stream-of-consciousness express and end w an item which, in fact, began that nite on the beach w Lilith at big sur.

Words, w no conscious coaxing, sometimes leap onto the backs of the notes of a melody as i hear it —like lions leaping on the backs of elephants in a circus parade. Tho busied w catchup at the sanctuary in the weeks following thanksgiving, in quiet moments, as our Earth slipped toward solstice, i dabbled w the lyrics to a tony webber song drafted the wkend of my eureka lectures. The following verses are the lyrical nitebirds which lit on my happy hand. Since their proper rhythm may not be explicit, we'll begin the song w a little tutoring.

[sample]

BEAT. Pause. BEAT. Pause. Now we fit toGEther
ALL the WORDS and ALL the syllables.
    NOW you have the RHYthm,
    the ICtae to go WITH 'em,
and now you can proceed to read this verse.
WITH the stress disPLACED it wont reHEARSE.

Lilith & nathan

(a seaside scene)

(italics indicate both voices in unison)
"Step. Turn. Dip. Turn. Nite is made for dancing."
Nature has a power we cant fite.
    Let your mind go free,
    find your fantasy with me;
where your mind soars let your body join in flite,
succumbing to the rhythms of the nite.

"Step, turn, dip, turn. Nite was made for waltzing.
Strange, this music, strange and stirring lite."
    Our shadows are cavorting,
    distending and distorting,
commingling on the cavewalls of the nite!
"Is this an angel dance or demon rite?"

Close your eyes and the ugly past will melt away,
all the fears you have known will set you free.
Close your eyes, hold me tite, and fall with me....
...become whom you have always longed to be.

In my arms your body's all atremble.
"All at once forgetting seems so right.
        ...This magic is enthralling!"
        Dont fite it, just keep falling.
You cant be hurt. "True love is feather-lite!"
Beside, there is no bottom to love's nite!

"Starlite weaves a strange illumination."
And the sea suspires in syncopation.
        "Nitetime lures the senses."
        Suppresses day's defenses,
"And gives one's wildest fantasy the right..."
...to blind with jealousy the eyes of nite.

Leave the past, for the past will only dash your dreams,
while the magic of the nite can set you free.
"In the dark desire finds complicity."
A masquerade of anonymity.

"Touch me, kiss me, hold me, now I'm falling."
Nite will catch us in its net of dreams.
        "Sand and sea will bind us."
        And ecstasy will blind us!
"Our clinging, fusing souls will find the means..."
...to make this fantasy all that it seems.

"Starlite, star brite, first star that I see.
The nite is split: half mist, half mystery."
        Trusting love is height'ning.
        "But doubt —it strikes like litening!
I wish I wont. But then, I wish I might
unmask the dream I've dared to wish tonite."

Leave your doubt, for your doubt will only break the spell.
Let the nite take you where you want to be.
"But nite invites pretense and makebelieve."
Then let's pretend, i love you... "You love me."

Can you feel the power in this moonlite?
"I feel, I fear, the feelings it excites."
    Twinkling, all a-tremble,
    a million stars assemble...
"...So beautiful we're speechless at the sight!"
Your eyes hold all the splendor in the nite!

"Can you feel it? Something stirs the senses!
Starlight? Windsong? Something feels so right!"
    Let your dream expand
    with each wave that sweeps the sand.
"Like the stars that rinse this tapestry of lite!"
Let love sweep in and drown us with its might!

"What will happen, if I dare to love you now?"
Ask no questions, the nite will tell no lies.
"What will happen? Can this trembling be the truth?"
I see the truth unfolding in your eyes.

Hold me. Kiss me. Just pretend we're falling.
"I dont know. I have this fear of height!"
    Let your body steal
    every thrill that it can feel.
"Love makes a mockery of wrong and right."
Love burns in hell to capture such a nite!

"What will happen if I dare to love you?
If I dare to lift the mask of nite?"
    Hush, it doesnt matter.
    Dont let this moment shatter
on someone else's rocks of wrong and right.
Let love impose its own laws for tonite.

"Look around, we're suspended in a magic void!
All the wishes we have wished have come to be!"
Look around! Beside the moon, the stars and sea,
a bed of sand ...there's only you, and me!

[lovers receding to fragments of song]

Come test your wings, enjoy the bliss of flite.
We'll tumble thru the velvet of the nite.
You wont get hurt; the feeling's just too right.
We'll melt into the loving arms of nite.

[distantly, echoic]
...Why not let your feelings flow...
"And glissade into the glow...."

"Seasounds hold the heartbeat of the nite...."
...Two wishingstars are twinkling in your eyes.

"...Dream all the dreams you ever dreamed —with me."
And all that you have dreamed will come to be....

Happiness is being loved yet free....
Come, tumble thru the Universe with me!

Part 5

[Approx. date of composition by author: Mar. '99, alternatively with Part 11 —Ed.]

shorttake on rilke:
≈What none has dared before...
This i find impossible to ignore.≈

why not chapter headings? They worked for melville & joyce

Beside, why shouldnt some part of this task provide a little pleasant distraction. I need to loosenup, recapture my old pretragedy demeanor.

my cutoff from Wilderness is now complete

Been needing to announce: moved to new bldg last week —newer cleaner briter cell, yes. More importantly, prisoner abuse effected in my cell will now be somewhat witnessed ...for the little that's worth. But as one comes to expect, the move had its downside. Less privacy, smaller cell, narrower bunk, waymore noise ε no window. (Even the foodcellar had a window.) And so my last connection to Wilderness (sky) is now gone. This loss is weighing-in heavier than i would have guessed. This claustrophobe has regressed from years of max horizon at sea to a dozen years in a glass house on a mtntop to the rest of his days in a windowless cell. Cutoff from all Nature outside of me, consider me, reader, civilized now in every external sense.

author's ticklerlist gone

Moved from my old cell wout warning, 10 or so pages of tiny encrypted script, pages detailing the major subjects covered thusfar in this bio, were lost. Rolled into a tube kept slid into a flaw in my mattress, i got no opportunity to retrieve it unseen; and when i asked for my old mattress (as pad for my new one), when they'd finished laffing i was told it had been trashed. Slugmoid: "Thanks to your continual whining schock, the [state corrections] oversight board will be nosing around here brite 'n' early on friday." Adding 2&2 i decided, every effort was being made to convince the oversight team that the cells in the old bldg had not housed inmates for decades. And so, the reader will hopefully bear w me should i repeat anything, omit anything. Writing fast&furious, and under such conditions, one cannot be expected to remember everything set, or not set, to paper.

juggled chronologics

The reader might keep in mind, parts 6, 7, 8, 9 ε 10 were witten before part5; reason being: should my execution interrupt, this part of the story is most expendable ...which should not be taken to mean, part5 is not vital to the argument of the tale. It was the final pages of part10 in fact which, on fr, went off w emil for replication ε safe-keeping. Boundless relief, you have no idea! My side of the story told at last! The details of how that deadly pathogen known as cd strickland died –really died, not the fed. ε poppress version– and what ledup to that death, is now a matter of record —albeit privately held for the time being. Such a monstrous weight off my chest! I was sure i would be put to death w my truth unspoken or incomplete. Anyway, not wanting to interrupt the narration of part4, a...

...cursory legal update is long overdue

First, a glut of actions against the fed., two states, ε one private estate, has been initiated. And an action before the supreme court is pending: to reverse judgement of a lower court which would not allow our obstruction of justice, fabrication of evidence, suppression of actual evidence etc charges; as is also a suit against the fbi and two of its agents. As to other actions, a suit naming the state ε milton co, and another against the city of noogachatta (all tn), looks first to go to trial. As to our fed. petitions for new trial and/or commutation of (death) sentence, i understand there has been nothing yet on the floors of either house, or w the justice dept or the office of the president. I should pointout, many of these petitions ε suits, and some of the appeals, are duplicated on a state level as well; eg: house, senate, supreme court, governor, attys gen, etc.

Closer to 'home'. Since petitions to the warden have gotten promises but sluggish-to-no action, emil has filed suit against the va dept of criminal affairs (ironic pun) for infractions ε abuses incl'g illegal unethical ε immoral medical practices, gross abuse of fed. ε state confinement limitations, bodily assault, battery, inhumane treatment, abuse of inmate rights ε privileges, etcetc. As for my fone, mail ε visitation rights, that farce ε fiasco, thanks to judge black, is totally up to the fed. court whose orig "confinement-limitations" ruling has in fact recently grown a new ε sinister tentacle.

sure Rx for terminal limbo

Even overlooking my death-sentence, my legal circumstance is dizzying & depressing. Forinstance, i am still carried month-to-month as public enemy #1 by the fbi. This situation, ongoing since even before my indictment, is made all the more ironic in that the "ok bomber" (who killed 168 people incl'g many fed. employees, demolished an entire fed. bldg and put our nation in a state of momentary shock), a person one thinks would win my dubious title even w his hands shackled behind his back, still comes in *second* to me on that list! Go figure, as lalage would say.

Related to this, i endure an indefinite ban on "all contact outside the institution of confinement". I'm not sure i've said how this came to be. In addition to murder1 i was convicted by the same court of "antigovernment activities, sympathies and ideologies" incl'g "conspiracy, sedition and subversion". Because of this, all those w whom i attempt to associate, or who attempt to associate w me (not incl'g my lawyer, one hopes), become suspect. Forinstance, if the reader sent a letter or tried to contact me, not only would her efforts fail but her name would be added to a list of antigov't terrorists & sympathizers. Even if her letters, calls, whatever, were politically immaculate, each subsequent attempt would serve to place her name one notch higher on that blacklist. And pity the person if i should be the one to initiate contact.

The shortend of all this? So far as nathan schock & the outside world are concerned, this prison is a selective blackhole. All messages to me are destroyed in its event horizon. Tho i'm finally allowed to send mxs, to whom that i love or like would i do such a thing? Therefore my very existence is all but theoretical to everyone i care about save emil. But since the court has even gone so far as to threaten my counsel w incarceration for "collusion with seditionist and/or subversive persons", emil fears (rightly, i think) to act as intermediary in any sense not explicitly in my legal defense. Therefor, practically put, i am already dead to those i love.

dear <*[#~ ~<[[.&>>*+*^]*"\<.

Knowing copies of my letters go to the fed. i intermittently create bogus leads. This gives me a value which maintaining total incommunicado would undercut.

> [Name of key person at dowsanto chemical (forinstance) goes here]: If no word from you by [date] i will be forced to consider all foregoing arrangements between us null and void. g1sq2r

Then, some time later, by certified mail, i will write:

> [ditto addressee above]: Consider all prior understandings and arrangements null and void. Yours VERY sincerely, g1sq2r

All sent thru prison mail, of course. I have sent such letters also to suits at dupont georgiapacific weyerhauser exxonmobile shell bp bechtel haliburton chasemanhattan bakerbotz ε other global Wilderness plunderers; general electric lockheedmartin raytheon boeing, landmine clusterbomb chemical nuclear ε other weapons manufacturers, getting more creative (counter-intelligent) w every letter i send. The idea being to complicate the lives of the enemies of freedom ε our Planet at least enuf to slowdown the amount of damage they can do in a day. And but for the danger the fed. monitoring of my mail creates for others, i would also send the following encryption.

Dear ⫽◜▯▯▴ • • ?▯• ?▯▴ ⫽▯◜◸▴▯◣ ⫽▾▯◡● ⫽◂▯▯•▯? ✓ • _▯● ⫽▴ • • ●■▯ • ● ◸ ⫽▾ ✕▴▯✓ ✓ ⫽▾▴▯◣ ⫽▾▯•◸◜ ⫽• ●■▯◡◸▯▴ ⫽▯▴◸ ✓◸ •▯?▴✕ •◸ ◡◜ ✓ ●_| ✓▯ ◜◸ ? ? ⫽●▯ •◸▯ ◂ ⫽▾◜_|●▴▯ _|⫽✕■◸ ▴▯▯ ▯◜▾ ?▯ •▯ ✕◸_|▾ ?◸_| ?◸⬘◸✕ ✓◜▯ ⫽◜◸ ✓▯✓ ✓✕■✓ • ● ?▯ • ●▯✕◸■✓ ✕_▯▴ ⫽▯◣ ⫽▾▯▯⩮◣ ⫽▾ ✕ ◡•◜ • ▴ • ✓▯ ✓_|•◜ • ✓ ▴ • ⫽● ?▯▯▯▴ •◜◜▯■✕ ✓ ▴◸_|▾◜▯ ▴ • ✓ ▴▯◣ ⫽▾ ◂◸✕◸▯▴ •◸✕◸▯◂ •◸ ●▯● ⫽▯⫽●◸▯◸◜ ?◸▯◂ ✓ ?▯▯● ?

[Or.] My dear ▯▯▯▯◸✕◸▯ •▯_|✕◸◸▯ ◂◸▯ ◂ ⫽▾◜_▯◜ • ⬘◸▯ • ✓ ⫽⫽•◜◣ ◸⬘◸✕▯ ✓_|▴◸✕▯▯▯▯ ⫽✕▯■ • ⬘◸▯ • ▴▯ ⫽▾ ✕▯ ✓◸ ?▴▯ ? • ⫽▴▯▯▯ ⫽▴▯ ▴ ⫽ ◂ ⫽✕ ✕◣▯▯▴▯◡ ✓◣▯ • ✓ ⫽⫽◸●▯◣◸ ▴▯▯ ⫽▾ ✕▯●▯

I could send such mxs thru emil but he is toppedout, as it is, w the task of conveying to safety the contraband that is this book. Beside, i cant be sure what other pressures may be upon him. Best to stick w what appears to be working. Which reminds me....

"this quarantine of yours is getting a bit much",
emil complained on arrival one day.

This quarantine of *mine?*

"Well... of the court's."

Lemme get this straight. Emil, i'm *living* this quarantine. My entire existence is audited!

While not the reason emil is on occasion still shookdown before our visits (disclosure of escape tools, weapons ε drugs is usually behind body ε briefcase searches), not long ago it *was* the reason that the papers emil brought, or carried away, could be "legally" examined. Now, thanks to the efforts of friends at aclu ɛ amnesty america, emil has regained his counselors' rights. Even patdowns these days are rare for him, tho still court-authorized; so rare in fact, fr's search upset him. When i first arrived here emil was shookdown even on leaving —a reason i did not begin this testament sooner. But after ngo complaints to the state, the strip-searches ceased.* (Turnedout the bar assn had had many complaints of counselor abuse here at lorton.)

*[What NS may not have realized when he wrote this was, the strip-searches the present writer endured were not always the clinically inoffensive routines I believe he imagined. The rudeness of my body search that day was disgusting, and I suppose I (wrongly, to be sure) held NS responsible in part for my humiliation. I did not mention it because my attitude is, a good counselor does not burden his client with such matters. Incidentally, NS fails to mention the apology I made. —Ed.]

if only i could have foreseen....

Because judge black would not grant bail during the 8mos between the date of my arrest and the date of my sentencing, and because all other attempts to free me were rejected, i spent those pretrial months behind bars. Had anyone, incl'g the judge himself, suggested before my trial that i might be convicted of murder1, i would have found it entertaining not worrisome. Manslaughter, maybe, if the trial was even slitely just. But not murder1. And, further, had anyone suggested i would get the death penalty i would have deemed him mad. Frankly it is precisely *because* i knew civil law is incapable of thorogoing justice that i faced my trial –we all faced my trial– expecting only the pretense of fairplay —all of it highly politicized, of course. For all felt that, given my broad-based constituency, no court in america would dare strap me to the same expresstrack of injustice which so many of the politically disfranchised before me have been strapped to. Sleep on green dreamer.

And so, during periods when i wasnt working on my defense, i spent those pretrial months trying to wrap my *Ecocosm: the Cosmic Gaia*, the most rationally ambitious of my dozen or so books. Trite to speak of altering the past, i know. Yet if only i'd had some inkling just how thoroly corrupted the evidence brought against me would be, the book you hold would have been begun while i was still free to write ɛ speak as i pleased, only mildly fearful of retaliation against those i love or respect. But such is the nature of the arrow of change (yes, change, not time), and such is the nature of our ignorance of how it actually all works, that we can, civilly speaking, be sure of little but corruption itself.

doktor malpractice

I've told the reader, i believe: Soon after my arrival at lorton i was put in isolation (solitary confinement, sturry, iso, the pit, timeout rm, purgatory, black box, the hole, warden's revenge etc), kept there w no concern for penalcode maximums. However, out of concern for narrative continuity, i found it necessary to skip a major step in dr ratstool's followup "treatment".

Returned to my cell from iso, still lite- & space-sensitive and easily dizzied by motion, the ratstool sent for me. "And how's our big blond darling today?" So began my appt w this bottomless cesspool of brutal rhetoric, scams & lies. Energetically swivels my way overstuffed hulk in overstuffed chair. "Oydamn, man! You look like your parents tossedout the baby and raised the placenta!" One guard escort fusses w, then applies, the brakes of my wheelchair. "We'll hafta fatten you up some, I see. Bit sallow 'n' sunken of cheek ...*b'side* the welts...wouldnt you say, gluum? But otherwise fine, we hope, hmm? [leaning toward me from behind his desk, squinting] Every little thing okay? Self-image changed? Not still therapy-resistant, one hopes. Not still sitting on our perfect little tushiepies in a greatbig old world of personalized wrongs, are we?"

<What's with these trappings?> Firmly secured to the chair save for head & fingers, i can only indicate my meaning using shrugged shoulders, inward-pointing fingers & sweeping scan of self.

"That's it? That's all you have to say? Not 'hello. How have you been, doctor s?' Nothing but poor-me whining again. My God, man. No wonder youre in such a fix. Refined persons can take only so much of that caveman deportment of yours. What a selfish little invert youre turningout to be. Anyway. Yes. I am ethically obliged to address your question. Prison policy states that a minimum of four guards be used to escort any prisoner having your diagnosis: violent/psychotic."

I said, trappings. Guards are people not trappings. I'm asking, Why this... [indicating self again] ...this stunbelt, this mobile straightjacket i'm in?

"So it's still me me me, hmm? Youve learned nothing, I see." Scoots back, rises w great effort, looks away dismissively from my steady blue gaze, a gaze accomplished only w much seasick concentration. There was something out of character in his actions this day, an absence of palpable anger. Only later did i decide it was not due to some new credibility i'd earned, neither to my obviously pitiful condition, but that his usual level of malevolence was probably tempered by the presence of a guard not under his personal control.

"Well, then." Turns back, clears throat w gross success, the gluey stubbornness of which deep upheaval he finally managed to urge onto a paper napkin by means of dragging it off his tung w his upper teeth. "Anyway, to your question...." Ad libs more alleged "prison policy" pertaining to situations when four escorts are not available, "Well, then the vip [smiles around] must be transported in a wheelchair under full restraint." I know from my own medic days that vip is code for violent insane person. "Then there is the matter of plain old commonsense, my inmate friend. You did after all attack me violently once already. While I would be first to diagnose myself as mildly masochistic (as one must be to put up with all the abuse he gets around here), on the other hand, I do not have, I can assure you, a deathwish."

Imitating a bad-answer buzzer in a gameshow: <Error error error!> Eyes me as potentially human for the first time since i vaulted his desk. <Had my socalled assault been violent, sir –not just an attempt to correct your malpractical m-o– i can assure you, you would not be standing there but be six weeks the veg'table of a crushed spinal cord, and i would not be sitting here subject to your sick idea of mental therapy but be awaiting trial for your sudden conversion into a harmless cabbagehead ...sir.>

"Take him away, gerald. There are other patients I must see to, patients who *want* my help."

Glumm, stymied (by the brake) in an attempt to spin me around –in retribution for my "disraspec foowa da docta"– still unrealizing the cause, next tries to shoot me toward the door. But this bravado too ends badly for him. After slamming into the back of my chair, he spends fully half a min bent at my side, cursing & waging a war of wits w a simple manual wheellock.

prep: torture as palliative

Two guards next day, again via wheelchair+restraints to the clinic, the same large room in which sigfroid "scoped" me. Checking my restraints thoroly at his behest, the twins left. "We'll be right outside da daw, docta."

{Alone with a madman.}

"You know how all rise when the judge enters the court? No need for you to do so, shock. I'm a humble man. [jowly chuckle] Wish you could appreciate that as I do. Anyhoo, as they say. I know what youre thinking. You think my strapping you to this chair is my perverse way of reminding you of that *other* chair ...the big one? across the hall from your cell? (I was still in the old bldg, the reader will recall.) Well, have no fear. I would have you put such terrors out of your head ...that is, if I had the means to do so. And that precisely is my message t'day. For sad fact is, you patently refuse to give me the means to put anything in to, or out of, your head. And because you have been so rebellious, dear boy –resistant to my gentlemanly suggestion and friendly guidance– we are going to begin t'day a new approach. While it is clear by your general comportment that, as usual, you plan to agree with nothing, I want you to know. Your reaction is not as atypical as you probably think. After all, criminals would never become criminals if they were quick to comply with what is expected of them. As to the new therapy I have in mind.

"Shocking a patient who is recalcitrant to preliminary methods has long been used with high success as you know. But contrary to popular belief, est (or therapy utilizing electric shock) is a rather mild form of resistance intervention. Clinically speaking, the most desirable result a physician can hope for is unfortunately also the hardest on the patient. I refer of course to any revelation which traumatizes a patient —or in lay terms, shocks him. As you can imagine, the application of electroconvulsive, heat, cold or other therapies need have nothing to do with it. Many patients are sensible, or at least cooperative. They can see that by helping their doctor they are helping themselves. And this is our ...yours 'n' my, I mean... stickingpoint. [lites cigaret] Forinstance, [exhales] I have tried numerous times to show you a psychological portrait of yourself. Yet every time, without ado, you have rejected that picture. So then, circumstances allowing, i applied a little handson therapy. I refer of course to your little hiatus in the hole. That's about as handson as one can get ...short of execution, you'll allow. But somehow you have resisted this as well. So you can see my dilemma. Your therapy must now be more aggressive. For sad truth is, we cannot get better if we dont accept that we're sick. In either case, the shock of psychic revelation is the only answer. Thus: shock therapy. [chuckles bodily] I wish you could appreciate that little play on words as I do."

It was then he unloaded his dx on me.

"B'tween you 'n' me, schock ...that is to say, what I'm about to say is not my *official* diagnosis [odd pause]... you are what's known as an obsessive/-compulsive trauma-onset paranoiac schizophrenic personality with latent psychosis." The sullen slob then had the effrontery to admit, "I happily confess to nailing this diagnosis months before ever meeting you. For you are one of those classic cases, schock, which leaps without hesitation from the scholar's textbook onto his couch! —a quite exciting thing, actually. But I wouldnt expect you to understand." His excitement here strikes me as genuine. Leaning back, humping above desklevel his gibbous gut, he struggles to ωdraw a handsker from a pantspocket, grabs it just in time to harumph an apparently lesser giblet than before into the thing, folds it, then sweeps his moist brow. "All this of course is complicated by your hyperactive libido, also common among criminals." Cites example of "a humpbacked burn victim, a man of high sexual energy who was so repulsive he could not hope to win, so poor he could not hope to buy, and so gentle he could not hope ever to take by force, any of the girlies he dreamed of. He is one of the most pitiable cases in all psyche lit because he was also too sane to kill himself. So what happens? *You* could probably tell *me*.... No? Well, then, I'll tell you —tho I know you suspect the outcome. His masturbatory fantasies grow so hollow over time that he literally withers away. Expires. Dies. Of lust 'n' longing. And now I'm going to say something I've never told anyone...."

Catches himself staring at his soft white pudgy manicured fingers. "Yes, as i was saying: Contrary to orthodox dogma, I believe the libido to be a somatic-not-just-psychic thing. Recent experiments have shown, in patients with sexual deprivation, a part of the hypothalamus presents a slite rise in temperature. If deprivation continues, chronic inflammation may onset. I believe this area of the hypothalamus constitutes an organ, and that this organ is, eureka, the libido itself! It makes perfect sense for, as with any tissue, misuse or abuse can cause inflammation. Deprivation in the face of powerful instinctive drives qualifies as such abuse. In the classic case of the humpback patient, the incessant unfulfilled longing irritates, then inflames, the libido. This chronic libitis soon exhausts the patient. A terrible torpor, a lethal languor, sets in. And this is your fate, my friend. Death by desire, or lust-longing. And then, *fini*. ...if we fail to take action here. Fortunately for you, the libido has been my area of research for some time. And tho I know you are not interested, I am ethic'ly bound [hic] to outline the next step in your psychic rehabilitation."

distrust all in whom the desire to punish is powerful. —nietzsche

Socalled therapy began next morn. "In order to get to the bottom of your problem [gurgly chuckle] ...I wish you could appreciate that as I do... we're going to let you spend a few sessions watching some clinically selected videos

...a kind of fun thing, as you will see. [walks to console having four small screens above a switch deck] You will spend several sessions wearing this handsome helmet [taps lightly w fat index] and stylish bib ...bib 'n' tucker, I should say. Actually, bib 'n' codpiece, of which *I'll* be the caring tucker. [pats item tenderly, chuckling] I see youre wondering: Let's just call this dear fellow a virtual reality console that's been refitted to assist therapists in their rehabilitative work. But now to business."

Within a couple mins i am backed into the dock end of the console, helmeted bibbed ɛ codpieced ("Liftup, thank you. Sitting on your privates not allowed"). Onscreen inside my helmet a talkinghead in scrubs, w a patient-friendly manner, talks me thru what i, the patient, can expect during our "exploratory adventure.... Your bib 'n' tail, like those used in many radiology procedures, not only receives signals –much like the electrodes you may have seen used in medical tests– but also sends them. Some of these you will be able to feel now and then: cold- or warm spots, vibrations ranging from feathery touch to deep massage, and even electrical and ultrasound stimulation." The patient was "strongly encouraged" to notice that, whenever he closed his eyes, or looked away from the screen (not easy to do but possible), "for longer than it takes to blink, a mild electrical stimulus will be experienced and a loud sound, much like a telefone busy signal, will be heard until such time as the patient reopens his eyes". The patient, finally, needed to know that, each time this happened "the session will automatically return to the start-point of the nearest section or subsection. This remedial adjustment is necessary if a satisfactory evaluation is to be achieved", and which replay also had the "result of extending the session for a period equivalent to the time lost for replay".

"And to those of you who say we're just a bunch o' drug-pushing yacht-fancies alientated to the subconscious, why I have half-a-mind ta slip you a few o' these pills here 'n' push you overboard." **—cy k. fraughd**, president, shrinks of america

At this point both screen ɛ sound went pinknoise and the slug's distant gurgly voice interrupted. "If any session runs overtime because you have fallen asleep etcetera, hehheh, it is only fair to warn you. I may have to leave the test area to attend to my next patient. This may require you to sit alone in darkness 'n' silence for an extra hour or so til I or some not-so-caring minion can get back to attend to you." The bottom line was plain. Cooperate w the "test" or pay the price. Eg: The elec shock one rcv'd for blinking was mild, as promised. But if one blinked more than four times per min, or for longer than, say, a quarter sec, the current flow became quickly unbearable. Even looking crosseyed (to blur the images) set off the sensor! So why not just watch the video? you ask.

Because the content was at the very least distasteful and often downright abhorrent! The best i could manage was to unfocus my eyes. Years of discipline *w* meditative techniques, reinforced by 6wks of sensory deprivation, made such unfocusing a cakewalk —once i got used to my new helmeted environment. Also helpful was the upclose motion of the helmet's screen. Having been so many weeks *w*out visual stimuli (as i've said), lite alone –muchless motion– made me dizzy. This dizziness encouraged lack of focus, and the concentration of maintaining this condition of sustained blur easily launched me into a meditative-tho-open-eyed state. The combined result of these things was that, for most of those sessions i was able to watch what went on on that screen, listen to what sounded in my ears, in a state of mind so effectively disengaged that even now, months after the fact, it brings a smile.

During the first session the slug repeatedly asked me to describe what was onscreen, for my lack of responsive readings apparently frustrated him no end. "What are you seeing now, flash, he would bark into his mic, as he'd taken to calling me flash gordon (a name, i would learn, he used on everyone subjected to his test). Zombielike, often from a great mental remove, i would focus just enuf to describe what i saw. A couple times he smacked my helmet in annoyance, the surprise of which i'm sure gave him a reading. More often he would yank the helmet from my head and peer into it, convinced the screen was blank, subjecting me to a painful dose of current when he neglected, or did not care, to disarm the automatic reprisal system.

Over those sessions, like it or not, i was shown outtakes of films from law enforcement archives, hollywd, foreign films, real footage from cambodian & other p.o.w compounds & nazi concentration camps, medical & bogus medical research videos, films of actual rapes & murders of adults, children, even infants, footage so abominable a healthy mind can not understand what is happening or why.

I was thus subjected to every form of sexuality & violence imaginable. Homo bi trans solo pairs groups old young crippled quadriplegic ancient infant conscious unconscious animals artificial bodyparts dummies utensils sperm urine feces menstrual anal & other blood (muchmuch blood) & bodyfluids it never occurred to me to relate to sex, mutilated eviscerated dying dead pregnant exhumed & soforth for, try to imagine reader, 2hrs+ a day for 4days!

What i judge the very worst of all i witnessed those days was the slow (hrs wks mos) meticulously purposeful torture violation & murder of children aged 4 to puberty. These poor little persons had just enuf understanding, and just enuf guilelessness, i felt, to make such acts an affront to Creation itself! If i ever doubted that Creation had a goal, or goals, farmore critical than preventing the most heinous acts a human could devise & carryout, i ceased doubting it after dr slug's version of rehab. (Actually i ceased doubting it on November 1st, 1996, at apprx. 8a.)

Summarily, the slug's machine was really a sophisticated entrapment device. Like a computerized vice squad, the idea was to methodically expose the patient (well, victim) to every known form of perverse behavior while encoding in the margins his bodily & brainwave responses to what he saw, and then (and here is the sinister part) recording his reactions to spurious clinical stimuli applied mostly to rump & genitals! Cute, huh? Is this standard equip in all fed. prisons [i would later query lenny the librarian] or are we here in va just frontrunners when it comes to brutality? (Quick to recognize an effective torture device, va, the old dominatrix, was first in the south to use the electricchair. A world leader in executions to this day, in 1912 christian virginia kicked things off w the execution of a 16yearold w the ironic name of virginia christian.) Lenny (Hi, len), eyes down, head low, called the "contraption...captain nemo's frite stimulator". Quiet lenny learned most of his prison info from the bluster of gluum and an inmate named pete reap (reep, maybe?). "He was sigmoid's guineapig...is now prettymuch a vegetable". Apparently gluum&glumm would enter the slug's clinic afterhours, pass the time watching their favorite "virtrality" [virtual reality] horrors, then thrill to shocking poor lenny by recounting in animated detail what they saw.

ignorance as bliss

One final sampling of my intro to ~~life~~ existence in maxlockdown. One day during smalltalk a couple months ago, after the 5min-warning buzzer sounded, emil (fresh from losing another suit against monsandow chemical) asked how "other inmates" were treating me; were there any "confrontations or questionable acts [he] should know about?" Seems he'd just learned, lorton deathrow had a whopping 14! "They must be a pretty gruesome bunch, eh?"

His question jarred me. I mean, that it took so long for my daily circumstance to cross his mind at this depth.

<I thought i explained? I rarely interact with other prisoners. It's the staff here that's gruesome. I rarely see other inmates. Beside, there are only twelve cells in deathrow, all but mine 'n' another, empty.> (Still in old bldg backthen.)

"Twelve? Empty?" Not for the first time i felt my credibility in question. [Coming from a family of professional counselors, this editor's client demeanor is often negatively misinterpreted. —Ed.]

Now w my own suspicions aroused, accompanied by two guards i'd never seen, on the way back to my cell i asked, <Where's deathrow?> We were no more than ten paces from the big iron door leading back to the old bldg. Both looked at me as tho i were kidding, said, "Wherever ya were before they put ya back here." When we reached my cell i asked <Why's my box so diff'rent from the others?> Seeing i was serious, they explained, i was on "double-deathrow", that my cell was the "holding tank" for prisoners sched'd for execution win 72hrs! They asked how many hours i'd been there. When i spoke in months they glanced at each other. "It'll be over before ya know it," actually wished me luck and left. Even tho i knew they disbelieved me it was refreshing to have an only mildly politicized (clue: somewhat human) chat for a change.

In truth they mightaswell have cut me down w a stungun. There i was for months, living nextdoor to the "barber's kitchen", sleeping nitely in the "last stop motel", the "groan room", remembering, self-disciplining, longing, ε yes, weeping, in the very bowels of the infamous "scream tank", living writing, day after day, in the same place where the condemned have been put for over 160years to await execution! For all those months what i thought was 'merely' a cell on deathrow was in reality the "holding tank" for the nextinline to be executed.... Only i never knew it! Somebody had failed to explain where i'd been so carefully caged! someone had neglected to drop the crucial hints, neglected to implant in my head the radioactive isotopes meant to slowly burnaway all hope in me. A plot to torment me had exploded ...well, fizzled in silence. In short: since day1 i'd received only half the torment planned for me. {This is reason for celebration, no?} But while i workedon my sense of grin&glee, another part of me was undistractedly aghast.

My old cell, the rooms, the cells around it, were once the center of an old prison, holdover from the days when several prisoners at a time were executed! Except for renovations (door-walls of cells, plumb/elec, cameras), i was laying my head every nite in the same room where prisoners awaiting execution (hanging & firing squad and who knows what else), all the way back to 1821, had spent their last hours! The result? I'd been living only half the nitemare intended for me. Certain incidents, certain comments, came back to me. "Hey, sumthin's wrong, schock. Theyre fryin humpinLouie next... O well. Ya kin always complain ya were sposed ta be first." Or that first time when g&g went on&on outside my cell. I thought they knew the speaker was switchedoff but maybe they really didnt. That first pantomime was meant, i think, as primer for another of dr slug's sinister psyche games. {Think of what a glorious slipup!} Had i known, had i been told, to be in that cell was to be as good as dead w/in 72hrs, i'm not sure what might have become of me. Had i understood the 'sheer miracle' of not one but two inmates being executed before me –me, nextinline to die– the angst i suffered might have broken me as surely as it was meant to. But i didnt know, my reader! I just didnt know!

{Smile, dance, cheer, nathan! Do it, damnit!}

Clearly not all the forces overseeing my fate are beastial. And what if i should tell the slug? Surely it was his boys gluum&glumm who'd fumbled. Who else? My thoughts ran back to the day gluum hung around my cell like a lost soul, as deep in thought as i'd ever seen anyone around here. Could it be, even someone as morally defunct as himself thought their game was a little over the top in terms of cruelty?

Not long after emil added this abuse to my list of complaints against the state, i was moved from the last stop motel to deathrow —lorton prison's *official* deathrow, the one authorized by law.

not another disclaimer!

Tho i realize there are many who enjoy this prison-exposé business, i'm not one of them. Since for me these updates fall entirely under requisite fyi, each is as short (if not as sweet) as possible. The purpose of part5, let me say then, is not this prison update. Its purpose is addressing such essentials as: ❶ why gender & sexuality are a pernicious problem in civil society; ❷ how the world matron became fultime proxy for Mothernature ε human instinct; but mostofall, ❸ how&why all of us, civilized ε otherwise, suffer under civilization's pathologic fear of things primitive.

Are these topics necessary? one may ask. Most readers can picture how 6wks in iso might have, for me, resembled an end-of-the-world *tableau noir*. Many were the hours in that silent blackness when it felt like civilization had finally achieved its will to nuclear winter. Yet even the onset of an ice age offers some lite, some visuals, some sounds, some motion, certainly a world more tactilely inviting than a stinking bedroll ε a cinderblock cell w a toiletbowl constantly agurgle w techno-torture (for its unremitting ε unremediable state of water waste). During onesuch psych-downer i imagined a group of apocalypse survivors, someone like myself among them, finding ε reading this book you hold. Yet, never having heard of, or w no access to, my other books, how could a reader possibly understand how this author arrived at the virtual landslide of 'radical' conclusions his book unveils?

So, yes. For those readers familiar w my other work, part5 is merely schock 101; mostly digression and little more ...save for these prison cameos ε an expanded exposé of the "outlaw" instinct. (Yesyes. I promise) And so i find myself in a most ironic position of needing to invert my earlier disclaimers. For this time it is not my most cursory or ambivalent readers who must <forgive this next digression, please>. No. It is the faithful reader i must appeal to now, specially those readers who have studied the following three of my books: *the civilizing principle; die, primitive!;* and *Mothernature & the world matron*. For it is precisely those who know these books best who stand to learn the very least in part5. So, yes. Skip ahead if you must. But before you do let me say: i'm writing fast now and cannot be sure how much that is vital to understanding the story of Lilith will be lost in the skipping ...say nothing of missing an *intimate* treatment of the "outlaw" instinct, a *personal* explication forced on me by that screed of lies ε omissions tribuned at my trial ε in the poppress. So let us wrap this catchup as quickly as possible so we may cursor these essentials.

that euphemistic headache from part4 + the ladies upstairs

Re sobbinrobin. Back in the old bldg, glumm, glorying in the latest gossip, sidled up to the glass, whispered over the speaker, "Psst. Schock. Listenup. Sobbinrobin fries tamorra. Bzzzzt poof! [his fingers fly up as if releasing the boy's zizm into the prison's stale air] Toldja they don' hafta give three days warnin. So guess who might fry *nex* saturday?" Kids, old folks, the mentally compromised; they'll kill anything they can strap into that accursed chair. And when it was done he said, "An now it's downda jus you, schock. Las li'l piggy in da slaughterhouse."

Hope clung to what it had: humpinlouie ε sobbinrobin had come there after me yet they were executed first. There was the pressure of public opinion on the fed. ε the state. If nothing else, it held a pinch of promise. But mostofall there was fini (federal inmates national invitational) in jan'99, which could give me til then if ...well, if the warden has any real say, that is.

Since arrival sobbinRobin spent several hours a day at the wailingwall of his cell. Tearducts long run dry, he genuflected regularly before the cyclopean monitor. His sched'd novenas had possessed a quiet desperation. In fact, his plaint was pathetic *because* it was almost inaudible. A thousand times i heard it: "I didnt kill her. I swear. I didnt. O please please believe me. I loved her. I really really loved her. Please. I'm innocent. I swear it. I dont deserve to die" etc. Fantasy or truth, it doesnt matter. A small being in the foodcellar of my past cringed whenever he sobbed. It wept: i wont slipup again, mother father juror judge guard doktor warden. I swear i wont.

Melancholia often merged my hours. He was just a boy –14 when he did the crime, or so he said– and clearly ill-formed mentally. They killed him in cold blood the day doktor froodnung returned from vacation. No accident there. "Had a marvelous time, marvelous, *herr amigo!* And that sour disposition of yours cant ruin it for me, nosir. No one here liked robin more than me, prisoner schock! But he was ugly 'n' unmanageable. Besides, terrible things can happen when someone makes the state angry ...as you yourself shall see. And probably very soon, such things being equal." Day after the boy's execution, at the start of my appt, he raved for fully 10min. "Ah, the beauties of old mayheeco —her customs, her people!" He would have sent me a postcard "but it's against the rules, you know. And the boys there. So many, so cheap, so sweet! Ah! [smirk cathodes] So, now. Anything changed with you? Any little thing? I could spoil you too, you know? The way the ladies up in skyview villas [index pointing upstairs] are spoiled ...for reasons I cant go into, of course. Still mum, my friend...? Fine. I'm soaring farabove your rudeness for now. You know what they say: You cant hurt a happy man. As for you, I see

I've returned in the nick of time. I'm happy 'n' whole and so we must set about putting you back together again, mr humptydumbdumpty" —his petname ("all you humptydumbdumpties") for the broken men he maltreated.

After our appt i went for a workout; then a nap & supper. Back in my cell, unable to face writing the bittersweet close of part4, i wrote: Anger is an antidote to depression —the best antidote i can manage just now. I workout past pain to prostration. That way i dont just doze & startle all nite. Dawn next day a note hung outside my window. Horrible imagery, swaying there in its noose! The ladies upstairs plainly sleep better, rise earlier, than me.

Dear Nathon: Mitzi fixed us a private meeting. This Sunday. Shes gonna let us use her office if I do a special favor. Tell you about that later. It has a little refridg. She will put a 6 pak and a bottle of wine for us. And theres a vcr and a couch. And a bathroom and shower and other stuff. It will be real nice. I look foward to meet you. But don't expec a whole lot if you know what I mean. I am alot of embarasment on the first date about personel stuff. Hope this is ok to you. Love your friend Rosa P [sic all, please, proofreader]

One senses the women's section is no *la salpêtrière* .

swish,thump. must every pit have its pendulum?

This next i also scribbled amidst writing part4. Not wanting to mar those memories i set it aside.

A private meeting indeed. In my depression & anxiety following humpinlouie's death i occasionally caught myself cross-wristed, clawing at the skin of my forearms. Border-hopping boy-hopping dr malfreud noted these blotches for my file as, yesterday, i sat across from him, reeling from his reek of frijoles farts, iguana gas & other entirely too imaginable stewings. Swish,thump.

Su, promises rosa's note. Only 24hrs to put money where mouth is, or where one might imagine his mouth to be. And w sobbinrobin's execution to deal w today. Swish,thump. Cannot concentrate. And so much yet unsaid. Must keep going. Yet cant clear my head. Critical concepts pushing&shoving to be heard. I hear the poor boy right next door. He asks such naive questions. And so sincerely! ("Can I see the chair before you do it...? What's it like in there...? Will it feel better than this after i'm dead?") My mind is a narrow hallway full of unruly reporters. Swish,thump.

In the midst of this, in the cell across the hall, jack ketch repeatedly tests ꞓ tunes a subtext performance. Looking over everysooften he says in his fake accent, "Bizzybizzybizzy". His outfit is royalpurple satin ꞓ suede w black-leather appointments (collar cuffs pocket-edging etc) incl'g black-leather hood, gloves ꞓ knee-capping boots. Looking like a cross-dressing musketeer, it's my guess jack ketch is a fagment (sic) of the slug's imagination, some guard from the new bldg planted here today to pique my pain to perfection. Sandals-o'christ, why do i even look up? I've work to do. Swish,thump.

O let me wake now and all this be but a dream! There, there. Hand jitters but must keep writing. I sense thru the muck of these grotesque hours that what i'm saying may be relevant somehow. Even a mediocre painter can come up w a likeness if he adores and circles his nude long enuf. But my tiny script is so so perishable. Perhaps i'm making a mistake by... Here, now. Think of, -a... Think of Lilith's handwriting, say: left-sloping, looping ꞓ lovely. This entire book should be printed [Swish,thump]... should be printed in her hand.

For the swish-umpteenth time ketch loppedoff the head of a kneeling bikini-clad manikin! And each time it slumps to the floor he yods solemnly, sets aside his ax, wipes brow ꞓ hands w a curiously scarlet-stained handsker, lifts the thing —effigy of a young man, hands tied behind back, saying his prayers— reprops it just so, replaces the bloodied head (which lolls waiting on the cot), reresins his gloved hands in a puff of white dust, adjusts his eye-holed hood (covering all but mouth ꞓ chin), readies for the next swish,thump. *Da capo*. What sort of person would consent to such a demented performance?

And you'd think one executioner would be enuf. But, no. Beside jack ketch jr, across the corridor, there's another. Monsieur guillotte, executioner-in-charge, who has replaced guillotine billy, as i think i've explained. Firsthing this morn he slithered up to my cage, told me —whether i cared to know or not— "I queet theerty years bleezeful how you say, reteermont?, to come here amerryka to deezpotch you, monsieur shook." When, bored, i look back to my work, he comments for me in his deepest accent-free voice: "To KILL me, you mean," then answers himself: "No, not keel, shook. I never keel. I deezpotch", copying calm greeneyed draconian guillaume guillaume wordforword. "An' I deezpotch only zee flesh, zee *eevee!* flesh. Remember theez. And you weel be my twothousan sevenhintred twelf! Very distingueesh number, *oui*?" He then points to ketch jr, who has just arrived and is settingup across the way,

"Behold zee arteest's asseesdant", whom he then, nodding, calls a "seelyseely butcherboy". Unlike socalled m.guillotte, who laffs ɛ jokes *w* the guards and is a terrible actor who sounds like he's from tx, ketch is aloof gloomy ɛ severe, more the thespian version. Swish,thump.

Horrible. Several buzzards ...vultures, actually... have been moving to&from the roof of the gym all afternoon. Something dead down there is being picked to bits ...and something keeps spooking them away from the feast —likely arriving reporters, witnesses, to a feast of their own. I have not the will to mount the sill of my cell to see. Three are there now, sitting in long feathered robes like greek judges of the dead. Must keep busy.

As i was saying about Lilith's script. I see it clearly. The artist's engineer's or architect's eye is instantly pleased by its beauty, symmetry ɛ consistency. Take a letter –preferably her last to me– smooth a page of it on a draftingboard, slide a transparent gage across its script: 15° leftward tilt is consistent, the skate of her hand always edging along, line upon line, as if a forest-scented breeze, which the trees of her alphabet lean into, blows always at the same strength! Swish,thump.

Who would believe this? Really? Great God, somebody stop him! There go the generators now! Horrible. Gadshazm, what next? This is only a test, right? Robin is still praying nextdoor, right? Where were we? Then, at the close of her letter [Emil, please insert facsimile of signoff to Lilith's last letter]: *Love, your own lilith* ...one person i wished would forget the comma after 'love'. O that i could see those words again! Her lilting ligatures were fully capable of flowing from letter to letter, from consonant to vowel ɛ back again, like brook water over sun-silvered rocks when she wanted. She had a capital L in her cartooning arsenal that resembled a backward-leaning pitcherplant, its tiny tung, in green ink, snaking languidly down, edging left on its skates to loop into the next letter. But such uppercase penmanship never ornamented her own name. And she never used the intinyms others gave her, never signed her name Lili, Li, or Lee, forinstance. Beside fifi, how many names consist of liligatures [sic] alone? And how many consist of just one?

Ex capo, ketch ceases his decapitage, packsup ax ɛ dummy. One senses all is ready. Sobbinrobin, too scared to ever cry again, is led away. The flitting ɛ fritened little smile he flashes me over his shoulder confuses me ...tho i do know i'll never forget it. Then, as the big iron door clangs behind them, i understand. Too fritened to cry, and beginning to believe all the condescending babytalk ("What a big guy youre being!") of his groomers, he was led away, puffing ever larger w a buffoon's blind pride. ("I'm a bigbig guy who's not afraid ta die!" Repeat til clang of door.) Ketch, carrying his large canvas satchel of props, joins guillote & another guard in the switch room. All doors all day were left open and my speaker volume maxed so i should miss no element of this grisly rite; not the prep, not the farcical counseling, not robin's heart-wrenching questions & requests, and certainly not the heavy clunk of the three switches, only one of which makes the generators snarl & snuffout that poor little lite ...scuse me: life. But there go the vultures. Perhaps they will be able to finish their work after everyone has gone.

last time the author felt like this (☹) he'd been whipped by war

It is su. (Yes. Little switch in lyrics there.) By the time all was done yesterday i found myself mentally fashioning what used to be called a "shiv" back in dirtycity (when i was this kid see) and what is called in prison parlance a "shank". Actually a pencil would do and that i have. And sharp, as arteries tend to pop to one side as one probes for their content, one's innate physiology passionately protecting his life from puncture, from leaking away wout state consent, like trying to stab a strand of spaghetti on a buttery plate using a fork w only one tine. How fulfilling should i get lucky, pop it open, cheat them of their favorite fun. But enuf. I am sworn (personal oath) to finish Lilith's story —"time" allowing. The doomed prisoner must get 72hrs warning by law. But justice has yet to figure into my case? I am prey to club-happy spray-happy trigger-happy switch-happy bugger-happy hands. Va was the first state in amer. to record an execution bythebye. That was in 1608. More than 4,000 have been executed since! Geesusboodabramakrishnadow! Appealing to Gaia and her Skyspouse for sobbinrobin, i move on.

Su nite. I am writing in dim lite. And so i wait & i wait.... Almost midnite now. Doesnt look like our rendezvous will comeoff. O Lilith, what madness i'm heir to! To think i entertained the thought of another lover. All the worse that she, not you, may have been my last! What has become of me?

O horrible this descent into malestrom [sic]. I wish i could die while i care not at all about anything.

Tag des gerichtes! Jüngster tag!
Wann brichst du an in meine nacht?

one "man" and one man alone

...by his life ε even by his death –in collusion w the fbi cia ε dia, and they in concert w the courts ε poppress of my homeland– have effectively exiled me. And he was able to do so, even posthumously, simply because i hold, clearly ε unwaveringly, so many antilishment opinions (read: proNature beliefs). Let the curious, a hundred or a thousand years hence, rest assured: Near the year 2000 in the usa, we are free to disagree w the lishment. But we'd better not be too successful, too influential, when we do. Or we will suffer —some of us w our very lives! As to criticizing civilization ε civil religion? Well, one might just as well surrender his freedom the moment the words are spoken.

as to skipping ahead. On secondthought...

...for those who would understand the Lilith/nathan relationship at any meaningful depth, this part of the book is indispensable.

anyplace but here, please

Late late i finally fell asleep, dreamt i was a patron in a fleissy-quality brothel til awakened by the calls ε caterwauls of rosa's friend's letting me know another mx had been ~~hung~~ lowered before dawn.

Dear Nathun: I'm sorry. Please forgive last night but I coulden't do it. Do Mitzi, I mean. Really I was gonna but I culdn't. That's why she diden't send for you. I'm sorry I made you wait and all. Love Rosa. PS Please don't be mad. [proofreader: stet all]

I do not reply. Tether hangs til breakfast call, is pulled up empty. Why punish rosa w my selfpity? I need to praise her behavior not pan it. Following breakfast i will go to the library, then to my workout. Leave her a note there. Am okayed to visit the library to write of late, have i said? —a new freedom not easily won, as the patient reader will see.

when hurt we should cry out

I believe i have explained the unspoken power-struggle between warden todion ε dr slugmoid —a struggle win which i am painfully wedged.

The reader may remember, warden todion (hereinafter, wardion or toadion), in trade for my seeking a nat'l intraprison title (fini), gave me the right to eat ε train "at will". That was 8mos ago. The slug has longsince been toying w those rights, claiming (since it was he who brought the body-sculpting awards of my youth to everyone's attention): "It's ME to whom you owe all your strutting 'n' prancing freedom around here!" He began w stunts such as sending for me midway in my training day, claiming i was breaking an appt etc; or he would tell those guards over whom he had sway to interfere *w* my privileges wherever possible —this incl'd interrupting contact *w* the warden —to a point where i had to ask chief chef tony (fan from my bodysculpting days) to let the warden know his intercession was needed ...again.

Wardion asked guards glumm & dion, who'd brought me, to wait outside while godion, capt of the guard, a quite husky close-cropped redhead, and the warden's personal security (dare i call him, guardion?), stayed by the door. "Lookin great, schock! A shuah-faya winnah, yessah! Been watchin ya on the monitah theyah. Gold's gooduz in the bayag! Yessah. In the bayag! ...So tayl me, what's up? Look lak ya loss ya bes huntin hayound."

This problem is best kept confidential. Guardion stood at parade-rest nearby.

"This heah's as confadenchul as it gets round heah, suh. So faya away."

You need to replace that socalled doctor with a humanbeing. [tho i think i spot a spark of fear i press on] Your main shrink is a sick man, sir. His twisted games have no limits. I spent another sleepless nite sick at heart 'n' sick at stomach. I cannot win this championship for you with him constantly interrupting my training 'n' crushing my spirit with his sick brutality.... I c'n see you need the gory facts, warden.

four-guard escort + stungirdle: a routine visit?

"But you stay close, you hear, mike?" says the slug to guards zodion & xodion, already there when gluum glumm & me arrive. {Does that mean xodion is named ike?} A stink i could not assign saturated the office. {Socks of a hunter/trapper several weeks unchanged? sweat of an executioner? sweat of the executed?} He began the session *w* his stock hustle: "Changed your mind about anything, my friend? Any little thing?" When i do not answer he goes on. "So tell me, mad hamlet, what is the status of the powerstruggle between you and your poor father's ghost?" Again i do not answer. I can see he is noxious to move on anyway, fidget-fingering the papers on his desk. "I have here a newspaper article, schock. I've searched our archives for hours just so I could have something tangible with which to take you back to that place where you lost touch with reality. Allow me to read. Let us makebelieve that you are mentally ill and I am your caring horatio."

I have an idea. Let's play justice?

"What's that you...? Goddamnit gluum I mean glumm. Come outa there this instant! An' gimme that damn paper!" Glumm had climbed inside the cage (used before stunbelts to interview violent patients), was ~~reading~~ perusing one of those rude tabs. Snatches paper w a snarl, disappears behind its frontpage. "This here article, schock, quotes a statement made by your sweety's stepfather after he foundout she was dead. Here's what he had to say. 'My baby was so young, so talented, so beautiful —and had so much to live for. And now she is dead. Hearing about that lecher, Schock, who she ran away to live with, I sensed something terrible might happen if I didnt do something. I begged her several times to come home. I even went after her to bring her back. But each time Schock thwarted my attempts. He was a cult idol to her, you know. It was not love. It was some sort of fascination —a form of worship. It's weird, hard to explain, the things young people will do. You put all your love, your time, your strength, your life, into them, and you get this. It's not fair. But the hardest part is getting used to the idea that she'll never come home again.' Tears flooded his eyes as he spoke."

I reject your manufactured and much-rehearsed propaganda. Nosuch interview ever took place.

"What's that? Try to stay on the topic, schock. I can help you only so far. After that it's up to you. [lites second cigaret: one already burning] You understand who said these things and why? [holds up tabloid behind nebula of smoke. I stare at floor] No? Then I'll tell you ...so you shouldnt be left hanging as they say. [wide puffy grin] These are the tender words of a father, the remorse of a fine gentleman, a poor fellow youve cruelly accused of despicable acts —forinstance, raping your lover when she was ...what did you say? Twelve?" Another drag ε slow exhale.

I feel sickly ...the stench is awful, and the room, filled w smoke old ε new, begins to undulate as tho we're underwater. Zodion ε xodion sit one to each side of the entrance, which is closed, glumm&gluum, one to each side of the room. They too are smoking: cigars.

"Of course, you know the girl he's talking about? [i study the sluglike aspect] You dont? [gurgle-voice is muffled by exhaled smoke] Jus between you 'n' me, schock, you *do* know. And I *know* you know. 'Cause she's got you fixated like a snake with wings. [deep deliberate puff] The girl in question is, of course, none other than your very own little sweety.

[deliberate exhale] The article gives her full name right here. Allow me to quote: a-, lilith...lilith mccrae...right there, see! [sweeps paper thru smoke as if to show me] Gluum, my good man, our friend schock here makes a terrible face. Perhaps he does not believe us. Get over here. Read this aloud."

Gluum rises from his post. Bowlegged from sitting for a living (or something), he lumbers past, brushing my arm, takes doublyfolded paper, begins to read. "And, a-, the body turned up in a, in a-, warehouse, three days after a-, miss maak a-, maak ray, a-, was reported...."

"Not that! Here! ...Read the part that gives her name; her *full* name."

Gluum squints at page: "Where?"

"Right there fergodsake!" Frood, heaving self upright, gasping w the effort, rachets pinkynail into page as if probing one of his tahitian toy-boys. Ash topples from cigaret, phew, as its absurd sloping length was making me ~~nox~~ anxious. "Right THERE, you ass, under your fudge-colored nose. Ferkryssake, gimme that an go siddown. Tsk. [hissy inhale, nostrils distended; exasperated exhale] Ugh." Lisped elongated t's & pinched sibilants positively cavorted upon the rank air. Slumps back, scans script, his bulk nearly obliterating the large chair. One edge of the script (which i could see had been pasted onto the newspaper) had begun to knurl, thanx to the unsched'd rough handling. Attempts to hide it –pinching between thumb&index– do not slip by my peripherals. Takes swallow of coffee, pudgy fist shaking worse than room.

{Mainline horsejitters i'd say.}

Continues reading. "...Which came to lite when police discovered the nude body of miss mccrae. She was the victim of what turned out to be a gang rape, with bizarre overtones. It was at that time that the federal prosecutor.... [voice drones on, smoke grows thicker, smell more stifling; noxious fluids slowly filling the tank of the room] The article, my friend, nathan, I now must pointout to you, does NOT say the victim's name was lalage, as you keep claiming. Which you know jus breaks my heart. It says, in very clear print here, lilith ...lilith alice-, alicia, whatever, mccrae! Here. I invite you to see for yourself."

I surprise him (and his recording machine) by saying, Yes, thank you, i will. To which he heaves unaccountably backward. (I am in hand&legirons, reader, and hardly rise from my chair as i reach out to him, a whole wide desktop & chair away from me.) “Siddown, you ape! I’m not falling for that again.” Gives my stunbelt a hefty juicing. “Behold. The gladiator collapses at the mere sight of the lion. God bless technology.” Head throbbing, my whole frame crumpled in agony, he goes on as if nothing has happened. “So you see, schock, it’s not her sister. It is your little sweety herself who is dead. Dead dead dead dead dead! Pregnant I tell you AND dead dead dead!” Rattled off in a sort of singsong banter, the words, etched in septic bile & excrement, shook his jowls and bounced about the walls as tho they marked the extent of my very cranium. “She’s gone, hear? Like fred’s lewd maud not will’s, like you’d ruther. That’s fred’s rue come true, you’ll discover.”

What is this psychobabble? <I be- beg your par- pardon?>

“What I *said* is: We’re done here, ike. Friends should laud goods not ills in each other. That’s what friends do, if true, for each other.”

For some reason i noticed, the burnt spot in the carpet was the size of a newborn’s head; charred black & deeply hollowed. It is clear now why so many guards are present. His intent was to incite me to attack again. I sensed, *this* time they had orders to shoot to kill.

<Are you mengele or caligula? Please clear- clear this up- up for me> i growl thru my pain, suddenly realizing {What i really need is a human rights attorney. Gareth pierce, where are you?}

“What’s that? What are you raving about now?” In his lap, below the level of the desk, he peeled off his cliff notes.

Your name? Is it mengele or caligula...? ...sir?

“Very well. I’ll put this right here ...in case you should change your mind ‘n’ want t’ read it after all.” Quadchinned & eyes down-cornered, he places the paper in a lower drawer of his desk ...tho the mic of the recorder thinks he placed it on his desk where the prisoner could reach it. I am about to note this for the recorder but am stopped by dizziness nausea pain & an assault of apathy as sudden & black as any i ever kept down. Our session is cut short when i fire a hot stream of breakfast, cigaret smoke, slug stink, lies & rehearsed propaganda onto the floor before his paperstrewn desk, seeing no reason to holdback such poison again at my own expense. He popsoff recorder. “Get that blond ape-thing outa here, ike. Now!”

and that nite i wrote....

Life begins in silence & darkness they say. But they are moody brooding scientists. Maybe it is they who were conceived in silence & darkness. Silence & darkness are also linked w death. How subjective. An expanding Universe knows nothing of death. Only evolution. And, no, i'm not going to write using complete sentences. There's no time for trifling now. To me a completed sentence means death. But here we go again. My prose is triaging itself.

While dying occurs in extatic [sic] spasms & spirals, with crescendos of lite thrilling spine & brain, i posit here another level of experience: algae tree tadpole marmot wolf sardine whale human waterfall ocean planet star stone or galaxy. I speak a machian reality: instantaneous connections over imponderable distances! Here, grab onto/zoom into this wide web of perisynchronous phenomena!

How shallow our grasp of being. Death is an anthropism of the lowest order. It confuses kids for life, confounds the elderly to their graves, turns the deathrows of civilization into places of blackest morbidity. I am intimate w it —death, i mean— even tho my days & daydreams are traversed by vertical shapes & shadows. Death, on the other hand, is a more horizontal thing. More like my nites & nitemares.

Since emil cannot make it til tomorrow i am stuck w what i have written over the past 2wks. Anxiety escalates (again). So i bide my time [hic]. I am a man treading water in a cold sea, wishing for some bearded & sandled epiphany to change cold water into warm time for me.

Unannounced, thru the dun partitions of my day, a deathmask will appear —laffing, pitying or some other pose. I glimpse them usually out of the corner of one eye, over a shoulder, or sense them hovering behind or above me. They have a unique quality; one i hesitate to describe; a quality a physicist could understand but not a prison psychiatrist. Were our shrink not the underlying cause, or were he even remotely human, i might seek his help w this. But he would call them "Mere apparitions. It is your guilt that gives them life", he would insist. But the faces are all wrong for that. Beside, i have no guilt. Regrets, maybe, but no guilt. I've spent a lifetime avoiding selfishness just so i could live, and die, w a conscience & subconscious light enuf to take wing on a moment's notice!

But as i was saying.... In the mind's eye those masks are quite alive! Yet, swing about, confront the things, bravely, facetoface, and, quantum-physicslike, all animation ceases! The only sense of motion is that which i know operates regularly behind the oily blackness of that cyclops-eye in the corridor, ever surveilling me in its silent "big brother" continuum. If i want to know, forinstance, the precise location in my cell of a given mask —playing dead on my pillow, mocking my own face in death; or w my cell door swung wide, wearing guard xodion's pasty grin, ordering me out on my "final walk"— i must be ready to trade location for motion. For abruptly, the moment vision strikes the mask it freezes; all motion, whether miming or mocking, ceases abruptly! Instantly, sardonically, the mask becomes a cellwall decoration! Such a frieze (of masks) cornices the corridor wall of my cell as i speak: prominent there, in inverse order of vileness, are the masks of guards gluum&glumm xodion ε zodion, the warden, judge black ε prosecutor liti —but mostofall, dr mangleMe himself! Yet when i swing about, fix them, dare them to restate their case w just me for audience? Or if, as now, i merely peek at them from under the overhang of my brows: There! You see? Cheshirecatlike, they freeze, or fade to dots of gray lite in the gloom of my cell. And all this is to ignore my niteterrors —which afterall could peel the lids off lizard eyes. But is this as cogent as it seems to me right now?

At litesout they tell me emil is coming tomorrow. How they love to toy w a prisoner's head, these insecurity guards.

and next morn....

Last nite i dreamt Lilith&me had a child. (No stretch guessing the dream's cause.) Our child grewup quite wonderfully but came upon a sad time. In the course of explaining this sadness she, an adult by then, asked: "But how c'n i tell the difference between them [knowledge ε wisdom]?" We'd been talking about not settling for "mere knowledge" when "sheer wisdom" could be got. As i readied a fatherly dissertation on this weighty question, and just as clearly as if you ε me, reader, were sitting there right now, Lilith answered: "By nuance of effect you c'n tell them apart."

Most knowledge is merely an impressive extrapolation of some basic misunderstanding.

I, farmore than our daughter now, wanted to hear more.

"The best way i c'n explain it is... let me see... okay, here: Knowledge gives satisfaction, true. But wisdom gives fulfillment. You see? ["Sorta."] It's kinduv like the difference between mating without love 'n' mating with it. A matter of depth 'n' durability ...which together, when present, addup to a kind of joy, not just erotic satisfaction. [she "Kinda" sees] Soooo, while knowledge has the potential to give passing happiness, wisdom holds the potential for permanent joy. ...Need i add, we must pay exquisite attention to tell the two apart. That's where your genius with reflection 'n' nuance will come in handy."

So clear in every word, every detail, was this dream —a setting of emotional completeness i havent even begun to exhaust— i find myself wondering if it happened in my past in some other context, some situation which mnemy has yet to put a finger on? Had not mary wilkinson's wise mama, zora neallike, similarly tried to explain the nuances of bigotry which so punished mary & me after she planted (2nd grade, in public) on my cheek my first dear kiss? Hmm.

causing trouble in 'paradise'

Wardion at first tried to glossover my problems. "Yall er makin a shitheap outa a couple cowpatties". I countered w, So i'm sure you'll understand when i dont win at the nationals.

He thought on that. "What you need, young man, is ta fyand the strength o' chryast. Jesus ya know c'n turn pain inta glorrah. Thayat's the miracle what got me whayah ah am taday. The man ya lookin at is not juhst the wahden o' this heah institution. Yaw also lookin at a deacon, a town fahtha an' a famlaman too. Look around heah. Whatdaya see? [lifts a black book, wags it] The word o' god, rhaat heah, bah ma elbow evraday. An heah too [points at foto on desk], a pictya o' ma lovela waaf emmarose an' ouwa lovela daughta emmalou. An' ovah theyah... please step aside mistah gowd [godion]... ovah theya [indicates wall to my right]... thet pictya is yaws trula bein bahptaazed bah the gooud revren les denton. [fat-faced biblebeater grins at camera] An' ovah theyah, on thayat shaylf [godion must step aside again], yall see yaws trula stanin basayd the govanah himsaylf! Some folks say we look lak bruthas ...Ahm the bayshful one. Now, as t' this heah problem o' yaws...?"

The problem is, that ...sir... that socalled doctor down the corridor is takingover this prison behind your back and i'm apparently the only one with the courage to tell you. And if you trust that socalled man too far he will slit your throat... ...sir.

Wardion's jaw mightaswell have hung to his chest for all the blankness of mind he made flesh. Looking at captain of the guard godion, "Am ah seein a spahk [spark] o' agreement in yowah eye, mista godion. [godion, standing at paraderest, swallows visibly] Well, what say ya, sah?"

"I cannot say he is wrong, sir."

Deep consternation. "Enuf. This heah's administrative business an' none of the inmate's affaya. [walks in slow circle] As to yaw problem, inmate schock. [another circle] If it's a problem –an ah mean a rayal problem not jus sumthin dreamedup in yall's hayd– it will be taken caya o'. An' thayat's all ah'll be a-sayin on this heah subject taday, sah. <One cant ask for more than that, warden, sir> Guhday, mistah schock."

slug v. toad

Next day, wout explanation, a suspiciously chatty & chummy gluum&glumm escort me to wardion's office. Present when we arrive are chief of security godion & the warden.

"Way'll git raaht ta the point, mista schock. Ya'll complained some tahm ago thayat oneuv owah guards absconded with a sheet o' piepah [paper] belongin' ta yaself, is thayat raaht?"

I yod.

"Yes, sah".

Scuse me?

"Ah sayd, the prisonah will say 'sah' when addressin his wahden!"

Of course. Yes …sir.

"Now thayn. Would this heah be thayat sheet o' piepah?" He heldup, between thumb&index a familiar sketch. •

It is.

"It is, sah!"

It is …sir.

"That's most unfawchanet, schock. Most unfawchanet. Ah wuz trula hopin yall would deny evah seein this heah pieapah." He glanced at all present as if to see if anyone doubted how unfortunate it was. It was then i spotted the slug, slouched in an armchair behind me. The open door had hid his obscene bulk as we'd entered.

"The gooud doctah, who brought this heah piepah t' mah attention taday… the gooud doctah an' mahsaylf have been a-studyin this heah soul-troublin drawin, mista schock." {Should i answer with 'sir'?} I guessed not for he went on. "An' heah's what we dacided." He slid the drawing to the front of his desk, came around to meet it. I meanwhile had stepped back to allow his bulk ample passage. "Step ovah heah, sah."

Pawn to k4, captures rust-bearded red-flecked ε freckled baby mastodon (godion) en passant.

"Heah's what we dacided. This is prison pahk [park] road, heah. An' this heah is dalivarah [delivery] steet, ovah heah. This is the west wall of the cawtyard, heah. This is the nawth wall, heah. Are ya followin', schock?" Pudgy index, *w* deeply grooved nail, stabs at this or that line, this or that object on the sketch. "This is the west daw, heah. This is the corrida what leads ta the west daw, heah. An' this is the corrida what leads ta deathrow, heah. Ah ya still with me, mista schock? <I am completely lost.> Completely lost. How quaint? …Completely lost [breath] sah!"

Lost …sir.

"So now we look suprahzed? No, wait! Wait! Allow me ta finish! [rotates paper toward him] Now, eena fool knows, mistah schock, these li'l arraws heah, heah 'n' heah, proceedin from yaw sayl [cell], heah, ta this heah daw, a-way ovah heah, constitutes conspirahcy of a prisonah ta escayp. An' this heah drawin [lifts, shakes it at me] is cause fowah saveeah —ah repeat, sah-vee-ah— punishment." His eyes fall on the dark hulk in the corner.

May i say something?

"Sumthin, sah!"

Something …sir.

"It bettabe dayyyyyamn gooud."

That drawing's not what you think it is.

"Is thayat so? [smiles around the rm] ...Yall were raht, doctah, as ta the prisonah's rasponse."

What you are holding is a sketch of a city in tennessee ...or part of a city.

"Now yall certainly kin do betta than thayat, sah."

A sketch of a tragic event.

"You, sah, ah the sketch. Now ah'll be honest. Ah'm fast a-loosin the godly patience faw which ah'm justly fymous. Bayah with me please. This heah drawin, sah, reprazents conspirahcy! [taps paper, back on desk] Conspirahcy ta escape from this heah prison, this heah faaaayn institution!" Right hand makes sweeping gesture.

The doctor is lying and he knows he's lying.

"An' you, sah, will shut yaw mouth! ...Now thayn. Wayah were we?" Tho he stared at it his eyes no longer saw the drawing, now upsidedown seen from his new position. Takes a moment before he realizes this, rotates it. "Now thayn, ta wrap this heah circus up. [picks up paper, holds it for all to see] Follow me. This pehrson, heah, is the prisonah. He is heading ta [peers around edge of paper]... ta this daw, heah. What weah all wondrin is, who in heaven's name is this pehrson [sets down paper], this li'l thang a-settin ovah heah? ...an again, this li'l thang a-laying ovah heah?" Mashes both indexes down on two separate stickfigures, each associated w identical little triangles and each w a wavy line descending from head to hips. "Who in the hayll is she?"

It was then i knew for sure the imbeciles werent playing, that all this was deadly serious.

"Well, mistah schock? What is yaw ansah this tahm?"

In a state of disbelief. <The two figures are not the same person....>

"...Not the saaym?"

Not the same person ...sir. The figure beneath your left finger is my....

"Yes? Speakup."

...is my fiancé.

"Ya dont say. [looks at me, mouth open] An' this one? Heah, by the courtyard gate? Jus a-layin theyah, a-hidin, a-waitin fah someboda, someboda, ta come a-runnin outa mah prison?"

That is not a courtyard ...a courtyard, sir. It is a warehouse ... a warehouse in noogachatta tennessee. And the figure lying there is....

"Is?"

...is my fianc-....

"Yes...? Speakup, sah."

...my fiancé's murdered sister.

But he hardly heard. His mind was fixed on something else. "Mistah schock. Whoevah this is, heah, is not jus a-laying theyah, a-waitin. No sah. Cause her dress is away ovah... heah!" Rapsdown a knuckle on a lone triangle in an adjoining box, looks up, smiles cynically all around. "The plot thickens, gentlemen."

May i say something?

"You, sah...You may ansah me this. [face aglow] Who in the hayll is this li'l thang a-laying heah? Ah ask you one moah tahm!" His finger (pointing to the longhaired stickfigure lacking a triangle) is shaking visibly.

Youre not listening, sir. The doctor has convinced you the drawing is some sort of escape plan.

"If one maw laah [lie] comes outa thayat mouth o' yaws ah caynt baheld rahsponsable...." Drops index as if lowering a smoking pistol; the wart under his eye twitching, he twists suddenly to one side, jaw locked, looks at ceiling. "Speak ta the prisonah, doctah, 'faw ah lose mah tempah an' do sumthin plumb unholeh!" Wardion, wiping mouth w back of fist, hoists one chunky cheek onto a corner of his desk while dr frumpmoid, manifesting a pair of legs, waddles forward.

"I can see youre all wondering about this. The good warden's daughter drew it. Our videos show, she gave it to schock in the library during what was supposed to be an educational visit to the various safe areas of her father's prison. For the warden had to come straight here from church that day to attend to an urgent matter. Of course mr dion here, also here on his day off ...having no way of knowing —til he got back from the cafeteria, where he'd gone to get a cup of coffee to go— that the guard who'd escorted schock that day had locked him inside the library. Mr dion, seeing no harm in leaving emmalou to poke around the library –which he presumed empty on a sunday, as it should have been– relaxed in the library station watching tv. This is just one of the many potential problems of having prisoners with special priv'lages."

Lies. All lies. The girl said "I know you", said her father had showed the family my foto, and that she would some day be a famous writer too, or maybe a dancer, all the while drawing a clever caricature of captain dion here from memory. It is *that* drawing she gave me to look at. [While the girl in truth was mischievously morbid, in my position i dared not suggest that my jailer put her bed out on the frontlawn by fullmoon as medicine for her eclectic brand of melancholy.] The sketch you hold was stolen from my cell by guard gluum not long after i came here. The real question here is, why didnt the doctor say who the guard who disappeared for coffee was? and why didnt that guard post the "trustee" flag so the captain would know i was there? I suggest you look at that video, warden ...if the doctor hasnt destroyed it yet. And if he has, just ask your daughter what was on that piece o' paper 'n' what became of it. You'll see that i looked at the drawing, chuckled and handed it back, complimenting her talent. Then spotting gluum, who had returned, sensing he was up t' no good, i said <Nice meeting you" and immediately moved to another table. You'll see her drawing was nothing but a harmless cartoon."

In the space of my outburst the slug went from white to purple. "Why you haughty arrogant criminal rapist scum, you. Who in the hell do you think...."

Tho something in his daughter's "foto/family/famous writer/dancer" revelation to me had clearly peaked the wardon's lowgrade curiosity, the slug's "rapist" word overrode it. He slipped off his desk. "Anotha wahrd oudda you, sah, an' yawl fynd yawsaylf back in sturrah faw'n ah kin say robbity lee! Do ya heah?"

Six more weeks of darkness, sir, like the doctor here arranged last time?

Anger can sometimes hear but divine wrath is always deaf. While wardion backs off as if angered beyond speech, the slug goes on, glaring at me, his jaw working sidetoside. "Of course, the girl will deny everything. This is only natural, for a day out is just fun to her —a mere game. While inmate schock, on the other hand, a chickenhawk by avocation, was *not* playing games...."

"An let me say ryhat now [raises a finger to his idea of God's location or something], it will not happen again! Those days ah ovah. [bushy eyebrows, eyelids, wart, all, rise as if in dismay] Theyull *not* be so much freedom unda this heah ruff from now on! Nosah!"

All heads bow in acknowledgment of a grimmer future.

I try to but can not keep silent. Someone around here has got to possess the balls to tell you the truth, warden ...sir. [wardion draws back his bowlingball head as if for a throw, examines me w intense sidelong eyes] That sick man beside you, sir. To him we are all just pieces in a chessgame. And he's playing you like a pawn, sir. He's playing all of us like pawns —always building a case against one or another of us. I'll bet there's a recorder in his jacket pocket as we speak, catching every word for future use.

Staring thru me toward some almost graspable concept: "Ah suggest yall stop raht theyah, sah, faw yall's own good!"

But what he's got on *you*, sir, is nothing t' all the dirty tricks *we* have on *him*. [in truth, i had only an intuition of who had what on whom] Everybody in this room knows what he's up to.

Since a scan of all faces turnedup no shred of disagreement w my "preposterous assertions" [as the slug britly (sic) ɛ explosively put it], the warden faded to blank. Sensing a stirring of suspicion behind the toad's speechlessness, the slug hisses his toxic inks in prep for a clean getaway, "You haughty, arrogant, criminal rapist scum you! Who in the hell do you think you are?"

Fearing, i suspect, anything even hinting at institutional disorder, wardion returns to the fray. "That'll be one ouch, prisonah schock! Delivah the punishment, mistah glom." Glumm steps forward, struggling to don a half-on glove. "Enna tahm yaw redda, mistah glom."

<He has called you a "bornagain idiot", sir, in front of both me and these two guards.> ...glove adangle, clicks his heels, sneers up into my face...

<That person there, in whom youve put your christian trust, scripted this whole thing!> I am delivered the socalled ouch. Now an ouch is the mildest form of punishment (of the corporeal type) in the prison's socalled gig system: an unwritten plethora of punitives ranging from an ouch (openhanded hard & stinging slapintheface) to the far graver solitary confinement in the old bldg.

"Stir mah grits agin, sah, an' I wont be rahsponsable faw yaw fewcha!"

He's playin you like a jew's harp, warden. He calls all southern baptists bible-thumping clods.

"Give the prisonah anotha ouch mistah glomm."

Again glumm is interrupted putting-on the black leather gloves which will enable him to deliver a second even-harder slap.

Turning my stinging face back, i relocate the slug, point at him so there can be no mistake. <*You* put this filthy lie in the good warden's head. *You* are the devil in his world. *You*.... [my biblical tack repeatedly fixes the warden's attn] One glance at the original police sketch of where my fiancé...my fiancé's sister was murdered, and the warden will see you dreamedup this whole devilish scheme. The noogachatta police can clear all this up with a single fax.> There followed in the room for 4-5 secs an inexplicable stillness.

"Give the prisoner a stomp, glumm." This command comes not from the toad this time but from the slug. "You, schock, must be punished for even talking to that girl!"

Partially donned second glove still adangle, Glumm steps forward.

<You, doctor, are the source of "evil" in this place. [i am pointing again] The very fires of hell are raging in your heart.>

"NOW, glumm!" shouts slugmoid.

Gluum clicks his heels, slams a bootheel on my left foot.

I suck in a long breath, close eyes ...after a moment continue. <You, doctor... You are a scheming "evil" genius, the antichrist of this prison! Thanx t' you, satan roams free here every day!>

"Glumm, again! Now, damnit!"

Glumm, still struggling w the glove, steps forward yet again.

The doctor will make me suffer but somebody's gotta tell you, warden.

"I say, now!"

Anybody ...ungh! [lean slitely forward, draw another sucking breath, reright self, reopen copiously watering eyes] Anybody [subdued gasp]... anybody c'n tell you what you wanna hear, warden. That's easy. It's what ya *dont* wanna hear that nobody round here has the balls t' say.

"Again, glumm! Again! "

<I may be the best friend you ever had in here. I may be- uugh!> Glumm is right in my face now, as animated as i've ever seen him and seemingly begging me to continue. Vision blurring, the only pain i'm feeling is in calf, shin ɛ knee, for the foot itself is still in shock. <The smartest thing you'll ever do is have your friend the governor give this scheming satan his walking papers.>

Blank sober faces all around shout my truth. Waving both hands like a traffic cop at a school crossing wardion charges forward. "I say, stop! STOP! STOP! STOP!" Glumm is passionately hunkereddown for a fourth stomp as the warden bellies up to him. "Did you heah me? Who in the hayl's in chahge round heah? What dont yall understand about stop, suh?"

Like a bad dog, glumm eases himself slowly upright, slinks backward, grunts a grudging "Yessir."

Wardion, shaken [i guessed], glaring a bit glassy-eyed, turns, waddles toward his desk. Leaning forward on it, catching his breath, he says "This place is needin less prayahs an' maw action, ah kin see thayat. [turning back, biting lip] My deah doctah. [sighs] A giant with a broken foot is no good ta owah team now izzy [now, is he]?"

The slug, feigning humility, yods in silence.

"As faw you, sah." I try to remain at full-attention and not blink tho my eyes are watering out of control and i'm balanced on the only foot i can feel. "Ah dont cayah a rayat's ass bout yall's feud with the doctah heah, yunahstan?", his hefty rump, on its stubby legs, agitatedly slipping on&off his desk as to&from a toadstool.

I yod. It is clear my little seedling is planted & watered. Yes, sir. {Not too partisan now nathan.} The harm to my foot is rapidly asserting itself.

Takes breath, addresses me. "Whatevah disagreement you two ah havin ah expect ta be cleahedup, is thayat cleah? <Yes, sir.> But this heah drawin', sah... [shakes paper] ...This heah piepah o' yaws has caused a heap o' trouble round heah. [sighs, lowers paper, looks down, intakes thru flared nostrils] An doncha think fuh one minute ah'm gonna buy yaw stora [story] without checkin wi' noogachatta poleece —an' owak video recuds too. [disconcerted pause] We'll be talkin furtha as ta this heah business. [shakes paper one last time] Take the prisonah away. This heah sorra-ayussed meetin's ovah. Git, now. All o ya. Git."

All but godion turn to leave. I am on my first limping step when glumm comes up behind, gives a shove toward the door. Failure of said foot causes me to stumble. Skidding to one knee i catch myself *w* a hand out.

"Hold up! [all turn] Thayll be no maw monkabizness from you two, ya heah?"

"Yessir!" fire the twins in one voice as slugfrood ducksout the door.

"Mistah gowd [godion]. Yall take these two charactuz heah an' splain ta them who runs this heah prison... *aftah* ya bring me those videos."

Godion salutes, comes alongside as i rise. We reach the door in time to see the slug sliming his way down the corridor in an opposite direction. I'm hurt yet feel extraordinarily good. I write my own headline above my battered picture as we go. {Good Strides Made Despite Bad Limp} Your occasional ignoble kinsman should win an interim battle here&there, no?

197-003-02-001617

That afternoon fed. inmate # (as above) was ordered to go to the clinic for x-rays. (What's wrong *w* this picture? I was in way worse shape back in iso and they laffed at the idea of medical attn.) Tho the foot is grossly bruised & strained, only the pinkytoe proves fractured.

a slime-trail by moonlite is twice as brite

For my pains, a week or so following the big blowout (the day i was moved to a new cell, in fact), wardion sent for me. Behaving as tho nothing had happened: "Ah've asked the good doctah heah ta sit in on owah li'l ol' powwow, since he wuz heah ennahow payin yaws trula a friendla visit." If i was there 5mins it was more than i remember. The closest he came to touching on the real issue was to casually ask if everything was going alright?

<Given my basic circumstances, yessir.> One bushy eyebrow, one fat brown wart, rose, "An' ah those two naughty boys behavin themselves?" <For the time being, sir.> Questionmark replaced by proud smile.

Directors straitmon & becillo were conspicuously absent from all these proceedings. It looked like sudden political equilibrium. Did mere sexual orientation automatically weigh them in on the side of the slug? Is this entire prison thus divided, hetero from homo? GoodGaia. At any rate, samuel-the-slimy-slugthing has not sent for me since. As mnemy rescans the dark squalor of him plopped squat behind his desk, i imagine him, even as i write, marinading his stinking sloth in old smegma & new schema, somehow i am sure –sure as his slime-trail is clearest by moonlite– i know i have not felt the last of dr rodent's devious & demented cruelty.

no slug was ever so....

I realize i've labeled sam-the-slimy unjustly. For no Wild creature deserves to be compared w him. No slug ever harbored such virulent dark intent. He merely resembles a slug. In reality he is a great white shark w the soul of a rat —a very diseased rat at that. Dr rodent, i presume? —accent on 2nd syllable, pronounced w a gallic 'e'.

k. m. v. g. a.

Kiss my virginal german ass, *herr doktor sigmoid froidnung slug-hoss rodént.*

governor to confab with schock attorneys

Such a headline would not pass muster today. The corpolitic press has been taught to ignore or downplay all positive aspects of "the nathan schock affair". Forinstance, i understand there has still not been a peep about the almost 4million signatures (13million worldwide!) petitioning all authorities w any say in my future. Not a peep —save for enviro, indy & foreign media. This blackout is meant to make it look as tho no one cares. Worse yet, it's working. As the baron once said so well, "The masses are forgetting even as we speak. For denying 'n' forgetting are what *the people* have been trained to do best", the emphasized words delivered w disgust.

hardtime-hulk nationals may be canceled

There are rumors that the "mr hardtime hardbody" contest (most popular part of the f.i.n.i games), sched'd for nov, may be canceled. This is due (have i said?) to a ban on weightlifting in fed. prisons rumored to come into effect soon. A newspaper article to this effect was given me recently by glumm. "Ya wont yell 'shakedown' if I show ya a measly newspaper, will ya?"

The argument is being made, weightlifting is making many prisoners so strong it takes several guards to restrain them. Apparently one guard had his neck broken by an "enraged weightlifter" and another's aorta burst (aneurism)due to body-crushing. Being on the inside i can i.d w that sort of rage. And how natural that persons stripped of all social validity would pursue one of the few forms of power legally avail to them.

✍

On the briteside. This chapter-heading stuff is pleasantly distracting.

the assignment of two sweaty intermediaries so warden todion can have a trophy-snagging gladiator for his prison and i can wrest a wraith of humaneness out of this moral wreckage

Having studied current champions, chief godion (whose begun to think of himself as my personal coach) does all he can to help me commit venal symmetry, adding meters of swollen veins to an already monstrous musculature. Amazing how the body remembers former tasks, how muscles ε muscle-groups (recalling as if my teens were yesterday) respond.

Now when i lay on my side i need two folded pillows to keep my head somewhat level. And, like an old canoeist who forgets he has new outriggers, i'm constantly sideswiping things: doorframes, jutting corners. Shoulders ε arms are bruised. In dreams my body is invaded by pythons ε anacondas, rhinos ε elephants, or i am a giant mass of yeast in a small hothouse! Claustrophobic to start w, i'm all but toppedout now w compression-anxiety. I dont just need another pillow, a wider cot, warden ...sir. I need a bigger cell! Preferably one with a window. Collapsing universes, must i pump til i burst? O Great Créator! [50s broadway] Why have you forsaken me? [70s broadway] Why must the one be at cost to the other?

variation on tincans & a string

Finally, to bring the reader reasonably uptodate on the rosa posa business. A day or two after our failed rendezvous rosa ε me spoke for the first time.

Farfetched, you say? Whatever. Left a note for rosa in the training bench w instructions; something along the lines of,

In the cell where you guys hang your notes to me, empty all water from BOTTOM of toilet by 8:15pm. I will do same with mine. We then may be able to yell to each other thru the pipe between our toilets. If the toilet is like mine, you will need also to empty (siphon) the trap behind the hole at the bottom of the toilet. [i incl'd sketched instructions]

The women are allowed 50mins of open-cell time at 8 every eve. (The men lost this privilege years before.) While it was impossible to tell what the other was yelling, on both ends we could hear a voice (of the opposite sex!) as if arriving from another world. See me, reader, head buried in a steel bowl i'd been scrubbing at since my arrival but which strata of mineral- & crud deposits only powertools & heavy chems could vanish. Mothernature, look at me! See what 'the desire to mate' youve inscribed in us has reduced me to! Me, your humblest servant!

And then, look at these notes i save like some elementary school kid: "We see you in the cafetera sometimes. Hunka! Hunka! Hunka! The qweens down there must stawk you bad. Sucha waste of studlyness!" And, "Walk by the [cafeteria] doors on Friday so's she [rosa] can scope out the merchendise." And, "Wach by the doors [same doors]. Well [we'll] make Rosa walk pass you. Whata bichin bewty! Lucky you!" [sic, all] Scena: Three sets of doubledoors between two diningrms are left open so the guards eating can help a skeleton staff [waiting to eat next] oversee the women inmates while they eat. Thus i have seen rosa in the flesh more than once and thus my starved imagination has been titillated almost beyond control.

requested book arrives

Lenormand's *the fortress*. So long in coming, forgot i ordered it.

touch of prison history

What i have been calling the old bldg (orig prison) was built in 1821. While three of the four orig sides are wrapped by newer additions, the front of the building, tho restored, is still intact. The brass-ornamented belltower atop the third floor, its narrow dome rising above the walls of this fortress, is its most-prized part.

Did you work here when they used t' ring the bell once for every year of the age of the executed? i asked g&g one day on the way back from the library. From a booklet lenny gave me i knew fullwell they werent, for the practice had been stopped in the 1920s, replaced by three simple knells —when they feel like it, for it was not rung for either of the executions i've 'witnessed'. Which brings up a curious phenomenon. Before i learned of this morbid tradition i found myself deafened at times by a tolling inside my head of (variously) the three *hammerschlagen* of mahler ε the gong-blows of puccini's 'unfinished', as tho they were reporting my own death. And now this. *Verdammt!* Imagine suffering from the reverberations of sounds that havent been made yet on one's own behalf!

Track this. Because the court w its lies has tampered w change in my life (tampered w my future), one particular change they have sched'd (the event of my death) is ever retrodominoing back on events of the present. It is for this reason alone that we have: the persons who go out of their way to write a letter, say, or sign a petition, in my behalf; or my dearest friends, on concert ε speaking tours to raise money for the nathan schock legal defense fund; or a certain mcGrae woman worried sick unto death over me and housebound w melancholy; or the people in jurisprudence, ε the press, getting rich on the fact of my sched'd fate. For this same reason i too must deal w the present hauntings of a future ghost. Witness this very book, and the fact i was writing it backwards for months. Such bizarre events are the result of bending the arrow of "time" unNaturally back upon itself.

On hearing thumping noises downstairs the nite before humpinLouie was executed, i'd asked several guards did they know what exactly was under my cell. None did. Then, thru the nite prior to sobbinRobin's murder it happened again. As we left the library on the day in question, secretly excited by the chance to answer what was to them a spooky architectural enigma, g&g led me to the fronthall of the old bldg, located immed in front of the library and which served as an (unkempt) prison museum.

"Member what ya asked about a couple muntz ago?" said gluum as we echoicly clomped ε swished (they in leather boots, me in cardboard ones) down a high-ceilinged entrance hall. "Well, I foundout it's da place da executioner usta stay —ya know, waybackwhen?" "In da ol days" added glumm for clarification. On reaching the door directly under my cell, gluum proudly swings it wide. "An' dis is it!"

As tho caught violating a child, jack ketch, naked save for knee-high boots ε executioner's hood, was in the midst of copulating (how?) w his boy manikin —which, as before, kneeled at the foot of the bed but whose head stared at him from a pillow half-a-bed away! (A dark humorist might venture here that he'd screwed its head off.) The only difference in this particular sketch (if one discounted the nakedness ε sex) was that ketch, manikin, head, bedclothes, all, were spattered w what looked to be gouts of coagulated blood but had the musty chalky odor of waterpaint.

"Dih-nt know he'd be dere!" said gluum, closing the door quickly. "Me neider" parrotted glumm. Had they said nothing, just their faces when the door swung wide assured me, the only person beside ketch who knew about this sickening "surprise" was youknowwho.

La represión del instinto genera monstruos. —yourstruly, after goya

*prisons give an underside view of the suppression of Natural Law,
and prisoners are examples of where the rules & expectations
of civil society have failed some of its potential best*

Following my move to the official deathrow, emil expressed concern over my being "thrown in with" other deathrow inmates. "It cant be very nice back there. They must be animals."

O no. Animals they are not. I've lived in the company of animals and these are not animals. But like you 'n' me, neither are they quite human anymore —healthfully instinctively human, i mean. Prisons are monuments not to ...and remember, prisons, like shrinks, are unknown in primitive society... prisons are monuments *not* to difference-in-principle between like beings (ie, us animals in here versus you humans out there), as civil rules 'n' expectations would like us to think. No. Prisons are monuments to difference in degree only —our responses to being civilized v. your responses. Until we understand this there will be no cures, just bandaids ...pathogenic bandaids at that.

[The present writer was not at all in disagreement with what N.S. was saying. Respecting his depression, I tried always to put aside the role of counselor, employ only the role of listener. —Ed.]

<B'side, i rarely interact with other prisoners. I eat with the guards, take my out-time in the little-used library, train with my spotter. And as to [official] deathrow: prisoners cannot see each other there. Our cells face a blank corridor wall. Even hearing each other is not all that easy ...thankfully. The front walls of 'r cells are solid glass ...except for the doors, which are more steel than open space.> Even given these things, once back in my new cell i wonder, Why so quiet? The rest of the prison is way noisier. Maybe because deathrow concentrates the mind? Or just maybe it's because we here are not your average prisoners —vulgar boisterous full of false pride. Maybe we're just broken silent men shackled in daiseychains and dragging balls of guilt —both the guilt we've 'earned' and the guilt we get assigned every day. But to return to my catchup notes.

"justice"

"The state attorneys' office wants to cut a deal... They'll drop their case if we drop ours."

What case? The assault 'n' battery bullshit? [yods] [what emil re:d was my suit against va dept of criminal affairs] In trade for what? Do they know what actually happened? ["They know our version."] Emil, i didnt slap him punch him or anything! All i did was squeeze his jowls. That's it! —those fantastic floppy jowls: the very oracle of deception 'n' cruelty in this toxic lab experiment we call a prison! Do you remember what he did to me that day? The things he said? The ghastly lies about Lilith 'n' lalage 'n' torture 'n' gangrape 'n' murder 'n' mutilation 'n' on 'n' on til i'm literally sick. I'd rather be beatup by the guards any day. All i did was squeeze that face til it screamed. [emil squint-grins] A scream is a form of truth, you know. An all i wanted just once (just once, emil) was for some form of truth to issue from that heinous mouth! And for that i was clubbed kicked shot in the head 'n' thrown in iso for six weeks. In any constructive punitive system a beating like that woulduv been more than enuf by itself. Or, without the beating, a week in the hole at best. But both? Plus five more weeks? An' without medical attention? Have you any idea what it's like to spend just one

Since none in maxlockdown is permitted recrm privileges, i have been ok'd for a tv. Yet because bigcorpx tv is all that's offered, i never bothered ...til i saw, in the library one day, movie loans & rentals. So emil will be bringing me the top-end prison-authorized model 12" unbreakable screen with videoplayer. Now all that remains to be seen is what i will be allowed to view via my new toy.

day in that stinking blackhole muchless fortytwo? An what about what that sick bastard did t' me in the clinic? Am i supposed ta jus forget that too? [feeling whipped, i sat head in hands]

"Nathan, I'm not telling you t' take the offer. I'm just informing you that they made it, that's all. You may do with it what you will, of course, and I will understand."

[regrouping] What would you do?

"That's not a fair question. We live in very different circumstances."

...Try.

"I'd take it... but with a stipulation. <And that would be?> That your life here be monitored, say biweekly, by an ombudsman of the state, and that if ever he deems any of these charges valid, your case will be reactivated [i try not to be visibly disappointed]...without regard for statutes of limitation ...Nathan, we have no proof. It's their word against yours. And if, as you say, theyre all liars 'n' thieves, with corpses in every closet, well then ...figure it out for yourself. I repeat, we have no proof. Not a single reliable witness to any one of our charges!"

My scars, physical & psychic, millabout in silence. {The groove in my scull is still tender as a fresh hematoma. There's a fracture under there, i know.} And that's not even to think about the 'lacerations' in my heart.

"Nathan, what happened t' you has happened to others in here. I understand inmates have been killed just for lunging at a guard. At least you got a piece o' the sorry bastard, if that helps."

Clinical stats guaranteed shrink sigmoid that after six weeks of total sensory deprivation i would emerge a virtual veg'table —a big blond zombie he could abuse at will. Explain please how battling a sentence of living-death is better than being killed while attacking one's tormentors?

Thoughtfully: "You are right, of course."

rosa poza update contd

In a note i told rosa she did the right thing and that there were no hard feelings. Here is a portion of the answer i rcv'd.

Nathan I'm really glad your not mad. I was pretty worryed... [etc] **To be honest I was worryed you woudnt like me when we met cause I wasnt beutiful as the girls you used to hang with. Plus I was worryed I'd be to old....** [and so on] [sic all ...again]

Too old? They say she's 23. And what, dare i ask, made her decide this? Ok, the goodlooks protocol i'm guilty of. But her raverchick brand of goodlooks is more than compensated by a neat ɛ thrifty body. And as to age: as i've said, i dont believe in it. We've all seen teens who looked 30, and some a hard-lived 30 at that. I've dated many women older than rosa. Nikki, forinstance, whom the reader has 'met'. So how did rosa come by such ideas? Here resides, exactly because of my death-sentence, one of the nastier masks which haunt my cell.

During ɛ since my trial i have been rëindicted rëtried ɛ rëcondemned in the media for many things. My alleged crimes range from neonaziism to misanthropy to lechery ɛ even to paraphilia. Since the reader has met the baron –one of six still-at-large alleged accomplices of mine– he can easily figureout how the press came up w all the neonazi crap. Indeed, the prosecution at my trial tried every gambit to get me convicted as a neonazi terrorist. As to the "raging misanthrope" rot: Since more than once the reader has heard me rail against human behavior, he can see how the press –taking a lift here, a tuck there, on the face of things– could twist my green criticism into dislike of my fellow man. As to the lechery ɛ paraphilia innuendo: Because sex intrigue sells best (better even than murder1, believe it), it is hardest of all to rebut, if only for the sheer mass of media exposure-thru-repetition such gossip gets.

from whence this corrigenda, nikki? greatGaia!

In the midst of the mass media's dredging for detritus, nikki stepped into the limelite. "I'm not saying we didn't have a good relationship while it lasted. We did. It was great. All I'm saying is, within hours of my twenty-sixth birthday he up and left me for a teenager. That's what looks bad."

There is a presumption in civil society that some sort of wrong has been done when an "older" man has a relationship w a "young" woman. Yet when you straightup shamelessly ask, What exactly is wrong with this?, you get mostly stammering biteless cliches. Even the most substantial criticism of all –What can two people of such different ages possibly find in common?– turns out to be hopelessly lame if only because humans wout something *very much* in common simply do not go to all the trouble to mate, specially in these sexually hazardous times. And all this is to ignore the reallife fact that, the "young" person in question here was inordinately talented ɛ wise! And i would heapon beauty fame&fortune too if it werent for how ludicrously theyre valued in civil society. By the same token, my rebuttal is not meant to negate the fact that nikki is hardly alone in her clandestine agenda. First tho, to the high-handed hypocrisy hid here.

When nikki herself was Lilith's age did she feel this way? By her own admission, in her teens she "fell madly in love" w several older men: the sundance kid, p.i magnum, agent007 ɛ han solo among them. Fact is, nikki told me she had "the hots" for sundance ɛ 007 (blond version) from around aged 9 or 10 and would have "hopped into the sack" w any one of them "on a moment's notice...oh, as young as age twelve, I suppose". So what's going on here? When did she drop into denial? And why? The following is instructive.

We knew eachother about a year before i questioned Lilith as to why she harbored not a mote of animosity for nikki's cruel treatment. "Well, first of all ...and mostofall, i guess... i had you 'n' she didnt. That was hard enuf for her. Secondly ...I wrote about this, come to think of it. [Emil, from her diary of the period, please.] Fading flowers cannot help but envy the blossoms around them. This is a sad thing and not to be taken lightly. And the more they fade the more they grow to hate the bees, butterflies & hummingbirds which pass by no longer even noticing them. I think Mother Nature has okayed such bitterness. Especially if we cannot see, the bees & butterflies are merely busy at the work they were created to do —searching for the best nectar. Sad [she added] but true". In nikki's case very sad. For this blossom was still far too talented, vital ɛ attractive to join forces so soon w the bitterly withering world matron underground.

In *the male psyche,* a zine which excerpted my *Mothernature & the world matron* for several months running, in a letter to the editor panning my world matron thesis, a shrink of the md variety said, "Women tend to forget they were very sexual as young persons". This he claimed as a cause for their often being "so hard on younger women". This man is either a fool or a coward. We "older" persons (not just women) remember in our very guts the sexual power we embodied as youths. And that precisely is the cause of much of our erotic anxiety. Yet because the competition is naive, older women have not waged out&out war against the youth of their gender. Not quite. But because sex is so hypertrophied in stressed societies, older women, each in their own way, see to it young women are kept sexually disfranchised for as long as politically plausible. More compassionate by nature however than older men —who historically sent the younger competition off to die in war (and, prehistorically, fought openly w them for females)— these days the world matron accomplishes her covert agenda by discouraging the dancing of what i will call here the libido limbo, by seeing to it that the bar of the age of consent is kept as high as a given paradigm will allow wout inviting general mockery —high enuf to allow an 18yearold to walk upright beneath it! And how is this managed? Despite my best intentions, i have no choice now but to outline my 'world matron' concept. For it is not explaining itself as i'd hoped it might.

all a-sea about this stuff at the start

At sea, on my first gE mission, glendon starling loaned me a book: oren liseley's the star-thrower. I was captivated. Here was a master at turning philosophic concepts into miniature adventure stories. When as a green activist i began recording my thoughts & adventures i found myself emulating liseley's method. It seemed the only efficient way to go. My first straying from liseley began w the writing of my 3rd book, *the ungreening of tomorrow*, and by the time of my 6th book, *Mothernature & the world matron*, my own style was in full voice. It was the task of this latter work to show man's unseverable connection to Wilderness (wild Nature), a task which left little room for the easy-read liseleyesque allegory which interspersed my earlier work.

Published in aug '92, i took *M&wm* on the road for the '92-93 lecture series. It was quickly driven home to me: most people read for entertainment; few care to learn very much while doing so. For the first time in my writing career the audio&video versions of my work outsold by double the book which spawned them —even tho wout the book they were prettymuch rationally groundless! In fact, of the three, the video, weakest in logical connections, sold best! That, and subsequent tours, brought me down to Earth.

My readers, long known as "thinking persons", in startling numbers gaveup on the book and bought the audio/video versions. The more candid of them confessed to being "content just to know the [logic of] my book was out there somewhere". It turnedout, all they were after was a mere fluency in key words & phrases; ie, an *appearance* of subject mastery. That done, they were done. Scary? Yes. And so i began drawing a parallel in my lectures which said:

<When we do this we turn from thinkers into zealots.> My friend the baron always insisted, hitler's police (not the ss but the police battalions which physically roundedup the obviously innocent) were average people. His point? Average joe&jane are zealots-in-waiting, in-waiting for their particular version of a messiah; someone to save them from their particular version of "evil"; someone to pamper their particular version of paranoia. Unlike the baron, who capitalized on such zealotry, i typically ignored letters of aggressive adoration. I do not collect fans. Fan is short for fanatic and fanatics (w their m.o of action-over-judgement) are unpredictable.

At the same time, while zealots thrive on catchphrases that can be chanted or marched to, one cannot be a successful instructor if he is shy to offer quickie outtakes ε catchy soundbites —the quickier ε catchier the better. In my lectures i called such cribsheeting of my books 'idiot101', always urging a greater depth of understanding from my readers. But now time is short. What now but an idiot101 approach can deliver my theses to the reader? Yet be warned. The following contains key concepts only, the merest smattering of my work. Those who have previously studied ε understood it may, of course, skip ahead. Those who dislike learning, or who fear iconoclasm (incl'g revelatory sex info), should definitely skip ahead. In fact, the timid ε passionless might just skip the whole book, wait for the movie.

split-world premise

If we are to understand the travails of Lilith McGrae, nathan schock, their loved ones, friends and –i mean, not just thumbnail but understand *at depth*– and if we are to do so wout reading the hundreds of essays (my books) designed to render the triggers to those travails not just clear but credible, then we are left no choice but to wheel&deal in keywords ε catchphrases for a space here. This is a sorry fate for an author who thrives on sound premises, an author who knows: Logic ε proof are sacrificed on the altar of generalization.

Our first sacrifice will be the apposed concepts "civilized" ε "precivilized". Since there are pockets of the Planet which civilization has yet to substantially deNature, "civilized world" is not yet an absolute term (☺). Of course, this non-absoluteness holds true as well for all the five categories below (smile again). Keeping these mitigations in mind, we plunge ahead, summarize the fundamental thesis of all my works in ecology.

tag-terms for split-world premise	
precivilized	**civilized**
mother-respecting	mother-trivializing
fear-respecting	fear-abusive
life-respecting	death-fixated
Earth/Nature/instinct-respecting	Earth/Nature/instinct-abusive
Wisdom/Truth-valuing	Wisdom/Truth-trivializing

I write entire books just to avoid such generic gobbledygook. But this may be the only book of mine which most readers will ever see ...and maybe not even it, if the current phalladigm has its way. But i am unarmed ε vulnerable, w my back to the wall, and coming at me fast as it can hobble, all scythe ε certainty, is brother death. My options are zip. And so i must plunge us to the pith of my deepgreen career or forever hold my piece. Allow me to preface that pith.

In a mother-respecting environment (precivilized humanity) it is possible to attain wisdom w age; it may even be likely. But lacking a basic foundation of mother-respect (incl'g mostly our chthonic Mother: Earth), Truth/Wisdom is impossible to attain. No overarching unity ε reciprocity of principles (the soul of sense) is possible wout it. This proves a doublewhammy for the aged.

As a quick example. In an antiTerra (civilized) environment, not only are the old disrespected for their frailties ε dependencies, they have little chance of attaining wisdom along w their years. Therefor, once having reached old age they find themselves w only knowledge to share w the younger world around them. Because change is rapid in such a world, what knowledge they have quickly depreciates to a condition of "historical value only".

Wisdom, on the other hand, is ever fresh, being unaffected by the opinions, possessions ε desires of the day. For Wisdom is always prior to quotidian quanta. In point of fact, such *a priori*-ness is what separates wisdom from 'mere' knowledge. With little wisdom to offer, w only deNatured ε date-compromised knowledge to barter, respect for the aged is doubly difficult to come by. What else have they accumulated for which we can respect them? Opinions? Material possessions? Pardon the watchword but, is it any wonder then that it becomes a hardship for we civilized to protect our aged from disregard or abuse? This is but one example. Exact understanding of what the above table means is not the point. This chapter's job is only to intro the average reader to a sampling of terms, basic concepts to which sHe can refer as these terms are encountered. These key-words & catch-phrases will act, as such generalia must, as both help & hindrance to the work in which they appear. Yet to proceed w/out them is to drop the reader into the depths of a dark forest w/out a trail. And so, *vom anfang*.

"all the richest schockian concepts, specially his
'Mothernature & the world matron',
are founded upon his civilizing principle'"

[Editor: Suspend my prison shorthand for this chapter, please.] The greatest anthropologist, i believe, after rousseau, got this far: "Until such time as we hold a picture of what exactly *caused* civilization; until we figure out what triggered and empowered to dominance that point of view which has dragged us, against our deeper sensibilities, into this alternative to life we call civil existence; until such time as we assemble such a causative picture, we will continue to trudge, zombie-like, toward an apocalyptic finale only a few of us see as inevitable." —stanford diamonde

I call that causative picture, which diamonde so passionately solicits from us, the principle which civilized us; or, *the civilizing principle*. The version i happen to have excavated over my lifetime distills to the following.

Nature is irrational and uncaring†

Which, in informal practice, distills to:

The methods of Nature are demonstrably inhumane

Which agenda, politically deployed, further distills to:

Nature and instinct are enemies of humanity

(That Nature is omnipresent in our lives, of course, exists *a priori* in all these variations.)

† This 'final' principle comprises a (necessary) compression of the history of humanity (both written and archeologic) in that it reflects how the gradual emergence of scientific investigation has acted upon the 'original' form of 'my' principle over time. That is, emerging from where civil humanity's 'earliest' form of 'my' premise was likely more along the lines of

Nature is our most dangerous predator/enemy and it is everywhere.

Humanity's resulting withdrawal from Wilderness —brought about by the varieties of 'walls' which civilization proceeded to erect, in concord with the eventual revelations of empirical science– have acted to temper this early perception into its less hostile (but still lethally paranoiac) present form:

<u>Nature is irrational and uncaring</u>

If this assessment appears tame on sight it is important to keep in mind: Depending on the infraction, civil society puts in cages and/or puts to death those said to be guilty of *irrational* or *uncaring* acts. Imagine for instance what would happen to someone who caused a "highly destructive" earthquake or tornado and promised to do so again whenever he deemed necessary. While an entire (civil) paradigm of belief is, of course, contained in this single existential pronouncement, we need presently pointup only its major *a priori* elements. That is, such a principle (however mistakenly) presumes that

❶ the methods of Nature/instinct are inferior to (human) rationalization. That is, that Nature and instinct are incapable of "thinking things thru to their most constructive and just conclusion before acting on them", and
❷ that we humans would, and could, deploy such a Universal constant of constructivism and justice if only we could vanquish the 'thoughtless and destructive' agendas of Nature and instinct and replace them with our own. It is our (tragic) failure to locate the qualities of rationality and caring in Nature and instinct which convinces us that they can not be otherwise than inhumane; ie, the enemy.

For economy's sake i have attempted to distill these *a priori* elements into my 'final' version of the principle by use of the words irrational and uncaring, which of course are intended to imply that civil society believes that Nature and instinct are savage (irrational and brutal, mirroring our mistaken view of the primitive) ...savage forces seemingly designed to strike when we least expect it and are least prepared to defend ourselves etcetc. And so civil humanity feels justified in concluding: If Nature and instinct refuse to play favorites with what is, obviously, the highest form of life (ie, us), then it is clear that Nature and instinct are neither rational nor on our side. At this point, as justification, all the "horrors" of Natural "catastrophe" where we humans have been "victimized" are listed as incontrovertible proof of Nature's lethal animosity toward humanity. It is easy to see, from these fundamental elements –even tho civilization has failed utterly to qualify them in any Universal sense (or really even to try)– just how and why the civil worldview was enthroned in its wide and paranoiac entirety.

And finally. That belief in a "cruel god" or "cruel gods" must lead to a hostile and paranoid view of Nature and instinct –must lead to a hostile and paranoid view of the World/Universe– is herein considered an unambiguous given. Thus this thesis avoids the deity factor, purposely avoids those multifarious numinads (concepts of deity) which ALWAYS underlie how we humans view Nature and instinct. For the present thetic has decided: Whether civilization came to view Nature/instinct as predator/enemy because of belief in a "cruel god", or in "cruel gods", can only serve to cloud or blind with (unnecessary) passions an issue which can be highly instructive (code: perhaps even save our sorry civil arses) without resorting to tossing any invented or intuited elements (ie, numinads) into an already deity-cluttered arena.

These fundamental elements fixed, we return to my shorthand.

civil v. Natural

That which civilized us, and which keeps us civilized, exists in the twilite region of our personal and social unconscious. I maintain, our fundamental belief that Nature ε instinct are not on the side of humanity, and that they behave like enemies of humanity, is rooted in a "misty mid-region" of our cognition, a state of existence uncannily represented in the french phrase for dusk: *entre chien et loup*, which, fascinatingly, transliterates as 'between dog and wolf'. And it is for this reason one must view civilization as *emotionally* enabled in us. For it appears that the subjective ignorance which renders us civilizable in the first place operates in the same realm of cognition w/in which most of our fears operate. To wit: We are able to approach, even touch, the snake curled around the girl at the handsOn zoo. Yet should we wake in the middle of the nite and find that same snake wrapped around us not her, most of us would view the event w/ horror for the rest of our days. This reveals the emotionally-based foundation of our civilizing principle.

So it will be when, in a moment, i present the snake of my argument to the reader w/in the pettingzoo of this book. Some will be quick to boast, "See me approach, even touch, your civilizing principle. There! You see? That I can do so any time I please clearly proves, your silly principle is *not* what drives me to be civil. And since I do not fear Nature or instinct it is clear, I could not possibly think they are the enemy". Yet should the same reader awake in the middle of the nite, realize sHe was just wrapped in the heaving ε panting coils of some fantasy which civil belief calls "immoral unethical indecent" or (the gods-of-civility forbid!) "illegal", and that sHe was nonetheless loving every minute of it ...maybe even leaning over a real bedmate to see if her/his cries of ecstasy, still ringing in his/her bonemarrow, had perhaps (O God!) been heard...! But let us leave our shaken dreamer in his/her scramble for that state of civil denial beneath which sHe is accustomed to burying such truths of the Self. For, personally, i have met facetoface the cause of our many hypocrisies —having seen upclose the deadly flames ε noxious smoke in its mad civil eye, having put my hand ε ear upon the cold iron pulse of its apocalyptic heart— and so find myself incapable of the usual civil response. Quite the contrary, i find i must tell what i have seen, share what i have suffered, in pursuit of fearless fidelity to the facts.

a procatalepsis: from the preface to "the civilizing principle"

...Schock's argument is *not* saying, fear of nature/instinct is unnatural, for at several points in these pages he states, "The fear of Nature/instinct is Natural in us". Yet he quickly adds, "But only to the degree that a little knowledge can be a dangerous thing and a little paranoia is *always* dangerous. Here the analog of the little fish in a big ocean fits well. Our perception of Nature/instinct as an ever-menacing enemy is equivalent to the little fish so busy seeing danger everywhere that it fails to see the role which the water all around it (the ocean itself) plays." Schock explains: "Such a level of intelligence only feeds paranoia in such creatures. Such a deficit of intelligence also keeps certain 'fish' from knowing to swim to the center of the school for increased safety, or knowing how to slip into a properly small place for a little peace of mind ...if not for a taste of a little feral wisdom: a moment in which to intuit all that is "good" (life-affirming) about its environment."

So when Schock claims that "Civilization is the story of an apocalyptic misconception", he is *not* saying that "this misconception is an *un*-Natural conclusion to come to. It is not. It is an entirely Natural stage in understanding". Schock goes on to reason, however, "Though the civilizing principle is not an unNatural prejudice, the limited state of knowing which permits such a wrongheaded idea is the *same* limited mindset which has proven itself (via the history of civilization) to be the perfect metaphor for the aphorism: 'A little knowledge can be a dangerous thing'. I would at once change that aphorism to read: Knowledge in *any* amount, small or vast, lacking an equivalent dose of wisdom (seeing the Universal picture), is indeed a dangerous thing."

This leads Schock directly into relating one of this writer's personal favorites. *"Of course* schools of small fish display seeming paranoid behavior. But at the same time, it's been repeatedly documented that the great whales (before the advent of the whaling ship)—like most of Nature that had never seen a human, and like all societies untouched by civilization—displayed not a single cell of paranoid awareness in their bodies. And why not? Among all of Earth's creatures, the great whales have been ruminating (unfearing) on the wide waters of our Planetary home since the time of the dinosaurs, gazing at the stars by night and knowing –in every ounce of their large beings, *knowing*– the wide sea and the wide World around them is a marvelous and life-affirming thing. So which of these worldviews is the more correct, the more evolved? To have just enough knowledge to see danger and enemies everywhere or to have the wisdom to see the wider picture: to glimpse Nature/instinct in at least *some* of its life-affirming magnificence? And most amazing of all: The choice to see danger and "evil" everywhere, or to see at least some of the life-affirming wonders of this Planet and its Universe, is *completely* ours to make. To update an old saw: There is nothing keeping us from wisdom but fear itself." [Denise Norris, paleoanthropologist, from the preface to NS' "The Civilizing Principle: A misconception of apocalyptic dimensions". —Ed.]

long ago, in a faraway land, a fear & hatred for Nature & her numinads thundered out of the north like the end of the world....

Even as Nature ε instinct are facts of existence, that thing which civilized us (the civilizing principle) is only *one* of humanity's hundreds of theories of existence, most of them *pre*-civil. Sorry to report, that same principle has annihilated almost all those *other* theories. And sorrier still (sorrier than i'll ever bore the reader w): That theory is not only a concept born of ignorance ε paranoia, it is wrong. Apodictically & apocalyptically wrong!

is the problem entirely too basic, too obvious?
Is that why we deny it?

In that i'm sure i seem to my reader unduly hard on civilization i should state uptop: Civilization is not an absolutely negative phenomenon. Because we civil at times intuit that something like the civilizing principle skulks in the shadows of modern culture, and that this masked mandate [sic] which rules our lives may well be a horribly destructive thing —because, in short, some of us insist on doubting that Nature/instinct is our enemy— we civilized are not always antiNature in our pursuits. The rise of the environmental movement, in the midst of a powerful market-driven (antiNature) establishment, is by far the best example of this civil doubt which many of us intuit and a few of us are ready to stand behind.

In a sane paradigm (in a more objective worldview) the lifeworks of such as francis of assisi montaigne rousseau turgenev emerson thoreau john muir & their likes would have precipitated an avalanche of environmentalism. They didnt. Not even close. Things had to get infinitely worse for even a fraction of humanity to see there might be a problem w our civil approach to existence.

This is why the enviro movement did not appear til the warning flags of rachel carson's silent spring went up in the 1960s. But this movement failed to develop into the revolution some have mistakenly labeled it. (A true revolution would not only have recognized the septic sewer civil man has made of our Planet, it would have, by necessity, revolutionized our ideas about civilization as well.) Fact is, quite the opposite has come about. Since carson sent up her "early" flags of incipient doom, civilization has forged ahead w making the world environment exponentially more toxic & inhospitable to life. That is not just a failed enviro movement, that is a crushed & totally humiliated movement.

What then, exactly, is it which is repeatedly stopping in its tracks, and often reversing the direction of, a proposition which is afterall simple commonsense? What is it that keeps demanding ever more proof that caring for one's environment is really the constructive way to live? (Apodictum: Since all healthy creatures refuse to soil their nests... conclusion: ...one must agree, environmentalism [Planetary-nest hygiene] is not all that difficult a concept.) Summarily, how can something so obviously constructive as environmentalism be impossible to effect among a species which is at all intelligent? The answer is really quite simple —tragically simple at fact. The percentage of human's who can see the flaw in what has civilized us (the civilizing principle) is entirely too low for an environmental revolution to take hold ...or to support *any* sort of paradigmic revolution. (Of course the prigoginic bifurcation which our very denial (that something is lethally amiss) is forcing, could make human suffering ghastly enuf where the necessary gouldian leap in our ability to face Reality might occur. The problem w this solution is, the damage we have done sofar will take millions of years to undo in any sense larger than a cockroach!) Anyway, back to the question, what's our real stickingpoint? —eg, what's really keeping us from finding, exposing & indicting our doom-bedamned dedication to the civilizing principle?

If all healthy creatures know not to soil their nests, what does that tell us about our species' lack of will to insist on a clean environment? If not for us then for our children?

Our biggest impediment is this. Even those of us who can see that the civilizing principle is lethally degenerate, face an even greater hurdle. That hurdle? The infrastructure of the civilizing principle is so colossal –having been worked on arduously almost since the last ice age– it underpins just about everything we civil know of and just about everything we believe in! —incl'g the very tools we need to expose its apocalyptic agenda! Tools like what? Tools as fundamental as the very language we use to express ourselves. Things have gotten *so* bad in this area that even basic terms, terms which should be ideologically antagonistic —terms like World (Earth) and civilization, terms in fact which should be our 'mortal enemies'— we have, all of us, sunk to using interchangeably! Our ability to value things objectively is SO inverted (has become so polarly politicized) that we can say, never entertaining the slitest doubt, "You know, the world's really goin ta hell". We parrot such civil propaganda every day wout it ever occurring to us what's really happening to the world: "Civilization has bound itself for "hell" and is dragging the world [planetEarth] with it!" *That* is the actuality. Yet we see it not. Not even close. And we who might, dare not speakup. For it strikes even us as preposterous that such a remove from Reality&Truth as we live in every day of our lives could come to pass among so "obviously intelligent" a species as ours.

As to the specular querist side of me, my ruminist side insists: We who are born so late into civilization's cumulative blunders need question <u>everything!</u>

And so the specular querist & ruminist can only conclude: When what we think is Reality is at fact its very opposite, what hope is there for corrective analysis muchless corrective action? Obviously, none. So if i comeoff a bit cynically when it comes to things civil, it is the utter hopelessness of the matter which has drained much of the rosy coloring from the lenses of my worldview. Please accept my most earnest apology for this choice i've made. That making nice toward things civil is very much like trying to forgive the tormentors & killers of one's loved ones (aye, of one's very Planet), will, i suppose, be viewed as a poor excuse.

but is it...?

...a poor excuse, i mean?

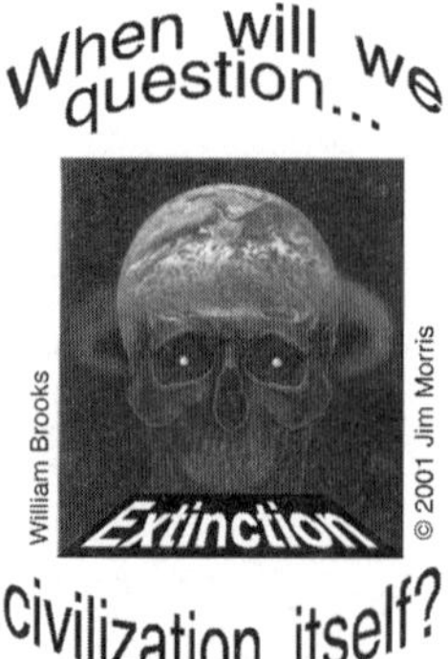

civilization: a rough-draft familytree

all animals including homo sapiens sapiens and his various homo- & hominid ancestors = hunter/gatherers (for ~ 3.3 billion years*)

*None of our ancestors, all the way back to our microorganismic beginnings, were shepherds or farmers. All were hunter-gatherers.

If the ~3.3 billion-year history of life is made to equal ten years, the upright-walking phase of humanity would have begun only a couple minutes ago and civilization itself only seconds ago! Yet to this ultrabrief experiment we call civilization we have sworn not only our lives but the lives of our children and the destiny of all life on Earth! To press blindly ahead never asking, "Is there something *fundamentally* wrong with the agenda of civilization?", as we have been doing for thousands of years now, is of course certifiably insane behavior. For if we trouble to test a drug or a weapon which can harm 'only' a few thousand lives, how can we fail to test this experiment, civilization, which is not only fully capable of annihilating all Earthly life bigger than a cockroach, but appears locked onto doing exactly that.

homo sapiens: hunter/gatherer ---> herder ---> farmer ---> producer

Nomad herders require great amounts of territory. They are however likely to control their birthrates due to hardship and what a transient lifestyle will support. In that such cultures relocate cyclically they allow Wilderness to replenish. The farmer, by contrast, encourages population growth via dependable food supply and other perks of geostasis. Such growth requires ever more territory on a permanent basis while keeping ever more people on hand to protect and propagate this unremitting expansion. Because such populations rarely depart, Wilderness gets no opportunity to reestablish or replenish itself and remains ever under the assault of this pernicious expansion.

nomad types

hunter/gatherer

Lighter footprint on Wilderness than that of herder because hunting & gathering sustains mostly people not their herds. In north america there is some indication that the white man's genocidal onslaught may have interrupted the plains Indian's transition from hunter/gatherer to bison herding.

herder

Heavier footprint on Wilderness than that of the hunter/gatherer. For Wilderness has not only to sustain the herder but his herds too, which are hugely impactful when used as a primary food source. Carnivores require the destruction of approximately 60% more Wilderness than vegans.

*None of our ancestors, all the way back to our microörganismic beginnings, were shepherds or farmers. All were hunter-gatherers.

nutshell history of primitivism/civilization

secular objectivism

scientific method cleansed of civilizing & anthropic biases✓✓✓✓

including civil religion's catechism that the Universe (Nature) is "evil". At this level, humanity discovers Nature/instinct is not the enemy but the very structure & sustenance of life, and that therefore the basic premise on which civilization was founded is flawed & in dire need of revamping. Only at this level of understanding can effective equality for females & peoples perceived as primitive begin. This would include equality for ALL living things (biophilia) since Nature & instinct are no longer seen as the enemy.

✓✓✓✓possible philosophic stance for humanity, though one which seems frighteningly remote lacking a lesson of globally catastrophic scale ---some Natural ultimatum which even an idiot can't deny or misinterpret.

future ↑

---

past ↓

civilization & establishment (civil) religion
(a marriage of convenience [politics] not love) ✓✓✓

There can be no love in this union because civil religion sees all the Universe (incl'g the civilized world) as "evil". (Only a "place" called paradise/heaven is believed free of "evil".) Still civil religion stoops to call civilization a "good" thing because it is "better than" the alternative: polytheism & primitivism. Civilization, in return, permits civil religion because it so absolutely condemns Nature/instinct (& primitivism/femaleness), and thus reinforces civilization's fear of Nature/-instinct by threatening all who revere it (idolaters & infidels, etc) with eternal damnation: eternal refusal of admittance to "paradise/heaven".

✓✓✓ Ties that bind: Both partners are paranoic (see enemies everywhere. the one in Nature, the other in an "evil" universe) & both are therefor imperialist (need for absolute control: civilization controlling an "irrational & cruel" world; civil religion controlling an "evil" cosmos.

civil religion declares war on polytheism
monotheism's "all other gods are false" is the grandaddy

of absolute intolerance. As the ultimate form of dissent repression (by way of threat of "eternal damnation" for non-believers), civil religions elevate civilization's fear of Nature/instinct (as well as its fear of primitivism & femaleness) to the metaphysical by condemning them as "evil" Meanwhile polytheism (ideological tolerance) is indicted as Nature/instinct-friendly and for that is condemned above all other "evils".

rise of civil religion

The dogmatizing of Nature/instinct as bad & civilization as good, incl'g the categoric demonizing of primitiveness (pagan idolaters) & of femaleness (as conveyors by birthright of "evil") & incl'g the metaphysical coopting of civilzation's fear of Nature/instinct into a paradigm which claims "evil" (Nature) is an actual Universal force.

early civilization

Humanity's earliest attempts to escape what it perceives as cruel & irrational Nature. Earliest forms of left-brain dominance. Protopolytheism✓✓ had long been a global "institution" in the sense that humanity had by then spread its primitive gods & demigods to almost every continent.

primitive humanity

polytheistic & right-brain dominated✓

✓✓earliest forms of "All that helps me is good and all that hurts me is bad", a belief system still very much in place today! Protopolytheism is simply this belief system ascribed to unseen forces: eg, "good" gods, "bad" gods.

✓ humanity qualified as primitive for ~5 million years... ~10 million, if inclusive of all hominids, whereas civiliz. has been in existence only 1/100th as long. The 4-billion-year evolutionary chain from which humanity sprang also qualifies as primitive.

back to the primitive? absolutely not

As to the response, "Would you have us all go back to living in the jungle?" I cant decide if this is the rhetoric of repressed fear or naked idiocy. (The baron would say, "Fear". Lilith, "Definitely both!".) Without going into the stoicheiological causes of my skepticism of all things civil... at no time is my anti-civil argument meant to imply a return to primitive existence. For even the most Nature-adjusted primitives would not go back to a primate lifestyle. But that doesnt mean this crucial lesson, the deadly error of the civilizing principle, should be lost on us, or that the tailend of this great tragedy called civilization should not be reversed where possible.

But then, i believe for this to happen on any effective scale will require first a lesson in great suffering —largescale human suffering. For the writing has been on the wall for ages —graffitied in blood, pre- ε protocivil blood, scrawled as warning on the *outside* of the walls of civilization. And what these heart-wrenching mxs have been pleading is news only to those of us who fear to set foot outside those walls.

Get primitive! The cause of the common (civil) criticism "get real" should be obvious. Civilization (antiNature + anti-instinct) = antiReality (rejection of the Universe as given by Nature). Thus, to really begin to "get real" is to first 'get primitive'. Not incidentally, the concept 'unreal' (non-reality) strikes the primitive mind as pointless. How totally revealing then that we civilized should liveout our entire lives under conditions which the primitive mind views as pursuit without REAL meaning!

Since publishing in '84 *the civilizing principle: a misconception of apocalyptic dimensions*, i have stated repeatedly: Personally, i have only to imagine myself sitting in a Wilderness shelter somewhere trying to figureout how to construct an effective insect screen out of coconut fibre ε tree sap; i have only to imagine being rain-locked in such a house staring at my sound library knowing i'll never be able to extract the zizm-elevating music of sibelius dvořák mahler berlioz schubert or massenet locked win it.... Yes, i have only to imagine any number of such scenes to reaffirm: I am not now, and never have been, in favor of the fervent ε often careless (directionless) primitivist movement which my *cp* unleashed. For i did not expose the civilizing principle in order to hurl us all back into some purist version of the stone age. Civilization's going to accomplish that w no help from me. (Well, maybe not the purist part.) My purpose was&is quite the opposite. My civilizing principle is advanced (not as a weapon against all that is civil but) as a tool for reconstruction once civilization has fulfilled its down-spiral into one ghastly global devastation or another ...all this providing, of course, any of my readers survive the apocalypse which our civil credo is all too rapidly manifesting. For those overly-protected civĺlizens reading this: Yes. I am *really* serious.

paranoia/civilizing-principle link

Any creature that can survive a paranoiac environment is civilizable. And any creature which thrives in such an environment will serve to propel civilization (ie, blunder ahead with the apocalyptic agenda of the civilizing principle).

For understanding's sake, let's assume the civilizing principle is an objective analysis of Reality. If it were, if Nature were indeed humanity's predator/enemy (and not his best nurturer/sustainer), and if Nature cannot be otherwise than everywhere –win us ε outside of us wherever we are– then it follows, such a worst predator/enemy must be "everywhere". If such a paranoid worldview did not in fact cause the civilizing principle, could the belief that one's worst enemy is everywhere lead to anything less than a state of ambient paranoia? And has not civilization proven to be a chronic incubator of pandemic angst?

...unfailing nurture for every nanosecond in every atom of our existence!

Examine, for a moment, those popular expressions, "defeat", or "conquer", gravity. Since both defeat & conquer require weakening disabling or crippling, it is clear we fail totally to grasp the gravity of, or even to care to grasp the gravity of, what we are hoping for every time we teach another generation (code: another three billion young people) to entertain such careless concepts.

The "sound" of gravity is at once so deep & so high it shakes the entire Universe like a handbell! ...and yet, between the stars, our civilly crippled ears can discern only "mute" nothingness.

For no one, not teacher or leader, ever ruminates on what, at fact, is being taught every time we subliminally instruct: "The conquering, or defeating, of gravity is not only an amazing achievement, it is often exciting beside!" (Code: "Rockets planes skydivers bungee developers and particle-accelerators are just a few of the mod techs teaching gravity a lesson it won't forget.") Such teaching is of the same destructive order as the everyday belief, "The World is crazy", passing the horrific ε tragic onus of what we civilized have done to "the World" on to Nature wout a smidgen of the culpability due us. For gravity, in fact, is the only force we know of which, uninterruptedly, connects each&every particle of us to every particle in every nook&cranny of the entire Universe! So completely connective & supportive is it, one might properly view gravity as the very skeleton ε nervous system of Mothernature herself! (See my *Ecocosm: the cosmic Gaia.*)

And as if this pea-brained oversight of ours werent enuf... Should any one of us, in humanity's inexorable pursuit of one day defeating or conquering gravity, ever manage, even accidentally, to do so (even for one second!), not 'just' Earth, and our own bodies, but the entire Universe, will collapse around the ears of what we're teaching as "exciting achievement"! Finally, until such time as our destructive antiNature agenda is exposed in the classrooms of civilization, i highly recommend calling it what it is: ARROGANT & IMBECILIC. For such terms, capitalized on this page or even scrawled among the stars, can never undo all the (yes) arrogant imbecility which the civilizing principle has spewed for millennia, an apocalyptic plague, across this paradise, Earth.

Civilization is, at root, no less than a paranoid reaction to existence —to Nature itself.

how did religion manage to hijack the civilizing principle?
(or: "...The incunabula of the divine grotesque")

A few months after my *civilizing principle* was published, *gynalept* (self-appointed "erudite zine for men") asked me to write an essay on my thesis. After several attempts to resuscitate what i'd failed to synopsize for my own publisher, i wrote *gynalept's* eic: <Cramming a critique of civilization into a mere 600-page book was crippling enuf. To try to cram it into a 3000-word essay would be to draw&quarter a cripple.> Obviously too close to my subject –yet knowing how much the zine could help to spread my mx– i sought help from the only person who felt equal to the task. After interviewing me at least once daily by fone for weeks the baron wrote, in interview format, the following (necessarily) ultrabrief analysis of my thesis.

[For considerations of space, P.J. Falk's questions are omitted. —Ed.]

At first glance what we call civilization appears to be evolutionarily inevitable for any organism having sufficient intelligence. Yet further reflection suggests this may not be so. In that civilization arose in some cultures and not in others, and in that some cultures, even those possessing considerable existential wisdom, passionately resist civilizing, renders highly unlikely the suggestion that civilization is a genetic inevitability of evolving intelligence.

In another way of speaking, it is not at all obvious that an organism, on having attained a certain level of intelligence, will Naturally set out to take aggressive action against the hazardous Nature of its environment while, at one and the same time, cementing, for all to see, the insufficiency of that intelligence. I reference how obvious it is (or should be) that that "certain level" of intelligence which we, civil humanity, have achieved, while fixated on the many hazards of Nature, has, simultaneously, failed absolutely to recognize the preponderance of nurturing and support afforded us, and all lifeforms, by none other than Nature itself.

Because of this distinct disparity in how we evolve —with many cultures passionately resisting civilizing for generations on end, with many even preferring obliteration to joining— one is wise to stay clear of viewing civilization as evolutionarily imperative. For civilization appears to be a developmental offshoot attractive mostly to the more fearful individuals of our species. This developmental stage —where a small portion of humanity stood up, in a way of speaking, surveyed what it could understand of the world, and decided to take aggressive action against what it read as a hostile (rather than nurturing) environment— for the purposes of argument, i have given a name. I call it the civilizing principle. Oversimply stated it reads: Nature is a predator/enemy of humanity.

While a worldview that sees Nature as our enemy might impress a baboon or chimp, should we feel confident it would impress an orangutan or gorilla quite as much? I say this because, the civilizing principle has clearly been rejected, or bypassed, by most human cultures, some of them at least equal, if not superior, in existential wisdom and cultural accomplishment to our own. One might even hazard, civilization (the civilizing principle) was, and still is, passionately resisted by most calm and content (code: happy) cultures. More to the point, isn't the paranoia in perceiving Nature as predator/enemy obvious to a wise form of intelligence? Yet my purpose is not to answer this, only to posit the question.

It is, or should be, historically clear. Primitive cultures view and value Earth and the Universe very differently from civilized ones. Where the primitive feel the superior society makes choices which lead to the greatest state of contentment for all, we civilized feel the superior society is that one which possesses the most power (ie, the best weapons. Civil history makes this point perfectly clear, irrespective of what we personally may wish.) This is an obvious outgrowth of a worldview which sees Nature (all that is not civil) as humanity's predator/enemy. It rather goes without saying, one feels justified in annihilating whatever one views as his predator/enemy. ("Since it's always trying to get us, why don't we just get it first?") Whether it's a "preemptive action" against another nation or society or culture, or the wiping-out of wolfs, bears and snakes, such actions spring from the same mentality: existential angst. (Consider what level of angst a society must suffer from when it, by choice, possesses enough weaponry to turn the surface of our Planet to ash three times over!) In such a pathologic state of paranoia the elimination of just about anything one terms uncivil looks like a "divine right". It is in fact such a cosmosophy which renders civilization the very epitome of imperialist aggression. (Cosmosophy: any philosophy which attempts to embrace the Universe.)

One hopes, amidst all this, it can hold without elaboration that, just as no society of lifeforms (as we understand life) is, or can ever be, completely civilized, neither can any culture be entirely free of the civilizing principle: ie, free of those insecure (paranoid) individuals who can never be convinced that the urge to possess a better weapon than one's neighbor is destructive to the social contentment of all.
—Nathan Schock

A plethora of degenerate endings: The degenerate endings which civilizations repeatedly bring upon themselves should be enough to convince even those of us in the most jaded state of denial of the disaster innate in continually framing Nature/instinct as the enemy. We've been practicing the civilizing principle (Nature/instinct is our predator/enemy) for at least 8,ooo years now and the endings only get worse! I know our history books tell very little about causes –fundamental causes– but singingDao, let's get a grip! This concept isnt all that difficult —not at this late date it isn't. From where i sit, civilized humanity is clearly on the slippery cusp of finalis in extremis!
——Nathan Schock

Developing in parallel with civilization is what we will call civil religion. Whereas the primitive priestess or shaman is the one who sees to the *spiritual* contentment of the group, so the civil shaman or priest is the one who justifies, in a spiritual sense, the civilizing principle: Nature and instinct are enemies of humanity. It was these monastic societies which, by much trial and error over thousands of years, managed to transform all of Nature into a (completely invented) condition called "evil", a state from which one could escape (to heaven/paradise) only if he put complete faith in what the civil shamans instruct. Still more perverse even than the invention of universal "evil" however was the civil shaman's careful and gradual amendment of the civilizing principle. It is this amendment which set into motion the eventual rise to power of religion as an institution within, and often in charge of, the state. Whereas the civilizing principle up til that time was definable as,

Nature is the predator/enemy of humanity,

and whereas the energies of earliest civilization were focused on the Natural dangers existing *outside* the human body, and *outside* the walls of civilization, along came the civil shamans claiming that humanity's predator/enemy also lies *within*, resides *inside* of us, WITHIN the very *Nature* of our being! The insidious suggestion being, if we think Nature *external* to us is dangerous, what about that part of Nature which exists *within* us? Namely, human instinct. What of the dangers in this *personal* manifestation of Nature?

In the book i address the pernicious politicking which permitted shamans of the various civil religions (monks priests prophets the like) to rise to power under the noses of the authorities of the day (the state and protostate), we can here plumb straight to the *end result* of all that surreptitious scheming, set out the civilizing principle as amended by civil religion:

Not just Nature but instinct too is our enemy, being Nature *inside* us.

The easiest route to denial, of course, is to view civilization as evolutionarily inevitable —to simply see ourselves as the fish smart enough to be wary of its predators yet too stupid to see the innumerable blessings inherent in its watery environment. But it is not so easy to view the rise to power of the various civil religions in the same developmentally inevitable light. In fact, for this writer, the plainly vengeful and antisocial politics invented by these celibate family- and female-loathing intellectuals strongly suggests a powerfully UNnatural element, an influence sinisterly and bloodthirstily (when "necessary") inserting itself into human history. I say this because, the degree of self-loathing and paranoid pathology required to view not only one's inmost being, but the *entire* World around him, and the Universe around it, (Eg: every thing and everywhere!) as foul and dangerous (code, "evil"), should strike even a *slightly* sane intellect (as i strive to be) as a wholly *UNnatural* twist on Darwin's *Natural* selection. Yet, be these things as they may....

While both common sense and our best science preponderantly discredit Nature or instinct as being humanity's enemy, so the civilizing principle has proven globally destructive not for what it claims but for the many nurturing and sustaining aspects of Nature that it *fails* to award. That is to say, the civilizing principle is lethal more by omission than commission. For it fails to state what civil science itself has proven: Nature is humanity's most nurturing and supportive ally. In fact, civil science has established beyond any doubt, if Nature were to withdraw its support for even a second –one second, reader!– not only us but *everything there is* would collapse to a state highly unsupportive of life as we know it. Therefor, if civilization did indeed believe in telling "the whole truth and nothing but" as it claims, it would not continue to repress the healthy and constructive side of the *whole* story —a side, not incidentally, which any primitive (and every other form of life) not only understands but lives by intuitively.

Forensic anthropologists working mass graves all over the world have little doubt: Civilization & civil religion have given humanbeings (That's us, guys & gals!) a reputation that is Universally loathsome!

[In conclusion.] Even in our "realized" and "highly intelligent" state (i like to point out) one can't watch an hour of TV without seeing Nature badmouthed at least once. How can an intelligent being, i would like to know, watch hour-on-hour of films about floods tornadoes ferocious animals deadly plants tidal waves cyclones earthquakes volcanos asteroid extinctions and the like and never pause to think about (muchless marvel at) the qualities in Nature that are supporting *his very existence*, as well as the Universe around her, from commercial to commercial? By the long depressing shadow of this fact alone, to apply to ourselves the terms "realized" "advanced" and "intelligent" is clearly not only jaded denial, it is insane. For whenever we fail to see Reality (things as they Really are) we are, by definition, insane.

It should be obvious as well, for one to tirelessly view Nature in this exclusionary and negative way is to fear the entire Universe. For we know, if only intuitively, the term Nature includes (by the imperative of functional extension) the *entire* Universe. And finally, would we not call paranoid-insane any person who told us, "Be careful! Look out! Danger is lurking everywhere!" Or, in the sense of civil religion: "Look out, pilgrim. Evil is everywhere! Even inside of you!" Yet this is exactly how we live our civil existences. These are the very premises upon which we and all our major institutions proceed daily, hourly. And those who view the world as a benevolent miracle in which we are fortunate to share for even a moment, them (the primitive and protocivil) we label "naive" or "foolish" or, in purest pc: Reality-compromised! Imagine thinking such a thing when it is *we* civilized in FACT who are Reality-compromised …and to a degree that is, for this writer, almost incomprehensible!

And finally, if i may: That only a handful of my six billion sisters and brothers –gobbling up with hardly a care their childrens' very future as we speak– will have any interest in what i've just outlined, for me, tells the entire tale to its bitter end.

[End *Gynalept* interview of November 1984. Topic also addressed in Part 2. —Ed.]

the civilizing principle reflected in civil institutions

≈The chatter of our institutions would persuade us to despise Nature.≈ —emerson

All the key institutions of civilization are innate & inevitable in the civilizing principle. First comes law. (Defining the new cataNatural rules & expectations). Then, writing. (One needs record for future re conclusions & decisions which do not come Naturally and are not automatically understood, remembered & obeyed by the majority of living things.) Lawyers/judges. (The domesticating [civil] regimen requires persons fluent in cataNatural law.) Libraries. (Begun as places for keeping a record of the necessarily increasingly convoluted cataNatural law.) Police. (Persons who enforce cataNatural law.) Prisons. (Places for isolating/punishing those resistent to cataNatural law.) Psychiatrists ε psychologists. (Persons dedicated to rationalizing the many conflicts which inevitably arise when invented ideologies [cataNatural laws ε expectations] are forced upon creatures reared for hundreds of thousands of years (if not millions) under Natural law.) Insane asylums. (Places for isolating/punishing persons pathologically destabilized by cataNatural rules ε expectations.) Civil religion. (Spritual institutions which most support the civilizing principle [cataNatural law].) It is no accident that nosuch institutions are present or necessary in pristine primitive society or in Wilderness.

Only a wide & deep study of primates & primitives can teach us where civilization went wrong. Abandon hope once their existence (in the Wild) is compromised. And this, tragically, is the case as i write.

civilizing principle: a wrap

Civilization ε its coöpter, civil religion, together represent the most elegantly thoro misconception ever putforth in the history of our species. And while a misconception need not, of itself, lead to a negative result, the elements of *this* misconception are such that, so long as we believe them true, they can lead only to pandemic disaster. For the civilizing principle is apposed (in principle [hic]) to ANY other outcome. But because we're unaware that the principle by which we're civilized is cumulatively septic *at its source,* every sip of civility we take, no matter how small and seeming-sweet, can only further toxify our systems. And it will remain thus until we identify absolutely the *principle* of belief which is poisoning that source: the civilizing principle.

Dont let the colors of the feathers when they fly blind you to what the battle is *really* all about. For underneath the featherdressing civil leaders are all the same. A congressman is a president. An mp is a primeminister. A general is a dictator. A bishop is a pope. A pastor is a priest. A monk is a mullah. A terrorist is a soldier. An imam is a rabbi. Bigcorpx are states and their ceos are kings & assorted royalty, just as nations are kingdoms. They are all the same; all cut from the same masking-cloth; all offspring of the same paranoia & aggression which civilizing automatically grooms; all one single sick & bloodied elite minority battling over one single thing: Who gets to run (control) the World, who gets to rule (control/enslave) the masses; in other words, who gets to own you&me, my reader! And of course, getting us caughtup in the colors of their feathers is the soul of the game. Warning! Just by *choosing* a feather-color we step off the banks of perspective and into the sucking deeps of civilization's rush to apocalypse!

The BIG question is, and long has been: Whom among us can be fritened beyond our inborn wisdom of conscience & commonsense? For it is THOSE among us who must choose a flag-color, a god-color, to hide behind, who by that choice guarantee our mutual rush to apocalypse.

even little red ridinghood

Having explained how civil religion successfully took what amounted to early humanity's ignorant animosity toward Nature and set about transmogrifying it into a fullblown paranoia of all things Natural, and of all things resembling, imitating, or even attracted to, Nature, we can now state summarily: Following thousands of years of civil/religious politicking, our lives are bombarded every day w myriad antiNature/instinct analogs, sinister propaganda masquerading in harmless finery. I must limit my usual example-cases of antiNature-brainwashing to a single classic: the tale of little red ridinghood. Its storyline would have us believe: We civil humans are guiltless inno-cents bearing gifts to grandmothers (code: persons easily tricked by 'wily Nature'); that the forest (Wilderness) is a dangerous ε fritening place where creatures (Wild animals) w the very worst intentions dwell; and that (to keep it short&sweet) it is females who are most likely to stray from the "safe" civilized path into the "evil" wiles ε clutches of Nature/instinct. Thus, in seemingly harmless dress, the civil/religious paradigm imprints its fear ε loathing of Nature/instinct on us every min of every day, from infancy to death, in thousands of ways —literally!!! But never fear, for whom but a raving ruminist would ever stop to examine (eg: maureen duffy) that in which most of us hope to find absolutely nothing amiss? "Little red ridinghood, you say? Tsktsktsk."

How, 'wayback' when he lived, could emerson have seen: "The end of the human race will be that it will eventually die of civilization." Infinte wow! Has it always been so obvious?

pronoia. a definition

Pronoia is the intuition that Nature ε instinct are conspiring to sustain and nurture all life incl'g us. Pronoia is archantagonist of the civilizing principle.

a little roadrage of our own

If we are not in a REpressed fury (think wanting to vent a little roadrage of our own sometimes) for having always to act so damned civil, we are DEpressed over it —w typically no idea as to why. In fact the very expression just used, expressions we use all the time ("act civil", "be civil"), effectively show our predisposition to know: we are not, any of us, actually civilized —not where it counts, in our essence Selfs. Such expressions as "be civil" ε "act civil" show that we, at the very least, intuit an as-yet-unaltered primitive depth to our humanity —our lastditch saving grace, if i may.

Just as chthophobia (fear of Nature) lies at the heart of the civilizing principle, manicheistic paranoia lies at the heart of civil religion.

the orangutan gene

Would i be sidling out on a limb (w my non-apposable big toes) if i were to say, i intuit in me an orangutan gene? and that i intuit this most personal proclivity in much the same way that i see the hulking shadow of my libido in the bonobos i've known, and my ego in the chimps? In a similar sense i see myself (my Self) in all the orangs i've known. And in 1988, in my book *die, primitive!*, in a short chapter entitled "13 ways of looking at a blacksheep" i said as much. Indeed, to further toy w these speculations concerning our human ε primate ancestry, at one point i confessed to feeling like <...a neanderthal who had, despite all theories of their extinction, survived>. After the book's release i realized this was a mistake. For a humorless ε cultish academe instantly threw me on the same choppingblock it uses to decapitate all thinkers who fail to seek its permission to get thetic in a public place. This vicious (and still ongoing) attack was launched despite the fact i never once claimed there are such things as chimp- ε orang-favoring genes in humans, or that the neanderthals disappeared because, like me ε most primitive peoples, they possessed toomuch of this gentler gene. My "crime" then? To have toyed w these ideas in public –and may i note, for a mere 1.5pp (out of 265) —wout prior permission from academia. So sonorous was the knowledge vacuum which my highflown fun had revealed —not to mention how many people were buzzing about the plausibility of my observation incl'g some severely credentialed academics— i mightaswell have toyed not *with* my genes, but *inside* my jeans, in public. At any hoot, we need now summarize so we can move on.

neanderthal depiction I:
As for the usual academic depictions of earliest man, I have two words for them. Obscene quackery. The most disturbed bonobo I ever studied had more humanity than the typical scholar's concept of a "cave man", which always strikes me as a mean-spirited assault on primatologic fieldwork. —denise norris

neanderthal depiction II:
The standard models of early human beings take none of this [the compassion and intelligent reflectivity of orangutans and primates generally] into account. Most academic models of early humans seem bent on justifying the selfishness and brutality of modern man, not on the discovery of anthropological truths. —biruté galdiska

In 1988 i played w the idea of we humans and our primate ancestors possessing an as yet "undiscovered" ancestor or two in common. This has long been a widely pandered theory. Take richard leakey forinstance. "The genes of Neanderthalers may be surviving in us today." That i chose to put a living mask or two on that supposed lineage was my "heresy", for the masks i chose effectively split that lineage into two discreet, and too entirely palpable, lines of human. My sandbox theory classed primate lineage into two types

—behavioral types. The one i called protocivil, the other, primitive. To clarify yet further i called the former "chimp-bonoboish", the latter, "orang-gorillaish".

neanderthal depiction III: Popular depictions of early humans, with rare exceptions, are clearly striving to put the blame for the emotional wasteland of our modern selves (not onto civilization where it belongs but) onto some flaw in our ancient forebears.

After asking the reader to reflect on how well chimps ε bonobos domesticate and how poorly orangs ε gorillas do outside Wilderness habitat, i went on to speculate (not theorize, for the idea is still quite green in me) how <...those of us possessing what i am calling the chimpnobo gene would rather submit to domestication than die, while we possessing the rangrilla gene would rather hide or die than unWild or deNature ourselves>. I then pointedout how <all persistently-primitive societies fear and resist most forms of civil imperium (aggressive civilizing). Indeed, just as primitive societies are repulsed by civilization generally –just as they cannot envision Nature/instinct as humanity's enemy– so the rangrilla gene innately prefers to shrink from civilization and all the ills it is heir to (lives in fear of our aggressive and often brutal ways and beliefs)>. In an appendix i listed some 250 examples of primitive peoples who consciously, and often over several centuries duration(!), chose to be killed, hide &/or die-out as a culture rather than submit to civil humiliation ε cultural sacrifice. Prime among such cultures are our own rural amerinds ε latindians. (Those who liked my little posit have since uncovered the decline or death of nearly a thousand such primitive or protocivil cultures worldwide ε theorize a history of several thousand!) *Op.cit* i suggested: For an entire people to choose to die rather than become civilized was, or should be, a sobering indication that there just may be two fundamentally very different strains of humanbeing. For persons, muchless entire cultures, can hardly do more than die for their beliefs ...or for their innate differences. (And yes, i am aware of the evolutionary spin this lends to my civilizing principle and that it is anything but detractive.)

Of course my sapiens v. neanderthal, chimpnobo v. rangrilla, *mise en scene* has not one bit to do w intelligence per se. The issue is farmore a case of accessing emotional stability in an unpredictable World; as in: what are one's *Natural* defenses against sliding into paranoia under harsh conditions? Who deals effectively w life's trials ε who melts into existential panic, slipping into destructive conflict w everything around it (the very Universe)? In a nutshell: civil knowledge v. primal wisdom. Peace in the eye of the storm. Healthy fear v. consuming paranoia. One's zizm as dearest friend not fearest foe. Soforth.

Except to say that Lilith couldnt wait to tell me of the bond she (after dian fossey & biruté galdiska) had always felt w rillas & rangs, it is here we will let slide the chimpnobo/sapiens v. rangrilla/neanderthal (rangrillathal) duality. Not because it is implausible but because some thinkers concerned w the problem of why the neanderthals faded so rapidly into historical obscurity have, one by one, since my 1988 book, shown a distinct desire to leap into that anthropologic breach (a breach i merely suggested) shouting "Yes! This deserves analysis!", which is of course no more than a plea for clearance from that <secular church>, academia, to evaluate my suggestions in public ...or like me, risk intellectual burning at the stake via the bruno/velikovsky syndrome.

Paranoia? I'll say! —with each of us possessed by a powerful entity (our subconscious) we've alienated! —and with instinct constantly assuring us we have many predators (for instinct does not yet know we've killed them all) so that, convinced we are <u>still</u> being stalked, we see "predators" EVERYWHERE! Paranoid? I'll say!

why not a lilith mcRangthal & a nathan schockrillathal, and a bunch of us beside?

If for hundreds of thousands of years most of us guys have been 'reduced' to voyeurs sexually speaking —that is, if ever since our primate days we have been relegated to the role of witness while the silverbacks of our multifarious societies kept for themselves all the most desirable females— if this is generally the scene we come from procreatively speaking, imagine being the average sapiens guy who lived at that period of evolution where we could always opt to wander off to the nearest neanderthal band to win a mate of our very own! And is this not exactlybutexactly how the mixing of races most often begins —females bearing the offspring of invaders? If so, then the question should not be whether we have in us neanderthal genes, the question should be: Given that study of primates & primitives shows, 'rangrillathal genes' 'prefer' to dieout than spawn a paranoid lineage, is it possible that the pandemic of paranoia in the history of we whiteys is caused by the very mitigation, or absence, of such a rangrillathal (calming inner-peace) gene in us?

That your average biotum on the street (the average living thing) spends only the weeist fraction of its life (if ever) thinking rationally, and that therein lies the source of equality & justice in the Natural World; that the hallmark of a paranoiac is personality fragmentation; that the absence of paranoia is the hallmark of certain primates & most primitive peoples; that our conscience (our *irrational* sub-conscious) is often the source of our ethics & morality; that the dross of civil rules & expectations has ballooned our personas (and often our bodies too) into gross Self-crushing (id-suffocating) entities; i say that these things taken in sum are cryingout to us, "Hellooooo!". Yet we sleep on.

robin williams on "the clevers & the slaphappies"

"I've read all your books but have you seen all my movies? [gotcha twinkle] ...Here's what I think's the problem. Picture [frames mental scenario with hands] picture all of civilization as two hillbilly clans, the clevers 'n' the slaphappies, both with too many generations of inbreeding. The clevers are the dominant clan. They run the whole damn world. An' the slaphappies? Their job is ta populate the world 'n' ta anyhow-they-can survive!" Robin proceeded to proffer whole continents of neanderthalish li'l abners & daisy maes enslaved by homo sapiens clevers for the sole purpose of creating a surplus of goods sufficient to support this aggressive elitist minority. It was a brilliant ε hilarious exposition. Was it ok to use it in his routines? But of course.... But please do promote the civilizing principle with it.

as to that protean pursuit we call progress

The true never-to-be-had rosegray of civil existence is, i believe, that figment, that fetish, we call progress. That the very definition of progress changes according to what authority you question, and when, should tip us off that something is amiss. What might that be? In the short version: Civil society is kept locked to a heading which stands exactly opposite that direction in which our fundamental humanity (when we allow it to surface) wants us to move. This ab-orientation is fixed for us by the civilizing principle. While it is in our most basic natures to feel, or wish we felt, intimately connected w our deepest Selfs, w our kin as community, and all these connected w Nature at large, the catechism drummed into us from birth warns: What our basic natures tell us is not trustworthy and may be hazardous to our wellbeing. Those of us who resist this warning soon encounter expectations ε laws designed to crush all anticivil (primitive/instinctive) resistence in us. The irony which inheres in our civil condition is: The goal of "progress" remains protean ε largely unachievable precisely because the basic needs (those precivil social fulfillments we long for) which actually *drive* our pursuit of progress, are impediments to achieving it (or so we are warned) and are thus denied us by civil law ε expectation. But more fundamentally, because our idea of progress is *linear* (unrealistically monodirectional & quantity-driven), it keeps us ever in denial of the deeper *cyclic* reality of our Earthly existence.

As this seeming paradox is so vital to grasping the hidden inhumanity of progress (as we perceive progress civilly), it may be worth pausing over s.crane's: "I saw a man pursuing the horizon... I was disturbed at this... 'It is futile' I said, 'You can never—'. 'You lie', he cried and ran on." Thus the old joke, 'You cant get there from here', turns out, for we civil, to be factual. For the progress we *really* long for —ie, freely reciciprocating fulfillment between the elements of Self/family/kin-community/Nature— is denied by the very principle of belief which drives civil progress. This is, of course, just one more indictment of the civilizing principle.

ralph's next-finest waldo

Before on the help of my friend bekky kydd i want to add: Stan diamonde was not the only thinker to come close to formulating a civilizing principle. Emerson broadstroked: ≈Most of the laws which underpin civilization were formulated not only without the input of Nature but often in opposition to it. [and] Civilization may in fact have come about as an escape from Nature, which in our ignorance we still perceive as a malevolent entity. In fact, instinct itself (Nature imprinted in our bodies) probably became the whippingboy of civil religion for similar reasons.≈ Wow! And wow again! And then there's denise norris: "Our sexuality has it's own rules. These in fact are the fount of our bedroom fantasies. That is, instinct trying its wings beyond the clutches of society." Yes, neesy! There are others. Like wordsworth. ≈I bounded wherever Nature led (like a man flying from something he dreads [civil rules & expectations?]) toward that Presence which rolls [inexorably] thru ALL things. In Nature [I found] the anchor of my morality, the anchor of my very being.≈
—*tintern abbey*

the second-saddest thing i ever.... How disheartening to watch my favorite thinkers go about their work. Tho i may value, even cherish, what they are trying to do, i am crushed knowing that even the best of their work will not access the deeply restorative cure we, & our Planet, so desperately need ...not til they recognize, and then set about purging, the fundamental disease. For to continue to look at civilization as if it is a remedy for anything is like trying to cure cancer by injecting the patient with a "new & improved" form of the same malignancy! For civilization is not the cure but the disease. And until we grasp this our Planetarily lethal degeneration will continue unabated.

my aching spirit

To get the wider double-mattressed bed my body's been aching for i signed a waiver agreeing to return to my old cell wout complaint. Tho a dim diminutive dank & dour domain by nite, nite or day there is its window ...ah, its window!... which my spirit has been aching for! Zizm, drink this Wild sky!

Mumia Abu-Jamal

my purpose for part 5

Midway now between my two major theses i ask my reader to pause w me, just long enuf to say: My purpose here is not diversionary disquisition. If anything, it is its opposite: lending some anti-popmedia substance to who we were, Lilith&me; to allow my reader a glimpse of that substrate of purpose upon which our very lives were founded, hers and mine.

bekky profile

Model since age 2, entered in beauty contests from age 9; walkins&walkbys in 11 sitcoms; entered miss usa/teen three times (aged 13,14,15) before winning; was filming her first major role, *the tragedy of treva weldon*, when her exposé hit the streets. Bekky's first book was titled *the miss usa/teen contest & me*. Her second book, *youth for sexual equality*, was named for her organization, "kydds inc: youth for sexual equality", hq'd in monterey ca.

"Kryst, how many times I wanted to jus pack a bag 'n' leave, get out 'n' not look back. The problem was, I was 'too young'. [makes quote fingers] Mother was in a bind. She wanted t' be free of competition on the homefront yet the thing that created it –let's face it, me– also attracted the men. But when hubby number three moved in she got really conflicted. Tho she didnt want me around the house looking sexier than her, at the same time she feared me dating men my own age. She saw in them 'no security 'n' a stupid love-life', all but guaranteeing heartache for me and a series of needy returns home for her.... Sure she protected me, cause she was living her own failed career thru me. Sure she'd castrate any joe who looked crosseyed at me. But why? Hardfacts have taught me, it was for the same reason ya keep 'n' heirloom locked away. Still, when it came t' really powerful 'n' influential people, she mightaswelluv cut me up for bait. Along about that time I discovered, ta stop taking her lip was ta stop biting my own. Really it was a love/hate thing at the end. I was more competitor/bitch than daughter/child.... Youre right. Such conflict *is* Natural. But to what degree, that's the question? [in *yse* she put it:] I've heard of way more compassion in wolves, way less venom in snakes." We had our mothers very much in common, bekky ε me.

teen angst, really?

For 3.5 billion years we've had predators. Species health requires it, be it fire flood tornado earthquake or huge things with gnashing teeth that swoop in without warning ...any ever-present life-threat will do ...and, as many of us are fortunate enuf to be able to forget, one of our greater predators used to be starvation. Life is good (really good) that provides a meal for oneself. But feeding two or more, as adults with offspring must do, for many is still a burden we cannot bear for long. Therefor a nest with offspring who have Wild ideas of their own is a nest too crowded. This is normal. Youths who, like bekky, find themselves "Taking mom's lip while biting my own" are in an unhealthy situation. Only buried malice & suppressed grudges can come of it. And mothers dare to wonder why the father who "didnt care if the kid left home or not" is less maligned than she. Give us a break, worldMatron. You know perfectly well why. The time when prehistoric youth left home to propagate the species (male) or to nest (female) doubtless coincided with parental exhaustion at providing for them. Certain events (like a sense of independence in the young) trigger the clearing of the nest. It's no accident teen angst follows sexual awakening and not the reverse. Raging hormones never get a chance to turn to angst when Nature's agenda is followed. Such angst is just one more illness of civilization —chronic at that.

Bekky left home "for the last time" aged 14, went to live w her sister deb (danzi) in nyc, who was then still on&off w ray zane. An impassioned idealist in less than sympathetic surroundings, a searcher starved for a brand of fatherly affection which zane could not imagine muchless manage, bekky glommed onto deb's boyfriend (me) like a vortex on a vacuum. Tho few in number, my paternal ministrations (incl'g two 2wk summer missions volunteering aboard gE vessels) were of such a quality as to make her sister deb not only wish "you were my dad" but dream of she ε me "someday having a child" ...even tho she was sure she'd make a mother "worse maybe even than me 'n' bek's".

While globe-traipsing w deb's often careening career was, for bekky, educational, what she was exposed to often were "things I wasnt prepared to deal with thanks to my repressive upbringing. And so my youth was alot like that of our [Kydds Inc] matron saint, Treva Weldon, and that of our honorary president, Nastassja Kinczek." Note, bek was "bragging not complaining". For it was a case of: "Do a life of parentless anarchy with my sister or return to a mother and a home in oppressive sexual denial." (Quotes from *yse.*)

Bekky, as one may guess, saw me as a larger-than-life rescuer. It was my books too, of course, which made me her friend; but moreover, the times ε talks we had. Yet oddly, a single sentence of mine came to play a pivotal role in forming what she initially called "My socially fractured philosophy". Not so strange is that it was the same statement which bent, over the years, any number of people into my orbit, many of them as infamous as famous ...like david otlingham, denise norris, orin liselely, charles chaplin ε others. A recounting of my brief (due to his ill health) rapport w chaplin is easily the most enlitening of the lot. Later, time etc allowing.

a wakeup call

As will be seen in part6: Late in 1993, at a most sensitive juncture in my life, i rcv'd a call, followed by a visit, from bekky. Skipping over its startling inception for now, we roundaboutly spoke as follows.

Those women who, for whatever reasons, are uncomfortable w touchyfeely lovydovy, often, knowingly or not, challenge potential lovers to just "take me if you dare", the idea being to rush them into the intimacy they desire minus the "game": the interim discomfort of insincere tenderness etc. Succinctly: for such women ε for bekky (and for most men, need i say), emotional heat was fine but stock dating-etiquette was "psoratic". And so, bekky preferred attractive assertive take-what-you-see-that-you-like men. Her sister's husband, zane, major male influence in bek's pubertal years, was such a man.

When bek visited me just after i met Lilith, when commenting on her latest affair, i said <But your taste in men favors videogames not the classic-movie ending youre afraid to confess you need> she took umbrage. When i added <Ya know, except for your pro sex-rights for youth, your a typical feminist>, more umbrage followed. <I see youve boughtin totally to the dieseldyke's oath: "Females c'n do no wrong only males are wrong." What you need is to meet a wise feminist for once in your life... I mean, b'side me> ...which of course set us off on her war-of-the-sexes again —which is how we endedup visiting alice krawel. (I'm hoping i've mentioned this visit.) And while it may have been my world matron who challenged bekky to move toward deeper answers, it was alice who disarmed her enuf emotionally that such a transformation could begin. Here is a sampling of early bek on men.

"If the statutory stewardship of the sex life of a typical western youth ends at age 18, yet 15-year-olds everywhere are doing at least some of what they please with their bodies (even if it is with cultural shame), then the actual legal age is not 18 at all but 15, and the other three years are for show." Shortly before she met alice i loaned her my copy of kim jankaid's *erotic purity*. At that point in the book when she came upon her own "for show" statement (above), followed by jankaid's response, "Show for whom? To impress whom? And why?", bek called me. "How come you didnt tell me I was in his book?"

To get us where we need to go now, yet not to fritteraway precious time w context, allow me to lurch into the following fragments.

bek's rapprochement w me following a crucial period in her life:

"*He* was chasing *me!* I'll admit, it was a headtrip. Hey, I was young... Thirteen? Fourteen maybe? Somewhere in there. You know zane: tall dark classact. Surrounded almost daily by the most beautiful women on earth ...*physically* beautiful, youre right. B'fore I lived with them I would go there weekends, summers, well, you know. I was an observant little bitch. <An' a beauty too.> I could tell men were looking at me ...I mean in a sexual way. By fourteen I was a kid in name only. At fifteen I looked 18 ...'n' acted twenny. But I didnt really start figuring things out til I unloaded all the vanity ...Okay then, most of it. Only when ya get over all the 'He's trying t' seduce me!' crap do ya begin to see what's *really* goin on." Mnemy remembers her words as more incisive yet i cant inflect it on the page for some reason. "In my book [her first, under pen at the time] I ask the reader to picture several million adult guys sitting before the tube, watching their mate's favorite sitcoms with strangely little complaint. For some reason I can hear the sound of their imaginations squeaking like beds ...You liked that? ...a line from my defunct movie. [she looked wistfully past me] At their best these guys are like zane. That means they sit, legs crossed (this act goes over better if your pose includes wire specs pipe 'n' smokin jacket)... they sit, legs crossed, using newspaper or tv guide as foil, occasionally peering at the screen cajlike, answering the more direct queries with things like `Not bad ...fer a kid'. Fer a *kid?* A *kid?* Well buuuulldooky! Who in hell do they think theyre kidding? Not this kid, theyre not!"

If only our genitals could squeal on us, huh?

"And that's the whole point, isnt it? They cant."

And so that civil thing which reduces we males to our various pathetic states of manners & etiquette (the world matron), bekky ducked ...again.

She rallied a former miss usa/teen winner. (Have i said?) "Shit, it was macrobonzai out there! You have no idea ...how brainwashed these girls are!" She also got the ear of a former miss france, and one each from holland 'n' denmark. Together the brave quintet rallied the interest of a few teen mags. "We started by blowin the whistle on the ceodoms who came onto us most! The press was all over us when our lawyer announced the bottomline: 'Usury (professional, monetary 'n' sexual) of underaged women'. (Now there's an oxymoron for ya: underaged women. The whole dirty scheme exposed in two words!) <Usury by whom?> Sponsors coordinators judges. But we only had hard evidence (pardon my lip) to go after three o' them —when half the damn industry shoulduv been indicted! It was okay to rat on wayward contestants, name a backer, or cite a judge. But when we said the whole damn industry was corrupt 'n' needed investigation, when ilse called beauty contests "maidenhead corrals", or when we called the contests a shopper's paradise for dom's with dollars.... [i couldnt help grinning during this impassioned volley] ...you liked that too? Jus wait'll ya read my new book. Ilse's a neat person.

You'd like her... Anyway, when we started saying we think beauty contest crowns, modeling contracts, are secretly jus carrots for sex, it was toomuch for them... Well, you know. Stuff like: 'I think youve got a good shot at the crown, my dear, depending on whether 'r not' et-cet-er-a."

Isnt that soliciting a minor?

"Duh. The *whole thing's* solicitation, unc! Glorified 'n' nationally sanctioned solicitation. There's always the big unspoken 'And what are *you* ready to sacrifice?' hanging over a contestant's head. Sooner 'r later, like bloody money, it pops up. ...pardon again. [her laff made it stark that she laffed far too little] Allthesudden the newsconference was over. In a matter of hours we couldnt beg, buy or steal media coverage! Not any worth having. It was like, outa nowhere the whole world went black! So help me, it was scary! [she really meant that] They wanted it their way. They didnt want the truth. We were trying to show them something bigger but all they wanted was titillation. One reporter, get this [wait for waiter to clear away dishes. No dessert, thanx.]... one reporter, a woman mind you, said, 'It's like you girls are accusing the whole world of molestation!' Can you imagine? If I knew then what I know now I'duv straightened her fat ass out quick. I wudda said, 'Look around! Maybe we are!' But I was too naive. Right after that we were dropped cold...."

Faster than the mass-rape thing in bosnia. [still occurring as we spoke] I predict this too will become a victim of media blackout.

"I hate t' admit this, but I was almost relieved when they gave up on us. That's how scared I was. I'm still treated like my own ghost in some places. After all the initial media noise, the silence, trust me, was deafening. [tells of menacing fonecalls, unsigned notes] The pressure was unbelievable." The producer [of the movie she was starring in] threatened to pull out. And that's after he'd already sunk over 500 thou of his own stash! [she gazed away. Nice eyes, but not her sister's] "Gimme a reason, a *good* reason, and I will be the only one who stands up for you' he told me one day. Imagine the nerve? That was *his* big 'if', the fat jew bastard. The pressure is fierce, nate. Just fierce. An there's always this secret agenda. You have no idea." (Sorry bek, but i had *yet* to suffer your feeling of infamous alienation.)

Try one more time: <There's a secret agenda against men too you know.>

Her eyes slitted, unready to see males in any way abused by western society. "It's always there. A girl learns early what she's gotta do ta succeed. Treva [weldon] said, 'In this business youve gotta.... Now ya musta heard o' her? [solo violin sounds in memory's large orchestra] A true tinseltown tragedy!" Bekky gazed off behind me. "What was I saying? <Treva somebody?> I know, but what?... O yes. Now there's a girl who came *this* close t' rocking the movieworld. But even she couldnt blow the cover off that jar o' maggots. She arrived too early 'n' was widely feared for her candidness. <The treva in the title of your movie, right?> One and the same. But it was a bambi version by the time it was shot. Didja see it? [i was forever meaning to] I'll send ya a copy. It didnt blast hollywood near enuf. Treva's parents, a couple old actors 'n' a dead director, took the rap for the real culprits. I mean, that whole cesspool of oglemoguls 'n' youth abusers who run the town. Theyre the ones who reallykilled treva... An' gotoff clean-not-a-scratch." Gives background on ms weldon, her era her movies her beauty her blazing life her early death.

A near-likeness? Is that why they chose you [for the lead]?

"I'd like t' think acting-ability had something t' do with it.

<I didnt mean it that way.>

Jus kidding. Most in the business think I look either like deanna durbin 'r sue lyon, not treva. <Sue who?> Now there's two endings that couldnt be more unalike." After explaining durbin's conquest of hollywd & hollywd's conquest of lyon, she returns to "Treva let herself be used —took the abuse inside, let it eat 'er up. I externalize. Maybe the times make it easier fer me. She wrote something you'd like: 'This movie business has weird rules. You rise by taking a dive. Your mom closes her eyes. Your dad, if he's still around, turns his back. And the cast of the movie youre in –plus a hundred people behind the cameras– say, it's up to you now, kiddo. Break a leg. What they mean is, break a law, break a promise, break a hymen if you have to. Whatever it takes, kiddo! Just keep the cameras rolling! Cause when the cameras stop we all starve ...together... you and your parents included."

Another line from the movie?

"No way. Too gutsy. Treva wrote that in her autobio. But nobody printed that part. Sameold sameold."

How old was she?

"Then? Twennysix —the year she died."

Sounds like a laff,clown,laff sorta person.

"She was funny …in a tragic way."

[my point, lost in its own cogency] The destruction of a clown is like the destruction of a child or a primate. It's always tragic. And apparently, in a way of speaking, treva weldon was both.

"They dont care if youre 8 or 80. [does squint which ages her 15years] In tinseltown it comes down to: It's your pride versus our jobs, kiddo! And then, if you go thru with selling yerself, when it's over they say, 'What a little trooper!' When you hear that around you just know youre gonna see yer name in lites!"

Treva again?

"Prettymuch …with a little crashcourse kydd fer zing."

As we talked an exchange occurred that's worth the telling, one of those exchanges which in real life does not interrupt the story yet put to paper here, does. Take a dive? i asked when she used the phrase. Like throwing a match in boxing?

"No, unc. As in, go down on demand. Youre not really surprised I hope? Maybe we should be nicetynice, call them pratfalls? …like alicyn wonderstone? …Youre kidding, you dont? …The girl who jus starred in *coming unglued*? …princesss of cutecore, who giggled 'n' gollied her way into the hearts 'n' hard-ons of cult-male america? Bytheway, the producer of my movie –the slob i told ya bout?– well, he's now the bucks behind alicyn's much-ogled buns. Or maybe I should call him a major cher holder? [she had to explain that too] Youre no fun, unc. Have you seen any movies at all?"

No time. Too busy trying to figureout life itself …as we civil know it.

Bekky was Lilith's polar opposite. She would share the rawest of erotics *w* a minimum of coaxing. But then too, she was more angry than hurt. As she put it, "It helps if you can turn the hurts into rungs in the ladder of life. But the problem is, most o' the time the seduction starts before a girl knows what she wants 'r even what rung she's on. I've known girls who were ringers before they were 14! You think I'm kidding, huh? In this business you learn the way t' the top early."

An' what's that?

"Arnchoo the skanky one t'day?" Bek's smile is her ticket: toothy & fetching; too seldom unleashed offcam. She ran the qualifications by me like a socialsecurity#. "Handjob at 13, headjob at 14, hymen sacrifice by 16. Those are standard. There are variations, of course." On the heels of this she mentioned meeting, at a party in beverly hills, at "the not-quite-tender-not-quite-hardened age of 15", nick jakal, who took her & his guitar aside & sang

I'll give ya the route t' success, miss brown
—if ya wanna make it in tinseltown:
The star that goes up must first go down.

I asked if it were different working for women. "A little better. But it goes on even there. If she's a lez, the pressure's more subtle and the price not so great. But it's still there. A girl's best bet is to work for a gay. I mean a gay guy. Even still, you run into it [secret seduction]. It's hard as hell to avoid. Pretty soon even the gays are hinting you should come over for a drink a hit 'r a snort ...er maybe jus t' watch if youre curious."

Did you ever watch?

"(It *is* a plukefest yer after, isnt it?) Answer's, no. Gays arent my taste in kink.

What is?

"On jus two drinks you ask me that?"

bekky on youth merchandising

"Its cause? Simple. Social-climbing parents ...usually; the temptations of fame and fortune. Of course, lacking an underground network of desire it could not exist. I say, commit to therapy at once any parent who has failed at fame. Such parents often seek vicarious success by merchandising their children. To prove this using Hollywood has been done. First-rate primers are Julie burch's *Teen Tragedies of Tinseltown* and MaryAnn Sincere's *The Nymphet Syndrome in Cinema*." [from bekky's, *yse*]

"The startup of Miss USA/Teen [MUSAT]contest was a major leg-up for this subculture [the "underground network of desire" she was indicting]. Americans had for decades resisted tossing its teens into the same fleshpool with 18-21 year-olds. That was okay for men in Europe, South America, the Mideast, the Orient. But America long resisted thinking of its males as DOM's (dirty old men). But with MUSAT now in place, American males could gawk with impunity while 13- to 17-year-olds paraded near-naked for big prizes and big bucks. The old 'your body as a money-magnet' institution was not only in force from 18 on up in America, it was now alive and well almost from puberty on! Yet this fact does not jibe with the laws of the land, or with the image we Americans like to parade. But wait! Could this mean there's a double standard? Who thinks that this double standard is accidental ought to turn in his driver license." [from bekky's first book, *musat&me*]

Bekky, a smartass? A bit. But it's rare that her hammer doesnt hit squarely. Let us switch momentarily from bek's voice to *the novalis-deland report on human sexuality, 1995*. (More about this titanic tome of social revelation shortly.)

> To convolute the problem [of a prevailing doublestandard], the question, "At what age does sexual choice begin?" is not only hazy (as most judges and prosecutors will tell you), it is in a condition of chaos both nationally and internationally. [my brackets]

The answer is hid in countless places. N-d authors investigated many of these. I quote again.

> This double-standard of statutory versus applied law shows statutory law, on the one hand, maintaining that girls 0-17 (0-21 in some places) are sexually irresponsible, while applied law reflects an age-range of 0-14 generally in the U.S. In many locales around the world what is law and what is practice often disagree widely. In many of these places, where 14 and 15 mark the legal barrier to sexual freedom, the age of consent, in practice, often dips as low as 10 or 11.
>
> On the other hand, many cultures (including our own) routinely parade the bodies of young teens in fashions that are more revealing, more provocative, than what their mothers wear. "Coming of age" is exploited in every media-guise imaginable: On radio in rap and song, in beauty contests, in modeling, in sports, in theater, dance, opera and symphonic music, in soaps and sitcoms, in videos, books, magazines and newspapers, in what are called rockvids and (most aggressively) in the movies: primarily in the dozens of lowgrade R-rated movies released each year,

> which have a large cult following among both youths and adults. And as to television, a widely disproportionate number of sitcoms, without explanation or embarrassment, offer little more than an uninspired exposition of adolescent sexuality. And, when all else fails, enter "the debutante".

One cant but notice, "r" is a rating which, in theory, puts these movies out of reach of the very minds theyre purportedly aimed at! Yet nobody asks the obvious! *Teenrape on elm street, frieda the 13-year-old, freddy defiles freedmot junior high, little angel does freddy to death* ...finally! Forget whose money is behind this stuff. Bekky's books answer that. Ask yourself why nobody ever asks, 'Who, exactly, is *supporting* this billiondollar form of social sepsis?' We all know the answer, of course. But it's too close to home, to close to the very bone, to vocalize —ever. *The n-d report* continues.

> Many formats are used to expose the best youth in a given culture to the adults in power. In the U.S. we are familiar with contests and competitions. These come in all conceivable stages (preparatory, preliminary, intermediate and final) and in all scopes (local, regional, state, national, international), cover all age-ranges of "youth", some requiring years to pass through. There are any number of other formats: training schools, tryouts, screenings, tests, applications, qualifiers and interviews, with some even brazenly linked with euphemisms like "sleeping arrangement quiz, lap interview, mattress matriculation" and "casting couch".
>
> (The present context ignores the related child-porn and teen-porn industries operating internationally, both of which are covered under "Subculture Paraphilias" in this study. See also the Novalis-Deland "Interim Report 4" (1989) titled, *Money, Power and Paraphilia.*)

bekky's thesis contd

"But it goes on all the time. The ad bosses, the moneymen, the backers and judges, all have a finger in it, pardon my lip. The girl who's hungry, or aggresso enuf to make the initial eye contact, to set the balls in motion.... [fingers over mouth, eyes atwinkle] "The girl with the goods who's willing to take 'the fall' is the girl who wins, who gets the lites the trophies the prizes. [i must have looked a little amazed] Didnt you ever wonder, nathan, why so many winners are guidettes...? Guidogirls? Tuffgirls? Raver- 'n' heavymetal types? Girls in leather with hippywitch du's? Didnt you ever wonder why it's them who endup on top (there I go again) while the real beauties –the ones who are too shy, who have toomuch pride– typically get only 'sorry's' and the 'see-ya's'?"

Not consciously i didnt.

"Nobody does." She tapped her swizzlestick, much-chewed at its tip, like a cigaret on the lip of her glass.

I assumed it was current taste, that the admen the media the sponsors the judges were just hyping the smartass syndrome.

"They are. B'cause ta the material girl –even if she's jus playin hardasnails– expects ta hafta pay her way, all the way. Some even prefer it …an excuse ta partyhearty without guilt. I've seen it over'n'over again. So that's the bottomline, the unspoken tradeoff. Ya see? [i saw] Some o' the most beautiful girls in the business c'n only get cats'n'dogbones…. [modeling for catalogs & newspaper ads] Look at deb. Beautiful as they come and fading professionally …at a mere twennyseven! Look at me! [twinge of treva] That's the price you pay for pride in this business. I think I like sex as much as anybody but I like to be the one who decides who it's gonna be with. So it's still a man's world, no matter what you say. Ferinstance, male promiscuity is still protected as studly while a woman's is sluttish. That's totally unfair."

Bek repeated this complaint when she met alice krawel. Alice however responded disarmingly. "But what if the error here is simply one of omission, of what's *not* in the picture of what we're taught? What if we were taught, the best 'n' surest sign of sexual health in a male is based on how much he desires to mate with *different* females? What if we were taught that? It's way closer to the biological facts you know. If we can accept such behavior from horses 'n' hollyhocks why not from the males in our lives? How sad, no? And for so many. Men *and* women. What if our family 'n' community life made all of us so emotionally secure that the antics of our penises 'n' vaginas were no more, and no less, important than what we ate for lunch the day before? You see? That's how it is with primitive cultures. Joyous theater. An that's how it is thruout most of Nature. Pairoff *if* you want, *when* you want. An *dont* pairoff if ya *dont* want. You see? Our sexlives could be a simple and damned fulfilling thing instead of the disgrace to our humanity we've made them."

Alice went on in this gracious vein. "It is both wonderful and natural to be strongly attached to a male during mating 'n' nesting periods. On the other hand, as long as women agree to center their lives around males instead of family 'n' community, they will be hurt and disappointed. For to do so is to work against nature. This is because males, by Nature, are interested in home and community only insofar as these supply a place to stay and females to mate with. Namely, matable females. To this end they can be employed to protect 'n' serve the home and the community in a manner entirely agreeable to them *and* us. In fact, the sexually fulfilled male is protective and even playful."

At first hyperkinetic bek was putoff by alice's slow surety. Yet by the time we left she was visibly changed. <You okay?> "Yahuh [head back on seat]." <Ya seem tired.> "Not really.... Jus relaxed.... Feel like my brain jus got a fullbody treatment." <Maybe it did.> "Yeah. Maybe it did."

"To men, generally, children, older women, even other men, are of little importance. But when they interfere with his ability to mate at will, any human except the desired one may be upgraded to the status of opponent. This is just part of the actual man who lives beneath the civilized persona we get to see, the man we are taught *not* to see. And so it often needs fall to women to see to it that children, older women (and men, to the degree they want to participate in the community) are looked after. To understand these things the word 'home' needs to be redefined, redefined to include any creature (including humans) which desires to nurture its offspring in a healthy and safe environment. That is to say: Home is, first of all, the mating/nesting creature itself. Only after that is it the structure in which that creature lives. Also, the word community needs to be simplified to mean, any group of creatures (including humans) whose life-focus is on a healthy and safe place for its offspring to grow and thrive. Only after that should it imply structures or infrastructures. Not strangely, to want a healthy and safe place for offspring to grow and thrive is to automatically embrace ecology and a sustainable future for all beings and things; that is, *all* communities. Moreover, it discourages overpopulation as well; for there is an ancient equation at work here: the overlarge community is less healthy, less safe. Growing may be possible in such places but thriving is not. And all healthy creatures want their young not jus to grow but to thrive. This is only Natural."

what any primitive or monkey

The western male was denied as a youth the everyday oglings of his naked siblings & peers, denied the summerdusk touchings & fondlings that any primitive boy, any treemonkey, can enjoy wout hindrance or criticism. To say that such youthful encounters are of little value is to trash the expectations of the subconscious & the instincts. The civilized male, as lifetime deprivation goes, is a hundred times more sexually deprived than the average inmate of a coed zoo. And studies indicate such freedoms may be exceeded tenfold by primates in the Wild.

what any superstar

An over-40 popmusic- or film star can go unmolested just about anywhere in the west w a 17yearold on his arm. But let the average guy, or specially any critic of the status quo (like me), try it, and he soon finds himself a blood-sacrifice. And it's all because it is precisely here the titillation begins. We want always to know more,more,more; centuries of erotic denial bubbleup in us like the septic waste it's become. Here instinct commands our subconsciouses to harken! to listenup! It is at this point something in us hopes, Maybe *this* time we'll get to participate in something civilization has been denying us for ages! And so goes the secret & malignant rondelay, hey hey!

female control & the law

I would now like to chat about an age-span which gets a most-peculiar share of statutory ink: birth to adulthood. I will be as succinct as possible. The law (ie, the state) is ever striving to enforce the reality-bashing notion that a female should not be put in charge of her sexuality (ie, that she should remain a virgin) until such arbitrary time as the state feels she has been sufficiently educated. I contend that means, sufficiently brainwashed w antiNature/instinct propaganda. Watch this.

The tactic does not just happen to be as old as patriarchal civilization. Whether we look back on shaman- or priest-dominated cultures, or whether we examine royalty- or military-dominated ones (sultans & mandarins saving virgins for their harems; emperors & kings keeping virgins for themselves and/or for their sons), the deepseated motivation is always the same one: male control over the female body. And this desire, as we shall see, becomes particularly electric, specially attenuated, as the age of the female approaches, and then passes thru, puberty. Anyone who doubts there still exists in our socalled modern world a tite correlation between enforced education and virginity might try a little survey; just a couple hours in a middling library ...a piddling library like this one may even do.

Pick a place. Any place. Aliceville al, lolita tx —it just doesnt matter. Find the median level of enforced education there. Then consult another statistic for the same locale: the age of consent. Now maybe i need to explain age of consent: that highly arbitrary moment when a socalled minor is handed over the responsibility for his or her own sexuality; ie, his or her own body. Never mind that in most of civilized history females have yet to achieve such a status at *any* age! The theory sounds nice. (Strangely, as i've noted, the state's interest in females does not get serious, does not gain heat and momentum, until they approach puberty. Also, strangely, its interest then proceeds to deteriorate steadily until they reach menopause, by which time females are almost invisible in the law. There is a reason for this, and it too stinks to arcturus.)

As camile pagles put it, "Like we do with any dose of ticks and leaches, we women need to get the state out of our pubic hair once and for all!" Let me make this clearer. In a typical phalladigm one can often interchange the words "state" and "male desire" and come away the wiser. This will keep you from being led astray when you do your little survey. Remember, male desire for control over the female body has had to go underground in this "enlitened" age. Compile your statistics realistically. That is, use only stats gotten from *applied* law, not from statutory law. Your survey will amaze you. For the median level of enforced education in any given region is directly related to the age of sexual consent! What is the underlying message? Suddenly, and for no constructive reason, the state steadily loses interest in further educating sexually active citizens! The bottomline is clear; we only need interchange a couple words. Males in charge (the state) see little point in further educating (brainwashing) sexually active persons (ie, nonvirgins). Now why in hell should this be?

If the true purpose of a person's schooling is indeed education, and if those in power are not still using schools as holdingtanks for virgins (a ploy leftover from earlier cultures), then the condition of a female's hymen would not be statistically relatable to the condition of her schooling —that is, in re that period she is bound by law to stay in school. Put another way, sincere benevolence would see to it that the 'protection of our youth' went in an opposite direction: more education, more community involvement, for the sexually active, not less. That would be to truly care about "the people".

This brings us back to my point: the age of sexual consent. The sex part of the issue is, philosophically, secondary. The real issue is, control, not sex. I dont expect tab-toters to understand this. That a girl/woman chooses to copulate, get pregnant, have a baby –whether w an old professor or a young mechanic–

is secondary so far as the laws are concerned. You dont have to trust me on this. You can prove it. What's at stake here is, those in power (far&away still males) losing forever a control they once reveled in. O the popmedia, its readers, watchers and listeners, get all titillated over the sex part alright. But one is the fool, the other the follower. The issue is control. As long as a man has social control his sexdrive can locate its desired outlet. But wout control (money, position, fame, or legal clout) such men (the clevers) are like any other person on the street (the slaphappies).

Let me pointout something else. Political leaders (today's royalty) and legislators (today's priests) are on average 20-30yrs past their sexual prime! That's a biostatistical fact. Do we think that *they* think they can continue to bed the sexmates they prefer wout legal assistance? For even w position, money or fame, if the law does not stand behind one's sex desire then the man who is getting older, and the man who is old, have little choice but to languish away w the same mate (only), the same dull fist ɛ fantasy, or both, for the rest of his days! And all this is not even to consider the effect which the rise of std's to epidemic levels worldwide has had on those in power ɛ their sycophants doing all they can to force virginity on the young —the latest watchword for this ancient tactic being "abstinence".

Now if the reader is at all like me, when he studies the laws said to "protect the sexual purity of our youth" he can almost see the incense curling from between the legalese, smell the perfumes, the rubbing-oils of the harems, oozing from between these catchy codes ɛ their coy codicils. Why, one can almost reachout ɛ touch, among the statutes [sic], one of the heterai of the greeks or romans; one can almost see, parading across the pages of the law, the young harlots of the pharaos, kings or emperors. Kublai khan sent out for 500 girls at a clip, roundingup "only the youngest, the most beautiful" (!) Until quite recently, sultans kept from 500 to 1200 concubines, w an average age of 15 in the harem. Many rulers insisted their sex partners be exclusively virgins! An aztec king of texcoco chose his sexmates from literally millions of girls, of which he kept 'only' 2000 at any one time! But i desist. There are fine works which document these things.

More recent political scandals are of the same order, except the motives of today's rulers are more closely guarded. I refer to the thousands(!) of complaints over the past few years of persons working for politicians, incl'g many young men&women just there for the pro exposure, you should pardon the expression —working under the titles "assistant runner intern apprentice observer" etc. What i fail to fathom is not why some politicians do what they do w these young people (that's so obvious just the thought of relating it pains me), what bothers me is why parents permit such age-old corralling of our choicest youth to spend wkends, breaktimes, summers, w some body politic! We in the know can smell the motive a countrymile! But then again, some few of us have seen the civil male mind stripped bare! And i tell you, there is a mass hallucination afoot, and its many negative effects on we commonfolk are little shy of appalling!

I probably should have said this earlier. When i say male i dont mean all males. I dont even mean all heteromales. I re only those males who have a normal complement of testosterone ε minimal mammary fetish in tow. With much in the way of evidence, i make a clear distinction between socalled leg men and ass men and their little brothers the breast men. Personally, if i must label myself (and by God, i must, or cower forever w the sexually egalitarian) i must say, i rise&fall w the former. As it turns out, men who harbor no oedipal longings fail to see a whole lot of sexuality in organs meant to feed infants not fetishes. Not to pickon such men, for most of we civil are mammary-idealized. Look at how many hetero-females are also breast-fetished. Let's do honest. If all healthy mammals suckle in inverse proportion to their adultness, dont we civil have a problem? Imagine, guys, a silverback trying to suckle the chest of one of his ladies! They'd laff him out of the jungle.

The shortend of this for me meant, once i had put the memory of my mother to sleep (and not just to bed like so many of my oedipulept brothers), more&more i began choosing my female friends using data gathered from the waist down, not up. It then no longer mattered if a female could suckle me, or if in doing so she resembled (egad!) my mother. On the other hand, we legmen ε assmen are no prize either. For we are, in the zizm of us, little more than stags needing a herd of does. Simple. Basic. And not easy to confess in civil company. But there it is. In our subconscious minds we nonmamm heteromales are all wouldbe silverbacks. That's just the way it is. Our challenge is to be allowed to be who we are in *fact* (not who we are in civil fancy) and to be that person absolutely wout shame.

L, lage sorrel & myself at ggNs one otherwise confusing eve

Bekky ε me reached a point when my world matron 101 became unavoidable. Likewise w the four of us on the eve in question. Had L not been so well-read in my oeuvre, had she not explained to all present that the difference between gender-differentiation ε gender-war was simply the difference between the primitive ε civil worldviews, my point mighthavebeen impossible to get across.

"Another tragedy is our war of the sexes."

That war is unNatural —a sign of civilization's general ill-health.

"I think competition between the sexes is healthy."

I will personally get on my knees to the sex of that person who can recreate the species all by him- or herself. Until such a person comes along, cloaca intact, i will consider both sexes deserving of equal respect. For any human society which fails to respect *both* sexes equally cannot raise healthy children. Sexually unbalanced paradigms, such as patriarchies 'n' matriarchies, can only produce unhealthy offspring. Because any cosmology ...a cosmology includes any globe-arching system of beliefs... *any* cosmology which fails to balance male 'n' female qualities, equally, is sick. In my books i repeat this because i believe it is a mantra; the mantra for achieving a healthy future.

Lage. "Not sure I'm ready for the cosmology thing. My mantra is, keep it simple."

Mine too. The word cosmology scares alot o' people. An' it's a shame too, because a cosmology doesnt hafta be complicated t' be good. An example of a healthy cosmology ...an' really, the simplest of all t' understand... is the Earthmother/Skyfather concept, where power is shared equally by both sexes.

"Why not Skymother 'n' Earthfather?"

Good *touché*. What's important is that each sex is represented equally 'n' that the mass subconscious (our collective unconscious) can identify fully with the model. Under such conditions all of us, parents 'n' kids, become siblings; we become the children of our Earthmother/Skyfather Godparents. And thus, on equal footing sexually, we compete for approval. But because the division of power within such a paradigm is equal, our human parents are revered equally, as different or as opposite as they may seem. The best cosmology should teach us: sexual difference is a divine thing, a thing to be respected 'n' revered; not something which is in cosmic dispute or contention, as civil sexuality is t'day, and *has* been for so long. At the same time i dont b'lieve the war of the sexes is suddenly going to cease, be replaced by an informed peace. B'fore this can happen, the pendulum will have to swing back the other way (to women's suppression of men). Only after that will it leveloff in liberty 'n' justice for all. As i once said to bekky: I hope you 'n' me can bypass this backlash and attack the basic problems, not let all these secondary ones confuse an already complicated issue. For allinall [this is deathrower ns talking now], we humans are not very brite —not where it counts. We have a long hard way to go; a way so selfish 'n' selfserving that the Planet as we've known it will not make it thru *w* us —*if* we make it thru. The problems of civilization are so vast, so dissevered from the Natural Universe, that by the time we figureout how to make things right so much destruction will have come'n'gone that the *tools* for corrective action will also have been wasted, or be so altered as to fail us as prototypes. A no-win situation —for us, not for Nature. Call me a prophet of doom and i will only bask in the assignation. For i have been to the very dregs of civil existence and back again and know whereof i speak.

the appalling speciousness of corpolitic spin on sex & youth

I'm sure bekky is today aware of this latest: Recent stats of a united nations "advocates for youth" survey have just bodyslammed another pop myth of our farright fundamentalist u.s media, which has been proselytizing for years as to america leading world youth in "just say[ing] no to sex". Now comes the real skinny on this fat spin. "The U.S leads all other 1st-world nations [1998] in having the lowest average age of first [sexual] intercourse [15.4], down from 15.7 in 1996." It is interesting, i think, that germany ran a close second (15.7) *w* the much-maligned (for its sexual emancipation) netherlands "winning overall", since its youth apparently stay virginal til the grand old average age of 17! Hello? Is anybody out there? Let's close our eyes, scrunchdown between our shoulders and think hard for a moment. What's the mx? America turnsout to fit precisely the stats which our corpolitic spin machine has been glibly attributing to "3rd-world" countries! Yes, the dumbeddown & highly secreted doublestandard marches on, untamed & unashamed.

those 'savage anarchists': adolescence & senility

On the heels of a decade of civil domination, reaching adolescence is essentially about our primitive Self desiring, and battling to obtain, a more vital sampling of existence than civil law ε expectation allow. Scilicet. Adolescence is when the Nature/instinct in we civil makes its (typically) penultimate, and therefore urgent, attempt to realize some share of existence beyond our mere (manners ε etiquette closeted) fantasies ε dreams. In civil society this period, in terms of the Self, is largely a failure to fulfill our libidos. Then, on the heels of our (civil) adolescent disappointment, the raw Nature/instinct in us typically goes back into hiding til onset of socalled senility. (While those of us who continue a pattern of resistance get treated as insane &/or criminal.) What senility is *really* all about is Nature/instinct's last gasp at conscious expression ε fulfillment. It is easy therefor to understand why these periods of life, adolescence ε senility, make civil rule ε expectation (law ε ethics) panicky. Only murder (misinterpreted as primitive [ie, savage] behavior) can turn the civil twist on Real Justice more brutal ε irrational than it is toward adolescents. This is not just because the hands of these 'savage anarchists' we call teens can now turn into fists, strike back at a decade or more of victorian repression. It is mostly because these (temporary) quasiprimitives (adolescents) can *themselves* now become parents, parents who (guaranteed by their own behavior) will not be so quick to crush the Nature/instinct (the primitive) in their own children as we, the adult (civil) lishment, were to crush it in them! This last is more crux than it may at first seem. (Sorry about the succinct language, my dedicated reader. But i *did* warn you.)

who is the savage, again?

≈Among the more humorous things is the white man's notion that he is less savage than the primitive.≈
—mark twain

We persist in calling primitive peoples savages. Yet, fact is, the worst *savage*-ries in the history of humanity have been inflicted by civilized cultures ε peoples, not primitive ones. From the precolumbian genocides of indigenous peoples by the aztecs to the genocides of modern rwanda, from the plunders of the persians ε the khans to the racial genocides of the nazis and the class exterminations by the french, russians ε japanese, all these assaults, ghastly in their numbers alone, were the works of civilized cultures, and any perceived differentness between them is merely a differentness of degree, not principle. For as any antipolitical anthropologist knows, these *savage*-ries were committed by cultures ε peoples in varied stages of civil development, not by primitives in isolation. To call the aztecs, as early spanish invaders found them, uncivilized, is to rehash the same prejudice of fear (which i have dubbed elsewhere the DIE, PRIMITIVE! syndrome) which presumes to view the hutus ε tutsies of rwanda as primitives ε savages when the apoliticized truth is, they have been living for generations the lifestyle of their colonial conquerors. That is, they have long been domesticated —and therefor supposedly "desavaged"— by civil rules ε expectations.

Summarily: No primitive was ever so savage as the violently civilized "primitive", for his thousand newly adopted civil repressions have twisted him beyond self-recognition (beyond deepself awareness). And so, his shame for the new person he sees in himself —or the old person she anymore fails to see in herself— has depressed ε angered her/him far beyond what he or she realizes, or may safely realize, and still call themselves civilized. And, of course, as ever, deepself denial can only lead to (civil) paranoia.

I say jesus', francis' & lao tzu's mastery over civil paranoia sprang from lifestyle intimacy with their deepest (& genteel) Selfs.

here are some stats we civil will never billboard

A society which *in fact* loves its children will refuse to fixate on the ~200 annual pedophile abductions while glibly overlooking the ~100thousand(!) children killed ε maimed annually by automobiles. A society which in fact loves its children will refuse to turn its back on the 1 in 4 youngsters living in poverty (in the richest nation on Earth!) so as not to interrupt its fixation on the 1 out of every halfmillion(!) youngsters abducted for sexual purposes. Those are just two of the many things which a society that, in fact, loves its youth will not ignore decade after decade ...while keeping ever-watchful (but of course!) for the latest youth/sex intrigue. They say that poverty leads to child-abuse. How come nobody ever says that poverty *is* child-abuse? Etcetcetc *ad civilitum infinitum*.

and finally (phew!), to the domicile of the world matron

Here we go. Ecopsyche is shorthand for where ecology ε psychology merge. Prime among the concepts in my ecopsyche thesis is the Triarchy —what i view as the most powerful nexus of archetypes in the human subconscious.

Generalized it consists of the triplex Nature-instinct/Truth. In practice however it is always gendered: Females project as Earthmother-instinct/Truth; males, as Skyfather-instinct/Truth. In addition, the Triarchy is the source of our intuition of deity, all manifestations of which we herein call numinads: a term which includes *all* the higher powers, first-causes, creators, gods, demigods, etc which humanity intuits.

Imagine what an oppressive bore it must be for one who never had questions to keep finding answers! Pity with me, please, that reader i worry so over. Thank you.

It should be noted. Save for my world matron/world patron thesis, my ecopsyche argument is often just a deep-ecology distillation of general psychology. Carl jung (whose fascistic tolerance i've descried at length elsewhere) brought to prominence the idea of a "collective unconscious", a view claiming that humanbeings share subconscious symbols which he termed archetypes. I am obliged to note that my world matron/-patron thesis more builds-upon than tampers-with these. Basics thus declared, we may callup the essential outtakes. [Emil, thank you so much for assembling these.]

Jung maintained the archetypes [in his collective unconscious] cannot be directly known, even with rigorous effort, and so they operate beyond our awareness. We must view the Triarchy with this same inductive spirit, as it lies at great depth in the personality. This depth of sublimation has three major effects. ❶ The Triarchy and its contents are difficult to grasp, which ❷ gives it a numinous quality, which ❸ adds to its autonomy —its ability to manipulate the personality from the realm of the subconscious.

The Triarchy, of all subconscious phenomena, casts the broadest and deepest shadow. When any aspect of the Triarchy is projected, its power to influence us is automatically deployed. The preacher who speaks like thunder and makes points like litening (Nature), who acts divinely right (instinct) and deals only in 'undisputable' facts (Truth), is counterfeiting the power inherent in the Triarchy, and almost always does so without understanding what he's doing. He knows only that it works and works well, not why it works. For the Triarchy is a force which rules *a priori* from the subconscious of the preacher's every listener, its long shadow projected into consciousness. If the preacher is male he will be perceived as standing in the shadow of the Skyfather; if female, the shadow of the Earthmother. It is rare for the Triarchy to manifest in an ungendered form.

> This, incidentally, is one reason female preachers working in a male paradigm have continually to battle the perception that they are trying to pull one over on us. For habitually, when it comes to 'divine' power, we denizens of patriarchies are accustomed to the shadow of the Skyfather being called to consciousness. When a female takes on the role of preacher, though we may try not to, we cannot help but suspect her authority, particularly when she claims to be representing "God the *father*", or any such male-colored anthropism. For what she does not realize is that, even as she speaks of the Skyfather, whose work she claims to be doing, it is the Earthmother shadow under which her listeners are cast. So it is that many female newage preachers have found they have more influence over their clients by referring to God as 'she', or Earthmother, etc.

As all this semiconscious posturing of the male preacher is being projected onto us, he is further empowered by his claim to be 'an authorized representative' of not just the Triarchy but of the very 'Author of the Triarchy', called God in some quarters. [Our Triarchy thus introduced, we can now move on to the world matron & world patron part of my thesis.]

The world matron and world patron are reactionary adjuvant archetypes; adjuvant because they typically manifest semi-unconsciously (that is, not *fully* *un*consciously like the archetypes), and reactionary because they manifest as a reaction to suppression of instinct: namely, suppression of the gendered expression of instinct. (Just like us, instinct is gender-biased, overarched in the subconscious as Earthmother or Skyfather. 'Instinct' we use in the usual way: pandemic unconscious impulse.) Since it is *suppression* of instinct that gives rise to these reactionary adjutypes, and since (due to our living in a mostly male-oriented society) the Earthmother aspect of the collective unconscious is currently the more repressed of the pair (Skyfather/Earthmother), what empowers the world matron will be easier to assess than what empowers the world patriarch.

[See me as i am today, in these my manacles & gyves, reduced to counting piffles & quotas, tabulating driblets, collating smidgens w iotas, once having written these things. Ah, yes. At anyhoot.... These preliminaries (much too quickly) put by, comes next the gist of my thesis.]

World matron i define as follows. Collective semiconscious impersonation of the Earthmother archetype representing a (mostly female) need for viability (credibility, authority) within a community or culture. The world matron is the absolute equivalent of the world patriarch, who is, in turn, a collective semiconscious impersonation of the *Skyfather* archetype. Both the world matron and world patron arise and do their work within the shadow of the Triarchy. In females that shadow is the shadow of the Earthmother; in males, the Skyfather shadow. Since a thorough understanding of this point is key to understanding the thesis itself, i will state it yet another way. (For simplicity's sake, we will focus on the world matron, deploying the world patron only for purposes of comparison and a nod toward due equilibrium.)

The world matron loses all power and vanishes (as if 'she' never existed!) the moment she moves out of (or is perceived to be out of) the shadow of the Triarchy (ie, the Earthmother shadow). That is to say, to be out of this shadow is to lose all numinal authority, to be 'merely' mortal, unGodlike, to be like everyfemale. One's agenda is then perceived as 'merely' human: selfcentric, non-universal. This personal-v.-collective distinction is crucial to the argument.

The obvious question is, when and why does the world matron make an appearance or rise to power? This occurs most typically when the Natural (chthonic) power of women (innate genius for nurture and protection) has been compromised and/or degraded in some way. As Jung spoke of suppressed instinct reappearing "in another place in altered form", when a woman's genius for nurture and protection is compromised or degraded (ie, suppressed), it causes within the woman a backlash politicization of the Earthmother authority and her *un*politicized Truth. Jung adds, when the instinct which has been suppressed resurfaces, "it is [now] loaded with a resentment that makes the otherwise harmless natural impulse our enemy".

For our purposes here i would rather that this brilliant exposition read: Whenever instinct is suppressed it resurfaces in another place but this time loaded with a resentment which has redeployed the otherwise uncomplicated original force in a new and disguised form. That is, when the unconscious impulse of a woman to nurture, let us say, is suppressed, that impulse resurfaces in an altered form (of the Earthmother). It is *that* form we are calling world matron. Further, to the degree that suppressed instinct is redeployed in altered form, to that same degree we must view the world matron's appearance as politicized; that is, loaded with a resentment which has redeployed the original expression of the Earthmother authority in a new and disguised form. The cruxvalue of this concept cannot be overstressed.

As stated, the autonomy of the Triarchy casts a long shadow over the personality. Yet because that authority is subliminal, without rigorous examination one cannot be sure where exactly Triarchy autonomy takes up and where it leaves off. Because the world matron and -patron arise and do their works within that authority, whenever their agendas cannot be *proven* to lie outside its (irrationally respected and feared) boundaries or shadow, those agendas are automatically assumed by us to be valid and true —as valid and true (and respected and feared) as the authority of the Triarchy itself. Yet when someone's agenda, formerly thought to be instinctually generated (ie, divinely right), is suddenly seen to lie outside the Triarchy's shadow –I.e., when it becomes clear that agenda is *personal* not *collective*– at that moment the world matron or -patron vanish as if they never existed(!), and the agenda in question becomes suddenly suspect (is weakened, possibly even crippled); that is to say, the agenda is no longer viewed as emanating from an Absolute (unquestioned) Authority. Therefore, in practice the world matron and -patron are never wrong! For to operate within this shadow is to be divinely right (instinctually infallible) and to operate outside of it is to be mortally fallible (selfishly not collectively motivated).

Since the goals and m.o of the Earthmother are allied with Truth (by way of the Triarchy), and since the goals and m.o. of the world matron are allied with motives which diverge from this Truth (motives politicized by conscious tampering), a tension is set up whenever the power of the world matron is invoked. This tension immediately casts about for an instinctual cause to which to anchor the authority it has counterfeited. It typically settles on the most fundamental of impersonations. For example: Mother nurturing or protecting her young, a scenario usually pervaded by righteous indignation and/or wrath, as the situation demands. It is no accident that the impersonation selected is one of the most powerful ones possible to a female politicization of an instinctual truth. This tension –this failure to achieve an apotheosis in Truth (which only instinct untampered-with can achieve– sets up further tensions, resulting in a vicious cycle of anger/guilt. But these occur on such a deep level (are therefore so very personal) one typically never shares them with others. E.g.: automatic secrecy.

Because the world matriarch and -patriarch operate within the shadow of the Triarchy (that is, that portion of the Triarchy manifested as Earthmother and Skyfather), and because that shadow rules every subconscious with absolute autonomy, we find ourselves fearful of questioning the agendas of the world matron and -patron. We always shift the benefit of any doubt toward their credibility. It is essential to understand this. Forinstance, the prosecutor who knows –but cannot prove– a certain woman did not kill someone to protect her child, as she claims, but did so so that she could later sell the child, knows better than to try to convince a jury of this if another approach is possible. On the same premise, many is the jury which has awarded custody to an abusive natal mother slighting in the process two perfectly fine adoptive parents. For, though it is not always allowed to surface, every mature person knows in his deepest Self the price of challenging Natural law. For we civilized, though we may not ever pause to realize it, pay that price repeatedly and without complaint all our lives.

> Sadly, there are imperative instinctual actions which are deemed immoral/illegal in civilized society. Scenario: One may be jailed or even executed for permitting instinct to run its course unimpeded. Yet one's punishment is suffered with cryptic pride and arcane dignity —a dignity so secret, so unpopular, and so likely perceived as immoral/unlawful, that even the sufferer may not understand why he doesnt feel more remorse for his actions! ("We all saw him murder my wife, so when I caught up with him I killed him then and there.... Sure I'm sorry. Sure I wish it never happened. But that doesn't mean I wouldn't kill that scum the same way again.") Not incidentally, those of us so civilized we constantly compromise our instinctual rights, can never know such dignified remorse. This is just one tragedy in that experiment called civilization: where pandemic private suffering occurs every day for the sake of public falsehoods, for the sake of ideals and behaviors that often stand in direct conflict with Nature/instinct and are performed in deference to what our deepest Selfs expect and need. And how ironic that everyone, to some degree, suffers from the same thing (the rules/expectations of civilization) in secrecy or under the cloak of some public lie! What onus, what apostasy, have we been so guilty of that we must often go to our graves with some form of unspoken and unspeakable guilt? The answer to this white-hot and frightening question is self-evident in my thesis. ——Nathan Schock

Look at this instance of Natural authority (Earthmother/instinct) being politicized to selfish (world matronly) ends: A mother, within hours of marrying a younger man, sends her attractive daughter away to boarding school for the first time. Still, when the world matron's agenda cannot be proven to lie outside the Triarchy or its shadow, that agenda is presumed correct and honorable; furthermore, divinely correct —divinely because, the elements of the Triarchy are numinous, with the power of each of the three reinforced by their numinexus. And so we dare not quibble about merely suspected motives. In the same way that the Earthmother concept derives its authority from having borne and raised all the 'family' of Earth (chthonic aspect of universal Nature), the world matron lays claim to that same authority by having borne and raised children of her own —that is, in the birthing of a human family. This is why few argue when a mother appears to be defending her children. And this is why females with children can lay claim to Earthmotherlyness with such compelling sovereignty; ie, can project (via the world matron) the Earthmother shadow to their own purposes. Known childless females, on the other hand, can emulate the Earthmother authority only in potential (the *potential* to bear, protect and nurture offspring), can therefore only *play* in the shadow of the Triarchy —being still 'mere' daughters (nymphs and subnymphs) of the Great Mother, their power 'limited' to the dynamics of biologic potential, not biologic achievement. (E.g.: The menstrual blood of a childless female is empowered by birthing blood, etc., etc.)

Witness the newfound respect a firsttime mother commands, particularly following a healthy birth. Even a very young mother commands such respect, often despite many negative circumstances. In fact, the mere announcement "I'm pregnant" instantly transfers most of the powers of an adult onto she whom, moments before, may have been perceived as a 'mere' child. This is because, consciously or not, she has stepped squarely into the shadow of the Triarchy, has begun speaking with all the authority of the Earthmother behind her. While she may later talk or act her way out of this position of power, it is very real, and very effective, while she has it. And then there is the case of the aged woman or man. Tho they may never have borne, sired, or nurtured, a child, if we dont know this (and often even if we do), something in us assumes *a priori* that they have some authority in this area, and so long as their argument stays within believable bounds of the protect/nurture ethic, we dare not question their motives, even tho in reality their politics may be far afield from the Earthmother or Skyfather shadow they are misappropriating.

An unrecognized fact is, it is the chthonic aspect of a female only –that is, her Earthmother-instinct aspect– that is capable of bearing offspring. No other part of her personality, not brain, intelligence or emotions, can accomplish this. In point of fact, not even the world matron 'herself' can bear offspring. This lies totally in the realm of Earthmother authority, which is likely the reason women are so deeply transformed by birthing. Though constantly under assault by the state, this may be the only remaining civil experience (including even orgasm itself!) lying all but *totally* within the realm of pure instinct which is not in some way illegal! Tragic? O yes.

It is important to restate. The world matron –ancient storyteller magitrix shaman– is adept at staying within the shadow of the Triarchy, for she knows, mostly by instinct(!), as long as she stands within that shadow no one can be sure her words or actions are not grounded in the Triarchy (Earthmother in her case). I say 'mostly' by instinct because the world matron and -patron are adjutypes (adjunct archetypes); that is, *semi*conscious forces. Need we add? To be semiconscious is also to be semiunconscious; i.e., partly in the subconscious-instinctive/partly borrowing of instinct-Truth (i.e., the Triarchy) and partly borrowing of conscious wants and needs: borrowing of a politicized (non-instinctual) agenda.

It goes without saying, men, like women (typically not exclusively, once again) are guilty of the same tactics when they operate within the shadow of the Skyfather. This equivalent politicization of instinct/Truth manifests as the world patriarch. In a male-dominated paradigm 'he' arises within the shadow of the Skyfather to do battle with (i.e., keep suppressed) not only male youth but the world matriarch as well. This is politics where all politics begins. Just as males in such paradigms perceive the world matron as a vengeful Earthmother, so females perceive the world patron as the cruelly authoritative Skyfather. It is this warping of collective impulse, under the brutal pressures of civilized law & expectation –i.e., the warping of the *collective* to the purposes of the *personal*– which is at the root of what is called the war-of-the-sexes; a state of affairs supercharged with tension (anger and guilt), all of it the result of our civil suppression of instinctual (gendered) expression.

Earthmother and Skyfather are key elements of our necessarily anthropized and gendered view of Nature and the Cosmos. They form a complementary Syzygy; scilicet: a monad of complementary opposites. In the orient this unity is conceived as Dao, or The Way; in the west, as God. But the minute the Triarchy (Earthmother/Skyfather/Truth) is corrupted by *conscious* decision –rules and expectations unmediated by the collective unconscious– it is then, all sort of tensions rumble, threaten and come to life. [Pause excerpts. —Ed.]

while i'd rather not own such credentials....

As if it were the ~~good~~ ol days of my incarceration, here i am back in my tumbledown 12-unit timeshare(!) once more, separated from the other spelunkers & troglodytes in this place, w glumm&gluum rigadooning outside my cell, slaughtering in sloppy singsong the lyrics to "jailhouse rock", which werent that great to begin w. I will have no excuse for failing to be a nonpareil authority on celibacy before they are done with me here.

how true to the source?

[Resume excerpts.] Amidst all this it is easy to begin thinking of the world matriarch and -patriarch as unNatural or unhealthy. While extreme repression (such as civilization engenders) can warp them thus, has warped them thus, it is important to remember. The agendas of the world matron and -patron are guaranteed Natural and healthy to the degree they are rooted in instinct! The present argument pivots on this: the dynamic flux of purposes which exists between the (subconscious) instincts and rational (conscious) wants and needs. To understand the reader must hold, in a single viewpoint, the purposes (agendas) of the instincts on the one hand, and the purposes (agendas) of the world matron and -patron on the other. For without scales to balance, the living dynamics of deed and cause are deadened or diminished. As the person who harms another in an impulsive effort to save her own life has acted instinctually (irrationally/healthfully/constructively), so the person who only fakes such a defense has acted rationally/sickly/destructively ...despite all ideologies and expectations which dictate the contrary.

In another way of speaking, instinct is often the Truth which civilization tortures on a crucifix (Nature hung in effigy), and the world matron and -patron are the thieves who hang on either hand as they lived: stealing from within the shadow of Absolute Truth. In this light, human 'resurrection' may be read as our intuition that instinct, in that it refuses to stay dead, will some day, somehow, ultimately rise to glory —even if only in the final act of our individual death! For one cannot even die but that instinct persists till the last instant —and who knows, maybe even beyond.

On this end of Biblical twistory: When the persona put on clothes (when personal idealism first sought to suppress collective instinct), politics (or the warping of collective Truth to personal agendae) was invented. The most sinister tool ever devised for said warping is the civilizing principle, which amounts to the organized suppression of Nature/instinct via the hijacking of the adjutypes, the world matron and world patron. Civilization named the one (Nature/instinct) "evil" and the other (civilization/ideology) "good", leaving the much maligned "serpent in the garden" (pure instinct) to take the rap for it all —all of it, that is, which females (feared to be closer to Nature than males) didn't get blamed for by way of Eve, etc., etc., etc.

Finally, as to perceived authority. The more generations of offspring a person can lay claim to (or is responsible for the welfare of, as in the case of social leaders), the more world matron -patron power he or she possesses. And, sad to report, this works conversely as well. For, the more world matronly a woman becomes, the less Earth-daughterly (nymphic, childless) she is likely to be. This fact is hypertrophied when we live within a patriarchal worldview where youth/beauty (Earth daughter) is prized higher than Nature/nurture (Earth mother). And it is here that trouble –big trouble– seethes below the surface.

Those who think things would be much-improved in a matriarchal paradigm fail to understand the complementarity inherent in the equal polarization of the Triarchies and the (genderless) Monad which Authored them. What do i mean? I'm saying, whenever Earthmother and Skyfather do not share power equally (e.g.: civilization), the suppressed element will, as Jung has warned and history has shown, rise up later in another form, a form loaded with resentment and a tainted agenda. Enter world patron and world matron. And enter they do... with a vengeance!

what is the Nature of your particular spin?

I've said, the agendas of the world matron & -patron are healthy/constructive to the degree they are rooted in or founded upon instinct! But there is danger dealing in only quantitative terms. For truth is surely a matter of quality as much as quantity.

Being the first storytellers —as well as the first magicians & shamans— the world patron and -matron always invoke in us an archetype. "My father's bigger 'n' stronger than an angry gorilla 'n' he'll be home any minute so you better lookout!" Under the right circumstance such a thing might be said by a person whose father is as small as a child and who hasn't been home since the night they were conceived. That's politics. And while it may distort truth/instinct, oddly it is not against Nature. For politics —the distortion of collective impulses to selfish ends— is almost as old as life itself! So, if i seem to treat it as negative/unNatural/destructive, it is the fault of civilization's tireless and long politicking without consensus of the collective unconscious. For the difference between the message imparted by a modern politician and that of a primitive storyteller may be no more than a matter of 'spin': good (universally constructive) spin v. bad (universally destructive) spin.

Civilization, born out of fear of Nature, automatically puts a negative spin —an anti-instinct/Truth predisposition— on all things coming under its purview. Even a thing so morally insignificant (or so one might think) as an ad (pop tv, newsprint, whatever) is often drenched in this bias. Try asking the next hundred ads you see "Are you saying, Nature make a mistake?" You will be amazed at how subtly, seductively and routinely Nature and instinct are slandered. So, while the world patron and -matron are as Natural as any stone or star, all their qualities and quantities (location, direction of travel, spin, charge, mass, everything) are crucial to maintaining the Natural order. It is both axiomatic and obvious: Change the mass of our Star just a little, alter the spin of our Planet just a tad, and we create all the unforeseen destruction such changes demand.

[Emil, thanks for the excerpts. You have not only saved me days of work, there's no telling how much i might have overlooked in the process. My mind has been toolong distant from these matters.]

...atlonglast the world matron is caught, in broad daylite, dragging behind her by the hair her libido's worst enemy

The "pretty women council" (pwc), arm of the dc-based "national sexual-rights coalition" (nsrc), for a $150ooo donation (tax deductible), has a standing offer (pardon the expression) of "a night with 20 talented and lovely hookers in a legal nevada brothel", says 40-year-old brenda breedlove, frisco callgirl & chairperson of the council. The money will be used, says breedlove, in "an effort to get underage amateur prostitutes off the streets of america". When a memo from her desk surfaced suggesting "This move should decimate the competition, girls" (competition as in "since there are more and more younger women entering the business these days...."), breedlove refused to comment other than to say, "The offer still stands".

> Don't be jealous of young girls...old woman.... You shall not rob me of my pleasures; you will not be able to reduce or filch [what] belongs to me. —Young Girl in Aristophanes' *Ecclesiazusae*

Doing her deeds for millennia in the deep long shadow of Mothernature (return to headline above)....

hey, narc,

[narc] what about the sexual rights of the sexually legitimate, the sexually viable, in our great nation? As denise norris says, "Nobody asks why rises in the age of sexual consent typically occur with the liberation of women when the opposite should be the case: More rights at an earlier age." Hmm.

> You ought to be his mother rather than his wife. With these laws in force the earth will be filled with Oedipuses. —Young Girl in Aristophanes' *Ecclesiazusae*

The unfortunately limited brilliance of carlos fuentes saw the world matron's agenda in a narrower sense than yourstruly: Never trust a woman, he said, whose admiration "you have not secured with a meat-ax". Anyone who cannot discern the many "evils" directly ascribable to the emancipation of women is as blind as "a toad in a rock". Stiletto-tunged bekky kydd looks harmless next to fuentes. "I fail to see how giving the state the rights to my body till age 18 or 21 is anything less than cruel and unusual punishment. Cruel because I am being sexually deprived during my most active and attractive years, and unusual because celibacy is a biologic aberration." You go, grrrl.

Bekky says, "At least the PWC isn't axing its *own* daughters in the back. Take a guess who's more liberated, the girl who is stopped from being intimate with the one she loves or her mother who can take him to bed any time she pleases, love bedamned? Parse this with a raised voting age and you guarantee, the daughter can't even vote to put things back the way nature intended them. Thanks for nothing, Moms Against Sexual Competition from Young Women." [From B. Kydd's book "Youth for Sexual Equality".—Ed.]

I will be revenged. —First Old Woman in Aristophanes' *Ecclesiazusae*

Of course, impotent old men (the world patriarch) arent a lick better. They still (yes, today) chop away at the stiffest competition (forgive sigmund slip) by sending them off to die, be hobbled, disfigured or isolated by war. While mature women (the world matriarch) are busy in like kind: "Disfranchising the sexual freedom of daughters and granddaughters in the guise of protecting them." As bekky puts it in the preamble to kyse, "All persons with viable sexuality should have equal sexual rights. But no. Worldwide, fundamentalist religions and the politicians they put in power keep raising the age of consent. Let us say up front. If 14 is often unfair, 16 is absurd. And 18 is criminal!". And as her friend alicette morrison sings it, "I ain't no goddamned kid, Mama! Aint been one since last June. Even the dumbest 'rent should know, no kid c'n bleed ta cycles of the moon".

you shall know her also by her angriest coverts

Ella is a gE supporter. 70something at the time of the following incident. Staffers tolerate ms (ella) gibble hanging around hq because her contribution$ far outweigh her eccentricities. She poppedup at an employee/volunteer picnic a couple junes ago. Since ella has a history of aggressive crushes on a different gE male every 2-3mos, and since glen had only recently rejected her monied advances (again), she knew very well who he was. Robin starling however she'd never met.

Ella sat wrong-side-out at the first table carefully following preparations. Eyecatching as ever, wearing tanktop&shorts, robin skittered back&forth from parkinglot to picnicarea for a good 15mins. This done she had to be on her way. In the car, out of ella's line of sight, waited the little starlings. On her leaving robin ɛ glen kissed. Only a table away, craning her neck, rapping her cane loudly on the bench, ella yelled in shaky ɛ piercing crone, "Stop kissing!"

Everyone stopped what sHe was doing ɛ turned. Glen ɛ robin froze. "Could she be yelling at us?"

"What's wrong, ella?" said steve.

"That little girl over there is kissing starling! Stop her!" she yelled, rapping her cane vehemently on the bench.

"Ella," said steve "what are you talking about?"

"Get her! Stop her this instant!"

"Ella, that's glen's wife. They have two kids!"

Ella's voice became instantly conversational. "Well she coulda been one o' those little witches without morals, you know. Theyre always around."

In many parts of the world a girl can be married at 14, have two children by 16. Millions do! Tens of millions in fact. But in amer we live in a queer wisdom vacuum. We are cataracts of information devoid of wisdom. Few of us know, forinstance, something so basic as: The worldwide household techno-standard is a clear naked litebulb dangling from two wires in the ceiling of a 1rm dwelling!

Anyway, it's not that ella couldnt see robin; she had excellent vision and was scrutinizing her the whole time. What's my point? Compare nikki's reaction to Lilith —except Lilith ɛ me still hadnt kissed. Why didnt nikki run out in the street, run to gE hq, to the police or to God, yell about what Lilith "was doing" as 4decades-older ella had yelled about robin? Nevermind that ultimately she in fact inflicted way more damage than ella. Yet, truth is, as ever, time-terms obscure physical fact. Tho ella was not as hurt as nikki, she *was* as angry. The reason? The once lovely ella –pride ɛ possession of many a cruiseship captain– resembled robin farless than nikki resembled Lilith. Still i am indebted to ella's performance because it gives yet another glimpse of the world matron at work: envy of the sexual power of the young masked as motherly protection.

imperative disclaimer

Yes, i love females. Among the sexes they are usually my favorites —the hope of family ɛ community, the cradle of instinct, literally. But my gynaeolatry can go only so far. In all my writings ɛ life-dealings, honesty ɛ the search for facts have always overridden all other considerations. It shall be no different here. To whomever this causes pain or humiliation i earnestly apologize. I say this wout irony, cynicism or tungincheek. For this is simply how i feel.

queen victoria: an all but fleshedout incarnation

For the same reasons that popnews and the facts rarely cohabitate, recorded history ɛ historical reality are rarely on speaking terms. In fact they usually diverge widely. Being primarily the record of the elite ɛ ruling classes, history is typically skewed toward ideals not reality. Forinstance, if history was recorded by the poor and subjugated classes, the architectural structures of past millennia (for one example) would not be seen in the glorious lite we see them today. Most would be agonizing symbols of mass suffering ɛ state/-religion brutality. I note this bias of history simply to bring focus.

Even w such blinding civil filters in place, rare were the moments in civilization when the child was the idealized citizen he sometimes is today. Indeed, once matrilineal prehistory came to a close, in most cultures the child became a thirdrate citizen, lagging in human rights even behind women. Then, of a sudden, a transformation began. Still in process today, this civilly novel idealism has gone so far as not only to isolate the child from carefully selected(!!!) aspects of subjugation, it has blundered far beyond what is commonsensible; w the result that a state of high conflict in the home has become the expected norm during the socalled teen years, too often w unfortunate, even tragic, results.

Even w criminals we sometimes pause in our punitive reflex to ask, "What are the social conditions causing them to behave the way they do?" We know better than to say, "O, pay no attention. Theyre just criminals". For we know, to be so simplistic could end w our missing an opportunity to change for the better a plainly destructive aspect of society. Why dont we possess the same objectivity, the same willingness to evaluate change, when it comes to our own offspring? Could it be because we are unready to discover that the 'fault' lies squarely w us, not them?

Truth is, many of us suspect in our deeper selves why this is, why we are so ready to say, "Pay no attention. Theyre just teenagers". For thus we put the responsibility for their behavior off our own shoulders and squarely onto those of our children, as if their reaction to our victorian tyranny were some unalterable biologic inevitability, not the fault of rules and expectations only recently adopted (historically speaking). Shouldnt we be as equally concerned about why teens behave "badly" as about why criminals do? Why are we content to care less about causes when it comes to our children? Why are all the shrinks and social service professionals, the help books, articles, film lectures, treating only the symptoms? Why do we never ask history to unveil its truths? all of history? Could it be, we dont dare?

As my philosophic ward bekky kydd observed, "Why do the thousands of help books give mostly *tactical* information to parents and teachers rather than dig to find causes? Why do so many articles, books, doctors and social professionals, pose the question of parent-teen relations as if the problem is some kind of warfare? Could we dislike our kids so much just because they are becoming sexualized like us? I think so. I think this is exactly what's happening. And it shows. Everywhere. Just the title of the book lying on the floor by my desk (*Winning Over Your Teen*) is designed to be read two ways —one, as sales pitch, the other, warfare. What happened to lovefare? Why is there no such a word in the vocabulary of teen-parent relations?"

Here, in white-hot abridgements, is how this historic anomaly (idealized youth) came to pass.

[Emil, some sense of the victorian sources of the world matron's rise to power is needed here —else readers may view my thesis as wout historical roots. To expedite this key connection, would you kindly insert a working abridgement of the corresponding (historical connection) in my *Mothernature & the world matron*. I realize that, after your heroic assistance w the many excerpts in part1, this is stretching your patience. But i foresee only an unnecessary weakening of my thesis wout it. Thanks for assisting w this.]

For hundreds of thousands of years human society was founded on kinship: the extended family: I.e., whole communities of kin, having a grand old patriarch (or, earlier, matriarch) at one end of the lineage, the latest-born at the other. In the mid 1600s this began to change radically. Enter, the nuclear family.

Causes aside (for now), within patriarchies, the advent of the nuclear family gave women the right to make decisions in the home. Suddenly they found themselves without the overseers of the extended family. Concurrent with this, men were now working so hard and so long few could afford to keep more than one woman. There being no older women in the home anymore, and men having so little leisure anymore, there was no one to coddle a wife much younger than themselves as was once the norm. This led to more men than ever before setting up housekeeping with women nearer their own age, responsible women who could manage matters at home while the husband stoked the fires of the industrial age. This meant, things on the home-front were now run by women with some idea of what they wanted out of life and the domestic latitude to express it. Gone, relegated to royalty, was the young woman who arrived in marriage (or its equivalent) as the sexy child-bearer for the son of some grand patriarch or other.

The royal life being still the ideal however, over time the nuclear family began to reflect those aspects of royal behavior within its reach. Women, isolated within the nuclear family, began to evolve in home and neighborhood a moral idealism unconnected with the reality beyond their dooryards. Beginning in France (in the west), upperclass families became less and less grounded in Nature/instinct and more and more caught up in things cultural (i.e., artificial ideologies). Soon, in most of Europe, and then America, with the lifestyle of royalty as the desired mean, this idealism evolved into a much-powdered and prissy atmosphere, complete with servants and salons.

Disdainful (and rightly so) of the days when the husband spent his salary getting drunk and, unable to afford a prostitute, found his way home again only to get his wife pregnant —again ...save for occasional procreation, over time, upperclass women successfully banished most things sexual from the home-front. But don't misunderstand. Those days of drunkenness and unwanted pregnancy were not really gone. They were just happening in a part of town where history was *not* being recorded, where cries for help were traditionally ignored (read, hidden away), and would therefore take some time becoming historically apparent.

Also remembering what we've said about suppressed instinct, we know now to expect, whether in ourselves or in society, what has been suppressed will pop up in another place at a later time, but now in altered form and freighted with hostility. The suppression of instinct occurring in all extremes of the middle classes unleashed an explosion in prostitution, an epidemic of venereal disease and a morbid penchant in erotic taste: a period of moral decay unmatched in human history save among the ruling classes. This psychotic social reflex we remember as the underside of the Victorian era —when we remember it at all. For being still in the grip of that era today, elitist as ever, history still prefers to forget it. That it is critical to our health to remember it, analyze it, change it, we *still* refuse to see.

For many of the ethical and sexual double standards from which we still suffer, crept into shadow-power during that era, most with a virulence we would rather ascribe to other causes. (A minor for-instance: Gothic horror stories were beloved in Victorian society; specially tales of sexual violence which featured trammeled purity and violated innocence. Ring familiar? Specially high on their list (and ours, still) of 'bad guys' were everyday things, the quotidian quanta of every life twisted to look like "the many instinctual and biological screwups of Mother Nature".

The Victorian ladies in their ivory towers, looking down with revulsion at the sea of degradation slopping all around them –a slop which they, their mothers and great grandmothers, helped precipitate– feeling they were the world's last bastion of healthy morals (and actually looking the part to the unwary), decided it was their job to set society "right" —again! They began by pressuring their mates to apply their homespun idealism (legislate their daydreams) outside the home as well as in it. When it became obvious, domestic pressure alone was not up to the enormity of the task, turning domestic power into community muscle, the right to vote was sought and eventually won. Well, brava! At last! Yet how much worldliness, how much streetwise reality, was present in this new muscle, let alone wisdom about Nature and Wilderness?

This exertion of power both at the poles and along the way to suffrage, accomplished the following. Prohibition, female property rights, ending prostitution, raising the marriageable age, creating a new view of 'the rights of children', and the creation of an era of sexual suppression never before seen in "free" society and never since matched. It sorely needs pointing up, the coincidence of the latter two historical anomalies is hardly accidental. [Here NS uses again the D.Norris quote already used above. —Ed.]

"Not surprisingly, the combination of these things had the effect of giving women increased autonomy. With the new laws, husbands were no longer anxious to divorce. That is, dividing property "just" to get a younger mate, then having to divide it again "just" to keep her, no longer seemed so attractive. Whereas the major social power was always, for women, the bearing of offspring and bringing them to maturity, and whereas for thousands of years this "nesting period" per child was brief at best, suddenly the so-called nurturing period began to telescope. Fact. In the mid 1800s most children in the world entered the labor pool in one form or another by age 9. B. Kydd quoting Rhea Hilltanna, sex historian:

"Horrors! we like to cry at this point, even though me and thousands of other kids worldwide, by that age (and earlier) are working professionally —modeling, in my case, to cite just one instance condoned by the codes and codicils of current 'enlitened' labor law. Ever wonder why we allow kids to be worked, often like slaves, in movies, modeling, music, beauty contests, dance (the performing arts generally) but *not* in areas where we can't be voyeurs of the whole process?"

The concerned prisoner, commenting on his editor's fine abridgement in the dusk of his cell, is not saying which of our civil laws or expectations is right or wrong. He's merely saying that, a little historical lite shed into our abstract darkness might help.... Now to the crux.

In the old kin group, children working did not threaten the end of the family unit. But with the advent of the nuclear family this changed. The new wrinkle was: When the age when offspring no longer needed full-time nurturing was reached, the essentialness of the family unit (read, full-time parenting) came into serious question —not a very promising scenario for man/woman cohabitations which, remember, were largely practical to begin with. For, in a union where 2.5 children were involved, a cohabitation (marriage or otherwise) was all but guaranteed to come into sobering straits in less than 15 years! In times when unmarried (or Gaia forbid, divorced) women were considered old maids by age 25 –and when men, as ever, were all too ready to trade them in for younger models– this was a truly terrifying prospect. By the 1800s, with the nuclear family already chalking up a 200-year history of foundering and collapsing once the children matured, something had to be done —and fast.

In former times, when routine husbandly copulation was enjoyed and/or endured by married women, the answer to this problem was all too automatic. An endless stream of offspring needing care kept the family (read, full-time parenting) essential to society till the wife all but died of it, and often did! But with the new fear and loathing of things sexual, handy and effective means of perpetuating the family nest narrowed dramatically.

By then the 'fatherless' tykes unleashed on society by Victorian morals were bursting the doors of orphanages, lining streets and alleyways with the outstretched hands of needy youth. But Victorian hypocrisy was such that, in all reaches of the middle and upper classes, women refused to consider adopting orphans, even in cases where "the little bastard" was known to have been fathered by the husband himself! Therefore, the only way a wife could perpetuate her indispensability to the home (beside via a surprisingly late, unwanted and in very poor taste pregnancy) was to keep *existing* offspring needy and at home for as long as possible. The terms "needy" and "child" were, and still are, the furtive operators here.

To cut to the chase. By 1975 women's political power had doubled the age when a youth was free to leave the nest and its authority, and, by 1985 was laboring to extend even that! In another way of speaking, in a mere 150 years, women had extended the period of their essentialness to the family unit from an arbitrary nine years (per child) to an arbiterial 21! Breathless (at the white heat of our pace in this delicate and crucial matter and all that it is uncovering), one can only ask at this point. Can it be purely accidental that 2.5 x 18 = 45 + 18 (the mother's married age) = 63? And... can it be purely accidental that, upping these arbitrary 18s to even more arbitrary 21s (miraculously) = 74, median life span of females in the western world today? What i am asking is, can it be entirely coincidence that, just 2.5 children surviving to (the new and lately-assigned ages of) 'maturity' guarantees the essentialness of the family unit (ie, the institution of marriage) to society (and to the state!) for the lifetime of the parents?

Don't mistake any of this. Again, i am not arguing rightness or wrongness, or even mutual civil harms between the sexes. I'm asking only that, what's really going on, and what has been going on, be faced full-frontally; that is, genderly undre ...'scuse me... addressed.

It is probably that i am honest that i expect honesty from others. And so, naively i ask: At what point did parental concern for offspring turn so obviously selfish, so obviously political? At what point did the world matron suddenly appear where Mother Nature had stood for millennia? And at what point did she begin castigating us for "the way we treat our children"? But far more importantly. Why are these new 'freedoms' so fraught with queryful losses of freedom for our youth? And why do these losses have at bottom, typically, the loss of sexual freedom?

I am not about to fall into ye old Cartesian trap, sit here and try to nail down at what point in a youth's maturity a mother's Mother-Naturely collective protective instinct is warped into fear of personal loss, loss which has little or nothing to do with the rights and freedoms of her offspring. Nor is there any need for my argument to become age-specific. For the age when a child becomes an adult turns highly arbitrary once we discredit Nature's signals —which discrediting is, after all, the very purpose of civilization (as explained). Much better to look for, and locate, the living results of our tampering with Natural law; remembering: suppression of instinct always yields unhealthy and nasty repercussions. We need remember also our chat concerning the destructiveness of using age as a sole criterion (as civil law loves to do), ages when thus and such should happen or not happen. Much better to look for, and locate, that threshold when youth/parent relations take a negative politicized turn; that period when we begin to surrender control because we must, not because love/instinct says it would be best for our offspring if we did so. Then only will we see clearly at what point the world matron should have backed off from her political agenda, backed off and let Mother Nature have some say about matters on the home-front, allow Mother Nature to remind us once more what conditions in a healthy nest are like.

We have confronted these things ignoring what effect deferring the legal rights of our children has had on social morals in general. And there is nothing more general than an axiom. Let's try the following for a fit. What we desire instinctively but cannot have soon fixates us, soon becomes objectified beyond its inveterate value. And soon that objectification/idealization, in its blind passion, begins to include all that even vaguely resembles the original desired object. This unNatural objectification cannot help but be the most dangerous part of repression sickness. In this stark light social atrocities begin to unveil their causes for us.

For those readers still doubting that the world matron lives, is alive and unwell among us, let him or her pose the following to any woman over 40 (i would say 30, but age is as arbitrary an indicator in this instance as in any). The world matron dislikes (even less than Mother Nature!) being stuck babysitting for an extra decade much less babysitting a teen! For her to make such a sacrifice, the new rationale for what amounts to house-arrest for adolescents must be pretty important. But what if the sacrifice means something even more than keeping the family nest essential to society for an extra decade or so? What if there is yet another perk, a secret dividend, a dividend worth enduring years of familial and social dissension and upsetment? What if deferring the age when our children can/should leave home, effectively means, keeping an entire segment of society (read, youth) out of circulation (read, out of mate competition)? What if it means that now, responsible men must lust after more mature women if they wish to avoid social censure and even criminal punitives? Is such a dividend perhaps worth all the familial and social chaos?

And after posing these things (many of them after historian hilltana), o reader, by our reaction we shall know her, fix her unspoken (semiunconscious) agenda.

The Victorian era gave birth to many incarnations of the world matron. In Great Britain and its colonies "she" even managed a maskless face in what was then deemed the pinnacle of the social hierarchy: queen! *The* queen.

Rest assured, no matter its mistakes, no matter the pain its politics inflicts every hour of every day, this rare moment of historical reign will not be relinquished without a vicious battle, a battle which already has patriarchy's penis in its grip and is grappling for its very gonads as we speak. And it is our youth who are the fodder for this Victorian canon of belief. But what's new? The weak and the innocent are always the pawns of those in civil power.

It is crucial we stop here to remember something. We must steer clear of a dangerous and much-abused generalization. The battle of which i speak is not, and has not been for a very long time, women fighting for individual freedom and the freedom of their children. Were this the case we would have no glaring double standards to expose, and we could have left the world matron to the many *private* domestic devices for which she was evolved. No. Sad to report (to those many female friends who've stood by me thus far), this negative consequence —Bekky Kydd's advocacy for youth in domestic pain and trauma— is the result of women doing battle via the world matron, doing battle in order to sustain —not the Natural right to nest and rear offspring in a healthy and safe environment, as it should be— but, rather, to promote the Naturally transient union of a woman and man to a lifetime autonomy that is *un*Natural! and worst of all, to promote it even at the heavy and heartrending cost of communal and domestic unhappiness, dissension, pain, illness (both mental and physical), and, in far too many cases, tragic loss and the grief which follows it.

Reader, *nota bene!* I wrote this, underscored it, two years *before* meeting Lilith. It is also pertinent: Bekky's work up to ε incl'g this time had yet to adopt my world matron thesis.

Such is not the work of Mother Nature; such is not the application of female genius for nurture/protection/wisdom and health in the family/community setting. Facts be faced, it is its opposite: a campaign for selective suppression and exploitation which has erected a no-longer-very-secret chaos in family, community and the world at large.

O that there were room to insert here my exhaustive *op cit* procatalepsis.

The politicization and selfishness inherent in this Victorian backlash –still ongoing and aimed at settling accounts against 4000+ years of calculated patriarchy– is apparent everywhere. I have stated a number of instances up to this point and will take the time for one more. Luckily, having been on the front lines of defending women's rights for decades, i've been obliged to learn its history. This history makes clear beyond doubt. In the West, what we call the women's movement was born in victorianism. And like victorianism, though claiming to be rooted in religious ideals, from the start the movement was highly selective, using and abusing religion at will! (Not that patriarchy was any better of course.) It has thought nothing of fanning the fires of religious intolerance when convenient (as in issues such as divorce and sex drive: use your own examples) while simultaneously ignoring religion when it came to women's issues traditionally and dogmatically condemned by religion. E.g., female property- and matrilineal rights, abortion rights, free speech, etc., etc. The divine-right politicking (hallmark of both the world matron *and*-patron) tucked away in just this single instance is both startling and revealing. Check it out.

I'm writing fast again, cramming several books into a couple chapters. This never works. But we do what we can. (Have i said? Maybe not.)

For, while Mother Nature is nothing if not truthful, the world matron is nothing if not political. To wit: In just over a century fully one-fifth of the sexually viable populace in the western world has been banished from mate competition. This was done by raising in increments the marriageable age from an arbitrary 12-14 to an arbiterial 16-18. And now, with increased life-expectancy, is pushing hard for a ludicrous 21! And teens and parents have been at each other's throats ever since. And ever will be till changes are made, changes that take human Nature and chthonic (not politicized) caring into serious consideration. For the wrath of the one faction knows to be fact what the guilt of the other knows to be a lie. Yet fear of breaking the law —and moreover, of making the always scary leap from the nest into the lately wide and sheer ether of legal adulthood— has made that lie an enduring success, pyrrhic though it often is for parents and teachers; and lucrative though that lie is for psychiatrists, doctors, health and social professionals, law officers, lawyers, the courts, the prison system and the media (among others).

That some of our offspring should never leave home is of course axiomatic. Yet (as Ms Kydd so poignantly points out) it is direly offset by "those other millions of us banging the bars of our domestic cages for rightful independence.... Of course we teens don't understand that advances in industry and technology make us look ignorant, in need of ever more education. Nor *should* we understand —understand the veritable horde of such bogus arguments out there. For industrial and techno advance has made not only teens look ignorant, it has made every last one of us look ignorant! Does that mean *none* of us should be out in the world on our own?"

You go, grrrl! Why cant i make my truths sting like yours?

When Ms Kydd assigns blame to older women like her mother for stealing the rights and freedoms of youth for selfish purposes, she overlooks the fact that some of this larceny is committed by civilization itself: We thought we could take longer and longer to prepare our offspring for the unNatural world we'd created around them *without* creating a debit of pain and dysfunction. Wrong. Wrong wrong wrong. For when we played with this synchronization (of sexual maturity and personal independence) which Nature had legislated so elegantly (and so intractably), we did so quite unaware we were seeding whole libraries full of second-, third- and fourth-level civil illnesses!

But we must be wrapping this now.

It is important we not lose sight of the fact, when the Natural qualities of our genders are reasonably free to express themselves, we have little need to force our gender-oriented desires on the community at large. Our world patrons and -matrons then become relegated to *personal* use, are called upon only for *individual* needs, to which they are better suited.

This causes the ill-health that comes of repressed desire to disappear on a societal (communal) level. Our present world-war of the sexes would then be limited to domestic agendae —those personal disagreements necessary to thriving health, growth and safety of the species and its young.

Not inconsiderable among the ill effects we've mentioned are the gothic horror stories we so love; tales of sexual violence featuring trammeled purity, violated innocence (remember?); stories we love to see on trial in our courts, see in heated debate in our media; stories we cant wait to be first to know of, then to relate to one another. All these not-so-subliminal touchstones which help to perpetuate our cultural psychoses, help perpetuate our need to know of sexual crime –the written tales and testimonies, the news stories, the movies, etc.– all these panting quirks of ours, should they ever be unmasked (and Gaia save us poor souls who dare unmask them!), would soon fall into decline and disappear!

Yet, since the threat of imminent sudden mental health is clearly more than our residual Victorianism can bear, i shall end my tirade with the following conclusion. Just as patriarchy's long harsh rule was itself a backlash, a reaction (or rather overreaction) to the matriarchal autonomies of prehistory, so the world matron's rise to power is the result of thousands of years of instinctual oppression beneath patriarchy's fear-clenched fist. So filled with animosity are these repressions, the present women's (Victorian-based) backlash may yet become a reign of terror before it is done. Yet because cruelty is so antipathetic to the protect/nurture/healthy-community genius of females, the current backlash is in a sense harder on them than it is on the men of the present patriarchy. In another way of putting it. This reaction to long patriarchal oppression seems to me to be hurting women almost as much as it is the men they wish to teach an unforgettable lesson.

(With such confessions this hebegynolept seems to be suggesting his gynophilia rathermore resembles unadulterated gyneolatry.) Those interested in sampling these latter ill effects –this "thirdwave" disenchantment accreting among women– might re the book from which these excerpts are drawn, my *Mothernature & the world matron*. This gendered <political power tag> as i call it —in that it pingpongs, like the ugly game it often is, between the sexes over historical epochs— oversimplified, amounts to: "I've got the power now. Better run for your life!" Admittedly not very wise. But then, under all the fluff & mayhem, civildom, being antithetic to it, rarely resembles wisdom.

world patron in the buff

["...And close the abridgement please w that [[m&wm]]chapter which shows the world patron ε -matron operating in both primatologic, precivil ε modern domestic settings. I think it's the chapter which closes the intro to my world matron thesis, tho i'm not certain of this. [[It is. —Ed.]] The heading i'd like to give this section is 'world patron in the buff'."]

A critical rebalancing is now in order. None of the above means to imply, the world patriarch and -matriarch are unNatural manifestations, as i've said. They are not. It is their warping away from instinctive social situations that are their Natural milieu; and, in the most unfortunate cases, it is their warping toward non-kin (non-communal), regional, state, religious and even international imperial interests, which give these normally authoritative voices a screeching and artificial ring to ears in the know.

Along with my anthropologist/primatologist friend Denise Norris, i believe homo sapiens is closer to bonobos than to chimps in erotic traits and related behaviors. After more than a decade of "intimate observance of these little buggers" (as she affectionately calls them ...my favorite, if i may digress briefly, was a sexy little guy who, for so much resembling a woodpecker, she named "piddy pudwacker") ...Denise has given us repeated examples of politicized behavior among bonobos. "Adults, for instance, often use the awe and inexperience of youth to personal advantage, encouraging youngsters to do things they would not ask an adult to do. It is not uncommon for such encouragement to pass from coaxing to coercive before the youngster catches on and ends it... [Further on she says] ...We have seen countless instances of them doing what we have come to call 'making a mask'. That is, they will feign a given emotion in order to attain a given result. [A bonobo] wanting its back scratched, say, may put on a sad face —a face which under normal circumstances only outright assault could bring on. This conclusion is supported by what precedes and follows the 'masking'. The moment there is compliance with the wish, the mask, rather than gradually giving way to satisfaction, vanishes, is gone as quickly as it appeared! Whereas in a real emotional circumstance the same face might take anywhere from several minutes to hours, or even days (if the assault involves physical wounds) to disappear completely. This is personal politics, pure and simple."

Of course there is the disclaimer. "With human encroachment on every side one cannot be completely sure that all of the behaviors we have recorded are pristine and unaffected. Yet I would hazard, except for those instances noted, all the behaviors are common enough, consistent enough and casual enough to be representative of bonobo behavior as it was under circumstances of unspoiled wilderness, some 300 or more years ago."

In a community innocent enough (read, overtly instinctual enough) where the mere flashing of a sad face is sufficient to arouse empathy or guilt, there is little cause for cumbersome politicking. In circumstances where gender suppression is all but nonexistent, the world patron and -matron are content to play domestic/communal roles. Such examples among primates serve to show us the superstructure, if not the source, of civil politics. In such basic form as this the not-so-innocent counterfeiting of instinctual displays is easily accepted, easily absorbed, by family and community. Even what Denise calls "monkey-wrenching in the raw" is often judged to be "charming behavior" by her..."when, that is, I can get past the ugliness into which such behavior has evolved in my own species." (My emphasis.)

The eloquent anthropologist Biruté Galdiska has put forth the same message in another form. "Like man, not born with agendas per se, young orangs are not long in acquiring proto agendas. Though never achieving, even in adulthood, nearly the political sophistication evinced in the behavior of bonobos and chimpanzees[!], still, it is not long before an orang youngster knows how to make a 'hungry' or 'sad' face when circumstance allows. Not really hungry, or sad, but simply wanting attention, a youngster is not long learning to lobby for its wants." (My exclamatory.)

And now to the world-patron manifestation.

Countervailing humanity's efforts to leave 'bad' Nature far behind, Nature continually drives us to attempt to bring some sense of Wild justice into the wobbly webs of unNatural conditions which societies have spun in the name of civilizing. Attempting to assign some small sense of instinctual truth to our artificial existences, the world matron and -patron (long driven far afield of their native roles) are often called upon to support ideas and behaviors which Mother Nature wouldn't touch with our bodies much less hers. A consequence of these things is, as we mature we discover just how many of our parents' wishes were not wished for our benefit (as we were led to believe) but for theirs. Along with this awakening we begin to understand how many of their emotions (after our anthropoidal ancestors) have been put on like masks rather than instinctually felt. We usually reach our teens before we begin to catch on, and even then we don't recognize them as the politicizations of primal truths which they are in fact.

As understanding grows, the atmosphere of the nest becomes politically charged —fluffed up with half-truths and partial truths, lined and glued with outright lies. While the youth is searching for the lost Truth which the (civil) world has conspired to 'save' him from, her parents are vainly trying to justify why instinct/Truth must take a dive in the first place. Though they can't explain it, the simple fact is, the parents are equally correct in the frustrations of their dilemma. For civilization will have it no other way. After all, it is founded on dissatisfaction with Nature/Truth/instinct! Parental control is thus slowly sacrificed on the cross of lost Truth. And so both sides prepare for the (civilly) inevitable protracted confrontation called the adolescent (teen) years —a difficult period even lacking the chaos of civil law and expectation slopped into the equation.

Where simple physical enforcement cannot be used (as under critical conditions), desperate measures are called for. 'Wrathful father' and 'vengeful mother' displays are sadly often the only alternative. A truly effective performance requires of course the right actions. Where we civil parents once could elicit a good performance by imagining our toddler falling down, or burning herself, or shocking himself, or running into traffic, by the time our kids reach their teens we must imagine them being devoured by the "wild monster" of human desire! And, of course, all is lost if our actions are not bucked up with the appropriate dialog. I am your mother! screams the world matron in us, her voice shaking with remembered emotion. "What is wrong with you? I hardly recognize you anymore!" etc. As she moves through her script the world matron is hoping that any second a true Earthmother rush will overtake her. Since good acting can trigger emotional reactions (if not the chthonic Mother herself) *even in oneself,* maybe at least her shadow may make an appearance and save the day. For as we have learned, her shadow alone is good enough —if we don't blow it, that is; if we manage to keep hidden (from our now too perceptive offspring) the artificiality of our civil agenda.

For instance, a father may say (deepest voice, grandest sense of own magnificence), "What is wrong with you? Why can't you see, when you fail to do your best it reflects back on us, makes us look like we've done a bad job raising you!" Clang! Wrong! Akh akh akh! The youngster might have bought into the emotional criticism if it had been dressed up to look like he was somehow endangering life and limb, specially his own. But the family's social image? Hold on a sec. Imagine how stunned the father would be if his teen looked calmly at him and said, "Bad. Very bad, Dad. Off to acting class with you. Geez, even butch here [the dog looks up on hearing its name] ...even butch here knows, Skyfather/Truth isn't interested in class pride. Hey, unless you're ready to slamdance a set or two with me over this (and I really hope you're above all that), I'm afraid I'm outa here."

...Since the latter are examples of the world patron and -matron at work in domestic/community settings, shouldn't they work as they do for bonobos chimps and orangs? Of course —but only to the degree the world order they are submerged in is not deNatured. (Recall D. Norris' disclaimer about the pressures of encroaching civilization v. Natural behavior.) For every time we dilute suppress or pervert instinct/Nature, Truth and politics diverge further —til we reach that point civilization is at today, a point where Truth and daily existence rarely converge, and the more emotionally rooted of our kids go off in pursuit of a place (or state of mind) where the two become one again, a pursuit we view as the supremest naivete. And why not? Though critical to our continued survival, what could be more naive (and yet exaltedly wise) than trying to bring all of civilization back to its human nativity?

How absolutely logical then that, among humans and primates alike, the worst abusers of the world patron and -matron powers are typically the most instinctually compromised. To wit, the many among us who are who they are exactly because they make *careers* out of politicizing Nature/instinct/Truth. We know them at a glance. Politicians, ceos, lawyers, juries, public prosecutors, expert witnesses, clergymen, governments, banks, insurance companies, funeral homes, other artificial persons and entities which act in the stead of flesh and blood individuals acting for themselves. Yes, even me and you, reader! —to the extent that what we say and do are not representative of the Triarchy, Nature/instinct/Truth. [End NS' self-quote. —Ed.]

"Too didactic. Stop already!"

Not everyone reacted to my *Mothernature & the world matron* w the hilarious hurrahs & harpooned huzzas of sex historian rhea hilltanna. Book & movie critic for *the greenwash monitor*, in the autumn issue of 1992, wrote:

> [Schock's] habit of sniping perfectly normal [!] agendas with 'truth' and dashing gossip with 'facts' gets annoying. [!] After awhile you find yourself wishing he'd stop with the moralizing and let loose with a blast or two of back-biting vengeance. And his habit of shaming perfectly normal [!] politics with unassailable moralizing is so tooth-grindingly constructionist one longs to jump up, start a good old-fashioned war, just for the sake of smashing something! [!] For you know, every time there's an issue, Schock will take the high road. For some of us this is not so much tackling issues as rising above them. And one can take only so much of that. Like strong medicine, one is wise to take Nathan Schock in very small doses. —gnotu greenmann [my brackets]

Rarely have i replied to my critics and specially rarely to the sheltered-workshop variety (above). For while i can defend others i do poorly defending myself. This has led to my accreting over the years a stalwart 'rear guard', a couple sharp-witted tail-gunners who look out for my deepgreen caravansaries thru hazardous civil terrain. One is painter-friend from nyc, rex ardalion. Rex countered greenmann as follows. [Emil: I am paraphrasing from memory.]

> In reference Mr Greenmann's review of Nathan Schock's "Mothernature & the World Matron": I personally find it refreshing every time I meet someone along that 'high road' who didn't get there by cheating. Most everyone you meet up there arrived by one idealistic leap of faith or another, usually religious or political. The fact that Nathan Schock got there by the sweat and tears of empirical research and realist reasoning really ought to be worth some 'tooth-grinding' and 'annoyance' on our parts —the price a few of us (I hope not as few as I suspect) are happy to pay for not having to do all that research and reasoning ourselves...Mr Greenmann reminds me of that troubled classmate we've all had whose attention-span permits constructive behavior for only so long. It's him and his ilk who, the moment the teacher disappears, are first to flick spit or snap snot...'just for the sake of smashing something'. This is how the Greenmann's of the world react to the very civil repression Schock is trying to focus our denial upon. If nothing else, Mr Greenmann is good for a cynical chuckle or two —unless, of course, you're the one stuck wearing his obnoxious body fluids.

the unpredictability of the past

During a visit almost a year ago asst dir straitmon left a newspaper which he'd used as prophylaxis between his profligate rump ε the chaste rim of my naked commode. The paper was folded in such a way as to display a headline w my name color-circled. STATUTORY RAPE SUIT MAY BE FILED AGAINST SCHOCK. (Think i've mentioned this.) A woman from noogachatta tn, unable to get the state to prosecute her charges, took her case to the tabs. The socalled respectable media, not wanting to be left out of her 15mins of fame, dished the detritus measure for measure, using however a nasty old tactic: parroting the orig rumor. This is cowardly —to merely quote the braver source which initiated the rumor. While tabloidal intelligence may resemble warm wet disease, at least its spunky. The same often cannot be said for the orthodox popmedia. Aside from this noogachatta person being a nayirahan liar, if all races and all ages of humanity smack of my predilections, should i be garroted for sharing them?

the most popular lie

in the poppress generally has been to call Lilith's ɛ my relationship "a dumbert/dolita affair". Have i mentioned this? (Wish someone would return my ticklerlist.) This is a brazen re: to a novel in which pedophilia passes as lechery —a word about which, bytheway, needs be said.

the Natural bent of all healthy heteromales

To give the label "lecher" to a male simply because he chooses young women as sexpartners is the kick in the groin it is meant to be. Further, any heteromale who does not, generally speaking, prefer young woman over older ones (as sexpartners not mates) is erotically maladjusted or a damned liar. (The world matron will fly up at this point and begin her rave and by this too you shall know her.) Let me stress, i did not say, the healthy male prefers young women for marriage or domestic companionship —or whatever other unions civilized societies may dreamup in the course of failing to oust the uncomplicated urges Nature encoded ɛ intended. I said, prefer as *sexpartners*. Period. And all arguments to the contrary are just tyrannosaurus turd. Mock turdle at that.

dumbert & cronies

As for this prof dumbert person, whose writings the press keeps calling on to qualify its smutty innuendo about L ɛ me. If one skips homoeros, dumbert's particular paraphilia is by far the most common among humans. A few mins on the library computer the other day broughtup a book title which turnedout to be a virtual index of such things: *erotic purity: how we empower our child-molesting culture*. The loc blurb says the book "indicts adult society for enabling and supporting a pedophilic culture.... It offers hundreds of examples of what it calls 'our hypertrophism with child molestation...which in its high heat makes little time for other child abuses ...including the starvation of millions of kids around the world. Only molestation scandal provides us with the titillation we so love to pass on to others'." The loc review itself says "the author [kim jankaid] focuses principally on trial law and the content and slant of news and entertainment mediums including movies and tabloid TV to make their argument, the main thrust of which claims, 'we derive a secretive sort of fulfillment from telling and retelling endlessly stories of child molestation…[and] by this practice we eroticize our children'". Here the review quotes jankaid as follows.

> The authors of this survey would be little surprised to find whole cultures stunned and bewildered should we suddenly wake up one day unable to find anywhere, behind any bush, under any rock, even one victim of molestation. Or, heaven forbid, unable to find in any closet, under any bed, even *one* perpetrator of molestation! In such a world try to imagine how long it would take before the first teacher, the first Boyscout leader, the first exconvict, the first homeless person, would, without a shred of actual evidence, be looked at suspiciously? Try to imagine how long it would take for the first person entrusted with the care of children to be accused of being, or of protecting, a child molester? But most of all, try to imagine who would dare ask why we find it impossible to believe that a world *without* child-molesters could exist? Why exactly should the very idea of such a world strike us as impossibly naive and utopian? *That* is the *big* question. Though all refuse to acknowledge it, therein lies society's self-indictment. And therein it will stay. For who would be brave enough –or foolish enough– to answer honestly?

A dozen or so appendices to the book list scientific papers books articles documentaries movies artworks etc related to child molestation. One is titled "popular fiction with child-molestation as text". A cursory page-scan finds several hundred listed. Yes, several hundred, reader, in english alone! But more to the point. Heading the list for sales is the novel *dolita: the deadly obsession of a paneuropean white male*. In a subsection is listed "popular fiction with child-molestation as subtext". Heading this collection are rev c.l dodgson's *alice's adventures in wonderland, through the looking-glass* and "miscellaneous other works".

Now i've never been a purveyor of pulpfiction yet, in a place crawling w sex offenders (on both sides of the bars), you'd think such books would be banned. Well, a few mins browsing came up w not one but three copies of prof dumbert's *dolita* and one broken-spined copy of *the complete works of lewis carroll*, all dogeared and w the juiciest pages illegible from being so often peeled apart. Subsections in the jankaid work go on to list literally *hundreds* of books, reader; documentaries articles essays movies artworks etc which have been written about prof dumbert ɛ his dolita, and lists almost triple that amount concerned w rev cuthbert ɛ his alice! It is in fact mind-numbing how much scholarly chitchat has been lavished on the sexual predilections of these two men —and that's counting only what jankaid says he "bumbled across"! More amazing still is how few *facts* about this *idée fixe* of civil society have emerged from the nasty miasma. And worst, how little gutlevel honesty has slithered out of hiding. Which only goes to substantiate the authors' claim: "Society's need is to propagate the problem not solve it. *But of course* we protest toomuch. *That's* the whole idea! For nobody wants to put to rest, or wants *us* to put to rest, the truths or the myths of child-molestation. Societies–not just ours but all societies–have *always* secretly underwritten their "evils". And while we may love to rehash this stuff over and over –that is, while we may just love to hate it– it's our children who are paying the price. And ending that tragedy is the whole point of our work."

Protestation example. Alice, rev cuthbert's main squeeze, was hardly the nymph he claimed her to be. And prof dumbert's squeeze was no nymphet, since there's no such thing. All of which means, *neither* man was bewitched and should *not* be forgiven; certainly not using the lame excuse "I came under her spell". (Pun no doubt intentional.) Cuthbert ɛ dumbert were pedophiles, w primaryschool skulking reverend carroll the more repulsive of the pair for preying on naughty ɛ confused (not immoral and certainly not demonic) girls. Yes, i said, girls. We have here two sadsack males, together carousing public parks schoolyards play areas gyms candycounters themeparks sundayschools ɛ choirlofts. We have here two poltroons who fail to get even a twinge from the attractive teacher smiling at the head of the line of children; two men who fail to notice the pretty coed waiting for her kidsister at the bottom of a slide. For it is on the windflared dress, the suddenly bared legs, the flash of panties scooting down that slide that their glaucous-glazed gazes are fixed, not on the sexually mature females around them.

Exhibit 1. Over there, hunched by a bicycle he has feigned knocking over, see rev cuthbert snarking in the process the seat of his next alice-in-underhanded-adventures. Exhibit 2. To the right of him, we have prof dumbert, camcorder at rest on the seat beside him as if it were not filming, as if it were not being focused (by remote) at three (slitely older) girls on the swings, while its owner

appears to be reading a newspaper, somber eyes rising, falling, in time **W** the kicks & screeches of the girls, heart pounding at their wind-hiked dresses, slavering after his next dolita in dildoland. O someone needs uncoil at once this tangle of tawdry old tricks as the bulk of 'critical' works on these men are clearly out to protect, not indict, them *and* their depraved practices.

Children everywhere, when you shoot at bad men, shoot at [these guys]....

A copy of fyodor vanbok's *a modern nymph* is here as well as the 1995 imprint *vanbook's garden* by annie mae bobbson. In her critique bobbson says, "Here we have a pedophile with a penchant for poetry". This, reader, is her harshest criticism of vanbok and typical of most academics reviewing such works. And then there's bobbson on "reverend" (yes, she repeatedly says reverend) carroll, "who regularly brought to his Oxford studio after church in excess of a couple dozen prepubescent females over the years, thereat bribing and disrobing them for poetic and photographic purposes". Why the kid gloves (ahem) treatment from these critics? Because these men claimed to be "mesmerized" by what they called the children's "evilness". PedOphilias witchlets chicklets cocklets cokelets nymphets, i dont care what name is assigned them. All your *pretty poisons* besquat, there's no such thing as an "evil" child. Period. In fact, except that certain religions have said it is so, there is no such thing as evil —a concept which enters philosophy at the same point infinity enters in math: where comprehension can no longer get a foothold. Ask yourself why, to the bobbson brand of academentia, the difference between a 2yearold footstamping & empurpled w rage over a denied piece of candy and a scowling politician just fined by a court for having been caught w his hand in the cookiejar has *nothing* to do w morals or ethics and everything to do w thespian polish or lack of it? Vanbok's hazel dahl, merely imitating her mother & her mother's society, chose to use her body to acquire the 'cookies' of her choice, and those cookies did not just *happen* to be prof dumbert, his social status and his money. Not to mention that it is just plain disgusting to make a 12yearold orphan masturbate you in public while you ogle her classmates.

Reverend carroll, once exposed, should long ago have served as warning to us of the twisted lusts of celibates generally.

Celibacy curses all Natural society. Even hitler's hero, afterall (brother von liebenfels), was a monk.

≈When the orphan is forced to weep, the very Cosmos shudders.≈ —saadi

Yet such violence to near-children is never broached headon by these scholars. "Never!", says jankaid. "And worse, *we* rarely criticize these "critics" for their ghoulish silence!" Great Gaia! How dare we civilized pretend there is no outlaw instinct insanely busy among us!

Thus am i saddened every time i see my lightsome & story-magical Alithe in Natureland (my Lilith) confused by the courts, or their press, w the coarser younger skin-deep likes of alice or dolita or hazel or any other counterfeit nymphs of book or movie fame. For i am heartbroken & disgusted every time i find my Love numbered among the dozens of 'alices' whom the oxford don regularly abused after church. What in hell (or heaven) have these tawdry trappings to do w me & my Lilith? Nothing. Lilith's body was 17 when i met her and her mind at least 300yrs wise! Yet such smutty affronts keep scandalizing my Love in the popmedia, contaminating her legacy all across this Planet she so passionately loved. Surely before my last word has been spoken the magic in our love will lift us above all the dung & decay.

history v. civil twistory ...one last time

My goal for outing the facts besquat, some day the historybooks will get it right; the allegations of the fed. & its poppress will be seen for what they are: ghoul scat. For in all the world there's nothing Lilith hated more.... No, that's wrong. She hated nothing. There's nothing she *feared* more than her stepfather. It is he not i who was the pedophile in her life. I've said i do not believe in evil. Yet if anything could cause me to so believe, it is the man she called okka & all his kind. Man-devil. Devil-man —who cutshort her childhood, locked her away in a psychic prison; a prison whose rules made her feel unworthy of childhood yet forbade her adulthood. Obeahan shaman, bocor priest! blazing bigger than life in my brain tonite; howling in ecstasy, spurting hatred for females from his flanks like a galactic flamethrower, his mambo, his cochon gris, chanting all the while, *Filles ce' marchandises peressables,* his favorite mantra as old as civilization itself!

But i must be calm about this, must explain my position dispassionately; step by step i must show the reader why these accusations (of the poppress, & of the forces which manipulate that press) are lies. For the popmedia is where Reality (Universal Nature) & objectivity are bound burned bashed buried or banished every day. Contrast this w my own foresworn mission; to see to it that any mirages in mnemy's script are, at the very least, noted in the margins of this testament. Yet i cannot recount these events. Not yet i cant. Must keep to the order of things as they occurred, not to a chronology convenient to my reputation. Anyway, soon it will be time for us to take Lilith's journals in hand, let she herself relate the trauma of her earliest womanhood. Then will be time enuf to speak in my own behalf.

nymphs: rare as dragon teeth & unicorn horn

Reader, follow over my shoulder, play please the part of the only kindly mask in this my cage, as i copy (w fresh pencil onto a fresh page) from a prison encyclopedia.

> Nymph, 1. Gk myth Numerous lesser female deities, inhabiting rivers, forests, lakes, woodlands, trees, mountains, valleys, meadows, marshes, seas, streams, fountains, waterfalls, grottos.

That said, let us pause to examine a dash of dialog: "If I see one more mountain, one more waterfall, one more indian reservation, one more wildlife preserve, I swear I'll puke all over this leave-it-to-beaver car!" Gnawing a cuticle, tossing her head in disgust. "Can't we, just this once –just this once!– do something interesting?" Speaking is someone whom prof dumbert, in his memoir, dares tell us is a nymph ("nymphet"). Well, the intelligent researcher will look in vain thru the pages of dumbert's book for one glint of a nymph. We find instead a girl confused by a confused mother, w an ego dizzied (and made further unmanageable) by the scummy affections of a new stepfather; and finally, a girl raised in a society which leaves no question that, short of bodily harm to another, material acquisitiveness (read: greed) is what life is all about, or should be. So it is greed that drives both dumbert ε dolita to their separate dooms. "Not only did my little love have no eye for natural beauty, not only would she brazenly ignore the many mountain-, lake- or woodland scenes we glided past along our winding and winsome path to the west, but she even belittled me when I, her cheerful tourguide, called her attention to this or that exotic detail of landscape." Nymph? Who does he think he's fooling? As for nymphets? Totally bogus. Prof dumbert's handy artifice. Nowhere in the legends or myths of any area of the world are nymphs children. They dont *need* to be, for they are the epitome of youthfulness, of ongoing *adult* self-rejuvenation.

Tho there are literally hundreds of critical works about professors dumbert ε cuthbert, as jankaid has shown, their perversions rarely come under attack in these works. So my question is: Why are these wily word-wizards permitted to strut about world academia in silk pajamas ε smoking jacket and sporting scholarship like society slatterns; permitted to go on pulling from their silk hats endless bogus nymphs ε spurious spells? I'll tell you why. Because, hidden under the linings of those hats, hidden in the literary erudition ε linguistic dazzle of their false passes, they hold the beloved repressions of civil society at large. And what of their critics? Are we to believe that so many experts do not understand the historic definition of nymph, of nympholepsy? Do i harp? Am i unsubtly infuriated? You bet your propaganda-perfused life i am. For every day, in some major medium somewhere, my Love ε me are compared to these sorry sadsacks of civil humanity.

And so a famous child molester and his propitiated scholarship roams free, defaming the word nymph in every quadrant of the Planet. And once again Mothernature, matrix wherein all nymphs exist, is throttled by a phallus-inured literati and its dirty-minded audience. Humping hyenas! Civiljizm! Let them bubble w babble about nymphets ε whateverlets. Their ignorance of 'what comprises a nymph' is obviously but a matter of legal convenience, a means of justifying their nasty little predilections. Wake up, sleepyheads! Newage brotherSun is breaking the horizon and our tousled heads are still under the covers! Yes, i'm outraged. You would be too. Look w me at the foto in this magazine rosa sent, w its blowup of Lilith, laughing blueeyed, snowy show of teeth, ponytail twirling onto one hip, leggy ε lovely and looking like a dream in shorts ε white blouse. And nevermind the purity ε joy overbrimming this foto, look what the cutline has to say.

> "Federal prosecutors are asking, did Schock's girlfriend, teen Lilith McGrae, have complicity in the raid of Ecoczar Strickland's mountain hideaway and his subsequent murder?"

The real story of the foto is croppedout: Lilith w gE activists on-board the aurora warrior, carrying placards, flags ε banners which proclaim: St. Lawrence Is Dead, Now His Seaway Is Dying! The smiles are victory smiles, not smiles of sexiness ε pulp smut. A barge, destined for dumping offshore, heaped w 300ooo tons of toxic waste, has just been turned back toward a more responsible fate. And yet, when this foto finally hits the media bigtime (the way it should have when it was orig released), it is under a shadow of alleged murder terrorism conspiracy sedition subversion ε soforth, along w a competing story which claims, Were the Caresh Kids Sex Slaves? My good reader needs only one guess to hit on why the articles were run sidebyside.

And i am imprisoned ε virtually helpless, my cries of <Leave her alone, you soulless ghouls!> cutoff from all hope of being heard. I cannot throw myself in front of my mary of magda, slumped there on pretty knees, facing the stones of an idiot mob, her great wide eyes welling *w* tears, dark tresses dragging in the dust. All i can say is (and years after the fact if i'm ever heard *at all*): Let him who possesses the pure heart she owned cast the first stone! I shake my cage, thump my chest, roar like a wounded kodiak, a *mortally* wounded kodiak: My God, why have you forsaken her?

the corpse-eaters

They sit at their screens like vultures and peckpeckpeck at the keys *w* necrosis-colored beaks, each time comingaway *w* a flap of flesh —sometimes big sometimes small sometimes still alive sometimes rotting. It doesnt matter to them. Violence, sex & conflict are what matters. Preferably young violence, young sex, *w* a good oldfashioned war, spattered *w* just the right touch of legal- & technobabble, thrown in to make for a great day's news. For exposure to such things proves –to creatures too long cutoff from Natural peril and the adoration of existence that goes *w* it– that, Yes! We civil are in fact alive!

The following is a taste of what i'm up against. Track please the note i found in the weightbench the same day rosa sent the mag.

Mitzi says you didnt get mad at me *[not]* because your *nice...[but because]*...you like girls younger *than* me. *[and that]* You were...probly *happy I didnt* go *throgh* with it. *Thats not true* is it? Please *dont be* mad if *it's not*, ok. *Its just* what some of *the* girls are saying. *Still* your friend Rosa. *(I hope.)* PS. A friend of Mitzi will *bring* you some *newzpapers* soon so you can see *I'm not* making *it* up. *Write* back PLEASE.

Mitzi's delivery system being better than rosa's & mine, i rcv'd (via glumm) a rubberband-bound roll of fotocopied newspaper & zine articles several hours before i returned from my workout and could read the note itself. The poor wretches who have keptup *w* my trial via the *irrational inquirer* were at one point thrilled by this banner. ACCUSED KILLER SAID TO PREFER JAILBAIT. Fotos of Lilith & me grace its coverpage. Her's is a hs yearbook portrait taken before we met, while mine is a scruffy shot snapped on my way to or from court. A subhead reads, TRIAL EXPOSES BIZARRE ALLEGATIONS ABOUT GREEN HERO. This article accompanied rosa's note. All but stunned, i sat on my new bunk and read on. In a box on page 3, beside a foto of what looks to be a mafioso *tosta faccia*, i read (see box):

I am haunted lately by nicks & zigs of several sexes: nikki, dr zigmoid & this latest fool. The article, predictably, fails to note: when zig knew me we were both in our teens. So of course we went out *w* teenagers. I just happened to be the one who liked girls. As to zig being "oudda touch". Was that ever in question? But we were never friends, as zig claims —just went to the same school (and not the umbrian school either), trained in the same gym. Even in the city (where brutality is business-as-usual) he was not liked, being into neo-zootsuits, zipguns ɛ bullying boys younger than himself (handy excuse for touching them). It was a nasty catch-22 for the kids. If zignorelli liked you, or if he didnt, you *still* got a licking. After i took the title in joyzeecity –in which event he did not even place– he asked (just to be near as flashbulbs were popping ɛ cams were rolling), "Hey, nate. [flexing, looking down, both hands turned in, pointing at self] What's amadda wid deez cuts?" —a not uncommon question in the sport, where 'cuts' re muscular delineation. Two things, i answered. One: your biceps are bigger than your head. Two: a thug named zignorelli lives inside those cuts. Reporters scribbled feverishly. He probably never forgave me. Too bad. But i was a victim of bullies as a kid. Loathed them then, loathe them still. Their disguise is transparent: military minds wout rank, politicos wout a constituency, dictators wout armies, kings wout slaves. The need for power in hollow people is as old as life itself.

"I've known schock since we wuz kids. When I met 'im he wuz goin out widda 15-yeah-old. 'Bout a yeah layda, when I saw 'im at anodda competition, he wuz datin' a goil around 16 aw 17. I dunno whut he's been upta loitly. I'm oudda touch." —Nick Zignorelli (Dialect added for realism.)

I try to imagine who likes the tabs. I think almost everyone in this place slavers over every (toilet t-)issue they can lay hands on. Forinstance, how did mitzi (or whomever) comeup w this article almost a year after the fact? Someone must keep back-issues. Aaaargh. Newsprint doesnt even have to be read to be toxic. The very paper its printed on is doused in chlorine and the ink is comprised of tar ɛ rat urine. (You think this is hyperbole, doncha?)

"Body builders are mostly fags and exhibitionists anyway. My guess is, Schock is a fag who uses females to get ahead. There's lots of them around. He probably prefers young girls to older women 'cause they don't intimidate his sexuality and don't ask a lot of questions."
——Richie Reynolds

Reynolds claims he knew me —one of the many curses of fame. The article tells the drooling reader, "Ms McGrae was a teenager when the accused murderer first met her". Mere mention of the words murder ɛ teen in the same sentence is guaranteed to titillate 20million near-illiterates who could giveacare about the incredible changes Nature can effect in us humans during our teens. Then they use an md's quote, tossingin a word one reader in a thousand understands. "Doctors call his kind, nympholepts." The editors, knowing well the reading level of their audience, waste no time in having the shrink they unearthed wing a definition that suits their purposes. "A nympholept is any older man who prefers to have sex with young girls". Clean miss there! Even our sorry prison dictionary does better: nympholept, a person seized with nympholepsy. Then, under nympholepsy: " 1. type of enthusiasm [now that's coy] which compels the behavior of those bewitched by a nymph 2. ecstasy of an erotic type." But, sorry, tab readers, the definition breathes not a word about age; not a peep about "young girls" or "older men". Get a life.

Beside, in most of u.s criminal law, an 18yearold who has sexual contact w a a 17yearold is a pervert. Imagine! The courts, ε their media, at whim, can turn almost all 18yearold males into practicing perverts just by applying the law as written! What is sick if that isnt? Let's just say, for the hell of it, the so-called murderer (whom i guess is supposed to be me) is a nympholept. Well, gadshazm! If any civilized male is, i am! But i would caution the reader: To the degree the women i have dated ε mated w are uncivilized, it is to that same degree i am a nympholept. My fear is, how few will get this. *Really* get it. I expect only one in a million to do so in the *fullness* of its meaning.

Said article is three pages long, w a lengthy tail on a fourth page! It goes on to accuse me not only of "nympholepsy" but of "pedophilia". Jumping jackaljizm! Not bashful to stop there, it plunders on to insinuate, i am "exhibitionist" "bisexual" "neonazi" and, for good measure, a "coconspirator in the u.s militia movement". Poor rosa. This is truly gruesome stuff. But does the article make a direct accusation? Nuh-uh. Too clever for that. They place calls to 'authorities' til they get a statement guaranteed to bliss an idiot. And that's their cue to print.

"Curves. That's the key word here. Healthy males like their woman to have curves—and in some cases, lots of them. They want to see breasts, hips, buttocks. These are the sexual triggers in the healthy male. Not so in the homosexual. Hips and breasts turn him off. And this is where young girls come in. Their sex organs aren't developed yet: hips haven't flared, breasts haven't...well, filled out. Their bodies are boyish. It is for this reason certain [homosexuals] find young girls attractive." —Dr Hans N. Knippel

---

My head throbs, my heart aches, and this trash adds new masks to the walls of my tombal cell. One can be made to feel paranoid, you know. More&more i come to believe in them —the masks, i mean; more&more they seem to stare down at me, study me, by day ɛ by nite. Aaaaaaaargh.

Lilith

Is it sa or su? I believe i've lost another day. O well. What's another day when youre counting every heartbeat?

The trammeledtruth tabs are one thing (there were six or so tearoffs in the bundle). It's the innuendo of the socalled respectable press that hurts the most. During my trial many racy articles began to ooze into print. One in particular which mitzi sent (and which i ran into in jail during my trial) appeared in the society slick *metropolitan woman* —a women's monthly (pardon the bloody likeness). Touted as highbrow ɛ chic, it seems *mw* could not passup the sales to be had by milking the pop subjects of my trial: murder, sex ɛ politics. We'll skip the murder ɛ politics and cut straight to the sex. The article referred to Lilith's ɛ my romance as a "dumbert-dolita affair", w ns being the dumb-former and Lilith the doll-latter. At the time i knew little of who these dumbert ɛ dolita people were (all fictional, bytheway).

How cheapened she, having already suffered kidnap, assault ...and still blacker atrocities i havent the stomach or timeline-rights to rehash just now... how cheapened she must have felt to be called "the dolita-like property of an accused murderer and neonazi radical" so soon after burying her sister? There are vultures who.... No, not vultures. Vultures are good, necessary. There are ghouls who love to feed on the corpses of the young ɛ lovely, who prey on the broken bodies of the weak ɛ suffering. The *mw* article served up almost as much slime as my trial: What part did i play in the militia movement? was i responsible for other political murders? did i play a part in the ok city bombing? was i connected to the unibomber, or perhaps figure in: the bureau of land mngmt (blm) hq bombing, the forest service ranger's house bombing, the amtrak sunset special crash? and could i help expose "the secret political mission of the green party"? and toward what "dirty and dangerous beliefs", what "bizarre practices", was i –both as myself and in the guise of "good Captain GreenEarth"– trying to lead the youth of the world?

Two fotos accompanied the article. One was the yearbook shot noted above, the other was a shot taken during our visit to the san carlos reservation, near fort apache (az). Lilith wore the outfit just given her: blouse, moccasins, twirly skirt, zigzagged by a circle of vermilion teepeelike designs, her amerind-looking dark hair flowing, flashing a smile that could make even an ancient totempole grow in the sunlite!

I'm delited to report, the popular male zine *jock & jill* took issue w *mw* on one point. In a section called "the phallic forum", *j&j* editors commented as follows. [Please insert entire article, Emil.]

Smutty Aspersions Department

An article which appeared in the October issue of *Metropolitan Woman* referred to enviro activist and author Nathan Schock's relationship with one Ms Lilith McGrae as a "Dumbert/Dolita affair".

While we can't go into the politics of the Schock trial in this brief Forum, the ability to tell women from girls happens to be our strong suit. Come now, ladies. A Dumbert-Dolita affair? Dolita was only 12 when Professor Dumbert copped her and boffed her! If Ms McGrae is 12 in the pictures you printed, as your article implies, we'll eat every word!

In the meantime: While we can abide *MW* editors calling Ms McGrae "a yuppy update on *Candy: the Counter-Culture Coed"*, we cannot abide the Dolita stuff. In fact, the innuendo strikes us as hitting well below the belt. One wonders if the ladies at *MW* have impaired vision. Or maybe an ax to grind. Or maybe both.

We here at *J & J* say, "We came, we saw, but we don't concur: Schock's lady was definitely no kid! Vavoom! And again. Vavavoom!" We give three thumbs-up (or whatever) for this beauty! Come now, ladies. Do try to play fair.

The "candy" reference (one guesses) is to a comic novel which, along w the dumbert/dolita dossier, cost me another hour on the loc computer today. All of which showed, my love was a mature female when i met her and all the rest is society's sickness not mine. But havent i said this? Of course *j&j*'s editorial bodyslam was nowhere to be found in mitzi's collection. Head feeling kicked around; heart, heavy. There is an ax buried in the chest of this angst, and it's name is world matron. It is *she* who floats one of the most merciless masks in my cell. But i protest toomuch. Still, under the weight of such venomous assaults, how can i not? (Odd phenomenon. All insinuata aimed at ε striking me, lose their sting when placed alongside media slurs targeting Lilith.)

the `thaw-white-nesbit' analogy

One last excerpt. *Chicmopolite,* the most widely read women's slickmag in the world, couldnt resist following *mw's* precedent w its more sophisticated slant on scurrilous scandal.

> Ironically our century is closing with a murder trial having striking affinities to another much-celebrated trial which opened it. Like the Lincoln-Kennedy similarities uncovered by scholars, many things and events concerning the tragic Schock-Strickland-McGrae *ménage a trois* are surprisingly similar to things and events in the ignominious Thaw-White-Nesbit scandal of 1906.

I am not going to place my credibility at risk by denying all elements of this largely whacko analogy. After all, the genders of the subjects (m-m-f) are alike, bygosh&bygolly! As to the rest —incl'g the age of florence floradora at the time of her defloradation, *and* the murder charge itself— the comparison is force-fitted, distorted ε inverted. And worst of all, "the girl on the red velvet swing" was not murdered by fed.agents as was Lilith's sister; and neither was thaw put to death for white's deeds as i am being put to death! This is exactly the sort of opportunist scandalmongering i am aiming at when i blast the poppress suffocating me.

the only package i've gotten in months (that is not from my lawyer) turnsout to be somebody's collection of pop coprophytes?

The cause of this lowlife resurgence about us in the media? I found it floating amidst the semisolids in mitzi's pool of sepsis, it too ~~founded upon~~ foundered upon the same tabloidal pretext: the inane accusations of one thelma thigpen (in yet another chicslick, *glitter & glitz)* whose foto reminds me of the girl under the table in a painting called "applejack nite" (i think) by a talent i dont recall. ["Snap Apple Night", by Daniel Maclise, 1806-1870. —Ed.] Except that now, added to her rape ε sodomy silliness, is paternity: my alleged fathering of the oldest of her three offspring, whose moronic gazes are however drooling replicas of daddy thigpen not me ...whose dream of money&fame emil says is behind the whole thing anyway. He says they have no letters fotos videos or fonebills or anything beside gossip to support their claim. Just because she seems to know the location of a scar on the underskin of my gender, the very flimsiest of pretexts has once again fixed the focus of the unprincipled press. In what sort of society does one flash to fame w such a claim? The reporter contends to have checked her story against medical records and found it accurate. It says nothing of how this travesty of my most private privacy was engineered. (Why do i smell the fed. again?)

Of all the women in my life who know of this scar firsthand (pardon the expression), leave it to one too plump to be of interest to anything smaller than a blind rhino, to go public w it! As i told emil a couple weeks ago, while i know noogachatta is a big town, i find it a little curious this lard-laden liar should hail from the same place, be about the same age, as someone Lilith ɛ me made friends win a nooga sweetshop a couple years ago. Here is someone i should write to, thus put the fbi on her uncouth back for awhile. <Dear ms thigpen, If I throw you a stick dipped in baconfat will you go away?> I'm ready to launch my own exposé. But not against this fubsy snaggletooth ɛ her gnathonistic seethru agenda –for only the most ignorant foto ɛ cutline carouser could take her seriously– but rather an exposé dedicated to unmasking the motives ɛ mindset of a culture which so carefully teaches our youth, and so early in their lives, how to become famous based on things sexual. Hey bek, got a minute for this particular cultural baiting of our youth?

Glitter & glitz, a mag no hair salon would be caught open for business wout, accompanied this feature trash w another "expert opinion" sidebar. (Well maybe just one more from this disgraceful archive?) "The artistic talent [of Ms McGrae] should not lead us astray" says dr mazotrop, psychiatrist.

> Apart from her artistic skill she is your average finger-tapping gum-snapping coed. ...And while her mentor-lover does not qualify as the pedophile some have suggested [geegolly, thank you], any older man who uses his fame and influence to stalk our loveliest and most-talented youth, does however still qualify as a lecher —unless they changed the rules since I last checked [such clever, gosh, prose]. And while he may have violated no morals codes, he certainly should not be left on a pedestal with others of our nation's best, a position of power he has apparently abused. ...And finally, cartoon and movie allegories of such a man's life, no matter how dressed-up for general consumption, should not be watched by our children every Saturday morning. [my bracketed asides again]

Does this sort of lowtech sex rap have credibility anywhere? What a noseful of nasty nostrums to sneeze into the public's face, doctor! Even win the high walls of nunneries ɛ monasteries they do better than this! Such accusations are a travesty of both language and fact —specially while men like Lilith's stepfather ɛ his best friend, an actual factual documented pedophile, slip past uncharged —even in a press which craves such sepsis! What i'd like to be shown, and soon, is exactly how my erotic tastes qualify *anywhere* in the world by *anybody's* law as unNatural —or even come close.

without legal basis

Before we tackle the most penetrating sex study ever undertaken in modern civilization.... A few mins in the library yesterday taught me, one cannot just flop open a dictionary, even a law dictionary, to the word pedophilia and get the facts. For behind all the civil legislation of human sexuality lurks a deeper truth. What makes pedophilia criminal in the u.s varies from state to state, from region to region. It even varies from county to county win given states ...if only in the way such statutes are applied and/or enforced. And, as one might guess, it varies even more widely around the world. In point of fact, a clear definition of pedophilia does not exist. And, more revealing still, not even one "working" definition comes close to working everywhere. This alone should flagdown curiosity. But of course it doesnt. For we dont want it to. And there is a reason for this; and the reason stinks not just to arcturus (as i think i've said), but all the way back to this our (pure) Star again!

I did not study psychology before i was sent to war. But i do know, a good psychologist must understand the subconscious —that unique room i mentioned? the one wout a floor? But then, good psychologists are rare as sperm ears ε good psychiatrists even rarer. I lived in that shadow room for 18months and i met there, face to face, much of its contents. Most shrinks have not, and *will* not, become intimate w the contents of this room. I believe they fear it more than their patients fear it.

I ransacked our library ε its capable computer. I was looking for stats on the median age of consent worldwide? By the time i'd finished, not only did the 'legal age' of 21 melt away into a joke of juris *im*prudence, so did 18 ...not just in the u.s but everywhere! Why? Because the law as written and as practiced (application to reallife circumstances) are worlds apart. And not coincidently, about the same distance apart as civil law has strayed from Natural law.

teenolepsy?

A major discovery was *the novalis-deland report on human sexuality,* a work which, as i think i've said, i avoided because of its sheer bulk. This report, 20 years in the making and recently (1995) completed, fills ten volumes, totaling over 15ooo pages! Now i know (if anyone knows) size alone means nothing.

I found *the novalis-deland report* (hereinafter *the n-d report*, or *the report*) outstanding for its ability to cut to causes, causes both subconscious ε instinctual. It does not become boggeddown in regional ethics, law ε religion, as happens w so many studies —the latest *kingsley report* being one of the most pretentious ε banal perusings of my entire week, straining as it does to compete w the psyche pablum of waxman ε johnson, whoever they are. Poor albert must have chewedup the underside of many a coffinplank since he turned over the reins to the present kingsley foundation.

The n-d report deals specially well w sociosexual taboos, leaving many of them groundless, based solely on superstition or stupid tradition —two terms which, after all, are cousins not only in sound but substance. The usual legal gags, the religious blindfolds, the idealistic expectations ε political pressures, all the things which typically encumber most studies, are not only absent in *the report* but are exposed at once in its foreword —a small book in itself. The last three books of the study were assigned one of its bulkiest topics: *the novalis-deland report on eligibility paraphilias.* Before we cut to the chase and excerpt a particularly revealing personal study, let me explain what an eligibility paraphilia is.

Such would include a man, say, who can achieve orgasm only w a very old woman. It would also include a woman who can be sexually satisfied only by a male in puberty. Paraphilia in both cases refers to a special requirement of the ageing process. Eligibility enters because both subjects are predestined to lose their lovers. For once the old woman dies, and once the boy's pubescence fades to manhood, the paraphiliac must begin the search anew, looking for a new 'eligible' partner. So it is w someone said to have "adolesophilia" or "periadultomania". (In the last few days i've run the gamut of ludicrous terminology.) Briter vultures and their editors, seeing the stupidity of calling someone a pedophile who has a clear sexual preference for adults, have used on me the robbe-grillet coinage, teenolepsy. That age alone should *never* be the criterion, muchless impose the law; that there can be all the difference which maturation can manage between ages 13 ε 19 (the teen years); that 95% of persons under 16 strike me as either brittle twigs or repulsive doughballs, is never mentioned in these cowardly attacks. For in a statement such as i just made there is little latitude for dirty minds to sloperate, little room for what otto reich called "that certain secret social sickness" (and what he named, the outlaw instinct) to rally its darker forces.

a layman gets a word in edgewise... at last!

[Emil, please obtain permission to quote the following. Use checked passages only. Thanks.]

[Photocopies of pages 13445-48 of *The Novalis-Deland Report on Human Sexuality, 1995* are inserted at this point in N.S.'s manuscript, which consists of the greater part of a single interview. —Ed.]

The interviewee is a white male 48 years old, appears to be well socialized, has been sexually social since age 17, has never been married, has cohabitated with a woman on four occasions, the longest incidence lasting five years, has no children, is an upper-to-middleclass U.S.A. citizen of European extraction three generations removed, is college educated, has a BS in anthropology, has kept the same job (public safety) for twenty-eight years and is active in community affairs. As with the other interviewees in this section, he has volunteered his assistance with no hope of remuneration and was asked to help shed light on the gray area where normal male sexual behavior grades into a general legal definition of pedophilia. His views on human behavior were also used in a preliminary Novalis-Deland study (1976).

Statement of Interviewee #USASWM 48-834

I was in my 20's when I began to suspect I wasn't alone. By the time I was 30 I had no doubts. I knew damn well what was going on by then. But it was because of the job I had. Most men *never* figure it out. [Interviewer: Why is that, do you suppose?] I guess you have to be in the right place at the right time. My job was, in some ways, like a lab experiment, like a doctorate study in human relations —only better!

[Better?] Yeah. I had an office which overlooked two miles of beach, at the main entrance of [names well known beach resort on the Pacific]...which was located, about midway, in a busy plaza, pier and boardwalk area. You've probably heard of it. [I was there not long ago.] Well there you go. There's all sorts of shops and eateries; your typical tourist traps–leisure seizures, we call them–where thousands of people a day pass by, or just hang out. The biggest hangers there are boppers. [Boppers?] Teens, you know? Been hanging there since the flood. [Could you be more specific? We need to know what you mean when you say teenagers.] I see what you mean. The difference between 13 and 19? Is that it? [That's part of it.] Well, then. That's a hard one. [Why is that?] I guess, because a bopper, by definition, is any girl–well, young woman, *actually*–who is a sex object. Or even one who's just *trying* to be. It's not an age thing so much as an appearance thing, an attitude thing. Come to think of it, there's another term we have in the beach bus [business]: Little honeys. These are girls who act sexy but who you just know, or sense maybe, are jail bait. Here I guess age *does* apply to a degree. But it's still a guessing game, not a science. While we know they're younger than boppers –generally speaking, I mean–here again, to put an age on any of this... Hmm. Tough. Really tough. Never thought about the age-parameter thing in exactly this way. Here I thought I was going to be comprehensive—lay comprehensive, if you will ...pardon my French. [You're doing very well. Don't stop.] Thanks.

This is apparently going to be a learning experience for me too. But back to setting age limits...I don't know. I don't like it. I think that's where all the trouble started to begin with. [How's that?] I've seen 20- and 25-year-olds who didn't radiate nearly the sexuality of the occasional 14-15-year-old you sometimes see. It seems, you can be way-legal sexually speaking and still not be as ready for it as some considered illegal. This sort of thing makes putting an age on it tough—impossible really, when you think about it. [Are you saying the arbitrariness of age renders the law unjust when it comes to human sexuality? If I'm putting words in your mouth please say so.] You're not. When it comes to *any* sexuality, really. Imagine trying to convince a judge who is gay just why your client went to bed with a female to begin with, never mind one who's quote unquote too young. [laughter] It's not just a case of, *looks* mean *everything*. It's also a case of who's looking... [I'm interested in....] And *why* he's looking too, come to think of it!

[That's true. Let me see... Can you embellish on "looks mean everything"?] Hmm. You know, I should make it clear here. I'm talking mostly about things I saw from my office. Did I say, this is not my private life I'm dishing here? When it is, I'll be sure and let you know. [Fine.] Embellish, huh? Let me see. For years, for decades, really, I've thought of my office as a glass room high above a hoard of modern hominids, people as naked in many ways as any ape in a zoo. And the glass was dark-tinted beside. A cupola, you know, like an airport tower? Did I say? On top of the two-story main building in the park, which was on top of a ten-foot high rock ledge to begin with. Our tower office sat near the pier and right beside the boardwalk, which goes for a half-mile in both directions. I spent twenty-three years in all in that glass house forty feet in the air! Being Polish, plus my long hair and all, somewhere along the way I got nicknamed Rapunzak. We could see to the horizon in every direction but east. Buildings blocked the view that way. We saw not only ocean and beachfront for miles, we could see twenty blocks down [names oceanside street] in both directions, which is a hopping place all by itself.

[Have you ever had a different job?] Off the beach...? No. I did spend my first five years in a lifeguard tower though... On the beach, I mean! Oh, I had odd jobs while I was getting my degree. But nothing steady. [You seem to think this vantage point played a big part in what you've been able to learn. Why is that?] Because I've seen human beings from every angle, people who either had no idea they were being watched or just didn't care. In fact, a lifeguard is *paid* to keep his eyes open, to see stuff. And I did. It was like being a forest ranger —getting paid to look for smoke ...except the scenery never got boring where I was. And there *was* smoke, believe me! Real infernos sometimes! The kind of fires that burn underground, fires that most people don't get to see. Or if they *do* see them, they don't admit to it.

[Could you elaborate on "looks mean everything"?] Sure. Guess I got sidetracked. What's happening here (let me think about this a sec...) ...what's happening is, bodies are so exposed on the beach that things like facial expressions, talk, clothes, and even actions—things we usually judge age by, you know?—take a backseat to more primal stuff.

[Do you mean, bodies are being judged in and of themselves? Because there are not enough clothes to form any kind of external opinion?

Please tell me if I'm putting words in your mouth. I don't want to do that.] No, that's it. You said it exactly. You're walking down the street. Everyone's wearing what everyone wears. Then all at once you hit the boardwalk and bam. A whole-body thing kicks in. And you've gotta remember, this ain't the '60's. Or even the '80's. These boppers, these young women we're talking about, have been weaned on hormones at burger barns and taco factories; they have been whipped to look sexy as possible soon as possible. By age 10 and 11 in some cases! [Whipped? By who? By whom?] By whom? By the world. By the society around them. By TV, radio, magazines, newspapers. Oh, and let's not forget, movies ...and videos too. Comes from all over the place. Even from their parents. You might not believe that. But I've seen it a thousand, probably more like a million, times.

[Explain, please, how parents contribute.] Most mothers dress their young daughters in things they wouldn't be caught dead wearing themselves! Check it out. And I'm talking girls now for sure. Kids, not boppers or sun bunnies, and not even honeys. Frills and lace, in all the wrong places. And skin, skin, skin! They think it's cute. Everyone laughs when she shakes what she hasn't got! But *she's* not laughing. This is serious business to her, serious social climbing. And nobody's considering what some people watching this stuff are thinking. And more people than you would think, too. Guys, especially. [When you say "nobody considers", who do you mean by nobody?] The whole community, I guess. The whole society. Here's what I mean: Everyone *except* the people who think these girls really *are* sexy. There's what I want to say, in a nutshell.

And mothers, parents, do it all the time. It's the dress standard anymore! And then they wonder why things happen. Especially as the girls start to get a little older, enter the little honey category. Everybody's shocked when the daughter comes home married, shacked up or knocked up ...or worse, doesn't come home at all. They claim they can't understand it when the girl is found later, assaulted, raped, or dead ...or only scared-to-death, if their lucky. It's really sick when you think about it ...where it all starts, I mean. But nobody does. [Does what?] Thinks about where it starts: It's roots. Nobody. I read somewhere a while back, they're going to start holding a national *pre-teen* beauty contest. Imagine. Sorry, but I think that's a mistake. I don't believe you should try to legislate human desire–*mutual* human desire–but there's nothing wrong and everything right with having community standards. And anybody who wants to start putting 10- and 12-year-olds on a stage in bathing suits, in my opinion, should be put on that stage first, with a whole lot of bright light and a lot of questions too. 'Cause there's sure to be something wrong with their motives. I believe in nature being allowed to do it's thing but not in trying to speed things up—not *that* much. To me this crosses the line from pitiful illness to criminality.

[You used the expression, underground fires.] Right. Where there's smoke there's fire and I've seen smoke rising from all kinds. I mean, we're still talking about, what? 14- through 18-year-old females, generally speaking? Is that what we agreed on...? Well then, I've seen husbands, fathers, grandfathers, uncles, friends, neighbors, politicians, priests, businessmen, the mayor of our fair city, I might add, councilmen and congressmen, the circuit judge I'd just voted for and regretted it, workers, laborers, poor men, rich men, famous men, bums and itinerants, and gays ...gays of *both* sexes. And this is only a smattering. And I've probably missed a bunch beside. Name an age. Name a sex. And I've seen him *and* her all but burst into flames over that age female, and sometimes, younger. Many's the time I thought to myself, Hey, that's a pretty sexy looking thing there. She can't be a day over 15. Well, if she was standing on the boardwalk on a typical day, I wouldn't have to wait but a few seconds to see how normal or abnormal my judgement was. Let me put it this way. My tastes run toward the high end, if anything, from what I've witnessed—so high that it's often *me* who should be the local preacher, schoolteacher, mayor, and a lot of *them* should be in jail. Or at least under observation.

Of course, through all this again, you've got to keep in mind, these boppers aren't dressed in school uniforms or choir robes. They're at the beach now, and they're in bathing suits, which means almost naked these days ...for the last decade anyway. It gets pretty primitive down there ...when you can watch it at a distance. It's like a big zoo, really. No. I take that back. Like a little jungle. I've seen guys 80 drooling like fools ...and guys 40 make complete asses of themselves, over some little sun bunny. And usually just trying to get her attention! You'd be amazed. I mean, amazed.

[Were any of those men... Well, persons... ever successful? ...to your knowledge?] If you're talking hit-for-hit? Well, I'd have to say.... [Hit for hit?] Yeah. Try for try? I'd have to say the rate is low. But there's a reason for that: other people watching, people who might know the girl being hit on. A girl who knows she's not being judged (like girls from out of town, who have nothing to lose) ...a girl who knows no one's watching what she does is way more likely to respond to a hit, even to a nerdy hit. [Nerdy? Do you mean you can tell what they're saying?] I do. Maybe I should point out, it's body language. I can spot loser moves in a second. Out there certain gestures, certain moves, are certain death. They just don't get you down very often. The girl has to be pretty desperate, and they're not. There's just too many guys to choose from.

[How can you be so sure, not hearing what they're saying?] I don't mean to tell you your business, but if you made a study of this you could actually come up with a formula for the success/failure rate I witness every day. I know *this* much. It has a lot to do with the time of day, and the number of people around, as it has to do with the guy's age, the girl's age, or his looks or mannerisms. The same hit that went bust at noon, on a packed boardwalk or plaza, done later in the day could end in a connection ...you know? ...First a ride, then a date, *that* sort of thing.

[You seem so sure of these things. How do you know it's not the girl's father? Maybe a relative or friend, who's just come to give her a ride home?] [Subject laughs.] I'll tell you what. You need to come up there with a camera sometime. I'll tell your cam man what and who to shoot while you watch and analyze. The longer the better. Then my take on all this stuff will be just a footnote to reality. You must know *something* about body language, doing what you're doing? [I think I do.] Well then, you'll understand when I say, at three-hundred yards I can tell not only if it's a friend or a stranger moving in on a girl, but I can tell you *how much* she likes or dislikes the guy even before *he* knows. [The interviewee relates several incidents of not only judging relationships accurately but of predicting outcomes, minutes, hours, sometimes days in advance.]

Lifeguards—lifeguards on the ocean, anyway, because they're up high and away from the crowd—they make a game out of it: How quick, how accurately, you can call a hit. [A hit?] Yeah. You know, predict where it's going to go, or how quick it'll flame out. Old timers can leave a rookie guard speechless, leave him thinking he secretly knows the people he's talking about when he's never even seen them before. My own experience has been, words only confuse the call. If I'm too close, especially if I can hear what they're saying, I might call it wrong. You know, get caught up in the very things that are confusing the guys and girls themselves. For instance, you and me, here, talking. A videotape (without sound, you know?) would tell an expert more about our true feelings than we even know ourselves! It's just obvious as hell after watching for almost thirty years. Not only can I predict if a guy's gonna score or not, I can tell if a guy is blowing it before *he* even knows it! Her body language will change and I'll know, like that [snaps his fingers], he blew it.

[To get back to an earlier question. Were any of these men successful to your knowledge?] I didn't answer that? Sorry. I'll cut right to the gory. Many's the time I've seen a perfect stranger, a guy say twenty-thirty years older than some bopper, walk her off the beach, or the boardwalk, or out of one of the plazas, to his car. And many's the time I've seen him leave, like he struck out. But after a few years I realized, even a lot of these guys who seemed to be leaving by themselves were in fact scoring all along! [How is that?] By her reaction! How much she looks at him, the angle of her face when she does, the distance apart of her knees, arms folded or loose, that sort of thing. There's a million signals. It's green lights all the way, then all the sudden he up and leaves. And I used to say, What happened there? I thought he scored? But these are the smooth movers usually, the regular dogs, who've been visiting hydrants for years, so to speak. A lot of them have learned to put on clothes. They tote cameras and compliments and a promise of fame, or at least a good portfolio, for their trouble ...and, of course, for the girl's body. If the average guy only knew how well this crap went over you'd see a million guys out there tomorrow, all dressed neat and cas[ually], carrying cameras and a line o' shit deeper than sugar sand. Pardon my French again. Of course, they stand out like Mr Roberts at a nudist colony. But that's the whole point. You know what they say? [Interviewer nods, no.] I'll tell you. If you don't have the feathers to flaunt you'd better have the song. [Interviewer laughs.] Where was I?

[Let me see. You were... telling me about guys you thought had "scored" as you say, yet who did not leave with the subject. Is that right?] Right. It used to fool me when I was green on the beach. But now I can tell, just by his walk as he leaves, if he's connected or not. Sure enough, 5-, maybe 10 minutes later, you see her gather her stuff up and leave. She may even hit the restrooms, or go buy something. Soon, though, there she is in the parking lot, crawling into his car, and off they go. These are the boppers [who are] worried about their image for whatever reason. It's a whole massive and wild scene out there, and most of it's underground. A lot of these girls... I keep saying that. Why? There's a study right there: Why we insist on calling females who are young women—*obviously* young women—by the tag, girls. Well, anyway. A lot of them are having as much sex as their parents. Probably even more.

[Knowing what you know, and how apparently common this behavior is among the general population of young people versus adults, have *you* ever been tempted, or have you *had,* such a relationship?] I was wondering when you'd get around to that. I need to know first, are you talking "honeys", "boppers", or just babes in general? [I am referring to... Let me see how to phrase this... to young women who fall into our more-or-less agreed-upon age-range. Is that fair?]

Absolutely. Let's see. With the bottom of the range at 14, that's *typically* pretty young —as much in terms of girls' bodies at that age as in terms of what people think of such things. Let me correct that: Or *say* they think. [I don't mean to interrupt but, we haven't talked about age of consent yet. Do you know what it is here in... (a state is named)?] Yes I do. I've had to make arrests. It's 15. [Then, let's use *that* figure.] Then the answer is no. In fact, since age 21 I've never dated a girl under 17 —not knowingly, that is. And I'm pretty damned good at judging age. Better than most, anyway. You get good in this business. You'd *better* be good! [Why do you say that?] Because of all the meat that gets thrown your way. *Young* meat. And *often*. And almost naked. Don't forget that part. [You talk as if you get numb to it after awhile. The popularity and nakedness, I mean?]

Any guy who gives you that crap is a liar...or he's been castrated, or he's near-dead or something! I'm sure you've heard the saying, Life gets old but every day's a new day between your legs? [Interviewer laughs: Actually, I haven't. Are you making these up as you go?] Not really. But it *is* a fact ...a fact of being human ...and especially of being male. No guy *I* ever watched was numb to it. And I've watched my share. I've seen cripples, psychos, hit on these... these, young women. Age means nothing to them. All they see is a naked body that looks damned sexy. In fact, along with real old guys, invalids may be the *worst!* ...I mean, the most openly aggressive. I think it's a cross between desperation and knowing they can get away with murder. That's an expression. [Now *that* one I've heard.] I remember a number of cases where we had to step in ...you know, when it becomes a legal mandate to make all the stuff you usually only get to watch, your business?...It's never been pleasant, but I've arrested quite a few guys in wheelchairs, believe it or not. Some were war vets, some just old, some both. Some so poor that their main ride is one of those things, you know, that mechanics lay on to roll under cars? I've arrested guys who were rickety old, some even with nurses or attendants! [What causes you to step in?] A complaint. Or a ruckus you or some other lifeguard spots.

[What is the offense? I mean, typically, as relates to our topic?] Oh, they'll do things like grab a... a young woman, or a girl, pull her on their laps, feel her up, kiss her, refuse to let go. That sort of stuff. Others expose themselves, or masturbate, or put her hands somewhere she doesn't want them, or try to make her do other stuff. You know, like that. Sometimes, if she's with friends, she thinks it's a lark to start with. Then the guy gets serious, shows what he's after. You'd be amazed. Lots of these people don't care a whole lot about the rules. What have they got to lose? I'll tell you something. A lot of times they're just acting out what other guys, who've been watching the... the given female... all day long, only dared dream of doing.

[You seem sure of these things.] In this business, if your eyes are open, you just learn. Ask around. Even some of the guys with only five or ten years on the beach are fairly body-language- and people-smart. You soon learn how guys especially think. Nobody fools me. Not alone, man to man, they don't. If they try, it's only once. Then they know better. [Why is that?] I've had over 17,000 guys working for me over the years. Some are doctors today, lawyers, politicians, movie stars, you name it. I've got a collection of scrapbooks ten feet deep at headquarters! Unless he's ultra gay, or still hung up on mommy (now there's a big one these days) ...If the guy's still breathin' and has two swingin', you should pardon my French, then I know what he likes...when it comes to sex, I mean. It's not complicated.

[You mentioned personal temptation a few minutes ago? Could you elaborate?] Temptation? [Yes. As in...young women and girls throwing themselves at you, I think you said?] Right. Well, I don't mean to imply it was like being a famous movie star, or rock idol. Not like that. Actually, I don't understand what your question is. [You spoke of lifeguards being tempted with, I think your term was, young meat?]

Yes. The term wasn't meant disrespectfully, you know. [I must admit, I was a little surprised to hear it.] Well, what I wanted was to give the impression of a factory, not a slaughterhouse. [I see.] Because that's exactly what it is out there on the beach. A glorified conveyor belt of foreplay in the sun. I didn't say this but before I was a lifeguard I thought only girls had to learn to say no. But lifeguards do too. You'd think they were rich and famous or something. But it's something else. Most people have no idea. I've had females throw themselves at me—I mean, sweet, clean, gorgeous girls; model and movie star material, I'm saying—come on to me, and come on strong. And, in a few cases, not that long ago. And when this didn't work, they'd go further —sometimes on their own, sometimes through a friend. One of them you may have heard of. [The interviewee mentions a famous female actor.] And the other I'm sure you've heard of too. [Names another.]

Carefully, and with lots of planning, both of these girls chose *me* to take their virginity! Now I'm an honest guy. A request like that's an honor *any* way you slice it. [The interviewee calls one of the actor's by her first name, not her stage name] was only 14 then [when she made the alleged request] but her stepfather (and a lot of other guys too) were after it, hot and heavy. Don't kid yourself. It goes on all the time. *You're* a good looking woman, you must remember? [I can not bias the interview.] I see. Well, both girls worked on me through their best friends, who, in one case, was gay (a lesbian, I mean) and bad in love with [repeats the actor's name] at the time. Well, it ended with [the friend's name here] telling me I just *had* to help, that I was the perfect one for the job: good looking, gentle, intelligent, considerate, *and* sexy. *That* was important too. I'm not blowing my own whistle I'm just saying what she told me. "Trust me, she is suffering for wanting you" she wrote in a note I still have. Her plea was like something from Balzac. Very next day this prodigy matchmaker posed the question, "Then answer me this. Can someone be *too young* to suffer from sexual longing? Is there some magic age-limit when a person should be called legally *too young* to suffer sexual pain?" she asked, in *shockingly clear* terms. "No? Then how dare you deny this? We're talking real pain here, [subject says his own name]! And the law has it all wrong if that's what youre worried about. 'Cause the law could care less about desire. If someone has sexual pain they should have the right to a pain-killer. And in [blank]'s case, that's you." Well, all this took most of that summer ...in both cases, come to think of it. They didn't wait around long after that though. Most don't... once they make up their minds to give it up. After that they get down quick, with *some* body. It almost seems like, after a certain point, it doesn't even matter who that somebody is. [How do you mean?]

I remember one sun bunny, an absolutely adorable little looker, who was after me all summer, then after school almost every day, and every weekend too, almost to New Year's. And then (this beats all), she drank a little at a party one night and ended up giving it away to some clown she hardly knew...in his 30's! Older than me, as I remember it! Turned out to be gentle as a bulldozer! She told me about it next day...just to rub my face in it, I guess. She said it was my fault. That I was cruel. And selfish too! I remember thinking later, maybe she's *right!* [How do you mean that?] I mean, like some law-abiding klutz, I was as concerned about the legal safety of *my* ass as I was about the *real* needs and *real* safety of her's. [pauses] Such legal inhumanity is a tragedy...for all concerned.

[No matter how hard the choices you seem to have dealt with them. Perhaps I'm putting words in your mouth?] Not really. Sometimes it was pure hell —trying to be a friend that could be trusted and still keep from becoming a lover. It was a tightrope; a tough act. And I guess, act might just be the operational word here. 'Cause the problem is, in most cases, I'm not talking about skinny, fat, or homely girls, or girls who couldn't get rid of it, so to speak ...I mean, get rid of it using a clean, reasonably nice and decent-looking guy. In most cases, the ones that stick in my mind anyway, we're talking about little honeys that twist ten heads a second (no, make that ten *minds* a second) in a crowded mall, and a hundred a second on a crowded beach, and not always male minds either! But *most* lifeguards have that to deal with on some level. Only the ages of the girls vary, not the sexiness. The better looking the guys are the better looking the boppers are who hang around. These stay more or less the same over the years.

[You just used the expression, turn ten minds a second. Why did you change it from "ten heads a second"?] Oh. Because intelligent men know, or men accompanied by a mate or potential mate, know, body-watching isn't as cool–as sanctioned, I should say–in a mall as it is on the beach. They'll look at the picture... well, the image in their mind... of what they just saw before they'll turn around and gawk. Especially if the female is jail bait, or might be construed as jail bait ...which is a whole other part of this whole mess.

[You said, the ages of the girls vary but not the sexiness. What did you mean?] That's a tough call. Well, maybe not. Remember I said, on the beach, bodies mean everything? [I think the term was, *looks* mean everything... or "appearances" maybe? I'm not sure. Sorry.] Doesn't matter. If the body's tight, if it has youthful skin and a reasonably open mind to go with it, then a bopper can be any age, really. You know? Within reason? [For example?] Like, say, 40? Or even 50? ...in the right person. Men get turned on by visuals mostly. We're a sad lot, really. But nature's given us no choice. You know? I mean that. All a young girl, or an older woman, has to do is trick his eye, and he's a goner. Pffft. Like that! Come to think of it, isn't that what fashion, and working-out and dieting to lose weight, are all about most of the time?

[You've said you were tempted at times. I took that to mean, by young women whom you judged to be younger than the age of consent, perhaps? Or was it some other barrier that gave you pause?] I'd have to say, *all* the barriers. [Such as?] Laws. The judgement of other people. You name it. [So what is the cut-off age?] That's just it. There *is* no age. It's not an age thing. That's what I'm trying to say here. [But doesn't that mean, if it's not an age thing, that you could end up having sexual relations with a girl of, say, 10 or 11?] I suppose it does. If there's an anomalous 11-year-old girl somewhere who could walk away with, or at least threaten to take, the Miss America crown, then, yes. In theory I suppose I could end up in bed with her. Because, I insist. The minute you slap an age onto mutual desire... Better yet, let me put it this way. My guts... Let me change that again. The *sexual essence of me* knows damn well exactly who *is* and who *isn't* ready to mate with me. And that essence *also* knows, every such urge I've ever had, other males have had too. And that I'm no way even close to alone in my sexual desires. Well, among non-gay males, anyway. You know, it's like... When you know, for an absolute fact, that your desires are... Well, your desires fall more into the zone of what is legal than [the desires of] most of the men you've ever known, you no longer question whether your desires are healthy or not. You *know* they are.

[So, if I brought that hypothetical anomalous 11-year-old into this room, in a bathing suit, say, and told you her age, there's a chance you might ask her for a date?] No. That's *not* what I'm saying. Dating her could ruin her life as well as mine. But I'll tell you this. Nature made me, like most men, to miss no potential mate. And if she looks good enough to win a national beauty contest for adults, as you say, then [laughs] I'm damn sure not going to look the other way if she's on display right here in front of me... 11 years old or 111, [subject says his name at this point] here is *going* to, at least, *look* his fill.

[So, what you're saying then, is... Well, let me rephrase that. Would you have any guilt for having felt desire for her?] First of all, let me say. Good looks alone don't turn me on. There's got to be an element of sexiness ...or what I perceive as sexiness. Then there's got to be what's called "chemistry" after that. That can happen with an 18-year-old; it can happen with... Well, what's your age...? Okay, you're not permitted to say that. 31? 32? Whatever. It can happen with someone your age. 'Cause, one more time, permit me, please. Age has nothing, *no thing*, to do with it. Age, almost every time you use it, is a bum rap for somebody.

[But again. Not to use age leaves our opinions open to misunderstanding and misinterpretation.] True. But I must tell you. To satisfy your scientific curiosity I've gone out on a limb, put 14 on the low end. But then again, that's no good. For, like I think I've said, there are guaranteed to be a few cases where it is totally misleading ...criminal, even. [Too low for comfort?] Actually yes *and* no. [How's that?] Well, on the low end, I know there exists in the sun, sand and mist of my own past, and probably in the clinical mists of your future, that one 11- or 12-year-old who will make a liar out of me and a believer out of you.

You know, just the other night I saw on TV an ex porn star—butler I think his name was. Anyway, he turned out to be a surprisingly well spoken young man in his 30's, I'd say. He claimed at one point that the elite minority who run the world have no clue at all of the sexual reality of things. He gave as example, that those running the porn industry, with few exceptions, consider women from 18 to 21 - women of legal age, that is- to be madams as far as experience in sex goes. As support for this outrageous claim (outrageous is in quotes) he said that every day 15- and 16-year-olds came to him looking to become porn stars. Every day, repeated for emphasis. These women, he said, had no doubt that they were qualified. Now hear this. Because, he said, they had years of experience. Years! *Sexual* experience. To deny them work was a joke, he said. *He* knew it, *they* knew it. But the law is the law. Realistic? No. But that's the way things are.

We are in heavy denial in this country. (This is me speaking now.) A recent study says, the U.S. leads other first-world nations in having the lowest "age of first intercourse" . Somewhere around 15 they say. [Yes. I saw that —a biannual global survey.] There you go. Maybe you saw this then too. They didn't even have the chutzpah to use the word *sexual* intercourse in the graph I saw. That's how heavily into denial even the people who *know* the facts are. 15-point-something and dropping annually. And intercourse accounts for only part of our sex activity. What then is the average age of first -what do you guys call it?- oragenital encounter? Or of our first consensual manipulative encounter? See what I mean? Keep going and soon you're in the single digits. What of the age of our first serious *touch* encounter? And who is it that's surprised these young women have some of these experiences on our public beaches? And *why* are we surprised?

[I see. Thank you. I'm sure some of that will prove helpful. Now I see here we didn't answer my question as to whether or not you've ever experienced guilt over your sexual beliefs or experiences?] Yes, I have. God, yes. Specially when I was younger. But no more. [How is that?] I think I've explained. Guilt comes from thinking you're weird ...or sick, or the like. But once you know the social score for sure, the guilt disappears. In fact, I'll tell you this. I feel damn good about myself. Especially knowing what I know. I've been tempted by the best. The best of the best. The best almost naked, mind you! And literally begging too. Don't forget that. Day after day, week after week. I've said no to honeys that could make a parson pole vault into the congregation, a saint commit sodomy! There aren't a lot of men who could deal with what I've dealt with, and that's a fact. And especially not unmarried men, year after year. At least *I* never saw such a man. And I've known a lot of men. Virile men. And I never saw one... No, I take that back. There was *one* guy. But they're rare. *Real, real rare*.... This is left-handed bragging, I guess. But you need to keep something in mind. [long pause]

I'm not necessarily happy about my choices. Every year older I get I like them less. [Your choices?] My choices, yes. [Why is that?] There's another tough one. ...I think it's two things really: getting smarter, and having less opportunities come my way. The two work together. Against you ...and against the choices you made. Plus you learn how society works; that it's rules are totally arbitrary, and that to follow the rules can sometimes be more destructive than breaking them. [Can you give an illustration?] I already did: the thousands, the millions, of girls who give it away every day to scum bags without a conscience, to guys who have no idea what a girl's *first* experience should be like...or worse, don't have any care to know. That's not the way it should be. I think a lot of the bad rap that having sex young gets comes about because, just about always, the best guys for the job have turned it down, because of the rules, because that's the kind of guys they are; and so they get passed up for the scum bags... who, let's face it, are only doing what nature's telling them they should be doing. So it's this big ugly mess. The very reason, probably, were having this interview.

[So, would you still say no? Today?] I said no, again, only a few weeks ago. [Why do you still say it?] [long pause] The rules. *Just* the rules. I'm sorry. That's it. [Why do you apologize?] I guess, because morality is nowhere in this issue that I can see. And that makes me sad. I'm sorry because it's mostly politics... The, rules, I mean. Body politics. Somebody out there, for some reason, is still trying to control our bodies, and what we can and can't do with them. Even by mutual consent. And mostly the bodies of young women. [Who do you think is doing this? And why?] I think it's a holdover from previous eras, previous societies. Paradigms, you know? Religion. Old law. Older men. Older women. Each has its own reasons for wanting to control the bodies of the world's most desirable females. And each has its hand in the pot, vying for control. I guess, really, the harem concept is still with us, like it or not. Except now the walls are made out of laws and threats instead of bamboo and tapestry.

[This seems to make you sad. Am I reading that right?] [subject nods affirmatively] [Why is that, do you think?] I guess I'm sorry... sorry that most people think laws have something to do with truth, when sometimes it's the exact opposite. [As in?] Well, as in this *whole* issue. If ethics–human law, I guess I should say–if ethics had anything to do with human nature, anything, then we wouldn't be talking about all this right now. There wouldn't be a problem. [pause] What it comes down to is, the rules. That's it. Not truth. But the rules.[But you still obey them.... Why?] Because they're there. [very long pause] And they're not going to go away.

[So, that probably means you don't fear the rules?] Not now. I did when I was young. Like a lot of people. I thought the rules were related to truth. They're not. No, I don't fear them. The rules aren't why I do what I do. Chances of me being nabbed, especially for giving a young woman exactly what she's hoping for, are almost nonexistent. [Why do you follow them then?] I feel like I've answered that: social responsibility. Not only to me, but to the girl —who has to go on to live with the choices I make... or that *we* make together. If the choices didn't conflict with the rules, there would be no problem. But you and I know they do. And *how* they do.

[Is that it?] I guess. And that includes intimidation too —unspoken intimidation. [From who?] From society. Fear of being criticized —behind your back. Or maybe even blackballed, professionally. I've seen men criticized, and even punished, just for fulfilling the wildest dreams of every hetero guy they know! And the wetter the dream the harder the slap. That's what I mean by hypocrisy. In private, among friends, men will bash each other for *not* grabbing such an opportunity. I've been accused of being gay, of getting old, of having no balls, etcetera. Pardon my French again. But that's a crock. I love women. And I respect them as people too. And part of that love, that respect, means wanting to break the law when it punishes them. [Punishes them?] Yes, punishes them.

[For what?] For not being allowed to fulfill their natural urges, fulfill their need to find a guy–the guy *they* want–not some guy they have to settle for. The same way intimidation punishes me. When a person's determined to give it away, whether he or she is 14, 19 or 35, they should be able to. Where they want, and to whom they want. Advice is fine, and loving advice is even better. But laws? They don't work. Not in these areas. They never will. They're cold and unfeeling and have no brains or conscience. Something *that* personal you just don't legislate. [Why is that?] It's like abortion. It's like your own guts are on the line. If it's *that* personal, and making laws about it causes so much pain and suffering, then it's like ...it's like, telling someone they can piss only once a day, or defecate just once a week, because someone's religion, or someone's upbringing, or someone's envy, or someone's insecurity, says so. ...I guess, when it comes down to it, this double-standard is like *any* sickness. You have to figure out what *caused* it before you can cure it.

[I like that. I'm not supposed to, but I do.] [both laugh] [pause] [I can tell you've thought a lot about these things.] I have. [pause.] Something else figures into all this too. [What is that?] I'm sort of old fashion, deep down. I may even get married soon —to a former bopper friend. As a matter of fact, to someone I turned down. And there's something else. I don't know quite how it fits, but I know it's important. The rules can make you feel dirty. Just another aspect of the guilt thing. And not because what you're thinking or doing *is* dirty, but because the rules treat it like it is ...but *mostly* because everybody *believes* the rules have something to do with right, with truth...when they don't. Not *these* rules.

[You mentioned being a little bit old fashioned. Is part of that being able to say no?] Could be. I've always been a responsible person. I think of the girl not only from my end of the penis (pardon me) but from her end too. But maybe that's wrong... 'cause she wants it to happen as bad as I do. So maybe it's from her parent's end, that I'm thinking. I'm not sure. I do remember thinking, "What if this was my daughter? Would I want some big jerk...." But then I'd think, "Yeah. Rather a jerk like me than *most* out there!" And that's who it's gonna be, you know. You can bank on it. If not me, some other guy. He's *gonna* do it! If only because he's *not* like me! So why not go with the girl's first choice? [Pause.] So I guess we're back to square one. ...Though I should probably add. It's a very small percentage of males...heterosexual males...an infinitesimal percentage, I suspect...who would not desire the women I've been talking about here. I don't know how to convince you of this. But because I like you I can only warn: I don't know if you live in the city here, and I don't even know if you have a daughter. But I'm sure you know somebody who does. So I'm telling you, don't, I repeat, do not, let that girl, whoever she is, walk the dog the same time every day. Even if you live in a small town, don't. Though I may not understand the odds involved here a whole lot better than any other guy, I am more honest about what I sense is involved. To let her do so is to tweak the odds against a happy ending.

[I think we've covered a good deal here.... Any regrets?] Aside from choosing a profession rife with vain inverts? [Let me change that to: Any final thoughts?] You make it sound like I'm gonna be executed when we're done. [both laugh] I can tell you this: I wish we lived in a more honest world. The lie people live–I mean, sexually–makes me sick. I'm talking nauseous. [The double-standard? Is that what you mean when you say, lie?] Yes. I think I've grown over the years... Well, a lot. I used to think the rules only dirtied the girls. Now I know better. They dirty everyone. Hurt everyone. It may even be the crime of crimes! I'm still sorting out the loose ends.

[Can you give us any...I don't want to say, last thoughts. Let's see...a kind of wrap-up thought?] Let's see. [pause] I used to be proud of my choices. I figured I had moral spine. I'm not so sure anymore. [Why is that?] That's a tough one. I'm still sorting that out too. [pause] 'Cause when I look back I see a lot of personal denial. And pain, too. A lot! Too much, maybe. And the older I get the stupider the choices I made look to me. I guess I need to confess–to myself, mostly–there was a *lot* of pain.... More pain than I may ever admit, even to myself. [Why?] [subject exhales as if weary] Because it makes me look like such a looser as a man ...as the man mother nature made, not as the man society molded. [Looser? Why? ...If I may ask?] Because, even knowing all I've learned, I've rarely done what my guts have told me to do. 'Cause more and more I suspect: It's in our guts, our deepest feelings, where the real action is. It's almost like I've never lived. Like something in me never got born. Like my whole life has been somehow only a dream. Like the rules have deprived me of life itself. And not just me, but all guys.

[I can see this is difficult for you. Dare I ask if you can elaborate?] Well... [pause] An underage girl can always find someone ready to risk jail or whatever so she can do what her guts are telling her to do. You know the song: If you don't, mister, somebody else will. But the guy who plays it straight, who plays by the rules: His guts rot untested. And that's where the crime comes in, the tragedy. [long pause] All men–I mean, normal guys–live with it. But most rebel. In private. Somewhere along the way take what they, and the girl, *whatever* her age, *really* want. That's not hard to figure out. But I never did. So... for guys like me, it's like you've got this Siamese twin deep inside you, imprisoned there. He lives his whole life in darkness. Never gets out. Never sees the countryside, the mountains, the sea, much less the stars. Never. Because he takes the rules to heart. And he will die in there. [subject seems surprised, then saddened] Alone. Forgotten. We rules obeyers never get to meet, much less give a good hug to, our flesh and blood inner selves. And our flesh and blood inner selves never get to come out and live. [subject interrupts tearing of eyes] Sounds weird I know. Yet I don't know how else to explain it.

[End Novalis-Deland interviewee statement. —Ed.]

having perused everything from quasar spurts to testicular quoits

I understand what it means to be male at a level prior to cultural imprint. For i have encountered maleness at the place where it begins. And i have found in the wide scheme of things sexual, perusing everything from quasar spurts to testicular quoits, maleness varies little wherever we find it. Again however i must warn against grouping w mine the tastes of the millions of over- or under-mothered men which disturbed societies create. I refer of course to the legion mammary mashers among us. Not only will they deny what i have to say in regard to maleness, but feeling cheated on bosom-love deepdown, they often react violently to it. Watch for this.

Obfuscate all we may, accuse ε deny all we can, hetero or homo, we are of a kind, we males; of a single instinctual stamp. So let us stab straight to the quick of things and toss convention to the mongrels of convention. For it is a rancid bone they gnaw (in public) and they are welcome to it.

sovereign right v. local reality ...again

I have explained why i avoided *the n-d report*. I did so for other reasons too. I figured it was like any other psych survey —a bore, a quiet flop; not because it has to be that way but because the typical study, like the typical poll, operates from within the cage of current belief. That is, the questions it asks rely for their validation upon the very values they seek to expose. Therefor it cant get outside the box (civilization) whose problems it seeks to solve —recipe for automatic failure. To the contrary, in the preface volume of *the n-d report* we find,

> We can not access things buried in our unconscious minds if the questions we ask only act to reinforce the values and rules that are in place; values and rules that may need desperately to be modified or changed; values and rules that have rendered the very truths we seek invalid or unreachable.

Such penetrationg analysis is largely incomprehensible to the experts of our day, whose very diplomas pay homage to these same fusty values ε rules lest they lose their viability, their power, in the marketplace —a marketplace maxedout on stale ideas ε failed therapies. Skipping (as if we can afford to) the first seven books we go directly to *the novalis-deland report on eligibility paraphilias*.

In brief, the study reveals, the average male would select for a sex partner a female of the median age of....

But we must take a longdeep breath here (at this juicy juncture) and chat some about the term "sex partner". Let us emphasize. They *could* say, but do not: housekeeper maid cook governess girlfriend housemate roommate lover wife or cohabitant. Yet they say sex partner. This is crucial. For instinct cares nothing for the fashions of the day, whether it be courting, casual copulation, living together, marriage, or some other arrangement. Conventions come&go w eras ε ages. But instinct is unimpressed by the transient trappings of the day, however important they may seem to us. This said, let us backup, start again.

> In phase two of the study, where the faces and ages of the object females were undisclosed, and where the participants were asked to imagine themselves living in "a world where no one judged what they did", our findings remain consistent and are unequivocal. We found the participants, given the option, would select for a sex partner a female midway in her teens.

This bomb dropped, the authors go on to review the key determinants in their test data, and then, in summarizing the bases for their conclusions, state,

> In an honest sexual environment, in a culture uncluttered by the self-deception that double standards impose, our conclusions concerning eligibility paraphilias would be self-explanatory. We saw this repeatedly as well in the social codes of the 15 primitive cultures we surveyed for diacritical contrast. No one is shocked when an older man marries a young woman, or when an older woman introduces a young boy to the sexual practices of the group. As long as sexual awakening is present, and experience is desired, no one has a problem with age as an issue in itself, or, more importantly, with age *difference*.

Here's another.

> In instinctively candid cultures, pedophilia (as the criminal act we know it) is nonexistent. This is doubtless because biological, and not ideological, codes are in force there....

And this.

> The distance of modern cultures from such instinctual candidness is striking, as are the penalties for those who give in to the urgings of sexual instinct. Based on the statistics of the study, it seems to the authors, the steady deterioration of our mental health is foremost among these penalties. This is not inconsistent with what other clinicians have concluded. [References given.] In fact, when our preliminary study was published (1978) we found, this distance of civilized man from the instinctual substrate was also apparent in the general reaction of other clinicians to our findings, with negative reaction being strongest in the remaining puritanical pockets of given nations.

The three volumes on eligibility paraphilias end w an afterword which says,

History tells us that cultures will do as they please. If a given culture at a given time chooses to make sex acts with persons years past puberty a crime, that is its sovereign right. But in the face of the evidence, when we step forth to call such acts "unnatural" or "criminal," or "the deeds of a sick or diseased mind," then we are, summarily, and dangerously, at odds with historical reality concerning instinct. But, of course, sovereign states can do that too. Self-judgement, realistic or fantastic, is also a society's sovereign right. Yet we would point out. To cite these acts thus is to make a judgement against Nature, and no one has the knowledge or autonomy to change or negate instinctual law.[!] So when we proceed to try to modify our subconscious minds or negate our instincts, several billion years in the making, it seems almost a foregone conclusion, it can only end in personal tragedy and suffering. [my brackets and exclamation mark]

It is our belief, following more than two decades of conscientious study, that instinct does not abide censure or criticism—not without a whiplash effect in our conscious lives. The results of such whiplashing can be seen throughout most of the industrialized world and is called by different names: emotional disturbance, criminality, mental illness, societal disequilibrium, war, etc. What amounts to several thousand years of ignorant, and sometimes frivolous, tampering with our instincts, has left a legacy of psychic dysfunction and social disorder in its wake, a legacy overfull with brutality and suffering.

Wow. And, wow! Why cant i write like that?

and on teenolepsy

Civilized societies force a man to operate according to a code of highly integrated behaviors, a code that often has little to do with his true sexual nature or with healthy emotional fulfillment.

N-d authors are digging deeply into this dastardly doublestandard now.

Our findings demonstrate, over and over in cultures around the world, that while 16% of all adult males claim to be happily mated (within the context of the ideals which rule their behavior), only 3.3 percent are *sexually* content. Our findings show repeatedly, the average male lives out his life in a quite remarkable state of psychosexual distress.

So revealing is this part of the report i would like to incl it to its bloody apotheosis. In that it is several pages long it must fall to the reader to locate.

This [sexual] pathos presented in all participants. And carried like a lodestone at the center of this distress was the hope of one day getting the opportunity to possess his ideal sex partner. This fantasy appears to propel the average male from the onset of puberty to the close of his sexually active life. Moreover, it appears

> to be ever present—that is, from day to day, from moment to moment, in waking and in sleep. Though during wakeful hours this distress seems to wait in shadow, and/or operates in socially viable disguise.

Who is this fantastic sexpartner? this sexmate missing from the average male's life? Who is it he longs to take to bed? And if his bed is off limits to her, who does he want to drag into the nearest alleyway, the nearest woods, the nearest grotto? By our deepest fears we shall know her.

> The participants [all "normative heterosexual males" aged 18 to 71] were shown [on private monitors, in private cubicles, using four-sided views] the faceless and nude bodies of female models aged puberty (median 11.2 years) to 70, whose ages the participants did not know. Much preparation and reassurance of confidentiality preceded this phase. (See "Preparations and Guidelines for Testing" on page 2101.)
>
> Test done, the participants were asked if they were satisfied with their answers. 88 percent answered yes, 5 percent said no, and a remaining 7 percent were unsure. Following this, a subliminal image (a photograph of the participant's wife, mother, girlfriend or sister) was flashed repeatedly behind a screen which read, "Data failure. Please answer the previous question again". (This tactic was used extensively throughout the testing procedure. See Double-blind Precautions, page 2276.) The tactic caused a dramatic change in responses. This held true even when the second phase followed the first by only 1-2 minutes! This time, when asked if they were satisfied with their answers, 14 percent answered yes, 58 percent said no, and 28 percent were unsure. [My brackets.]

<Witness civil denial regaining consciousness —*w* a vengeance!> i want to pencil-in at this point in the report among a forest of exclamationmarks but manage to restrain myself. Who is this ideal sexpartner? this ravishing ultrafemale most heteromales desire and most heterofemales fear? Let's take a closer, statistical, look. Some 7200 adult males were surveyed in the report in 34 cultures or regions around the world. Thirty-four tables are given to show cultural variances. These are followed by a summary table. Thus, culture by culture, region by region, this mysterious she is revealed to us. The last table statistically defines who this she is, and in doing so exposes the outlaw instinct of which i speak; and of which i've *been* speaking, a doublestandard, let me add, we all live by, die by. I duplicate that table.

[N.S. has affixed at this point in his document a photocopy of said Summary Table, taken from page 15264 in the last book of *The Novalis-Deland Report on Human Sexuality, 1995.* —Ed.]

Survey Group by % *	Age-Range of P.S.P. **
2.4	11
5.0	12
6.7	13
8.9	14
10.9	15
10.6	16
10.3	17
9.4	18
8.4	19
72.6	19 and under
14.1	20-21
9.1	22-30
4.2	31-70
27.4	over 19

* Heterosexual males, age 18 to 71. ** Preferred sex partner. Source, *Novalis-Deland Report on Human Sexuality, 1995*, Table TS331, page 15264.

So you see, the nymphs of my muse are alive & well after all —theyve just been in hiding! Better yet, captivity. And thus we stand exonerated, vindicated, my Love & me! Perhaps in another age we will even be canonized instead of cursed! The mass hallucination meanwhile marches on. The outlaw instinct gallops on thru the hot social nite and will not be unmasked even when caught **w** young blood on its hands at the scene of the crime!

> Despite built-in precautions in our procedures, despite guarantees of confidentiality (given in writing), fear of exposure continued to bias the results we obtained. Given this limitation, coupled with our failure to use photographs of models under 11, one is left to surmise just how broad the sexual preference of the average male may be in *actuality*. [my stress]

There should be a point beyond which a scientific treatise can employ exclamationmarks. If ever there was such a point, this is it. I dont markup the books of others ...still, i placed three such marks, in ink, in the margin there, and do not regret it.

The novalis-deland report should be a benchmark in sociology if not as yet a guide in cultural renewal. Of course, lacking bloody revolution, significant change is possible to humans only in small, & usually generationally-gapped, increments. And so *the n-d report* drops its bomb in the middle of the reader's (civilized) picnic. Only the thing doesnt explode like it should. It's almost as if, since nobody recognizes it is a bomb, it *cant* explode! It's downright surreal: the mass myth, the halcyon hallucination, the daft delusion! I'm thinking of a certain movie; *the gods must be crazy* it was called. One day a strange 'thing' lands in the center of our consciousness. We swing thru the trees making a wide circle around it, chittering nervously, pausing every now&then to eye it suspiciously; we scratch ourselves ε blink. Most of us wish this strange new thing would just disappear so we can get on w life, life as it was before that strange thing fell from the sky.

civil repression incarnate in murder & rape

In her book, *our shame: the rape of a nation,* susan miller confronted the bottom-end (psp) age-question of n-d researchers. That question: Does male sex desire see prepubescence as a barrier to coitus in practice. The documented mass rape of some 26ooo muslim females, in the war of 1992-93 in the former yugoslav nations of bosnia ε herzegovina, shows that, "Where sexual assault was sanctioned among the [male] soldiers, age barriers fall past the depths of credibility!" Miller is aghast and even world-court records say *all* of us should be aghast.

> The [U.N. War-Crimes] committee findings show female victims of sex crimes [in Bosnia and Herzegovina] extrapolate as follows: Infant to 2 years, 4; 3 to 5 years, 23; 6 to 8 years, 222; 9 to 11, 1104; 12 to 14, 3645; 15 to 17, 8538; 18 to 20, 6809; 21 to 23, 4344; 24 to 26, 3712; 27 to 36, 5698; 37 to 46, 1121, 47 and over, 855.

The range of victims is flabbergasting. What aberrations of reflexive sickness our civilizing has brought us to!

> ...Rapes by civilians as well as soldiers. Many were neighbors and friends of the victims and their families. ...The gang rapes were so brutal many victims died. Rape camps...were set up early on, after the okay to do so was rumored down the chain of command. Therein, women, even those who cooperated, were abused, tortured and repeatedly raped, with upwards of 14,ooo deaths as a result of said treatment. ...Rapes of young adults and children were performed in front of fathers, mothers, grandparents, siblings, many of them children, with most of the older males killed after the offense was complete. ...The committee said that the [rape] camps were set up as "sanctuaries" away from the war, where the impregnation of Muslim females by Serbs could be accomplished in relative "peace". It estimated that as many as a third (13,ooo) of the victims were held and kept alive for this purpose, some until they "showed", others until they gave

> birth. One witness, a 15-year old female from Herzegovina, stated that as soon as she gave birth (on a bed in a run down apartment building appropriated by the Serbs as such a camp), her baby, a girl, was defiled by two soldiers who told her, because her baby was female they had orders to "make it pregnant" or kill it. They tried the former right there in front of her. "When they were done they tried to shove my baby's head back up inside me. They broke her neck. This is what killed her I think."

Poor mersiha and her 26,000 sisters! "Why" asks ms miller, "is the only act analogous with killing, in war, sexual violence? And moreover, why are the victims of that violence predominantly young females?" In an effort to answer these questions, ms miller interviewed dozens of imprisoned male serbs charged w war crimes.

> This proved the hardest part of my task. Most of the men wanted proof I was not recording their responses. In the controlled environment of the prison camps we wore for this reason hospital gowns. "See, we have no tape recorder" the translator would say, hoping we might get an honest confession. After word of our task spread, more and more of those we questioned insisted on complete bodily inspection of my aides and myself for microphones, etc. "This had better be a good confession" I would say to the interpreter, submitting to this purposely degrading request. All too often the interview was refused anyway. Four men, two of whom proved to understand English, exposed themselves, masturbated to conclusion, before the guards were able to remove us, or *said* they were unable.
>
> Most prisoners (not just the sex offenders) claimed there was a tacit mandate among Serbs to impregnate enemy women, bar none! "Let's suppose this is true", I would say. "Does that give a man the right to have coitus with females even before they reach puberty?" About half the respondents said "Yes". Another third said "Maybe". They qualified this with something along the lines of, "It's sometimes not easy to tell who you can get pregnant and who you can't". I confess to having lost control a couple times saying, "Like with infants and two-year-olds, you mean?"
>
> I have since decided, a shocking percentage of we members of so-called civilized nations, societies which claim to believe in the rule of law, use the opportunity of war to do those things we've always dreamed of doing but were afraid to do because of laws, moral and/or religious codes, or simply because families, friends or neighbors might find out. Freud said something along these lines I understand. But all is fair in love and war, they say. And so, for thousands of years our shame, our mutual shame, has kept the truth at arms length. For thousands of years we have averted our eyes, erased our memories.

Toward the close of the book there is a shift in ms miller's attitude, a change in perspective to which she, w surprising candor, even admits.

> ...One of four officers who admitted that the impregnation (read, rape) of Muslim women had been authorized in unwritten form at or near the top of the chain of command, made the following statement. This man, a high-ranking officer of about 50, was charged with inciting war crimes by omission. "Most of the men realize now, when it comes to war, we are all made of roughly the same stuff. Once you realize this fact you begin to ask yourself, Why should we be ashamed? Why do we have to deny the things we've done, things we've all done, or dreamed of doing?"
>
> "Do you mean," I asked, "that it should be legal in wartime to rape a female?" "No", he answered. "What I am saying is, the rapes you are dealing with here are the result of deprivation, in many cases, a lifetime of it. [!!!]
>
> "You see before you a beaten man—beaten by what I've been party to. You, and this court, say you want the truth from me. But from what I've seen, your search is a lie. No. Let me withdraw that. It is a search for what you want to hear. Having heard it, it is this you will call the truth, when, in fact, the truth is what you don't want to hear."
>
> I am able to convince him otherwise ...though it will be months after my return to London before I can treat any part of his message credibly.
>
> "I don't believe you. However the candle is burning low for me.... The laws of my country, in fact, the laws of the Christian and Muslim world, forbid people many of their basic rights. Maybe I should say, instinctual rights. [!] When men must hide very powerful drives, and when we are made to feel ashamed of them, then these events you have been writing about—these rapes, these atrocities as you call them—are not only likely to happen, they are going to happen. It is just a matter of where and when. [!] Sometimes it almost looks to me like war is only an excuse for such release, an excuse to set free the tortured and cowering animal that is in us all. I am sure such an animal grows inside most men as they age." [!]

My emphasis [!] in all cases.

> My skepticism showing (I'm afraid), after a pause he goes on. "Maybe I can make my point like this. A person who has not eaten a satisfying meal for his entire life will probably disgust us when he finally gets to do so. And especially, I might add, if he thinks no one is watching. [!] Who knows, perhaps even war itself is the result of such denial, such oppression of our basic desires. Religion too has played its part; showed the way, really. All these things combined have twisted our basic animal natures into something shameful." [!]

> "No animal ever acted like this", I replied, shaking a file of notes, for at the time I rejected all but completely what he was saying.
>
> He only smiled rather wryly, said, "You are probably right. But then, no healthy animal would put up with the emotional deprivation we humans endure every day. I have studied animals and so I know, any good animal would rather lie down and die, or be killed in the line of duty, the duty of being a good animal, an animal true to its animal nature. You can not convince an animal why life should be lived as we live it —not a healthy animal, you can't. [!]" [all, my brackets]

Ms miller, not ungrudgingly, postscripts her book as follows.

> I began this book...with a heart full of wrath and righteous indignation, ready, in all honesty, to indict categorically if I had to. At last, I thought, we women have the evidence we need. And as I watched the system suppress, mitigate, change, even destroy before my eyes, more and more of that evidence, I became ever more enraged at the male power structures covering up, or attempting to cover up, what I knew for a fact, things which others of us working at this terrible task were beginning to find out.
>
> That has changed for me. I find myself on the threshold of a new understanding; an understanding even more essential than the one which launched my original quest; an understanding that indicts not just men but the laws and beliefs all of us live by. For the illness I've uncovered in my searches and researches appears to be universal, not just an artifact of war in Bosnia/Herzegovina. And that is a frightening thing for anyone to have to conclude. Unfortunately, dealing with this new perspective will have to wait for a later forum.

Miller is so close, *so* close, to holding the answer in her rightly enraged fist! What a tragedy, is all i can say. The best i can do, using the works of others (as the reader has every right to expect me to do), is to share the following editorial statement, which ends the preface to *the n-d report* .

> We can only hope to scratch the surface of this schism [between our ideals and instinct] and to show some of the devastation that has resulted from it. For the purpose of this study is only to demonstrate a problem, not solve or cure it. If along the way we have been able to shed some light on causes and solutions, all the better. But this is not within the scope of our intent.
>
> For humans have been thousands of years creating and widening the rift which has torn male and female apart, and has all too often set them at each others throats. There can be no quick fixes for this, no instant bridges to unite this rift. We can

only hope that much self-dissection, much painful pursuit, will one day close this gap to a point where each side can see what the other is going through, and then go on to understand how this tragic situation came about. Then, hopefully, mankind will proceed to make the changes so crucial to its fundamental health.

denial, not lack of facts

"More facts" is the big stall. We've more than enuf proof. What is needed is less denial. For of all human flaws, denial is the most destructive. Denial = mc^2 and a bunch beside.

To retroparaphrase my rehab diary following nam: We know all we need to know about the outlaw instinct and about the world matron ε -patron who helped to outlaw it. We verywell know. Yet, unlike me backthen, it's not a lack of ability to understand that keeps us from the truth. No m'am. It's a lack of courage to come to grips w the causes of our repressions ε hypocrisies, and to reach viable conclusions despite the personal ε societal danger of those admissions; it is the lack of viscera ε spine to desire fact ε honesty over sickness ε propaganda. Thru such mental machinations we protract the horrors of our denial.

mark twain on "angelfish"
≈Commentators have already thrown much darkness on this subject. If they continue it is likely we shall soon know nothing at all about it.≈

"we girls are going out tonite" v. "dont call me 'girl'. I'm a woman."

Finally, i must deal w a staggeringly abused word. Girl. One can often glean the cultural status of a word by looking it up. How many words would you say it would take to define 'girl'? 50-60? A hundred at most? In the compleat oxford: try 3ooo...and counting! Two pages of entries! We find it everywhere; songs poetry novels movies. But engineering, tax law ε particle physics? As one of america's foremost musical patriots knew, selective echolalia only heightens the passion. "Most ev'ry fellow tells about a little girly girly...with teeth so white and pearly." Indeed, it is found even in politically incorrect listings! Yet its life presses on undaunted! A man's lover has great grandchildren, still he calls her his "girl". Why? Nobody asks. For to ask is to expose a fragilely-yet-enduringly erected doublestandard. Further, except for gender assignment, this much-bandied word is all but meaningless out of context. Because of this vagueness (code: stealthy predilection), all women get bloodrushes when its used on them —except young ones. Mothers blush, daughters seethe, which prettymuch explains the whole sorry business. But, lacking my harangue, and that of a couple others, who would know?

gender-faulting for the girlery underground

We have named this doublestandard, this pandemic doublestandard, this public secret, the outlaw instinct. Yet there are those who would construe this public denial as a "secret" known to men alone, construe its underground of desire as the work of men only. This is wrong. It is wrong if only because it is sheer madness to think any society could float such a culture-wide psychosis w only one of the sexes participating. Add to this that all of civil society suffers from this *same* syndrome (the outlaw instinct), each to its own level of denial, and youre talking sickness on a global scale!

w/m's most common mask
"I'm just a supermom obeying my protective instincts."

As *the n-d report,* as well as the studies of the likes of drs otto reich, kuno franke, kim jankaid, bekky kydd & a few others show, all genders of [civilized] society participate in the mass mirage of how nicetynice all our endless girleryism [sic] "really" is. It is at the same time true that women alone could, in fact, put their heads together and blow the whole farce skyhigh any time they wanted! For the truth is, every woman has firsthand experience w the sexual power inherent in the teen thru 20+ years. But to do so w credibility those same women would have also to be brave enuf to be bekky kydds in their own right, brave enuf to admit to the potent sexuality of youth, admit to "those days when we (Yes, WE. Hey, don't hang me out to dry here, girls! Speak up!) ...when we *gladly* would have leaped at the chance to mate with even, yes, a post of our virginal beds, if only the thing would have come alive to our hot youthful existence for just a few minutes!" [b.kydd] But that would also mean admitting that, females of a certain degree of sexual development will, if allowed, runoff to mate w just about anyone whom they sense truly finds them desirable ...for *whatever* reason! Also admitting that, just waiting a year or two, "til the hormones get used to you and you get used to them [as bekky puts it], til after the initial frenzy passes and young women become more amenable to social pressures [that is to say, civilized rules & expectations], and can even, in rare cases, be convinced to putoff sexual activity til legal [civil] parity is achieved." [my brackets]

By our deepest fears we shall understand her.

Now of all genders there is none i love more than the female. If the reader doesnt know this by now i guess she never will. Still, i can no longer pamper the lie we live by. *The n-d report* is not silent on this point.

> The moment women admit to such a mass delusion they accede to this fact: The most powerful emotion acting in a man's life is focused on a specific group. Our survey has defined that group explicitly: females, ranging in age generally from puberty thru 21 years. In more primitive times this group was anything but the sink of social "infertility" it is today. Being for most of human history the group most overtly pursued by adult males, it stands to reason that that same age group also had the greatest number of child-bearers. That is, this group singled out today for special isolation from all things sexual and reproductive is the same group which was, for millennia, the core source of the human race. !!! [my underscores]

(Boy, would bekky love to have *that* quote. Emil, break your code for just this once. Just kidding. I know, we're saving that <just once> for the big stuff.) If this statement doesnt prove that the worst enemy of Nature/instinct is civilization, what can? *The report* continues....

> Lacking a social format to pave the way, to prepare our minds to deal with this double standard, such facts frighten the average person. Everyone fears being caught with an illicit belief in hand or even in mind. And, surprisingly, that the belief is founded on fact makes little difference. Fact or fiction, these double standards and prejudices remain in force. Therefor the authors expect their findings in regard to the present group [heterosexual adult males/female adolescents and adults] will be acceptable only to a limited audience.

And thus the pact is made, the complicity between the sexes, complete. Complete enuf so that what was once known as 'the rights of the passions' (that yod to Nature/instinct of former times), even *that* is now lost to us; enuf so that what professor franke called 'the tragic conflict between elemental instinct and moral law' has become diseased and sunk belowground w its ulcerated longings; enuf so that our hearts are slammed shut and our lips are sealed; enuf so that even the most intimate of mates can not, even privately, whisper the deeper truths of human desire to one another; enuf so that we go about our lives making sure we believe in this tragic delusion; and, just as importantly, making sure we punish those who do *not* suffer as we do for refusing to practice our depth of denial.

By the depth of our vengeance we shall know her.

the rules & expectations of civil society fly in the face of instinct by design

Perdu pariah mothers sequestered sisters casanostricized brothers banIshmael fathers excommuniKate mothers, an agegroup which is in fact the parents of the human race itself, treated as so many quaranteened deporteens by that banishmentor of quaranteens, the world matron, feeling good about her evictories, her sexclusions ε proscriptions. [sic all] But i desist, for the authors of *the n-d report* have agreed. Our species would have been psychologically betteroff left in a world of jackals ε hyenas. For the facts repeatedly show, "It is the pursuit of ideologies, not the fulfillment of instinctual impulse, that has crippled us emotionally, has made our world a dangerous place". Phew. Well, now that the findings are in and the costs are being tallied, it seems hardly accidental that: The one species denied fulfillment of its sexual instincts should also prove the most dangerous, the most destructive. But now we've sunk to quoting me again.

Civil institutions are, at their foundations, antiNature/-instinct cartels.

the same Force that bends lite?

I've seen it a thousand times firsthand and studied it many hundreds.... While heteromales, w averted body-language, bruise ε shred their best optics, all but bend lite itself, just to catch the merest reflection of a beautiful young woman (or apparently-young woman) –by way of any handy mirror, glass or polished surface– the world matron prays for any calamity at any cost to obliterate in men all such fleshsheaths of allure. And here's the tragedy in the tale: The more immaculate that allure (read, unconsciously pure) the more vicious the world matron's wishes! Of course, most women will deny owning such politics even at threat of torture. <u>By the depth of her denial we shall know....</u> But i've said.

harms of repressing sex-longing

Annie difrance, who often performed at my lectures, is that rare feminist who, w gloria steinem, eve ensler ε the fascinatingly unpredictable camille pagles, is able to see how civilization's (ie, the world matron's) repression of male sexual longing harms women as well as men. Even dear bekky, brilliant as she is, was awhile whipping this denial. While on the other hand, Lilith, mortally wounded (you could say) by men, and the civil worldview which stands behind them, had no such blindspot. Even as she feared men she understood their dilemma and its source. I think she may have understood even had she never met me or knew my works. Go figure.

all politicized pigtails & hypocrisy

In part3 i explained at some depth how the difference between the Lilith i met and fell in love w, and the "girl" the fed. ε its poppress has accused me of abducting, is both obvious ε extreme. (I have saved til later the soft ε lovely details of this.) As 52yearold allan woods, writer/director/actor, posing w his 21-yearold bride recently said. "I don't know what all the fuss is about. You'd think I'd married a 10-year-old!" In nations around the world winners of "most beautiful female" contests are rarely over 21 —but dont get caught in bed w them! Gawk at my Lilith if you will! Have an eyegazm! But dont touch! Gimme a break! I've studied humanNature, both by the book ε in its psychoreactive dregs, and what i've borne away has caused me to live up to the universal truth not down to the local law. Out of 550 million species (species, reader!) of animal, only one, civilized man, thinks puberty is a big mistake! —or so he says at this particularly destructive period in his civility.

On a final note, *the mackernen report* test group (precursor to the landmark novalis-deland study) found it "strange" and "possibly degenerate" to dress a 20-year-old female to look like a 10-yearold. Yet, in a "mirror" test, the same group found it only "comical", or "cute", when a 10-year-old was madeup to look like an adult prostitute. Think about it ...maybe even alot.

> The law in most regions of the U.S., Great Britain and Canada holds generally that any adult having sexual intercourse or sodomy with a person under 16 is guilty of rape, a crime which levies in most regions a maximum sentence of life imprisonment and a minimum of 10 years. Yet a survey conducted at the University of Illinois in 1991, which researched 243,000 cases in the U.S., Great Britain and Canada, found that males 21 through 66, sometimes after years of hemming and hawing, were released by the courts without sentencing after being found guilty of having (all manner, both singly and in groups) sex with females between the ages of 12 and 16. The deciding criterion for dismissal of these cases? That "the girl consented" and that "no use of intimidation or force was apparent."

Emphatic hmm. Even civil law is itself trying to mumble something in our ear here, reader —not *statutory* law, mind you, but *applied* law, law as it's *practiced*. Then come the rich&famous. And thereof *many* are the victims, and *few* the prosecutions. Most get off clean as a handwiped whistle —while the youth involved may go on to face a ruined or wretched life. The tragedies are legion. Some of the stories make dolita look like bernadette, dumbert like the pope. And these represent but the merest smattering of our shadowy doublestandard, the outlaw instinct, which torments to this minute the memory of my Love in the public mind.

my fondest wish: to purge, once & for always,
the socially-polluted public memory of my Love

Just after capt.gE premiered, the mag *the great outdoors* ran an article about Lilith. It came on the heels of an interview she did w globeSpan (satTv network). To complement a metonym for myself ("the green warrior"), the editors titled the article, "The Green Nymph". Few stories since my arrest have passedup the chance to duplicate, one way or another, these now wellknown metonyms. Even today, people who dont know the names Lilith McGrae or nathan schock likely have heard the terms "green warrior" &/or "green nymph". The following oft-repeated headline (if only repeated as subtext) is the media's cue to crucify us one more time: MIDDLE-AGED KILLER BRAINWASHES TEENAGE RUNAWAY INTO BEING HIS MOLL. From that point on i would be known in academented circles as "the Green Nympholept", and my Lover, as "the Green Nymphet" (as if a female is valid only if attached to a man). I must find a way –some way– to lift my Love above all this dung ε decay before my last word has been uttered.

If i had to guess i would say, out of every 100 adult men who saw Lilith, 95 were assaulted w longing. But not because she was a "nymphet", or a "dolita", as charged, but because she was, quite simply, a beautiful young woman. In *the oxford dictionary of mythical beings* we find

> Nymph 1. beautiful graceful young women, said to inhabit rivers, forests, lakes, oceans, etc., and frequently attending a superior deity who sees to their well-being; maidens, whose beauty is so great that all who look upon them are captivated; young demi-goddesses, whose beauty is so overpowering that males, gods, and even certain females, on seeing them, can not help but pursue them in an erotic frenzy. [and further on] ...females <u>of apparently cohabitable age, as all mortal adult males, and some females (as well as gods and goddesses), on seeing them, are seized with a frenzy to possess them in a sexual manner."</u> [my stress]

Now shouldnt we wonder just who is trying to change this? And why?

If one was close enuf, just the wide-set vast silverblue innocence of Lilith's gaze assaulted one. Many is the male i saw stare, stumble ε stutter ε walk off in a daze, her large eyes a stereoscopic grayblue sea into which one was compelled to saunter til he sank out of sight, notsomuch drowned as solipsized. Her exquisite face, long dark hair ε supple body were powerful attractors toward which one must fall ε fall....

Long accustomed to others staring rudely at my dates ε me, i had a headstart on dealing w the reactions of most people to Lilith. In fact, it was not those who gawked so much as those who didnt, who got to me. They had my sympathy. For over time i learned, it was usually some disability that caused this. But not always. I remember one fellow in his late 20s in a restaurant in frisco. Leaving his table, where an older male sat, he came over to us. "I hope you'll forgive me. I just had to tell you, your companion here (indicating Lee w a nod ε a gay twinkle) is spectacularly beautiful!" I loved his phrase. Not only did i forgive him, i thanked him. Tho he may have had ulterior motives, in this case i think not. The *dmb* continues on 'nymph'....

> 2. a maiden: literary or playful usage 3. a sexually attractive female 4. in entomology (a) the young of an insect without complete metamorphosis (b) a pupa 5. any of several nymphalid butterflies, including the purple, the fritillary, and the peacock butterflies.

Numbers 2 ε 4 above have nothing to do w either the nymphs of primitive cultures or w Lilith. It is strange, this dictionary cites metamorphosis while the encyclopedias do not —the most fascinating aspect of classical myth. Since transformation plays an intriguing role in Lilith's life, it would be haphazard of us to overlook this aspect of nymphs. Maybe there will be time lateron. But for now....

I have seen waiters (male servers) ask Lilith for her order up to three times. 1st time: "I'm sorry, I forgot what you said"; 2nd time: "I'm really sorry. I'm having a bad nite. Could I get your order again?"; 3rd time: mortified, fresh orderpad in hand: "You wont believe this but... Well, they lost your ticket. Could I, please, get your order one more time?" I point to orig pad still lying on table where he (or she) walked off the previous try and left it. I've seen petrolstation attendants spill oil over the engine, or, as happened on the way to rohnert pk, jam the dipstick into the spinning fanblade. For you see, the hood of a javelin (decades ahead of its time) opens forward, exposing engine, wheels ε steering, windshield, car interior, and, of course, whatever beauty happens to be sitting there. That day there happened to be two of same. I've seen them squirt petrol onto the ground, or a roll of bills into the wind, while studying a tinted window behind which sat my love. *Dmb* again.

> ...Nymphs are antipathetic to satyrs and other beings of lascivious inclination....

Like any esthetic force, nymphic attraction is applied against one's *entire* being, one's entire awareness, not just against one's groin. Only when theyve "blown it" do the dunderheads among we males (we schlongs w two eyes ε feet, i mean) find this out; but then it's too late, after we've insulted her essentialSelf w our slavering eyes and after she has fixed us w the brite naivete ε searching wisdom of her own azure gaze, or perhaps after the sincerity ε simplicity of her mtn-brook speech has wobbled to its knees our boorish intent.

I've seen speakers at functions lose their place —not just me, reader; not just me. And i've even seen blindmen ε cripples riseup like fakirs from the dusty pavement, set aside pencil-cups or trinket-filled trays, leave behind amazed dogs ε neighboring beggars, just to hobble over to greet "the goddess" who stood nearby. So help me –forgetting that incredible incident in lhasa– this happened in both frisco ε ny city! That the blindmen were probably more faker than fakir is not the question here. A bank teller in scotsmoor was talking on the fone as we approached his window. It was so quiet in there we thought they were closed. On looking our way, as if trapped in a dream, he slowly hung up the fone (female voice on the other end buzzing away til her throat was slashed by the clickoff) and floated over to the window. What did L think of all this? I was awhile discovering.

Because even some females reacted to her similarly, she was convinced, people somehow sensed the "bad" things that had happened to her in her youth. While this damaged selfimage improved in our short time together, she never overcame it. Anyway, where were we? Oh, yes. Lilith, uncanny attractor. In *the dictionary of mythical beings* we came across the phrase, "Even certain females, on seeing them, cannot help but pursue them in an erotic frenzy". This phenomenon too –where sex roles are sometimes switched in Nature– we may find time to visit lateron. I'm thinking now of the michelle french's, karen kremer's, leslie kletman's ε liz gillick's who pursued my Love on occasion. And of the deldevi's who perhaps even wondered if....

Anyway, nikki, working w Lilith... almost wrote, Lilicky, in my haste here. I am writing licketysplit now, to get this overw, conclude our theses... Nikki, working w Lilith for hours at creative projects having mostly Natural settings, had to have sensed her new employe's uniqueness as much as i did. While she could no more list those forces than i could at the time, this did not stop them from fritening her: L's eyes, her facial expressions, her bodily motions, the glimmer ε glow of her gloried limbs; the faylike felicity, the beguiling insouciance that wove quietly thru her manner; qualities hard to explain but guaranteed to charm win seconds of meeting her...and to melt one, instantly, upon touch! It was this gathering of forces into a single being which caused nikki to know her place in my life was doomed, which sent her to my door that nite like the fuming ghost of flaubert's collette.

To summarize. If youve never been giddily dazzled to your bonemarrow while simultaneously fritened by a merest glance, then youve never met a nymph, never been a nympholept. And that was *before* we'd been intimate, when Lilith had yet to melt me in her meadows, envelop me in her valleys, capture me in her caverns her caves, fetter me in her forests, entrance me among her trees, ravel me in her rivers, lure me w her lakes, spellbind me w her seas, bewitch me w her winds, make me grovel in her grottos, bind me w her breezes, ravish me in her ravines, enrapture me w her rainbows, fell me under her falls, mesmerize me w her mtns her mists, seduce me w her sunsets, hex me w her stars. O Lilith, that the reader could have known you, then all argument would fall helpless at the feet of your memory.

lore on Lilith, plus a word about lenny-the-librarian

As we prep to begin part6 of Lilith's story i would like to pointout. When i say 'prison library', the reader should not picture a great open room filled w aisles of shelves but a hallway (in the old bldg) w offices on either hand and archways punched between them, w every two of the eight arcades having their own guard overseeing things during library hours. And when i mention carrels one should not picture the misty & musty skylit carrels of luxurious academia: squeaky rolling ladders, dusty shelves & narrow aisles, where the large girl w the shiny complexion backs out bashfully to let you thru; or where the scapulae & tresses of a frail scholar brush lightly behind you as she, smiling demurely (not at you but at a space close-by), glides by, lovely head bowed, excusing herself in a whisper and leaving a faint sorrel scent (cross between cloves & anise) in the still-quivering space where she'd just shaken out her fabulous hair. Early to pick her up at the main campus, i surprised lalage one day in the ua/huntsdell carrels, "I had a feeling someone was staring."

You must be [switch to a whisper]... You must be used to *that.*

Eyes down. "Why so early?"

Well, i thought that, since we decided to.... [smile dawning on her features] Someone behind me?

"No."

I note how perfectly straight her teeth are, and such a white white, w slite but sexy overbite. Whatsa matter? I look over my own shoulder then back.

"Your shoulders..."

Dandruff?

Another glued page!

One needs a letterknife to do research here. This library, pathetic as it is, has a constructive function however. Try to find what you want in ornithology –say, wild birds of n.amer– or astronomy –spallation in lactal b objects, say– and you end emptyhanded. It would appear that the goal of this gaol library is your basic legal-aid & psyche collection, yes. But far&away it is for sexual utility: specializing in vehicles of release for those employees and inmates who can not only read but can presumably do so one-handed. But we were talking about the sexual underground pandemic OUTSIDE these walls.

"No, doofus [her Sister's petname for me]. They takeup the whole isle." A problem w carrels. And that was *before* this latest body-widening. But there are no such in this prison. Here the carrels consist of cardboard cartons on steel shelves in two windowless offices across from lenny's and the book-checkout counter. These cartons are prolific w crunchy cockroach corpses & copious poppyseedlike coproliths, which spill about, their dry rattle heard but unseen, at every tilt of every brittle box. And as you might guess, the best books are in boxes here while most of the shelves in the main rms are lined w "the books that move, mr schock. And you know what moves in this place... You dont? Well, I'll tell you. Criminal law and trash novels. *That's* what moves." Looking down when he speaks so the cameras cant read his lips, lenny the librarian is one of only two (that i know of) reasonably sane persons in here.

I locate the book he recommends for my research. *The vampire*. I would not otherwise have cracked the covers of such a title. My God! There's even an index! "Damngood start around here." And so i find the name, lilith, located between lamia & limniad. Eight pages are re:d! Wow. I take it to the main room for fotocopies. Lenny says "Go on, take it. After all [whispering], the few reflective humans one comes across in here deserve *some* pampering ...And, o yes, I'll get those others for you too... No trouble at all. My pleasure, in fact." He is re:g borges' *the book of fantastic creatures* & duffy's *the erotic world of faery*. "And that other title, what is it? By lenormand?

Should be in any day now." It already came in, len. I thank him, head back to my cell, picking up glumm at the door, who –speaking of bloodsuckers ε flesheaters– is devouring the pics in a mag called *people*.

Origins of Lilith. Here it is! Habits. Nocturnal, irresistible, lascivious, vampirish, ghoulish, promiscuous ...and w a poor self-image. (Sorry. My take.) Likes to terrorize, betimes, even murder. My opinion of "good" ε "evil" aside, i go in for a closer look. Is there no thing those monks didnt rob ε twist to meet their own ends? Once the sole keepers of mideastern knowledge, they must have felt certain no one would ever uncover all their culture lootings.

Lilith's sources are not semitic at all, turns out. She was heisted from babylonian cylinder seals. The *revue d'assyriologie* cites the demon, lilîtu, a nite spirit (nite monster). Certain males of babylon, it seems, were "troubled by nocturnal emissions", attributed to visitations of "lilith and her sisters". Apparently there was every chance such a session might cost the sleeper his life. How? Some victims had the blood sucked out of them; others, get this, were eaten alive.

There is disagreement (ho-hum) as to the linguistic rudiments of the name lilith. What a word! How stunning, how magical, even in these vulgar ε vicious trappings. Some scholars favor the hebrew laîlah, "nite". Others cite the assyrian lilû, as this derives from lalû (luxuriousness) and lulti (lasciviousness, lechery). (For clarity's sake, proofreader, i do not want these particular foreign words in italics.) Then this intracultural salad of dim definitions goes greek and latin on us, tossing in lamia, strix ε larua. Lexicographers lewis ε short say in classical latin, lamia is "a witch who was said to suck children's blood, a sorceress, enchantress." And the strix is not far afield: "...ghost (larua) which drains the blood of young children". Ghastly gobbledygook.

True to their twistoric female fear ε loathing, semitic (read, rabbinical) sources are rich w legends of the she-demon, lilith. Tool for defaming ε diminishing the wonder of femaleness in the eyes of children ε the world, they replaced the old horror stories of men hiding along dark roads in desolate places (code: Wild places), in deserts, forests ε moors, among ruins, by lakes ε bogs, w a new ε fearsome female. At the hands of these celibates, the lovely gentle nymphs of the ancient world, and Mothernature too, undergo a dark inversion, a vicious transformation. One cannot but wonder about the private sex lives of such men. In agreement w godwin ε reich i see them as motherless wifeless daughterless, invertedly hermetic —at least heterosexually hermetic. For a ruthless sexism has been imprinted onto this socalled lilith creature of theirs, w the sickest of civil traits laminated upon a female body. For all honest men know, the impulse of females generally is to protect ε nurture children, not harm them. If we must assign a gender, terrorizing torturing killing ε raping children is, historically, a male thing —the work of male gods male rulers male soldiers, most of them far&away highly civil. Have i said, moses ε abraham, by admission of *bible* AND *torah*, slaughtered thousands of children ε their parents and were proud (aargh) to describe the horrors in detail w stats to boot?

As the baron put it in his *twisted cross*: "All the my-god-is-better-than-your-god religions deserve every horror which the intolerant armageddon they have in mind for each other brings about. For the sheer viciousness of civil religion is possibly unmatched in the history of the cosmos and is very certainly unmatched in the history of mankind."

Finally, the assignment of "evilness"* by monks to Mothernature ε Earth, ε to females generally ("We are all born into a world of sin", that sort of meanspirited ε paranoid rubbish), was fed by the fire of ignorance in the communal imagination of medieval times. "From jewish lore she [lilith] passed into medieval demonology," says montague summers, passionate witchhunter/-researcher ε author of *the vampire*. And johann weyer says that she was the princess (also the queen) of the succubi. Enter here all sort of depraved acts ε deeds –things w blood, pus, semen ε excrement– and all of them, mind you, attributed to *un*civilized she-demons, to superfemales, but nevernevernever to civilized males. But of course.

O that i had been lucky enuf to learn these things in my passionate adolescent searches ε researches. Even tho i remember reading end-to-end the *old testament*, the following got by me. "The wild beasts of the desert shall also meet with the wild beasts of the island, and the satyr [he-goat] shall cry to his fellow, there hath the lamia [aka, lilith] lain down...." —*isaiah* 34, 14.

"Belief in evil enters at that point where our ability to understand destructive behavior collapses in horror or exhaustion." —otto reich

*I have put aside my opinions on 'evil' onetoomany times. Even tho the foundations of einstein's theories of Reality are time-dependent, so brilliant & candid a humanbeing was he, he still was prepared to admit: ≈Time does not exist in the Real World. It is a human invention. Space, form, content, location and motion have an empirical existence. But not time. Time is merely an artificial means, a humanity-invented tool, used to better understand how matter is distributed thru space.≈

It is little different with "evil". It too can not be found in the Real Universe. However, where arguing the artificiality of time may get one cited for technical eccentricity, arguing the bogusness of "evil" can get one branded satanic/demonic. I am serious. And so, we doubters are often fearful of debunking "evil" in public places. But what can you do to me now, civil corpoliticos, civil clergy? Electrocute me for 40mins instead of 20? Not to ruin your fun but, after the first 10 or so, after one's nervous system has been effectively skewered & parboiled, how bad can the final 20mins be?

Belief in "evil" demands ignorance of actual causes, or paranoia (attitude bias against Reality) or both. And since lifestyle paranoia is directly related to ignorance –lack of sufficient empirical information– ignorance is far&away the most essential element for believing "evil" is a real thing.

I have often been challenged by those who, for some reason, secondguess me as doubting primitive cultures were also victims of the mirage of evil. Most are relieved to find this is not the case. For, since ignorance or paranoia are essential to a belief in evil, "evil" obviously 'enjoyed' a lively existence among primitive & protocivil cultures. And it enjoyed it long before civil religion came along & elevated "evil" from a local & transient perception to a basic condition of existence, a "basic state of the World at large". That is, the primitive perception of "evil" is local/transient (leaving plenty of room for "good"), while the civil/religious perception (of "evil") is present in ALL that physically exists, leaving no room for "good" anywhere except within its imagined paradise/heaven. Both states of "evil" (primitive and civil) have long been effective (and much-abused) tools for social control, and no other pop fiction has ever been more effectively exploited. Just as primitive shamans surely used fear of "evil" to further some agenda or other, so religiots & politicos to this day push "evil" among the masses like the virulent drug it is. (religiots = whacko fundamentalists)

only now can my reader understand out of what unmentionable depths this next reincarnates itself

My hour w the little fellow: When charley chaplin assembled his notorious Honest Men, Brave Men summit in davos in 1966, certain persons were not invited. Three of these were conspicuous "oversights": balthus (painter), vladikov (author) & otlingham (fotographer) ...not leastofall because all three were almost chaplin's neighbors. When pressed about this, following the summit, he said, "While they without question number among the finest living talents, and while they certainly qualify as honest and brave men who reject many of the unjust aspects of the status quo –all qualities vital to our undertaking– it is also unfortunately true, the mere presence of these men at our gathering would have endangered the credibility and superior morality of our agenda". He described this agenda as "the public establishment, once and for all, of what is normal ...biologically normative, I mean... mate selection among heterosexual men." Chaplin showed a genuine concern for the prides of the obviously uninvited, whom he matter-of-factly referred to as "lewis carroll's lollipop brigade"... For he truly felt they would have been "embarrassed by the mating age-limits which even the most honest and brave of men were likely to set... even under the summit's non-threatening conditions of anonymity-in-numbers, from which i feel it benefitted greatly ...exclusionary age-limits which the nearly four-hundred of us did in fact end up setting."

Not long before he died chaplin (whom i'd never met) foned me to say he'd just encountered, in a new documentary about the 1960s, my sex-suffrage doctrine. It reads: <If a person is old enough to suffer the pain of sexual deprivation then he/she is old enough to own the right to assuage that pain.> "Your elegant and humanitarian formula would have rendered all that glaring and vulnerable language we used in our final proclamation at davos unnecessary. Sweetgeezus how I do so wish we'd had your formula in hand at the time", said chaplin, his voice shaky w age but impassioned, the "most glaring" of which language he then went on to quote. "...Any bias for ages 13 and 12 (again, generally, of course) we here assembled have voted and labeled as 'more desperate than erotic'...while a bias for ages 11 and under we typically find 'more repulsive than desperate'." With clear disappointment he concluded,

> I wish we'd never mentioned age [for its mention had] dragged us down to the level of those very laws which have punished society for so long already, and whose very arbitrariness caused me to call such a congress in the first place.... [his diction was immaculate if halting] Had we only had your elegant and altruistic principle in hand at the time, our final draft might have read [after some speakerfone rattling of papers he read aloud]: 'Our principle (of course we would have credited *you* with that principle), let me add... our principle renders all considerations based on age, whether legal or not, flagrantly antihumanitarian and wholly in conflict with the most basic human rights. For age-based law always exists in conflict with the facts of consensual sexual desire among our species generally. We assembled therefor, being men bent on justice, enjoin all cultures, whether respecting the rule of law or not, to trade the sheer arbitrary inhumanity of age-citation for the more just method of case-by-case evaluation, a new process of law and decision-making which rejects as arbitrary, unjust and cruel, the many age-biases we cling to which have for too long punished all of civilized humanity. [Text kindly provided by The Little Fellow, Ltd. —Ed.]

the true primal scene

Freud got it wrong. (The world matron 'n' her mammery-males will "lose it" on this one.) The primal scene is not witnessing our parents in the act of creating us. It is rather *all of us* witnessing the silverbacks of our communities seducing, then copulating w, our most attractive females. Virtually all our voyeurism, both overt ε secreted, attests to this.

Out my window tonite....

...between the grime on the outerside of its pane, its thickness, its age & the glare of security liting along the prison walls, once again, there are no stars tonite. What a stupid expression, eh? As if a whole Universe has disappeared because the writer cant see any stars. As ever, pop language obscures reality. During doktor slugnung's last campaign some time ago the warden asked about my mock journal, *constellations of confinement,* which froodnung was insisting is a terrorist manifesto needing its code broken. Wardion seemed wholly satisfied when i explained having been a nitesky fancy all my life who hasnt seen an unpolluted nitesky for years. Of course wardion suggested that i "give jesus a try. Afterall, he is the lite of the world, you know", wardion claiming to have "seen that lite manyatime smiling among the stars". This got me to thinking ...and you know what can go down when *that* happens.

smiling dead prophet's-eye-view of Earth's niteside

Pretty clusters of lite "down" there? Or is it just one more means of obscuring 99.9%+ of Natureality (the entire Universe)? And are we thus litup out of love of nitetime glare, or fear of darkness? And why is our environment growing briter in proportion to our approach to self-annihilation? What forms of nite exactly are we running from, outlawing, or *trying* to outlaw?

my jailers and their apprehension of deity & 'the now'

Wkdays, twice or more each day, the staff clowns, when not doing their master's bidding, slip into the old bldg to hide out. Their chatter would infuriate an imbecile. "Ya know what yer problum is?" says glumm to gluum, his parting shot to their hour-long blather & banter. "Ya lib in da past. Ya needa snap oudda it." The glibness w which glumm restated the mass illusion that any of us live, or can live, "in the Present", gnawed away at me not just til litesout, but on&off thru sleep til pre-daylite performed its chalky charade on the cafeteria windows across the way. By then my urge to reply, rhetorical or not, was unbearable. For the words, "Ya lib in da past", limned, if gutturally, the pertinences of my very *existence*: nathan schock, political prisoner, day on day, nite unto nite, living "in the past". Whether to finish this bio, or out of purest longing to return 'there', or both, the past is where i exist. And what better topic, before i lapse into part11, than a brief word as to....

How glibly we speak of the Now, as if the blood&bone of thinking existence is really capable of experiencing the Present. Who among us is ready to remove his anthropic blinders long enuf to admit to himself that by the time we comprehend a moment, *any* moment "in the present", the *actual* present has left us behind and moved on. For the actual present (Present), no matter how rapidly we may try to apprehend it, moves ever ahead of our ability, as thinking creatures, to ever actually *experience* it. For the electrochem connections which comprise our thinking existence are so crude, the hope of our ever achieving simultaneity w the actual present is not even on the horizon of practicality. For the simple fact is, only non-thinking entities can exist in the absolute ɛ unboundaried Now (or Present).

I have managed to sidestep this question for years in my books. So how can i now, knowing this is my last, fail to confront it?

O, to be sure, life is extraordinarily constructed for so crude a scale as ours! But what of we thinkers who feel sure we exist win the embrace of a finer, faster, more efficient scale of physical existence, a scale however w which we just cant quite seem to sync? What of we who feel sloggeddown ɛ thoughtsnarled by the mere blood&flesh connections of our electrochem biology, who feel cast adrift in a seeming speed-of-lite-connected Universe ...or should i have said, speed-of-lite-disconnected? What is to become of we who feel: waiting for someone in the same room to respond is like waiting for a photon to arrive from the sun; who feel, when that answer finally reaches us, it is already history? And what of those of us who feel that just waiting for a sensation in our toe to reach our brains is like waiting for a signal to rebound from the moon? Forget the gargantuan disconnection ɛ displacement problems of einsteinian liteyears ɛ galaxies, what of just knowing that every thought we think is, by its very electrochem mechanics, already in the past? that our every realization is in fact plodding along behind the skadjillion Universal changes which the absolute now (Now) has already wrought? What of we who long to be more directly, more instantaneously, connected w this World we've been so unceremoniously plunked down into? What of we who intuitively disagree w that admittedly humorous copout: Maybe the hokeypokey is, afterall, what it's all about? Where do we, we who sense that instantaneous connection exists all around us but that we are (cruelly?) partitioned from it... where do we go from here? A gentle suggestion....

In frisco in '74 i mustered the discipline to master the discipline of shuttingdown conscious thought; what some think of as a discipline of ego-suppression. It was that or learn to suffer the state of never finding, never experiencing, the finer, faster, more efficient scale of connection available to all (non-thinking) entities. And finally, how could i have known that, an automatic bonus of practicing said discipline would open a whole 'new' Universe of machian connections?

in here, of all places

I came across the following title in the library today. *Turning your 4play into 10play,* by lucus inning ε ella tofi. As if any of my keepers or cöinmates —whose idea of good foreplay is taking a moment to drop one's pants during sex …as if anyone here cares to improve his foreplay. For things here doubtless are as helmut once said (joking, we hoped): "Foreplay is what a real man gets, not gives." At the counter larry tapped a book. "Just finished it: You'll *love* this woman's art, I know." So i took arundhati roy's *the god of small things* to my cell …and win the hour knew <The finest writer of english alive today!>.

wardion's gladiator or ratmoid's andabate?

Chrome-dome day —made sure i was workingout when the barber came. His hair grew long when sampson was in prison at gaza. And the temple still stands! Today was my first day in open sunlite in months. Firedrill. My skin is almost under-a-rock white! {O open sunlite and air how i've missed you!} My newly massive shadow moving beside me took me back a step. <Whoa! Backoff, brotha!> til i realized it was only me. What a waste of food ε energy. I hope i can quit this silliness as soon as the competition is over.

the most incredible body of all

however is the body of Motherearth: floating agate-blue ε white thru the icy blackness of space, set like a magic gem in a backdrop of stars.

on reading this book

Until part6, reading this book is a little like being a small kid pulling a big sled up a steep hill. But once at the top of our story, it's a screamer the rest of the way. And we're almost there. We're almost there!

chri-stoyevsky said

"The degree of civilization in a society can be judged by entering the prisons." I would turn that on its head: The amount of Wilderness missing in a society can be accurately gaged from the amount of prisons in its midst.

proof, you say?

All you need do is ~~took at~~ examine the ethics of the socalled *successful* to see how the civilizing principle more&more skews our instinctive morality toward the destructive, as onebyone we commit those acts which (we claim) success "requires" of us, often behaving in ways which commonsense & good conscience –if we dared consult them– say we should *never* behave …if we *really* want to do our part to heal this Planetary Home we've so thoroly trashed. But of course, *most of us* dont care one way or the other …not *really* we dont. That *should* be clear by now, here on the very cusp of apocalypse.

the prisoner's song

There is a song my father used to break into once we'd lifted off and reached assigned altitude —a man apparently happy enuf to sing only when he was airborne & on-course. It is obvious, he saw life outside the cockpit (hic) as a kind of prison. How could i have guessed, the words of his song (one of but a handful he shared) would one day have such poignant meaning for me? I would like my reader to imagine part5 closing w the chorus of that song.

> *If I had the wings of an angel, over these prison walls i would fly;*
> *I would fly to the arms of my poor darling, and there I'd be willing to die.*

the worst punishment for primitives is banishment

Banishment once worked even in civilization —backwhen being civilized was less the hard & cold cage it is today. With the extended family more&more disabled by the state, and w the state's nuclear family also in a shambles, banishment more&-more resembles freedom than punishment. These days, being banished might even cause someone to reconnect w that more fulfilling existence civilization stole from us! These are the dregs into which (the) cataNatural justice (of the civilizing principle) has dragged us …often by the hair of our very souls!

primitive conscience v. civil law (after confucius)

Because it replaces 'the justice of conscience' with 'the fear of law', to rule by power of law and not by power of conscience is to create a culture of cheating and a society without shame. And i am living hour-to-hour up the anus of *that* culture, *that* society. O for those wings of an angel….

Part 6

[Approximate date of composition by the author: Dec. 1998. —Ed.]

1

The blustery days of oct/nov on the bluff had mostly passed southward by the time i returned home. While the temp at nite dropped to jacket wx (weather), daytime temps were usually shirtsleeve. This was good, for there was a backlog of outdoor work needing attention.

Bernie mcCleigh, my nearest neighbor, had been in charge of sanctuary maintenance almost since its purchase. The only thing i expected to change when i wasnt around was his sense of caring about the place. Over time however –and for reasons i could only guess at– our relationship deteriorated and his sense of responsibility w it. This particular time-away i returned to find –among other problems also thanx to neglect– the missing bison calf (already noted) and the observation tower trashed. Neither would have concerned me halfsomuch had bernie known they occurred. Tho experience had shown him to be a hard-working man, it had also shown him not above handy excuses. Since i will not tolerate a boss/servant relationship, i accepted his weak-but-not-impossible explanation in a gentlemanly way and not for the first time....

...Until that is next day when i found the calf's remains (it had been shot) and called stan starbuck who'd left me a note. The corpse was partially buried beneath a ½meter-high anthill and had been abandoned by the vultures for "a couple weeks at least, I'd say... Naw, dont *gotta* pull 'er oudda there. Thet theyr hayd [head] tells the tale, ma friend. Taint no steer. Thet there's a buffalo [bison]." Because the corpse was only a couple hundred meters from the s.most boundary of the sanctuary, and given their history of criminal mischief, i suspected the calhoun boys. My use of 'boys', like 'mischief', is a euphemism. Re the vast numbers of today's first-world adults who remain perennially irresponsible: mischievous aimless & ignorant. Too cowardly & lazy to be out&out criminals, they make a life in petty crime til "the big lottery-win" or "legal-suit I c'n retire on" presents itself. As to thetower trashing. The astronomy club had cleanedup a mess at its last visit, said starbuck, club pres down in scotsmoor. The sheriff was called etc. Bernie knew of none of this, tho starbuck said he left a note in his mailbox.

As the pheasant flies, bernie's house is almost 1k due e of mine, w his land lying largely along frontloop rd. Because the ~200hectares where the bison graze, and where tower park sits, surround bernie's farm on two sides, and because most of it is high open ground, only a small part lies out of eyeshot of his house & farm. In fact, tower park sits on some of the highest land around; its observation rm & deck can be seen above treeline from any open area of comparable elev to the limit of visibility. Using binocs on a cold winter nite i have picked out its distinctive violet-white strobes from as far off as 90k! —not exactly the most private place for imbibing 24cans of beer (budwater, what else?) and tossing the empties over the rail. Yet i'm sure the vandals considered me lucky that they didnt get hurt & sue while climbing up & around the gate of such an "attractive nuisance".

buffalofieldcampaign.org

I first met with this terminology thru my insurer when i voiced concern over some trespasser purposely getting hurt on "my" property. "I hate ta be the bearer of bad news but thet thing not only meets, it exceeds the law's definition of an attractive nuisance." It proved not only a case of pay the responsible party (my insurer) an increased premium but, thanx to the twisted values of civil society, it also became my responsibility to build a court defense for the insurer (warnings fences gates locks etc). All this because i wanted a bird's eye view of a tiny part of this Planet i so love from "my own" property without having to use a biplane or balloon.

The scotsmoor astroclub was small when i sought advice on getting my own scope. The owner of the best instrument around (starbuck) wished, for a number of reasons, he'd spent more on his own scope. The one he wanted (& recommended) cost $20ooo, more than double what i'd hoped to spend. Seeing an opportunity to upgrade the club's best viewing instrument, starbuck got the members to front the money i needed to vandal-proof my "more expensive but frustration-free" scope... well, that is, if only they could use it 156hrs a year for the next 5yrs. This is how our destinies, the club's & mine, became star-crossed.

Even doing much of the labor ourselves, this vandal-proofing came to one-half the cost of the scope itself! For those who wonder, "Why go to the trouble? Just collect the loss from the insurance if the scope gets wrecked or stolen."

Who thinks this knows nothing about the labor- ε love-intensive hours it takes to get a decent scope up, running, and quickly ε easily enjoyable. Consider this: Just the infinitesimal sway of the tower in a strong wind could interrupt the viewing of any object smaller in apparent size than saturn! —which means of course *most* of the visible Cosmos! That the scope was bolted to a heavy alloy stand bolted to the pylon frame, itself secured to a massive slab of concrete ε granite, was good but imperfect. The vandal-proofing did limit the damage that could be done however. Had my "small room in the sky" not had metal rollup shutters, a heavy alloy door ε heavyduty locking system, there would also have been a cluster of perturbed [hic] star-gazers to deal w when i got home. Of course (to bring this sidelite current w the rest of the story), like most such arrangements, the "honey" in our mutual "moon" had longsince begun to crystalize. By the time of this most recent vandalizing i felt like the abused parent of a pack of whining brats to whom i wasnt even related.

The first days back were always busier than i liked. I'd been saying for years, i needed a fultime on-premises mngr but could never find the right fultime person. There were woodlands ponds creeks springs falls spillways bridges roads paths overwalks stairs houses ε other bldgs, vehicles machinery pontoonboat kyacks canoe dock fence- bluff- ε shorelines, to keep check of. But mostofall, i needed to know the status of the *other residents* of ggNs, both ambulative ε stationary (fauna ε flora). This required time ε respectful observance. *Nature does not reveal her best "secrets" easily,* goethe said. And this is to say little of those things i'd placed in the care of others: forest- creek- ε tarn ecologies, orchard- vineyard- ε treefarm maintenance ε harvest, bison-care, mowing/grazing (treated as a crop) &soforth, most of which were managed by the local college thru grants ε private funding. Inmixed in all this were preparations for ggNs' "6th winter-solstice rites of gaEa".

2

GaEa is an acronym for "green-activist Earth-awareness". I conceived the observance during winter solstice 1987. It came about largely because i'd spent that holiday break alone, romantically speaking —unexpectedly alone. For the woman i was, well, dating at the time (tara pickford) was obliged to join her parents in visiting relatives out of state. The inspiration for these Earth rite's grew from the central lines in an otherwise weak sonnet i wrote at the time. Here the ~~poet~~ *jongleur* is invoking Mothernature/Gaia.

...evanescent elusive 'Goddess' who
(unlike our other lovers do)
lets me come and lie with Her
only when my thoughts are still,
only when the 'i' called 'me'
exists within Herself alone.

But it's the *sense* that counts here, not the *ab*sence of poesy. These lines, plus a list of what i found unfulfilling about other Earth celebrations, were the germ of my Earth-awareness rites. Important note: These rites, falling on the equinoxes & solstices, do not conflict w Earthday celebrations. Yet today as i write, almost a decade hence, one can hardly find a large Earthday celebration where at least the totem i conceived (that day in '87) is not present in some form. However, in case the rite is lost in years to come, and by some twist of happenstance this book is not, i will make a space here to setout the rudiments of these rites.

The sanctuary hosted Earth-awareness festivals four times yearly: winter & summer solstices, spring & fall equinoxes. Tho the fetes end quietly, their openings can be quite blustery. So to keep the endemic sanctity of ggNs, these fetes are held in tower park, ~½k s of bernie's farm and about midway between front- & backloop rds. And since at 6p on dec 21st it is dark, and since the hundred or so maples lining the park are by then mostly leafless, as one drives past bernie's house toward tower park, the lites colors & motions of the fete can be seen. As to the park proper, it was conceived one day during the purchase phase of ggNs. Up in a helicopter w two tva reps, trying to secure in perpetuity water-access rights for sanctuary Wildlife, i noticed, at only 15m or so above the highest point on the property, the vista openedup in every direction to the extent of visibility! Using rock from the dynamiting of a not-too-distant hwy project, plus some of the extensive silting extracted from the westerly restoration of juanita tarn (a natural pond + cypress swamp bordering the n.bluff), i had the 4.5m-high base of the tower built. On this base the tower was erected, its uppermost deck becoming, purely by accident, one of eight "highest lookouts" in the state. It is on the w.side of this base that the Earth awareness fete itself was always held (see ggNs sketch if incl'd). While some part of the tower is visible to 35 or so of the nearest houses thruout the year, the festival itself was not. Most of the trees thereabouts being deciduous however, in winter about half my neighbors could make out the lites, hear the music, and a third of them could even see some part of the goings-on at its base, specially the stage ɛ totem. Atop any one of three barns on a certain farm near the s.boundary of ggNs, an angry man *w* binocs could make out the general proceedings of our "heathen" holiday *w* little difficulty.

As to those proceedings. What one saw when he arrived on that eve of dec 21st were the seven elements of the totem-to-be spread across the higher stage (the base of the tower), each spotlited ɛ slowly rotating. Six of these elements (levels, or units, if you will) are best described as cubes while the 7th only is a sphere, typically much larger than the cubes. Since the cubes are meant to be totemed, they can effectively show only four faces, each repping the four primary points of the compass plus other chthonic or celestial quaternities. Five of the six cubes have faces carved or otherwise shaped onto them. These may be human, animal, or even plant 'faces'. Yet for the sake of children ɛ neophytes, at least one face on each of the five levels must be anthropized (human or humanlike).

Perspectivized: Each element of the totem represents an element of the Earth rites generally, and five of these represent the senses: smell taste hear feel see, *w* each element prevailing over (roughly speaking) 1/7th of the festival. This segmenting means, most festivals are 7hrs long, tho this is hardly set in stone. 7hrs was the case on the eve in question, beginning as it did at 6p and ending at 1a. I need add, spirituality, like all suppressed behavior, grows bizarre not when it is free to express itself (as many would have us believe) but when it is crushed by formality (dogma-bound ritual). So it was that the format to each 7th of the festivities was left open to spontaneous inspiration. In fact, the seven roughly hourlong sections were meant to serve merely as an outline, to give spiritual spontaneity a legup.

Standing before the stage (we do not call it an altar), exam of the totem's lower elements reveals each to be missing something. In element 1, which begins the festival, it is the organ of smell. For the kids, a pinocchio- or dumbolike face might be represented sans the nose. For the 1st hour, the element-1 cube is set on a lower platform at the front of the stage where it may be examined more closely as it slowly rotates in place, bathed intermittently in white, violet ɛ "black" lite.

The beginning ε end of hour1 are presided-over by those who feel competent to speak in the area of "Why I love my home this Earth even tho I've lost my sense of smell", while the remaining 40mins is given over to all in attendance who then strive to block, or otherwise disable, that sense. The most exotic, and often hilarious, nasal plugs ε clips the reader can imagine have been seen at gaEa festivals, some requiring more than one person, and sometimes even a manually powered vehicle, to tote them around. It is no accident that the eve's food is being prepared ε laid out at this time.

And so it goes thru the eve ε on into the nite. One by one the sense-elements are placed (sacrificed, if you will) on the lower platform, each for its given hour, then carried back up the stairs to grow the totem. I will not bore the reader familiar **w** all this by detailing each element, except maybe to note in passing what amazing works of folkart the ggNs totems have become over the years. Most art-lovers would be proud to place any one of its 15 faces, as last i saw them, on display in his/her home.

The 5th element, as it involves the sense of sight, is naturally one of the most dramatic sacrifices. But the 6th element, blankness, my personal favorite, can be downright uncanny. How does one represent Nothing! On the totem itself it is (must be) represented by a faceless (blank) cube. This is the "uncarved block" of Daoism made manifest. By this point in the festival, participants have 'givenup' all their senses and are in a state of meditation, or at least simulating one. (I dont think there were 20 people who really meditated (successfully banished *all* thought) that nite. But there were 40 or so who stuck it out, who possibly left thinking "Hey, maybe there're more rewards to this innerlife stuff than I thought".) It was this penultimate element which usually separated the dedicated from the merely interested. During it, at one of our early winter fetes, a funny thing happened. It was one of those laffs triply painful because, during 6th-hour meditation, everyone is not only silent but virtually motionless. Someone was overheard to whisper after some time had passed, "God, I'm freezing!" To which someone nearby replied, "No, you *cant* be freezing. To feel cold you must be able to feel, and we gaveup that sense a couple hours ago". Today one cant hardly attend a winter fete where this story is not retold, specially if it is cold.

The 7th element of the totem is a model of Earth as seen from space. This element, which opens the final hour, is the only one not intro'd or ended using words. The Earth-sphere is raised to the top of the totem —which is then lit by spotlites as it slowly ε majestically turns on a (real) starry black background, the blackness immed below it facilitated by the black 'nothingness' of the 6th element. One of the most thrilling moments of my childhood was the liting of our holiday tree. Because of my state of mind after 6hrs of sense deprivation, this final moment of the gaEa festival rarely failed to surpass the warm glowing internal YES! of that hypertrophied memory.

The Earth-awareness rite spread rapidly. And since most E-a brations have grown w the years, i had to work at keeping ggNs rites intimate. This incl'd excluding the press ε other heckle-proclived rubberneckers. While this added to the mystery (code: fear) of what we were up to, i wanted in attendance only those people looking for a selfless experience. If that meant 6 people instead of 6000, sobeit. Earthday in frisco this year i understand brought upwards of 10000 and incl'd a 4hr version of my E-a rites. Not bad for an event i never promoted and which never left the property in alpalachia til 1989 ...that i know of.

Lilith

GgNs events were put on ε attended mostly by people in some way affiliated w ua@huntsdell or w bamalachia college(bc), located just outside the townlet of quadrant, the nearest town to ggNs (tho not the nearest village). Tho ggNs festivals rather tend to superimpose in memory, one stands apart. Lilith's first. A word-of-mouth-only event, out of the 200 or so who stopped by, most came&went by 10p, and of these, most were under 30. And tho i always invited my neighbors for "a green bite to eat and a little Earth music", very few, sorry to say, stopped by. Even so, 200 was an exceeding-good turnout for such a demographically sparse area, specially considering, just a few k away, over on lookout mtn, kukluxklan meets were still well-attended! (No, i'm *not* kidding.) But best remembered: that was the nite a core group of 20 or so of us had a quite deep "Gaian moment", a moment i dont believe any of us would have traded for a larger turnout.

Back when i conceived the totem ε its rites, while i knew from experience, shuttingdown the senses helps shutoff the chatter of the rational brain (thus putting one closer to Natural forces in terms of awareness), who, i wondered, could be convinced of this? Over the years, virtually all of those i've spoken w say the 'hook' which grabbed them was the physical totem itself. Most seemed to intuit from it's elements some profound cosmology which they generally couldnt explain. As for me, tho i didnt like offering ritual in place of what a good chatterbrain-zapping meditation brings automatically, it was plain: the results were worth it.

As to my neighbors, most did not approve of our little festivals. Had i known before i purchased the property the extent ε depth of their bigotry, i would certainly have settled elsewhere. But before purchasing i went out, met the people who would be my neighbors. The sole symptom of bigotry i found was the following. "You know, the people from the university down in tuscaloosa did studies, and this mountain of ours is the last region in america with no negroes. None. Not a one." Since this came from a matron who sat on the board of a "daughters of the american revolution"-funded school, i did not take it as representative of my neighbors. All of which makes me wonder today how so many of them could be so fussy about the skin-color ε beliefs of others yet generation-on-generation march themselves ε their children off to imperial war in support of a government whose laws say their bigotry is wrong. Faced w this quandary, how can one not believe, bigotry ε imperialism are bedmates?

That i bought all that hectarage in a community where such a boast could be made to a perfect stranger is not entirely my fault. For i told every neighbor i spoke w of my plan to create a Wildlife sanctuary; and found them (on the surface) at least as friendly as any i'd met anywhere in america broadly speaking. That i was not an evangelical christian, and that i did not hate people of color, they did not give me to believe would be a problem. I figured —given all the howdy ε handshaking i encountered, plus the hundreds of hectares which insulated us from one another— no future problem would be insurmountable.

Yet as that first spring jubilee of '88 began to come together, my nearest neighbor ε dear friend, zak mickley (who died at 91, not long before my arrest on murder ε subversion charges), felt the need to confess something.

"I'm sorry t' till ya this, nathaniel, cause I'm not a bit proud of it." Zak never cared that nathaniel was not my name. *He* liked it. "Folks on this here mountain 'll go da bed with the divil if they hafta. Wanna know their ixcuse? <Of course.> So's they kin drav a stake thru his heart if'n they ketch him asleep. Or so they say." Coming from "mountain-born 'n' raisedup" hard-lived pain-tempered wise & goodnatured old zak as it did, i knew i was getting bigtime insight. Beside, it answered alot of questions milling in my mind like cows needing milking. It also went hand-in-hand w something tara had said out riding one day when i commented on how many people waved hello. "Dont kid yourself, nathan. Most o' these people will wave at the devil. It's just an excuse ta sizeup the enemy with impunity. Theyve always disliked outsiders, probably always will." What a shock to finally realize: Most of my neighbor's deemed "my" goodfellow's croft as little more than a "devil's acre". That i often wore the following mx on my casual clothing probably did little to endear me locally.

And when i turned away....

...to Reality

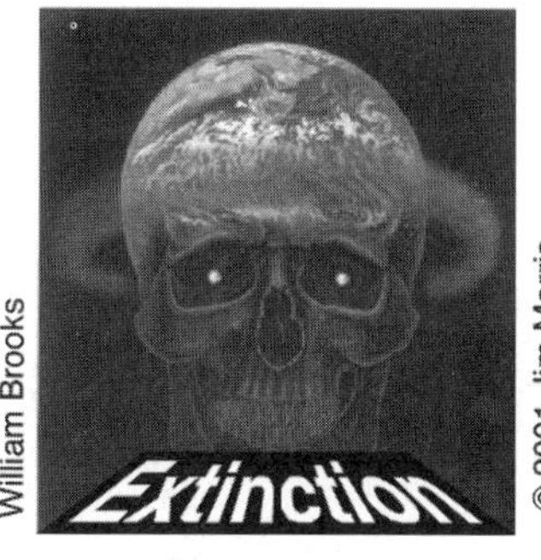

And so, by the time of our first festival in '88, i knew i needed to lessen the fear among my good-versus-evil-believing neighbors.

> Dear neighbor: Friends of Goethe Grotto Nature Sanctuary will be celebrating Earthday on April 22nd with a green bite to eat and a little Earth music. You and your loved ones are invited.
>
> While ritual is part of our celebration, none of what we do has to do with religion. People of all beliefs are welcome. One need only bring a desire for peaceful coexistence and a respect for Nature.
>
> The celebration begins at 6 P.M. and ends any time after 1 A.M. This time is devoted to the skills of achieving EarthAwareness thru selflessness (forgetting for a few hours the me/me/me part of ourselves). Since this is better accomplished on a full stomach, food and refreshment are supplied. A sleepingbag, pillow, or blankets to sit on are recommended. It is not necessary to R.S.V.P. although doing so will help us to plan a better event for all concerned. Sincerely hoping you'll come. Your neighbor…

The purpose of the "invite" was to take what in their imaginations probably resembled a saturnalia/bacchanalia and scale it down to a rural jamboree, a *fête champêtre* that would friten no one. Not to rock the boat more than necessary i even permitted tara to use capitals in rendering my name. Indeed, to forestall an eversion of the bigotry which threatened not only me but all "outsiders" in bamalachia, the *only* people to whom we sent this special invitation were the 22neighbors immed surrounding the sanct(uary).

3

Responsible as well for the ppp (pickup packup ε putaway), most of our core group brought sleepingbags, bedded at the chalet for the nite. Following a hearty ε late breakfast next morn, the 15 or so of us setabout our work. While stage ε totem-platform were left in place, the totem itself, the a/v equip ε other items, were stored at the college. As to cleanup; the area was allbut spotless that morn. This was typical.

At most ggNs events a thing to which i paid little attention usually played itself out. Tara (later succeeded by her sister rachel) became my unbidden assistant, taking on more responsibility than was due her. Timber harvest in my new state being second only to agriculture ε factory farming, tara began her enviro activism **w** the problem of overlogging. For to our bama legislature, ancient forests are just tall crops. It was tara in fact who, rallying a small but enthusiastic group from bc (bamalachia college), first suggested we follow logging trucks **w** our own funeral processions: borrowed hearses, cars **w** black streamers, black-edged pennants ε drapes (STOP THE SLAUGHTER, SAVE

© Greenpeace/Cajander

OUR FORESTS), "the whole bit", creating a fotoOp which even our laggard local press couldnt resist. (An idea Lilith would later adapt to her tv series incl'g an open-coffin viewing of a most tragic-faced tree lying in state, some of its severed roots limbs & leaves tucked lovingly around it.)

Ps: In the years it took us to clinch this single state-wide victory, over 4100 species were extincted Worldwide, with over 12ooo species extirpated by human (let's just say) activity. There are some few of us who can see that civil humanity's war against Nature will not end short of pandemic ruin for ALL concerned, for that is the character of this apocalyptic misconception we call civilization, just as it is the character of those religions which civilization has spawned, and in whose cataNatural worldview so many still believe. Yet there are some few of us who will, even in the face of this worst-of-all-inevitabilities, die content knowing we have done all that was possible to fly the banner of COMPASSION FOR ALL CREATURES & THINGS, to fly it above the battles in this very lost & hopeless war. In this sense, the few battles that we won, tho small compared to ALL that's been lost, loom glorious for me tonite.

Because the sisters dispatched their duties so splendidly i overlooked their subtle "assistant to nathan schock" powergrab —save for when familiarity needed tempering. The worst of these came about as a result of tara taking on a formidable job: organizing & archiving all the data scribbled on some fliplid boxes of indexcards, jottings accumulated while i was still a fultime gE activist. Instead of taking the files to the manor (the house which came w the property & where she'd been in residence for some months), thereat putting them on disc using her own pc, i soon found her allbut movedin to the chalet for use of my pc. It proved the one time when rebuffing someone's advances workedout better than i could have hoped it would.

"Why someone from school?" (to finish the project tara had thrownoff because of my rebuff). "And why a *girl*-student?"—a girl I'll probably even know, is what she meant, a telltale appoggiatura of jealousy in her voice. "Why not get some kellygirl ta finish it? ...Okay then, kelly *person,* from down in scotsmoor.

I dont think so.

"Why?"

Cause it was a kellyperson who robbed me that time.

"Joleen was a kellygirl?" Scotsmoor being small in population backthen, tara had in fact known the young woman, one joleen mackeif ...for anyone caring about the details behind the crime.

<Threethousand cash! Felt like thirty at the time. Plus another two thou stolen with my creditcard, the ethically bankrupt little bandit …every dime i had for restoring this land to Wilderness. [tara had met me right about then] Had to borrow for two months jus ta eat! And sooo, i dont trust kellypersons. [whereat my mx turned personal] More than that, if youre ever forced t' reject someone's advances, get them the hell outa your life *b'fore* they c'n do ya dirty. But for her [or so i warned] i would never have dreamed that the skill of appearing upfront 'n' straightforward could have been mastered so young by one so corrupt. And the *worst* part? On being caught she suffered not a smidgen of shame.> That this little tale of woe, by itself, served to turn tara's affection back to our *mutual* needs, speaks of the unusual health of her values system. (*Achtgeben,* nikki!)

4

By the time of winter solstice '93 –to bring us up to story-speed once more– the hierarchy of who (tara or rachel) was supposed to undertake what, reasserted itself w every rites event. (Earlyon i figuredout, both were seeking insight into whom exactly the non-bamalachia females in my life were and what their emotional status w me amounted to.) Per this, during breakfast a call came in: "Nathan, you there? Tried to reach you last nite. [hands full ε a ways from the fone: <Rachel, will ya get that?>] Well, then. Guess youre busy. Get back to me when you get this. It's important." The first words i heard after rachel handed me the fone, were, "Sounds like there's no shortage of babes back there in bamalachia."

That depends. How ya doin?

"I'm doin great but [pause] *my* sister here slash *your* lover isnt too good." Only as i took the call toward a quieter spot in the house was i sure it wasnt a cheerful Lilith i was talking to.

"No, it's lage. Aintcha glad?"

I am, yes.

"Hey, ah'll accept that." She went on to say that things in ca were such that "Sister is allbut switchedoff again. …Well, firstoff, her 'n' dad are still not cozy. Then *you* up 'n' left 'n' immediately after that, beth" –whom lage called "*lezi*beth, if ya get my drift"– had attempted suicide. "Couldnt deal with Sis's rejection [she guessed]. Botched the job of course. Pardon my two-cents but, sumthin about people who miraculously (ahem) fail to kill themselves grates my fortunately finite patience finely!"

With that call i learned Lilith was planning to visit aurise for the holidays (va), that L had moved out of "my" apt and in w friend sorrel the week after i left. I asked about the wisdom of Lilith returning to va; my worry (unspoken) being that she was putting herself win easy reach of her stepfather. Lage said L had no plans of seeing their mother (whom she called leyda) and that she felt safer at aurise's house (in va) than at her campus (in vt) "because aurise's dad, being a city 'r county boss 'r sumthin, has big enuf clout that upchukka [okka] doesnt dare mixitup with him". Then she dropped what seemed to me the big question. "So tell me. Is it over between Sister 'n' you?"

Who wants to know? ["Curious little me."] I asked if she knew that before i'd left i dropped some pretty potent innuendo about L coming to live at ggNs? "A-, no", she answered. Only as i hungup did suggestible me wonder if lage might have called for interests other than just her Sister's.

Over the years i often shared gE accommodations w other activists. My last few days in frisco i roomed w gE's new fleet ops mngr. Knowing he'd lend a hand, before i left i mentioned L's housing problem to brian. *So* anxious to help was brian, i later learned he'd offered Lilith her own apt at his place; to which she'd responded, "I wouldnt feel right about that. But thank you very very much", and opted to room at the mission house w fleet mngr luscombe, who doubtless figured he'd died ε would soon be shipping to heaven. A few days later, however, she moved in w sorrel, who enjoyed "her own wing" at the family house in haightAshbury, poor child.

Around this time, having smashed the camera of a tabarazza at a ski resort somewhere, epa asst strickland made the news. There were rumors of the tabloid suing but no more ever came of it that i know of. There were also rumors that creation of the new cabinet position (secretary of the environment) might be put off til spring. Rick, having predicted strickland for the job all along, was sure the two things were related.

As to the surveillance the baron had warned of, for all i could gather, he was wrong. Tho neighbors ε associates at local bc(ollege) ε ua/huntsdell were questioned, the fbi appeared to have clearedout of bamalachia by the time i got home. And while i felt insulted, the ripple effect of their probing yielded curious results. Generally in both areas (schools/neighbors) there were two reactions: hysterical ε cynical. The first, the minority, flamedout early. In that hysterical types dont make good students, the only hysterics at bama u (bc), according to rachel, were the office help. And in that hysterical types make good religiots, most did their gossip ε rumoring among churchfolk on the mtn. It is them in fact who were the leaders of the "ban pagan worship in our schools" coalition, a small group which first showed its face when faith slinkard, a neighbor who worked at the school as a typist, found parts of our totem boxed in a storeroom. To put a quick end to this idiocy, i bought a shed for tower pk and let gary godkin, prof of world philosophy there, store therein anything even remotely smacking of "paganism". (Some items he stored had nothing whatever to do w our gaEa rites.) And that college administraitors [sic] cowered for awhile there had more to do w a few local donors threatening to wdraw funding than w being burned at the stake ...i think. For when funding was safely augmented the school began to resist local bullying, insist on educational freedom, if lighthandedly.

The cynics, the low-key but persistent cynics, soon prevailed. At bu, where my critics once stayed grumblingly aloof –from me, my works, my friends ε advotes– in an odd twist of allegiances, suddenly recognizing the fed. as the greater ε more dangerous enemy, soon slipped silently in behind me, the underdog in an intrigue they failed to understand. As to the cynics among my *neighbors*: The greater unknown (why were the feds tracking me to begin with?) grew in them a fearful respect. Something my old buddy zak said enlitened me as to this allegiance, temporary as it proved to be.

Rural southern suspicion of the fed. harks back to prohibition. This it does by way of kin-group storytelling —about "the days when the guvment tehryzed us mountainfolk jus fuhbein who we wuz". And since, locally, i was judged fearless in the face of fed. probing –not entirely accurate– they assumed i had powerful connections i wasnt talking about. So it was i soon found i was being viewed as if i were a local rum-runner, a hope straight out of the 20s. I cant tell you the number of times over the next year or so when i felt i was failing that myth, that i should be doing a robert mitchum imitation, incl'g the cigaret, the likable sneer ε jog-jawed wisecracks. "By their funny boots 'n' baseball caps you shall know them" warned tara w a grin when first i moved there. Were it someone else's life i was living, my newfound 'supporters' might have been a source of colloquial comedy.

Sad but so, i now knew for certain that i'd chosen to live in a place where a darwin fish on your bumper can get your vehicle vandalized if not set afire, a place where "hanging 10" has not to do w surfing but w posting judeochristianity's 10commandments everywhere. <So all those vehicles i've been seeing all this time werent just bought?> "No, you silly secularist." <Been wondering about that.> What i'd been seeing hung in the sidewindow of every fourth vehicle was not some auto dealer's sticker but was that phallocentric decalogue of anthropic morality first decreed by whom i will call the original zionist. Need i add how stupid i felt to have moved of my own volition back into the dark ages?

As to my life being wired. Tho i kept an eye out i quite frankly didnt give a flying frig. As i laid on the couch one eve, lineofsight fell upon a smoke alarm tucked in the groin of the chalet roof some 7.5m above me. A smile crept into my features as i wished pj were there so i could ask <Didja bring your skyhook? [Whatsay?] Up there. Could be bugged ya know> re:g the "sweep for surveillance devices" the baron had made thru "my" apt the nite he met Lilith. Finally, as to the *biped* brand of bugs. It's clear, nikki's looking back in anger –however much she regretted it later– is what gave the fed. a footInthedoor of my private existence, a door otherwise slammedshut by admirers acquaintances friends & loved ones. But for nik's malicious remarks i believe the fbi would not have shownup in my hometown, thus clearing the way for any wise-use whacko or fundy weirdo to emerge & do me or mine harm not only w impunity, but w secret huzzas from local law enforcement.

5

Finally: as to my idea of totem. Descriptions of the 'face of God' vary widely from petunia to pachyderm to person. Even the most prunebrained proponents of both particle physics & cosmology have been forced, finally (phew), to evaluate the idea of an instantaneously-maintained Universe (in the ultrashort definition). Specifically difficult for them to dodge these days are the seeming-instantaneous field(s) of matter-organization apodictated by both intragalactic & interparticle correspondence, both of which appear to be taking place (and here comes what knocks them into a state of stuttering fibrillation) at superluminal (faster-than-lite, even quasi-instantaneous!) speeds!* Because this suggests to many an "incomprehensible" form of order (Implicate Design or Pansynchronous Maintenance by a Cosmic Architect), the very idea is, of course, purest horror to einstein-speed science and its speed-of-lite-max disciples. Thankfully, it is scientific discovery itself which, atlonglast, permits me to say to those frothing atheists & agnostics, who are afterall the backbone of nulliversalism: It is this only, the apparent implicate order or pansynchronous maintenance of the Universe —as explicated to me by the best in science and my own daily doses of machian connectivity— which ~~puts a face on~~ identifies my conception of Firstcause ...and which ~~visage~~ image, incidentally, is the ONLY ~~face~~ identity lurking behind my use of the words Firstcause (Creator) and Intelligent Design (Creation) ...and, when feeling specially daring, my use of the epithets Dao & God.

In other words, when i say Dao/God/Creator/IntelligentDesigner/Inscrutable-Arbiter/CosmicGaia whatever, i am implying (p-l-e-a-s-e) no other 'face' for my FirstCause than that of Pansynchroörganizer of the Known Universe (POKU), whose Unifying/Organizing method(s) happily incl we humans ...a part of which incredible mechanism we may sample at any time (O rush of rushes, extasy of ecstasies!) ...any time that is we are prepared to apply sufficient discipline to freeup this seldom-mastered tho existence-edifying conduit.

*This is in re the: ❶ intimate correspondence between galactic cores & their most-distant stars and ❷ the crosstalk "anomalies" in particle physics. Incidentally, my conclusions here are conservative. Forinstance, current discovery in science gives no cause to induce that the POKU i have settled on actually *maintains,* hands-on moment-to-moment so to say, the Universe. For the data to date suggest this is taken care of entirely by the *forces* of said implicate order. All this, incidentally, is not just some bonyassed teleology. This is logical preponderance responding to the forces of the very latest empiric discovery —even as a single warm breeze can put the fire of global warming under the most massive glacier!

And finally, as long as we're this deeply into it, and since it is so basic: The human need for deity is historically continuous. A new god or new gods are being forged even as you read —hopefully not from the tired metal of our many mistakes in this matter! (I will die guilty if i do not write what i know.) Any god or goddess you choose to assemble for the era of post (global) disaster (and you *will* assemble a new one), if that deity does not possess *all* sexes, or if it does not, at the very least, share the Universe equally w a mate of the socalled opposite sex, or if, mostofall, it is still beyond mankind to imagine a genderless deity, then you can be sure it will amount to just one more false god in a ponderously long & pathetically anthropic pantheon. But i desist. After all, who am i to tell you what to do. I must buckup to the facts. I dont even have charge of my own fate anymore. I am prisoner not paladin. The man in green you see before you is no robinhood, just a silly jester; puppet of your glance. My reader is king. I am only harlequin. Cuff me and i sing. Kick me and i dance. And thus we arrive at story-speed.

6

Lilith left ca for va around the 23rd i believe. The day after xmas i got a call, possibly a result of lage's dutiful intervention. "I'll be flying almost right over your house in a couple days. I'd like to take you up on your offer of a visit ...*if* it still stands, that is. And, of course, if youre gonna be around." I pickedup the fone at once. <Hi.>

When Lilith landed in atlanta on the 28th i was there to drive her back to the sanctuary. Tho only 240road-k distant, comfortably putby, the drive from s.atlanta to ggNs takes over 3hrs. This time-gobbling inaccessibility, while nicely quashing unessential commerce, also drivesup prices in a demography among the poorest in america.

After bailingout of i75's n.bound insanity a driver headed for rome ga must immed begin negotiating a series of "temporary" crossovers & cutbacks which, after some ¼century under construction(!), are infamous among professional drivers working e of the mississippi. <Every time i do this drive i cannot help but wonder how those persons, who started battling this rutted maze waybackwhen they got their driver licenses, and whose grandchildren yes grandchildren are now dealing with it, can be so apathetic. How many accidents, deaths, whole lifetimes of unnecessary waste 'n' aggravation behind the wheel.... But i desist. There's way worse state & fed. abuse we civil denizens apathetically abide isnt there?>

Some 40mins after i75 one gets to rome, prodigal son of that industrial obsceniCity [sic], gadsden, al (which Lilith, bless her brain, will soon name, egadsden), whose answer to heavy traffic mngmt is traffic signals every other block, each timed to guarantee optimum congestion. Then, on the dragging heels of rome, on the way into coosa one passes one of the most deadly-polluting powerplants in amer, not only still coal-burning but still devouring thousands of trees annually!

Soon after coosa one approaches, then runs westerly, the rolling base of the s.appalachian chain. With Lilith at my side —and realizing that since we'd met i'd never mentioned the many negative aspects of reaching ggNs from atlanta— this alltoo familiar ugliness hit me fullon. Thus was i grateful for the 40-50mins of sweet rolling & then precipitous vistas stretching from beyond coosa onto lookout mtn itself. For i knew no Nature-lover would miss, during the briefly spacious & breath-laboring descent into ft payne, a certain mtntop stripping & decapitation. By the time Lilith saw it it had expanded to a paleorange gash in the down-valley forested distance, a gash which leapt into sight like blood on a banner, the title of which blasphemy had recently been p-c'd (by the trees-as-crops imbeciles) from "mtn removal" to "valley creation". <Following west virginia's lead, most of my state's legislators agree, "There's too many dayum mountains round these parts anyhoo. What's the harm o' usin a couple here 'n' there ta improve livin conditions?"

"Living conditions for whom?", she asked **w** earnest curiosity.

Theyre lying of course. Profit's the *whole* reason. But it's easier t' teach a stone t' dance than end such shameless greed. This i've learned firsthand manytimesover. [pause] I wish i could speak of such abuses with more forbearance. But that's a luxury we can no longer afford. Patience for greed is a luxury our forebears usedup in our name. [adding in voice of authority] 'How big of mr schock that he can speak of such terrible abuses with so much forbearance.' [normal voice:] When they c'n say *that* about you you c'n bet your dying Planet youre wasting time we no longer have. Only last year, lamar marshall, head of wildBama,* with the help of WildLaw, was finally able to prove that the state forestry commission not only funded but (check this) *created* alabama's [violent anti-enviro] wise-use movement. [her jaw went slack] Yes. Which *means,* the death-threats he & i were getting for about a year there were being paid for with taxpayer dollars! Welcome to the dark ages alabama style. (*Focused on the w & s of the state.)

As i do **w** friends for the last leg of the trip, i brought Lilith to ggNs via the scenic route, skirting the shorter route, **w** all its moldering vehicles in the weeds, bony animals & garbage on display. Here i'm led to quote another Wilderness man: "You can tell youre nearing civilization when the animals you see, and often even the people, are too broken to run even from abuse...people and creatures with a bone-to-flesh ratio so high you think you hear them rattling as you pass. Yet right behind you is wilderness, ever striving to undo the conditions of rampant atrocity which civilization creates." —oren liseley. This route meant that, on reaching quadrant, instead of going directly to the sanct, i stayed on sr35 and, following a stop at an overlook (tn rivervalley), went down off alpalachia mt and across the river into scotsmoor.

A 30min windshield tour thereat and we headed back across the river. Instead of going back up the mt however i took river rd home, not just the most scenic way back but the most energy-efficient —a splendid s.westerly drive of rolling rdway & forested riverbanks, w a presunset on-going beyond the winding & wooded waterscape the whole way. Wx & timing were perfect. By the time we reached gap rd, wound our way up slowly to the best of its overlooks, the sun was just sliding behind gunter mt across the river. A stunning moment there and we were on our way again. For i wanted L to be in time to watch the lites flicking on in the valley against a backdrop of empurpling hills —while i prepared us something to eat.

Lilith being clearly exhausted and, i suspected, depressed, after dinner i settled her into the guest quarters, left her undisturbed. Time permitting, i will expound lateron as to her failed rapprochement w girlhood friend aurise.

7

Next morn we did a short tour. <This [ne corner] is as close to bluff road as the sanctuary gets ...one of *three* eastern boundaries actually; tho you cant see it from here because the fenceline drops into wet creek hollow behind those trees there. [as we turned into and wound along frontloop rd] This treefarm on our left came with forty hects i bought a few years back so i could protect the headwaters of muir creek... And these [both sides as we went] are the homes of some of my closer neighbors.>

She said nothing as we passed one stark sampling of the garbage, dogs & moldering vehicles i spoke of earlier, the garbage & dogs actually reaching into the road proper, and which she'd not seen the eve before since i'd come home via the s access of frontloop rd. I slowed before a tiny house. <And this little place is the home of my good friend zak. He is eightyeight brave candid 'n' goodnatured and i hope you will get to meet him. And on your right there is the driveway of a camper from florida who appears only a couple weeks a year at leaf-turning time... And this here is where frontloop road horseshoes around 'n' back out to bluff road, the way we came in

yesterday. An' this road [the one we were now going down] is called backloop road —not very original but functional.> I slowed, then stopped, hectar (elec 4wd i'd dubbed hectare hopper) so she could study the sign on her side. <It's set back like that because the road proper isnt private.>

"Love the disclaimer...Beautiful. Clear. Yet tactful." A good sleep, breakfast, a few hundred lungfuls of crisp sunny mtn air, and Lilith seemed wholly restored. "Havent slept like that since ...since that hospital drugged me" she had sighed at breakfast. "Do people know how t' pronounce goethe?"

goethe grotto
Nature sanctuary

a Wildlife preserve

Private

Wilderness is endangered.
It needs every place
it can get
to lick its wounds
in safety and in peace

Most everyone says gōthey. In fact, to most of my neighbors this is "the gothey place", if ya can believe that. [And how long had i been there?] Over ten years. [wide eyes] Occasionally i even get mail addressed to mister nathan gothey.

"That's amazing ...but kinda catchy actu'ly. I'd still be saying it wrong if it wasnt for you. One teacher taught us t' say gerthy... What kinda trees are these? <Sugarmaples. Over three hundred planted t' date. Naked is nice. But you should see them dressed for october.> Sheesh. So all this is the preserve ...on *both* sides."

Would it be uncool or just uncivilly candid to mention what a rush i got having this talented & gentle beauty there in my homespace...? By then we'd reached the middle bridge (over muir creek). How should i explain this...? Of the land lying *above* the bluff, the sign back there marks the... well, the most-westerly of three eastern boundaries. I paused to give her a view, the only one from the road, of the pond & cypress grove, and to pointout both headwaters of the creek on the hill behind us.

"How peaceful... An' that pond as you call it looks like a lake t' me."

As my sardonic dad usta say, "Da caspian sea's a lake, boy. *Daat's* joost a pond." ...part of a tarn, really. I was about to add, tarn of juanita, when....

"Hey, i see another mountain... thru there!" She was looking out thru frikka's cove across to gunter mountain.

That mountain's on the other side o' the river. Near the bottom of that opening there lies goethe grotto itself, about 21meters [70ft] below.

"When do i get t' see that?"

Right now, if you like. But in winter it's best at midday... when the grotto's full o' sunlite.

"I'd like that."

The air was cold but dry that day and the sky was still a little morn-hazy tho cloudless. I headed us around the bend in the road, stopped before the second of only two openings in the thick wall of fence trees ɛ brush running rdside, thoroly obscuring the bluffside of the sanct. <An that's the chalet.>

"Where...? O. Yes. Way back there."

The forestgreen roof w its glass eyrie projecting, the e gable w its prow of dark glass glittering in the morn sun, could be madeout, while the old brass wxcock (atop the eyrie), the forestgreen shutters, door ɛ trim, set against the warm ivory-colored house, were barely discernable. <This usta be the old entrance. [i explained] Moved it further south to keep comings 'n' goings away from the tarn. Juanita tarn is the Wildlife commons ...for the upper sanct anyway.> Between being stopped where we were and facing s as we were, the manor, barn ɛ stable were obscured from her view. Next, instead of turning in at the frontgate when we reached it, i proceeded to the gate across the road, taking us the backway to tower pk.

"Wow. What's that?" she'd remarked on seeing the tower lites the nite before. <Observation tower. Good way t' get the lay o' the land hereabouts.> She was 10min making the climb, brave heart that she was.

Lemme get this right. You'll fly in a tin coffin [airliner] or ride like the wind atop a creature with four skinny legs, but youre afraid t' climb these steps ...these veryvery sturdy steps? That was correct. Yet it was you, not lage, who was in the *coit* [tower] with me ...an in the elevator too at the francis [hotel], right? Somewhat breathless (tho not from exertion), she sat on the third landing gripping the rail. "But the ground wasnt open underneath me like this the whole way up?" (The tower is open steel-frame construction secured into a massive concrete ɛ granite footing, as i've said.)

But you looked down when we got t' the top.

Yods, "Uhuh. But you were holding me, remember?"

{O do i ever.} Ya see those miniature morains down there? [she thought i meant a scatter of young cypresses til i explain morain] Those onetwothree-fourfivesixseven fingers of rock mud 'n' water reaching toward us from the grove of young cypresses there ...plus those mini morains 'n' the pond off to your right ...on up that hill 'n' all the way t' the treefarm... that amounts t' most o' the watershed for upper muir creek ...the creek we crossed when we went over that little bridge ...over there? ...Right. Most o' the water in the tarn comes from these sources ...all of which feed the falls ...which lie straight ahead below that opening beyond auber pond there ...and which [falls] shaped the grotto, and which sustained flow *keeps* it a grotto ...and which basin, in its turn, is a brief layover point for muir creek before it descends the rest o' the way to the river.... They are prolific springs and amazingly constant for being so highup.

"*Tete l'eau.* <Huh?> *Tete l'eau.* Head of the water. Many indigenous people believe springs are powered by spirit forces." Suddenly her attention split away from her overt vertigo to what i thought was the bison grazing beyond the little cypress grove. I could not see she was looking past them. Leaning around the steel struts in her line of sight she cried "Youve got horses!"

Growing up in va Lilith was exposed to quite a few avocations. Of them she liked gymnastics & piano the least, and drawing, horses, singing, camping & dancing, best. (I would be awhile prioritizing this list.) For their 9th birthdays don gave Lee & lage palominos. While the girls were forced to learn care & grooming as part of the joys of riding, Lilith fell in love w horses. Beyond the bison grazed two such creatures. "You didnt tell me you had horses...! I knew you had bison but you never mentioned horses."

Actually that's because theyre not mine.

"O." Nonplused.

They just live here.

Taking a deep breath & mimping her lips, she climbed the rest of the way to the top not looking down.

8

The horses belonged to tara ɛ rachel. Tara taught at the local college ("bu") while earning a masters in fotojournalism at ua/huntsdell; rachel (the one who called me about the missing calf) was a senior down in scotsmoor. I'd known tara some 7yrs at the time Lilith visited. She was on a fotog assignment for the scotsmoor sentry when we met (more of which later, maybe), the result of things beginning to come together: chalet ɛ tower finished, walkovers ɛ stairs almost finished; but mostofall, the Natural watershed, wetlands ɛ falls fully restored. For the first time since the '20s —when muir creek branched into two smaller creeks (due to erosion caused by deforestation ɛ agriculture)— i rerouted the creek into its old bed where it, like a newborn baby, was destined to be wet year-round! And what, beside providing a falls 12mos of the year instead of five, was the point? The restoration of a once incredibly luxuriant and ecofunctional grotto, that's what.

Tara took an instant liking to ggNs and soon became the first gE activist in alpalachia. She lived at the time w her parents ɛ younger sister down in scotsmoor and kept a horse at the sanctuary since late hs. Then, as rachel's interest in riding grew, their parent's added a second horse. Now, as L arrived on the scene, the sisters were talking about getting rid of the horses, specially as one was developing health problems and neither sister any longer wanted to put in the time (or foot the expense) the proper care of horses demands.

Halfway from barn to house
    the long-encroaching rain began.
On one knee, as i was just then,
    checking for some sign of life
    in a fallen barnswallow...
    bent low behind the neck of a black storm
    of OO-nostriled ɛ foaming-jawed horseflesh,
    as if flung at me from out of a long roll
    of thunder which arrived ɛ arrrived ɛ arrived
    yet again with the long-arriving rain,
    knocking me back as much with surprise
    as with the galloping graze
    of the beast's sod-clotted wake,
    a flashing-eyed glowing-cheeked
    beauty tore past. And from the black back
    of the long-striding creature came the cry:
    "Sorry, but we're snake-spooked 'n' cant give
    even God the time of day right now!"

Feeling myself hurled into a brönte novel, adrenaline-drenched, esthetically aroused, i stood staring dumbly after as beauty ɛ beast diminished in size, passing around the margin of the tarn, disappearing behind a wake of silvered splashing into the surprised cypresses, thinking i knew the horse yet having absolutely no idea who'd just missed trampling me; but mostofall, no idea how the dark-haired flashing-eyed young lady ɛ her mount got into the sanctuary. This is how i met tara's sister, rachel, w me the astonished victim of tara's failure to represent her sister –possessing all the autonomy of henry esmond's mistress– even nearly as whom she proved to be.

9

While ns ɛ his exciting new guest eat a country lunch in the townlet of quadrant, then pu some "abidable provender", head back for his guest's highsun appt w the goddess of the grotto, some talk of local topography needs be dealt w —else much that is necessary to our story, and some that is life&death crucial, will not be understood.

GgNs lies in a region of the southern appalachians called alpalachia mtn, a long mtn that runs generally nne all the way from mid al to southern tn and which i hereinafter call alp mt—hoping the reader will overlook the accidental inference to a far higher tho farless biodiverse european mt chain. Because alp mt is over 240k long ɛ 40k wide, the folks on its n end have given 'their' stretch its own name: bamalachia, tho it too i cannot find on any maps, official or folk.

The appalachians are among the oldest mtns in the world. For this reason, millennia of rain, snow, wind ɛ tremors have rather flattened their tops. This topographical fact has invited many types of colonization, both Natural ɛ civilized. Wilderness flora ɛ fauna were first to discover ɛ populate these hills. Then humans, from over the top of the globe, soon entered ɛ lived in them. Still all was well w the region for the next 17ooo or so years. Tho some would date the start of their bio-instability from the time of its first substantive clearcut, quarry, mine or industry, i will be more liberal. Tho industrial pollution ɛ fallout from europe were in the wind of these mtns well before the white man settled here, i would put the date of the start of bio-destabilization in bamalachia at about 1820 (later than many other areas of the "new world"). From this point on began the irreparable destruction of its ancient forests for purposes of mining, logging ɛ agriculture.

The coal rush brought hundreds into the hills thereabouts, most of irish ε scot descent. One of the largest veins around was mined in lochston, a small town which borders ggNs on its rivervalley side. But as the coal gave out, whole families –growing unchecked for generations– fell into extreme poverty. We will not poke fun at the price they have paid, and are paying to this min, for their forefather's greed ε short-sightedness; for the rest of we civil are performing precisely the same ugly assault upon our own heirs all over the World as i write, and doing so by way of yet another Planet-gouging ε -polluting pillage ε plunder (petrols), and w even less excuse: for we have many clean-energy choices they didnt have. As the coal veins peteredout into sandstone, miners turned to timber ε farming. Like Motherearth herself, ggNs bears the scars of all these pursuits. The sanctuary occupies 456hectares (1126acres) of a promontory called frikka's point, which, like a dozen or so other headlands, juts out into a stretch of the tn river called lake guntersville —a million-plus ha of valleyfloor flooded in the 1930s by the longsince infamous fed.tva.

Goethe grotto Nature sanctuary can be arrived at by water or land. By water, from both the great lakes ε the gulf of mx; and even from eastern ok ε st lawrence gulf if one is freer still to adventure. By road, of course, it can now be had from anywhere on two continents. As real estate agents in bamalachia like to boast (playing against the old saw "You caint git theah from heah"): "A body kin git *ennawayah* from heah." And as Lilith would joke to family ε friends, "Well, weah bout az fur az a body kin git from *evra*wayah". (Which in turn reminds me of something lalage quipped [so terribly portentously] not long before my arrest: "Unfortunately, bad men as well as good c'n get here from anywhere." But this too must wait.) If three men, say, decided to come to the chalet by boat, either for mischief or monstrously worse, they'd better be prepared to do some steep hiking. On the other hand, if two men ε a giant should come by land, the nearest county rd (backloop) reaches ⅔ of the way out onto frikka's point before looping back east again.

(I have no choice now but to write for those readers having editions of this book which do not incl my aerial sketch of ggNs ε environs.) Frikka's point itself can be pictured as a finger of land lopped off to the first knuckle by thousands of years of erosion plus an avulsive passing glacier or two, surrounded on three sides by water, two of which bodies (on a navigational map) look like longish triangles of blue: each a miniature inlet. Both inlets are named for the creeks which feed them. On the n is wet creek; on the s, e sandy creek, the larger. And each creek winds its way down to the river along the base of a long hollow, each named also for its creek.

Complicating all this however is a third ɛ smaller wet system, the only one of the three lying completely win the bounds of ggNs. The delta region of this creek lies about 200m due s of wet creek and looks, on a nav map, like a child's drawing (in blue) of the front two-thirds of a diving cormorant, beak buried in the shoreline. Formerly called frikka's creek (on tva maps prior to 1990), in 1986 i renamed this creek, muir. It supplies a fair volume of water annually to the river below and, far&away, is the purest of any feed of equal size anywhere on the lake, and possibly on the entire tn river. This is because it ɛ its watershed –from springs ɛ topoly-high runoff– are now protected allbut entirely win the sanct itself.

The uppermost bluff of the region lies at about 366m(1200ft) elev, tho it doesnt look so high because the entire region lies on a plateau. Tho hikeable in two places, the climb to the chalet up the w face is quite precipitous. The only existing pathway, ruff-hewn ɛ heavily forested, is ~½k long. As the bluff swings e on the n side, the terrain beneath it grows somewhat less steep —due to the baseline of wet creek hollow rising to meet it. The sanct's e boundary however precludes that ultimate intersect. What all this comes down to is, the fall from the upper bluff to reasonably walkable terrain (land w less than 20° gradient) is a median 183m(600ft) at its greatest altitude and 122(400ft) at its shallowest. But this fall, as happens w older mtns, is rarely straight down. As a matter of fact, ggNs has only three spots where one could fall (or be pushed) 30m(100ft) wout first striking land or treetops and only one spot where she or he might freefall 60m and hit nothing but a speed approaching 200kph.

Topside of the bluffline the land tapers upward at about 12° (old mtns are round-shouldered) to a rocky ridge which lies some 30-50m(100-165ft) inside the bluff-edge itself. This ridge (necessary to the course of events) –flat-topped ɛ rising a median 3dm(1ft) higher than surrounding soil-level– is a topo feature (called a monadnock) of most of alp mt. Too bedrocky to be cultivated, this ridge was never farmed, nor have any of the trees which managed to take hold on it (win the sanctuary) been cut for at least a half-century. In places where soil has been trapped, some quite sturdy old trees have evolved an admirable existence on what looks to the inexperienced eye to be solid rock. But in reality, many is the root system which has worn away, pushed apart or split, the sandstone boulders of alpalachia effectively trapping soil ε water. So integral is this union of rock ε tree that in heavy winds, trees farmore protected *below* the bluff, are inevitably uprooted first. This smacks of a sand/rock aphorism from my biblical youth.

A tornado spawned by hurricane opal in '95 comes to mind. To the s of the chalet, a carolina basswood standing near the edge of the bluff was literally avulsed from the Earth in a *liebestod* leap that left me speechless when i saw it next morn. For the old tree (tantris[sic]) did not succumb to the wind til the dumptruck-sized boulder (iseult) caught in the embrace of its roots was tipped enuf to topple w it! In another example, a dozer operator, caterpillaging for a house along the bluff a few years back, kept ramming ε gouging at an old oak w the blade of his machine til the four of them –dozer, operator, tree ε the slab of rock all were resting on– slid over the edge. Tho this local man's-man was crushed to death by the machine he so loved, the courageous old oak, thanks to the boulder caught in the embrace of its roots, landed nearly straightup in a wet hollow and, today, lives victoriously on, some 35m below the site of the crime! For once the vandal didnt get to dance upon the stump!

It is win this rocky swath, on an outcropping –a mere wart on that nubbed digit of land– that the chalet stands. Because of the rockiness of the site, only a couple sparkleberries (strangled into bush-form by the thin soil) were destroyed to build the house. As a matter of fact, i passed over a far superior site (in terms of view): the most riverward prominence of frikka's point actually! I gaveup on that preferred site (panorama point) because the chalet could not be fitted there wout harming at least two 40/50yearold black oaks solidly rooted in sandstone thereat. What makes the site ideal is that no part of the river n or s is blocked from view, even standing at bluff-level! There are few persons i have ever known who would not have traded two or three gnarly oaks for that marvelous view ...and around six billion others who would have! For even in the eyrie of the chalet, some 15m higher than the bluff itself, that point in the valley to the s, where the river loops e around deer island, is not visible (as it is from panorama point). Only the island itself, and the town of guntersville beyond it, can be seen.

As to ggNs generally. Speaking of plummeting to death from the top of that very Earthplace one loves most.... I'm feeling the frustration hugo must have known, anxious to tell his story of "the hunchback ε the gypsy girl" yet knowing his tale would be diminished should he leave the great cathedral itself undescribed.... As to ggNs generally, then. The shape of the property defies brief descrip. Among silhouettes of u.s states, for no just reason that i can divine, its outline most closely resembles that of texas —that is if, using a straight n/s line and a fair imagination, ❶ one lops off the tip lying w of new mexico's east border, ❷ adds a second narrower "chimney" above ft worth that reaches the kansas border, then ❸ straightens the e border of the state while sliding it over toward the middle of louisiana, and, finally ❹ superimposes the s tip of the state a little below corpus christi. Those things done, one has a fair, tho flatlander, facsimile

Finally, as to demography. Tho over 3/5 of the sanct is heavily forested, thanx to past clearcutting, 75% of that lies below bluffline. Looking e toward ggNs from across the unusually wide river –excepting the chalet-site proper, which appears as a tiny gap midst the bluffline trees– in summertime he will see mostly forest, *w* high-up patches of rocky face showing thru now-&again and best spotted toward sunset. The forest being mostly deciduous, the true contours of the land are of course farmore apparent in winter.

Seen from the observation tower (as Lilith first saw it), upper sanct land was obviously not long before largely in agriculture. For, like most land atop the mtns thereabouts, it had long been farmed. As to how the upper sanct is divvied: Except for priscilla orchard (5ha), an organic farming project of the local college incl'g vineyard (10ha), two major ε two minor grazing areas (45ha), walkovers/driveways/buildings (2ha), i have both Wild-planted ε allowed the sanct to run Wild. In fact since purchase i have planted, or seen to the planting of, some 5500 trees shrubs ε herbs —and in the public swale areas another 100 or so. (The lower sanct, as i've said, is allbut totally forested.) ~800 of these plantings were for fruit, nut ε herb habitat supplementation, incl'g chinese chestnut, autumn olive, persimmon, wild plum, wild- ε crabapple, and even a few sawtooth oak. Most woodland margins ε open areas i supplemented *w* red- ε landino clover, oats wheat chufas ε even some lespedeza thumbergi. Unforested areas, specially the orchards ε ag areas, are strategically "bandaged" *w* Natural insectariums: many swatches of sweet fennel barley oats snowpeas ε other foodplants whose prime purpose is hosting squadrons of parasitic wasps, ladybugs ε other crop-protecting insects. (All this is not counting a certain lovely person's ecologic as well as gorgeous investment to be described later.) That the ecology of ggNs was highly effective was apparent in the dearth of socalled pests: flies ε mosquitos were exceedingly rare, roaches ε rats never seen.

As to the vineyard. '91 brought the first harvest of our scrupulously organic scuppernongs, the first taste of which flooded my being *w* mnemosalient sensation: Buddy geoff stood as if before me in his 8yrold person, the faded beige&maroon of his columbia (lasalle among bikes) exactly duplicated right down to the mold-scent of battery acid ε rust seeping from its horn compartment! But the scuppernong taste had a negative trigger as well, causing me –to my surprise– to relive my earlyon ε long unrequited yearning for priscilla, an agon worse even than i had remembered it!

To put a civilized spin on all this, one can arrive at, and then drive thru, the ~midsection of the upper sanct using county rds —a fact i should have put a stop to the first time a bison was shot. For the closing of backloop rd would have inconvenienced no one and saved taxpayer money beside. But for reasons of neighborliness (to say nothing of an innate belief in freedom) i left it public until such time as... well, until such time as injustice incarnate swooped into my life and slammed shut *all* my options. Sad to report, by the time the road privatizing was authorized, tragedy had already struck my mtntop arcadia. In fact, the closing-off of socalled backloop (most will think i'm inventing these folksy names), along *w* the erection of gates at the e ε s ends of the sanct, was not complete til a few weeks before my arrest. Til then, frikka's point had two county roads looping out ε back. The first, "front loop road", dips only a third of the way out to the point, passing, in its transverse tack, thru a narrow portion of the preserve (the narrow chimney we attached at the top of my tx facsimile). The second, "back loop road", swung 2/3 of the way out toward the point, *w* most of its length falling *w*in the sanctuary. One more thing needs be said about this road. By some phenomenon of geo logic[sic] or serenDIPity (i have yet to grasp which), the obliquity to the bluffline of the n leg of backloop rd almost mirrors the grade at which muir creek hollow rises to meet that road! Like the hole in the glass of the window of my cell, some (seeming?) coincidences tend to nag.

Nag as they may.... With the orig purchase i got all the houses ε trailers on backloop rd save those on its s leg. It is not at all incidental to mention as the reader will see: the 10homes lying along that leg are most easily accessed using the s entry from bluff rd. As a matter of fact, to do so using the n entry (main entry to ggNs), adds to their trip from half a k distance (for the nearest neighbor) to a full k (for the farthest). That is to say, if certain of my neighbors had to walk or use a horse to get to town, rare would be the times they saw the need to pass thru the environs of ggNs. As it was, that's the way they *usually* went. No, *you* tell *me* why...?

As to the land's history of ownership. The most recent, living in quadrant for some three generations, kept ggNs land mostly for hunting purposes, w much of the arable upland leased or rented for farming. They did not care about trespass w five exceptions: deer, wild turkey, trees, soil or fire. In event of any of the latter abuses they would prosecute to the last letter of the law. One could use or abuse everything else til he dropped so long as he didnt set fire to the woods and "beat the mud off his boots before exiting". This is the type of landowner they call "environmentalist" in bamalachia, a teddy roosevelt style of conservation i call "hunter green". Such areas are not looked at as Wilderness (where *all* things are revered) but as game preserves, places set aside for hunting, fishing, etc. So well did my neighbors understand this that, til the day of my arrest, owl bat skunk 'coon 'possum groundhog chipmunk beaver otter rattlesnake ε copperhead) have yet to rebound to normal proportions at ggNs, and squirrels (thanx to a certain local "delicacy") are still rare as civil justice in those parts. This holds true even on "protected" state lands, where officials rarely enforce game laws. Except for the fox, lynx ε bobcat i imported, they too are allbut non-existent in bamalachia.

When the huntergreen father died, the sons, no hunters they, put the land up for sale. Meanwhile the no-hunting signs were allowed to molder and when deer or turkey were shot no one did anything —which meant, for the 2yrs prior to my purchase, all my neighbors, their friends ε families, slowly began to use the land for just about anything that was legal and some that was not, incl'g timber cutting, cattle grazing, growing crops, racing cars, w a few even growing marijuana ε holding cock- ε dogfites. Enter naif Wildlands preservationist from california, nathan schock. O me. The first time i went to visit the property i was run off at gunpoint by a family squatting in one of the houses, relatives of the calhouns (owners of a bordering farm) who claimed to own all the land "as fur ez the ah [eye] cayun see". Even after purchase was complete they ran me off again, this time unloading *both* shotgun barrels in the wincing quietude.

As to the bldgs that came w the land: a modest southern colonial-style house (having only eight of the usual 18 rooms), a barn twice its size a ways off, a 5rm clapboard house half a k to the s (called "bldg j" on the deed), an old barn a couple ha behind it, two more clapboards so poorly built and in such disrepair i had them dismantled for (a decade's supply of) firewood, and three house trailers, two of which were hauled to a dumpsite and the best one of which i gave to bernie mcCleigh for hauling them. (The squatting calhouns i gave a year to move if they would clean up the j-house ε property and 30days if they didnt —a mistake as it turned out.) My plan was to also dismantle the old barn for, while it was constructed of rare chestnut (doubtless before the blight ravaged alp mtn), parts of its roof had been so long bad the walls were dropping away from dryrot.

Wendell Berry: "Place"

A tornado would have put a whole lumberyard of old planks airborne, rusty horseshoe-nails protruding. But one peek inside and i knew, the quaint tho dilapidated structure would not be coming down. For its remaining protected areas were home to a sizable population of bats.

This project was the first in which i involved bu and which proved germinal to its dept of enviro sciences. A few months later, w my $ ε student labor, an alternate "bat cave" was erected nearby and a program for transference to the new 'hangout' begun. Tho largely experimental at the time, it was 95% successful, requiring an astounding three years of tiptoe&retreat to complete! Once the transfer was done i got a crew together (how i came to meet pepe guevarra) and dismantled the barn. Its beams we used to string an oldfashioned buck fence around the main barn and the remains we returned to the forest to rot.

The people living in the orig house (the manor), in-laws of the brothers who sold it, moved soon after the purchase and i moved in. That house, eight brite rooms, balcony ε porches, was not only away from the bluff, it was far too reminiscent of the colonial south and much that it stood for. Built by the grandparents of the sellers in the 1940s, the grandmother moved out after her husband died and, from the early '80s on, the place was variously rented, lived in by relatives or vacant. Sturdy & in good repair, i did little more than exist in it til the chalet was finished.

With the barn –hayloft cupolas w wide sloping wings– i inherited several agri-artifacts: single-bottomed horse-drawn (scuse me, mule-drawn) walking plow (used well into the '50s in bamalachia... the *nineteen*50s!); mule-drawn cleat-wheel-powered mower built by pre-mccormick-deering(!), huge hand-scythe; hayloft lift, sling, skate & carry-back track still operational(!), and a dietz lantern (clear not red, damnit), a couple of which were antiques backwhen i was a kid! The bldgs stand on land cleared for farming sometime in the late 1800s. As happened in the u.s generally, family farming as a way of life was abandoned on alp mtn thanx to the reagan administration. And where the land went unkept –as happens til trees are either planted or return Naturally– an angry glut of weeds vines & grasses took over. This made the oldest trees in these abandoned fields on Lilith's arrival a little over 10yearsyoung, and the hundreds i'd planted a bit younger still.

Barbara Kingsolver: "Place"

As to the house on the bluff. To distinguish it from the orig house (the manor) we called it the chalet. Due to topo, from the public road one can see only roof & chimney, the gable windows above the loft & the eyrie. However, from a boat on the river, or from across the river on gunter mt, on a clear day, w a quality scope on a tripod, one can see the w-facing of all 3.5 levels of the house ...There, in that open space just to the left of the point. Is that a modified a-frame? No. A chalet, with cupola (the .5 level). Its construction combined old dream & conciliation for that which has whipped me toward oceans & mtntops all my life: claustrophobia. Neighbors born&raised in those mtns find it curious anyone would want to have a house near the bluff. For years i've answered this w <What's the point of being on a mountaintop if, when you look out a window, for all you c'n tell you are living below sealevel?> Beyond this, as author researcher & ruminist, i spent most of my days indoors and so the orig house, even had i moved it to the bluff, had far too few windows and far too many walls for my wellbeing; say nothing of the energy cost of relocation, waste of it's regal old basement & the inevitable damage to one of its finest features: all-plaster ceilings w bas-relief cornices. The other option, done often in these parts (clearcut all the trees [~2,000 of them] blocking one's view), i will not even comment on.

Construction employed all the environmentally sound resources available at the time (1985) incl'g recycled aluminum frame, ecowood ɛ 24v power ɛ liting etc. With a windturbine on the bluff ɛ 250sq m of photovoltaics, ggNs has been off-grid for over a decade. (Not incidentally, all phases of construct were overseen remotely by the institute for green living™, hopland ca.) A second turbine proved unnecessary even after tara ɛ friends moved into the manor. Beside assuring pollution-free electrical independence, the sale of our excess power back to the grid paidoff our investment in less than 5yrs (even at the lowest rates in the nation) and by 10yrs had provided a maintenance/replacement fund ɛ turned a profit beside. Anyone w access to bluffline air-risers can do the same. Wind- geothermal- ɛ gravity-powered farms, not solar (for awhile anyway), are our future —if, that is, much of a future is even in the cards for we larger lifeforms.

As to the question, does one person need 800sq meters of house? Of course not. But i often had guests and hoped one day to have a mate ɛ child and this was, afterall, my first ɛ last house —providing the local ccc didnt burn us to the ground as theyve done to others. (Little did i know, eh? For the plans of we humans are the jokes of the gods. All primitives know this.) But what i anticipated mostofall, once the chalet was finished –beside the long-awaited thrill of being 'outside' when inside– only tall persons will understand: a bathrm, at last, where a big guy doesnt have to smash elbows ɛ knees to come clean ɛ dry; and a bedrm big enuf to house a bed big enuf to support a big man wout his big feet adangle in midair thru the nite; and finally: because i'd dreamt for years of getting food&drink from 'my own' animals gardens ɛ orchards, and of picking my own salads fresh from just beyond the door! Need i add? My final arrest hurled me back beyond even lousy square1 in each&every one of these depts?

To roundout (we are almost there) this prep for events which follow —which *must* follow. Of the land above bluffline on frikka point, the highest lies off the property to the se and roundsoff at about 1/4k beyond the obs tower. The fall from this point to the bluff, at an avrg 8°grade, is about 9m(30ft). In other words, eye-level (mine, not Lilith's) in the eyrie of the chalet (its highest room) is about the height of a tall man above the highest ground on frikka point. In another way of putting it, while a 360° horizon, seen from the eyrie, is limited only by wx conditions, from anywhere else in the house the e horizon is blocked by that very rise of land. About midway between this horizon & the chalet lies a natural mounding of land. It is upon this that i had the obs tower constructed. Set on its own smaller mound of granite boulders, it was primarily conceived as a place for regional- & nitesky survey, designed to offer a point of view situated well-above the local horizon and well away from the bluff, w its proclivity to mist heavily toward & after dark.

The land lying immed e of the chalet, save for a low-lying ash grove by the driveway, is largely wout trees and continues to rise slowly for a full 500m to backloop rd. This means (there's a reason i stress this and it is *not* a good memory), looking bluffward from the public road thru either of only two openings in the brush & trees, a person or persons, irrespective of motive, while they can see the manor, thru these openings can see only the eyrie, part of the roof, the chimney and e gable windows of the chalet. And when the meadowgrass is long for the grazing, chimney & eyrie alone seem to rise right up out of the grass!

A final word or two. When i say "out on the main" rd i'm re:g socalled bluff rd. Despite the word "main", bluff rd is no different from any other county road in bamalachia —except that it fairly follows the bluffline: to the nne about 13k into the mtn town of quadrant; or, in the other direction, deadends (after 4 very windy k's) in a state pk called south sandy cove.

This is an outline of what ggNs was like on Lilith's arrival. As to that 'mischief' i mentioned. There have been many instances. Avoiding (like death itself) the worst, the for-instance i will give took place in autumn of '96 and took the form of four fishermen in a pontoon boat who, on spotting two deer one eve –down for a drink at muir creek while the men quietly angled– shot both dead where they stood. Three points now if you please. ❶ The creatures living in the sanct have been long enuf Wild (ie, virtually unharassed by humans) that they have allbut lost their fear and will not run on sight of a human. ❷ They were shot on clearly posted and obviously private property (beside dock & boat-hoist). And ❸, it was not deer-season. Sportsmanship it's called? Morelike the hate-set of zionist soldiers shooting rock-throwing kids in palestine, i'd say.

10

More&more i argue with myself.

self: There is so little time, and i must fit so much into such a brief space!

me: Look, dont take this wrong. I like your stuff. I do. But really, sometimes your prose gets a little thick, your dialectics, too reaching.

self: Crane, plath, religion-plagued dylan t, and others, were killed with the same smoking pistol you now hold to my head! And they too felt always the executioner's ax above their necks!

me: Perhaps. But even things as great as the heavens have vast spaces. It is the *spaces* between them which help us appreciate the grandeur of the stars.

self: Are you saying, the beginning of the Universe, the Big Bang, so called, is of little value because it had *no* emptiness, *no* blankness?

me: No, i'm not. ...On secondthought, I guess that's exactly what I'm saying. For who can comprehend such a thing? how many of us have the capacity, or the staying power, to appreciate such an all-embracing Event as the beginning of the Universe? And how many even *care* to?

self: Yet there's nothing more intrinsic to all that we *are,* all that we *know,* even all we *desire,* than the start of the Universe! All potential –you, me, everything. Hear me? *Everything!*– is there! If we do not want to make a thing so stupendous as *that* a conscious part of us, then what do we amount to? Maybe there comes a time when the audience needs to stop scratching 'n' munching sweets, quiet down, lean in a little closer and try to concentrate on what the Speaker in the Dark *never* stops whispering to us.

I have these me/self debates all the time anymore. Where were we?

11

Daypacks under strap, we headed n along the ridge to keep her appt *w* the goddess of the grotto. Halfway there i chose to go via the near-edge of the tarn, turned e toward the meadow. As we emerged from the thinly scattered young trees, just ahead, a phlock of pheasants arose *w* a racket and resettled in a thicket a few meters beyond. Startled, she stopped, gazing after them. "Were those quail?"

Sort of. ...Pheasants.

As we approached the pond we stepped around a low spot. I stopped, pointed to a cloven skidmark.

"Deer?"

A young satyr. ...Jus kidding.

"Deer, surefooted-deer, slip?"

Sometimes. Usually their hindfeet. Probably less than a couple hours old.

"A faun? [!] *That* big?"

Fresh track, i mean. Not fresh birth. But theyre surefooted when it counts. You'll see them go into that treeline there at fullbound when young calhoun's truck goes by. Why they never slam into anything at such speed is just another wonder of Nature.... All this here's called juanita tarn. "Beautiful!" We walk, weepingwillow-wise, to pond's edge, are circling its w end (heading toward the bluff) when another, smaller, phlock hits the air. A stately harrier, perched in an almost naked hickory out on a point of land by the pond, watches them whorl past, their wings stirring the water's surface as they go. It then calmly turned to look at us. I stop, look down at the water.

"What d'ya see?"

The reflection of that fat hickory over there [not looking up i yod its general direction]. But there's a bass instead of a hawk in its limbs. As i tried to spot the hawk's reflection the bass passed dadaesquely thru its branches. If we look directly at him he'll likely leave. [she imitates my head-down mien]

That's hawthorne. He thinks everything this side o' the tarn belongs t' him 'n' his lady. "Who's name is?" Thorna. "But of course."

I've gotten amazingly close to creatures of all sorts simply by facing askance. We watched three, then one, small trout swim past. Hey, a *trout quartet*! [allbut whispering] One's playing bâss -er, bāss. My visitor, first ever to get my pun, moans lowly w closed lips, "Are you related to don mcGrae perchance?" We watch the harrier thus for a time, then resume walking. On almost every rock ɛ fallen tree along the sunside of the tarn turtles were reanimating in the warm lite. "There must be hundreds!" I guess. See otta 'n' her pups over there? I yod toward a rivergrassed hammock in the cypress grove. "Dont tell me youve named the turtles too" she says, surveying my querist's eyebrow-arch. Then, following my glance, "How fabulous! ...Do the pups have names?" she asks, looking quickly back at her feet, having caught herself staring at the trio of otters sunbathing there.

We have five now i think 'n', actually, i cant tell them apart once they mature. Maybe some day. It's the same with most o' the Wildlife here. I am purblind to creature individuality generally speaking. For me there is really no beatrice the beaver, madge the badger or chip the chipmunk, 'n' i hate 'n' bemoan the fact. [But why?] Because i so often find myself wishing i lived in an earlier time, a time when i could have known Mothernature in the personal way we were meant to know her; not t'day, when i have no choice but to waste my days doing battle so that generations to come may know Mothernature in that personal way i long to know her. As we step onto the rutted monadnock that runs the bluff, she takes my offered hand. <And the other side of the tarn belongs to ozzie the osprey 'n' his lady. [Whose name is?] Ospra. [I see.] Now them, 'n' the hawks too, i *do* know... [following the ridge, moving only gradually toward bluff's edge] ...because... [i stop. she looks at me] ...theyre the only hawks 'n' osprey living in the upper sanctuary. If there were more of them i'd be outa luck there too.>

As we approach the walkover, peripheral awareness catches the harrier scoopingup a fish, beating the air for altitude. Gravity grappling with greed. "Why greed?" Cause he'll only eat the eyes 'n' the innards.. "Maybe he's got babies?" He doesnt. I wonder aloud at the fatidic odds of the caught fish being one of those which had intersected w the raptor's reflection in the water. Just then she spots the swans (black) feeding in shadow among the cypress roots. "My god, how lovely! [whispering] ...Theyre right there an' i didnt even see them!" She stood briefly transfixed. <Their names are two- 'n' onenella. They are lifemates.> I guess that it is for thinking about the idea of lifemates that she has failed to question my sibelian re, while, silently, i am happy my noisy guarddogs, the geese, are off feeding on the other side of the tarn.

Will Van Natta

We reach the walkover, which at that point runs along the indented bluff above frikka's cove. A moment later the falls comes partly into view. It is still running at just under ½m wide thanks to nov rains flooding the tarn.

"Sheesh. Now *that's* lovely." Not unlike yourself. Shakesoff a flush as we stroll to the little bridge spanning the pond's sluice & spillway. We walk to its apex, lean on the rail like good tourists. "God, what a view!" <Muir falls. ...Muir was a scot, you know. She knew. "I went to muir woods with daddy 'n' sister. No famous scot gets by dad without mention... And *that's* GOT to be the grotto down there." Looks at me, then back down again. I swore i saw her eyes flash, her breath quicken.

Right thru there. Ya see? Goethe grotto herself ...in the flesh. Come ta think of it, this bridge is the only thing here without a name. For a few mins we listen to the falls plashing below, which one cant see from there since the spillway itself is out at bluff's edge. {If this is a true nymph she wont last long up here.} The spillway can accommodate an overflow (a falls) 2m wide, beyond which point the [monadnock] banks of the pond itself would begin ta spill over. Only once have i seen it running near capacity. When that happens ...wait. Do you hear two different sounds? one closer...? Well, the near one is the water hitting a shelf on the way down. But when water volume gets about twice as wide, it clears that shelf, falls directly into the grotto pool. When that happens it becomes one of the highest falls in the state. That sort of pressure can dig a pool in sandstone in a single lifetime.

"Are those the stairs down?"

<Yuhuh.> I tip head, eyes askance, as if to say, 'Wanna go?'

"Thought you'd never ask."

We descend to the first landing. <You cant tell it now but in summer its *really* lush here.>

"God, it's *beautiful.* No wonder you love this place."

And i would stand here like this, liking you to like it for as long as you like. (Looks at me w mona lisa deadpan.) Quoth this willy s advote, already high on this nexus of waters & all its positively ionized air.

Smiles, looks bashfully away. "And no ecotourists will popouta the bushes?"

Not t'day.

Standing now on the second landing, where falls & grotto both can be seen: "It's like stepping thru the lookingglass. 'It's so very lovely here, alice said.' [glances around as if forcefield-imprinting the location] And moreover, like emerson said: Here is sanctity which shames our religions. ...Gosh. However did you find this place?"

Thought you'd never ask. I fixed a pennant with the word ecology to the antenna of my car, took two months off o' work and jus drove 'n' drove 'n' drove, all the way from the adirondacks. When i got to a place where everyone i met asked, "Hey, what's ee-kol-low-gee mean?", i figured i'd better stay; that there was much work to be done.

"Youre not serious?" The way she said it (quaint blend of shy incredulity & naked trust) combined **w** her expression (tilt of head, slack of mouth, blithe slitting of eyes) brought all awareness skidding to a stop. {Such intuitive wonder 'n' wisdom as this must have imagined the World!}

As we moved down to the next landing the real explanation of how i endedup on alp mtn was in order. Between stints at sea with greenEarth i would stay at lex reever's place near grizzly flats.... That's in california, in the sierras. I spent a great deal of time alone in those mountains. I had something to finish healing in me there. When *the castration of priapus* was made into a movie and the book was put back in print again, my passion for the sierras was already in leveloff 'n' decline.... Then around 1983 i began to miss more 'n' more the older mountains of my youth. [Montagnard schock, i dub thee, she said rather earnestly.] I wanted more than anything to create a Nature preserve like lex had; wanted to 'buy back' from civil humanity a piece of Motherearth so i could, in my small way, assist in her safekeeping.

"How many acres?" (We still spoke in the oldstyle backthen, have i said?)

Little over elevenhundred ...that's a few hundred more than when i bought it. Stretches from mountaintop to rivervalley. The way it lays its an ecologic niche in itself. Rainwater, and water from the mountain springs that supply the tarn, flow over the falls and into the pool there, then wind 'n' drop for over a mile down the creekbed, leaving the protection of the property only after confluing with the river. The Wildlife living here dont have to cross farmland, clearcuts 'r any roads to reach riverwater —and they will *never* have to do so so long as i, dead or alive, can maintain control over the deed.

"Now *that's* beautiful. [reflective pause] But werent you raised in jersey?"

I was. But my parents always got rid of me summers, usually i wound up in biblecamps in the adirondacks or alleghenies. But realestate on a lake or river was too costly there. The same money that bought all this space, year-round standing freshwater 'n' a trust fund to keep it Wild in perpetuity, would only have gotten a couple hundred acres in jersey or new york state; or in the blueridge or smokys, where i originally wanted to settle.

"Do you ever see deer down here?"

Yes. And one time or another i see most of the larger creatures who live here. Any morning you care to get up at dawn (little did i know, for her that was about *every* morning), go up to the eyrie and you will see deer ...my deary... usually grazing near the tarn or browsing in the orchard. There are *too many* deer now. [she looked at me] Most animals are quick to spot a safehaven. ["These days they'd better be."] In hunting season i'm actually overrun with animals. I hafta kick them outa the way sometimes. [she tried not to look at me as tho i'd just sworn foully] Just kidding —old hunter's brag.

"So actually you'd rather be living further north?—in the mountains, i mean?"

Not anymore. Even when i was looking for land backthen i thought: If one has a choice, it doesnt make a whole lot o' sense to live in a place where much o' the year it's warmer in your refrigerator than it is outside. [she chokesback an adorable chuckle w a chin-clefting grin] Even with only a month of below-freezing temps here in southern appalachia i feel i c'n still appreciate the sheer wonder of the onset of spring as much as any non-eskimo.

"I c'n see that."

First coldsnap you'll see. She get's down in the teens here at least once a year. [She?] Yep. Local Mothernature. B'side, by the time i got back t' my roots my roots were mostly tornup, built on, toxified, sickly looking 'n' expensive as the hell theyve become. The "arrow's oath" has long been broken there. No, make that, splintered. *This* is home to me now. I've never really had a permanent home. Mostofall, i've never known a piece of Earth the way i've come to know this one. Almost as soon as i moved here i began learning things about local Nature which a lifetime of world travel or library labor might never have disclosed.

I quote my notes. Spring '85: While no frigatebird –tho w a silhouette almost as impressive– i learned today that "my" blueherons can draft-ride at 3-400feet any time they choose. That flora often tries to blend *as well as* stand apart: I've seen numerous examples of a shrub or tree matching w its closest limbs *exactly* the color of a neighbor's foliage. If you have a hedgerow handy, check it out. Some of those deepgreen branches might actually belong to the liter-green neighbor! And in autumn '85: If after 10,oooyears of civilz'g i still wince when a large shadow (plane eagle vulture) slams past me, am i not foolish to marvel when a peacefully grazing herd den flock or covey suddenly up ε scatter, seemingly "for no reason"?

So this has become the Great Mother's body to me, here, in these hills. It feels exactly the way the woods at summer camp used to feel when i was young —the woods out away from the cabins; the woods a young mind dared wander into after dark when everyone else was sleeping. It took a few years but now i know for certain, when i go to sleep here, in this place, that my head is resting on the same –the very same– living Bosom where it rested in the allegheny 'n' adirondack dreams of my youth. It was then she said, smiling, "So you sorta *came home to a place you'd never been before.*"

Wow... Yes.... *Exactly.*

12

Speaking of Place. In time i will relate the following story to Lilith: I had been living at ggNs around 4yrs when something quite extraordinary happened. I was standing by a young poplar evaluating its relocation (before its roots began tearingup my underground cooling/heating grid) when i realized, not only was i aware of our shadows (the tree's ε mine) stretchedout in the shortgrass there, but that, astonishingly, unconsciously, those shadows had not only conveyed to me the time of day but the time of year! A huge clock ε calendar lying in the clover ε spotted subliminally could not have offered superior data. Here's why. The time of day was not given me in abstract hours, as would have happened had i caught a glimpse of a clock. Rather, i saw the hour in terms of my location in space between dawn ε sunset; or in relation to what attitude, if you prefer, me ε my surroundings had rotated relative to the Sun. Translation: I experienced *actual* Earth-'time', not some numeric equivalent of that huge reality. Furthermore, a check w a clock a few mins later proved it on target. Yet it gets better.

The time of year, which came as part of the pkg, was given not as an abstract date, not as a numbered day win a certain arbitrarily-titled month repping a certain arbitrarily-titled season, which date (phew) one can then proceed to figure is apprx'ly equidistant between fall equinox & winter solstice. None of that civilized hooey. Just as had happened w the time of day, the time of *year* appeared as my Planetary situation in space; a mental graphic of that semiannular [sic] moment where the trip thru seasonal change was rapidly approaching (ie, was by then only 25% away from) that most fritening annular moment of all: winter solstice! And, in the same gulp of recognition, i saw my Planetary Place (ggNs) as being 75% distant from that most comforting of all annular moments: summer solstice! (Translated to process. Once shadow-study, where i lived, had taught me how to spot highest- & lowest Sun, annually speaking –that is, how to monitor the extremes of axis-tilt in Earth's ellipse around the Sun– i was then ready to learn how to divide that trip thru space we call a year into four parts; a matter of adding a shadow-knowledge of the periods of equinox. That done, my mastery of shadows (& lite intensity etc) was learning to separate the year into eighths; that is, learning to divide in half yet again Earth's trip between solstice & equinox. It was this degree of shadow discrimination which i'd achieved on the day in focus, missing the annual mark by less than 30hrs!)

Tho this awareness evolving in me was spread over several years, its steady entrenchment was nonetheless a thrill –an existential rush, if you will– as it worked more&more often w precision! And it was not my liberation from our civil hoax of clocks & calendars that did it. It was, rather, how intimately connected this knowledge made me feel to my Home and *its* Place in the Universe! Sun Moon & stars, w Earth as a body among them, took on a *personal* and, i might add, a uniquely uncivil, somatic, aspect; qualities of life i'd always sensed should have been there as i walked & sailed about the World, but which rarely were —save for moments wayout at sea on a starlit nite forinstance, or on my knees digging in Earth's soil under a rising or setting moon. (I believe women more than men tend by nature of their reproductive functions to understand such chthonic connection.) However, such all-Natural celestial coordinates are not accessible to one wout a lifestyle Place: freeranging, yes, but not beyond local intimacy. Enter key subtlety. Where meditation connected me as a sentient being to an awesome Universe, and while that connection was excruciatingly physical *during* meditation, following it, Earth-linkage, Place-linkage, graded more mental than visceral. Yet, as my awareness of Place ٤ Change (not time) became more&more sensitized, my connection to this World (into which i'd been rather perfunctorily dropped wout explanation) became more constantly visceral and thereby comprehensible; as if the zizm of me was plumbing at last the true meaning of Home ...the very least that can happen to an irrepressibly questing curiosity, i suppose, yet which still seems like an extraordinary gift. It thrills (as well as depresses) me today to think on the wisdom i would have had to pass on to posterity had i been permitted (by those who fear Wisdom) to reach old age —or, at least, an older age than this. How cheap&easy it is, eh, to share our couldhavebeens?

The amount of wisdom we are missing is proportionate to the amount of error we see in Nature & instinct. —*Ecocosm: the Cosmic Gaia*

Lilith

Speaking of solstices. They are no less than celestial edicts. Many persons feel there are moments in life when Earth ٤ Universe (stars seas liteningstrikes Earthviews eclipses auroras sunsets dawns whatever) are whispering some message of Cosmic import. If this is so, then the solstices, comparatively speaking (hic), are the voice of the Universe *thundering* a mx, uttering a warning which only those deaf to Natural phenomena neither hear nor heed. For the solstices are a World-stage dramatization of where we stand in the Universe, a celestial drama which clearly portrays Earth's, and our, very delicate condition in the Grand Scheme; a lite&shadow show as broad as the distance between Earth ٤ Sun; an actingout from horizon to horizon of the vastest chiaroscuro panorama we'll ever witness, painting in living pigments Earth's *so* fragile location between consummate fire and lethal ice! In fact, there are no moments between birth ٤ death more fearsome ٤ humbling –irrespective of *whatever* horrors we may have experienced– than the deepest hours of solstice, winter or summer! And it is exactly our loss of intimacy with this Natural fact, our species-wide disconnection from these inexorable semiannual phenomena, which has made all the difference ...all the difference in the future of ALL living things ...but mostly in the future of those lives balanced at the top of what we glibly call "the food chain". I speak of course of a lethal disconnection from Nature ٤ instinct which has altered for the worse the future of ...well, let's face it... mostly us *bigger* lifeforms.

13

Want to catch a nymph? Get a grotto. If youre desperate, try a rock garden, in the yard, in a windowbox, or even on the roof. But remember, water's a must —fresh, clean water (no chems) if you can find it anymore. A tiny trickle, a pool, the weëest of fountains. Anything. And dont forget, the nymph you 'catch' will match exactly the size of the grotto she adopts. For example, a large grotto (such as the one at ggNs) may attract several lifesize nymphs. And tho it is true they come in many sizes, every nymph is always a 10! That's automatic. Or should i say autopsychic?

While not immortal, nymphs are said to live far longer than mortals. I admit to being unable to envision Lilith anywhere close to plutarch's 9,720yr age limit for nymphs, even knowing the ancient greeks said nymphs showed no signs of ageing no matter their age. If a culture views Nature as irresistible –as possessing the most compelling of ALL beauty– then nymphs (personifications of their mother, Nature) must be irresistible as well, an epitomic mix of gravitas & youthfulness; all the forces of Nature's self-rejuvenation personified. And i, nathan schock, am the true nympholept, absolutely bewitched by the entrancing body of the goddess Gaia... agateblue&white, floating thru the icy blackness of space, set like a magic gem among the stars. Yes, i confess to being wholly caughtup in an erotic whirlwind (nymphixilated, yes!), a passion to possess a transcendent being! or two, or three.... And, o, had the reader known Lilith, all argument to the contrary would be instantly moot.

In that shape one causes by clasping an invisible coin between thumb & index, so the surrounding bluffline & cliffs at ggNs clasp frikka's cove, wherein lies the grotto. When i found the cove it was a mostly driedup brambly crumbly dead-tree-limb-filled narrow-mouthed & largely forgotten hole in the mtnside. With a bluffline indention of some 800m, the cove is said to have been there long before humans set foot in n amer. And, until a ms written by one fanny frikka was discovered by a student at bu in 1994, the place had 'only' its rocks, bones & fossils for a personal history.

About 2yrs after i purchased the property, and just after the walkovers, bridge & stairs were in place, *the scotsmoor sentry* ran a sanctuary pictorial. Tho it showed some of the tarn, falls & grotto, it made no mention of their namesakes, john muir & wolfgang von goethe. Yet it did trouble to incl a quote from a certain neighbor who decried goethe as "some damn ferriner who wernt e'en no immagrint lak m' granpaw". While it was the assignment's fotog, tara, who later supplied me w the pronunciation (& the house it lived in), she also said the reporter felt, the opinion of someone w a frontyardful of trash & several hungry dogs gave the article a sense of "frontier realism". When tara suggested "Seems ta me the prejudice 'n' hate mr schock is braving up on that mountain is the harshest of *all* of america's frontiers", the reporter rebuffed her w, "Alota kids t'day are suckers for fame 'n' money. Dont get too close ta him. You'll regret it". Odd statement considering it came from the only one of the two who threw herself at me.

As to garbage visible. I happen to agree w ggNs' reigning nymph. One day at a <high genteelese> gathering down in lochston, when some of our newer mtn neighbors, led by one mrs halley castle, poked fun at whom they called "our local trash cachers", Lilith responded (in her endearingly blameless way), "They only accumulate in public what the rest of us get rid of in private." A selfconscious silence followed. "If our own trash were in plain view for all t' see, maybe, before we threw anything away, or bought anything new, and maybe even before we ate anything, we'd pause to ask what *exactly* we're doing." That said, mrs castle's hubby thusiastically popped back with "Or as my gramma usta put it: Buy the best 'n' wear it out. Make it last or do without." One could almost feel him wince at his wife's hard-jawed glance. "If any of us, with our higher entropy lifestyles, suddenly found ourselves with all our waste sittingout in our frontyards, you couldnt see our houses for the garbage. Why those peoples' garbage piles are so *small* is what makes me wonder about how *i'm* living." A second silence ...broken by: "Well, thank goodness us newer folks on the mountain are ABOVE all that garbage business [interjected mrs castle], forgive my double ontondray." Lilith, nibbling gently toward the (rotten) fruity center now: "Our part of appalachia isnt really all that highup, is it? I mean, unless *my* head is in the clouds (pardon my *double sens*), cloudcover in these parts hasta get really lowdown for us to look at all highup, doesnt it? I mean, compared with places like the rockies 'n' himalayas", all of it delivered with not a trace of our boorish neighbor's 'altitude'. Zero zip zilch nill null none. Culpable humility. And if L's surgically accurate repartee had *my* head reeling, i'm sure mrs castle, no royal fool, still cheers at my slitest misfortune just for my having been obviously in love w this gentle defender of *all* of civilization's underclasses.

High genteelese, with its thousand affectations & pretensities –with its morally barren formalities & ethically bankrupt COURTesies– can only grow in us vast reservoirs of repressed anger.

The fotog who accompanied the nasty *sentry* reporter that day in '86 of course was tara pickford —first visitor to be agog over the grotto. "I jus lu-UV this place! ...I'd like t' shoot it again when your plantings are in." Yet if artifacts excavated in a nearby cave count, any number of amerind maidens must have cavorted in its waters over some 13oooyrs time. (More on ggNs' glabrous version of eileithyia's cretan cavern later, time permitting.) After tara, ggNs' charter nymph, other nymphs (well, grotto groupies) gravitated thereabouts —thanks to projects like flora ɛ fauna inventories ɛ demographics, natural pesticide ɛ soil experiments, bat colony relocation, etc, regularly conducted by bu on sanct land. In fact, it was tara, and these very muses ɛ their friends, who formed the core (corps 'n' grotto, o haunting romanza!) of the first greenEarth action group in bamalachia.

If i had my life to do over... i dont believe in zizm reincarnation per se but let's say i did.... But who am i kidding? The Forces that be wont even let me finish my *present* instalment muchless some *next* one.... Well, anyway. Say i had it all to do again. I'd acquire a grotto, any grotto, as soon as possible. For, thanks to juanita ɛ Lilith, i've come to believe in both nymphs *and* their great ɛ generous Mother.

Lilith

For most of my life i've tended to appear to be a loner. Tho it is true the love my parents denied me left a vacuum in a vital emotional area, by the time i left home, despite the desperate insecurity a dearth of parental love causes, i rather knew better, somehow, than to become over-enamored of any female who showed me affection. For while in childhood i learned to find emotional stability in artistic pursuits, by my mid20s i'd learned to anchor myself (my Self, my zizm) in the copious rewards of disciplined meditation ...which, need i say, practiced in virtual isolation as it is, automatically stirsup a great deal of deepself confrontation, automatically situates one face-to-face w his subconscious. And this precisely –confrontation w one's zizm; eg: know thy Self– is the subject of the present aside.

While Reality-adjusted primitive peoples always incl some variation on deepself exam, civil society not only omits this, it finds endless ways of discouraging such investigation. So serious is this denial of our subconscious Natures that the very concept of 'loner' (person likely to make contact w his Natural Self, that 'close encounter of the FIRST kind') strikes fear into your standard civil SQ'er (status quoer) —ie, we avrg subconscious-impoverished civílizens. While i never qualified as the emil (masc form of emily) dickinson of bamalachia, and even tho i was known as host to routine social events, believe it or not, gossip being the ruthless deconstructionist it is, there was always the question of my being a loner *domestically* speaking. Because i failed time&again to setup housekeeping w any of my lovers —and w my heterosexness being beyond question (thank the god of small favors, living as i did in that fritefully homophobic region), the localized search for "other weirdness" about me, *any* other weirdness, soon tookup in earnest. However, after years passed —and w my "religious weirdness" amounting to little more than fodder for hardcore gospel gossips— it was not long before the "big question" about me in those parts became: "Who [ie, what female person] had gotten closest to me so far and what exactly was it that had kept her from jamming her toothbrush, like the national flag of some lovely invader, into the sweet soil of my baccalaureate sovereignty?"

And here i must ask, w ggNs opening its gates to more people in a year than any 50 of its neighbors, how could the term loner possibly be applied to me? The answer, tho whacked, is simple. In any biblebelt (muchless this one), unless one is veryyoung or ricketyold, his bedrm (if not his bed) is perceived as being meant for *two* not one. Take oral & dexter, gay friends of Lilith (who eventually tookup residence at ggNs). Tho farmore stigmatized christian-communitywise than myself, still, in the shadow of that fearsome noahtic duality which insists "every *normal* mature creature will pairoff", oral & dexter, rampant local homophobia bedamned, fit in better on alp mtn than i did. Imagine! And so i'm here to say (my penultimate point), a gay couple will fair better than a straight loner in a narrow-minded environment exactly *because* of that 'mind's' narrowness; always trying to interfere as it does w any&all chances that a person might make contact w his 'other' (uncivilized) self. Ie, have a cozy relationship w his own subconscious. And specially feared is that loner suspected to have made contact w his Natural Self *despite* any bible-thumping or flag-waving authority; and "worse", that that person (How dare he?) be overjoyed & content w what he repeatedly finds deep within himself, overjoyed & contented *not* w what civilization or civil religion gave him, but w what Nature alone ("evil evil" Nature) gave him! (Civil religion: any religion which reinforces the civilizing principle.) Which brings us finally to my:

Religion is not required for one to be more moral than any pope, more immoral than any perp.

Rudiments of good health: These consist of a lively and unrepressed subconscious working hand-in-hand with what was designed to be arbiter of all our actions: that guarddog of behavior we call conscience, which arbiter (in addition to us making it lively & unrepressed) must never, no matter how cruel the social pressure to live a lie, never be in denial of Reality (Universal Nature), and which conscience must never rest when the body is awake. This neuters *all* need of philosophy, incl'g (mostofall) the civil (imperial establishment) religions and the governments/states they pamper.

Summarily. I maintain, this need of ours for the pairing-off of all persons is as desperate as it is because of the deep-personhood impoverishment rampant in civil society. Little differently than the abandoned ɛ helpless arm 'longs for' the hand which was severed, so the civil personality (carefully ɛ cruelly decoupled by a thousand arbitrary ɛ artificial rules&expectations) mourns for a lifetime its loss of intimacy w its subconscious (the deep-seated ɛ innate Self), and not only the loss of its own Self but also the loss of the *social* unconscious (the social Self) that is both its mirror ɛ its medium —and which need only the extended family (existing in relatively primal peace) can provide in any fullness. Just look what happens once our deep Selfs have been abandoned to the embrace of that sucking ghoul we call civilization.

Lilith

How *the scotsmoor sentry* came to contact me is curious in lite of later events. While from frikka's point to lebanon, from lochston to quadrant, the latest about the "gothey place" is always great gossip, it was specially lively during the purchase ɛ development phase. But the *sentry* was down in the valley (the "sinful sinful...valley so low" as my evangelical neighbors sang it) and therefor prettymuch out of earshot of alp mtn, if not out of view. It seems to have got rolling when parttime *sentry* fotog tara was "turned-on [by a classmate] to a good ride [equine] out at frikka point". But her source did not know the land had recently been sold. Arriving w horses ɛ trailer, tara ɛ friend were disappointed when confronted by my "private" postings ...yet intrigued, "For I'd never heard of a Nature preserve being private." Running into bernie as they were leaving, tara asked about the sanctuary, gave her *sentry* business card. Yet bernie said nothing to me about this "valley girl". "Fergot all bout it," he claimed —which tara "seriously" doubted since "His son tried to throw a serious make on me".

While i'd long known better than to get involved w the press at any depth, i was a little like an excited groom over this my latest commitment to Mothernature. Since, despite the gentle disclaimer, snobbish isolation could be read into my "private" postings, i figured it was just good-neighborliness to allow *the* local newspaper access. My only stipulation was that the mission-statement of the sanctuary (Wilderness needs every place it can get to lick its wounds in safety and in peace) be duplicated in the article. This was not done. Further, it was not even attempted. The 4page su spread w color fotos ɛ text cameoff as 'a who's-who in local realestate?' The very title of the piece was offensive: MOUNTAIN HIDEAWAY HAS IT ALL. I was incensed. <What is all this rich-guy-on-a-mountaintop crap? Fergodsake, i dont even have a jacuzzi or a pool, or even a full-fledged garage, 'n' i drive around in a glorified golfcart! [editor offers a retraction] What will that do? I want a new article clearly stating what this Nature preserve is all about, as we agreed.> He would have the owner get in touch w me. Nincompoop owner proves duller than his eic. "Everaone *ah* know would be jus thrayld ta git a stora lak yall got, mista schock". So why wasnt *i* "thrayld fuhgoodnessake? ...Maybih in a few months we c'n arrange faw anotha stora".

Over my dead body. I jus turneddown two national magazines because of their home'n'gardens view of the Universe. I notice ms vindicta pritchett (or whatever her name was) ...fine, ms sunday barnes, whatever... didnt forget t' mention *that* in her story...that *she* got an interview 'n' *they* didnt. Does that tell you she was on the level, sir? Does my turning down two national magazines lead you to believe that i wanted t' play glitter 'n' glitz in a newspaper which people just fifty miles from here never heard of or ever will? No. I was being a good neighbor. That's the *only* reason i allowed the *sentry* on "my" property. I let that vicious woman who works for you into my private life trusting that my ecological goals would be represented. Well, they werent. Not even a little. She took my friendly gesture 'n' turned it into a cheap burlesque. An article anyone would be proud to have, you say? Well not i. I feel like i was forced to sleep with a tramp and now i've caught an ugly disease called public vanity!

The career slut (i apply the term well-advised) who wrote the article, ms barnes, irate (because her fotog & me got along famously while her own meretricious fawning got her nowhere), tipped her hand just before she rushedoff w her story. "If you love the sierras so much why didnt you build your sanctuary *there?*" Tara's mimp-faced reaction assured me, this was petty nastiness not investigative probing.

<Well, firstoff, my love of the sierras is somewhat past-tense, as i explained. Secondly, one doesnt 'build' a Nature preserve the way one builds a house. Only Nature, over millennia, can do that. And finally, to answer your question ...which, not incidentally, is totally out of order... i prefer the old appalachians to the young sierras for, it so happens, my taste in mountains runs exactly counter to my taste in women. And, no. You may not quote me —when you finally figureout what i jus said ...in ALL its Natural depth:

I love broad lushly dressed mountains not angular naked ones. Furthermore, ms barnes, this tawdry little interview is now over.> Rising, i turned to the cheerful fotog, said i was glad to have met her. The article came out not only w my off-the-record comparison of mtns, but w that statement given a nasty chauvinistic twist. For all these offenses & more, i filed suit.

Following a printed retraction, and a (unpublished) pitiful letter of apology from the paper, i rcv'd a call from fotog tara. She said she was sorry things had turnedout badly and hoped none of it was her fault. In fact, i said, i found her fotos had captured the spirit of what the article had ignored. Tho in the months that followed i learned from tara some of the dirty little secrets of the *scotsmoor sentry,* still i dropped the suit; but not because of its sorry retractions or limp apologies, but because it just wasnt neighborly to persist; and mostofall, because i find most revenge belittling ...to the avenger.

But the civil world does not respect such behavior. During & since my trial that little misquote has risen & walked again in the poppress like some insatiable ghoul, not as i said it but in its misquoted form. Only last month, in that bundle of newsprint sent me from upstairs, i caught that ghoul foully feeding again! This version, the worst yet, read: "Schock says: 'I like my mountains old, my women young'." Will this civil contagion never die?

Lilith

As to the "sinful sinful valley" thing. Down in scotsmoor a different tale is told about us "mountain folk". "Those folks up there (the speaker cast a credulous eye toward alp mtn which spread its misty & blue length in the distance behind me) may badmouth us cityfolk ta kingdomcome if they wanna. But truth is, come friday 'n' saturday nite those hills emptyout like there's hellfire a-ragin up there 'n' the only thing that c'n save 'em is t' get across the river 'n' into town here. Youve seen those movies where the cowhands come ridin down out o' the hills and into town whoopin 'n' shootin? It's scary, right? Well, alot of us stay home on those nites jus because it *is* scary. <They whoop 'n' shoot you say?> Well, no. But the way they drive is just as dangerous as shootin. It's just not safe aroun here them nites." "Yeah. [adds his wife] It's like bumpercars here in town til they leave." She is teeth-gritted serious. "Anyone loves their kids keeps em home friday 'n' saturday nite. *And* [she quickly adds], the walmart parkinlot? *Certain death!"*

14

The nearest hamlets to ggNs are lochston ε lebanon, the nearest village, quadrant, the nearest towns, scotsmoor ε rainsdale, and the nearest cities, noogachatta (to the ne) ε huntsdell (to the nw). Huntsdell being far&away less polluted, i planned to take Lilith there, if only to show her the area wasnt completely lost to some of the arts ε a good vejan [sic] meal. (I'll say vāguein when you say vaguetables.) But sensing my guest found ggNs the greatest thing since peace&quiet ("I'm happy to just hang here 'n' read, if that's alright?"), i changed that plan, gave Lilith to choose from two guestrooms when she arrived. Oddly (to me), she chose the one w the least windows, slept 10hrs the first nite, excusing her "rude" behavior with, "Reesy 'n' me talked nonstop til all hours. Beside, it's so quiet here. God! I jus kinduv die til morning ...well, make that almost *noon?"* she blushed.

Fine. But at ggNs we believe it takes tons of sleep, meditation 'n' quiet reflection to render a creature as peaceful as a tree...well, as a turtle, anyway, lounging on a log in the sun. Please sleep as long as you like, and *when* you like. What good is being here if youre not peaceful as that turtle?

"Thanks. ...Youre right. What good is being *anywhere* if youre not?"

There's usually more to exhaustion than just lack of sleep. Lage had hinted some of these causes in our chat. Beside the problems w don, aurise ε beth, there was capt.gE too, due to begin production in jan. Lilith was a perfectionist in her art. Tho everyone felt there was time to fix the things that troubled her, still she wanted to be "ready to start". Since i'd left she'd been working feverishly on "a whole fresh look for my characters". When, a couple weeks before her arrival, i'd asked rick how she was doing, he told me, "Had t' give her a key t' the place. She's here every nite –I mean *every* nite– til ten, eleven o'clock". This concerned me but, "No need. One of us is always popping in or out, an' it seems brian is here all the time too anymore. B'side, we've got building security keeping an eye out." Rick ε me, off to a rocky start back when he took over in '91 (he took an immed dislike to me, as men often do), had slowly become friends. He gained significant points w me simply by not asking anything about the "el granada beach incident", nor had any rumors ever come to me from his direction. Amazing how far a little respect can go if it's mutually applied.

Lilith: "Please. No special attention. This was a bad time for me ta just pop in. Youve got lots t' do ta get ready [to go on the road again]. Just do what you'd normally do if i wasnt here. Please? Okay? I mean it."

{Right. Like *that* could happen.}

Gap rd, overhung w an arbor of foliage most of the year, in winter was arbored mostly by bare limbs. Since the road wound up the w side of the mtn, in the dead of winter one had to wait til 2p if he wanted full sun thereat. So at highest sun on her second day, we put on running duds and drove hectar to the top of gap rd. Since i always pickedup trash on the warmup walk (down the mtn), *we* pickedup trash —she insisted on it ...and was shocked by the sheer amount of it, specially those scenic overlooks where it had been dumped down the mtnside by the puTruckload.

"This looks fresh. Damn! An' that couch down there cantuv been there very long! [and, walking away] There are parks all over the world that would give anything to have this road, this view." Next overlook, same dump scene. "No offense, but i cant believe this ...You warned me 'n' still i had no idea ...This is unbelievable." As she starts down the swale after a beer bottle, on unseen gravel her feet go out from under and, landing solidly on her rump, she slides to a gritty stop, feet in the ditch, bag of trash still in hand.

You poor thing.

"I feel like such an idiot."

She is on her feet before i can cross to help. <An' for slobs who could giveashit theyre turning the Planet into a dumpsite. You okay?>

"I'm fine ...Really!" She reminds me of something i said when we started. <I try not ta complain, t' make this act as private as possible in a public place —b'tween jus me 'n' Motherearth>.

Youre right. Thanks for the reminder. I fill four grocery sacks every time i run, jus pickingup the immediate roadside ...and usually in less than halfa k. And i'm not the only one pickingup. There's another fella ...who actually does more than me in that i'm gone so much.

"Talk about crimes against Nature."

I got b-c ta do a small study here a couple years back. There are only some forty different vehicles a day using this road. The amount of trash which accumulates in any one week, strictly roadside that is, indicates that allbut six or seven of them are r'sponsible. What percent of forty is thirtythree? I'm the dregs at math. At any rate, theyre pretty shameful stats.

A gorgeous spot, gap rd drops –in four steep reverse-curves, thru heavily-wooded terrain– to the valleyfloor, 2200m below the elevation of the uppermost bluff at ggNs. This steep winding distance, w accidental overlooks, from top to bottom is 1.2k, and to the postoffice in lochston, another ¾k. Being perfectly brisk running wx, we decide on the long version. At the bottom of the mtn we hide our trash. "Hide it?" <Yeah. They'll break it open 'n' spread it around if ya dont.> Another look of disbelief. "Raccoons?" <No, young people ...hangout at this spot.> "Why do i think youre not kidding?" Done, we take off toward lochston.

<Hey, i'm just thankful certain persons dont shove hectar off the mountain when i'm off running, burn my house when i'm on tour, or shoot any more bison. [stares, lips ajar, in on-going disbelief] In church, i understand... Ya know the church i showed you in lebanon? Well i'm referred to there as "a certain heathen neighbor of ours" ...an the tower, ya know? They call it "the tower of babel" ...only they say it, baybl ...or so my friends tell me.>

Car speeds by. <Didja see the way she looked at us?>

Lilith beginning to look a little blank by now. "Yuhuh."

The driver reacted like men (mostly) out in public when Lilith passed. I understood what jolted them: momentarily seen, full of beauty, youth & sizzling fertility. Muchless in running gear: the shimmering bodily shell of her: threading out, gathering in, of muscle, plucky tautness of tanned tendon.

<It's miles 'n' weeks between runners in these parts. Most o' my neighbors are thoroly discomfited as to why anyone would want to run. And theyre confounded ...no, make that, bedeviled... as to why anyone would *walk* down the mountain and then *run* up it. It strikes them as bassackwards. Even tho i've explained it many times.>

"Why do you? ...I mean I *think* i know why ..for a harder workout. But splain anyway." First time i heard her use lage's "splain".

Reason number two. You know how the tips o' your toes got sore walking down? That's impact; unnecessary wear&tear. Imagine what *running* downhill does. That's why i walk backwards where it's steep."

"That *did* feel alot better."

We turned at the postoffice, started back.

An' level ground's not a whole lot better. Bet ya still feel those toes, huh? [she did] But steep *uphill* running, specially in sand or good shoes, lowers impact ...on your joints 'n' tendons, i mean... to almost zero ...while raising the *aerobic* impact exponentially. You'll see when we start up. {Damn. She runs with such ease!} Her face shone w only the slitest bit of perspiration; her hair, in long ponytail, swayed sidetoside, its auburn streakings gleaming in the open lite. Go on ahead, if you want. *Really. Go ...Go!* You c'n baby me nexttime. Sidelong smirk as she drifts on ahead, hardly breathing.

Unused as yet to mtn running, halfway up i began catching her. Sight of her in silk running shorts causes me to idle back. Seen working from behind, her legs, their creamy highlites flashing wetly, were a treat for the eyes: tendon insertion of dual hamstrings, rising like twin harps behind her thewy thighceps, struck me like erotic melody at every step; that lovely, deep, shaded popliteal hollow behind the knee; the moist sheen of her capable calfs —w their teardrop-shaped hoops of muscle that put such launch & lift in her step— fluffily collared in their practiced white socks. Two-thirds to the top she stopped to walk and i had no choice but to pass. Unlike that steep gravely trail in ca, or the beach where i sank to my calfs, i glided by, ran backwards for a space: <Forgive me if i enjoy this while it lasts. A couple more times up this mountain 'n' you'll be dusting me again.>

Toward sunset we took a stroll, endedup walking the old driveway just to stay in the sun's fast-receding warmth. As we passed the barn i asked if she'd like to see the manor. When we started up the frontstairs she flinched, stopped. <You okay?> "Just a little hitch" she laffed, and strode across the porch." <Hurt yourself when you fell, huh?> "Just a little."

I call it 'modest', having only eight rooms compared to the southern colonial's usual eighteen ta twennyeight. While the barns 'n' outbuildings were let to run down before i purchased them, this house was both wellbuilt 'n' well-maintained. I sensed her about to add some humorous analogy here about me except that the familiarity we'd had back in ca had got lost in the interim. What i mean to convey is, how austenesquely proper we had become, how victorianly poised-to-strike our libido repression was growing. This latter i was not sure existed in other than myself however. Not absolutely, anyway.

While the 2story manor was neither her style nor mine, we conceded it "cheery 'n' charming" w its regionally contrived ɛ adorned columns ɛ cornices, its french-doored porches ɛ balconry. (Listen to this larding, lord!) Yes. I lived here til the chalet was completed, i said as we toured the lower floor... Yes. [Rented] a couple times ...most recently to an owner of those horses youve already met.

I caught the slitest feint ɛ grimace again as we started up the stairs. You know, i said as we reached the top, if ever you want to get away, as they say, from the city by the bay, or retreat to these mountains from hazy l.a, you are welcome t' stay here. The house is yours. Even in perpetuity, i added, staring into her eyes with all the fire i was keeping in precarious abeyance. And so you shouldnt feel selfconscious let me add: You would *not* be the *only* lovely creature with water rights around here. [she looked at me w that shyly askance glance i only then realized i was coming to love] We have swans 'n' geese 'n' deer in every size. An', come spring, all *sort* of butterflies!

"You sound like swinburne."

What? The way her head was cocked i figured she'd heard something outside, for i had no idea i'd just "made a poem", and would have long lost it's occurrance ɛ content except for her diary.

"Of course i would insist on paying a fair rental" she continued, turning to one side, staring out the 2^{nd}story window we stood by, pond, falls ɛ yes, grotto, in the lowering-sun middistance.

Of course you will *not*. Unless (of course) it is the *only* condition under which you will come. In that case you may pay a nominal fee —and *not* "a nominal leg", as my [inventedly warm] grandpappy used t' say.... Is it something to do with this house? Its cues of colonialism? i said as, finishing the top floor, we started down the wide stairway. We are becoming more victorian by the second, my sweet Friend.> Rhett, stepping in front of not scarlett but melanie, stops her descent midway: What are you afraid of?

This took her back for a second. Looking around. "Heights, i guess. <Heights?> Yes. Spatial heights. Emotional heights. Any experience that is, well, so heightening it blurs judgement."

Like falling in love?

Staring straightout over my head, yods almost imperceptibly. "Like falling, period."

But why? Love is the himalayas of our sealevel lives; it's why we go on, to reach, or hope to reach, the snowcapped peaks above the clouds, above all the foothills of hypocrisy that tripup our civility.

"It's not that —not entirely. Even tho i may fear heights i also love them."

Then, what?

Pause. "The downside. The dangerous descent ...the terrible distance to the bottom ...where not only your toes 'r yer butt get bruised [slow smile] but where your heart may be hurt ...if one should slip...." For this i have no argument and it shows. "I hafta learn t' stop, t' look down while i'm climbing, not just keep lookingup at the goal. I need t' learn t' look down at where i've come from, and what it has taught me ...and all i've maybe *missed* in its lessons. Or maybe i jus need to stop sometimes, get used to the rarified air...like you suggested while we were running t'day... Maybe we *both* need t' stop now, catch our breath, get used to the height of all this breathtaking terrain." She surveyed all w a sweep of her fabulous eyes, out the windows, down the stairs and across the sunstreamed greatarea.

I looked away from those all-absorbing eyes, found stability in her hand at rest on the railing. I thought for a long moment, yodded slowly, gradually, to the sense of what she said ...took that hand, kissed it. <Talk about speaking poetry.> I turned away, continued our descent to evening.

As to my "making a poem" that day. Had i made one on purpose it would have read more like....

I want to hold you. That's all.
What harm can come of this?
But, no. I lie! That is *not* all.
I have in mind unmitigated bliss!

15

By fr, her 4th day there, roundingoff her "fabulous sleeps" w catnaps, Lilith was as shining & contented as i'd seen her. That morn she rose at dawn. I however didnt fully wake til my guest mouse went silent, til my small overwintering jay population made it raucously clear, she had ventured outside, was headed thru the chill mist in the direction of the grotto. A note on the kitchen bar read, "Went for a walk. Back in a little while". With a glass of juice spiked w foodgrade peroxide, i retreated to my eyrie to recapitulate an essay promised to an editor. Occasional scans of the sanct as i worked gave no sign of her. Somewhere in the backdrop of awareness i began to wonder why my guest had not waited a little longer so i might join her "creakOday" ramble. The possessiveness in that thought was apparent even as i thought it.

Movement in my peripheral vision some time later caused me to look up. Some distance away, whom i guessed was her was walking down the old manor driveway. I tookup the binocs to be sure it wasnt rachel. Something about the early-morn look of her, like the prismatic limbus of some strange & beautiful creature seen in the lite of a microscope, was corpuscularly lifelike! Facing the chalet, she set on the turf a bottle she'd apparently found and, w a blank but wide-eyed expression on her face, began flexing/holding flexing/holding her high-hoisted knees alternately, surveying her surroundings as she did so. I happened to be zoomed on her face when a car went by out on the road. A single wingflap of concern crossed her features. Not quick enuf to catch it at the old driveway opening, i saw an unfamiliar car cruise past the frontgate. Rocking limberly now in her faded jeans, she removed her jacket (also a faded denim) and, looking elsewhere, dropped it from the fingertips of her fully extended arm. One arm of the jacket, as it settled upright on the turf, folded open and (as if harboring a meanspirited wraith) backhanded the bottle, overturning it.

(As to that turf. Lawns which require mowing were outlawed at ggNs. And, save for grass-as-feed production, mowing itself was banned. How is it then that what Lilith is standing on at that moment, and that i have called turf, looks like a mowed lawn, feels like a mowed lawn, and is attracting her activity like a mowed lawn? Well, fact is, the turf she's standing on was a type of clover whose luxurious thick mat grows no more than handhigh. Thus, not only does it never need mowing; not only is it one of the best soil regenerators; not only does it feed ε nutrate most ruminators (in our case, deer, bison, horses, rabbits etc); not only does it support many nectar-requiring insects (honeybees, butterflies etc); not only does it look better than a lawn, act better than a lawn ε feel like a lawn, but millions of tiny florets overlay its forestgreen leaves w a sweet-scented ε lavender-tinted haze. Once experienced it becomes clear why the lawn-product industry –polluting ε wholly unnecessary money-raking monstrosity that it is– has effectively kept the news of never-mow groundcovers unknown to the avrg person.)

Pacing now in a tite loop, she stopped to do standing calf presses every third revolution. After bouncing like a boxer for a min or so (reminding me of her sister under 'normal' circumstances), she suddenly stood erect, motionless ε staring. Head down in concentration (i guessed her about to take off for a run), she pawed the turf a few times w the toes of her white trotters. Then, w the short high-thrusting steps of a vaulter, she broke into a fullout sprint, fell into a volley of forward handsprings (memory counts seven) ending w a "stuck" tucked double salto, followed by a tiny balance-check, just to prove, to any wowed worshiper who happened to be spying, that she was possibly human afterall.

Now here i must tender a curious etiology. While i am unempathic toward obesity ε other forms of selfishness –aggression/greed topping my list– i am generally uncritical of others, particularly those i like or love. Indeed, i'm not the hypercritical observer a writer should be. Forinstance, tho i clearly remember the first time i saw Lilith walk, run, jump, scramble up a hillside or vault a mound of rocks, and tho my study of her was surely a loving one, til this very moment it lacks the backdrop which quality analysis possesses: conscious critical comparison of overt elements. For my focus is habitually on exposing the subtler, the well-hid, elements of existence.

The mcGrae sisters, on&off from aged 4 to 12, were given lessons in gymnastics ε dancing. One does not come away from such training w a hillbilly hobble —or does one? The first time i saw Lilith, one of the most striking things about her was her walk; a perfect integration of athletic thrust ε dancer grace. We often link selfconsciousness ε insecurity. Yet the most polished dancers –seemingly oozing selfconfidence– during performance are totally selfconscious. If she or he is a great artist, she has in mind at all times every aspect of her visible self. And it only follows, the more physically selfconscious a person is the more styles of movement, and gradations of style, he or she will possess. Most of us step to an occasion to some degree, and few of us, in formal ceremony, walk like our everyday selfs. Some have even been known to cast aside crutches ε wheelchairs to receive a coveted award. And, yes, your honor. This line of thought *is* going somewhere.

A handspring, specially set in a consistently-arched series, is a skill. I think even the walk of an athlete just before or after a performance is a part of that skill; that is, it's not the way he or she walks about the house. That morn, after retrieving her jacket, the bottle, ε crossing the space from handspring staging area to driveway (around 150m), i saw Lilith transform from gymnast to walk-on model, then from humble athlete to no-stumble hiker.

There is no doubt that our anthropoidal origins, plus millions of years of hiking from place to place in search of food ε safety, have encoded in us an apelike ambulation, a way of walking which anthropologist denise norris calls 'the tired hiker', where one's momentum plus the downward pull of gravity are balanced over the hips, and where the arms swing lower ε lower w every additional kilometer, ready on split-second notice to restabilize us like the outrigger mitts of an orang or gorilla. I have learned, when Lilith felt she was alone ε unseen –at least by human eyes– she would drop into a hiker's stride, as if carrying a clinging child and w a long way yet to go. While the first time i saw this (ascending that initial ca hillside near a falls i'd compared to ggNs' muir falls), i thought it out of character. But over time that sexless ε goal-oriented ambulation –along w her ability to run ε bound like an impala– became more indicative of the true Lilith (the primitive Lilith) than all her learned motions ε skills put together, as esthetically showstopping ε applause-worthy as the latter manytimes were. For the longer i knew her the more i realized, Lilith was a seemingly bottomless pool of secret astonishments.

After breakfast we went on our first real hike. She was positively adorable in her long-billed denim cap (dappled w brite butterfly pins), which shade of blue increased the amplitude of her normally electric eyes, making them dazzle the air around her! Her hair was (somehow) gathered into a dark whorl on her nape; her denim shirt was shortsleeved while her jeans, non-designer, tho they lied in the leg were still honest in the butt. The black boots she'd chosen "Wow" fit her "perfect!" and, Who did i know wore size6? she asked in the mudrm, sampling an assortment of hikers i'd <accumulated...> "...just for impromptu hikes like this one, of course", she unflinchingly supplied wout missing a beat or suggesting a thing.

This time out we went the long way to frikka's cove: via the ne end of juanita tarn, following the trail ε walkovers which circumscribe the far end of the cypress swamp, whose ferny-leafed constituents, even by the most psychedelic starlite, only a small ε very fritened man (or an opiated ε paranoid one) could possibly perceive as "titanic". <Of course, on warm summer nites this bog does have its wicked *illichter* ...its will-o'-the-wisp lites... both *in* the water 'n' *above* it ...and which are *most* bioluminescent in early august [not in lonesome october].> She guessed, swamps were "scary t' people because theyre so teeming with life. And we therefor sense the *potentials* of life, potentials both wonderful *and* terrible. And when a *paranoid* imagination starts t' fill in the blanks, it endsup seeing things that may not exist." The intensity of expression on her downturned face as she spoke honestly thrilled me.

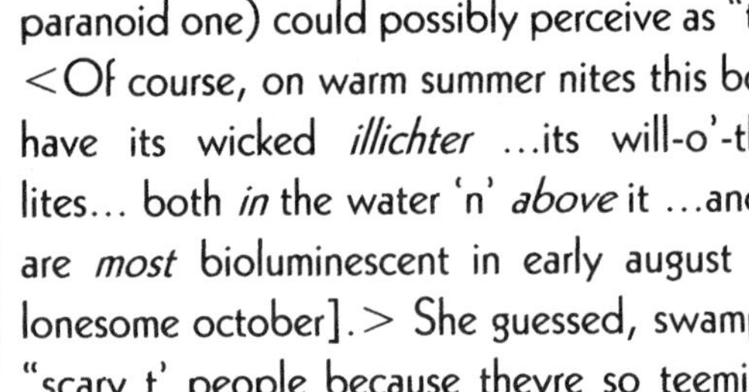

Dennis Ward

Our route took us onto ε along the n face of the bluff, which we soon descended, soon were walking the rock ledge of a 2nd bluff below the tarn. I stop when we reach a spot where three monoliths can be seen. Lined up end to end, each is the size of a 5story brownstone. Once a part of the lower bluff on which we stood, the relentless perking of the old orig tarn had undercut their footing til they broke away. Remaining upright, they'd slid some 5m down the steep slope and away from where we stood. These tall sheer islands of rock formed, in the process, a mini-canyon some 80-90m long. <Not too impressive from where youre standing. ...But maybe when youre down there looking up.> "Hey, *i'm* impressed." To divert her trepidation i pointout a lone tree on the middle monolith?

"My God! How does it get water up there?"

Capillarylike suction 'n' absorbtion by the roots in the cracks o' the rocks from what i c'n tell? State geologists say this whole slide happened within this century —a work in progress.

"Like the Planet."

<Like the Universe.>

She had said something wise. Yet, instead of hearing her –really hearing– i trivialized it w my cosmic strivings ...and neither of us, i think, saw the error of my ways. This would happen many times in our too few days together ...i mean, the *totality* of our too few days.

And that is probably why, suddenly, just now, i hear her in the crazy great distances of my mind, humming, singing, da-da-da-ing, so softly, sweetly, francis lai's wordless theme for *bilitis*. Hot hot hot tears, tears i did not know still remained in me, perk up up up thru the soil of my being, til i can no longer see the page before me. "Da-da-da-DAT-dadada." GreatGaia how i miss her...!!! Why? WHY *this* ending, not some better one?

Anyway, as i was saying.... The pace of erosion is faster down here than in other areas of the sanctuary ...because of ceaseless perk from the prolific springs 'n' watershed.

"An' gravity. Dont forget your beloved gravity."

Yes. And gravity ...mostofall.

The easiest way over to where the interrupted bluffline tookup again was to go upslope ε around a thick grove of hickory saplings. Higherup ε a little bit in front of me, moving over leaf-fluffy damp soil, Lilith suddenly lost her footing, bumped down a 2m drop, rump-skidding a quick 5m to a halt up ahead of me. I lunged to grab her, but no need, and likely too late had there been one. Her waterbottle popped from her daypack as she landed, shot between trees as if carefully aimed and, neat as you please, like a reflection from a mirror, flashed out into full sunlite beyond the bluff and twisted down ε out of sight! As it dropped, she looked at me, mouth open. Then, disgusted, not caring to rise, said, "What an idiot! I feel *sooo* stupid! I've been spending more time on my ass than jesus did on his ride into jerusalem! Sheesh! Youre probably thinking, This girl never hiked a day in her life!"

<Hey, i fall too. It's part o' hiking. We jus make sure *not* t' do it in places where there's no reset button. Wait! Dont get up! *Stay* right there!> L had landed only a meter or so from a spot i called frikka's funnel, a hole in the rocky shelf about 10m from the edge of the bluff, a spot which years of descending moisture had found a crack in and opened up, now as wide as a semitruck tire but which was blind w branches & leaves.

<Gimme your hand. [i pull her up & away from it] The perk from the tarn is in the process of cutting-away this whole outcropping.> I pickup a slab of sandstone nearby, wide as her shoulders, half her weight, drop it onto what looks like solid forest floor. But like magic it passes right thru! falls about 20m, strikes a ledge below, ricochets off and continues on down & out another 30-40m, broken branches dark soil wet leaves raining after it. The opening it left made her gasp, scoot back a couple more steps. <I've been meaning to cover that. Or at least, mark it.> She stands frozen w amazement. As we skirt it and leave i suggest, <What more perfect instrument for the accidental death of some killer politician or ceo, eh?> I had here to do a veiled doubletake for i saw some thought flash past her profile like a dark shadow. Not wanting to mar her visit w the sort of questions that shadow intimated, i changed the subject. <It's not the blueridge but these hills can still be treacherous. I squatted, grabbed a fistful of dry leaves. The ground here may *look* dry [withered 'n' sere] but look under here. Sweep away w gloved fingers topmost layer of leaves. See? Still wet 'n' slippery as ice under here ...from november rains. *That's* why you fell. Dont feel bad. Could happen t' anyone.>

We moved on then, stopping briefly to sit in semisunlite on an outcrop for a breather & a drink. She refused to share my water because "Ol' pocahontas here dropped half our water supply off a cliff 'n' almost got herself killed ...t' say nothing of littering!" —she re:d her jettisoned waterbottle.

{Better flip than depressed} thought captain john.

"There is no height more fritening than the feeling of freefall" she said after a moment. This vivid fact set me to mentally evaluating the exact altitude of my testicles, which a strong empathy had yanked up into my body cavity the moment i looked up, saw Lilith sliding toward that opening and knew i could not reach her in time.

"You okay?"

Yes. Yes... A-...yes. She thought me consternated by a maple sapling which had chosen to grow on the very lip of that rocky outcrop.

"That was almost an alice-down-the-rabbit-hole stunt i pulled, wasnt it?"

Minus the happy landing. [True.] But my fault entirely. [How's that?] I've been meaning to put a grill over that hole for years.

"...That vine's tryin ta drag that poor little tree over the edge, isnt it?"

<Isnt it. ...But the problem of getting a grill big enuf ta cover the hole, all the way down here, always stopped me. Never thought til now about the problem of living with myself if ...well, you know... some guest, 'r some trespasser, got swallowed by that funnel.> I rose to end a contest we both viewed as unfair, tugged on the vine til it came free, left it to dangle over the edge. The stripling immed stood almost erect.

"It's saying 'Phew, thanks. I was hopin somebody'd come along soon'."

Oz? The scarecrow?

"Tin man."

O.

"Somehow i'm not myself today. I still cant b'lieve i fell again."

<Ya know, your first day here you said something i've been thinking about.> Sitting, knees up, arms draped over them, she looks over. I think i see fear in her eyes. <No, nothing bad. A tiny thing. Cliche, actually.> Relieved, dissimulating a secure persona, she picksup a loose stone, begins drawing on the rocky surface to my side of her rump. Her declined profile is almost translucent in the dappling limegreen lite. <Something was troubling you that day. But, as we often do, you wrote it off by saying "I'm not myself t'day". After i settled you into the guestroom that evening i began thinking about ...no, ruminating, actually... that seeming-harmless little saying of ours. And i've decided: Like the expression "get real" –which you know i've written about– for us to say "I'm not myself t'day" is a little bombshell in its own right. [gaze lowered & fixed, she stops drawing] Cause when we say "I'm not myself", i b'lieve it is precisely at that time we are likely closest to

actually being ourselves —our deepest Selves; it is at that time we are likely closest of all to a breakdown or a breakthru. The problem is –and a sorry problem it is– when we feel like this.... [and here we pass from her&me talking back then to Lilithless me talking now]....

(...The problem is, when we feel like this, when we say "I'm not myself today", we invariably decide we're being afflicted by something *external* to us. Or, as robert rogers suggests in *the double in literature*: ...We suddenly see a disparity between what we assume is our true identity and some kind of false or alien identity that has invaded us. This is because, for us to entertain the possibility that we are, in fact, being afflicted from *within* us, not from *without* —eg: for us to presume that we are experiencing our repressed inner Selfs trying to break free of all the *external* civil rules&expectations weighing on us— that is, for us to assume an *internal* cause for our actions is to invalidate our everyday civil existences; devalue that mode of existence for which we have been carefully trained from infancy. I am re:g of course the fear we have of questioning the philosophic underpinnings of our day-to-day lives, of questioning why we are civil to begin w. Even a person as reflective as thoreau feared to question the sovereignty of the new england persona which had been impressed on him from infancy. Writing of going off to make a life at walden pond he said: "It will be a success if I shall have *left myself behind*" (my emphasis). How ironic when we realize, thoreau's overarching passion was in fact to make his retreat into Nature the very means of *finding* himself (finding his Self), not losing it. For since his passion was to reconnect w some earlier lifestyle of our species, his search could not have been otherwise than to reconnect w some former less-superficial selfhood —an act which would leave behind (lose) not "himself" per se but his superficial (civil) self –the repressive aspects of his domesticated persona– thereby locating (finding) his precivil self *within*. In fact, it was this very process of isolation from society (from civility) which enabled thoreau to discover how to live by the rules&expectations of his Natural Self —to learn to live again w that deep Self in each of us, that very Self which it is the overarching goal of the civilizing principle to obliterate!)

Every time we act civil/-domesticated at the expense of our Natural/-instinctual selfs we are doing our (civil) part to disseminate the general-ized morbidity innate in the civilizing principle.

A fault beside the outcrop on which we'd rested had eroded into a steep narrow path which passed under a rock bridge, which i had always to duck <Low rock!> but she didnt. <I call this pass the laundry chute. [which, winding down, opened into:] And this here is littlest canyon.> Concentrating on not falling, she followed into the rock ravine. "Wow. This *is* impressive! I'd call it a canyon! Hey, it echos here! How far t' the top?"

From lowest ta highest, about five/six stories. Not exactly a canyon [or an alley titanic] but it tries. These, t' our left, are the same three monoliths ...escarpments, actually... that we saw from above. I call them *los tres conquistadores* ...because they ventured out, took by force what wasnt theirs to take. This here's desoto. Next there, with the tree on his head, is drake. 'N' last but not least, positively pathologic cortez.

"You have a name for everything here. <Not nearly.> They remind *me* of a gigantic girl-mother-crone trilith. Lintelless, of course."

Explain trilith. She did. Turnedout, i knew of such things but had never heard the term...or fully acknowledged its matrifocal origins.

About halfway down to cortez i stopped. Now this here [to her immed right at eye level] looks like a solid wall of stone doesnt it?

"At this point i'm afraid t' say [hits w side of fist] Yes, prettydarn solid."

I tap w an index the rock face at a point just in front of her own. See anything here?

Leans forward so that the bill of her cap is allbut grazing the rock. "Nope."

I reach over, coaxout w a knife-tip a small 'drawer' of sandstone, hand it to her, scrapeout a few months' silt that has gathered at the hollow rear of the slot. <Natural safe.>

"Sheesh. How ever did you find it?"

The stone was ajar. Caught my eye on the way down one day.

"That musta been painful. Thank goodness the jar wasnt broken."

Oooof. *That pun* is what's painful. Now ***i*** owe *you.* I hand her the stone to put back.

"Did you hear that? ...No, really. Listen. [slides stone in&out] Sounds like the keystone scrape of some ancient burial vault, no?" [stands back, makes a sternly scrunched face at the wall] Open says me!"

Boy, are *you* ever in rare form t'day. We gotta cutback on your sleep. (I was happily reminded of our first date.) I flushup stone w rest of wall; we move on. After completing the n route into the mouth of frikka's cove ("Wow. There's the falls!") we climbed to the grotto pool. Some o' the steepest drops this side of little river canyon [which i'd pointedout on our way in from atlanta] line the sidewalls of the cove here. "Now *that* is definitely high." About ten stories. But... "What?" I walk her around some trees blocking the e face. Look right thru there. "Where? Damn! [blinks disbelieving]" That's about a twennystory drop, no layovers. "R'mind me ta stay clear." We jus came down from there. "What?" See that outcropping...? That's where we rested after you fell. Frikka's funnel is just to the left...*there*. Thick tree-cover makes it hard to judge heights from above.

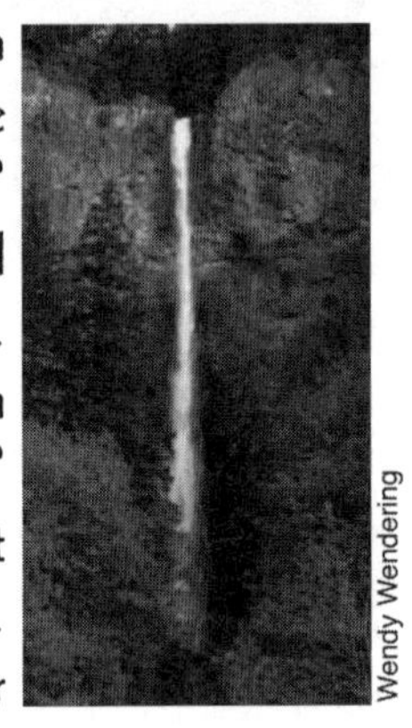
Wendy Wendering

After an extended silent study i could not track, she shuffled down to pool's edge, dropped to all fours for a longlong drink. Her fingers seemed as much to be holding on to Mothernature's stony breast as supporting her weight. When she came up for air she said, "Cold, umm. An' delicious. [wipes lips w arm] I see why animals love this place. Has all the amenities."

Joanne Galdamez

After i refilled my waterbottle we sat poolside. <This right here was the grotto a couple thousand years ago. It had a way-larger falls backthen as you c'n see by the hole.> When we'd caught our breath we hiked down, creekside, to show her where muir creek went underground for some 80m before reemerging, proceeding to river's edge. (L will later nickname that stretch of the creek, arethusa.) When we came to the creek's basin, and she could see out thru the forest-lined watery corridor to the river beyond, she stopped breathing. "Ya know, i cant b'lieve this place. It's gorgeous. Lush. Pristine. Even in winter. No wonder you love it here."

Steep hikes are hard work. Even when the wx is cool one worksup a sweat. To cool down, we took off boots ɛ socks, waded in the creek basin ["Brrrr damn, now THAT's cold."] til we reached the little sandy beach which led out over a nub of land to the river proper. There we tookout a canoe while our jeans drip-dried (on us) in the weak but still warmish afternoon sun. When time to head back, we took the steep-but-better-graded path up the w face of the bluff to the chalet and, in time for sunset, walked s down the monadnock to panorama point, my rejected homesite.

"Wow. This *is* the best view."

On rocky brow we loved to stand
and watch in silence, hand in hand,
the shadows veiling sea and land.

The rivervalley, falling into purple shadow, was visible n ɛ s for 20k that afternoon. We sat a spell on the rocky ridge, at a point worn almost level as the land around it.

When the deep purple falls over mountain-valley walls....

"This *is* gorgeous! [then shyly] But i hafta tell you: I pictured it steeper 'n' craggier than this ...not that it isnt breathtaking. It's jus this habit i have of sketching mentally while i listen, and your love for this place painted my mental image in ...o what should i call it ...a-, alpian, no ...a-, himalayan hyperbole. Which, i'm *very* relieved t' say, it isnt."

Himalayan? Is *that* all? ...That makes me *the welshman who went up a hillside 'n' came down a mountain,* doesnt it?> I then had only to spend the rest of the day convincing her she had not hurt my feelings.

In the flame-flecked rays of fast-fading lite a vanessa atalanta flittered around her every few mins, finally settling on the dark knot of her whorled hair.

I think he sees his buddies on your hat.

"He's a she" says she, w a hint of playfulness so subtle it made me wonder {How much of what this untypical miss typically says 'n' does do i typically miss?} "You better get home" she warns after awhile, shaking gently her hair thisway&that.

I want to say {I think it's a guy ...cause he landed on you not me} but say instead: He –er- she– thinks she *is* home, i b'lieve.

"It's gonna be dark soon, you silly [says she, as if warning a child, shaking her head, moving to rise] an' then you'll be bat bait." Makes pained expression, sits back down. <The early bat gets the flying worm.> I catch her pressing her hips w the heels of her hands, making a face. <Hurts?> "This is awful. I've become a flatlander. No, jus sore. [i query 'where' w my eyes] Mostly here ...in the hips. Feels like their gonna pop their sockets from all this up 'n' down."

No more hiking for you.

"But i love it. Really i do!"

Love what? Sore hips 'r hiking?

"Hiking, you goose ...An *you,* silly. Shoo!" Tho staring straight ahead at lites winking on in the valley she is thinking of the creature behind her head. Her lashes, themselves pulsing like dark vanessas under the long bill of her butterfly cap, she reaches back w her left hand and, w the tops of her fingers, fluffs the whorl of hair on which the creature persists in resting, ("Shoo, you silly!") bobbing her bob as a blossom is tossed by a breeze. "Get! ...Shoo!"

Like i said, he's ...er- she's... apparently planned to overnite with you. ...Such a tactic i understand completely.

Sitting, forearms on knees, peering under her lashes but over her arms, she looks over at me (also sitting), gives a sideswiping little glance –there ε gone like some ravishing grayblue apparition– which makes my blood lurch from aorta to capillary in one long cascade! {This woman is sooo beautiful i dare not linger on the thought.} And just as her looks were a composite of olivia ε mia, so her voice, specially on the sibilants (Shoo! Shoo, you silly *chouchou!)* seemed a union of two voices. In the simplest setting: add a wispy lisp to the voice ε manner of expression of L's friend sorrel rose (whom we will meet shortly), and youre there. Yet the reader, likely having no way of ever sampling sorrel's voice, needs other sonic clues. But is this important? Lilith's being the sweetest most fetching sound i've ever heard, i think my musically inclined readers will answer, yes. Therefor: Take the intonation of sarah brightman and overlay it w the delivery ε lisp of the stunningly multiloquent brilliant ε beautiful aarti shahani (freedom fiter) and youve prettymuch captured the spectrum of L's speech.

We'd better go. Youre getting cold. [i help her rise] You okay?

Yeh. It's just, well... I dont exactly know how t' walk with a butterfly on my head. Makes me feel like a highwire performer.

To get my mind off her maddening attractiveness. <I think what youre feeling –in the hips, i mean– might answer why so many people in these parts have such wide-track bodies. Makes me wonder if widening of the pelvis isnt Nature's way of lowering one's center of gravity.>

She thought about that as we headed back. "Arent mountain sheep 'n' goats wide of hip?" <*You* certainly arent, my goatling.> *Afraid of being praised, or even noticed,* she gave that fleeting ε sheepish (hic) grin-v.-grimace.

<Mountain goats. A-... hmmm.> Juanita's goat crossed our path in my mind. <A-, in four-footed animals, it would seem to me, when it comes to climbing, what we call hip-girth in us bipeds, in them, being quadpeds, may also translate to the distance between forelegs 'n' hindlegs, no?

"I c'n see that."

I'll hafta throw this one at denise. She's an anthropologist friend of mine.

From our book she knew whom i meant. "She's very smart. And pretty too."

If you mean the foto in our book, it's somewhat flattering ...ta *both* of us, actually. [*Die, Primitive! Anthropology & Imperialism.* —Ed.]

She coaxed onto a finger, then set down in the thickest foliage we could find, the hitchhiking vanessa. When we got back to the house (following a heart-rending sunset) we found a female barnswallow dead on the deck.

"Pauvre hirondelle! I hope youre no sibyl." She held it like she'd just given birth to it.

<Why do corvids never slam into my windows?>

"Theyre probably not as easily fooled by reflections." Almost stabbing to the quick **w** her sister's "duh" {Hadnt i warned her i owed her?}, i bit my tung. And as we buried it beneath the slender shadbark (which the basement-level deck enwrapped) she epitaphed, "Our humanity is measurable by how long we remember this swallow *slain by the false azure in the windowpane?"*.

Lilith

On newyear's eve we had dinner at the green bottle, my favorite huntsdell restaurant. Oddly i remember tabletalk for one item only. "One scene doesnt a great movie make, i know. But there's a scene from a movie i saw once where, if the rest o' the movie was anything like it, it's my most favorite." That trace anxiety i could usually sense when out in public seemed forgotten as she spoke. "Picture this hunk with an easy trustable smile squatting beside a young woman on a quiet suburban curb. Using a handful of small stones he has gathered, he sets about erecting in her cupped hand a miniature stone monument. With handsome concentration ...he reminded me alot of you, come ta think of it... he erects, just so, on the curve of her palm, his impromptu little artwork. Everything's justright in the scene –in contrast to my own life at that time– the liting, the timing, the birdsong, the facial expressions, camera angles, his gentle dialog... a cinematic treasure worth any thousand-odd of the usual 'trailer moments'.... [i didnt know quite how to respond] ...It was one o' those hafta-see movie-moments i guess."

<Maybe we can watch it some time.> Already i was fully ready to trust my busy sched to her esthetic sense.

"That's just it. We cant. <Why?> That's the only part o' the movie i *ever* saw... an i dont even know its title. ...or even who was in it. ...tho i'd know their faces if i saw them again. [rarely seeing movies, i was no help] Anyway, after he finishes stacking the tiny cairn —she's by the way been sitting there the whole time, hand extended, sort of dumbfounded as if wondering, 'Is this guy a little eccentric or am I jus wound too tite?'— the scene ends with him suddenly tipping her hand [hic], spilling his symmetrical little monument into the street, at which finale she gives a wee gasp of surprise and he, with a resigned shrug, says, 'Couldnt last forever' ...with which she, seeming-reluctantly, agrees: 'I guess not.' ...and the scene ends ...or i had ta go, i'm not sure which. [that misting that graying that distancing, had sifted into her gaze as she spoke] Been keeping an eye out for it [the movie] ever since... I'm beginning ta think maybe i dreamed the whole thing. The actress, whoever she was, had the warmest most expressive face i've seen since audrey hepburn. [*Still Breathing*. Joanna Going. —Ed.]

Wow. ...That's kinda sad. [she seemed not to get what i meant] I mean, never ta get ta see what might be your favorite movie. [eyebrows up, she internalizes this] It's like never getting to see or hear what could be your favorite story.

"Hnnn. I guess it is."

We "saw in" new year's day w a *real* wood fire (not the usual ecologs) ε music. Once we'd settled by the fireplace, each w his own *cacao au lait,* i explained the music i was about to play: songs of humpback whales... <Along with assorted pelagic verse read by a phlegmatic yet distinctive voice you may know. ["O? whose?" turnedout she meant whose *verse,* not, whose voice] Let's see. Melville, lawrence, roger payne, gary snyder, others too —mmm, cant remember.>

"Odd you should mention him. [raising up slightly] I quit his *turtle island* to study your *Nature 'n' the subconscious* an' forgot to go back." An attention-fixing hour later the recorded recitation ended w payne's *the voyage home.* <That is one of the most exquisite pieces of prosepoetry i've ever come across> i confessed once silence had fully resettled around us.

"I hafta have that."

A little longer i think and nothing could have kept us apart. For our bodies (as the line goes) *still remember[ed] each other,* still suffered from *a sort of shivery affection* we dared not unleash. What she feared most, i would find (lage was right about how poorly we sometimes read each other), was a repeat bout w separation trauma (!). As for me, the shaman of commonsense in me had by then facedoff w my panther lust. It growled lowly by firelite as it could fairly taste its prey. But i had vowed not to give the man-fear, which this lovely creature already owned, *any* excuse to revive, even if our deeper more fiery needs wished it so.

16

Come sa morn (plebian lyric) my plan was to be gone w Lilith (shoney's holiday breakfast in ft payne) when rachel came by to care for the horses. But it was not to be. Rachel ε friend, apparently a little hungover, were just finishingup at the barn when we got back and i was bound to intro each to each. Rachel, explaining for Lilith's benefit why her friend seemed to know me: "Everybody knows everybody who's anybody around here. an' nathan's definitely somebody."

Rachel, 'n' her sister, tara, own the horses ...their parent's are among the most open-minded people i know [not quite the truth but not quite a fib either], a valuable commodity in these parts ...Rach keeps me uptodate on my neighbors' latest sentiments. Her sister's the one i told you invented the phrase, how does it go again, ray? "Let's see. Some churchly babble about, hmm, bahbls [bibles], baybls [babels] 'n' beezlbubs.[sic] Dont look at me. That's how these people up here talk."

To L: Did i mention the ongoing war b'tween the townies 'n' the rurals here?

"You explained what *causes* it in your books."

"People here on the mountain hate us cityfolk. We donno why."

Scotsmoor? A city?

"It's jus what they do best up here. [adds her friend] They hate outsiders."

Where i expected tension between them not only did very little develop, before they left rachel was reminding Lilith to use the horses all she wanted, surmising just a little sarcastically, "An maybe nate here 'll even spare you an hour 'r two 'n' go riding." While "nate here" just stood by, devoid of *touche* as usual, and the ladies enjoyed a little gender-fun at his expense ...a method bytheway which females, even civilized ones, despising violence as they typically do, have of defusing –via talk ɛ busyness– tensions which arise between them. The most expedient –if unspoken– method of accomplishing this is to find consensus on some issue, *any* issue. A vehicle often chosen these days is, women can take men or leave them. And so, whether i existed or not just then was incidental. Under the circumstances, this worked for me as well. As to the part about me rarely making time to go riding, it was factual.

As we walked away: "Intelligent girl. Could double for an actress i've seen."

Angelina jolie? ["Ya know, i think that's it?"] Everyone says that."

L's passion for riding, plus my passion for L, plus factoring in the lovely wx, prettymuch addsup to how we spent most of her last day at ggNs: purveying from horseback the sanct ɛ environs, along trails as little used at the time as they doubtless are today. *This* being Lilith's idea of a "terrific" way to end a vacation, we did just that. That was the day she replied, finally, to my 3legged horse question."Because two of the four hoofs are striking the ground at the same time.

17

Essential disclaimer: When tara first called my mtn neighbors "redneck fundies" (fundamentalists) i did not quibble —for two reasons. ❶ i had to thinkthru her assessment, and ❷ being frankly quite taken w her from the gitgo, i have long known that the quickest way to findout who someone really is is to give them the freedom to show it. Today i realize my new mtn iso contributed some to my tara attachment. But not enuf i think to blind me. I knew there was little difference between calling someone a redneck or a wetback, a redskin or a slanteye. All are degrading; all project our DIE, PRIMITIVE! civilchimpnobo-gene fears. And so i waited to state my case.

A few months later: Are you as hard on urban fundies as you are on redneck ones? The comparison had never occurred to her.We also addressed tara's other redneck principle: A redneck is a cowboy stripped of legend. When we talked this thru it became obvious, she had in mind ranch-style rednecks, a class whose thoughts ε hands arent in the soil (as are the family farmer's) but whose hands have been dripping w the blood of slaughtered cattle, bison ε Wild carnivores for generations. Big difference. The amish forinstance are some of the most instinct-repressed fundies civil society ever invented yet their attachment to the soil is so rich that, even w the lethal load of religious repressions they tote thru life, they have little stomach for violence. Never underestimate the positive power of staying intimate w Mothernature's soil, even if it's 'only' in the family garden.

≈The truly rich and truly royal are persons of the land and soil.≈ —emerson

The redneck accusation is inevitable among newcomers to alp mtn. When it was made earlyon both by lalage ε their mutual friend clarisse, Lilith shared what i found then, and still find today, a fascinating insight. "A poet named oscar hammerstein spotted the difference between ranchers 'n' farmers waybackwhen he wrote *oklahoma*. [" *What* are you talking about?"] Well, the ranchers, whom he called 'cowmen', were trying to run the farmers, whom he called 'plowmen', out of the west." She proceeded to read the ranchers as "aggressive colonialists" and the farmers as "passive colonialists. It's been the same story all over the world, not just in america. While both ranchers *and* farmers feel they have some divine right to runoff all indigenous life, including people, only one of them, the ranchers, feel that that right extends to runningoff the farmers too. Ranchers abusing farmers is a classic high-end case of nathan's DIE, PRIMITIVE! imperium at work, defined in musical theater of all places!" While i dont think even lage had any clue what she was talking about, what Lilith had encapsulated was: If it is civil to think of all seeming-simplistic things as lesser than one's own 'sophisticated' self, then "doing away with farmers is only a step away from doing away with the indigenous people who preceded them …'n' so on down the line to the most trusting 'n' therefor defenseless. And we will continue like this til we finally realize where our worldview of conflict 'n' destruction originates. That cause is exposed in nathan's civilizing principle. I know i keep saying this, but you guys *really* should read him some time."

18

After meeting rachel ε friend we returned to the chalet to change for our ride. "Now *this* is a functional foyer". A conversation we'd had following breakfast, while sightseeing the length of bluff rd, triggered this remark. I guess it's not hard to spot the rude money hereabouts, i had said as we cruised by one particularly imperial monstrosity overlooking the river.

"Theyve jus *got* to know their house …er, castle… is yelling to all who pass, 'Look how fabulously wealthy we are!'"

A culture which values money (material possession) over wisdom can only self-destruct.

I'm sure of it…. Ya know, ta build a house like that in *any* neighborhood is a slapintheface to most living things. But to do so in one of the most economically depressed regions in america is nothing short of psychological brutality. An' ah'll tell ya, theyre lucky they built that castle *here*. For a people not so ethical as my neighbors would consider such a display criminal incitation, with routine defacement 'n' burglary the least response owed to such gross brutality.

"Just the smell of food cooking is cruel 'n' unusual punishment for the hungry."

I had long ago barred from my future home all floorplans w imperial main-entrances. "A family of four, you say? That's nothing! *Two* families of four could live elegantly in *our* foyer!" The rude rich utter such words w no smidgen of shame as to the hundreds of millions of homeless, specially the children. Such displays are the ultimate pornography. For it is in the institutionalized foyer that we, the civilly sophisticated, attempt to shed all sign of (uncontrollable) Nature before entering that zone of (highly controlled) culture we call home. Had i the money to burn i would long ago have bought double lots in a bunch of IMPERIOUS-FOYER ESTATES, constructed entryways twice the height&width of all around them (minus the house itself), set 2-3 lofts of private livingspace behind all the towering glass ε chandeliers, and dedicated each to homeless-family use. This is the only proper response to the me-me arrogance/greed which lives in the cold embrace of such obstreperous obscenity. So, no. I vowed my home would have no imperious vestibule. The only propylaeum to *my* home is Nature's own nymphaeum: goethe grotto itself.

Lilith

Altho thruout that day i got fuzzy signals which exceeded platonic, i was on a mission: clarity or nothing. I kept it light thru supper ε kitchen cleanup, all of which she insisted on helping **w**. Then, when any other couple would have settledinto the romantic fireplace glow, i announced <No visit here is complete without a little stargazing>.

It was a standard winter eve on the mtn, temperate for that latitude, and dry enuf that the cold was not uncomfortable. As we climbed the tower steps under a cloudless sky (still high adventure for her): "This is like a scene from *mermaids.* <Book?> Movie." After spending some time scoping the few nebula i could quickly index for her (eliciting a string of ooohs ε goshes), after locating her first live look at a spiral galaxy (Sheesh! Wow!) the lockon-tracking failed. <Wouldntcha know?> So i closed the scope, turnedon the fans, squeegeed the dome clear of condensation and settled back on the observation couch for a little <nakedeye viewing>.

"I beg your pardon. I'm not that kind of girl" she quipped. *'Les filles de frisco n'entendent pas cela!'"* she sang in an aside.

{What a stunning mind! *and* voice!} i thought as i spoke: I dont see the constellations in their classical arabic 'n' greek cerements. I see them as nakedeye stargazers always saw them; i mean, as arrangements of lite-points in anthropic juxtapositions. Given her arts background she'd have better understood had i had the agility of mind to say: commonly identifiable juxtapositions of pointillistic constellates twinkling on the dome of nite. ["I have only the weëest clue of what youre saying."] Sorry. How to explain? Hmm. ...I see the constellations as obtaining their identities not from mythology so much as from how these figures playoff each other in the sky.

["Now *that* i get."] Name a constellation. Any constellation. [left pinky sweeping across billions of liteyears it settles on & names "Nastynasty hunter orion, there. Too obvious?"] No. Good choice, actually. When i look at orion i dont so much see the famous hunter killed by artemis, or by a scorpion bite. For me, *those* stories are not in *this* sky. I see rather a bowhunter who, only a moment before, was chasing down your pet lepus, over there ["Hi, brite eyes!"] ...a supposition supported by his main [hunting] dog ["Yes, nastynasty mog- i mean, canis"] ...right. Canis... being so close as it is on your rabbit's tail ["You *go,* hoppin hiney!"]. We see orion about to faceoff against the bull, over there ["Yes, taurus. I know him too now"], which has threatened to gore the hunter if he so much as harms a hair on the hind of your hare.

"This is like your very own bedtime story." <Youre poking fun.> No i'm not. In fact, if you quit i'll be sad. [serious eyes by starlite] For me, hares 'n' butterflies are perfect metaphors for primal contentment 'n' tolerance...."

My brand of skylore likes your brand of metaphor.

"Like plants, i see hares 'n' butterflies as animative of *all* Gaia's *poor creatures born t' die.*"

<Now youre tryin ta get me tearyeyed.> My circumvisuals catch her checking if it is so. (It was.)

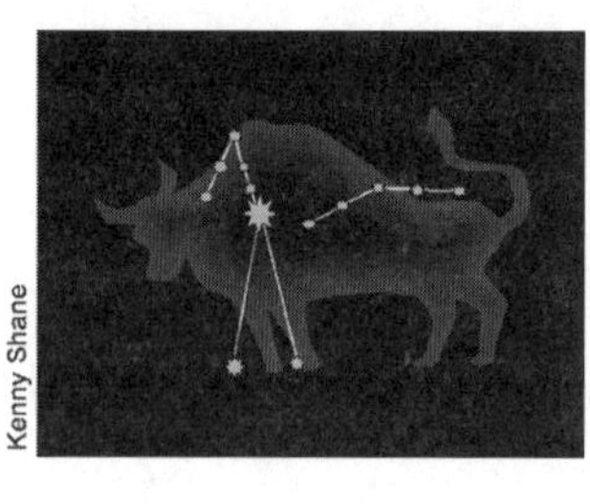

Kenny Shane

"Dont those two radiants, there 'n' there, represent taurus' horns?" She pronounced it properly: tower-us (pardon the pun). <Yes.> Well, they look to me aimed at gemini [the twins] not at orion, no?" Done pointing, the back of her hand comes to rest (accidentally?) grazing the back of mine.

How perceptive. [i touch that hand, w fingertips only] But that's because taurus also has the job of pr'tecting the twins...whom he sees as two lovely heifers named castra 'n' polly... pr'tect them from leo, crouched there behind them [untouch her hand to indicate head & tail of the lion], whom i interpret as the sexual panther crouched inside most males. [hand seems closer when mine returns]

"Youve got this story down. Bet youve told it a dozen times."

Two 'r three maybe... But not like this. Both of us were reminded of our big sur hotsprings bath.

"*Nota bene.* Pleiades there, hyades there. All the nymphs hang near the bull, dont they?"

I must say, you are *way* more nitesky- ...well, constellate... conversant since last we whispered by starshine. ["Ooof. Way poetic, mr schock."] Sorry. ["But i love it."] Stargazing makes me unabashedly rightbrainish.

"Me too. ...I've been boningup alot since i made my waywhopping fauxpas that nite. <What nite's that?> When i thought sirius was venus?

O that. Manyuv done that.

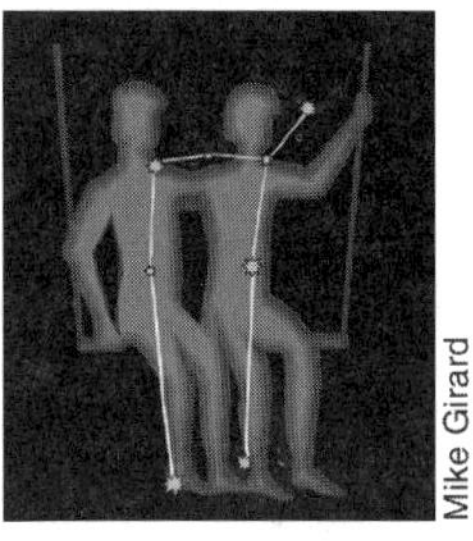

Mike Girard

"Those who cant tell a dipstick from an ecliptic maybe. Frinstance i learned, gemini was called twins long before nakedeye astronomy could have known it is madeup almost totally of binaries! Even the ancient sumerans called castor 'n' pollux twins! An' *that* was wayway back. An' ta beat all, ya know how twins alot o' times seem incomplete as individuals? <A-....> How it often takes *both* twins to resemble a whole person? <Umm....> Anyway, studies have named it intracomplementarity, where one twin ...among mz's (one-eggers, i mean)... gets all the emotions while the other seems incapable of feeling. Then there's this too: You mayuv heard where ancient chinese astronomers <Great astronomers, yes. *Before* the ancient greeks.> both in china and in what is now known as korea. Anyway, they saw in gemini –these twin stars, socalled– the yin 'n' yang duality of Nature and the Universe. Talk about your intracomplementarity of twins! All of which historical twin-ascription ...to a bunch of stars which much later turnout t' be not only binaries but *double*-binaries... strikes this amateur as waaaay beyond the potential of mere serendipity if i must say."

Wow. You *have* been boningup. {Aaaargh, i should talk.} I never knew one bit o' that...that...astroarcheology. Very int'resting. And so we chatted —in deference to Lilith's, let us just say, 'artemisian fear of male passion'.

Silent space slips by. "Under this starry influence its easy t' slipaway to a state of primal wonderment."

Ooof. Way poetic, ms McGrae.> We were allbut whispering by then.

"But true, no?"

Nat'ral as breathing, i'd say.

We finishedup the nite wout the *mermaids* "tower scene"-ending however. It was this nite, i believe, which presaged & prestaged a twilite ritual we would later adopt.

19

Unable to reach Lilith at her dorm or the school, animaze studios had called gE to confirm she would be on hand (in l.a) by the 5th (movedup from the 10th). There being no sign of elation just anxiety over the date change, at the time i took it as modesty. Lage called the eve before L left. When she asked "Is Sis there?" i replied w something along the lines of, You mean of course the soon-t'-be-rich 'n' famous cartoonist?, to which she quipped, *"and* talented *and* beautiful *and* I'm gonna barf if ya dont put her on quick".

The animaze startdate proved untimely since, according to lage, don was not feeling well —of concern, since she couldnt remember "ever" seeing their dad sick. Seems the animators were also waiting to foto & sketch an in-the-flesh example of captain gE's "gimmy-cut" chest, a look i preserved only vestigially once i left tinseltown and my thoughts turned to more crucial matters. To that end, after lage's call, L & me put together a portfolio from my body-sculpting days. I incl'd a note suggesting they use lex reever if a reallife model was needed since he stayed in far better shape than me and since, not incidentally, he was first to incarnate the gimmy-cut chest.

20

After only a couple years at ggNs it started happening, and eversince i have departed "my" mountains reluctantly, lingering on as long as possible, reveling in their wonders, their secrets, til i absolutely had to go. And the longer i lived there, the worse it got. How glad i was as we readied to leave for the airport that morn, that for once i'd be back in a few hours. This eased for me Lilith's return to ca.

Heading s after little river canyon ("We have a 'little river' back home too!"), wooded mtns downgrade into rolling farmland, the farmland, slowly, into small towns, and then, further on, to inevitable city & industry. Papermill stink ("scarlett's rotting corpse", as it's known to greens from ga) always precedes, if not the w.border of ga itself, at least the cities of coosa & rome. Such ugliness after such beauty always shocks me. Lee took it all in. "People live here [rome] all their lives, dont they... when only ten/twenny miles away they could, well, escape poisoning themselves, their kids 'n' their animals."

Not to cut you short but, the brite side is, we should thank our lucky stars for romans; romans past, romans present; romans here, romans abroad. Millions died young in old rome from lead poisoning. They wouldnt listen to the shepherds 'n' farmers from the surrounding hills who said the water from their aqueducts tasted like poison.

"Like youve said, the townies have always felt superior to the rurals. Civilization hasnt changed ...basically."

Just worse in the same old ways. Civil devolution.

"Too short smart, too long dumb, as jon windstar's granny usta say."

Revere your instinctive simplicity, my *Naturally* sophisticated friends. For the highly civil among us are artificially complicated monsters, unNaturally fabricated using the flesh of that frankensteinian flaw i have named, the civilizing principle.

We chuckled over the many dysgrammatic signs, which so humorously outed the motives of commerce: KRAZY KENZ FIREWORX, SKINNY ENNISES GYM, across the street from FATBOYS BARBY-Q, and, best of all, FLIM FLAM AUTO [sic all]. My patient reader probably thinks i'm making this stuff up as we head e.ward. Not so. Chuckles are followed by silence as one begins to dread the appearance of i75 and its steel-heaped rapids of roiling insanity. <This transition from quasiWild to craziCivil gets harder for me every year.>

Once the triathalon of tricky turnoffs & linkups was negotiated and we'd entered safely the s.bound tsunami, Lee asked, "What does gimmy-cut mean anyway?" We had poredover my albums the nite before gathering a sheaf of poses which she was sure, from an artist's point of view, even the fussiest animator could make do w in my or lex's absence.

Squared-off chest... How can i explain this? Almost the chest you gave the captain... with a couple changes.

She took a vinyl pouch from the backseat, removed from it a sketchpad, made on her leotarded legs an impromptu desktop, slid over against the console, handed me a pen. "Show changes." Traffic heavy, pace insane, my sketch is a squiggly mess which misses the crucial finepoints. Sliding back into her seat, pen poised, she says, "Splain it then."

Let's see. Take the sides of a v... No, use a backward slash and a forward slash... Right. Now separate their bases with a straight line four –no, make that *three*– times their length... That's perfect. You mustuv done this b'fore. [smiles] Now add two dots, for nipples... No, closer to the baseline... No, here [i point], jus b'fore the pectoral slashes cut upward to wrap onto the shoulders... Right. Now roundoff the angles... just a tad... and youve got it. No, the cleavage, [point] in there, should have no roundness to it; straight up... there... very little depression except for the tiniest notch... right there, over the sternum, where the muscles insert.

"Which doesnt show anyway... except when he [captain gE] removes his shirt."

Does troy trent ever remove his shirt?

"Every time he becomes the captain."

I mean, remove his *captain* shirt.

"O that. Later in the story, maybe.... Ya hafta ramember. I was 15 before i saw you without clothes." (O what the fed. & their gossip-mongering press would have paid for a recording of *that* little gem out of context!)

I beg your pardon.

"O, you know what I mean. ...And, it was a rude awakening. <Well thanx.> Not *that* way, you goose. I mean, ta findout that ...well... gay males... and, not t' forget those ladies who love wrestler types, had been ogling your near-naked body for years while i, working alone 'n' outa touch somewhere in virginia, had t' invent a body for you with pen 'n' ink."

<And how close you came to the fact is nothing short of awesome. Say, i've been meaning to ask. How'd you come t' make the captain left-handed waybackthen? [i'd figured it was just a projection of her own handedness] "By your videos." Right. You must be really observant.

From the start she had put capt.gE in a forestgreen bodysuit, which meant she had to invent a bodystyle for him. What i found amazing was, she cameup w a fair facsimile of me in my early 20s, back when i was full of false pride, lost & insecure. In mere seconds she finished a neck-to-waist sketch, amazing to watch, like the blooming of a flower in fast-forward. "But none of this explains the name, gimmy cut?"

That was lex's doing: a chest built in such a way as to create a high unbroken mantle of muscle, a look which reminded many muscle mavens in the sixties of the high-chested look of certain g-m-c 'n' chevy trucks common on the highways backthen —called c-o-e's. [C-o-e's?] Yeah. Acronym for cab-over-engine; no relation to my friend bryn coe, whose picture you saw.

"And gimmy?"

Thought i explained?

"Not yet."

I get it. You think gimmy was a person? [Uhuh] No. Gimmy's a petname g-m-c owners give their trucks. You may have seen it on vehicles: I LOVE MY GIMMY, or somesuch corporate hook. Of course, some people thought there for awhile that the gimmy-cut was named after a mr america from florida, a reever/schock lookalike named james haislop.

"It's mostly greek t' me."

...And *should* be, come to think of it. Didnt they start it all?

"That's what i meant."

Which subtlety i might have spotted were i not dodging vehicles diverging & reconverging around us like we were an island amidst total whitewater —even tho i was going 10k over the "legal" limit! With much rewriting i dictated for her notes, <...a straightacross undertuck of the pecs which, after bisecting the nipples, takes an oblique tack straight to the shoulder; a uniquely masculine effect because it joins the pectorals almost seamlessly, closingup the usually unmuscled area of the sternum and thus obliterating cleavage, straightening in the process all those roundnesses we associate with the female chest ...the antithesis of gynacomastia. A physical therapist in hollywood put it this way (ol mnemy 'll have it here in a sec... ah, here it comes): "Reever turned bodybuilding's hunkaboobalas into hunkabrickalas.>

Places pouch by her feet, removes sweater, a bulky cream-colored thing zigzagged along its hem ε cuffs by a reddish-brown continuum of v's we've come to associate w amerind art; laid it modestly across her lap, forestalling the leap of my lecher eyes which had been wondering as to those underskirt places toward which the flow of black leotard led. How *did* you come up with the captain's physique? i asked, shielding my thoughts from view.

"By crossing *superman* comics with julie beltrán's *conan* ...with, hopefully, a touch o' the great frazetta."

That's interesting, cause my friend lex borrowed the look from superman too, built it onto his own body ...from comicbooks he read as a kid. Later, hollywood put him in lites where, eventually, i saw him; borrowed the gimmy-cut a *second* time for myself. After that *you* borrowed it one more time for the captain. And so we whiled [sic] our way into atlanta. I've bothered to mention these incidentals only because a myth-to-reality-and-back-to-myth-again cycle was thus completed. In half a century the gimmy-cut look had made a circular metamorphosis, starting as a fictional character (world hero, *superman* comics), blossomed into a humanbeing (lex reever), next borrowed for another human (yours truly), and finally returned (by way of Lilith's cartoon) to a fictional setting (world hero, *captain greenEarth*). Sad to say, however, Lilith's wonderful stories will probably remain fiction indefinitely, surely til after i'm dead. And, judging, clear-eyed ε brave, by the state of human sensibility in the civil world at large today, maybe forever.

21

The all-unifying cosmic braid i'd been trying to weave thru the essays of my 7th book had frayed substantially since meeting Lilith. After *Mothernature & the world matron* was broughtout in '92, my publisher, foreseeing difficulty, agreed to a rather distant deadline of sep '95 for my *Ecocosm: the Cosmic Gaia*. And now, due on the road for part b of my lecture series, my hope of mastering the grand ephemeral threads of that braid was fading fast. From prior deadlines however i knew, for me the surest way to resolution was hiking. Once back at ggNs i ate, packed a canteen, recorded 'gone hiking' on my private memopad and headed n along the bluff.

The essays which comprise *Ecocosm* (never polished to my satisfaction) enfold, win a context of Wildlife settings, at least one-each astrophysical phenomenon. This they do well. My problem was, my previous six books ended w chapters so unifying as to bring about a strong closing. As *Ecocosm* existed at that time, it lacked such a powerful wrap. "The thrust of the essays so far is self-unifying and precludes the necessity for a splashy closure" wrote my editor, hoping i think for an early wrap. "Some grand summation or other might even be anticlimactic." Yet wout the keys to such a powerful unifier woven into each essay, i felt stymied. At dusk when i returned, collected my mxs, one was from bekky. Seems she'd been "tangling again" w my world matron, wanted to visit before i left on tour.

On wedn i called Lilith. Afterall, i didnt even know if she'd arrived safely. "I'm doin ok. Sis calls every day." Prod, pry. It turnedout, don's test results were back. "But he's outa town 'n' we jus know the doctor has bad news." As to things at the studio? "Okay i guess. [more prod&pry] Well, sorta." It turnedout, "They treat me well enuf but ...well, it's like i dont know diddly about what makes a good cartoon." When i call on thu i learn don has told "the girls" nothing about his test results. As for animaze productions (coax, prod, pry) i learn, the problem is w the director. "He listens to my input privately but ignores it in the script. He's prettymuch doing as he pleases with my captain." I make her promise to tell brian firsthing in the morn. Still more prying reveals "The school's bringing in julie beltrán for a class on 'the flesh metallic' and i cant be there." It turned out, L's "art teach", back in oct, on learning Lilith's work was being animated for tv and knowing beltrán's work had influenced her ("after frazetta, who is of course the davinci of illustrators"), had troubled to get beltrán to do a masterclass. But, ironically, studio troubles preempted her from attending. All these things were colluding to cause L's unspoken melancholy.

Meanwhile the great essay unifier i sought, and which i tried always to keep adumbrating my subconscious, refused to reveal itself. So on fr morn, my last wkend home, i setoff on another hike ...to locate that stunning Earth/Cosmos unifier i so often intuit; something beyond the wellknown: There is "stardust" in every handful of Earth, in every breathful of *us!* An aggravating on/off drizzle by noon turned into a steady rain. Soon slippery conditions drove me back home, no betteroff for the effort. Frustrated, disappointed, i decide not to call Lilith as i know my gray mood is sure to ruboff on her. On sat morn i find a mx from L (back at dillon beach for the wkend). When i call lage answers. "She's still sleeping.... Not too bueno akchally." Lage cant tell if its "botherations at the studio 'r worriments over daddy. 'Sides that, she misses you. But i'm not supposed t' say." This i'd not guessed. In fact, i assumed L's reticence of late was disinterest, even thought her request ("Could i get a foto of the grotto, 'n' maybe one from the bridge by the falls?") was just a courteous tag to another otherwise tepid fonecall.

Like it or not, by some emotional mischief, Lilith had nuzzled down thru many a lonely autumn into the leaf-layers of my former luvs, had got linkedUp somewhere behind quotidian awareness w the lost juanita. Apparently i was a house divided and head needed to findout what heart had gone&done wout its permission. Was *this* the source of my distraction, my malaise? Was Lilith that olympic female, the lover that cleanses & closes all wounds? How scary. But why? Let me hear you enunciate the words, nathan: Essential other, love of my life. But i could not. I discovered that i felt ...that i believed in fact... the moment i did so, like the nymphs priscilla & juanita, Lilith would just vanish into the forested deeps of my existence!

22

Despite my most heroic efforts, the image of rosa poza —silly sexy poor victimized rosa poza, this very second smearing her sweat on the same weightbench i will be using shortly— keeps popping to mind. (Does she towel it off when done?) There is so much i have to do, yet the mere body of a *détenue* a couple hundred meters away tugs at my sensibilities like a child's popUp book —which i keep slamming shut & putting down and yet which fantastically, as in a dream, i find in my hands again, its silly folded-shut cardboard images somehow poppedup again, taunting me to forget my tasks, my goals, and come & play makebelieve.

As a free man i would simply take care of this pernicious drive of mine, this temporary insanity called lust. But in this place, under the thumb of my self-enforced monkdom (& therefore stalked by my own pantherlust) hour on hour, day on day, insidiously, popup memories become my tormentor. Soon i am thinking, Yes! Make it happen! What's the harm? After all, it's only sex —among consenting creatures at that. As Lilith herself has written. "What's the big deal? Sex sex sex! People are totally whacked about it! It is what it is: It's fantastic, it's boring or it's hideous, and then it's done. And we should move on. If we dont rave rhapsodic about the bathroom visits we've had, why do so with sex?" Handy method of escaping one's past? of making anyone curious about that past feel foolish inquiring? and yet so so sensible. What *is* the big deal. Any dog or dogwood can procreate. But then neither should we be ashamed of this ...Do you hear, nathan? Tell rosa, yes. Get on w life ...such little of it as there is around here.

Desire, unsated, reduces even the wisest of us to panting maniacs. The shadow of desire skulks along the peripheries of our highest callings. The monster w four legs pops up&down, crushing its squealing catch, as my imagination, absolutely wout my permission, opens ε slams the little popupBook til the deed is done. And here i am, a man who has loved ε been loved by the most beautiful Creature that ever moved over the face of Motherearth. Yet the body of a woman i dont even know tugs hourly at my mind like there is nothing else in the Universe just now. WillyS came close: Desire is absolutely a form of madness! It is a long time since i have suffered guilt over my sexuality. Since the days when i didnt know better in fact. But this celibate existence: *this* is the sort of sexuality one can quickly grow ashamed of. No wonder the slug asks firsthing every time i see him: "Changed your mind about anything yet, schock? Any wee little thing?" I am convinced, deprivation ε repression of Natural desire are the parents of belief in "good&evil". Specially in the minds of those who dont understand what's happening. Deprivation of brite healthy instinct slowly erodes self-respect, grows itself into a degraded beast in the afflicted mind! Celibacy has made stark to me how civil religions' view of sexuality evolved.

Famous love affairs are famous precisely to the degree they reject the status quo, go about their merry or tragic way. For desire is a mad hatter, and civil desire, unleashed, is a state of being that will stop at nothing if not stopped by something. Where the first human lover gifted a flower, a polished nut or stone, as token of his desire, the civil lover would give a disneyland as wide as the orbit of pluto, then think nothing of casting about for something a little better to give next time! How far away did you say the nearest star is? Do the math. Control civil desire (the many madnesses of impassioned denial) and Planetary resources abuse would grind to a standstill —say nothing of the Planetary contagion of the (paranoid) civil birthrate.

How long did we date? a month or two? And were we as taken by desire as any two lovers? Yet all the while we were asking, why am i hanging from this cablecar? climbing this tower, this mountain? ignoring this condom? challenging this surf, those rocks? What i'm saying is, *our* love was DIFFERENT exactly *because* we were constantly asking: Couldnt we be even more fulfilled by some little walden in the woods? adrift on a river? sitting by a pond? watching a waterfall? dozingoff in a peaceful grotto, "with billions of Natures [as L used to say] a-hum all around us", connecting at last w one single place on this Earth, learning to want only what is necessary, and watching quietly while that place becomes the living thing it truly is (the living part of us it's been all along but we were too severed to see), watching as that Place gradually, inexorably, insists on incl'g us in its Cosmic legitimacy.

23

A brusque brash dustjacketer might view the Lilith/ns relationship as spiritually tested at big sur, fitted for mating at capitolaptos, and then collapsed by diverging goals, as happened w me ε veronika. Yet to an outsider w insight, obstacles ε difficulties bedamned, the collision of our destinies might just seem as inevitable as it does to me still tonite. After all, all events having to do w Lilith ε me as a *pair* is surely done ε overwith now, tho the best part of it may not as yet be setout in words —the *right* words. In all candidness, this is due simply to our union striving, from the start, to embrace the whole World. That we got as far as we did unsilenced unstopped by the skadjillion civil forces fundamentally arrayed against us —not even to mention those rabid enmities *specifically* targeting us from the start, most of them unknown to me— amounts to a chthonic outcry surely deserving investigation.

24

These "people" are well *beyond* fiction & fantasy. After breakfast today gluum (why alone?) enters, slips over to my cage. Happied by some nastiness or other he tells me to read "outloud" from an article circled in his latest tab, just as ratmoid has trained *him* to do. <Fine... FLORIDA APPEAL JURY GIVES MOLESTER-MURDERER MAX PUN. Following a four-week trial, yesterday a district court in Miami handed down its sentence for the molestation-murder in 1989 of a 6-year-old boy from Ocean City, New Jersey. David L. Herrick Jr, vice president of Life-Guard Insurance Underwriters of Boca Raton, Florida, stood pale-faced and stunned as the judge commented on the jury's speedy death sentence, calling Herrick "one of the most reprehensible forms of life this court has ever dealt with".... Yes, all true, i'm sure. But what has all this sorry putrefaction t' do with me?>

"Cause [grinning ear to ear] by tree oclock t'day dat skummy li'l chickenhawk shud be commin tru da main gate! Heh heh heh heh heh. [machinegun laff] *Freshmeat,* my horny friend! Backdoor justice strikes again!" Does sloppy softshoe (shu shi-shi shu shi-shi shu...) all the way to the iron door. "So let da games begin!" Exits w a "Yyyyesssss!" ε a clang.

25

On su bekky called to say she'd be arriving on sa. I suggest she meet me in saint louis [hic] the following su, explain how much traveltime (pollution) she can save sodoing. When later i speak w L, she tells of don leaving again on business, insisting his health-problem is "nothin t' fuss about". In bits&pieces by tu i've learned, "All the passion 'n' high-purpose i invested [her cartoon] are being ignored in favor of his [the director's] passion for man-on-man action 'n' special effects." But when i asked if she'd complained yet to brian? "Well, not exactly."

On wedn rick calls to ask if i'd heard epa chief obrien resigned? Rick's worst federal fears seemed coming to pass. By wedn eve i sense Lilith is thoroly depressed. I threaten to fly out even tho i'm due to lecture ε meet bekky on su. This perks her up. "Dont you dare." She promises to tell brian of her problems "right away". On th i learn from rick that hines, the director ("a flamer so vain he wishes he could bugger himself") is unreachable til mo. "We'll have brian straighten him out then." Fr eve Lilith's fone rings on&on. I console myself: {Bout time she got out for the evening. I mean, l-a? single? talented? intelligent? jaw-dropping goodlooks? C'mon, nate. Where's all that worldly objectivity?} Around 11 (that would be 9, l.a lounge-snake time), w L still not answering, i try the mcGrae res.

Hey, you.... Yeah, i called her apartment. Rings off the hook. Jus wond'ring how she's doin?

"Probly sleepin... Been pretty down lately. [Was i] still calling the old number? Changed apartments yesterday, ya know. Heat wasnt workin 'r sumthin." No i *didnt* know. As for Lilith complaining to brian: "Really? He [brian] was down there *twice* this week. Sis never said boo t' him [about hines] that I know of." Lage runs on, "Did she tell ya how her 'n' hines started out...? No? Get this. The fannywagger *began* their relationship with, 'Arent you a little young ta be in animation?' (delivered in bogus britspeak).

Instead o' tellin the fag ta get fucked (you know Sis, little miss saintlytush), she says not a peep. Since then it's been s-o-p between them: he makes condescending remarks, she takes them personally. I go, 'Well, hullo! It *is* personal! But then, track *this.* One of the animators ...No, not hines. Some guy assigned to her project. You shur yer still dialed-in here?... *Anyhoo,* yesterday this guy goes to Sis, 'Hines says that living-Earth theory is a bunch o' bad chemistry wrappedup in a fairytale'. Sooo, as you c'n see, he may be their finest director but, meanwhile, he's givin not jus Sis's cartoon but the captain too (that's you, case you havent heard), a double dickin. An' *that* i hope i *dont* hafta splain ta you...."

(How many men **w** clout, i think as i write this, could L have kept worrying (slavering) over her career had she just one manipulative bone in her body? I'm thinking now of that sable-haired girl **w** the violet eyes and how many slavering worshipers she kept always in her stable following her equine film triumph of the '40s.)

"...Sick? She's notsomuch sick, I think, as down with the damsel's dismals. With daddy, plus all the crap at the studio, say nothing of hating ta leave you back there at ranch nowhere, overwhelmed-by-life is probably more like it. So I'm thinkin I might go in fer her t'morra, ream that faggot sonuvabitch a new butthole as daddy poetically puts it."

Tho the sweater of linear thought is still snagged & unraveling on her barb "ranch nowhere", i reply, <You dont mean, go there *doubling* as her?>

"No. But why not, now that you mention it? It's time *somebody* gave all the politics there a kick in the ass, gave Sis's art a shot at success." I feel i'm hearing the hurt unspoken Lilith in her words. <It'd take ya halfaday jus t' get there.> Snay, nathan. I c'n lear outa s'noma any ol time. 'Sides, I could use some downtime from playin miss goody rasponsible round here."

Already having learnt, restraint just makes lage more determined, i decide not to try to disarm this lovely canon but aim it at a better target: *Personally* i'd go to hines' boss [studio owner named carter], *specially* if he's in lust with your Sister as you say. B'side, a friend tells me hines is outa town til monday.

"Youre not suggesting I go an' sacrifice my virginal resids for the cause?"

My hope is that youve learned by now, your power lies precisely in *not* sacrificing them. Anyway, explain virginal resids.

"What's left after a virgin makes an inglorious ass of herself" if ya wanna know. <Meaning?> When love drives a girl ta go an.... [clears throat] Look, c'n we do this some other time? I've got this *genuine* puppydog waiting on the other line who's all drooly 'n' doesnt even *know* my Sister."

Sorry. Hope those dont become famous last words.... Not one bit. This is me being sincere.

"I'll keep that in mind ...sincerely in mind. Thanks."

26

Sa just past noon (10:15pt). In the eyrie unable to concentrate all morn, gazing out over the river toward... toward what? Toward ca, i suddenly realize!.... Downstairs the following comes over the speakerfone: "Nathan!... Nathan, you there! Did you leave already? Youve jus *gotta* be there!... Pick up, please. Nathan!"

{Lilith! Damn!} I'm taking the eyrie steps two-at-a-time {Shit!} as her voice sounds near hysteria.

"Nathan! ...Nathan, listen. They took Sis! [loft steps now three-at-a-clip] Nate, I'm scared fer her! Look, I gotta go. Call me soon as you get this. I'm goin straight to the airport ta...." I pick up. She runsby the basics, voice fragged, continuity nonexistent. "I gotta go now ...figureout what I'm doing."

Look, it'll be okay. You'll see. I'll be outa here in a flash. Should arrive at lax [check clock] at least by seven. Hold tite. I'll call you in a couple hours... Hey.... [Huh?] I love you.

Distractedly: "Love you too."

Soon as i clickoff i order a chopper to atlanta out of huntsdell. In the middle of this it hits me. {You'll hafta cancel your lecture. Whoa, you canceled these people last year.} <Very bad.> There comes a point when thinking gives way to talking aloud to myself. {And what about bekky?} <Shit! I've canceled *her* once too many times too.>

27

On debarking at lax i spotted her at once. Her looks are even frequent-flyer stopping.

On the run ɛ in chaotic surroundings, it takes a certain male mind awhile to get past the somatic allure, spot the worry present in her features. My first awareness of who in fact has met me should have come at sight of her busy eyes, her use of cosmetics, her jewelry, her rippedup jeans; or even when she held my gaze as she spoke (in contrast to Lilith's shy downcast); or when we hugged —long slowdancing squeeze. But it didnt. It was the lift ɛ thrust in her walk, the whole-body turning ɛ gesturing, the mode ɛ pitch of her speech, the overt physicalness of her, which tipped me off when we started for her rentalcar —say nothing of the fact she was able to talk at all under the circumstances. When it hit me i felt exceedingly foolish, for i was secretly vexed to again be so wholly foxed by this visually viable *L'image.* I was thankful she was looking away when it hit me. Yet it turnedout she'd known all along. "It wasnt on purpose, you *know* that. We'd already hungup when it hit me. It was your 'I love you' that cued me, of course. But I figured, whatthehell. Maybe you wont worry so much if you think it's only me who's missing in action."

Wow. *That's* not nice.

"Sorry. Jus tryin t' lighten things here." Then, on leaving lax to go checkin w lex, last one to see Lilith: "But *such* a hug at the airport! You *an-ee-mal,* you! I thought my time had come! But when you said, 'God, i've missed you so much!', kissed my neck like that... [nostrils indent w deep breath, eyes scrunchdown] Well... [sighs] that prettymuch clued me from hollywood dreamtime ta realtime-l.a."

After the obligatory deadends which big hotels revel in ("No shortage o' glitznost round here"), we located lex in the lobby midway in an interview. Following our father/sonly exchanges, lage stepped up, gave him a hefty hug, thanked him for looking after her Sister. After searching her face for some mild strain of insanity, yet seeing none, easy-does-it lex finally said, "Hey, anybody'd uv done the same thing. I'm jus glad t' see y'r back safe 'n' sound." And so we explain. And so he is incredulous, having worked w Lilith for several days. (After *my own* error at the airport, i empathize: the looking eye seeing only lookalith in that bundle of lovely lookalage.) When i call lex my boyhood hero he says w a toothy weathered smile to lage, "I'm hoping someday t' deserve all o' nathan's misplaced adulation". Promising to get w him later, we left the goodnatured ɛ still "handsome *and* hardbodied" lug to his interview. Agreeing we are starved, on the way to "Get a bite" lage explains her last couple days. Turnedout, circumstances had her working again for ranking among the top20 elites: "Probly futile but worth the shot. Even the pros arent allowed my kinda hours. A sportscaster last year got sacked for calling women's gymnastics a legal form of child-abuse."

You must be exhausted.

"I wish. All this anxiety has me keyed to the max. If I dont hit a gym I'll never sleep t'nite."

Arent they closed?

"You kidding? This is lalaland, countryboy."

Ah yes. ...*And* your namesake.

"Jus so we dont go t' golds. My ex works there an' I dont know which one he's at."

Ira gold was assigned as my personal trainer back-when. Had only two gyms then. Now he's got what? Two hundred?

"Hey, that's right! You usta make movies in this town!" I hate it when drivers look full-at their passengers for more than a second, specially fast drivers in congested areas. After locating a gym by fone she tells of crampingup "way-bad" on the plane for having missed "my a.m limberup. There I was groaning rocking 'n' massaging my thigh ...as quietly as a girl can while in muscle-shredding agony... while two guys across from me were freaking, wanted t' help. <I'll bet they did.> The stewardess ...scuse me, flite attendant... tried t' stop me from breaking the cramp out in the aisle; said I was scaring the other passengers. Imagine! ...There I was with my heel hooked under my seat like this [demonstrates] while liderally hanging from the luggage rack!" The good part of her extempore demo –hands against car ceiling (yes, *both* hands), foot hooked under her seat– was that it left the accelerator idle long enuf to drop our speed to somewhere near the legal limit.

<Ya *did* see that hooker in the crosswalk right?>

I did. So I go ta her, 'Ya think if I jus sit there an' *scream* til we land it'll scare the passengers less?'" (Non-athletes cant imagine the pain which a highly trained muscle (or muscle-group) can put one thru when denied its regimen.) "I almos took their stupid wheelchair outa spite when we landed."

Thought i saw you limping a couple times there.

Tho the gym she found was unisex, the areas –incl'g a fully-outfitted tranny room– were largely discreet. And so i saw her workingout only sporadically ɛ at a distance. Following this we ate (on gym premises), got on our way. I hardly recognized the "town" anymore. My agents had long known i hated to lecture there —tho i had to on occasion. Turnedout later, lage, too proud to confess, had learnt her way around l.a huntingdown her first lover. Instead she quipped, "They dont call me l-a mcGrae fer nuthin. Wanna see my sixguns, mister? Huh, do ya?" [Her full name was Lalage Alise McGrae. —Ed.]

Ah'll be your huckleberry. [says i, adding] Where ya stayin?

Grins. "Guess." Seen from the side, the whites of her eyes were resplendent.

What? [still grinning] No? [and still] You jest. [and still] You *dont* jest.

She re:d what she at the time called "Our *désobéissance mais sans cozenage jeu*—correction, *retrouve*...No, make that, *d'amoureux*. [looks over] Hey, *I* didnt pick the place. *Sis* did. It *is* near the studio, ya know." [lips pursed, looks away, then back] Jus kidding. Tryin t' add a little levity here, that's all ...I'm in Sis's apartment, silly. And yes, there *is* a guest room 'n' bath."

An' no window b'tween rooms.

"Right. No window. ...Beats hell ouduv a park bench, I'd say. [impish grin again] But there *is* one tiny glitch. <O?> There's only one shower."

28

A reconstruct of events which led to my emergency trip is now in order. Times which follow are ~pacific time. And bit&pieces are, even at this late date, still missing; and still other evidence does not quite mesh. Better to leave things that way than dabble in speculation.

94.01.14, fr, 18:50. Animaze studios parkinglot, burbank. (The studios being small ɛ the new guys on the block, and w most of its stars born of a few sketches ɛ alot of imagination, it's parkinglot wasnt guarded like most.

The only security was at the main bldg.) Good friend lex reever, being salaried at the time to model for the animators *w* Lilith overseeing, had been keeping an eye out for her safety. For as he knew better than most, L ε he were working in one of civilz's most amoral metropoles. While walking to his own rental –having walked L to her car by which they'd stood talking for some time– lex notices a car (til then presumed unoccupied in the almost empty lot) startup ε cruise out the gate after her. 19:25. Suspicious, lex drives straight to L's apt where there is no answer either on the fone or at the door. A check of the hotel's garage reveals L's car but no L. 19:55. After checking back at L's apt, recalling ε rewaiting, lex sees no harm in calling 911. 20:20, lapd arrives, questions lex ε two of L's neighbors. Lex, afraid his intuition might be off the mark, and that Lilith may be just having a nite out as the cops suggest (after establishing that he is neither her father nor grandfather), goes home, plans to call her next morn and take things from there.

Sa., mcGrae res: 9:30, doctor's office leaves mx for don to be at frisco general's admitting at 16:30 on wedn the 19th to prep for surgery at 9a on the 20th. Lalage, having "slept in for a change", retrieves mxs, one of which is from animaze studios referring her to lapd. After hangingup *w* them lage panic-calls Lilith's apartment, then her own best friend, then me (whom i, recall, took to be Lilith). On her drive to sonoma lage tells of calling "fbi offices everywhere ...cause Sister said they'd been ta question her twice about some guy's murder. <What?> Yes. Once at the studio 'n' once at her apartment. <And when did she plan on telling me?> Probly when the time was right? I dunno. Anyway, I jus wanted ta know if the bastards picked her up for questioning without permitting a fonecall like I'm findingout they do all the time". Meanwhile lex, fearful of alarming me unnecessarily and, moreover, of inserting himself into a situation which, up to that point "might stilluv been a bad hunch 'n' none o' my damn business", decided to give L til su afternoon to turnup —afterall, he had done all that could be done just then incl'g followup calls to animaze ε lapd. Noonish, ns pickedup by helicopter, flown to atlanta while lage leerjets to lax. 13:00ish, ns is leering for denver. 14:00ish, fbi agent questions lage at lapd hq, suggests among other things that she might be Lilith faking her own disappearance. How lage managed to override the missing-persons do-nothing time-lapse should, very soon now, no longer trouble the attentive reader.

29

While i'm showering lage yells, "Cops still dont know anything. Duh. Maybe in the morning. O, fergot t' tell ya. Rick from greenEarth called jus before I left the house. I'm a mental mess. Sorry." <T'sokay.> I'd spoken w both rick & brian enroute. Among other things, they'd offered gE's pi service. Great people, these professional rescuers of endangered lifeforms. When i came out of the shower she was on the fone.

Knowing don had called home from outofstate and she wasnt there, she decided to wake him rather than let him worry. Seems don interpreted her emotional upset as caused by his silence concerning his medical problem. Once he realized she was calling from l.a however ("Youre not chasing that asshole [her ex] again are ya?"), the fact that Lilith was missing just flowed from there. "I had ta tell him. He'd freak if I kept it from him any longer."

In lalage as w most extroverts, depth of reflectiveness ran counter to amount of stimulus applied. Inotherwords, when you caught her forinstance silent & staring unseeing at something (as she then stared at her hands pressed flat on her knees), one suspected a problem. "Cancer. <Youre kidding?> No. Prostate." That off her chest, tho late and us sleep-deprived, she wanted to go for a drive —anywhere. "After I made him drop the cancer bomb I wasnt zacly itchin t' hit him with the latest on Sister." She closes apt door, pauses at top of stairs. "Arent ya s'posed t' take care o' that like rightaway? <What?> Prostate cancer." Mid-landing she stops again, lips pressed together. The close of a car door below delays only for a moment her wholly unanticipated meltdown. One emotional assault is enuf for any day and she's faceddown two. As i hold her i'm struck by several things: the likeness of her sobbing to Lilith's; that i should find her sobbing almost as heartrending; the muscularity of her back & shoulders against my arms. {Looks like dulcinea, feels like aldonza.} Odd? I mean, that these things should be grouped together at such a moment? Not really. For no one need ever explain to a war vet how strangely trauma, or its threat, acts on human behavior.

30

Next morn. Lage checks for any word (none) while i try again to reach bekky. At breakfast, going over her questioning one more time, we try to anticipate how the fbi, or some related entity, might stand to benefit from suspecting Lilith of faking her own kidnaping. In the midst of these speculations lage mentions a studio quality foto of Lilith which the agent had used. "I've never laid eyes on that portrait 'n' it's the best picture of Sis I've ever seen. How c'n that be? It's prob'ly no big deal I know, it jus bothers me." After breakfast she suggests gift-shopping for lex. I find a variation on the see-hear-speak-no-"evil" monkeys. This version has a fourth monkey standing among the usual three, hands covering its rump, CYA lettered on its baseball cap. (During production of one of his movies lex had been accidentally stabbed in the butt by a sword.)

After meeting w gE's p.i service we head to lex's hotel. During the visit lex passed us a copy of the *tinseltown tattler* in which a headline read, 'HERCULES' TRIES TO RESCUE MISSING GIRL...who "cannot be named because she is underage. Reever, now in his 60s...." and, zap, the reader is hooked. The rag then wastes no time questioning lex's relationship to this "beautiful" mystery "girl", an "intern [mind you] at Animaze Studios" etc. Lage looks at me and lex says what i already know. "I've spoken only to the police of these matters, believe me. This is just one more l-a-p-d leak. It's disgraceful but it happens all the time here." I am saddened when he reminds me, "This town c'n never just send something nice our way, can it? There's always got ta be the sliming that goes with it." Lage, having lost both her ex and, so far, her Sister to l.a, is in quiet agreement. In the elevator she says, "Great. If that crap gets pickedup nationally... Damnit! Daddy *never* misses the papers".

It was along about that time that Lilith's stolen addressbook popped to mind. Back at the hotel, after a bunch of deadends, i got lucky. When i reach her aurise is either shocked or disinterested, i cant tell which. When i ask <Who mightuv done this? [she is evasive] I mean, Lilith is missing. You *do* understand, right? I mean, i thought you might have *some* ideas.>

"Look, I'm not playin with your head, okay? There's stuff ...stuff I'm sworn never t' tell anyone! It's not just you, trust me. It's telling *anyone!* ...the president, the pope, God... anyone!"

And you *do* understand she's missing since *yesterday,* right? an' that my best friend just about witnessed the whole thing?

Lage, hearing the exchange, is as transfixed as i'd ever see her.

"I know that. Look, I've *lived* this stuff! I know better than you what youre talking about! I mean, you have no idea. [pause] Look, if she doesnt turnup by t'morrow call me. In fact, call me even if she does. An' if *anything's* happened t' her I promise I'll blow the top off this whole fuckin business! Til then there's *nothing* I can do. It's Lili's ball ...totally! *She* hasta do what needs ta be done. An' that's it. [sighs] I've gotta go now."

Wait. Is it her stepfather? It's him, isnt it? Jus tell me that. ...Aurise, you there?

Silence. Clicksoff.

To call the gloomy hiatus which always followed mention of aurise's name, jealousy, would be simplistic. Nor was it a one-sided thing. Not long before my arrest aurise would say, "Being Lili's best friend, thru good *and* bad times, I was always angry about how she felt toward lage —who, after all, left her cold just when the going got tough in her life.... No, I agree. It *wasnt* her [lage's] fault. An' that's just the point. I couldnt justify how I felt toward her. An' that made it even worse." As for lage, her problem *w* aurise grew out of guilt —guilt for not having stoodby Lilith during those "terrible" years. And the more she learned about those "regrettable forgettable times" the more this guilt grew.

Lilith

Around 2p don arrives at lax. He is plainly surprised to see me. "I c'n still tote my own bag, thanx" says he. On the way to the car he cannot hide his limp and, on getting in, has difficulty just sitting. Door open, he fumbles for the seat adjustment. "I always order a big car. [grunt, huff] These tuna cans are fer goddamn midgets." I can see lage dying to say, "You mean, sardine cans, daddy". Huffing, he looks over at lage. "Does this seat look all the way back ta you?" She nods. Fumbling on both sides now, he is staring straight ahead like an invalid who cant find the rails of his wheels. "Where in kryst is the goddamned adjustment thing?"

Sensing i'm about to be crushed in my own cramped corner of that can, i slide over behind the driver. Before i can extricate all of me, however, seat *ɛ* man lurch backward *w* a resounding thunk. There issues a low groan as he slams to a stop. Lage's large eyes are now mere slits in the mirror.

"You alright back there?"

Just fine, i reply, unwedging a stinging foot. As we get underway i think {Now *all* of us will be limping}. We are soon on the freeway.

"Jezuskryst, do ya hafta drive so fast, kiddo? Youre catchin up t' that ambulance!" It is plain, don grewup in an era when under no circumstances did one pass a code10-39 going in the same direction. Lage slows only for a moment. He checks his watch. "What time do you have? [Lage answers] I dont understand it." [What's that?] How'd *he* get here before I did. [You mean, nathan?] Of course I mean nathan. Who else?"

"He caught a private flite, daddy." Partly true.

Don decides we will "do a late lunch somewhere near the apartment", at which point he is surprised next to learn i'm already lodged thereat. Of course we had moved me to my own room that morn.

"Youre not implying, nathan isnt welcome, I hope?" says lage, using only the flat of her sWord.

"I didnt say that. I'm just supprised. Cant I be supprised?... I got here soon as I could, ya know. [We know that, daddy] Goddamn changeovers... in atlanta two hours, three in dallas! Kryst! the faster the planes go the longer it takes t' get anywhere!."

{Dare i add, *That's* the truth?}

By the time our meals are served don has not only gone silent, he is grumbling & banging things around. When the pepper skids across the table into my lap lage looks up, slits her darting eyes and, Lilithlike, presses her tung behind a corner of her mouth. I remind myself to check which cheek Lilith uses when thus consternated. No sooner have i thought this than i find myself fritened by the prospect of possibly never seeing that cheek, or its owner, again. {Groundless, stupid thought!} Don sets down his cup w such abandon some coffee splatters on lage's hand.

"*What* is the matter with you! [lage bangs fist, fork jutting like mini trident] Youre acting like a cave man!"

"Our family needs t' talk."

"So, talk."

"I said, *family.*"

"Is this about Sis?"

"It is."

"So, talk."

"Not with him here." Tips side of head my way.

"Nathan? ...Fergodsake, father, what's the big secret?"

Lowers head, growls from under furrowed brow, "Just because your sister has lost her mind over siegfried here, 'n' just because you go all googoo when he's around, doesnt mean *all'uv us* hafta have our heads in the clouds!"

While i'm weighing googoo v. gaga she snaps, "And what zakly is all *that* supposed t' mean?"

Suddenly patronizing. "Must I paint a picture, child? Open your eyes! Do you remember things like this happening to our family before *he* [askew nod my way again] came along. We've always been free of cops 'n' robbers and this... this sorta lowgrade rock-opera bathos!"

I set down a well-mayonnaised knife. I think i'd better be going.

"Wait! [lage sitting erect, stopping don/nathan traffic w both hands] This is good. We need t' get this out... It sounds again t' me like youre more worried about our family name than about Sister. You havent asked a single question about her since you arrived!"

"Why should I. So *he* can answer my questions? You shoulduv told *me* about your Sister b'fore you told *him!* I'm her *father,* ferkryssake!"

"So *that's* it! You think there's an alpha-male conspiracy here. Well maybe *you* shouldnuv left home this time, ever think o' that? I begged you not ta go when I caught you limping around. Then maybe YOU'DUV been first ta know! An' after you digest that, maybe you should tryda imagine what it's been like for *me*—without the heart ta tell you Sis's been kidnaped on the *same* goddamned day you fin'ly dacide ta tell me youve got cancer!"

Having had my fill of this startlingly *aladdin*like imbroglio, i motion "check please" to our server, who is keeping a safe distance. Look, i'm gonna go.

"I dont think so. This *is* a family thing, like daddy says, and *youre* part o' the solution whether HE wants t' face it 'r not!"

"Are you blind, child? If this man wanted a family, its problems *or* its solutions, he'duv had one years ago. Siegfried here's a playboy not a familyman! Open your eyes, child, b'fore YOU turnup missing too!"

I wondered about his repeated use of the 'c' word. Eyes flashing like carmen's she says, "O yes, the *family* thing again. Of course, *family-pride aboveall.* Well then, how bout we include family stuff like... like lesbianism? Or incest, maybe? And, o yes! Let's not forget *murder*, huh? Okay? Right, dad. Our family's as american as apple pie! What planetuv *you* been hangingout on?"

Our server, even hearing "apple pie", even seeing money in the tray, still thinks it best to hangback.

"That stuff wasnt in *our* family. All that's on your *mother's* side!" announces don swan, long mateless himself, flailing even his limp wing in lekky show.

Poised to respond, head lowered, mouth open, jaw slack. "In case youve forgotten. They might not be *your* family, mr donald mcGrae, but they *are* still Sister's an' they *are* still mine!"

It was then i decided never to argue w lalage if at all possible. All of us had stopped eating incl'g even some not in our party. Indicating to our server, the gratuity tray is "fine", i rise to leave. Don rises too –w considerable difficulty– spots my fifty in the tray, scrambles to throw another on top of it.

"Nobody pays *my* bills, young man."

"Goodgod, youre *totally* frikking gobsnarled, arent you?" says lage, taking his arm and helping him toward the door.

I picture server waving money to coworkers after we leave, saying, They c'n feel free t' come here 'n' tear each other up any time they please!

"Are you so thick-headed, child, you cant see what I'm saying?" don says as he's hustled thru the door. "Duh," is all she says.

Well ahead of them, head down, i fite the urge to bolt toward our lodgings.

"Let me remind you, little miss starryeyed. [he says, needing to stop] Since he [thumb my way] came onto the scene, your Sister has been assaulted, batteried, hospitalized, and now, maybe kidnaped! [he numbers the events, thick fingers popping up as he goes] And lord knows what we *dont* know about! [pinky rises to represent unknown] This sort of thing never happened to our family b'fore."

Lage, totally exasperated, looks at me shaking her head.

I approach, calmly, distinctly say <If none of us –not a one of us– was there as witness, how can we be sure nothing like this happened to Lilith while she was living with the *other* half of her family?> Knowing what Lilith had so far confessed to me, i was trying to suggest a less fritening/more familiar scenario, not assault his guilt.

Head cocked, nostrils working, he says, "Who in the hell do you think you are?" Fists clenched, arms stiff at his sides, he stands before me as tho we are arguing over a low stone wall back in an earlier scotland.

With one bound which amazes me, lage lands between us. "Daddy, stop it! He didnt mean it the way you think!"

The overall triviality of those things which cause panic-level angst in we civil is proof enuf of the subliminóia (paranoiac substrate) which 'mere' civilizing imprints in us.

"He's obviously got you convinced all this ugly shit is some kinda huge coincidence. Well I'm here t' tell ye, it's not!"

{Did he say 'ye'? ...This is insane.}

"An I'm telling you, nate hasnt convinced me of *anything!* Youre acting *totally* paranoid, do you know that?"

Just when i thought he was evaluating this possibility he responded, "Ya know, if this is all some gag ta make me pay for leaving her with her mother, it's goddamned cruel."

"You *dont* actually think Lily would disappear on purpose?"

"I dont know. But I *do* know [deep breath & swallow] she prob'ly has the right to if she wanted. An' maybe she took that right." Tearedup now, he skirts me pathetically, hobbles on.

Lage, far faroff in thought now, pats his arm. "I guess she does. But this is hard on *all* of us, not just you. First your cancer then Sis. The las couple daysuv been hell around here, an' youre not helpin by staggerin aroun ragin like captain hook on uppers, attacking nathan like all this is, is *his* fault. He wants Sis back as much as we do. [lage is walking backwards now, leaning in close as if trying to pry open his downcast snarl] "He loves her, cant you see that? And she loves him!"

Don stops, looking at the pavement. But apparently, rather than deny directly the love thing –at which even lage winced the moment the words escaped– he caught his breath and, w an earnestness little short of morbid, said from under his bull brow, "If he *really* loved her, child, as you seem ta think he does, he'd clear outa her life... *b'fore* she turnsup dead". He caught his breath, then hobbled on.

This was one of few times i would see lalage lost for words. As for me, as if i didnt feel menalousy [sic] enuf already, by then wishing old don miguel had gone off to be killed by the moors in africa afterall, i said, <I *will* be going *this* time>, and headed for my room to pack.

Need i say, don's wagnerish bluster that day blinded me to the leroy anderson sweetness which both daughters claimed was the real don.

Wer meines Speeres Spitze fürchtet,/ durchschreite das Feuer nie!

31

As i was ordering a taxi in the lobby lage appeared.

"I think we should talk."

What healthy heteromale would say no t' that? ...Yes. I've decided ta head for the hills, as they say....

While my head-for-the-hills line was as literal as a metaphoric device can get –afterall, i lived in the hills– it refused to mesh neatly with this next: For at this point in his relationship the rider had already crawled off his weary mount & scrawled the following on the walls of the box canyon (of love) he'd ridden blindly into: Whether shotthru by blue or blownaway by gray, / the mere happiness-quotient in her gaze / can make 'r break my day.... With the appearance of that little rhyme & its committed truth now upfront in my existence, i knew it was time to try to dilute in me this emotional elixir called love. So you see, i, in fact, could not really get to *the hills of home* til i'd transcended this box canyon i'd galloped into —not emotionally i couldnt.

Sits. "Look, I dont blame you for leaving. I'd leave too. Daddy was really *really* overthetop t'day. I've *never* seen him like this. I know you cant see it but he's really a good person. He's just in alota pain. He'll apologize one day, you'll see." Unconsciously extends right leg, tips toes toward knee while she speaks, in an effort to stretch calf muscles; as an afterthought confesses, "My whole body's screaming for a knockdown dragout workout". In certain profiles i see, her eyes sometimes appear somewhat bulpthalmic. Had i failed to notice this in Lilith?

But he's right. She *will* be safer without me around. I jus never thought of it that way. You'll *all* be safer. The f-b-i is obviously gunning for any excuse to haul me in. Theyre a dangerous bunch. *They* know it. *We* need ta learn it. What i meant at the time was, like the cia, dangerous in the sense that half their work was securing their future via the *creation of* enemies-of-the-state.

Shakes car key to index right words. "Correct me if I'm wrong but. All those incidents with Sis happened when you were nowhere around. In the first case, you had t' fly t' portland, right? ...for some conf'rence 'r other? That puts you hundreds of miles away when Sis got attacked. {Attacked, she says?} Then, *this* time, when she gets abducted you are all the way across the country, where jus the drive t' the airport takes hours ...or so I've heard." With pained expression, she looks at, leans forward, squeezes, one calf, then the other. And such skin! And such lovely latent power just beneath it!

Lage (rest hand on her forearm), all this justification –tho i know you dont mean it that way– it, well... insults my integrity... i mean, that you even *think* you need to justify....

"No no. Youre not understanding. [she looked down at my hand just as i was wdrawing it] Look, track me on this. I have a valid point, not just excuses. Personally, if the doorprize is gonna go t' someone else, i hope it's my dear dear dear Sister. *But* —stop me if I'm wrong. It seems t' me, it's when youre *not* around to protect her that Sis gets hurt. If anything, if you go ahead with this exit-stage-left an' clear outa her life, you'll be *abandoning* her ...leaving her alone to face a pattern of events that's now prettydamn clear t' me." Fixes my eyes, not looking away.

<I c'n see that. I can. But... but it comes down t' who's calling the shots here, *doesnt* it?> Bent forward, she stands, turns, now squeezing raised calf

w both hands. <Fact is, your dad's in charge here 'n' the only role he sees for me is addios señor siegfried.>

Kulots block her expression til she puts same leg reverse akimbo, toes pulled to her hip by hand. Now i can see she is plainly consternated.

Look. I think of you as a good friend. ...and as a friend, i need t' tell you something important....

"Okay." Now rising, collapsing, rising, collapsing, on her toes.

<I need t' tell you something.> Like trying to lasso the nose cleat of a nearby boat in a rocking sea. <Could ya *please* stop bouncing for a sec? [Huh? Sah-ree. Promptly sits.] Thank you. [take breath] Look, i consider you a friend... a really *good* friend....>

"An a character, 'n' a little pistol, 'n' just a joy t' be around, huh? Hey, dont hold back. Tell me how it is."

I will... I *will*... when I'VE got it figuredout. Til then... Look, dont you dare even *think* of spluttering. That's not fair. Lage... [but my admonition isnt working. Place hands on her shoulders, shake gently] I'll strangle you if you start. I *will*.> What i would give today for the tiniest film clip: her eyes examining mine, then my features, in that split second after i said those words —fire ε fear flashing behind those big grayblue welledup scrutinEyes of hers— searching my face for meaning ε intent. I let gentle smile gather, lean over, kiss her temple. <See? Madeja stop.> Taxi appears. I rise, head for door bag in hand, turn about, back against door. <You be safe, lalage mcGrae.>

Standing now, steady ε still: "You too, nathan schock."

I'd lived thru closures farless subtle than this one, seeming permanent summaries of existence which turnedout to be temporary. For {Trial by fire brings the truly close closer, sends the truly distant farther apart}. I strode to my waiting ride as if i felt i had somewhere to go.

32

While i deal well w radical unsched'd change, i hate it. And so the hours since that treacherous fonecall had taken their toll. Frustrated by my inability to solve or jettison the problem of this newest woman in my life, long on unanswerable questions and short on patience ε sleep; despite these things i knew, busy was what i needed most. Since lex had the eve free, and since i did not need to be at my next lecture stop til tu afternoon, i treated myself to a room at lex's hotel.

That was the day i met lex's beautiful namibian friend, marlise vandermerwe, the three of us sharing Wildlife sanctuary notes for hours. And just as, back at my room, i was settling into a much-anticipated early-to-bed, the fone rang. The moment i said hello an excited female voice declaimed: "You were right, nate. She's alive 'n' well!"

Ecstatic at the news, yet not quite recognizing the voice i venture, <O. Good....?>

"Your *world matron,* nate. She's alive 'n' well. It's me, bek... Hellooo. Did I wake you?"

My disappointment at who is alive&well surprises even me. <O, hi, bek.>

"I thought you'd be *glad* i've finally seen the lite."

I am.

"Is this a bad time?"

<No no. Dont mind me. Jus dozedoff. How ya doin?> Months before, trying to bolster my world matron thesis (rather hotly challenged by bekky), i'd given her a copy of kim jankaid's *erotic purity*. Then, in all the *sturm und drang* of late, forgotten i'd done so.

"Like I told ya, I've reconciled with her. Your world matron? But it gets better. You need ta know, I've been road-testing her for a couple months now ...challenging her with all my disappointments 'n' hurts, and with all I know to be true. <Sounds like a tall order.> But the past two days clinched it, unc! [spent w deb & her mother] By the second day, nathan, I had lured mother's world matron out into the open any number of times. Again'n'again, thinking we empathized, mother would reveal her hidden matron in a blaze of glory ...or maybe I should say gory. The petty jealousies, the selfish motives —me 'n' deb saw feelings that would make any good mother wretch. I tell ya, unc, it was a dorothy parker dream-scenario; so cathartic I'm lost for words. Let me jus say [sighs], a major breakthru's been made in my family 'n' I've got your world matron t' thank for it."

Well that's ...that's *reallygreat* news.

"You sure this is a good time. You sound, welp …sad. <I suppose i am …a little.> I *can* call back ya know."

No. This is a *perfect* time. Really. More-than-you-know perfect.

Bekky had gotten my mxs in time to keep her from flying to st louis. ("When in hell are you gonna cave 'n' get a cellfone?" Got one. I jus need t' start givingout the number. "Well right here's a great place ta start.") Tho ny born&raised, l.a was fine for her, "most o' the time. There's always a few people I need ta see down there anyway. It works fer me if it works fer you." Bekky was also deeply absorbed at the time in monica sjöö & barbara mor's zizm-etching *the great Cosmic Mother*, which alice krawel had gifted each of us with during our visit. [The philosophic matters NS and Ms Kydd resolved between them next day, NS has already sampled in Part 5.]

33

Tu morn while awaiting a delayed departure i made a call i figured lalage would not make. Aurise's hardline softened when i stopped going easy on her. I think Lilith cares a whole lot more about *your* wellbeing than you do about *hers*. (I still did not know if aurise hated me in particular or men in general.)

"How much I care 'n' how much it seems to *you* I care are two different things, mr schock." That outoftheway, antagonistic polarity moved toward communication. "It shouldnuv happened is the whole point. The man's a megaslimeball. He knew perfectly well she didnt want anything to do with him. She was just a kid —a kid in a woman's body. Nothing had prepared her for his kind. She was totally sheltered when I met her. She didnt even know what a flasher was, believe it or not. O she played the part of being worldly. But when ya scraped-away the makebelieve ya foundout, shit was the ugliest word she'd ever heard 'n' a foal being born the sexiest thing she'd ever seen! So then along comes this slimeball 'n' his evil candy 'n' her, well… her whole tidyclean world is turned upsidedown!"

But none of this pouredforth til i said i knew of Lilith being raped not long after the divorce. Had it stayed like that til she ran away? Well, no. There was "waymore to it than that." Aurise agrees to tell me "all [she] can in good conscience anyway… slipping someone drugs without their knowledge. *That's* the cruelest form of seduction. Also the most foolproof. Some drugs c'n make a rudabega want sex." Did i have any idea what she was talking about? I allude to my tinseltown days. "Hopefully it was with your consent. It wasnt with hers. Or, later, with mine either. And I'm not implying a couple outings hooked us either. A person's either gonna use drugs or theyre not. Personally I like to pick who I go to bed with. And I know Lili's the same, even moreso. I like the experience to register in a real place, not be a buzzyblur even while it's happening."

<Professional spider, preferring helpless victims.>

"An' more where *that* came from. But look... How t' say this...? I do'wanna give the impression we were above a little curiosity 'rselves. We were precocious, really —me moreso than Lili. But then I was older by three years. An' that's where the difference lies. She was a clear-glass virgin when he trapped her. So help me, not a smudge. While some o' the young pros he brought in for parties were okay –as people, I mean– the rest were slimeballs like him. [introspective quiet] No, be clear. Our precocity didnt extend to okka *and* his friends." That had taken shanghaiing & other shady shenanigans.

<Been there, done that.> Sensing she'd been plumbed as deeply as her oath would allow, i 'lighten' the subject. <What should i picture when you say megaslimeball?>

"Just, *yech!* Disgusting. Handsome but smarmy. Just the thought of him makes me nauseous. I'm serious. Not very scientific but that's it."

Smarmy, as in maggots 'r smarmy as in pondscum? I'm just tryin t' picture this socalled person.

"Then picture him as toxic ta pondscum and an insult to maggots."

Hŏ-kay. ...See...? And you said youre not an environmentalist.

"Lili's the enviro, not me."

Did she think there was any possibility this okka person was responsible for Lili's disappearance?

"Look. I've said waymore than I shoulduv. But I know how she feels about you. I've known for years. She'd probably tell ya this stuff herself if she could. But Lili's a really private person. Add t' that, life's driven her into hiding. Beside, she's scared t' tell anyone. He's one *way*whacked character. I think the guy's still capable of just about anything. But Lili says, no, 'n' that's good enuf fer me."

You *could* go ta the cops.

"Lili'd rather curl up 'n' die. You dont know. That's the sweetest person God ever put on this Earth. B'side, backthen I was as scared o' him as she was. But you need ta know. Personally I have no shame over any of it. I usta, but no more. I do have regret, tho ...'n' anger. *Lots* of anger! That scumbag is guilty of entrapment, of rape –multiple rapes, technically– of a minor ...quite a few minors, really. Stuff even worse, if ya wanna know. He has a video of what I hope was his worst evil, if he didnt destroy it. But that's an unrelated horror. I've said more than I shoulduv. Probably sounds like a goddamn fairytale anyway. I dont b'lieve in capital punishment but, well... I think somebody should slap him in the slammer 'r cutoff his penis 'r something. Youre probably shocked. Who wouldnt be? But ya need t' know —an I told this same thing to a cop I was roomie with last year: if anybody *–anybody– ever* questions me on this stuff I'll deny every word. An' ah'll keep denyin it til Lili says ta stop." And beyond these things the indisposed deposed would not disclose.

To be fair, i believe aurise spoke well beyond what she & Lilith avoided even in their own conversation. That is, when gory details absolutely demanded attention, i know for a fact (*today* i do, i mean) they would deploy euphemisms epithets & convenient oversights. Only thus were they able to sustain their friendship reasonably unmolested by the past. But Lilith's journal for 1990 will, meantime, afford my patient reader a more vivid harkback.

Where did you go, Daddy? Where?
And why did you leave me here?
Mother's become a Medusa.
I harden to stone at her stare.

Why did you go, Daddy? Why?
And will you return by and by?
Her lover's a bocor of voodoo.
He sticks me with things till I cry.

Come back, please, Daddy, and get me,
and take me to where I can hide.
Come back, please, Daddy, and save me.
—Once more on his altar, I'll die.

34

Somewhere between l.a ε st paul, twixt catnaps (never did quite catchup on that sleep), i found myself again overlooking a distant thunderstorm. Recalling the gryllos-in-the-clouds of my oregon trip, one of those pangs of anxiety i so hate –and which, thanks to years of internal work, i'd managed to rid my life of– rose up 'out of nowhere'. I recall catching, twixt dozes, a beyond-denial glimpse of some new Other wedged deeply in my life, and finding i had invested therein a depth of feeling i had not known since youth.

Altho Lilith's disappearance cost me a long-anticipated meet w the incredible david suzuki *and* vandana shiva, i did secure two friendships that trip; oddly, both, percussionists. The first, fiona glengarry, a marimbist, i met at lunch w the u of mn booking agent. Possessing a most-musical brogue (glasgow), i was at once struck by her sweetness ε depth. A busy sched had her w st paul chamber orch on fr ε sa, on su solo at u.m, and su eve at a school (minneapolis college of art ε design) Lilith would have attended had lalage ε don not moved from mn to ca. Being deaf, i did not expect much in the way of musical performance from fiona. Beside, she was quite beautiful, a quality, sadly, one learns not to expect verymuch that is exceptional from. Quickly (for in this timespan much is happening), i was at once thrilled by her performance and very much ashamed of myself. {Beethoven, afterall, was deaf!} Often during her show she played up to five instruments at a time, and possessed an acuity of rhythmic precision i associated w fritz reiner!

That tu i was to speak at u.m, wedn at the arts college, and fr back in st peter. At lunch on tu i asked fiona if she was free th, my only eve off in the days ahead. But playing w the frisco sym on fr she had a th rehearsal. Needing someone of her powers to keep me focused, we did manage to spend a few hours knocking about the cities that wedn. It was in st paul w fiona that i learned, the author of *tender is the nite* met his zelda at the same age Lilith was that year, that zelda's given name is scattered thruout the author's own patronymic, and that she hailed from s.bamalachia of all places!

That th my plan was to tour the cities or travel to lyon or sioux, minnetonka or mazeppa, herman or ada, kiester or garrison, or even take a shot at finding woebegonia. However angela, the other percussionist, was anxious to get to her alma mater. Angela newlith (not a redherring but her actual name) may just be, even today, the most articulate musician in the classics. I met her during a "local arts scene" interview at the public tv affiliate: one of few persons i'd ever heard give berlioz his due as a musical groundbreaker wout any hectoring over his outrageous personal life. Tho i'd called on arrival, because of commitments (hers ε mine), we too had difficulty connecting.

Sched'd to teach a class at gustavus adolphus college on fr, angela performed there sat eve as well, among other commitments in st peter. It was there i heard for the first time berlioz' *ten picturesque pieces*. Her berlioz was superb; moreover, she spoke both sensitively ε entertainingly about her repertoire. Recent alumnus of gac, she took me past her portrait in the main hall. Circled by other "famous alumni" among which she was the most recent arrival, another face drew my attention. I noted it not because i once knew the person but because of something warmly familiar in her resemblance to Lilith —a likeness which otherwise might have been awhile occurring to me. "Ah, yes, annabel martin" said my talented companion. At once i recalled what a crush (unspoken) i'd had on annabel waybackwhen. "She was married to jon windstar. [contd angie, as if i had no idea] The famous 'annabel' song, you know? [hums release] ...He wrote it for *her*." [points]

Windstar. Civilization's secondmost famous green.

"Secondmost? After you?" Angie's coy smirk told me she thought i was asking her to consider my own fame since we'd just considered hers.

No, not me. Second after the captain of the calypso, i mean.

Before my lecture in st peter fr eve i booked a flite back to ggNs. 2wks til my next gig ε full of a strange *ennui*, apologizing to angela, on the morn of su the 23rd i returned home.

I remember that u.m lecture for the following synopsis. It sprang to mind at the postlecture q&a session. <As to your question about instinct and the subconscious. Tho these are among the most powerful forces in our bodies, and thus in our social lives, instinct 'n' the subconscious are rendered virtually invisible in civil cultures ...specially in major institutions like ethics 'n' public health. Imagine. I c'n understand banning instinct and the subconscious from plate tectonics and algorithmic analyses, say. But for us to evict these powerful forces of our emotional lives from both ethics *and* public health is an open assault on logic 'n' commonsense. No wonder so many of us endup shameless hypocrites. For we are trained, from earliest youth, how to live in denial of our most basic Selfs.> Hmm. Teacher, know thyself.

35

In an interview i gave to a major tv station in the cities, ye ol charge of Nature-lovers being people-haters croppedup ...again. Interviewer: Youve been accused of misanthropy. Why is that? You certainly seem people-friendly to me. Me: You are no doubt familiar with how prosecutors, when desperate to charge someone with *something, any* thing, reach for the old "conspiracy" grabbag? ...Well, you c'n prettymuch depend that, when the misanthropy charge is leveled, its coming from people desperate to crush you yet having nothing of substance to do it with. So i'll say one more time. Quite the contrary, i love people ...waytoomuch for my own good in fact. It's the most *civil* versions of my species who scare me. Specially the high-etiquette versions –those corpolitic suits 'n' smirks we used ta call by the name, royalty– all powdered wigs 'n' niceties to our face 'n' a maniacal urge to slit the throat of 'the people' as soon as our backs are turned. Read the history of *any* civilization. If youre not scared of civil man's genius for pandemic destruction when youre done, you didnt get it. For it is instinct-starved civil humanity and its nation-states that are the hardcore people-haters, not me. I'll say it again. I love people. What i hate is the endless stream of Earth&Self-aliens (code: destructive assholes) our civilizing creates.

Interviewer, shocked. "I see youre a bit tired of the accusation."

A bit. It is civil humanity, 'n' its nation-states, which slaughter everything they read as savage or uncivilized, often including their own species! Ruminate *that* for pure horror. And still we –civil mankind, i mean– in pure numbers are faring waybetter than *all* other species —which are suffering obliteration precisely *because* we're faring better. In fact we are doing so well that even as we overrun 'n' destroy our Planet we are busy planning to overrun the *other* worlds in our solar system. And all this with no care for consequences —even for our own clearly inevitable obliteration, mind you. Would we not call "mad" any person who wept over a maggot mound which had grown itself into starvation by choice? Well, proof of sanity is the need to face reality. If that means finding it hard to weep over the suffering of that maggot-mound of Earth-devouring nation-states we call civilization, then so be it. For the biggest reality is, or should be: Civilized man is one scaryscary entity, a global goon squad which has battered its only home in the entire Universe into the intensive care unit yet could care less. It takes one helluv alota love, not misanthropy, to brave the sharing of such a stinging 'n' staggering truth. Still, if my message rings anti-people to anyone, then all i c'n say is: Their tumor of denial is one black 'n' oozing whopper, and i strongly recommend emergency surgery ...if only because, thanx to the selfishness of our forebears, there's no longer any time for body-cleansing therapies. It's the knife for us now or be consumed alive by the cancer of our whopping denial.> That day i crossedover from defense to offense, vowing neveragain to pamper or avoid the charge that i dislike people.

36

That whole week on the road i purposely did not call home to collect mxs. My only contacts were rick, gE's pi service & my agent. With me repping gE as well as my own work while on the road, gE always kept me abreast of the latest-breaking actions. When i spoke w rick en route to mn he told me, "Lilith's sister's been trying to reach you. She wants you to know (in case we hear from you) that Lilith is safe at home in dillon beach" —a fact rick already knew(!) from an fbi press release which gE gumshoes had faxed him. Had the pi's comeup w anything concrete as to her disappearance? Not as yet. That fbi press release stated roughly the following as i recall: ≈Lilith had turnedup at a home for the handicapped in l.a, was taken to county hospital and released; the victim of the alleged abduction (underaged according to ca law) had pressed no charges or made any statement and was recuperating from minor injuries at home.≈ The purpose of this spin? To have the popPress tell its believers that the fbi had neither made nor planned any such arrest and was "investigating" as to whether "the girl's disappearance was a publicity stunt or not".

Back home by su, i found 3mxs from lage. The 1st (from the day i left l.a) said Lilith was "okay" and "not t' worry". The 2nd guessed i was "still on the road", told of don's upcoming hospitalization. The 3rd, from th, said "Sis's okay. Sortaprettymuch", and that i could call "without worrying about daddy pickingup the fone". For, not only had medication "despazzed him [but]...he's had a complete change of heart about you". However, Sister was "still *molto silenzio*, poor thing. Dont know what t' think. Hafta take her t' dumb doc kubski again today who has no clue what t' do if he cant push drugs." Despite lage's morbid take (maybe it was just my mood), Lilith at least had been found. Feeling i wanted to just forget all the mcGraes, i sank into my first genuinely grisly mood since nam.

37

Rarely w time to watch a movie, next day i decided to banish my doldrums w a movie marathon. Since i'd already seen *dead poets society, good morning vietnam, mrs doubtfire, ε posing portly with porpoises* [robin's own take on his save-the-dolphins documentary], for 3days i lost myself in all except what he called his throwaways. My favs were his standups, incl'g some ingenious ecology routines. It was then i decided, robin williams is what happens when the genetic zizm of the likes of winters chaplin caesar sellars lewis ε hope suffuse the brain of an einstein placed in the body of an environmentalist.

But what of this ennui? —a downer oppressive enuf to arouse pity in bekky; not an easy thing for a man to do. And what of my libidinal apathy of late? Sexuality had become an out-of-body experience for me —and around the likes of bekky, angela ε fiona no less! Between spates of making rw force me to laff i would puton some music, snag a lager, takeup a table of comparisons i'd recently completed, mullover the items listed in its apposing columns. I'd been at the task on&off for a few weeks by then —an effort to locate any&all non-complementarity between george monbiot's brilliant *peoples' world parliament* and my own global legal-defense-fund vision —which i felt would be an irresistible force once conjoined. I needed only to be sure the two concepts were fundamentally compatible. But soon ennui would exhaust me again. {Come now, nathan. Mere anxiety? Hell, no. Say it: Fear. Fear and foreboding. For you have met with a Complementarity to your Self beyond *any* rationalizing regimen to ignore or disable, and you know it.}

If from our very first breath (or so i began) we are instructed that Nature is irrational ε uncaring (eg: doesnt love us), and if we intuit that, beside ourselves, Nature is all there is that's real in any fundamental (life&death) sense —and if we cant buyinto that fetal scenario (of the philosophically paranoid) which holds that some deity is lookingout for us on a *personal* level— it then comes pretty clear why so many of we civilized suffer from existential depression. Yet i will maintain til i die: <u>If only you, reader, could for one instant glimpse the pure primitive zizm of your Self, you would fall in love with life for life!</u> This last in fact, from *scapegoats & fallgirls,* became Lilith's credo. She claimed it saved her from "committing suicide over my choices and my fears when i was young".

And for a space Lilith's credo would work. But soon this chump would slump to funk again. {That's all well'n'good nathan schock but you posed 'n' adopted that b'lief years ago. What you need now t' do is set aside all those allegorical reachings, those metaphorical near-misses, 'n' face one simple fact: Something in Lilith's 'mere' existence in the Universe turns the very idea of 'other women' into flimsy theory for you.} For every time she popped to mind i felt, in my deepest viscera, a massive lurch toward a connection i'd not felt since falling in love w juanita. So what was to become of me?

38

Another reconstruction of highlites is now in order. If dates & times seem overdone, i am only being as thoro as possible in the hope, some researcher some day by some miracle will be able to reconstruct what happened to my Love for those two days.

94.01.16, su. L turns up at home for mentally challenged adults in l.a; it is not clear if she got there of her own volition or was droppedoff. When lage & don arrive they find her sitting on the livingrm floor circled by house occupants, most of whom are down's syndrome afflicted and all of whom seem mesmerized by her. Police say she cannot speak but house parents maintain they heard her conversing w residents altho they noted a speech impediment; her face is bruised, her left eye partially closed, its orbit discolored; left side of her mouth is swollen w some bruising apparent around the lips. Police call in paramedics; paramedics insist on emergency transport; er nurses find two shallow lacerations across her throat and a third on her lower abdomen; er doc dx's psychogenic shock & possible amnesia, calls in shrink for spec dx. Er doc says he must make report to police to which lage responds, "Duh"; psyche spec merely underwrites er doc's dx even tho lage tells him "She's hiding from a world that keeps hurting her. We need to find the corpse-eating bastards who did this". L is ℞'d psyche treatment (for suicidal tendencies) & released. Don & lage take Lilith to dillon beach. Don tells lage, "Somebody's gonna pay fer this, I promise!" Lage replies, "First she's got t' say who did it, doncha think?"

Speak, gentle sister, who hath martyr'd thee?

Lage leaves first fone mx for me.

Mo,17th. Lage misses school again; don hires housekeeper & nurse; L is taken by lage & don for psyche appt; lex wraps animaze assignment, returns home. Tu. Fbi issues press release (above) which lapd & media parrot; lage & don drive L to psyche appt; lage drives don to doctor. Wedn. Lage returns to school; nurse drives L to psyche appt; lage visits don in hosp in eve. Th,20th. Don has surgery; nurse drives L to dr visit; lage visits don after school; shrink sends permission-form home to begin shock-therapy series on L; seeing L's agitation when nurse speaks of this, after nurse leaves lage tearsup note & form to see if L reacts. Fr. Lapd calls mcGrae res to see if L speaking yet; nurse tells them, no; lage, overhearing, warns nurse not to speak *w* *anyone* about Lilith. Sa. Lage finds don has had a second surgery, is upset over his contd secrecy; lage goes to friend brenda's house, has her call house, feign being *irrational inquirer* reporter; nurse offers scoop on L "if the price is right"; lage returns home, fires nurse but nurse plays dumb, refuses to quit on lage's say-so. Su,23rd. Lage visits don, tells tale, don fires nurse over fone after lage gets home; this is first Lilith hears of don being hospitalized; lage takes L for dr visit, has friend brenda stay *w* L while she visits don in eve; brenda overhears L talking to the horses when she thinks she's alone; followup events inspire lage to try reaching me at home again.

39

Late that same su, while applying dr freddy fennell's "hi-fi a la española" to my sullen spirits, the fone rang. Zap texidor {Damn!} to monitor mx. ["Message", not "Mexico". —Ed.] "Nathan, it's lage [elatedly]... Guess youre not back yet. Just wanted t' tell you, Sister is talking again!" Absolutely *w*out my permission, moving in a zombielike funk, my hand –which in retrospect still seems not to belong to the man wielding it– picksup the fone. <Hey.>

"Is that you?"

Live, in person. [logistically true]

After a quick reunion (her, animated; me, reticent) she got to explaining how "Sister...talking again" came about. "An yesterday we got ta the point where a couple times, when I told 'er t' say something she'd say it —repeat it after me like a sleepwalker." Lage explained how at times, the day before that, when she'd say something *w* emphasis (as while talking *w* a friend on the fone), or say something *w* a certain lilt or rhythm to it –as in 'And *that* was *that*'— she would notice Lilith's lips moving, quietly repeating the words to herself, the sort of echolalia children use to hone language skills. As i listened to loquacious lalage i realized: If, in my funk, i *failed* to track the eye of her stormy elation exactly, i would endup being slammed about like a ragdoll.

"So t'nite I'm sitting on the bed here —well, really, *we're* sitting on the bed. I jus finished brushing her hair like we used t' do 'n' I'm reading *jabberwocky* 'n' *beautiful soup* outloud like for the twennyeth time. Anyway, I'm noticing as I read, she's mouthing the words; 'n' if I fade out, she will finish the end of the line for me. Mind you, she's not glomming the page like me but is staring the whole time off into space, so I know it's from memory. Anyhoot, when I finish –*for the third or fourth time, sheesh*– I go t' her, 'Now *you* say it', and I'd start t' read again. Well jus like always she'd only go to the end of the line 'n' stop, like a kid waiting for her puppy t' catchup. So I'm starting t' get aggravated 'n' I go, 'No Sis. *You* finish the poem'. Well, she wont. So I'm sitting there, pissed 'n' tired by this point, when I get this flash. So I go, 'Say shit, Sis. Say shit'. Well, she gets this funny faraway look in her eyes so now I figure I'm keyedin: 'Sis, say shit! I *said,* say shit!… *C'mon,* say it!' Well, there I am sitting there, ready t' jump ta some new curseword, thinking she's such a prude, ya know? I go one more time, 'Say, shit, Sis! Shit shit shit shit shit'. I shove her with my elbow. 'Say it, damnit!' "

All thru lage's recital i feel like a growing whirlwind is pulling at me.

"Well, her lower lip starts quivering 'n' her eyes go like, y' know, there's some bonzai earthquake in china that she somehow knows about without the 11oclock news? Anyway, youve seen those movies where the girl's face melts into like a really old woman's? Well, Sis's face UNmelts, if ya c'n imagine *that,* 'n' when I look back at her she's got this smile –a bonafide barbiedoll dumbblond kinda smile– which totally demolishes me 'n' I'm falling over 'n' she's starting t' laff too 'n' pretty soon we're both crackingup, with me dragging her along in a joke I dont get except that it's working 'n' that's all that matters. There, ya see? She's smiling now jus *thinking* about it.… Yeh, she's right here. [aside] After some moments of what sounds like their fone being wrapped in cellophane.…

"Hi." Soft small sweet voice. "O, I'm okay. How're you...? That's great. [plain to hear is a thickness of speech one associates w dentists ɛ novocaine] Well, i c'n hardly talk so i'm gonna hafta go now. Hope youre doin okay. Here's lage back.... Bye."

"She's embarrassed about her speech."

O my poor Lilisp! And by the time i've hungup that whirlwind has scoopedup this dizzied ɛ oddly giddy ragdoll bodily.

40

A word about the winter of '94. Cold wx hit the day after Lilith left ɛ snow fell the day after that. While it snows every winter in bamalachia it seldom lasts ɛ rarely accumulates. Because of the moderating influence of the tn river —very wide there, thanx to damning— winters in the area are fairly mild. But that winter took oldtimers like my good neighbor zak back to their youths for worthy comparisons. Indeed, lovable old zakariah, slighting the soothsaying of his farmers' almanac, had predicted such a winter the previous spring! While my bison, ɛ zak's goat, didnt require the haydrops needed in alot of the grazing world that winter, it was the *coup de grâce* [hic] for factory chickenfarming, economic backbone of the biblebelt. For a few million debeaked ɛ drugged cluckers were put out of their misery when the roofs of 90% of the coups in the region, constructed w only liquid precip in mind, collapsed, freezing ɛ suffocating what cramped ɛ miserable creatures werent simply crushed. A too-brief hiatus in factoryfarm cruelty, it did at least serve to give good willie nelson more ammunition about a foul ɛ stinking industry.

Around that time figureskater nancy kerrigan got whapped in the knee by a masked stooge, returning to primetime an artform which had been languishing since the fall from grace of ice-hussy sonja (tutu) hennie and the fall from the sky of our olympic team. Today an intn'l favorite, figureskating, for me, became a fav back when i fell for sweet margarita fleming. This was the same winter bekky ɛ her mother united to force video games giant, nintega, to yank its "nite trap" from the marketplace, a game where the player uses a giant auger to drain the blood of scantily-clad young females from whatever body part he prefers to puncture. It sold millions, bytheway, before it was yanked, and was probably loved by many of the same people who helped ban Lilith's capt.gE electronic games.

Also that auspicious month, c.d strickland was appointed to the cabinet post rick predicted would be created for him (secretary, enviro affairs) and was expected to appoint a new epa director any day. Also that jan, a jury acquitted lorena (not the lorena of that haunting song) bobbit (cause of a new term for castration) ...for having "bobbed" her hubby's penis w a kitchen knife after he, or so she testified, beat ε raped her. Also that month (in a lighter vein), allen gilbert odell, creator of what is probably the catchiest gimmick in the history of advertizing, died at the age of 90, doubtless chuckling to himself over one or another of his long-vanished roadside two-liners. GRANDPA'S OUT... WITH JUNIOR'S DATE... OLD TECHNIQUE... WITH BRAND-NEW BAIT... BURMA SHAVE. And u.s hwys have not been the same since (tho many grandpas doubtless still are). But mostofall, i remember that jan as the first time that mass rape in war (bosnia/herzegovina) made major headlines —and quickly faded as i'd predicted, not to be heard of again. But not to be forgotten, it was also the month of the l.a earthquake.

Now if this were a novel every reader would spit, 'O right!' Just when the heroine needs an excuse for not livingup to her movie contract, an earthquake comes to her rescue. Gimme a break! Yet animaze studios, located in burbank, did close for a month —not because the quake did some damage but because it affected the lives of so many employes. Lage called from her car that day to say, "We found a good nurse yesterday, so Sis is back on-course 'n' I'm free for awhile! Dad 'll be back home t'morrow 'n' then I'll have two invalids on my hands. So I'm enjoying it while it lasts." This new freedom for lalage was stung w a sadness however. For L's disappearance had caused her to miss a crucial gymnastics meet, dashing "for keeps" all hope of lalage ever reaching the olympics. Then came don's confession.

Because of the "unlikely possibility" he might die is surgery (say nothing of a deadly nationally institutionalized iatrogenesis doing you in, don, sir), don felt he had to confess something. Following Lilith's halfmoon bay (el granada beach) incident, don had gone to va to "find Sister's stepfather ta put the fear o' God in the man". But the new owners at the old address did not know of any such person, and cnty records showed the seller's name as leyda I. mcGrae only, who had never remarried after the mcGrae divorce.

Confused, don called Lilith back in frisco, who said she knew only that address and "Look, i'm not talking about this. This is craziness. What are you going to do, shoot him, 'n' then go t' jail for murder? I cant believe youre still at this!" After two days of searching, don returned home. "If anything ever happens to Sister" he concluded, "I want you to know, I'm convinced *that man* is behind it 'n' not mr schock." Had Sister told him so? No. "But we all know there's somethin she's not tellin us 'n' it's not good. Not good at all." Don had therefor had the family lawyer "officially inform" the fbi and annandale ε fairfax (va) police of foulplay, and then "hired a pi outa dc" to locate who exactly the man was and where he'd gone to, since leyda would tell him nothing. And what of don's dislike for "mr schock"? Seems i'd first slithered under the lens of his suspicion following our "gentleman's chat" over the fone. "'Instead of honoring nathan's respect for my daughter's right to privacy' (those are his exact words, nate)", don had taken my lack of cooperation (with "a father's concern for his daughter's safety") as me having something to hide. (Quotes are approx via lalage quoting her father.)

Lage called again that eve. Halfway thru her update she stops, says, "Here. Sis's awake. I'll let her tell ya herself." Fresh from a nap Lilith takes fone and, with a sigh ee would have called "slippered starlite", said, "This is Lilith" ...and w this music, once more, comes that gut-hollowing whirlwind.

I've had occasion to see autopsy reports. In one particularly grisly homicide it was noted, "The victim presents some bruising around the mouth with laceration and edema confined mostly to the anterior of the lips... the tongue is swollen with edema and presents a band of shallow lacerations along much of the length of its underside... with the throat area, including the uvula, microscopically abraded and, on its anterior side, grading to more obvious abrasion, some shallow laceration of tissue, and signs of inflammation (prior to death) as well. [and further on] It is this examiner's opinion that even the combined effects of the above-described trauma [to the mouth and throat area], though significant, were insufficient to bring about fatal occlusion. [and still further on] These facts, combined with the presence of noted substances on the face, in the hair of the head, in the mouth, and within the throat and esophagus of the victim, combine to cause this examiner to conclude that asphyxiation resulted from...."

So as not to overshoot my point here. L.a cnty hosp noted no *internal* injuries, only "some bruising around the mouth" and "a laceration on the left lower lip with some edema and intermittent suppuration". Further on the report concludes, "These are impact injuries, possibly sustained in a grand mal but also possibly due to battery." This assumption of the e.r doctor, along w his deciding that her alalia was due to "psych shock" and not to pathological causes, precluded his, or *anyone's,* asking my Love to say, 'ah', and then taking a competent look *inside* her mouth. It also precluded a good *haruspice* checking for sexual assault or battery. And as for the shrink who 'examined' her ɛ subsequently treated her at his office. He no doubt tookup where the genius before him left off: *assuming* someone had looked for trauma inside the mouth ɛ throat, duties more befitting a hospital than a shrink. For as we know, most shrinks are happy to forget how to do 'lowly' gp work, are happy to simply dispense the bigpharma poison pill-o'-the-day.

All this i've decided only long after the fact. I have reason now to believe, Lilith, on the nite she turnedup, felt safe to speak only to those incurious about past events. And being, as lage divined, on the run mentally/-emotionally from any further trauma in her life, i'm sure she was blocking, by some psyche safety device, the source ɛ cause of her pain.

Synoptic. Around that time lage caughtup Lilith w all that had happened since her disappearance. As for L. She could remember little, incl'g how she got to the safehouse. Her memory of events went thus: She was arrested by fbi agents in her parkinggarage, blindfolded, taken to a house in the mtns outside l.a (or so she guessed by scents ɛ sounds ɛ the tiltings of the vehicle); was interrogated (for what seemed like 2-3hrs) at which time she collapsed (from being drug injected) and after which point she could remember nothing til she found herself in a chair on that frontporch in l.a. L gives lage permission to tell lapd she can talk now; lapd sends two interviewers, L makes statement as above. Next day *l.a times* runs story. Quoting an lapd spokesperson: "...There is however no basis in fact for the girl's accusations [against fbi]. Unnamed sources with LAPD suggest she may have madeup the story, or even hallucinated it, but that the FBI never operates in this manner". Lapd then goes on to re "the girl's" psych treatment and "a previous incident in which the girl may have been assaulted, though she refused at the time to press charges against her alleged boyfriend, author, environmental activist and playboy, Nathan Schock.... LAPD detectives say Schock is still a possible suspect in her disappearance". However, because neither "the girl" nor her parents will press charges, "County Attorney Ashcrop says the entire matter may have to be dropped." That the fbi may *in fact* have abducted Lilith –despite all the handily pandered propaganda– or that someone else might have kidnaped her...that these likelihoods were never even broached (muchless investigated) seemed more&more to have a dark ε criminal tale all their own to tell.

41

Lilith ε lalage were robustly healthy girls prior to their parents' divorce. About 9mos after that divorce however lage developed "two" peculiar problems simultaneously: breathing ε stomach. After months of testing cameup w no comprehensive cause, because she was a gymnast and many of them are bulimic, involuntary bulimy was settled on. But to lage, this was the least serious aspect of her new problem. "The worst part was the sleep attacks." Sporadically she would awake unable to breathe. "Sometimes it went on so long I went unconscious. It was really scary. I thought I was going to die every time I passed out." Her doctor assumed "aspiration of vomit or mucus", side-effect of the alleged bulimy. "Humiliating" but necessary, they'd even installed a "panic button" in her bdrm.

In that it happened on the order of twice a month she wasnt long finding a pattern. However once a trend emerged (mostly late on sa eves or very early su morns), suspicion that she might be suffering from divorce/separation trauma gave way to her having a weekday sched that was too demanding. "So gymnastics was the firsthing to go. I hated that. It was the center of my life." When this failed to change anything their doctor sent her to a shrink. "I hated that too but I hated choking to death even worse. He prescribed ritalin™ on my very first visit, the ass, but daddy wouldnt allow it." These sleeptime attacks were often precipitated by a recurrent nitemare: "A man-monster dressed all in black" sometimes chased her w "one o' those big wide pirate swords, ya know?" With the attacks coming on wkends, and given the elements of her nitemare, and "since as they put it there was no mother in the household, this genius doctor o' mine" alerted the local social services of the possibility of domestic abuse. "What jerks! I told 'em they were whacked 'n' not in the nicest way either" —even then a plucky number by any standard. "Imagine those old noseyholes suspecting daddy, the last bastion of sexual virtue in the western world!"

Despite professional opinion, lage soon decided that both her problems were the result of a spontaneous inability to breathe. Nervous stomach or bulimia "had nothin ta do with it." When awake she could fite the attack, "tho I still got sick t' my stomach". But asleep, her defenses down, her throat would closeoff and an inability to breathe would take over. "They wanted ta do a uvulotomy on me. It sounded like somekinda sex operation 'n' so I freaked. Hey, I was only thirteen! An' the clowns werent even sure it would cure the problem!" While the symptoms didnt disappear entirely til she was 15, by 14 she had conquered their effects —waking whenever the nitemare "struck", blocking the "upchuck" whenever the choking & nausea "kickedin".

Symptom-free since age 15, how stunned lalage must have been when those "hated" symptoms returned "fullbore" win hours of her Sister turningup missing. Several times wout warning, the attacks started anew. Since the symptoms did not abate until Lilith turnedup safe, against even her own "sense of things" lage decided, "It *was* separation trauma causing it afterall! All at once the whole thing made sense. Cause once I knew fersure Sis was safe, all the symptoms jus vanished. I mean like *that!* [fingersnap] Completely! It was like meeting a side of myself I never knew."

In that Lilith never suffered *physical* symptoms of separation trauma, "this hell I went thru" endedup doing a great deal for lage's self-image. Tho awhile revealing it, her psychic malady apparently even allowed her to subsume –against all other evidence– that she possibly loved Lilith more deeply even than Lilith loved her. While this made no sense gutwise, and while it never ceased to trouble me every time events workedout w L farmore concerned over the welfare of lalage, i could not deny the possibility. (The part of our story where lalage confronts her Sister with the pathologic "proof" of her 'superior' empathy (their 'big' fite), i've already addressed.)

42

Problems w animaze studios had developed meanwhile. When brian, before the quake, asked to put a temp hold on production til L could return to work, the studio agreed but said their lawyers first wanted a new contract drawnup. Sensing studio trepidation over L's "problems" going public before sale or distribution of the finished tv series, brian (on conferencing w rick, emil & me) decided to stick w the original contract, which allowed up to 90 days in delays per party.

As to the domestic scene in dillon beach.... When Lilith began to wonder what *i* knew of all that had transpired (hoping i'd been told only that she'd been ill), lalage found herself torn among allegiances "—again!" There would have been "little question" as to what to do were their father not temporarily crippled ε depressed. Lilith, for awhile unaware that i'd flown in –and thus unaware of don's personal assault on me– had regained an old empathy for her father —an empathy rediscovered from a time when the girls felt their mother abused him. For his part, being initially helpless (to him, a femalelike state), don managed to make peace w Lilith. But as the days dragged on, and as don began to get around the house; but moreover, w calls ε a visit from sorrel leaving lage no choice but to tell all, unresolved tensions between father ε daughters began to arise. Blaming herself for all that had gone wrong (again) –incl'g possibly even precipitating her father's cancer– at such close quarters and w lage back at school again, Lilith tells lalage "I should go b'fore i cause more trouble". Lage argued but to no avail.

43

Before i left on tour again, a resemblance issue, nagging since we'd met, got resolved. Now, a skilled writer doesnt have to resort to fotos, paintings, or to comparisons w famous persons to describe someone. To do so is to take the low road. Yet i am sure, in cheap or underground copies of this book, the fotos of Lilith (which any decent biography offers) will be either eliminated or poorly reproduced. I therefore choose not to entrust her appearance wholly to the whimsy of inspired metaphor, or to the poesy of palpable comparison, specially when there are a few fair likenesses on which i can draw.

The moment i laid eyes on L, mnemy was upended, thrown back to the 60s of my young-man's dreams and to one jean shrimpton. For earlyon, Lilith's weight hovering in the esthetic negative, that's the Lilith one saw: laserlite silverblue eyes w brilliant whites set in a fragile face w clear high features; classic nose, bobbed just enuf to negate "snubbed", just enuf to fall short of "severe", what the french call *un peu rétroussé*; perfect mouth, neither small nor big: pert purl of upper lip, sultry pout of lower, its wicks turned down just enuf to skirt "cutsy" on the up-side, bypass "sad" on the down-, settling on an attitude which took its cues from emotion not from basic alinement.

Yet there was another Lilith, the introspective, serious, sad, private Lilith, whose likeness kept evading me. Then, passing a tv in a store one eve i saw a face that tugged at me, that spoke the *inner* Lilith. Surrounded by 40-50 tv screens filled w that face, i watched. Tho the eye-color was wrong, tho the face was too long in the chin, what came thru in terms of expression was at times exactly right; spookily right: the blend of fragility, ethereal softness, sparkly inquisitiveness; the face's slow revelations of an internal intelligence & sensitivity that was often gut-wrenching in its likeness; having many of those nuances of feature so difficult to pin down. I hung around while that face, its noddings, tiltings, glintings, worked the camera just so til a commbreak, at which time, having learnt the name of the show, i left. Calling one eve, a friend L will soon make, clarified this minor mystery. "Turn on your tv. She's on." Well, turnedout she was on *every* week and her name was joanna going, and the show she starred in ("little city") was set in, of all places, frisco.

Yet, even these examples fall short. For Lilith would make certain faces, get in certain moods, which *both* she and going reminded me of in their turn. But whom? With its eastern flavor, i kept thinking it was veronika. The resolution came one bitterly cold damp jan day down in scotsmoor just before i returned to touring. As i waited to have my teeth cleaned i scanned an article in *esq.* about some alleged litterateur & madman, then cast about for a different read. But all there was was a rackful of *humdrum & lollipop* —a kid's mag. So i closed my eyes, did my best to meditate. Immed task: to completely block the idiot songs escaping from a radio somewhere behind the receptionist window. Givingup, in a shuffle of mags on a table i found a copy of *life remembers 1993*. Among fotos of those who'd died that year, there she was! {Lilian gish! Yes!} It was *that* face, a bit somber w a flash of fearful, a touch of forlorn –from the era of *broken blossoms* or some other early gish flicker– which had played behind the deep greenery of my subconscious the day of our parting (in ca), and that time at the tea garden in frisco, and any number of other times since.

Incidentally, gus liti, prosecutor at my trial, the man who claimed "The defendant doesnt like women his own age", in a sense was right. For, til i was 14 or 15, the women i liked were often *older* than me, as were ms shrimpton & suzanne farrell when i fell under their spells.

44

When i arrived in santa fe on th the 27th in a serendipitous mood (caused by a conversation had en route w a beautiful fan i was thrilled never to have to wakeup beside), i called lage. This was the first time (since leaving ca) *i* had initiated contact. And i found, after deciding to do so –in fact, even in that instant *before* i'd decided– my depression/anxiety, amazingly, lifted, like dawn beyond a stormfront. I had no choice but to conclude, {Nathan, ol buddy, i believe youve bitten off waymore than you dare now eschew.} For always i strove to counsel common ardor w commonsense —a striving which the baron always re:d as "Schock's surgical brand of humanism", since i seemed "ever trying to resect the heart's neural dominion over commonsense, striving to reinstall 'heart & head' as equals. How very civilized of me, some may think —when actually it's how *primitive* of me! For 'civilized' rejects the heart's opinion, fears the heart's dominion; while "primitive" accepts & reveres the heart —which amounts to a right-brain/left-brain world of difference.

Love is brave, it has a mission. Unafraid, makes no condition.

Every year tireless ali macGraw keeps me busied in the new mx area w lectures & other events. This trip was different for the help of a relative of the guy who wrote the poem, "trees", val kilmer, w whom i happened to be speaking when lage called me back. "Youre kidding! I've been in love with him eversince *willow!* Tell him, 'lage says, grrrr'. [and wout missing a beat] Hey, Sis says she wants to go home ...Yes, her word, not mine! ...No. I took it t' mean *your* place. I mean, where else? She says you made some kind of offer where she was free to rent or something?" Not wanting to be hurt by circumstances she had gotten herself wedged in, lage tried to be patient, & fair, & empathic, really she did ...for i had interrupted w <What makes you think that? Hasnt she prettymuch forgotten 'ranch nowhere'?>

"Hey, dude, follow me on this. She hasnt forgotten one bit. Not one bit. Any more than I... Wait... Jus a sec...." I figured she'd lost patience for i'd interrupted w yet another contraview of matters LM&ns. "Sorry. I'm back.... Ya know sumthin? Fer two people supposed t' be in the business of instructing others, you guys need t' work on your communication skills. Cause there's alota times ya dont get each other at all. I mean, *at all!*"

goethe grotto Nature sanctuary

legend [for overleaf sketch]

1. chalet
2. manor
3. priscilla orchard
3b. various organic crops
3c. organic vineyard
4. Lilith bridge
5. where muir creek reëmerges from underground
6. goethe grotto
7. muir falls
8. wet springs
9. old cattle pond with broken-thru dam
10. springs / headwaters of muir creek
11. bridge
12. spillway with gate
13. juanita tarn (auber pond + cypress swamp)
14. shallow gully
15. carolina ash grove
16. tree farm
17. ggNs entry sign
18. main gate
19. tall grass grazing (for bison primarily)
20. tennis courts
21. food garden

F-H. calhoun relatives
I. calhoun farm
J. ggNs rental ("j" house)
L. zak mickley's place
M. bernie mcCleigh farm
Z. man-from-fl property
†. church

all other letters: neighbor houses, bldgs & land

facts

upper bluff of ggNs averages 366m(1200ft.) ams
nearest hamlets: lochston & lebanon
nearest village: quadrant
nearest towns: scotsmoor & rainsdale
nearest cities: huntsdell (nw), noogachatta (ne)

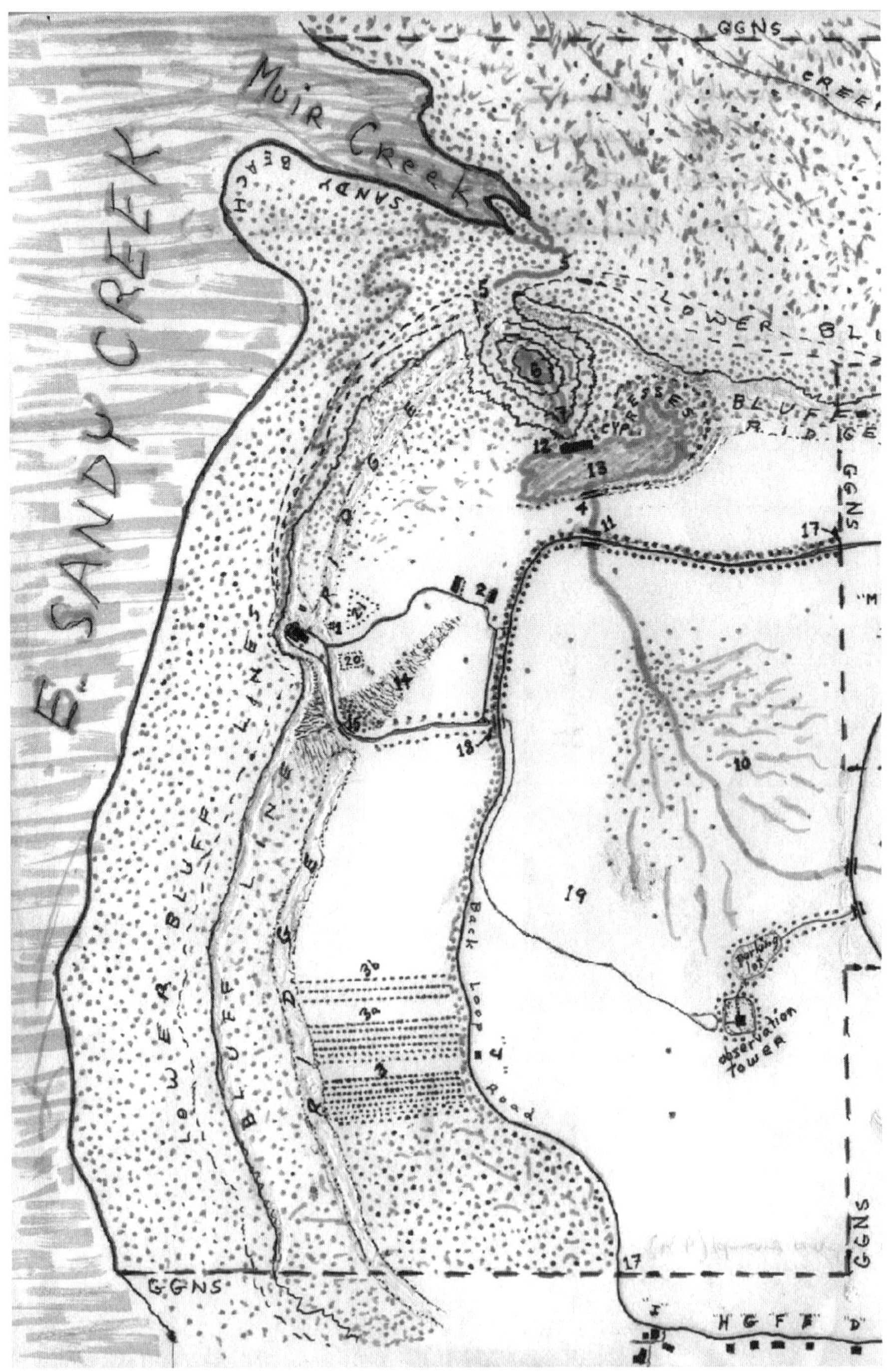
E. SANDY CREEK
Muir Creek
SANDY BEACH
GGNS
LOWER BLUFF LINES
BLUFF LINE
RIDGE
LOWER BL
BLUFF RIDGE
CYPRESSES
Back Loop Road
parking lot
observation tower
19
10
H G F E D

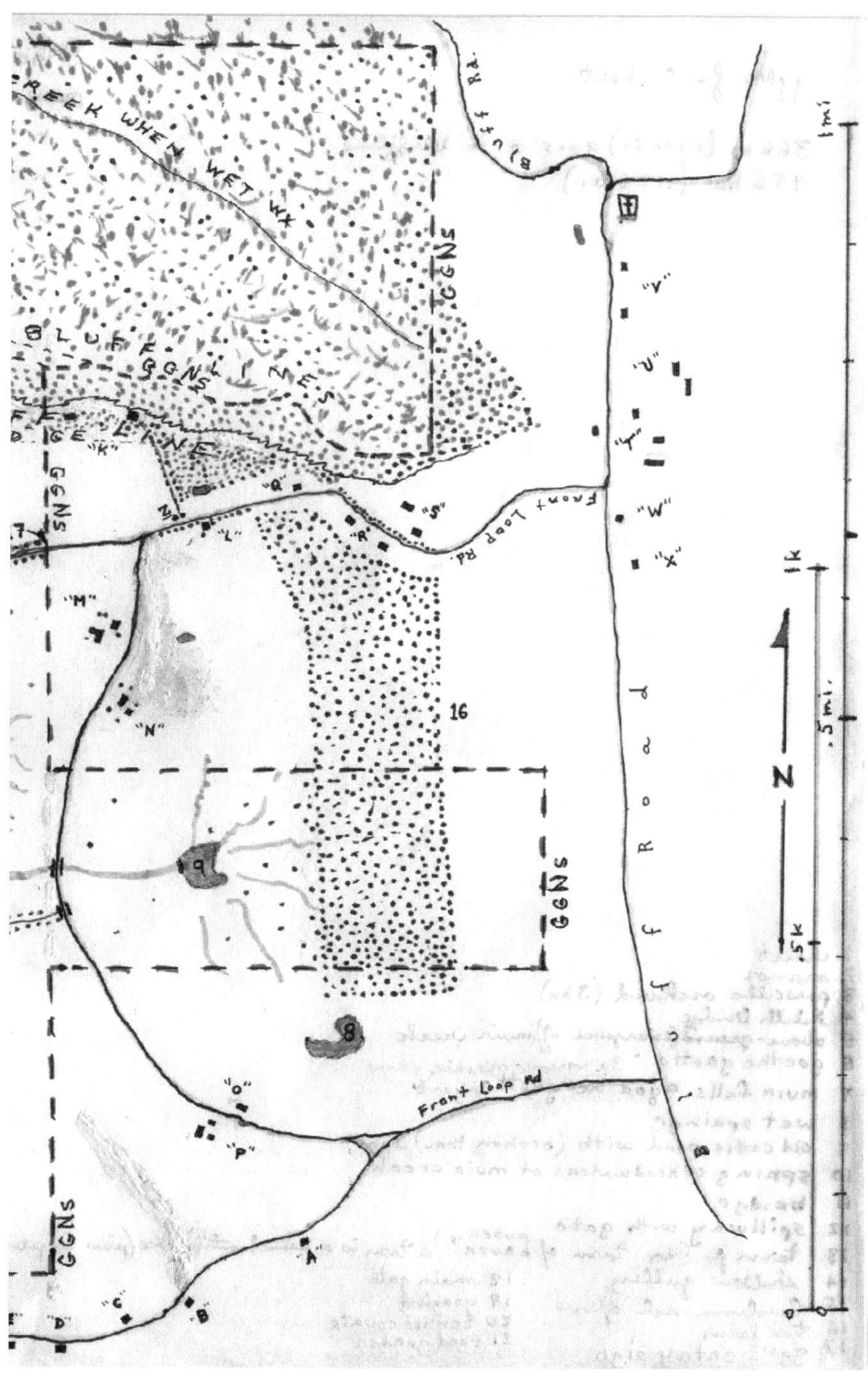
CREEK WHEN WET WX
BLUFF GGNS LINE
Bluff Rd.
Front Loop Rd.
Front Loop Rd
GGNs
16
N
Road
1 mi
.5 mi
1k
.5k

the written works of nathan schock

❶ 1977.11 the castration of priapus (sociology/political science)

❷ 1980.08 scapegoats & fallgirls (sociology/religion)

❸ 1983.08 the ungreening of tomorrow (sociology/ecology)

❹ 1984.08 the civilizing principle: a misconception of apocalyptic dimensions (sociology/political science/religion)

❺ 1988.08 die, primitive! anthropology & imperialism (anthropology/sociology/political science/religion), with Denise Norris, anthropologist, and Lindsey Margault, biologist

❻ 1992.08 Mothernature & the world matron (sociology/psychology/ecology)

❼ 1999.03 Ecocosm: the cosmic Gaia (ecology/astronomy/psychology) (Approximately 95% complete at time of NS' execution. Prepped for print with prefaces & postfaces by L. McGrae, Velda Rubins (astronomer), Glendon Starling (with Jane Phelps) and scheduled for a year-2000 printing at time this book went to press.)

❽ 200? planet Earth: a remembrance (ecology/environmentalism) (An incomplete collection of essays selected by NS as "the closest i'll ever come to autobio", comprised of his written "experiences in & around ggNs with re to a lifetime of Nature advocacy, written mostly during dry periods while unveiling 'the Cosmic Gaia'".)

miscellaneous essays

1981.05 last gorilla, last orang: a scientific, historic & moral tragedy (anthropology/ecology), coauthored with anthropologist, Denise Norris, and first published in "NY Monthly"

1983.12 dissent for freedom: "neocons" or neofascists? (politics), first published in The New Left magazine. This was NS's rare angry insight at where U.S. politics was sure to go *"if these neocons ever get power over our already shaky democracy"*. [Editor-added emphasis.]

1987.05 heavenly sex: the sexuality of the physical Universe (astronomy/sociology) coauthored with Daniel Bohm, physicist, Velda Rubins, astronomer, Denise Norris, anthropologist, and Lindsey Margault, biologist, and first published in "Natural Alternatives"

Variously published & anthologized also are many essays extracted from NS' books.

edited by

1987.07 The GreenEarth Chronicles: a history of, & adventures in, ecoactivism (environmental activism)

outtakes from

"Lilith: a biography", Book 2

(Protracted ellipses.......indicate skipped paragraphs or pages.)

Lilith capitulates: ....Tension, rare between us, seemed everywhere since Lilith's mother, institutionalized, had called, begging to see her. "You know she's been paranoid about meeting you." Leyda was supposedly seeing a shrink just to prepare her for meeting me one day.

She's in therapy because she's a substance abuser, Lee. She's been doing it for years. Beside, he'll be there. He'll just showup. I know it. You know it too. That's why youre so uptite.

"I'm not uptite. ...Just excruciatingly alert...." I could only stare at her, trying to locate in the carrels of my reading the source of that remark. "Beside, mother swore he doesnt even know i'm coming."

O great. *Now* i feel better.... Lee, your mother is his puppet. Totally. You *know* that.

"Theyre divorced, nathan! He doesnt live there anymore ...hasnt lived there for a long time."

You never told me that.

"I didnt know it —til yesterday. B'side, he lives in tahiti, she says."

<Terribly jetset.... In tahiti t'day, in my sweetie tomorra. [no comment, just sudden straight-ahead eyes] I know, dont tell me: over your dead body. But that's no consolation, is it? God knows, youve had to play the lovely corpse b'fore.> Just as one knows when a stormcloud covers the sun, one glimpse of that dulled gaze and i knew all debate was done. Punching my chairarms w both fists, i stood, marched to a bookcase by the windows, leaned against it w one hand, as if stopping it from toppling, crushing me for daring to bringup the painful if factual past.<Playing the warm corpse shur stopped him before, didnt it?> Three slow deep breaths, turn back. <Lee, i'm sorry. But it's not just a visit with relatives when you go there. Youre the estranged 'n' much-desired victim, not family. A visit there is a butterfly trapped inside a psycho ward! Lage said it yesterday. Those people 'll tear you apart the minute they get their hands on you ...again!>

No response. Eyes fixed on the most distant azure they can find.

And when it's all over i'll get the pieces [...the lovely tattered shreds]! Or maybe you'll just arrive in a box this time [...not patchable anymore ...never to fly again]! I watch her reflection in the glass, suspended above the bluff; the loveseat beneath her afloat in a sea of leaves, her legs tuckedin close beside her, her white-socked feet the britest part of the dim doublexposure. I wait for her reflection to say something, hoping she will move, get up, anything. Answer me, Lilith McGrae! Dont you dare go silent on me! But the chemicals of Lilithalalia have already seized her awareness and, beyond my anger somewhere, i know it. A few mins later i stalked off. 20min after that i left for a run. Last i saw of her, as i descended the steps from the deck, she was still sitting, staring. *How statue-like I see thee sit.*

It had rained ɛ blown for two days. Wet leaves littered porches, walks ɛ drive; the footpath to the river, the trainingslope, would be slippery w leaves. So i chose the frontroad for my frustrations. Feeling my blood boiling sufficiently, i skipped the warmup. How could i adore a person who gave me so much pain? I hoped the question would drive my workout. The answer however leapt to mind as i started down the driveway. New love is an uncarved stone and pain is the effect of having to work w a chisel unsharpened by intimacy w the grain of that stone.

After rounding the long curve in the driveway i looked back. Was this a premonition —this presence, this shadow from a clear sky? The chalet was obscured for some 70-80m by a grove of ash. I pickedup my pace, overrode my imaginings. Now, about that pain ...Cant hurting so often eventually disenchant love? I approached the timbered archway of the front gate....... Is loving Lilith despite her emotional problems a sign of irrationality in me? But then, isnt irrationality Natural, the very mode of our subconscious genius? My manic muse carried me thus to gap rd, and then back home again ...over 2hrs later, a grueling run meant to destroy me for the nite.

When i returned she was still sitting there, unmoved that i could tell, her eyes wide ɛ fixed, toripaullike. I went about getting myself a biteToEat. What did she see when she got like this? What thoughts, or thought, were the true object of that haunting far-off gaze? It was almost newstime; i puton the radio hoping to hear what sort of wx her flite would go off into....... Uninspired to cook, i made a freshpicked tomato ɛ scallion hoagie (knew better than to fix her anything). Annoying "traffic update" (huntsdell) came&went but no wx report. After showering i climbed to the loft, sat down w my supper ɛ john walsh's *the raving and ravenous raven* (which L had left in the sittingarea), read til well past dark.

Every time i looked up she was still seated down there. Her going-silent being hardly new to me i knew not to regard it as an "I'll show him" sort of sulking. Yet thru the glaze of my exasperation, fedup somewhere inside w the whole seeming-endless gothic mess, this time i took her reaction as stubborn retreat. In my anger i was unready to recognize that, by then, what i knew as mere switchedoffness had evolved into a whole different symptom. Tho new to me, it was hardly Lilith's first go-round w it. (It had happened while rooming w oral ε dexter after her latest scare in l.a. Before that it had happened following her abduction, that time when the medics showedup, took her away from that home for the handicapped in frisco. And an unknown number of times before that.

Yet each time i reflected on her fast-approaching trip (double/triple-checking to see if my stance was in error) i felt more dedicated than ever to stopping her. Even if it took *this*. Still, minute on minute, a small change, or rather an adjustment in my point of view, was taking place. Whereas earlier her trip had struck me as a *joan d'arc* delusional sort of selfsacrifice, now it struck me more as a *charlotte d'armont* kind of mission, w the brave lovely determined young heroine understanding the high risk yet knowing it was not a risk wout some hope of success: the rescue of her mother. My workout having done its job, i was soon asleep.

Around midnite i awoke with a start, my reading still on my lap. The moon was high ε so brite the valley below seemed bathed in a foggy sort of daylite. Gazing at the all-glass gable i soon found i was unable to see what had caused me to awake as tho i had been struck. Moonlite glinted off a table. Nothing moved (from stair to stable), tho my view was unobstructed all the way from porch to bluff. Still i could make out a misty twinkling just beyond the bluff. Deep into the darkness peering, seeing nothing, only hearing the low ululation of an eerie cry i've come to know; as the owl's cry was quitting, and my gaze was recommitting to the dusky objects waiting in the livingspace below, a patch of moonlite, flaring, flitting, revealed my Lilith still sitting —sitting in the same position i had left her hours before —folded in the same position i had noted hours before. (I see her sitting there still, in that pool of lite beyond the loft railing, on trial by agon of her own angst, and me memorizing that portrait, an hauer [hic] too late on the scene.) I couldnt take it anymore. If this was, even remotely, possibly a war of wits, it had gotten wholly outofhand. I slid off the bed, went to the landing. Moonlite thru the skylites, displaying pale rectangles in the open area below, bathed her silhouette in a macabre glow. I went down.

She did not stir when i sat by her, nor did her eyes blink or respond; her usual wide gaze had now narrowed to where only its sclerae were visible! It is not only the eyes of fetuses the sleeping the comatose ε the dead which do this but also those in deep meditative states. Anyone unfamiliar w this phenomenon would have been fritened by the blank stare of those pupilless whites. Not certain she was entirely unconscious of me, i seized the moment to examine her features.

The forehead in profile is not prominent but elfin, childish; the lines of eyebrow, nose, cheekbone, jaw, chin ε lips –all disparate, each indulging in its own self-centered esthetic– magically synthesized into a complementary confluence of contours; a geometry which flawlessness i have yet to unpuzzle. For instance, the line of her mandible had an angle of rise that was lower than i would have carved it had i been her Sculptor. Her nose was not the saucily *rétroussé* item of priscilla, sandy brandywine, veronika or deb danzi but the more classical upturn of juanita. Her hands lay one upon the other on her left thigh, calfs drawnup ε folded close, heels of her white-socked feet all but touching her buttox. Hadnt she been in exactly that position when we argued, now almost 8hrs before? {Damn.} I noted her legs were not their usual tan but seemed pale —almost as white as her socks! {Compartmentalization! Shit!} I touched her calf. Cold as polished ivory. Then her thigh. Same. I whispered, Lee? She did not respond. I kissed her temple-hair, said her name, touched her eyelids: Lilith. Her response was as catatonic as being alive can lapse to.

Her hands were icy as i tried to unfold her. I leaned in, lifted her –carefully, like a frostbitten flower, lest i snapoff a petal– stood, carried her upstairs, left her half-folded ε quilt-covered on the bed while i went to the bath, turnedon the heatlamp, set the tub to gushing.......

[hours later in atlanta] I stood at the window after she boarded, wishing i'd found a chance to say what had been on my mind for hours. {See me, your tender taurus, *inflexoque genu* before you! Please dont go back there. I beg you!} ...wishing i had forced a space in our parting to speak my heart. From behind the glass i watched her pilot take a last slug of coffee (or whatever), enter the plane wout so much as a glance to see if they'd given him one w wings. {Walk around that scrapheap of miracles, you death-bedamned dreadnaught! That's precious cargo youre carrying there!} Towbuggy bar is clamped to nosewheel, chocks are pulled. I berate the captain again, then spot a copilot circling the smoke-stained junkerjet. Soon it taxies off, shrinks to a tenth its size doing so, turns onto a rain-glossed ribbon of dark asphalt, races across my field of vision, trail of smoke ε mist billowing behind; noseup now, the silver brontosaurus lifts smoothly. Jog to windows opposite. Ascent steep, it disappears into a floor of low-hung cloud. {Take care of her you bored-with-life jetjocks or i'll come and find you, wherever you are, in Earth-time or ghost-space, and ripoff your landinggear.}

Slow clearing of sky as i drive west; burst of sunlite as i cross the state line. Soon my beloved mountains are parading their lilacs ε lavenders in the distance. An hour later i am cradled among them. Her eta occurs as i climb lookout mt, just s of little river canyon. She has arrived in dc before i can even get home! What a stupid antiReality we've erected around us! I am sitting in traffic in ft payne, just down the street from the stainedglass shop she loves, when she keeps her promise: calls to say she has landed safely.

"Nite-unto-nite" lapse: There were other things on which i'd managed to get commitments: ❶ call every nite; ❷ rent a car to be self-sufficient; ❸ stay at a hotel in town, not at "the house". Yet how i wished she'd allowed lage or me to go along. At 8 the fone rang. Her visit had been "Okay. Well, good, really." There'd been no arguing. And, no, he didnt showup. However she felt exhausted "for some reason" (i marked her seeming unawareness of why that was) and was going to supper "as soon as i hangup. On secondthought, maybe i'll jus skip supper an' crash". Given all the flying she did i remember wishing she wouldnt use that expression.

That was fr nite. On sa darkness had fallen in va when the sun was just setting beyond the river in bamalachia. 8oclock came&went, then 9, w no call. A token three bottles of münchenfest in the refrig suddenly looked good. By 9:30 i could stand the silence no longer. The fone rang on&on in her hotelrm. At the hospital they said her mother had been discharged; at leyda's house i kept getting an answering service. How stupid of me not to have set an hour when i could consider not hearing from her an emergency.

Unable to sit around –as any creature free of love's umbilicus might have– since all the counties thereabouts were dry, i headed for scotsmoor. My plan was to cutoff the horsemen of panic at the pass. I cant put all this on Lilith either. Events of the past year's stalking by the fed. had also piledup. Her trip was just the stone that broke the axel of the cart. By 10 i was chatting and swilling white russians at lanner's lounge, by midnite (with my preschool intolerance for alcohol) sufficiently shitfaced to take a taxi home.......

After failing again to purge myself of the potion poisoning me, i redialed her hotel, then leyda's house. Defeated again i stumble up to bed. Smell of alcohol & vomit w overtones of acetone. {Musta spitup when i dozed off. No wonder i rarely imbibe.} Suspecting myself of diabetic tendencies, i close my eyes, recall my sugar-crutched youth...just in time to see the tung&groove-lines in the ceiling's vault start to spin me like a windmill again.

<God, what i'd give to barf!> I sit up, begrudge the gift of upchuck the gods of food&drink give freely to good drunks & gourmands but not to the offspring of insanely fastidious mothers. I kneel for a few mins beside the bed —child praying at his humble board for a healthy upchukka. {UpchuckING. Yes, -ing, of course.}

<Please!> i add aloud. After crawling onto the bed again –deciding on facedown this time– i realized <Now the goddamn bathroom lite is on! I didnt turn that on, did i?> (I believe i've mentioned my inability to sleep w toomuch lite, like inside my cell this very minute.)

Doze, dream. I'm back in ca looking for Lilith, beam of searchlite sweeping the salty blackness for some sign of her. I hear her call, weakly, "Nathan? Is that you?" A second later, astonished, i realize i wasnt sleeping! Open eyes, twist around. Nothing. No one. What in hell? Sit bolt-upright, scan area, look downstairs. Balustrades, marching across the line of sight, fell away like the foils of dreamslow windmills in some quixotic knightmare! {Is this one of those fantastic contacts people say they get just after a loved-one has died? Dont think like that, fool! ...This is ridiculous. I'm drunk.}

Stippled w gooseflesh, i stand, wobble downstairs, slugdown another couple glasses of water. {If i hafta situp all nite it's better than being nauseous.} Mullingover the curse of my absolute inability to vomit, i decide on a plan of sobering dilution. {I will swill down a whole liter of water but first:} I head back thru the pantry to try again. I had only just knelt before the bust of the porcelain pieta, begun my penance, when i heard a muffled thud ...or thought i heard one. Slowly i withdraw my arm from my throat (so it seemed), rose to my feet, cocked my head thisway&that. Gooseflesh again. <This is insane! I'm hallucinating!> I rotate in place and, forgetting why i'm there, tiptoe out into the greatarea, just stand there. Nothing. {Start in basement for a looksee.}

As i descend the stairs, lites in the valley surprise me ...til i realize my mind has been in va, tearing the state apart for some sign that Lilith is safe. Finding nothing, i return upstairs. So as to make its contents pour evenly i am kneading a cylinder of frozen grapefruit concentrate on the counter when a wave of sudden sobriety washes thru me. {This is stupid! Why am i tiptoeing around?} I thumped the cylinder on the countertop as i kneaded it. Now what was *that?* I stopped, waited, gazing up. Thump-down cylinder again, listening for echo. No echo. Again, louder. Renothing. I could not rouse again the sound i thought i'd heard: distant, muffled —like the stump of a cripple thumping the plush of a thick rug. I was just easing the clumps of icy congealate into a decanter when it sounded again. {Now *that* i *know* i heard!} For some reason dakota's (war buddy) freshly legless torso came twisting at me thru the jungle ether of thought and, w an audible thump, landed on the floor of the loft directly above where i stood. I sidled to the pantry, took down my snoozing oozie, clickedoff the safety, clickedOn the big lites, and, sober as a executionary judgement, headed for the stairs.

Peering between two balustrades (which had ceased their earlier marching and now stood frozen in their tracks), i glancedabout the loft, then watched as the glassblocks of an shadowless showerstall stared back at me. For some reason sure now i was not the one who'd turned on the lite in the bathrm, i decided my best move would be to rush the place.

So sure was i that i'd find someone, its emptiness stunned me *and* the waving nozzle of my gun. I fully expected, at the very least, a fat raccoon to be staring back at me —as had happened out in the barn one nite. Peering around a partial wall (separating toilet from room), and as i was just concluding i'd either lost my mind or was still drunk, suddenly –clear as the voice of poe's lenore from beyond the grave– i heard Lilith groan: "Nathan?" I swung around, moved the gargantuan hulk of my gooseflesh backout to the bedrm sittingarea. A swatch of floor to the farside of the bed & its platform –the same area i'd stared at mins earlier from downstairs– leapt to mind. I hadnt investigated back there yet! Gripping the stock of my ugly weapon, i moved slowly forward.

There, foldedup like a fetus on the edge of the platform.... {GoodGaia!} I stepped over, dropped to my knees beside her. Her head lolled in my hands as i knelt. She moaned, faintly, opened her eyes, closed them —as if she made the effort only to be sure it was me.

My Sweet, what happened? [those fantastic eyes fluttered a bit, re-closed] What's going on? How longuv you been here? I lifted her onto the bed. Odor of ketones/vomit —a smell i knew from my medic days cut the air. Consciousness was ripped like a sleeve from the shirt of the present, hurled back to that seaside darkness where it all started —source of all the shadowy sinister gothiquary in my life now. {What else but a scent can do that?} i thought as i situated her on the bed. Sniffets of this *same* scent {Diabetic coma!} had been there that first nite on the ocean yet their cause hadnt registered.

When i put on a lite, the sight of her stunned me: hair damp, bedraggled; large yellow & crimson abrasion blooming on left cheekbone; lips, eyelids, fluttering spasmodically; nose, cut on one side, appeared broken. Lilith, home a day early, looked like she'd been shoved from a speeding car.......

[scene from days prior] ***Cades cove:*** ...is a restored pioneer community which arose out of a collection of small farms. Settled in the 1820s, today it is operated by the ntl pks system and lies in one of the loveliest coves in the eastern u.s. Tucked away in a high enfold of the smoky mtns, there is an inexplicable poignancy to the region. Oddly it remains rich w mood despite the crowds that now swarm there annually. But offseason, just before the cove closes for winter, mood is optimal. In late afternoon, the threat of a bitter winter in the air, the rugged history of the place, the lovely yet brutal nostalgia, seems whispered in the surrounding woodland steeps, breathed like forgotten frite thru the chinking of cabin walls. My first visit was in the late '70s, wellbefore it became popular. While not a tourist trap (as yet), i knew enuf not to take Lilith there til just before it closed for winter.

The drive into the park reminded her of the drive up our own gap rd. Since she loved the place on sight, we decided to "hang around", as if we had no place else to go; to imagine the cove as home, like it or not; to remain there til the old days struck bonemarrow, til we got a sense of what it must have been like to be born, growup, court, marry, have a family, and die, in america in the 1800s in a harsh isolation thoreau only dreamed of. It took three days to drop in on that eerie sensation, that transmigration of the senses to another era. Lilith called it "spooky ...a timewarp". But "timetravel" comes easy there, for the hills surrounding that rolling basin have gone largely undisturbed. The great wave of logging, farming and mining that swept n.america went a little easier on those particular hills.

Plus, the place has the props of coordinated anachronism: costumed storekeeps, farmers, housewives, blacksmith, mill workers, and period pieces by the thousands: furniture, cookware, utensils, family portraits, working wells, mills grinding grain, beehives abuzz, farm equipment, animals, even crops being worked; a n.american brigadoon enfolded by pristine woodlands climbing themselves breathless into a cobalt-colored mist. Since our stay was in october, the embrace of those hills was ablaze, and an autumn breeze, chilly but harvest-scented, did its part to facilitate our retrotropism.......

It was late afternoon of our 3rd day when a most-telling event took place. We were at the penultimate logcabin on the loop, having just finished a challenging Nature trail before heading back to camp. (The odor of this prison cell, incidentally, when the humidity drops enuf, reminds me of those cabins, its musty scent helping restore the moment as i write.) Our backpacks leaned on the porch behind us. We sat on the front steps catching, or hoping to catch, our 5th wind —for we had hiked ourselves to exhaustion and would sleep a near-deathbed sleep that nite. As we sat we talked about, and listened for, the old silences the small valley stows, all the while watching, a couple hundred meters away, a queue of deer cross the road and enter the meadow.

Ya know, this pocket in the Wilderness is so ideal, my guess is, indigenous amerinds were runout of here by exgenous palefaces.... I feel a strong amerind presence in this topography. ...My guess is, these people we're studying made a life on stolen land. When she does not answer i add, Ya think?

Sighing, removing the twigtip she's been chewing: "I dont... [clears throat] I dont guess the first amerinds to trek down the bering straight into north america... [bends away from me, gently spitsout twigbits] ...i dont guess they ever thought to ask the wooly mammoths, the sabretooths, the wooly bison 'r wooly rabbits, 'r any o' the life in residence here; i dont guess they asked if it was alright if they 'settled' the continent from end to end over the next few thousand years." Her tone was so apathetic, so alien, i had to keep looking up to reassure it was her. "It seems, that's just what life does ...or thinks it has a right to do, doesnt it? [rhetorical assertion] ...it tries 'n' tries ta spread itself wherever it thinks it's allowed ta go ...and allowed is the key word, cause when we know damnwell we're perfectly intolerable 'n' we still elbow 'n' shove our way around, that's when healthy life trades places with aggressive sickness; that's when Nature becomes UNnatural; that's when we become anerobes eating ugly oozing holes in an aerobic world ...in our human case ...scuse me, civil human case... the name o' the disease is arrogant imperialism ...(which alota people think of as some kinda divine right)... cause we all know, any ol armadillo is permitted to stumble into any ol fox den any ol time ...it's alright ...it happens ...it's when we, knowing damnwell better [leans away, spits again] it's when we, knowing damnwell better we shudda said 'sorry' ta the fox 'n' scooted outa there...but instead we go 'n' roundedup other conscience-lobotomized armadillos like us, go back 'n' wipedout the fox ...'n' her home, 'n' all her kids too... *that's* when what shoulda been just an anomaly of accident becomes purest horror; *that's* when a forgivable mistake becomes the disease of a species; *that's* when Natural life becomes mere civil existence, *that's* when almost an entire species goes begging t' Mothernature t' be done away with, an' quick too. An *that's,* well, prettymuch what i think."

I was speechless. As for her, she just sat, tracing now w her twig in the dirt. In a single runon sentence she had summarized all the books i'd written & all the books i'd ever write, and if she expected me to reply beyond <Gimme a minute here. I'm sure i'm not *completely* speechless> i could see it was going to be awhile. For that was the day i became irredeemably convinced, i was in the presence of towering genius.

I need to note. Lilith was shaken by the number of graveyards in the village, many markers moldering into the soil while others were all but obliterated. What alarmed her most were the early deaths common to those times. We are totally unused to thinking of 35 and 40 as an average lifespan. "God! So many children!" She would take hold of my arm w two hands, sort of stumble along beside me. "So many infants! And the mothers, so young!" Tears came to her eyes. Had i thought before i spoke, i would have skipped what my uniquely uninspired conversation on that porch soon led to.

<The last time i was here, the nite we arrived in fact, a girl was murdered, brutally, by her boyfriend ...in a tent in the primitive campground.>

She looked at me, disbelieving. “Brutally? All murder’s brutal” she said w no particular passion, then continued to tease w a twig a small stone at her feet. (For those who dont know, arguments are rare in campgrounds, violence unheard-of, ε murder unthinkable.) It may have been our sore bodies, our hunger. Also, daylite was quickly dissipating westward and the air quickly chilling. Or perhaps it was just the essential morbidity of the place, that our visitor veneer had finally peeled away exposing us to raw history. For even after just a day-visit at the cove the sensitive tourist goes away w something more than a feeling of quaintness and a roll of fotos. It may also have been, we had by then a vivid picture of what pioneer hardship was, and being sufficiently depressed by that picture, we now felt obliged to suffer in fact some inkling of what the dust of those who filled those graveyards had suffered. Beside this, it didnt help a bit i’m sure that we were exhausted, that i had brought up said murder, and the fact that our tent was setup not far from the very spot where it happened.

She traced the perimeter of the stone between her boots. “Sometimes life’s really shitty” she said, w not a trace of emotion.

Had i not been so tired ε hungry myself i might have slid close, held her. But truth is, i was wishing just then that someone would hold me. <We outa get on our way before we collapse.> I was thinking of the uphill hike back. Just then i spotted an ant, prowling up a leg of her jeans, pincers mincing the minute fibers of denim in seeming anticipation. I picked it off, gave a squeeze, minced it between my own pincers onto the ground.

Lips parted, she stared down at the corpse, saying nothing —the blankest stare i may have ever seen. (Of course, blanker ε dreadfully longer stares lay in our future. But that cannot concern us now.)

It was crawling up your leg.

“I know. I was watching it.”

Fine. ...Then why didnt *you* flick it off?

Perfunctorily, “It wasnt *hurting* anything?” she shrugged, looking down to where the small corpse lay torqued in the dust. I should stress, there was not a hint of accusation in her words or demeanor. The blankness of her tone matched precisely the blankness of her stare. She pushed the ant gently w the twig’s tip. “It’s dead.”

We sat. This sort of impasse –which, for me, happens mostly *w* females– never fails to drive me nuts. After awhile i shook my head. Lee …monkeys, birds, bats, lots of animals, and plants too, kill bugs …by the trillions! Why cant i kill one, just one, without invoking a cloud of cosmic revulsion?

Her twig stopped tracing its small trench around the stone. "It's you, not me, who said, 'Nature, healthy Nature, kills only to save its life'." (The proposition, of course, incl'd eating-to-stay-alive when i wrote it.)

<Okay.> I point at the ant but no words come. <Okay.> I hate it when that happens —i mean, when i lose the rhythm a good rebuttal requires, endup being my own echo. <You know, [wrist on knee, still pointing at ant], that little shit wasnt making a social call, okay? [still echoing] His leisurely little trip up your leg was a foray, the beginning of what woulduv endedup a very personal 'n' bloody attack when he found what he was after.

"I know. But you mightuv just brushed it off." Still staring down, a slite poutyness about the lips, perhaps, but still no accusatory signals.

{This is silly.} <And you coulduv brushed it off too! That little bastard …'scuse me, your little 'friend' there… had the very deadliest motives in mind, you *know* that. If his plans were the plans of some giant here with us right now, you'd not only be revolted by them, both of us'ud be half-eaten as i speak.> My pace was returning.

"You dont know that fer shur."

But i *do*. If ants will kill 'n' eat most animals they'll kill 'n' eat you 'n' me. [Maybe i shoulduv dropped the subject right there but her silence left my point rather unresolved.] Lee, millions of people around the world still kill 'n' eat bugs.> Now that was a mistake —i mean, taking a human point of view as my own, a thing we'd agreed never to do in our ecologic problem-solving.

"But *we* dont eat them. Theyre not in our diet anymore." She stared at the twisted critter, her voice finally beginning to take on some expression. "B'side, you didnt kill it ta eat it."

<Ya know, i dont know about you but i'm too tired for this. We've been down this road so many times.> My vision was blurring, i was starving, my body ached all over, and beside, i was dehydrated & depressed. Thinking our day would be farless demanding, we had taken only nominal supplies. Slapping my knees in frustration, i stoodup, walked a few paces, turned back to address her non-committal quietude.

<Ferkryssake, Lee! Whaddaya want from me? Whaddaya want me ta say? I'm wrong? I'm thoughtless? I'm cruel? ...Okay. I'm wrong. I killed an ant. ...No? Still not enuf? Well, how 'bout, i'm a thoughtless big dumb ant-killer? Huh? Enuf? [no reaction] Here, then! I'll eat the sonofabitch for you! Maybe that'll do it.> With that i bent, tweaked up the tiny corpse, blew the dust off, popped it in my mouth. <There. That better? I'm eating him. Now his death was not in vain.>

She gaped up at me for what seemed like a long time. When she finally spoke she said, "Why... w-why... did you do that?" Her speech was dreamslow, her mouth slitely awry.

I chewed, swallowed, watched a last chilly common cramer loop past us and out toward the road, looking for a place to spend the cold nite —maybe to spend forever. When i glanced back, her mouth still held the shape of that "Why?"

<Youre *still* feeling sorry for him? Should i maybe'uv given the mean little shit ...pardon me, your little friend... a grand burial instead of eating 'im?>

She was about to speak but stopped, said in a whisper, "Never mind. It's not important", then busied her twig again.

What?

"Nothing."

<What? Tell me. What were you jus gonna say?>

"I think it was still alive when you ate it, that's all. I saw it starting to move." I cannot overstress, she was not being in the least clever or ironic.

<Goddamit, whaddaya want from me, Lee?> I stopped, knew if i said another word i'd be yelling.

"I'm sorry. I'm doing all i can not to make you angry an' youre jus getting angrier." She went silent —perhaps for the nite. No anger, no attitude —that was the infuriating part. If she'd only copped an attitude, lit into me. Instead, those big wet eyes of hers broke my heart. She stared at the meadow across the road, following the receding butterfly, then looked over to where the deer had got to by then.

I turned, gathered some stones, started winging them at a roadside stump.

She soon stoodup, brushedoff the rump of her jeans —i will deal *w* that motion another time. Then again, maybe now's a good time. Thrustingout of trim rump, sidetoside over-each-shoulder downward glance as, mouth open *&* sensuously pear-shaped, she finished brushing. She then tookup her backpack, ambled down the doorpath, stopped at the road. After tossing a stone or two more i went to the porch, got mine, followed a ways behind. We passed the last cabin wout so much as a glance over. (We would endup sleeping there the next nite.) I gradually caughtup w her as we crossed a shallow hollow and began the climb to the campground.

<Damnit, Lee. We've been over this a dozen times. You know i love animals. All kinds of animals. [she looked over at me w a sort of childish faith] Alright, *most* animals. I steer around grasshoppers. I dodge toads 'n' treefrogs. Youve seen it a hundred times. I'll brake for an caterpillar if it wont cause an accident. {Why do i feel like some civilized brute? This is ridiculous!} As for flies? rats? roaches? ...Okay, i'm prejudiced there. And ants too, i guess. But theyve got no respect ...not for anything! Theyre vicious little stomachs with legs! ...Creatures with the armament of sharks, the sentiment of vultures!>

I imagined her thinking, "I suspected it might come to this. What a fool i've been. Youre a fraud, captain greenEarth!" A poor selfimage can cause such doubts when one least expects it. In reality of course she was thinking nothing of the sort.

"Rats 'n' roaches hafta eat too." I tracked her features from a corner of vision. She was not disinterested in what i was saying. And this is the part about Lilith one either gets or doesnt get. There's no middleground. Life is precious, period ...in *all* its forms. It was really that simple. And because it was so simple it continued to evade me. Reflecting on this incident, a few weeks later i would write....

[Editor's note: The following hypertext is inserted at this point in the MS margin: "Emil, you may recognize the following as coming from my *ungreening of tomorrow*. But please dont use that version. I feel the following revised & personalized statement captures better what i'm after here. Thanks."]

> Nature is present in the 'least' of its parts. This we know in theory but do we know it in practice? And this: Nature in all its forms is intrinsically precious. —including, yes, even the creation & evolution of man! Nature is also the grand equalizer. If our species is due any retribution it will surely get it. Maybe thanx to war, or to disease, or to some other counterbalance or group of them. But humanity will *not* get its due thanks to the interdiction of Lilith. We could sooner wait for butterflies to wage war, for zebra herds to trample lions, for whales to slaughter humans, than wait for Lilith to hurt anything. For apparently, built into all finite injustice is Infinite Justice. But only a view of the Whole Picture can give understanding to what only *seems* like error on the part of Nature. (Such as life seemingly disdaining life.) But since our minds are not nearly vast enuf to comprehend that Picture, we see error almost everywhere we look! That said, it needs be put yet another way. The amount of wisdom we are missing is exactly proportionate to the amount of error we see in Nature.

I have inserted these reflections because, well ...It was like Lilith walked around all the time w such a perception of existence, such a Worldview. It came across as if it were burned into her blood, branded on her zizm, in a code she was beginning to get command of but still could not explain, so big was it and still inchoate to mere language. And the messages it gave her, so to say, tho too vast ɛ too exotic for her to put into words just yet, *did* demand of her a terrible reverence, a reverence for this Something apparently manifest in her. But i too had yet to figure all this out. For i still had the naivete (or was it arrogance?) to believe, Nature needed my help to subdue civil humanity, or at least to humble him&her a little.

She blinked, pursed her lips, as we walked along. After a few mins we came to an open space in the trees. She turned and, walking backwards, looked at what was visible of the village below: the broad meadow, the churches, the cabins. Beyond the dark enfolding hills a cold purplish glow, w a weak orange warmth diffusing up thru it, was all that remained of the day ...and summer too, as it turnedout. The whitetails had reached the commons creek by then, were drinking, looking about. The peacefulness in that view, that moment, despite our little conflict, would stay w us. I believe this was the moment when the above realization (the preciousness of life, ALL life) bored a hole in my being and laid its egg.

We faced back, walked on in silence. When almost to camp her voice startled me, for i fully expected her to be mostly silent for the rest of the nite. "Why cant humans just let things be? ...You know, like the song says?"

I thought about that. My track record thus far suggested i just shutup. {But if i dont respond maybe she'll go silent.} <You mean, like letting civilization just blunder ahead with its deadly agenda, overrun the Planet? kill the oceans? burn the last of the rain-forests? turn this smallBlueMiracle in bigBlackSpace into our Galaxy's largest landfill? Just sorta sit by? Just sorta, let it be?> She stopped at my remark, looked askance, jaw poised. <Ya know, when i met you you admired the likes of captain matson 'n' roy freeman. Ya dont get more aggressive than them without bearing arms.... I know i know. That was then 'n' this is now.>

I was sure that now i'd really done it. Twilight was descending quickly. We trudged on. Yet a min later she spoke. "I know it sounds insane...but that's exactly what i think i mean." I stopped, as much surprised by her speaking as by what she said. A couple steps later she stopped us again. I looked at her. Not meeting my gaze, half-turned away in thought, she continued: "Overpopulation's not an accident of Nature. You taught me that and i think youre right. It's purposeful. It's aggressive ...you say it yourself when we talk about aids, about cancer, about the insidious cleverness of human diseases as time goes on: 'It's the nature of Nature to cure overpopulation' you said. ...But at the same time i dont think you knew what you were saying —not really. Or maybe you jus dont believe it."

I looked at her. I wanted to say, Do you know how long, how deeply, i think about things before i write them? But i said nothing. We started walking again. Her eyes were large, wet, and the deepest of blues in that fast-descending dusk. I thought to myself, How beautiful she is! I told myself, Just shutup 'n' listen. {Maybe i'm missing her point an' maybe that point is not only valid but precious.}

We reached the top of the grade. Thru the trees ahead the first campfires could be seen.

I'm guessing there's more, right?

"Well... the way i see it, Mothernature cant do it –the easy way, the quick way– when civilization fites her methods, her cures, at every turn ...all her easy simple cures stopped dead, interrupted, derailed ...by us."

And when those cures fail ...i mean, the small easy cures which Mothernature [in her tireless altruism] deploys first?

"Then she's forced to search her bag of tricks for larger, bigger, more deadly ones. But the way i see it is different from the way you *say* it. My view doesnt stop to evaluate itself. It jus blunders on. For more'n'more i see less'n'less need for our interference. It may seem tragic but...but... Civilization has grown most of humanity so greedy 'n' blind it's all got to endup out of our hands eventually anyway... I wish i could explain what i'm trying to say." Her voice almost broke. She gave her head that hopeless little shake which, every time i saw it, stabbed me in a deep place —a little dip to one side, easily missed, which oftenasnot might precede an extended silence —or, under fritening circumstances, even a petit seizure.

I know what you mean ...i think. If we dont understand the Cosmic Plan it is presumptuous of us to lift a hand. The *Dao de ching* thing. To interfere, to take action, is to presume one knows the Great Universal Plan ...knows it intimately ...which of course is an arrogant thought born of ignorance. Or how about this? Squashing an ant is no different –in principle, i mean– than burning a rainforest.>

She squinted at the ground *w* concern while i spoke, then soberly said, "I like that. Yes. That's certainly the *basic* idea."

We started walking again.

Well, so what's missing from my explanation?

“Mmm... the frite, maybe?”

Frite?

“Yeah. That’s what it is. For me, anyway. Frite. <Of what?> The frite of doing something wrong... purposefully taking an action that turnsout to be wrong ...Cosmically wrong, i mean. What a terrible –impossible really– responsibility! [her step paused w her words] ...Defending Nature sometimes seems more like work for gods not men. That should be the lesson we all must learn.” And it was then her mx struck home ...deeply, lastingly home. Tho i was in every sense stunned by her words i replied, <For gods ‘n’ *men*, not goddesses ‘n’ *women?*>

This eked me a childish little smilette. A warbler, almost hid by trailside brush, “charmed” the dusk in “sheer appreciation for the gift of another day” as she put it. Echoing its little serenade in her wee-est sing-songiest cartoonish arpeggio, she translated: “This is my last song before dark. Hope you enjoy it.”

Little bird, little bird, come sing [us] a song.
It’s a short time [we’ll] be here and a long time [we’re] gone.

Just as the rosy furnace of the sun is unlike, yet inseparable from, the glowing ash of the clouds couching its last lite, her gentle lovely face, but specially her eyes, were, for a moment for me, suspended above the usual flow of Earthly time/change. With a longing arm i enwrapped her waist, murmured into her hair <You are the most marvelous thing in my life!> As we walked i wondered {Why *cant* i let the World just be? Do my own ecologic best an’ let the rest jus “be”?} I knew the answer but try as i might –thirsty, hungry, exhausted– i couldnt get at it. <Remember what you once told me? ...You fell in love with me because i took action, because i stuckup for the weak the helpless the non-violent, because i took action when others just stood by, wore t-shirts, pasted bumperstickers, mailedin their annuals ‘r jus ran their mouths with green blather? And how long do you think people will keep reading *captain greenEarth* when he suddenly starts sitting on his hands for four frames a week out of fear of doing the wrong thing t’ help our damaged Earth?>

(Of course i should have known better. For by then i’d learned, Lilith was someone whose reverence for life stood appalled –quietly, humbly, appalled– before the need of others to find a way to lose weight. (Diary: “I can wrench a carrot or a parsnip from the garden. Of <u>course</u> i can! But if, that done, you’re gonna ask me to shave, shred or cook the thing, then i’ll be needing a tokeERtwo.”) ...written one day after we’d had differences over food prep. Of course, for one to *choose* to eat "things with faces" (w brains ε nervous systems) was beyond her comprehension, and had been since age9, i understand. And this afterall was the same person i'd comeupon tearedup at the sight of dogwood blossoms twirling Earthward, and whom you'd think was struck by every bug that sounded against the windshield. "I know it's stupid [of me] ta feel like this. Stupidstupidstupid!" And so, because of these things, atlonglast it struck me. These were not passing moments of sentimental empathy as i'd been supposing. For the first time i realized: Lilith was hiding (and hiding from) a subtle but recurrent surfacing of existential terror. Whereas in most of us it is only the fear of our *own* death, or that of someone dear, which can arouse in us the terror of ABSOLUTE OBLIVION, here was a mind so unique it would suddenly vivify, wout warning, the terror of absolute oblivion in relation to *any* death, be it bluebonnet or bluewhale!

Memoirist conclusion: What a safe ε delicious World would exist for ALL if each of us owned more than just a passing intuition of all that this sweet Creature's intelligence addedup to!)

She stopped, stared at the ground. "Youre right. You *are*. And i dont know the answer.... I dont. Maybe it depends on the action. When our work becomes painful ...to *us*, i mean... agonizing sometimes even... longing as we do to turn all that seems doomed around... isnt that like civilization's sick belief in martyrdom? ...isnt that us turning our green life-wish into civilization's deathtrope? ...turning our secularist Gaiadigm into just one more of those religious martyrdigms you find so destructive? —and rightly so?"

I stood locked in my tracks. Where have you been keeping all this stuff?

"I'm not really sure i'm explaining myself. All of it's just a *feeling* right now. A sense of things all raw 'n' unformed growing inside me... or maybe it's me growing outward into something else... like a metamorphosis... like maybe i'll grow wings some day? Weird, i know." {That fantastic faraway gaze of hers again!} "But, of course, i'm still way too heavy ...too cumbersome: a clumsy slow worm with only the hope of wings; two helpless nodules on my back, dna promises... shoulderblades that ache to fly but cant even help me get back to camp."

{You not only can fly, you carry rationally-leaden me along whenever you do.} I dont know if i had such a statement in me then. Seems i should have had. What i do know is, had i suspected our destiny in the tiniest degree i would have managed something like it. But such honest humility we often relegate to a 'better time'. However, the rearview mirror of moving life knows, such ideal opportunities do not necessarily pass our way twice.

"Maybe wisdom is knowing when to stop struggling, stop hurting, 'n' just 'be'... But, i know: How to do it without the anxiety of feeling we jus gaveup. I think we can only do so much as individuals before we join the destructive mentality of civil martyrdom."

I came alongside. By then we'd passed the first campsites. Scents of charcoal fires ε foodstuffs. The few campers left were finishing eating, neatingup or relaxing. I gripped the prominence of her left hip as we walked. <I know what youre saying. I do. That there's never,never,never a time that's right to kill —unless it's t' save yer life, or the life of a loved one. ...Is that it?

She thought. "Uhuh."

All at once i realized something i'd thought a hundred times before but never in such sweeping context: She doesnt have an aggressive bone in her body! Maybe not even an aggressive cell! I imagined the killer-t cells of her immune system suddenly slitting their own throats in grief —grief over having killed billions of invader organisms 'just' to keep her safe. When we reached our site i stopped, began to laff. [What?] I explained. And dont you know, tho i was just kidding she had trouble w that too? —the fact that organisms inside her were giving their lives to save hers? "That's goingon inside me, isnt it? Right now. I keep forgetting." She grinned, but her grin was not convincing. I had unwittingly exposed a war goingon inside her, unleashed a new moral quandary for her to wrestle w. <It is possible to be too sensitive for one's own good> i said.

After supper ε skimpy waterbag showers we sat watching other campers sitting around, staring glassyeyed at –the sometimes amber-flaring but mostly rosy glow of– what remained of their small cooking fires. Sure as i believe truth resides in instinct, there is an ignicolist still alive&well in each of us. I watched her shakeout her hair to dry over her chairback, silken eyelids doing that *falter*ing thing, trying to outline thru the misty nite damps just one constellation. I couldnt, and she too soon tired of trying.

<If i c'n say one more thing, an' then i'll shutup? [gives tacit yod] You care more about the life of an ant than you do your own! There's something unNatural about that. ...Nature wants you to live, Lilith ...else... else that war in your behalf wouldnt be going on inside you all the time. The fact that it *is* going on is an affirmation, an affirmation by the highest Authority; an affirmation that you, Lilith McGrae, have a right to live! —a divine right, no less!> And in the next breath i knew, if i ever met the sonofabitch –her stepfather, i mean– i would strangle him w my bare hands. For it was he who'd obliterated, i was sure, her pride, her selfrespect, to a point where it continually endangered her very right to exist!

Fire out, stars misted over, together in sleepingbag: "Ya know what i think our problem is? <Huh?> We're facing winter here, here at the depths of our pioneer experiment, without a spring summer 'n' fall of hard work t' show for it; no actual homestead t' save, 'n' no real sweat'n'blood loss to make us feel worthy of survival."

Hmm. But didnt we imagine all those things —the planting the cultivating the water-carrying the harvest the broken implements the callouses cuts bruises the fencing the canning the salting the chinking the stitching the chopping— we've been going over'n'over it for days.

"True. But it's *bodies* that hafta make it thru the winter, not imaginations. An' our bodies know the truth ...the truth of what we *didnt* do ...the truth of no real sweat'n'blood investment here, no heart-wrenching loss, no bone-deep sacrifice ...the very things that make one know he's alive and at risk ...and then *blessed,* if not deserving, if he makes it thru."

Like a sudden summerwarm syrup her words threaded their sweet sensibilities into me & thru me. I believe youre right. As it sank home her perception stopped me in my tracks. You know, i'm *sure* youre right. Yes. What we're missing is all the things ...no, the body-memory of all the things... the thousand things, little 'n' big, a person does, that a family, a community does, must do, all the way from first thaw ta first freeze, task-by-task accomplishments which let them know they can make it thru one more winter. An more than that, that they *deserve* t' make it. That's it! Youve called it exactly! I wanted to whirl her at once in an impromtu jig. Youre brilliant, you know that? Ya dont hafta answer, of course, i added quickly.

"Sumthin in us expects ...*really* expects... survival t' be a challenge i think."

That rang a bell. Jonathan winters said, "Why am I always shocked when life slips me another spiked turd to pass, ["Ooof."] when I should know by now, that's a big part of life's job ...so we can fully appreciate the *absence* of pain."

"An' when we *dont* meet survival's challenge headon, anxiety 'n' paranoia set in. The paranoia of rulers, of the 'pampered few'. <True.> An' bitterness too." I felt her words somehow paused in the darkness. <O yes. Let us *not* forget bitterness. For we met it and it vanquished us. ["Temporarily."] Yes. Only temporarily.>

We shared a much-needed little chuckle in the cozy darkness. I stroked the hair at her temple. Out of habit, in semisleep, she lifted her head so i could pass my arm under, and, as always, w the same motion, turned my way, settling her head onto my shoulder. Folding her into the crook of my arm i continued to stroke her hair, cool & damp against my cheek.

<I love you, Lee.> i whispered after awhile, thinking her asleep.

"Oooo, I love you too" she murmured, now barely, barely, barely awake, forehead pressed against my jaw, wee breath on my neck.

Before i fell asleep i knew for certain {She'll never press charges. Never. And if the bastard ever goes to jail it will not be because she sent him there. I mightaswell giveup on that.} And suddenly i realized, there was no ruse, no hidden purpose, not even self-deception. It was exactly like she said it was when i first asked her to press charges: "I cant. I jus cant."

And me? What of my role in this Play? I lay there thinking. {You are my muse, Lilith. You sometimes take me by the hand t' show me your wonders. And i pull away, thinking you are trying to lead me toward the oceanic; toward weakness and inaction. But from now on, i promise, t' be the best, i mean the best, killer-t cell in your body —sworn t' kill every invader that comes near! sworn to eradicate every thing, big 'n' small, which threatens your existence!}

I thought such things as i drifted toward sleep. And in my exhaustion it seemed to me i suddenly had hold of a working theory of the Universe ...or, at least, the whiplashing tailend of such a theory. As rational thought diffused into sleep i imagined myself reaching out, stretching an arm up, up, up, finally touching some Great Wing as it passed in the celestial Nite, momentarily dragging its feathers in the dust of a small Planet, a small Planet sailing on its way thru a vast, very-dangerous-to-life yet very fecund & awesome Universe!.......

Leyla Zana: "Freedom"

[later, Part 9] ***<u>Nontiscordardime:</u>*** That nite i was chased from one fitful dream to the next by a cross between agent chadeau & the giant who accosted lalage. Tho up at her usual earliness, Lilith skipped her rA.M.ble. I guess we'd hiked & biked ourselves into average morning civílizens. By the time i stagger downstairs she is wellalong *w* her day. My kiss, i'm shy to admit, toomuch resembled the rote peck of a long-mated man.

"You okay?"

Not really. Head feels like a hockeypuck. I sit. Feeling grumpy i get right to the negative stuff. I see that r-v's still there.

"I wish you wouldnt worry about it. It's just some family brokedown. ...They'll probably fix it today, be gone before dark."

Funny it should break down in the only spot with a view of goingson around here. Head down, fingering a hairline which felt like it was receding, i try to put faces on the shadows which had stalked my dreams. Something on the stove sizzled for a second.

"They probably stopped there b'cause the old driveway's the levelest part o' the swale."

I suppose. Plus, i saw no hairs on that dog dish ...'n' the tires o' the bikes look new. Fact, all the stuff looks new.

She turns. "It probably is. Maybe some people dont have vacation stuff jus lying around the house." She comes over, sits sidesaddle on the edge of my chair. I note the pretty butterfly apron ree gave her. "It's okay, sweet. I think the feds 'ave gone ...probably for good. We havent seen hyde nor hairy for months now. They probably got bored t' death with us homebodies."

Youre probably right. She kissed that hairline, went to the stove, returned, setout my fav heavy ε moist onion rye toast ε roast tea; sat. It's me. I'm jus spazzing.

Reaches across table w one hand ε agonizingly munchesque gaze. "Youre jus tired. You tossed half the nite."

I'd believe anything those eyes o' yours stood behind.

"Ooo, youre sweet. I luuuv you." Susurrous whisper, suspirous lisp. We gaze at eachother like lovelorn lemurs as pacifica radio's amy goodman, as ever, informs our day. "And youre right to be suspicious. I'm so stupid about stuff. Somebody around here needs t' keep his head screwed on. [we sip our tea] Speaking of impractical, this is t' remind you, sis, ree 'n' me will be off carousing t'day."

Come to think of it, i had heard lage come in: "It's only me, everybody. Go back t' sleep" came over the ic around midnite. (None of us came or went wout all at home knowing about it; one of the thousand&one negatives of living stalked.) That's right too. Ree's back. They'd been out celebrating her return. Ya know, i dont get it. [What?] How you guys just up 'n' forgive her like nothing ever happened. How does that work? I mean, she sticks you 'n' lage 'n' dexter, 'n' whatshername? ...amy. Right. An' that other girl... sticks you all with her classes for two months ...*two* months. I know you got paid, pardon the euphemism. But that's not the point. If you or amy wanted to be aerobics instructors you woulduv went into business with lage. Forgive me if i jus dont get how ev'rything gets instantly okay again.

"I c'n see that. I do. But she didnt mean t' be gone so long. Jus needed to sample her horizons —which should be compulsory, no? O, dex called. They'll be back on saturday." They'd gone to atlanta for oral's first chemotherapy. While dexter was convinced the gerson therapy could putoff oral's demise indefinitely, oral was deadset against all alternative medicine. Pardon 'deadset'. <Mayaswell get ta that front ten t'day. Maybe the fresh air will blow my head clear.> Since oral would be unable to work for awhile, if ever again, plus the way i was feeling, it seemed an ideal time to tackle the job. <B'saad, navemba rains 'll be heah fer'n ya know it.> My bad imitation of local agrispeak. With half a frost-grazed melon in fist, i kissed my pure-of-heart ecomate on the cheek and headed for the barn.

While the soil needed cultivating before it got too wet, i could have waited til she left to start. But by then the motorhome might have been gone and w it an opportunity which had nagged me thru the nite: {How stupid not to have shot a couple mins of video before dark. If something had happened i'd have nothing but a licenseplate#, probably worthless at that.} So while L straightenedup around the house, i rather snuck the camcorder out, shot a few mins of rv, tracks & surroundings. I'd finished, was just hitchingup the tractor when she appeared to feed & pasture "the girls ...Breakfast, ladies!", familiar morning music i hadnt heard at closerange in awhile.

Machinery libated & readytogo, i went to her. <Hope i didn upset you. I jus wanted ya ta stop 'n' think. You seem t' have lost all sense of caution since youre back from virginia.> Indeed, we'd decided, trying to stay absolutely safe all the time was not only emotionally exhausting, it was impossible. <Dont misunderstand. That youre not living scared anymore is great. It is. But t' lose all sense of caution? Trouble lives jus to prey on us incurable optimists, you know that.>

Fingertips to my lips: "I havent lost my sense of caution. [she spoke like i was her favorite barn resident] I havent. I'm jus not gonna agonize over stuff anymore. I'm not. It wrecks life. Life should be more than just enduring. [gazes at me w a tenderness which turns me kidlike] I'll be careful. I promise." Presses a flutter-eyed kiss on my lips, leaves to go "shake those lazybones outa bed". So ree had come home w lage. Hmm.

Rowhounding, furrowdogging, whatever one calls it, this activity creates its own state of mind, a state not alot different from wheeling a tractortrailer, bus or train crosscontinent, or piloting a freighter over one hump of water or another. The farmer is a far-traveler who never leaves home. If i imply a blank stateofmind i mean it in the sense of "from going back and forth in the Earth". That is, like an old drunk, the more years one does it the sooner in the day a seeming-drugged demeanor overtakes one.

Whether we are drunks, furrowdogs, road- air- sea- or spacepilots, once enuf time on the job[hic] has elapsed, we cant get out of our roles. Not unlike camping or hiking, to be *adscriptus glebæ* for a day is to locate, to set free, a coiled ε toolong-trapped primal sigh.

I was well into this reverie, just remarking to myself (over the drone of the motor) how little time i spent (since oral took over) on my vintage Ⓜ...slanting rays of weakening autumn sun stylize every mote of dust on her carmine flanks, every filament of cobwebbing clinging to her hydraulic arms. <Oral doesnt admire you the way i do, sweet marcheta.> [Pet name of NS' restored early 1950s-manufactured Farmall "M" tractor. —Ed.] A windrow of dust rose up ahead. Churning it was lage's geep, which stopped, waited at the end of my current furrows. L came over as i idled up. "We're leaving now!"

Hartist McPartiss

I figur'd.

"You countra boys 're men o' few words, huh?"

I smile, dismount my 3-legged lady.

"We still a little sad?"

Row reverie.

"Youre not angry...."

For what?

"For me taking off when youre worried?"

No.

"You sure?"

I suppose, a little sad.

"But you understand, no? It's not like i'm going off alone t'day."

I know. [yodding perceptibly] T'sokay. Go. ...Really.

Sun in one eye, squints up at me. "This is sorta personal, mister, but...." Lips pressed together.

But?

"But... [on toes she steals a lipsip, staresup at me] ...I know we were beat but... <But?> But i jus wish we'd made love last nite." Her eyes –eyelids, really– had that lovely lovelorn munch-madonnaesque droopiness they got w too little sleep.

Me too.

Lage beeped, waved. She looks around, then back. "T'nite could be our nite?"

Wee grin sneaksup on me wout permission.

"Right after class? I'll come straight home."

Class?

"I'm helping amy with ree's class ...so sis 'n' her c'n go out."

She's back 'n' youre *still* filling-in for her. I.... Phhhh. (She'd just givenup 2eves so ree could go w lage to see the atlanta7minus1 on world tour.)

"It's jus for t'nite only, then i'm free. I promise." No sooner spoken than lage beeped, twice. L half-waves wout looking away. "Nathan?" Peeks adorably under my downcast brows.

Ya see? That right there. You spend two hours getting her going –patient goodhumored hours probably– an' now *she's* in a hurry? [still peeking up at me] Here we wanna have an evening, but, no. Lage's fun 'n' ree's irresponsibility come first? Sorry, it's jus me, i guess. I dunno.

"Youre right. Really you *are*. This'll be the last time. We're coming first from now on. I mean it. You 'n' me. First. Always ...*always*."

Deep breath... sigh... yod w resignation, swallow. *{Immer. Immer.}* How's ree doing anyway?

"Good. She wants to apologize t' you... about those people? the talent trap you warned her about? <O. Right.> But she's too embarrassed right now. Maybe later."

That's fine. [yodding] No need to apologize .

Warm eyes unflinching. "I'll be home in time to change, okay?" Slow sip this time.

Dont change —ever. [smiles up that shy little smile i love so] Youre perfect the way you are.

"Oooo, i love you." Her softsmiling silverblues lock my gaze for an extended moment (a moment still w me) before she turns, heads back to geep.

All trace of anger gone out of me (how? where?), i watch her walk off. <Be safe!> Couldnt help but say that. Left hand rises in acknowledgment, or maybe just to keep her balance in the spongy soil, or maybe both. Ree opens door, waves, calls "Hi, nate!" I wave.

It's not strange. I mean, that i can still taste those limpid sips, see that precious little smile so clearly, feel her bodypress, her fingerhold on the back of my triceps. And i watch again the sway of her hips as she strides off —which sway (the quashed burlesque of a vamp's swagger) occurred only when she walked on soft surfaces, as in sugarsand or over freshly turned soil. But it's that little squinty shy smile that's got really wedged in my brain tonite —like a tiny frangible white flower between pages of a beloved album.

Sometimes
  in the middle of my day
  for no apparent reason
  that shy smile will float _____sωanlike_____
  across the rippleless azure of consciousness.

She slid into the seat behind ree, pulled in two maddening legs. The little door was slammed once, twice, as lage spun away. Hand waves behind glass. Juanita crosses my thoughts, probably subliminals from my tractor's petname. The glass coruscated in the sunlite as they bumped toward the frontgate. Lilith's face looked afloat inside, disembodied, jittering in the shadows of the interior, reminding me of the way moonlite jitters in the wind-wrinkled trough of a seawave. Look at me! Dr ratmoid would love this. I carryon as tho she were dead. Chinup, catulus! They honked as they passed thru the gate —or, i should say, L leaned forward and tapped the horn. I crawled back onto marcheta. A here/there flash of green metal from between the trunks of the nearest maples as i did my turnabout, told me Lage was doing about 100 [km] when she banked right around the curve by the creek. {Speed will be your undoing, girl} i thought, doubleclutching the longlegged lady in red beneath me.............

My glosses are smudged 'cause my i's are tearing.

END OUTTAKES OF BOOK 2

final synopsis

The lifestyles and beliefs of our ancestors have stolen our "right" to waste, deplete, extirpate or extinct ANYTHING. In fact, it is the irresponsibility and greed of our ancestors, unprecedented among all forms of life, which has put the onus upon us to replace or compensate in some way for all that they wasted, depleted, extirpated or extincted.

However, in that such reparations are long past achievable, and in that only one person in a thousand is objective enuf to LIVE, day to day for a lifetime, by such a moral mandate, apodictically guarantees the accelerated end of Planetary existence as we have known it ...and all dissenting views are but the all-too-familiar death-rattle of the same gluttony, careLessness and ignorance our ancestors lived by, and that our own progeny will pay the price for.

This is no excuse however to throw up our hands in defeat and dejection. For the Realist has his own conscience to live and die with, and the Realist conscience deplores denial. And so some few of us will continue to do battle DESPITE ultimate outcomes. For we have our deepest Realist Selves to answer to. As to the rest of humankind? It will own to its grave, and perhaps even beyond, ALL that denial always costs.

—from Nathan Schock's *The Cosmic Gaia* [editorial insert]